PHOENIX HEART

THE COMPLETE SERIES

SARAH K. L. WILSON

EPISODE ONE: ASHES

SEASON ONE

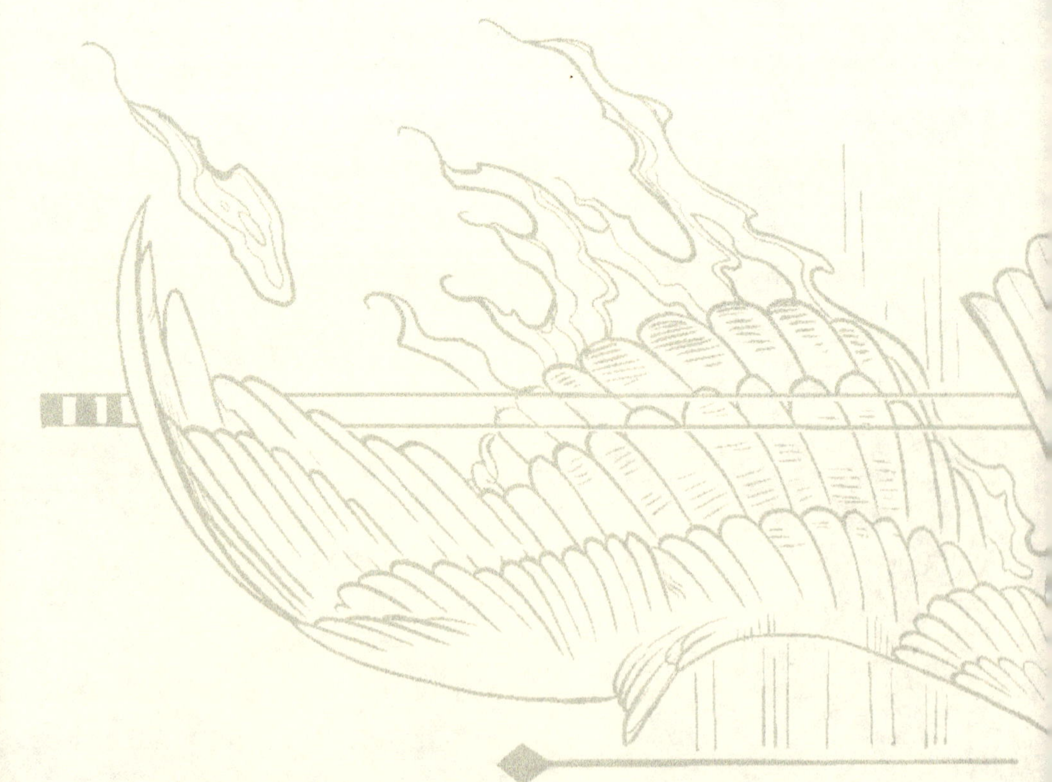

1

The best part of being voiceless is that I'm great at listening. I hear everything people say, and I hear the things they don't say.

The worst part is how hard it is to warn people when they are making mistakes.

My cousin Mally was making a mistake, but since she was across the bustling common room from me, I couldn't just call to her with a convenient excuse to come over here like my aunt Danna might. I could try to sign, but she'd have to be looking at me for that to work.

Instead, I gritted my teeth and finished cleaning the pine table while the wind outside howled its destructive intent and rain lashed against the small diamond-paned windows of the Hog's Head Inn.

This morning when I'd risen, the sky had been dark and portentous with clouds bubbling over the horizon like the foaming head on the house brew behind our bar. By noon, the good folk of our seaside town had begun tying down everything that could blow away. By suppertime, everyone was hunkered at home or here in the warm firelight of the inn.

Brave laughter and boisterous talk betrayed them, though. Voices betray people all the time. They think they are using them as shields to hide their fear, or anger, or disgust but they're like wet parchment. One good swipe and the defense is gone.

I don't have that problem.

I have no words to hold up to hide myself from the world. But I also have no words to slip on my tongue and accidentally reveal my true heart.

The loud boasting of the sailors my cousin was flirting with betrayed the fear they felt for their boat, hastily docked when the rain began to whip the shore like a broken cur. Even the dancing fire and warm stew couldn't fully drive the grip of fear from their hearts.

The calls of "More mead!" from Tyndale the blacksmith – my cousin's betrothed – were meant to hide his growing irritation at her flirtation. And that flirtation was meant to disguise the panic she was feeling as she realized she'd never leave our village now that she was getting married.

And despite the loud tune of the pipes playing over the howl of the wind, despite my aunt Danna's booming laughter as she poured at the bar, despite the stomp of feet and the clapping of hands as couples took up the dance, we were all just little people teetering on the edge of being swept away by the hand of nature, by her feckless rage, by her defiant flinging of water and air against our rocky shores.

I shivered. I was scaring myself again. I did that sometimes. I glanced at Fon reading a scroll by lantern light behind the bar. He kept chewing his lower lip and I wanted to chew mine, too. It was that kind of night.

I was the only one to notice Tyndale stand up with a dark look on his face as he wiped mead from his lips with the back of his hand and squared his shoulders. And I couldn't give a cry of warning as he made his way purposefully between the dancers with black murder in his eyes.

I dropped my rag and hurried to intercept him, but crowds don't part for voiceless kitchen girls the way they part for burly blacksmiths and I wasn't even halfway to him when paused and drew in a breath.

One of the sailors had his hand on Mally's waist, fingers splayed across her back. She was winking at him wickedly and laughing. Some barmaids might do that to get an extra coin, but I knew my cousin – who was just a year younger than me. This was what she lived for. She loved it when they wanted her and loved it when they fought. She loved it when her winks caused more trouble than a decree of war from a king. And since she wasn't married *yet* she was going to keep tugging that neckline down over her ample figure and tossing her curling chestnut locks over her shoulder and winking like she was the goddess who caused the storm outside. Because this was her favorite game, and it was almost over.

No one was ready for Tyndale's reaction except me. I saw it building all night.

"Get your stinking fishy hands off my betrothed!" he roared, face red and mottled.

The pipes stopped.

The dancers spun to a halt.

The sailor got to his feet.

Violence lingered just out of earshot. I could feel it there, ready to pounce.

And the inn door crashed open and we all jumped. My breath caught in my throat like a fishbone and my cousin Fon behind the counter let out a squeak of surprise.

The door swung drunkenly on its hinges, squeaking, pummeled by the wind as my Uncle Llynd and cousin Gandy hurried inside. Rain and fierce wind whipped around them, soaking the floor, slashing through their clothing, and driving across the wooden floor. Their hair hung in sodden clumps as water cascaded from their clothing.

Usually, they stood watch just outside the inn to keep trouble out. But right now, Cousin Gandy was supporting a man as tall as he was. The man was shrouded in a dark cloak, his face half-covered with a bright woven scarf. He clasped at his belly where blood poured between his fingers, shockingly scarlet. Everything he wore was too fine for this place – the cloth and ornamentation suggesting a faraway place. I swallowed down a wave of sudden fear. Foreigners brought trouble on their heels.

In Uncle Llynd's arms, a dark-skinned woman hung limp like a dead fish, her face grey in the bright light of the inn but splashed with the crimson of fresh blood. Her hair was dark and didn't disguise the subtle peaks of her ears or the sharpened features of her elfin face.

I'd only ever heard of the elfin before – never seen one with my own eyes.

Someone screamed – a little too late, as if their fear had only just caught up with them.

"Sweet fires preserve us," one of the pipers moaned.

The door banged against the wall again, a plaything of the wind, straining at its hinges. I hurried to fight it closed as my aunt Danna rushed out from behind the bar.

"Inn's as packed as a barrel of saltfish," she said authoritatively. "Put them in the girls' room." She caught my eye. "Sersha. Go with them."

I gave the door one last push, leaning all my weight against it until I heard the click of the latch, and then hurried after them, soaked to my skin and shivering after that single brush with the storm.

"I told you that wind was an ill one," one of the sailors muttered. The common room was so still that it carried over us all like a curse. "It carries with it malediction on all who are touched by the fingers of its wrath."

He couldn't have imagined then how right he would turn out to be.

2

We sleep in the back of the inn, in a few rooms clustered tightly together – one for my uncle and aunt, one for my two boy cousins, and two for the girls since there are five of them and me. By the time I caught up, my uncle was already draping the unconscious woman over my woolen blanket and Cousin Gandy was settling the man onto Mally's cot.

"Help her," the man whispered, so faintly that I barely caught the words. I doubted anyone else had. I usually heard things they didn't, since I spend all my time listening.

"We'll fetch supplies," Uncle Llynd said and I nodded distractedly as I checked the woman first.

She was still alive – shockingly – but her breath was thready and faint, her heartbeat slow. It was easy to see why. She'd been hit on the head hard enough that under that glossy black hair I found her skull was sunken in.

I gasped, my hand trembling as it pulled away. There would be no healing this. We could only make her comfortable and wait. I drew in a wavering breath, trying to steady myself. It wouldn't help anything to have my fingers shaking with horror.

When they settled, I opened the clasp of her cloak, freeing her throat, and carefully undid a few of the buttons of her high collar before tucking a blanket around her.

She whispered something in a language I did not know, and I felt a pang in my heart. There would be no one to understand her last words. No one to speak back words of comfort to her. With luck, she'd never know that, and she'd slip away quietly without feeling the pain of the mortal wound she'd suffered. It seemed too cruel to think that – but the alternative would be crueler yet. No one should die in agony. No one should die alone.

I swallowed down the urge to cry for her and put a second blanket over her motionless form. At least she could be warm and comfortable. I could give her that last gift.

I wiped my wet eyes.

Her friend needed tending.

He was out cold by the time I turned to him and I began to open his jacket and shirt so I could see his belly wound at the same moment that Aunt Danna came in with the supplies.

"I'll go for the midwife. Fon will see to the bar while I'm gone. And Mally will see to the customers," she said with a wry smile that held both judgment of her daughter's actions and pride intermingled. "And you'll tend these two, Sersha."

We had no healer in Landsfall. Just a midwife for births and deaths. And everything else was seen to as we could. He wouldn't be the first patient I'd tended. People liked it when I tended the sick. There was a superstition that the voiceless made the best healers because anything said to them in the throes of illness would stay secret.

I nodded my agreement and took the hot water and bowl from her, adding the herbs she handed me to the hot water. These frenta leaves made a strong astringent to clean the wound. That was good. She'd also brought feverfew and boneknit which I could give him if he woke again.

I dipped a cloth and set to work. I needed to clean the wound enough to see what we were dealing with. His breath hitched and I paused until it evened before working at the edges of the wound again. It looked clean – like a sharp blade had been run right through him. There was no hair or dirt in the wound that I could see.

I caught Aunt Danna's eye to try to show her the wound, signing that she should look but she waved the idea away.

"Yes, do whatever you need to with it, Sersha." She cleared her throat awkwardly. "I talked with Fon last night."

I froze for a moment and then went back to work. Why was she bringing this up now when I needed to focus?

My aunt always ran her ideas past my oldest cousin instead of Uncle Llynd. Maybe because Uncle Llynd said almost as little as I did no matter what he was asked. It meant talking to him was a lot like talking to yourself. He wouldn't even sign with me, just ignored me, and grunted if someone mentioned it.

"Fon doesn't think they'll take you at the Academy."

I gritted my teeth. I'd been counting on going. It was the only way I'd ever have a future beyond washing dishes and tables and making soup in the back room of the Hog's Head Inn. I could have even lived with that life if it had been permanent, but it wouldn't be.

Because as generous as Aunt Danna was, she had seven children. And even with Fon and Mally settled elsewhere, that left five more to settle. One would get the inn – probably Gandy who was next in age to Mally – and I was one too many to feed and house. Once he had a family of his own, there would be plenty of hands for cooking and cleaning here. And I'd be asked to find my own way to make room for them.

I shook my head in denial as I probed the wound. There was no bad smell to it.

Could it be possible this man was so lucky that the blade hadn't ruptured any organs? Maybe his luck would hold and he'd recover from this.

"Fon doesn't think they'll want you anywhere else either, Sersha. You need to be able to talk to do almost anything well – even serve pies from a cart. And you can't speak." She was trying to be kind – I could tell – but her words left wounds on my heart. It always came down to what I couldn't do instead of all the things I *could* do. "And why waste the money on your journey just to see you disappointed? You'll just have to stay here with us at the Hog's Head Inn. With Mally getting married next moon, I'll move Nessy into front of house and we'll all be so happy to have you running the back. You know what you're doing. It will give Nessy time to find her feet in Mally's place."

My heart made a painful little stutter. Because she wasn't wrong. It would work for now. And all my daydreams had always glossed over how I couldn't speak. They'd always highlighted what I *could* do which was work and listen. And in those dreams, the potential employers in the city had been pleased with my hard work and attentiveness and my voicelessness hadn't caused them to even blink. The real world was different. People noticed every discrepancy and picked at it like a loose thread in a shirt. It made things worse and worse and yet they couldn't help but keep on picking.

I eased the man onto his side and checked his back. His skin was shockingly pale and well-muscled for a man so slender, but there was no wound there. So perhaps the one he did have was shallow. The blade hadn't gone all the way through. I could stitch it, and hope for the best. He'd lost a lot of blood, though. That was worrisome. And I didn't know if I'd cleaned the wound in time. It could still become infected and give him a fever.

I bit my lip as I worked and tried not to think about how Fon would leave next week for his apprenticeship as a scribe for the Academy. You didn't get to be a real student, but you *did* get to learn to read and write, and you got to transcribe for the real scholars and work in the libraries. And if you were lucky, they kept you and paid you for the rest of your life and offered a pension when you were eighty – if you lived that long. One of the Academy Masters had selected Fon from among the hopefuls in the countryside to go and train with them.

And now I would remain at the inn until I faded into nothing more than a background for everyone else's lives.

"And you needn't fear, Sersha," my aunt said, setting a hand on my shoulder as I reached for the needle and thread that we kept in the little crate beside our cots. I'd almost forgotten she was there. "We know full well that the village lads aren't keen to marry you, but my girls are all full of energy and sass and they'll marry quickly. You'll be needed here for as long as you can stay. You shouldn't fear that you won't be."

Which was very generous. And so very, very heart-wrenchingly wrong.

Because my life had a ticking clock. Gandy would marry next year or the year after. And then I'd be one too many for this house. And all my aunt's generous heart and kindness wouldn't be enough to feed and house one extra person. I should just be grateful that she'd been doing it since I was a toddler and my parents were killed by raiders. She'd raised me with Fon – the same age as me minus a single moon – as if I were her own. But we both knew I wasn't that. I could never be that.

I was as unheeded as my voice. And being ignored was the thing I feared most.

My aunt left at the same moment that my needle bit into the skin of the unconscious man, my tears of disappointment washing his blood away as I worked to close his wound.

Whoever he was, he had more of a future than I did – even with this wound in his side.

I had just tied off the thread when the door opened with a loud creak.

3

Mother Mynta, the local midwife, wasn't much of one for privacy or politeness. Neither was useful to her.

"Danna found me at the Ranga birth," she said tiredly, wringing her long braid out so the water splashed across the floor. I frowned at that. I would be the one to have to clean it up – just like everything else. "Twins. Second one was breech. What a struggle." She yawned. "I've been up two days and nights in a row, and I want my bed, so, let's look to it then, shall we?"

I got up and led her to the woman, pointing to the dent in her head. Mynta grunted.

"No hope for her, Sersha," she said, confirming my fears. "The blankets are a kindness. If she wakes enough to take a dose, try to convince your aunt to give her some of the good stuff from behind the bar – dulls the pain. That's the best that can be done. Poor thing. Foreign. We won't even know what name to put on her stone. Let's see the other one, then."

She knelt by Mally's cot and examined the man there, checking his forehead for fever and then checking the wound I'd stitched. It was the first time I'd really had a good look at him.

He wasn't much older than me – nineteen or twenty maybe – with longish brown hair hanging wet around his pale face and more freckles than any person ought to have across his nose and cheeks and chest. I unwound the cloth that had been covering his face from his neck – it had fallen there in the commotion of getting him into the bed. His hands were surprisingly soft looking – like he hadn't even done dishes, never mind a man's work. And yet there was something about his face that made me think he was as likely to wink as Mally was – some kind of lingering good humor.

"A lordling, unless I miss my guess," Mynta said. "Maybe he'll give us the woman's name if he survives this. Maybe there will be a coin or two for your aunt and uncle in it, too. So, use your best herbs and let your aunt add that to his bill if he recovers. If he doesn't, the jacket will fetch enough to cover the expense."

I gasped. She didn't really mean we should rob the dead, did she?

"Don't look at me like that, girl." Mynta shook her head tiredly, rubbing her wrinkled forehead as if she could wipe away both her tiredness and years in a single motion. "Healers know that life is for the living and the dead are past caring. Try to keep him alive, and mayhap it won't come to that. Strip off these wet clothes and get him in dry blankets. And watch for fever. Your stitching is neat, and you chose right to do it quickly. He seems to have stopped bleeding so much, but who knows if something was nicked inside or if the wound is tainted. Did you clean it?"

I nodded.

She seemed pleased at that. "Then get feverfew into him as soon as you can, and willow bark tea, and make sure he's dry and rested. Someone needs to sit with him all night and it can't be me. I'm so tired I might fall asleep right now."

I nodded at that, too. She looked like she was already half asleep.

She fussed with his jacket, almost as if she was deciding if it really would cover my aunt's expenses at helping him, and then she paused, drawing something from the pocket. It was a small silver disk wrapped in a piece of parchment, wet and blurred from the rain with a picture drawn on it of something that looked a bit like a constellation. I'd seen that pattern before.

I was sure of it.

But where?

There was writing above it, too, but neither of us knew our letters.

"Maybe you should let it dry out," Mynta said slowly. "He might need it for something."

I nodded as she examined the disk. It was the size of my palm and so shiny you could see your face in it.

"Been a while since I saw a mirror," Mynta said wistfully. "The years have not been kind."

I shook my head at that, and she laughed harshly, laying the mirror beside the parchment on the little bedside table.

"Best not to look into it, Sersha. Women are better off not knowing what we look like." And with that, she eased herself back to her feet, moaning and sighing as she rose and tottered out of the room, calling over her shoulder, "I'll return in the morning if the inn is still standing."

And then she was gone, leaving me with the two strangers in my care.

I stared at them helplessly for a moment and then set to work, stripping off wet clothing and hanging them on the little string in the corner that we used to dry our dresses.

It gave me something to do other than feel bad for myself.

I had no future. I needed to accept that. I could at least make my present count for something.

But every time I looked at the fine stitching on the jacket I was hanging up, at the silver embroidery worked across the chest and sleeves, at the silky lining inside, I thought of the apprentices in the city who would have labored over the jacket. Every time my eyes stole toward the mirror on the table, I thought of the silversmith and the apprentices who would carry water for him and pump the bellows. And I couldn't help but think that there must be a place for me in this world somewhere, if I could just carve it out.

A place where I could be useful.

And as the night grew long, I looked often at the faces of the strangers and wondered what their place might be. Had they been seafarers? Or nobles riding on some glorious adventure?

Perhaps the townsfolk knew the answer, but no one else came all night as the darkness descended and the storm blew on, rattling the timbers of the roof and making my heart leap into my throat.

The candle clock said it was past midnight when the man moaned the first time. A spear of despair struck through me when I felt his head.

Fever.

And after that, the next hours were spent bathing his head and chest with cool water and hoping he could fight off what ailed him.

Twice, I stole into the quiet kitchen to boil water for feverfew tea and gather fresh rags. The rest of the inn had settled into a fitful slumber and there was no one to note what I did or didn't do.

I tried to get feverfew into the man's lips, but he sputtered and spat and refused it, leaving a sour worry in my mouth. If I couldn't get him to take his medicine, the fever would keep raging.

But in this, as in everything, I felt helpless.

It was a little before dawn when the storm broke and the wind began to settle. I opened the shutter and looked out into the grey of pre-dawn, letting the coolness bathe some of my exhaustion away.

A terrible, gurgling moan came from my bed.

I hurried over to the cot where the woman lay. I reached for her hand as she thrashed in the blankets. It was moments like this that I most wished I could talk – could comfort with words where looks just felt like not enough.

Instead, I stroked her hair and blew quiet shushing sounds – that much I could do. She settled for a moment, her eyes gazing at me blankly, and then her hand thrust toward mine and her fingers uncurled their death grip as the first rays of dawn washed over her dark face.

For a moment, her eyes seemed to focus on mine as she shoved something in my hand, and then they went blank and she fell back into the blankets, her eyes glazed with the fog of death.

I swallowed, blinking back sudden tears, and opened my palm.

It was full of black ashes.

4

I didn't have the heart to get rid of the ashes.

I stared at them in my palm for long minutes. This woman had been someone important. She'd lived a life that probably didn't involve washing an endless stream of dishes or peeling potatoes for soup. And when it was over, all she'd had to hand on to the next person was a handful of ashes. A clump of black flakes and grey dust that made my palm itch a little.

I blinked away tears and after long moments, I brought my breathing back under control and put the ashes in the pocket of my dress. I felt silly doing it. And yet there had been something about the way she'd given them to me that felt like a last request.

Throwing them away would be wrong.

Burying them with her would be just as bad.

And I couldn't have explained why, I just knew it in my heart.

The storm had faded to a heavy mist when we brought her body out to the stable and stitched the blanket around her as we always do for our dead.

"Bury her when the mist clears," Uncle Llynd advised practically and strode back to his job watching the front of the inn.

My aunt Danna went back inside, too, worried about Mistress Mynta. She'd arrived just after dawn to take a turn watching the patients, but her eyes were still heavy with exhaustion.

It was my turn to sleep.

But I didn't want to go back into the inn to my bed where this woman had just died. I didn't want to have to think about how meaningless my life was – and how quickly it could be snatched away.

Instead, I found a place in the straw of the stable, curled into a ball, and slept the morning away there.

"He's getting worse," Mistress Mynta told me, in late afternoon when I roused myself to spell her off of her duties. The thin pallet that was usually on my cot was hanging outside to air out. She'd been kind enough to clean the bedding for me. "I managed to get a little tea into him, but you need to try again as soon as you can. I've already brewed feverfew and willow. I even put a little honey in it for the flavor. Get him to drink something. I need to check on the newborn twins."

And then she was off again. I took up the cloth to wash his lined forehead and dutifully watched him.

Who was he out in the wide world? Was he carrying some important message? Or perhaps he *was* the important thing – a prince perhaps, or a knight. Maybe they'd been waylaid by usurpers to the crown. Or maybe by brigands. Maybe he alone knew a secret too dark to let out.

Or maybe she was the precious thing and he'd taken that wound trying to protect her. Maybe, when he woke and found her dead, he would go mad with grief.

I reached into my pocket and felt at the ashes there, stroking them between my fingers. What secret could ashes possibly hold? And what significance? They must have meant something for the foreign woman to have given them to me. Unless she was so far removed from sanity that she didn't know what she was doing. Maybe she was simply clutching them because they were in her hand when she was struck over the head. The young man must have brought her a long way before they stumbled to Uncle Llynd at our door. No one had seen a ship or horses. We always noticed things that were out of place in this town. There was so little variety that a change stuck out like a blue horse.

I was pulled out of my daydream by a sharp pain in my chest.

I clutched my palm to the pain, smearing black ash across the front of my dress. Sparks! It would be hard to wash that out.

A second pain flared, worse than the first and hot – like I was burning on the inside.

I bit my lip and sucked in a long breath, gasping as the agony filled me, leaving my head spinning and nausea rising up through my throat. I lunged for the bucket in the corner just in time to empty myself.

And still, it seared through me.

I was on fire on the inside.

I was burning up.

I was going to die.

Little half-breaths were rippling out of my throat as I stumbled through the door and out into the hall, past the shocked face of my youngest cousin Marra and out through the bustling kitchen.

There was a crash. Mally had dropped a plate. I pushed past her, not caring about dishes when the pain was so intense.

"Sersha? Are you hurt?"

I shoved the door open and stumbled out into the heavy fog, running as if I could get away from the pain if I just ran fast enough. I hit the side of Old Duggan's shed and spun, uncertain where I was as I clawed at my chest.

Make it stop.

Make it stop.

My pulse roared in my ears as the flames licked me from within.

I stumbled uphill, kicking rocks, smashing into branches, scratching at my chest, my throat, my chin. The pain burned and burned and burned, filling me up until nothing else was inside me but that.

Behind, I heard voices calling, but they were faint, and I couldn't have answered anyway.

Tears rolled down my face as I clambered up the crown of the hill and collapsed on the ground, clutching at my chest. Darkness descended, leaving me shrouded in the black of night.

I would die here.

This was the end.

And it didn't even matter that this was my death. I had no future, anyway.

No future?

A voice – raw and almost spitting – spoke to me, and it seemed to be coming from inside my chest. I looked down by instinct. Light glowed from my torso with such brilliance that it pierced through my dress and lit the ground nearby, making the fog glow.

What in the –?

Who has no future?

I was going insane. I had no voice – but now I had one in my head.

No voice? I hear your voice loud and clear in your heart. It is very bright indeed. But where is Veela?

You can ... you can hear me think?

I can hear you feel *and that is even stronger. Who are you, little human?*

My heart was racing so fast that it felt tight and tense like the string of a bow. What was happening to me?

I needed to calm down. I was Sersha. I was a simple village girl in the coastal town of Landsfall.

Sersha. The voice said the name as if it was savoring it, but then I felt a burst of panic inside me, sharp and jagged. But *I* wasn't feeling panicked. It was as if the feeling was independent of me.

I am the one who is panicked! The voice sounded just as erratic as the feeling. *Where is Veela? Where?*

Who was Veela?

Veela is a Flame Rider, powerful among her people, one hundred years my friend and companion. She is strong of spirit and firm of purpose.

Was she an elfin? An elfin with short dark hair, a slight build, and really rich wine-colored clothes?

Yes! The voice sounded eager now.

An elfin with a young man for a friend who had been stabbed with a sword?

Perhaps. And now it sounded wary.

I tried very hard not to think of Veela. Not to think of her wounded in my cot. Not to think of the ashes in her hand.

Noooo!

The voice sounded like the howl of a wolf as it ripped through my heart and mind. My head felt like it would split in two. I gripped it in both hands as the howl went on and on.

She gave you something, the voice said, a little breathlessly when it was done, as if part of it were still howling while the rest was speaking to me.

Ashes. A handful of ashes.

The howling stuttered to a stop and there was a pause that felt heavy, as if it carried something in its quiet.

The master passes the ashes down to her successor and so the Phoenix is reborn in a new heart. And some of who the new Flame Rider is bleeds into the Phoenix as he loses the flavor of his old Flame Rider.

Flame Rider? What was that?

Untouched by flame. Unburned by fire. Bound by ash and oath to her phoenix. That is the Flame Rider. And I have lost mine. She has taken the great journey to the beyond without me.

I'd never been able to apologize to anyone before. But I felt like I should now.

I wish I could have saved her.

There is a deep well of compassion within you.

I wished I could have taken her place.

The voice paused as if considering that. And when he spoke again, he sounded like he could barely think the words.

She chose well. She did. You are deep of heart and true in courage. We shall soar together, little hawk. The Phoenix and the Flame Rider.

He was a phoenix? Like the bright burning birds of legend? I looked around me, wishing I could catch a glimpse of bright flames of a flutter of a wing.

I am within you.

And you'll stay here then? In my heart? Burning up?

The rumbling in my chest felt like a sorrowful laugh.

You are my home now, little hawk. But do not fear the fire. It will not burn you up – or not any more than fires of the heart always do.

What could that possibly mean? Fires of the heart?

Passions. Obsessions. Visions. Surely you have known people who burn to create or to excel. It burns them up – but not in a bad way. Without the burning, there would be no soaring.

I took a long breath. It wasn't going to kill me. Or at least not right away. I could breathe. I could take a moment to calm down.

Cup your hands and hold them out in front of you.

I did as I was asked, cupping each hand, and raising it in front of me.

No, no, hold them together. We're both being reborn here.

We were being what?

I shifted my hands so that they formed a bowl and as soon as I did, a glowing egg appeared in them. It seemed to be made of molten fire.

I gasped, nearly dropping the egg.

Steady now. This hurts me, too. I must let go of Veela, my true friend, to embrace you.

Then he shouldn't let go.

Where she has gone, I cannot follow.

I swallowed a lump in my throat. I knew what it was like to be abandoned by those you loved. My parents hadn't wanted to leave me. But they'd had to go when they were taken from this life.

We must be reborn, the phoenix breathed and then the egg cracked like a branch snapping and something that looked like fiery honey poured out of it. I was sure it would burn my hands. I began to pull away.

Keep steady, now!

I gritted my teeth and kept my hands in place and then, struggling out of the thick, flaming honey, emerged a bright, blazing bird.

5

The bird shook himself, splashing molten honey droplets in every direction. His scarlet feathers were edged in bright flame and his black eyes held tiny flames of their own. He was not just beautiful but also deadly. His beak and talons were sharper than any bird's I'd ever seen.

Bird? A phoenix is no bird.

He looked awfully bird-like not to be a type of bird.

You look awfully ape-like not to be a type of ape, but you don't hear me mentioning it.

What in all the world was an ape?

Better that you don't know.

A streak of red fire spilled from his eye and down his cheek.

I reached for it, gently, so gently, wiping it away.

I feel as though there is a hole in my heart. Even now that I am new and fresh, he said.

I bit my lip, wiping a second tear from his eye. He was just like me. Hurting. Alone.

Broken. Bereft.

He preened his feathers sadly and then leapt from my hands to a rock on the grass beside me. I sank to my knees with him. If I could take his hurt I would.

If I could take yours, I would, too.

I smiled slightly. But I was not the one who was hurting. He tilted his head slightly to the side.

Aren't you? It feels as though you are.

The night was cold, the ground soaked and muddy from the storm, but it felt wrong for this magical creature to perch on the sodden ground and I'd thought that phoenixes would be bigger.

You try being reborn and attaining your normal size in a single day. Demanding, aren't you, little hawk?

But there was a shudder in his teasing that sounded as though he was disguising pain.

In the distance, I still heard voices calling for me, but they were growing fainter. Perhaps people were giving up trying to find me in the thick fog.

I should probably go and show them that I was safe and unhurt. But I didn't want to leave him here. He was hurting and all alone. He deserved to at least have one friend here to comfort him.

Are you my friend, then, little hawk?

I could be. I would be if he would let me.

And I am yours. You are a true friend to me and so I make this vow. I will be bound to you until you die and I leave to journey without you. Until the end of your days and the last burst of your energy, I shall be your boon companion.

There was a bitter tinge to his words as if he was thinking of the last person he'd said that to.

My mouth felt dry at his words. They were too big. They were too much. No one should vow to be with me forever. No one *would* if they knew what that meant.

I know what it means, and you're wrong. The words aren't too big. They're too small. If I could promise you more than this, I would.

But why make any promise? He was a free phoenix. He could fly off and let the winds take him wherever he would.

I cannot. You hold my heart.

I held nothing. And if he should pick to bind himself to anyone, maybe he should think about getting to know them first.

I told you, you hold my heart. There is nothing deeper than that. I cannot know anyone better than I will know you. I cannot wish anyone more happiness than I will wish for you.

I opened my hands, spreading my fingers wide. There was no heart in them.

I felt the echo of a laugh inside my chest.

I see smears of ash on your chest and face. That is my heart, little hawk. You wear it on cheek and breast like warpaint, like a talisman to ward off evil. And it is right that you have chosen to display me so boldly, for now, I rise to the challenge and pledge myself in return.

And was I meant to pledge the same thing?

You could – but I will die with the dawn. And your display of my ashes is more than enough.

My breath caught in my throat. He would die with the dawn? This gorgeous bright creature would only live for a single night? It felt like a crime. Like it couldn't be right.

I shivered at the thought.

You are cold. When a phoenix is your friend, you should never be cold. How will we go on righteous quests together if you freeze to death?

How did he expect to quest at all in the length of a single night?

Worry not about that.

I supposed I should at least be glad that he'd never find out I was not good at quests, not good at much of anything beyond tending the sick, cooking, and cleaning.

Sit on this rock. The ground is too wet for sitting.

He fluttered up into the air and I complied. The rock was wide and slightly slanted so that all the rain ran off. I could stretch out across it entirely if I wanted to. But I was cold to the bone. I needed to huddle in on myself to keep warm.

To my surprise, the phoenix swooped through the air and landed on my lap. Was he bigger now? He felt heavy. And hot. Hot enough that suddenly my shivering was gone. I leaned into the heat, letting it wash over me.

I must sing the song of remembrance for Veela. It will take me until dawn, but it must be done. Stay with me.

I really shouldn't. I should go down and set my family's minds at ease. I should let them know I was not hurt or missing. I should go back to work tending the injured stranger.

Judicus Franzer Irault.

Who?

Veela's companion was Judicus Franzer Irault. That must be who you are tending.

Yes, him. I definitely shouldn't be settling down on the rock with my head pillowed on my arm and my body wrapped around a burning bird.

Phoenix. Get that right or I'll launch into the sky and leave you here to shiver.

There was a slight teasing tone to his mental voice, but I corrected myself anyway.

Phoenix.

But I couldn't leave him here to mourn alone. Especially not when he was about to spend the rest of his life for this one thing. It seemed – sacred. Honorable.

Respect blossomed within as I settled myself to wait with him.

His song started low and quiet – a mournful keening that made my heart weep. And as he continued, the song, slowly built on itself, higher and louder, unearthly and yet lovely. I wanted to talk more to him, and yet I didn't want to interrupt what sounded like deep sorrow mixed with memories.

My eyelids were drooping, despite my hardest efforts to keep awake. I felt safe. I felt like someone was listening to me for the first time in my life. I never wanted to let go of that feeling.

I hear you, little hawk. I hear your heart.

It was so, so good, that I didn't think I could stand it.

And then the singing turned to a wild dirge of despair and passion. It might rip me apart. My tears began to flow with his fiery ones as the music rose, fire and water, human and phoenix, we were bound in this moment as one.

In self-defense, my mind shut off and I fell deeply into sleep.

I woke to a whisper in my mind.

Dawn comes quickly. Rise, my little hawk.

6

I sat up, horrified at the dull glow on the very edge of the horizon.

I'd wasted the night sleeping. A lump formed in my throat.

And where was the brokenhearted phoenix?

He wasn't curled up beside me anymore. I stood up, frantic.

Over here. And my name is Kazmerev.

Kazmerev. It was a name with an adventure inside it.

My breath stuck in my chest at the sight of him. He stood beside the rock, but now he was the size of a horse. His dark feathers flickered, flames edging them, gusting into brilliance as little gouts of flame burst from the tips. Now, rather than small and innocent, he looked huge and deadly.

And he was about to go. About to leave me.

Sorrow plummeted through my heart. It had been so good to be heard by him. It had been so good to be near his warmth and sit with him in his sorrow. I *liked* him. So much.

I shall miss you, too, little hawk.

Sersha. I wanted him to know my name, at least.

I shall miss you, Sersha. May the dawn bring new hope.

Tension wrung my stomach as the mist slowly lightened and turned gold and then light flared bright and golden, slicing through the mist. The moment it hit him, he vanished in a puff of what looked like ash. Frantic, I tried to catch the little feathers of ash floating down but as quickly as I caught them, they faded into nothing.

My eyes stung with tears as the mist around me burned off the ground and the light warmed the rock and the grass.

One night of magic.

And I'd slept through it all.

Sersha, you will never have a future because you can't even seize the moment when it drops right into your lap. You don't speak up for what you want even when you *do* have a voice.

I forced that voice of blame down. It would do me no good now.

Swiping away the hot tears, I gritted my jaw.

Enough.

Self-pity didn't help. Letting myself mourn for something I thought was impossible yesterday would just ruin the few glorious minutes I'd had. I should treasure them instead. It was like owning a pearl necklace for a day. Couldn't you just enjoy it instead of being angry that you couldn't keep it?

I would try to embrace gratitude instead of loss. I would try for joy.

I sniffed, drawing my despair back within and squaring my shoulders. There was work to do. I had shirked for too long.

I peered down from the hill, trying to see where I'd ended up outside of town. I was on one of the hills inland, looking over our sleeping town. The mist had fully retreated from the hills and as I watched, it burned off the town, revealing glowing smoke trails from every chimney reaching ambitiously toward the bright sky. The edge of the sea shone like silver – so bright it hurt my eyes and left little dark specks across my vision.

Wait.

Those were not specks caused by light. Those were boats.

Strange boats.

Almost at our shore.

My breath caught in my throat and I picked up my skirts and ran.

Raiders.

There were raiders here and the girl without the voice was the only one who had seen them. My feet felt loud as they struck the ground, each step like a drumbeat – but they weren't nearly loud enough.

We hadn't seen raiders since I was a little child. Not since my own parents were killed in a raid. Not since I lost my voice.

My heart was beating faster than my feet could fly and my lungs couldn't catch up. Panic clawed up my throat and I forced it back by sheer willpower.

I didn't remember the raiders killing my parents or taking my voice and Aunt Danna said that was a small miracle and that I shouldn't think on it. Not now. Not ever.

I thought about it now as I raced for the town.

Push, Sersha, push! Run with all your might!

If I didn't run hard and fast who might lose parents today? Who might lose a voice or a hand or their livelihood? There was never much in our little town for raiders to take – no chapel here with golden edged books or silver-plated relics. No lord here with fine fabrics and stocks of weapons. No merchants here with oils and spices. There were only the fishermen and the potter and the blacksmith and the ale at the inn.

Our family's inn.

My muscles burned as I ran and my throat burned with them with the aching longing to speak, to yell, to scream my warning.

If only the phoenix had not died with the dawn. He could have warned them all. Maybe he even could have fought for us. Could phoenixes fight? I hadn't asked Kazmarev.

I reached the edge of the empty town. We didn't post regular guards. Why bother in a sleepy town like ours?

A rooster crowed, lonely and with regret, as though he had slept through his most important night just like me.

A few houses over, the butcher's dog howled, and someone called for his quiet. There were the sounds of wood being split for morning cook fires, of sleepy people stepping out to use the back house. A baby cried somewhere.

And over it all the harshness of my breath sawed across my ears as I ran headlong, lungs screaming with strain, toward the center of town. The well was there. And so was the warning bell.

I'd never rung it before.

They rang it on feast days and the change of the year, but that was a coveted honor. I'd heard it ring the night of the fire, too. We'd lost half the stables that night and a horse.

I needed to ring it now.

I needed to get there before the raiders got to us.

I reached the bell at the same moment that my cousin Mally – startled and wide-eyed – leaned against the well beside it. She carried a pair of buckets on a pole and she dropped them when she saw me.

I wouldn't have stopped to explain this to her even if I had a voice. This was too desperate. Too urgent.

"Sersha! We've all been looking for you! Where were you all night?"

The bell was on the top of a small wooden tower and the rope was tied just out of reach, up one of the three tower legs. If it was left where anyone could handle it, then the children would ring it.

I clambered up the leg of the tower, struggling for enough purchase to catch the rope.

"What are you doing, Sersha? Have you lost your mind?"

I ignored Mally, snatching the rope with one clawing hand, and pulling with all my might.

Bling Blang

Bling Blang

My heart was hammering faster than the bell when my cousin reached for me.

"You've gone crazy! First, you run off and now the bell? What's gotten into you, Sersha? I told Mama that it was a bad idea to tell you about staying here. Wait, I told her. Wait until he goes. She'll just get upset."

I dodged her grip on my arm, but she managed to grab my skirt and tug me down from my precarious place at the bell.

I spun, looking her in the eye with my best no-nonsense look.

Her gasp told me she understood that I thought this was important, that I shouldn't be stopped.

I needn't have bothered.

A scream ripped through the town, followed by a roar of voices.

7

"Sersha! Sersha, come on!" My cousin tugged at my dress, stumbling in her frantic efforts to pull me after her. I found my balance in the mud and grabbed her hand, running with her toward the Hog's Head Inn as screams rippled out from the edge of the village.

The sign of the Hog's Head squeaked as it swung frantically in the stirring winds, dislodging a crow with an angry squawk as my uncle Llynd and cousin Gandy slammed the door behind them. They both gripped heavy cudgels and Llynd held a meat cleaver in his left hand.

"Inside," Uncle Llynd grunted when he saw us, not bothering to stop as he trotted toward the screams. His bluff face was set against the violence ahead. Gandy's mouth was screwed up in concentration. This would be the first fight he'd been in that didn't involve dragging drunken patrons off each other.

My stomach did a flip at the sight of them ready for battle and my gaze dragged after them as if I could keep them safe just by watching.

"Hurry, Sersha!" Mally reminded me, her tugs frantic. "Mama will need our help barring the doors and shuttering the windows!"

We scrambled inside only to nearly be knocked back again by Aunt Danna. She held a cast iron pan in both her fists, her face set with determination.

"Girls!" She puffed out a relieved breath. "Mally, get these windows shuttered and then get the other pan! Sersha, go check that the little girls are not leaving their room and check on that injured man."

"Madam innkeeper?" someone from the stairs called down. "Are we in danger?"

"No, no," Aunt Danna said, her voice changing from fierce determination to forced cheerfulness. "We'll be fine here, just stay in your room. I'll send Sersha up with tea in a moment."

Of course, it would be me. This was one of those moments when it was handy to have staff who couldn't panic your patrons by saying the wrong thing. I frowned at that. I didn't like being used.

I hurried into the back to obey.

My youngest cousins were playing happily on the floor of their bedroom and I made signs to tell them to stay put. They ignored me but seemed interested in staying where they were, so I moved on.

The injured man lay still in Mally's bed.

Judicus Franzer Irault. That's what Kazmarev had called him.

I checked his wound. It was angry looking and very swollen, but when I sniffed it, I smelled no rot. The wound had not turned bad, but unless we could beat back whatever was making it swell, he wouldn't be moving from this bed.

Carefully, I cleaned the skin again and rebandaged the wound, and then checked his forehead. He was burning up. I wet a cloth, wrung it out, and put it on his forehead. He needed more feverfew tea. I'd have to brew that.

I paused for a moment, scanning his pale face, looking for signs of anything I was missing. His expression was drawn and his cheeks sunken.

Did he know his companion had died? Did he know what that meant for her phoenix friend?

I drew in a worried breath and bit my lip. Were those raiders after him? Was that what drew them to our shores after so many years?

A sheen of sweat coated his brow.

And then all at once, his eyes shot open and his hand grabbed my wrist. I froze, my hand still in the act of bathing his forehead.

"Ashani masai tanarentak," he whispered and then shook his head violently and said, "the ai'sletta. In this town. There's a medallion in my pocket. Take it."

I shook my head. He was delirious.

"Take it," he begged me. "The ai'sletta must be kept safe. Take the medallion and use it to find ..."

He passed out again and I let out a long breath. He must not know where he was. There was no ai'sletta here – whatever that was. We were just common folk.

But I checked his coat pocket anyway. And I drew out a bronze medallion. On one side it held a small turquoise stone and on the other, there was a pattern that looked like a constellation.

I squinted as I looked at it, shocked to realize that the pattern really did look familiar. I just couldn't remember where I'd seen it before. Was it a star constellation? No.

I shook my head. There was no time for Ai'sletta's right now anyway. I tucked the medallion in my pocket. And hurried away to brew him more feverfew and take tea up to the frantic guests above.

I was halfway up the stairs with a tray when something crashed into the door of the inn, making the whole place shudder.

My tray crashed to the ground, crockery breaking and tea spilling everywhere. A second crash and I fell against the wall, barely breaking my fall. I bit my tongue and tasted blood.

The raiders had reached the inn.

8

I reached for the tray, my hand shaking as I scrambled to collect shards of pottery from the hot spill. My aunt's voice cut through my panic.

"Sersha! The children. Defend the children!"

I dropped the shards, rushing down the steps and stumbling around the corner into the kitchen, nearly bumping into Mally as she rounded the corner, the second cast iron pan in her capable hands.

"Mally!" my aunt called. Her voice held an edge. She was barely holding in her own fear.

The sound of splintering wood made my heart speed. They were at our door.

"Right here!" my cousin called calmly, joining her mother in front of the door, pan raised. The bar across the door shook as something crashed into the inn a third time.

My mouth was dry, hands shaking. But I must be brave, too. I turned and raced into the kitchen, snatched up a knife, and hurried into the back rooms.

The small girls were still playing on the floor. At the sight of my knife, they froze. I put my index finger over my lips to quiet them and beckoned them to my room. It would be easier to protect everyone if I kept them all in one place. And that meant keeping them in the sick room.

Four sets of owlish eyes stared at me as they crowded together into the corner beside my bed. I swallowed. I must not fail them.

There was a cry from the common room and an explosion of splintering wood and shouts crashed across my hearing. I raised the kitchen knife and squared my stance.

Feet thundered as Mally's screams echoed through the halls. And then there was so much noise it was hard to pick out one sound from the next. Feet were on the stairs, in the common room, in the kitchen, in the hall. Battlecries rang out and screams of terror and pain. The clang of metal on metal and sickening crashes and thumps.

My heart was in my throat and the point of my knife wavered as my stomach did flip flops.

My cousin Fon's voice was loud in the kitchen – but his words were unintelligible and ended abruptly.

The raiders were right outside the door.

I swallowed, sweat breaking out on my forehead. I glanced behind me a second time. Four small children clutched each other, silent tears tracking down their faces. One knife was in my hands. It wasn't enough. I couldn't keep them safe on my own.

I heard the girl's door down the hall open with a crash as it hit the wall inside. Then my aunt and uncle's. Something rattled our door handle and then with a splintering pop, the door flew inward, smashing against the wall.

I gritted my teeth, knife raised, as the raider flowed into the room like a living shadow.

If I'd had a voice, I would have been screaming defiance. Or maybe just screaming.

I'd never seen a man like this before. He was deathly pale, their skin sallow in a way that suggested illness. A dark cloak flapped around him and his swords were perfectly straight with no curve to them at all. Worse, his face was masked by cloth drawn over mouth and nose so that I was left wondering at what manner of face might lie beneath the swaths of cloth. Only his yellow eyes showed above the mask.

My mouth was drier than good firewood, and my thoughts skittered across my mind like water on a hot pan, but I kept the knife up. I would slash and hack until there was nothing left of me.

Behind me, one of the girls' sobs became audible.

The man tilted his head to the side. When he spoke, the words sounded like ripping cloth.

"Akenash atrenna. Akenash Ai'sletta. Akenash."

If I'd had a voice, I would have warned him away. I would have spoken words of bravado and courage.

Since I had none, I could merely stare at him, mutely, my eyes speaking for me.

Don't give an inch Sersha. Don't let him know you are afraid.

I gritted my teeth.

He strode forward, hands so quick they made lightning look sluggish. He lifted me up by the front of the dress before I could gasp, his other hand batting away my clumsy knife attack.

Behind me, one of my small cousins screamed like a bird driven from a perch with the throw of a stone.

"Ai'sletta!" the raider repeated. "Ka."

I was trembling all over as he shook me and to my horror, two more men stepped into the room, one of them reaching for my little cousin Lis as she sobbed, frozen in place by terror. She was just six.

I flexed my knife hand, trying again to fight back, but the raider struck a blow so hard that my knife flew from my hand, clattering to the floor.

I'd lost before I'd started. And so had my little cousins.

Tears welled up in my eyes as they screamed.

My breath felt like it was ripping my chest apart.

And then something that looked like a dark purple rope skittered past us. It reached up, branching, one branch shooting toward the raider reaching for Lis, the other toward the neck of the one holding me. The ropes twisted sinuously up, wrapping themselves around my attacker and the other raider.

Foreign words poured from their mouths, but now they sounded more like pleas than threats. The ropes flexed, shaking the raiders so hard that I was thrown free. I fell to the ground. Clawing my way back up in time to see three men motionless on the floor. The ropes were slithering back to a point behind me. I spun to find my patient pushed up on one arm, eyes drooping, and face pale.

He said something in a language I didn't know and when I stared at him blankly, he shifted to something I could understand.

"Help me up. I cannot stand on my own."

I wanted to object that he was too injured, but his green eyes flashed, and he nodded slightly toward my small cousins.

"Don't risk children when you have a rope worker of Vetara in your midst."

Hastily, I scrambled to his side and helped him stand. He really couldn't stand on his own. He could barely stand with my arm under him. I wavered under the weight, stumbling forward as he shuffled beside me, head lolling forward and dark hair falling to half-cover his eyes. We wobbled into the empty hall, my gaze flicking over each broken door.

I looked over my shoulder to my huddled cousins, sobbing in the corner. They needed an adult with them. But I'd seen how Judicus had killed those raiders with the black ropes – magic? – and I knew he might be the only hope to drive these raiders back. Without his help, our town was no match against trained warriors, and we would just die together when the next men came through the broken door. My cousin's best hope was in Judicus and I could not help huddled back there with them.

I signed to them to hide and wait for help and then turned back to my charge.

We shuffled into the chaos of the kitchen. Bowls and spoons had been flung around the room as if the person hurrying through had just been trying to create chaos and nothing more. Someone had spilled the pea soup across the hearth and they were already darkening where they came close the flames. It would take all day to clean this mess.

Underneath the wreck of the table lay my cousin Fon. I clasped a hand over my mouth and looked away, blinking back dry tears at what I'd seen in his glassy eyes. He would never take that job as an apprentice at the academy.

"Nice place you have here," Judicus muttered. "I can see why you're so keen to keep it intact."

Maybe it was a good thing I was voiceless right now. It kept me from snapping at him. I drew in a long, shuddering breath. I needed to hold myself together. I needed to get Judicus to where he could help.

Mally cried out in the common room, a panicked sound to her voice and Judicus seemed to focus on the sound, leaning toward it. I steered him in that direction, stumbling a little under his weight. He wasn't a large man. But he wasn't carrying any of his own weight, he'd put it all on my shoulders.

We shoved through the door and I bit the inside of my cheek to keep from crying out, too. My aunt Danna lay motionless next to the door, her cast iron pan wedged in the wreckage of the inn door. Someone in the rooms above us was screaming hysterically.

But it was Mally I was worried for. She was wedged in the back corner of the common room, swinging her frying pan wildly as a group of raiders surrounded her, swords drawn. One of them lunged just enough to taunt her, laughing when she swung her pan toward him.

Fear gripped my heart with icy hands. I had to keep blinking to push the tears away so I could see.

Judicus muttered something grim sounding and then he spread his palm and dark ropes poured from it onto the ground, spreading out like roots, clawing across the floor, over Aunt Danna, over a raider slumped on the floor a few steps from where she lay, and up the legs and backs of the men surrounding Mally.

Mally shrank further back, her face growing pale as a raider lunged forward. One of the ropes coiled swiftly around his neck and he was yanked back toward us with a jerk. The rope shook him like a cloth doll, but even as my mouth fell open at the sight, four more ropes were twisting around the remaining raiders, tightening around their necks so that they choked, flailing against the pull.

It shook them worse than a ship in a grand storm and then dropped them, broken and limp, to the floor.

Mally let out a shuddering breath and dropped her pan, racing to her mother.

"Mama?"

"The door," Judicus said, his voice weak and thready. "Take me out to the street. There will be more. They're coming for the Ai'sletta just as I am. They must be stopped."

I wanted to ask what the Ai'sletta was. I wanted to ask why they were all here in our little town all of a sudden. No one had ever been here before searching for an ai'sletta. What had changed about that now?

But I couldn't ask my questions, so I bit my lip and supported him with an arm around his waist as we stumbled forward.

"Mally?"

I let out a shuddering breath at Aunt Danna's voice. She was alive.

"Go find your little sisters." Her voice was shaky. "They're with Sersha. Go on now, I'll be right as rain in a moment."

Her voice sounded strained, but she was speaking. I glanced back at Mally who met my eyes with grim judgment. But if I hadn't left the girls in the back there would have been no one to save her life. There was no time to feel gratitude for what had been saved. A crash from the floor above reminded me of that. This wasn't over. Not even close.

We lurched out the door into the madness beyond.

9

The Hog's Head Inn was in the center of town. Stumbling out the door gave us an immediate ability to see just how bad things were. The bell tower had been knocked over, and the bell had a big crack running up its side.

Across the street, Tyndale's forge was lost in flame along with the bakery to one side of it. Old Ferris was trying to put out the fire on the roof of the fishmonger on the other side of it, but the wind was whipping up the flames like a goodwife with a bowl of batter. It spun and whirled, spreading as fast as he could throw water across the blaze.

There were bodies in the street. I didn't want to look at them. I didn't want to know whose they were. I shuddered remembering Fon laid out on the kitchen floor. I didn't want to see anyone else like that.

We'd barely taken a step out of the door when a roar met my ears.

Uncle Llynd charged out from an alley, Gandy on one side of him and Tyndale on the other, his blacksmith's hammer raised high. Behind them, a scattered group of townsfolk followed, roaring with them.

They plunged across the street to where a knot of raiders emerged from Jensen's house, his teenage daughter caught between them.

I'd watched roosters attack before and this collision looked like that. A sudden screeching roar, movements so fast you couldn't catch them all, a flurry of fury and terror. A weapon flew through the air – one of the too-straight swords – and a bellow cut of abruptly.

It was over faster than I thought possible, poor Nella sobbing on her knees, and those who had tried to steal her from us lying around her in heaps.

Not all the heaps on the ground were raiders, though. One was Carsden from the docks. The flower of blood on his jerkin was proof he'd been heart-stabbed.

My uncle looked winded, his eyes wide and nostrils flaring like a frightened horse. There was blood on one side of his head, and he'd lost his knife.

With a long battle cry, a knot of raiders sprinted out from behind the stable, swords out, their eyes fixed on my uncle and the other men from our town. Tyndale raised his hammer and Gandry the cudgel he held, but their eyes were wide with the understanding that they were too few for this fight. Twenty raiders thundered toward them – all armed with their straight swords, all screaming defiance at the cluster of village men with their mismatched weapons and wide eyes.

"Here we go, then. Get ready to catch me," Judicus whispered, winking at me, and then the black ropes poured out of his hand again, rolling over the ground, twisting as they went as if the rope was weaving itself from shadow and light and nothing else at all. It slid toward the raiders noiselessly, wrapping up their bodies as they ran and jerking them backward like a child might jerk a toy dog on a string.

One by one they screamed and fell, gagging and thrashing against the bonds. One of them cried out, "Vetara!" and ran in terror. He was the only one to survive the encounter.

As the last one of the raiders collapsed to the ground, Judicus fell heavily against me, his eyes fluttering shut, and face etched with exhaustion. His ropes dissolved to nothing. My feet shuffled as I tried to hold up his weight, sliding in the mud.

He was heavy for someone so thin and his pale face looked young, vulnerable.

And yet the power he had wielded – the ropes pouring from his hands – was impressive.

"Rope Worker," Gandy gasped and there was a murmur from the men around him.

"We need to find the rest," Tyndale gasped, his huge muscles shaking as he spoke. How hard must he have fought to be shaking now? I'd seen him hammer all day with those twenty-pound hammers and never seen him shake.

A long horn blast made them all freeze. And then a second.

"Two for retreat," my uncle gasped. "They've heard about the rope worker."

How did he know that?

"I hope they haven't heard he's collapsed," Gandy muttered. "Maybe it's him they came for."

I bit my lip.

It wasn't Judicus that they were looking for. They were looking for the same thing he was looking for – the Ai'sletta – whatever or whoever that was.

I just hoped it wasn't a phoenix.

10

By the time the fires were put out, the lone raider who had survived in the upper floor of the inn dispatched, and the dead collected, it was nearly sunset.

There had been far too many dead.

Those of us still living huddled in the common room of the Hog's Head Inn as the village head man of our town – Old Canvers – tried to form some kind of plan. The inn had stone walls, making it the sturdiest building in the town now that the forge was burned down. It shouldn't have held everyone in town. It should have been far too small. We were all trying not to think about that.

The raiders – though they had retreated – were still on the shore. We could see their fires between our homes and buildings. And that meant they would return soon and what would we do then?

"We could flee," Old Ferris suggested. "Take what horses are left and head into the hills."

There were murmurs of agreement. It was the most popular suggestion among the seventy or so people who remained alive.

I reached into my pocket nervously and my hand hit the medallion. I felt my cheeks growing hot. This couldn't be the ai'sletta that they wanted ... could it? What if I had it all along? What if I could have prevented this?

My heart hammered in my chest.

But no, I was panicking for no reason. Judicus had said this medallion would help find the ai'sletta, not that it *was* the thing he was searching for. I was too tired. It was addling my mind.

"Five," Uncle Llynd said and then paused until everyone looked at him before he continued. "That's all the horse we have. Five. And even if we use them as pack horses, they'll barely carry enough supplies to get this many people to the next town down the coast. And that's if we aren't followed."

Despairing looks flashed across our faces as we looked from one to another. There wasn't a person left who wasn't soot-marked. Not a single set of shoulders not drooping. We'd fought the fires until they were low enough not to spread again. We'd dragged the dead to the edge of town. There hadn't been time yet to dig enough graves. But we would have to finish that, too.

To one side of the inn, Tyndale clutched Mally to him, her cheeks streaked with tracks of tears. He'd lost everything in that fire. His entire future. There would be no wedding now.

Aunt Danna's head was wrapped with a long white bandage, her frizzled hair sticking out around its swaths. Her jaw was set grimly, and she kept stealing small glances at the bar where Fon should be ready to pour drinks for customers.

"All the children are in the rooms upstairs sleeping," she said firmly, swiping a tear from her cheek.

The sound of little feet tapping out hurried rhythms belied those words, but no one bothered to correct her. We'd dug so many graves our hands were raw and bleeding from it and I wasn't the only one with eyes stinging at today's memories when she said the word "children."

"And there is food enough in the inn. We can fill the empty casks in the cellar with water if we're quick about it. We can hold up in here."

"And what?" Old Ferris asked. "Sleep in the common room and hope that the raiders just decide they'll wander off now?"

"They're looking for something," Aunt Danna said with a defiant glint in her eye. "This ai'sletta they kept screaming about. We'll give it to them."

I made a squeaking sound in the back of my throat and she turned eyes of pity on me.

"I know you've worked hard to keep him alive, niece, but he's a stranger to us. It's not worth seeing our own people suffer and die just to protect a stranger."

I made fierce signs with my hands. No. No.

But if I'd had a voice, I would remind her that it was his magic that saved them all. His magic that drove the raiders back.

"Might not be a good idea to give up the one person who was able to defeat them," Old Canvers said stubbornly.

"He's collapsed now," Aunt Danna said. "That used up the last of his power. He won't be helping us now. And even if he was strong, how do we know he's our friend. We'll give him to the raiders. It's our best bad choice."

If I could speak, I'd tell them it didn't matter because he wasn't the ai'sletta. And I was pretty sure my phoenix was. But he was dead now, too.

But they didn't call me voiceless for no reason. Even if I could speak, I wasn't sure anyone would listen.

"This is talk for adults. And you have work to do," Aunt Danna said briskly. "Fon," she started to say, and then a look of devastation passed over her and she turned to Gandy instead. "Gandy. See to filling the casks with water. Take Tyndale with you. Mally, we have hungry mouths here. A carrot soup will do well enough. Sersha, tend our wounded guest. If we're going to trade him, then we need him alive. Go on now, all of you."

She shook her hands at us, and we scattered to obey.

My heart was heavy as a rock in my chest as I stumbled into the kitchen, nearly bumping into Mally.

"Don't look so sad, Sersha," she said but even as she teased me, her mouth twisted bitterly, and she wrung her hands as she looked at the ruined kitchen. "Your patient's pretty, but not pretty enough to die for."

My mouth fell open.

And not because of her callous jest.

I hadn't realized it until just this moment, but now it was pretty clear why that constellation on the back of the medallion had looked so familiar. It was the exact same shape as the birthmarks on Mally's cheek – like a triangle with a curving tail.

I knew what the Ai'sletta really was … or rather who.

She was my cousin.

11

I was still gasping like a fish pulled from the deep as I made the feverfew tea, nearly slamming into Mally as I took it off the hearth.

"Watch it, Sersha!" she said, teeth gritted in annoyance. Her eyes were red-rimmed from crying.

I gaped at her. I'd nearly burned the Ai'sletta, whatever that was.

I shut my mouth with a click and hurried past her to our room where Judicus had been set back on Mally's bed.

He moaned, his body twitching as he did. I hurried over to check him. He was feverish, and he'd been that way for far too long and whatever strength he'd used to fight for our town had taken its toll. He needed this fever to break.

Carefully, I eased his head up and his eyes flickered open a little. This was a time when it would be nice to speak, to tell him that he needed to sit up and drink. Instead, I tested the tea, being sure it wasn't too hot, and then brought it to his lips, tipping it into his mouth as he spluttered and coughed between swallows.

It took a while to get enough down to help him and I wasn't even sure if he was conscious until I laid his head on the pillow and he began to mutter.

"Comes to a close. It all ends. All, all, all."

He wasn't wrong. On the other side of the wall, the townspeople were planning his betrayal.

My mouth formed a firm line. There had to be another way. There just had to be.

I refused to give up on that yet.

I checked his wound as he kept muttering incoherently. The swelling had gone down, and it smelled fine. I frowned. What was his fever from if not the wound?

I changed the dressing, and his words formed a sentence again.

"Find the Ai'sletta. She's our only hope. Save us all."

I felt the blood drain from my face. The only hope to save us all? My flirtatious cousin Mally?

That seemed ... unlikely. Maybe I'd read her birthmark wrong.

I fished out the silver disk and the scrap of parchment, looking at the symbol drawn on the smeared surface and then I compared it to the medallion. They were exactly like her cluster of birthmarks. Exactly.

I swallowed and looked again at the mirror. And this time, with no one dying beside me, I ignored Mynta's advice and really looked.

I'd never seen my own face before. I looked quite grim. But that was mostly because I wasn't sure we'd live through the night.

My eyes were startlingly bright and large. The rest of my face was plain enough – my nose was straight without the saucy upturn of Mally's. In fact, my face actually didn't look much like my cousin's. There was a ghost of resemblance to Aunt Danna in the determined set of my mouth, but that was all. Mynta was right. There was no blessing to a woman in knowing what she looked like. I was wasting time looking at my own face.

I put the mirror away. It was as useless as the note. Even if I – and I alone – knew what Mally was, who did it benefit? We would not give her to the raiders. Not even in return for sparing the rest of the town. It might save Judicus from being traded to them – but I doubted that. My aunt was the one pushing to have us trade his life four ours, and she would only be more determined if she thought it would save Mally from a similar fate.

It wasn't hard for someone like me not to utter a word – and that was exactly what I'd do about this.

But as I drew the blanket up over Judicus' chest, I realized I didn't want him to die, either. I didn't know much about him except that he was willing to fight for the sake of strangers. He hadn't ordered me to help him out of the inn so he could flee. And he hadn't used what magic he had to get away. He'd used it to fight for us. A man like that didn't deserve to be handed to his enemies.

And he was barely older than me, his smooth cheeks nearly beardless. Did he have a mother like Aunt Danna out there somewhere worried about him?

His eyes popped open and he grabbed my collar.

I gasped at the intensity in his eyes.

"Where am I?" His hand shook.

I shook my head. This part was always the hardest. When people didn't know. When they made wrong guesses about why I wouldn't talk to them.

"Answer me!"

I lifted my hands in a pacifying gesture and pointed to his wound.

"A Calicarn sword," he muttered. "Where is ... the elf I was traveling with. Is she here?"

I shook my head.

He collapsed back onto the bed, releasing my collar.

"I can't die yet. Can't die yet." His eyes found mine and there was so much vulnerability in their depths that I took a step forward, hardly thinking about it. "I need your help. Please, help me."

I nodded my agreement. I was trying to help. I just didn't know how to do it.

I opened my mouth, but I knew no sound would come out. Instead, tears of frustration leaked from the sides of my eyes. The world was not made for people who listened more than they spoke.

"Voiceless," he gasped, understanding dawning on his face. "A secret keeper. If we live through this and you help me, you can be *my* secret keeper."

What was a secret keeper? I bathed his head with cool water, and he sunk back into sleep seeming content with that. But my stomach was roiling with nerves.

There had to be a way to save everyone – him and the town. I'd failed the woman with him, and I'd failed the phoenix. I didn't want to fail anyone else.

If only I'd had the ashes tonight instead of last night, maybe the phoenix could have helped. But he had died with the dawn.

My heart lurched in bitter pain at the thought. If something as magnificent as that fiery bird could die so easily, what did that mean for someone plain and ordinary like me?

I reached a hand into my pocket, stroking the remnants of ash in my pocket as if they were the feathers of the glorious bird who had lived only hours ago.

Opening the shutter, I looked out into the last rays of the sunset and thought about how sad it was that I'd only met Kazmerev hours before he was gone. And now, I would likely die tonight. Neither of us would make much of a mark with our passing.

The last light of the sun faded as darkness descended and with it fear. The raiders would come. And we weren't ready for them – not to fight, not to run, and I was not ready to offer up an innocent man to keep us safe.

Little Hawk?

I gasped at the voice in my heart. But he was dead. I had watched him die. There was muffled laughter in my mind.

Do you not know how phoenixes work, little hawk? We die each dawn, and then as dark descends, we rise. Up from the ashes. Up from the depths! Up from despair, we rise!

But there was no sign of him in my hands. No small bird. No egg.

I'm far too large for that now. Look up.

I craned my head out the window and looked up, gasping at what I saw. Kazmerev drifted down from the roof of the inn and landed in front of me in the stable yard. His feathers – flame-lined and brilliant – burned into my sight. I'd never seen something so gloriously beautiful before. He was like the sunset itself.

Only the sunset? I was certain I was prettier than that.

Like the dawn, too.

Oh. That's disappointing. I'd hoped I put them both to shame.

He put them both to shame.

Now, that's better.

I couldn't help the smile turning the corners of my lips up. I'd thought the world was darkness. I hadn't realized that light might appear.

There was still a hint of sadness to his mental voice, and yet there was also a feeling of tentative reaching, as if he were trying to coax me out.

Do not doubt, little hawk. We shall soar together – someday. Only give me a little time as I try to patch up my broken heart.

I would help him with that – if I could. I'd never lost anyone I'd known for a hundred years. But I had lost my parents and today I had lost a cousin. I knew that grief could strike at any time and leave you breathless all over again.

Perhaps a quick flight over the sea would help me breathe.

It would be hard to do with raiders outside our village perched on the edge of the sea.

Come out and join me, little hawk. My heart aches with mourning.

That was all he needed to say because my heart was aching, too.

12

Come out of that stone building. It's impossible to speak to you through rock and stone.

The frustration in his voice was endearing. Carefully, I slipped out of Judicus' room and through the kitchen where Mally was finishing up the soup.

The darkness outside enveloped me, leaving me shivering as the cold air sucked the warmth from my body and the ground around me. I needed to be careful of raiders. They were here somewhere. They could be just steps away – and yet Kazmerev needed me. I could feel the ache of his heart. It was like a wound that needed binding up and the part of me that helped to heal couldn't leave it alone to fester.

You ease the pain just by existing.

I felt a little shiver at that thought. I'd never meant that much to anyone before.

You hold my heart in yours, Flame Rider. A Phoenix cannot rise out of the ash unless he is connected to someone's heart. Your tender heart raises me from the ashes.

I stepped through the stable yard and out to the back of the inn, and there he was in front of me in all his fiery glory. He was the size of a small horse. I bit my lip. Someone was going to see him.

Phoenixes are meant to be noticed.

And that would terrify the town folk.

Why? You are not terrified.

That's because I'd seen him born. I'd seen him hatch from the egg and glow in front of my eyes. I'd felt him in my heart. I felt *who* he was, not just what he was – that he was aching with hurt but under that he was something genuine and good.

I felt you too, before I returned as your phoenix, I felt you.

Wait. *My* phoenix?

I told you – we can only rise from the heart of another.

Did he mean ... but no. I could feel the wash of sadness rushing over him like a wave. He did not mean that he would stay with me.

Not in the way that you mean.

My heart wasn't sinking. Because that wouldn't be fair.

I led him quietly through the stable yard to the darkness beyond. I'd never seen Landsfall so still before. Not a single candle glow marred the darkened street. Not a light burned beyond the flicker dancing in the windows of the Hog's Head Inn. I saw that someone sat up in the thatch of the inn with a bow and a lantern, but he was facing the opposite way and didn't seem to notice us slinking away into the night.

Which didn't say much for the watch the town was keeping. I was leading a massive fiery bird, after all. It was hard to hide someone like that.

Perhaps now would be a good time to mention that only you can see me.

What?

I spun to look at him. He was following me, looking a little sheepish and a little like a songbird hopping along the ground in search of seeds.

It's hard enough to be a fiery bird – bright and beautiful - but it's even harder to be so reliant on someone else.

What did he mean? He hopped past me, past the bakery at the end of the street, and then fluttered to perch on the peak of the bakery's roof.

I stood where I could see him up there. The thatch didn't even sag. Was he ... not real? Was he a dream of mine?

He lifted his glorious flaming head, little ripples of fire dancing down his dark feathers, and then a song ripped from his mouth, keening sad and sweet.

He was mourning Veela again.

I wrapped my arms around my chest.

I could understand that. There was no limit on grief. There was no time that one must stop or move on.

But I was vulnerable here, out where anyone might attack at any time.

I was at risk and my whole town was at risk the longer I stayed out here because they would notice I was missing, and someone would grow worried and try to find me. If that happened, they would leave the safety of the stone-walled inn and be vulnerable.

I bit my lip.

I should go. Now.

But he was aching and hurting.

I couldn't force him to mourn alone.

I let out a huff of anxiety and then steeled my nerve. I was his only friend still living. He needed me.

I strode to the wall of the bakery and grasped the window frame with care. It had been a long time since I'd climbed up onto the thatch anywhere. Not since I was a child helping to rethatch roofs in the spring.

I shook my head as my hands found their clumsy purchase and I scrambled up onto the roof, trying not to think about looking down, trying not to think about what the guards in the inn's thatch would do if they saw me – would they shoot? – trying not to think about falling.

I shuffled carefully across the thatch until I was crouched beside him. And as he keened again, I reached out and stroked his fiery wing. I should have known he wasn't real when the thatch didn't light on fire.

I'm real.

I should have known he couldn't stay when he vanished with the dawn.

I will not stay in this town – but neither will you. You see, it's not that I will stay with you, Flame Rider, but rather that you will stay with me.

Wasn't that the same thing?

Of course not. You are my anchor to this world. I am your wings. I will fly you into the unknown and you will keep me from going straight on up to join the stars in their cold dance.

I kept stroking him. He was grief-stricken. He didn't know what he was saying. He'd already said he couldn't stay.

I can't. Phoenixes can't stay in one place. It's against our nature. But being one with our person in oath and life – that we can do. You will come with me when I leave this place, Sersha. You will stay with me.

With what money? With what clothing or food? The idea – while charming – was utterly impossible.

Nothing is impossible with me.

He was still singing his mourning song, but his thoughts were buoyant with hope. It felt almost addictive.

It has always been so for the Flame Rider. There are stashes. Places with supplies. Your needs will be met.

And what did I bring to this uneven partnership?

Everything. You make everything possible with the breath of your lungs and beating of your heart – until, someday – when you give my ash to another.

I felt in my pocket, not stopping the gentle stroking of his wing as I checked for his ash. A little burst of panic rose in my chest. It was gone.

Of course it is gone. I am living before you. It will return when I die with the dawn.

What if I lost it? I felt a sudden panic.

It doesn't work that way. You can't lose me now.

I swallowed uncomfortably. Did it hurt to die?

Every single time.

There was a long pause.

But you wouldn't believe how it feels to be raised.

Something shuffled below us on the cobbles. I held my breath, trying to hear past the phoenix's keening song.

A flash of metal met my gaze. A weapon. I followed it with my eyes and found the raider – streaked in black ash – who clutched that weapon. He slipped down the street like a shadow, and at his back were a dozen others.

13

There was a scuffling sound from another street over.

More of them.

My heart was in my throat. I couldn't scream a warning, and if I moved at all, they would see me and kill me. Some of them held short bows. It would be easy enough to shoot me out of the thatch. I turned worried eyes toward where the guard on the Hog's Head Inn was waiting in the thatch. Another man had joined him, passing him a mug. In the light of their lantern, I could see that neither of them was looking this way.

My face went cold as the blood drained away from it. They weren't going to see this raider attack. It was going to be too late.

I spun to look at Kazmerev. Would he help? Could he?

He tilted his head to one side.

How do you want me to help?

His keening came to a stop as he regarded me.

He was a phoenix, a fiery bird of legend, surely, he could help somehow.

How?

My eyes went wide. I hadn't expected that response. Well, he could swoop at them and blind them, perhaps.

No one can see me but you, remember?

He could set them on fire.

Look at the thatch.

It was untouched. But he must be able to do something! What did other Flame Riders do when they were attacked?

Ah! That! Well, you can throw balls of fire from your hands and with practice, you can get quite good at aiming them. You can shoot sparks from your fingers. You can dance in the flames untouched and ride on my back into the sky.

No, I couldn't do that. Veela might have, but I could not – except maybe the riding thing.

I'm still a bit small for that, though I am growing back to my proper size.

He was right. He was almost half again as big as he had been when he leapt from the inn roof just a half a turn ago.

The sound of leather creaking below me reminded me I needed to do something. Now.

Could he at least carry me as far as the inn to warn them all?

Better to carry you into the night, little hawk. You have no cloak, but I can be your warmth in the night until we get you to a cache.

Run away? Was he kidding? I would not leave those who needed me. I hadn't thought he would, either.

You are my Flame Rider now. My allegiance is to you.

What about Judicus?

He seemed to almost shrug. *I like the boy, but your safety is more important.*

No. No, that simply wouldn't do. I stood on the thatch, wobbling in a way that made my belly twist, but I refused to back down. I planted my hands on my hips.

We were not abandoning my family and town. We were not abandoning the boy who had worked so hard to save Kazmerev's Veela. I felt his twinge of pain at her name, but I pressed on. We just weren't going to abandon them.

I felt the hot tears tracking down my cheeks before I could stop them. I was so powerless. Even now, even with this new friend, I couldn't help anyone.

He ducked his head, shying away from me, a feeling of hurt in his thoughts.

It's just too soon. I can't lose you, too.

My heart melted within me.

He wasn't cruel and heartless He had a wound like Judicus' but Kazmerev's was in his heart.

It hurts so much. I can't do it again. Please.

I swallowed, my gaze flicking between the raiders creeping down the streets like an army of beetles and the bright burning bird trembling in front of me.

If I was going to save everyone else, I needed to find a way to give him courage again. But how did I do that? I'd been scared my whole life. Scared that people wouldn't understand me. Scared that no one would marry me, and my cousins would tire of me and I'd have no home or family or place in this world. Scared that nothing I did would ever be enough.

How did you give someone else courage when you had none of your own?

He was my first true friend. The first to ever truly hear me. The first to know the fears that blossomed in my heart. I didn't want to lose him either. But I also didn't want to hide in the shadows – and I didn't want that for him. He was a flaming, bright light. He was majestic and powerful. He shouldn't be reduced to cowering in the shadows. He should soar.

The raiders moved further up the street. Just a few more buildings and they would reach the inn.

Kazmerev spread his wings, shrugging them as if to shake out the feathers and I felt a swell of something inside him.

He could do this. He could be strong again.

The raiders paused, making hand signals to one another. They were readying themselves to charge.

I wouldn't leave Kazmerev when he left this place. I would do exactly what he asked and go with him, without a coin or proper cloak or anything else, I would still go.

But first I had to make sure my people made it through this night.

I could feel him softening to me – but I wouldn't ask him to go with me. He was right. He'd already lost his best friend. I shouldn't ask him to give more than that.

I gave his wing one last caress and then slipped down the thatch toward the edge of the bakery roof. Just because I wasn't asking him for help didn't mean that I wouldn't act. I could still warn them. Even if it meant risking myself.

I leapt from the edge of the roof, landing on the dirt road below in a crouch. My ankles and knees hurt from the drop, but I was fine. Sucking in a deep breath of air, I sprinted toward the inn.

I was halfway to the raiders when a voice called in my mind.

I will give you what I can, little hawk.

My heart leapt.

I was just beginning to smile when ahead of me, the men on the thatch called out a warning and the inn door opened spilling orange firelight across the street like a washerwoman emptying her cauldron.

"We have what you're looking for!" Aunt Danna's voice rang out.

Oh no. What had she done?

14

They spilled out of the inn, weapons held high, Judicus propped up between Uncle Llynd and Gandy. My breath was caught so hard in my throat that I felt like I might choke.

No.

They shouldn't be doing this.

I sprinted down the street. There had to be a way to tell them that they were making a huge mistake.

I wasn't a quiet runner, and yet none of the raiders turned. They were as riveted by the scene coming from the inn as I was. Upon the roof above the tableau, two townsmen held their bows, arrows strung and drawn, pointed at the raiders. The shutters were closed, windows nailed shut, but the inn door stood open. It felt like they'd constructed a shield with a big slot down the center. What was the point?

But the bravado in my aunt Danna's voice told me what the point was. She was certain this gamble would work.

"I have hot soup and cider. Take what you came for, eat, and then go. You don't need to kill us. You don't need to take anything else. We're welcoming you here," she said firmly, as if they were just more of her children and if she spoke with authority they would buckle at her words.

There was silence for the space of a heartbeat and then one of the raiders stepped from the shadows and into the light. He was swathed so deeply in hood and cloak that I could only make out the outline of a man under all that cloth. He could have been any age. He could have been something utterly inhuman.

He spoke like a human, though. And he spoke our language in a low voice not much louder than a hiss.

"We aren't here for the rope worker. We can find one like him anywhere. Besides, with the blow Leedar struck, he won't live the week out. He's dead and he just doesn't know it."

The way Judicus's head lolled from where he was propped up, his analysis seemed justified. But I knew better. His wound was not infected. It would heal – provided no one cut him open again.

"Then why are you here?" Aunt Danna's voice didn't shake, but I knew she was holding on by her iron will alone. It was probably why she was speaking instead of our head man. She refused to bend for anyone. She was stronger than anyone in our town – even now after the death of her oldest boy.

"Ai'sletta. We seek the ai'sletta."

"And we're offering him to you," Aunt Danna said, shaking Judicus as if to emphasize her point. He flopped bonelessly and I flinched. All that movement wasn't good for his healing wound.

The laugh of the raiders was like something waiting for you in the dark. It spoke of pain and fear, of brutal killing and leaving the remains for the ravens. I shivered at the sound.

The raider spread his arms wide as if he was making a proclamation. "Little chicken hiding in your chicken coop, we will draw back and let you talk. In one hour, we will return and then you give us the ai'sletta or we kill you all down to the last child."

Did they know what they were looking for? They hadn't been fooled by Judicus, but could something else fool them? I had a bad feeling that they knew at least as much as he did – that they were looking for a "she."

I pressed myself to the nearest wall as they melted back into the shadows. The hardened mud of the cooper's walls was dusty against my grip, but I squeezed my eyes closed as tightly as they would go, my breath coming out of me in little gasps. The raiders were going to find me here.

I dared to open my eyes just a tiny bit. What if they saw the gleam of my eyes reflected in the moonlight? What if they stopped to dispatch me on their way to wait the hour out?

What if they didn't, and I waited with my family only to watch everyone I'd ever known butchered before my eyes?

I felt a pang in my heart as if it were burning and I didn't know if it was the fear or the phoenix doing it.

It's me.

Dark shadows slipped down the street, passing me by narrowly as they whispered in their own language. I caught the word *ai'sletta* and nothing more.

They had only just passed when Kazmerev landed on the dirt street in a burst of golden sparks. He'd grown again.

I flinched at the sight of him. He was so bright – and so beautiful with his dark feathers edged with a cherry red glow and little golden flames licking up and down them hungrily. How could it be possible that no one saw him but me?

I've changed my mind. If I do not help you, it's clear that you will kill yourself trying to do this without me.

How could he help? He'd already said he could not.

I can help you. All the things you'd hoped I could do – those are your powers, your grim duties, your heavy burden to bear.

Heavy burden?

You want to throw fire and watch your enemy burn. Is that not a burden? You want to fly into a mass of men with weapons and swords. Is that duty not grim enough for you? Battles are not games. Death is no friend to any man, no matter what he says on the matter. It's no friend to me, though I dance with it every dawn.

I swallowed. He was right, wasn't he? It was fighting these raiders that had left Judicus so ill and Veela dead.

And even when you are not the one torn apart, you are doing the tearing – and that is just as bad in its own way. But I relent. Sorrowful as my heart is, I will not wound it again with your needless death. Come, call on my strength, and craft your grim workings.

Hope burst in my heart at the thought of standing in that spill of orange light and defending my people and town. I could do it. He would help me. I just needed him to tell me *how* to do it.

That knowing is not for me but for the Flame Rider.

That was not very helpful.

I do not know how you channel my heart of fire to make me visible to others or how you harness my strength to fling flames or make pillars of fire.

My heart – soaring a moment before – crashed to the ground.

Then there was nothing for it but to go and die with my people. It was a nice thought that he might help me – a kind gesture – but it was no good.

Swiping hot tears aside, I stepped out, walking right past the glowing scarlet phoenix and down the street. It was hard to act like he wasn't there when sparks kept popping and sizzling from the ends of each of his feathers and flames roared up in little gouts when he moved, bathing him in waves of fire. But I was wasting the hour of life I had left in talking to him. He either could not or would not help me. He was only a distraction from the real choice ahead of me.

Should I tell the town about Mally or keep that to myself? That was the question, and I needed an answer before I got to the inn door.

Somehow, the thought of betraying her only made my tears flow hotter and faster than ever.

15

Wait. *Wait, little hawk!*

I ignored him. I felt betrayed that he'd known this the whole time and never mentioned it. He knew I was wasting my time asking him for help and instead of just telling me that he strung me along letting me hope he'd change his mind and help me. I could have been spending that time doing something useful.

It's possible that I regret that.

I ran into the pool of orange light, skidding to a stop in front of my Aunt Danna. She stood with her spine straight, looking out into the darkness as the other townsfolk dragged Judicus back into the inn.

"Should we take him back to bed?" Gandy called.

"Just leave him on the floor behind the bar," Aunt Danna said in a calm, almost sunny tone. I knew that tone. It was the one she used when she was trying to disguise despair. "He won't be any safer in a bed."

And he wouldn't live long enough for it to matter. That's what she was thinking. Her eyes focused on me, narrowing, and her mouth formed a thin line. There was a note of warning in her voice.

"Where have you been, Sersha?"

I signed to her that I'd been down the street.

She shook her head but there was a gleam in her eyes that made my heart speed up. Those were the eyes of someone looking for a way out. Any way out.

"You wouldn't happen to know who this ai'sletta is that they want so much, would you, niece?"

I was not lulled by the false note of cheerfulness in her voice. This was a challenge. I felt the blood rushing to my cheeks. Because I did know. And I couldn't keep my own body from betraying that secret.

"I thought you might," she said, her voice growing even sunnier. "I thought to myself, 'Who doesn't quite fit in our village? Who here is just a little bit different? Who has a tormented past? Who comes from somewhere else? Who might be the one they are searching for?' And one name came to mind."

I shook my head, desperate to deny her words.

What was she thinking? She had raised me herself! But grief did strange things to people and her son's body was still warm in its grave.

She grabbed my shoulder in a hand like a vice and leaned in calmly, friendly, as if we were just chatting in the night while raiders waited for an answer.

"And even if I'm wrong, what is one life for sixty?" she whispered. "And which one life is worth spending on this?"

I looked her directly in the eyes and I saw the purpose there. My aunt Danna was not a bad woman. But she was a practical one. And cold certainty washed over me as I realized she was right. I was the correct sacrifice for this. I was the perfect choice to be offered in exchange for the village. I had no future. I had no clear purpose. But in this, I could give all the rest of them a future. It was cold and heartless – and logical.

And she didn't even know that it meant saving the life and future of her own beloved daughter. If she did know, she would give me up even quicker. Because while my aunt was kind to me and generous in her own way, there was nothing and no one she loved more than her natural-born children. And she'd already lost one today.

Ice flowed through my veins.

I did not fight as she turned me toward the inn.

What are you doing?

I was letting them give me up.

Crimson light danced across the wall and door of the Hog's Head Inn in front of me. But it was light only I could see – the light of a phoenix flapping his wings with irritation.

He should just go away. He couldn't help me. He should spend the rest of his night flying and letting the wind soar past his feathers one last time.

I was wrong.

It was too late for regrets. Perhaps someone else would pick up his ashes. Maybe one of the raiders.

It doesn't work like that.

There was a note of anxiety in his voice now and it ached with a strong burn in my chest.

It had worked like that for me.

His reply sounded desperate.

It needs to be the right kind of person, the right kind of heart. Like a seed in soil, the ashes will not hatch in just any heart.

Then he'd better hope that someone in the village had that heart. Maybe Judicus would take the ash. He knew what it was.

He's a ropeworker. They can't be Flame Riders, too.

Either way, it was no longer my problem. I needed to set my mind toward death. It was all I had left.

16

Aunt Danna brought me into the inn and sat me on Fon's usual chair behind the bar.

"Watch her," she said to Mally, tossing a meaningful look at her daughter. "Don't let her get up from the chair."

Mally nodded. She was no fool. She knew exactly what my aunt was doing.

My cheeks felt hot. They were already talking about me like a thing and not a person. That's what you did with people right before you did something terrible to them. I knew that. I'd seen it before. You called someone "that woman" right before you kicked her out of the house into the world with no money or chances. You said, "that old man" right before you swindled him into selling something valuable for a pittance. You called a woman a filthy name before you tried to take advantage of her. I lived in an inn. I'd seen it all.

I choked on the thought, coughing intensely. I was already a thing.

You aren't a thing to me. If you would just calm down and listen! I can help you.

Everyone else was packed in the common room like fish in a barrel. The air felt close and thick. I struggled to breathe it. It didn't help that my heart wouldn't stop galloping like a horse that jumped the fence. I should run. I should just jump up and run.

But I knew I wouldn't even if I hadn't been put on this chair and watched over by a thoughtful Mally with a barrel stave in her hand. I didn't hate my town enough to want to see them die violently. Not even if it meant I would be the one to die.

I shivered and then forced that thought away. I tried to think instead of the twins delivered yesterday. They would be upstairs probably sleeping or nursing and utterly innocent. I was doing this for them and all the children sleeping above me. For them, it was worth it.

I have never met someone so quick to throw herself into the flames!

As if she could read my earlier thoughts, Mally came over to me with a length of baling twine.

"I think maybe it would be better to tie those hands," she said, her mouth twisting with distaste as Gandy dragged Judicus across the floor and dropped him at my feet. I tried to look down at him but Mally gripped my chin between her fingers and pulled my face up. "It's you that they're after and it's you that they'll get."

I shook my head and she rolled her eyes. She was just like her mother. All the confidence in the world on the outside to hide that she was shaking underneath.

"Don't roll your eyes at me, Sersha. If they're here for someone who doesn't fit, then mama is right. It's you." She pulled the twine tight around my wrists and it bit into my skin. I bit down on my lip against the pain.

It wasn't me that the raiders were looking for. Maybe she should know that.

I signed to her a second *no* a little awkwardly as she cinched the last knot around my wrists, and then I made another sign. *It's you*, I told her with my hands.

Her face flushed a bright pink. "Don't say that."

I reached into my pocket awkwardly, my fingers barely grasping the chain of the medallion before I pulled it out and held it out to her.

She took it uncertainly, frowning.

I made the sign again. *It's you.*

At least she should know. Maybe someone else would come for her someday. She should know that they might.

She was shaking, her face bright red and her eyes welling up as she looked at the medallion herself and then jammed it into her apron pocket and crossed her arms over her chest.

"Stop lying to me. This stolen necklace doesn't prove anything."

She stomped away, shoulders heaving. She knew, somehow, that I was right. At least I'd warned her. At least she would know.

I looked down at Judicus. He stirred, eyes fluttering open and then closing again.

Maybe I'd get lucky, and he'd wake up in time to fight the raiders.

Or maybe you'll listen to me! Please, please listen!

I ignored Kazmerev. He needed to go, too. He didn't have to stay for this.

Aunt Danna cleared her throat. She was standing on a bench, looking over the white-faced townsfolk.

"As much as it pains me, we have to do what's best for the town," she said, leveling her gaze at everyone one by one. There were already nods at her words. "We'll give them my niece Sersha. She's who they are looking for."

Every eye turned to me and I felt my face growing hot. Mouths thinned and eyes turned down. They knew it might not be true. They would do it anyway. As long as it wasn't their family, they didn't care who was given over. I understood that. And it still cut me to the quick. I'd grown up with these people. I'd helped most of them at some time or another. I had never known any other home.

"Maybe we should look for this thing that they want. Maybe it's not a person," someone said. I couldn't tell who from where I was.

"Do any of you know what it is?" Aunt Danna asked. Her question was met only by silence. "Well, neither do I. So, we can only guess that it's the one thing that doesn't belong here."

There were murmurs, but they were murmurs of agreement. Ice shot through my heart.

"What about the magician?" a woman called – Goodwife Floeiv. "Can we wait for him to wake up again? He could defend us."

"He's taken with fever. And we only have an hour," the head man said grimly. He wouldn't meet anyone's eyes. He knew as surely as I did what they would choose to do.

"Why wait for the hour to be up," Tyndale asked from where he stood, soot-stained, wide shoulders slumped. "We know what we need to do. Call the raiders now and let's be done with it."

My aunt Danna's mouth turned up slightly at the corners and her eyes flashed at his words, but she said nothing. She looked amused. But I knew better. She was angry. It was fine for her to offer me up like a chicken for the pot, but for someone outside the family to do it – well, that bothered her. At least there was that. I almost barked a laugh at such a small blessing.

Even if you are not listening, I will try to tell you. I don't really know how a Flame Rider accesses my strength, but I know a little. I know it involves embracing the flames around your heart and letting them burn.

"Go ahead and do it, Tyndale," Aunt Danna said with her slight smile. Irritated, but not likely to stop him. She was treating him with care. She must still be hoping he would marry her daughter and give Mally a good future.

Aunt Danna raised an eyebrow in a superior manner and Tyndale shuffled slightly before squaring his shoulders and pushing through the crowd to the door.

You have to want it, not fight it. You have to open your heart.

The time for opening my heart was almost at an end.

The door swung open and as Tyndale stepped into the night, all I saw through the open door was the blaze of bright feathers.

Please. Please try. Don't give up.

But everyone else had given up on me. Why fight it? Why push when no one else would push for me?

I will push for you. I should have fought for you from the beginning. Let me fight for you now. Will you not forgive me?

That made my heart come to a stuttering start. Wouldn't I forgive him? Was I so stingy as to withhold forgiveness from a creature only I could see just to spite him? Was that to be my last act?

I glanced at my cousin and the hard expression on her face. She wouldn't even look at me. And I knew that under that, she felt guilty that they were going to give me up to the raiders and she wondered if I told her the truth – if maybe I wasn't being given up to save the town, but rather to save her. And yet, she wouldn't give me one look of kindness.

I didn't want to be that way. Not now. Not ever.

Kazmerev shouldn't even have to ask for forgiveness. I should have offered it openly and from the start.

I was sorry, too.

I opened my heart to him at the same moment that Aunt Danna stepped down from her bench, crossed to me, and grabbed my upper arm in her grip.

I forgave him completely. And I wished him well. Perhaps the next one to lift his ashes from the ground would do right by him. I wanted that for him.

I hoped that in time, he could forgive me, too.

Of course I forgive you, little hawk.

My lips quirked up in a slight smile as Aunt Danna helped me stand.

"It's for the best, Sersha," she said, leading me from the chair toward the door.

I paused at the sound of a groan from behind me. Judicus pushed himself up onto all fours, panting hard.

There was nothing he could do to stop this. He was too weak, too hurt. But at least he would live. I'd managed to help him that far.

"She's here!" Tyndale roared into the night. "Come and get her!"

A cry from down the street answered him and it sounded like triumph.

The blood in my face rushed away leaving me lightheaded. When I'd said I had no future, I'd been right.

17

An ache like the beginning of a fire started in my heart, searing through me so painfully that if Aunt Danna wasn't holding me up, I would have fallen to my knees.

Don't fight it! Embrace the pain!

I tried to unclench my body, to let my mind absorb the hurt flowing through my chest and heart. It felt like I was on fire. I clenched my jaw against it. How could you not fight pain? How could you not battle against it with every beat of your heart?

For the same reason that you aren't fighting risk and death. For love. Hold onto me, little hawk. Hold onto me through the pain.

We stepped out the door and into the night, and I don't know what everyone else saw in the circle of orange light pouring from the door of the inn, but I saw Tyndale shaking and my Aunt Danna's grim face and a line of dark figures advancing with one hurrying ahead of the rest – but I also saw Kazmerev.

He fluttered down from the inn roof – larger than a huge plow horse – as large as a wagon. And he was fire and embers, falling ash and bright sparks. His eye was fixed on me and when our gazes caught, he burst into brighter flame.

I was wrong to doubt you. Let me stand with you here. Let me shelter you under my wing.

Warmth filled me along with the pain, because even though I couldn't stop what was coming next, at least I had a friend to go through it with me. And it meant so much to me to know that he was willing to stand here and be with me through the grimmest moment of my life, even though it would cost him in sorrow and pain. I'd watched him mourn Veela. I knew it would hurt him for me to die, too. And yet, here he stood.

I held my head a little higher as the lead raider met Aunt Danna in the stark light of our lanterns. There was a shuffling from behind me as the townspeople stepped out the door to stand behind us. I risked a look over my shoulder to see Mally step up and wrap a hand around Tyndale's arm, her barrel stave still in her other hand. Her eyes were red like she'd been crying.

"You have the Ai'sletta?" the lead raider asked.

"What will you do with her?" Aunt Danna said. I wondered if knowing would change her mind about this or if she was just stretching it out to show the raider he didn't call all the shots here.

"We are the Hand of Rats. Our faces cloaked in the night. Our actions cloaked in secrecy. What we do hereafter is not for you to know."

"You burned my village," Aunt Danna said firmly. "You killed my friends. You are taking my niece away. I think you owe me the truth."

He laughed a dry, ashy laugh. "The Ai'sletta threatens us with light and order. These are two things we cannot abide. We will kill her. But fear not, loving aunt. We shall do it quickly and then we shall be gone."

So, they did know they were looking for a girl.

Coughing like someone was trying to cough up every breath they'd ever had resounded from behind me and I twisted to look. Judicus clung to the doorframe of the inn, doubled over, his face red as he coughed and coughed. He was pale and sweaty, but his eyes were fixed on Mally, wide and afraid. He knew. He must have seen her birthmark. Would he say something?

Fear tore through me at the thought. If he did, everyone would die. Tyndale and Uncle Llynd would fight to their deaths to defend Mally and everyone else would join them. He must not speak.

Right now, he could not.

"Let's do this quickly," the raider said with a sneer, but there was fear in his tone as he drew his sword. I was good at listening. It was what I did best. I could hear what no one else could. He was afraid of Judicus. Afraid he'd recover and stop this before it began.

Aunt Danna's hand was shaking as she let go of my arm. She met my eyes with steely determination, clearly certain that she would have to force me to walk forward. She was wrong.

I took a step toward the raider on my own.

Kazmerev had said this took love. He wasn't wrong. I thought of the little ones sleeping upstairs in the inn and I took a second step.

"Why doesn't she speak?" the raider asked as I took a third step toward him. It was all I could do to keep my knees from trembling.

"She is voiceless." Was that regret in Aunt Danna's voice? I would hold on to that. Brave front aside, she was sorry for what she was doing.

I was near enough now to see the glint in the raider's eyes at her words. Under his veil, he was probably smirking.

"Kneel," he said aloud.

I knelt on the ground, letting the squelch of the mud remind me that the earth I knelt on was the earth I'd lived on all my life and when this life was gone, it would embrace me.

Draw on the flame, little hawk. It is not too late to soar!

The raider leaned down and whispered to me and I realized with a chill, that he knew he could confess because I could not speak his secrets.

"When I've taken your head, I will kill every soul in this village. What a fool you are to come willingly when it will do nothing for your people."

Fear shot through me. My sacrifice would be for nothing.

Oh. No. That's too much! Don't draw that much!

I barely heard Kazmerev. Panic bubbled up inside me. My sacrifice would be for nothing. My family and friends would die anyway. My little cousins and the twins born yesterday and ...

Fire filled my mind, blazed from my heart. I felt my hands pull apart as the bindings around them fell to the ground and I raised a hand at the same moment that the raider lifted his sword above his head in a double-handed grip.

Blazing heat ripped through my body, racing out my hand and scorching through the air with a sound like fabric tearing. It lanced out in an amber streak, shot through his sword, through his arms, and licked across his face. He was a living torch in the blink of an eye, his sword falling to the ground in a splash of molten metal. He opened his mouth and then the fire flashed so bright I couldn't see and when I looked back there was nothing there but ash.

The street was silent for a heartbeat.

And then a battle cry ripped through every raider throat.

They charged toward me as one.

18

I leapt to my feet, hands flung up as if I could ward them off. Could I? My heart was beating so hard that I couldn't hear anything else. My vision seemed to pulse with black as if fear was robbing me of sight.

When I say jump, jump.

A glint from one of the weapons leveled at me told m I didn't have time to act.

Jump.

I jumped as high as I could.

My legs felt hot as they were swept out from under me. My breath was in my throat. My eyes were blinded by light. I blinked hard, trying to sit up.

Don't squirm!

And all I saw was bright flames. Wind whipped past my hair as I realized that I *was* sitting. I was sitting on the back of a soaring phoenix as he climbed up and up into the air.

He let out a long keen like the cry of an eagle and turned, banking into a wide circle. I should have fallen off. I should have slid through his semi-transparent body of flame. But I didn't.

And you won't. The Flame Rider is linked to the phoenix on a life-force level. I will not drop you. I will not leave you. We are bound now by flame and ash. You have formed our bond.

Was he sorry that I did? I felt nervous at the thought.

You ease my pain with your presence. His thoughts were awed. *You help temper the agony of my loss. I've never done this before. Veela was my only other rider. I've never lived through another loss. You ease it in a way I thought was impossible.*

Tears pricked my eyes. I hadn't expected it to feel like this.

I felt ... safe.

And yet I was anything but. I reached out and dug my fingers into his flame, but while there was a sense of resistance, he felt insubstantial. Was he visible now?

You are making me visible.

We swooped down low toward the ground at the same moment that something swiped through the air beside me. A dark arrow ripped past and then another.

I caught a glimpse of my family and friends frozen where they stood, mouths hanging open as they watched Kazmerev careening toward them, flames unfurling at his back.

The raiders reacted with trained precision. They had their bows out and arrows flying immediately.

Kazmerev twisted in the air, avoiding the bolts, and I reached to grab at him by instinct.

I lifted a hand, hoping to shoot fire at the raiders, but nothing happened. I shook my palm and tried again.

Nothing.

My stomach dropped. Was that it? I'd run out of the ability to fight? Then my people were still dead. I'd done nothing to help them!

Calm. You are new at this. It won't come easy.

They were shooting arrows at us! We couldn't just accept that! We had to fight.

We were in between them now, soaring just feet over the ground. I covered my face with my arms as Kazmerev flapped, his wings setting the edge of the head man's house on fire as he swept past. I thought he couldn't light the buildings! This was getting worse and worse!

I can when you make me visible.

A sword swiped through the air beside us and Kazmerev flapped hard to gain height. We swept up into the air, leaving the raiders in chaos, their faces etched with frustration and anger.

I leaned into his hard climb, realizing finally how high up we were and how easily I could fall.

I won't let you fall.

Good thing I wasn't afraid of heights.

We were turning again, but it would be no use unless I could access that fire again. I tried to feel for it in my heart, but all I felt was racing joy and nervous anticipation, pulsing and dancing through me. I was flying. I was up in the air and I was flying.

And someone had chosen to fly with me.

I told you it was about love. Love of others. Love for your phoenix.

I melted into that sacred feeling, hoping it would be enough. We raced toward the ground and it was all I could do not to close my eyes tight as we hurtled down the street toward where the raiders were regrouping and fitting arrows to bowstrings.

We were out of options. I had to think of something – anything.

An arrow struck me, and I fell forward, eyes closing in pain. I reached for the shaft in my arm at the same moment that Kazmerev seemed to panic within me.

Oh no!

I tumbled down to the ground as he disappeared from under me. The ground rose up and hit me hard. I rolled across it, moaning in pain where the arrow shaft hit the ground.

But I wasn't worried for myself.

Was he hurt? Was he dead?

I scrambled to my feet, fighting the waves of agonizing pain.

The fire was gone from my heart.

The phoenix was back in the sky but no one was looking up anymore, they were all looking at me.

The nearest raider raised his sword and charged.

I gasped, backing up until my shoulders hit the building wall behind me, but the raider followed, leaping forward, his bright blade crashing in a deadly arc.

It stopped dead. Here it came, the killing blow. I gritted my teeth and tried not to flinch.

And then he was yanked away, pulled across the ground, panic in his wide eyes.

I clutched my throat with one hand, shocked.

A dark rope of magic dragged him, flailing. It was looped around his neck, choking the life out of him.

And just like that, he was gone. They were all gone.

I clutched the wall, panting in fear and exertion.

Across the street from me, Kazmerev lighted on the roof of the inn above the terrified townspeople frozen in fear.

It was a good first ride.

I swallowed, looking around. Every raider lay dead where he had stood only moments before and in the doorway of the inn, Judicus lowered his hand.

"I think that before I pass out again," he said calmly. "I should tell you all three things. First, the Flame Rider is not the chosen one. She is merely a very gifted person who has been claimed by a phoenix. Please don't give her to the Hand of Rats while I'm unconscious. Second, the Ai'sletta is among you – the chosen one prophesied of old. She's that comely barmaid with the curling dark hair who likes to dump me behind the bar like a sack of potatoes. And third, if you try to kill me, the ai'sletta, or my new Flame Rider again, I will have you all fed to the drakkon alive. And now I think I shall pass out again."

He slumped slowly down the doorframe, eyes rolling into the back of his head.

I thought I might have gasped. Everyone else did.

A good speech, Kazmerev commented. *A bit short, but that's how it goes when you're losing consciousness.*

He said I was his.

Oh yes, did I not mention that? He sounded far too innocent with that bland mental voice. *Any rider of mine is part of Judicus' magical coterie. When he wakes up, he'll have a lot to say about that. But for now, your village is safe. I don't see a single living raider in the streets or shores. And I see very well indeed.*

All I could see was a phoenix who had saved us all. I wished I could hug him.

They'll think you're crazy hugging an invisible friend.

I wished I could tell him how grateful I was.

I will be sure to ask you to tell me that when everything is settled. I'll want to hear it in detail. But we have the rest of our lives to be grateful, so why don't you get some rest? I'm going to stretch these wings.

I wasn't alone anymore.

I cleared my throat awkwardly and hurried to help the others. When Judicus woke, I'd have a lot of questions for him, but right now, I had a feeling that everyone else had a lot of questions for me. I would answer the ones that I could. But the rest would have to wait for later.

I had a lot of *later* left to come.

EPISODE TWO: SECRET KEEPER

SEASON ONE

19

Dawn came and with it the sense that I'd lost something precious. I would never love the light of day the way I had before. Not now that Kazmerev ruled my nights and emptiness my days.

"The ground is too hard," Nessy complained beside me in the gathering light. The village had decided to bury the dead immediately. If more raiders came, we didn't want them counting bodies and knowing what we'd done. Easier to look innocent with the evidence covered up. "I don't know how they expect us to dig graves when it's still tight with frost. We might as well be hacking at ice."

She was exaggerating. We'd buried Veela and we could bury these raiders. I kept working alongside the others, carving a place for them in the hillside. I couldn't really dig with one arm bandaged and stitched, but I could help carry buckets of clay and help move things out of the way of wheelbarrows. My arm ached where the arrow had grazed it – but that was all it had done. At least it hadn't lodged in the flesh and left me with a ruined arm. This wound would heal quickly once it could rest. And if it couldn't rest it would still heal, just with an angry scar. That's how flesh wounds were.

I didn't like the furtive glances the townsfolk kept stealing at me. No one wanted to work beside me except for Nessy and when I hurried to bring them tools or clear the ground nearby for wheelbarrows, the townsfolk moved too, keeping the distance between us.

"Fire," I'd heard whispered and "phoenix." And I couldn't tell if they thought that my efforts to save our village had succeeded or doomed us all. Some of those eyes glittered with wariness – eyes that had never really looked at me before.

Just as bad, their glances couldn't help but drift by me as they watched Tyndale and Mally arguing very publicly beside us.

"You can't go anywhere with him no matter what he says," Tyndale said for what felt like the hundredth time. I could probably set a rhythm to him saying that and dig this whole hillside out in time with it. The dawn light painted his features in stark relief. "He's making this up. None of us have ever heard of this thing he says you are."

"Ai'sletta," Mally said. She wasn't saying much. She never did when she was really mad – and she was really mad at him. I could see how her eyes were flashing whenever she looked at him. "It means Chosen One."

"Chosen by him, maybe. But you're *my* betrothed and I'm not giving you up."

He was wasting his time. With her chin jutted out like that, Mally had already made her decision. She was going. She'd break their betrothal. She'd walk away from him. She didn't love him enough to stay.

I felt sick at the thought as I carved my own part of the hillside up with the heavy work of digging into clay with one arm. No one loved me like that. No one would beg me to stay anywhere. None of these people – my family, my town – had so much as objected when Aunt Danna suggested offering me to the raiders. If they'd taken me away or killed me, the town would have breathed a sigh of relief. Even now, when we were burying the ones who attacked us instead of burying our own, they still gave me a wide berth.

I gritted my teeth as Tyndale paused and his sad speech cut into my heart in a way that kept it from being able to harden.

"Please, Mally." And with those words, he suddenly wasn't fighting. He was pleading. "You were going to marry me. We were going to have children together. A home. Just like we promised each other. Please."

I risked a glance in her direction. She was looking away, her face inscrutable. The only sound in the air was the sound of picks and shovels on hard clay.

When she finally spoke, the whole town was waiting to hear her words. "I guess we won't now."

She dropped her shovel as if she didn't need it and walked away, leaving the rest of us to bury those who had come looking for her.

I sighed as Tyndale picked up her shovel and with the energy of a man with nothing to lose, tore into the hillside.

I wasn't the only one keeping her gaze to herself and blinking back tears when Uncle Llynd and Gandy arrived a moment later bringing the last of the dead in a wheelbarrow. We'd already buried our own. We'd done that first. And said proper words over them. I shivered at the sight of these raiders. They could have been the rest of us, although I didn't think the raiders would have been kind enough to dig graves.

But if it hadn't been for Kazmerev and Judicus Franzer Irault, that would have been us for sure.

As if I'd spoken his name, the rope worker appeared before me, the wind battering his dark cloak and swirling it around him. Someone had cleaned his fine coat and shirt, but they hadn't been able to fully remove the bloodstains from it or had time to patch the hole where the sword had been buried into his side.

He stood there, swaying for a moment before he found me in the crowd. One finger crooked as he beckoned to me. He was barely on his feet, his dark eyes ringed with purple.

I planted my shovel in the ground and hurried to obey. This is what I'd been waiting for – some sign from him of what came next. Kazmerev had said we'd be part of his coterie now and we'd travel away from here, but he hadn't known more than that, and Judicus had been too ill to tell me.

Now, my hands tingled, and my mouth felt dry at the idea that I was finally going to hear it for myself. I stole a furtive glance over my shoulder and saw the town watching me like they'd watched Mally and Tyndale and I knew one thing for sure – whatever came next, I couldn't stay in my village. Not now. In fact, the sooner I left the better. And that thought left a cold stone in my belly that made me feel like I needed to sit down.

A few days ago, I'd been willing to be an apprentice to anyone who would have me just to get out of this town but now that I had my chance, I was beginning to realize something worrisome: I wasn't ready.

20

I chewed on my lip, suddenly both anxious and excited. I almost felt like I could feel change in the air, like a shift of the wind or a turn of the tide.

"Can we speak together?" Judicus asked me gently.

He had an odd scar running down his temple, old and aged. I'd hardly noticed it in the close sickroom, but here in the light of morning it stood out. At my nod, he tried to turn, clutching his belly.

I slipped my arm under his shoulder and helped him walk. He still shouldn't be out of bed. He needed weeks more to recover. But I understood his urgency. There were more raiders out there. The town's best chance of survival was for us to leave. And this was my chance, too, if I dared to take it.

His face flushed pink in the gathering light. "Or, I suppose I shouldn't say speak."

He looked flustered and I offered him an ironic smile. People always stuttered over how to approach the fact that I couldn't speak to them. Whether my voicelessness was magically induced, or the result of the trauma that had happened to me as a child, I didn't know. It didn't matter to me. I was fine living without a voice and it didn't need fixing – or blushing about.

"I'll learn your signs if I'm given enough time to try," he said, much more confidently. "And, of course, I can understand yes and no."

I nodded at that, laughing silently to myself.

"I sound like a fool," he said ruefully, running a hand through his hair. "But that's why we need to talk. Can we sit together?"

I nodded again, steering him toward a clearing between the hillside and the town where we usually cleaned fish. There was room all around it, so no one would eavesdrop on what he was saying. And there would be somewhere for him to sit. He shouldn't be walking so far.

He settled on the fish cleaning bench and ran a hand over his face again. Maybe he was just as worried as I was.

"I promised you that you would be my secret keeper," he said, looking at me with concern in his eyes. "But you don't have to come with me if you don't want."

I shook my head. I *did* have to go with him. Scared or not. Ready or not. After riding a phoenix through town, I certainly couldn't stay here. No one here wanted that kind of power anywhere nearby. They knew it would draw trouble. So did I.

"It's the ai'sletta that the raiders are after – though I don't know how they knew she was here. It was *my* theory. *My* research." His brow furrowed. "Unless I was followed, but Veela would have noticed. I'm sure of it. She didn't say anything about being followed."

He bit his lip looking away and then back to me.

"Because you are Kazmerev's new Flame Rider, you can have a place in my coterie. Do you want that?"

I nodded firmly. I didn't have a choice. I tried to keep my hands in my skirts so he wouldn't see them shaking.

"Does Kazmerev want that?"

I nodded again, trying a slight smile to put him at his ease.

He sighed and looked like he was trying to compose his thoughts.

"I feel bad dragging you into this mess." He shot a side-eyed look at me and I kept my face straight. As far as I was concerned, this was all very straight-forward, and he was making it more complicated than it needed to be. "Seriously, you don't have to join me. There's ... I think there's more at work in all of this than just raiders attacking a town and saying they want the ai'sletta. No one would judge you for staying here."

I rolled my eyes and he blushed again.

"Okay, I guess you've decided you're with me. Right?" He ran a nervous hand through his hair.

I nodded patiently.

"I suppose I should at least give you some kind of background if you're going to stay with me. I'm from Calicarn." He paused, watching me. A little bird began to sing as blithely as if this wasn't the most important conversation of my life.

I nodded gravely. All I knew about Calicarn was that it was two full nations south of us. It didn't matter. He could be taking me to the other side of the world and it wouldn't matter. I glanced back at the hillside and caught more than one person leaning on a shovel and looking in our direction. I couldn't stay here.

"Our Grand Hadri has a Hunt every five years and if you're young and noble you can round up a group of people to go with you on the Hunt – talented helpers are in the coterie and there can be guards or armsmen with the party, too. Are you with me so far?"

I nodded but my mind was full of questions. What was a Grand Hadri? And did that mean Judicus was a noble? He certainly dressed like one.

"This year, we were supposed to find the ai'sletta. No one expected us to do it. They've been hunting for her for two generations. But I had a theory. A lot of theories. And they led me all the way up here to find the barmaid."

I smirked. Mally wouldn't want to be called that.

He looked guilty. "Here's the thing. I need to get her back to the Grand Hadri with me. But the minute anyone knows who she is, her life will be in danger. So, we have to go in secret and with great care."

I was burning to ask him why this Grand Hadri wanted her. I'd have to be patient because he'd already moved on. Patience was something you learned when you had no voice.

"And, of course, I owe it to you to teach you what I know of Flame Riders. But you don't actually have to join my coterie. It was Veela who swore to me, not Kazmerev. So, you aren't tied to me if you don't want to be, and I'll be honest – you don't want to be." He was rambling. It was a thing people did to protect themselves as if many words could form a shield between themselves and discomfort. He squared his shoulders like he didn't want to say this part. "I'm a mostly un-trained rope worker with limited funds, no transportation, a name that is in ruins in my own land, and absolutely no connection in other lands. A complete wild card. You'd be better off with almost anything. The most I can offer you is an equal share of both danger and reward. I'm ... well, I'm not very good at this."

He looked so downhearted. His head slumped down into his hands and his eyes were tightly shut.

I touched his shoulder and when he still didn't look up, I tightened my grip until he did. Then I pointed at myself and then put my hand on his chest.

I was going with him no matter how little confidence he had in himself. I couldn't stay here. Kazmerev had been clear that *he* wouldn't stay either, and the two of us were as tied together as if we had been married. If I had to go, I'd rather go with Judicus. He'd proven himself to be honorable and kind and I'd never met someone like that in Landsfall. Even this conversation where he was treating me like a full equal who should get a say in her future – well, that was new.

And oddly, his lack of confidence seemed to make me feel stronger – like I had to stand a little taller so I could help him. I could do this. I could.

I watched him shyly as he looked down at my hand and then nodded, pushing his long hair back.

"Okay. Then, I guess I'll make my side of the vow. You can't say the words for yours, but if you agree to stick by me and be part of my coterie then hold my hand while I make the vow and it will count for both of us."

I took his hand firmly in mine. He was so worried that it made me afraid he'd change his mind. I held on tightly so he couldn't squirm away as he said his vow.

His voice had a small hitch as he said, "My honor to keep you. My wealth to succor you. My conscience to guide you. My glory is yours."

Not a bad vow. I squeezed his hand and smiled encouragingly, and he blew a long breath out before letting go of my hand.

"Well, I guess what's done is done. We're tied now, secret keeper," he gave me a rueful smile. "So, I guess now that you're bound to share my counsel and keep my secrets – did I mention that's what a secret keeper is? My closest advisor?" I shook my head, but I was secretly pleased. I was just glad it wasn't a reference to my voicelessness. "Well, I can tell you I'm worried. I've never seen raiders attack like they did here. I've never heard of them looking for the ai'sletta before. And I have a bad feeling they're going to hunt us all the way down the coast. There are other things I should tell you. So many." He looked around him as if he was suddenly worried someone might be listening and when his eyes caught on a solitary raven hopping from a tree to peck at the ground, he shook his head. "But not here. Not in this town. I'll tell you when we leave this place."

21

I don't know everything a Secret Keeper does, but I know Judicus seemed a lot lighter after he told me that much.

"Come on. We need to go convince your family," he said when he was done. I didn't think Mally would need much convincing after this morning, but I thought the rest of her family might feel differently.

We found her with my aunt Danna.

"Already done burying all the dead?" my aunt asked me with a pointed look. She wasn't happy to see us. Mally was working beside her cleaning the common room of the inn and we'd walked right into an argument. I could tell by the way they both had identical flashing eyes and innocent looks on their faces.

I shook my head and gestured to Judicus, indicating he had something to say.

"The raiders will be back, honored innkeeper," he said to my aunt and his accent seemed just a little thicker. Was he doing that on purpose? "But only if I and the ai'sletta remain here. We need to leave. As soon as possible."

"Mally can stay right here," my aunt said, her words tight and sharp. I knew better than to push her when she was in a mood like this but Judicus didn't.

"She can't," he said simply. "Those who survived will be finding reinforcements. They'll be back. Maybe even tonight. I can hold them off when I'm well and strong, but I used up a lot of my strength last night and I'm not healed. I won't be able to keep them off of us forever."

"Then Sersha will," my aunt said, her voice even pricklier as if she could discourage conversation with it. "She surprised us all with that display last night, but she's always been a good girl. She'll be loyal to her family and her town."

"*Sersha* is still learning," Judicus said, shooting a look my way. Had he heard my name before this? I wasn't sure. But I was glad he knew it now. "She won't be able to hold them off forever, either. Especially now that the element of surprise has been lost. We need to leave. Tonight, or tomorrow morning."

"If you can't keep them safe in a nice stone inn, then you can't keep them safe out on the road," my aunt Danna said in a sing-song voice. I took a step back. I'd learned to fear that voice. There was no coming back from that voice.

"I don't think you understand," Judicus began.

I tugged his arm. If he thought raiders were dangerous, he had no idea how bad Aunt Danna could be when she used the sing-song voice.

"Mally." Aunt Danna said, hammering her words out like Tyndale hammered iron. "Is marrying Tyndale. She is staying here. She will have children. She will live a long and happy life. And *we* will protect her."

And then she turned her back as if that was all there was to the discussion.

I caught a side glance from Mally. Her chin jutted out and her arms were crossed. And despite the fact that her eyes stayed almost entirely on Aunt Danna, I was pretty sure she planned to go with us. Judicus didn't need to convince Aunt Danna – not when Mally's mind was made up.

I tugged Judicus back to our room and laid him down on Mally's bed and started to brew tea. He sank back gratefully, gasping as I offered the tea and checked his bandages. He was bleeding again. All that walking and talking had been too much effort. I shook my head at him and pointed to his wound.

"I know," he said, his eyes fluttering shut. "I'm in bad shape. But we can't stay here."

I nodded my understanding.

"Do you think she'll come with us if we can slip her out from under her mother's nose?" he asked me.

I nodded and then tried to indicate with gestures that he had no horse. It took a while to make him understand.

"Veela and I came on one, but yes, I don't think it's here anymore," he agreed. "That's okay. I planned to take a boat from among those the raiders brought here. Do you think you can gather supplies? Blankets? Herbs for pain? Maybe a kettle?"

He looked at me helplessly as I nodded. Veela must have been the practical one. If we were going to set out in a boat, we'd need so much more than blankets and herbs. And I was going to have my work cut out for me gathering it all under Aunt Danna's nose.

I bathed his head with a cool cloth and then slipped from his room when he dozed off to sleep. Would he survive a boat ride? It would probably be gentler than riding a horse, but if we hit rough seas, they would still jostle him. And any jostling might aggravate his wound.

Worry curled in my chest. We had raiders to worry about. And an uncertain future. His wound complicated both those things.

I was still frowning in thought when I closed the door behind me and turned right into Aunt Danna, standing with her arms crossed over her chest.

"Well, Sersha," she said with a quirked eyebrow. "You aren't planning to leave us just yet, are you?"

I shook my head no and she seemed to soften.

"But you are going to leave?"

I agreed and she nodded, her eyes narrowing. "That's probably for the best. A lot has happened in these past days and I think it's best for everyone if you head along your way."

I wasn't going to get an apology from her for offering me up as a sacrificial lamb. That was for sure.

I thought I might be willing to forgive her anyway. Especially now as I looked into her uncertain eyes. She was trying to disguise the look in them with bold words and bluster, but there was fear underneath. We took care of our family. She'd taken care of me when my parents died. Was she afraid I wouldn't do my part now? That I would put them in danger?

"I'll make a deal with you, Sersha," she said grimly. "I'll help you gather all the supplies you need as long as you promise me, you'll take that boy and leave here tomorrow morning."

I nodded fervently.

"And that you'll leave Mally behind," she said, her voice hard as iron. "If he wants someone to be called ai'sletta and go far away with him it can be you. No one will know the difference anyway."

I hesitated.

Her face darkened with fury. "At least promise me that you won't try to convince her to come with you. Promise me you'll leave her to my advice and counsel.

That I could do. I nodded my agreement.

But I doubted Judicus could be convinced of that. I was his secret keeper, but for some reason I couldn't fathom, Mally meant more than that to him. She meant enough to come up here and risk his life for. Being voiceless, I was spared having to tell my aunt what she should have already known – that nothing would be the same in Landsfall ever again.

22

I didn't have time to tell Judicus what was happening, and I wasn't sure how I would even if I'd had the opportunity. It would be a while until he learned my signs well enough to communicate larger ideas with me.

Judicus slept the day away – and no wonder. That wound he'd suffered would take time and energy to heal and I didn't know what cost he paid for the magic he used defending our town.

I checked on him twice during the day in between taking a nap and gathering what things Aunt Danna said I could take with me. She wasn't stingy. She allowed for two wheels of cheese and dried meat wrapped in oilcloth, road rations of fat and dried berries, two waterskins, two blankets, fire-starting equipment, a pot – all the basics. Even so, once they were packed into four leather bags, they seemed a meager thing to take of the life I'd had. I stood awkwardly over them, one hand clutching the other arm when the sun dipped low and Kazmerev was born again in my heart.

My relief at seeing him again was enough to almost send me to my knees. Bright feathers bloomed from the darkness, blushing scarlet from his plum body and then slowly ripening to burnished gold at the tips of his feathers. He felt like warmth in my heart.

I'm very happy to see you, too. I feel ... fresh and new in your service.

I stumbled out of the stables where the bags were stashed to find him in the quiet outside the places of people. All the villagers were inside the inn again. No one could shake the feeling that the raiders might return at any time. No one wanted to go home yet – not when that might be deadly.

A guard had been posted on the inn roof – but he wasn't looking in the courtyard. I stole out into the silky night, careful not to walk toward the finished graves, but in the other direction, inland.

Was Kazmerev unhurt? He'd had to leave so suddenly last night. I reached carefully for him and he ducked his head so I could touch the silky feathers there.

I am reborn safe and sound. Don't fear for me. He sounded cautious. *I followed the raiders who fled, watching to see where they went. They were regrouping south of here. They will come back to this town.* He paused again. He must be afraid to bring this up after I was so set to defend my town last time. *The best thing for your people is for us to leave.*

So everyone kept telling me.

And Judicus? Will he come with us?

Yes. We were still a part of his coterie.

Kazmerev seemed pleased. He tossed his head and little sparks flickered off with the scent of woodsmoke.

Then go get him. It's time.

But we were leaving in the morning. It was planned.

We travel at night. It's safer, and I can guard you from above. In the day, how will I watch your back, little hawk? You are as one newly fledged and with no voice of your own. You shouldn't travel when I cannot watch you. And the sooner we set out the further we can travel before I die the phoenix death once more.

I felt torn. He made perfect sense, but I'd also promised Aunt Danna we'd leave in the morning. I hadn't said goodbye. I hadn't slept except in tiny snatches in three days. I wasn't ready to travel. I was ready to sleep.

I understand. Everyone is cranky without sleep – not that I would know. I am either dead or alive. There is no in-between. He sounded angry.

I felt my cheeks growing hot.

No, no need for embarrassment. You can't be expected to remember little details like when I'm alive or when I'm dead. You can sleep now. Here. I will wake you when the night is half full and you can go rouse Judicus then.

He was angry. And I didn't know what to do about it. I was just trying to make everyone happy.

You can't make everyone happy. Pick a person. Make that person happy. The rest will have to live with disappointment.

He clearly meant he wanted me to pick him. I was about to explain that things weren't that simple when a lantern light bobbed out of the darkness and Mally seized me by the back of the neck.

"If you think you're leaving without me you can think again," she hissed.

I held up my hands to placate her.

"I'm the ai'sletta that the rope worker was looking for." She tossed her curls as if she wanted me to know how confident she was, but I saw the gleam of worry in her eye.

This is the ai'sletta of prophecy? I wasn't sure if Kazmerev sounded more awed or more offended.

I didn't know any prophecies, but I knew Mally. She didn't like being excluded. And she could be vicious if she thought you were trying to take something of hers.

With my hands, I asked her about Tyndale.

She rolled her eyes. "There are other men. Maybe I'll even come back for him. Who knows?"

I gave her a worried look.

"Don't judge, Sersha. If he really loves me, he can wait. He's not the one the raiders are looking for."

And that was why she was coming with us. I saw the glint of fear in her eye. Sometimes with Mally, you have to listen for all the things she isn't saying.

"I'm going to wake the rope worker," she said calmly, pinching my arm. I batted her hand away. "You go get the bags and meet us at the docks. We're taking a boat."

She was gone without waiting to see if I agreed or not.

That is the ai'sletta of prophecy? That pinching gull?

I almost laughed at his thoughts. A gull. That was too mild of a word. Mally could be quite cunning.

Hmm. But if she harms you, she'll find I do more than singe her edges. I'm angry – angry all the time when I think of Veela and how she died. I wouldn't mind burning something.

She wouldn't harm me. And Kazmerev had better not burn her. Mally would just make my life a misery. I tried not to think about that as I gathered the bags of what Aunt Danna had let me take. There would be no goodbyes. And there would be no sleep.

I peeked out of the stables and looked longingly around the town. Landsfall was the only place I remembered living. I knew every nook of the place. And now I was going to leave in the night without a goodbye. It felt like running out on a friend.

Listen. Let your heart feel mine.

I paused outside the stable and let my eyes drift to him standing on the thatched roof, his glorious fire caressing every feather and gleaming in his bright, knowing eyes. The eye on the side nearest me looked right down into my eyes.

I will not leave you. I will not abandon you. You will never need to say goodbye to me.

My eyes pricked with tears as his words turned lighter.

And as for the ai'sletta – if she pinches you again, I will peck her toes. He seemed irritated. *Even if it lowers me to her level, and I never thought I'd sink that low.*

I nodded my head, grateful, and adjusted the bags hanging from my shoulders. They were heavy and I was not ready for this.

We're never ready for adventures, Sersha. But sometimes they are just what we need.

Adventures, it seemed, were very uncomfortable.

23

By the time I had gathered our bags and worked my way out to the docks, Mally was already there dragging a reluctant Judicus with her.

"If we don't leave now, I'm not going at all," she said, her jaw set and determined. She was exactly like Aunt Danna when she wanted to be.

"Look, surely we can be reasonable about this," Judicus was saying, his hands held up as if he could ward her off. "We do need to leave, but we can wait until the morning. You can say your goodbyes to your family and your friends. You might not see them for a very long time. Isn't that a good reason to wait?"

"It's a good reason to go," Mally said, looking over her shoulder, as if she could already see Aunt Danna striding after her. "Before they find a way to tie me to this town and I never get to leave."

"We will need some supplies," Judicus protested. "We can't eat hopes or drink dreams."

"Sersha has all the supplies we need, don't you, Sersha?" Mally asked as she searched through the boats tied to the docks. Some were fisherman's boats – left here when the fishermen fled to the inn during the raid. Some were foreign – boats of raiders that they couldn't afford to crew when they fled here missing so many of their number. She hurried along the docks testing one after another. Most were damaged – whether intentionally or accidentally – from the chaos before.

I held up the leather bags awkwardly and tried to will Kazmerev to be seen so Judicus could see we were both there. He looked relieved.

"It's good to see you both," he said, running a nervous hand through his hair.

He looks ill. I think I agree with him. You should wait for him to rest more.

"I must admit, I'm barely keeping to my feet," Judicus said, as if telling me a great secret. "And I could really use another night of sleep, but your cousin might be right. Maybe now is the best time to –"

"This one," Mally called from beside a small fishing sloop. It had two sets of oars and a single mast with a sail. It didn't have water in the hull – an improvement on the others – and the sail was rolled neatly which suggested the owner took good care of it, but it wasn't a raider boat. Taking it would be stealing. "Don't look at me like that, Sersha. It's not stealing. Tyndale will pay the fisherman if he's still alive."

Tyndale. Who she was abandoning. Was he supposed to sit here and pine for her and pay her debts? Or did she expect him to marry someone else and still pay for a boat?

I shook my head, crossing my arms over my chest.

I also do not approve of theft. I will not endorse it. Kazmerev sounded put out. He ruffled his feathers irritably, his eye never leaving Mally.

"Can you swim, rope worker? Sersha and I can, though I'm much faster," Mally said blithely. "Not that I think we'll have to, but if a disaster strikes it would be good to know."

"Of course, I can swim," Judicus said absently.

"Not everyone can."

"Can Kazmerev see any raiders nearby?" Judicus asked me nervously. It was a good question and I nearly sighed with relief.

Could he go check? It might simplify things down here.

I'll look.

Kazmerev leapt into the sky and my heart made a little lurch. I wanted to fly up there with him away from ground quarrels that might lead to a stolen boat and the way my belly was rolling and flopping at the idea of running from Landsfall in the middle of the night.

You will again, I swear it. We'll fly together.

He made a wide circle, looking in every direction.

I'll put you on my shoulders tomorrow and fly you as far and wide as you want to go – but I think that if you want to travel with Judicus you might need to stay with him. He is barely standing. He needs a groundling to help him walk.

He was right. When I looked at Judicus he was swaying on his feet. He wasn't well enough for much more standing. With care, I took his hand and led him into the boat to the prow. Mally was checking the oars and making sure her bags were in a good place.

I took Judicus' bag gently from him and put it in the hull so he could rest against it.

"Thank you," he said softly. There was pain in that voice.

"No rest for him. He needs to row. There's no wind," Mally announced.

I shook my head at her and positioned myself at the first set of oars, staring at them grimly. I couldn't row well with my arm injured but I wasn't sure what else to do. She was going to get our ally killed and then she really would be trapped here.

She rolled her eyes. "Sersha, always the martyr."

"Sersha?" Judicus asked faintly. I glanced over my shoulder at him. "Does Kazmerev see anything?"

Tell him I see fires down the shore but now for a few hours by boat. Nothing inland but the town. Nothing north. Is the next town north very far?

I wasn't sure there was a next town north. Our supplies came from the south or inland.

There should be more north of here.

But I also couldn't tell Judicus all of that. I tried to sign to Mally and she snorted. "I'm busy getting ready to sail, Sersha, and you know that if my mother notices we're gone she won't let me go, so stop trying to distract me. We can chat later."

I had not realized how I would partake in your voicelessness. Veela was my voice to other humans.

I feel my cheeks flare red. I'd dragged him into this with me. It wasn't fair. And then suddenly he was there, landing whisper-soft on the gunwale of the boat and leaning in so that his huge head brushes cheek to cheek with mine.

I am pleased to share this with you. I am pleased to join you in it.

He gently butted his feathered head against me.

I was stunned.

He said he was *pleased*. He'd lost his voice now that he was bound to me and he was ... pleased?

I'm pleased with you and that is all that matters. Now, do not fear, little hawk, I will fly above, and I will keep us safe. Watch over Judicus Franzer Irault and try to keep that gull back from him and we'll find a way clear of this place and our enemies.

He launched himself upward in a flurry of sparks. I blinked my vision clear and when I turned over my shoulder to look at Judicus, he was fast asleep, his mouth hanging open. His injury really had taken a lot out of him.

Before I'd even turned back again, the boat lurched forward and shuddered. I spun in my seat and met Mally's grin.

"And we're off," she said, grabbing her own oars. "South, I think. I'm sick of the cold and that's clearly where he comes from. We'll row out a little and then set the sail. I think I can manage that much."

I shook a finger, a clear warning sign, and she rolled her eyes.

"If you think I'm going to let you choose the direction we go, you're crazy, Sersha. This is my escape, and we're doing it my way."

I tried again, pointing to the south and running a finger across my throat. If there were fires there, there was trouble there.

Mally ignored the warning and began to row without another word. Stunned by her thoughtless bravery, I stared at her for long minutes. The world smelled of water and seaweed and the balmy breezes that sometimes rolled over Landsfall like a thick wool blanket. It also smelled a little bit of fear.

Somewhere in the distance an owl hooted from the shore, its call barely audible over the splash splash of the waves on the shore.

I bit my lip. How close were those fires?

Not close. And this boat doesn't look very fast.

Was there some other way I could warn her?

I suppose you could try to overpower her.

And then what?

Set your own course?

But I didn't know where to go, either.

Hopefully, Judicus would wake before we reached those fires Kazmerev had seen and then I could convince him to listen. Hopefully, Mally *would* listen to him.

Hopefully, I hadn't just started a journey with two crazy people and one friend who would be gone with the dawn.

But I will remain alive in your heart.

There was that.

And it would have to be enough.

24

I was leaning over in my seat, half asleep, when I heard voices. I blinked fully awake. Across from me, Mally put a finger to her lips, tilting her head to the side as she listened. She kept one hand on a rope she held attached to the boom and another on the tiller. She'd been right, she seemed able to sail the boat – though where she'd learned that was a mystery to me. Tyndale was no sailor, and neither were any of the people in our family. Could a friend have taught her?

She tapped her lips again, emphasizing the need for silence. The only sound came from waves lapping against the hull.

Kazmerev was supposed to warn me if we were close to people.

You shouldn't be close to anyone there. From the air, I see nothing. The fires are still further down the coast.

And yet, I still heard them. Their voices were faint, but they echoed over the calm water.

"It won't be easy to get them to attack again. They didn't like the surprise that he was a rope worker."

"I thought you stabbed him. How did he get to the town when he was that injured? He should have died on the road, and the woman, too."

I clamped a hand over my mouth. These were the people who attacked Judicus!

He woke, as if summoned by my thoughts, shuffling in the boat to sit up. I placed a finger over my lips. It was so dark that I couldn't see individual people along the shore, just a vague outline of land and sea.

Their next words were snatched away.

"Where are we?" Judicus groaned, waking.

"South," Mally said in a low tone. "About two hours from Landsfall by boat."

Judicus cursed quietly, sitting up. "Are you crazy? We'll have to backtrack the whole way. We can't go south! The raiders are there."

I felt like rolling my eyes. Well, obviously. But no one was listening to me.

"South is where you're from and it's where we're going, isn't it?" Mally said with a sniff. "It's the middle of the night. If we stay quiet, we'll slide right past any raiders and be on our way. You don't know what's north. There could be more raiders there, too. And the roads inland would take too long with all of us on foot. I don't think you're up to walking."

Would we have to go on foot? I wondered if Kazmerev could carry all three of us.

Not far. Maybe a short hop. I could carry you and one other a long distance, but that takes a lot of strength and practice from my Flame Rider since you'd be manifesting my physical presence enough to carry another person. For the first few months, we should stick to just the two of us. We need time to adjust to each other.

That made a lot of sense.

I smiled slightly, imagining I was on his back right now with my hand buried in his bright-lined feathers and his wings spread into the wind. My heartbeat sped just thinking about it and a little hard lump formed in the back of my throat.

I think so, too. As soon as we don't have to watch for enemies, we'll fly together again. I will teach you the ways of the Flame Riders.

I'd like to hear more about them, too. I knew so little.

I shall regale you with their great tales and stories, the histories of when my people have tangled with yours.

I was so busy listening to him that I hadn't noticed how long Judicus was silent until he hissed his reply to Mally.

"You've put us in real trouble, Ai'sletta. If we go back, we'll have to fight the wind and get past those voices." So, he had heard the voices. He must know then that the ones who had stabbed him were lurking on the shore. "And we don't know if there are more raiders down the shore."

I nodded my head as if to try to tell him that there were indeed more raiders further south, but he wasn't looking. His head was in his hands as he thought.

I swiveled back to Mally and tried to convince her with signs that there were people further south. She waved a hand through the air, irritated. She didn't want me distracting from her plan.

"If you're going to travel with us, Sersha," she whispered. "The least you can do is keep rowing. And just so the pair of you know, if you think this journey is hard on you, it's just as hard on me. I'm the one who had to leave Tyndale behind, but you don't see me moaning about it constantly."

Remind me why you put up with this from her?

She was my cousin. She wasn't all bad. We'd been friends our whole lives.

If this is what "friend" means to you then I am not your friend. We'll need a new word for what we are because I don't plan to treat you like this.

He sounded angry again.

Of course I'm angry! She's treating my Flame Rider like a common servant.

I'd be lucky to find a job as a common servant. That kind of regular pay without being a burden on your family was a real step up.

I could feel his mental eye roll.

Now that you are my rider, there will be no more talk of servants.

But ...

None.

"Can Kazmerev carry all three of us?" Judicus asked, looking up at me. It took me a moment to pull myself back to our conversation. Even in the faint light, he looked like he was barely keeping himself conscious. He ought to have more healing tea, but there was no way to brew it in a boat.

I absolutely cannot. I could feel his feathers puffing in irritation. *Judicus Franzer Irault should remember he's speaking to a phoenix, not some farm ox he found on the side of the road.*

I leaned forward to feel Judicus's forehead. How sick was he? Was the fever back? He gently caught my hand and turned it aside.

"Can he?" he asked again.

I shook my head sadly and tried to indicate with signs that there were many fires south of here.

He sighed. "I can't see your hands in the darkness and even if I could, I don't know what you're saying, Sersha. I promise I will ask the ai'sletta to help me learn your signs so we can speak, and we'll keep light with us so I can see. You must be very frustrated."

I was. But I was more worried about running into that party of raiders. I bit my lip and tried again.

"I'm sorry," he said again, still not understanding. "I promise we will try. For now, we'll follow the ai'sletta's plan. Our best hope is to get as far away from the voices that claimed they were responsible for stabbing me before they try to do it again. I don't much care for being stabbed."

He huffed a wry laugh and Mally joined him.

"Exactly," she said, satisfied with our decision. "Now, head down Sersha, so I can shift this sail, and let the poor man pass out again. You and I will get us down the coast and in the morning, you can talk all you want with your hands and I will translate."

At least I won't have to be there for that. I have a bad feeling that she's quite loose with the translation.

Sometimes I couldn't tell if Mally knew she was doing foolish things and just didn't care, or if she really didn't realize what she was doing but her confidence fooled you into thinking she did. Whichever it was, it could be deadly to have that kind of confidence in this situation.

I bit my lip and wondered if Kazmerev could help us at all.

Usually, I could help by warning that there are fires ahead and getting closer by the minute. I think I also see movement on the water.

Great. That was just great.

But since no one will listen to us, I think you and I need to prepare for danger, Sersha. Are you ready to fight raiders with me again?

25

The clouds are getting too thick. That's what Kazmerev had said an hour ago and at first, I was worried he meant that they got in the way of flying, but now I realized the real problem – they got in the way of seeing.

I haven't seen your boat in an hour. I can't get low enough. Can you see?

Honestly, I couldn't see either. I'd tried to tap Mally's leg and then her arm to ask her if she could see well enough to guide the boat and she'd just shaken me off while shushing me.

"They're going to hear us, Sersha. Is that what you want?" she whispered fiercely.

And that's when I knew I'd made a terrible mistake. I shouldn't have gotten into a boat with Mally at the helm. I shouldn't have let Judicus do it, either.

Honestly, it might be best that she left her betrothed behind. She doesn't seem to play well with others.

I slipped to the front of the boat and shook Judicus awake.

"What? Who is it?" he sounded only half awake.

"Leave him alone, Sersha!" Mally hissed. "I'm more than able to sail this boat without consulting the rope worker for every high wave."

"Sersha?" I couldn't even see Judicus's face in the darkness. I leaned back so he wouldn't sit up and bump his head on mine, but that was the best I could do.

All joking aside, I'm getting anxious up here, Sersha. Kazmerev sounded more than nervous. *I tried to get low enough to find you and one of my wings dipped into the sea. It's fog all the way down to the water.*

That wasn't good. And I couldn't even tell Judicus. I bit my lip and tried to think. Could I draw Kazmerev to where we were? Could he help us tell Judicus what was happening?

No. Wait for him. He'll figure it out.

He seemed deadly calm. Which was utterly different from the anger he kept letting out. Why be angry at everything else but not at this?

The anger is my grief, the only way I have to express my loss. This is a problem that needs solving. Immediately.

I waited long moments until Judicus spoke again, this time with eerie calm.

"Mally," he said slowly. "I feel that I do you an injustice asking this, and yet I am very nervous about what your answer might be. Have you – by any chance – sailed us right into a bank of fog and then continued to sail, not knowing where land is, not dropping an anchor, and not waking me to tell me of this predicament?"

"We're fine," Mally said confidently. "It's just weather."

And that's about when Judicus realized he'd also made a huge mistake.

"What have I done," he moaned.

I waited. After a minute he'd realize – like I did – that there was really nothing we could do now except take down the sail, drop the anchor, and wait it out. At least there wasn't much breeze in the fog.

Whoa now! Kazmerev said and then he made a sound I didn't know that sounded almost like a combination of a bird screeching and a human being cursing.

What was he seeing? What had happened?

His mental voice was clipped.

Sudden wind. Can see. Ships. So many ships.

What? What should we do?

Get that sail down! You're going to crash!

At that exact moment, a wind hit the sail, slamming the boom to one side and dragging Mally with it. She clung to the rope, nearly falling out of the boat as it leaned precariously to that side.

Her shriek – more anger than fear – cut through the air.

I was glad that I couldn't speak, because I wouldn't be able to hold my tongue now. With all my strength, I jammed myself to the other side of the boat, trying to even out her weight.

Judicus, being gifted with a voice, let out a startled yell and then we hit another boat – well, boat was too small of a word for it. We hit a ship with our boat.

There was a crunching sound and a sudden lurch that rattled my teeth together and made my head feel like it had been cleaved open. Pain rolled through my neck.

Cold, inky water bit my feet, swirling up in the darkness to reach my ankles and shins and knees.

"She's going down," Judicus yelled, scrambling backward, gathering our leather bags of supplies and holding them up out of the water. Our boat tilted to one side, leaning painfully as the bow was lost to the depths.

Kazmerev! Was he close enough? Help!

Coming. Coming. Coming. He sounded as panicked as I felt. *Hold on! I've lost sight of you again.*

I couldn't see well enough in the inky darkness to see anything other than a vague outline of the ship we'd hit. There were shouts from above, but the exact words were blocked out by Mally's cursing.

There was a sound like something huge swallowing and then the boat and everything I had was swallowed by the waves.

I opened my mouth – to scream perhaps – and I suddenly found myself neck-deep in water, trying to swim. The wound in my arm burned and my panicked breathing made my lungs burn right along with it.

I tried to turn in the water, searching for Judicus, when Mally's loud cursing abruptly stopped, and something grabbed the collar of my dress and dragged up upward.

26

There was a scream from above and I felt the brush of something warm against the back of my neck.

Kazmerev! He was here to save me.

I reached for him with my heart, all my hopes stretching up with me.

I began to smile and then – like a knife slicing through soft earth – the clouds parted, and a beam of dawn struck me.

I felt like I almost heard a bird-like shriek and then Kazmerev was gone. My heart fell.

"Bring them aboard and let's take a look," a gravelly voice said, and my vision was temporarily blocked by a flurry of dark shapes hauling me forward, the timbers of a ship, and a variety of boots.

My heart was pounding, and I felt as agitated as the shrieking gulls swirling around us. All it had taken was a breath to lose the boat and Kazmerev.

I was dropped unceremoniously to the deck beside Mally whose lips were slightly purple in the pale dawn light. Her skin pebbled with cold, and her hands wrapped around herself as if she could clutch her warmth to herself. Our supplies were dumped beside her and water spilled out of the sodden leather bags, spilling across the rough wood of the decking.

I bit my lip.

"It's them," someone said. "That's the rope worker."

Judicus groaned and they all stepped back. I took a chance and peered around Mally to where he was slumped on the deck, dark hair plastered against his face. He looked half-drowned even though I knew he couldn't be. It must be his wound. He wasn't even close to healed and the sudden movements needed to scramble out of a sinking boat followed by being dragged and hauled upward must have hurt his side.

Yes. Right there. Fresh blood stained his linen shirt.

I started to move to help, and a hand clamped on my shoulder.

"You're not going anywhere," the same gravelly voice said.

I pointed to Judicus's injury and the man laughed at me, grabbing me by the chin and forcing me to look up at him. The lower half of his face was wrapped in a swath of oilcloth with a pair of leather buckled straps keeping the cloth up and a deep hood surrounding it all. Only his eyes were visible, set in weather-beaten skin that crinkled around their edges. They were steely and hard – hard enough that I didn't want to make him angry unless it was my only option.

"Cat got your tongue?" he asked – my least favorite expression. It's moments like this when I want to curse people and tell them exactly what I think that I am grateful to be voiceless. I'm glad there's something to keep me from ripping them apart – because I could. Oh, I could. I've practiced all those words and speeches in my head. I know exactly what I'd say. I know how it would make me feel powerful. And it's best not to say any of it at all.

Words are their own kind of magic and even against enemies, they need to be used sparingly. They are arrows. Once loosed, they don't come back without striking.

"Well? Speak or we'll give you reason to speak." A sharp dagger appeared in his hand, flicking at the cloth of my sodden dress near my belly. I bit my cheek, trying not to panic.

"She's voiceless," Mally said from beside me and I almost sagged with relief at her help. There was never any guarantee with her. She might help you when you needed it – or she might not, and I could never figure out which path she'd take until she took it. "She won't be able to answer your questions."

"Is that so?" the man said. I could just see over his shoulder that his whole crew was looking at us, peering around each other to get an eyeful. "And why are you sailing with a mortally injured ropeworker and a voiceless girl, pretty, pretty maid?"

He didn't look at Mally when he said that. His eyes were still on mine. I gritted my teeth. Raiders killed my parents. Raiders were what haunted my nightmares. But I didn't dare let him see that in my eyes. I knew what anger could do to you. Even the kind that roared through Kazmerev in waves of grieving. It could burn your strength of mind away and leave you hollow.

"She's who the ropeworker was looking for," Mally said casually. "He called her 'ai'sletta.' Whatever that means. But she can't go with him alone. She needs someone to interpret her hand signs and that's me."

My stomach dropped.

Well, I *thought* she had decided to help. It turned out she was helping herself – shifting any suspicion or concern in my direction instead of hers. Great. Now they really wouldn't let me help Judicus – not if they thought I was valuable in some way. And they thought I was the one they came searching for. What would they do to me now?

I shook my head, heart racing and the raider holding me grabbed my shirtfront and shook me.

"Do you deny it?" he asked.

I nodded firmly.

The raider glanced aside and I followed his gaze to Judicus on the deck. His face was ghostly pale and the spot of blood on his side was growing.

"Why else would he be fleeing on a fishing boat in the middle of the night?" Mally asked. "Why would he be so desperate that he'd sail right into the middle of all your ships."

She gestured and I followed the line of her hand to see what she was pointing at.

In the cloak of night and fog, we'd sailed right into the middle of a group of raider boats at anchor. Now that the fog was clearing, I could count six masts emerging from the mist. Great. Just great. Even if we could somehow get away from this one, there were five others to chase us down and snatch us up.

I clenched my jaw and my fists. This was not a time to surrender or lose hope.

"He's not much of a sailor," the raider laughed, his accent so thick that I nearly missed his words. His crew's snickers filled the air as I risked another glance in Judicus's direction. He'd likely torn his stitches. Hopefully, he hadn't done worse damage than that.

Stupid, stupid, Sersha.

I should have found some way to stop Mally from sailing us here. I should have jumped on her and overpowered her. It had just felt like such an overreaction at the time. But now, what was I going to do to help Judicus and to get us out of this mess? Especially now that we had been captured by the very people we were fleeing.

I was so used to just going along with people that even contradicting them felt like a big statement. It had never occurred to me to take back control and force Mally to do things my way. And now I was seeing what all my politeness had earned me.

The man holding my wrist and chin seemed to be considering Mally's words. It was hard to tell with his face covered, but his eyes flicked back and forth between us.

"Put them in the bow and tie them securely. We'll make for Finger Point and see if the mistress likes their story."

"And the village?" a voice asked.

"We have no other business there if the ones we seek are already aboard," the gravelly-voiced raider said. "Signal the others to lift anchor. We'll set a course and be on our way."

I caught Mally's eye, and she winked as if to tell me not to spoil her ruse – which was crazy because if I could have denied what she was saying any more firmly, I already would have. No one was going to listen to me. They never did.

"Tie the ai'sletta extra tightly," the raider said. "If we return without her, we don't get paid."

Great. Just great.

27

They tied my hands in front of me – very tightly, as if they thought I'd be able to slip away at a moment's notice. I schooled my face to acceptance, forcing my frustration away. I'd had a few moments of self-pity, but I couldn't stay there. That wouldn't help anyone.

I wished I had my hands, not just to check Judicus's wounds but also to scold Mally for first of all getting us into this situation and second of all for placing the entire blame of it on me. But maybe it was better that I couldn't do that right now. Better to get a hold of myself. Things could be worse. We could have gone down with our boat.

"We'll need supplies to bandage him again," Mally told our captors, pointing to where I was trying to tend Judicus's wound. One of his stitches had come free and the healing skin had split open again, leaking blood. Without bandages or supplies, it was going to be hard to stitch him. I shot Mally a sour look – I hadn't entirely mastered calm yet. She returned it with complete innocence. "Isn't that what you want Sersha?"

Of course, it was what I wanted, but I just shook my head. Calm. Sersha. Calm. Get control of your frustration.

"Thank you," Mally told the raider when he returned. "Do you ever take that scarf down?"

"No," the raider said shortly, shoving the bandages at me. Clearly, he knew who was really doing the work.

"Not even for a little while?" she asked and when he stomped away, she snickered. "See, Sersha? They're easy. Let them think you're an idiot and they won't pay any attention to you at all."

I wanted to tell her that playing with raiders wasn't going to get her in my good books. I wanted to tell her I was worried about Judicus – that it wasn't good for his healing to be on this adventure. I wanted to tell her that she should have listened to me when I tried to convince her that sailing south was a bad idea.

I glanced up and found her looking out across the bow and into the wind, her jaw jutting out and her tied hands clasped together. She looked upset. Not just angry or irritated but genuinely afraid.

Even if I hadn't been voiceless, I would have swallowed all my words at that look. We were all human. We all made mistakes.

I sighed and went back to work binding Judicus's wounds. I managed to stop his bleeding and get everything clean and rebandaged, even with my hands bound, and by the time I was done I was exhausted. I slumped down beside him and looked around us.

The raiders had dumped us in the bow of their small sailing ship. They'd left one raider to guard us, but he was keeping his distance. The rest worked busily around the boat.

The boat they held us on was in the lead with the others following close behind through the last scraps of mist. A crosswind was picking up, blowing the sea into a frenzy and smashing the starboard side of our boat with wave upon frothy wave. White spray flew through the air keeping us constantly damp and the scent of salt was heavy in the air. Almost, I was glad we'd been caught by the raiders. If we'd stayed in the fishing boat, it would be swamped by now.

Almost.

Mally gave up on looking noble and brave and came to squat with me over Judicus's unconscious body.

"What I think we both need to know," she said, "is what the ai'sletta is supposed to be and why everyone wants her so badly."

I gave her a dry look.

"Well, I'd say it was me that needed to know," she whispered unapologetically, "but now that I've told everyone that you're her, I think you'll need to know what they expect. I can't quite tell if the raiders came because they want her dead or because they want to make her their queen."

I gave her a second dry look. She was getting good at interpreting those.

"And yes," she whispered with a smirk. "If the queen thing is real, I'll be taking that back."

I hesitated a moment before nodding my agreement. I hated to admit it, but she was right. We needed to know that. As soon as possible. Really, we should have pressed Judicus for details earlier but the whole part about saving the town from another raid had seemed more urgent.

We'd accomplished that, at least. These raiders were sailing in the exact opposite direction. Landsfall would be safe from raids. They'd have time to rebuild. Our family would be safe.

If we'd headed north, all these ships would have had to go past – or even *through* – Landsfall. I looked at the rising light in the distance and tried very hard not to imagine what would have come next.

I didn't want to admit it to myself, but maybe Mally's mistake hadn't been a total disaster.

"See? My choice wasn't a total disaster," she said, smiling out across the ocean as if she could read my mind.

I bit my lip, willing myself to calm again.

"We're leading them away from the family. And Tyndale. You keep thinking it was so easy for me to leave him behind, but it wasn't. It wasn't."

I felt my eyebrows rising. I really had thought it was easy for her to leave him behind. She had acted like she didn't care. The glassiness to her gaze now said otherwise.

"And I took a knife off that raider when I was asking him about his scarf, so I can cut these bonds and we can all run – as soon as Judicus wakes up," she said easily.

My eyes widened and she smirked. "What?"

So – she hadn't just been toying with him. She'd lifted a knife somehow without being noticed. That was impressive. I'd always thought my cousin was an expert at stirring up trouble. But where had she learned the skills for it?

At midday, they offered us flatbread and water. Judicus still hadn't woken. I tried to keep him sheltered from the worst of the sun, but there wasn't much I could do. His body was worn out and the magic he'd used had drained him. He'd wake when he was ready.

But I couldn't help the lump of worry growing in my throat. We were in a lot of trouble. Escape – even with that knife – was unlikely. And judging by how the raiders were talking, they planned to bring us to someone even worse than they were.

They flowed from job to job around the boat, never showing their faces, never removing their hot black clothing, speaking often in their clipped, harsh language. I watched them, hoping they'd show some opening, but there was nothing.

My only hope was that the sun would set and Kazmerev would have a good idea – because right now, I didn't have any of my own.

In the distance, a settlement appeared along the shore. Our ship changed tack, angling toward it, and I bit my lip. Settlements meant more guards and prisons with locks. This was not good for us.

A tear began to form in my eye when I heard someone whisper my name almost inaudibly.

"Sersha?"

It was Judicus.

28

"Shh," Mally said, lying down on the deck beside him. "Sersha, you stay up where you can see and watch."

It was good advice. She could say more than I could with my nods and the limited signs I could use with my hands bound. I knelt in front of them, appearing to look out over the sea, but just blocking them from view.

"Now, listen up, dark and mysterious stranger," Mally whispered.

"You know perfectly well that my name is Judicus Franzer Irault." His voice was weak and irritable.

"Fine, *Judicus Franzer Irault*," Mally whispered. "While you're awake we need to discuss something."

"Yes. Like why you sailed us into a cluster of enemy ships. Have you betrayed us, ai'sletta?"

"That. That's what we need to discuss," Mally said, and her tone said she'd take no nonsense. "What is an ai'sletta and what do people expect from her? These raiders are taking us to someone. I don't know who. And that someone is going to have expectations for Sersha. We need to know what they are."

"Sersha? Why would they ... wait. You told them she was the ai'sletta." He ran a hand over his face and froze, clearly in pain from the movement. I leaned over to tug his hand back down and shook my head. He needed to keep the arm still so the wound could heal again.

I glanced behind me and saw one of the raiders watching us with steely eyes. The leader. I didn't like how his eyes stayed locked on mine while Mally and Judicus continued whispering. What *did* they want with the ai'sletta?

"Mally." Judicus's voice was tight. "Please take this kindly, as it is intended." And then his voice became more fierce. "But for the love of my sanity, would you please stop running off and dragging us all with you? You are more trouble than a wolf pup pet."

Mally was ominously silent for a moment. I tried to indicate with my eyes that she really needed to agree, but then I was afraid the leader would notice, and I had to look over my shoulder again to make sure he wasn't coming.

No sign of it yet. The raiders were occupied quickly trimming sail and manning the rudder. They were far more adept at this than Mally had been and the boat flew over the water like Kazmerev in the sky, barely slapping the peaks of the waves despite the strong wind picking up and snatching sound in ragged tatters.

"I will consider it," Mally said eventually, her words half lost to the wind.

Judicus seemed to sag with relief. I strained my ears trying to hear what he said next. "Look, the ai'sletta is important. For a lot of reasons. Ai'sletta means Chosen One."

"Chosen for what?" Mally didn't sound like she knew whether she liked that or not.

"Well, that's the thing," he said, looking a little abashed. "Well, the ai'sletta was foretold a thousand years ago and when she first came, she destroyed the nations of Valetio and Cassavara and set up the nation-state of Calicarn. Which is where I am from, incidentally."

"So why are you looking for a woman who is dead and gone?" Mally whispered.

"Because a new ai'sletta has the potential to be born every generation through the same bloodlines. But you know how bloodlines can be – tricky. It's hard to keep track of exactly everyone who might be genetically descended from someone, so every five years, Calicarn rounds up our best and brightest to go looking. The last time we found one was forty years ago."

"And you didn't think to keep track of her descendants?" Mally scoffed. I barely heard more than "descendants," so I was surprised when Judicus answered.

"Of course, they did," he said. "But any descendant of the *original* ai'sletta could be the one. So, you have to be good at genealogies and maps and guessing and remembering weird little bits of history. Which is why we don't find the ai'sletta very often."

I wanted to know what happened to the last ai'sletta. I nudged Mally and she looked at me quizzically. I tried to sign but my hands were too limited. At least Mally was clever. She figured it out anyway.

"What happened to the one found forty years ago?" she asked.

If anything, Judicus turned a brighter red. "Well, we aren't the only ones looking for her."

"Who else is looking?" Mally asked.

His whisper was so faint, I could barely make it out. "The Hand of Rats."

"And who are they?" Mally prompted. She was much less patient than I was.

I looked around, but none of the raiders appeared to be watching us. If they could hear us, I couldn't tell.

"Traditionally, they keep their faces covered when they are away from their homelands, so the demons don't see their faces and trick them into hell after they depart this life."

So, the raiders really were after Mally. The boat shook suddenly, in the grip of a massive wave. It felt like it was punctuating his words. I glanced out across the water and saw the raiders on the other boats struggling to keep their courses. In the distance, heavy breakers pounded the shore.

I swallowed.

But Mally snickered in response. “Really? Demons?”

Judicus hadn’t answered her question, but Mally was too busy sitting up so she could look around at our captors to realize that. She had a speculative look on her face. I knew she was wondering what they looked like without the scarves and if they really were afraid to show their faces.

I nudged her.

“What?” she asked.

I raised my eyebrows.

“Oh, yes.” She turned back to Judicus. “Sersha wants to know what happened to that woman.”

“They found her first,” he said, his eyes meeting mine. He was too pale, pain and weariness grinding him down, but there was more than that in his eyes. He shook his head slightly as if asking me not to press. But we both needed to hear this.

I poked Mally again.

“That’s not an answer, skinny boy,” Mally said, acting flippantly, as she always did when she was scared.

His whisper was so quiet we had to make him repeat himself but, eventually, we caught the edges of it.

“They killed her,” he said at the same time a massive wave hit again and shook our boat like a rug being cleaned.

Well, that was great. Just great. No wonder they were all looking at me in between battling this angry wind. They were wondering what size of hole they’d need to dig for my grave.

29

They killed her.

The words kept echoing in my head as the settlement on the edge of the coast came into view. I'd thought it was a village at first, but the light refracting off the water had played tricks with my eyes.

What we were seeing was a group of large tents and enough raiders around them to double what we had on the boats. As we drew closer, I could make them out working around the camp like a hill of ants. Some were bringing in wood for the fires while others were preparing food, mending gear, and doing some small smith work – and all with their faces bound up in thick cloth. It made them a fearsome sight and it made my stomach dip and roll. How did you relate to people with covered faces? How did you know what they really meant when they spoke?

I clenched my bound hands together and tried not to think all the questions that kept flooding over me. They came anyway, unbidden. I wished I could voice them aloud, if only to dispel them from my heart.

Would they wait to kill the ai'sletta or do it right away?

Would they wait until after dark? And if they did, could Kazmerev help me escape?

"Can't you get us free?" Mally whispered to Judicus when our guard was occupied with orders from their leader. "You killed so many of them back at Landsfall."

Judicus snorted. "Could I kill everyone on this boat? Maybe. And then I'd pass out for the next few days because I'm out of energy. I might even die. That effort in the town nearly sapped me of life and I'm still injured. Why do you think I keep slipping out of consciousness? If I did that, I'd leave you here still surrounded by the rest of our enemies and now with the added burden of my unconscious body. And that's assuming you would worry about me at all."

I gave him a reproving look.

"Not you, Sersha," he said mollifying me. "But Mally has shown she has an ... adaptable ... conscience."

"I'm practical," Mally said, jaw thrust out again. But that glassy look in her eyes was tears. I knew the signs. She was afraid. And she didn't want to be alone without us.

I put a hand on her shoulder, and she shook it off irritably – but I knew her. She hated being vulnerable. She hated pity. But she wouldn't be so prickly if she wasn't scared for her life. I didn't blame her. I was scared, too.

"We bide our time," Judicus whispered. "And if things get truly bad, then I'll act as best as I can and pay the price."

I clenched my jaw. If he did that, he'd be a dead man and we wouldn't be far behind him. I was practical enough to understand that. What would be better would be if he and I could come up with a plan to work together, but I feared trying to plan under the eyes of our guards. That would require Mally translating between us and it would be harder to keep our communications secret with my wide hand gestures to alert the guards. I would also have to bide my time.

I'd learned patience over the years. Both people and ideas needed patience like young plants needed sunshine. They'd sprout when they were ready.

Even so, I missed Kazmerev. Having someone to talk to was like a spring of fresh clear water on a long hot day. Losing it felt like having that same water ripped from your hands. If he died with the dawn, then I died, too. I wasn't fully alive when he wasn't here.

I stole a glance at the sun as if I could will it to move more quickly across the sky, but it stood stubbornly still. I'd need to be patient with that, too.

Eventually, our boat tied up along a long crude pier. How long had the raiders been here? Long enough to create this, unless it had been here before them.

That worried me. The attack two nights ago had been our first warning of raiders – but there were enough here to overwhelm Landsfall. Why hadn't all of them come? Had they been spread out and scattered to other towns? Or were the rest of them newly arrived? When had they had time to construct this docking place for their boats?

I didn't know a lot about boats, but these ones were small, holding maybe a dozen people and limited supplies. It was hard to believe that they'd traveled very far in these – certainly not from across the sea – but I'd always been told the raiders lived in a land across the water. None of this was making much sense to me.

I noticed Judicus watching it all, too, his face pale and slightly green. That might be from his wound. Or it might be that he was drawing the same conclusion I was – that we'd stumbled into something bigger than a small random raiding party and we were in big trouble now.

Mally, for her part, was surprisingly quiet, her large green eyes flicking over the other boats as ours was tied up to the dock and a rough plank was extended to the boat. The raiders began to disembark, and we were urged to our feet and guided to the plank.

I offered my arm to Judicus for support. He leaned heavily on me, his steps slow and pained. He ought to be in bed for a week and kept on clear broth and herb teas. He absolutely should not be stumbling his way across a rocking plank with only a bound prisoner for support.

I bit my lip and was thankful yet again for my voicelessness. If I'd had a voice, I would have had to decide how to use it, and speaking up – or not speaking up – was a terrible responsibility.

People forgot the power of words. Or they misused them. Or they didn't use them when they should. I only had actions to show my intent or to help or hinder. Perhaps it was better to start there, where the harm or help was more obvious and less like a snake twisting in your hand.

The raiders might as well have been voiceless, too, for all they were saying to us. They led us into their tent village, their eyes forward and mouths shut. To my surprise, no one called a greeting or ran to meet them. Though some paused in their work to watch.

That, to me, was not a good sign. People didn't stand around staring owlishly at anything good. Were they planning to execute us immediately? A trickle of sweat worked its way between my shoulder blades.

Their camp was tidy and well ordered. I'd expected it to look and smell foreign and I was almost disappointed by how familiar it looked. Rough canvas tents, fish cooking on the fires, basic tools, the smell of wet wool, and chaffaray plant. All sights and smells you could find in our village. If we took down their masks, would they look just like us?

We were brought up to the largest tent in the encampment. It was plain and rough as the rest, but two people stood outside the tent, faces uncovered, hands on long spears with tufts of feathers up at the tips. Their hard faces were no more comfort than the masks and I flinched away from their sharp glares.

The lead raider approached the closed tent flap as the others pulled us into a rough line facing the tent.

After a moment, the tent flap opened with the sound of wind-snapped cloth and a dark figure stepped forward. Her face was bare, and her blonde curls tumbled down her back.

I almost gasped. She was barely older than I was.

Her eyes narrowed on us and her smile was just beginning to turn her lips up in one corner when Judicus finally raised his tired head. His gasp echoed loudly in the silence. He sounded like someone hit him and I looked over quickly, prepared to catch him, but it was only shock etched on his expression.

"Cassanetta Lightland?" he asked.

30

"Judicus Franzer Irault," she said, and her close-lipped smile was cat-like. "I told you I would win this year."

"Win?" Mally said, and I heard that note of threat in her voice.

"Didn't the son of the Lord of Chaos tell you it's a little competition with us to find the ai'sletta? He didn't steal away with the pair of you in the dark of night out of goodwill. Goodwill isn't something that rope workers know anything about, do they Judicus?"

"Are you in league with the Hand of Rats now, Lady Lightland?" Judicus asked warily.

"Our interests align," she agreed, looking to the raider leader. "I'd like to speak to our guests if that can be arranged, Horacen."

I made note of his name – Horacen. It seemed familiar somehow.

"Wolf?" Judicus asked, looking at the leader. "Is that what the name means?"

"All their leaders are known as Horacen," Lady Lightland said. "They don't show their names to strangers any more than their faces, do you Horacen?"

The raider seemed unimpressed. I thought maybe he was frowning under his mask.

He didn't reply, simply turning and walking away, snapping his fingers as he left. At that motion, his raiders gathered around the prisoners, giving Lady Lightland what she'd requested, even if Horacen wouldn't acknowledge her condescending tone.

"I see you've made friends, as always," Judicus said, his smile turning mocking.

"Everyone is the friend of a woman with gold to spend," Lady Lightland said, but her eyes were hard. "And none is the friend of a rope worker with a dark past. But this is not the place to discuss this. Bring them into my tent."

She turned, striding through the door of the tent as the raiders nudged us forward.

Her quarters weren't empty. Four men in maroon and silver livery stood just inside the door and four more ringed the large white tent. They carried bronze-tipped spears like the men guarding outside the tent door. How interesting. Why did she need all these guards if she were among friends?

Inside, sprawled across camp chairs, were an assortment of young people in fine clothing, their hair styled in ways I was unfamiliar with. One had a braid dangling down one side of her pale head, the other side shaved to the skin. Another man had bright medallions strung between locks of hair. Friends of hers, perhaps?

Or maybe this was her coterie. My eyes narrowed. If she was Judicus's rival in a "game" and if Judicus had a coterie of skilled people – though his currently only contained Kazmerev and me – then perhaps these people were Lady Lightland's coterie. One of them turned a palm up and let a few dark threads spiral over it as if to show us he was a ropeworker. But what skilled rope worker needed to brag about it?

My eyes narrowed further. I didn't trust this coterie.

Lady Lightland spun, her eyes gleaming for a moment, and then she smiled again. I was starting to hate her smiles.

"Do you know Galen Floren Topocos?" she asked lightly. "You aren't the only rope worker seeking glory, Judcus Franzer Irault. I have one of my own."

Like he was a pet. Or a milk cow.

I felt my eyes growing larger, but Mally had a considering look on her face. I tried to imagine how this would appear to her. Maybe like a negotiation? After all, she bore Judicus no loyalty. Maybe she'd see this as a way to increase her value.

I hoped for better, but I knew my cousin. And though I enjoyed her intelligence and wit, I knew perfectly well that her loyalty was to herself alone. She'd easily slide away from any entanglements meant to hold her in one place. One look at how she'd ended things with Tyndale was enough evidence of that.

I needed to think of a way to remind her that it was better to stick with those you trust.

"And you have no Flame Rider now that dear Veela is gone. No coterie. No one but these village girls."

Mally opened her mouth and I stepped on her foot, ignoring the angry look she shot me. Now was not the time to argue and certainly not the time to reveal our one hidden trick – Kazmerev. We'd need him to help us escape this, but secrecy would be his best chance to help.

"You wouldn't know, Lady Lightland," Judicus said, and his tone might have seemed light to a stranger but to me, it sounded very dangerous, like a trap not yet sprung. "After all, you're the one who attacked Veela and me, aren't you?"

"Did you see who stabbed you?" Her tone was light, but I heard the real worry behind it.

"I know that I didn't tell you I'd been stabbed – and yet here you are knowing all about it." His face had gone paler. Maybe he hadn't been sure until right now. Maybe the first he really knew of it were those voices on the beach.

Her lips compressed firmly together. "Well. We don't need extra people running around claiming they know who or where the ai'sletta is. We don't even need you and your research anymore, Judicus. Three of you have come into this tent, but we only need one to leave with us."

I wanted to ask her what she expected the rest of us to do – vanish? Even if she killed us, she'd have to take us out of this tent eventually. Fortunately, running my mouth wasn't an option. I would only make things worse, and I could already feel the sweat making a line between my shoulder blades.

If she could just decide to let us live until Kazmerev was reborn. It was an hour at most. I clenched my jaw, thinking as fast as I could. If she didn't know which of us was the ai'sletta – and she must not know – then we could string her along and stall by refusing to say which of us it was. She'd need Judicus to confirm the truth and she wouldn't risk killing the wrong one.

We just had to keep our mouths shut for a few hours and Kazmerev would come and save us.

Which was apparently too much to ask.

"Me," Mally said, suddenly, like it was a race. "I'm the ai'sletta."

If I could have groaned – I would have.

31

"Well, that was easy enough," Lady Lightland said, and her smile was cold as a snake in winter. "Come here, child."

What a ridiculous thing to say. Mally was almost the same age as the blonde woman – dressed more simply, certainly. Bound with ropes, sure, but not a child.

Mally grimaced. But she obeyed.

My cousin was no fool.

She held her wrists out with a raised eyebrow and quick as the flip of a coin, Lady Lightland had a dagger out and had cut through the rope.

Interesting. She was skilled with the blade. The way she flipped it in her grip and put it back in the sheath spoke of years of practice and training. I felt my mouth go dry at that. Whatever she was up to next wouldn't be good.

"Give these others to the Hand of the Rat and let the raiders deal with them as they please," she said to the men in livery near the tent door.

One of them was already moving toward us when Judicus spoke up. "So trusting, Cassanetta. Where's the schemer I've grown so fond of? Where's the girl who hunted and chased me from village to village and eventually stole all my research out from under my nose?"

"I would have stolen your soul, too, if it wasn't for that dreadful elven and her flame creature," Lady Lightland said, her lips twisting. "But as much as I'd love to reminisce and pull out that research of yours to show you how I corrected your commas, I'm afraid I have more important things to do. Like reading the heart of the ai'sletta. And arranging for your quick interment."

"No need to bury the living," Judicus said, holding his hands up. The guard nearest him grunted and pulled him to his feet.

I didn't wait for the one next to me to tug. I found my feet on my own, head down, the picture of submission. If we fought, they'd fight and we'd be unconscious when Kazmerev came to save us. I needed my wits about me and a body ready to flee.

"But perhaps you'd like to double-check this work, too," Judicus said, his smile turning sly. "I found the ai'sletta – oh I certainly did, but why would I bring a voiceless girl with her, do you think?"

Lady Lightland frowned as if he had made a good point.

"Wouldn't it make more sense," he asked, "that I would bring the ai'sletta and her interpreter."

I kept my face carefully blank. The longer he could pull off this ruse, the better.

"And are you the ai'sletta, girl?" she asked me.

I shrugged. It seemed safer than a definitive statement.

She watched us both for a long moment and then shook her head. "No. The Judicus Franzer Irault I know wouldn't put the real ai'sletta in danger. The voiceless one is a fraud, and the girl who spoke first is the true ai'sletta. Take them out and kill them. Oh, and do it before it gets dark. Just in case one of them can contact that elven woman's fire bird. We don't want to deal with it on top of everything else."

Judicus opened his mouth and then shut it again with a snap. He was probably hoping what I was hoping – that we could just get out of here without being killed. There was no point arguing about it – we'd already tried that, and it hadn't worked. Now, we just needed to *do*.

Her armsmen – or whatever the men in livery were – dragged us out of the tent and then threw us to the ground. I fell awkwardly on the stony earth, twisting a wrist. My arm burned from where it had been stabbed and I was worried the injury had opened. Beside me, Judicus lay on the stones, pale and gasping. Being thrown right onto his injury had stolen his breath. I scrambled to my feet and stood over him as he recovered himself.

Carefully, I offered my bound hands and helped him up as a pair of dark-clad raiders drew near, swords raised. They kept us there, blades to our necks until their leader sauntered over. He was eating some kind of spiced meat, carefully slipping tidbits under the folds of his thick covering.

"And so, you are returned to me," he said and I was certain there was a smile on his covered face. "And we are moving inland. I'm told the lady wants you killed. And before dark, no less. But your lifeless bodies will be sent before my people to terrify the villages to the east of here. What do you think, will it work?"

I thought it would, though I wouldn't have said so even if I could. I was waiting. Eventually, Judicus had to realize he needed to use his magic, right? Because even if he was waiting to use it as the very last of last resorts, this seemed like the time.

I clenched my jaw hard and tried to support his weight as Horacen finished his meat.

"What do you think, boy?" he asked Judicus, grabbing his head by the hair and jerking his face up to look the raider in the eyes.

"Do you think it will tell them to surrender?"

"Perhaps," Judicus agreed.

Horacen smiled. "But I won't be dictated to. Not even by the one who pays the gold coins for this endeavor."

Well, that explained what relationship he had with Lady Lightland.

"Take these two to the edge of camp. Feed and clean them," he told his men. "I'll kill them when I am ready and not before then."

"We've slipped from the fire," Judicus whispered gratefully, as the raiders dragged us after them. I wasn't so sure about that. We seemed to have slipped out of the fire and directly into the melting pot.

32

We ate raider food in silence. It was surprisingly good – fish wrapped in flatbread. I'd misjudged these people based only on the fact of harsh accents, hidden visages, and the fact that they'd killed my parents without mercy. It turned out that didn't mean that their food was terrible. I'd been wrong about that. I'd been wrong about a lot of things.

"At least it's not rat," Judicus had muttered. Which meant, of course, that he was judging them, too.

I'd never known the Hand of the Rat as anything other than just raiders. We had tales of them from generations back – darkly clothed, hidden people who snuck into villages at night, stealing and killing indiscriminately. Like how they'd slaughtered my parents. They were the thing of warning and nightmares. Of locked doors and whispered fears.

And now here they were, planning to move inland. What other towns would be sacked by them? What other children would be left orphans?

Thinking about it made my skin itch. And I felt responsible to stop it.

Before, fighting them had been about saving my village and my family – my people. Who were my people now? Kazmerev, obviously. Mally because she was blood. And Judicus because we'd made that vow. What about these other villages? Were they my people, too?

Maybe leaving here wouldn't be as simple as just running away. Maybe I owed it to everyone to try to stop this invasion before it began.

With my mind churning, I tried to sign to Judicus that we needed a plan, but he shook his head not comprehending. I'd have to wait for him to get there on his own. I tried not to grind my teeth in frustration. Being voiceless often meant having to be patient with how slow everyone else was. There wasn't another option.

"I didn't tell you everything," he said as he ate the food we'd been given – some kind of boiled grain in a bowl. It tasted of an herb I didn't know. I liked it. "The ai'sletta is more than power and more than a tool to be used to build nations."

I had hoped so. Otherwise, what he was doing in looking for Mally was just cruel. I didn't think Judicus was a cruel man. He looked around us before continuing.

"Some say that the coming of the ai'sletta means a time of change – a turning of nations. That those in power will be brought low and the people will rise again."

That sounded like the kinds of things people said around a campfire to bring them hope. It didn't sound like the kind of thing that was real. And had he considered that sometimes the guy who lived next to you was just as awful as whoever was in charge? Tyndale had been even more willing to throw me to the wolves than Aunt Danna had when the raiders were outside our doors and they thought it was my life or theirs.

"I don't plan to hand her over to those in power," Judicus whispered. "I don't plan to let them use her for their own ends. That's what has happened every other time. This time will be different. This time, she's going to change the world."

He looked off into the distance, his eyes slightly glassy, while I tried to figure out how he combined that kind of hopeful optimism with my cousin Mally.

I couldn't put the two together.

"I know it sounds crazy."

He wasn't wrong about that.

"But I've read everything there is to read about this. I know she's more than she seems. She can do this. This time, when evil is overthrown it won't come back to bite us. Not like with my father."

That was more like it. At least he had this tangled up in some kind of dream of the past. Those could cloud your mind. I could see dreaming of an ai'sletta even after meeting Mally if you believed she could change.

I liked Mally well enough, even if she had her failings. We'd been almost sisters my whole life. But *I* wouldn't count on her to change the world. And maybe I could hold Judicus's hand when he realized that. Maybe the two of them needed me more than they realized. I seemed to be the only one of the three of us with any common sense.

I tried not to find it frustrating that I couldn't communicate any of this to Judicus. I'd learned a long time ago that frustration brought you nowhere. Patience was key. But this time, I was finding it hard to be patient. I needed to teach him to listen to the signs of my gestures. And I needed to teach him very soon.

"It's less than an hour until sunset," Judicus said after a while, finally turning his mind to a plan and his eyes back to me. The raiders had returned to their camp and the only one near us was a lonely picket keeping watch from so far away that I could barely hear it when he sneezed. The air was abnormally warm for this late spring – almost comfortable. "As soon as the sun dips low, you need to call Kazmerev. I'll use the ropes to set us free and dispatch the sentry – but after that, I'll be useless. I'm barely staying upright as it is and that much rope work sucks the energy out of a man." He paused. "Along with other costs."

I wanted to know what those other costs were, but he stared into the middle distance for a long minute as if weighing all those costs before turning to me again.

I shook my head gently. Kazmerev had said he couldn't carry more than me until I was ready. He wouldn't be able to help us.

"You'll have to ask Kazmerev to carry the two of us out of here and after I regain consciousness, we'll figure out a way to break Mally out. She'll be safe enough with Cassanetta until she's brought to the Grand Hadri. Lady Lightland won't want to give up her chance at that prize. Plus, she has my notes. She must realize how valuable Mally is."

I shook my head again, this time more firmly. We needed a plan that didn't involve Kazmerev having to carry both of us. Because that just wouldn't work.

And I wasn't as sure as he was that Mally was safe. She was headstrong and tended to speak her mind and other people didn't seem to understand that underneath all that she was just a girl who was frightened and trying to figure out how to live her life. All that bravado disguised a lot of uncertainty. What if they punished her for it? What if they punished her for our escape? I didn't like this plan.

I swallowed, looking at the red sun hanging low in the sky. Kazmerev would be reborn soon. And Judicus would want us to act. How could I tell him we couldn't do what he wanted?

I shifted uncomfortably and tried to get his attention.

"I'm going to sleep until the sun sets," he said without opening his eyes. "Wake me when Kazmerev arrives. I need every scrap of energy I can find."

I nudged him. He needed to listen to my arguments.

"Not to put too fine a point on it, Sersha," he said with a yawn, "but you should eat more. Your elbows are very sharp."

I sighed and then drew in a long breath.

Patience, Sersha. Patience.

He was snoring by the time I'd composed myself. The frustrating thing about trying to communicate when you are voiceless is not that you can't speak – it's that no one is paying attention. I'd have to come up with my own plan.

Even more frustrating was not knowing how this rope worker magic worked. What were Judicus's limitations? Was there a way to tell how much energy he needed to use? A range on how far it could reach? Could it untie us? Could it capture enemies or only kill them?

I wanted to sigh in frustration, but I would have to wait until I had Mally back to interpret before I could ask him any of these questions – or the hundreds of others I had. Right now, a plan was more important than figuring out how rope workers worked.

I was still thinking it through when the sun dipped into darkness and cold spread across the ground where I huddled next to Judicus. The scent of pine needles filled my nose at the same time the earth in front of me seemed to erupt in flames and out of the fire my glorious phoenix emerged, wings spread wide.

I breathed a sigh of relief, letting it wash all the way through me and deep into my bones.

Kazmerev.

His name was like home to me. His fire burned hot and powerful. I could survive anything if he was near.

Sersha. You're alive.

His voice was equally relieved. He cocked his head to the side.

There was something just a touch different about him as he was reborn today. Something that seemed to be listening to every nuance of my mental voice.

They tied you to a tree. His own mental voice sounded furious. *They don't tie my Flame Rider to a tree.*

It would be okay. Judicus was going to wake up in a moment and set us free and do something about that guard.

That will knock Judicus flat on his back.

And then he would expect Kazmerev to carry us to safety.

A fresh ripple of fire ran down Kazmerev's wings and he ruffled his feathers irritably.

I can't carry both of you unless your mind is already stronger than it was two days ago.

I knew that. But there was only one way to find out – we'd have to try. And if it didn't work, then we'd do the only other thing I'd come up with while I was waiting.

I sure hoped it worked. Because these were my people now – Kazmerev, Judicus, and Mally and it was up to me to fight for their safety.

This. This right here is why I am born in your heart each evening. There's faithfulness and hope here. There's kindness and gentle patience. It tastes like cinnamon. Have you ever tasted cinnamon?

I smiled. I'd never tasted cinnamon.

Someday you will. And I will be there to watch you smile over that, too. Well, wake the boy, and let's try this hair-brained scheme. But if he gets you hurt, I'll abandon him and take care of your safety. You may be thinking of all these people as your own, but there's only one person for me. You know that, right?

I knew it. And while it filled my thirsty soul, it was also part of the reason I was so worried about this. But there were no other options.

I took a deep breath and jabbed Judicus with my pointy elbow.

33

"Mmmph." I had to put my hand over Judicus's mouth to disguise his grunts as he woke. "Not enough time," he muttered after he dragged my hand from his lips. "Not enough time."

I was feeling the effects of no sleep, too. What wouldn't I give for four hours of sleep and a cup of tea? But there was no time for regrets. If we were going to run, this was our chance. We needed Kazmerev with us for as long and far as we could before his death the next morning.

Just a day ago the idea horrified you and now you speak of my deaths so casually.

My cheeks heated with my chagrin. Guilt flickered in me like a fire. After all, he'd told me it hurt. He told me it was unwanted. I should speak with more respect about his daily ordeal.

I'm teasing you. Your cheeks go as red as my feathers, little hawk.

"Are you ready?" Judicus asked in a whisper.

In the gathering gloom, small things were scampering and an owl was hooting happily to himself. We were about to break that peace. I couldn't help the bubble of anxiety that burst in my chest as I nodded.

"It's hard to tell what you're saying when it's dark," he complained. But that was hardly my fault. "Okay. I'm going to untie you. Don't move until I tell you the guard is disabled."

I felt the flick of something cold against my wrists – cold like an eel pulled up from the depths. It slid over one wrist and then my bonds tugged apart and fell to the side.

I hurried to massage my wrists, rubbing them to get my circulation going again. Judicus was doing the same.

"Here we –"

His words cut off and he slumped to the ground. I didn't even catch him in time. I could only hope he'd done something about the nearest patrol before he fell or we'd have guards here before we could twitch. Hurriedly, I checked to be sure he was breathing.

I swallowed down relief when I felt his breath against my palm. Could Kazmerev get low so I could pull Judicus onto his back?

I can.

He was there in a heartbeat, crouching down low on the ground, bright dancing fire against the rich purple of the closing night.

I was nearly blinded by the glory of him. I had to keep my eyes squinted as I lifted Judicus, hauling him up from under the arms and pulling him onto Kazmerev's back as my phoenix friend crouched low and wiggled to get underneath. Fortunately, Judicus was light. Any more muscle on those bones and I wouldn't have been able to move him.

Now, how did I secure him in place? The ropes?

I told you before. I don't need those things. Magical creature, remember? Now, hop on.

I hopped on.

And through.

His back couldn't hold me. My mouth dropped open, and I slammed to the ground on my bottom. Ouch!

My heart pounded in my throat as I tried to listen for any sound we'd been heard. There were faint laughter and voices coming from the camp and the sounds of dishes tapping together as they were cleaned. No sound of alarm yet.

I breathed out a sigh of relief. Now, why had Kazmerev suddenly lost his physical solidity? I turned to examine him. Judicus was still on his back. He hadn't smashed through to the ground.

It's okay. Steady now.

Confused, I pulled myself to my feet looking frantically around us a second time. No one had seen. Kazmerev would be invisible to them and in the darkness, no one would notice Judicus hovering at waist level. He must have taken down the sentries. He must have, right?

Stop panicking. Try again. Think of me as solid – but not solid enough to make me visible.

I tried again – more carefully this time – and my leg went through his back a second time. Little sizzling feelings of anxiety rolled through me.

Try harder.

I could do this. I could. It was okay.

I took a deep breath, closed my eyes, thought of him as solid with everything that I was, and stepped again.

I met with a solid back. I was about to breathe a sigh of relief when a cry came from the camp.

"Fire! Fire!"

My eyes flew open. Everything around me was bright as day. The nearby sentries lay on the ground – probably just unconscious – I was pretty sure I could see one breathing – but I'd made Kazmerev too visible! He was lighting everything up!

A nearby tree puffed into flame, lighting like a torch.

Kazmerev stretched his wings, half-screeching half-cursing in my head.

We could do this. We could do it.

But as he leapt into the air my strength failed me and I fell through. The second my bottom smacked the hard ground for a second time, the light was gone and only I could see a phoenix – purple with golden flames dancing along his feathers – sweep up into the darkness of night.

I scrambled to my feet, bit my lip, and blinked away the tears from the pain flaring from my tailbone. I'd bruised it for sure. But there was no time to worry about it. No time to think at all.

We'd just have to go with the alternate plan.

Calls and shouts rang from the camp and there'd be a raider here to check on the prisoners or the fire, or something at any moment. I forced myself not to look back, sank into a running stance, and then ran as hard and fast as I could.

Little hawk? Where are you? You aren't on my back!

I was here. I was running.

You're supposed to be with me!

Now he was the one who had to stop panicking so that he didn't drop Judicus. I tried to pour confidence and courage into our connection, but my concentration broke almost immediately.

It was much tougher to run through the woods at night than I thought. I stumbled, went down, and took a branch to the face. My cheek and lip stung but I forced myself up again, running again, my hand hitting a tree.

Pain flared through me. My breath heaved in my chest. This was impossible.

To your right. There's a path.

That's where they'd look for me first. No paths.

Then stop hitting trees!

I bounced off another tree and barely bit back a groan and pain flared through my hip. At this rate, I'd be nothing but a huge bruise. My thoughts skittered over my brain like water on a hot pan.

Just run. Stop worrying. Just run.

And you'll be caught. They're gaining on you!

My breath rasped in my throat and then Kazmerev was there, right above me, the light of his feathers glowing just enough to light a path for me through the thick trees.

I clambered and ducked, wove and darted, my breath coming in huge gasps as my heart galloped twice as fast as me. But I could see enough to run.

Thank you, friend. Thank you.

He chirped and a puff of sparks kicked up around me.

Behind us, in the camp, I heard a very distinct female voice rise above all the other sounds.

"Bring me the prisoners. A hundred gold crowns for the pair of them!"

34

A hundred gold crowns? Did she have any idea what someone could buy with that kind of money? A pair of fine horses. Enough clothing to last the rest of your life. A full field for farming with the supplies to plant it and tend it.

I was still making a list when Kazmerev interrupted.

They're gaining on you. Don't go any further to the right or you'll end up along the sea and a boat's already launching. They'll see anything that moves on that rocky shore.

I tried to keep to my feet without moving too close to the shore. The way was rocky here with so many dips and rises that I seemed to be moving more vertically than horizontally. I needed to get inland again.

Kazmerev's mental voice sounded clipped and urgent. *Don't do that. You'll cross the trail and you're moving so much slower than them that they'll catch up immediately. We need to get you on my back so I can take care of you.*

We'd already tried that. I didn't know how to make him solid enough to hold me and also not be visible.

Then we should try again. And if it doesn't work, you need to leave Judicus here and I will fly you to safety.

There was almost a whine to his words at the end – like the twang of a string under tension or the sharp whine of a nervous dog. I felt spikes of nerves, too.

Ugh. Don't compare me to a dog. I am worried about you, Sersha. And consider this. If something happens to you, I will vanish, and no one will be able to take care of Judicus. Hide him somewhere in the brush. He won't be found. Then save yourself first and come back for him when you are able to. There's no need for heroics tonight.

He made a lot of sense, but not about the heroics part. I should stash Judicus here somewhere safe. And then I should go back and get Mally while they were distracted looking for me. There'd never be a better time for that.

Your self-sacrifice is admirable – and so is your courage – but you're crazy. Utterly insane. You're my heart – please don't count that as so small a thing.

Now, where to set Judicus down? Could Kazmerev see a good place from the air? Or should I find one here on the ground?

Neither of us should be finding places. We need to get you as far from here as possible. They're gaining on you.

Maybe if I found a good place for him, I could hide there too, until this first wave of raiders passed and then I could sneak back in their wake. Maybe Kazmerev would even agree to carry me.

Into unknown danger against my better judgment?

Yes.

No!

He was being unreasonable.

Here!

It was a low point in the rolling landscape where two dead trees had fallen over the dip in the earth, crossing each other. One was an evergreen tree, and the branches and needles were a thick mess disguising this little dip.

It's the first place they'll look!

I scrambled down toward it, awkwardly crawling through the branches. I didn't think anyone would bother going to all this effort unless they were sure someone was here. I'd just wait until they passed. And then I'd hide Judicus very carefully. Could Kazmerev bring him down here?

Only if you agree to listen to me, my little hawk. Please.

My breath heaved in my chest from the exertion as I drew myself back out of the cave under the fallen trees. It was going to take all my strength to get Judicus in there.

I'd listen to Kazmerev while I worked.

No.

What?

No. You won't. I'm putting my foot down. Or my wing. Or something. I am not your horse.

What? I froze. I'd never called him a horse.

No, but you're treating me like one.

In the distance, I heard a crashing sound. Someone was getting close. I drew further into the branches. I was not treating Kazmerev like a horse. If he was a horse, I'd be riding him right now with Judicus in front of me and I'd be twice as far away as I was right now.

I thought I heard a mental snort.

On the road you didn't want to take? A horse would not do well on the terrain you've found for yourself. Remember how you were stumbling in the dark? That would be the horse.

I felt my chin jutting out stubbornly.

Wait.

I felt my face growing hot. Maybe I was as bad as Mally. Maybe I'd plunged into danger just like her without thinking it through.

Listen.

And he'd seen it all and he knew I was a fool. He'd hold it against me. Humiliation scorched me.

I won't poke fun, but you must listen.

I listened.

You hold my heart. I die each morning and rise when the sun falls just to see your face again.

I couldn't help it. Even hiding here in this tangle of trees, that made my heart feel almost as warm as my hot cheeks.

Your loyalty and stubbornness are born in me – an echo of who you are that grows with every rebirth. You're making me just as loyal and just as stubborn. And I don't mind because I like who you are.

I blinked back the tears stinging my eyes, trying to focus on wiggling deeper into the tree mass so that I wouldn't have to think too hard about what he was saying. It was too much.

I will not leave you. I will not have you go on without me. I will bear your loads. I will share your pain. I will carry your friends and accept your plans and wishes.

Warmth infused my heart.

But.

I couldn't tell why the "but" hurt. He was already giving me so much that knowing there was a limit on it shouldn't sting the way it did. And yet it did. Had I already pushed him to the limit of what he could take from me? Everyone rolled their eyes at me or just ignored my signs when they didn't want to hear me. Maybe they hadn't listened because I had nothing valuable to give.

But you are carrying my future, too. You are making my *decisions, too. I am bound to you. I cannot fly away – and I will not, so don't let that worry you. But I think I should have a say in what we do. I am not your horse. I am not your slave. I want to be your partner. And your friend.*

I felt my cheeks growing hot. He was right. I'd done that – just assumed he'd go along with my ideas the way Judicus assumed that about me. I'd assumed that he would do as I asked. I'd treated him like a horse.

Humiliation filled me. I wanted to hide my face.

No need for that. But please – can we be partners? Friends?

Yes. It was what I wanted, too. I didn't mean ... I didn't think ... it had been an error on my part to tell him what to do when I should have worked with him and asked him to help me figure out what to do.

You were wrong. You have so much to give. I just want to give to you, too.

How did you say thank you when the gift was too great?

You do it just like that. And now, I would like to suggest two things.

Only two?

One is quite urgent.

And what is that?

I would like to suggest you use your flame to burn the raider currently creeping up on you from behind. He's lifting the tree branches and raising his sword as we speak.

I whipped around and met the eyes of the raider.

35

The scent of his rancid breath blew across my face – those swaths of cloth didn't prevent it – and the raider jabbed his sword toward me. It was only the thick branches that saved me. They slowed his thrust as I wiggled away from the blade.

You won't be able to get away from this without fighting back.

I hated killing. I didn't want to do it. Better to knock him unconscious as Judicus had done with the rope worker magic! Though, I still didn't know how that worked.

Not like your access to my flames does. Come on! Defend yourself.

The raider growled and my heart sped in panic. My breathing was ragged as I lifted a hand, squeezed my eyes together, and *hoped.*

I think he's not going to hurt you now, Sersha. Kazmerev's voice seemed calmer. *Open your eyes.*

I opened my eyes and gasped. In front of me, the tree was ablaze and if there had been a man in front of me, nothing was left of him now.

My breathing restarted, aching and panicked. I'd killed him. There'd been a man there a moment ago and now there was nothing but a smoking emptiness. I felt numb right through.

Get out of there.

I scrambled to obey, clawing my way back through the unburned trees, keeping clear of the fire licking over the tangled evergreens.

Get ready to jump.

Heart in my throat, I readied myself.

Now!

I leapt. Warmth flooded over me as I landed on the back of a very solid phoenix. My breath *wuffed* out in relief.

But where was Judicus?

That's the other thing I wanted to talk about. I stashed him somewhere safe. If I'm going to agree to help you double back for your cousin, you are not doing it alone. We'll go back for Judicus – just like you planned, but I found a place that will be harder to reach than your little tree cave.

I felt my face heating. In the end, the tree cave had done little more than slow the raider. But what hiding place could he have found that was better than that?

I want to be clear that I am not a bird, Kazmerev said as he flew us up above the trees. *I am a phoenix. It's different.*

Of course, it was. He was not a bird. He was magnificent.

Exactly. He seemed to warm at that. *Nevertheless, I left him in the branches of a very tall tree. In ... ahem ... an eagle's nest. Don't worry, I wedged him in place. He won't fall off.*

I didn't want to tell him what a bad idea that was. Not when we were getting along so well. He almost didn't seem furious right now.

I'm still furious. I'm angry all the time. I can't help it.

I was angry for him.

See? It's that which holds me fast. And it's your constant presence, just here sitting with me in the depths of this grief that makes it bearable.

We flew low over the trees as guilt ate at me, raw and painful. I'd killed that raider. I kept thinking of him as a man, but with the face scarf up, he could have been a woman. I had no way to know. He could have had children. Been kind to puppies. Given to the poor. He might have been a great artist or craftsman. And I'd snuffed it all out.

He was going to grab you and make you his captive. And then you'd be dead, and Judicus and me, too. You did what you had to do.

I reacted in fear. Maybe there was another way that I hadn't thought of.

And maybe I will grow gills and swim.

Either way, I could never take it back. That fire slipped from my hand so easily and took his life. And I hadn't even thought it through.

Stop chastising yourself. We are almost at their camp.

In the darkness, no one looked up at the girl who would have looked like she was sailing through the air on the back of nothing at all.

I felt relieved by that – stealthiness would mean I wouldn't have to fight anyone – but worried when I looked down.

In the distance, three of the boats had set sail in three different directions. Ship's lights marked them out against the inky water.

Whatever is in those boats will be lost to us if we go down into the camp. Are you certain of your choice?

There was only one thing I wanted from them – Mally. And she was in their tents.

That's all I needed to know. Let's take on this righteous quest, little hawk. Together.

I could sense the purpose behind his mental voice and it fed into my own focus and courage.

I looked down at the disorder below. It looked like a henhouse after a cat got in. People ran here and there, darting in and out of tents. Lights spread out through the trees in every direction. The tree I'd accidentally lit on fire still burned, spreading to the trees nearby. Raiders fought to bring their tents down and pull their possessions out of the fire's path. They ran frantically, pouring buckets of water and scrambling to move what was in camp to the boats – but it was a large camp. It wouldn't be packed up too quickly.

The key would be to get down unseen and get into Lady Lightland's tent and out again without being detected.

I can wait for you on the edge of camp. We need to get you practicing so you can put two people on my back. This would be easier if we could just fly in and fly out again.

Could he let me down on the edge of camp but then soar above me? I didn't like leaving him behind.

I don't like being separated from you, either.

We would just have to focus and do this right.

There was a darker spot where the camp met the docks close to the large tent we'd met Lady Lightland in. If I had to guess, I'd say Mally was still in there. It was the first place we should look. And that meant we should try to settle down in the nearby darkness.

I don't like the idea of you going in alone. Keep me invisible and I'll come in with you.

Could I use the flame thing again?

If you have to. As long as I'm close. I was right overhead when you blasted that raider in the trees.

That was good to know. There were limitations.

I have to be within about five of my wingspans for you to be able to channel my flame. Or at least, that's how it was for Veela.

Ideally, I would have another Flame Rider teach me how to do this.

Ideally, yes. But Flame Riders are secretive and hard to find. It will take us some traveling to discover any, though I will watch for sign of them as we travel. For now, we will have to find our way together, as one running through a strange forest in the night.

I winced at that. I still hurt all over – especially my face.

We dropped down into the dark patch and I took a long breath, gathering my nerves and settling my racing heart.

All I had to do was sneak in, find Mally, sneak out. It would be fine.

I reached out and touched Kazmerev's feathers. I needed the warmth and support. I just needed to know someone was with me. His warmth lit the courage within me, strengthening my heart.

I'm right here. I'm not going anywhere.

I leaned my forehead briefly against his warm feathers, drew in a long breath, and then slipped into the night.

36

It was likely the chaos of the camp that made it possible to slip in at all. They were looking for someone trying to escape, not someone trying to sneak back in.

There were no guards picketed that I could see and the raiders on the dock were busier loading one of the boats than doing anything else. Four boats chasing one pair of people seemed like too much. But I wasn't going to argue. Not when that made it possible to steal right up to the edge of the tent where we'd met Lady Lightfoot and sink to my knees, pressing my face to the crack where the tent wall met the ground.

The tent was fully lit. And mostly empty. Only one figure remained, slumped under a blanket. Bits of rope dangled out of the blanket from where I'd guess her hands were.

I gasped.

Mally.

She was here just like I'd thought.

I stood, sneaking around the side and toward an entrance. There were no guards at the door of the tent. No more of the laughing coterie that had been with Lady Lightland. Did they really take our escape so seriously that none of them had stayed with her? Or had they hurt her so badly she couldn't move or run?

Fear seized my heart. They wouldn't have killed her, would they?

No. They need her alive.

But would they badly hurt her?

They stabbed Judicus in the side. They hurt Veela badly enough that she never recovered to wish me goodbye.

I bit my lip at his words, fighting down tears of sympathy. These were not kind people we were dealing with. These were enemies. But I couldn't help but be suspicious that they had made this so easy for me.

It does seem too easy.

Too easy or just easy enough?

Nothing in life is easy enough. Don't go in the tent.

But I'd come all this way. I needed to see if that was Mally – and if it wasn't then I needed to move to the next tent and the next tent until I found her. I wasn't leaving empty-handed.

And if she was hurt, she needed me more than ever. People always thought that because she put on such a tough show that she couldn't be hurt, but I knew better. She was just a girl, like me. She wasn't superhuman.

At least take a weapon.

Someone had conveniently left a knife stuck in a log beside the tent. It looked like they'd been putting points on roasting sticks before that. Would that be a good enough weapon?

Better than nothing, I suppose, but I don't like this. And remember my fire. Use it if you must. Don't be squeamish about fighting enemies because they will not hesitate to destroy you.

Well, I didn't like this, but if we all stuck to doing only what we liked, nothing would ever happen.

I held the knife in a strong grip, took a long breath, and slipped between the tent flaps. I stole across the dirt floor, and knelt down beside the pallet on the floor, reaching toward the bound hands in front of me.

It was her! Her exact size. Her soft white hands.

The blanket was over her face. I drew it back.

"Ha!" the word hit me like a blow, and I tumbled backward, the knife falling from my grip.

The ropes slipped from the soft hands of Lady Lightland's rope worker - Galen Floren Topocos.

No. It couldn't be.

His too-red mouth curved into a devious smile as he leapt to his feet, hands out and fingers spread wide.

"They all thought I was a fool to try a gambit like this, but I knew the moment I saw you that you were a dog."

He must have seen my offended expression, but he only laughed, black shadows springing to life in his hands.

"Don't take offense. People are either dogs or cats. The other girl is a cat. She goes her own way. You're a dog. You'll keep coming back, faithful and patient, to serve and protect. Won't you? I know it's true. If it wasn't, you wouldn't be here, and we wouldn't even be talking."

I darted a glance toward the tent flap, and he leapt quickly to block my path, hands still outspread.

"For someone who travels with a rope worker, you seem remarkably ignorant to what we can do."

He could say that again. If one of them would just tell me instead of constantly hinting at it – well, that would be great!

Flames! Hit him with the flames.

I raised a hand. But could I really kill someone who was only *saying* threatening things? He hadn't done anything to me yet. And he knew where Mally was.

Attack him! We can talk about the ethics of it after it's done!

"You won't be leaving this tent until I agree to let you," Galen Floren Topocos said. "But don't look so sad, you aren't missing anything. Your friend isn't even here. The minute the alarm was sounded, Lady Lightland took her out on a boat. They're faster anyway, and that way there would never be a chance to catch her before she brought your friend to the Grand Hadri and collected the reward. If that's what she decides to do in the end ..."

Could Kazmerev still hear me?

I can hear you.

Could he tell if this was true? Was Mally really on one of those boats? Had Lady Lightland taken her away?

In the dark, it will be hard to tell – especially with them scattered in every direction. Worry about yourself. Use the fire.

"So now, what will we do with you?" Galen Floren Topocos said, rolling his head from side to side as if he was preparing for a physical fight.

I felt my knees grow weak. I wasn't able to fight him. He wasn't a big man – just as thin and wispy looking as Judicus was – but he was still a lot bigger than me. The only option would be to burn him with fire, but I was still aching about having done that a few minutes ago. There had to be some other way that didn't end with someone dead.

There are three ships sailing in each direction and a party heading inland on horse. Maybe a dozen in that group. Can't count numbers on the boats. Too hard from here, but likely eight to twelve people on each of those. If they were planning an inland raid, what made them scatter like that?

Could it be something Mally said?

Kazmerev seemed to be considering that. *Maybe you're right. Maybe you can get an answer from this rope worker.*

The rope worker clenched his fists and little flickers of shadowy black rope spilled from his fists, dangled a few inches down, and then just clawed at the air as if waiting to be released. "Your cousin seemed to think you had something special to offer us. Oh yes, she revealed that you are cousins. And she told us you have a friend who comes when you're in trouble. You're in trouble now, girl. Where's that friend?"

There it is. Mally told them about me. Flame Riders are rare. Not as rare as the ai'sletta, but rare enough. He wants you.

Wants? How?

"Perhaps you'd like to ask me about what it means to be in a *real* coterie," he said. "Perhaps you'd like to have a future. I can give you those things if you tie yourself to me."

Uh oh. That didn't sound good. He wanted oaths as Judicus had.

I don't think it is oaths he wants. He wants something worse than that. I've looked and looked, Sersha, but I can't figure out which group Mally's in. They must be hiding her, knowing we can see from the air. It's clever – and a lot of effort to disguise their path. They fear you. And I want to get back to where you are. I don't like where this rope worker is headed.

"I know you do not speak," the rope worker continued and the ropes in his hands spooled out a little further. "You don't need to. Just hold your wrists out to me and my ropes will coil around them and up into your heart and I will tie a knot around half of it and it will be mine."

No. Nope. Not happening.

I took a step back.

What's going on?

He wanted to tie my heart up with his ropes!

No! Attack. Now.

I tried to think, but all I could feel was how hard my heart was racing. I couldn't form a strong thought. I couldn't think of another way. Resigned, I bit my lip and lifted my hands to call the flame. Nothing happened. Was Kazmerev too far away?

I'm coming!

He must have flown away checking the boats. He must be too far away for me to call on his flames.

The black ropes shot forward, spiraling around my wrists.

"The moment people find out you're a rope worker," Galen Floren Topocos said, "they always ask if it's evil. And, of course, it is. Evil is disrupting the proper course of the world, which is what we do. Evil is bending the world to your will instead of being bent by it. Which, of course, we do."

That didn't sound right. That sounded like power. Power and evil weren't the same thing. The same axe could chop wood for a fire to warm us or splinter the beam of a man's house and bring down his roof. It was how it was applied that was good or evil.

I shook my head and tried to call the flames. Please, please, please.

Nothing happened.

Keep trying!

The black ropes slowly curled up my arms, brushing under my armpits with their waving threads. It was almost like a loving caress, but when I tried to jerk my arms away, the ropes bit into the flesh.

"Rope work," Galen said, "takes focus. You must know exactly what you want. Then you must carve away all other desires. It can take years to learn that part. It's a lot like spinning. You have to card the wool first, aligning all the fibers. The mental discipline and focus that takes isn't possible for everyone. Not even everyone born with the threads of ability."

He seemed to be enjoying telling me this as I squirmed and fought in the double embrace of his ropes.

"And then you must spin. You focus the threads of your hopes and desires and thoughts and the health of your heart, the power of your mind, the strength in your bones. And you spin that into threads – and when you are very powerful, into thick ropes. And with those ropes, you can weave or unweave little bits of this thing we think of as the world. And, of course, the world is spun, too. It's as malleable as thought."

The threads were getting too close. They spidered across my collarbones, reaching inward. Could he really pierce my heart?

The traitorous organ sped up, as if trying to get every last beat in before the end. I was breathing too fast, trying to shoot flames with every other breath but nothing was happening. Right when I needed my access to the flames the most, it had left me.

When I say jump, jump.

Please, get here in time.

Galen's eyes were glassy as he took a step toward me, his voice almost sing-song now. "Almost there. Almost. We'll spin for you a new heart. A heart that loves properly. A heart that loves *me*."

I couldn't breathe. I couldn't think. It was the end.

Galen's mouth tilted up in the corners in a dreamy smile and then I felt his rope bite my flesh, sinking into my chest. I opened my mouth in soundless agony, wanting now more than ever to be able to scream my terror.

Jump.

I obeyed, putting every scrap of energy and focus into the leap.

With a *fump* fire burst through the tent, lighting the edges.

I was swept onto Kazmerev's back, head whirling, lungs gasping for breath. Only his magic could have gripped me tight enough in that moment as the ropes spun around me, gripping hard, digging in tightly.

For a heartbeat, Kazmerev was flapping hard to gain the air again and I was gripping his feathers in desperate fists while Galen hung below us, suspended by the ropes he'd woven around my arms and into my chest.

And then his threads lost their purchase. They slid from my chest and down my arms and into the depths of the sky.

I heard his panicked scream going on far longer than I expected. Long enough that I shut my eyes tight and buried my face into Kazmerev's feathers. I wanted to scream, too. I wanted this to be over.

And then it was.

Don't look down.

I didn't look down. I took deep, heaving breaths as I buried my face in burning feathers, breathing in the sweet campfire scent of Kazmerev, not caring how my skin was so hot it felt like it might burst into flames.

Kazmerev. My one true friend. He'd come for me.

I am very fond of you, too, little hawk.

What were we going to do? My thoughts were shaking. I kept thinking of that long fall and Galen Floren Topocos's scream going on and on.

I suggest we circle the camp once and then fly north and after a while, maybe you can try to calm down enough to make me invisible again. Then we'll double back and get Judicus down from the tree.

Judicus. A rope worker. Like the one who had tried to literally steal my heart.

They aren't the same.

Like the one who had fallen to his death on the rocks below.

Maybe. I wouldn't be too sure. Rope workers are hard to kill.

Why? They were only human. And it seemed his power was dependent on concentration and that it robbed the rest of him of vigor.

True enough. But they are also fueled by an unrealistic confidence in their own view of the world – and that can be very hard to shake.

I took a deep breath and buried my face further into his feathers. I needed a moment. A moment not to think about rope workers or how we were going to get Judicus out of that tree or which group we should follow to save Mally. Just a moment to calm down and tell myself I was safe.

You are safe. You're with me.

I was. I was with him and with Kazmerev I was safe.

EPISODE THREE: BRIGHT FEATHER

SEASON ONE

37

We found Judicus exactly where Kazmerev left him – in an eagle's nest up a huge poplar tree. His arms and legs splayed out of the nest. His eyes were closed.

How were we going to get him out of there? The tree seemed too delicate to hold my weight as well as his and someone would need to wake him and pull him onto Kazmerev's back. How had he even got the boy up there?

I flew up beside the nest and tilted until he rolled into it.

My stomach lurched at that. What if he'd kept rolling right past the nest?

I would have caught him.

It still made me feel ill.

Don't fuss, little hawk. He'll wake soon and when he does, he can ride on my back and I'll bring him down.

If he woke before dawn.

Yes.

If he didn't panic and fall off the nest.

Yes.

And until then I'd need to wait right here, ready to catch him.

We'll circle while you gather your thoughts.

He lifted in the air to circle the tree. But it wasn't Judicus I was watching as I gathered my thoughts.

First, it was the dark figures moving through the trees and back toward their camp. They moved in straight lines, purposeful and determined.

Then, it was the ships out on the moonlit sea growing smaller by the minute. Any chance we had of catching up with Mally was sailing away.

But it was the fire that finally made me bite my lip in despair. It was licking further into the wilderness, moving along the path of the wind from both the first tree I'd accidentally lit on fire and the second. And it was getting closer and closer to the eagle's nest.

We couldn't wait until Judicus woke up on his own. And we couldn't wait until dawn or I'd lose Kazmerev's help.

Then what will you do? Reach over and shake him awake? And what? Tell him to sit quietly while we try to get him down with raiders all through the trees?

I could shake Judicus awake and then Kazmerev could put me down and go back for the rope worker.

If you think I'm letting you off my back again tonight, you can think again. The last time I did, you almost were killed. And the time before that, too. It's a disturbing reoccurrence.

But it was our only option.

Not the only one. Come on, little hawk. It's time to dig deep. I need to be able to carry both you and Judicus. And I need to do it soon.

But I couldn't. I'd tried twice and failed.

So, try again. There is more to you than doubts and fears. You are deep and full of courage. Reach deep now and find it.

If my heart failed and one of us fell through him here because I couldn't keep him substantial, we'd be killed.

So, don't fail. His bright feathers seemed to flash at that.

I didn't even know how to try.

How do you make me visible?

I focused on him and how near he was and that he was real to me.

So, do that again, but also focus on how solid I am under you. Focus on how strong I am to carry you.

I swallowed down a wave of fear but just as I did, another gust of flame was driven by the strong winds. Trees burst into flames, growing closer and closer to the nest.

I bit my lip. We had to try.

Focus!

Kazmerev sailed toward the tree, seeming to slow as we neared it and carving a slow circle around it.

Leap from my back to the nest, wake your boy, and then as the nest collapses I'll catch you both. Come, little hawk, you were born to fly or I would not be born of your heart.

That was a poor plan. I was already shaking my head when he flew a second circle.

Look below us. The jackals circle.

What was a jackal?

On the ground, between the trees, warriors were gathering – faces covered, weapons in hand. They'd seen my glorious phoenix friend. They were here for us. One of them was running his hands over the base of the poplar as if trying to decide if he could climb it.

It was now or never.

On Kazmerev's next sweep around, I clenched my fists and belly. I was going to have to leap.

I liked riding on Kazmerev's back. I felt safe and strong in his feathers – capable of anything. I liked the rush of flight and the freedom of not being tied in one place. But jumping from him and falling a distance – or even not falling but just jumping with all that air under my dangling feet – made me ill. I couldn't do it. I couldn't.

When I was born the first time, I felt that same way about taking my first leap. I was not ready.

I wasn't ready either. I clenched my fists around his feathers, glued my eyes shut, and tried to catch my breath. It was raw and painful just at the thought of leaping and my heart was racing, racing, racing like the raider boats across the waves.

I can help. Do not fear.

He tilted to one side and then suddenly I was tumbling – not for far – but if I could have screamed, I would have screamed then. My mouth opened in silent terror.

This was not helping! This was – it was the opposite of helping!

I took the leap, landing on the eagle's nest. The nest swayed wildly in the top branches of the tree and my belly dropped again.

See? I'm very helpful.

Sweating with fear, I shook Judicus, trying to hold onto him and one of the far-too-slender branches sticking up past the eagle's nest. I was going to kill Kazmerev.

No need. I shall die on my own with the dawn.

He sounded almost jubilant. I shook my head angrily. He shouldn't have just dropped me into this!

It's the best way to learn to fly. Like most things, the best way to learn is by trying.

The best way to accidentally die, was more like it.

I'll catch you if you start to fall. You're worrying over nothing.

I shook Judicus again and his eyes snapped open this time.

"Where are ... Sersha? Are we on a ship?"

I shook my head, but the movement was too much. My stomach lurched with fear and disorientation.

I turned my head to the side and the whole nest started to tilt as I vomited off the side.

Those lurking below yelled up at us – one a cry of irritation and the other one of triumph. They knew they had me now.

And at that moment, the entire nest fell apart.

38

Branches skittered under my feet now that whatever magic the bird had woven to hold them together was gone. I lost my balance, slamming face-first into the collapsing nest.

Judicus whuffed an exclamation as my weight hit him across the chest and I closed my arms around his warmth and held on tight. We slipped to the side, caught by one of the branches for a brief moment, and then the last sticks under me crumpled and the air whooshed up around me.

My stomach lurched.

This was it.

There was no point, fighting it anymore. We were falling and we'd be broken or dead in a moment, surrounded by enemies. Judicus screamed directly into my ear – far more high-pitched than I'd expected.

What an odd last thought to go to my grave with.

Warmth rushed up to meet me and I clenched my jaw. I hoped it didn't hurt.

Open your eyes.

We were suspended over the ground, just an arm's length from our enemies below.

My heart was beating wildly. I blinked back spots of blackness and clung to Judicus.

"Nngh." He spoke for both of us.

I felt my eyes going so wide that they felt scorched by the heat of my phoenix. We weren't dead. He'd caught us!

I told you I'd never let you fall. Hold on tightly.

It was all I could do to let go of Judicus with one hand and force my fingers to open long enough to grab a hold of Kazmerev's burning feathers.

"Don't let go," Judicus gasped at the same moment that one of the raiders reached for us.

"It's a phoenix," the raider said with awe in his voice, but I didn't have time to even twist and try to see how they were reacting.

Kazmerev's glorious flame-tipped wings spread out and pulled the air with a mighty series of flaps and we lifted up, caught a draft, and soared up over the ruined eagles' nest, over the tips of the swaying trees and up into the clear sky.

My heart fell into my belly and I swallowed down a spike of fear, clinging to his back and trying to remember that I loved flying – I loved the exhilaration of reaching for the heavens.

"I should warn you that I get very sick when flying," Judicus said in a weak voice. "Veela found it frustrating."

No, she didn't. I found it frustrating. It's as unnatural as breathing water instead of air. And it keeps you from doing anything fun – Judicus is no fun at all.

I shot a worried look at Judicus. In the light of Kazmerev's feathers, he looked drawn. Maybe we should set down somewhere.

We will do nothing of the sort. Look down.

The tree we'd been in was surrounded by raiders. One of them tried to loose an arrow at us. In the darkness, I could not see where it had gone.

Yikes. I swallowed down a burst of fear and wiped my sweaty palm on my skirt.

Beyond them, the fire had taken what was left of the campsite and spread up to the trail beyond. Raiders scrambled to fill the last of the boats and even those pursuing us were already abandoning the tree to hurry to the shoreline.

Ooops. I bit my lip guiltily. I hadn't meant to set the forest on fire. I'd only meant to escape.

All actions have consequences. Sometimes the most innocent of choices leads to destruction.

My belly flipped at the thought. And now what? I was without supplies. I had an injured man with me. I didn't know which way Mally went. There were raiders everywhere. What now?

What disastrous innocent choice should I make next?

Now we fly as far and fast as we can to get away from this fire before dawn. Once I die, you will be slow and vulnerable. We must get you somewhere safe first.

But where? I wanted to continue down the coast. With at least half the boats headed along the shore, that was the most likely place for Mally to be.

The wind is wrong for that. Look.

He was right. The wind whipped along the shore, fanning small flames into hungry waves, swallowing bushes and trees whole. Acrid yellow smoke rose from the edge of the fire. I coughed, realizing that the air around us was beginning to scorch.

I can't outfly that spread. We could go back toward your village.

Which would only lead the raiders back there. Besides, my village had been very clear that I wasn't welcome there. And Aunt Danna might very well skin me if she realized Mally wasn't with me.

She would? The violence of that woman!

It was only an expression.

I don't like that expression. Don't use it again.

If I promised not to, could we get back to the problem?

Yes.

I was happy to promise that. I was not happy that the only direction left to us was inland. There were already raiders scattered there and I didn't know how far it might be before we found other people. I had no water, no food, no blankets – nothing.

Easy now. One worry at a time. Let's get away from this fire.

He banked to the side, flying us inland and through a blanket of smoke.

"Where are we going?" Judicus mumbled, but he was weak, too weak to do anything but slump with his chin on my shoulder as we rode. I felt a stickiness to his side that seeped into the sleeve of my dress. He was bleeding again. And I had no supplies to help him.

He coughed on smoke and so did I, clinging to both Kazmerev and Judicus as I doubled over with coughing – one I clutched for the safety he gave me and the other to keep him alive. We just had to get out of this mess, one way or the other, and find some place for Judicus to rest and heal. That was all. We just needed to do that.

Hold on, I'm going to get you out of the smoke.

I held on as tightly as I could, but I was starting to find it harder to think, harder to get a clean breath at all. What was I doing? I couldn't quite remember.

Sersha? Sersha!

39

My head cleared when the smoke did, but the scent of it lingered, filling my nose as we raced away from the flames. Judicus remained heavy and slumped against me, and I clung to him and to Kazmerev as we flew inland.

You're doing well. You've been able to make me solid enough to carry two. And that's very good. As soon as you can do that without making me visible, too, we'll be able to do this without drawing attention.

We were drawing a lot of attention. Every time we crossed a road or ducked too close over a farm, I heard a cry of alarm. It might be the dead of night, but the sight of flames in the sky was enough to wake some people up.

Consider it an early warning for them. If they see the flames, they'll prepare and if the fire gets this far, they'll be glad that they did.

It was more populated than I'd imagined. We crossed almost half a dozen scattered farmsteads or trapper cabins in our path. Why didn't we just stop at one?

I don't feel safe landing at one. At least if we land at a real village, you should have enough eyes on you that they won't just kill you on sight for having ridden a creature of flame.

I didn't want to be killed, so I agreed. But with every hour that we slipped further inland, we were an hour further away from wherever they were taking Mally. With every hour we didn't find a place to set down, we were an hour further from help for Judicus.

We don't know how far the raiders will go in the morning. I don't want to leave you too close to them alone with an injured man.

And dawn was growing closer. I felt it in my bones. With each passing minute, Kazmerev grew a little brighter, a little angrier, a little more indrawn as he mused on his loss.

It's not all me. I take on your characteristics, remember? And you are worried. Your worry is making my flames burn blue.

My eyebrows rose. His flames really were blue-edged. That was my worry?

Well, it certainly isn't mine. I've been in spots worse than this before.

I sighed and tried to calm myself but chasing after calm only made it fly away faster.

There's a tiny village on the mountainside up ahead, Kazmerev said before I even caught sight of it. His eyesight was better than mine. *Stay with me and your eyesight will improve to match. For now, I think we need to land at that village.*

Would it be safe?

I glanced behind me, but the fire was far distant now, nothing more than an orange glow against the darkness of the thick sky.

We're out of options now. Dawn is fast approaching.

He began his descent, cupping his wings and I clung to his feathers, watching the blue edge of the flames flicker as I tried not to panic and make his blue flames grow even bluer.

It will be okay. Find help. Stay out of trouble. I'll be back at dusk and together we'll figure out what to do next. There's nothing that we can't figure out when we're together.

I was still trying to think of something to say in return when he landed roughly on the grassy field in the center of the huddled buildings, skidding over dew-wet grass, his wings burning off the dew with a hiss. Before I could open my mouth, he disappeared, leaving me to fall on the ground, still clutching Judicus.

My hip bone screamed an alarm of pain at the rough landing.

My phoenix was gone. And with him, my sense of confidence evaporated like water under the hot sun.

Gone. Gone. Gone.

If there was a worst part of being a Flame Rider, then this was it, because I felt like half a girl when he was away.

I sighed and turned back to my rope worker friend. Gingerly, I checked him over. He didn't seem broken – but how would I even know? The rope worker was living on borrowed time.

I gripped him under the shoulders – this was becoming a far-too-familiar habit – and dragged him toward the door of the nearest building. The yard around it was chewed up with hooves. Someone must be here. Right?

Panting and huffing, I got Judicus as far as the door before rapping on it as hard as I could.

No answer.

I tried again.

Still no answer.

At the third knock, another door opened from across the village and a voice barked out, "Who calls before dawn?"

A spark flared to life and the lantern was held high above the speaker's head.

"I told you, Sersha," my Aunt Donna said from the doorway, "Whatever you do, don't take Mally. But you just had to go and take my daughter."

My mouth fell open and I stared at her in shock.

What was she doing here? How had she traveled so far, so fast?

"Well? Are you going to stand there staring all morning or are you coming in for breakfast?" she groused.

I shut my mouth with a click and turned to drag Judicus in the other direction toward my Aunt Danna and whatever hard words she might say.

40

Before I'd moved a step, Aunt Danna was there, helping me to lift Judicus and carry him into the cabin. Her lantern rocked from where she hung it by the door, making the darkness of early morning dance with its beams and the first half-gold light of early morning.

"You look like you haven't slept in days," she commented, and I tried not to frown at how close she'd come to the mark. I hadn't slept properly since I saw her. And even then, it had only been in fits and starts the first few days. "You're young, but you can still burn out. You aren't an eternal fire like your phoenix friend."

We brought Judicus into the small cabin and laid him on the only bed – still warm – under Aunt Danna's blanket.

She shoved a satchel in my hands. "See to him while I fix tea and porridge."

Tea! The thought of it made my mouth water. Blinking back tears, I lifted Judicus' shirt and began the work of recleaning and bandaging his wound. It was getting better – though there were ridges of scar tissue and clotted dried blood that formed an angry line where they hadn't broken open again. He was going to have a really noticeable scar after all these reinjuries. I frowned as I checked it, but there was no swelling or heat in the skin around the injury. He'd escaped the worst of it – again.

"You're good at stitching them up, Sersha," Aunt Danna said coolly. "If only you were as good at keeping them out of trouble. But that's men for you. Always up to some kind of trouble."

I found that hard to believe about Uncle Llynd. He was the steadiest man I knew. He could stand where the hearth irons sat, and no one might notice the difference.

I glanced surreptitiously around us.

"Just me," Aunt Danna said from the fire. "I left in a hurry. Made good time on the roads. I'd hoped to get Mally back before she went too far. But I don't sail, so I didn't want to take a boat. Wouldn't do to run into another boat in the night – or whatever other fool thing you can do wrong at sea." I felt my cheeks grow hot. If Mally had been more like her mother, we wouldn't be in this mess. Maybe Aunt Danna could have predicted all that and prevented it if she'd been there. "Figured you'd need to come ashore eventually. I wasn't wrong. But here you are and no Mally. Should I assume that's something to do with the glow of fires south of here?"

South? I could have sworn we were going directly inland! I could have sworn we were headed east. But Kazmerev had only said he'd been heading inland – not which direction he'd headed. And he'd been trying to avoid the fires and the raiders. And trying to find a village for Judicus. Maybe he'd swung further north than he'd meant to.

But even so, Aunt Danna had come a long way for a woman with no boat or horse.

"I took the horse that brought the rope worker to us," she said, without looking at me, as if she could read my thoughts. Her chin was thrust out just like Mally's. "And thank goodness I did. Look at the poor rope worker. He'll need to ride. You can't be making him boat and fly – and don't even try to tell me you didn't fly here – in that state. Sersha, Sersha, Sersha. From now on, you travel with me."

I grimaced. Not much got past Aunt Danna.

"Porridge is almost ready and it's getting light outside," Aunt Danna said. "Once we've eaten, we'll leave."

I shook my head.

"I'll brook no nonsense," Aunt Danna began, and then she looked out the window, sighed, and for a moment I thought she might cry. She was worried about Mally. Even I could see that. After a minute, she spoke again. "Does your phoenix come back later?"

I nodded.

She sighed and offered me some porridge. "There's only one bed, but once you've eaten, I can probably fix you a spot from a hammock I saw in one of the other cabins. I don't know what this place is. Never heard of it before. But it was empty when I arrived and it's empty yet. Maybe the two of you can sleep and I'll watch over you and then tomorrow we'll go after my girl. Does that seem fair?"

I nodded and began to eat, trying to pretend I didn't notice her red eyes or how she'd treated me as she always did – not quite like furniture but also not quite like someone able to explain what or why things were happening. I wasn't used to that anymore. Not after Kazmerev and Judicus. I didn't think I could go back to it.

But I didn't have the strength to argue.

By the time I'd finished eating, Aunt Danna had strung up a hammock and set a warm blanket over it. I washed my wooden bowl in a bucket beside the door, kicked off my muddy boots, crawled into the hammock, and let the warmth of the sun wash over me and lull me to sleep.

If I dreamed, it was only of open skies and warm feathers beneath me, and I didn't wake until the yelling woke me.

"Shh!" Aunt Danna said, a hand over my mouth. My eye popped open, but it was full dark.

Sersha! Sersha I was so worried! Why didn't you wake up!

What was wrong?

Judicus sat up with a start from his place in the bed. His curse slashed through the room.

"They're here," he said grimly. "They've come for us."

41

"Both of you, be quiet," Aunt Danna said, stuffing the blankets onto the hammock I'd been sleeping in and then slipping it from its hooks and rolling it up neatly.

She jammed the bundle into my hands and whispered, "Tie this tightly."

"What are we doing here? Are we back in Landsfall?" Judicus whispered, disoriented.

"Shh!" Aunt Danna slung a leather satchel over her shoulder and another one over mine as I finished tying up the blankets and then grabbed Judicus' arm and pulled him to a door at the back of the cabin.

Voices filled the abandoned village.

"Someone has been here. My hammock is missing!"

"Search the cabins."

"Are those horse tracks?"

Aunt Danna cursed quietly and dragged Judicus out the door, scrambling over a grassy berm. By the time I had the door shut silently behind us and joined them, he was huffing and breathless.

"Was that a little yellow shield painted on the door?" Judicus gasped.

"Shhh!"

"Do you know what that means?"

"Shhh!"

The horse was tethered there beside a tree and Aunt Danna threw the pad and pack saddle over his back, cinching it like she'd done it every day of her life. Bear of a woman that she was, she lifted Judicus onto the horse in the awkward spot between the crossbucks. He drooped over the horse's withers, his energy already spent.

"Hold onto the mane," Aunt Danna whispered, pushing his hands into it and tying our burdens deftly to the packsaddle.

I was shifting my weight from one foot to the other, my impatience getting to be too much for me.

Kazmerev?

I'm here. Watching.

I glanced up and saw him there, circling, seeming to slip from draft to draft of air with barely the smallest motion in his wing to keep him aloft. My breath froze in my lungs for a heartbeat, and I let myself just look. He was breathtaking.

A quick yank from Aunt Danna pulled me back to my senses. My cheeks went hot.

Don't be ashamed. Any human with a solid head on their shoulders would be stunned by my beauty. I'm a glorious creature of legend. It's right that it steals your breath and leaves you speechless.

Everything left me speechless, I thought wryly as I stumbled along behind the packhorse. This time, I kept my wits about me, listening.

They're searching the village. I don't know who they are, but I would avoid them. They stumbled in with baskets of berries and loud voices. They didn't expect company. But they are odd. I don't trust them.

Odd how?

I ... I don't know. There's just something not right about them.

Had they heard the horse? Were they following?

I see no pursuit.

Had they left anyone ahead of us?

I see none ahead.

I frowned and hurried up to Aunt Danna at the head of the horse. I signed to her that the road was safe.

"If you want to ride your flaming bird, I won't stop you," she whispered coldly. "If you want to take your rope worker and leave me here, I won't stop you from that, either."

I did want to do those things. I didn't like the idea that we were losing time and we could go a lot faster on Kazmerev's back. Even with a fire raging in the distance.

I don't see signs of fire anymore. The change of wind direction must have pushed the fire against the sea.

"But I think you'd do better to travel with me, Sersha," Aunt Danna said smugly. "After all, I have all the supplies and you can't stop in a village for seven days."

"Yellow shield," Judicus gasped.

I tilted my head in question. We were back on the trail and around a turn. No one was following us, and yet Aunt Danna couldn't know that, but she was speaking very boldly as if she did.

"Well, you have to stay in quarantine for the next seven days. Those men at the plague camp were sent there because they can't be cured. It's why the place exists. We could have caught it by sleeping in their homes."

I gaped at her. She had known that and said nothing.

One of her eyebrows went up. "You didn't think I wouldn't find a way to keep you once I caught you again, niece? Until my Mally is found and safe I am not letting go of you. I am not leaving your side. You're my ticket to getting my girl back."

I bit my lip, wanting to shake myself. I'd trusted her. I'd thought it was safe to go where she wanted and do as she asked. I'd thought it was all safe and here I was, trapped. And maybe sick.

"I doubt either of you are sick," she said blithely. "Or me, for that matter. But the villages will burn you if you go under their roofs before the seven days are up or if you start to show the spots the disease sufferers show. That's why they send them to the colony. They only get to go back if the spots are gone."

I felt like I was going to be ill. I was poorly supplied. My closest human ally drained of life. On the run. Possibly ill. I was all those things. Oh, and I was also a hammock thief.

It was all too much.

I set my eyes forward and walked without looking at my aunt.

I will watch from above, little hawk. And don't you worry about disease. Flame Riders are immune to diseases. You can burn it off.

Burn it off?

You know how you can throw my fire?

Yes. I did.

You can also make light or burn off illness in your body or keep yourself warm – all by directing my fire as you please.

Eventually. When I learned all of that.

That's right. He seemed smug.

But I'd have to do that pretty quickly if I was ill right now. I didn't know the way yet.

Oh, your body would figure it out pretty quickly – just like a fever.

I could just about murder Aunt Danna. I gritted my teeth and walked as fast as I could, keeping pace with the horse. Seven days. We were stuck with her for at least seven days and nights.

Then let's make the most of them. I will tell you of my life as a phoenix and you can tell me of your life as a young human and I will spiral over your head and watch your path. Perhaps in seven days, Judicus will be well, and we will fly from here so hot and fast that our trail stays fiery hours after we are gone.

It was a nice thought, but try though I may, my spirits just kept sinking. The harder I fought to get away, the more my old life clawed up and grabbed me again. I was starting to think I would never be free at all.

42

We traveled three nights like that. Me in silence – no surprise there. Aunt Danna in *stony* silence – no surprise there, either. That woman could out-stubborn a rock. Judicus sleeping almost all the time. Kazmerev chatty and gorgeous, burning bright in the night and dying with the dawn. He was the light in the darkness and the hope in my heart.

On the first morning, when Judicus moaned his way to consciousness, Aunt Danna had remarked, "It's a shame you aren't voiceless like Sersha. You'd make for a better traveling companion."

And Judicus, in a rare bout of temper, had sent out his ropes, lightning-fast, and wrapped one around Aunt Danna's neck.

"You don't ever speak about Sersha like that. Ever. What do you think, Sersha? Do I choke her life out now or wait until later?" he'd gritted out.

I shook my head furiously and then he slumped over again, unconscious from his use of power. I'd huffed and made him comfortable, shaking my head furiously at both him and Aunt Danna and their foolishness until Aunt Danna put a hand on my arm and when I froze, she leaned in.

"What would you do?" she asked. "If it was your girl, what would you do?"

I stared right back. One thing I'd do was not completely slow the process of saving her. If Aunt Danna would just give up this crazy idea of going after Mally with us, then Judicus and I could fly on Kamerev's back and be ten times as fast.

You could still do that. Leave them here and come with me, and we'll go get her together. Or at least find out where she is and circle back here to tell them.

I'd bit my lip at the thought. It was a good one. So, why hadn't I thought of it?

On the second morning, right after Kazmerev died and the world went dull again, we'd made camp and settled Judicus. He'd slept continuously – except for breaks to relieve himself or take a little food – since his spat with Aunt Danna, but his wound was closed now and hadn't reopened. I was feeling confident about it. That, at least, would mend even if he was running himself ragged.

"When she was born the midwife was taken with a vision," Aunt Danna said, not looking at me. "'She'll be ripped from you before her time,' old mother Sonsy told me that night. 'And the Hand of the Rat will come and the Scourge of High Places will be at their back. And they will snatch her away and make her in their image and you will know true fear.'"

I looked at her, finally. She was pale and drawn. Fear left her hands shaking. And she should be fearful. The Hand of the Rat already had her girl and whoever this Scourge was could be right behind them.

I should have left on my own then. But I kept looking between them – Aunt Danna and Judicus. Judicus and Aunt Danna. Would one kill the other while I was gone? And what about my vow to Judicus? I was supposed to be in his coterie. And even if he'd been ill for the entire time I'd known him, I'd made the promise to stick with him. Could I really fly away and leave him here?

When night fell on the third night, Kazmerev wanted to know the same thing.

When are we leaving, Sersha? We are dragging our feet and slow as a snail in a flower garden. We could have found your cousin already if we left these two here. Coterie or no coterie, you aren't doing Judicus any favors waiting here with him on this lonely road when you could be saving your cousin.

I was stuck in quarantine for four more days after being near those plague victims.

So, we keep out of villages and cities then. It won't be hard. And it's only for four days.

If I hadn't been voiceless, maybe I would have tried to convince Aunt Danna of this with words. I *did* try to sign to her, but she only said, "It's too dark, Sersha."

Frustration tasted like acid in my mouth. We were dragging our heels. First the flight that went too far north.

I was just avoiding the smoke so Judicus wouldn't die of asphyxiation.

I wasn't blaming him. But it *still* took us off course.

Then finding Aunt Danna which had led first to having to toe the line with her methods and second to Judicus burning out his hard-earned energy squabbling with her. And now here we were – wandering this lonely people-free trail and slowly, oh so slowly, winding our way south when we ought to be flying every night on Kazmerev's back.

I ground my teeth at the thought of it. Out there somewhere the raiders or Lady Lightland's coterie had Mally. And they thought that because I was mute and Judicus was injured that we couldn't do anything about it. But we could, if we just decided to.

You're not ready to carry three people yet.

But I didn't need to. I could go with just Judicus and leave Aunt Danna to follow.

Frankly, he's dead weight right now.

Then I could leave them both and strike out on my own.

When you don't know the way? When you have no abilities to get your cousin back? We need Judicus. And right now, your aunt and her longsuffering horse are also very helpful.

And yet I was losing time.

Is it a race? Oh wait, I suppose it is. But what do you think will happen? Do you think she will turn to the dark and go with their goals of using her prophesied role for ... whatever it is they want ... after just a few days?

I didn't know. But that was the whole point. I *didn't know* which meant anything could be happening while I spent night after night walking beside the world's slowest horse, listening to the frogs sing, and wishing I was flying with Kazmerev.

Ha! You just miss flying. Admit it. You love the feeling of the breeze beneath your wings, every tilt and lean embracing you in harmony with the flow of the winds that swath our world, clothe it in clouds, and carry forth the rains and snows where they are needed.

He was waxing poetic about flying.

So are you – with every grinding squeak of your teeth.

That was when Judicus finally woke up.

43

"Where are we?" he asked with a moan, sitting up.

"On the road south," Aunt Danna said coolly. But I knew she was glad he'd woken up. She'd been waiting for this moment. I knew that because every time he so much as twitched she made sure she was nearby. "We're keeping you out of trouble and you should be grateful I'm willing to do that much after the stunt you pulled. No one uses magic on me. Are we clear?"

"You insulted Sersha," he said mulishly and my heart sped. It felt so ... gratifying ... to have someone speak up for me. But at the same time, I didn't dare let him use his ropes again. He needed to recover his strength.

Hastily, I snatched the lantern from where Aunt Danna had it hung on the side of the baggage and I held it up. Was Kazmerev sure I could light this?

It's like the fire – but subtle. Be subtle!

He was nearly too late with his warning and even with it when I focused on the wick and screwed up my face it lit with such a pop of flame that one of the panes in the side of the lantern flew right out, shattered by the heat.

Aunt Danna made a sound an awful lot like a squeak and Judicus cursed quietly before recovering himself and gravely saying, "Thank you, Sersha."

I lifted the lantern so he could see my face and hand. Maybe he couldn't read my signs, but this was important. I tried my best to sign his rope magic – an opening of the hand, and a writhing of the fingers before making a throwing motion and then a hasty wagging of my finger. There was to be no more of that.

"No more magic?" he asked, looking bemused.

"If only," Aunt Danna said dryly, frowning at the lantern.

I mimed sleep.

"You want to sleep?" Judicus asked.

I shook my head and pointed to him.

"You want me to rest?"

I nodded.

"And what will you do?"

I pointed upward and mimed a bird flying with my hand, pointing south.

"You want to go south after Mally yourself?" he guessed.

At my nod, he sighed, and Aunt Danna firmly said, "No."

It was my turn to frown, but she didn't stop there.

"And what would you do to recover her, Sersha? Do you suddenly have warrior skills none of us know about? Or cartography skills? You've never left Landsfall before. You'll be so lost in a fortnight that there will be no recovering you."

"It's nearly impossible for a Flame Rider to get truly lost," Judicus said, his voice thick with scorn. "Or do you suddenly have the gift of flight without *us* knowing it?"

Aunt Danna's mouth narrowed in fury until I thought she might really develop the gift of flight right there just to spite him.

I made a pacifying motion, but it was too late.

"See what you've done?" Aunt Danna said to him. "You've put these ideas into their heads. First Mally. Then Sersha. They think they're more than they are. It's going to end in trouble. What do you think will happen when Sersha gets to a big city? How is she supposed to find her cousin? She doesn't know what she's doing. She doesn't have any money. She can't even ask questions. Better to send a toddler out to fish the sea."

I felt like I'd been slapped, and I recoiled from her harsh words, my face heating so hot I was afraid I might light on fire like the lantern.

"Enough!" Judicus roared with so much energy that I was afraid he'd start weaving ropes again. "Sersha is part of my coterie. And as such, you will respect her."

"Coterie, is it? Like in the stories?" Aunt Danna laughed. "How adorable. And what does your coterie do out there? Do they play at being little nobles like you until you grow bored and kick them off to the streets to beg?"

"I think you're still failing to understand what Sersha is," Judicus said tightly.

Aunt Danna scoffed. "Oh, I think I know what she is."

"Do you? Did you watch the royal Flame Rider Trodark Redwing defend the city of Grosenbeg in the Tranch War?" His voice was rising as he spoke. It shook, as with great passion. "Were you there when the Flamerarch roared over Briccatore, their hands filled with fury, their talons stretched out like the plows of the gods to rip us to pieces? Was it you who was there when they descended and tore the Black Death of the Coast to pieces?"

I gasped, shocked to see there were silver trails of tears on his face.

"I was there," he snarled. "I saw every moment of it. I watched as they shredded everything I ever loved and put it to the flames, so don't lecture me on what a Flame Rider *is*. I lived after in a time when any scrap you could beg was a hard-sought blessing. So, don't tell me about poverty. I've watched the mighty fall and the lowly rise. I've watched evil toppled and renewed. I've seen the seasons of kingdoms turn. If Sersha wants to go look for your daughter on her own, then fine. She has my blessing. Better out there on her own than burdened with your prejudice and made small by your insults. And better me left with you to bear the brunt of your cold heart than her left to shrink under your frosty dictates."

He slumped over, coughing and coughing until I was afraid he'd never catch his breath but all Aunt Danna did was look at me and say, "See what you've done."

I did see. But I also saw that Judicus had stood up for me. And that he believed there was more to me than just a girl with no voice. And the knowing of it lit a flame in me brighter than the lantern I held, brighter even than the flames racing along my phoenix's feathers.

44

"Meet me at the Forked Refuge along the coast of Flamafi, south of here," Judicus said when the coughing stopped. "It will take me and your aunt about two weeks on the road to travel that far. By then, you and Kazmerev should have found Mally wherever she might be. Don't try to rescue her on your own. Just find her and shadow her until we can join you and then we'll work on a plan together. I'll have restored my magic by then and be ready to help."

I quickly made my no magic signs. He laughed grimly.

"I promise. I won't use magic until then. I'll spend my time recovering."

"And do you expect me to tend you and care for your weakened state for those two weeks?" my aunt Danna said. "Think again, rope worker."

I quickened my pace, stepped around the packhorse to the side where Aunt Danna was, and stepped in front of her, crossing my arms over my chest and planting my feet. When she tried to move around me, I moved with her, blocking her path.

"What, Sersha?" she asked irritably.

"I think," Judicus said carefully. "That Sersha is trying to remind you that she and I could just fly away right now and never go after your daughter. That we could go back to Briccatore and live our lives without ever thinking of her again. That we could go find an inn – which wouldn't be hard with Kazmerev flying us – and stay there until I recover, eating fine foods and resting. We owe Mally nothing. And yet, we are willing to risk injury and hardship to go after her."

Aunt Danna threw up her hands. "Fine. I won't force him away and I'll travel with him. Is that what you want to hear?"

I nodded. But inside, I was sad. I had hoped for better from Aunt Danna. She'd been like a mother to me all my life. But it turned out she only liked me in the kitchens working behind closed doors. She wasn't very happy with me in the skies with Kazmerev or making decisions that she didn't like.

I shook my head to myself. There was no fixing that. Instead, I laid a hand of goodbye on Judicus' arm. I wouldn't take more supplies than absolutely necessary. Hurriedly, I took a single waterskin from the bags and slung the strap crosswise over my body. A tiny bit of the pemmican in the bags went into my belt pouch and I checked again that my flint and knife were there. Kazmerev and I were quick and we could forage and find something to eat.

I require no food of this earth. But I am proud of you, Sersha. It takes strength to stand and demand responsibility rather than being carried along by the current.

I felt my cheeks heating from his compliment as I laid a hand on Judicus' arm in a brief goodbye.

He slipped a few coins into my hand.

"Take these. You'll need supplies when you get to a village. Prioritize that. No sense dying of thirst because you had no waterskin."

My aunt huffed. She still wasn't pleased with us.

"No stopping in a village until your seven days are up," she reminded me.

Judicus caught my eye again. "Remember. The Forked Refuge. Along the Flamafi Coast."

I nodded and gave him the lantern.

"Don't flame out before I see you again," he said with a tired smile.

I glanced at Aunt Danna, but she looked away. She had no interest in a goodbye. And I could not say goodbye unless she agreed to hear it from me. I sighed.

If I was someone in a storybook I might have whistled or called out a phrase like, "Wings to the Wind!" and then Kazmerev would descend from the clouds.

Instead, I just looked up and reached for him with my heart.

He was there in an instant.

Jump.

I jumped – and for one glorious moment, my whole world was hot purple feathers tipped in scarlet and gold and the softness of pillowy down underneath. I closed my eyes and breathed the scent of burning birch and cloves. It felt like going home.

For me as well.

The wind whipped around my face as we climbed up through the air to race above the treetops and something in my chest that had been weighing me down tore loose. I was not afraid to fly. The rush of it filled me, like the sail on the boat Mally chose. It rippled through me and filled to overflowing those empty places inside.

I opened my eyes and let the sensation of the wind rushing past my face and through my hair lull me and the woodsmoke scent of Kazmerev comfort me. My belly barely wobbled even as we banked, tilting far to one side in our circular swoop.

Below, in the dark trees, a single lantern spot was all I saw of Judicus and Aunt Danna.

For a moment, I was afraid. I was on my own now, my decisions my own. The consequences of my choices mine alone to bear.

Not alone. Never alone.

It would be alright. I would find Mally and meet them at the Forked Refuge. Wherever that was.

I've heard that name before, though I have not been there. I'm not well familiar with your northern lands.

Then we'd both learn something together. This might actually be fun, too.

I pretty much have a fun time all the time, Kazmerev teased and then he sobered. *I'm glad you won your freedom again, Sersha, but just a small reminder – it's nearly dawn. We need to find a safe place for you to pass the day.*

I felt my cheeks going hot. I probably should have stayed with Aunt Danna and Judicus for the day. But if I went back to them now and waited for the sunset, well, I'd feel awfully ridiculous. And maybe they wouldn't agree to let me leave again.

I think I see the perfect spot. I'll keep you warm there until dawn. We can fly again when the sun sets.

I should probably argue that it would be more responsible to go back to Judicus – but I didn't want to. I wanted to sink into his warm feathers a little more and get some much-needed sleep.

45

I woke with a start. The hilltop we'd settled on had warmed in the sun and I'd overslept in the comfort of it. Now, I woke as the shadows lengthened and dusk descended. I was already regretting not taking more of the supplies. I missed having a blanket and I could use a good combing. I hastily fixed my braid and then waited, breathing deeply until the last rays of the sun slipped over the horizon.

I felt him arrive – like a burst of joy in my heart.

Sersha. His voice was warmth and happiness.

Kazmerev.

He bloomed from my chest – as if he really was reborn in my heart and then he was right there in all his brilliant glory, preening his feathers.

Ready to fly, glorious phoenix?

Ready for anything!

I slid onto his broad feathered back, marveling at how easy it came now – as if I'd been launching myself onto the back of a magical phoenix since I was born. He smelled of foreign spices and charred wood and I drank it in, letting his warmth wash over me in welcome.

I had missed him.

The days are cold and empty without you.

I thought he was dead during the days.

Even the dead may dream of love and light.

I leaned my cheek into his feathers, soaking him in. But I couldn't stay like that forever. Eventually, we lifted off, leaping into the cold night air. Cold didn't bother me. Not when I could fly with my phoenix.

We started in a lazy circle, ready to head to the south. Moving in a wide loop. I wished it wasn't night. This view must be spectacular in the day. But in the bright moonlight, it was still a delight. The proud mountains rose strong and tall in the distance. The green trees formed a different kind of black and the water shone the light of the moon back to her face.

It was a beautiful night to be out flying. I didn't want to miss a moment of it.

I wanted to fly so far and fast that we left everything behind us. Angry aunts. Raiders. The responsibility to help Judicus and save Mally. My voicelessness. Everything.

Then let's do that.

Just for a little while. Just for today.

DO I sound like I'm disagreeing? Because I am not. Flight is the great gift – the beauty of feather and wind, zephyr and spirit. A tangle of earth and heavens and bright, searing spirit.

I clutched his feathers, and he sprang to further life under me, his wings catching the wind like never before and propelling us with such force through the air that I couldn't help the silent whoop of delight that echoed through my mind and heart.

This was life. The air in my face. The wind under our wings. The taste of life everywhere.

We soared in our wide loop, drinking it in together – the balmy air, the moonlit night, and the shared joy of our friendship. And it felt just a little bit like paradise.

It was long minutes before the heady ride began to clear my head and I remembered my duty.

Time for us to sweep south and head toward where we'd last seen Mally. There was the sea in the distance, and the darker land burned blacker-than-black in reaching fingers across the landscape. And there was the road under us – and a bobbing torch that must be Aunt Danna and Judicus. They were hardly any further south than we were. I looked past them at the landscape we'd cover today and then stopped. Was my sense of perspective wrong? Had I no sense of distance at all?

Right in front of them – at the other side of the bend they were already turning around – a large number of torches and fires were lit. Where had they come from?

My grip on Kazmerev's feathers grew tighter as the joy of the flight whooshed away.

You have a good sense of direction. You aren't wrong, Sersha. That's a group of people right there a single bend away. What should we do?

We needed to fly down and warn Judicus.

Too late.

As we watched a pair of torches closed in on their single lantern and drew them into the large camp. My heart flew into my throat. Now what?

Maybe they are friends?

Do you really think so?

It never hurts to hope. But we won't know unless we go in there and find out.

I licked my lips nervously, trying to see details of the camp. It looked familiar. Far too familiar.

Do those tents have burned edges?

Had we just dropped Judicus right back in raider hands? My heart was racing so fast now that I couldn't seem to slow it down.

I know what you're going to say.

That was helpful. Maybe he could tell me.

You're going to say you want to go into that camp to check things out and rescue them if they're in trouble.

That did sound like me.

You're going to try to make me wait here.

Well, he was a bright burning phoenix.

But last time when that happened, you almost were killed.

Because nothing screams anonymity like a phoenix so bright you saw purple afterimages for months after looking at him.

Well, now you're just flattering me. He seemed pleased. *But compliments aside, I'm putting my foot down. No sneaking into that camp alone. No leaving me behind. If you're going to do this, then we're doing it together.*

What if I slipped up and made him visible by accident?

You didn't do that when we were flying together.

But there was no pressure then!

You didn't do it last time when we were attacked.

That was different. I had allies then.

And what am I, then? He sounded hurt.

I hurried to soothe it.

You're the best phoenix alive and my best friend.

The sense that came through our connection told me that if phoenixes could smile, he'd be grinning ear to ear at that.

I'll take that compliment. And I'll take you into the camp with me. No need for payment. No questions asked. I'm just that kind of a gentleman.

What was that supposed to mean?

That I'm getting my way one way or another.

I couldn't help but laugh at that. I was still chuckling at it when we set down on the grass just outside the well-lit camp. I wasn't ready to sneak in. But then again, I'd never been ready for any of this. I gritted my teeth and strode forward.

Here we go.

46

It was hard to be patient. It should be easy by now. People had been pushing me aside my whole life. They'd been making me wait while they decided whether to pay attention to my signs and expressions. I couldn't stay someone's hand with a sharp word or set them back in their place with a growl. I couldn't lure them to my way of thinking with honeyed words or dismiss a thought with words that sweep away. Truth and patience had always been my only allies when assertions, flattery, manipulations, and defensiveness were not mine to possess.

And yet I was struggling for patience now.

I crouched in the bushes, listening as the patrols ringed the camp. It was smaller than I thought originally – only five tents and the people to go with them. Three fires. Someone had cooked stew on one of the fires and when people went off patrol, they visited that fire and ate. It was at that fire that men and women huddled and sharpened weapons or spoke in low voices together.

They looked worried and nervous. They spoke very little.

And no wonder. Because in one of the tents, people were moaning. Occasionally someone would speak in a low, guttural tone and then an agonized gasp or cry would tear through the tent wall.

Every time it did, I shifted my weight, the urge to do something almost overwhelming in its power.

Don't move until you're sure you can sneak in. We must be certain that you won't be caught, too.

But what if I wasn't certain? What if it took all night?

Then it takes all night.

And then what? What if the people gasping in that tent didn't have all night? What if they were Aunt Danna and Judicus?

I don't know. Can you recognize any of the guards? Or the livery?

I couldn't. These guards were wearing livery, I could see that, and it was vaguely reminiscent of Lady Lightland's but I'd been busy noticing her and the rope worker with her when we'd been her captives. I'd been occupied trying not to die then. I hadn't paid attention to what was on the uniforms.

I should have paid better attention.

I bit my lip and watched as the guards made another ring around the tents. The fires were burning lower and with less light, the shadows of the guards danced over the tents less often and the light inside the tents danced even more. The largest tent – the one with all the gasps and moans – was lit from within by a lantern and the shadows within danced and writhed like trapped souls.

Sweat formed along my brow despite the cool of the night and I buried my hand wrist-deep into Kazmerev's feathers trying to chase away the feelings it drove through me. I didn't dare succumb to fear. And yet, I could feel nothing else.

The hours were wearing on and my joints were stiff. I'd been crouched here in the darkness for too long. If I didn't move soon, I would miss my chance. I needed Kazmerev. I needed his help.

Someone burst from the tent I'd been watching, bringing the lantern with him and another figure followed close on his heels. My breath caught in my chest.

The first one shuffled slightly, his hands clutching a knife and a rope – two items that made me even more jumpy. The other one walked like a crow in little fits and starts as if he couldn't decide where to place his feet. His shoulders were hunched despite being not much older than I was.

He turned, suddenly, his lantern jostling with the movement and sending little dancing shadows in every direction.

"No more of that. They won't talk fast enough for it to help and then we'll just miss the rendezvous. I vote we sleep for the rest of the night and then in the morning, we can travel as far as we dare and pick up the questioning again at night."

"Mmm," the older one said. "Two more will add to the burden."

"We can leave guards behind with the horse and some of the tents. Travel lighter," the first said dismissively, walking again in his peculiar, half-strutting, almost-hopping manner.

They didn't stop for stew, moving directly to one of the other tents instead and slipping inside.

I counted my breaths and after twenty breaths their lantern went out.

One of the guards blew two low notes and two of the fires were abandoned as the remaining guards filled the other three tents. Only two were left on watch, circling.

I tried to calm the excited hitch of my breathing.

If I was going to act, now was the time.

Give them a few minutes to grow bored. You know how boring circling can be if there is no prey to watch.

I didn't know, so I'd have to take his word for it.

We'll have to circle more often together so you can feel the boredom for yourself.

All I was likely to feel was exhilaration. The fact that I could fly with him at all still gave me little shivers of excitement.

If you had to choose between flying with me or having a voice again, which would you pick?

I didn't even have to think about that one. I'd choose to fly. Speaking was for the birds.

So is flying, Kazmerev teased. *Just saying.*

I smiled in the darkness, but my heart was racing. At any moment it would be time to sneak in and I had to be ready. The guards were about to cross the point where both would be parallel to me before one started working his way from the fires back toward this side of the ring around the camp. I waited ... waited.

I think ... now.

I stood up as silently as I could.

Time to do this.

47

I raced across to the tent, heart pounding so hard it flooded my hearing.

But I wasn't alone. Kazmerev stayed right beside me, bright eyes looking in every direction.

There's a stone in front of your foot.

I avoided it just in time to avoid stubbing my toe.

Duck into the tent!

I slipped into the dark opening, my vision suddenly gone as the tent flap closed behind me. Outside the tent, I heard footsteps as the guard passed but it took three more breaths to calm down enough that each breath didn't saw loudly in and out of my lungs.

Fear tinged all my senses – but I still couldn't see well enough to make anything out.

Wait for your eyes to adjust. If you light a lantern they'll see if from outside.

I nodded, agreeing. Could Kazmerev see anything?

I think this is Judicus.

There was a moan from beside me that sounded like Judicus.

He's hurt.

And Kazmerev could see that?

The tent isn't dark for me. My flames light it. You could see it all, too, if you let me become solid.

And then the whole tent would go up in flames.

True enough. Your aunt is across from him.

There were no sounds coming from her and I bit the inside of my cheek. She couldn't be dead, right? She just couldn't be.

She's not. She's simply under iron self-control.

I almost sighed with relief.

There's a third one here, too. An old man.

So – they were here, and they were under guard. We'd confirmed that much. Now, we just needed to get them out of here. I'd already shown I could carry two on Kazmerev's back. I'd just load up Judicus and Aunt Danna and we'd take off.

And the third man?

I didn't know him.

Does that matter?

He could be a bad guy, too, for all I knew.

Or he could be as innocent as your friends.

Did that make it my job to take care of him – just because I didn't know if he was good of bad?

I hate to be the one to break it to you, but yes. It is your job to take care of him, too.

My cheeks burned, because of course, I knew that. And I felt guilty that I'd even asked. Of course, I had to figure out how to free him.

If you saw him ... well, it wouldn't be a question. He's hurt. Bad.

He was? What about Aunt Danna and Judicus?

Kazmerev didn't answer.

Kazmerev?

Let's just get a plan together.

I swallowed and tried to think. I could load two of them onto Kazmerev's back and then help the third one hobble away. Who looked like they could walk?

Wait –

The door of the tent burst open before Kazmerev could finish and a lantern flared to life.

"Caught you," a scratchy voice said.

It was the man who walked like a raven. I raised my hand, ready to call fire if I needed to, but he clucked his tongue, "Tsk tsk."

And then his own hand shot up and through the night something dark shot out.

I gasped at the same moment that Kazmerev made a sound halfway between a bird's shriek and a man's curse.

The "something dark" was the size of Kazmerev.

I stumbled back from it as it flapped in my face, feathers fluttering against my skin. I crashed into a bed. To my horror, there was a man on it, bound and bleeding. I pushed away from where I'd crashed into him. His skin was searing hot. In the light of the lantern, his eyes were swollen shut but he muttered, "Run" through lips thickened with beating.

I gasped again and looked up. Three things struck me at once.

First, Aunt Danna and Judicus looked a lot the same as the man – just as roughed up and swollen – though they were gagged and bound, as well.

Second, the crow man looked gleeful as if he'd caught me, too.

And third, the dark thing between me and the door of the tent was like a reverse mirror image of Kazmerev. Where he was bright, it was dark. Where he was dark, it was bright. It stretched its violet-tipped wings and shrieked at the same time that I called the fire to my open palm.

My fire streaked out, striking toward the crow-man – but not soon enough. A matching beam of darkness shot out of his palm. Our beams struck between us and shattered, sparks raining down into the tent.

Jump! Kazmerev demanded and without thinking, I obeyed.

I landed square on his back at the same moment that he shot up into the air, hit the tent roof, and shrieked to me. *Make me solid!*

I did it without hesitating and he burned through the tent, streaking through the night like a shooting star.

My breath was in my throat as I twisted to look back. Had we hurt the others? Had we lit the tent on fire? Was the dark phoenix pursuing us?

No. Yes. Yes.

I stifled a groan. Nothing had happened the way I'd hoped and now Judicus and Aunt Danna were in worse trouble! How were we going to save them now?

Hold on, Kazmerev told me in a tight mental voice. *It's about to get wild here.*

Wilder than this?

48

I clutched Kazmerev's feathers, my heart pounding, my breath trapped in my lungs unable to get out. I felt hot all over.

And then suddenly, we rolled to the side and completely around so that I was upside down and then back to right side up again.

If I could have screamed, I would have. Instead, I tried not to blackout, clinging to his feathers as fearful tears streamed down my face.

Don't cry. Don't cry. It's okay.

I made the mistake of looking back over my shoulder.

The dark bird was right behind us. And there was a rider on his back, too. The bird's wide beak opened – gleaming in the light of Kazmerev's feathers – and then he snapped at Kazmerev's tail, snatching a single bright feather in his sharp beak.

Kazmerev screeched, spinning in the air again and I clung to him, trying to remember to breathe.

That *creature* stole his feather. Stole it!

Try to grab it on the way by!

What?

Grab it!

He swooped over them and with one quivering hand I reached out and grabbed for the feather. The creature's mouth opened – probably to rip my arm off! – but with it, his grip loosened, and I snatched the feather and drew it in to wedge it between Kazmerev and me as he fell away from the other bird, plummeting toward the dark earth.

It was coming up so fast.

We were going to die.

No.

We were going to die.

No. Trust me.

And then his wings spread out and caught the air with a feeling like the snap of a sail. We soared up into the air like a rock thrown from a sling. I looked over my shoulder, hair swirling around me, sparks whipping up along the feathers of my sweet phoenix. The dark bird was still on our tail.

A Stryxex.

A what?

That strange creature is a Stryxex. I've only ever heard of them. I've never even known of anyone who has seen one. They're a thing of legends.

They were very vindictive for legends.

They aren't supposed to be real.

They were very violent for things that weren't real.

I don't know how to defeat it.

Behind us, the man on the back of the bird whooped. I was pretty sure it was the crow man. Was he like the equivalent to a Flame Rider but for a Stryxex?

I think so.

Kazmerev sounded strained. And no wonder! He was flapping hard and then diving into updrafts, trying to take advantage of anything he could find to propel us forward. He needed to put me on the ground. I was only slowing him down.

No time. Hold on tight.

We swooped high up into the sky, narrowly avoided a bar of something worse than dark – something that looked almost like an absence of light. Was I supposed to be doing that? Fighting back with fire?

I looked behind me at the wrong moment – Kazmerev dipped low so suddenly that my stomach was in my throat and my neck had to snap forward again. I blinked away stars and darkness, concentrating on holding on and breathing.

Just breathe. It will be okay.

We sailed toward a hill. I didn't even know where we were going. I'd lost any sense of direction. And then we were skimming along the ground, ducking and dodging, as dark beams shot around us.

Kazmerev rolled again and then dropped very low so that his belly was almost touching the water of a low lake.

Uh oh –

His words cut off at the same moment that the first gold-tinted the sky.

Water closed over me so suddenly that I didn't have time to take a breath. I emerged into the dawn coughing and sputtering, batting at the water. My lungs were screaming. My head spinning. My throat aching with pain.

I managed to clear my lungs enough to breathe and there I was – treading water in a clear blue lake.

No. No. No.

Cold filled me, shooting down my limbs and through my head. I treaded water for a moment, listening. Above me was a loud cry like a bird screaming and then nothing.

After a minute, I let out my breath. I needed to find the shore. And get warm again. I needed to get back and rescue Judicus and Aunt Danna. I swam, trying to push memories of them from my mind, but I couldn't. They'd been *beaten.* They needed me. And – and I didn't know. I was too tired to know.

I didn't even think to look for the Stryxex again until I was nearly to the shore. I stumbled up through the mud, my wet clothes clinging to me and weighing me down, and then turned a slow circle watching the sky and the shoreline and the trees around me.

I saw nothing. I saw no one. If they'd seen me go down, they weren't showing themselves now. Maybe without glowing Kazmerev, I was just too hard to see.

But maybe not and they might be back at any time.

I hurried to the trees and scrambled under the low hanging branches of a spruce tree. It blocked the worst of the wind, but it wouldn't be enough.

With stiff fingers and shaking limbs, I dragged dead branches and clumps of dried grass to one spot and set a rough fire up, drawing my knife and flint from my belt pouch and awkwardly striking and striking, trying to make a spark.

There. A spark. I almost collapsed with relief. My fingers were already too stiff to easily get my knife and flint back in my belt. It took long minutes to manage it and then I was back to the fire, tending, coaxing, blowing over it – and ahhhh there it was.

Relief stretched through me at the flames. My eyes closed, but I forced them open again. I couldn't rest yet. I'd die of hypothermia. Carefully, I stripped off my wet clothes and hung them on the spruce branches, huddling by the growing flames before I finally collapsed beside the fire.

I'd failed. We'd rescued no one. We'd let them know we were out there. I'd learned nothing about our enemy – except they had creatures as powerful as Kazmerev fighting us – and I was stranded out here for the day with no idea where I was, soaking wet, and with no way to rescue my friends.

It couldn't get any worse than this. I'd ruined everything.

I wanted to cry, but I had no energy for even that. Instead, I closed my eyes and hoped it *didn't* get any worse than this because I couldn't handle even one more thing.

I promptly fell asleep.

49

I woke to warmth and opened my eyes sleepily, expecting Kazmerev to be there.

But it was still day. Late afternoon – if I had to guess. The fire was out. The sky was cloudy. And yet I was warm.

I struggled up to a seated position, and then rose to gather up my clothing which had dried as I slept. But as I dressed again, my mind kept going back to how I had been warm – in my underthings, sleeping on the cold ground. It made no sense.

I felt my forehead, but I didn't feel hot to my own touch. So, no fever.

I was, however, incredibly thirsty.

I stumbled down to the water's edge, drank from the clear lake, refilled my waterskin, and crouched there for a moment, thinking. Judging by the sun, Kazmerev wouldn't be reborn for a few hours, at least. I couldn't go anywhere before he returned.

I pulled up some water plants with edible roots – rushy things that smelled of the fecund edges of the lake. I rekindled my fire and cooked the pale roots while I thought.

I needed a plan. Urgency ate at me, driving other thoughts from my mind.

I would not be able to sneak back into that camp. They would be expecting that. That Stryxex had been terrifying. And I did not know anything about it. Did it also die in the day like a phoenix? Or would it be there all the time? If it died in the day, then perhaps I should make my move then.

But I was just one fragile young woman. How could I possibly fight six or seven men even without the Stryxex? I tapped my lips and thought.

Perhaps, Judicus could fight them. But they'd hurt him again. I didn't know precisely how his magic worked, but it certainly seemed to sap him of strength. At most, he could maybe stop a few of them. And then what? He and Aunt Danna and that other prisoner were in no shape to run. And the other prisoner had been burning hot – perhaps with fever. How far would he get trying to flee in that state?

I paused at that. Was that why I was so hot? Had I caught something from him when I touched him? Or had I caught the plague from the village? This was the fifth day. If I was to catch it, I should know soon.

I swallowed down worry. I felt fine other than being warm. I shouldn't worry about illness until I felt ill. There was no point in borrowing trouble.

So. I needed a plan to slow or stop my enemies and I needed a plan to get three people and myself out of that camp afterward and far enough away that we couldn't be recaptured again immediately. And I had to decide if it were better to do that at night or in the day.

But no matter how I turned the problem around in my head, I couldn't find a solution to it. I was outnumbered. I was outclassed. Even if I set the whole place on fire, I couldn't see how we could escape without being caught up in the fire, too.

I was still shaking my head when the sun set. I felt a tickle of joy in my heart – so at odds with the despair I was feeling at my circumstances that I was momentarily stunned by it. I reached for that thread of joy, feeling it blossom as I prodded at it, flowering full and then bursting forth. It shot through me with warm hope and out into the world beyond me. That's how a phoenix hatched – a resurrection of joy, a rebirth of hope, a glorious breath of fresh life.

He burst into the air – a ball of bright feathers and sparkling eyes – circled overhead once, and then settled down beside me in a flutter of wings.

I reached for him, reveling in the warmth of his flaming feathers and marveling again at how his flames did not burn me or die out though they danced and flickered like fire.

You are still alive, he said, relief in his mental voice. *I worried about you.*

He could worry when he was dead to this world?

No, but I worried as I died and worried as I was born again to new life. But here you are. You did not even get too cold – though you're still welcome to snuggle close to me.

I shuffled over. I hadn't been cold – and I still wasn't with this abnormal warmth settling over me – but that didn't mean that I didn't want the comfort that someone nearby could give.

Warm? You are unusually warm?

He sounded like he thought my answer was significant. Was he worried I was sick?

No, I just didn't think that would happen so soon. It's a good sign. Flame Riders are often warm. They take on some of the fire of the phoenix within. But that usually comes later – after a lot of other skills manifest and the phoenix and rider merge into a deeper level of understanding.

Well, we did flee from a Stryxex last night. And those were quite the flying tricks he'd made. Maybe that was what had drawn us together.

Ha! I like how you think. Perhaps we'll have to fly like that more often – for the sake of study, of course.

I felt my jaw clenching at the thought. I wasn't sure I could handle more like that right away.

Do not fear. This is a good sign. We are growing closer. Your heart is more closely tuned with mine.

My heart wanted to save my friends from the people with the Stryxex.

And so it should. Mine wants that, too.

But I'd thought and thought, and I had no plan at all.

Easy now. Don't give up before we've even tried. That's the problem for most people. They see a problem and talk themselves out of finding a solution before they even try because it just looks too hard. Don't be like that, Sersha. Don't talk yourself out of trying. We are creatures of flame. We will burn away lies and injustice and reach into the ashes to find life again.

I liked that.

And that is why you burn so hot. What we need to do is go and find out what we missed while I slept the dreamless sleep.

Perhaps. And on the way, he needed to tell me everything he knew about Stryxex. I tried not to shudder at the thought of them but if we were going to fight one, then we needed to know what we were fighting.

A nightmare. That's what we're fighting, little hawk. A thing of dreamlessness forever. It is everything I am not and the only way to rid the world of its evil is to watch it burn.

And with those ominous words still ringing in my mind, I climbed onto his back and held on tight as he launched into the sky.

50

We'd flown further than I thought last night. I didn't recognize any of the landscape around us as we flew up, up, up so high in the sky that my perspective shifted and everything beneath became tiny.

My heart was beating irrhythmically, stuttering and stopping as I looked at how small everything appeared below me. It reminded me that there was nothing holding me to my phoenix's back except for his kindness.

I could almost feel the flows of air shifting us slightly with every movement as if we were balanced on a taut thread.

Flying, Sersha, has a lot to do with trust. Trust me. Let me carry you and don't doubt that I will do it well.

I tried not to doubt, but it still made my heart stay up in my throat, beating in my ears.

We caught an updraft and I'm letting it take us. There are different winds up here. Faster ones. We can go further, quicker if we let them propel us toward our destination.

It all made perfect sense – but perfect sense didn't help the sense of instability that made me sweat all over.

I tried to distract myself.

There. I could make out the coastline and then the dark scar of burn from the fire. Which meant the cabin where the plague-infested spent their quarantine must be northeast of that. And the road where Aunt Danna and Judicus were captured must be the one wandering southeast from there.

Well done. And it seems you have another phoenix trait, little hawk.

Was it worry? I had plenty of that.

Night vision. The moon is but a sliver of a crescent tonight and yet you see that winding road and the dark patch of the burn.

I swallowed. Did that come from the burning heat under my skin?

They must be related. You've gained them both very quickly. Aren't you pleased? They should be a boon to you – a help when I am not near.

But how did that work? How could I have access to his magic if he wasn't there?

How am I born alive again from your heart? Is it my magic that births me or yours? Is it your magic that fuels you or mine? I think you're asking the wrong question. The moment you accepted my ashes we became one. We're as intertangled as a pair of vines stretching between two trees.

Then I supposed it was a good thing that I wasn't afraid of commitment. If I was, I'd be running like the wind.

Running from your own heart?

I would have thought of a clever answer to that, but my eyes were running up and down the road. I couldn't see a camp or signs of people anywhere. Maybe this night vision wasn't as good as we thought.

There. Do you see it just over my left wing? A tiny glow on the road?

There was certainly something there – but it was just one fire and three tents. What had happened to the rest?

We'll aim for that spot and find out.

And that reminded me – I needed to know everything he could tell me about Stryxex.

Everything?

Leave nothing out.

They smell terrible.

You can leave that part out.

Their table manners leave much to be desired.

Now was not the time for joking.

It's always the time for joking – particularly when it isn't the time to joke. But I see your point. He considered for a moment. *Stryxex are a legendary creature. Where Phoenixes are living light, the Stryxex are living darkness. Where we are the heat of flames, they are the cold of death. Where we are bright, they are the absence of light.*

And they carried riders.

That I had never heard tell of until today. I will not lie to you, little hawk, this terrifies me. There are not many Flame Riders out there. If there is a new enemy now – one who is our opposite – then we could be matched phoenix for Stryxex. And what will we do to overcome them?

Aren't they kind of the same threat as a phoenix might be if the phoenix were bad?

Phoenixes aren't bad.

What? Never?

Never.

I didn't believe him. People were sometimes bad. Often, in fact. He must have noticed.

People are people. Phoenixes are phoenixes. We are not bad. If we slip into evil, we simply cease to be. The dawn will rise, and we will crumble to ash – never to be reborn.

But your Flame Rider – could they not turn bad and turn you evil with them?

If your heart slips into darkness, little hawk, then when the dawn comes, I will slip into ash and never again be born from your heart.

Wow. Harsh.

Not harsh. Just. And right. It is why we will dedicate ourselves to righteousness and to questing for the good of others. Those who are busy working for good find it harder to slip into evil. Idleness makes it easy. So does wanting what you don't have.

Okay ... so ... no idleness.

No idleness.

And what were we going to do about these Stryxex and ... Dark Riders or whatever they were?

I like that name. And I don't know. We're outnumbered. Two to one.

But were we? I had the funniest feeling about that old man. The one who had been hot to the touch before I suddenly developed the ability to be warm with Kazmerev's heat and see through the darkness. I'd felt something – almost like he was a friend, though I couldn't explain how I felt that.

Was it possible that he was somehow a Flame Rider? Could Kazmerev have failed to see his phoenix?

I would have seen. I would have known. I was right there.

He hadn't known about the Stryxex.

That's like saying you didn't know about a unicorn. It's a thing of legend. Not only do you not expect to see it – you doubt your own eyes when you do.

Were there unicorns out there?

Kazmerev made an irritated sound in my mind.

Just focus. We're almost there.

We flew a circle over the camp, slowly lowering ourselves closer and closer to the ground. My eyes scanned the ground below, and I was still surprised to realize how well they saw in the dark. It wasn't that it had stopped being dark – it was still inky black. It was just that I could see in that inky water as easily as if it was noon.

And I didn't see anyone – just the banked fire and three tents set up and a picket of horses.

It felt like a trap.

Something *wooshed* through the air right past my ear.

Arrow! Kazmerev roared. He spun into a tight summersault and flew straight upward.

Fear shot through me – making him so solid that the tips of the tents lit even from a wingspan away. The campsite flooded with orange light as it went up in flames.

51

We shot into the air faster than the arrow, corkscrewing up in a tight spiral, sparks spitting all around us.

Calm! You need to calm down!

I needed to calm down? What about whoever shot the arrow?

Look down.

My stomach lurched with displeasure as I clung to Kazmerev with knees and fists while twisting so I could look down his body, through the splayed flames of his tailfeathers, and to the ground.

One tent collapsed, completely engulfed in flames. An archer sprang from another, beating at the flames with a piece of sacking, his arrows falling from the quiver on his back onto the ground.

A second tent went up in a puff of fire. A man dashed their wash water over the blaze. Someone was yelling from where the horses were picketed and someone else called back to him there. Horses screamed – they hated fire – and curses flew loudly up into the sky.

Five men. Horses. Three tents – and no one else had come out of the tents. Were they burning even now? Dying under the canvas?

Horror filled me. What had I done?

No! Be calm. Look.

I *was* looking! I was seeing burning and flames and not enough people.

And that tent just collapsed to nothing. It was a ruse. They didn't even have baggage in it. The only people in a tent came out with the archer. They're shy by one guard, both Dark Riders, and their prisoners. These are just the people they left behind.

Unless they were in that last tent.

We'll circle and watch. But we'll do it from higher up. I do not react well to arrows.

Neither did I.

We circled and watched, watched and circled, but the men never so much as looked at the collapsed tents. They *did* fold up the remaining tent, gather their supplies, and pack the horses. The occasional curse was loud enough for me to hear, but with Kazmerev invisible again, they couldn't see us in the air no matter how often they craned their necks up to look for us.

See? Kazmerev said eventually. *Decoy.*

It had been a trap – not a very good one. Why try to trap us like that at all?

I don't think they were trying to trap us. I think the Dark Riders are trying to get our friends somewhere quickly before they're rescued. They were willing to ride three to a Stryxex to make that happen.

Could Kazmerev carry three?

I can. You can't yet.

Maybe I could now. I was getting better.

So you are.

But that left just one question. Where were they? And how were we going to find them? We could follow the horses and these soldiers, but they would travel much slower than we would and there was no way to know if they were meeting up somewhere.

We could go back to our mission to save Mally and trust Judicus and your aunt to rescue themselves.

They hadn't looked like they were doing very well. How easy would it be to escape if you were beaten and wounded and surrounded by anti-phoenixes?

Not easy.

We were their only true hope. And even we weren't really ready.

Well, their Stryxex limited how many they could take. It's three guards and three prisoners.

Unless ... they wouldn't have killed the prisoners, would they?

My mouth felt very dry suddenly. I swallowed.

I don't think so. Why keep them at all if they were planning to kill them? They must be going to take them somewhere or to someone.

But they could be going anywhere. Across the sea, back to the north, south like Mally, or even inland to the east. And we couldn't tell which way. Flying magical creatures left no track or trail. The guards below might say – but they had proven hostile. We had no information to guess on. They could have gone any of a hundred different directions. And if we chose wrong, we wouldn't know until it was too late.

The horses and what was left of their riders started down the long snaking road and as I watched them travel, my heart plummeted. I might as well turn around and go home.

Not necessarily.

What did he mean?

There's a little trick I know that might come in handy right about now.

52

We were flying yet another wide circle around the original campsite. We'd been doing it for hours and every circle got wider and wider and with every one, it seemed more and more impossible that we'd ever succeed.

It wasn't going to work.

It is going to work. I thought you said you'd learned patience from all those years of people mistreating you and ignoring you.

Well, I guess I hadn't learned enough of it because I was feeling – not impatient – despairing. I was feeling despairing. I'd failed them all and they were all counting on me.

I like you, Sersha. I like that you love your people – whether that's your family or your town and now even crazy Judicus out to redeem his family name.

Out to what? He kept on talking as if that little detail didn't matter.

And I – of all people – know what it is to burn with passion and desperation. To want things you can't have. To fight and live and die for them. Again and again. But do you want to know one thing that I've learned from thousands of deaths?

I did want to know. Yes.

I've learned that letting yourself be completely consumed by your emotions – or even by guilt – does not heal wounds. It does not fix problems. It does not save loved ones. It's a pit as deep as a grave.

I felt a twinge of even more guilt at that. I forgot sometimes that every time I stewed on something, I was dragging him into it with me. I was not alone. I was matched to this glorious burning phoenix and I owed him more than a steady stream of discouragement.

Don't think I'm not still mourning Veela. I wake every morning delighted to find you, but still devastated to learn again that she will never rise from the dead with me – at least not in this world. My minutes and hours are still dipped in the sadness of that – in the hollow echo of where another heart once was. And yet. And yet I have begun the painful lesson of letting sorrow wash over me without being consumed by it. I have learned to take joy in your heart and to rise with the determination to live my nights for more than my own sorrows.

I am sorry, Kazmerev.

You are forgiven and also beloved for as long as fires burn, and the stars wink down from the sky.

A warm glow burned in my chest as I dashed away a tear, drawing in a long, steadying breath. No despair. We could do this. His trick would work somehow.

I'm glad you think so, his voice sounded like he was repressing a laugh, *because it is working right now.*

It was?

I caught a whiff of them in the air – the slightest trace and yet I've scented it.

I didn't think birds could smell.

He made an irritated sound. *For the hundredth time, Sersha, a phoenix is not a bird because it flies, any more than you are a lizard because you shuffle along the ground.*

What was a lizard?

A long green creature with four legs and a powerful tail.

That's a dragon.

He huffed a laugh. *My Flame Rider believes in dragons but not lizards.*

Dragons were in stories. I'd never heard a story about something called a lizard.

Just wait until you see one and those dragon stories won't sound quite so romantic anymore.

Why? Did they stink?

How would I know? Birds can't smell.

It was my turn to laugh, and the laugh seemed to loosen something in my chest. I bit my lip and let myself hope.

We'd find them. And we'd rescue them. Somehow.

First, we find them. Then we make a plan – but I want a promise from you.

Anything.

Don't go running in without me. Wait for me to be alive to make your plans. Wait for me before you go rushing in. We're a team. And you promised me we would act like one.

Of course, I said. And I meant it. We were a team, and we could do this.

There! I smell them again. We're on the right track.

We were angling south and slightly to the west as if we planned to move toward the sea eventually. My heart was in my throat. How far ahead of us might they be?

As much as a full day – but perhaps the Stryxex are alive in the day. Perhaps they do not die as I do.

I swallowed down fear at the thought. What would I do if I found them in the day and they were there but Kazmerev was not?

That's why you have to wait for me.

I agreed with his thoughts on that. Even with both of us there, we'd be vastly outnumbered. Two Stryxex. Two Dark Riders.

I let him fly and mulled the problem over in my mind. When you were outnumbered, you needed to set a trap. To set a trap, you needed to know what your opponent was going to do based on what you baited the trap with. What did I have for bait?

Us. They want us.

How could we be bait without getting caught?

That's the trick. That's the question.

We flew through the night, the cool air streaming through my hair and around my face. And I tried to watch carefully where we were going and what landscape was passing under us. It was easier now that I could see, but it was still strange to try to make sense of the landscape below us. It was so very … big. There seemed to be no end.

When I stood on the ground, I could see only the trees and hills around me. On a high hill, maybe I would see a lot farther – but even then, it was just a tiny piece. A little chunk of the world. Up here – up here I was seeing so *much* that it was hard to take it all in. One patch of water looked so different when it was ahead of you, or below you or behind you, morphing in shape and size depending on your perspective. And so, navigating by them was hard. The ocean helped, but the coastline also changed and morphed. And the trees were all the same. Even the different ones looked just like a dozen other different ones.

How did Kazmerev do it?

I feel the air – it rolls across the landscape in currents and dips and I can … sense it. It's like a map. I can follow currents and see which roll into which others and how they roll out across the land. It makes it easier to navigate.

Were some currents faster?

Yes.

Could we take a current that would get us to the Stryxex faster?

Yes, but then we might lose their trail.

Hmmm. That made sense. If only we knew where they were going. Then we could take that slipstream and meet them there.

But we didn't know. And we were still no closer to knowing when dawn grew close. Kazmerev dropped suddenly, wings up above his head. His bright feathers were just brushing the grass below when he whispered, "Until tomorrow, little hawk," and then vanished.

And just like every morning since I'd met him, I was left standing on the dewy grass, alone and also lonely.

53

We carried on like that for two more days and nights. During the day, I ate, slept, and cleaned myself in whatever water sources were nearby. If there had been a village, we could have set down in it – I was past the quarantine limit for the plague and the warmth I'd been worried about had slipped away – but we avoided villages, following the scent and gleaning food where we could to supplement the tiny stash in my belt pouch. At night, we flew and flew fast.

I felt – constantly – an ache in my belly from being so twisted up with worry. It felt like every movement was too slow, every hour too short. Our friends needed us.

On the dawn of the third day, we reached the sea far to the south of where we'd started and I sat there after Kazmerev died, clutching my chest with one fist and feeling like the whole world was tightening around me – which was crazy since that very world had never seemed so large as it did when I was flying. But that was the thing. It was the very largeness of it all that made it feel so impossible to find my friends again. And it was the thought of not finding them that squeezed me like a knotted rope tied around my midsection and being pulled in two directions.

On top of that, I was lonely.

I spent my nights flying with Kazmerev. And I loved his company, I loved his strong spirit and bright outlook. I loved his wisdom and generosity.

But I'd never realized how much I enjoyed sitting with others while I ate or doing the little things for them that I did – washing their dishes, preparing their tea, arranging things to make them more comfortable, listening to their many babbling voices. I had never realized how much I counted on other people, either – counted on them to be there when I needed someone to lean on or help me.

I was lonely.

And for the first time in my life, I was realizing that I didn't do well entirely on my own. I needed to be needed by someone. I needed to contribute. I missed those things.

I strolled down the beach, looking for a sheltered place to sleep and listening to the seagulls. Somewhere along this coast, Judicus was probably listening to them. And so was Aunt Danna. And so was Mally. They'd each been kidnapped and yet we were still all connected, all walking the same sand. All watching the same sky.

How odd that I'd lost people to two kidnappings in a row! Or was it odd?

I paused, my brow furrowing. Could it be possible that they were working together? Lady Lightland had hired the raiders to attack us. I was pretty sure of that after listening to her talk to them. And she had a coterie of highly skilled people. One of them had been a rope worker like Judicus. So was it crazy to think that the others might be Dark Riders on Stryxex? Could they be part of her coterie?

I went to sleep wondering about that.

I woke before sunset, unable to sleep anymore as an idea finally began to sprout within my mind. I walked down the beach, carrying my boots because the tide was out and the beach here was sandy and easier to walk on bare feet. The sun slid slowly to the horizon and I thought about Lady Lightland.

Of course, she would want to find Judicus. She'd shown that things with him were personal. And our escape would have bothered her. She was the kind of woman who liked things to go her way – who only saw one way to a goal and refused to take second best. She would have wanted to know where Judicus was – and even better – to have him with her or properly dead and out of the way. And I could see why they would have picked up Aunt Danna in that same net.

They would want me, too. Kazmerev was right. We would make the perfect bait. Wherever we were – that's where they would go – if they knew where that was. But baiting them would be easy. The hard part would be not getting caught and also getting our friends free.

Maybe if we split up. Could Kazmerev draw them away while I snuck into their tents?

For some reason, I had a sudden memory of heat. Why was heat important? Why was it sticking out in my mind right now?

And then the sun dipped and Kazmerev was born and for a moment the sheer joy of his birth was enough to knock all worry from my head. I wrapped my arms around him the moment he materialized, burying my face into his burning feathers. The scent of burning birch had never smelled so good.

Little hawk! Are you okay?

I missed you.

It's nice to be missed.

I want to hold onto you forever.

Then please, do.

I almost laughed as I slid onto his back and we leapt up into the air.

He wobbled slightly under me and just like always, my belly wobbled with his movements. It was always such an odd thing to feel him moving under me – to be going up and down in the air instead of standing or sitting or lying on the solid ground. It was even different than floating in the water because water pushed and pressed against you – even if it was only a little – but up here, above it all, it sometimes felt like nothing kept me moored in one place at all.

It's just you and me – and magic.

I laughed at that as a shower of sparks shed from his back and swirled up around us and it reminded me. Heat.

The old man had been very hot.

What if I made him part of the trap? What if we made them think he was a Flame Rider, too? Could we use that as a ruse to get them away?

Fire. That would be the key. If we set fires very quickly – either around the camp or on a trail leading away from the camp – that would distract them, right?

But would it distract everyone?

I didn't know. But I could creep into the camp and –

Again? You've tried that twice and both times it was a bad idea. The first time you had to kill the rope worker. The second time you were overwhelmed. Even if you light fires and lure people out, what if they don't all go? What if none of them do? We don't know what these Stryxex and Dark Riders might be capable of. Perhaps they are immune to fire.

Immune to fire! Imagine.

I am immune to fire. Is it so unbelievable? He sounded irritated.

I ran a hand over his feathers as far up his neck as I could reach. Of course, he was immune to fire. He was *fire* and everything beautiful and glorious that fires were. But that wouldn't mean that people would be. And those Dark Riders were people.

You are.

Wait. What?

Why do you think you can ride me without burning up? While we are linked, no flame may touch you. But I do not know if that applies to Stryxex and Dark Riders. They are not made of flame and they are not like me.

Wait. Go back to the part where I can't be burned by fire. Is that all the time or just when I'm riding you?

He ignored my question. *I think we should assume they might be protected against it in some ways but probably still vulnerable to it since they're not made of flame. That way we won't falter. Which is why I don't think this should be a trap. I think we should just burst down from the sky and demand our friends back – set flame to anyone who doesn't listen and fight the rest.*

Wait ... can we go back to where I can't be burned?

It's a solid plan. I like it.

I didn't like it at all. It seemed needlessly reckless. But any time I wanted to talk about it again, Kazmerev said, *Do you have a better plan?*

I did not.

Eventually, I stopped trying to talk about it. Whatever plan we made would have to account for where we finally caught up to them, anyway.

We started to see villages while it was still early in the night. They were lit like tiny smoldering freckles across the earth.

First, just one appeared, and then a few, and then dozens, and then there, blazing like a bonfire and rippling orange out across the shifting sea was a full-blown city.

Had we lost their trail? I was worried.

No. Kazmerev seemed to shift nervously under me. *It leads straight to that city.*

Maybe we should go around the city and pick it up on the other side.

I like that plan.

Kazmerev circled the city on the ocean side as I studied it from above. I'd never seen a city before. It was bigger than I expected. I tried not to feel impressed by it, but even from the air, I had the feeling I could get lost inside those warren-like streets. Even with the sun down, the docks were crawling with people sliding into small boats or tying them up, walking alone, or with others, or just sitting along the docks.

Larger ships were anchored out away from the docks. None of them looked like raider ships – or at least, none of them had decks teeming with people wearing face coverings. And how else would I know they were raider ships?

The sounds of the city drifted to us, snatches of music, the rumble of many spoken voices all at once. Occasionally, the sounds of night birds pierced over the background buzz. A fly bit at my arm and I slapped it away. It felt no bigger or smaller than I did beside this massive city.

I breathed lightly as we flew around it to the other side. I had the oddest worry that someone, somewhere, might see me up here. Relief filled me when we reached the other side – until Kazmerev spoke.

Their trail doesn't come this way.

He circled, looping inland now to circle back up around the land side of the city. The view was just as spectacular from this side, but I couldn't enjoy it. I was too worried about where their trail might go. When, at last, we reached the coast again, my heart froze.

The trail doesn't lead out of the city.

We both looked toward the glow of so many people. There would be no raid on a camp. There would be no clever fire to distract them. Our friends were in there somewhere. And we'd have to go in that mass of people and buildings and things I'd never dealt with to find them.

I felt my heart sinking.

I swallowed.

People weren't kind to strangers. I knew this.

They were particularly unkind to strangers who could not speak.

Could I go in there, knowing that? And if I did, how could I possibly get to my friends and free them? I couldn't ask questions. I couldn't ask for directions. I couldn't even lie.

I'll be with you. I won't leave your side. Remember, they won't be able to see me and I will not leave you.

I found comfort in those words, but they were the only comfort I felt as I looked at that massive city. I didn't even know its name – but I knew it would try to eat me alive.

54

Kazmerev wanted to set me down just outside the city walls but I knew that the guards stationed at the gate – we could see them next to the glowing braziers they warmed themselves with – would want to know who I was and why I had come to their city. And I could tell them none of that.

Instead, we opted to try diving into a dark alley inside the gates. Hopefully, no one would notice a girl floating down from the sky in the darkness there.

I slid from his back to stand in the alley and frowned. It smelled of waste in the alley. I shivered as Kazmerev leapt back into the sky. It felt odd to be walking again – like my legs weren't quite the right shape for it. Odder still to be near people – I was certainly no longer used to that.

But I couldn't sit around dwelling on those things. Everyone was counting on me.

I crept down the alley and slid out into the streets. It was darker in the city from on the ground. The lights were further apart, the laughter I heard sounded more vicious, the eyes of people who noticed me seemed more predatory.

You're just nervous.

But no one stopped me as I made my way down the main street, keeping to the middle of the road where it was easy to see what was coming next and hurrying to get further into the city. Was I on the right trail?

Yes. They came this way.

I risked a glance upward and was filled with relief at the sight of Kazmerev there, hovering above me – a bright flame in the darkness. I could do this, as long as he was with me.

I hurried onward.

The scent leads toward the heart of the city.

It was both a good thing and a bad thing. Good – because we hadn't lost the scent. Bad, because I had a long way to go, and it was taking much, much longer by foot.

Within an hour I'd moved from the rougher outskirts of the city to a more prosperous area where all but the inns were shuttered for the night, leaving a single light burning outside their doors. Small snatches of music and chatter rolled out the doorways of the inns, but it was mild chatter, mild music. It wasn't rough like it had been in the outer parts of the city.

I was worried about Kazmerev. What if there were other phoenixes here? What if he was seen?

No one has noticed me. Not the guards. Not citizens. I smell no other phoenixes – or any other magical creature except the Stryxex

My legs ached when I reached the point where the city changed again. There was a short wall and a flight of steps up to it, and when I climbed the steps the streets were set with carefully placed, leveled stones and the houses were gated off by small walls. There were no shops – closed or otherwise. No inns to be seen at all. The silence here worried me.

Had we lost the trail?

Not at all. It leads straight here. Turn right at this street.

I turned down the street to a dark row of short walls. Behind them loomed higher buildings.

The trail disappears at this building. Let's look inside.

I didn't see the gate.

I'll hop you over the wall.

Before I could object, his talons closed gently around me, lifting me from the ground and over the short wall into a garden.

My heart raced at the sudden sense that I should not be here. This place would be guarded, and I could be caught. I bit my lip and hurried into the garden, ducking under a tree with low branches to catch my breath.

It would be okay. They didn't know I was here. They couldn't catch me if they didn't know.

Just look. Don't try to save anyone. Just try to see where the Stryxex are.

If I was a massive bird made of the absence of light, where would I be?

They aren't birds –

I know. I know. They're Stryxex.

If they were birds, they would be nestled in the branches of the trees, Kazmerev huffed.

Sense of cold crept over me and I caught my breath and held it.

They'd be sleeping with a head under a wing until morning – unless they were night birds, of course. But these aren't birds at all.

Though they certainly did sleep at night, I thought – and the thought felt far away as if it belonged to someone else. Someone who wasn't standing here, trying not to breathe or move or panic and run. Someone who was really, really hoping that her suddenly racing heart wasn't going to give her away. No one could hear that outside my chest, right? I hoped not.

What's going on?

Well, I could report that the Stryxex did not sleep in trees.

Oh?

Or at least not on top of them. They slept under them. And they did, in fact, tuck their heads under their wings. Which did not seem like nearly enough protection when I was standing here within arm's reach of them. One of them shifted.

It was all I could do not to turn and run. Inside my head, I was screaming with all my might.

55

I eased my weight back onto my heel. Don't panic. Don't panic.

They're there? Under the tree?

I was almost afraid to say yes in my mind. Could they hear me?

I slowly stepped back and the head of the nearest one whipped up.

I froze.

What's happening?

Its dark eye shut after a moment and it tucked its head back under its wing. My knees were jelly. I needed to go lie down somewhere. But I couldn't do that. Instead, I stood – motionless – in this awkward position, trying not to breathe too loudly, my eyes fixed on the two dark shapes. The edges of them wavered like hot sand under the sun and the very edges of their darkness seemed to almost glow blue.

My mouth was very dry.

You can't stay there. You have to get out. I'm coming.

No! There were two of them and they were just as strong and fast as he was. We couldn't afford to fight them.

They are less powerful without their riders.

How do you know?

I'm guessing. Because that's how phoenixes work.

But I wasn't willing to risk his life on a guess. And they hadn't died for the night – they'd gone to sleep. So that meant that in at least one way they were not like phoenixes.

You make a solid point. So ... creep away slowly but be careful. It is almost dawn and I may vanish at any moment.

I took another step back, ducking partly under a thick branch of leaves and the head emerged again, looking around for long minutes until it finally tucked under his wing again.

I let out a long, slow breath. No moving, then. No breathing. No thinking. I'd just wait here.

I don't like that. Kazmerev sounded panicky. *I don't like it at all.*

But what else could I do? I'd have to wait here until morning and hope they couldn't see me. I was stuck – bent over and waiting, every muscle screaming – until then.

You could try to run.

Have you seen prey run from birds? It never ends well! Have you seen their beaks? Their talons? Because I'm getting a great view from here.

They are not *birds.*

But I couldn't shake the image of a mouse scurrying across a road only to be plucked from it by a descending owl. I'd watched that happen once. I wouldn't want to watch it again from the mouse's perspective.

I want to act, Sersha. I do not want to wait.

I felt his irritation, and it made my own only grow stronger. But no. I couldn't give in to it. I had to take long breaths and wait.

My leg began to shake. I couldn't stop it. I watched the Stryxex with wide eyes, sure they would notice the trembling at any moment.

And then another sound hit my ear – the sound of a gate swinging.

"She said to have it dug by dawn. They want him buried before they ship out," a voice said through a yawn.

"In the garden? There's no room here for bodies," another voice complained. "The whole place is trees and flowers."

"Pick a place away from the trees. Those bird things make me nervous."

See? I wasn't the only one who thought of them as birds.

Do you really want to be compared to this unwashed creature?

I did not.

"There are flowers here, though," the second voice said.

"You're willing to torture a man but not damage the flowers? What's wrong with you?"

"It just seems wrong is all."

They were silent after that except for grunts of exertion and the occasional curse. I tried to focus on that to keep the strain of my own muscles out of my mind. By the time they were done, I was nearly crying from the effort. I needed to move. I needed it so badly.

I heard the gate swing again, but the gravediggers were still there.

"Toss him in the grave," a light voice said. Lady Lightland!

My heart sped with excitement. We'd found her! And just as quickly it crashed to the ground. Who was she "tossing" into a grave?

It couldn't be Judicus, could it?

"Are your Stryxex ready to ride?" she asked quietly over the shuffling sounds of people obeying her.

I shifted slightly to try to peek at her through the branches but at my movement, the Stryxex closest to me flinched. I bit my lip and stopped again. No movement, Sersha. I *should* be good at being quiet.

"They will be after dawn. Give them until then."

"I'm anxious to be gone from here, Kraden Moren. The sooner we get our prize to the Grand Hadri, the better."

"And if he plucks her from your grasp when you deliver her to him? If he uses her for his own ends?"

Lady Lightland laughed. "Isn't that the point? She will make him great – and he will make me great. And already I have put a barb in the rose, a poison in the wine – a hook set for the fish."

"And will you be telling us about that hook?" Kraden Moren – the Dark Rider – asked wryly.

"What fun would it be without the surprise?" she asked lightly.

"Your friend Judicus was certainly surprised."

"Wasn't he?" her words were already fading as she left the garden. "Come with me, boys. I'll send someone else to cover the grave. The ship's captain won't wait until next bell."

The grave. The thought of it bit at me as the last sounds of them slipped from the garden.

I needed to know who they were burying. I needed to be sure it wasn't Judicus.

You need to get out of there. Kazmerev's words were almost like a whine.

The tension of them rippled through me. I bit my lip.

Please, just run. Dawn approaches.

It would be okay. I'd just –

Please –

Soft light crept over the sky as a blaze of gold ripped across the horizon.

Kazmerev's death rippled through my heart at the same moment that the Stryxex unfolded.

56

I held my breath, but I couldn't stop the racing of my heart. Every nerve of my body felt like it was sizzling with fear.

They surged forward, scrambling through the branches, wings knocking tiny twigs to the ground. I bit my tongue as one barreled into me so hard that I flew backward and smacked the trunk of the tree. I lay there, too terrified to move for a long moment, but the Stryxex didn't return. Through the branches, I watched as they leapt into the sky.

I picked myself up with care. Nothing broken. My tongue was bleeding, but it would heal.

I took a long, shuddering breath, and limped out to where the grave had been dug in the soft earth of the garden. They hadn't bothered to make it very deep. The pile of earth covering the shoots of spring growth wasn't nearly as big as it should have been.

With terror in my heart, I crept to the grave and looked in.

Please don't be Judicus. Please don't be Judicus. And don't be Mally either.

The old man from the tent lay in the hastily dug grave.

Pity surged through my heart. No one deserved to die alone and be buried in a garden without loved ones to mourn them.

I should be used to death by now and to danger and to the ridiculousness of all of it. But I wasn't. My eyes prickled as I looked in the direction Lady Lightland had left.

I should run now. I should chase after Lady Lightland so she could lead me to where Mally and Judicus were. I should leave before she slipped through my fingers.

But I had to check on the old man.

I wasn't sure when I'd started crying, but the tears were flowing down my cheeks by the time I reached down and shook him.

Wake up. You're not allowed to be dead. Not when I failed to keep you alive.

And then I felt it – the barest whisper of breath. I held my hand over his parted lips. Warmth. He wasn't dead yet. They'd beat him. They'd hurt him. They'd left him for dead. And they were going to bury him alive.

I looked anxiously back the way Lady Lightland had left and then back to the grave. You couldn't see this spot from the house. There were too many trees. I had to make a choice. Help this old man or go after my friends. I wanted to go after them. They were so close, so very close. I didn't want to chase blindly after them again. I didn't want to lose all the ground I'd gained. I didn't want to risk that one of them would end up in a shallow grave like this.

But this man was right in front of me, still hot and burning up. I pressed a hand to his forehead and his eyelashes fluttered slightly. I swallowed down a lump in my throat.

They had no right to do this to him. They had no right to leave him like this.

I made up my mind.

Fury gave me strength. I grabbed the man under his armpits – he was lighter than I would have guessed – and dragged him from his own grave to the hidden spot under the tree where the Stryxex slept.

Live! I told him with my mind. Please, live.

I tried to shove back into him all the fire I had in me. If I could make Kazmerev alive, couldn't I make him alive? Couldn't I? I knew I sounded crazy. I knew it. But I couldn't stop trying.

His eyes fluttered open and to my shock, his hand reached out and grabbed mine. He shoved something hot into it. Where had that come from? How had he held it through all of this?

"Stryxex," he said, in a weak, thready voice. He gasped in a rattling breath before speaking again. "They're back. They're hunting."

I wanted to ask him what they were hunting.

"Do you hear me, girl?"

I nodded but he didn't seem to see. His eyes were glassy, and they focused on a point somewhere behind me as if he'd lost the ability to see me.

"Tell me you hear me."

I hear you! I was screaming in my head.

"They're hunting phoenixes. They killed Arturo. Ripped him to shreds. His heat – it's still in my heart. A last echo of him with me." He sounded like he was rambling. "I put everything I could into the feather. But you'll need a rope worker to read it. Find a rope worker. Stop them. Before it's too late."

I opened my palm and saw what he'd put into it – a feather as long as my hand, glowing a hot bright red. It didn't burn me – but was that because I was a Flame Rider or because it wouldn't burn anyone? I didn't know. It was strung on a long leather thong. I threw it over my head and tucked the bright feather into my dress.

By the time I'd turned back to him, his eyes had fluttered shut again.

"Three days," he whispered to me then. "The message will be gone from the feather in three –"

His breath hitched – and never came.

Come back! I wanted to scream. Come back!

But he wasn't coming back.

My heart pounded in my chest.

He'd been a Flame Rider after all, hadn't he? I *knew* there was something about him!

But they'd killed his phoenix – killed him in some way that didn't leave a handful of ash behind. Was that why the man was burning up?

He wasn't burning up now. He felt cold suddenly.

Cold as the dead, I realized.

With a shuddering gasp, I realized what I had to do.

Hurriedly, I returned him to his grave, crossing his arms gently over him.

He'd given me three days. Three days to rescue Judicus and read whatever had been put on the feather. I couldn't do it in time.

But I had to. For Kazmerev. For all the phoenixes out there just like him.

I bit my lip, brushed off my skirts, and slipped along the garden wall toward where the creaking hinge was. I had one goal in mind. Find Judicus. Now. Before it was too late.

57

I crept through the gate to the street beyond where a pair of horses stamped in their harnesses before a heavy coach. Chests were strapped to the top of it and as I slipped out the gate, I saw Lady Lightland's profile as she entered the coach. She tapped the side of it as she entered and closed the door behind her.

A flash of inspiration struck me, and I sprinted from the gate to the back of the coach at the same moment that it started forward. Two steps and I was within reach, my heart pounding, breath caught in my throat. I took a final leap and grabbed a hold at the back of the coach, my toe catching the tiny step-hold at the back. These spots were meant for guards, but there were no guards on this coach. If my luck held, they wouldn't catch me here and she'd lead me right to where she was going.

I barely breathed as the coach rolled down the street.

Don't notice me. Don't notice me.

A serving girl across the street watched me with narrowed eyes from where she was entering a large house on the other side. I put my head down and hoped she wouldn't stop.

Everything and everyone here was clean – so clean that I felt my travel stains and rumpled hair. So brisk and crisp that I felt my sleepy exhaustion. I wasn't used to stones set into streets under wheels or carefully dressed stone on the houses and gates of the street. Nothing was like the village I grew up in.

But I didn't have time for gawking. I straightened and tried to look official – like I was meant to be there.

This was my only chance to find them – and now I was on a clock. Three days to find them. Three days to get this feather to Judicus. Why hadn't the old man handed it to them when they were captives together? Maybe he hadn't been conscious for long enough to do it.

The coach turned down a narrow side street and I had to tuck myself in tight to the side of the coach to keep from scraping against barrels and crates stacked beside the buildings here. A shortcut.

I was breathless when we emerged, my forearms aching from pulling myself in so tightly.

This street was in a merchant district and already it was full of people who looked a lot more like me and all of them were hurrying with arms full or distracted looks on their faces as they set up merchant stalls or hurriedly swept off the stoops of the shops lining the streets.

The driver cracked the whip and the coach leapt forward to the angry squawks and curses of those around us, but I wasn't paying attention to them. I slipped to peek in the back window of the carriage. It was mostly covered by a curtain, but there was a sliver of light. Did she have the prisoners with her? I held my breath and stole a look.

Lady Lightland was alone, looking out the open side of the coach with an impatient expression on her perfect face. She looked almost as jumpy as me, as if she, too, had a deadline to meet.

I bit my lip and pulled away from the window. My friends must be at her destination. I just needed to hold on. My hands were getting sweaty.

I held on for three more turns.

We were quickly approaching the city walls. I hadn't realized how near them we were. We had to be headed to the ship Lady Lightland had arranged, right? And what would I do then? Could I creep onto the ship? Would she catch me? Or should I wait here and simply note the name of her ship until Kazmerev was reborn and then go after it with him?

Tension vibrated through me, tainting every thought with worry.

We passed through the city gates. I hadn't expected so many people. A cart loaded with sheep passed, blocking the way for long seconds. Should I get off here and follow on foot? Would it reduce the chances of being discovered? The carriage passed the gates with a wave from the city guard.

And then the decision was gone from me as the carriage sped up to a fast trot and the carriage jostled and jolted as it went.

It was all I could do to hold on as it rattled along the winding road that ran along a short cliff beside the ocean. From my perch at the back of the carriage, I could see the docks far to my right and the boats moving to and from ships. A curving, low ship – sleek and fast-looking – was anchored just out from the cliff, the name "Falchion" painted on the stern.

I was still admiring it when the carriage came to a sudden stop.

My breath caught in my throat.

Hide, hide, Sersha!

I leapt from the carriage, not sure which way to go. There was no cover nearby. I could hide around the side of the carriage – but which side?

The driver leapt to the side nearest the ocean, and I scrambled around to the other side, my breathing loud in my throat.

You should have thought, Sersha! You should have thought this through!

Voices drifted to me.

"Come down and help launch the boat, Carver, and then you can return the carriage. I'll compensate you for expenses when you meet me in Briccatore," Lady Lightland commanded.

Carver must be the driver. And now I knew where they were headed. Briccatore.

If I was a fighter, perhaps I would have launched myself at them. But could I justify attacking, assaulting, and possibly murdering them? Even if they'd stolen my friends? I didn't think so. Besides, I'd still have to contend with the people on their ship – because that must be where my friends were. It had to be, right?

I bit my lip and the moment they were out of sight I crept forward and snuck a look over the edge of the cliff. Lady Lightland and the driver were halfway down narrow stairs cut into the rock. The stairs edged along the cliff and ended in a small jetty where a rowboat was tied. A pair of sailors waited with the boat, one of them holding a basket, seemingly immune to the spray of the sea slapping against the jetty.

There was no way to get to the jetty without alerting them I was here. There was no way to sneak onto the boat and no other way to get out to the ship.

I bit my lip, feeling the tension of it all. My friends were so close – so close! And I felt so powerless to help them.

I opened the carriage with frantic hands, searching for something – anything – that might give me an idea. There was nothing within but the seat cushions.

Frustrated, I made my way to the driver's seat. He had a small basket that held a half-loaf of bread, an apple, and two pennies. I left the food and coins. I wasn't a thief.

Frustration burned in my throat.

There was nothing here to help me. Nothing.

As I watched, the boat launched with Lady Lightland in it.

The sailors heaved on the ropes and my heart sank.

I'd missed my chance and I didn't know what to do.

58

Blinking back tears, I reached into my shirt and clutched the bright feather. Three days. It was all I had, and I didn't know what to do. I couldn't fly to the ship without Kazmerev. I couldn't swim fast enough to arrive before the boat. I couldn't do anything at all.

Despair washed over me like the deep waves smashing against the cliffs below. What should I do?

If only Kazmerev was here to help me. If only Judicus could give advice. If only it wasn't just me trying to figure it out alone all the time.

I clutched the feather, blinked back my tears, and tried to think.

Oddly – as if holding the feather helped my vision, I could see Lady Lightland's face clear as day. She was staring up at me on the clifftop with a puzzled look on her face.

I let go of the feather and her features blurred again.

Did this feather help me see farther?

I grabbed it in my fist again, enjoying the way the scarlet feather warmed my palm and I looked out toward the ship – and just like that every detail sprang to life and I could see the sailors' expressions of concentration as they readied the ship. I could see the ropes and lines, taut and ready, two men ready beside the rail to receive the lady.

I nearly gasped at the sight of one of them – the Dark Rider! In horror, I realized that I could see the edges of something circling above the boat – the edges of wings and talons. The Stryxex! Even if Kazmerev was here, they'd be over the boat, guarding it. They were nearly invisible in the light of day, their features transparent except for those odd edges that bent the light in a way you could pick out if you knew what you were looking for.

Knowing now that they were hunting phoenixes, the mere sight of them froze my breath in my chest. Would they recognize me? Would they know Kazmerev was attached to me? Would they lie in wait nearby until dark when he returned?

I tore my eyes from the Stryxex and looked back to the ship and there – in a huddle in the bow – I saw them. Aunt Danna – one eye blackened – hunched angrily beside a defiant Mally, her chin raised and hair swirling behind her. There was a large purple bruise on her chin and her lower lip trembled.

They were alive! And they were standing up, which must mean they were strong enough for at least that.

Hope surged within me.

Beside them, Judicus stood, hands tied, pale face tilted to one side as he looked up at me. And then his brow furrowed – almost as if he could see me, too, and his lips parted as if he'd like to speak.

The ship rocked slightly as Lady Lightland was hauled up to the deck, but I wasn't looking at her. My eyes were on Judicus.

If only I could talk to him. If only I could tell him how desperate I was to get to him. How I needed him to read the feather. How I wanted him free. I tried to project all of that to him, even though I knew it was useless, even though I knew there was nothing he could do.

And then suddenly, his eyes met mine exactly and he nodded sharply.

I gasped as black threads spun out from his hands, snapping his bonds.

One of his guards leapt back and Lady Lightland's mouth was open like she was giving orders, her hands gesturing wildly.

And then Judicus leapt up to the railing around the ship at the same moment that the huge white sails snapped open and caught the wind.

For a moment, he balanced there – the ship surging forward, him on his toes, arms spread wide – and then he looked at me again and leapt into the black sea.

The white boil where he'd hit the water was already astern by the time it made a noticable ring.

And if our enemies were shouting or cursing, there was nothing they could do.

My eyes snapped to Lady Lightland, but she was shaking her head and turning to Mally and Aunt Danna. Her people crowded around them, daring them to do something, weapons drawn in case they did.

They didn't move.

And already they were sailing away at full sail. It was too late.

But I couldn't hope yet – not when no head had come back up to the surface.

Where are you, Judicus? Where?

The small boat rowed over to the disappearing ring of bubbles, splashing around it. But they didn't haul anyone out of the water, and they were already shaking their heads when the coach driver finally reached the top of the cliff and noticed me.

"Hey! You!"

He fumbled for the sword at his side, and I spun. Nowhere to hide. His legs were twice as long as mine. I had no weapon. I couldn't run or fight.

I was still debating what to do when something snatched at my foot, like a rope tangled around my ankle.

I opened my mouth in a noiseless scream as I was yanked off the cliff and into the sea below as silently as one of the Stryxex circling the distant ship.

My skirts flapped around me as I sailed through the air, pawing for the sky.

I tasted blood – probably from biting my own lip, and then with a slap that felt like the angriest giant in the world had come for revenge, I hit the sea. Brackish water swirled around me, stinging my eyes and clouding my vision.

I was pulled through the water so quickly that all I felt were bubbles caressing my cheeks and arms and legs as they rushed past me toward the surface.

I held my breath, clenched my teeth, and hoped Kazmerev would be found by someone – somehow.

What had caught me? What manner of strange and wild creature could pull me from the very shore?

The tentacle holding my foot spun me around as I reached the bottom of the sea. My feet hit the sand and I tried to run as bubbles raced past, clouding my vision but I was too tangled, too caught.

And then something black closed over my face and without thinking, I opened my mouth in terror, losing the last of my air.

This was it. This was how I was going to die.

I closed my eyes.

I didn't die.

Fresh air filled my lungs and my eyes shot open.

I was in a bubble – a bubble held in a net of black lace. And in it with me, was Judicus.

"There you are," he said with a smile.

EPISODE FOUR: ROPE WORKER

SEASON ONE

59

Bright sea spray caught the sun, forming a rainbow of color off to one side of the bow. I wanted to enjoy the feeling of it, but tension twisted my belly.

"Stop fretting, Sersha," Judicus said from where he sat cross-legged, staring at the bright feather in his hands. His face was a pale green that complimented the bottle green jacket he'd bought for himself before we departed on *The Volente* and one side of his face was mottled with bruises. Most of the damage he'd sustained in captivity was covered by his clothing – masses of dark bruises he wouldn't let me look at – but those bruises on his face were impossible to hide.

"They'll heal. They don't need help," he'd said, shrugging me off when I tried to examine them the moment we cleared the sea. I'd left them alone, but my fingers itched to tend them.

I didn't know how he'd purchased our passage, or the clothing he'd acquired for both of us, or the equipment, I'd tried to ask with my hands, but he studiously ignored the question, so it remained a mystery.

I squinted at the ocean and wished for the hundredth time that we could simply fly on Kazmerev's back.

"It's better on a ship," Judicus said, his eyes rolling slightly as he fought against his seasickness again. It made him speak more slowly as if he were trying to breathe through his mouth. "A ship sails day and night. A phoenix only flies at night."

I looked around us worriedly, but no one was watching. The sailors were busy working the sails and tidying the deck. The other passengers weren't on deck so early. We'd chosen a place in the bow where the ropes were coiled, and the sea spray left us constantly misted and it seemed to keep unwanted ears away.

It was dawn and my beloved phoenix, Kazmerev, had faded from this world again. I clutched a fist to my chest – to my heart – where he slept, dead to this world, and watched the ocean, trying not to shudder as I remembered what it had felt like to almost drown beneath those waves.

It had only been the bubble formed of Judicus's magic that had saved us. He'd walked us down the coast until we were too far away for the men in the boat to find us and then he'd stumbled up out of the water – with my help – found us these fine clothes and passage on this ship and then promptly passed out in his assigned hammock.

By the time he woke in the night, I was practically hopping up and down. We'd lost a full day and there were only three to untangle the puzzle in the feather. At least our ship was sailing in the right direction.

"You're sure there are only two days to unravel this?" Judicus asked, looking up at me with a drawn expression. He was a poor traveler. He grew ill from boats and ill from flying. Maybe he even was ill on horseback. I had no way to know since he'd spent most of his time on horseback unconscious. He'd spent most of his time since I met him unconscious, though it wasn't exactly his fault. I'd grown so used to it that I wasn't sure what I'd do with a healthy, energetic Judicus.

I nodded in reply.

"It's a complicated bit of magic. I don't know if I can loosen it in just two days," he said, but he sounded more intrigued than upset. His eyes hadn't left the feather since I handed it to him last night and tried to explain what it was.

Kazmerev had been just as fascinated.

I've never seen this before, he'd said to me. *I've heard legends of feathers enchanted with riddles, but never before have I seen one. The old man must have been a powerful Flame Rider before his phoenix died.*

I still didn't understand that part. Kazmerev died every dawn but was raised to life again at sunset. How could a phoenix die and not rise?

He can be corrupted. Only the righteous rise again. Or, he can have passed to the beyond for some other reason – a death that severs the soul's connection to this world and forces us to the life beyond, perhaps. Or perhaps the hope in his rider's heart died.

That could happen?

Many people lose hope.

But if I lost hope, would I lose Kazmerev? The thought seared me like a painful brand.

You would. Keep your hope alive, little hawk. It is more powerful than you know.

I scrubbed nervously at the back of my neck as I watched Judicus. I was uncomfortable in these new clothes – they were far too rich. He'd bought me thin stockings of a wool so fine they clung perfectly to my shape. Tall leather boots protected my legs up and over the knee. My skirts were warm and practical but were full and cut in a flattering way and the sleeves of my bodice had a decorative puff as if I were a lady and not the daughter of villagers. I was afraid it made people look at me more and I wanted to be looked at less.

"Patience, Sersha," Judicus said in a wavering voice – but I knew it wavered from his nausea not from lack of confidence. He seemed very at home sitting here and studying a magic feather. "I'll figure it out. I always do. It was I who found Mally, wasn't it? That was a tricky puzzle if there ever was one and I was the first to solve it."

I looked around, worried someone was listening, but to my relief, everyone was too busy to keep their eyes on "that seasick lord and his mute sister" which was what she'd caught them calling her and Judicus.

"It's a knot made of magic, kind of like a blacksmith's puzzle. Have you seen those? The ones with two horseshoes chained together and a ring around the chain, or the ones with a series of rings and a pair of pins?"

I nodded to him. Tyndale made those when he was bored in the darkest depths of winter and sometimes he brought them to Uncle Llynd to try with the understanding that Tyndale could eat and drink for free until the puzzle was solved.

"I think that if I just ..."

His brow furrowed and then slipped into disappointment. It must not have worked.

I shook my head and he looked up. "Oh. You're bored. I suppose you can't see what I'm doing."

I nodded. Could he help me see it?

But no, he reached into his pocket and pulled out an oilskin, and handed it to me. Wrapped inside was a detailed map.

"Here. You can learn some geography while we travel. That can only help. We're here, leaving the city of Halvered and we're headed to Briccatore in the south. See it here?"

My eyes studied the map, tracing the scrolling letters for the names of places and the jagged coastline we'd be following all the way south down to Briccatore.

With my finger, I traced a looping letter near my home village.

"Wildrock," Judicus said, pointing to the letter I was tracing. That's what people call your country. Did you know that?"

I shook my head. I knew Landsfall. But not Wildrock. I tapped the map where it should be but Judiucs laughed.

"If they put every village on the map, it wouldn't fit them all. It's just cities and important landmarks. But I think studying this will help you – and it will give you something to do while I try to solve this puzzle."

I lifted two fingers.

"I know," he said, looking even greener. "Two days. I have to solve this puzzle in two days."

He turned back to it, and I tried to keep my eyes on the map and to concentrate, but what if he didn't succeed? How would we stop the Stryxex from hunting down and killing phoenixes? I would do anything to protect Kazmerev. Even give up on ever regaining Mally.

The thought of that drew me up short. I shouldn't think that way. She was important, too. And she was relying on us.

But now I had two impossible things to do, and I felt helpless in the face of them.

60

We were each so absorbed in our tasks that we hardly noticed the passing of time as the rest of the crew changed the watches and rang a bell to let everyone know they were doing it. We barely noticed the strolling of other passengers walking by us as they took a turn around the deck before retreating below again. We hardly noticed the ship's captain as he came over, stared at us a few moments, shook his head, and then left again. To him, it would have looked like Judicus was staring feverishly at a dark feather and like I was engrossed in a map beside him.

I'd learned a lot. Not how to read the names of the places on the map – but I'd learned the coastline well and learned the dips and weaves of the roads and where the cities and countries were. I'd need Judicus to tell me their names later, but I was fairly sure he was right and that this would help me to think about where we were going and how we could get there.

Judicus had made no further progress, though he'd become slightly less green as he muttered over the feather.

"A cross knot, perhaps? No. What if I tug this end? No? How can one wrap a thing in a rope worker's knot without being a rope worker?"

I had brought him food and water twice and had checked on him, tapping his arm and cocking my head to ask if he had the energy to keep going. He just waved a hand vaguely as if dismissing the question.

"Staring at a puzzle and tugging at strings requires minimal effort."

I hoped that was true because our hours seemed to be melting away.

We'd both avoided the company of others. Me, because I couldn't speak to them and that always made things awkward with new people. Judicus, because he was too seasick. Just moving from this spot seemed to make it worse.

I had just begun to grow complacent when the ship bell began to ring for dinner. A shadow loomed suddenly, and a hand reached out and snatched Judicus' feather from him.

I surged to my feet, the map falling to the ground and Judicus scrambled to grab it before the winds whipped it away. But maps could be replaced. The feather could not.

It gleamed bright on a weather-worn palm, and a large man in a trim jacket and high leather boots looked down at me. His dark hair was threaded with silver and little wings of white were over each ear, running down behind them. His skin was very dark, but not the dark of natural-born dark skin but the darkness of someone who had started brown and become browner and browner under a sneering sun. Little light squint lines around his eyes and mouth highlighted that and his chin was dusted in light stubble. I judged him to be nearly the age of Aunt Danna – early in his forties, perhaps. He had the powerful frame of an older man who had been physical all his life and so was still strong despite a bit of extra thickness that came with age.

He was frowning at us.

"And what do you have here, little thieves?" he asked.

I crossed my arms over my chest. *He* was the thief, not us.

"Do you know what this is?" he asked me, turning his body to me and not to Judicus who was pulling himself up awkwardly, still hunched over his healing wound, purple bruises, and rolling stomach.

I glared into his eyes and tried to snatch the feather back.

He was shockingly fast. He grabbed my wrist and held it so I couldn't pull it back.

"Answer me," he said quietly.

"Leave Sersha alone," Judicus said imperiously, dusting off his jacket. The map had disappeared into one of his pockets. He'd straightened and composed himself so that I could barely even notice the green in his face. "She does not speak, but I will offer you the courtesy. Why have you trespassed on our time and property?"

He sounded like a prince or a great ruler.

The man barked a short laugh.

"Hot. She is hot to the touch."

Judicus' face turned blank. "You should not be touching her enough to know that. Let her hand free, or you'll be swimming back to shore on your own."

I swallowed down a bubble of fear. We couldn't afford to let Judicus spend his energy that way. We needed every scrap of it to solve the puzzle. And we couldn't let anything happen to the feather.

"Do you know this is a phoenix feather?" the man asked in a low voice, looking over his shoulder as he spoke. "Not only is it that, but it is from Arturo – a phoenix of my acquaintance."

I gasped. He could tell that? It looked almost indistinguishable from Kazmerev's feathers to me.

"Was he accompanied by an old man?" Judicus asked grimly. "An old man a little shorter than me with grim eyes who rambled half-consciously about something bent on destroying all phoenixes?"

I almost sighed with relief at this speech. Because I wasn't sure if Judicus knew why I needed him to solve the puzzle of the feather. I'd been able to explain the time limit – three days – to him but explaining all the rest with hand gestures had stretched our ability to communicate to the limit. The old man must have spoken to him while they were in custody together. He must have told him about his fears. Or maybe Judicus was just so clever that he'd put all that together himself.

"Hallimore." The powerful man released my wrist and ran his hand over his face. "Where is he now?"

I shook my head sadly.

"Dead," Judicus interpreted.

"He gave you this?" the man's gaze was fixed on Judicus.

"He gave it to Sersha. Was he a friend of yours?"

The man swiveled to regard me. "Yes. Sersha. That makes sense."

It did? I frowned. What made sense of that to him? I thought the man had given it to me because I was the only one there when he was dying.

"I'll take it then. Since I am his friend."

I shook my head emphatically and held up my two fingers.

"What is she trying to say?" the man asked Judicus.

Judicus leaned against the ship rail looking as if he was lounging, but I knew it was an act. His green face gave him away. Fortunately, people don't want to be around seasickness victims, so no one was interrupting.

"She's telling you that your friend – Hallimore – told us there were only two more days before the puzzle and message disappear."

"What message?" He looked at the feather now, turning it over and over in his hands.

"The one that's hidden with a ropework knot," Judicus said dryly. "The one I was attempting to untangle before you came and so rudely interrupted." He opened his hand. "If you'd care to return it, I can get back to work. Unless you have the gift of rope working and I somehow do not detect it?"

He let those words trail off and the man grunted. "And who are you?"

"Judicus Franzer Irault." Judicus said in a low tone that did not carry. His eyes were hooded but the look in them was dark and burning.

The man startled, taking a step back as if unconscious he was doing it. He looked Judicus up and down suspiciously and Judicus sighed, looking at me.

"You'll find they do that a lot, Sersha," he said. "They all think I'll turn rabid and rip their throats out."

And to my surprise, the man nodded at that, as if it was the most obvious thing in the world.

61

The man bent his head slightly and said, "And I am Gundt Hellebar. And I'll take charge of you, little sister."

I tilted my head and to my shock he made a sign with his hand that looked like one wing flapping, starting at his heart and moving outward. He placed his other hand – cupped – over it.

"We Flame Riders watch out for one another. You must be freshly minted if you did not know what I was immediately at our touch or know who Hallimore was. And that makes it my sworn duty to train and protect you until you no longer require my guidance."

Judicus snatched the feather from his grip, but he hardly noticed, so intent was he on me.

"We'll get you properly outfitted when the ship makes port and every night you can train with Huxabrand and me. We're not like other orders – there aren't many of us and we're so nomadic that you don't get your choice. You're stuck with me, I'm afraid. I'm the Guarding Flame."

I cocked my head, urging him to go on.

He smiled. "We'll need to work on some kind of signs. That won't be a problem. Our phoenixes can talk for the more complicated parts and that should make it easier to sign. This is where the nomadic part is handy. If someone hatches fresh, they usually stumble into one of us eventually."

I didn't know how to say "but what if I don't want your teaching" or "but I'm trying to save my cousin" or anything else, and his jaw was set, his features firm. He was certain in this course. I wouldn't be able to change his mind.

"I'm afraid not," said Judicus not even looking up.

"Try saying that again," Gundt said mildly but there was iron behind his words.

"She's sworn to my coterie," Judicus said and he sounded like an arrogant young lord for the first time since I'd met him. "She comes with me and you can't change that."

Gundt's face flushed. "You swore her very quickly, whelp. You took her loyalty when she was still fresh-hatched."

Judicus was blushing now, too, color finally showing in cheeks made pale from the rocking boat. "I did nothing wrong."

His hands were shaking. I'd never seen him furious before and I'd been with him when Mally crashed our boat.

"Sersha is under my protection," he said, modulating his voice. "She's sworn to my coterie. And if you think I'll let some stranger show up, and just claim her then you're wrong. I don't know you, Hellebar. I don't know your family. I don't know your hold. If you're honorable, then I don't know that. I have no way to know. But I do know she's safe with me – or at least safe *from* me – so she stays with me unless she says otherwise."

He was out of breath from that speech and to my surprise, I realized he was taller than the other man when he was standing up straight like he was now. He almost loomed.

They both turned to me and I pointed at Judicus. He'd been ill for most of the time I'd known him. Ill and miserable. But he'd been respectful and trustworthy and fair and Kazmerev liked him. I was sticking with him and that was all there was to it.

Gundt ran his hand through his hair again. He should be careful with that. He might go bald. Uncle Llynd had started going bald after too much tugging and pulling at his hair when he was feeling overwhelmed.

"I am bound by the oaths to train her as the Guarding Flame, regardless of her oaths to you. I can't let her fly off without proper instruction. It's not safe for her. It's not kind to her phoenix. Would you let a babe wander in the woods on their own?"

Judicus lifted an eyebrow. "Sersha is grown."

"Not in this, she is not."

"Her phoenix is older than the hills."

Gundt crossed his arms over his chest.

Judicus looked to me, again showing his respect in this. "Will you accept his teaching, Sersha?"

I didn't know what I was agreeing to. I looked the man over carefully, trying to judge him. His hands were marked with white scars. He had one on his neck, too. He might have been attractive to women his age, but he only looked old to me. Would he be able to keep up? Would he dig in his heels when Judicus and I tried to save phoenixes and Mally?

I frowned.

But on the other hand, I couldn't help but feel a little thrill at the idea of someone like me – someone who understood phoenixes and what they were like. Could he teach me all the skills Kazmerev kept hinting I might have? Could he help me understand how to be the best possible Flame Rider for Kazmerev? If he could, did I dare say no to that?

"The training is not onerous," Gundt said, holding his hands up as if trying to make peace. "You'll be taught our traditions. Given to understand where help can be found. Shown ways to make use of what you are learning so you don't accidentally light the roof of your home on fire or fall to your death from the back of your phoenix. His former rider cannot teach you since that Flame Rider has passed into the beyond where God alone knows what comes next. This is a kindness I am offering, not a burden." He paused. "I say offering, but I am not offering so much as ordering. I'm bound by oath to help. If you flee, I will pursue. Where you go, I will go, until you have passed the test of flame and shown me you can be trusted to stay alive and safe without guidance. You, also, will be sworn to this duty. If you meet a stray on the road you'll be bound to help the same as I."

So, Judicus offered me a choice and this man didn't.

"You make it sound so appealing," Judicus drawled.

"Did they give you a choice, rope worker?" Gundt asked, his eyes never leaving mine. "When they saw you could weave the threads of this world, did they just let you run wild, or did someone take you in hand – for the sake of your own life and the safety of all of us?"

Judicus grunted. He had no argument.

I nodded reluctantly. I supposed there was no getting rid of him. But would he try to delay us? Would he get in the way?

"Sersha says you can come with us," Judicus said. "So, you can. You aren't part of my coterie, but Sersha is, so your training will have to be secondary to her oaths."

Gundt ducked his head in silent acknowledgment.

"We're busy chasing after her kidnapped cousin." I found it interesting that he left out the ai'sletta part. He was keeping some things to himself. "And we're trying to solve this riddle before it's too late."

"Then I'll help you with both those things," Gundt said, nodding at the feather puzzle. "Try unwinding a Deadman's Hitch. That's what most phoenix riders use to tie things they don't want untied."

But he still wasn't looking at Judicus, not even when Judicus leaned down again and set to the feather with all is concentration. Not even when Judicus swore and said, "I think you're right."

Not even when other people began to wander back up on the deck, their dinner eaten, their bellies full.

He didn't look away until I did first and then he said, "It's almost dusk. Will you fly with me tonight, little sister?"

62

Judicus shot a warning glance at me, as if begging me to be cautious around our new, unknown friend. I nodded very slightly to him before nodding more obviously to Gundt.

"Here, come away a little with me," he said. "We can talk about what you already know while Irault over there works on the knot."

His voice took on a note of disdain when he referred to Judicus – a note I did not like. I frowned at that but allowed him to guide me to the side.

"You received ash from someone dying," he said confidently.

I nodded.

"And a phoenix bloomed in your heart."

I nodded again.

"How long ago?"

I hadn't been counting. I screwed up my face and tried to count now. What was it, ten? Eleven days?

I showed him my fingers, wiggling them slightly to show my uncertainty.

"Not long," he agreed. "Have you flown?"

I nodded and mimed throwing a beam of fire.

His eyebrows rose.

"So far already." He looked around us, making sure no one heard. "Can you carry another?"

I nodded my head toward Judicus.

Gundt gave a low whistle. "That's good. And can you stay invisible while carrying him?"

At this, I was forced to shake my head.

"Then maybe we can start there. Your friend certainly looks like he could use a break from sailing." He gave me a weak smile. "But before we do anything else, do you know what you need to keep your phoenix alive?"

I did know. Kazmerev had been very clear. I needed hope and I needed a pure heart. But you couldn't sign those things.

"Has your phoenix mentioned how important your intentions are?"

I nodded my head. Had he ever. He cared so much about righteousness, that I worried it made him less practical.

"Phoenixes cannot go to evil. They may only thrive in good."

I knew that, but I let him repeat to me the things I already knew – about how my phoenix would die every dawn and be reborn from my heart, how if I lost my hope or stopped following the path of righteousness, I would lose him utterly. How he was my equal, not a horse or a pet.

It was all good, but I knew this part, so my eyes drifted often to Judicus, which was how I saw his look of shock and then his furtive look in every direction. He hung the cord of leather back around his neck and hid the feather under his shirt. Just like I had done.

He'd solved something. I just knew it.

But when he caught me looking, he pressed his finger to his lips and slipped away toward the hatch leading below decks. What wasn't he telling me? Why was he being so mysterious?

"Pure of heart," Gundt was saying. "That's what you must be."

I nodded to that, but my mind was full of questions. Why did only phoenixes require that? And how did you become pure of heart?

"You're probably wondering what I'm doing on this ship," Gundt said looking a bit guilty for a moment. "We were delivering supplies to the far north caches when Huxabrand was injured. She needs to rest before we can do any distance flying. Which is why we'll have to take it easy tonight."

And that was fine by me. I was both mistrustful and excited where he was concerned. When he was one teaching me all these basic things – what more might there be to learn? Could he help me find my way – and maybe even get good at this? I had visions of myself riding Kazmerev as we sailed into danger and easily used a great, fiery magic to defend innocents and save the city.

"It would likely be best for us just to get acquainted tonight anyway and practice flying in a formation once we know each other well. It's harder than you think."

I doubted that since it would be entirely Kazmerev and not me at all who would be doing the work.

He sounded nervous suddenly, rubbing at a dark green bracer that poked out from under his sleeve. "I know we've been thrown together, and I've been very insistent, but I hope we can be friends. I haven't ... well, I've never been the Guarding Flame before for anyone else. I guess maybe I'm not very good at it."

It felt so odd to have a huge man confessing this to me that I set a hand on his arm and gave him a reassuring smile. I didn't know what was going on between him and Judicus, but so far, he'd been kind enough to me. I didn't see why this couldn't work. Somehow. And I certainly wasn't going to let it get in the way of my fight for Mally or for phoenixes everywhere.

He smiled back and for one tiny moment, I thought this might actually work.

And then the sun set.

63

Deep joy tore through me and I reached for Kazmerev, only to freeze. Gundt stood frozen beside me, a look on his face that was halfway between concentration and rapture. It was a private expression – one not meant for me. I should have looked away, but before I could, I saw a bloom of bright pink like a summer flower puff out from his chest in a flame the size of my fist.

The flame billowed, and then multiplied, and then bright golden flames rippled out, and like lightning striking they crackled out in a sudden flash and there was a full-grown phoenix perched on the ship's rail beside him.

Not a single person on the decks turned to look – as if they couldn't see the bright, rippling feathers or the glittering falcon eye watching them all. And, of course, they couldn't. Just like the ship wasn't tilting at all from the weight of a great bird perched on the rail.

My heart stuttered, unsure how to feel. I'd just watched what happened to me every night happen to someone else. And it was glorious and beautiful and terrifying all at once.

I caught Gundt's eye by accident and saw his wry smile before I looked away, blushing furiously as if I had caught him half dressed. I didn't know why it felt like I shouldn't have seen that, but it did.

I turned my back to him before I opened my own heart again. Kazmerev leapt forth with a stutter of joy and confusion.

Are you hurt? Are you – oh.

I shook myself and recovered enough to look up and see my phoenix friend reeling back from the phoenix on the rail and I looked at them side by side – both impossibly beautiful and searingly bright, both powerful and magical and ... indescribable. I could see the differences. Gundt's phoenix's gracile curves were slightly more feminine, slightly less sharp, slightly more curving.

Flame to flame, I greet you, ancient fire.

For the first time since I met Kazmerev, none of his attention seemed to be on me,

Mmm. I see you, phoenix.

I could hear her, too! I felt my eyes growing wide and stole a look at Gundt who looked like he was biting his own tongue within his cheek to keep from looking smug. He must have known I'd be able to see and hear his phoenix – just like he could see mine.

I am Kazmerev, Bright Flame, Bound in Oath and Heart to Sersha of Landsfall.

My eyes narrowed on Gundt. Was my privacy over now? Would he hear my every thought? I hadn't planned on sharing Kazmerev and I didn't want to.

What is this, Gundt? The female phoenix asked. *What strays have you picked up now?*

She wasn't even answering my phoenix's pretty greeting. I gritted my teeth. He deserved better than that!

Easy now, little hawk. She does not need to greet me until she is ready.

Then I didn't need to greet her until I was ready. I felt – snubbed. No, worse than that. I felt like she'd snubbed my Kazmerev and it made something inside me burn hot and fast.

Easy. Easy. Don't light the ship aflame.

And I was going to, if I wasn't careful. I could feel the heat of my fury making my skin tingle.

Gundt was saying something to Huxabrand but I wasn't listening. I stalked away to the very narrowest part of the bow, my back to them. What was I thinking? I should never have agreed to this. I couldn't go flying, anyway. Not with all these people on the ship. They'd notice if I just started floating up into the air.

I didn't know why I wanted to cry or why I wished I had a private place on this ship to hide. But I did and I *did*. It was as if all the emotions of the past days and days of fleeing and of seeing magic I'd never experienced before and of travel and uncertainty and being constantly surrounded by enemies were all catching up to me at once.

Disappointment comes from the difference between our expectations and reality. Did you possibly expect more?

And I hated Gundt for pushing his will onto me and forcing his presence. And I hated his smug phoenix for shunning mine. And I just wanted to be left alone.

Sersha.

I shied away from his voice. I wanted to be alone.

Sersha, it's me. It's okay.

I felt him there behind my back, cupping a wing around me so I was completely enshrouded in guarding flames.

Someone cleared a throat behind me.

Gundt.

I didn't realize I'd been crying until I heard that. I dashed the tears from my eyes and turned very carefully. Kazmerev turned with me, keeping me cupped in his wing. When we faced them again, Gundt was frowning.

He made a curt gesture with his fingers. His phoenix ducked her head slightly, looking almost embarrassed.

Flame to flame, I greet you, ancient fire.

Oh. She was greeting Kazmerev. I sniffled, feeling a little less lost.

I am Huxabrand, Smoke Trail, Bound in Oath and Heart to Gundt Hellebar.

"And?" Gundt said, like a parent urging a child.

And I submit my humblest apologies for the rudeness of my refusal to greet you.

Kazmerev ruffled his feathers but when he spoke it was calm.

My Flame Rider is new to this. I will die a thousand deaths to keep back one of her tears.

Huxabrand shuffled uncertainly, moving her head so only one eye looked at us.

But I will accept your apology.

He looked from me to Gundt and back again as if weighing what he would say next.

Are you safe with him, little hawk?

I thought so.

I would prefer to take you out for a view of the sea right now, but you are drawing eyes already.

I sniffed and looked out at the deck where a woman was whispering to one of the sailors, casting worried looks in my direction. Hastily, I uncrossed my arms and raised my chin, trying to look relaxed.

If you are safe, I ought to take a flight with Huxabrand. Tradition is for two phoenixes meeting to share the winds and the taste of sky.

I had no idea what that meant, but I was not his keeper, and I would hate for us to be rude to the other phoenix, though I was still stinging from how she had snubbed him. It wasn't because … it wasn't because of me, was it?

Is that what you think?

I glanced up at the humor in his tone. His eyes sparkled.

She's merely putting a male phoenix in his place, making him come to her as a supplicant to remind him he's no worthy mate to one as fine as her.

I had thought all phoenixes were born of righteousness and pure hearts.

So we are.

Where did her haughtiness fit into that?

He laughed mentally.

It fits in the mating dances of the ages.

I heard the snap of a fiery beak from Huxabrand's direction.

Don't let it trouble you.

I hoped he was careful. And I hoped it wasn't really a mating dance. I didn't like the other phoenix. At all.

Fly with me, Flame of Dusk, Kazmerev said in a charming tone I hadn't heard before, and then he launched into the air, a dazzling flame shot into the velvet purple of the night.

Huxabrand – whatever she thought of him – followed and in a moment, they were already shrinking as they rose high over us.

Gundt cleared his throat awkwardly and I turned back to him.

"I apologize for my friend."

I nodded awkwardly.

"There are things I should teach you – but I think perhaps now is not the time." He finished the sentence with a questioning tone on the end and I nodded. I wasn't in the mood to learn anything. "You should know that I can't hear what you say to your phoenix – to Kazmerev. Though I can hear what he says. Your privacy still remains – to an extent."

I hadn't realized how worried I was about that until relief flooded over me.

He gave me a sorry half-smile and offered, "Shall I help you to your cabin?"

It was a kind gesture, but I shook my head. I didn't want to be closed in a box right now. I had a lot to think about and I still hoped that eventually Kazmerev would return to explain more.

I felt nothing but relief when he gave me a brief bow and strode away.

This was all too much for me. And now there was another phoenix. And the way she treated Kazmerev like his words couldn't be heard felt far too much like how everyone treated me. I didn't like it.

I didn't like it at all.

64

I was still watching the small balls of light above when my eyes began to droop. Kazmerev and Huxabrand flew complicated patterns over us and their constant movement lulled my mind so that I found myself sitting on this tiny piece of neglected decking and then leaning back onto the coils of rope stored there, and then slowly drifting off.

I awoke to someone shaking my arm. My eyes snapped open, heart racing at the threat. It was only Judicus, looking furtively from side to side, one finger over his lips as if he thought I'd suddenly start making noise and betray him.

I sat up, rubbing the sleep from my eyes. It had become cold while I slept, and gooseflesh dotted my arms, though surprisingly the cold didn't bother me. Around us, there was no sound but the slap of water against ship and the occasional murmur of the few sailors left to man the ship.

I was surprised they'd let me sleep up on deck, but I supposed it was no concern of theirs where their passengers slept as long as they weren't in the way.

"I got it," Judicus whispered. His eyes glowed in the light of the ship's lanterns. "I undid the knot."

What did it say? What was the message? I was instantly awake and leaning forward, eager to hear what he might say.

"It did this," he whispered, drawing the feather from his shirt. He shielded it with his body, but even so, the feather was glowing more brightly than ever before.

I gasped as I realized that on the bright feather, black words were scrawled, and three dark symbols seemed burned onto it.

"Can you read?" Judicus whispered.

I shook my head.

"It says 'Choose Wisely.' I think that means that we pick one of these and if we're right we get the message and if we're wrong, we don't."

I swallowed and looked at the three dark marks. A feather. A claw. A flame.

I looked back at Judicus and he shrugged. "They're all phoenix things. I guess a true Flame Rider would know which to choose." But I didn't. And this was very odd. How had Hallimore made this magic feather? How had he spun the magic for this riddle? Judicus answered my mental question without any sign from me. He did that a lot. "A rope worker could have made him the feather and the rope seals – ready to put your words into it and then snap closed at a word. Which means the making of this won't hold any clues on how to open it. But perhaps as a Flame Rider one of these signs speaks more to you?"

I reached out and touched the feather, marveling at this strange magic.

"Forget the feather," he said impatiently. "It's a common tool. I could make one given enough time. It's the signs we must judge. They are all related to phoenixes and I can't tell which is correct. Perhaps that's the reason they were chosen – only a true Flame Rider would know which to choose."

I tapped my chin. What could they represent? Why would a flame be any more like Kazmerev than a feather? Or a talon?

We could ask Gundt. I looked toward the hatch to below decks and Judicus guessed my thoughts.

"I don't trust him. He says all the right things, but doesn't it seem just a little too fortuitous that he's suddenly here when we really could use his help? Offering to help you with no strings attached? Everyone has strings. Even I wanted you in my coterie. I didn't want to lose Kazmerev. I like you and I wanted good things for you – but even I have selfish motivations. What are his motives? Why is he here? I don't want him to know I've opened this until we've heard the message."

I agreed with him about Gundt. Even if he had been kind to me. Even if it made me feel so hopeful to be around someone who might understand this new life I'd taken on. Even if I kind of hoped he was everything he claimed to be and more.

But what if we guessed wrong and never got the message? What if he could help us?

"Besides, we need to open this tonight. If there are any other puzzles to solve, we can't wait until the last minute to solve them."

I leaned my head to one side undecided. I would like to ask Kazmerev. I didn't want to guess. But if I did that, then Huxabrand would hear him which would be the same thing as telling Gundt, which Judicus was asking me not to do. Oh, but this was a tangled thing!

"Just think about it, Sersha," he begged, looking so hopeful and boyish that it was impossible to say no. "Maybe there's an easy answer."

I chewed the end of a finger and thought about it. A talon. Violence. Ripping. Tearing. Was there any other way to see it? But that wasn't how I thought of Kazmerev. That wasn't even how I thought of Huxabrand. They were more than the potential for violence or power. They were more than tearing things to pieces.

I glanced at Judicus. He was leaning back on my rope pile, eyes sliding closed. He must be tired after that long day and night working on the feather – and all that after a daring escape and shopping for clothing – which he claimed was worse than being beaten for information.

"Really," he'd said. "If you don't believe me, you can try both in a row and offer your opinion."

I slid the feather from his grasp so it wouldn't blow away and stared at the symbols again.

I'd ruled out the talon. But what about the other two?

The feather was more mild. All it made me think about was flight. Flight was inherent to a phoenix.

But so was the flame. I mean, that was what made him different than just a bird, wasn't it? It was his power, his magic.

I sat there a long time looking between the symbols, but I couldn't decide.

Above me, the phoenixes danced, bright flames on the dark sky - more lovely than lightning bugs, more heart-breakingly beautiful than the northern lights that danced in winter deep.

Out there, somewhere, Mally was waiting. And out there, all around us in every direction, miles and miles away, there were dozens, or maybe hundreds, or maybe even thousands of phoenixes who needed our help to protect them from this hunt.

And what was it about them that made them so precious? What was it about Kazmerev? It wasn't his great power. It wasn't his magic. It wasn't even his ability to rise from the dead. It was he himself - my good friend. My kind ally.

As I lay back on the ropes beside Judicus, I held up the feather in front of me and I bit my lip and let my finger press down on the feather.

Because it was the phoenix himself I loved. It wasn't the power. It wasn't the magic. It was him.

Always him.

65

I realized my mistake immediately. I should have woken Judicus or Gundt. Or called Kazmerev.

My only excuse was that in my sleepiness, it hadn't occurred to me that the answer to our question might be a voice. Or that it might be temporary.

The message locked in the feather was the voice of the old man – Hallimore. I recognized it immediately. And it was speaking into my head – as Kazmerev did.

"I hope this works," Hallimore said, pausing to cough. "It's my one chance before they're back. They've caught me. They've killed Arturo. I ... No, I need to stay focused. Focus." He was rambling and his voice was thick, like he was barely holding on to consciousness. Had he recorded this in between beatings? "The Stryxex are here. They are not legends as we thought but living horrors. They consumed Arturo like a lion consumes its prey and there was nothing left and now they are intent on finding every Flame Rider cache. They already know where they are. That is not what they want from me. From me, they want a way to contact those I have served as Guarding Flame. I will not tell them. So, I will not live for long. They follow a bright lady who gives them their commands and this lady seeks something called the 'ai'sletta.' A powerful weapon to reshape the world as she pleases. And she pleases that there be no more phoenixes. The riders of the Stryxex say that she sees the phoenixes as an evil aberration – for they die and do not stay dead. And so, she plans to –" His words cut off, then return, too garbled by coughing to understand. They clear after a moment. "They are bringing me south. To Briccatore. They kept mentioning the Festival of Moons – as if they had to be there in time for that. And something about a rising star. I don't know why. I will try to leave this message to a true Flame Rider. You must warn the others. You must go to Briccatore and stop them. Trust no one. And beware – there was talk of a Flame Rider who had turned on us all. A traitor. You must find the others before he does."

The words faded away and then abruptly the glowing feather faded to darkness.

My heart was pounding in my chest as I tried to repeat the important parts to myself so I wouldn't forget. Caches. Stryxex. Bright Lady. Festival of Moons. Rising Star. Briccatore.

We were already headed south. We were going in the right direction.

I tried to assure myself with that, but I did not feel sure. I felt like I couldn't calm down. There was a Flame Rider who was a traitor and hunting down other Flame Riders. What should I make of that? Especially now when someone had just appeared and named himself "Guarding Flame" to me? That coincidence was just a little too convenient, wasn't it?

A stab of fear shot through me at that thought.

I lay back on the ropes beside the snoring Judicus and watched Kazmerev fly so high above that he seemed like a tiny firefly. How was I going to protect him from all of this?

The words of Hallimore rang in my head "they consumed Arturo."

I dared not do anything that might let that happen to Kazmerev.

And yet, I couldn't hide anything from him. We'd have to shake off this new Flame Rider and his phoenix. We'd have to go our own way. But how would I tell Judicus?

I realized with sudden clarity how frustrating my position was. Because for the first time, someone really could speak complex thoughts for me. Kazmerev could listen to me and repeat them to Huxabrand and Gundt would hear them in his mind. I could have told the entire contents of the letter. I could have laid it all out and he could tell Judicus.

But I couldn't trust him. I didn't dare.

Frustration filled me and with it an intense longing for what I'd only just realized I could have. But not with Gundt and Huxabrand – maybe not with anyone if I didn't know which phoenix and Flame Rider I could trust.

I bit my lip and thought furiously. I needed to find a way to tell Kazmerev all of this without giving it away to Huxabrand.

Around me, the waves smacked steadily against the bow of the ship and we climbed them and descended again, climbed and descended with the scent of the sea heavy on the air and the sense of my great responsibility heavy on my heart.

I had a heavy burden laid on me now. A burden even stronger than saving Mally because an entire race was depending on me to get out the warning – the race of phoenixes. If I failed them, who would warn them? The old man had given his last strength and his life trying to get out the warning.

And saving Mally was tied up in that, too. She was the ai'sletta. She was the weapon that the Bright Lady planned to use.

I swallowed down worry and scrubbed my face with a troubled hand.

You are troubled.

I hadn't realized Kazmerev had landed until he was right there beside me.

I sensed it from afar and returned to you.

I wanted to sink into his strength. I wanted to tell him everything. But there, lingering just behind him was Huxabrand watching us with head cocked to the side.

Were they friends now?

They both bobbed their heads slightly in a way that suggested laughter.

We have danced the flame together in the way honored by tradition, Kazmerev said. *We have set aside misconceptions. We will fly together. We will share the sky and burn brightly side by side.*

Was that a yes?

Yes.

And could we speak alone? Could we have any kind of privacy again?

We have no need. Huxabrand has our trust.

She didn't have my trust.

Kazmerev snorted a laugh. *You're a suspicious one, little hawk. But you don't need to be.*

We did need to be. But how could I tell him when she could just listen to my thoughts?

She can't hear you, remember?

But she could hear him. And because of that, I couldn't tell him.

We are bonded together by the ties of oaths and heart. You cannot keep things from me.

Not from him. Just from her. When the ship went to shore, we could go our own way and then our thoughts would be private, and I could tell him everything. He could wait until then.

You don't need to keep secrets. Huxabrand is a friend.

Why did he have to be so insistent about that? Why couldn't he just trust me?

Behind him, the female phoenix shifted as if growing anxious from what we were saying.

I felt like I was being foolish and they could both see it. But I wasn't, was I? Because Judicus didn't trust Gundt either. That's why he'd kept his discovery hidden.

I bit my lip, so many thoughts whirling in my head that I couldn't make sense of them all. They whirled around and around so that one moment I thought I should entrust what I discovered to them and one moment I thought I should keep it to myself.

Kazmerev seemed suddenly cooler than usual, his fire less hot, his eye sharper.

You found the message, he guessed. *And you won't tell me what it is because you don't trust Gundt.*

Huxabrand's fire flared at that, as if she were angry with me. And that alone locked my jaw tighter as if my very bones were afraid the secret might slip from my silent tongue.

You won't tell us? Kazmerev sounded hurt. *Little hawk?*

And then a dark figure stepped around the pair of phoenixes and loomed over me.

"Tell us what?"

66

He looked so intent, so stern. And I understood why. He didn't want me to keep secrets from him. He thought of himself as something like a guide or a teacher for me.

And I understood the hurt look in Kazmerev's eyes. He expected more from me – deserved more from me.

So why won't you give it?

That stung.

I understood the superior look in Huxabrand's eye. She knew she was better than me.

She's not going to hurt you. Kazmerev sounded like he was trying to calm a frightened child. *You misunderstood what she was doing. She wasn't trying to isolate you or me or treat us with contempt. It's not like that. It's – you humans flirt, right? You know that sometimes things between men and women are not all that they seem on the surface.*

I'd certainly seen Mally bend and twist men up until they were at each other's throats and then soothe it all with a smile and a laugh.

Like that. It's like that. Huxabrand is shockingly lovely. Beautiful even among a people so beautiful that we dazzle your eyes.

She looked so much like him that if I didn't know him well, I'd have to squint to see the differences.

Human eyes struggle to pick up on the details. Even with your night-enhanced vision.

"Why are you talking about how phoenixes look?" Gundt asked with what sounded like impossible patience.

So, she expected me to ... well, this is embarrassing, but she expected attention. Right? Unwanted attention. It's what she usually gets.

Was his fire burning hotter?

Please, don't mention it. It's very awkward to have to spell this out. I – well, I was very forward introducing myself like that without the proper ritual and dance back and forth and she was simply reminding me of my place.

His *place?* No, I didn't like that. Not at all.

Stop being so protective about me. He sounded frustrated. *It's my job to be protective of* you.

"Easy now," Gundt said, stepping between us, hands up as if he was settling a dispute.

I didn't appreciate the interference. This was between Kazmerev and me.

Of course, it is between us. Please, don't be upset.

My heart hiccupped. Our friendship – his and mine – was the deepest thing I had. The only thing I had. Having people come in from outside and disrupt that … well, it made me feel like I needed to protect it. Like I needed to get away. Like I needed to be anywhere but here.

I was shaking all over and I couldn't control it.

Shhh, little hawk. It will be okay.

It might have been okay like he said. But then Huxabrand spoke and I heard her. *Why is she being so dramatic? Doesn't she understand phoenixes?*

And suddenly I felt like they were all in a group together and I was the outsider looking in. An outsider in my own life, in my own friendship with Kazmerev.

I felt betrayed.

I feel betrayed, too, little hawk. You won't trust me with your secret.

And like a knife in the heart, Huxabrand spoke, too. *Of course, you feel betrayed. This human is unreasonable.*

Tears stung my eyes, and I opened my mouth as if I could answer, hurt wanting to bubble to the surface, loneliness coming from nowhere to swallow me up.

I'm sorry, I –

Dawn shattered his voice and fragmented him. He vanished in a puff of black smoke and even the smoke looked distressed as it spread and diluted until there was nothing left.

I bit back a shuddering sob. We'd fought. We'd fought and hadn't found peace and now he was gone. And would he even come back? Could he be reborn in my heart when we were at odds?

I nearly jumped when Gundt cleared his throat. He pulled awkwardly at his collar.

"He'll be back," he said as if he could read my mind. "At dusk, he'll be back."

I caught his gaze with mine, eyes wide, trying to indicate that I needed something to hold onto. He understood, somehow.

"I've fought with Huxabrand before. She can be … high spirited. Headstrong. Fiery." He coughed a laugh. "Which goes without saying, of course. Sometimes I think that I never married because she's too much of a handful to add a family in there as well. Not that Flame Riders marry – we usually don't. It's too hard with a phoenix who always must be moving." He shook his head like he knew he was rambling and was trying to stop. His next words were so full of assurance that they made my tears stop. "She always comes back. Even when she's furious with me. Even when she has a good reason to stay away. She comes back. She's in my heart.

The only thing that could ever banish her is evil. Don't grow evil and he will stay with you."

I blinked back tears and put my hand on his arm for a brief moment. A silent thank you.

Perhaps I should trust him after all.

The first drops of rain started with that thought and Judicus sprang awake, scrambling to his feet and searching the ship's deck frantically.

"The feather," he gasped. "What happened to the feather?"

67

I opened my hand and showed him the dark feather in my palm.

"You solved the riddle," Judicus gasped.

"There was a riddle?" Gundt asked, looking from one face to the other.

"A feather, a flame, and a talon," Judicus said. "You had to choose one."

He was being so open with Gundt now. Where was that openness hours ago? It was Judicus' mistrust that had fueled my own and now he was just letting it go.

"Any Flame Rider would know the answer to that," Gundt said simply. "The feather. The phoenix is not his power, the talon. Nor his magic, the flame. He is valuable because he is."

I smiled at him shyly. That was the same conclusion I had come to.

"Did you access the message then?" Judicus asked.

I nodded.

"That was what we were just discussing," Gundt said carefully. "She does not want to tell her phoenix what she heard because she does not trust me."

"What?" Judicus looked between us, his expression softening at the heat flaring in my cheeks.

"I can hear him," Gundt said. "So, if she tells him, she will have told me."

Judicus whistled a long, low whistle. "I see the problem." He gave me a long look. "And she can't tell us any other way. I'm guessing your signs won't be up to the task?"

I nodded, sadly.

"And you cannot write."

I nodded again.

The rain intensified. Sheets of it began to pour down, hitting the deck and drenching us in moments. There was a shout, and someone began to ring a bell.

One of the sailors hurried up to the bow.

"You can't stay here in a storm. Get below with you!"

Which was how we found ourselves below decks, huddled in one cabin. Gundt and Judicus were wearing Gundt's spare clothing – brought from where his bag had been stashed – and I was still wet as a drowned rat. I tried a little sadly to wring my skirts out while the men watched, awkward. Gundt had nothing that would fit me.

We all felt that same feeling of an impasse. Gundt wouldn't leave since he was my Guarding Flame. But Judicus and I didn't know if we could trust him. Judicus wouldn't say it outright, but he kept looking at me as if to be sure I still agreed with him.

It felt strange to be so suspicious when I'd trusted Judicus so easily – but this was different. We'd been betrayed and chased so much since then and I couldn't just forget that.

Instead, we sat in dour silence as the waves beat at the sides of the ship. It tossed and rolled on the sea like a child's toy. Judicus was ill almost immediately and took to the only cot, moaning and clutching his belly or head. There was not much that could be done for him except to share a worried look with Gundt.

Once, Gundt tried to leave the cabin and was immediately shouted back in by the ship's captain.

"Are you a fool? Get back inside. No passenger is to leave quarters! My sailors have enough to contend with!"

So, he came back in and sat himself on the bench screwed to the wall to keep it from toppling and I sat on the other side of it, and we kept a half of an eye on each other and half an eye on poor Judicus who looked like he might die of aversion to the sea.

I felt the burden of my fight with Kazmerev weighing me down and it was all I could do to hold in the tears that threatened to sweep over me. I wished I hadn't let him die like that. I wish he hadn't felt betrayed. I was just trying to be safe. To do the right thing.

I stole occasional glances at Gundt out of the corner of my eye. I did want to trust him. I did. But what if I chose wrong?

After an hour he let out a long sigh.

"I can't think of a way to show you that you can trust me, Sersha," he said. "But if we sit here like this all day, we will only grow more and more miserable."

The lantern hanging in the center of the cabin flickered as the ship took a particularly bad roll on the waves and Judicus moaned in distress.

"The storm is getting worse. We should keep our minds on other things," he said. Was he a little pale, too? Perhaps he liked these waves no more than Judicus did. "The rope worker said you cannot read or write."

I nodded grimly.

"Perhaps, I could teach you that." He suggested. "Perhaps you would like to learn. And perhaps as I am teaching you to read, you might teach me your signs and perhaps we'll be able to communicate a little better. Trust, I find, grows best in the soil of truth."

Which was how I found myself learning to read, beside a man I wasn't sure I could trust, in the middle of a ferocious storm.

I should have been sleeping. But there were only two cots and it felt wrong to sleep while Judicus was in agony and Gundt was stuck in our cabin with us.

Instead, I poured over the words and letters he showed me in a small book he produced from his pocket, and for each one he taught me I made its sign and he practiced that.

I thought that perhaps the book was written in his own hand. After some time with it, I was confident it was a journal of his travels. Carefully, he stepped me through the sounds of the letters and how they blurred together. Since I couldn't make the sounds of them, he made them over and over, and the rumble of his deep voice began to feel soothing.

Perhaps I should trust him.

Or, perhaps he was doing all this to get my guard down and I really *shouldn't* trust him.

I needed to decide today. Before I saw Kazmerev tonight. Because if I was going to trust Gundt then I could wholeheartedly apologize to my phoenix and tell him everything. But if I wasn't going to trust Gundt then I must brace myself for more of Kazmerev's disappointment and my own broken heart.

Those thoughts plagued me as I listened and learned and started to decipher the letters before me. As my eyes traced the graceful flow of an "f" I was thinking of how I'd taken so many risks, what was just one more? As they flowed through the snaking "s" I thought of how even trusting the wrong person and letting them disappoint you might be more kind than distrusting someone who deserved your trust.

And by the time my head was hurting with all the letters I had almost talked myself around to trusting Gundt. I paused, looking at him as he read to me, willing him to look up so I could indicate that I was sorry – that I was willing to try things with him.

He looked up and I could see he had something he wanted to say, too.

"Trust is a risk. But not trusting makes you rot away, curling in on yourself. Please, just trust that I am here to help you."

He looked like he wanted to say more, but a cry from above arrested us both.

The bell began to ring furiously, and the ship canted sharply to the side.

"Stay here," Gundt said, lurching to his feet. "I'll see if they need help."

68

He hadn't even reached the door when it was wrenched open, and someone threw something inside. I heard the sound of breaking glass even over the storm and the shouts outside and then a figure burst into the room, sword flashing.

Something wafted into my lungs, choking me. I wretched, gasping for clean air, clawing away from the noxious smell.

On the far side of the cabin, where the glass jar had broken, a puff of colored smoke rose right under Judicus. He fell from his hammock, landing on hands and knees, coughing and gasping.

Our air was tainted. We needed to do something.

I fumbled for my belt knife, but I was already too late. Weight slammed into me, pinning me against the wall. A thick hand rose and clamped around my neck.

Panicked, I fought against his grip as his leather glove bit into my throat. I couldn't breathe. I couldn't see anything but his contorted face filling my vision.

Kazmerev!

Kazmerev!

There was a hollow smacking sound and then the hand left my throat and the man slumped to the ground. Gundt stood over him, sword raised.

"He's wearing a green bracer," Judicus said, gasping.

Gundt nodded, adding, "And that's Kopovain powder that we're smelling. It will render you immobile if you breathe it for too long. Hurry, we need to get out."

Judicus stumbled toward the door, nodding, and Gundt steadied me with an arm and then helped me out of the cabin.

Outside seemed no better, people were yelling and screaming through the corridor. Something cold washed over my feet. Water, I realized. Our ship was taking on water.

As if my thoughts had triggered it, the ship lurched further to the side, knocking me into the wood beam. I stumbled, falling to my knees in the brackish waters. I bit down on my lip and tasted blood. Around us, people were screaming.

"They've barred the hatch!" Someone cried. "The sailors are taking the ship boats!"

There was a hammering sound – or was that my heart? I looked down one passage and then back down the other and all I saw were desperate, wet people. Merchants perhaps. Or lower nobility. A few craftsmen. No children, thank the heavens.

And no sailors.

It was only afternoon. By the time Kazmerev rose again, it would be too late for me.

Strong arms hauled me to my feet, and I turned to see Gundt braced against the passage wall, holding his sword in one fist and me in the other.

"Back in the cabin," he barked, his eyes flicking from one person trapped here with us to the next.

"But the gas," Judicus started to say.

"Back." Gundt's words were harsh, and face tight, and when I followed his gaze, I could see why. People close to one hatch were battering it with any piece of wood or weapon they could find, but the ones nearest us were watching us as if they were about to attack. Shivers ran up and down my spine at the looks on their faces. "Now."

I nodded.

It was like climbing a steep hill to get back into the cabin, but we clawed our way in, coughing on the colored smoke. Gundt pulled the door closed behind us and barred it.

"I should have known he'd follow me here. I should have been ready," he muttered.

"What are you doing?" Judicus gasped.

I caught Gundt's gaze. He'd been my enemy all along, hadn't he? And I'd almost trusted him.

Judicus came to the same conclusion. He reached out and snatched Gundt's left sleeve back. Beneath it was a bracer just like the one worn by the man on the deck. The one I'd glimpsed before when I didn't realize they meant something.

My heart thudded in my ears.

"You're wearing one, too," Judicus said, breathlessly. He gagged, dry heaving, but kept his feet, his eyes burning and fixed on Gundt.

I drew my sword.

"No. Wait," Gundt said, raising his hands.

"You'd better talk fast," Judicus said in a low voice. "The smoke is still rising."

"I can explain everything but not in here." Gundt spoke between his teeth. His eyes had taken on a new fire. "The Kopovain powder will disable you. And then the sea will swallow us up. We need you to break a hole in the hull, rope worker. Now."

"And then?" Judicus said tersely.

"And then we swim for it."

Judicus's head was already shaking. "I'll be so exhausted, I won't be able to swim."

"There's no other way out," Gundt growled.

"I'd be putting our lives in your hands. And you're our enemy. The bracer marks you as such."

I didn't understand that. I tried to catch Judicus' eye.

He paused, remembering me. He never treated me like I was ornamental.

I was coughing on the powder, my fingertips starting to tingle as he quickly spoke.

"It's the sign of the Greensleeves, Sersha. They don't just search for the ai'sletta during the Hunt. They search all the time. He's one of them. But how did he know we were after the ai'sletta? He could only have known if he was told by Lady Lightland. He claimed he was friends with Hallimore and yet he consorts with his killer."

"Wait. What?" Gundt asked, his expression shocked. He cut off, coughing. "We have to go now. We can sort this out later."

"I can't do it," Judicus said with a shaking voice. "I can't put our lives in your hands. I can't trust you. Don't trust him, Sersha."

Yes, my heart was screaming. I won't. We can't.

The ship shifted again and then suddenly there was another scream, and the ground was knocked out from under me, the cabin suddenly filling with water as it rolled so that what used to be up was down and what used to be down was up.

I kicked and thrashed, but I couldn't find my way to the surface.

And then the lantern went out and the cabin was plunged in darkness.

69

"Sersha? Sersha!" Gundt's frantic voice rang out as my head broke the surface of the water and I sucked in a huge breath.

Someone grabbed my collar and plunged me beneath the water again. I sputtered, fighting against their grip. Panic washed over me, dark and inky.

And then something lit everything up and I almost sucked in a lungful of water when the side of the ship burst outward in an explosion of debris and splinters of wood of every size shot outward. My vision seemed to ripple and then a cloud of debris filled the water around us.

My heart raced but my limbs felt frozen, like they didn't know how to move anymore.

A rough tug dragged me forward and then shook me. I followed the motion to see Gundt, pointing upward toward a lighter patch in the dark water, his expression urgent in the fading light of the – magic? – whatever it was that broke up the side of the ship. Gundt pointed a second time and gave me a shove and before hauling a limp, dangling Judicus toward the surface.

I fought the pull of the depths to follow them – my skirts and heavy belt fighting against me. I didn't dare shrug them off. I'd need the flint and map and knife in that belt – especially now that it was all I had.

But they hampered me, fighting my movements.

I just needed to reach the surface. I just needed to breathe.

My hands were numb. I couldn't feel them. My feet, too. It must have been that last breath of the toxic powder clouding my ability to move. I could only swim and hope my limbs were doing what I told them to do – hope they were propelling me through the water.

Hope.

The thought of it ripped through me. I felt like it was leaking away. And I didn't dare lose it. Not even for a second.

My lungs screamed, desperate for air.

And then I reached the surface, relief washing over me with the feeling of air on my face. I gasped in a deep breath.

The surface was not the salvation I had hoped for.

Calls and moans broke through the pounding sound of surf on rocks. Thunder boomed through the air and lightning lit the sky in a bright flash that stood out against the deep darkness of the storm. I thrashed in the water looking for Gundt or Judicus. All I saw was the round hull of the ship rising from the waves like the belly of a dead cow in a marsh.

There was a dull sound coming from it as if someone was hitting the inside of a bowl with a wooden spoon. I didn't want to think about what – or who – was making that sound, trapped in the sinking ship.

I shuddered.

My hands weren't responding the way they should, the fingers clumsy, my motions jerky and spasming. The gas. It had affected me worse than I'd thought.

I needed some safe place to swim for.

Not the rocks ahead. As I watched them, I saw the dark figure of someone swimming. He was lifted by a great wave and smashed against the jagged rocks. He did not surface again.

Not there.

The rocks must have been what sunk our ship. Perhaps, in the heavy rain of the storm, we had lost our way.

There was so much wreckage in the water – too much, I would have thought, for just one ship. Too many people bobbing in the water. As I watched, someone dragged a barrel out from another man, plunging his head beneath the water with a rough hand. Bubbles surfaced, but the dunked man did not and his attacker swam free, barrel beneath him.

I swallowed, treading water against the drag of my clothing. My breath was coming too fast. My feet didn't feel right.

I fell beneath the surface, losing the strength to keep my head up. I needed to fight or I would drown.

Fight, Sersha. Fight!

I pulled twice as hard with my hands, surfacing again, but barely. My legs weren't responding to me. I didn't know if they were kicking at all.

I slipped back under, clawing my way back up to sputter and cough on the surface of the water.

I was going to die like this.

I was going to die and then what would happen to Kazmerev? He would be lost with me. I never had thought to ask him if phoenixes could make more phoenixes or if there were just those that already existed slowly winking out one by one.

It felt oddly important. Or maybe I was so close to death that I couldn't hold on to normal thoughts anymore.

My mind drifted oddly as if it wasn't part of this life and death struggle, as if it had already gone on without me.

This time when I slumped below the water, I didn't have the strength to resurface. I fought and clawed, but the water closed over my head, and I sank below the waves, my hair swirling around me.

Nothing but water and darkness and the end.

The end.

I should have told Gundt about the message. Even if I didn't know if I could trust him. Even if that armband meant he was hunting Mally. I should have told him about the threat to the phoenixes. Because now no one would know. It would die with me. And Kazmerev would die with me thinking I had betrayed him.

I'd failed them all.

Darkness closed over me.

70

Pain seared through my skull and I was dragged back up to the surface. I'd been pulled up by my hair. I felt the pull of fingers in the roots of it, but I couldn't feel my hands. I couldn't turn to look. I could only drink in the sweet, sweet air in between green waves crashing over my head. Drops of rain hit the sea so hard and fast that they splashed back up, soaking me so thoroughly that I could not blink the water out of my eyes fast enough to see.

And then something grabbed me under the arms, and I was hauled up and onto a piece of wreckage into the air above. I clung to it with clumsy arms.

"There you are. Hold on now," Gundt's deep voice was comforting but it sounded tense, like he was barely holding on to sanity, too. "Here now. Hold onto Judicus. You're both too cold."

He gave me a little nudge and I found the rope worker pale as a fish's belly lying across what I thought might be a portion of wall. I huddled against him – grateful for even the scrap of warmth and then I remembered. I couldn't be poisoned for long. Or cold for long. I just had to find the fire within.

"Reach inside and feel the good things Kazmerev has given to you and feel grateful for them," Gundt instructed, strain in his voice as he worked to maneuver our floating wreckage.

Grateful? In the middle of this storm? Was he kidding?

I shook, my teeth chattering and body shuddering in the cold. Beside me, Judicus barely seemed to be breathing. I felt his face. His skin was frigid to the touch.

"It will work, but it's hard to do the first few times. Reach in deep and find it. It will burn off the residual poison and warm you from the cold."

Gundt was using a shattered board to paddle us between floating debris but though his arms strained to fight the water, the surf kept trying to pull us toward the rocks. He shot them worried glances, throwing his whole strength into pulling us away from them. As I watched, debris from our ship's wreck smashed against the rocks, breaking into fragments. No wonder he was working so hard.

I looked around, trying to see how I could help.

"Don't worry about paddling. I'll manage that. Worry about warming the rope worker before we lose him," Gundt called over the waves. "You and I can survive this. He won't without help."

I bit my lip and drew myself carefully towards Judicus. The wreckage was precarious, tipping in every direction. Judicus had tilted his face away from the pouring rain but he wasn't shivering. He was limp and cold as death. I wrapped an arm around him but I didn't know how to be warm enough to help him. I didn't know what I was doing. Was it really so simple as feeling grateful for my phoenix?

"Trust me," Gundt called over the waves.

And that was the thing. I didn't trust him. Him and his mysterious arrival. Him and his convenient offers to teach me. Him and his suspicious armband.

And yet.

He'd pulled me from the water. He was fighting to get us to safety.

And if he really didn't care about us, or if he was our enemy, would he care about Judicus? Would he be urging me to help him? Lady Lightland didn't care about Judicus. She wanted him dead. If Gundt wanted us dead, he wouldn't have had to lift a finger. He could have just sat and watched it happen. We were only alive because he'd saved us.

I had to trust him.

And I thought that maybe I *could* trust him.

I took a deep breath, wrapped my arm tighter around Judicus, cradling his lolling head against my chest, and thought about Kazmerev who loved me and who had given his future to me. I thought about the phoenix who listened to my heart when no one else heard me at all. I thought about his steady kindness and faithfulness.

I squeezed my eyes shut. Warmth filled me until the cold and rain didn't seem to touch my skin and my chattering teeth stilled, my limbs grew lax, and my shivering stopped. I closed my eyes, sinking into the gratitude.

"There you are. He's looking better," Gundt called.

I opened my eyes to see a little color creeping back into Judicus's face.

"Keep it up," Gundt advised. "I'm making for the lee side of the rocks. We should be safer there."

It felt like a long time until he cleared the rocks and let the eddies swirl us to the back side of their dark jagged edges. Something in him seemed relieved to be past them and he relaxed enough to talk.

"Another ship is wrecked here, too," he said. "Look, you can see there's too much wreckage to just be ours. And that mast wedged between those two rocks is not ours, either."

He pointed and I followed his finger to where an unfamiliar banner – torn and waterlogged – hung from the end of a broken mast lodged in the rocks.

"If there are survivors, they'll be on the lee side, too. But brace yourself. We may not find friends there."

I looked at him quizzically. Why go where there might be enemies?

He caught my look and gave me a rueful smile.

"We've no choice in the matter – not really. Until the storm calms, the sea will fight against me and I don't have the strength to fight the surf all the way to shore. I can't even see it in this downpour. Best to shelter as much as we can and wait for nightfall and then we can beg our phoenixes' forgiveness and ask them to fly us to safety."

And by 'we' he must mean me because I was the only one at odds with her phoenix. I would have blushed, but I was already flush from heat as I warmed Judicus.

The heat was clearing the remaining dregs of toxin from my blood. My vision was sharper again. My breathing normal. My hands and feet tingled as the blood returned to them. I could focus.

The rocks still blocked all visibility to the side we were aiming for. We had to swing wide around them to reach that other side.

I craned my neck, trying to glimpse the other side of them, but I couldn't catch a glimpse. We'd round the corner soon and see for ourselves.

I took a long steady breath and watched Gundt for a moment. He'd proven faithful. He'd proven I could trust him. Surprise tasted like a summer berry on my lips.

He noticed me watching him after a moment and offered his own opinion. "You're safe, Sersha. The worst is over."

I wanted to believe him.

I almost did.

And then we rounded the corner of the rocks. Our piece of wreckage slipped so easily into that horseshoe-shaped shore worn into the back of the ship-killing shoal of rocks that I barely noticed who was waiting for us.

When I did, my breath caught in my throat and all the warmth of gratitude fled like a snuffed-out candle.

71

I had expected the wreckage. I had expected the huddled survivors.

I had not expected Lady Lightland.

Or Aunt Danna.

Or Mally.

Lady Lightland held a pair of knives in her hands – one to each of their throats.

My mouth formed an "O" at the same moment that Gundt shoved my head down.

"It's too late to hide!" a tinkling voice rang over the water.

I wiggled out from his grasp and peered over the side of the wreckage.

They had done better than we had. They had four ship's boats – plus two that still held sailors from our boat tying up on the rocks on the other side of the bay.

Fury filled me at the sight of those sailors. They'd abandoned us and taken the boats. The villains! Even now, they could be dragging poor souls from the water into the safety of those solid boats, but instead, they huddled here on the rocks, hoarding them for themselves.

Lady Lightland's soldiers and crew had already lit a fire with driftwood and established a guarded perimeter on the strange, uniformly shaped beach.

There was no sign of the Stryxex. Perhaps they had gone out to bring back help for Lady Lightland. If they could only carry one extra person each, she wouldn't have wanted to abandon everyone else while she went to freedom, would she? Or maybe she did want that, and they'd flat out told her no. Or maybe they hadn't been near when the ship wrecked. Maybe they'd be back at any moment.

I shook my head and focused.

"That woman is dangerous," Gundt whispered to me. "Whatever you do, don't let her know you're a Flame Rider. She'll try to take you, break you down, and make you serve her. You'll lose your phoenix and your life."

Well – that made me trust Gundt more than ever. Any enemy of Lady Lightland's was a friend of mine.

"She'll try to threaten me and Judicus to make you obey. Don't listen to her," Gundt said in a low tone. "I can take care of myself, and Judicus just proved that he can, too."

I glanced over at the leader of my coterie. He didn't look like he could take care of anyone and especially not himself. His magic was more powerful than anything I could imagine, but it left him crippled and ill – missing out on most of life entirely. I didn't envy him for it.

I looked back at the people on the leeward side of the rocks. Mally was glaring at me as if trying to communicate something with her eyes. I couldn't tell what it was – except that she didn't want me there. Only Mally would glare at you for tracking her down and trying to save her after she was kidnapped.

But oddly, Aunt Danna was looking at me the exact same way – not as if we had come to help but as if we were the opposite of help – which I guessed we were. After all, Judicus was unconscious again, and both the phoenixes were gone right now.

I shied away from looking too closely at Aunt Danna. She was bruised and bloody – one of her eyes swollen shut. The sight of it made my breath hitch. Mally – on the other hand – looked unharmed. Her long chestnut curls had been hacked off shorter than her shoulders and she'd been dressed in very fine clothing – embroidered trousers, a brocaded silk jacket with a frothy white shirt under it, tall polished boots, and a flounced cape.

I looked from her to Gundt and he grunted.

"They don't look very happy to see us, do they, girl? But we have no choice. We can't make it to land, and we can't stay on this wreckage. It's barely holding together now. One good wave will tip it and we might lose Judicus. Better to try to talk our way in with these people and those poor captives of theirs, until nightfall. Even if they don't like us here, I doubt they'll cut us down."

I lifted an eyebrow. *Talk* our way? I wouldn't be doing that.

He frowned at me and then cursed. "I'll do the talking. And hopefully, you're wrong. Hopefully, they won't try to kill us, because I don't think I can win in a fight against all of them."

He'd misread my expression. It wasn't that I was worried we would lose in a fight – it was that I suddenly had twice as much to lose.

I felt my other eyebrow rising, though. He thought he could take some of these guards in a fight. He patted his sword – still hanging on his belt despite everything, with the kind of calm assurance of someone who knew how to use it. That was interesting. When I'd envisioned Flame Riders, I'd envisioned people like me who needed a phoenix to escape who they were – whose big hearts were the biggest treasure they had. I hadn't envisioned tough warriors with their wet jackets straining around muscled shoulders and arms. If I'd been twenty years older, I might have even found that quite attractive. Instead, I just found it puzzling.

The more I saw of Gundt, the more it puzzled me that he was out here and with me. Shouldn't he be off doing something a bit more exalted or important?

But I had no time to dwell on that. Not with Aunt Danna and Mally threatened like that. I watched Gundt speculatively. Was there a way I could tell him that we needed to save them? That they were my relatives? My mind rushed over the signs we'd practiced today. They'd been practical, useful signs about eating and inns and rivers running. Nothing that said, "Can you risk your life to save my relatives, please?"

We'd almost reached the little beach. I kept glancing nervously to Aunt Danna and Mally. They hadn't moved since we arrived. And Lady Lightland's blades were very close to the delicate skin of their throats.

"It's too late to fight, if that's what you're thinking," Lady Lightland's voice called out across the remaining distance. "One false move and someone gets a second smile."

Gundt growled but said nothing until his boots hit the rocky shore. Then he and I scrambled off the wreckage, hauling Judicus with us. I hated doing that. It put him in danger, too. Even if the wreckage was close to sinking, it was safer than a beach with Lady Lightland on it.

"Cassanetta," Gundt said as he set Judicus down on a dry patch of rock.

He knew her by her given name. My breath hitched in my throat.

"Still running with the Greensleeves?" she asked. Which meant she knew him better than we did. A stab of cold shot through me that had nothing to do with the chill waves.

"Faithful in life. Faithful in honor," he said as if it was a proper response to that comment.

"I hear that not all are faithful," she said with a taunting lilt in her voice, cocking her head to one side. "I heard there was a little philosophical matter that morphed into something wrong and split up that secret society of yours."

Was that why one of them had attacked us?

"And where did you hear that?" Gundt asked carefully. He wasn't moving toward her except to put his body between us and her. Not friends, then.

"From the Greensleeve I hired to kill you back in Halvered." She sniffed. "He wasn't worth my wasted gold, it seems."

That explained the man with the powder attack!

"Now why would you do such a cruel thing, Cassanetta?" Gundt said. I reached for his sleeve and tugged on it. Why did he know her by her first name? Why was he talking to her like this?

He shrugged off my hand and my heart froze. Was he here to sell us out after all? Had he saved us from the waves only to sell us to her? You didn't have to like a person to profit from them. Just because she'd ordered him killed, that didn't make me safe.

"You didn't think that I'd spare you, did you Gundt? Why would you think such a thing?" she taunted. "Is it because you're my brother?"

72

Gundt roared, startling me. I fell back, clutching at Judicus as the other Flame Rider hurtled forward, drawing his sword. Lady Lightland's guards raced to intercept him and the sound of steel on steel rang through the air.

What was he thinking? He was going to get himself killed. There were too many of them for him to fight himself. Eight ... nine ... ten. I gave up counting and I drew my own weapon, standing over Judicus, ready to defend him if I needed to. But I wasn't going to rush into battle – not only because I wasn't skilled enough to help but also because Lady Lightland still had her blades against the throats of my cousin and aunt.

Lady Lightland. Gundt's sister.

Or so she claimed.

I shook my head. There was too much to take in. Too much to absorb. I felt overwhelmed.

I looked toward the horizon, but I saw no hint of how far off sunset was and in the insanity of the last few hours, I had lost track of time. It should be afternoon. Shouldn't it?

Gundt's blade rang off the swords of the guards and I bit down on my lip, wishing I could call out to him to stop. There were too many of them. He was going to die like this and for what?

I bit my lip, frustrated.

"Go ahead. Get some of that anger out, Gundt," Lady Lightland called. "But if you get close to the captives. I'll just kill them. Look."

To my horror, her blade at Aunt Danna's throat flicked up and cut a line across her cheek. Aunt Danna hissed, eyes bright and furious. And that was when Mally reacted.

"You promised you wouldn't. You promised that if I found the blessing, then you wouldn't." Her words were bold, chin thrust out despite the knife at her throat.

The sound of swords cut off as Gundt withdrew. He stood in a ring of guards, chest heaving. No one was dead. One man clutched a forearm, and another limped slightly. He had a slash on one leg but he didn't seem to be noticing. His eyes were on Mally as if he'd only just noticed her.

"The blessing?" he asked in a breathless tone, his eyes wild.

Lady Lightland smiled. "See? Even my much older, much more foolish brother has heard of the blessing. Even he knows what you can become, Ai'sletta."

Gundt gasped. Down the beach, the sailors who had heard were making signs of reverence.

Mally's secret was out.

"Now, look within my precious, and find that blessing," Lady Lightland purred. "Surely now, with a mad man attacking your guards, with your mother's very life in the balance, surely now you can find it."

"I don't even know what it's supposed to be," Mally said, her lip trembling. Her show of aggression melted into vulnerability and I felt a stab of fear shoot through my leg. Not good. If Mally was letting go of her armor then things were really bad.

I took a careful step to the side, hoping to edge nearer. Something caught my ankle and I glanced down to see it was Judicus' hand. He looked up at me and winked and then went limp again.

How long had he been faking for? That was good, right? He was a secret weapon just waiting for the right time – if he still had the strength to do anything at all.

"You don't mean that *she's* the ai'sletta?" Gundt asked and there was something about his voice that drew every eye to him. His face was limned in reverence and the moment that his sister said, "Yes," he dropped to his knees, sword raised in both hands as if he were offering it to Mally.

Darkness and madness! The fool. Frustration roiled through me. If he really cared about her, he should be trying to free her, not making empty gestures of reverence.

Furious, I took a step forward.

No reverence for me.

I knew exactly what Mally was – a young woman with a knife at her mother's throat. And I knew what she wasn't – invulnerable.

I strode to where he knelt before anyone had time to react. The guards surrounding him were gaping while Lady Lightland laughed, her eyes only for her brother. Which left none to watch me.

"See, Ai'sletta?" Lady Lightland said in a tinkling voice. "See? You really can use it. What are the odds that my brother – sworn to find the ai'sletta and protect her with his life – oh yes, that's what his ridiculous little club does, though they've never actually managed it – what are the odds that he would stumble upon you here? What are the odds that his ship would break up right behind yours?"

I snatched his sword from his hands. I would have grabbed his collar and hauled him up, but my hands were too full of sword and knife, so I planted a light kick on his rear, forcing him to stand to avoid another blow. He spun in fury and gaped when he saw it was me. Angrily, I shoved the sword back in his hands.

"Oh, it's you. The mute," Lady Lightland said in a bored tone, noticing me for the first time. "And now you're defending my useless brother like you keep defending that tarnished rope worker, Judicus Franzer Irault. Do you really think your cousin wants to go back to your pokey little village? Tell her, Ai'sletta."

"I don't want to go back," Mally said, meeting my eyes savagely.

But I couldn't tell if she meant she wanted to stay with Lady Lightland, or if she was just trying to keep me out of trouble and either way, this was ridiculous. Like I would leave her here. Like I would just walk away. The desperate, meaningful looks my Aunt Danna kept shooting at me told me that she, at least, needed me to get Mally free from here. She, at least, was still counting on me.

I hadn't been paying attention to the sailors until now. I'd been too focused on my family and my friends and the woman who I figured I could call my enemy without any fear of being proven wrong. They had arranged themselves in a rough knot, leaving Lady Lightland and her people between them and us. But now, one of them spoke.

"What is the ai'sletta supposed to do, then? What's this blessing she has? Can she get us to safety?"

"Luck," Lady Lightland said. "She can turn the tides just by being there."

And suddenly, everything started to make sense.

73

That's why she was so valuable to anyone who wanted to use her to make an empire. Imagine having Lady Luck herself there to turn the tides of your battle? And we'd already seen the results, hadn't we? Why else would our ship have crashed in the same place as hers? Why else would I have pulled Judicus up from death's door again and again when she was near? Why else would her mother have been stolen and brought to her by the very people who held her captive? Why else had raiders come to snatch her only to peacefully leave when she was on her way?

But it worked the other way, too, didn't it? For her boat had smashed right into another boat in the darkness – and what were the chances of that? Judicus had come to her village just in time for Lady Lightland to send her raiders there. Not every example of her luck turning things was for the best, was it?

Maybe our arrival right now was another thing she would place on the bad side of the scales. Maybe she was mentally cursing us for being here at all.

"And you're going to give her to the Grand Hadri so he can conquer the world?" Gundt asked in a quiet voice – too quiet, as if he were testing his sister. "And then you can be the Ducana of Lightland with his blessing?"

"Perhaps," Lady Lightland said with a closed-lipped smile and a glance over her shoulder at the watching sailors. Or perhaps not."

"I think ... not," Gundt said and lunged toward his sister. He was blocked before he could get close, the guards swarming him, but he was holding his own with the blade, knocking them back like this was a brawl in the common room with a few boys too deep in their cups, not a real fight at all.

I had to put my own blade up to block an accidental blow, but they weren't trying to attack me – thank goodness. I edged around them, trying to get toward Mally. It was harder to find a clear place than I'd hoped. The beach was narrow and rocky with only a small strip of gravel surrounding the towering center rock.

It looked almost like a shrine – but who would set a shrine in the middle of the sea?

Lady Lightland looked side to side, worried suddenly, and Mally shut her eyes, screwing up her face in concentration.

She must have been trying to find that luck inside her – that blessing – but some people make their own luck – like Aunt Danna.

I'd been wondering why Aunt Danna was so quiet. She wasn't one to keep her thoughts to herself.

A look of concentration filled her face and I realized that in her bound hands, she held a dagger. She must have slipped it from Lady Lightland's belt during all this distraction. She had it halfway up before Lady Lightland noticed. Aunt Danna plunged the knife toward her at the same moment that Lady Lightland screamed.

And then everything was happening at once.

Mally stumbled backward, Lady Lightland's knife no longer at her throat. She fell back against the rocks in a strange nook there that almost looked carved, her hands splayed against the rocks.

Aunt Danna's lunge sent her dagger slashing along Lady Lightland's side at the same time that the other girl roared, slicing out with her dagger and slitting my aunt's throat.

A silent scream tore through me and I rushed forward, dodging behind a grasping guard.

My aunt slumped to the ground and Lady Lightland fell to one knee.

Not Aunt Danna! No!

Aunt Danna was a rock. A living piece of immovable certainty. She couldn't be gone. She couldn't.

I was almost upon her when I was hit from the side and knocked off my feet. One of her guards had noticed me.

I was only seeing sand and sky and then I hit the earth hard and lost my knife. It took me a moment to blink back the pain and scan the area around me. Screams and grunts shattered the air.

My ribs ached and dark spots danced across my vision, but I forced myself to my knees. I had to get to my cousin. I wasn't even sure why, but I knew somehow that if I didn't get to her, we'd lose her again.

I found my feet at the same moment that Lady Lightland did the same. Her eyes were wide as she looked over my shoulder and then my eyes widened, too. Behind her, the sailors stood frozen in the act of charging forward. Darkness wrapped around them in wide ropes.

Judicus!

I spun and saw Gundt still battling Lady Lightland's guards, but now half of them were wrapped up, too. Past them, on that last little lip of beach, Judicus stood, swaying, face pale, hands held up as he worked his ropes.

"Judicus Franzer Irault," Lady Lightland spat. "Always in the exact place I don't want you to be."

"Cassanetta," he acknowledged. But he said nothing more. He sounded like he couldn't – like he was barely holding on as it was.

"You think you've won, don't you?" Cassnetta said, and she was laughing, I realized. Slashed along the side, bleeding, her people tangled up in magic, and she was laughing. "That's adorable."

I took a stumbling step toward Mally and then my eyes went wide.

She was still and drained of color, looking at the body of her dead mother, her eyes glazed with tears and her breath coming far too fast. But that wasn't what shocked me. That was normal. My own eyes were wet with unshed tears.

What wasn't normal was that her fingers were sunk into the rock, into perfectly circular cuts that had slid into the rock like a pushed door. I squinted and realized they were encircled by some kind of faded carving – and so was the alcove she was standing. How many hundreds of years – thousands of years? – must that rock have been beaten at by tides and seas to be so worn I could hardly see the bas relief anymore?

What luck would it take for your hands to accidentally find those exact spots?

I hurried to Mally's side and she looked up at me, mouth working but no words came out. I reached for her at the same moment that Lady Lightland spoke.

"You've underestimated the ai'sletta. And you've underestimated me. Do you really think we crashed on these rocks by accident?"

And then the ground began to shake beneath us.

74

"Do you really think I wasn't orchestrating this from the beginning?" Lady Lightland asked as the ground continued to shake.

I fell to my knees, hitting the sand. It gritted against my knees and for a moment I lost track of everything and then the sound of water flowing surprised me. I clambered to my feet, fighting my sodden dress and feeling my way up the worn rock beside Mally. She was sobbing, keening like a wounded animal.

I hadn't noticed when the rain stopped – though it had. It was still windy and gloomy enough not to make it obvious that the deluge had passed. And the sound I was hearing was not the constant battering of waves. It sounded like a waterfall, like water pouring off of something.

I looked out to sea – confused and then gasped.

Our island was rising. Water flowed off the edge of the rock. Little pebbles and shale from the beach rained down with it and as I watched, Judicus scrambled back from the broken edge, his ungainly long limbs pinwheeling as he fought for solid rock.

He found it, clinging to the vertical side of the dark stone.

My heart froze within me.

What was happening?

Someone screamed – and I realized it was one of the guards falling off the edge and then another. I couldn't take it all in, it was happening so fast. Judicus fought for a handhold. Gundt fought a guard as they both tried to stand on one narrow spit of rock. I reached for Mally – desperate not to lose her, too – but she snatched her hand back, unwilling to let me touch her.

My heart was in my throat. I gripped the rock nearby, breath speeding as my eyes flicked from face to face. The only face I couldn't look at – wouldn't look at – was Aunt Danna's though I caught a single look at her glassy eyes and bile rose in my throat.

Another scream as someone failed to find purchase. Not a sailor. They were still held in place by Judicus's ropes.

I pressed my back firmly against the rock.

What now?

Lady Lightland balanced on the edge of the hard stone on light feet, her golden hair streaming around her, her arms lifted.

Tiny stones cascaded from around her perch but she didn't so much as blink at them.

"Ai'sletta, I told you that you would work marvels. And all it will take is a little sacrifice. A little determination."

Did she not realize she had killed Mally's mother? That my aunt still lay at her feet? I didn't let myself think about how it had happened. Wouldn't allow myself to think about my cousins – motherless now. About myself, no longer with access to someone who had known and loved my parents. I fought down a lump in my throat.

And then I saw them.

They rose out of the sea, looking as if they had been formed of stone. Water poured off every crack and ripple of their forms. They looked like monsters of the sea, shaped by the hand of a giant carver and set to life by magic. But whoever had carved these stone figures had taken liberties. Wide mouths filled half their forms and were layered with stone teeth. Whorls and ripples replaced real legs or fins and tiny eyes were nothing more than slits.

What was this madness? My eyes were so wide they couldn't open any more than they already were. A gasp was stuck in my throat.

There were so many more than I could easily count. They marched steadily from the sea.

But all Mally had done was touch two places in the wall. That was all! She couldn't have known this would happen.

"The Creatures of Sydonon," Gundt gasped. "I thought they were legend."

"Are they legend?" his sister asked, "Are they lost to us? Or did it only require a little luck brought to the ancient altar of Sydonon to raise them once more from the depths?"

Without warning, one of her men attacked Gundt and all questions were lost to his grunts as he fought the enemy back. Were her guards crazy? Why bother to fight now? When we were on the backs of stone creatures?

I looked out over their rocky backs, my eyes growing wider and wider and then – just a little further out where the waves beat white lines on the horizon, there was something else.

Sails, I thought. Sails glowing a light pink color against the darkened sky.

Who in the world could that be? For just a moment, I wondered if it could be someone coming to save us. And then I remembered there had been no one to save us any other time. Why would there be someone now?

Aunt Danna had wanted to save Mally. And look what had happened to her!

There was no one to fight for us except ourselves.

I was still frowning when the island shuddered again and then began to rock side to side, almost like a tray set on the back of a horse.

There was a scrabbling sound and then Judicus made a low, panicked sound. I saw as his fingers began to slip and I didn't even think. I ran along the wobbling stone, skidding when I fell and skinned my knee, but I was up again, stumbling forward when the rock leaned a second time.

I caught his flailing hand as he started to tumble down the rock, my other hand grabbing a stony outcropping. The rock bit into my hand. Pain flashed through me. I couldn't hold on. I couldn't.

Screams rang out behind me, but I couldn't turn to look. Every scrap of my energy was spent in holding Judicus in place.

"I lost them," he gasped, a look of horror on his face. "All those people."

I wanted to scream to him not to talk, just to climb. But I couldn't. I wouldn't have been able to even if I wasn't voiceless because it took all my energy to hold him and even then, he was slipping.

Another wave of screams that faded out as if someone had ... don't think of it, Sersha. Don't.

Just hold on, Sersha.

I couldn't do it.

I heard Judicus groan but now my eyes were shut, and I couldn't watch. I couldn't breathe.

Another scream and a sound like something hitting a solid surface. My belly churned.

How many people had died today? Inside sinking ships, dashed on the rocks, slipping under the sea and now, falling to their deaths? How many?

I didn't want to lose Judicus, too.

His hand slipped. I strained to hold him tighter, my other arm and feet scrambling to find better leverage to hold him up.

I gasped, tears blurring my sight. There was nothing else to hold on to.

I was going to lose him.

I couldn't look.

And then I was stumbling back as someone else grabbed a hold of Judicus and pulled. I landed on my seat, eyes springing open. Gundt fell beside me, panting as he pulled Judicus the rest of the way up the edge.

Gundt.

Who we hadn't trusted.

And who just saved our lives.

Again.

And then there was a scream like an angry bird and something that wasn't quite darkness but was definitely not light descended, talons outstretched, beak opened in a scream.

75

No, no, no! Not again!

They were going to take Mally *again*. I knew it in my bones.

I abandoned Judicus to Gundt and scrambled to my feet, clawing at the rock as I tried to stand before the Stryxex reached us. I felt my nails shredding, but I couldn't look to see how bad they were. I slid and skidded over the rocks, swaying as they fought the movement of the rocks below.

My eyes locked on Mally. I wasn't going to let them snatch her again, not after everything we'd gone through to get her back. She needed me. She needed us. I wasn't armed. I had no way to stop them – and yet I couldn't just stand there powerless again and watch her get swept away.

She glanced at me, wide-eyed, and then her eyes narrowed.

"Leave me be, Sersha. Everyone around me just dies."

She was crying, her body shaking in great heaving sobs. But there was no one between us – no one to stop me from going to her. The sailors had fallen when Judicus did. His magic had failed when his life hung in the balance and he'd lost his grip on them. And Lady Lightland's guards were either stunned or had fallen from the shaking rock.

"Don't come for me," Mally said in a trembling voice.

I shook my head, taking another shaky step. The ground rocked precariously, and I nearly lost my balance. I had to rip my eyes from my cousin to concentrate on what I was doing. My breath sucked in sharply through my lips.

I just had to get to her. I just had to touch her – stop her from doing something mad.

If only I had a voice. If only I could use my words like tools to curl her heart back toward me. If only I could shape them to shape her. But I had no words and the emotion I tried to put into my firm gaze was not enough.

Please, I thought. Please.

She shook her head. "If I'm luck, then I'm bad luck. Look at Mama."

Her voice broke and she doubled over gasping to breathe. She kept looking and looking at her mother's body. She needed family right now. She needed me.

I stumbled another step.

And then something slammed into me, pinning me against the rock. Feathers that weren't feathers brushed against me and I felt like I was choking on something – something that wasn't air, that wafted off the Stryxex like frigid smoke.

I gasped, clawing against it, fighting to see.

The person sitting on the back of the Stryxex was familiar – one of the Dark Riders. As my eyes widened, he yanked a leather cover over his nose and mouth, obscuring his features, and then he barked something in an unfamiliar tongue.

"Take her," Lady Lightland said, shoving a sobbing Mally at him. She seemed shaken. Maybe losing her guard and bringing up some kind of dark magical creatures hadn't been in the plan.

He reached for her, tugging her into place behind him on the back of the dark bird that wasn't a bird.

I reached for her, fighting at the press of the bird, but I was pinned to the rock by his heavy body and all my struggles did was draw a furious squawk from the Stryxex.

"We need to fly," Lady Lightland said. And then she disappeared from view. I couldn't see anything but feathers and sky and Mally squashed up against the Dark Rider. But the other Stryxex must be here to carry Lady Lightland.

Mally twisted to look back at me.

"I'm sorry, Sersha," she said thickly. "But you have to stop chasing after me. It's better this way. I don't want you to die, too."

I lifted my one hand, signing a no, signing that she needed to stay with me, but she just shook her head.

"Don't follow me," she said and then I was smashed harder against the wall and I had to shut my eyes against the flap of feathers.

Pain filled me and added pressure. I couldn't breathe. I couldn't breathe. Feathers pushed and shoved and scraped against my face and arms.

And then suddenly they were gone, and I fell to my knees on the rock, heaving in great breaths.

Hands hauled me upward and I looked into Judicus's wide eyes and open mouth.

He shut it with a click.

"Are you hurt?"

I shook my head. I was covered in cuts and bruises but nothing that should slow us down.

"She's gone," he said, snapping his head toward where the Stryxex were winging their way upward. His expression was just as miserable as I was sure mine was.

A ball formed in my throat. I couldn't seem to swallow.

Gone. Again.

So soon.

"And we can't stay here, either," Gundt said from behind Judicus. He wasn't looking at us. His eyes were looking out in the distance.

I followed his gaze to where the white sails I'd seen before had grown larger.

He pivoted, looking in another direction and I followed his gaze to realize that we were hovering above shallow water now, almost to the shore I hadn't realized was here.

"Shore?" Judicus said in shock. "That should be miles away still."

"An island, I think," Gundt said grimly. But he wasn't looking at the island. He was looking at the stone creatures silently moving across the land. "How do you stop stone?"

He turned to meet my eyes and I shook my head with him. I didn't know. And I'd lost my cousin again – and my aunt. And I just didn't know what to do. I felt my heart curling up tight, forcing out everything but that lonely, solitary sadness.

I'd lost them both.

I'd failed again.

76

"Well, if you can find the animus in it – the life force – that can help," Judicus said calmly. How was he calm right now? "Then it's a matter of disabling it. It would have been helpful if the shrine had remained intact. There might have been inscriptions to explain or something. These creatures are old. Their magic is ancient. I can feel along it if I try, but it ..."

His words trailed off and his brow furrowed as he watched behind us, clearly trying to piece out the puzzle of how to follow these trails of magic. It was as if he hadn't even noticed that the rocks around us were falling apart. The big chunk Lady Lightland had been standing on broke apart from the rest and tumbled free, followed by scattered smaller pieces. The chunk we were on rocked on whatever supported it from underneath.

Aunt Danna fell with the rock. My breath caught in my throat, grief searing across me like fire.

She wouldn't be buried properly. She wouldn't be laid with our ancestors in the old Landsfall graveyard. It wasn't right.

Gundt gripped our shoulders and drew us into the dip in the rock that was like a worn alcove.

"Sunset must be almost here," he murmured, watching the sky.

"... what they are or why they would lift the island up, is anyone's guess. Perhaps it was just above them," Judicus said. He was still puzzling out the mystery of the magic. "Maybe they lifted it by accident."

"Perhaps we should turn our minds to escape," Gundt said pointedly.

Judicus flashed him a look. "What do you think I'm doing? The only way to stop this is to figure it out and cut it off at the source. What might these rock creatures do if they walked over a village like Sersha's?"

I swallowed. I hadn't thought of that. I'd been so focused on trying to get to safety that the thought of what else these magical things might do had simply not occurred to me.

Gundt sighed. "Okay, rope worker. You think of that and we'll try to find a way to escape. "Sersha, can you – "

His words cut off as the sun went down and from our hearts, two phoenixes hatched. I wasn't looking at his. I only had eyes for Kazmerev. He unfurled from my heart in a puff of inky smoke – the scent of it acrid and stinging. I'd never seen him like this.

I could barely see his bright feathers, they were so shrouded in smoke, never seen his bright eyes hold so much fury.

Little hawk.

I wrung my hands.

"No time for that. We need to fly before there's nothing left of this rock," Gundt said. "Come on, Judicus, you can ride with us."

He started to tug at Judicus but the ropeworker shrugged him off, eyes distant as he focused on the faraway problem. Was he still spinning ropes to try to see his way to the heart of these stone creatures' lair? "I'll fly with Sersha and Kazmerev."

Gundt grabbed him again, firmer this time. "Judicus Franzer Irault."

That got Judicus's attention. He froze at the same moment that the rock holding the wall beside us crumbled away, leaving us with pinwheeling arms, struggling to keep our balance as the small fragment of rock we were left standing on jostled and heaved. Whatever bore it was moving at speed and beneath us, the dark world blurred.

"You ride with me," Gundt said firmly, and – still gripping Judicus's arm – he leapt.

Huxabrand unfurled under them, scarlet and bright, her gilded tailfeathers flashing at us as she plunged upward.

And that left Kazmerev and me.

I swallowed. I knew he was angry. I knew I couldn't make it up to him. I knew I was completely guilty. That I should have trusted him and trusted that he knew what he was doing with Gundt and Huxabrand. I swallowed nervously as I fought to keep my footing on the rocking bit of stone.

I didn't want to leave you. I didn't want to leave you with this darkness on your heart. That was the worst of deaths.

The stone heaved and I shifted my weight, trying to keep my balance and then it slipped out from under me and I was tumbling, tumbling toward the ground. I caught a glimpse of the earth beneath. My improved eyesight was a curse. I saw – far too clearly – how the earth below moved and heaved, rippling like the land itself was no more substantial than ocean. There were so many rock creatures swimming across the ground that they looked as if they, too, were a sea.

I was going to fall among them and if the ground did not break me, then their rock feet would trample me into paste.

I just wished I'd had time to make things right with Kazmerev.

And then – soft and light as breathing – warm feathers were under me.

The soles of my feet scraped against moving rock backs as we suddenly shot upward. My heart was in my throat as one of the rock figures leapt like a fish into the air, nearly plucking my brindled phoenix from the air. He was smoke and shining, piercing light and the dusk of death.

And then we were flying, shooting upward, soaring over and beneath us was a wave of moving stone and at its back the very surf of the sea battered it.

I gasped.

You can apologize now.

I was so wrong. I was so sorry.

You can tell me that you don't deserve me now.

I did not deserve him.

You can remember, now, that I pledged my life and loyalty to you and that you did the same to me and that you owe me your confidences. You owe me your trust. You owe me better than what you gave.

I did. I do.

You can trust me.

I do. I trust you with everything.

His feathers flared a bright scarlet as the last of the black smoke disappeared from around him.

Well ... okay then.

There was a long pause and I realized I was crying. I sniffled, blinking back my tears. Forgiveness felt a lot like happiness.

In that case, let's go see how Huxabrand likes being puked all over.

77

But Judicus was not airsick – or if he was, he wasn't showing it. He was riding behind Gundt on Huxabrand, his back to Gundt's. The Flame Rider had tied his belt around the pair of them and it was a good thing since Judicus's concentration was entirely focused on the sea and the rising tide of stone behind us. His brow screwed up in concentration and his mouth twisted into a scowl that almost made his thin face attractive.

Don't go thinking that. Judicus is your coterie leader – not a romantic option.

Well, Huxabrand wasn't a romantic option for him, either.

I have not been entertaining such a thought.

Huxabrand's mental voice jumped in. *Can the two of you not be quiet? The rope worker is trying to stop an ancient army.*

Kazmerev snapped his beak shut as if he'd been speaking aloud and was proving how quiet he could be.

Sure, he wasn't entertaining those thoughts.

I won't validate that with an answer.

I said, silence. Huxabrand was bossier than her human.

I didn't want to be silent. If I was silent, I was going to have to think about Aunt Danna. If I was silent, I was going to have to remember that I'd watched her die and done nothing about it. But what could I have done? If I was silent, I'd have to remember that Mally thought it was her fault.

We needed to go after her. I needed to make sure she didn't have to grieve alone.

But she'd told me not to come. She'd told me not to follow her. And besides, what if Judicus could really stop these creatures? What if he could prevent them from rolling over the countryside, stomping farms and people into nothing. I could only imagine the terror of that. Someone had to prevent it. And I couldn't just abandon him if he could do that. And there was still the matter of the Stryxex trying to wipe all phoenixes off the face of the earth.

Wait. What? Kazmerev said, stunned, but I didn't have time to answer because suddenly Judicus's eyes went wide, and a snarl ripped through his teeth.

I turned to look behind us and saw two things at once – the tide was coming in faster and higher than any tide I'd ever seen, washing up over the rock figures, bubbling and swirling and foaming like a living thing. As I watched it rise, Judicus's groan turned into the crescendo of a keening wail.

And behind that tide the white sails I'd seen were racing toward us and up from their decks, three small figures rose toward us glowing bright in the growing dark of night. I peered at them, eyes squinting, trying to make out what they might be.

Judicus screamed, ripping my thoughts away with the agony in his voice that tore through the air like lightning.

Smoke and flames! Kazmerev cursed.

Try being the one carrying him! Huxabrand's voice dripped with irritation.

Judicus screamed again – long and chilling – and then collapsed against the rope. Gundt swayed on Huxabrand's back, struggling to balance a limp Judicus tied behind him. He twisted, trying to grab the younger man and hold onto him as Huxabrand spiraled downward in a controlled descent. We needed to get to them to help them keep from crashing.

They were going to be trampled on the ground!

Kazmerev raced toward them, chasing them, but as we descended I realized there was a good reason Judicus had fainted. He'd succeeded. Somehow, he had stopped this stone army.

They stood, frozen in mid-stride, as the frothing tide receded.

We landed beside Huxabrand and I leapt from Kazmerev's back to check on Judicus. On every side, we were surrounded by high stone statues. They towered over me, taller than the Hog's Head Inn, their animal faces carved in such exquisite detail that every tooth and whisker was plain to see. I gasped, feeling like a mushroom in a forest of redwoods. But they weren't moving.

We were safe.

Safe.

I helped Gundt untie himself and ran a hand over Judicus's forehead. Had he given too much? Had he killed himself?

"He tries to do too much," Gundt said dryly. "He is not the only one who can fight."

He wasn't, but he was the best. No one else could have stopped those rock creatures. No one else would have even tried.

My heart was in my throat as I looked him over, but he seemed fine – just worn out.

"Check him, quickly," Gundt said in a tight voice.

I settled Judicus in a comfortable position on the grass. We'd have to set up camp here until he could move again. It would feel terrifying to camp among these stone creatures – frozen or not – but I didn't see how we could move him in this state.

"Sersha? Can he be left for now?" Gundt asked, almost as if he'd forgotten that I couldn't explain in detail.

I risked a look up at him, but he wasn't looking at me. His jaw was clenched as he braced himself, staring into the sky. I followed his gaze and gasped.

Flying toward us were three phoenixes. Their Flame Riders were dressed identically and on their faces were identical looks of fury.

"Here comes trouble," Gundt said, pulling me up to stand beside him in front of Judicus. "Whatever you do – don't tell them anything."

He must have been really rattled to have forgotten who he was talking to.

He glanced at me, suddenly realizing what he'd been saying. He rubbed his chin awkwardly.

"Just – just trust me, okay? I have your best interest in mind. I think I've proved that."

I hoped he was telling me the truth – though I'd need an explanation for his sister and this Greensleeves thing. I hoped Judicus would get his energy back quickly and Mally would be safe being used as a good luck charm for Gundt's sister and that Kazmerev and I would be able to find her and save all the phoenixes. I hoped for a lot of things. And hoping always meant you had a lot to lose.

Then hope in me, little hawk. I will never leave you. I will never betray you. Set your heart on that.

And somehow, it was enough.

EPISODE FIVE: GRAND HADRI

SEASON ONE

78

Phoenixes can land in a space that seems impossibly small. If one was a dragon of myth, or even just a real bird the size they were, then they wouldn't fit in the spaces they could squeeze into for a landing. I was pretty sure that was because they were more spiritual than physical. They were only limited by their riders, not by their bodies.

You're no limit, little hawk. You are freedom and warm zephyrs caressing my pinions as I soar.

"Crowd in close to Judicus," Gundt advised me, drawing in beside me so we were almost touching as the strange phoenixes and their riders landed.

Stone statues loomed over us and crowded around us, moonlight spilling around them and I licked my lips nervously as the bright figures descended. I would have thought that there was only one way for a creature of flame to look. I would have been wrong. While Kazmerev was dark purple with scarlet and gold accents – sometimes flaring to a molten crimson, and while Huxabrand had bright pink highlights to her flames, these phoenixes were of their own varieties, too.

There were three of them.

The one who landed first was such a light gold color that it hurt the eyes to look at him. An impressive man with a sharp black coat that spilled to his knees and heavy leather belts crisscrossed over his chest leapt from that phoenix almost as soon as it landed. His skin was weather-worn but his features were almost delicate.

As soon as he'd dismounted, a second phoenix landed. This one was a burnt orange color with little tendrils of black smoke clinging to it. The shaggy man who leapt from its back suited the burnt orange. He lumbered to stand with the other man as they waited for the third phoenix – a ruddy creature of red flames and the occasional orange highlight – to set down beside them. The middle-aged woman who descended from its back was dressed to match the other two. She wore a cylindrical black fur hat on her head that disguised short grey hair.

With the phoenixes burning so brightly behind them and beside them, their faces were half brightly lit, and half cloaked in shadow, giving them an eerie look that left me shifting back and forth nervously.

Gundt reached out and laid a hand on my arm to still me.

I was struck by the silence. Phoenixes are silent almost all the time except when they speak mentally and the occasional audible shriek – though now that I thought about it, that might be no more audible than they were visible. Maybe it was only we who could see them who heard it.

No, we can be heard. Sometimes, we must *be heard.*

I was used to silence. I was always close to silent myself. But this silence was eerie. It felt like the silence of judgment.

No phoenix voices rose in greeting.

No human voices rose to say anything at all.

Gundt crossed his arms over his chest and stood a little straighter and I had the oddest feeling that he was standing like a wall between me and them.

Long moments passed.

And then Judicus groaned from his place on the ground, and I sank into a crouch to look at him. He rolled onto his side, both hands cradling his head. I placed a hand gently on his shoulder and stroked it, hoping to calm him.

"Gundt Hellebar." I was shocked that it was the older woman who spoke first. She hadn't seemed like the leader of this group. "And with a Fledgling, no less."

I could almost hear the capital "F" in "Fledgling." I assumed that was me.

Gundt only grunted.

"Your green sleeves are showing," the delicate man said mockingly.

Gundt didn't even bother to grunt at that.

So. They knew him. And he didn't like them.

But weren't all Flame Riders good? Didn't they have to be? Or their phoenix would disappear?

I felt Kazmerev shift behind me like he wanted to say something. Why didn't he speak?

He shifted again.

To my surprise, it was Huxabrand who spoke.

Flame to flame, I greet you, ancient fires.

What? No song and dance this time? No making the other phoenixes bend to her before she'd greet them?

I felt Kazmerev shift again, and this time I felt the edge of humor from him – but he was holding himself back, purposefully silent before these other phoenixes. I didn't like that. I wasn't used to him being near me but not speaking to me. I reached for him with my heart and felt his reassurance. And then he shifted to move so that he was close enough that his hot feathers touched me. I sighed at the feeling. He wasn't ignoring me. He wasn't leaving me. He was silent for another reason.

There was a long pause. All the humans were motionless as if they were about to draw weapons and then, when I thought Gundt would explode if he didn't take a breath, the new phoenixes answered, three voices speaking in unison.

Flame to flame, I greet you, ancient fires.

Kazmerev replied so quickly that they were barely finished before he began.

Flame to flame, I greet you, ancient fires.

The humans around me relaxed. The delicate one ran a hand over his face as if great disaster had just been averted.

"We all get to live another day," he laughed but there was no humor in his laugh.

I looked from one to another, confused.

Remind me to tell you later what happens if phoenixes refuse to greet each other, Kazmerev murmured in my mind.

They didn't like being snubbed? But Huxabrand had snubbed Kazmerev and he hadn't minded.

He didn't answer me, clearly not wanting the others to hear his answer, but for a moment, his flame went a brighter red as if he were blushing.

"Well, if we aren't going to kill each other, then I suppose we ought to offer up the message we were sent with," the bulky man said, peering around him at the statue. "Though it hardly seems as potent after seeing this stone army. Are you waging war on the worlds of men now, Gundt the Fatherless?"

"Are you looking to find yourself in a heap wondering what hit you, Refrento?" Gundt replied and while it sounded affable and as if they were joking, there was an edge under their words.

"We're here for Captain Rackham," the older woman said.

And just like that, everyone was silent again.

79

Who was Captain Rackham?

I don't know, Kazmerev murmured – the first thing he'd been willing to say to me. That was good. Maybe he'd answer more questions.

Who were these Flame Riders?

No other answer.

I shook my head. I was the only one who didn't know what was happening and yet Kazmerev couldn't fill me in without telling these new phoenixes everything. For the first time since meeting him, I felt voiceless again.

He shifted uncomfortably, his feathers going darker and his flame lowering. Maybe he felt bad about that. I felt bad, too.

"The captain invites you to meet him on his ship," Refrento said.

The word "invites" didn't sound like an invitation.

"And if we refuse?" Gundt asked, waiting. There was tension in every line of his body."

The woman barked a laugh. "Have we miscommunicated? Do you not know who the captain is?"

"Of course, he does," Refrento said. He walked to the side, examining one of the stone creatures frozen in place. His hands ran over it, as if memorizing its shape. I shuddered. Those had been alive and moving only minutes ago. "And he knows this ancient magic was seen alive and crawling across the ground. Were you involved in the raising of it, Gundt Hellebar?"

"No. It was the ropeworker who expended himself stopping this. Shouldn't *Captain Rackham,*" he said the name as if it was a joke, "have a better way of expressing his gratitude for that than detaining us?"

"If you know he should be grateful then you know who he is," the grey-haired woman said. "And you know this isn't just an invitation. Bring your rope worker. We leave. Now."

To my surprise, Gundt didn't argue. He merely grunted and leaned down beside me.

"I can take Judicus."

I shook my head. It was better if he was with me and Kazmerev. Especially if anyone attacked us. Gundt could fight back. I couldn't.

"It will be okay," he whispered, though he looked pale. "Trust me. I'll explain everything as soon as I can. Do you believe me?"

I bit my lip. But after everything that had just happened, how could I refuse him? I nodded my head.

"We'll get your cousin back and keep her safe," he said, and it sounded like a vow. "And I will not fail you as your Guarding Flame."

I nodded again, blinking back tears as I looked back the way we came toward wherever my Aunt Danna's body had fallen.

"We'll come back and set a marker for your aunt," he said, following my gaze. "And I will keep you safe until we can do all those things. You have my word."

I nodded again and offered a tremulous smile.

"Would you stop babying that Fledgling and get moving?" the delicately featured man said from the back of his phoenix.

Gundt looked over his shoulder for long enough to growl – actually growl like a wolf – and then he faced me again, all hints of hostility fading into gentleness like he was afraid I'd fall apart if he dealt with me too harshly. Maybe I would. I felt like I was barely hanging on after the shipwreck, and then my aunt's murder, and then an army of stone figures that had somehow been stopped.

"Here, Kazmerev," he said, addressing my phoenix. "Let's load Judicus onto your back. Sersha wants you to carry him."

Kazmerev shifted silently but lowered his back enough for Gundt to sling Judicus over it, belly down.

I hopped up behind him and held on to both Judicus and Kazmerev, burying my fingers into my now silent phoenix's feathers and trying not to be too afraid of whatever this captain we were flying toward would be like. He sounded like a thug. He sounded like one of the raiders.

Kazmerev blazed just a little brighter as if he was trying to protect us with his heat and light, trying to reassure us that he was still burning bright and hot.

"Ready?" the female Flame Rider asked with a wry twist to her mouth.

"Ready enough," Gundt agreed. "Any reason you and the captain are so far north, Dalissa Fenwan?"

She smiled mysteriously. "That's for us to know and for you to find out, Gundt Hellebar."

They were already mounting their own phoenixes and I drew in a long breath. I wasn't ready to leap into another adventure again – but once again, I had no choice.

Our phoenixes leapt into the air.

Kazmerev flew much slower with Judicus on his back, letting his wing tips almost touch the backs of the stone figures and then the treetops and then the bare earth, he was so keen to keep us safe. After a moment, the rest of them outpaced us. Gundt flew at a pace with them, his head turning to keep an eye on us every few minutes.

One more moment, Kazmerev said.

I waited for whatever he was waiting for and I clung to Judicus as I did. One of his hands reached and clutched mine. To my surprise, I felt a small tingling. I held on anyway. What was tingling compared to armies of stone and earth and our enemies bringing us back to a ship with them?

Ahh, Kazmerev said finally. The rest had outdistanced us, though we were still flying steadily behind them. *Now I need to talk and talk quickly while they're out of range.*

There was a range?

It's like talking. They can hear the murmur of my voice, but not the actual words. If we get closer, they will hear me again.

That made sense.

I know these phoenixes by reputation. They are very honored and renowned. Yxella, Utterbexen, Frissei. They would set me ablaze if they thought I stepped wrong.

Wasn't he always ablaze?

Not in the way they would make me.

What was all that with the greeting?

If they had refused to greet us in return it would be a challenge. From Huxibrand it was a challenge to do better – a flirtatious challenge if you will. Good-humored, perhaps a little dangerous, but only to my reputation and sense of merit. She would not have harmed me. But with these phoenixes, had they not returned our greeting, it would have been a fight to the death right then and there.

But I thought phoenixes were good!

Of course we are. But good people can disagree about what good means. And both sides would have thought we were fighting for what is right. The only difference is that you and I would have been right and they would have been horribly mistaken.

I shivered. I hadn't realized how important that greeting was. We could all be dead.

I will never let anyone harm you, little hawk. I will set the world ablaze to keep you safe if I must.

I smiled at the warmth he sent through our mental link. It seemed to feed something inside me, making me stronger, washing away my exhaustion and fear.

But back to the situation at hand, I have heard of these riders. Refrento was military before he birthed a phoenix from his heart. An officer. Dalissa is a renowned advisor to the Grand Hadri. The third is Duche Olliman. A noble. Of high reputation as being an effective leader of his people and lands. I did not know he was a Flame Rider. When last I saw Frissei she was born of the heart of a young warrior from the south. I mourn her warrior's passing.

So, they were important people. Famous, even. But what did that have to do with us and who was this Captain Rackham?

Captain Rackham is also well known for being the greatest fighter of pirates in all of Calicarn. They say that when he raises his sails the ladies swoon and those with black hearts tremble.

I didn't do much swooning. I left that to Judicus. Who was still making my fingers tingle.

Last time Captain Rackham sailed, he started a war with the Oolibern Islands. In the end, Calicarn won that battle and took over the Oolibern trade routes.

That sounded dangerous. Didn't he get in trouble if he went around starting wars?

It's hard to get in trouble when you rule the nation.

What?

Captain Rackham is the not-so-secret alternate identity of the Grand Hadri.

I felt my mouth fall open.

80

Shh now, we're about to arrive, Kazmerev said, already circling to come around the three red-sailed ships.

They bucked over the dark waves, curves gleaming in the moonlight, lanterns lit on the masts and strung along crisscrossing lines to light the decks. Even with my superior vision, it was hard to pick out all the sailors at work. The ships were so large that they made the one we'd sailed on look like a local dory.

I clenched my jaw as we rejoined the other phoenixes, circling a second time. I was feeling very tired. Perhaps surviving a shipwreck, battling for our lives, and then barely managing to flee a crumbling island had taken a lot out of me. I could really use a warm bed. And a blanket. Yes, I'd like that.

Below us, a bell rang. Was that because we'd been seen?

Our escort is declaring that we have arrived, Kazmerev said carefully. Which meant those three phoenixes must be visible and they could hear him again.

Escort? The phoenix voice I heard sounded a bit high-strung. *Insolence! But what do you expect from backwater loners? You've forgotten your dignity.*

Rude. I didn't like these new phoenixes at all.

I probably would have said something but at that moment Judicus gave a long, death-like gasp and I scrambled to check on him. To my shock, he was waking up, scrambling up from his belly to sit in front of me.

"I'm up, I'm up," he said in a dazed manner.

Worried, I set a hand on his forehead. No fever. He wasn't ill. But how had he recovered so quickly?

"Thank you for the energy you've lent me, Sersha," he said gravely and at my puzzled look he amended, "Oh, I'm so sorry, I thought you'd given that to me intentionally, but was it an accident?"

I nodded.

"Oh. Oh dear. Well, if you want to avoid giving me energy when I'm recovering, don't touch my bare skin. My ropes will draw whatever they can from you until I awaken."

That sounded awfully handy. For him. But then again, I had been holding his hand while he slept – taking an intimacy he hadn't realized he was offering so it was only reasonable that he had taken something in return.

"Are we flying again?"

Tell him to keep it down, Kazmerev murmured.

I tapped Judicus's shoulder and put a finger to my lips.

"Oh, sweet land and seas, that's not another ship, is it?" Judicus whispered.

I pulled a face and nodded.

The first of the phoenixes was descending. Utterbexen – the smoky one.

"When we reach land again, I would like to request that no one drag me onto any more ships for the foreseeable future," he moaned.

Which I thought was reasonable to request after the last time.

Utterbexen landed and then with a puff he was gone, leaving his rider on the deck. What in the ... was he hurt?

There isn't room for him on the deck. He's retreated to his manifestor's heart, Kazmerev explained.

They could do that? Shock shot through me. That didn't seem kind. He was a living thing. He shouldn't be imprisoned. Not in someone's heart or anywhere else.

Kazmerev said nothing but I could almost feel his agreement in the air between us.

Quiet, children, the high-strung voice said again.

I was really starting not to like that phoenix.

The light gold phoenix descended and landed sharply on the deck, vanishing just like the other had. I shook my head.

Nope. I wasn't happy with that. Kazmerev had better not descend on me like that.

To my surprise, it was Gundt who descended next. Huxabrand landed sharply on the deck, but unlike the others, she waited for Gundt to dismount and then shot back up into the air to circle over the ship.

What terrible manners! The phoenix I didn't like said. *Well, down you go, Kazmerev. And try not to act like you were born yesterday.*

I was born only hours ago.

I could almost feel the other phoenix's eye roll. I definitely heard Huxabrand's disguised snicker.

Yes, that's very literal of you.

But despite her cranky words, we were descending. And no, I didn't like this. I didn't want to go down there. Maybe we should just stay in the air.

And do what? Wait until I die, and you fall into the sea?

"Wait. Oh, no, wait. I don't like this," Judicus voiced my worries aloud. "That banner is Captain Rackham's!"

But we were already falling from the sky toward the deck.

"No. No. I really don't recommend –"

Our feet hit the deck and I tumbled off of Kazmerev awkwardly with Judicus right behind. Kazmerev's great dark eye winked at me and then he shot back up into the sky.

I felt bereft without him. And utterly vulnerable even though Gundt moved to shield me almost immediately.

We were standing on the wooden planking of a ship, the deck rolling and heaving under our feet in a way that made me ill and must be utterly devastating to Judicus. I could smell the sea and the left-over burnt smell of phoenixes and I wished it was just the fire and sulfur that I smelled and none of the sea because I was so sick of the ocean and the disasters we kept falling into on its dark, heaving breast.

"I wish I was still unconscious," Judicus said thickly.

In front of us, arrayed in a curving line, were six men in long green coats which were embroidered heavily with gold. They wore cylindrical hats like Dalissa and curved swords were strapped at the waist while a long, carved staff was held by each of them.

There was a door set in the deck between them and as Dalissa landed beside us, the door opened, and a grim-looking man in the same bottle-green uniform ducked on his way out of it.

"Captain Rackham will see you now," he said in a deep, pitiless voice. And it sounded more like a death sentence than an invitation.

I felt Judicus flinch beside me. What would make him flinch? I'd watched him face down so many enemies without blinking an eye, but a *meeting* worried him that much?

I bit my lip as Dalissa Fenwen led the way through the hatch, the other two phoenix riders closing in behind us as if to show that if we didn't follow, we'd be made to follow.

Don't worry, little hawk. I'm right here. And I will burn that ship to cinders – Grand Hadri or no Grand Hadri – if you are put in danger.

It was a comforting thought.

81

Though the ship was large, even large ships don't have large cabins. This one was packed with people and one end of it was filled with a low desk. Behind the desk, a man sat, leaning so far over the desk that I almost thought his body might be absorbing it. He was a hulking brute of a man – so dominant, so powerful, that in his presence I barely noticed the guards clustered to either side of him or the ornate scrollwork in the wooden paneling and around the circular window behind his back.

Small alcoves held treasures and icons, and someone had gone to the trouble of setting a thick woven rug in front of the desk. Its crimson and purple wool shocked the eyes but also suggested that the owner thought nothing too grand was enough.

The Flame Riders who had brought us made dramatic bows and quickly moved to the sides of the low-ceilinged cabin and to my surprise, the captain flicked his fingers in annoyance.

"Is this the court of Briccatore that I must endure constant formality?"

I was horrified when his eyes settled on me. They narrowed speculatively.

Perhaps I ought to bow? But he wasn't my sovereign. Or did women curtsy? Dalissa had not curtseyed and Judicus did not bow, though Gundt made a cursory attempt at one.

"I'm a ship's captain, not a Lord," the captain said with a twinkle in his eye as if he took pleasure in pretending he was a captain while everyone else knew he was a king.

I didn't like games like that. This was a situation where Mally would be more comfortable. She probably would have winked.

"There are rumors that a young woman is shaking up the north, bringing raiders to our shores, and snatching people away in the night. Is this the girl?" he asked, eyes still fixed on me and behind their glittering brightness, there was masked violence.

He thought I was Lady Lightland.

"Nothing could be further from the truth ... Captain," Gundt said, adopting the story they were playing at.

"Oh, indeed," the captain said, with a smirk. "Is that your story, illegitimate son of the Lady Lightland?"

I felt my brow crinkling.

"The first Lady Lightland," Judicus whispered to me. "The mother, not the sister."

That's why the others kept insulting him, then. As if a man could help his birth! We did nothing to bring ourselves into this world and had no say in who our babyhoods were entrusted to.

My story," Gundt said with a twist to his lips, "such as it is, involves House Lightland – but it involves my half-sister, not this Fledgling."

He gestured at me but didn't turn to look at me and once again I felt like he was trying to protect me by offering himself up instead.

The Grand Hadri smiled at that and I didn't like the light in his eyes or the way they seemed to sparkle the most when he thought he was unsettling us. I straightened my back and made sure he didn't see me slouch. I'd never bend to people like this.

Do not bend.

But how did Flame Riders follow someone so clearly unhinged when they were supposedly good?

Even the good can be deceived and persuaded by clever words and tangled-up motives.

I shivered and then froze when the Grand Hadri's eyes landed on me again.

"So, just a trainee. And yet she does not speak for herself."

Why did it always come to that? Were words so essential that no one would ever trust me unless they heard my voice?

Fools, all of them.

"She is voiceless. She does not use her voice to turn the tides of man or sail them into the teeth of war," Judicus said quietly. "Unlike some I could name."

Someone gasped – I didn't know who – and everyone else seemed to freeze as if the entire cabin had been suddenly coated in ice.

The Grand Hadri's face went from the pleasure of a cat toying with a mouse to frigid anger.

"I know that voice," he said in what was almost a growl. "It's the voice of one who has been granted so much mercy it must strain the patience of even God himself."

Judicus said nothing but he seemed to stand even taller as Gundt stepped to the side and out of the way of this duel of wills and gazes between Judicus and the Grand Hadri.

"Is that you, Judicus Franzer Irault? Oldest son of the Mad Lord of the Dead? Heir of the Seed of Chaos?"

"I go where I must," Judicus said quietly.

"And where did you go in the north, I wonder?" the Grand Hadri asked. "Were you traveling with this girl? Are you perhaps the voice behind the voiceless stirring up my enemies? Reports tell me there are raiders that reach their icy fingers miles into lands I've claimed as my own."

"What ship's captain lays claim to lands?" Judicus asked with one eyebrow raised ironically. "What simple sailor calls me his enemy? I know of none."

If we were frozen before, we were like rock now – unable to even move.

The Grand Hadri stared at Judicus for so long that I wondered if he was frozen, too.

And then he barked a laugh.

"Never let it be said that my enemies are dull or slow," he said. "Let it be said instead that they are mighty and swift and still I am better than all of them."

"If we've given up the mummery that you're a ship's captain," Judicus said – and I was shocked that he was still treating the Grand Hadri like an equal even now that he wasn't pretending. "Then I should confess I was coming to see you ... uncle."

82

"I'm touched," the Grand Hadri said, placing a hand on his heart.

I shivered. In any thoughts I'd had of kings or emperors, they had always been remote, distant rulers who passed down wise judgment or gave powerful orders but who sat apart from the people, clothed in dignity and grace. What I'd never envisioned was this – a massive, seething man whose passions whirled him around and whose eyes were more scheming and weighing than those of a peddler at his last stop in the north.

"My brother's only son is coming to me after all these years. And here, I already have your sister in my courts. She plays a lovely viol, did you know this?"

"I knew it." Judicus' face flushed hot, and I saw his hands were trembling. What about his sister playing the viol made him so angry?

"I had a mind to find her a husband. She's of the right age," the Grand Hadri said casually. But there was nothing like casualness about this conversation.

"And if she prefers not to marry?" Judicus asked.

The Grand Hadri's smile returned. "A dynastic marriage for my niece would be useful to me. But perhaps there is a service her brother could do for me instead. Hmm?"

Beside me, Judicus stiffened, but Gundt seemed to relax a little as if finally knowing what this ruler wanted made him less tense.

"But first," the Grand Hadri said, "tell me why you were coming to visit me, Judicus Franzer Irault. It doesn't have anything to do with the fact that you're traveling with a cult member and a voiceless girl, does it?"

Judicus cleared his throat, and I took the moment of the pause to look furtively around us. The guards remained impassive, but the Flame Riders were interesting. The worried glances they exchanged told me this conversation was not what they expected – and maybe not something they liked.

See? They are still good, Kazmerev said. *They may simply not realize that throwing their loyalty in with us is the best thing they can do.*

Huxabrand laughed. She must be staying close with Kazmerev. *You are the most arrogant phoenix I have ever met, Kazmerev Bright Flame.*

I ignored the pair of them. I had to focus on what Judicus would say here.

"Did you know that a stone army rose up out of the sea only hours ago and nearly marched across your kingdom?" Judicus asked quietly.

"Are they still a threat to me?"

"I dispatched them."

"How altruistic. In that case, no, I care not. I do, however, care to have my question answered. Who are these people traveling with you?"

"They are my coterie," Judicus said, claiming us both.

"Oh, are they now," the Grand Hadri said, raising an eyebrow. He made a curt gesture with one hand and one of the guards took a decanter and goblet from a side table and brought them to him. "No one may raise a coterie without my permission."

"Unless they are raising one to seek the ai'sletta," Judicus countered.

The Grand Hadri barked a laugh, nearly spilling the drink he was pouring for himself.

"Indeed, nephew. But that comes with a timeline, does it not? A timeline of one year. And what will you do if you have not found her in the year?" Every time he spoke, I liked him less. "No one has found the ai'sletta in generations."

I shifted my weight nervously. I didn't like them talking about the ai'sletta. I didn't like the idea that this ruler might hear my cousin's name. I didn't trust him.

"That's what I was coming to tell you," Judicus said mildly. "We found her."

I clenched my jaw. Great. Now he knew.

"And where is she?" the Grand Hadri asked, his disbelief apparent.

Gundt cleared his throat, shifting his weight.

"You have something to add, Greensleeve?" the Grand Hadri asked.

"With respect, noble one," Gundt said, "there has been no ai'sletta found for many generations."

The Grand Hadri snorted. "And if there were, it would be your job to protect her. Are you protecting her now by denying her existence?"

I swallowed. It was hard to fool this man.

"She was snatched from me by Lady Lightland," Judicus interrupted, pulling attention away from Gundt again. Did he do that on purpose? To protect us? "On my way to bring her to you, I lost her."

The Grand Hadri tapped his chin, looking from one of us to the next as if considering us. I wondered if I should tell him what I'd learned. Could he help the phoenixes stay safe? Would he? He didn't seem very altruistic.

I wasn't sure if he'd even blink if I told him Stryxex had emerged and were hunting phoenixes.

Just one phoenix, Kazmerev said. *I hardly count as more than one.*

But the note from Hallimore had laid out that they had found the caches. That they were destroying them and laying traps for any Flame Riders who went to them. That they were trying to eliminate phoenixes entirely.

What?

Oh. In all the excitement, I'd forgotten to tell Kazmerev the secret.

But ... but they can't.

I wasn't sure if that was denial or if he thought it was fact. After all, they'd killed Hallimore's mount, Arturo. Killed him for good, not just for the day.

I didn't know how I sensed it, but I could feel a sudden freeze – not just in Kazmerev but in Huxabrand, too.

Kazmerev began to keen quietly in the back of my head, but it was Huxabrand's voice that spoke.

The Stryxex are back, and they are hunting phoenixes with a plan to kill us all.

At first, I thought she was just repeating what I'd told her, but then Gundt's head whipped up and his eyes met mine. Oh. She had been telling him.

Not only that, but when I peeked from my peripheral at the other Flame Riders the looks of horror on their faces confirmed what I'd wondered. They'd heard it, too.

"I think I have a solution," the Grand Hadri said mildly.

My eyes widened, heart speeding up. He'd heard, too? Was nothing private anymore?

But no. He was looking at Judicus. And I wasn't sure if I was more afraid at the horrified fear in every Flame Rider in the room, or the look the Grand Hadri was aiming at my friend.

83

"You, Judicus Franzer Irault," the Grand Hadri said, "will travel with all speed and the aid of your coterie to recover the ai'sletta and bring her to me."

My belly did a flip flop. That's what we'd been planning all along, so why did it sound so bad, now?

Gundt shifted his weight, silently, eyes looking down. I could tell he wasn't happy. But what could he do?

"You, Gundt Hellebar, illegitimate son of Lady Lightland, will answer directly to Irault."

At that Gundt's eyes shot up. His jaw was rigid with what must be fury at this constant reminder he wasn't a legitimate heir of his family. In Landsfall, no one worried too much about that kind of thing. If a child was being raised by parents who loved them, no one asked questions about who had conceived them or why. We knew who their parents were – the ones clothing and feeding them. And if a man died and his oldest wasn't technically his blood, no one so much as shrugged at the fact that the oldest was still named heir and the line carried through him. We had a looser way of things. A kinder way, I thought.

"Oh yes," the Grand Hadri went on, his lip curling. "I don't trust my nephew. He bears his father's name. He bears his father's look in his face and in that rail-thin body which is so useless for war or adventure." Well, that wasn't called for! "Inviting him into my trust is like inviting in a snake. His magic is too wild to be raised to the place of Calicarn Trust. He'll forever be a wild rope worker. His father was wild, too. Too wild to leave him lands or a title worth having, but instead, tarring him heavily with shame."

I glanced at Judicus. His fists were white from clenching them so hard and he bit his lip so that a tiny trickle of blood ran down his chin. But he didn't flinch. And

I didn't think it was shame or hurt that had him fighting for control. Not when his eyes were aflame with fury.

The Grand Hadri paused, looking around the room to weigh the reaction to his words. He seemed satisfied – maybe even reveling in the shock in the room – when he continued.

"But I am putting him in charge of this little expedition anyway. Because he will be motivated. Succeed and bring me the ai'sletta and your family's shame will be washed away," he told Judicus. "I will tear down the statue in Triumph Square and erase from history the censure to your father's name. I will give your mother and sister the estate and income they might have had, removing the guards who have stood there since the day your father was torn down. Won't that be nice? They can retire from city life and no longer be shunned by the others of their class. Or." He paused again, but this time he had eyes only for Judicus and those eyes were hungry. "Or, I can marry your sister to an enemy who will use her mercilessly for his own ends but still gain me some slight advantage. And I can turn your mother out from the last place that will have her. And I can make them both so destitute and ruined that you will wish you had killed them with your own hand. And because you do not doubt me even in the slightest, you will agree to this."

Gundt cleared his throat and the Grand Hadri gestured to him to speak.

"My half-sister is a renowned high Lady with many resources at her disposal," Gundt said carefully. "And she currently possesses the ai'sletta. To retrieve the chosen one for you will not be easy."

"You'll have letters of marque in my service," the Grand Hadri said, smiling with only one side of his mouth. "They'll make you my privateers, make you above the law, give you access to places you wouldn't have had access to before. And of course, I'll send you with an escort."

I lifted an eyebrow. An escort? Would he send guards? How could we travel quickly if his guards were slowing us down? Lady Lightland had the Stryxex. She could move day or night, flying quickly to her goal. But wasn't her goal to bring the ai'sletta to the Grand Hadri? If he really wanted Mally, all he had to do was wait. But we hadn't told him that.

My eyes flicked to Gundt and Judicus. Neither of them was saying anything and I wondered if we were all thinking the same thing – that we had no intention now – or ever – of letting Mally get into the hands of this man.

Or was Judicus thinking of his sister and mother?

A chill shot through me. How could he not be? How could he not hold them as more important than Mally who had offered him nothing but trouble?

I bit my lip as the Grand Hadri spoke again.

"My Flame Riders will go with you as an escort." I felt the Flame Riders stiffen. "They'll provide help in acquiring the ai'sletta, and they will be my second insurance that you will bring her to me as quickly as possible. My trust goes with you, Flame Riders," he said.

I risked a glance from them to him and back and I was surprised at what I saw. I'd expected reluctance or interest or simply acceptance. Instead, they looked wary. Was it us they were uncertain of? Or the task itself? Or the Grand Hadri? They were wise to be wary. If he treated his relatives so harshly, how would he treat someone else?

"I'll have your oath of obedience now," the Grand Hadri said lightly as if he was asking for a refill on his wine.

The others – Flame Riders, Judicus, and Gundt stammered an oath they all seemed to know. An oath that bound them to find the ai'sletta and bring her to the Grand Hadri.

And I said nothing. Both because I could not and because I would not.

And I wondered what my role might be now that I was the only one who was not bound.

84

"Leave me now," the Grand Hadri said. "And do not tell me of the hardships you have suffered or the difficulty you have endured, for I do not care. Merely take what supplies you need from the ship's stores and get into the sky as quickly as possible. We dare not waste another hour … not when so many have already been wasted."

Which was how we found ourselves an hour later, mounted on phoenixes and flying in a silent formation toward the shore. We'd been given supplies and each of us had a bag strapped to a back or slung across our bodies. Our phoenixes were not mounts with saddles or saddlebags and if we wanted to carry gear, we had to carry it ourselves.

Gundt had left the Grand Hadri's presence with sullen rage behind his eyes. He'd said nothing to anyone since then except to lean toward me for a brief moment to whisper in my ear, "Keep trusting. We'll talk soon."

Despite everything, despite all my misgivings, I *did* trust him and even more so now that he was clearly angry about what we'd been pulled into. He seemed to be the only one other than Kazmerev who wanted Mally's freedom and safety as much as I did.

Judicus had left the Grand Hadri's presence wiping his mouth and swearing under his breath. Fortunately, only Refrento had tried to talk to him.

"We can take turns carrying the noble," he'd said and Judicus had cursed even louder, shaking off his friendly hand.

"I ride with Sersha or not at all," he'd said grimly. His face was like death.

I found I was both nervous that we were going to get in even greater trouble if he didn't calm down and also flattered. He trusted me. He knew that Kazmerev and I wouldn't let him down.

And now he slept, head slumped over my shoulder, arms limp where they were wrapped around me. I held his wrists to keep him in place and held onto Kazmerev with my knees – not that he'd ever drop me.

I never would.

I longed to talk to him and plan with him – but the other phoenixes had all woken up and anything beyond the basics was impossible with them listening to Kazmerev's side of the conversation.

I wanted to talk about what we could do to keep Judicus's sister and mother safe while still not betraying Mally.

Yes, was all Kazmerev would say to that.

I wanted to talk about how we could slip free of these other Flame Riders.

Unlikely, was all he'd allow himself to say.

I wanted to talk about how I trusted Gundt now. How I was sorry I hadn't earlier.

I understand.

How I was worried for Judicus. How he'd somehow taken some of my energy.

I know.

How even though I trusted him, I was worried that he was going to be so torn in his loyalties that he'd somehow betray that trust.

He won't.

How I was sad about Aunt Danna and I missed her. Even if she'd never really treated me like I could make my own decisions. Even if she'd seen no more future for me than washing dishes in her kitchen – even then, I just missed her. I just didn't like a world she wasn't in.

Death comes for each of us, and we must face it in our own way. Your aunt gave her life for her daughter. She made a strong choice – a choice born of love and self-sacrifice. There is great honor in that – and a future, I think, for her on the other side.

I liked that, and I liked hearing more than one-word answers from him.

Though I am bound, yet my heart feels with you.

I understood. Even if it made us both voiceless right now.

We flew until just before dawn and then collapsed in a clearing. We'd been heading south along the coast – blindly – aiming toward the nearest city.

"We'll find word of them there," Refrento had said and with Gundt refusing to speak and Judicus fast asleep, no one had offered a different opinion.

We were within sight of the city when the darkness started to lighten, but not close enough to walk the distance in a day, so we set up rough shelters in the clearing along the road, started a fire – it's easy to start a fire when everyone there could open a palm and let it fall into the tinder – and pulled out the blankets and kettle in time to settle in before our phoenixes vanished.

I helped Judicus into the shelter Gundt had made and had him tucked into a blanket before Kazmerev disappeared. When he left, I collapsed on the ground, my strength failing me, too.

A strong hand came down on my shoulder.

"Come, Sersha," Gundt said, "Rest now."

He led me into the shelter made of boughs and helped me settle down next to Judicus, wrapping me in one of the blankets. He was almost like a father in how he was treating me, gently helping me without any judgment.

"I'll take first watch," he said, but if he said anything else, I didn't hear it because I was already fast asleep.

85

I took my watch second when Gundt came to wake me, stopping to check on Judicus. His cut lip gleamed in the afternoon light and there were dark circles under his eyes, but other than that he seemed fine. We needed rest. Rest and a whole day in one place to clean our clothes, eat properly, and sleep.

Instead, I splashed canteen water on my face and joined Duche Olliman on watch. He'd made tea. He offered me some and I accepted it, fascinated as he made a tiny ceremony out of pouring it for us both.

"Gundt is your Guarding Flame," he said quietly as we sipped our tea.

Around us, birds sang in the trees and insects buzzed, but the others all slept, and the road was silent.

I nodded and sipped, grateful for the fragrant green tea. It must be from a private stash of his.

"It is good someone found you," he said neutrally, though I got the impression that he meant it would have been better if that someone was one of the others. "Lone Flame Riders can hurt themselves and their phoenixes."

I gave him a long dry look. I would be safer alone than with these others. I had no respect for anyone who blindly followed corrupted authority.

"We are not wicked just because we come at cross purposes to you, young woman," he said acidly.

I tried very hard not to smirk at that. It was hard not to when he was only a little older than me and trying so hard to look important.

He sipped his tea delicately before continuing, "Gundt isn't much of one for words, so I think it is unlikely he has told you the story of the Flame Riders – how we came to be and why we exist. Is that true?"

Considering how I would not trust him at first, he hadn't had much time to teach me anything, but he'd tried to understand my signs while this man wanted to tell me all about himself. Two very different approaches.

Of the two, I preferred Gundt's but we had a long watch ahead and the day was warm and quiet without a cloud in sight, only the warm sun bathing the earth and the earth reflecting back that warmth and adding to it the scent of grasses and flowers.

I nodded, contentedly, happy to hear his story if he wanted to tell it.

"Long ago in a place far from here," he began. Because all stories start long ago but in an undetermined place so that no one can check to be sure they are true. "A great general was laying siege to the countryside of his rival. He was a cruel and dark person with no pity in his heart or respect for anyone – whether young or old, innocent or comely, he did not care. It was a time of great sorrow for the people. Many died quickly and terribly. Among the many terrible things he did, he used fire as a weapon. He would set great blazes across the earth that ate up crops and homes, animals and people, leaving nothing behind where once life was.

"One day, he set to blaze a countryside where a man lived and worked beside his aged parents and his young child. His wife had died in childbirth and he had only these few left, but he was happy with them, though the work each day was long and arduous, their love gave him great peace.

"But their story does not end with peace. They fled the flames, running from their home, but they had no animals on which to ride swiftly, for they were very poor, and there was no lake or pond or ocean nearby in which they could huddle, so they ran instead through the thick forest, hoping to reach the mountain nearby where the trees are far apart and perhaps the flames would not climb too high. All the forest was filled with others trying to escape. I do not wish to detail the tragedy of that day as it is grim and terrible. Let me only say that by the time the man had reached the base of the mountain, both his parents were lost to him, as were all the other villagers, so there was only the man and his young child – a boy of seven.

"The flames leapt up before him, consuming the land ahead and behind until there was only a small patch of ground around them that was not yet burned. The desperate father whispered sweet words into his terrified son's ear as he tucked him into a small dip in the ground and then laid his own body over the boy.

"'Do not fear my son, for I shall never leave you,' he said. 'And even if I pass from this life, I will rise again in your heart.' When the flames passed over and the forest cooled, the boy found that his father had died, and he wailed in sadness for he alone lived and had lost those he loved best.

"But when night fell, his heart felt so full that he thought that perhaps it would shatter and run out across the ground like a broken egg, but to his surprise, instead it birthed a phoenix. The phoenix burst from the ashes of his father that were clutched in his hands and it came forth as an egg which then hatched and grew before his eyes.

"It was the soul of his father, risen up from the dead to protect him.

"But death is a great adversary and though the father could hold it back in the night, when dawn came, it consumed him just as the fires had consumed his body. And yet, when the blazing sun fled again at dusk, he would return again, reborn.

"In this way, he led his son to safety and in this way, he comforted the boy's sad heart, and in this way, he raised the boy up until he was a young man and with the strength and magic of the love of his father, he slew the general and set the land free.

"And so, the first phoenix was born."

I found myself blinking away tears. I wanted to ask what the name of the phoenix had been, but Duche Olliman did not say.

"Each phoenix that lives now has a story like that. They gave themselves long ago out of love and sacrifice, though most do not remember the story of how this came about. Through the millennia, they have lived, passed on to the next person who needs their love and shelter and the next after that and the next after that. My own friend phoenix, Frissei, was passed to me from a member of my guard as the man lay dying in my arms. He prevented an assassination attempt on my father. I did not even know he carried a phoenix with him until he thrust a handful of ashes into my palm."

He was silent a long time. And I was silent with him. I reached out and took his hand and he let me hold it for a moment as we sipped our tea and watched the butterflies hover from flower to flower. After a long time, he took his hand back and shook himself.

"Do not judge us too harshly, Fledgling. You do not know our stories. We are each doing the best good we can in the way we know how."

And to my surprise, I found that I believed him.

86

Gundt woke in the late afternoon and Judicus with him. The pair looked far too casual as they moved about the camp, tidying and gathering wood for the evening meal. Gundt collected the waterskins.

"I'll fill them in the creek," he told us. "Help me with this, Sersha. It's a lot of water for one man to carry."

I stood, brushing myself off, and hurried to join him.

"Don't be too long, older brother," Duche Olliman said. "When Refrento awakens, he has promised to cook his spiced beans for us. They are already soaking."

Gundt grunted and shoved half the empty waterskins at me. I hurried to catch up as he broke a purposeful trail through the undergrowth and brush.

It took us long enough to find the creek that I was almost worried we were lost when a low whistle broke the quiet of the forest.

Gundt grunted again and then we emerged on a flat black rock fringed in reeds where the creek formed a shallow, whirling pool. From the thick grass nearby, Judicus emerged. He grinned.

"Good ear, Gundt."

"You'd better hope your whistle didn't carry, rope worker. I tried to make this look casual."

I looked from one to the other and asked them what was happening in signs.

"We don't have to discuss it to know that none of us likes this letter of marque or the task the Grand Hadri has set us," Gundt said in a low voice, looking side to side to be sure no one had followed. "But this might be our only chance to talk. Look." He cleared his throat awkwardly. He looked like someone had jammed thorns down the collar of his jacket.

"If you're about to apologize for not being forthcoming – for not telling us your half-sister is Lady Lightland or that you are a sworn Greensleeve, then save the breath," Judicus said mildly. "It's clear you're no closer with Cassanetta than I am.

Knowing you've got a blood connection with her changes nothing. As long as there's nothing more we need to know then I am satisfied."

Gundt grunted. He was doing that a lot lately. "I will inherit nothing at her father's death. They do not claim me, nor have they had a hand in either my decisions or my fortunes. My mother, God rest her, was fond of me, but now that she has passed, I am not welcome to their home."

Judicus nodded. I laid a sympathetic hand on Gundt's arm.

"As to the other thing," he said, and I knew he was upset because he hadn't shaken my hand off to prove he didn't need my help. "I am sworn to protect the ai'sletta and sworn to search for her. Which should make you feel safer, Sersha," he said looking at me. "And though it might not do the same for you, Judicus," he said, "you should at least realize I am a man of honor. If we can think of a plan to save your sister and mother along with our nation's best hope, then I will listen."

Judicus was deadly calm. I had begun to realize that he was often calm when he was upset.

"I'm fond of Mally – despite how she is both a symbol and a very flawed girl at the same time. But I'm much fonder of my sister and my mother." Gundt ground his teeth loudly enough that I could hear them and Judicus quirked an eyebrow at him. "What? Did you expect me to say, 'I'll do anything to save the ai'sletta. Even if it means hurting my own family?' Is that what you expected?"

Gundt's voice was laced with fury. "I thought you were a good man. Self-sacrificing. Loyal."

Judicus leaned forward so that his pale face was only inches from Gundt's. "I. Am."

Uh oh. This was not going well. I laid a hand on each one's shoulder.

They both looked at me with identical looks of surprise and I raised my eyebrows.

After a moment, Judicus coughed awkwardly, his face growing scarlet. "And of course, she's your family, too, Sersha."

I nodded, but I tried to convey compassion with my eyes.

"And when the time comes, it will be you alone who can save her from us," Gundt told me. "Because you didn't take the vow. And the vow was laced with a sting."

I cocked my head to the side.

Gundt shook his head. "I don't know what kind of sting, but I felt the cold bite of magic."

"Not rope work," Judicus said, though he was nodding, too.

"Then maybe the rumor is true," Gundt said. "Maybe an oath to a king of Briccatore is truly binding in the ancient sense."

"It wasn't so with my father," Judicus muttered.

"Your father was no king."

Judicus lunged and I didn't know what they were talking about, but I had to stop them.

I wrenched at Judicus as he wrapped his hands around Gundt's neck and throttled him. Gundt wasn't fighting back. He just let it happen. When I finally dragged Judicus off of him, he coughed, long and ragged.

This time I stepped between them shaking my head and signing, enough, enough, enough between them.

They seemed to understand.

"He shouldn't have said that about my father," Judicus said with a trembling lower lip and while I didn't understand what the insult was, I nodded gently and looked at Gundt.

"He's right. I apologize."

"And I shouldn't have choked him," Judicus said, deflating.

"Also correct."

Judicus scooped up the waterskins and began to fill them, and I was pretty sure it was to hide his face so we wouldn't see him blinking angry tears away.

We both let him do it for a moment and then Gundt spoke again through a raw throat.

"I swear to you, Judicus, that I will try to find every way possible to save your family while also honoring my vow to protect the ai'sletta. I will spend my own life, if this is what it takes."

Judicus turned to him sharply and yes, there were silver tear trails on his cheeks.

Gundt nodded, chewing his lip and looking shamefaced. "I will not ask you to risk them. I only ask that you help us try to do the impossible – try to help them and the ai'sletta both."

"Yes. Okay," Judicus said, and his shoulders heaved again as he turned back to fill the waterskins and he choked on a sob.

Gundt turned back to me. "When the time comes and an opportunity arises to keep your kinswoman from the Grand Hadri, take it. And I will do everything I can to stay out of your way."

So now, it was up to me.

87

The spicy beans were better than I'd expected. The conversation was not.

The moment the sun set, the Flame Riders insisted we join them around the fire. The excuse was the beans, but what they really wanted to know was why we thought the Stryxex were real and why we thought they were hunting phoenixes.

Kazmerev was born in the midst of their grilling and to my relief, he relayed our story as simply as possible and then spoke for me as they asked questions.

"There was no way you could have saved Hallimore?" Dalissa Fenwan had asked, her wrinkled face troubled as she regarded me.

"And you were sure Arturo was gone?" Refrento pressed, as if I would have failed to see a massive phoenix made of flame and light.

"You're sure you saw these Stryxex? Who else saw them?" Duche Olliman asked.

I realized Duche was a title when the others stopped addressing him by it.

It is like a Duke or a Canta, Kazmerev explained to me as the others were debating whether to believe us. With three humans and two phoenixes testifying to the facts, it was hard to dismiss them entirely, but no one wanted to believe that legends had arisen and were trying to kill them.

"We'll have to stop at all the caches," Dalissa said eventually. Worry marred her face. "We can't afford not to check them out. And we must leave word for anyone else."

"It won't be enough." Refrento was the most emotional of them and when he glared at me like that it made me want to freeze in place. "What about the ones like her who are too new to know their own strength. What about them?"

Dalissa shook her head. "We can't do everything Refrento. We can only do as we can."

Refrento pointed a meaty finger at Gundt. "You should be making her do heat exercises. She should be meditating. If she's being hunted, she needs to be prepared."

"I'm a Guarding Flame," Gundt said easily from where he was rolling his blanket. "Not a nursemaid."

I looked at him, worried. Were there things I should be doing? Was I slacking, somehow?

He winked at me and shook his head. Whatever they were, he didn't think I needed to be doing them. But now I was worried. Gundt had a different approach to most things than I did. What if he wasn't teaching me the way he should? Should I beg one of these others to teach me?

Sersha, stop.

They were right that we were threatened and running out of time.

Sersha, Gundt is a good teacher. Trust him.

Gundt looked up and met my eyes and there was a little hurt in them. I felt my face go hot.

"See? Even the girl knows this goes beyond you, Gundt," Refrento said. "Hand her over to us and we'll take on the duty of training her, brother. You can go about your business after we finish the Grand Hadri's task."

"Is that what you want, Sersha?" Gundt asked quietly, but everyone was so quiet that it felt like they were all hanging on my answer.

I shook my head no.

"Then best finish eating and packing your things. We leave before the hour is over. I'll take my charge into the town to find what information I can," Gundt told the others.

"No," Dalissa said. "We'll all go together. We all need a real bed and a bath and more Flame Riders means more people to scout for information. I have a friend who owns the Figleaf Inn on the quarry side. Let's spend the night and morning looking for what information we can find and gather there for an afternoon of rest. I'll pay."

And then, without asking anyone if they agreed, she dashed the fire out and grabbed her own things before launching into the air. To my shock, Duche Olliman was only a few strides behind.

Rude.

She couldn't just order us all around like that!

Sersha, Kazmerev said gently. *It would seem that voicelessness has not taught you how to hold your tongue.*

They couldn't hear me. Only he could.

Please, make it easier for me. It is hard not to respond.

I felt my face growing hot – again.

I should have thought of that, but I was too embarrassed to apologize even when we took our places on his back, Judicus sitting jauntily behind me as if this was a pleasure ride and not vital travel.

I was too embarrassed for the whole flight to say a word in my mind – which might have been best because it gave me the chance to practice holding my mental tongue.

But when we arrived at the city, I could hold my thoughts in no longer.

I had thought the last city we'd seen was huge. It was like Landsfall compared to Rafinnette. This place boggled the mind. Nothing could be so large, could it?

I could get lost here and wander for days.

My jaw dropped open as I watched it unfurl ahead of us.

"There's the quarry," Judicus said, pointing just past the wall of the city on the far side. "And the high houses, and the guild chapters, the river and the docks, the barracks stacked up like bricks."

Sersha, Kazmerev interrupted, *Gundt is trying to get your attention.*

I glanced to the side to see Gundt on Huxabrand. The female phoenix's eye flashed in the moonlight.

Yes, I'm telling her, she said irritably.

Gundt's eyes met mine and he nodded at me like he was trying to give me courage.

Gundt knows we can't go flying into cities while we're visible, Huxabrand said. *And Sersha is very visible up there. So is Judicus. She needs to learn not to be.*

Can Gundt tell her how to be? Kazmerev said. *I do not know the ways of riders – or if I did, I have forgotten them. When I was reborn as a new phoenix for Sersha, I lost many of my memories.*

Gundt says that's normal.

They were talking over me. It made my cheeks flame even though people had been talking over me all my life.

It's not the same, little hawk.

What's not the same? Huxabrand wanted to know.

She feels that we are overlooking her.

Really? He had to tell her that? I did not trust Huxabrand with my emotions.

Good, Huxabrand said. *Because Gundt is saying she has to learn to be quiet. Quiet with her mind – easy to forget. If she can do that then she can make you all invisible while she's riding you.*

I'd always been easy to overlook and forget. The trick was to figure out how to be *seen* not how to be ignored.

I think she'll find this difficult, Kazmerev cautioned. *Perhaps we shouldn't rely on it.*

Wait? Why did he have so little confidence in me? He'd just heard me saying how easy it was to overlook me. I gritted my teeth and concentrated on how I was always overlooked and not seen. This would work.

You are making me shine brighter, little hawk, Kazmerev cautioned.

I wanted to curse when I opened my eyes and realized he was right.

It's not those who feel sorry for themselves who walk without drawing attention to themselves. It's those who are very confident that they are valued and loved who do not need *to grasp at people's attention.*

Was I blushing before? I was blushing now.

Perhaps we should try again later, Kazmerev suggested.

It shouldn't be so difficult, Huxabrand protested, but when I glanced at Gundt he nodded at me, and then Huxabrand sighed.

Fine. He says fine, she can try again later, though really, she should be able to do this. Doesn't she feel safe with you, Kazmerev? You make me *feel safe.*

Was that phoenix flirting? I looked back and forth between them.

Kazmerev made a sound that was like a human clearing their throat and Huxabrand's mental laughter rang between us.

I was grateful when Judicus broke in. "If you're all finished with whatever private conversation you are having, and if we are skirting around the city instead of flying directly toward it as the others did, then can I recommend we try the area near the eastern gate? There is a district there known as the Spice District but what spices are sold behind the careful facades of the merchants there are not all of the permitted varieties, if you catch my meaning. If I was hiding someone I had kidnapped, low on allies, and seeking refuge, that is where I would go."

I was surprised when Kazmerev relayed that to Gundt and even more surprised when Huxabrand said, *Besides which, Gundt's family keeps a small suite of rooms over one of the mercantiles in the Spice District. She could be staying there.*

Was it too convenient that we were just thinking of this now, or had Gundt already been thinking that when we set out and just failed to tell the others? Based on how he wouldn't meet my eyes, I thought it might be the latter.

"Oh, lovely, you're flying toward the Spice Gate, nicely done," Judicus said. "Cassanetta would have had to recruit new guards and where better than among the criminal element?"

I was only half listening to him. Something had nudged at the edge of my concentration. What was it?

There it was again. I hadn't imagined it. But what was I noticing? With so many things to look at, and these new revelations about what Gundt knew and wasn't saying, it seemed impossible to pick what didn't belong.

There it was again. I caught a full glimpse this time and froze on Kazmerev's back.

Stryxex.

They were here in the city of Rafinnette.

88

Now would be a good time to be invisible! Huxabrand suggested as we plummeted to the gate.

Gate. Gate. Gate, Kazmerev gasped, and I understood why. He didn't want to think about anything else – like about how the Stryxex were zipping toward us, eyes glinting in the moonlight. I also didn't want to think about that. Or about how there were five of them. And I'd only ever seen two before.

"Please tell me those aren't Stryxex," Judicus whispered in my ear.

But, of course, I couldn't.

Hide. Hide, Huxabrand was chanting, but I couldn't hide. I didn't know how to make us invisible.

We hit the ground outside the city walls with a *fump* of dust. I stumbled as my feet were suddenly under me and Kazmerev was gone. Behind me, Judicus grunted letting go of me as we hit the ground and rolled.

When we stopped rolling and I was able to sit up my heart was in my throat.

Kazmerev? Kaz?

No reply.

Where was he? What had happened to him? Panic clawed at me.

A dark shadow dropped beside us and I put a hand over my mouth. Beside me, Judicus hissed, leaping in front of me protectively, but the figure turned slightly, revealing his profile picked out in the moonlight. Gundt.

"They were tracking the phoenixes. I think they can smell them. We should be safe if we can get inside the city. I don't think they want normal people to see them yet."

But we didn't know that. It was all guessing. And now Kazmerev was just gone!

"Come on. Let me do the talking at the gates."

"I have as much pull as you do, Flame Rider," Judicus said, his voice low. "And unlike you, I am good at speaking with people and not making them my enemies."

"Are you? My half-sister didn't seem very fond of you. Neither did *Captain Rackham.*"

After a moment, Judicus whispered. "Fine. You do the talking."

He seemed upset, but I couldn't focus on that for long. I was worried. I didn't like Kazmerev being gone, and I didn't understand where he went. When he was alive, he was with me ... wasn't he? I mean those other phoenixes disappeared and then reappeared but he hadn't said anything before he was just gone. That didn't feel like him. He hadn't said anything to Gundt or Huxabrand either.

"Sersha," Gundt whispered, "Are you okay?"

I shook my head. What if Kazmerev was hurt or ... what if he was dead? Really dead? Like in the way where I couldn't bring him back?

"We're almost at the gate. We'll talk on the other side."

I chewed my lip and wrapped my arms around myself. I didn't like this. I was barely listening when Gundt talked us through the gate. The guard didn't seem to mind his curt responses. I should have been tracking where we were going as we slid into the night of the Spice District. But I was so distracted that within a few turns I was hopelessly lost. I knew that Judicus and Gundt were looming over me, walking so close I could touch either of them very easily if I wanted to. Without a word exchanged, they were guarding me. And I should have been grateful and watchful and helpful. Instead, anxiety ate at me.

"Sersha," Gundt whispered. "Kazmerev vanished to protect you. He's inside waiting to come out again, okay? He forgot how to do it, but he remembered when he saw the other phoenixes earlier. That happens with phoenixes reborn into new hearts. They forget things. He'll be back, just you watch. He's a bright flame. He'd never leave you unless it was to protect you."

But it wasn't okay because I didn't feel him in there and I didn't think Gundt knew what he was talking about.

I barely paid attention as Gundt paid a man a shining coin at a small tavern and spoke in hushed tones about his sister. I still wasn't focused when Judicus leaned in close, whispering about nothing in my ear and smirking to make anyone who saw us think we were a couple flirting rather than two people on the hunt.

We slipped out of the tavern again.

"She was here," Gundt murmured. "They saw her, but they don't know which way she went. I can get into the townhouse, but not until tomorrow unless we want to break in?"

There was a long silence and Gundt said, "Well?"

We were standing in a huddle beside the tavern. No one could overhear us.

"We should go now," Judicus whispered. "We can search her apartment. I can ... I have ways of tracking if I use a little energy. And if we're going to an inn right afterward, maybe Sersha will lend me just a little more and I can mark the trail to start tomorrow evening. I don't like the idea of wasting time. Any time. What about it, Sersha?"

"Lend you energy?" Gundt asked in a low tone. He didn't sound pleased.

"It was an accident," Judicus said, turning to me. "I'm sorry. I didn't mean to take it before. I'll always ask in the future. I didn't ..."

"You took something of hers without asking?" Gundt asked, looming over Judicus. "Some of her life?"

"Not everyone can offer that," Judicus stammered. "And to do it you have to be wide open. I didn't know I was –"

"No excuse!" Gundt roared, raising a fist.

I dove between them, setting one hand on Gundt's fist and holding up one hand to Judicus. Had they almost come to blows? This was ridiculous.

Where was Kazmerev? I needed him for this!

If he ever left without telling me again, I was going to ... I was going to. Well, I didn't know but it would be something he would remember!

I thought I heard a whistle from up above and I looked up to see a Stryxex perched on the roof, its dark eyes looking right at us. This one had no rider.

Fear froze me. I gasped as both Judicus and Gundt looked up at the legendary creature with me.

"Uh oh," Judicus said.

89

He grabbed me by the collar and had me back into the tavern in a heartbeat, Gundt just behind him.

"Here now, we're closing up!" the bartender said gruffly. "No more drinks."

"Do you rent rooms above?" Gundt asked at the same moment that I heard the rustle of feathers from outside the door.

Kazmerev, you picked the worst time to hide! It is not helping! I tried to talk to him with my mind. If he wasn't dead, he must be near, right? Those other phoenixes had emerged again when the coast was clear. If he really was hiding in my heart, could he not hear me?

"We do not, young man and I would thank you to leave," the bartender said at the same moment that a big man stood up from where he was sitting beside the fire and strode over to us. He glared at Judicus.

Judicus raised his hands. "No trouble here."

"Leave or we call the Watch," he said with a growl.

"Do you have a back door?" Gundt asked as two more toughs emerged from the back.

"No," the bartender said, lifting a crossbow from behind the bar.

"No trouble," Gundt said, raising his own hands. He pushed past Judicus and me, almost slamming the door open as he pulled his short sword in the same motion.

It slowed him long enough for Judicus to bound in front of him, hands flaring to life with black ropes pouring from his palms. Even moving that quickly, he was almost too slow.

The Stryxex leapt forward, feet extended. Only my enhanced phoenix vision could really see the edges of his dark wings and fierce talons. Judicus must have seen them, too, because his black ropes shot out, twisting around the outstretched feet and trussing them like a bird to sell at market.

I gasped as the bird lost its balance and fell, hitting the cobbles of the street hard. Behind me, the door of the tavern slammed shut. And then Gundt was leaping forward, sword swooshing through the air – and straight to the cobbles. It should have struck the creature's neck. And yet it hadn't. I gasped and he seemed stunned, his mouth falling open.

"Quick. I can't hold it for long!" Judicus cried as the bird thrashed. And then, out of nowhere, Huxabrand bloomed from Gundt's heart. The moment she burst to life – a bright star in the black night, Gundt opened his hand and a bar of white fire tinted around the edges with rose pink gushed from his hand and splashed across the Stryxex. It gave one long, ungodly shriek, and then it disappeared, leaving nothing but the stink of burned feathers and a cloud of acrid smoke.

"They're in the city," Gundt said, catching Judicus as he reeled, stumbling from his use of power. "We can't stay here."

"What do you suggest?" Judicus snapped. "Going out to the countryside?"

"It's still night. We go to the townhouse. We get the scent. We get out of here."

"Without the others?"

"They'll catch up." His voice seemed too loud in the night.

"Without supplies?"

"We have these packs." Gundt seemed less certain this time.

"Without rest?"

Gundt swore.

"We're more vulnerable without the others," Judicus protested, scanning the sky with palms still spread wide. "We might not like them or trust them, but we need them. Especially if we're going to be chased and hunted by these creatures. Let's go to the townhouse, collect any clues – in and out, fast and hard, and then hurry to the Figleaf Inn and hunker down in a defensive position until the rest of them can join us."

"There are Stryxex everywhere. My skin crawls with them," Gundt said, but it didn't sound like an objection.

"What do you think, Sersha?" Judicus asked graciously.

I made sure they were both looking before I nodded and offered Judicus my arm.

"Not yet. I won't take energy unless I have to. And unless I have your permission."

I opened my hand and very deliberately offered it to him.

"Is that your way of telling me I have your permission?"

I nodded again.

Gundt sighed.

"I guess it's her energy to give," he said with a frown. "Bring Kazmerev back, Sersha. We need his eyes. Huxabrand needs him at her side."

I shook my head.

"We need him. I know it's more dangerous for him. That he's safer in your heart. But you have to let him free," Gundt urged.

"Stop being an idiot and tell her how to do it," Judicus said calmly. He wasn't watching us, so he couldn't see my cheeks heat at his words. I wouldn't have put it like that, but I was still grateful he'd said it. Sometimes, I could almost swear he was reading my mind.

Gundt coughed awkwardly like he hadn't realized that I didn't know how. "Okay, try it while we move. You take the rear, ropeworker. Give a grunt if you see something or if you think you might collapse. I'll hold onto Sersha so she can look within."

"This *is* my coterie," Judicus protested.

"But tonight, this is *my* quest," Gundt said with finality in his voice. He grabbed my arm and pulled me along with him. I saw the reflection of Huxabrand's light on the dark cobbles ahead. It was well past midnight, and we were the only ones still out in the street unless there were villains lurking in the shadows. "Huxabrand will take point. Now, close your eyes if you must, Sersha, but whether you do or not you need to turn your thoughts inward. Think about your own heart and will. Think about the phoenix you have hidden within and call him forth."

It sounded so simple. And at the same time – it didn't explain anything at all.

I clenched my jaw and turned my thoughts inward, trying to think the way he told me.

Kazmerev? Are you there?

Nothing.

Kazmerev? I need you!

How did you think of fire inside you? How did you call to someone who felt a million miles away?

I didn't feel full of a phoenix. I felt hollow and lonely.

I reached inside, thinking about what it felt like to find his ashes in my hands for the first time – of the feeling of sadness that had washed over me when Veela pressed them in my hands. Of the fire that burned in my heart – burning, burning, burning.

I felt it again. My hand clawed at my chest. My mouth opened, and we were lucky I couldn't scream because I'd be screaming and screaming.

I felt myself dragged against someone's chest but my eyes were clenched with the pain and I couldn't see who it was, couldn't think, couldn't hardly breathe.

"Sersha ..." the rest was lost to pain. Their words washing against each other like broken wreckage from a shipwreck. "Let go ... come on ... enough. How many? ... All the way around? ... split up."

And then darkness and burning. And I couldn't find him within. There was only the pain and the fire and me. I did not know if the minutes were long or short, but they felt like years.

And then it was over.

And I was gasping for breath and just grateful, grateful, grateful for the feeling of cool air on my face and the sound of a familiar voice in my mind.

What were you trying to do, little hawk? Get yourself killed?

Kazmerev.

He was here. It would be okay. He was here.

"Sersha? Can you hear me?" Judicus sounded breathless.

I opened my eyes, and his face was right there, leaning over mine, pale in the light of a lantern. There was sweat across his brow, but his bright eyes were completely focused on me. The scrutiny made me feel uncomfortable. Was I lying on his lap?

I was.

How embarrassing.

I struggled to sit free of him, and he let me go, hands hovering inches from me as if afraid I would fall again.

Sersha, are you okay?

I thought I was. Was he okay? There was strain in his voice. But he was right here beside us, bright eyes watching me and he seemed fine.

Fledglings. They're impossible, Huxabrand said from very close by.

Something crashed against a nearby wall and the lantern shook. With a start, I pulled myself free to look around us. Gundt rushed into the room – some kind of bedroom by the look of it – with Huxabrand hopping through the narrow door right behind him.

"Oh good. She's up," he said briefly. "I found the track myself. Huxabrand swears she could sniff it out anywhere. It's the Stryxex. They stink to high heaven to a phoenix nose – especially if there's more than one of them."

"What if Mally isn't with the Stryxex," Judicus asked quietly. He was looking me all over like he was afraid I was more hurt than he could see. I waved a hand and frowned to tell him I was fine, but he still inspected me and again, that kind of close scrutiny made my cheeks flame.

The agonizing pain had left me, though I still felt a little unsteady.

You were burning yourself up from within.

"She will be," Gundt said. "Trust me. My sister would never let them free of her once she had her grip on them. But that's not our problem right now. Our problem is that there is another Stryxex outside and this one is cunning. If we don't act soon, it will burst right through the wall."

90

"Does no one in this city notice giant birds attacking their houses?" Judicus muttered. "These northern cities are far too used to destruction."

He was right. The whole house was shaking. Surely one of the neighboring houses should notice, right?

Fear not, we shall tear him to pieces, only speak the word.

The two of them flew out the door Huxabrand had entered through, eagerness in their every movement.

"I guess the neighbors will find out in a moment. The phoenixes want to engage the creature," Gundt said.

"By all means," Judicus waved a distracted hand. "Surely they'll have to stop with the dawn, and it's nearly morning."

Dawn. And I'd lose him again after all that.

Fear not, little hawk. We fight your enemy. We wheel and strike.

My heart was in my chest. I didn't like him fighting while I waited to see if he would be hurt. I wanted to be with him. I wanted to help him.

"They've begun the fight," Gundt said. "Let's get Sersha out of here while the Stryxex are distracted."

I tried to sign that I was fine, that they didn't need to worry about me, but they were so considerate in how they led me down the stairs to a backdoor and out – opening all the doors and watching in every direction as if they were my personal guards – that it felt ungrateful not to go along with it.

"Will that happen to her again?" Judicus whispered when we were out of the house and into an alley beyond. Above us, the only sign of a phoenix battle was the bright lights flashing overhead.

I hoped Kazmerev wasn't hurt. How would he fight a Stryxex without my flames to help?

It's two against one treacherous beast. Don't be so anxious. We will shred the creature. Huxabrand just took a chunk out of its tail. This is what we were made for – righteous work.

But I couldn't calm down even as we pelted down the alley and out into the open street, working our way from the smaller street to a wide main way dotted with darkened fountains. The streets were nearly empty in the middle of the night, though I heard the occasional call of the Watch.

Shockingly, none of them seemed to realize an aerial battle was being fought in their skies.

"She'll be fine. It's just hard to learn new skills while you're moving," Gundt assured Judicus. "But this is going to take forever. How far away is this inn?"

I wasn't listening. My face was tilted up to the sky.

There they were!

Huxabrand swooped toward something I could barely make out and as she struck, talons out, Kazmerev struck from the other direction. They ripped the Stryxex between them, but at the same moment, something pulled at Kazmerev's wing. He swung precariously to the side and I gasped.

He fell, plummeting, twisting at the last moment to pull himself up and shoot back into the sky.

It was a tight match – phoenix versus Stryxex. And then – out of nowhere – a bright yellow phoenix dove into the fray and there was a sound like ripping cloth as the three phoenixes swooped, dove, struck, and struck again. A shriek like a huge bird tore through the night and then, nothing.

My hands were trembling at my sides.

Kazmerev?

I'm fine. We're all fine.

The light gold phoenix dropped to the earth slightly ahead of the others and to my surprise, Duche Olliman leapt from his back and hurried to us.

"No inn today, I don't think," he said grimly. "You spoke true. That was a Stryxex of legend. I found two others when I went to check the cache in the city. They'd made ... a nest of sorts there."

"A nest?" Gundt asked, sheathing his sword. He looked wary.

Olliman looked away, his face tight. "We won't recover anything from the room. Or anyone."

"How many?" Gundt sounded grim.

"At least a dozen dead. As far as we could tell. There wasn't much of them to find." His voice was husky. "Dalissa sent me to look for you. We need to get as far from here as we can, or we'll be so embroiled in fighting that we'll lose the trail. Did you discover where they went?"

"I found a scent trail. We can follow it," Gundt said. "But what of the city? What of the other riders here?"

"There are none left," Olliman said harshly. "And we don't dare leave anyone here to warn others who arrive. There are too many here for the five of us to defeat, and if we stay to try we'll lose the trail and the ai'sletta."

"If we leave no warning, more phoenixes will die," Gundt said sharply.

"If we leave someone here, *that person* will die," Olliman argued.

I tugged on Gundt's sleeve and he swiveled to me, his eyes bright with intensity from arguing with Olliman.

I held my palm up like a landscape and used my other fist to make a bursting motion.

He nodded. "They'll spread across the landscape."

I pointed at him and Olliman and made the same motion. We needed to disperse and warn people in every direction.

"There aren't enough of us to spread out and warn others," Olliman said, understanding. "There are barely enough of us to recover the ai'sletta, if she is accompanied by these creatures." He looked over his shoulder. "Frankly, some of us should return to Captain Rackam. He should not be left on the open water with such a threat nearby." He paused. One of us will go to him. The others will join you down the trail. Which way does it go?"

"Hard west. Follows the Grand Hadri's Highway from what I can tell," Gundt said.

"If you start flying now, you might be able to reach the town of Band End by morning. We'll try to catch up but if we fall behind, find an inn there and we'll join you during the day."

"Agreed," Gundt said – as if it were really so simple.

91

We made it almost to the town before the phoenixes died.

It was a tense ride with everyone as silent as me. Even the phoenixes were silent except for the occasional check to be sure we were holding up.

It will be okay, Sersha. It will be okay, little hawk. We will find your cousin. We will outrun these Stryxex.

Kazmerev would break into my thoughts every so often with one of those assurances, but though I adored him for his thoughtfulness, and though I wanted to believe him, I was still as tense and rigid as an oak board all through the flight.

There were Stryxex behind us and Stryxex ahead and how could we possibly rescue Mally with so many enemies on every side?

Judicus was a silent burden behind me, and he adjusted his seat often, trying to read his map by the light of the moon. Knowing him, it was more than boredom that drove his study. I could only hope he was hatching some kind of plan.

At one point he muttered, "Ciuade, ciuade," as if that meant something to him.

When Kazmerev died, we kept going on foot. My heart ached for him. I felt lonelier than ever, surrounded by the long shadows of morning. Any of them might hold an enemy. I didn't realize I was shivering until Judicus took my hand and held it between his.

"Here, let me warm this. You're too cold," he said, and it felt both kind and attentive and made me feel awkward all at once.

I felt even more awkward when Gundt looked back at our linked hands and shook his head without saying a word. I knew that's what he'd do before he did it. The man couldn't understand friendship. And why would he when he was bound for life to an insane phoenix with her nose so far in the air she couldn't see her own talons?

That was unkind.

I was just tired.

We were almost to the town after hours of walking – it had seemed a lot closer when we were flying – when I smelled smoke.

Gundt threw a hand up, face wrinkling in concentration. After a moment he pointed to where he smelled it. It was up hill and into the trees, but as we moved toward the line of forest, we found a trail worn into the grass.

Gundt paused.

"I have a bad feeling about this."

"So do I," Judicus whispered. "We're close to the ancient ruins of Ciuade. I have heard many tales of the place. No one should linger nearby. I don't think that treasure hunters go there anymore – not now that it's been stripped down so far. You'd need crazy luck to find anything there now, but there might be other vagabonds. Or there could be something worse." He paused, swallowing visibly. "We could wait. Wait until nightfall when your phoenixes are back. Wait until there are more of us."

I bit my lip. Because waiting was fine. It was fine, but what if we missed our opportunity because we waited? Or what if this was a false trail and we wasted time backtracking to it only because we thought something was here that we could have eliminated by quickly checking it out?

Gundt seemed to feel the same way.

"You two stay here. If I don't come back in a turn of the hour, go on to the inn without me and wait for the others."

Judicus licked his lips like he was thinking about reminding Gundt that he was the one in charge of our coterie – again – but Gundt gave a very subtle nod to me. They were still worried about me. Which was crazy!

"It's a plan," Judicus said. "But if you see a ruined city – best that you don't go in. It's haunted by things no mortal should see – or so the texts say."

"I'll be back quickly." Gundt left his pack with us and disappeared into the woods.

"It's okay," Judicus said when Gundt was gone. "Probably just hunters or other travelers. Or something."

I frowned. Why would travelers stay in the forest when a town with a real inn was so close?

Every sound in the forest made my skin crawl. It felt like there were Stryxex everywhere waiting to pounce.

To my relief, Judicus took out the map and opened it up to show me.

"Look, here's Rafinnette. Here's where that crazy island was with the altar on it," he pointed as he spoke. "I think this little dot is meant to be the town ahead. If we travel further inland, the road swoops to the south and toward Bricatorre. See?"

I pointed to the small marking close to the dot he thought was a town.

"I don't know what that mark means, either," he admitted. "It looks like it's right where we are standing, but that's maps for you. They play with distances. It could still be miles away or even on the other side of the road. I *think* it could be a sign for Ciuade, though. If it is – well, no one should put that on a map unless they are trying to avoid it. At least there's a warning. The maker of these maps uses this wavy line as a way of saying 'don't go there' but he uses that for old quarries as well as places rumored to be haunted or rapids in rivers. To him, it just means generalized danger. See how he places the wave symbol under whatever this one is?"

I peered at the sign. It looked almost like a snake to me.

"I need more detailed maps," Judicus said with a sigh. "These ones cover the whole country, which is nice, but I'd like to really narrow in on the details, you know? It's hard to make proper decisions about travel if you don't know whether you're avoiding a deadly mine shaft that drops into nothing or just a rumor about a mysterious woman who collects mushrooms." He laughed nervously. "Or the legendary city from which all rope workers originally came."

I huffed a laugh and caught him grinning with me. And for just a moment I thought about how I now had more friends than I'd ever had before. How they cared about me. How I had a place with them. It made me feel so warm, so full of belonging and appreciation – like nothing in the world could ever touch me.

Judicus took my hand again, almost on impulse and he was smiling when he said, "Sersha. I've been thinking ..."

And then I heard a scream.

And I knew that scream.

"Mally," Judicus whispered, suddenly paler than normal.

We were both back on our feet before the scream ended.

92

We took one look at each other and Judicus turned to follow, but I snatched his hand.

"Gundt will need our help," he hissed. "Even if it's Ciuade, we can't leave Mally if that's her in there."

But that wasn't why I had grabbed him. I squeezed his hand trying to make him understand.

He shook his head as he realized. "No, I'm not taking your energy. We don't know what's happening and you haven't slept since yesterday. You're too tired. Maybe ... maybe it's nothing."

But we both knew it wasn't nothing. I drew my belt knife just in case and Judicus drew his sword. The dark circles under his eyes combined with the blade gleaming in the dawn light made him look like a rakish villain.

"I just hope it isn't Ciuade," he muttered. "The legends of that place are gruesome."

I followed him wordlessly – of course.

The track went uphill, and we had to bend half double to follow it, but when we reached the top, we had a clear view of the other side.

Judicus pressed himself backward against a tree the moment we reached the top. He tugged me against him to keep me from trying to push past. I followed his finger as he pointed.

"Look, it *is* a ruin," he whispered. "Merciful heavens, don't let it be the city."

And it was certainly ruins. Though what had been ruined was hard to tell. The trees had grown up and had grown mature so that they towered not just around the ruins, but through them, until rubble looked like natural hills and half-walls looked like more fallen trees.

Half of a face lay stuck into the ground ahead of us, half its nose and one of its ears buried in the dirt and pine needles. A tree grew around it, curving with the form of the head so that it wrapped around the brow, nearly disguising the crown that had been carved into the stone. The tree was thicker than my waist and Judicus's waist put together. How long ago had this place been destroyed?

"When rope work was discovered – those who touched the threads didn't know how to do it safely," Judicus whispered. "There were ...accidents."

One single stone eye looked right at us from the ruined statue's head. It was polished so that it shone and reflected and showed me myself huddled against Judicus, my eyes wide and long brown hair in disarray. The way Judicus had me tucked against him made him look protective. I was so taken aback that it took me a moment to realize what else the eye showed – Gundt a few trees away, looking down from a low branch, lips pressed together and shaking his head as he looked right at me.

Well, what did he expect? We'd heard screams! Of course, we were going to come and join him here.

Judicus took a trembling step forward and Gundt tried to hiss for him to stop. But the rope worker's eyes were huge as he dropped my hand and stumbled toward the statue, hands up, palms open.

"It's Liandra Keerana Fleris. The first rope worker. She who found the threads that weave all things together."

He was staring in awe at the statue.

I tried to grab his arm, but he was too quick, hurrying now to where the head was so he could run his hands over it.

"Merciful heavens, it's a Lens. No one talks about that, Sersha. It's a Lens!"

I looked back at Gundt, trying to show him with my expression that this was not the plan. His own expression was equally distressed as he slid down from his perch and snuck across the ground toward where Judicus was admiring the head.

It seemed there was a crumbling wall behind the head and a pair of feet sticking out from the foliage – stone feet, of course, belonging to the half-head of this Lens.

Gundt signaled to me and we crept around the head, watching. If we couldn't stop Judicus, we could at least make sure this place wasn't going to swallow him up.

I kept hearing Mally's cry in my head again and again and I couldn't help the urgency that filled me now, willing me to act – to somehow save her from distress. It leaked into my actions, making me quick and jerky and it leaked into my thoughts, the distress making them slow and muddled. She was in there somewhere – in this place that Judicus had feared. And what was happening to her to make her scream like that?

There was no one on the other side of the head. Just the crumbling wall and a massive doorway with the door shut. It was a gorgeous masterpiece all by itself – tarnished silver hammered over wood. Someone had taken the time to carve an entire garden's worth of flowers over the door in intricate detail – some of them no larger than my pinkie finger. It was wide enough for three carts to go through at once and just as tall. But over the masterpiece someone else had gouged letters into the metal, hammering them in with chisel and a heavy hand.

"None shall pass lest the curse fall."

I looked at Gundt and his lined face was troubled.

"I guess if the door is barred, we should go over the wall," Judicus said from behind me.

I turned to him, eyes wide, and he shrugged.

"What? That was Mally screaming. We're not just going to leave her in there because of a vague warning, are we?"

But I wondered if maybe we should.

93

I didn't like the way the shadows moved within the ruins. They moved like they were alive, but when I looked directly at them, I saw nothing out of the ordinary.

We climbed over the crumbled wall.

"Stay behind me, Sersha," Gundt said, keeping his sword high.

But as we passed between broken buildings that must have once been homes, huge conifer trees growing up and through what remained of them, we saw no people at all. Nothing but those strange shadows that tried to slide away from your eyes.

Another long, wailing scream made the hair on my neck stand up and I eased my weight onto my toes, ready to run, but not sure if I should be running towards or running away from it. Judicus slipped forward, past Gundt's outstretched hand, hurrying soundlessly across the pine needle-covered street. We hurried to follow as he ran around a building and then spun right back and threw himself against a crumbling wall, spread flat against it.

His eyes were wide.

Gundt tried to push me to join him before creeping around the building himself, but I refused to go. If there was something to be seen, I was going to see it.

I crept up just behind him and my mouth fell open as I looked.

We stood on the edge of a crater. It was as if a wide portion of the ground – a rough circle about the size of most main city squares – had been cut out like a round of pie dough and then smashed into the earth. Rough carved earth and stone formed sheer cliffs all the way around it, grown over now with creepers and tiny striving plants except for the far side from us where the ground had torn a little less neatly and had left a rough, rocky path down to the lowered circle.

There was a small building with a domed roof inside made of stone – a temple if I had to guess. A tree grew right through the dome, leaving spiderwebbed cracks all around. It was a mighty redwood and from where I leaned over the edge, I could see the tops of its noble branches and the nest of eagles nearly at the top of the tree.

These ruins had been here a very long time.

It would have been beautiful and maybe even peaceful – a place to sit and contemplate life and the brevity of human accomplishment beside the lengthy scroll of years – if it hadn't been for the screaming.

This time when Mally screamed, my eyes found her right away.

Just outside the temple, someone had built a round altar and the top of the altar was a wheel surrounded by bladed weapons pointed inward on tall columns. It could spin so that the blades whirled around whatever, or whoever, was in the center– as it was doing now.

I didn't know what it had been there for originally, and I wondered if the people below knew, but what it was doing now was spinning around Mally who was chained in place so that she was nicked by one of the blades every time because avoiding one only put you in the path of the next. I thought the cuts were shallow, but even that many shallow cuts could be too much. Her blood sprayed out, splattering the watchers, the altar, and the stones all around.

How horrific.

But wasn't she their good luck charm? Wasn't she meant to save them all? Or at least give them power, which to the evil among us seems like the same thing?

Gundt growled between his teeth, shot to his feet, and began to jog around the lip of the cliff.

It was a bad idea. His sudden movement kicked up the eagle from his nest, who shrieked as he launched into the sky. And just as I feared it would, it also drew the eyes of every one of Mally's captors.

I could not hear their words, but I could see their fingers point at him. And that's when I saw the second thing – a group of soldiers in uniforms that I did not recognize were standing with a picket of horses on the far side of the cliff.

They saw Gundt, too. And they didn't waste time calling or pointing. Five of them broke off from the rest, charging toward him.

I felt a hand on my shoulder and then Judicus was whispering in my ear.

"Crawl back from the edge before they see us, too."

It was a good plan. It should have saved us from notice.

But as we turned to sneak away, a second group of people slid from the buildings around us, faces wrapped in black.

I hadn't been wrong. The shadows *were* moving – they'd been filled with people.

Raiders.

Here.

Miles to the south of where we'd seen them last but still just as deadly.

94

One of them spoke in his own language and Judicus replied back. I forgot how educated he was sometimes – it made me feel doubly voiceless.

"You'll come with us," the raider said in my language, his words rough as his men surrounded us.

Judicus swallowed and I saw the little flickers of his eyes as he assessed the men surrounding us, assessed the cliff behind us, and noted Gundt, and the sound of ringing steel as the Flame Rider fought back against the soldiers further along the rim of the cliff.

Slowly, Judicus raised his hands.

"That's right. Horacen will speak with you," the raider said. And I was glad I couldn't see his expression because his words sounded leering and cruel.

"I get the feeling it's not talking he wants to do," Judicus said as we walked with their spears against the small of our backs.

"He doesn't speak much, no," the raider agreed.

"I bet he likes cutting people up," Judicus added casually.

"It is one of his finer skills," the raider said.

Sweat broke out across my brow. What was Judicus thinking? Was he trying to make light of this? We'd massively failed. And it was morning. There was no hope of a phoenix saving us.

He probably should have fought these raiders with his rope work while he could so we could escape.

But his eyes kept flicking down the cliff to where Mally was crying out every few minutes and I knew the truth. He wouldn't abandon her to save his own skin – not when she was in that much trouble. Not even when he didn't like her much.

There was a sadness in his eyes, and I wondered if he felt as indebted to Aunt Danna as I did – if he felt like he owed her after she nursed him through the forest.

Or maybe, as usual, he was just that noble. The real kind of noble, not the kind that you were born into that meant money and privilege. The kind that made you do the right thing when no one would expect it of you.

I'd lived for years behind the bar and in the kitchen of the Hog's Head Inn. And I'd dreamed of seeing the world, of becoming more. And here I was, surrounded by raiders, having not just seen more of the world than anyone in my village ever saw, having not just seen it from above as only a privileged few ever would, but seeing things that no one even thought were real. Seeing legends come to life and magical ruins and strange peoples.

And in all of that, I'd learned something – something I was holding onto even as these barbaric raiders pushed me along with the razor-sharp tips of their spears. I had learned that a kind heart and a determination to do what's right is more valuable than magic. It was more precious and rare than strange artifacts or creatures made of nothing but shadow and magic.

He was right not to flee again. We couldn't flee forever. We couldn't chase forever. And maybe we hadn't picked this spot or this confrontation, but it felt – somehow – as if it were inevitable that we'd take our stand in this abandoned, cursed place.

They led us all the way around to where the earth sloped down into the basin. I couldn't help but notice how they nodded to the soldiers they encountered as if they were all friends and not supposedly the armies of the men who lived here and the armies of invaders. If Mally's screams and all Lady Lightland's previous actions hadn't been enough, that would have told me that something very suspicious was happening here.

Rough steps had been carved into the ragged edge where the top earth met the bottom of the basin. We were pushed into single file and then forced down the steps.

Judicus glanced back at me constantly, checking to make sure I was safe, until he was cuffed by the raider in front of him.

"Eyes forward."

My eyes were not forward, I was watching the basin below, noting every detail as it slowly grew larger before our eyes.

Everything was built or had grown to a massive scale from those towering redwoods to the columned and domed temple and the large arches surrounding a stone courtyard in front of it where the wheel of blades had been carefully placed.

If this was where ropework had originated, then I wasn't surprised that people feared it. This was not a happy place. Not a good place. Not at all.

I picked out Lady Lightland first. Her two Stryxex riders flanked her. But what made me very nervous was that she looked uncomfortable – maybe even a little wide-eyed – and so did her riders. I'd watched her slit my aunt's throat with barely a flinch, watched her raise an army of stone creatures, watched her order my death. And *now* she was looking nervous?

I bit my own lip and kept looking.

There was a clump of raiders to her left, watching Mally spin with arms folded over their chests. I recognized Horacen immediately. He had a wolf head stitched on the chest of his black clothing and he stood exactly as I remembered. Seeing him here with Lady Lightland was certainly no surprise.

But seeing the Grand Hadri's soldiers in a careful square formation on her right? That was a shock. Even though I'd seen the men and pickets above on the rim, I hadn't stopped to think about why they were here. What could bring soldiers of this land who were meant to defend it and these enemy raiders to the same place without bloodshed?

Ah. There was my answer. One of the men in uniform wore a gilt-edged helm, his grizzled face shaved clean, and a tuft of red horsehair tied to the pommel of his sword. He'd be a general, then. He could have ordered his soldiers to come here. His eyes were fixed on Gundt as his men dragged our friend toward him.

I swallowed at my first clear look at Gundt. He hung between two soldiers, his feet dragging in the pine needles behind him. There was no sign of his short sword anywhere.

Not good.

Not good at all.

There were four of us if you counted Mally. Two were injured now. All four captive.

Even if the other privateer Flame Riders made it this far, they weren't going to be flying in on phoenixes to rescue us – not until nightfall.

And I wasn't sure we'd live until then.

Against us were a powerful lady, a general, a raider ... and who were those two?

Two people in finery stood a little to the side, hands raised to cover nose and mouth delicately. They were both older than middle age. Both grey-haired. But they wore different colors with different sigils embroidered on the front panel and the older woman wore a heavy veil to obscure her features, while the man was bareheaded and cold in demeanor.

Nobles.

What manner of madness was this? Nobles, a general, raiders and Stryxex. It was like a coup being planned against the Grand Hadri. But did they really think they could get away with that?

And beside the whirling wheel, I noticed another figure for the first time. He stood beside Mally's device of torture, a look of concentration on his face and his hands held out as if he was manipulating something. After a moment, I realized a long narrow black thread poured from his fingertips into the wheel. Was he the one spinning it?

My eyes went huge at the same moment that I heard Judicus mutter an ugly curse. He'd seen the man, too. And as I realized what I was seeing, I realized he looked a lot like Judicus – pale of skin, his coat long and billowing, they could be cousins.

Or maybe that was just how all rope workers looked.

I barely remembered the one I had killed in Lady Lightland's pavilion. The thought of him made my throat feel tight. I didn't think I'd be sending bars of flames into anyone today. I didn't think I was going to get out of this alive at all.

Something dark crossed over the sun, leaving goosebumps to rise across my skin as the air suddenly went colder.

And when I looked up, I felt colder still.
Descending upon us was a cloud of what I at first took for birds.
They were not birds.
My breath froze in my chest as I realized what they really were.
Stryxex.

95

The descent of the Stryxex took all eyes off of us.

Even mine.

We froze where we were, standing just at the base of the stairs where they opened into the basin. Even the ropeworker spinning Mally's wheel dropped his hands and her wheel wobbled to a stop.

A look of horror filled the general's face and even from so far away, I could hear his words slice through the air, "What have you done?"

I didn't understand at first. Didn't understand why all his men seemed equally horrified.

After all, there were two Stryxex riders standing with Lady Lightland. Had they not seen them when they arrived.

It wasn't until the Stryxex settled just in front of the wheel – three ranks of three of them – that I realized they had come with prisoners.

Their leader – a rider with a grizzled face and reddish hair, leapt from his Stryxex, wobbling slightly as he tried to find his footing. Half his face was awash with blood. The others looked just as worn. The Stryxex – when I looked closely – were missing feathers. One moved awkwardly, and I realized one of its feet was gone entirely. And their riders were just as battered. The one nearest me fell bonelessly from his Stryxex and hit the earth. There were five arrows sticking out of his back. No one even bothered to run to him to help.

But they were not alone.

They had captives with them that they dragged from the backs of their Stryxex and threw to the ground in front of the two older people in the fancy clothing.

Were they the leaders here, then, and not the general or Lady Lightland?

"Counselors," the redhead said in a gravelly voice. "Your prizes. Delivered as requested."

"We asked for assurances that you could overthrow the throne," the female counselor said. "We did not ask for prisoners."

I glanced at Judicus and he mouthed the words, "Advisors. Grand Hadri."

Two of his advisors, then. Traitors. I was right about the coup attempt.

I swallowed as the redheaded man laughed.

"I think you'll find some *assurance*," his mouth twisted at that word, "in this."

He ripped the sack off the head of the first prisoner and then went down the line ripping the sacks from their heads. I gasped.

Refrento was the first man. There was a red wound where one of his eyes had been.

I bit my lip as my vision grew blurry for a moment. Oh no.

Dalissa Fenwan was the second. She swayed, started to slump, and was cuffed hard on the cheek for her weakness. Refrento leaned to the side, supporting her as she fell against him.

My hands were sweating, breath coming too fast as the third hood was removed.

Duche Olliman. Blood, dried and black, coated his chin. I feared for what that meant. Me, more than anyone else, because I knew what it was to have no voice.

My eyes prickled with tears and it was all I could do to hold them back. Our allies. Our friends. The only people who knew where we were and could possibly rescue us – and they had already been defeated.

But who was the fourth person?

A tiny cry sounded, and Lady Lightland's hand flew to her mouth. She must have realized who it was even though I could not.

I swallowed down my fear – what could be so bad that it would draw that kind of reaction from the most cold-hearted woman I'd ever met?

Fear lit her eyes.

And then, with a smirk, the redheaded Stryxex rider yanked the sack from over the head of the fourth figure and silence fell across the basin.

The man, bound hand and foot, still seemed to loom as he leaned forward and said, in a voice like a lion, "And now, what will you do, little mice? Now, what will you do when you've brought the lion to your dinner table?"

I bit my cheek so hard that blood rushed into my mouth as I realized there really was no one left who knew where we were because the man on his knees was Captain Rackham, the Grand Hadri of the Calicarn Empire, he who had sworn us as privateers. And he who was being betrayed before our eyes by his advisors, his generals, and his own soldiers.

96

The moment passed and the raiders pushed us forward.

"Come on now," the nearest one said. "You're missing the party."

And though my brain was scrambling for a solution – some scrap of something that could get us out of this mess – nothing was coming to me. It was as if every thread that had led us to this point was tangled together now, forming a net I hadn't realized was weaving to capture us as surely as a fish in the sea.

Out of the corner of my eye, I noticed Mally moving. I kept my eyes dead ahead, refusing to notice in case it drew attention to her.

"You captured the Grand Hadri himself?" one of the advisors asked – though it was obviously not a real question. He was right before them, after all. There could be no doubt. "But how?"

"We told you that our Stryxex were powerful," the redhead said, leering down at the Grand Hadri. When I wasn't looking, he had drawn a sword and pressed the blade to the ruler's throat.

I was trying to keep my eyes on him now, as we were marched toward him, the raiders using their spears to make the point that they wanted us moving. But as we moved, I was keeping track of Mally out of the corner of my eye. She'd slipped out of her bonds somehow and laid the manacles silently on the bottom of the cage. Everything she touched was streaked in red and blood ran freely from her many wounds, but determination filled her every movement.

We were almost upon the group when she slipped from the cage entirely and it was our sudden arrival that masked her slinking behind us and into the dome-roofed temple.

I kept my eyes ahead and my expression careful. There was only one way out of this basin unless you could fly. Could she slip up that narrow walkway, too?

Maybe.

If there was enough distraction down here that even the soldiers guarding the horse pickets were distracted, then maybe she could slip past everyone.

I held my breath and hoped.

We had caught up with Gundt, and he was tossed – bloody and stumbling – to the ground beside the other Flame Riders. He tried to surge back to his feet and was clubbed on the head with the hilt of a sword, leaving him gasping on all fours. He retched. They hit him again, and this time he collapsed on the ground.

I flinched from the sight of their cruelty, my heart wrapped up in Gundt and his pain. This wasn't right. They shouldn't be doing any of this. The horror of it was too much – so much that I thought that even Lady Lightland was finding it to be more than she'd expected. Her face was very pale.

"We're committed now," the female advisor said from beneath her veil. "The six of us are committed to this course of action. There is no turning back now that we have taken this step."

The general's mouth twisted at her words, but the eyes of Horacen – the leader of the Hand of the Rat – glittered with excitement.

"We are ready to begin," he said. "Shall we strike tonight?"

"I need to move my armies back," the general said quietly. "I'd like to spare as many as I can. Your raiders will stick to the approved paths to Briccatore. No deviations. No accidents. This is meant to throw the nobility into disarray, to root out who in the army is with us and who must be sent to the slaughter. It is not meant to slaughter the population."

"There will always be those who die in wars," the Grand Hadri said. He flinched when the blade was put against his throat a second time, this time it drew a tiny drop of blood and I froze.

I'd never heard of the Grand Hadri before I met Judicus. I'd never heard of Flame Riders, or the Hand of the Rat, or Stryxex. But even girls from villages knew what happened when rulers were pulled down. It meant war, which meant famine and poverty for everyone – even people far away awaiting trade ships and sons to return. It meant deaths – not just of powerful people brought low – but deaths of those caught up in the confusion of war, of those who just happened to live or to be standing in the wrong place at the wrong time. It meant waste – the waste of crops burned in fields. The waste of animals slaughtered for armies to eat, the waste of people dead or robbed for no reason but some other person's whim.

And all at once, two things ignited inside me. One was rage that these fools would gather here and doom everyone else for their own ambition. And the other was frustration. Because this time right now, *of all times,* was the time when someone with a clever word might make a difference and stop this. And I could not speak all the words bubbling up and tumbling through my heart and head.

And before I could so much as look at Judicus, he reached out and squeezed my hand and then pushed past the surprised raiders surrounding us. He angled to the side until he was between the prisoners and the conspirators so that I could not even see him through the thick bodies of the raiders who were pressing forward to get a good look at him.

And when he spoke, his voice was pitched loud like an orator – exactly how I would pitch mine if I could speak as I'd wished.

"Listen to my words, sons and daughters of Briccatore, listen, soldiers of honor, listen you from far shores," and to my utter surprise, they did seem to be listening to him.

"Don't give us that time-honored opening, Irault," Lady Lightland drawled as if she was the only one there who didn't care what was happening. I knew better. I'd been watching her and even now her gaze would stick when it passed over the fallen form of her half-brother. "Just because it means we have to hear you out doesn't mean we won't kill you when you're done. Shouldn't you be dead already? I left you to the mercies of the sea."

But Lady Lightland was no longer the one in charge of this and the male advisor shushed her.

"Quiet, my lady. The oration has begun, and tradition says that any who begin in such a manner must be allowed to say their piece, even prisoners condemned to death as this one is now that I know who he is," he sounded almost gracious except for that casual comment about how he was happy to kill Judicus. "Go on now, Judicus Franzer Irault, son of the Lord of Chaos. Speak your piece before we slit your throat."

"I am indeed Chaos's son," Judicus said, still in orator's voice. "I have seen the depths of darkness and I have risen from the ashes of a dead man."

I was so intent on his words that it took me a heartbeat before I realized that the raiders weren't watching me anymore, and no one else was, either. I could sneak off just like Mally and no one would ever know. It would be easy. I could regroup and come back for Judicus and Gundt. If they were still alive.

Or.

I bit my lip and thought of all those children dying from war. All those people with their crops burning and their homes destroyed. I thought of Aunt Danna giving everything for her girl and how these people would ask for the chance to do the same thing if they knew how to do that.

So, I could try to save myself and the ai'sletta, too.

Or I could try for something more.

And for a moment I felt a tingle of fire in my fingertips, almost as if Kazmerev were watching me and trying to tell me that he'd be with me, if only I would *try*.

97

I slipped backward, one step, two steps, and sidled toward where the Grand Hadri was on his knees with a blade to his throat. Judicus, shifted his weight as he spoke, seemingly naturally, but I caught the barest fraction of his eye as he did it. He saw what I was doing, and he was trying to help.

"You remember my father, may his tale burn bright forever," he said. "You remember how he would not suffer injustice when he found it through the ranks of the people. How he rooted it out from the lowest beggar to the greatest prince, toppling even the ruler of the country itself – Grand Hadri Jemisin Falca Greniline. He dragged him from his bed and cut off his head on the palace steps and from him he seized both city and country."

He did? I shook off my surprise at that and focused on what I was doing.

I was right behind the Grand Hadri, but I couldn't act. The redhead still lingered back with the prisoners, his blade to the Grand Hadri's throat. The bloody side of his face was toward me and I could tell he couldn't see well from that side, but if I moved he'd notice.

I swallowed and looked up at Judicus. I could see in his eyes the moment he realized my predicament. He leaned forward, speaking in such a low tone now that this audience leaned forward, too, hoping to hear better. The redhead leaned with them, but he was still here, still paying attention.

"And what did he do to the hidden Hand of the Rats who he found in the secret wing of the palace? What did he do to their emissary of the red hair and ruddy beard? What else ran red that night?"

And I didn't know if the story was true or if he was making it up right there, but the sword tip dipped in the redhead's hand and he took a subconscious step forward, eyes locked onto Judicus.

"What happened when it was found out that man was a traitor to his people, that he had sold them as surely as our ruler had sold us?"

The redheaded raider took another step, "Lies!"

And then he took two more and now they were all watching him as he made his way toward Judicus, the bound prisoners forgotten.

I sprang into action.

Quickly, I hurried down the line, deftly nipping the bonds of the Flame Riders as Judicus continued to speak. This speech was his sacrifice for us all. I didn't think he'd survive it. It was made to infuriate the powerful and with their own rage, to turn their purpose against them.

"Oh, but he had," Judicus said. "He'd sold them for a golden palace and a wife of his choosing – such a small bribe for such a great thing. And when my father heard of it, he slit his throat, too, and every man with him. And they dragged the corpses to the docks and set them on a ship bound for their homelands where the sailors leapt from ship to boat and lit them as a pyre to be found by their people."

His speech was just long enough for me. I severed the knots at the Grand Hadri's wrists and heels while the Flame Riders I'd freed were still frozen in shock.

"And now we've come for what is ours," Horacen growled and the redheaded Stryxex rider growled with him and for the first time I realized that was who these Stryxex riders were – the Hand of the Rat. Mounted raiders. A chill flowed through me. "And you'll die for what your father did."

The redheaded rider leapt forward, slashing toward Judicus with his sword.

Black ropes shot from Judicus's hands as he turned the blows and around him, his enemies fumbled for weapons, their shouts echoing through the basin.

There was a growl from in front of me as the Grand Hadri surged to his feet and then fell back down with a muffled cry. And then Refrento was in front of me, single eye blazing with passion.

"Get him out of here," he whispered, shoving the Grand Hadri at me as the other Flame Riders formed a wall in front of us. "We'll deal with the traitors."

I looked from him to the Grand Hadri who he wrenched back to his feet and shoved into my arms. His leg, I realized, was dangling at an odd angle from the knee down and his black boots and black trousers were disguising how soaked they were in blood. He couldn't stand on his own, certainly couldn't fight.

I looked to Gundt – still clutching his head as he lay on the ground moaning, and back to Judicus fighting five armed men now with his ropes, while more scrambled for weapons and a chance to find an opening against him.

The rope worker who had been tormenting Mally streaked past, hands held out as he joined the attack.

And for the first time in my life, I didn't know what the right thing to do was. I didn't even know what I wanted to do. I didn't have enough hands. There wasn't enough of me – and it had nothing to do with my voice.

If there was one person – other than Kazmerev – that I wanted to live, one person who had shown again and again that he was *for* me, it was Judicus. And to help anyone else, I'd have to turn my back on him.

"You can't save everyone," Refrento insisted, pathos in the one eye he had left. I couldn't even look at the other one. He shoved me toward the temple where Mally had disappeared, "but if you can keep him alive, you can save the most."

98

The Grand Hadri was a heavy man.

But everything in me roared up like a flame to meet the challenge. Heat rose up, giving me the strength to heave his arm over my shoulder and half-lead, half-haul him toward the temple.

I stole a glance over my shoulder as steel met steel and saw fire blossom from Refrento's hand even though his phoenix was dead within him. It roared through a pair of raiders and the soldiers behind them, catching the veil of the female advisor on fire. My mouth fell open, wondering why he hadn't struck before, and then just as fast as the inferno had begun, it guttered out. He must only have so much strength with his phoenix dead. He dropped his hand, looking frantic, and then a blade fell and Refrento fell with it, clutching his throat. He was dead before he hit the pine needles.

Further back, a web of black ropes flung a soldier so far in the air he nearly hit a bird. He smacked into the cliff face and fell as heavy as a stone. I faced forward again, feet sliding and pulling with every ounce of strength that I had.

If only it were night. If only we had our phoenixes. What would happen to Refrento's phoenix now? Would there be ashes clutched in his hand?

Was this what it felt like to feel your heart break? Was it this hollow, aching gap inside?

"I can fight," the Grand Hadri said thickly. Whatever had given him the strength to speak against his enemies before was leaking out with the blood leaving a thick smear of gore behind us. "I can."

What would we do when we got to the temple? I had nothing but my belt knife. I had no way to fight and defend him – and I was losing the fight against exhaustion. The Grand Hadri was twice my size and far, far too heavy.

Fear choked me, making my breath stick in my throat. I risked another look over my shoulder. Bodies littered the ground everywhere. The screams of the living mixed with the silence of the dead in a grisly tapestry. Dalissa lay on top of Refrento. Her head lay a pace away. I hadn't even seen her fall. Duche Olliman was the last one standing between us and our enemies.

His hands splayed open as they charged at him and fire whipped out from his palms in rolling waves like a rope whipped in the hand. It splashed across a Stryxex rider, clawing both him and his bird from the ground and scorching them to the skin. The scream of the Stryxex pierced through me like a sword.

Another Stryxex screamed, diving from the sky with talons open. It caught Olliman by the shoulders just as I was turning back to look at our path.

I gasped as my vision was suddenly filled with a scarlet-stained Mally. Her shallow cuts were still bleeding as she ran out the door of the temple, freezing as she looked over the battlefield in front of her.

She had something clutched in her hands – something odd that, like the Stryxex, seemed to turn light away from it. It was a circlet with a single black cabochon gem the size of a chicken egg that would sit over the forehead.

"No!" the scream ripped out from behind me and I turned to see Lady Lightland reaching toward us, hand outstretched. She was too far away to reach us, held back by the burning turf and bodies between her allies and the few of us. "Don't, Ai'sletta! You must not!"

I couldn't see Judicus back there anymore. I could only see his ropes clawing out blindly like the legs of a dying spider. Or were those the ropes from the other rope worker? I didn't know, but something seized painfully in my heart at the thought of Judicus gasping for life and failing to find a breath.

I turned back to Mally, desperate for help or hope of any kind.

She smiled in a forced way and tilted her chin up defiantly.

"The Dark Diadem," the Grand Hadri said, his voice so faint I barely heard it. "Beloved of the Night."

And then Mally very precisely set the diadem on her head.

And darkness fell like a curtain blocking out the sun.

I gasped as all fell silent except Mally who said, "It's lucky I found it, don't you think?"

And then my Kazmerev was bursting forth, tumbling from my chest like a volcano erupting in feathers of flame. He roared to life with a *fump* of fire puffing up when someone threw lamp oil over it. Above me, a sister explosion of flame erupted as Frissei sprang to life and the Stryxex holding Olliman screamed in terror.

With deliberate calm, I thrust the Grand Hadri into Mally's arms.

"Who is this?" she asked but I didn't try to sign an answer, I spun in place, hands blazing with heat even before I opened them and let the fire flow through me and into the soldier with his spear raised over Gundt, into the raider leaping through the air, his knife aimed toward Judicus's back, into the male advisor whose mouth was open in horror.

My phoenix was reborn.

And with him, my hope.

Fly with me, little hawk, there is righteous work to do here!

EPISODE ONE: "FLIGHT OF RUNES"

SEASON TWO

99

I blinked at the afterimage of what had just happened as if blinking a dream away.

But it wasn't gone. Mally was still wearing the Dark Diadem on her tumbled curls, blood streaking her face and bare arms. She clutched the Grand Hadri against her – the ruler of Calicarn – his face drawn with agony and his leg dragging at a terrible angle.

The world was still pitch black – no moon, no stars, no light but the terrible brightness of Kazmerev, my beloved phoenix, and Frissei flaring above us like apocalyptic suns.

The three men I'd burned with fire – the soldier, raider, and advisor – lay slumped on the earth, their bodies still ablaze.

I gulped down air. The horror inside stuttering for a moment before I realized I couldn't stay like this. My friends were still in danger. The battle had really only just begun.

Everything seemed to be happening in slow motion. My eyes scanned across the world around me, only catching glimpses in the thick blackness. How was I supposed to make choices when I just couldn't see?

I forced myself forward on shaking limbs anyway, but the ground was shaking, shaking in a way I didn't understand. My only thoughts were of Gundt slumped on the ground and Judicus out there somewhere in the darkness fighting a half-dozen raiders. Huxabrand stuck in Gundt's heart until he recovered enough for her to flare to life.

I'd help them one at a time. That was the sensible choice.

I reached Gundt first, falling to my knees beside his semi-conscious body. He mumbled something I couldn't understand as I tried to drag him up. It was at times like these I wished I had a voice and a way to comfort others. He moaned, but his eyes were still closed, the wound on the back of his head leaking blood. Could a man survive a blow like that? I felt ill with wondering.

Watch out! Kazmerev warned and as fast as I could look up, he was there, wrenching a raider from the ground right in front of me. The man thrust a spear inches from my face as he was torn away, ripped into the air.

I sucked in my scream. No time for panic. Not now that he was rushing up into the sky in the talons of my beloved phoenix.

That was close!

Kazmerev's bright wings conjured enough light to bathe Gundt's pale face in orange for one brilliant moment. I tried to haul him up on my own, but Olliman was already beside me, his chin still dripping with dark blood, his eyes aching and hollow. I was certain he'd been tortured along with the Grand Hadri and the other Flame Riders when the Stryxex had kidnapped them and brought them to this place. He opened his mouth for one horrible moment and then spat and closed it again with a look of concentrated pain. Our eyes met in shared misery. Neither of us could speak and I felt his pain at the realization as if it were my own. There is nothing wonderful about being voiceless, even if sometimes I pretend there is.

Olliman shook his head, as if agreeing with me that my sympathies would have to wait, and took Gundt gently from my hands his stronger muscles able to lift the man up and onto his shoulder even though he bowed and stumbled under the weight. His phoenix would help. It would be okay.

Frissei is occupied right now.

Olliman's eyes met mine, desperation meeting its twin as he nodded. I risked a glance to the side to see Frissei tangled in darkness as he fought a Stryxex. There was a scream from its rider, but Frissei was under the creature, tearing with his bright golden beak while at the same time being torn, his dazzling feathers raining down as if the coffers of heaven had opened over us.

I met Olliman's eyes again and almost missed the raider creeping up on me except that he was reflected in the fires there.

I spun, hand outstretched, and my fire blazed out, catching the masked raider in the chest and throwing him backward. No one should have such killing power – certainly not me – but I was grateful for it in this moment. The raider hit another like him, knocking the man back, and then the ground trembled again under us, and something like a crack formed by my foot. I danced back.

I had to find Judicus. I had to get everyone to the same place. No one else knew enough of where everyone was to make that happen.

Could Kazmerev tell Frissei where Mally and the Grand Hadri were so Olliman could join them?

Frissei, tell your man that the ai'sletta and the Grand Hadri are in the temple, Kazmerev said, and he sounded choked. I searched the sky to find him high, high up. A scream echoed from his location, and I couldn't tell if it was a person he was dropping to their death or another Stryxex.

Frissei gave a bird-like shriek, too occupied to tell anyone anything, but Olliman was already turning toward the temple as Frissei exploded suddenly in golden light.

It bathed everything in sudden brightness like a flash of lightning and in that instant, I saw we were still surrounded by enemies, that they were closing in on the temple, too, that Judicus yet lived and was grappling – against all odds – with a knife-wielding Lady Lightland and, to my horror, that tiny threads of something were working their way up through the cracks in the ground around us.

This time I did gasp as one of them thrust up to the height of a man, grabbed the remains of Frissei, wrapped around him like a tentacle on something our fishermen pulled from the deepest channels of the sea, and shook.

Frissei, Kazmerev gasped, horror filling his mental voice, and then the light was gone again, and we were once more wrapped in darkness.

100

A dull scream echoed beside me in the darkness, chilling me to the core. Where was my night vision when I needed it most? I could only barely make out the edges of things, and even that felt like my eyes adjusting to the darkness after a bright light had been shone in them.

This is not natural night. Kazmerev's voice was strained. "*This is magical and terrifying.*

How was I going to find Judicus in the dark? The obvious answer would be to shoot flames from my hands, but that could kill him or any other innocents in my path.

I'll swoop down as soon as I can get this Stryxex off my back. I didn't like how tight his voice sounded.

Kazmerev?

He shouldn't risk himself.

Something bright and crimson flared in the sky in a way that made my stomach twist.

Kazmerev?

Nothing.

Fear shot through me as I turned slowly in the darkness.

Something bumped my shoulder and I spun. I was all I could do not to scream before another bright crimson flare edged everything in red light and a hand clasped my arm.

It was Judicus, looking the worse for wear, his clothing shredded, and his dark hair matted with blood and mud. He must have won his battle with the other rope worker or simply slipped away in the darkness. If I could ask him, I would. The idea that the other magic worker might be creeping up on us sent little shivers of fear through me. His face was so dirty I couldn't tell how badly he might be wounded, but his eyes were bright as stars as he whispered, "Sersha? Help me with her."

I looked down, aghast. He had an unconscious Lady Lightland by one arm, and he was dragging her across the ground.

No. I was not going to do that. It was a bad idea.

Something brushed my other arm and I turned more carefully this time. Was there someone else hoping to get my help?

A tentacle waved, sliding along my arm a second time.

My eyes widened and I hissed in a gasp, leaping away from the arm. It had felt like polished stone.

"Hurry," Judicus said and this time I did, grabbing Lady Lightland's other arm and helping him drag her across the grass. Her head hung down limply, the hair tangling under her body and pulling painfully at her head. I wouldn't want to be carried that way, but I also wouldn't want to be left out here, alone, where tentacles clawed up from the ground.

Another high-pitched scream was cut off somewhere near us and I heard a faraway voice calling, "Sersha? If you're still out there you'd better run! I'm closing this door at the count of ten."

I wanted to groan. That was Mally with everything. A tiny branch of peace extended but behind it, there were always deadlines, conditions, and no mercy.

Scarlet light flared again and in the edges of it, I thought I saw the figures of dark-clad raiders dancing back from grasping tentacles.

Kazmerev? Still nothing from my phoenix. He was worrying me.

I met Judicus's eyes for a bare moment before we both heaved, managing a stumbling-near run as we dragged Cassanetta behind us and Mally's voice rang out across the valley.

"Ten," she called.

My toe caught on something, but I didn't dare look down. No time.

"Nine!"

Sersha. I'm so sorry.

Kazmerev! What's happening? I called to my phoenix, frustration lacing my words as I was both blind and voiceless in this heavy darkness. Was he hurt? Why was he apologizing?

"I hate to say it," Judicus said mildly. But his voice had the faint sound of someone struggling with a burden too heavy.

Sersha, I must retreat. They're too many.

I looked up and my heart seized in my chest as he flared again, bright and scarlet. He was surrounded by four Stryxex and they dove and struck, ripping at him from every direction. I caught a glimpse of the red-haired rider on the back of one of them, his face shrouded by his veil even while his red hair glowed like an ember in the darkness.

Go, Kazmerev, go!

But he wasn't going. I gritted my teeth against waves of mindless fear for him. They could do no good.

"Eight!"

"Sersha," Judicus was saying as we stumbled together like two poorly matched draft horses. I could only tell that we'd made progress because Mally's voice was louder as she counted down against the heartless moment when she'd lock us out. "I don't wish to tell you your business, but I think now would be the time to absorb your phoenix so he can live to fight another day, yes?"

His words hit me like a bucket of cold water. Yes. But how? I couldn't remember. I could remember the others doing it and I remembered how to bring him back. But how did I get him to go into my heart and be safe? I froze. My mind offered nothing up as a solution.

"Seven."

"Don't stop pulling!" Judicus urged.

I threw my shoulder into the work, but I was gasping on sobs now because I couldn't remember. I had to remember. Lightning thoughts sizzled and faded half-formed in my mind and still, they gave me nothing. Above me, I could see every feather being ripped from my Kazmerev.

Please, I begged him in my mind. Go. Save yourself. Please!

Nothing.

"Six."

My shin smashed against a stair at the same moment Lady Lightland tugged back. What in the –?

"Five."

Kazmerev burst into flame again – bright gold and scarlet and then I saw the tentacle gripping Lady Lightland's leg and at the same moment I saw dozens of them clawing up from the ground, some with the living and even the dead clutched in their curls. They rose as high as the massive tree at the center of the valley, so high that if they all belonged to one creature then it must be larger than the valley itself. I'd never seen anything like them before. I barely bit back a scream as Judicus yanked on Cassanetta with a manly roar.

She slipped from the tentacle as he yelled," Sersha!"

I threw all my weight in with him, climbing the steps two at a time while Mally yelled out, "Four, three, two, one," with no pauses in between.

We darted through the stone door as she was already closing it, dragging the broken doll of Lady Lightland behind us. The door almost closed on her leg as we fell into the dark recesses of the temple and in that moment I finally remembered.

I closed my eyes, and pullllled my phoenix into my heart and I heard his voice as I did it.

You need me. Don't ...

And then he was safe within for at least as long as I was safe, and I hoped he could forgive me for dragging him into my heart against his will and trapping him in this dark temple.

And if I could just get my breath to stop sawing through my lungs, that would be very helpful.

A light sparked, and to my surprise, I saw the Grand Hadri holding up an ancient bowl lamp filled with oil and carved with grasping tentacles. His face was white and slick with sweat, but he seemed in full control of himself as he spoke.

"Well now," he said. "I suppose you've succeeded in the task I gave you, Flame Riders. And you, too, Judicus Franzer Irault. You've delivered the ai'sletta."

The look on Mally's face could have killed.

101

"You've *delivered* me?" Mally's eyes flashed, matching the black gem on her crown. "I'm not a plaything to be passed back and forth."

"You're the ai'sletta," the Grand Hadri said coolly despite a visage so pale it was almost green. "Your only value is working for a great ruler, such as the Grand Hadri of Calicarn. Alone, you'll rot and die in a tiny village somewhere, known by no one and of no more value than any other village woman."

Well, that explained a lot about whether I should trust the Grand Hadri. I put him out of my mind and hurried to help Judicus who was lowering a bar over the door. The ground shook under us and I looked at him in mute appeal. Would this temple hold up?

"I don't know," he said with forced calm. I was beginning to recognize that was how he dealt with disaster. "It might come down on our heads or it might be crumpled in those stone tentacles outside. I don't think I could prevent either from happening. They seem to be similar to the stone creatures that rise from the sea, but if they are, then I need time to find their source if I'm to disable them – which I am not sure is even possible. Perhaps, they are a permanent feature of this land."

Something struck the door hard enough to jar it and we both looked at the bar in the flickering light of the lamp. I saw the same sinking expression on his face that must have been on mine. That bar wouldn't hold for long.

Which meant I had to be fast. Quickly, I hurried to where Gundt was slumped on the ground. Behind me, Mally was still arguing with the Grand Hadri.

"I won't be used as a prop to make you look good, just like I wouldn't be used by her," she said, pointing at Lady Lightland's unconscious body.

"I think you were used by her very well," the Grand Hadri said, his voice tight and a bit fierce. He must be in agony with that leg, and yet his entire focus was on my cousin. "It's your essence she tapped to bring us all here. The core of who you are that rallied a coup around her, made it possible for her to kidnap me – her rightful ruler – brought raiders to this land and the strange creatures they ride in the night, and woke an ancient evil. Your luck – your twisting of fate and chance – did all of that. Is it so terrible that I want to use you to twist it back?"

I shook my head. If I had a voice, I'd tell them both to be quiet and focus on the wounded or getting us somewhere safer than this temple. Without the ability to speak, all I could do was take my own advice.

Olliman joined me to look over Gundt, looking as worried as I felt. In the flickering light of the strange lamp, his face was ghoulish with drying blood from the way he'd been tortured before we even began to fight. I ignored it for now. One victim at a time. Olliman was still mobile. That meant Gundt first.

I checked him with quick hands. The head wound was bleeding profusely and clearly the source of his lack of consciousness, but it didn't seem deep. I'd just have to hope it wasn't a cracked skull. He was so hot to the touch it hurt my fingers – a good sign. Perhaps he was burning off the injury the way Kazmerev said Flame Riders could. All we could do for him now was bandage his wound and to my surprise, Olliman had already found a basin of tepid water and a stack of dusty cloths. Carefully and quickly, I cleaned Gundt's head wound and wrapped it in cloth.

The Grand Hadri and Mally had escalated to shouting by the time I was done.

I turned to Olliman, still ignoring their dramatics for what really mattered. He met my eyes, and I could barely hold his agonized gaze. I reached out and gently squeezed his hand and to my surprise he squeezed back, tears leaking from the corners of his eyes. I could feel in that squeeze all the questions he couldn't ask and wanted to put to me and all the answers and comforts I wanted to give and couldn't. Because that was the thing. They'd taken his tongue and now he was voiceless, too.

And I couldn't tell him that he'd survive and that he could still have friendships and goals. I couldn't tell him how different things are when the veneer of speech is lost to a person. I couldn't tell him that in some ways it helped you realize who your real friends were and what was true under all those words. All I could do was offer a kind touch and hope he could keep finding hope in his heart – for his sake and the sake of his phoenix.

And I remembered the story he'd told me about the first phoenix – the father bent on keeping his son safe – and I hoped he'd remember it, too, and remember he was not alone.

Carefully, I let go of his hand and slowly moved to wash his face. He let me, ruefully submitting to my healer's touch. With no supplies, there was little I could do but clean and inspect.

As I worked, I listened.

Judicus had clearly had enough. His voice slipped into a crack in the shouting like a prybar between two rocks.

"Mally," he said evenly. "Uncle. I beg of you, listen to me. Outside this ancient temple, a creature of stone is arising with tentacles large as trees and it is this creature that shakes our temple."

"Why should that matter to me?" Mally said with a sniff. "Either it kills me, or this man does, or the stupid girl on the floor who you just had to rescue does. But

I'm not submitting to any of it. I'm the ai'sletta. I'm the Chosen One. I'm not here to serve. I'm here to rule. See the crown? Rule."

I could see her face in my mind's eye. I didn't have to turn to see the thrust of her chin, the defiant glare, the flashing eyes. I knew that sound of her voice meant she was scared. And scared for Mally always meant belligerent.

"This is hardly your affair, Judicus Franzer Irault," the Grand Hadri said. "And unless you want to see the full measure of my authority brought to bear, you will keep out of the conversations of your betters."

I gently gestured to Olliman to open his mouth, grimacing as I did. I didn't want to see the wound and there was little I could do to help it anyway, but someone should look.

He opened his mouth up enough to reveal a cloth stuffed inside. Gently, I removed it and checked the site, grimacing in sympathy. His torturers had done what was necessary to keep him from bleeding to death, but the resultant wound was – horrific. I lost the conversation behind me as I tilted my head side to side being sure I hadn't missed anything. He was likely in a hideous amount of pain. Added to that, he'd lost two people he had worked closely with and probably his phoenix, too. That he was functioning at all was a marvel. I'd likely be a heap on the ground, weeping my heart out.

I wanted to call Kazmerev back. Just so I could know he was there. I felt my arms snaking around me protectively, my head bending down, my own tears starting.

And then Olliman tapped my elbow gently. When I looked up, he shook his head very subtly and gave me a rueful close-mouthed smile. I looked into his eyes for a long moment, sharing with him a touch that promised I'd help him and promised he wasn't going to fall off the edge just yet.

With a sigh, I offered him a fresh cloth for his mouth, and he took it gravely. I patted him gently on the shoulder and then turned again. There were more injuries to see to before we could move from this place and even with limited supplies, I was the only one here to tend them.

I turned to check Mally next. Some of those cuts had been vicious, but when I looked across the lamp-lit room, she was gone.

102

I caught a glimpse of Mally slinking behind a tapestry at the far end of the temple. I hadn't even studied the temple before. There were no windows. There was only one door. The rest was open with an altar in the center which was generously decorated with interwoven tentacles, had a few shelves around the edges, and offered many small oil lamps like the one the Grand Hadri had lit. He was propped up on the altar, his bad leg laid out in front of him, cursing at Judicus in a quiet voice.

I needed to either see to him or Lady Lightland next. I didn't want to touch Cassanetta. It was an ungracious attitude, and I knew it, but I'd rather deal with the angry ruler than the woman who had cut my aunt's throat in front of me.

I thought I might hear Mally's sobs coming faintly from behind the tapestry. I paused, looking between the crumbling tapestry – it covered the wall floor to ceiling and seemed to depict a very faded octopus – to Cassanetta, to the Grand Hadri.

I was spared having to decide when Olliman tapped me on the shoulder and indicated he would look at Cassanetta, directing me to our ruler.

I drew in a deep breath, took half the remaining cloths we'd found, and hurried over.

"You have to get the crown off her head, Judicus," the Grand Hadri said between clenched teeth. "Do that and your sister will be spared."

"It would seem that the path to sparing my sister grows ever longer," Judicus said wryly.

I reached for the Grand Hadri's leg and he batted me away.

"Let Sersha look at your leg," Judicus said. I was surprised he wasn't more drained from his use of magic. It usually left him wrung out and empty and he had used a lot of it in the valley defending us. But as the building shook again I noticed that a little of the hunch was out of his shoulders and his face under the grime and blood was flushed rather than pale. How odd. "She's a healer and you're broken."

The Grand Hadri scowled at me. "No one touches the Grand Hadri of Calicarn without express permission."

"Do they touch Captain Rackham if he's injured?"

The Grand Hadri grunted.

"I'd appreciate it if you'd see to his leg, Sersha," Judicus said to me, turning long enough to smile gently. He was always gracious to me. "Despite his complaints, we need him mobile if we're to escape this place, and we need him with us if we want to prevent a war in Calicarn and an even worse ruler taking over the land and his throne."

I sent a pointed look at Cassanetta and Judicus nodded. "Yes, as ... unmeasured as my uncle is, Cassanetta and her conspiracy are worse."

"Worse!" the Grand Hadri began, but his objection was wrenched from him as the building shook again and he had to grit his teeth against the pain of his broken leg rocking across the altar.

Something bashed against the door and the sound of something creaking sent a thrill of terror down my spine. I hurried to remove the Grand Hadri's boot, ignoring his curses. Judicus was right. He wouldn't be going anywhere unless it was set. It would grow infected if left like this. The bone was sticking through the flesh.

"I swear, voiceless girl, if you do this wrong, I will kill every relative you have in the worst possible ways. I'll remove your hands at the wrists. I'll ..."

I dropped his leg and stepped back at his howl.

"What did you stop for?" he bellowed.

"I suspect," Judicus said mildly, pulling his oilcloth-covered map from his pocket and examining it, "she stopped because you threatened to take her hands. You may be Grand Hadri of Calicarn and you may command five divisions of ships, four great armies, and the whole of the Flamerarch but you were also the fool who went sailing off improperly guarded on his ship for a lark, and you're the one who was kidnapped by his enemies in their coup attempt and you're the one now with a bit of bone sticking through his skin while a stone octopus the size of your Spring Palace tries to break through the door of this temple and you're cursing the only healer within this valley rather than just letting her do her work." He turned to me, polite as ever, and said, "I understand if you'd rather not tend him, Sersha, but if you can ignore his threats, I think you'll find it is more valuable to us to keep him alive."

I lifted an eyebrow, questioning and Judicus ran a hand through his hair flushing redder and redder under the dirt and blood.

"Yes, even when he threatens us both and acts the fool. And even though he dragged my father from his throne, killed him, erected a statue enshrining the act forever in the center square of Briccatore, took my mother and sister as hostages, and dragged my family name through the mud – yes, even then I think it better to keep him alive."

I shrugged and went to work. I didn't have half the things I needed to tend to this properly. No thread to stitch the skin. No herbs to keep fever at bay. We'd even lost our waterskins in the fight outside this miserable temple, but with Olliman's silent help – for he came when he was finished assuring himself that Cassanetta was neither dead nor dying – we managed to set the screaming potentate's leg and splint it with broken shelving we pulled from the walls, we two children of flame and silence.

A sort of brotherhood – or siblinghood was forming between Olliman and me. It pained me to think of it because he should not have to share this fate with me, and his tongue must be in agony still and there was nothing I could do about it. I could see in his eyes that he had not expected to live this long and also that he was deeply troubled by something else. He kept looking toward the door and I thought at first that he was worried about Frissei who had vanished during the fight and was likely mortally wounded or dead but after we finished with the Grand Hadri and we paused to regard one another as if to say "what next," I realized what was making him so jumpy.

Out there beyond the doors were the bodies of his friends Dalissa Fenwan and Refrento. And it was nightfall, or at least dark. And that meant that in their palms they would hold the ashes of Yxella and Utterbexen and if no one went and retrieved those ashes, their phoenixes would be lost forever.

I swallowed as I realized what his eyes flicking to the door and back meant. He wanted us to go out there and get them. And while there was no part of me that wanted to go, I couldn't refuse him.

I let out a long gust of air and closed my eyes and when I opened them, he was smiling.

Time to go do the impossible. Of course.

103

"Absolutely not." Judicus had guessed our intentions before we even made it to the door. He leaned in close, whispering. "Sersha, please. I rely on you to be the sensible one. Look around you. I have two people passed out on the ground, one in tears wearing a forbidden crown, and one with a broken leg and you want me to let the only two able-bodied people out into that madness? Have you lost your mind?"

I shook my head and tried to show a phoenix rising with my hand.

He sighed, rubbing his forehead. "Listen. Yes. Their phoenixes died. And you two want to go collect the ashes. I understand that. But this valley is the lost city of Ciuade. The heart of rope work. I had no idea – no one ever mentions it – that it's also the heart of the cult of the Tattered Ribbons, but it must be, right? They worship octopuses and darkness – I know, it's a little far from the sea and you'd expect to find them along the coast, but here we are – and I think it's pretty obvious that a temple full of octopus tentacles buried everywhere that also holds a crown of darkness which, once put on the head of the ai'sletta, awakens a massive octopus – well, it's probably their kind of place, right?"

I look at Olliman and back.

"And I hate to state the obvious, but I feel like someone needs to right now," he said a little breathlessly as if trying to get it all out at once. "There must be some reason that our enemies did not try to make their stand in this temple, too, and in my mind, it can only be that they did not want to pin themselves down so that the creature could kill anything that went out that door as soon as the door opened."

As if to emphasize his words, the ground shook again and this time the entire structure seemed to jar terribly to the side. The Grand Hadri bit off a scream of pain – the shudder of the altar against his broken leg would have been a terrible agony – and from the floor where Gundt was laid, a moan rose over the other sounds of the room.

"Please," I beg of you," Judicus pled, and I really should have done something about his face because it was still dirty when I'd cleaned everyone else – even my enemies. And I really wished I could bring Kazmerev back – even for just a moment – to ask him what to do. And I felt like I was going to combust right there with everyone watching because what was worse? To risk them all or to risk the two phoenixes? And wasn't it risking my own phoenix to go running out there?

I almost called Kazmerev up even though the room was too small and thick. I almost asked him for help, but I knew he wouldn't fit within the walls of the temple and so to call him would be to either burn the rest of them to death or subject him to the horrors of clawing stone tentacles – or whatever those things were – and Stryxex.

A scream burst through the air, and I spun – knowing immediately it was Mally – and as I stared at the tapestry and realized in one horrible moment that the scream had sounded far away, the door behind me creaked. I turned and to my horror, Olliman was forcing it open, face set with determination.

Judicus had been flung aside, but he pawed his way back up, hands open as black ropes fell from them to the ground. He was both too late and just fast enough.

Too late to stop Olliman who had the door open and was already out, racing into the dark.

Too late to stop the tentacle that shot out and ripped him from the ground, rising out of sight into the moonless night above.

Just in time to slam the stone door closed behind the other Flame Rider with the strength of his magic and to slam the bar down over the door again.

He ran a hand over his face and said with quiet authority, "I think that should settle the decision about whether to go outside, though I have little confidence that any of you will condescend to listen to me. But here is a thought to digest. All of us still alive want the ai'sletta alive and all of us just heard her scream, so perhaps it is time to put foolishness aside long enough to follow her into whatever mischief she's caused this time, what do you think?"

104

I was shaking when I nodded my agreement, my eyes still lingering on the closed door where Olliman had been only moments before. I barely knew the man and yet I felt his loss like the cut of a knife. We had been the same for a short time – united in challenge and determination. And because of that, he felt like a brother to me and one I had just lost, at that.

"Judicus," the deep voice was thick, and I spun to see Gundt hauling himself to his feet, swaying against his injury.

I scrambled to his side, supporting him.

"Sersha," he acknowledged, his eyes racing around the room, lingering for a moment on the Grand Hadri and then again on Lady Lightland. He wiped his face with a hand and drew in a long breath. "The ai'sletta?"

"She was here a moment ago, but she slipped away," Judicus said. "We were just discussing how to go after her."

Gundt grunted and I could tell by his eyes that he was sizing up the situation as the building shook once again. This time, little bits of plaster fell from the ceiling, pattering against the floor.

"We need to hurry," Judicus said. "How steady are you on your feet, Greensleeve?"

"I'll manage," was all Gundt said and with barely another word he made his way to Cassanetta, and then, squatting down with a slight sway and a pause to collect himself, he threw her slight form over one shoulder and stood again. He stumbled against the wall, caught himself, and for one terrible moment I thought he was going to collapse and then he righted himself and let out another long breath.

"Think you can do the same, nephew?" the Grand Hadri asked snidely.

"I think that you'd better get moving or we'll have to leave you here," Judicus said calmly, but I saw his hand flexing as he strode away toward the tapestry, and I realized I was seeing Judicus in a temper. He was always so controlled that it was leashed most of the time – a very large dog held in a cage until the right moment – but that leash was fraying at the edge.

Gundt fell in behind him. He had a look of deep concentration as if every step was a struggle, but he didn't waver.

"I guess that leaves you and me, girl," the Grand Hadri said. "You can call me Captain Rackham."

I wouldn't be calling him anything.

He held his arm out like he expected me to just slip in under it and bear his weight and I just couldn't do it. The revulsion that rose in me at seeing him sitting there expecting the world to be handed to him, expecting me to be the one to hand it over, expecting that his sweaty weight was just going to be mine to bear – it was almost a physical thing. I thought I might vomit.

I clung to the thought of Kazmerev. I should call him back. I should ask for his help.

And then what? Would I ask him to do what my entire being was revolting against? Would I ask him to bear the entitled weight of Captain Rackham?

I shook my head. I wouldn't do that. He should never bear a burden I would not bear myself.

"What's the hold up?" Captain Rackham asked, dropping his arm but leaning forward as if he could threaten me when he couldn't stand on his own two feet.

"I suspect she is waiting to be asked," Judicus said in a clipped voice from the other side of the room, without looking back, and then he wrenched the tapestry and the whole thing came down in a dusty *fump* revealing a gaping passageway lit along the walls with oil lamps and angled downward.

"Please," Captain Rackham said with a look that he probably thought was charming and I found … not.

I looked to Judicus but he was already striding down the passage, Gundt following behind him with a set to his shoulders that told of barely managing to stay on his own feet.

I grimaced and moved close enough to let the ruler of Calicarn lean on me. We couldn't stay here. And I couldn't leave a man to his death, even if I didn't like the idea of him touching me and didn't know why.

"You resent me," he said in a low tone as he shifted his weight onto me.

I didn't want to talk about this. Or more specifically, I didn't want to be talked at about this.

"You think I've been harsh to your friends."

Of course, I did. And I didn't want to hear a lecture about it. Not now with his heavy weight leaning on me and my back hurting as I helped him limp across the room. Not now with the temple shaking apart around us. Not now with the fresh memory of Olliman rushing out to try to save the remains of the two phoenixes and bring them to new Flame Riders. It was because of this man that raiders were spreading like darkness across the earth. Because of him that my cousin was threatened. Because of him that Judicus's sister and mother were held hostage to force him to this man's will.

I gritted my teeth and supported Captain Rackham's weight as he kept talking, seemingly ignorant that the plaster above us was falling more heavily onto the ground and the temple was beginning to make a crumbling sound.

"You forget that I'm a ruler among men because I am injured and at the mercy of you – a foreign, voiceless girl."

I wasn't sure anyone could forget that when he kept reminding them. I fought to contain a grunt of exertion as he adjusted his weight on me. He was a powerfully built man, but not a timid one. He leaned very weightily on me, not at all shy about making someone else carry his mass. I wished there was another way, even as my traitor heart told me that Kazmerev might be able to squeeze in here and he might be able to bear both the Grand Hadri and me on his back. Or he might not. It would be cruel to call him up without knowing.

"You don't seem to understand what's going on here, and why should you with only Judicus Franzer Irault to advise you. Let me explain. The ai'sletta is just a woman running loose and turning luck in her palm. She has no power or ability beyond what is offered to her by others. And that means she needs someone like me to take her and steer her into the right goals and aims."

We were into the passageway now, and I didn't know if the others could hear us, but I could see Gundt's retreating back. He was still on his feet, though he was silent – likely fighting the pain and dizziness of his head wound to carry Cassanetta. If he could carry the woman we all had reason to hate, while suffering himself, then I could certainly support the Grand Hadri.

"And she needs me because I know more than any of you. I know that we have to get that Diadem of Darkness off her head for one thing – or at least we do if we want the tentacled creature to stop trying to tear this temple stone from stone. She needs me because you Flame Riders are only good for one thing and that is finding and fetching."

I froze at his words and shot a glare up at him.

"Keep walking," he ordered as if he simply didn't care that he'd insulted me. "Rope Workers, similarly, are very useful tools, but the ai'sletta won't help them at all. The odds are usually in a rope worker's favor, so her proximity can only harm that, not help that. So, she is more valuable both to and with me than she is with you and your coterie."

He seemed happy with that, as if justifying himself with his own words ought to be enough for me. As if I couldn't see through their gruel-thinness. As if they weren't as transparent to me as dragonfly wings. I'd seen enough people in my day trying to construct castles for themselves with their carefully buttressed arguments, and precisely laid statements and their fitted emotional appeals. They seemed to think that my lack of similar verbal clothing meant I was vulnerable to believing all their tattered shreds of reason rather than the exact opposite – that I could see them for who they were without the garnishes of human creativity.

I didn't like the feeling of the dank walls around us as we descended into the tunnel behind the tapestry. The walls were made of smoothed earth with nothing but the oil lamp holders – which Mally must have lit, right? – set into them. My mouth went dry wondering what kind of a thing had carved such a neat, tubular burrow – like a worm tunneling through the earth.

"On top of that, I'm not sure if you understood, but that was a coup attempt back there. We need to get back to Briccatore immediately to stop it. The nobles who were conspiring against me – while low in stature – are still powerful when counted together and allied with the Hand of the Rat. And for that reason, I need the ai'sletta to turn luck to my side."

He certainly could talk. I wished I didn't have to listen. I didn't want to turn Mally over to him any more than I wanted to give her to his enemies. I was nervous about the raiders. They seemed to be without honor and liable to bite at any turn. But I had just learned something valuable – that I was just as afraid of these people, my supposed allies. And especially their leader with his many words.

"Regardless of where you think your loyalties lie," Captain Rackham went on blithely, "You're wrong. You made an oath to me, and it is to me you will look for your orders."

I would have liked to remind him that I made no oath and that we were falling behind those who had.

"But I will sweeten the pot," he said with a grunt. We were barely in the tunnel, and he was already running out of energy. "I will offer you this – serve me and make sure the ai'sletta is mine alone and I will offer you a place in my court.

I would have liked to indicate to him with my face alone that his offer was not being entertained, but at that moment, the temple behind us collapsed with a sound like a huge tree cut in a forest. And with its collapse, a wind ran down the tunnel and huffed out every light.

We were well and truly trapped.

105

"Judicus!" Captain Rackham shouted. My ears rang from his yell as we stumbled under his weight, careening into the wall. I hissed in a gasp of pain at the same moment that he yelled again. "Judicus!"

He was going to make me deaf as well as blind and voiceless. Desperate, I tried to claw out from under his bulk, but he gripped my arm in his clawed fingers.

"I'll kill you." He sounded breathless. "I'll kill you if you leave me. Judicus!"

There was no answer except my wild heartbeat flooding my ears with the sound of my own fear.

"He threw me in the dungeon down in the dark. He threw me there when he killed the Grand Hadri and crowned himself."

Captain Rackham was talking gibberish. Which meant it was up to me to do something here. And the only thing I could think to do was to call my phoenix.

"He was a king killer. The worst of betrayers. The Lord of Chaos. The Mad Lord of the Dead. My own brother. And he named *me* the betrayer and threw me in that pit of madness and despair. I'll kill them. I'll kill them all."

I swallowed and tried to block him out. I couldn't take this man's panic attacks and threats any more than I could take his domineering and bragging. With his leg that badly broken, I could probably avoid any attack – not that I thought he was talking to me. He was somewhere in his memories, and I was no part of what he was reliving. But people in that state might do anything.

I reached deep inside myself and called. Kazmerev?

And just like that, he was there, blooming from my heart and into the tiny space until he filled it and with him came gladness thick and full, a gladness so deep I could drown in it.

Sersha, he murmured. *You're safe.*

And I was now, because my phoenix was with me. I reached for all the hope I had and offered it to him and to my surprise it felt more like it was doubling in my heart rather than being received.

Together, we multiply hope. Together, we divide sorrows. But what is this? You are trapped in a small space.

And so, I was. I could see through the darkness again in his presence. Whatever I'd lost in the artificial night was back again. We were in an earthen corridor, the way behind us was a tumble of ruined stone, the way before us likewise enshrouded. But to one side there seemed to be a crack in the earth. Curiously, I stepped toward it.

"In the dark. The key is in the dark," Captain Rackham was muttering. He'd slumped to the ground and had thrown an arm over his eyes. "The key to fixing it before it happens again, before I go mad, too."

That ship had sailed already.

You should have called me back sooner, Kazmerev said. *But where are the others?*

I tried to recall what had happened as fast as I could while I poked my head through the crack in the earth. It seemed to be another passage on the other side of it. A passage made of stonework. How very strange. Could I squeeze through the crack? Yes. But what about Kazmerev and Captain Rackham.

You have made a fundamental error, Sersha, Kazmerev said reprovingly. *You didn't call me because you thought I wouldn't fit, but my dear little hawk, I am born of Spirit, and I can fit any space I must. Of course, I fit here. And of course, I will go through that crack with you. I can dwell anywhere your heart is, for it is within you that I live.*

My cheeks felt hot. I'd been a fool.

We are all fools sometimes. But now, the real question.

How to get out.

No. I sense fresh air through that passage. I'm certain we can get out. My worry is this ruler among men. What should we do with him?

We'd have to bring him with us.

The man with the broken leg who is crying in the dark?

I thought phoenixes were always good. He couldn't be considering ... leaving him, could he?

I am suggesting you go and put some sense into him.

If I could speak, I could have done that. I could have reminded him of who he was. I could have built for him a new self out of words as people so often did. But without that, how could I put fresh life into him?

You'll have to use truth and not sophistry.

I didn't even have that!

Don't be silly, Sersha. You're the most truth-filled person I know.

He always did this to me. He'd thrust some grand, difficult goal onto me that I had to perform, and I always did it because disappointing him felt – well, it felt intolerable. But right now, I just wanted someone to comfort me and tell me I was doing a good job and it would be okay. I didn't want to be challenged *again* and told I had more to do.

Would you rather I pretend you can just abandon him? Fine. Go ahead, Sersha. Just leave him here.

I sighed and turned back to the Grand Hadri, reaching down to touch his arm.

"Don't touch me," he hissed. "It took him in the dark. He was never the same."

I wanted to roll my eyes. What was I supposed to do with him? But Kazmerev was right. I couldn't just leave him. I cast around, looking for an idea and my eyes landed on one of the oil pots. On instinct, I reached for it and lifted it down, taking care to light it with the fire I could draw from Kazmerev before tapping Rackham again and offering him the pot.

"A light," he said, and his eyes seemed to focus finally.

I nodded and I wondered that I'd never noticed before how broken he was under his bravado – how grim and threatening and terrified.

He seemed to shake himself, starting with a shiver and then letting it run through his whole body like a wet dog trying to dry himself. He winced when his leg moved, but he held onto the pot and after a moment he nodded.

"Yes. You're right, Flame Rider. We have light. We have breath. We can't just sit here when there is so much to do. I have a kingdom to preserve and enemies to defeat. And right now, we must escape this tunnel tomb."

I nodded wordlessly and offered him a hand.

"If you ever so much as breathe a word of what you might have heard me say ..."

He began to say more but with my free hand, I pointed to my mouth and shook my head. It was all I could do not to roll my eyes. It seemed to me that the measure of a person might lie in whether they could remember enough about the people around them to keep track of which ones couldn't talk. If they couldn't remember that what else were they forgetting?

He nodded, a bit ruefully, perhaps, and as I led him to the crack in the wall he said, "Let's just hope it doesn't lead to the Ciuade catacombs. There are legends about that place and if they're true, then we would have been better off with that stone squid thing my nephew was so worried about."

I just hoped the way out was short. If it wasn't, I couldn't be sure I wouldn't leave him somewhere and then lose my phoenix because my heart had turned to darkness.

I will keep you from the worst in your nature.

On the contrary. Leaving him here might be one of my better impulses.

106

It was a tight squeeze through the crack and tighter still for Rackham who trembled with pain at any touch to his leg. He really shouldn't be moving it at all. He should be resting and lying down, but I could hardly abandon him here in the dark – especially after hearing his fears bubble up through his lips – and staying in one place hoping someone else would save us was a fool's choice.

I was already thirsty and hungry with no hope of food or water any time soon. And who knew where these tunnels went or how long it would take to navigate them?

This one was made of dressed stone, and it seemed that someone had taken great time in constructing it – which led me to wonder why the temple had the worm-like tunnel leading from behind its tapestry when it could have been built into this more civilized tunnel.

We tracked the tunnel backward towards where the original one had started – or at least I hoped that was the way we were tracking it. Without consulting one another, we made our way toward that end. I wished I could ask Kazmerev to fly up and look down on us and tell us where to go, but he was as imprisoned as we were within the walls of this underground maze.

I can fly ahead of you or behind you, but I cannot go far from where you are without risking ill effects in you and I will not risk that.

What kind of ill effects?

You are benefiting now from my light and my heat. What will you do when you lose that? The small oil lamp will not be enough.

A chill of fear went through me. Because I still didn't know enough about phoenixes. The crown Mally had placed on her head had brought a magical night where there should not have been one. I still didn't know where she'd found it. Surely, you wouldn't leave such a thing lying around for just anyone to crown themselves.

Perhaps her luck guided her to a hidden cabinet. Or the base of the altar. Perhaps it was guarded by a hidden catch or the need for blood to open it, or some other arcane defense. As ai'sletta, nothing like that can keep her out. Her hands unerringly find the mechanisms, she stumbles into things both too glorious and too terrible for her.

I shivered at his analysis. She'd always be in danger. There could be no happy ending for her.

But imagine the adventures she'll have!

If she lives that long. No, thank you. I would pass on that if it was offered to me.

She wasn't given that option. Not when the raiders came.

It felt like we'd traveled a long way in the darkness, but it couldn't have been that long because this ran parallel to the other tunnel, right?

I'm not entirely sure ...

When the tunnel changed, it seemed to change suddenly. It went from plain stone walls to a mosaic tiled along the side of the room.

What is this?

My footsteps slowed as I looked with him. Whoever had done this tile work had been a master of the art – or just very inspired. The picture we were looking at was of a man-shaped figure with dark tendrils reaching from his hands into a great pit full of darkness. His face was hidden by a scarf or mask but in tile, you wouldn't have seen it anyway.

My hand ran along the tiles, feeling how age had worn their edges smooth. This was not new.

"I've never heard of this," Rackham said, and his words were so thick that I stopped to look at him. Sweat slicked his pale forehead and face. We needed to find him a place to rest – and soon. He wasn't doing well.

But even knowing that urgency, I couldn't tear my eyes from it. As we trailed down the tunnel, the mosaic of the man merged into a depiction of a cluster of dark islands.

"Howling lands," Rackham said, running his finger over the tiles. "That's their shape."

That's where the raiders come from – or so rumor has it. But how he would know their shape, I don't know. I have not met a phoenix who has flown there.

The mural merged now into a picture of a dark, twisting figure. Even set in tile, I could tell it was a Stryxex, as if the tiles could suck out the light just as that abominable creature could. The tiles changed colors the further they were from the Stryxex, as if the ones close to the image had been leeched of light. Small runes I could not read decorated the edges of the mural. Perhaps they explained the story, but if they did, I would never know.

As we traveled further, a Stryxex leapt from the hands of a red-robed figure, and in his hands, he held a mound of grey. The background behind them was made of light gold tiles as if it were dawn set in stone and couldn't help the way my stomach lurched uncomfortably at how alike that was to the birth of my own phoenix, only where Kazmerev was born with the light and died with the day, this dark monstrosity was kindled in the light of dawn.

I'd seen far worse things than this mural – seen them not even hours ago – and yet these images chilled me just as badly. Chilled me even more as we followed along, as if walking backward through time and saw another figure with a sword, slashing it through what looked like the flaming body of a scarlet and gold phoenix. I was still shaking from the grisly sight of the grey tiles depicting smoke pouring from his wound when I saw the next portrayal – people depicted in a long line following the red-cloaked figure. They trailed along, showing faces of every color, dressed in male and female clothing. Some large, some small, some children if this depiction was true. And as we reached the end of the line we saw that they were walking into a door set in the legs of a statue and I realized, to my surprise, that it was the ruined statue we'd seen above – or seen parts of it above. And that long before this place was the site of this tentacled temple, it must have been the site of something else. Something just as deep and dark as the other thing.

On either side of the statue, figures stood with hands outstretched and black, twisting ropes running from them to the statue.

"Rope workers," Rackham said, "I've never trusted them."

And then he slumped to the floor, groaning when his broken leg struck the ground.

He'd passed out. His face was grey and sweating. Fearful, I pulled his clothing aside to look at his leg. His boot was full of blood and his bandage soaked through.

The realization struck me with force. I might have accidentally killed the ruler of Calicarn.

107

He's not dead. I don't think he's dead,* Kazmerev said. *Good people don't accidentally kill kings.*

Well, which was it? Was he not dead or did he not think he was dead?

I wasn't even making sense to myself. I put the boot down and tried to think about what Judicus would do and not about how badly I wished he was here and how I felt just a tiny bit resentful that he left me with the Grand Hadri while he went off after Mally, separating us in the first place.

He would stay calm. That's what he'd do. I took in a long breath.

Stay calm? That's not a plan. That's a delay.

I took in another long breath.

I don't like to mention it, but I sense something up ahead.

What did he sense?

Living things. Fire.

Judicus. The others. We could find them.

Not necessarily.

I was not calm, but I didn't think any number of breaths were going to calm me now. My thoughts still scattered at any attempt to think of a plan.

Fear not, little hawk. Just strap the man to my back and I will carry him unconscious or not.

And what? Let him bleed out?

Don't take on yourself burdens that aren't yours. You have no supplies to fix him with. He will live or he will die as all men do and it is not your job to save him. You are not God.

But it felt like my job. And hadn't Kazmerev said that Flame Riders could heal themselves?

Themselves. Yes. The fire burns off sickness. And infection. But healing someone else? That's not something that you can do.

But I could try, right? I took a step toward Kazmerev and rested a hand along his feathered cheek. He had my confidence. His strength could do things that seemed impossible.

I'm flattered but it really won't work.

I smiled gently and then turned back to the Grand Hadri and put my hands on either side of his face, and looked into it. I was going to try anyway. I had to.

He wasn't as old as I thought. All that brash talk and his heavily muscled body had made me think he was, but unconscious, he looked younger than Gundt. Maybe in his late thirties. He must have been a lot younger than Judicus's father. His aquiline nose was bent from a break. His cheeks were black with the beginning of a beard – it looked even darker next to skin as pale as Judicus's – and his eyelashes formed a fringe that was almost delicate compared to the rough-hewn features of the rest of his face.

What was he under all those words he used as weapons? Who was he? Could he be as vulnerable as me, or was he corrupt and self-serving all the way through?

You'll probably kill him if you try to do anything. You'll accidentally burn him up.

And then I'd be evil and lose Kazmerev.

No, it would be an accident, but you'd be haunted by the horror of it. Please, listen to me and don't do it. Magic doesn't come just because you call. Miracles don't happen just because you want them.

But magic had come when I called for Kazmerev. And he was my miracle.

He seemed flustered by that.

Sersha, my little hawk, fly with me and leave this man here for now. We'll scout ahead and find help and then return for him.

But then he'd be dead by the time we returned.

Better dead by chance than dead by your hand. Come fly with me.

He was so appealing. So convincing.

But I had to try. Because something in me always had to try. The part of me that could give up had broken along the way.

I reached inside myself where I usually found the fire, but this time, I wasn't looking for fire. I was looking for warmth. I found it deep, deep within.

I closed my own eyes, concentrated on my touch on either side of his face and imagined my warmth going into him and burning up fever and infection, imagined the fire of it stitching his bone and muscle and skin back together. I thought of how he must have been in so much pain and yet he'd hardly even groaned, and I thought of drawing on that brutish strength and gathering it up and using it to mend his whole self.

I was hot with it, woozy and feverish as if just thinking of the heat was making it overcome me. Maybe I was more injured by our battles than I'd thought.

And then the warmth was gone and with it both my feverish sickness and my confidence.

What a little fool I was to think I could heal with magic.

Open your eyes.

I obeyed, reluctantly. He was right. We would have to move on.

Look down. At his leg.

It looked the same as ever – except maybe just a little straighter? But he wasn't dead. I hadn't burned him to a cinder. He was breathing – maybe a little easier, as if the touch of another human had comforted him.

I think you should check his wound.

If nothing else, I could make him more comfortable.

Gently, I unwound the soaked bandage, length by length.

When I saw it, I gasped. His leg was whole. I prodded the bone gently along his shin. It seemed unbroken. I could hardly breathe. Had I really ... Could it possibly be ...?

Kazmerev's laugh was something between a rumble and a sigh.

I looked up at him, and I couldn't help but smile and he seemed to be glowing twice as bright.

With pride. I glow with pride for you, little hawk.

He butted his fiery head into my chest, tenderly and carefully but with a kind of exuberant joy that I was feeling, too. We did that. We fixed someone.

We did.

I felt lightheaded at the idea of it, but the joy buried that and filled me instead with happy tears. For a full minute, I clung to Kazmerev, sinking my face into his warm, flame-lined feathers. He was so beautiful. And look what he could turn that beauty into? Healing.

I'd had only ashes before he came, and he'd turned them all into beauty. I'd had only mourning and he'd given me joy.

Easy, little hawk. We still have to find out why I sense living things nearby.

And I still had to figure out why Rackham was still unconscious. But for one more moment, I was just happy beyond anything I'd ever hoped for. Kazmerev didn't just fill me with a renewed sense of belonging and healing – he gave me the chance to pass that on to someone else and now I never wanted to stop.

Even people who are your enemies as this king might be?

Even them.

And his proud glow filled me full in a way nothing ever had before.

108

I think it took a lot out of him when you healed him. I still don't know how you did it, Sersha. You amaze me with the depths of your compassion and what you can do with it. My dear Vella would not have accomplished such a thing and nor has any rider I've ever heard of.

I felt my cheeks growing very hot as I tried to pull the Grand Hadri's boot back on. He really was just a man like any other. What a strange thing to think about a king who – when he wasn't stuck underground with me – could kill or destroy almost anyone he wanted on no more than a whim.

And yet you cared about him enough that you were able to change your magic into something that heals.

It wasn't me. It was probably something a lot of Flame Riders did and just kept a secret.

It's not.

It wasn't anything special.

It is. Just like you. Don't forget that all of this – who I am now, what power of mine you can access and bend to your will – it all comes out of your heart, out of who you are.

And now my cheeks were really burning. I pushed the ideas aside. It felt too arrogant to dwell on them and yet I was so pleased by this that I was afraid of ruining it by acknowledging it.

But we had a new problem. What should I do with an unconscious king? I was just about to ask Kazmerev that question when Rackham's eyes popped open.

"What happened? Where are we?" His questions were curt, snappy. He rubbed his face with a hand and almost pushed me aside as he scrambled to his feet. I ducked backward, climbing up and swaying slightly. It really had burned up my energy to help him.

He's rude. He gives you no thanks at all. What arrogance.

Well, he *was* a king.

Rackham looked around us, ran a hand over the rope workers in the mural, seemed to remember it, stomped his foot in his soaked boot as if testing it, frowned, and then looked at me.

"I don't suppose you can tell me what I missed or how my leg is now well, so perhaps we should carry on."

Still no gratitude. I spit smoke in his direction. He is not worthy of you my little hawk. And that makes your gift even greater.

Kazmerev shook out his feathers irritably as if shaking off flies and it was hard not to laugh at that when he did it right beside the king of Calicarn while the man strode away from me. If he could see Kazmerev he might not be so blasé about the dangers here or about his healing. Meanwhile, I was still worried about that bone. Who knew whether I knit it fully or only just enough? He should treat it gingerly. If he broke it again, I couldn't guarantee I could heal him like that twice.

I think you could. But you should stop him. He's headed straight toward where I sense life and we don't know if those are friends or foes.

He was also striding into the darkness, not bothering with a light.

Shaking my head, I grabbed the oil lamp and hurried after him. His fingers trailed along the mural, leaving clear lines in the dusty depiction. There was something to that mural I wasn't understanding. Something that told about phoenixes and Stryxex. I needed time to ponder it.

I need time to forget it. What a grisly thing to spend months or even years lying out across this hidden room.

I was having trouble catching up with the Grand Hadri. His strides were longer and even at a half trot, I couldn't seem to gain any ground. I was already out of breath and in need of a rest. Healing, it seemed, had its cost to the healer.

The oil lamp shook as I turned a trot into a reluctant jog and if I could curse, I probably would because I didn't even need the lamp. I had Kazmerev. I was only holding it for the Grand Hadri and he was taking my company for granted.

I think, perhaps, Sersha, that you are going to have to stop letting people do that. Stop letting them assume they can just arrange you where they want you like a doll.

And how would I do that? Should I speak up? Ha.

You speak with your actions and your intentions. You speak with what you do not stop. You've been speaking very loudly since the moment I met you. And I love your compassion. I love that you love to serve others. But stop letting them push you over and walk over your fallen body and then pretend like you're hard done by and had no other choice. You can have another choice. You can start to refuse to be their footpath.

I could do that. I *would* do that. If he would help me.

I will certainly help you. You bear my honor.

And just like that, I had almost caught up to Rackham. I breathed a sigh of relief as I turned a slight corner and found him just outside a stone door. I reached toward him, hoping to halt him before he did something foolish.

Before I could, he pulled the door open. Light splashed into the tunnel from a room beyond with a huge pit of fire in its center. Someone had tossed the room. Bits of torn fabric and broken wood decorated the floor and piled around the edges of the mural that covered them. A mural of stylized phoenixes under a layer of stylized Stryxex and all of them under a great octopus with waving tentacles.

But that wasn't the important part. The really pressing part was the living Stryxex hovering across the underground hall just past the fire ... and the dozen black-veiled raiders who had just looked up from what they were doing to see who had opened the door.

109

The Grand Hadri stood in the doorway stunned. I didn't have time for his shock. I pushed him aside, slipped under his arm, and slammed my weight against the heavy door, closing it with a thud.

There was no bar or latch. My heart was in my throat. Think, Sersha, think. On the other side of that door are more enemies than you can possibly defend against. Flight was our only option.

Could Kazmerev carry us?

It would be a tight squeeze. Treacherous in its own way. You could be crushed, or you could fall if we reach a part of the tunnels that I'm too large for, or –

Let's go! I cut him off, grabbing Rackham's collar in my hand, and moved to stand behind him.

"Leave off," Rackham said, irritably, trying to shake my hand off.

I clung to his collar. We needed to be positioned correctly for Kazmerev to get underneath us. Was Kaz ready?

"We must flee," Rackham said, patting his sides as if he expected a weapon to appear and trying to shake off my grip on his collar a second time.

Behind us, the door began to open, stone on stone. Rackham launched as if planning to run but I held his collar tightly.

"For the love of – what are you -?"

But his words were cut off as Kazmerev materialized under us and we were lifted in the air onto his back. For just a heartbeat – like every time – I reveled in his warmth and beauty, the licking flames on the edges of his feather, the gorgeous purplish-black of his feathers, the brightness of his flashing eyes and sleek beak, and then we were moving, slipping down the hall in a bobbing fashion as Kazmerev flew as best as he could in the restrictive space.

I like it when you call me Kaz. It sounds ... right.

Behind us, someone yelled in a language I didn't understand, "Akenash atrenna! Akenash!"

Something struck the stone behind us with a clatter, and I shoved Rackham down as I leaned down with him. We might still be shot in the back, but we didn't need to make it easy for them.

"Let go of my collar," he hissed.

Try to keep him still. This isn't easy, Kazmerev growled.

I risked a glance behind us. The bobbing motion of flying in this tight space made it hard to see without growing as ill as Judicus, but still, I could just make out how they were pouring into the tunnel in a wave of black, weapons being drawn, arrows notched. The Stryxex was at their backs and the way it reared up and turned showed how eager it was to rush past them and into our tail. We'd have to go faster.

One of the raiders launched a second arrow to a scream of, "Kash trva Aknazareai!"

I slammed my body down and over Rackham, ignoring his curse. This time I felt the wind of the arrow rush past. We needed to be faster.

We need to find a bend, a turn, anything.

But there had hardly been any bends other than that very gradual one. Our only hope was to out-fly them.

With two on my back and our energy depleted from healing the useless king? It's a terrible task you've set me, Sersha.

Less terrible than me dying by an arrow and his ashes being picked up by someone else? Maybe this arrogant king he loved so much?

Nothing is less terrible than that.

To my surprise, we flew in silence. Rackham had the sense to shut the torrent that usually came from his mouth. It was a gesture I wished he'd performed some time ago. Kazmerev was concentrating on flying. And silence was my gift. A gift, I was starting to realize, that had as many blessings to it as curses because at least I wouldn't have to look a fool later because I'd spoken without knowledge.

We were past the mural now and hurtling toward the rent on the side of the passage we'd entered through. The air felt cooler this way and I clung to Kazmerev, grateful for his warmth in this endless night.

I relaxed my hold on the Grand Hadri. He was breathing more easily now that our enemies were dropping away behind us.

"How far do you plan to fly before we stop?" he whispered and then he seemed to catch himself with a sigh. I could give him no answers, and yet he couldn't stop asking. "Have you done this before?"

This time he glanced back at me for an answer. In the silence, I heard a distant shout. Our enemies were falling behind us, but that didn't mean we were safe.

I shook my head. I hadn't rescued kings, flown underground, or worried my friends were crushed under rock before. And on top of that, it seemed like a silly thing to confirm. Did he know other people who had done this?

He shook his head. "You must think me a fool."

I said nothing – and this time I wouldn't have said anything even if I could. It's not wise to tell kings they are fools. Even I knew that. I focused my concentration past him to where we were going. We had just passed the rent in the side of the tunnel. I didn't know what came next, only that we were racing deeper into the earth and at any moment we might hit a collapse of rock that cut us off and forced us to turn and fight. And then what would we do?

We'll do something desperate. We'll wheel and try to gain speed to plunge through their ranks. If we survive the rush, then on the other side we can try to get to whatever door they used to enter these tunnels and we'll risk the stone octopus on the other side.

It was a good plan. I almost wondered if we should try it right now.

No.

It seemed more thought-out than plunging further into the unknown.

By my estimate, my plan would mean almost certain death for us. It's the only plan I have and we'll use it if we must, but I'd rather keep looking for a better one.

I could burn a few of those raiders.

Most certainly, though we both know you would hesitate to harm another, even with your life on the line. Besides, even if you succeed in burning them all without eating an arrow or being mortally wounded by one of their other weapons, there is still the matter of the Stryxex, and while he is not my equal in speed or intelligence, he does have a certain wrenching violence that would make things ... mortally challenging.

I liked how he didn't say we were dead already.

I waited a heartbeat.

I did not like that he had no comforting quip.

I'm working on one. While I also fly us out of danger. While I also try not to kill the king as he works out how to relieve me of a feather.

He what?

And yes, he was examining one of Kazmerev's feathers a little too roughly. Without thinking, I reached forward and slapped his hand. He froze and I froze, too.

Uh oh.

He would not forget that when we reached the surface – if we did – and then what? Would he punish me? Or Judicus? Or Judicus's innocent sister? I hadn't thought before I acted and now I was in a bind.

I bit my lip, worried, but after a long moment he relaxed, and I let myself take a breath.

"Flame Rider," the Grand Hadri said carefully. "I fear I have made a grave error."

If he means he senses I want to char him like a nice cut of meat, he is correct.

"I have mistaken our situation."

Kazmerev said nothing to that. The passage seemed to be growing narrower. Something in my gut tightened at the sight of that. Were we going to have to spin and rush them like we thought?

Behind me, a terrible almost-scream broke the silence.

"And I have mistaken you," the Grand Hadri said, to my utter surprise. "I beg your forgiveness."

Fortunately, I was spared having to answer. I wasn't sure you could deny a king forgiveness, but I certainly would have wanted to delay.

I waited for Kazmerev's lecture on how I must forgive and keep my heart innocent, but it didn't come.

Kazmerev? I waited for another beat. He was still flying – so why wasn't he answering? Kaz?

I think we're in trouble.

110

Just as he said that, the ground fell away and what had seemed like a tunnel opened up into a massive water-carved cavern. A winding staircase strung along the edge like a piece of fabric tacked in place before the tailor could set the seam. It looked perilous from here, but just as perilous was the yawning cavern and the way my phoenix dropped over it like a stone.

I didn't know such places could exist beneath the earth.

"Dear sweet mothers," the Grand Hadri gasped. "But how could this have been kept a secret all these years?"

How, indeed. I didn't know what door the raiders had used to enter these tunnels, but the parallel tunnel had not been well disguised. Any wandering adventurer or prospector could have found it. I half expected to see carts of mined ore and blackened miners, but the cavern echoed hollowly, a belly that could never be filled. It was – I thought – nearly as large as a city, with its own grand architecture of curving striated stone that both surrounded the cavern and made stern lines across the cavern floor. There was no doubt in my mind that the place had been formed by water – the trickle of it had worn away the edges of the stone giving everything a curvaceous feeling – but there was no water here now.

"Perhaps, it was flooded," he said, musing to himself as his eyes followed the same curve mine did.

But both of us froze when we heard a distant cry from somewhere far below. A woman's voice, I thought, though it was hard to be sure.

I swallowed. We'd have to go and see. What if it were Mally? Or Huxabrand?

"*Agreed,* Kazmerev said.

But as we turned over the updraft coming from the cavern, coasting down in a spiral, I saw no signs of lights or people, only us and our bright phoenix light flickering over the rock.

"*I can go lower, and we'll scan the ground from a little closer.*

It was a good idea. Another cry rang out from below – faint and reedy.

But this time it was answered from above. And my blood seemed to freeze in my chest at the shriek of the Stryxex flying overhead. It plunged down on us and as I twisted, I saw a hint of red hair despite how the creature was swathed in shadow. It seemed to almost suck the light from the sky.

"*Brace yourself!*

I grabbed the Grand Hadri with both arms in a bear hug, tightening my knees around Kazmerev as he twisted – not that he would drop us, his magic prevented that, but who knew what the ruler would do when he wasn't in charge? Kazmerev suddenly flipped upside down and then curved back upward. He was using his rushing strategy in the air. I clenched my jaw tightly, trying not to scream at the sudden speed and the way the world lurched around me so that all I could see clearly was Kazmerev's feathers and flames. The walls past that were nothing but a blur of darkness and vague shapes.

"*Ready your fires!*

The Grand Hadri's yell of fear sliced through my ears, but I clung to him with one arm, the other reaching out, ready.

And then the eye-wrenching, gut-twisting sight of the Stryxex was there right in front of me – so close, too close.

"*Flame!* Kazmerev cried in my mind.

I let loose with all I had, letting the bar of white-hot heat shoot from my palm and out to where the red-haired rider clung to his abomination.

The Stryxex twisted in the air, enough to keep his rider from feeling the bite of the flame, but not enough to dodge. The flames ripped into his chest, scorching him with a smell like burning garbage. He screamed, a terrible, gut-trembling scream, but now we'd closed with him and as we passed, he reached out his neck, its form disguised by how it twisted light away, and he clamped his jaws into Kazmerev's wing and tore at it.

I didn't know if I was hearing Kazmerev with the ears of my mind but all I heard was his scream. And I thought I might be screaming with him. I clung to his back with my knees and to the yelling Grand Hadri with my arm as we plunged toward the earth, the burning Stryxex clinging to Kazmerev's wing as his other wing desperately flapped, trying to right us.

We were going too fast. We were going to crash.

We tumbled awkwardly, crashing against one wall. Kazmerev took that hit on his healthy wing which collapsed toward his body with the blow. We crashed against the next wall and this time Rackham grunted in agony and my arms hit hard enough that the bone in the center of it flared with pain. Had I broken it? It felt like it was still there, just hurt.

The crash drew the Stryxex's body alongside ours, though his tight grip on Kazmerev's neck didn't loosen and then he was right beside us, crashing into the next wall with us, and I didn't hesitate, the moment that the raider came near, I snatched for the long dagger kept at his waist even while Rackham reached for the raider with powerful arms, grabbing him in a throttle and yanking him from the back of the Stryxex.

I hadn't warned him. I couldn't hold three.
The breath gusted out of me, and the solidity gusted out of Kazmerev.
And then we were falling through the air with nothing and no one to catch us.

111

I reached for the Grand Hadri but he was too far away. My heart was pounding. It didn't feel real. And then I smacked feathers, face-first, and sucked in a sulfur breath of relief.

Caught you.

We were diving. I scrambled to sit. No time to process what had happened. No time for fear, though I felt its acid reach through every limb and tasted it on the back of my tongue.

Can you hold three?

We were ducking down again, speeding to try to pass the falling king and his falling opponent. The Stryxex was there first. It wavered, flying badly, still smoking, but it plucked them both up, on in each clawed foot, and then flapped awkwardly but powerfully away from us.

Oh no.

Kazmerev was already rushing toward the creature – but what would we do when we got there? If we fought, it could drop the Grand Hadri.

It can anyway.

If we didn't fight, it would leave with him in its grip.

The creature lurched and then fell again, dropping like a stone before suddenly catching itself with open wings.

I heard an echoing cry from above. The raiders had arrived and taken to the ragged stairs. If they survived the stairs, we could worry about them then.

Or if their bows get into range.

For now, we needed to make a choice.

I have an idea – but it's risky.

I could handle risk.

Crazy even.

I could handle crazy. What else would you call all this?

The Stryxex was climbing again, up and away from us. We needed to act now or lose the Grand Hadri.

How much do you want to keep him?

Judicus had left him to me. I wouldn't disappoint him.

I can fly you over top of the bird. Then you leap from my back and throw your fire and while he's distracted, I will swoop down, pluck the king from his grip, and then catch you.

He was kidding, right?

Just a short solo flight.

I couldn't. No one could. It was insane.

I thought you were fine with crazy. It's that or abandon him. I can't rip him from the Stryxex's grip while you're on my back and vulnerable to the creature's beak, and if you blast the Stryxex with fire from afar, he might drop the king.

I gritted my teeth and shut my eyes. This wasn't the kind of job for me. I wasn't a physical hero. I was just a sensible girl from a small village who was used to hard work and listening.

Then listen to me now. We must decide immediately. Will you try, or no?

I couldn't say yes. I was too afraid.

I will catch you. I will always catch you. Wherever you fall, no matter how far, I'm with you. But now is the time to show me that you have as much faith in me as I have in you.

I would do it. I would do it for him, not for the Grand Hadri.

Good girl.

We were already moving, slicing through the air like a ship through the sea. Kazmerev was faster than the Stryxex.

Of course! Phoenixes are proud creatures. The Stryxex are only a dim shadow of who we are, like the blink of the eyes after the light is gone.

Why did that ring so true and also make me think I was missing something? Something about Stryxex being after images?

But no. There was no time to think about that.

We were above him now and it was my time. I had to jump.

Wait for it. Almost there.

I couldn't do it. I couldn't.

Be more than the scared village girl. Have faith in me.

I couldn't.

Now.

This had better work.

I leapt from his back, and I felt like my heart was leaping with me, all faith, all trust, just letting go and believing he would catch me.

Kazmerev flared brighter as if my very faith was fueling him.

It is.

And I was falling, my heart in my throat, and I couldn't think. I could barely see. My body had moved so my back was toward the ground, my arms and legs drifting out around me and my hair rushing past my face.

The fire!

I couldn't find it on my first try and even with my second I hardly knew where it was going.

To the right! The right.

Which way was right? I couldn't seem to see. I caught a glimpse of Kazmerev wrenching the Grand Hadri from the Stryxex. The man let out a gut-wrenching scream. And then my fire was on track, slicing into the Stryxex. His bellow blocked out all else.

I was going to hit the ground, wasn't I?

I was going to hit the – my flame disappeared in a *whuff* at my lack of faith and then suddenly my phoenix was there, catching me in the embrace of *his* talons, but sharp as they were, burning flame as they were, they were also feather-soft as they caught me. I sucked in a long breath of relief, barely able to bring the breath in through my trembling lungs.

Beside me, a moaning Grand Hadri was cupped in Kazmerev's other hand.

But for now, I was safe.

I was safe with my beloved phoenix the savior of my whole world. It would all be okay.

It will be, little hawk. It always will be. I'll never let you go.

I leaned into that as we dove, nearly touching the rock ground.

I'm your hope and your faith and your best friend.

A sound like rock scraping far away came to me. And I had just enough time to wonder what it was when light filled the air and Kazmerev disappeared.

And I was falling again, but this time, there was no one to catch me.

112

The ground came up and hit me – fast and hard. I'd lost the lamp ages ago and the fall threw me into a shadow. I could see bright golden light beyond me, but here behind this stalagmite, the world was still inky black. I wheezed in a breath – painfully – and pulled myself to my hands and knees. I hadn't hit too hard, I didn't think. I'd taken a good slam to my chin, rattling my jaw, and had the air knocked out of me. But as I stopped to collect myself, I didn't think I was badly hurt.

My breath came back, sawing painfully through my lungs. I couldn't wait here recovering. Not for too long. But the blood was pounding in my head so loudly that I couldn't hear anything past my own pulse and though there was light somewhere beyond, I was seeing everything through a buzz of dancing white lights.

What had made the sun come out so immediately? And what time was it? Was it be sunset or dawn or midday? How long would I have to wait for Kazmerev to reappear?

I shook the thought clear. I couldn't sit here thinking. I needed to get up.

I forced myself up on shaky legs. Not far from me, someone groaned.

The Grand Hadri.

I stumbled across to where he lay in a heap, half in and half out of the shadow. His back was in the light, his shirt and coat shredded to pieces, along with the skin of his back. When Kazmerev had ripped him from the Stryxex, the creature's claws had torn him up.

I swallowed, feeling suddenly lightheaded.

No, Sersha. No. This was not my wound. I did not have the right or the luxury to be ill from it.

Pulling in a steadying breath, I moved to the shadow so I could see his face. It was barely illuminated, only enough for me to glimpse the outline of his face as he huffed with pain, desperately fighting to keep his consciousness.

Without Kazmerev here, I couldn't hope to heal him. And I had no supplies to tend him. And out there somewhere was the Stryxex. I'd hit it with fire, but I had been too busy falling to see what happened next. For all I knew, it might be slinking through the shadows nearby, its rider readying his bow.

Panic clawed at me, but I forced it away with all my willpower. No.

While we were both still alive there was hope.

Who knew? Maybe Judicus had fought himself free of the tunnel collapse. Maybe, even now, he was searching for us.

I knew – without really knowing how I knew – that he would search. He would never just abandon us. And neither would Gundt. Not even if he feared for the ai'sletta and secretly thought it would be better to keep her from the Grand Hadri, he would still look for me.

Across the massive gallery, I heard the sounds of movement and froze. The raiders. I'd forgotten they were here, too, slowly making their way down the rickety stairs.

A curse bubbled up in my mind, but I forced it down, too.

Think, Sersha, think.

"Sersha," the Grand Hadri gasped out. He sounded like he was battling with himself. Perhaps he was trying not to scream. "You tried well. In the end, you tried well."

It wasn't the end for me. And I hoped it wasn't the end for him, either.

I nodded, not sure what else to do. My mind was racing, but no way out of this was coming to me. We couldn't go up the stairs. Certainly not with him like this.

"How bad is it?" the Grand Hadri asked. I shook my head grimly, face set and unmovable.

I couldn't heal him without Kazmerev. I couldn't defend him either.

He sighed. "I feared it was so. Since you are here, you'll hear my last confessions."

I tried to frown more deeply to indicate how much that displeased me. He wasn't dead yet and if I could just think of a solution, maybe he'd live. He had to hold on until it was dark again. His wound was bad – but surely not so bad that he couldn't do that. For all we knew – and we really didn't know – it might be close to sunset.

"Don't frown," he said, and his words seemed to cost him. "You hate me because of Judicus. Likely, he told you how I beheaded his father in front of him."

What? I could feel my eyes widening and I couldn't stop it. Knowing that, why had my rope worker even tried to save him? Why had he tried to get the ai'sletta for him?

I shuddered with second-hand horror, drawing back from the wounded man without meaning to.

"Likely," the Grand Hadri said with a moan. "He's told you all kinds of terrible stories of how I have kept his mother and sister close, pawns to hold him tight to me. How I gave him only one choice – train to be a rope worker and work for me. Or see them perish. I'm sure he did. I'm sure he explained why his desperate gamble to find the ai'sletta means more to him than just a coterie of his own and funding from the crown – how it means his freedom and his family's safety."

He had told me none of that. And wasn't that so Judicus? To keep his own worries and pain deep inside and save me from the burden of them?

"You should know I wouldn't have killed them."

Except he'd killed Judicus' father – by his own confession – so what made the rest of his family different?

There was scuffling across the gallery. How long until the raiders reached the bottom? And what then?

"I just didn't want him to be his father. I just couldn't bear to kill him, too."

He was raving like a madman.

"That's my confession. That I was cruel to be kind."

It wasn't much of a confession. It sounded like words crafted to make armor to protect him from his own guilt. People did that all the time.

I set my finger to my lips. If he had nothing of value to say, he should be silent and not draw the attention of the raiders.

"I will not be silent. There is relief in finally speaking these things."

Not for me, there wasn't.

"I didn't want to kill him. I didn't. But he read and read, and studied, and in the end, he decided we were oppressed and kept down by a tyrant and oh so coolly he set up a coup, and he killed the Grand Hadri, and took his place, and jailed me for my betrayal. And it was all like a history book to him – dispassionate. Workmanlike. Scholarly. I think that's what hurt most, that he didn't hate the Grand Hadri who came before him, and he didn't hate me. He just thought things were going wrong and that it was somehow his business to fix it. I could have forgiven him if he'd hated me. I could have spared him. But we couldn't forgive with such a monster at the reins. Not me. Not those who freed me from prison. Not the people. I did it for us – for them."

Sometimes I wondered if my silence made people feel safe and if that was why they spoke to me, or if it made them feel guilty and that was the reason. Whichever it was, there was something about me that made them pour out the words of their sins across the ground and flood up my soul with the knowing of them and I wished I could burn it all off like a fever burns off sickness, but now they belonged to me, too, and I felt tainted by them.

"If I am to die," he whispered, "As seems likely given my injuries and the prevalence of our enemies, then I must lay out my secrets to you. We've been seeking the ai'sletta for so long – but in the past three generations, it hasn't just been about glory anymore. It's been about survival. The Grand Hadri has spies – every nation does, but these spies are my own network alone, passed in secret from Hadri to Hadri and gifted through the crown. And our spies across the seas were coming back with rumors about the raiders – that they're more than just people of the sea now. That they have aligned themselves with those who ride on black wings. And the rumor whispered from lip to ear, was that they were making these creatures in a way that could only be stopped by the ai'sletta. Do you see now why we need her? You saw that thing of darkness who scored my back and broke my body. You saw that painted mural. It confirms it all."

In my mind, I saw the mural on the wall above. What did those rumors have to do with a long-buried mural?

"If I'm overthrown and killed – and it seems I am – then this knowledge will be lost. Surely you can see it."

I nodded and he slumped with relief.

"You must take her to their lands. I know, I know, don't look at me like that. Of course, I know it's impossible. But you must. And you must guard her until she can do what she must."

I opened my hands quickly. Trying to express my question.

"I don't know what it is. But maybe she will when she sees it. I thought we had more time. Much more time. I wasn't even sure we'd find her in my generation, wasn't sure the rumors weren't just the whisperings of an ill wind."

And yet here we were. I wanted to sit down. Needed to. When I sat, it was heavily, burdened by more weight on me. Save the phoenixes. Stop the Stryxex. Save Mally from being used. Use her. So many demands and just one Sersha to try to meet them. I wanted to put my head in my hands and just sit for a while, but across the gallery, I heard the muffled sounds of our pursuers. They would certainly find us here. And then what? Death?

"And now you must leave me," he whispered.

I shook my head. Obviously, I wasn't going to leave him.

"You must," he insisted, his voice rising. "For if you do not, who will pass my words on? Go to the palace in Briccatore and look for Jensen and the Crown and Seal. Tell him that you seek the reversal of error, and he will pave your way."

I was shaking my head, but his hand snaked out and grabbed my wrist.

"Promise me," he begged, pent-up passion making his voice ragged. "Please."

One of the best parts of not being able to speak was that I didn't have to be coerced into promises I wasn't ready to make, vows I didn't agree with, or assurances I did not feel.

"It's not natural for me to beg," he said, and his face seemed older somehow at this confession. "But who else will I turn to? Please."

If I said yes, I'd be binding Judicus and Kazmerev and even Mally into something they hadn't agreed to. And if I said no, I'd leave a dying man in his despair.

I wanted to tell him I'd consider it. I wanted to say I would ask the others. I didn't want to make a vow.

He reached out and clasped my forearm as if we were making a legal agreement and then he said, "In my power as Grand Hadri of Calicarn, humbled though I am, I both command and adjure you to fulfill this request of mine and to immediately flee this place and leave me to my fate."

And while I'd denied him my assent, I couldn't deny the courage in his eyes. I squeezed his arm and fled into the shadows.

113

I was surprised how shaken I was by leaving the Grand Hadri to his fate. Guilt clawed at me – though what I thought I could do with no weapon, no phoenix, no friends, and not even a voice to negotiate with, I didn't know.

I slipped through the shadows, darting from one stalagmite to the next, gripping the gritty edges of them with trembling fingers as I hurried away. There had to be another way out of this cavern, or failing that, perhaps there was a way back up the staircase the raiders came down. Now that I wasn't listening to the Grand Hadri – now that I'd abandoned him to his enemies – other worries were flooding in. Day was here. The artificial night was past. What did that mean for Mally? Had she removed her crown – or had it been taken from her? Were my friends trapped – or even dead? And how would I get to them?

Perhaps if I could retrace my steps through this must-scented gallery, trace our flight through the caverns, go out through the door the raiders took into this system of caves, and then brave the stone octopus, go back to the temple and ... what? Dig through the rubble to where Judicus and the others were? With my bare hands?

I couldn't stop shaking. The enormity of it all – of how impossible it would be – felt like it was crushing me. And yet I couldn't stop trying, fighting, running. Because, eventually, the night would fall and Kazmerev would be there, and he would know what to do. He would. He always did. I just had to keep trusting that.

In the distance, I heard a yell – a painfully familiar one. The raiders had found the Grand Hadri. I hadn't even liked the man, and yet tears smarted my eyes at his cry of pain. Judicus had left him with me, and I failed him. I failed them all.

I let myself offer up one shuddering sob and then I screwed up my face and forced it all down. Crying now – breaking down – that wouldn't help anyone. I had to keep my head. I had to keep out of sight. I had to stop sniveling and get on with it like I had all my life.

Thinking like that shouldn't have cheered me up, but it did.

I'd faced worse.

I would be fine.

I wasn't sure either of those things were true, but I was going to keep on believing them anyway.

I nodded my head, and spun, hurrying into the darkness – and ran full into something warm and soft. I gasped and the other thing – person, it turned out to be – gasped with me.

I swallowed down a scream as arms tangled around me and then a whisper shushed me, right beside my ear.

"Sersha." It was barely audible. "Sersha, is it really you? It's me. Judicus."

He smelled of woodsmoke and dust and I'd never smelled anything so comforting.

"You're alive," he whispered as if he was trying to convince himself. "You're actually alive. We dug and dug but we couldn't get through. The rocks were too big."

I put a finger over his lips, but he peeled it away. I couldn't quite see his face – just the barest outline of it but he looked distraught. I didn't want him captured.

"We saw. I know the raiders are down here. We saw them coming down the ladder. And we saw the Stryxex disappear through the roof."

I whuffed a sigh of relief at that. Even an injured Stryxex was a terror to me. If it had fled, that gave us time for Mally to wear that crown again. Time for Kazmerev to return.

I tried to mime putting the crown on and Judicus shook his head. "It stopped working when she passed out. And we tried it on me and Gundt and it didn't work."

I froze. Mally had passed out?

"Come. I'll show you."

His eyes raked over me as if he was searching for injuries. His expression was tense, but that was all I could tell in the shadows. That feeling was confirmed when I took his warm hand in mine and let him lead me through the darkness. He seemed to almost relax at my touch as if he needed someone to hold him, too. Someone to tell him, too, that it would be okay.

But we couldn't leave the Grand Hadri. I pulled him to a stop and gestured back the way we came. He shook his head. I gestured again more emphatically. He must not understand.

"The Grand Hadri," he said eventually, and now there was enough light to see his features twist in pain. "Is he dead?"

I shrugged, shaking my head. He might be by now.

"Are the raiders upon him?"

I nodded.

"Then can't you see, Sersha, we don't dare go back for him. There are only you and me and Gundt to get two unconscious women out of here. We can barely manage that without fighting at the same time."

I tugged on his sleeve, and he ran a hand over his pained expression before sighing and nodded.

"You're right. We'll look."

Sneaking back was just as hard as sneaking away had been. Every step on the rippled stone felt like it might betray us. But this time was different. This time I had hope. This time I had a friend.

We were almost back to where I'd started when Judicus's hand clamped on my shoulder and we both froze. We were half-hidden in a dark shadow but even so, we were terribly exposed as a pair of raiders marched by with a blanket held between them. To my relief, the effort kept their eyes steadily forward. But on the blanket, limp, eyes wide and staring, lay the Grand Hadri.

I fought to stay as still as I could, not to flinch, not to gasp, not to turn and vomit. He had been right all along that his time was close and now he was surely dead and only I knew what he'd been trying to achieve.

We stood together in absolute silence, motionless, as our enemies passed by and I clung to the warm hand in mine as if it were a rope over a chasm. I had the oddest sensation that Judicus was clinging to me in the exact same way.

114

The Grand Hadri's plea to me rang in the long moments that I huddled there with Judicus. I hadn't vowed anything to him – and yet it felt like a vow – and a terrible one at that. To cross to the lands of the raiders. To bring Mally. To stop the birth of the Stryxex. Just the thought of it made me ill. What would Kazmerev think when he woke?

Eventually, the feet of the raiders passed. It seemed they were headed back to the stairs, not searching for more than the Grand Hadri, as if he were their only goal. Perhaps he was. They hadn't shown much interest in the rest of us other than as obstacles in the way of his retrieval. Except Mally. She'd been important to them. It was good they didn't know she was here somewhere.

Judicus tugged gently on my hand, leading me away, and I let him. My mind was full of the Grand Hadri. Of healing him. Of watching him snatched away by Stryxex. Of his demands. Of his back torn as he bled on the ground. I shuddered and to my surprise, Judicus put his arm around me – somewhat hesitantly – as if he thought his long, skinny limb might guard me from trouble. It put me in mind of a mother goose with a gosling tucked under a wing. I leaned into him gratefully.

What was he feeling now? Was he worried or did he only feel relief at the end of the life of a man who had admitted to tormenting him?

We reached a jagged part of the rock far more quickly than I expected and ducked inside, Judicus dropping his hold on me as if he'd been caught stealing.

The two women – Mally and Cassanetta – lay side by side. Someone had carefully set Mally's crown beside her.

Stationed between them and the rest of the gallery was Gundt, crouched defensively as if he were prepared to strike.

He relaxed at the sight of us. Drawing himself back to a more normal stance.

"Well?" he whispered to Judicus.

"Dead," Judicus said, shaking his head.

"Heaven send mercy," Gundt said but he didn't sound particularly sorry – more worried. He looked at me then, awkwardly, relief lighting his lined features. "Are you hurt, Fledgling?"

I shook my head. My body ached and my jaw was screaming where it hit the ground and my ribs pinched painfully if I took too deep of a breath, but none of that needed tending to right now.

He nodded as if he understood all of that without my telling him.

"You managed yourself well up there," he said, nodding at the roof. He must have seen us fighting, too. "I think you wounded the Stryxex badly enough that it will need to recover before it comes after us. Hard to say. I only caught the last few seconds. Huxabrand was carrying the girls and I was distracted when the ai'sletta fainted."

His words snapped me back to reality and my hand flew up over my mouth. Mally.

I hurried over to her, checking her for wounds. It was harder than it looked. She was so covered in drying blood from all the little cuts her captors had given her before she escaped that it disguised anything new. I checked her thoroughly, but the only new wound was a head wound.

"She was hit hard when the rocks came down on us," Gundt said grimly. "But she's a tough one and she was managing to stay upright, and then all of a sudden ..." He gestured with his hands as if it was too much to say aloud that his revered ai'sletta had fainted before his eyes.

I nodded along. I didn't think the head wound was enough to have made her faint and I didn't see any other injuries to account for it unless it was just losing all this blood. Either way, there was nothing to be done. I shook my head helplessly to indicate that and Judicus sighed.

"We'll have to go on without the phoenix's help. Can the pair of you manage Mally between you? I can carry Cassanetta. She's half the weight of your cousin."

"I think you should carry her with Sersha and I will bear the ai'sletta," Gundt said but Judicus waved him away.

"We won't have this discussion again, Flame Rider. You're as injured as Mally is – even if you say you've been partially healed by your phoenix. It is sensible that everyone should do the most they can, and that means I carry our prisoner and the pair of you carry Sersha's cousin. It will be hard enough as it is without argument."

I agreed with that sentiment. I agreed even more once she was slung across my shoulders.

"And here we are, then," Gundt said as we balanced her between us. "I was worried for you, Fledgling. We tried to dig you out but couldn't budge the rock."

I nodded, smiling to show I thought he did well. No need to carry guilt for something that was none of his fault.

"We've been following the rope worker's lead." He nodded toward Judicus, and to my surprise, the leader of our coterie had his eyes shut.

He took a deep breath, and then dark ropes fell from his hands and skittered across the ground like purposeful snakes, questing outward.

Gundt was silent, waiting, as if he'd seen this before and I was content to be quiet with him but after a while he whispered, "I think proximity to the crown makes him more resilient. The rope work doesn't take as much out of him."

I raised my eyebrows. Interesting. The Grand Hadri had thought Mally would have the opposite effect on a rope worker. He'd been wrong. What else had he been wrong about?

It was long moments before Judicus looked up and when he did there was relief painting his face.

"This way," he said.

115

I hadn't realized how heavy an unconscious girl was until we were an hour into stumbling in the semi-darkness.

"We need water soon," Judicus said eventually.

Gundt merely grunted.

"We need night so the phoenixes can help."

Another grunt.

"We need a clear path out of here without enemies."

This time the other Flame Rider answered him, "While you're wishing, why not wish there's no stone octopus up there."

"Oh," Judicus said absently. "I'm not worried about that."

"You aren't?" Gundt was surprised enough that he froze, leaving me to stumble when I was forced to stop with him. My body ached more the second it was stopped, as if the interruption in motion was a signal for every muscle to send me their complaints. "What do you mean you aren't worried about it? Do you think it has moved on to ravage the countryside?"

"Doubtful," Judicus said through gritted teeth. His feet slid a little when he stepped, and I could tell the burden of Lady Lightland was a lot for him to bear even if he wasn't complaining.

The gallery had narrowed to a passage once more – this one formed of water and very narrow in some places while broader in others. It split often into little bends and curves that ended in nothing. Navigating it took concentration and a firm determination not to panic that you might get lost. I was having trouble with both, even after Judicus lit a flickering oil lamp – the strange tentacle-decorated things were everywhere, more evidence that these caves were somehow connected to the rest of this place.

"The creature is there to protect the temple and the artifacts contained within and around it. It won't leave the valley unless it must, but I was never worried about it. I was worried about gathering in the injured somewhere safe and then I was worried about chasing down the ai'sletta when she so foolishly wandered off, but I was never worried about the octopus. I can handle such a creature."

"Then why did you not handle it?" Gundt asked with the kind of carefulness that tells you a person's temper is not far from flaring. "It killed Olliman after we sought shelter."

The sound of Olliman's name brought with it a burst of pain. That last fellowship we had shared made his death more painful. I blinked and saw his face seared into my memory, grim determination filling his eyes, and his lips sealed tightly over his missing tongue. I stumbled as tears glazed my eyes and it was all I could do to blink them back enough to watch my steps once more.

We were moving again and the ground beneath was sloped relentlessly downward. Both Gundt and I grunted frequently under Mally's weight, her head leaned on my shoulder and her slumped body was hard to keep upright. I couldn't tell what was wrong with her and that worried me more than the terrible difficulty of moving her.

On top of that, Gundt had given me her crown to hold onto and the little spikes in the top of it bit into my hip from where I'd tied it to my belt, adding pain to exhaustion and frustration. We couldn't bear these burdens for long – but I tried not to focus on that, knowing it would only make the difficulty worse.

Judicus moved in a way that might have been a shrug if he hadn't been so burdened.

"Disabling the cursed creature would have sapped all my energy and left Sersha and the ai'sletta alone with four unconscious people and raiders on all sides. I thought it was better to leave the temporary protection of the magical beast in place."

"You thought it was better," Gundt echoed, tonelessly. My hands were starting to slip and twice he'd had to readjust Mally to take more of her weight. That we were still going at all was amazing.

"Yes," Judicus said, and he sounded distracted. "Do you think the cult would have thought to leave a boat for the river?"

"You thought it was better not to disable the octopus even when Olliman ran out the door."

"We've already covered this ground, Gundt. Yes. I thought it was better. Now, do you see a boat? Did the Cult of the Tattered Ribbons use boats?"

"I've never heard of this cult before," Gundt said, and now he just sounded tired – like he'd finally reached the end of his rope. We were close to the end of mine, too. Maybe we should just sit for a while. Maybe we should find a place to defend and hold onto it until nightfall when our phoenixes would return. Trying to move with the burden of these others was just too much to ask. "And why would we want a boat?"

"I don't think most people have heard of the Tattered Ribboners," Judicus said, and he still sounded like his mind was absent. "From what I can tell, they were very well hidden. Perhaps Sersha will have more to tell when Huxabrand and Kazmerev return to us, but until then, I'm operating just with what information we have, and it seems to me that they kept their secrets from the history books, from the ruling class – or those counselors would not have met there – from the rope workers who both revere this place and forbid entry to it, and from the public who have not come in search of treasures. It's an odd thing to have such facility with secrecy. In my experience, most people offer up secrets in the same way they offer up platitudes – far too often. And a people like that, are a people who would be prepared, so I'm going to assume they will have left a boat."

"A boat," Gundt repeated. And I knew he wanted to ask again what we'd do with a boat here in a cave – just like I wanted to – but he was too tired for it. We all were.

"For quick escape," Judicus explained, and he sounded pleased. "I read about something like this in the Chronicles of the Freenen people, but I thought it was only a legend of course. Who would have thought that anyone would actually do it?"

He paused, as if waiting for Gundt to repeat his words again, but the older Flame Rider was clearly too tired to bother anymore. Judicus looked at me and I smiled tiredly, but I couldn't give him what he wanted, either.

He rallied. "But it seems they have. What do you think?"

And saying that, he hitched Cassanetta higher on his shoulder, and with a grunt, he stepped to the side.

Below him, the cave opened and widened to where our flickering lamp revealed within a ring of orange light, a small jetty set in the stone beside a very slow, very fetid smelling pool. Tied to the jetty, was a small boat carved in tentacles.

"I think that every good hideaway has a secret escape," Judicus continued happily. "And we've found the one for this place."

"And I've found you," a voice said from the shadows.

My heart caught in my throat as the red-haired raider stepped out from the shadows.

116

He had a weapon – that was the first thing I noticed. After that, I was just trying to stay upright. Gundt shoved Mally into my arms, lunging forward to meet our attacker, and I became completely occupied with keeping my cousin from falling bonelessly to the ground. In the end, I had to lower her slowly, while chaos erupted in front of me.

"Get her into the boat," Gundt called to me.

I glanced up long enough to see him locked in a tangle with the red-haired Stryxex rider. I tried to drag Mally, but she wouldn't budge. She was too heavy, and I was too scared. My hands kept slipping.

Gundt grunted behind me and then something sounded like meat being hit against a butcher block and someone – I couldn't tell which of them – cried out in masculine-sounding pain.

Judicus was there suddenly, lifting Mally's shoulders so I could get her feet. His ropes of power tangled around my cousin, helping us draw her to the little craft. It was small – barely big enough for four, never mind five. There was only one oar.

We laid her on the floor of the boat beside where Judicus had laid Cassanetta. It was a marvel to me that he was still going to such great lengths to save Lady Lightland's life when she'd tried to kill us both and was part of a coup attempt on the Grand Hadri, but perhaps I was the only one of us who thought no information could be worth all this effort.

I was still huffing with exertion when Gundt's bellow of agonized fury shuddered through me and then Judicus's hand was on my arm, guiding me into the boat.

"Take the oar," he said. "Try to keep it in the center of the channel. If you hear water rushing, try to make it to the side. I hope there are no waterfalls. I hope not, but I don't know. I just know that running water always flows somewhere and this stuff must flow, too. We'll follow when we can. The minute night falls, work with Kazmerev and get these two to safety."

I clenched my jaw. As if I wouldn't go back for them. I would.

"Don't you dare think of coming back for us," he said, calm as a summer breeze. "As a member of my coterie, this is my order to you. Seek safety. Seek shelter. Don't come back. Wait for us at the end of the water – wherever it goes. We'll find you."

Something screamed in the distance and to my utter shock, Judicus reached around his neck, wrenched a chain from it, and slung it over my head.

"If you need help, show this around and someone will help you."

And then he was running, sprinting toward where Gundt's cries of pain were punctuated by the shrieks of the wounded Stryxex. It dove toward the other Flame Rider, but Judicus's black ropes were already there, tangling it up like a trap set for a rabbit. Judicus risked a single glance over his shoulder, caught my eye and his lips formed the word, "Go."

And then I was pushing my boat off and launching it into the darkness.

The water moved with deceptive speed, appearing calm and balmy, but fighting against us with every swell and roll. It dragged us along, just another piece of debris caught in its mighty purpose.

I glanced behind me, catching a last glimpse of Judicus throwing himself into the fray and of Gundt springing back to his feet, arm out as if he were going to hug the enemy into submission, and then the placid river bent slightly, and I lost all sight of them except for the occasional cry that split the air like an axe in dry wood.

I also entirely lost the ability to control my boat. To my horror, whatever current held it was a powerful jailer, and neither rowing, nor shoving with the haft like a pole, was even budging the boat. It was anchored in the current like a sword in its hilt and I could no more shift it than I could shift the sword.

Even worse, it was picking up speed.

Our boat plunged around the corner of the rock and to my horror, something followed.

A dark shadow shrieked from behind us.

I twisted from my seat, looking just in time to see the riderless Stryxex as my night vision caught the outline of its wings cupping the air to either side of its burned body. The feathers across its chest and left side were shorn off white stubs from the flame I'd wielded and where skin could be seen it was red and bubbling. I swallowed down my gorge at the sight, marred as it was by the dullness of my vision in the pitch black.

In a minute, it would be on us, swooping down to pluck us from the boat and dash us onto the rocks.

But that assumed he could get to us before we plunged off the edge of what was coming up – and I could not tell if the rushing water was pushing us toward a tiny lip of rock that would be nothing more than a little tummy-flip drop or a full waterfall but the roar ahead was not comforting and the darkness gave me no hints and the paddle – the useless, soul-forsaken paddle. Well, I might as well throw it overboard for all it was doing.

I dropped it in the boat beside Mally, slipping as her crown fell under my leg. Stupid thing.

I scrambled to where she was in the little boat, grabbed her in my arms, and then jammed her crown on my head for good measure – maybe it would stay put and we could keep it. Cassanetta was on her own.

The moment the crown slammed on my head, my night vision was ripped away like a curtain shutting over a window.

I gasped at the same time the Stryxex shrieked, and then we were falling over the edge and my heart was in my throat.

117

Pain exploded in my chest in a strange way that was streaked all through with joy.

The cavern blossomed with scarlet-and-gold light so that the water falling all around me looked more like molten gold and ruby drops than water.

Sersha!

Kazmerev! My phoenix!

Kazmerev caught me on his back, giving a cry somewhere between a man's yell and a bird's shriek. We plummeted parallel to the waterfall, me with my arms clutching Mally, and him with his talons outstretched until he plucked Lady Lightland from the air.

This happens a great deal more than I like. Veela rarely woke me in such a state of crisis.

Veela, it seemed, was better at managing the affairs of her life so they did not spiral into complete chaos. I wish I'd known her properly.

As do I.

He cupped his wings and we leveled off, turning a death-drop into a swoop and I searched the cavern for any sign of the Stryxex. It was a wide cavern with a large pool at the bottom that outflowed into another narrow river. I saw now what I'd missed before – a ladder leading down the side of the waterfall and a second jetty with a second boat. There must have been a place to tie up the first boat – a place I'd missed and been unable to navigate with a boat full of injured women.

There was a rustling flap in the darkness near where the cavern narrowed for the river, but the Stryxex was hiding too well to be seen. I didn't like that. It left little chills running up and down my neck. What I couldn't see, I couldn't defend against.

I'm with you now. I will defend you.

A noble thought, but we had two others to defend, too. And behind us, somewhere, Gundt and Judicus battled the redhaired raider.

We'll chase down the Stryxex. It won't get away.

But not yet. First, we needed to check on the two injured women and settle them properly on his back. We couldn't fly and fight with Lady Lightland clutched in one of his talons.

I'm not overly concerned with her welfare.

But Judicus had been. And he was the leader of our coterie.

There was a long pause.

Yes. You're right, of course.

Reluctantly, he set us down along the edge of the pool. The rocky edges were smooth and nearly flat, worn by centuries of water flowing. It made the place feel almost man-made except for the eeriness of the darkness and the black rock. I checked over Mally with care. She'd hit her head pretty good, hadn't she? Could I heal her like I'd healed Gundt?

What if you do it wrong? Get a leg wrong and a man won't walk. Get a head wound wrong ...

He had a point. But we were still outnumbered, still on the run, still desperately trying to get out from under the ground and beyond just my fear for my cousin's health, there was also the practical problem of how to keep moving her around with her unconscious – a dead weight on our small group.

Remember how much energy it took for you to heal the Grand Hadri? If you use that now, we won't have that for other things – not to hold off Stryxex or to fly with multiple people on my back – or anything else. Congratulations on managing three, by the way. That's new.

I paused at that. I hadn't even realized we'd done it until it was done.

But back to the problem of managing all my responsibilities at once.

This, like so many things in life, was a matter of balancing. What mattered most? I could leave them both here right now, hop on Kazmerev's back and fly to freedom. We could keep following the river or backtrack up the waterfall and to where I'd seen open sky. We would be fine, but only if we abandoned everything else.

Love you as I do, hope of my heart, I would never lead you into heartlessness.

And I wasn't asking him to. I felt a little ashamed for thinking it, but I did have to think it all through. Because the next option would be to heal Mally – or leave her alone – and then to fly free with just her, leaving Lady Cassanetta here on the bank of the pond. It wouldn't be killing her. It just wouldn't be aiding her anymore, and she was, after all, my enemy. And I'd done the same when the Grand Hadri had asked it of me. She was, after all, the one who killed Veela. What did we owe to her?

We were silent for long minutes, pondering, and to my surprise, Kamerev said nothing about this. There were no lectures on doing the right thing. There were no comments on how I was better than that. Just silence. As if he wanted to be rid of the one who had snatched his friend away from him as badly as I did.

The choice about Mally was obvious – cousin, friend, or not, she was still not my enemy, and she deserved my compassion. But what about my enemy? What about Cassanetta? Even knowing what she'd done and was planning to do. Why had Judicus helped her all this time? Did he want information from her, or was he so moved by compassion for an enemy that he risked his own life for her?

Perhaps it wasn't about who she was to deserve my mercy. Perhaps it was about who I was.

I sighed and leaned over her and Mally, a hand on each one, and I chose.

With all my heart, I hoped for healing and reached down deep into the warmth of the fire within me.

It roared and crackled within my mind, burning away my uncertainty, burning away the barriers, leaving me stark and cleaned by flames and far more exposed than I wanted to be.

I can see you still.

I wished he could not, for there was no hiding the selfish impulses of my heart.

And there is no hiding the goodness, beating strong and powerful through you – as gilded a heart as any that has been.

I clung to him and to those words and kept on burning.

118

By the time my cousin blinked her eyes open, and Lady Lightland began to stir, I felt like I was nothing but fire anymore.

I pulled it back into myself, finger by finger, like eating living flames. The pain in my head shot through me, licking at every defense and exposing my heart for what it was. And it wasn't the pain I shrunk from, but the knowledge. There is nothing quite so painful as being forced to see what we'd hoped to deny and being forced to admit what we'd hoped to hide. There is nothing that stings quite like the deep knowing that comes from seeing how we can never wear our guises in quite the same way again.

Easy now, little hawk. You are safe on the drafts and breezes. Glide free and do not falter for there is no judgment from me to you.

I sucked in a long breath and barely got it in before a slap rang through my head and my cheek burned. I was still blinking, tasting blood when Kazmerev flared up, burning like the heart of a campfire where the flames are almost white they're so light, and then *poof* he was gone.

I blinked against stars and then someone pulled my hair with painful sharpness, leaving me blinking against the thick blackness around me and batting at whatever tangled in my hair. And then just as quickly as he'd vanished, Kazmerev was blossoming painfully from my heart and the room lit to show my cousin, arms crossed over her chest and crown jammed hard on her head.

I willed Kazmerev to light the cavern for everyone and flung up a hand to keep him from burning Mally to a cinder. Wasn't it he who had scorned me for even imagining leaving her here?

That was before she slapped you! That was before she stole that crown.

Anyone who knew her at all would have expected that. I was just too distracted to remember to duck the minute she was conscious.

"It's mine, Sersha," my cousin said, lifting her nose in the air. "I might not ride around on a phoenix or have a bunch of friends who get me out of trouble, but the crown is mine by right.

I lifted my other hand – this time, to try to tell her I wasn't challenging her, that the crown was hers. That whatever she wanted was hers. I was not petty. I didn't need to fight for trinkets – even magical ones.

On the other side of me, Cassanetta groaned and Mally stomped over to her. I threw myself between them.

"Don't you dare come between us," Mally said, and her lower lip was shuddering. "It's just us here, isn't it?"

She looked around the room, quick as an owl with his head spinning around, and then sent her gaze back to me with double the focus. "No one but us and the girl who murdered my mother. I can drown her, and they'll never know. We'll say it's an accident." She laughed harshly. "Well, I will, and you don't have the words to deny me that."

I shook my head firmly. Choosing to murder someone was even worse than abandoning them to their fate like I'd considered doing.

Is it, though? It seems about the same. It certainly has the same ending.

I didn't want to hear that. It was another thing I didn't want to acknowledge.

"Come on, Sersha," Mally said. "Give me this one thing. I don't ask for much. I didn't ask you to follow me or stick your neck out for me. I just wanted you to stay out of the way. And you should have listened. And now I'm asking for the same thing. Just. Stay. Out. Of. My Way."

I swallowed and I couldn't seem to summon the effort to stop her as she reached past me and grabbed Lady Lightland by the collar and dragged her up. Whatever healing I'd given Cassanetta hadn't been as effective as Mally's. Her eyes flickered open and then fluttered shut. They opened again, but now they could barely focus. I must not have had enough energy to heal them both.

Or.

Or what?

Or she's more badly injured than you thought.

Or that.

"Look at me," Mally said to Cassanetta. And her voice was terribly flat – the kind of flat she used because screaming wasn't enough. "Look at me before I kill you like my mother looked at you before you killed her. Look at me and hope that I won't kill every person even remotely linked to you by blood or affection. And know, as my mother did, that I will. That nothing you can do can change it. That you are dying, and soon you'll be dead. And once you are, I will kill them all and I will make it take a long time and hurt so much that eventually, I will stop hurting, too."

Her words were thick by the end. Thick and heavy with tears.

I put a hand on her arm. She shrugged it off. I tried again, this time, more firmly and she slapped it away.

"Leave off, Sersha. This is between the two of us."

I wanted to tell her that I understood. I wanted to say that you couldn't heal by cutting someone else. That you couldn't mend by ripping them. That you couldn't retrieve the past by stealing their future.

But words were a weapon denied me – and a salve I could not wield.

So, I did the only thing I could think of.

I wound up and slapped Mally across her face just like she'd slapped me.

119

Perhaps I would have blushed furiously and apologized. Or, perhaps I would have taken that moment to enjoy the stunned look on Mally's face – as if her own handkerchief had suddenly slapped her senseless. But I was spared having to sort out my own emotions as a fresh light flared bright above us and a shout rang down.

"Sersha? Kazmerev!"

It was Gundt on the back of Huxabrand. She looped down, landing gracefully on the rock shelf at the same moment that Mally shook her head at me and lunged past to grab Lady Lightland by the throat. And then I was distracted, trying to pull my cousin off our mutual enemy. I hadn't spent all that energy healing her just to see her die at Mally's enraged hands.

"Enough!" Judicus bellowed.

And to my relief he was suddenly beside me, helping me pull our ai'sletta away from the woman who'd murdered her mother.

We held her for a moment, everyone panting and trying to catch their breath. Judicus's eyes were wild, black hair in disarray. We never had washed the blood and dirt from his face and it was streaked with clean lines where sweat had carved runnels through the mess.

Mally was just as wide-eyed, though cleaner. As soon as she caught her breath, she sniffed and yanked her arm free from me so she could run her hands through her chestnut hair. I still couldn't get used to how short it was.

Gundt cursed quietly under his breath, but he was slumped over his phoenix, favoring a wound to the side, his face pale and set in grim lines.

I hurried to him as Lady Lightland began to laugh.

"She doesn't know," Cassanetta said with a weak voice. "Which is funny, don't you think Judicus Franzer Irault?"

"What don't I know?" Mally demanded, her lip quivering with high emotion. "What's been happening?"

Her face was flushed in the light of our phoenixes, but Cassanetta's head lolled forward again and her voice took on a thready quality.

"She doesn't know she shouldn't kill me. Can't."

I was by Gundt's side now and I reached for him, but he flinched back, his hand catching mine before I could tend to his wound.

"It's bad," he said tightly. "The raider got a slash in, and he disappeared into the shadows. When Huxabrand materialized he was gone."

I was going to just heal him anyway. I was used to doing things without permission since I couldn't usually ask, but I paused, realizing that wasn't true.

Could Kazmerev ask for me?

Kazmerev danced from foot to foot, he'd been inspecting Huxabrand like he was worried about her while Mally breathed threats at Judicus. Was Huxabrand hurt, too?

She is well, Kazmerev assured me. *Huxabrand, Sersha was able to heal both the Grand Hadri – before he was taken – and her cousin Mally, though the healing didn't seem to take with Lady Lightland quite as well. I doubt she has the strength for more, but she is offering to heal Gundt if he'll allow it.*

Gundt looked at me in surprise. "A rare talent that. I've heard of it only a handful of times before. And it's a generous offer. Thank you for it, Sersha." I reached for him, but he shook his head. "Patience. First, let's see if we need to fly again. I can live with this wound however bad it is but we will need all your strength if we must flee further."

I'm worried you cannot, Huxabrand said, tossing her head anxiously.

"You could always heal me later if we need to preserve your strength right now," Gundt said, but I couldn't help but notice the sweat forming along his brow. The pain must be intense.

That's what I tried to tell her, Kazmerev said irritably. *If she listened, then we wouldn't have to deal with the enraged ai'sletta.*

Neither Gundt nor Huxabrand said anything to that, but despite one being human and the other phoenix, they wore identical expressions of agreement and Gundt grunted. I supposed even a dedicated Greensleeve had to realize our ai'sletta was no noble, biddable specimen.

I sighed. I had only been trying to help when I healed her.

Your heart is good, Kazmerev agreed.

Which wasn't the same as saying that I'd done the right thing.

"Tell her," Cassanetta said through her faint, wheezing laughter and my attention snapped back to her.

Judicus flushed red.

"Tell me what?" Mally asked and she was quivering with fury. "Tell me what could possibly keep me from taking my revenge? She wanted you dead, too, you know. She tried to kill you so many times."

"I'm aware," Judicus said quietly. "I'm well aware of all Cassanetta has done. And I'm aware that revenge – even revenge that feels righteous at the time, has implications we can't fully understand. It's best not taken lightly."

"Then I'll take it heavily," Mally said, striding to where a loose chunk of rock was washed up on the shore. She plucked it up and hefted the weight in her hand. "I'll take it as heavily as the original crime."

Judicus sighed. "Wait. You are the ai'sletta and Cassanetta is right. The prophecy says that if you shed blood your power will be gone."

The rock lowered in Mally's hand. "I'd lose this?"

"Yes."

The rock lifted again. "I'd lose the reason people keep trying to kill me?"

"Yeesss," Judicus drew out the word warily.

"I'd lose the reason they keep threatening my family and friends?"

"Yes," he said sounding resigned.

She'd lose the way to save us from a calamity only the Grand Hadri knew about.

I didn't realize Kazmerev had repeated that until Gundt cleared his throat. He must be in a lot of pain. His voice was strained with it and shuddering around the edges.

"Sersha learned of a threat that only the ai'sletta can save us from. Apparently, it's an urgent thing."

Mally seemed unmoved. She looked between the rock and Lady Lightland and back again as if the idea that we all might be doomed if she killed someone hardly outweighed her need to avenge herself. And then suddenly, as if it had just occurred to her, she shoved the rock into Judicus's hand.

"Then you will do it for me," she said simply.

"I will not." He looked tired. He looked tired a lot. It made me want to tuck him under a blanket beside a fire while I made him tea.

"Why not?"

"Because I don't murder people when I don't have to," Judicus said gently. "And neither will Sersha and neither will Gundt."

He had so much faith in us. It made me feel tingly all over.

"Why not Gundt?" Mally demanded.

"Because he's my blood," Cassanetta said bitterly. "And that still means something to people like him."

Her green eyes flicked to me next.

"Why not Sersha?"

In answer, I strode forward, and I took her rock. She seemed to sag with relief until I threw it into the pond. It made a satisfying splash – but probably not as satisfying as Cassanetta's cry of pain would have been. I wanted revenge as badly as Mally did. But I had Kazmerev. And every time he was reborn it was a reminder of all that had been given to me. How could I take a life – not in self-defense but just because I could – when I'd been given one? How could I take a future when mine was reborn each evening?

Good girl.

Judicus coughed. "At any rate, you can have your revenge when her execution is ordered by the next Grand Hadri. Properly. In a way that fits the law."

"And what makes you think he'll do it?" Mally asked, a tear tracking down her cheek. It was a tear of rage – a fact we all seemed to know without it being spoken aloud.

Judicus's tone was dry as a desert when he answered. "I think I know my own mind."

120

"Your own ... wait, you're going to be the next Grand Hadri?" Mally asked, surprise shedding her anger and pain like a man sheds layers when he enters a warm inn after a day in the cold. "Is this true?"

She looked around at us and I shrugged – how should I know? It was plausible. He was the nephew of the former Grand Hadri – but he was hated by the populace because of his father, and I wasn't sure that would help his claim much.

Gundt looked away uncomfortably when her gaze met his and he coughed into his hand. He was here for the ai'sletta and for me. Who the Grand Hadri was now or later seemed of little consequence to him.

When Mally turned to Lady Lightland she laughed again, looked around blearily, and then said, "Well, I suppose he would have been if we weren't taking over Calicarn and deposing the rulers and advisors and military. Now, he's probably just going to be executed if anyone finds out who he is."

And just like that, the bubble burst for me, because I was thinking of Judicus's mother and sister. What would they do? Could they flee the city in time? I didn't know what that involved but it seemed to me that they'd need to be warned. And who else would need to be warned? Who else would be in danger?

I looked up sharply and caught Judicus' eyes on me. They were both wary and torn as if the same ideas were going through his mind.

I wished I could tell him I'd stick by him.

But will you stick by him? You know you need to get the ai'sletta to the lands of the raiders to prevent a great disaster from occurring. You know you need to stop the Stryxex from massacring all phoenixes. Neither of those things allows for loyalty to Judicus and his plight right now.

We were in his coterie. Of course, we would stick with him.

This goes beyond coteries.

Huxabrand shifted slightly and I heard her voice in my mind.

The fate of all phoenixes has to take precedence over any other loyalty. No, Gundt, even over the ai'sletta.

She sounded fierce and when she was done she snapped her beak for emphasis. Gundt was frowning. He liked all this as little as I did.

But my eyes locked on Judicus's again, radiating sympathy.

I wished I could offer him promises, empty though they might be.

I won't lie for you. We can't promise him anything.

We'd made promises when he brought me into his coterie. And I hadn't asked Kazmerev to lie.

He's the one who made promises. And that means this will be even more difficult for him. He's going to have to choose – come with you and probably Gundt.

Definitely Gundt, Huxabrand put in and I risked a glance at her proud form and the stricken look on her rider's face. He was listening to all of this with the concentration of someone barely holding onto consciousness.

Kazmerev kept speaking as if she hadn't interrupted him. "*He can choose to protect the ai'sletta as she crosses the sea and thwarts the plans of the raiders. Or, he can stay here and fight for a crown against a multitude of unknown enemies. Which do you think he'll choose?*

He'd choose whichever was most honorable. I held his solemn gaze and I saw that he realized I was having a silent conversation without him. He tilted his head to the side, sadly. Somehow, he realized I was just as torn as he was.

"Well, this is ridiculous, and I won't stand for it," Mally said, and I wanted to hug her because I was feeling the exact same way. "I didn't ask for it. I don't want it. And I'm not even sure I'm willing to go on with it. Killing her means I'm done with this magic and craziness, and I can do what I want? Great. Someone hand me a knife."

She held out her hand and the crown on her head made the gesture look massively dramatic.

"You can't, Mally," Judicus said, finally dragging his eyes from mine. He sounded so, so tired.

"And why can't I?" She was shaking, tears in her eyes, and I both recognized the hurt in them and also knew that if I tried to do anything about it, it would only make it worse.

"Because none of us can do what we want now. Do you think Gundt wants to go to the lands of the raiders on what must be a suicide mission? Do you think he wants to face down Stryxex risking both himself and Sersha?"

She shrugged.

He kept going. "Do you think Sersha wants to fly into danger chasing after a cousin who gets into one scrape after another?"

Mally's lower lip jutted out just a little further. He shouldn't put that on her. Sure, she'd made some decisions, but most of this had been forced on her.

"Do you think I want to leave Cassanetta alive? I have reason to believe she killed my friend Veela. I have reason to believe her actions have doomed my uncle, my mother, and my sister. She's destroying my entire world. But leaving aside the fact that I do not murder people simply because they have hurt me, I should also note that Lady Lightland will have information about the conspiracy that is destroying my land. She'll have names. She'll have ways to talk with them. It would be utterly foolish to kill her and lose all of that. And so, I am going to ask you for the impossible, Mally. I'm going to ask you to be reasonable. Delay your revenge. Take a bath and wash the blood off, don't fly into a murderous rage again, and trust that eventually justice will be done and that I will see it done for you."

"Justice," Cassanetta scoffed, but her scoff was cut off by a burst of lung-ripping coughs. She really had been so hurt that my attempt to heal her had only taken the edge off.

Mally, on the other hand, looked thoughtful, and after a long pause, she said flippantly, "Well, if I'm going to bathe you could at least turn around."

And that seemed to be all she'd commit to, so we turned around and left her to the private mourning and misery that I was certain she was hiding from us, and I wished everyone had a phoenix to burn their sorrows and purify them in the ashes.

And perhaps, one day all phoenixes will share their hearts with riders like you who care for others as they care for themselves. If they do, then they'll be as lucky as I am and just as grateful.

121

We rested.

It was a strange thing to do when we were still likely to be set upon by enemies at any moment, but Judicus had taken one look at Gundt and me and said with authority in his voice, "The pair of you need rest. If we're going to survive this place, we need your phoenixes and if you're too tired to manifest them, that's a problem. Rest."

He extended a hand, wrapped Lady Lightland in black ropes of magic, and told her, "You can rest, too, Cassanetta. We won't harm you today."

And then he collapsed beside her – which made sense to me since he had to make sure Mally didn't murder her. But I worried for him. He was flat on the rocks, spreadeagle, his mouth open, eyes shut, and in moments a rattling snore was coming from him. How did anyone sleep like that?

I shook my head and found Lady Lightland glaring at me. I looked away quickly. Gundt couldn't refuse me now.

He slipped down from Huxabrand, but to my surprise, he clung to her like a lover, his hands tangled in her feathers, his face buried in their depths. It felt wrong to come close, like I'd be intruding.

It's not intruding to heal, Kazmerev said.

Quick on his heels, Huxabrand said, *If you can heal him, please help.*

I'd never expected Huxabrand to say "please" to me. That alone was enough to shock me into movement despite how exhausted I was. I stumbled toward them, Kazmerev sticking by my side so that I could lean on him. I hadn't realized I was so exhausted until we stopped moving.

Gundt didn't even turn to me. One hand clutched his belly and the other was tangled in Huxabrand's feathers. He made a sound between a grunt and a moan as I leaned over him.

He was in more trouble than I thought. His wound was spewing blood and it was starting to smell foul. The slash had caught his guts.

Huxabrand tossed her head anxiously as if to highlight my thoughts. She was worried, too.

I put a hand on his shoulder and focused. He needed healing. He needed to be knit together. I felt for the wound with my mind and focused on fixing it.

I felt like flames were licking through me and perhaps I was starting to feel this better now that it was my third time, or maybe the sensation was in proportion with the severity of the wound. Whichever it was, this time healing caused fiery agony to sear across my heart. And for a moment, I couldn't see, couldn't hear, couldn't do anything but clench every muscle as I fought against the flames roaring through me.

When the flames had burned everything away, I slowly relaxed, one muscle at a time. Letting go felt almost impossible. Come on, Sersha. One muscle at a time. Relax. It's over.

When, at last, I opened my eyes, I found Gundt there, breathing in huge gulps of air.

He moved his hand and looked down and I gazed at his wound with him. There was still blood on the skin and soaking through shirt and jacket and breeches, but the skin was red and tight as if it were healed over but not well, closed, but still tender. It was the best I could do.

"It's good," he said, trying to reassure me. He breathed raggedly as if he, too, could not relax after that. "Trust me, Fledgling. It is far better than the wound."

It would leave a scar, though.

Flame Riders do not flinch from scars, Kazmerev said.

Gunt flexed a hand, wiped the sweat from his face with a sleeve and then attempted a weak smile. "I'm not upset about the scar, Fledgling. Thank you for your help."

He slumped down to his knees and then to the ground, and like Judicus, he slipped into sleep on the bare stone.

Huxabrand shuffled closer, draping her wing over him as if she would protect him from all comers. The sight was so sweet that it pierced me to the core. I couldn't watch. It made my heart throb.

And so, I found myself making my way to where Mally was dressing again in her tattered clothing, the blood gone, her hair soaking wet, and her face streaked in tears. Her cuts had been shallow, though plentiful and they still leaked light pink into the water she'd washed with. We didn't have bandages, but even if we did, we'd have to wrap her from head to toe.

We sat side by side in silence.

"You're the worst, Sersha," she said eventually, thickly.

I put an arm around her.

"You should have stayed in Landsfall. You shouldn't have a phoenix. You should be washing dishes in the inn."

And I wasn't angry at her because I knew that what she wasn't saying was that she wished she was there, too, and that neither of us had left and that her mother was there bullying us both into living our lives in the way she had set for us. And though I didn't wish for that, I did wish I could take her pain.

"But I guess I'll go save the world with you now that you've dragged me into it," she said eventually with a noisy sniff. "Just don't take my crown again. It looks terrible on you."

And then she fell asleep with her head on my shoulder, and I was alone in the darkness with my phoenix.

You have the oddest family, he said. *Or at least you did before. I am your family now.*

Thank goodness for that. I could have kissed him just for that one assurance.

No need for kisses. Just remember that we are family the next time I suggest something for your own good and don't take it so hard.

He shuffled close to me, and I closed my eyes against his warmth and soon I was breathing deep and even, with everyone else.

122

I woke to the sound of something moving. I was the only one awake. I drew in a long breath, looking around and even the phoenixes were asleep, their heads each identically tucked under a wing. I'd never seen a phoenix sleep before. It was surprisingly beautiful like watching a fire at peace.

The sound came again, and I froze. Lapping water. Something skidding on stone. It was a heartbeat before I realized there was a lantern bobbing, mostly hidden by a hood.

Someone had slipped up the underground river. They weren't coming from the falls above but from the caverns further and deeper in.

That had to mean the river wasn't very long, if they'd had time to rally and come from that direction. I swallowed, unsure what to do.

The phoenixes had faded to invisibility as we slept and Judicus's lamp had gone out, and it was only my flawed night vision I was seeing with. It was not enough to do more than show me the outlines of multiple dark figures creeping out of low boats. The non-phoenix riders would be all but blind. Could I wake Kazmerev and keep him invisible?

I'm here. He didn't seem to be visible. No one screamed or noticed him.

A moment later, Huxabrand's head came out from under her wing. Her movements were slow and furtive as she stretched. I could just barely see Gundt slip up into her feathers.

We'd need to wake and be moving before they got here and before they realized we were onto them. Mally's head was still on my shoulder. I could grab her and get her on Kamerev's back but what about Judicus?

Can you get Judicus and Lady Lightland? Kazmerev asked.

Not without the enemy noticing, Huxabrand replied.

Get Mally, Sersha. We should put her on my back. She's who they'll be after.

No time for more planning than that. I clamped a hand over Mally's mouth but even so, the raiders froze at her muffled protests.

Uh oh.

Move! Move! Move! Kazmerev chanted in my mind, and I threw everything I had into my actions, grabbing Mally and physically hauling her onto his back as Huxabrand leapt toward Judicus and Lady Lightland.

"They've seen us," someone called from the shadows.

"*Aishen savro. Sakhenine despranto elanta.*"

And then they were among us, swords flashing in the light of Huxabrand who had suddenly burst into visibility.

"Up, up!" Gundt called to me. He had no blade to defend himself, but his hand was thrust out and flames burst from his palm.

It was a half a second before I realized he was saying that to us and not to Huxabrand.

Kazmerev leapt and my own hand came out, but when I reached for the fire, it guttered in my hand.

You used too much power healing.

"Burn them!" Mally screamed. "What are you waiting for, Sersha? Burn them all."

Go! Gundt says go without us! Huxabrand called and without discussing it, Kazmerev gained height.

But no. We needed to stay. We needed to fight. We couldn't leave our friends.

Get the ai'sletta out!

The pink-toned phoenix was insistent, but it was all happening too quickly as if a tornado had descended and was whipping around us. I couldn't keep track of everything happening at once. An arrow streaked past, bright in the red of Kazmerev's glowing feathers. I'd forgotten I couldn't keep him invisible with riders on his back.

The raiders poured forward – twenty or thirty men, their faces covered and their clothing black. Underneath, I knew they were muscle and purpose, veterans of years of raiding. One Flame Rider and phoenix couldn't hold off that many. Not even with Judicus helping.

Our rope worker was on his feet, his ropes already snaking out, tripping the first wave of raiders. They snaked back, striking at heels and calves as he disabled them almost as quickly as they poured over the rock. But even that was not enough. Already they were standing again.

I couldn't leave him. Not like this. Not again.

Go! Huxabrand howled in my mind.

Judicus met my eyes and I saw his mouth working in harmony with her words, "Go."

And I didn't want to go. I didn't want to leave them, but already we were moving, sailing over the heads of the raiders, out past their ships, and then over the lapping of the black pool. We had to stop. We had to go back for them.

We can't.

I held my palm up again, calling the flames, and again, nothing happened.

You wore yourself out giving to others. We all have limits.

But these were not mine. They couldn't be. I couldn't afford to flee when I had to fight.

We must go.

He turned, flowing like water in all his fiery beauty. Mally leaned low over his neck, whooping with the excitement, one hand – cleverly – keeping the crown fixed in place. You could always trust Mally to know what was best for Mally.

I cursed in my head, and I felt Kazmerev flinch, but he hadn't done this to me before and he didn't have the right to do it now. I wasn't willing to go.

You have to be willing. We have no other options.

I wanted to stay and fight.

I looked over my shoulder to see Judicus overwhelmed under a wave of black figures, his dark ropes snaking in every direction, but their press of bodies was so great that I couldn't see him behind them. Huxabrand circled above, Lady Lightland screaming from one of her talons and Gundt slumped over her neck, hurt again, his hand spewing flames.

This wasn't right.

I blinked against tears, feeling as if I was being torn in two between my phoenix's cruel demand and the needs of my friends.

Cruel?

I wouldn't leave. He couldn't make me.

Take them far from here, brother, Huxabrand called, and then an arrow ripped through her. She bucked, flames spilling down from the injury, and then we turned a corner, and she was lost to me.

No. No. This is not how it ends I just found them. I couldn't lose them.

I tried to slap Kazmerev. To make him stop. But my hand only passed harmlessly through his flames and my sobs hitched in my throat as we shot down the dark passageway, weaving and darting like a pike in the reeds but I saw little of it for my eyes were clouded by tears and my heart by betrayal.

I have not betrayed you, my phoenix said.

But it felt like a betrayal, and I would not dignify his lie with a response.

123

We soared down the narrow tunnel over the river and I clung to Kazmerev's feathers, torn by a mix of desperately needing him and feeling as though I wished he were somewhere else. I did not like someone else making decisions for me. Not anymore. It felt far too much like the many years that my aunt and cousins had decided for me. It felt like being made a thing instead of a person.

That is not my intent. Surely, you can hear my heart. I want only your safety and your future. And the others want the ai'sletta kept safe.

It wasn't up to them!

It isn't up to you.

To my surprise, the tunnel was not very long. It opened up before long into a black sky beyond, but I could smell fresh air as we exited the cavern over a river. It sprawled out, serpent-like, over a wide plain, and around it lights reflected over the water.

The sky remained unnaturally dark, not a star or moon in the sky, but the sprawling city ahead was bright and twinkling with lights, and surrounding it were shoals of lights that confused me. What was I seeing?

You see an army camped to one side of the city and a fleet of ships in the wider river where this little tributary meets the Brazoinne river. You see the road of Briccatore lit with the friendship torches as they always are at night. Before us sprawls the might of Calicarn and the threat to it that you heard explained to you – the coup and the raiders coming for fat Briccatore and the city sitting there waiting to be snatched up like a ripe apple.

I swallowed as I realized he was right. We were already reaching the point where our tributary fell from the mountains to the larger river and below us, the first lights of the city were beginning to show.

I can't fly over the city unless you make me invisible. We should land by the river.

We should return for the others.

That will not happen. But we can decide how to flee this place once we land. Perhaps you can hire a riverboat.

With what money?

Or hide until nightfall when I can carry you away.

He wasn't even listening to me. And it was shocking how painful that was – as if he'd broken something between us that I'd grown to rely on.

You must not be a child about this. I am my own being with my own choices and I have chosen to save your life.

The word child stung and I let it sit on my heart, festering, as he swooped over the river and landed in the reeds on the other side. Small fishing boats were pulled up on the shore all along this part of the river and while I saw no people moving, it felt uncomfortably populated. I was not the place to have a screaming fight with my phoenix – not that I was able to scream anyway. I was just a passenger on his back and in my own life. He hadn't liked me treating him like a pet and not a person – and I didn't like him treating me the same way.

Don't let bitterness warp everything like that – you know perfectly well it is not so. I care for you, or I would not have ripped you from trouble. I care for you still and together we will find the next step. I will be with you wherever hope blooms in your heart.

I slid from his back into the rustling reeds and Mally slid down with me.

"Well, it's a relief to be out of trouble," she said and then she pulled the crown from her head and like magic, the world went from black as the pupil of a person's eye to a bright sunny day.

And with the change, my phoenix melted away, leaving nothing but a trail of smoke and the scent of regret in the air.

"I guess I shouldn't wear this where anyone will see it, or it's going to get snatched," Mally said idly as if she made the sun rise every day and not just on this one.

I wanted to scream at her, too. I hadn't been done with Kazmerev. I wasn't done with any of this! She was just choosing *for* me like everyone thought they ought to. Judicus choosing to fight in my place. Gundt choosing to prioritize the ai'sletta over my desire to choose him and Judicus. Kazmerev in league with him on that.

I reached for the crown, frustration twisting my face, but Mally batted my hand away.

"We had a deal, Sersha. You don't wear the crown and I agree to save the world. So, let's start saving it, shall we?"

She straightened her shoulders, smoothed down the close trousers over her hips, and began to stride toward the city as if it wasn't about to be laid siege to, as if it wasn't about to see government upheaval, as if we had coin to pay for food and lodging, and if she had any idea where she should be going.

I looked after her, frustration filling me. But what else was there to do but follow? I was just one girl, floating like a single leaf on the current of this mad world. And all I could do was cling tightly to what I *could* affect, what I *could* save, what I *could* protect. And I had to keep feeding the hope in my heart so that I never lost my beloved phoenix.

It was with him in my heart that I let out my breath and followed her into the streets of Briccatore.

EPISODE TWO: "CITY OF SECRETS"

SEASON TWO

124

Saffron, fish, river water, perfumes, sweat.

The scents of the city were nothing I'd experienced before. Gone was the fresh sharpness of the forest around my village. Gone the simple, individual smells of the smithy – acidic metal and smoke – or the fishmonger – fish – or the baker – bread – or the inn – soup and beer. Here in this mass of people, the scents tangled and mixed and distracted me in an uproarious stew of humanity.

My cousin tugged me into the mass of people filling the streets, her eyes bright and cheeks flushed. The city suited her. I'd never seen her look so much herself. It made me feel a twinge of something – guilt? Wistfulness? She couldn't stay here. Not when she was ai'sletta and destined to somehow save the world from a threat we didn't fully understand. And yet, I could tell this was her kind of place. The sort of place where a girl who thrived on drama and willful certainty could flourish.

Alarm mixed with wonder was in every voice we passed. Mally's eyes twinkled as she watched people stop and stare at the sky and I knew that she was thinking, "I did that."

To one side, a hawker cried he had amulets and talismans to hold back the wrath of heaven and to the other, another man called that the temple would receive all who wished to assuage their consciences with a sum of silver or copper. Each of them looked different from the next. While I was brown – brown skin, brown hair, brown eyes, these two were opposite either direction. One was shaded the palest of ivories flushed with pink and the other was the darkest hue I'd seen in a man. It wouldn't be a problem blending in here. Even Mally's green eyes and cropped chestnut hair had matches in the crowd. I felt both relieved and worried about that. How would Judicus find us if he arrived in the city? Our descriptions wouldn't help to locate us. We shouldn't stray too far.

Someone seized me by the free arm and shook me – an elderly woman swathed in colorful scarves, her eyes ringed in fine lines.

"Did you see it, girl? The sky turned black as pitch. In the middle of the day. But, of course, you saw it. Lasted for hours. And for the second time, too. You should flee this place, girl. A strong thing like you. Flee, for we're cursed! The ravens gather to feast on the carcass of Briccatore. Eh? Eh?"

"She's mute," Mally said, giving the woman a cynical look. "And she isn't going to give you a coin so you might as well find someone else to offer gloomy predictions to."

"Well she's not blind, is she? She can see we're in trouble. And who are you?" the woman shot back. "Her keeper?"

Mally gave me a saucy grin. "I suppose I must be. Come along, Sersha."

And then she was dragging me through the crowd again. People began to tear their eyes from the sky, but I sensed worry in their movements, and they seemed quiet – though together they were still too loud for me. How did anyone live in this chaos? It felt like I couldn't catch a breath. Every time I did, I knew it was air filtered through hundreds of other lungs and I shuddered.

I watched as a mother hustled little children into a doorway, her glances over her shoulder tight and strained. Saw a hawker begin to pack up his cart with fast hands. I was not the only one on edge.

"So much fuss over a little darkness," Mally said, rolling her eyes. But she seemed energized by it o as if their fear sparked excitement. After all, she'd caused it just by putting on and taking off a crown.

My brow furrowed as I glanced over her. Where had she put the Diadem of Darkness – the crown that had caused all this trouble in the first place?

She tapped her thigh and winked at me, and I realized that without me knowing, she'd slipped it under her shirt and jacket. It made a bulge at her middle, but though I could tell she was hiding something there, I couldn't tell what it was.

It was standing there, looking at her that I realized what a sight she looked, and she must have thought the same thing about me.

"You're a wreck," she said. "And I mean that in whatever way most indicates that you look like a ship moldering at the bottom of the sea. We need to find an inn and get cleaned up. No one will talk to us like this. And I'm assuming there's someone here we want to talk to, right?"

I nodded. But I shot a quick glance the way we came and made signs to Mally. I wanted to go back and wait for Judicus and Gundt.

"Nonsense," she said. "They'll find us."

I signed to say that I thought that unlikely given the size of the city and that we should wait where we landed. Reasoning with Mally always took patience and repetition.

"You're such a bore, Sersha. I'm not waiting for them, and you should know I think they're trouble. We're better off on our own."

She tugged at me, but I stood my ground. We were starting to draw attention out here in the street arguing. I saw more than one person with wide eyes staring at us as they passed. Mally must have noticed because she licked her lips nervously.

"Look. You must know some step we have to take here, right? Someone we need to talk to? Something we need to do?"

I nodded. Was she really agreeing to help do something useful without being coerced into it?

"And we can't do it when we draw every eye to what a shambles we are."

I shrugged. She did have a point. We were already drawing attention.

"And if your 'friends' are worth anything they can probably find you on their own. And if they can't, then I'd still help you, only I'll be a lot happier because they won't be around to complicate things," she said, tugging me toward a door that was a small inn based on the bed carved into the swinging sign. Beside it – so tight they shared a wall – was a dry goods store. "Besides, we're pressed for time. I'd say we have a few days here at most before hell rains down on this city and I'd like to be gone by then, wouldn't you?"

And she did have a point. I'd seen the enemies closing in as well as she had and soon – very soon – the raiders would storm across Briccatore and the city would be enmired in war. We had very little time to find the Grand Hadri's spies.

I nodded my agreement and to my surprise, she smiled.

"It's really not that hard to just stay out of my way, Sersha. If you'd done that from the start, we wouldn't be in this mess."

Which was really the opposite of the truth. I glanced warily back toward the river and hoped Judicus and Gundt were alive and headed this way. I didn't want to leave them. I didn't want to do this with only Mally for company. But it seemed I didn't have a choice.

125

To my shock, Mally had coins. Where she had found them or how – I did not ask, I simply followed her silently as she bought me a plain, serviceable dress of charcoal wool and herself a somewhat nicer dress in cherry red wool from the dry goods store along with a pair of linen shifts for each of us and a small sewing kit.

I watched her, wide-eyed. This practical Mally who had the foresight to steal coins from her captors and then use them for sensible things was not a Mally I recognized. I liked it.

I followed her from there to the inn where she purchased us a very tiny room – more of a closet really – for the night, a bath each, and a dinner of chicken stew.

"We can afford to spend one night here before we save the world," she told me as we crowded into the tiny room together. We couldn't both stand at once, but there were two beds under the peaked thatch roof and a window at one end of the room that least kept it from being panic-inducing. "I'll take the first bath. You can start on fitting the dresses."

We both had history stitching our own clothing and altering them as needed. A girl didn't grow up in a tiny town without learning the basics, so I carefully set to work as she left for the baths, stitching to take in the bust and hips on the dress she'd bought for me and letting them out on the dress she'd bought for herself. They were good quality and warm and would wear well and I had to admit that it would be nice to have a change of clothing again. I'd lost everything in the flurry of the last few days, and I was dirty and ragged. The hem of my dress was torn from flight.

I paused, looking at it as memories of the ruined city and the stone octopus flooded back. Would it come here or would it wait at the temple like Judicus thought it would? I missed him in an almost physical way. He always knew what to do next. He always had a plan. Even when we were apart I had been working to get back to wherever he was. Working on something without him felt like a betrayal and it sat uncomfortably inside me like a greasy dinner.

Eventually, though, I set my worried thoughts aside. Even I had to admit that a bath and a hot meal couldn't hurt if we were about to start running again. It had been a long time since I'd had either.

Besides, as long as it was day, I was stuck here without Kazmerev or any idea where to start in looking for the Grand Hadri's spy network. He'd given me a name and told me to go to the palace and look for the Crown and Seal. But how would I get in? And how would I explain myself when I couldn't speak or write? Solving that problem would take time and thought.

I also had to find Judicus' family and warn them to flee. But I didn't know where they would be either. I was chewing the inside of my cheek worrying about that when Mally returned, snatched the red dress from my hands, and proceeded to dress, throwing her old clothes in a heap in the corner.

"I should have bought a comb," she muttered as she combed through her hair. "After your bath, we'll go see the city and if you have any idea where we need to go, you can tell me then."

I waited to agree, but she didn't look up, so after a moment I left to find the inn's baths. The frustrating thing about Mally was that she never listened to anyone but herself. And it seemed that despite everything she'd gone through, she'd decided to keep being that way. If she didn't want to listen to me, she'd just ignore my signs or refuse to look at me. And there was nothing I could do about it.

Resigned, I found the steaming room where the baths were kept warm by serving girls and I stripped down to bathe.

It wasn't until I was in the water that I noticed something hanging from my neck. Surprised, I lifted it to inspect, as the waters lapped around me. It was a medallion on the end of what appeared to be a gold chain. The medallion was also gold, tarnished where it was engraved with a small mouse holding a spear, and around the rim were words. I could not read them, but I did pick out some of the letters Gundt had taught me. Three words. Almost all the same size. The first started with an "M." Maybe it said mouse.

I blinked back tears, feeling forlorn, as I watched it spin in the air, dangling from the chain. I'd never had such an expensive – or odd – piece of jewelry in my life. And it looked just exactly like the one who'd given it to me. Only Judicus would wear a medallion with a mouse on it, and only he would choose one who also bore a spear. It was both ridiculous and somewhat endearing – just like him. And for some reason, just looking at it made my chest feel tight and my eyes tear up.

They'd survive the caves, wouldn't they?

I could only hope they would.

The door opened and shut, and I glanced up to see a serving girl come in and then another female guest – the bathing rooms were, fortunately, divided for men and women.

I went back to studying the medallion before finally shaking my head and scrubbing myself from top to bottom before turning to clean my dress with the same water. Waste not, want not. I'd need the old dress as backup, even if I had a new one to change into.

I was just dressing when I heard a whisper in my ear.

"Midnight. In the stable."

I spun, but all I saw was the edge of a skirt leaving the room. I dropped the dress I was cleaning and hurried to the door, looking out into the hall, but in the gust of steam that came out of the bathing room, I could see nothing. Whoever had spoken to me was gone.

126

Mally had insisted we go out immediately.

"The stew won't be ready for an hour and there's no point wasting time here. What are we looking for, anyway?"

I indicated we would be looking for the palace and she smirked. "Really? You want to go to the palace when you know there's going to be an attack on it at any moment."

I signed that perhaps we should warn the guard and she scoffed. "Absolutely not. I think we both know we can't trust authorities anymore. Our best bet is not to be noticed and to get on with whatever thing we need to do to save the world. You say it's over the sea, right?"

I nodded.

It was on the stairs that I noticed the first strange thing, though I thought little of it at the time.

A maid carrying a large load of wash tripped on the top step, dropping her basket. It flew through the air and landed right-side-up at the bottom of the stairs. Meanwhile, she cartwheeled down the stairs, screaming as she went, and landed on her bottom right in the laundry basket. Everyone froze, hearts in our chests, breath stoppered in our lungs. It wasn't until she groaned and picked herself up again that we let out our breath and carried on.

I thought it was just a coincidence. A strange thing that happened for no reason.

We were back on the street when I saw the next thing like it.

Mally pushed through shoals of people toward where the buildings rose higher, and the crowds grew thicker. Red sunset glows surrounded everyone and with them, little bursts of hope flared in my heart. Soon it would be dark, and I would get to see Kazmerev again. I couldn't wait.

I wanted to talk to him. I wanted his confidence that we could do this. Most of all, I needed him to help me make this plan.

"I don't see why we aren't looking for a ship if we have to cross the sea," Mally said but she kept pushing forward. And she was right. We *would* need a ship, but first, we needed to find the contact the Grand Hadri had sent me for.

I was glancing in the direction of the dock when I saw the second strange thing. A man carrying a wooden box stumbled on a stone no bigger than my thumb. He lost the crate and for a moment seemed to be held in the air and then he fell to the side just as a cart went by and somehow – unbelievably – he tangled in the harness of the oxen. There was a terrible snapping sound, and someone screamed.

I didn't realize I'd frozen, staring horrified at the people rushing to pull his lifeless body from the tangle of cart and harness until Mally tugged on my arm.

"Come on," she said, looking a little green. "We can't do anything for him. Bad luck, don't you think? It's like the opposite of what happened to the maid."

And after that, it seemed like coincidences were all I saw. A child plucked a gold coin from a gutter with a cry of delight. Someone else was yelling that his horse had dropped dead in the street, a fine, healthy horse that had been well only moments ago.

It wasn't until we were nearly at a place called "Triumph Square" – a place I'd heard the Grand Hadri and Judicus mention. Wasn't it the place where a statue was placed depicting his father in a way he didn't like? – that Mally had enough.

A woman fell in the street in front of us and to the shock of onlookers, she delivered a baby right there with hardly a gasp. Another woman rushed out of a shop, gathering up mother and babe to be cared for in her home when Mally laid a hand on my arm, a sick expression on her face.

"I think I need to lie down," she said, her eyes haunted.

I signed a question. Was she hurt? Troubled?

She made a curt dismissing gesture.

"We both need sleep, Sersha. Stop always fighting nature."

And with that grim explanation, she steered me back the way we'd come through the crowds to the inn where we ate our chicken stew in silence and went to bed in similar silence.

My mind was racing as we lay in the darkness of the small room, side by side. I could hear Mally's breathing sawing through the air as if she was trying to suppress sobs – until finally, it softened into sleep. What had Mally found so concerning about today's events that it kept her awake and on the edge of emotional collapse? Did she know something I did not?

I was still troubled when I woke sometime later, and the answer popped into my head. Hadn't Cassanetta said that the ai'sletta changed luck? What else would you call what we'd seen today but the oddest stream of luck – both good and bad – turning on people? Did Mally realize she might be the source of it?

I shivered at the thought. But even knowing my cousin was likely shifting the course of fate around us, I was even more concerned to see the sun had not set. How was I supposed to keep a midnight appointment if there was no midnight?

I snuck down to the stable anyway, hoping to find the person who had scheduled a meeting with me. Perhaps they would think, as I did, that it was worth meeting even without the sun to tell us it was midnight.

Most of the inn and the hostlers had gone to bed despite the unmoving sun and the horses whickered lightly in their stalls.

I waited. And waited.

And I fell asleep in the straw.

When I woke, someone had stuffed a note in my hand.

For all the good it did me when I couldn't read it.

The note had one word on it. It started with a "P."

"P-A-L-A-C-E," I read in my mind, sounding out each letter as Gundt had taught me. But together they meant nothing. "Pal. Pala. Palakey." It made no sense.

Frustrated, I returned to my room and slept a few more hours in the bed.

I had lived my whole life silently until a few weeks ago. And I had never felt so alone as I did now. I'd grown spoiled. Used to being listened to. Used to being able to speak in my mind to Kazmerev. Used to being included in everything and now here I was back in the world that excluded me as much as it could.

I did not like it.

I rose frustrated and certain that until I found my phoenix again, I would not be able to rest. It turned out that I needed him more than I'd ever realized.

127

It took hours to convince Mally to try to go out into the city again. Hours where she bought us more to eat and then braided her hair elaborately only to pull it loose again.

Eventually, she sighed. "Stop looking at me like a goat I've milked, Sersha. We'll go out and see the sights, if it means so much to you."

Of course, it wasn't sightseeing that interested me. It was the chance to find the Grand Hadri's spies. At any moment, the raiders might invade this city. At any moment, we might be on the run again and before that happened, we needed to find out where we were going. Only they knew that. Only they could confirm the things the Grand Hadri had said to me.

The sky was still red and gold by the time we reached the wall surrounding the palace courtyard. The guard there – his features thrown into stark relief in the bright light – scowled up at the sky but turned his attentions on us the moment we tried to walk through the gate.

"Hold up, now," he said kindly enough. "What business do you have, mistresses?"

"I'd like to see the palace," Mally said. "My cousin works in it scrubbing floors. Quiet girl, but good for hard work."

She shot me a smirk. Clearly, she was drawing on her thoughts about me as she conjured up this cousin. But it was clever enough. It sounded real.

"Servants' door is around back but they aren't letting visitors in. I could let you leave a message if you have one." The guard was kind, gesturing to indicate a small wooden box with a slot on the top.

"I can't write," Mally said, but she thrust one hip out and tucked her chin in coyly. "Perhaps you could write for me."

"I have more important things to do than that, mistress," the guard said, flushing. I suspected he also could not write. "Best look for her at her residence if you have no note."

He went back to examining the sky.

"Is something the matter?" Mally asked innocently, trying to angle herself further through the gate while she distracted him.

His hand shot out to stop her and he shook his head with the kind of smile that said he admired her attempt, but it wasn't going to work.

"Sun should have set hours ago. Didn't you notice?"

Mally stilled, her eyes wide, "I was busy."

"So, we have bigger problems than people visiting their cousins," the guard said grimly. "Try another day when the sky is right and not sending chills up and down the spines of any guard with half a brain."

He was right. Almost a full day and the sun hadn't moved. Not in all the time we were bathing or walking or sleeping or searching. Would Mally have to put the crown on again to fix it? It made me feel a little ill to think that she might have that much responsibility now. Would she have to keep an hourglass at hand and watch it carefully so she could put the crown on and take it off to keep days and nights in place? That was madness, wasn't it? Perhaps this was just bad luck like the rest. But something told me it was not just bad luck.

Worse yet, no night meant no Kazmerev. I reached out to grab Mally, suddenly feeling a wave of nausea so intense I could not seem to stand up straight. She caught my hand before I could clutch at her.

"Calm down, Sersha," she said, rolling her eyes. "Seriously, how do you expect to navigate the city if you panic at every little thing."

But it wasn't a little thing. It was a huge thing. I should have panicked about it earlier but I'd been too caught up in finally getting to sleep in a bed and in trying to figure out why someone wanted to talk to me. I'd hoped that it would just right itself and that at any moment Kazmerev would sail back out of my heart, bright and bold and happy as he always was.

But there was no night and that meant no Kazmerev and also no Huxabrand reborn for Gundt. It meant that Judicus and Gundt could be days away instead of mere hours. We were truly on our own.

And probably Mally had broken the sky.

I was breathing too quickly. Little black stars danced across my vision.

"Sersha," Mally whispered urgently, pulling me away from the gate where she could lean me against the palace walls.

The walls were made of mosaiced bricks. They were edged in flowers and trees topped with wide fronds. I tried to focus on them but all I could feel was sharp-edged panic.

I couldn't do this. Not by myself. I couldn't be alone again. I'd finally found friends. A family. And now I just wanted them all back. I'd give up saving the world. I'd give up saving all phoenixes if I could just have them back.

"Sersha."

It was all her fault. Again.

First, crashing into raiders.

Now, breaking the sky.

But I'd done it, too, hadn't I? I'd worn it once. Maybe she could just put the crown on to fix it. Or maybe I could.

I signed putting on a crown and Mally laughed. "I'd be a fool to do that. Don't you see? This is perfect. If we stop time, we can be away from here before nightfall, and if that happens, no one can start a war before we're ready."

That was an insane thought. Life would go on, night or day.

I made a mad grab for her skirts but all I found was cloth and her legs.

"Really, Sersha, that's indecent," she said, her voice mocking. "You don't think I have it with me, do you?"

And she didn't even have it with her! Anyone could steal it. Anyone could have it already!

"You really need to stop being so panicky. It's like dealing with a child," Mally said. "I think I should buy you a drink."

She grabbed my hand and started to haul me across the street. I almost gasped when I saw the sigil on the sign above the door she was hustling me toward. It was very clearly a crown laid on a wax seal.

"Go to the palace," the Grand Hadri had told me. "Look for Jensen at the Crown and Seal."

And now here it was, right in front of my eyes. Talk about luck.

128

I did not have much experience with inns outside of The Hog's Head Inn where I grew up – but I had a lot of experience with The Hog's Head. This place was not like it, just as the inn we were staying at was not like it. While The Hog's Head had been homey and warm, bustling with life and children, the place where we were staying felt impersonal and drafty, and this inn we were entering felt colder still.

There was a small fire banked in the very clean common room and patrons drinking at the chest-high bar and private tables, but their murmurs were quiet, and their heads bent low, their clothing so fine that I immediately blushed, though my new dress was perfectly serviceable. They reminded me, somehow, of Judicus, even though they were neat and tidy and he was usually rumpled. The Crown and Seal was clearly an inn for nobles, and the man scowling at us from behind the long bar was the innkeeper.

"Servants' entrance is around back. So are deliveries," the man behind the bar said. He was bald and thin with a set of scored markings on one cheek – deliberate, I thought, and more decorative than the result of an enemy or accident.

"We aren't servants," Mally said frostily. "In fact, we'd like a drink."

"Keep the riff-raff out, would you, Jensen?" a cloaked man down at the end of the bar said, his voice low. I couldn't make out his face, it was buried so deeply in his hood, but though my cheeks were aflame, my heart soared.

Jensen. This was who I'd come to find.

I was already seeing why everyone wanted to be near Mally. By blind luck, she'd led me directly to the one man I needed in a city of thousands. A person could use that. Imagine looking for a lost artifact with her along? Or a missing person? Or, I realized belatedly, a way to save the world. That was sobering. It brought my attention back to what we were doing.

"Get your drink where girls like you do," the man in the cloak said and he pulled the cloak back from his hip just enough to show a dagger which was as long as my forearm.

I tugged Mally toward the door. We could use the servants' entrance. It wouldn't harm anything. Besides, maybe I could sign to her what was going on while we found it.

But she had planted both feet, refusing to move.

Of course.

I wanted to put my hand over my eyes.

"And where would a girl like me get a drink?" she asked, her eyes blazing.

A chair scraped across the floor on the other side of the fire and a nobleman in crisp blue clothing edged in silver thread cleared his throat. He wore a fancy sword decorated with gold frogging.

The nobleman spoke clearly. "No need to stir up trouble, Prexav. Let the girl have her drink and be off."

I tugged on Mally again. If we made a scene then Jensen would never talk to us. And then my promise to the Grand Hadri would be for nothing.

Mally shrugged off my hands a second time, but this time I spun in front of her, signing rapidly.

I signed that we needed to go around back. That it was important. That it had to do with the king.

I hoped she'd caught that last part. I'd never signed king before and it's always hard to try a new sign for something. Sometimes people guess immediately. Sometimes it's not as obvious.

She ignored me but the troublesome man at the bar stood and sauntered toward us. To my surprise, he was carrying a white flower in his gloved hand. An oleander. It smelled beautiful.

I was even more surprised when he offered it to me.

"A gift, my lady, for clearly being the sensible one burdened with the management of this madwoman."

Mally threw back her head, which had the added benefit of bringing other aspects of her physicality into prominence. I'd seen that move work on Tyndale before. But though she opened her mouth to speak, the man was already disappearing through the front door. It was well oiled – like everything about this inn – and did not squeak or shudder as he left in a flurry of dark cloak and black leather.

"Well," Mally huffed.

"I'll tell you what, girls," the innkeeper said diffidently. "Come around the back instead and I'll give you each a cup of ale on the house. You'll find no better offer."

I tugged on Mally again, and this time she seemed to deflate as if all her fight had walked out with the cloaked man.

"Agreed," she said miserably.

I led her back out to the street, where the sun still hung awkwardly just above the horizon as if it were hovering on the doorstep of a home it had visited, unwilling to say goodbye.

We found the small alley at the back of the inn. It led to a tiny door and from there to a courtyard.

"We aren't servants, Sersha," Mally said, fuming, as we went. "We're as good as anyone else."

Which was fine, but besides the point. We weren't wanted there, and we had other business to attend to. Like talking to the Grand Hadri's spy. I'd never wanted to be anywhere I wasn't wanted, and well-polished inns were no exception.

"If I'd stayed with Lady Lightland no one would ever talk to me like that," Mally said. I stopped for long enough to force her to stop, too. "What?"

I gave her my longest, driest look.

"Okay, yes, I'd probably be dead," Mally said overdramatically. "Or used forever for what I am while everyone I loved was tortured. Is that what you want me to say?"

I nodded and started walking again.

"But I *would* be surrounded by wealth and nobility, and no one would look down their noses at me. For a girl from Landsfall who was raised in an inn, that's something. I wanted that, Sersha. I wanted a little glory and some nice things. Is that so wrong?"

It wasn't wrong. It just wasn't for us. We had to do the things no one else would do. If we didn't, we'd lose even what we had, small as she may consider it to be. That's what I was learning – either you fought for what you valued or it slipped away. Hoping, waiting, wanting: those things weren't enough.

Mally was still talking, "And if Lady Lightland hadn't killed my mother, I would have been happy enough to get those things from her. I'll never get another offer like that, you know."

We'd reached the back of the inn by the time her rant ended. I wrinkled my nose. Something smelled familiar.

Oleander.

I'd just taken a step backward when the man in the black cloak stepped out from the shadow beside the servants' door.

"Lady Lightland, is it?" he said to Mally, reaching out to seize her arm. "Now, what do you have to do with *her*?"

129

"Nothing, obviously," Mally said, talking before she should, as she always did. If I was allowed to open my mouth and say just one thing, do you think it would be "I love you" or some great wise comment that would be passed from one pair of lips to another and engraved upon stone? No, it would not be. It would be to tell Mally to think before she spoke for just once in her life. Instead, she opened her eyes wide and followed it with, "And what is it to you, anyway?"

"It's a lot to me. That name could get you strung up right now."

She quirked a half-smile, flirting, of all things. "Is that you being fresh?"

Reaching out quickly, she pulled his hood down, revealing a face much younger than I'd expected. The boy was our age. Younger even than Judicus – eighteen or nineteen at most – and angry. His thick eyebrows knit furiously together. They were dark brown and shocking beside the light gold hair that hung around his face where it had escaped the knot at the back of his head.

"You wish," he said, leaning forward. He still had her wrist in his grip. I'd worry except that they were clearly playing silly games, and no one was going to get hurt. Or at least not physically. It was possible a heart would be broken.

I sighed and pushed past them both to where the bald innkeeper was coming out the back door with a pewter mug in each hand. He looked at Mally and her new companion, shook his head, and offered me a mug.

"Well, girl, you could use this if you're with her."

I nodded emphatically and he shook his head with a chuckle. Behind us, the banter continued. I'd heard it all before with Mally. I could practically play her part if I had the voice or the inclination.

"Pity you can't speak," Jensen said, "or maybe I'd get the real story of why you're here."

I tried to mime putting a crown on my head. If this was Jensen, then he was who I needed to speak to.

"A hat?" he asked me, setting Mally's drink on a barrel beside him and crossing his arms. "I can help you with that if you need it, girl."

I shook my head, trying again.

"A cloak?"

Mally paused her flirting, though she was so close to Prexav that I couldn't have slipped a thick blanket between them.

"If you're talking about a crown, Sersha, you know better."

"A crown," Jensen said, his eyes narrowing. "You want to see the Grand Hadri? The palace allows petitioners twice a month and the next judgment is not for a week."

I shook my head and tried again. First the crown, then pointing to myself, then to him.

"I can't get you in there any sooner and I'm needed back in my inn."

Frustrated, I turned to Mally and signed that I needed to speak to him.

"She wants to talk to you," Mally said and then turned back to her flirting.

"We are talking, though we aren't getting far," Jensen said, rubbing the back of his neck. "Sorry, girl. Can you write?"

I shook my head and tugged at Mally's sleeve.

"What?" her voice was sharp, irritated at being pulled away again.

I tried to sign that the Grand Hadri wanted me to talk to Jensen. That he was a spy. She rolled her eyes.

"It's too complicated, Sersha. I don't know what you're saying. We'll find you one of those phoenix people later."

"You'll what?" now her companion stiffened, his hands dropping hers, the playful light vanishing from his eyes.

"Flame Riders or whatever they call themselves," Mally said impatiently. "She can talk with one of them."

Jensen and Prexav exchanged a look then – one that sent a little burst of cold down my spine.

"You've known Flame Riders, then?" Jensen asked casually, but he hadn't relaxed yet. His voice was asking a mild question. His body was warning that the wrong answer meant violence.

I put a hand in warning on Mally's arm.

"Well, there was that Gundt fellow. Useless, I thought, except that he seemed to be able to hear her. You can decide if that's a blessing or a curse," she said, and then turned back to her would-be-lover. "Let's not worry about phoenixes. I think you were telling me about watching the stars from a hayloft. I'd love to have someone explain the southern stars to me. I've never been. South."

The pauses between her words made me blush.

"Why would he have understood the voiceless girl?" the blond man – Prexav, Jensen had called him – asked. His smile had double dimples. I wondered if she realized he was unleashing it to loosen her tongue. It seemed like a waste. Mally's tongue was looser than a rope flapping in the wind.

"Because she has a phoenix friend, too, and they're all in cahoots in their 'we're so important as we save the world' game they play," she said, rolling her eyes. "Personally, I'd be more interested in seeing your stars."

"Maybe another time," he said, gently shuffling her to the side, and stepping right past her to place himself in front of me and then offer a low bow.

I stepped backward, surprised, and found myself with my back against the wall, my drink slopping over my knuckles.

"Lady," he said, "I'm honored. And I hope you won't find it too forward of me when I tell you that you will always have a friend in Prexav Bassica."

"I think you might have the wrong girl," Mally said exaggeratedly. "Sersha isn't like you and me."

"Ah," Prexav said, a glowing smile on his face, "but that is where you are wrong. She's exactly like me. Or at least, she will be when the sun finishes setting."

130

"Wait," Mally said, and I couldn't tell if she was surprised or irritated. "You're a phoenix rider, too?"

"Flame Rider," he corrected while Jensen snorted and went back into the inn.

I wanted to curse. I wanted to go after him. I wanted to tell him about the Grand Hadri and beg him to share what he knew but I couldn't. Not until nightfall.

If that ever came again.

"Another one?" Mally said, exasperated. "You people are everywhere. Honestly, I'm surprised the whole world isn't lit up all the time. Maybe that's why it looks like sunset. Maybe the sun has actually gone down but there are so many of you phoenix people that the sky is permanently flaming."

He was still ignoring her, his eyes looking me up and down as if he'd found a treasure. "You're lucky to have found me. There are few of us in Briccatore not sworn to the Flamerarch and you would not want to run in with them. Do you have a Guiding Flame already?"

I nodded and he looked a little disappointed. Was it possible he was hoping to be my Guiding Flame? My cheeks flushed at the thought of it. Somehow the idea of him teaching me everything about riding a phoenix felt a lot more ... intimate ... than learning from Gundt.

"*I'm* the lucky one," Mally corrected. "I'm the reason you've found each other. The only reason."

And I almost laughed then because she looked so outraged – and she was right it must be her insane luck that brought us to where the spy was *and* a phoenix rider and yet there was no way to prove it.

"Well," he said, smiling his double-dimple smile. It really was pretty – though far too showy for me. I liked my men a little on the pale side with a worried brow. Wait. I did? "Since our luck is here, you can both eat with me, and then when night falls, we can talk together about whatever your business is here in Briccatore."

"I don't think night is coming," Mally said as Prexav put an arm around me and swept me into the inn with him.

I looked over my shoulder at Mally, trying to indicate that this really wasn't my fault but that I couldn't afford to lose him when there was a chance he could speak for me.

It was lost on her. She was huffing and shaking her head as she followed us, like a dog heeling her master. I recognized the signs. She would make us both pay for this.

"I'm treating the ladies to the lamb, Jensen," he said as we passed the kitchen and went through to a small, private dining room. "Sit, sit."

We obeyed, sitting around the wooden farm table. There were eight chairs and there was no window – which seemed strange. After a moment, I realized there was also no decoration or hangings, no stacks of things in corners or on shelves. There was only the table and the chairs and the lamp on the table with just the one door in and out. Interesting. Wouldn't this be the exact place you'd have in your inn for spies to meet? A place where eavesdropping could only be done through the door and never while the innkeeper was watching it from without?

"I fear your sister may be right," Prexav said. "This sunset may be magical, blocking us from our rightful place on the backs of our phoenixes.

"I'm her cousin," Mally said, and he went on as if he hadn't heard.

"But don't fear. If it continues, the Flamerarch will do something about it. They can't bear not to see their phoenixes rise any more than independents like us can. You are independent, right? You don't owe your allegiance to a band of Flame Riders?"

I shook my head and he nodded happily as a serving girl came in the room and passed around bowls of lamb and thickly buttered bread before retiring and closing the snug door behind her.

"And are you a Fledgling?" he pressed.

I nodded my agreement and just agreeing to it made me miss Gundt all over again – and worry about Judicus. Had he survived? Would he be able to lead them out of the caverns?

"But you have a Guiding Flame?" he pressed and there was a note of wariness as if he was afraid of stepping on toes. His smile broadened at my nod though it quickly vanished. "He should be here. Is he detained?"

I nodded again.

"Hurt?"

I shrugged and tried to indicate my worry as I took a bite of the food. Mally was nearly halfway through hers already.

"Fear not, when the sun sets we'll figure it out," the other Flame Rider said. "Have you been to Briccatore before?"

I shook my head.

"Then it will be my pleasure to guide you through it."

I wasn't sure I liked all this attention. It didn't seem right. I was no Mally to dazzle the eyes and heart and without Kazmerev nearby no one could be certain my claim to him was true. I offered a wry half-smile, but I was low on trust. Who was to say that this Prexav was a good man? Who was to say I could trust him?

I ate warily as he gossiped about Flame Riders I'd never heard of on quests I didn't understand.

"But no matter what, you know you have a place with us," he said encouragingly. "Flame Riders never turn their backs on one another."

Which wasn't true in my case. After all, I'd turned my back on Olliman and let him die for me. I'd turned my back on Judicus and Gundt – unwillingly, but still ...

"I am curious why your sister –"

"Cousin," Mally corrected.

"Why your cousin was speaking of Lady Lightland when you came around the corner," Prexav said without missing a beat. "The thing is, she's key to some things here. Things I would use your help on if you're willing."

Mally cleared her throat. "If you want answers to your questions then you can stop treating me like I'm just someone who tags behind Sersha. You were interested enough in me before you realized she's tied to a big flaming bird. Even if you're both phoenix riders and have so much in common, you can't just ignore me."

"My apologies," Prexav said mildly but his eyes were still on me. Something flickered in them, and I realized with a start that he was torn and that he'd just chosen duty over pleasure. He did want to talk to Mally but he was holding that part of him back, pursuing his duty to talk to me with dogged intensity. So. Why was speaking to me a duty? Was there more here than met the eye?

Frustrated, Mally pushed her bowl away and stood. "I think we should go, Sersha." She shook out her skirts dramatically. "What's the point of staying around blockheads who don't even have the vision to see what is happening around them. You could say you were the ai'sletta and they wouldn't notice, they're so involved in 'phoenix this' and 'Flame Rider that.'"

I looked worriedly between the two. I couldn't afford a dramatic scene from Mally or it would put in danger my contact with Jensen and with the ai'sletta. I needed both those things to stay intact.

"If you truly were the ai'sletta," Prexav told her with a smirk, still not looking at her. Clearly, he did not believe that was likely, and yet I could see the iron will he was exercising to keep from falling back into their easy banter. "I would spill my secrets to you as a waterfall spills its contents into the river below."

I leapt to my feet and was within inches of getting my hands over Mally's mouth, but she was too fast for me. She threw herself into the chair opposite him, dragged it noisily forward and said, "Good. Because I am the ai'sletta and I think you can offer me more than a cold shoulder, don't you?"

If I could say just one thing. Just one thing, that's what I'd tell her: to stop telling everyone her secret.

131

"Of course you are." Prexav was laughing as my cousin fumed, her face going bright red. His cheeks were flushed, too, and I wondered if he thought this was an elaborate lie to get his attention and if he might just be a little flattered. "Of course, you're the woman of prophecy who everyone's been looking for. Because you'd just stroll in here and announce it to us."

I put my face in my hands. There was nothing you could do about Mally anymore than you could do something about the wind or the rain. They happened. You endured it. That was it.

If I had words, maybe I could vouch for her. Or maybe I couldn't. Maybe they wouldn't have taken my word anyway. Maybe they would have thrown us out and never listened to the Grand Hadri's message or anything else.

By the time I looked up, Prexav was staring at me. I'd expected him to be staring at Mally who was beside me speaking with a voice full of outrage.

"But I am. I really am."

Instead, he held his hand out across the table and said, "Take my hand."

Mally reached for it, and he shook his head, nodding at me. I took his hand. It was very warm as if he were feverish, confirming that he really was a phoenix rider. Only Gundt was that hot to the touch. Another human would be weak and sweating if they were like that.

"She called you Sersha. Is that your name?"

I nodded and he nodded with me.

"You're hot, Sersha. But not sweating."

I snorted. He was doing the same mental math I was.

"And now you're going to chat about the weather?" Mally asked, throwing up her hands. "I confess the truth of who I am, and it means nothing to you. What do I have to do? Bring the night back."

I might start sweating if she revealed any more secrets.

Prexav eyes were locked on mine and he smiled, his dimples flashing me again. "No fever. So, I trust you really are a Flame Rider with a connection to a phoenix and your cousin isn't entirely a liar. Yes?"

I nodded, but I couldn't help my wry expression. I wouldn't trust Mally's word, either, if I didn't know her. I didn't trust it half the time when I did know her. Mally was usually out for Mally. Although it was a little unfair to her that she was finally trying to help other people and still no one trusted her.

And a little unfair to all of us that she was just spilling her secrets everywhere like a seed bag with a rip.

"The word of a Flame Rider can be trusted," Prexav said. "Even if she doesn't talk." He cleared his throat. "Well then. You need to come with me so Ceghan can take a look at you."

"I don't think so," Mally said, but I was already rising. This was the closest we were going to get to being trusted. "I don't know this Ceghan and I don't plan to be inspected by her."

"None of us does, and yet here we are," Prexav said flippantly but I noticed he very obviously was not meeting Mally's eye. He was trying to keep her from realizing how attracted to her he was, even after everything. I was certain of it. "Give me a moment."

He left the room but neither Mally nor I could help peering after him, our heads stuck out from around the door like eavesdropping children. We caught him whispering fervently in Jensen's ear. Doubtless, explaining his intentions. I wish he had been that forthcoming with us, but I was no stranger to the need to earn trust.

"You don't really plan to go with him, do you?" Mally whispered.

I tried to sign that I did and that I thought she should, too.

"And if you do, then when it's nightfall you'll spill everything to him and hope he can help us?" she pressed.

I agreed. But this wasn't my fault. She'd started it. And now, if we didn't stick with him, he would still know our secret and we'd know none of his.

"Well. I don't trust him," she said, crossing her arms, but eventually, as I stared at her, wondering if she could possibly be so stupid, she let them fall and without looking at me, she confessed. "But, I suppose I started spilling secrets first."

That was practically an apology from Mally. I reached out and squeezed her hand gratefully.

"He'd better be taking us somewhere nearby," was all she said to that.

It turned out, that Prexav did live nearby. And that was where he was taking us.

He took us by way of a string of alleyways behind some very fancy manor homes located near the palace. They led to a winding switch-back staircase behind a towering stone building. That, in turn, led us to a rooftop where a dovecote was located. The dovecote was empty. But it disguised a trapdoor which opened into a hidden attic far larger than I would have guessed – maybe the entire span of the eldritch home below it.

Open beams covered in thatch spread over us. Wide beams and a wattle ceiling formed the floor. Someone – likely Prexav – had formed islands and bridges between them out of boards laid over the beams so that though the space was large, only the parts with stitched-together floors were usable.

These he had draped with silks and tapestries so that they were more like individual private islands connected by bridges than actual rooms or even one large room. And each island was replete with furniture – all small enough to be hauled up the tiny staircase and through the dovecote – from folding chairs made of light wood and tight silk, to a hammock filled with cushions where he must sleep. Strings of glass beads and lanterns hung riotously, decked in every color from emerald to citrine – some lit, despite the danger of leaving open flame where no one attended it – and some empty.

It was to this strange place he led us and then welcomed us as if to a palace.

"Mind your voices," he said quietly. "Those below would be rudely awakened to learn that heaven dwells just over their heads."

And then he waggled his eyebrows playfully.

I shook my head at his teasing, but it only made him grin more.

"And now what?" Mally hissed.

Prexav turned and this time I caught him actually looking at her – really looking and clearly admiring. His face flushed hot, and his smile was entirely unfeigned as if he was being served his favorite flavor of pie.

Mally appeared not to notice. Her flush was all fury. "What happens now that you've taken us to your secret hideaway?"

"Now, *I* decide what to do with you," a fresh voice said and over one of the bridges, a girl was approaching, dressed almost identically to Prexav, her long flowing hair matching his in golden waves. Her eyebrows just as dark and drawn together. There were no dimples, though. But only because there wasn't a trace of humor on her storm-cloud face. "Hopefully, I decide that you live."

132

Whatever Ceghan's judgment of us was going to be, it was not going to be fast. She made us tea first, undeterred by Mally's frustrated whisper of, "You brought us to your *sister*? Really?"

And as the tea brewed, other people began to slink in.

The first was an old man, so bent I couldn't tell what his original height had been. He seemed to fade before my eyes so that I almost forgot he was there at all. I had to concentrate to remember and pay attention. He took a folding chair beside what had been three crates and was now a bookshelf and began to write in a tiny journal with a crisp hand. I could not read his writing, but he didn't seem to care if I tried, for he neither hunched over it nor protected it at all but rather smiled kindly at us as Prexav introduced us to him. I noticed his name was not given to us.

Neither were we given the name of the woman who came next, carrying a basket of rolls and fussing over Ceghan and the tea before taking her seat on a one-person hammock seat. Jensen, I already knew.

The longer it took to assemble everyone, the more nervous I found myself as I peered out the tiny round window. It had slanted shutters to keep anyone from looking in, but it easily showed me that the sunset was still endless. And maybe it would always be that way until Mally put the crown back on.

Only Mally would hide something important enough to govern night and day somewhere in a strange city and expect it to still be there when she returned. My guts twisted in knots every time I thought of that. It was my own fault. I should have insisted she make a plan for it with me or that she keep it on her person. I should know by now that what made logical sense to me wouldn't be a consideration for her.

The others whispered pleasantly together as if glad of each other's company though they gave nothing away to us about who they were or what they were doing. I felt as though I were driftwood washed up on the wrong shore. I missed my friends and the safety of being near them. Where were Gundt and Judicus? Probably still along the river somewhere if they'd survived. And what would they do if they were wounded? I should never have left them. I should have found a way to insist that Kazmerev stay.

"He's certainly making a big deal out of your arrival," Ceghan told Mally in a whisper that was clearly meant to carry. "He always does with pretty girls."

Prexav turned and winked at his sister.

Mally was resentfully helping with the tea even though I could tell she thought it should be my job. Usually, I would help. But I was trying not to vomit now that I was getting closer and closer to panic. What would I do if I never saw Kazmerev again? How would I carry on?

You couldn't just have a best friend one minute and have them ripped away the next and not feel the agony of it.

To my surprise, a hand touched my bouncing knee and I looked up into the sympathetic eyes of Prexav.

"Don't fret. Night will fall. It must. Even miracles cannot last forever."

"See?" Ceghan whispered to Mally.

"Sersha?" Mally said – no whisper this time because of her surprise and Ceghan threw her hand up over my cousin's mouth.

"Shh! Do you want to get caught?"

"He likes *Sersha*?"

"Well, they're Flame Riders, aren't they? The only reason you're here is that he thinks she has something important to say. We haven't seen a lone Flame Rider in a long time and there are rumors they are being hunted in the countryside."

But I wasn't worried. I'd seen how Prexav looked at Mally and I recognized the expression on his face when he spoke to me. I was in his brotherhood of Flame Riders. But I was not a girl he was pursuing. Which was a relief. I couldn't handle romantic overtures at a time like this.

"It will be fine," Prexav told me again, this time reaching out to squeeze my hand reassuringly before turning to Ceghan. "No need to frighten them with worrisome stories."

"I'm not frightened," Mally said, jutting out her chin. "Just surprised. Does that mean you don't know that the Stryxex are back and they're killing phoenixes?"

A cup fell from Ceghan's hand but before it could hit the ground, Jensen snatched it from the air.

"Say that again," Jensen said calmly but something about his tone turned my belly to ice.

"Stryxex," Mally said, tossing her hair. "You know, big black things that are like what you'd get if phoenixes turned evil."

"Yes," he said, but it clearly meant, "Go on."

"They're everywhere now and targeting phoenix rider places – whatever those are called and smashing them to bits or something. I didn't catch the details."

"But does your mute friend know the details?" Jensen asked and I didn't like the sharp look in his eyes as he rounded on me. The hash marks of his tattoo stood out starkly and I wondered if that meant he was going pale underneath them.

"Probably," Mally said. "But we won't know until your phoenix people can talk to her phoenix people. I only found out because Gundt wouldn't stop going on about it when we were separated from her."

"Gundt Hellebrand?" Ceghan asked casually as she poured tea. She was pouring far too slowly for it to be a truly casual question.

"I suppose," Mally said. "I didn't catch his name, but he has a phoenix and he's pretty cranky. He wouldn't stop berating Judicus when we lost Sersha and the Grand Hadri."

And now all eyes were on her, owlishly large. I saw her realize it as her face went from irritated to smug. I closed my eyes. I couldn't bear to watch. It was like seeing someone tumble from a roof and break their leg right before your eyes. If I could speak for just one day. Just one hour. I wouldn't even need that long – just long enough to beg her to stop spilling our secrets everywhere.

"He was there, too, of course," she said. "The Grand Hadri. He wanted me to work with him. Because I'm the ai'sletta. But I told you that already."

And then she took a casual sip of tea from the cup on the tray closest to her and looked out the window like a hunter who had already set out the bait and was just waiting for the prey to walk into her trap.

I put my face into my hands and wished I'd been born to a different family.

133

"It has to be true," Jensen said eventually. "It has to be. She has no reason to lie so foolishly. She must know the consequences for that."

Everyone's regard of Mally seemed to intensify and it was just like her to look superior instead of flinching.

"She must know she'll be used – maybe even tortured – if the wrong people discover who she is."

Still, she didn't flinch. But this wasn't a surprise to her, was it? She had been tortured – mentally, if not physically. She'd watched her own mother die.

"And you saw the sun. It is frozen in the sky. But what does that mean for The Plan? What does that mean for the colonies?"

The old man's head snapped up at that and he shook it so subtly I wasn't sure anyone but me caught the gesture. He pulled a book from the shelf beside him – an ancient one written by several different hands -and began to flip through it agitatedly.

"Why does it *have* to be true?" the woman who had brought bread asked. Her words were kind and open and yet I found the others quieted whenever she spoke. I'd begun to realize that despite her plain exterior and peasant clothing, she might be their leader.

"How could she know all those names if she were lying?" Jensen asked.

"Anyone can know names," the woman said.

"I know that Judicus is the Grand Hadri's nephew," Mally said.

"Everyone knows that." The woman waved her hand.

"I know he'll be Grand Hadri if it turns out the Grand Hadri is dead," she pushed.

"And they can deduce that, too," the woman agreed.

"And I know that Cassanetta Lightland has turned two ministers and a general to her cause of overthrowing them both and that's why the armies are withdrawing from defense of the city rather than rallying around it," she said triumphantly.

The woman's mouth shut with a click.

"What else do you know?" Jensen asked in a low, dangerous voice, and I wished so hard that she would just stop talking. That she would know when to hold her own counsel. I tried to sign it to her, but she wasn't looking – intentionally, I thought.

I stood up, all the energy in me pent up and desperate for release. I strode across the room to the bookshelf beside the old man and bent over the trinkets on top of it, trying to pretend I wasn't as agitated as he was.

"Sersha knows more," Mally said firmly. "And she'll tell Prexav, when the sun goes down."

"When the sun goes down. When the sun goes down." Jensen rubbed his hands over his bald head. "Everything is depending on it and yet, look! The sun does not go down."

"Well, I just need to get to the inn again and I can deal with that." Mally waved her hand, sipping her tea again.

Everyone froze, staring at her.

"What?" she said, innocently. But she wasn't a fool, and I knew she had done that on purpose. She finally had their attention again and she loved it. "I keep telling you I'm the ai'sletta but no one listens."

"If you can make the sun set, do it now," Prexav said, crossing his arms over his chest and I wondered if the way he seemed to almost vibrate when standing still was normal for him or if he was feeling as agitated as I was at the lack of phoenixes.

"I can't," Mally said. "I need something. Something I hid in the inn."

He made an exasperated sound – not his first if he spent much time with Mally.

"Is the Grand Hadri really dead?" the older woman asked. It took me a moment to realize she was looking at me.

I shrugged, but in a way that suggested it was likely.

"You saw him?" she asked me.

I nodded.

"He told you something?"

I nodded again.

"Something to tell us?"

I pointed at Jensen, and she raised an eyebrow.

"I think that she's not lying," the woman said eventually. "Fine. We expected to have to move soon. We thought we had days, but that is life, my girls and boys. It does not dance to your tune, you dance to its tune, or you're dragged along by the hair wishing you'd danced, yes? We've lost the boss. We'll lose more if we don't act fast and then The Plan might as well be a child's dream.

"So, here's what we'll do. Ceghan, you and Jensen take the talker to her inn and come back with whatever she has stashed there. She can fix the sun when she returns. Jastomen, we'll need you to get word out. Anyone you can find – get them spreading the word. We launch tonight. We have no other options. Prexav. You stay here with the cousin. When the sun is fixed, she can tell you the rest through her phoenix. If it's urgent, you know how to find us."

I moved to stand next to Mally, trying to communicate that I went where she did. My cousin shifted her weight to stand closer to me, too. She agreed.

"Not a chance, voiceless girl," the woman said.

"Sersha," Prexav corrected.

She tipped her head to him as if conceding. "Not a chance, Sersha. As brutal as it may sound, I still don't trust your flighty cousin who spills her secrets as a vein spills blood. You'll be our hostage until she fixes the sky. After that, we'll talk. We've chosen to believe your stories. But trust goes both ways and now you'll have to trust us, so find a comfy chair and settle in for the ride."

I frowned, but in her place, I would feel the same way. And if they wanted to separate us, there was nothing I could do to stop it. Not without Kazmerev.

"You can read this," the old man – Jastomen – said kindly as he passed me. He pushed the tattered book into my hands and pointed very subtly at the mouse medallion that had slipped out of my dress. "Mighty though Small," he said with a wink, and then he was gone.

And then they were all gone and that left only me and Prexav and he was staring at the medallion around my neck like it was going to burst into flames.

134

"Where did you get that?" he asked and then waved his hand dismissively as if he either knew I couldn't answer or didn't need me to. "I didn't realize. Please, accept my apologies."

He gave me a hasty half-bow, his cheeks flushed so red that I thought he might be ill. But when he straightened, he did not seem ill, merely very anxious. He studied me worriedly, and I made a gesture that I hoped he'd understand as saying there was nothing to forgive.

"Even those of us who have never met Judicus Franzer Irault still have heard of him," he said in a hushed tone. "We know his medallion and what it means."

Well, *I* didn't know what it meant. If only people would start telling me things instead of leaving me to fumble in the dark to find them out. I tucked the medallion back into my bodice. I didn't want anyone else drawing conclusions.

"Please know, I would never willingly incur his wrath," Prexav said and he looked more worried than he had when we told him something had happened to the ruler of his city.

My brow furrowed. I knew Judicus. Thoughtful, considerate Judicus. I knew he was fair and kind and a bit absentminded and that he'd been either recovering or injured for most of the time I'd known him. Was that, perhaps, why I couldn't see whatever it was striking fear into this man's heart?

"You must be very close to him indeed to wear his medallion." Prexav sounded tentative. "A wife perhaps?"

He looked so wary that I quickly shook my head. And now *I* was blushing. What would it be like to be Judicus's wife? It would involve learning better cures for seasickness, for a start. And probably a life on the run.

"Then his betrothed, for certain," Prexav said, nodding to himself. "Pray, do not be offended by my advances earlier. We rarely meet other young Flame Riders – especially pretty ones with kind eyes – and I fear I was shameless in trying to make the most of the opportunity. I would never have done so if I realized your loyalties were already claimed."

But things weren't as he thought, and I had no way to tell him so. It felt like I should. Like I was making some kind of claim on Judicus that I had no right to make just through this stranger's words. My cheeks grew hotter.

Words! They made me crazy for not having them and they made others crazy for having them. Because now Prexav had made himself an elaborate fiction he fully believed out of nothing but words and surmises and because I had no words of my own, I could not shatter it.

I felt – as I so often did – that I was weaponless in a battle everyone else was fighting. By their words, they chose the grounds, made the hits, scored the points, drew blood. Without the same advantage, I felt powerless.

"And, of course, no one would provoke our generation's most powerful and reclusive rope worker," he said grimly.

Wait. What? I knew Judicus was good – but the most powerful of his generation? That, I had not expected.

"You can tell him that for me," Prexav said fervently. He stopped awkwardly, hearing that in his mind, and then shook his head. "I'm so sorry. I didn't mean that. I'm just tired. Please, eat something and make yourself comfortable with the books."

He left the platform swiftly, his feet whisper-quiet along the bridge as he practically ran from me, leaving me in his odd little room, alone and utterly confused.

I examined the medallion one more time. Who would have thought a little mouse would make people so crazy? I could imagine Judicus running a bewildered hand through his hair as he sorted this mess out.

"Oh," he'd say. "No, I don't think I'm the most powerful. That's so and so who I knew in my youth."

Or maybe he'd admit he was and then immediately vomit. That sounded like him, too.

Both those thoughts just made me miss him more.

I turned to the room. Flame Riding and spycraft did not pay. That was my first thought upon inspecting it. For though the colors of the hanging silks and hammocks were bright, and though the curios were shiny, nothing in this room was any finer than what I grew up with at the Hog's Head Inn. Everything here was just like Prexav, a distracting surface hiding something I didn't understand. Everything, that was, except the books. They seemed solid enough.

I sat in the chair that Jastomen had occupied and opened up the little book he'd given me. I couldn't read it properly, but I did know the signs for dates. We'd get casks at the inn or other items with dates scrawled on them and knowing what was fresh and what was not could be the difference between happy patrons and patrons lined up out back to use the privy. I could read dates.

Which was how I realized that the book was very, very old. The most recent entries were made before I was even born – perhaps twenty years ago. The oldest were more than a hundred and fifty years old. I traced the edges of the paper with a fingertip, marveling at the age of the book and picking out the letters Gundt had taught me, trying to form their sounds in my mind.

If ever I saw him again, I'd ask him to teach me more. If I could read and write, I'd be less adrift in this world where my silent voice kept me boxed in from the magical lies everyone else told each other.

"Reading the prophecies?" Prexav asked from the entry between silk hangings.

I shook my head.

"It looks like you are."

I shook my head again. He frowned and put down the bundle of things he'd been carrying to stride across the makeshift room and look at the book in my hands.

"Is it possible that you cannot read?" I nodded, awkwardly and for the first time since he saw the medallion, he smiled. "Then let me read them to you while you dress. I brought you some of my sister's things. A simple wool dress is hardly enough protection if we need to fly or fight once the sun sinks low. There's a screen beside the tea set."

And then, without waiting for me to acknowledge anything more, he turned his back and began to read aloud.

"Evening and morning will come swift on each other's heels, the black fox chasing the white fox until they pause in their chase for her advent, they pant and wait and look to see her arrival, they anticipate the end of an age."

I didn't know about the ends of ages, but I did know these clothes he'd brought me were very fine indeed. There were tall stockings, beautifully made leather boots, a dress split for riding, a pair of soft breeches to wear under it, and a deep cloak with a large hood. There was even a wide belt with a crisp new pouch. I wondered how much Ceghan would hate me for wearing her clothing.

"And so it will be in the last day that those with bold hearts and the milk of compassion will rise up before her and they will come to the place of darkness and with bold hands will take hold of it and plunge it within."

I began to dress anyway, shedding my cheap woolen dress for this silky lace-lined finery.

"And healing will come in flames and the darkness will be burnt in the bright light of a new dawn." Prexav paused in his reading. "That's what I don't like about prophesy. It's all so vague. You'd have to have either the best or the worst luck for any of it to come true. But don't you think it's weird that the sun is stuck in place like the white fox pausing as it chases the black fox?"

I did think that was strange, but I was still buckling my new belt and trying not to be too in love with the fine cut and feel of these clothes. Perhaps Prexav and Ceghan were richer than I thought if they could afford such finery.

"Listen to this next one. It's dated forty years later. *'The day of disaster will strike suddenly. A coin golden and high that does not blink. A red ribbon flowing from the mouth that once spoke. A black veil over a single eye. And when you see the signs flee. And may all who are innocent flee. And may those who know flee toward trouble for only by the words of this prophesy may they stop the stones.'* See? It's weird and creepy. And yet there are people who set so much stock in this book that they're forever training themselves in compassion and boldness, so they'll be ready."

I stepped out from behind the screen, and he smiled. "They do fit. I thought they would."

I thought he was about to say more because he opened his mouth but there was a crash from without and then the older woman stumbled back into the makeshift room.

Blood was running down her chin.

She reached toward Prexav as if desperate and her mouth opened to speak but then she crashed to her knees, her eyes rolling back in her head. She fell to the floor as heavy as the dead.

I scrambled to her side, shuddering, desperately trying everything I knew to help. What had been done to her? And what message had she tried to pass on that failed?

Prexav leapt past me, his wicked dagger flashing in his hand. If there was trouble on her heels, he'd find it. But there would be no saving the woman. Her heart had stopped as she fell and the stream of blood trickling from her mouth had slowed. The dead didn't bleed.

I pushed myself back from her, swallowing down bile and horror. She'd left here alive not an hour ago. She'd been so full of life. And now – now, look at her.

I bit my lip. I should be mourning how fleeting life was and that this poor woman had suffered as she died. I should be shedding tears for a life lost.

But instead, I was thinking of the words Prexav had just read. The gold coin. The red ribbon. The day of disaster.

It couldn't just be coincidence. It was happening. Right here, right now in Briccatore.

And I was powerless to tell anyone.

135

My hands were covered in blood. Her blood. I stared at it stupidly.

She was past my help – past anyone's help. I found a knife was jammed in her upper back, right in her lungs. It was a plain knife. No indication of its owner. No way to tell who had done it or why.

I didn't realize how badly I was shaking until Prexav flew back in through the door and stopped suddenly, his eyes wide and knife drawn. Before he closed the door, a reverberating crash sounded outside, reverberating through the city. A second one sounded from somewhere further away.

He froze.

"The gongs. The city is under attack."

Our eyes met in horror. And I knew that the armies had withdrawn long enough for the raiders to be here, to leave the city open for attack. To leave it trussed up as bait like a rabbit to lure in wolves.

"We have to go," he said, rushing to a little crate at the side of the room. He pulled a leather satchel from it, threw it over one shoulder, and then shoved an empty one at me. "Grab scarves, blankets, food, whatever you see that we can use. Expect to be gone for weeks."

Weeks? What was he talking about?

He made an exasperated sound in the back of this throat, wrenched the satchel open, and began to fill it himself with a decorative woven blanket from one of the chairs, a pair of books from the makeshift shelves, a small hand mirror, food from the tea tray, including all the buns that had been brought by the dead woman.

The poor dead woman. My gaze lingered on her. Would anyone know where she was? Would they know to bury her? Would there be anyone left to do the job when the attack was over?

My eyes were glassy before I realized it. Prexav pulled the prophecy book from my grip and shoved it into the satchel, too, threw a few more items into it, which my blurry eyes didn't register, and then buckled the satchel shut and threw it over my shoulder.

He put a hand on my shoulder.

"Your mourning is an honor to both Shasasa and to you. But we have no time for it now. No one could have known she was a spy for the Grand Hadri. And if they did, then they know all of us and we will be as dead as she is unless we flee in time."

He was right, and yet all I could think of now was Mally, out there somewhere with no idea of the danger.

"Stop fretting," he said, grabbing my hand. "I'm certain your cousin can take care of herself as easily as my sister can."

And then he was tugging me through the door and onto the wooden walkway and for just one terrible moment of vertigo, I wobbled there until I realized that the city beneath us was pure chaos.

People ran in every direction on the streets below, horses dancing between them and then thundering down straight stretches. A block of marching soldiers in uniform ran in neat ranks down one street, pushing civilians aside like strands of beads in a doorway. From the other direction, I saw the Grand Hadri's palace where figures in thick leather had climbed to ring the wall.

"Look," Prexav said, and he almost seemed gleeful to see them. "The Flamerarch is as grounded as we are right now. Who owns the air now, Flamerarch? Who controls the skies now?"

Those were the fabled Flamearch? Hadn't Judicus said he witnessed them rain fire down? They must be Flame Riders – but organized and somehow not friends of the charming spy I'd joined ranks with. I would have shaken my head at Prexav, but he was already pulling me down the rickety stairs to the alley below.

"If we get split up, head to the docks," he said as he pulled me along.

His hand was warm and firm, and he gripped mine like he had no intention of letting me go. I pulled back on it so that he'd pay attention and then shook my head, pointing in the direction of our inn near the river. I wasn't leaving Mally here.

"She'll be fine. If we get split up, find the ship called *Pleasant Squall* and tell them."

He paused, looked back at me as people jostled all around him, and then shook his head, remembering again that I couldn't speak. People always forgot. I didn't see how they could when it was all they ever seemed to bother to know about me. I have a soft heart and I'm good with herbs. I like tea, and frankly, I haven't had a good cup in a while other than the one his sister just brewed. I like yellow flowers and I don't like loud noises. I'm fond of children and good with maps. I'm handy with a needle, a decent cook, and even handier with wounds and illnesses, and yet the only thing anyone outside Landsfall ever saw was that I couldn't speak to them. And for just a flash of a moment, I felt sad and guilty because Aunt Danna had been right when she said it would have been better for me to stay in Landsfall than go to the city. She'd been right because if I hadn't had Kazmerev bloom within me that's all anyone would ever have seen and if I'd gone to the city on my own, it would have ended in heartbreak.

"Just show them your medallion and they'll take you," he said plunging onward.

But I wouldn't do that without Mally. Kazmerev had said to stand up for myself even if he wasn't there and even if I couldn't speak. He's said my actions were more important than my words. And he'd been right.

I wasn't going anywhere without my cousin. Not again.

The next time the crowd surged, I wrenched my hand from Prexav's and spun back toward the inn. I heard him behind me calling, "Sersha!" but I wasn't going to stop. I wasn't going to be led away. I wasn't going to spend weeks trying to get to her again. Not this time.

There was nothing else as important as that.

"Sersha!"

Something brushed my hand. Prexav. If he grabbed me again, I would be forced to go with him and I would not do that.

"Wait. Sersha. We need to get to the ship. They'll meet us there. You'll never find her in this crowd," Prexav said, practically yelling in my ear as people jostled us from every side.

Someone knocked into my shoulder. I spun around and found myself face to face with Prexav as he breathed heavily, face flushed, head tilted down until we were practically cheek to cheek so he could yell in my ear. "Please, be reasonable!"

And then all of a sudden, I heard another voice – a familiar voice – raise itself over the clamor.

"That's usually my line," the voice said, and I turned, gaping to see the ragged, drawn face of Judicus Franzer Irault just inches from mine.

Our eyes met and I smiled, and his weary smile seemed to light up the whole street so that to me it went from sunset to dawn.

"Sersha," he said and there was blood streaking one side of his face and a bandage made of Gundt's cloak over one eye and he was filthy and stinking and *here*. And I'd never wanted to leave him. I felt that doubly so now.

"Son of Chaos," Prexas said, and he sounded like he was going to choke.

I ignored him and instead, I reached up and plucked the medallion from my neck and offered to back to its owner.

"Keep it," Judicus said wearily. Bracing an arm around me to deflect the people who jostled and tugged as they streamed by every side around our little human island. "It suits you more than it does me. And before you introduce me to the troublemaker who addresses me as an enemy, tell me – did Mally break the sun again?"

And it was nice to be around someone who understood exactly what we were dealing with. So nice that I almost cried with relief as I snorted and nodded in a gesture of "what else did you expect?"

136

"Where is she?"

I wanted to be the one to ask the questions. I wanted to ask how bad the injury to his eye was. I wanted to ask if he was hurt. I wanted to ask where Gundt was. Instead, I gritted my teeth as Prexav spoke.

"She's with my sister and Jensen of The Crown and Seal."

Judicus shot him a look I'd never seen in the face of the leader of my coterie. It was sharp and deadly.

"Alive?" he asked.

Prexav threw up his hands. "Of course, alive! Of course! What do you think is happening here, traitor? The city is under attack."

"I know." I hadn't thought of Judicus as a particularly intimidating person. Perhaps because I'd met him when he was mortally wounded. And it didn't help that he was still hunched, though he stood half a head taller than Prexav. I knew he was powerful – I'd seen what he could do with his rope work, but I wouldn't have thought he was ... scary.

Until Prexav backed up half a step into the rushing madness of the crowd and put a hand to the hilt of his knife almost unconsciously.

"I was just taking Sersha to safety. A ship."

"A ship," Judicus repeated, his voice clipped and his one eye burning like a phoenix. "And now?" he asked, looking at me and his eye softened when it fell on me.

I shook my head. I wasn't going anywhere without him.

He sighed and it seemed like relief before he suddenly stopped, and his face grew hard again. "I'll not hold you to the bonds, Sersha. You're free to leave my coterie to go with him if that's your desire."

I was already shaking my head so hard it blurred my vision.

"She's in your *coterie*?" Prexav asked, as if Judicus had just announced I was the new Grand Hadri.

"You seem woefully underinformed, my friend." Judicus spared him a short glance but then he returned his full attention to me as if it were just the two of us on the street and not shoals of people. "I'm hurrying to my sister, Sersha. Gundt is waiting for us in an apt location with ... our other companion." He shot Prexav another tight look. Clearly, he didn't have Mally's problem with spilling secrets. "Will you come with me to secure her safety?"

I nodded quickly.

"And once she's safe we'll see to Mally." He sounded definite about that – as if it were a sure thing.

The gong rang again over the city, reverberating through the crowd. It drowned out anything more he might have said, overwhelming shouts and demands, shrieks, and fearful calls. This time, it struck twice and the faces of those around me turned from worry to terror.

Judicus cursed, beginning to move, but Prexav grabbed his sleeve.

"By the time you find your sister, our ship will have sailed with Sersha's cousin on it. And the palace won't let you in while the city is under attack. You're wasting your time."

Interesting that Prexav knew where Judicus' sister lived while I did not.

Judicus looked toward the palace and then back to me as if torn and in that moment of indecision, Prexav grabbed his sleeve. His face was inches from the rope worker's, yelling over the noise of the crowd.

"I won't pretend I'm your friend, Son of Chaos. But though I don't want to be your enemy unless I must, I care about Sersha's safety. The ship will sail with or without us and it will sail with Mally and my sister on it. If she doesn't come with me she'll be trapped here and I can't spare another moment on this reunion."

Judicus paused for a moment, cocked his head to the side, and said, "Are you Harmon's son? The Flame Rider who served Captain Rackham aboard ship? What was that? Ten years ago?"

Prexav colored, standing a little taller, but he looked confused when he replied. "What if I am?"

Judicus smiled cheerfully. "Good. You're coming with me, too."

And then he plunged into the crowd not even waiting to see if we'd follow. I was going to follow, of course. Where he went, I would go. But it was totally different than having my hand taken by Prexav. There was no demand here, just an assurance that I'd follow him.

I kind of wish he'd taken my hand anyway. Just to remind me he was there.

"You're crazy if you think I'll be drawn into your schemes, Irault!" Prexav said as we plunged through the crowds. He was keeping pace with me right at Judicus's heels.

Judicus took the stairs out of the plaza two at a time. I could hardly keep up with him. He didn't pause, didn't wait, just kept forging ahead through the masses of people.

"I won't betray the Grand Hadri." Prexav ran beside me, keeping up despite his verbal protests.

We mounted the last step and Judicus spun, slamming Prexav against a shop wall. A clay pot holding reeds shuddered beside them. The two young men were face to face, Judicus's nose barely a hair away from Prexav's. I took a step back.

Surely people were watching. Surely, they'd notice this. I glanced around, waiting for someone to yell or try to break them up.

But no one noticed. No one cared. Everyone was fleeing or quickly boarding up shop windows and doors. One shop over, a man sat a dancing horse, its feet splaying over the cobbles as it stamped at anyone who came near. Every spare bit of attention in the street was on the horse as those rushing past tried to keep from being kicked or trampled.

"You're still following me," Judicus said, his mild tone at odds with his firm actions. "Which means you have decided to come along despite your words. Each word you speak is meant to barb me, but I feel no jabs, Bassica. I can see you're torn. You rightfully understand that Sersha is important, and you want to protect her. You rightfully understand that the king you once served is gone, and an enemy is at the gates. But you misunderstand me. I am neither a traitor, nor the son of a traitor, and my only aim is to save my sister from being ravished and killed when this city falls. You surely must realize that were I to die the crown would pass to her."

"If she can defend it," Prexav gritted out.

"Indeed. But while she doubtless could not, she is still going to be killed for the blood in her veins – the blood your father swore to serve." Judicus barely paused. "The blood that perhaps you swore to serve. So. The faster you stop getting in my way, the faster we all get her to safety and return to your escape plan."

"Or?" Prexav asked.

For a moment Judicus frowned and then his eye widened, and he said, "If we all live through this we can talk about 'or'"

137

I had expected a mad dash to the palace and then being let in by the guards and escorted to wherever Judicus's sister was housed. I had not expected that we wouldn't bother with gates. We were inside through a secret entrance along the wall before I could so much as breathe the wrong way, though Prexav's quiet curses were enough to tell me that he hadn't known about the entrance.

Judicus had found it with a tendril of black rope work and opened it the same way – a magic trick for a magic worker.

The passage led into the cellars. Which was not a problem since those led to a network of more secret passages, dusty, dark, and lit only by candles. I didn't need the candles with my night vision – and it seemed Prexav didn't either – but I was growing tense. By now, Mally should have found the crown. By now, she should have put it on. Yes, the spies with her had said they'd wait until we were all together, but that was before the city was attacked and besides, I'd never expected Mally to wait.

Mally was not the waiting kind.

By now, I'd have expected her to ignore them all, jam it on her head and declare herself the queen of the night.

It bothered me that she hadn't.

And what was worse, I had a terrible gnawing guilt that I should be going after her and not Judicus's sister. What if she really did board the ship before we could get to her and then she sailed away? What if the sun never set again and I was forced to follow however I could without Kazmerev?

Fortunately, I didn't have the option of sharing my fears and so they sat in my belly like a handful of starving mice, chewing at me until I could hardly breathe.

By the time we came out somewhere in the palace, I was looking for anything to distract me from guilt.

Judicus led us quickly through silent halls, narrow and close as if he knew the labyrinthine layout by memory – which, clearly, he did.

I couldn't have asked for a better distraction. It took effort not to stare at everything in the richly appointed hall. The walls were tiled mosaics, blue and white and gold, patterned with fanciful lions and dragons – both creatures of myth – set into the tiles by an expert hand. Arches frequently split up the monotony of the long corridors and these were tiled with pink and orange mandala designs. Between the tiling and the decorative urns and tables, mirrors, and bead curtains, I felt like I'd been caught up in a whirlwind of color and design. It was too much for the mind to take in all at once.

"This is where the Grand Hadri houses lesser nobility when he invites them to stay," Prexev whispered to me.

But where were they? There were no hurrying people, no feet running, or murmurs behind the doors. No whispers – or even screams – and from so far in the thick-walled palace, I couldn't even hear the gongs. Incense was thick in the air and the smell of oleander and green things was everywhere, but not a living thing stirred in the halls.

I was just about to tug on Judicus's arm to try to point it out, when he finally turned and wrenched open a door.

The room beyond was chaos. It was a sitting room, as bedecked in brocaded cushions, settees, and woven rugs as the halls had been, but garments were scattered across the floor and trinkets had fallen from tables as if someone had left in a hurry.

"Mother?" Judicus called. "Kristiana?"

He ran to what appeared to be a bedroom in one direction, still calling and then out of that one, to one opposite. I took a moment to look around the room. Opulent, yes, but where was the personality? It wasn't a plain room, but it looked just like the halls as if those dwelling inside hadn't been permitted to change anything about this place. Perhaps they weren't just trapped here but were treated like glorified prisoners, too. I thought of Judicus on the road, accepting of hardship, seemingly uninterested in opulence or comfort. Could that be a reaction from having lived like this once himself?

When he returned to the sitting room, he was wide-eyed and panting. There was no one else here.

"The nobility must be assembled somewhere," Prexav said. He looked troubled now, too. "This is not what I expected with the city under attack."

"If they've harmed my sister," Judicus's voice was low, and he did not say more, just led us from the room and back out to the fancy hall. The bright colors and crowded décor felt oppressive now as if the loud walls might reach down and swallow me up. It didn't help that Judicus was no longer walking, or even trotting, but had broken out at a full sprint, tension present in his every movement.

I followed him down the corridor, Prexav right at my heels. His curses were quiet, but they came out at a steady stream.

I ran so hard and fast that I tasted blood in my efforts to catch up, but Judicus's legs were long, and he was so far ahead of us that I almost missed it when he ducked into a tiny corridor. I definitely wouldn't have noticed that he ducked behind a tapestry in that corridor if the movement of his passage hadn't left it rippling.

"I'm not here for a vendetta," Prexav muttered from behind me as we hurried up a rickety, dusty ladder.

Another passageway. My hands felt sweaty with nerves.

When we finally emerged, it was in a narrow, dark corridor that smelled stale and was coated in dust. It led to what must have been a balcony overlooking a grand hall. Judicus stopped dead there. He was so far in front of us that I could see nothing except the railing and the space widening before him, a white-domed ceiling overhead.

My eyes were locked on him as we caught up. I didn't like the rigid look of his hunched shoulders.

From beyond the balcony, a sound rose up. Chanting. A strange, almost angelic sound, as if a hundred voices had joined in one wish of blessing. It was not the sound of people under siege or a city attacked.

My brow was already furrowing as I slowed my run, snuck to the edge of the balcony, and laid my hands on the dusty ledge beside Judicus's so I could look down.

We barely fit on either side of him in this tiny nook in the ceiling dome. Clearly, it was meant to be hidden, the laced edge of the balcony blended in perfectly with the scalloped and laced decoration covering the domed ceiling.

There really were hundreds of people below us chanting that beautiful song. They were dressed in finer clothing than I'd ever seen before. A sea of wealth and high blood. And here I was, peeking down like a barn owl flown in the wrong door.

I felt my cheeks grow hot with an embarrassed flush. I shouldn't be here. I didn't have the right. At any moment one of them might look up and squint and see me here and they'd know it, too.

It was all I could do not to squirm.

In the center of the flower-like pattern of riotous color and soft, sweet chanting, was a young woman dressed entirely in white, her face young and pale, her hair thick and black and wavy like an ocean tide before a storm.

She looked up just then, but if she saw us, she did nothing to acknowledge it. She sank, instead, to her knees.

I looked at Judicus expecting surprise or curiosity on his face, but what I saw instead was stunned horror.

Were they going to kill her?

I turned back hoping that what I'd taken for a special ceremony was not actually something much more sinister.

But no.

A pair of men carried a golden crown on a pillow between them. The light crown was surrounded by hanging pearl drops on chains and they flowed down artfully as the men lifted it from the pillow and held it up to the indrawn breath of the audience. They paused dramatically and then lowered it onto the girl's head as the chant reached a crescendo.

Loud as it was, I heard but one voice in an anguished whisper.

"No!"

138

Judicus reached out like he could stop the ceremony, his hand clawing through the air, but before I could do anything, Prexav was there. He wrapped a hand around Judicus's mouth and another around his shoulders and hauled him backward.

"Sersha," he whispered, breathing wildly. "Help."

I hesitated. Judicus was fighting against Prexav, trying to get free. And it was to my coterie leader that my loyalties lay.

"If you love him at all, as a friend, as your leader," Prexav whispered hoarsely. "Then help."

And his eyes burned with intensity. And that settled it. Because I knew that look. It was the look I wore every time I tried to keep Mally out of trouble.

I grabbed Judicus's hand with one of mine and with the other shoulder, I leaned in against his chest and shoved.

Between the two of us, we got him back from the balcony and back into the tight dark corridor. His chest was heaving, eyes wide. He gulped in air as if he were drowning, making tiny, agonized sounds on the inhale.

"That's her. Kristiana." Prexav told me.

I startled. Had they just crowned Judicus's sister the next Grand Hadri?

"Calm down, Irault," Prexav whispered. "I'm going to take my hand from your mouth. If you aren't quiet when I do, you might get us all killed. We shouldn't be here. Especially not you, if they're crowning her. You know this." A pause. "You *must* know this."

The moment his hand was gone Judicus's whisper tore harshly through the air. "I'll kill them all."

"And what? Kill her, too?" Prexav pushed.

"Never." His whisper was raw.

"That's what will happen if you try to interfere. They'll use her as a hostage against you. Or use your mother. I didn't see her down there, but she's somewhere. And then they'll kill them both with you."

Judicus ripped at his own hair. He really was going to make himself bald. "Haselhad and Florentin, Gaspard and Prevva, Kastar and Tranjen. Do you know what it means?"

"That the Grand Hadri's advisors have all turned on him," Prexav said calmly.

Judicus's eyes widened, and he let go of his hair long enough to look up. "You know."

"We suspected. We *are* his spies, after all. Why do you think Sersha sought us out?"

And now it was Judicus's chance to look surprised as he looked from Prexav to me and back. What did he think I was doing with Prexav? Had he believed there was some romance here? Or that I just picked up followers wherever I went? I was not him.

Judicus shook his head as if he couldn't think about that right now.

"I can't let them do this to her."

"Make her their ruler?"

"Use her."

"It's done. You can't stop them now. And now that it's done, she either rules or she dies."

"With enemies at her gates and her population in terror. Terror leads to atrocity. Every time." Judicus sounded anguished.

"Think," Prexav said, and I put a hand on Judicus's arm trying to show I was with him. Whatever happened next, I was with him. Even if I didn't understand the politics of all this. He took my hand in his almost mashing the bones he was trying to hold on so tight. "Think. They took her, even though she's not directly in line. They crowned her. They need a pawn. It means you're a dead man if they catch sight of you. And Kristiana is worse than dead if they see you. And if, by some miracle, the Grand Hadri survived, they will kill him on sight. Your only option is to flee."

"I can't leave her alone." He bit his lower lip looking away. "I can't leave her behind."

"They won't kill her immediately. If they meant to, then they would have done that rather than crowned her."

"But they'll use her."

"Of course. But what good will it do her to watch you die first? And you *will* die. The rumors say you're strong. But there are three armies outside the gates – and some or maybe all are allied to the men in that room. They have rope workers of their own. In that room. At least a dozen. Maybe twice that. And guards. And the Flamerarch, if the sun ever sets again. You are only one man. Wait. Bide your time. Return with allies."

"Allies," Judicus spat, as if he couldn't even say the word.

"Sersha. She's an ally of yours. So is this Gundt. Yes?"

"Yes," Judicus admitted reluctantly. But he was looking away, still intent on the dome beyond as if at any moment he would burst past us, run across, and leap from the balcony into the dome on threads of black rope and fight them all.

"Irault?" Prexav said, and he seemed uncertain, like he wasn't sure he should say what comes next. "If you do this. If you walk away. For now. Until you can come back in strength. If you do this, I pledge to return with you to free Kristiana."

Judicus whipped his head around, eyes bright. "You do?"

Prexav looked at me and then back at Judicus. "For Sersha's sake. Look. You're breaking her up. She's worried about you."

Judicus seemed to melt at that.

"For her sake, and for the Grand Hadri who I served, and for revenge in his name," Prexav said. "I swear it."

139

I was reasonably sure I was trying to sneak out of a palace with two madmen. Worse, they were two mad men who were clearly at odds with each other and only just managing to negotiate a tenuous peace over a vow to save the sister of one of them.

I kept looking between the two of them – Judicus hunched and pale and thin with a burning fire in his eyes like he was being set aflame from the inside out. Prexav, brown-skinned, light-haired, and animated, compactly built and muscular – the picture of health on the outside, but behind his eyes was something black that edged on disillusionment or even despair. Two men. Dark and light on the outside, light and dark on the inside.

And me, silent, between them.

I just kept thinking that though Mally wasn't right here with me, her luck must still be lingering, twisting fate, for what else would throw these two opposites together? What else would drive a beleaguered nation to crown a hostage girl queen? What would spin circumstances in just the right way that we would enter this fortress undetected and arrive at the moment the crown was placed on her head? Either it was the ai'sletta twisting the fate not just of herself but of the whole city, or it truly was circumstance. And I wasn't betting on circumstance.

We slipped through the palace the same way we'd slipped in, slowly retracing our steps in secret. No wonder it was so silent. Every soul within was busy crowning a Grand Hadri.

And as we worked backward through our steps, I was working backward mentally through my journey here. How many times had luck turned in my favor? Finding Hallimore as he was dying so he could give me the message about the phoenixes. That was luck. Happening to be on the same ship as Gundt who was both a Greensleeve and a Flame Rider. Luck. Running across Aunt Danna in the quarantine camp. Luck. Horacen sparing our lives when Lady Lightland wanted us dead. Luck. The tunnel collapsing and cutting off the Grand Hadri and me from the rest at just the right point that we walked past the mural. Luck.

Was each of these twistings of fate a result of having brushed against the ai'sletta? Perhaps, all these important people were right to seek her. If not to turn luck for them, then to keep her from wreaking havoc across the countryside.

And I was planning to lead her not just across this countryside, but that of a foreign land, too. I paused in my thinking and also in walking so that Prexav ran into me with a quiet curse.

"Almost there. Don't stop," he muttered.

I shook my head at myself. What did I care if we caused chaos in the land of the raiders? After all, they seemed bent on doing that to us generation after generation. And strange luck was better than mass slaughter. We just had to find Mally again and then live long enough to save the world and come back here to rescue Judicus's sister and hope she wanted to be rescued and didn't execute us all as her family had a habit of doing to people who threatened their rule or principles.

I didn't even notice Judicus's reaction to everything until we stepped from the dark tight passage and out into the sunset past the palace wall.

Orange tears lay wet on his cheeks. He swiped them away angrily, leaving smears of dust. I didn't meet his eyes. Not when I couldn't offer hope with my own. Not when looking would just highlight that I saw the most powerful man I knew broken on behalf of his sister.

Instead, I swallowed, and began to push through the crowd, leading the other two. Prexav caught up and took my arm for a moment, guiding me in a slightly different direction.

"This way," he murmured, and he seemed as shaken as the rest of us, his gaze flicking from one thing to the next as if he wasn't sure what to be on guard against.

I was so worried for the pair of them that it took me a full minute to realize that the gongs had stopped. There were no rushing citizens in the street. We were the only ones hurrying across the cobbles.

And by the time I noticed why, it was almost too late.

The palace and the streets surrounding it were fully encircled by armed men in the Grand Hadri's uniform. They spread in a wide ring, holding back the crowds, their stance stiff and formal. Even the breeze which tussled flags and the cloaks of regular people did not seem to touch them. I shivered at the sight of their stiff backs and severe lines.

And as we hurried from one alley to the next, the palace gates opened right in front of us, catching us mid-stride in the street.

I stumbled as, above us, the palace wall filled with massing bodies, like limpets filling gaps in the rocks as the tide receded. They assembled in an ominous line at the top of the wall.

A trumpet sounded, blasting louder than any trumpet I could have imagined – a clear, bold announcement searing through the air. It seared my heart with it – branding it with fear and perilous certainty.

And magnified over all else, a voice broke through from the palace wall, shouting and then echoed by criers on the edge of the crowds held back by the ring of parade soldiers.

"All Hail the Grand Hadri, long may she reign over us!"

And it was at that exact moment that the gate guards seemed to realize we were there.

140

My eyes met Judicus's in horror. His lips dropped open and I thought he might say something but before he could, shouting rang out around us. It slammed into us like a moving wall as the ring of guards, the people waiting within the palace walls, and everyone on top of the wall above us seemed to shout at once.

One of the guards pointed.

They'd spotted us. It was impossible not to. But there's something about dozens of hostile eyes turning on you at once and dozens of voices raised in approbation that sends terror through a person. My heart was in my throat, hands clammy and sweating, breath rasping, before we even started to run.

A guard broke from the cluster at the palace gates, hurtling toward us impossibly fast. Someone else followed. And then I lost track as a hand grabbed mine and yanked me away. My feet pounded on cobbles sending shivers up my shins, but I forced them to push, push, push. My breath sawed in my throat, the taste of blood in the back of my mouth. Everything around me was reduced to what I could see or hear between each shuddering smack of my feet.

So much for helping the phoenixes. So much for saving the world. So much for friends and hope. It was over now. We'd be caught and brought before the conspirators who had overthrown the Grand Hadri and maybe Judicus would be spared because his sister was now the Grand Hadri, but a foreign mute girl who couldn't defend herself? There would be no mercy for me.

I tried to hold back panic and focus on running instead. Thinking too much didn't make anyone faster. But I couldn't. The thoughts chased me, as unbidden and relentless as the guards.

I was going to be caught. I was going to be killed.

Like a slap in the face, the world went dark.

I gasped, and with my gasp fire blossomed in my heart, swirling up in a dance of flames that seemed to almost whoop with joy.

Kazmerev!

Thinking his name was almost like a prayer – personal but intense, a hand thrown out hoping to be saved. A heart lurching to life at the advent of unhoped-for news.

He did not disappoint.

He materialized under me, becoming solid in less than a heartbeat. I was just barely quick enough to jerk Judicus backward with the hand I was holding and grab him around the waist with the other hand before we were launched into the air.

Wind whipped under my feet. Joy blew through my heart echoing it.

Not wind. People. Running people chasing you. What is – oh. Flame to flame, I greet you, ancient fire!

He seemed to stutter in his hurry to get the words out.

Flame to flame, I greet you, ancient fire!

This voice boomed with a barely suppressed joviality, and I glanced to one side to see a grim Prexav trembling as he sat astride the biggest phoenix I'd seen yet. The magical creature was orange and so smoky that he almost looked shaggy. He tossed his head as he laughed.

I am Kazmerev, Bright Flame, Bound in Oath and Heart to Sersha of Landsfall.

I am Grevankin, Smoke Cloud, Bound in Oath to Prexav of Briccatore. But now, what's all this? You're being chased my dear boy.

"I know that!" Prexav's voice was testy, though I could barely hear it over the wind. "We're trying to get to the ai'sletta and flee the city."

The ai'sletta! A grand quest worthy of a phoenix. You've done well, my boy. I should rest more often if I wake to these kinds of surprises.

I glanced over my shoulder and froze. We were not the only fires in the sky. Over the palace flame after flame rose into view, dark figures clinging to the bright backs of phoenixes. There were at least a dozen. They must be the Flamerarch everyone kept speaking of. In front of me, I heard Judicus give a low curse. He'd seen them, too.

I sense Huxabrand not far from here, Kazmerev told me.

We should go to her. The quicker we found Gundt, the faster we could start to group together and flee this place.

He was already moving, angling into a new heading.

"I'm hopeful that you've asked Kazmerev to join Gundt," Judicus told me. And I knew he was afraid because his voice was as calm as still water. "With the Flamerarch launching, our moments are limited."

Limited? What could he mean by that?

Did you hear the Flamerarch greet me?

Of course not. Their soldiers had been chasing me.

They also did not greet Grevankin. You asked me once what would happen if a phoenix did not greet another immediately upon being seen. You may just find out.

That sounded ominous.

Have not a fear, little she-human, Grevankin boomed. I liked him already. *You are with me and noble Kazmerev. We will handle the phoenix problems and you can handle the human problems, and all will be well.*

I was pretty sure I heard Prexav muttering. He was not so certain.

Poor Prexav was cursed at birth with a rainy spirit, and he cannot see the shining sun for all the clouds he drags along behind him.

Yes, I was definitely loving Grevankin.

A flurry of bright pink and yellow flame erupted ahead of us and like a falling star falling in the wrong direction, Huxabrand rose, Gundt on her back, his sister trussed up behind him.

We were all here. Now, if we could only find Mally.

The Flamerarch is preparing to come after us, Kazmerev warned.

Kaz? I asked in my mind.

His tone softened. *Little Hawk.*

I missed you. I thought I might not see you again and I was afraid I wouldn't get to tell you how much you mean to me.

There will be time for that.

But there might not be. I plowed on. I needed him to know how much he mattered to me. I needed him to know that he had saved me from a life of futility in my village and then saved me again and again from death, capture, pain, and loneliness, that he was my true friend and my savior all wrapped into one. That even if I failed and died right now, I would never regret leaving Landsfall with him. I'd always be grateful for every time he'd been reborn in my heart.

I know it little hawk. I know your heart, for it is my home. Now, know mine. I will be your friend always until your life is snuffed like a candle wick. But that day won't be today.

141

A phoenix is a glorious, beautiful thing. A song of fire and smoke, of light and shadow, of bird-grace and brilliant mind and the strange brave trust that makes a thing of legend breathe.

But there had never been one after me before and I found the notion of it horrifying.

"That's the Flamerarch," Judicus said, looking over his shoulder and mine to see the phoenixes rising from the palace behind us. "I have watched them as they stood down hosts. I have watched them as they guarded those who tore my father from his throne and set up my uncle in his place."

I could hear the horror edging his voice. But phoenixes were only supposed to do what was good.

And if you don't realize yet that good is complicated, Kazmerev said, *that sometimes people think that they're doing right when they're wrong to the extreme, then you haven't understood good yet. You haven't understood why humility must be sewn into it and woven through its warp and woof.*

A sudden picture of the weaver at home – Marla of the rocky bay – sprang to mind. I'd seen her loom before. She worked there tirelessly making cloth for Landsfall, her shutter moving so fast I could hardly keep up with the flow of threads as they moved from raw strands into whole cloth.

Humility didn't seem like something Kazmerev would preach. He wasn't a primary example of it.

I've never found much of a reason to be humble. But even I know that it's the only way to prevent being burnt up.

"Perhaps, I can talk to them," Judicus said contemplatively.

I met his eyes, and let mine widen. He didn't think Gundt or Prexav should do that? Below us, a square spread out with a huge statue in the center. I hadn't seen this in my journey through town.

"Sometimes people surprise you," he said and now his mouth was firming into determination. I wanted to throw my hands in the air. He was supposedly the most powerful rope worker of his generation. So, of course, when faced with pursuit by an enemy he wanted to talk through their grievances. It was so … Judicus.

Triumph Square, Kazmerev told me. *The statue at the center is a bronze rendering of Judicus's father at the gibbet. His brother thought it would serve as a reminder to all.*

How horrifying.

I have always thought so. Veela thought that perhaps we could not understand because we were not human.

It wasn't a human thing. It was an arrogant thing.

See? Humility is a safeguard. That's what I was trying to convince you of.

"I just need to think of what to say," Judicus said. "What do you say to stop a war?"

I was staring so intently at the square around the gibbet, that I hardly noticed the small figures on the statue until we were nearly upon it.

Was that? It couldn't be –

And then we whirled in a sudden almost panicked flurry as Judicus's voice rang out.

"Come and reason together with us, Flamerarch. Surely phoenix should not be pitted against phoenix."

Kazmerev made his angry shriek sound I was starting to realize was a phoenix curse. *This is when I wish you could speak. Then you can tell him how foolish that was. We were not greeted by them and that means they plan to duel us.*

Duel?

Flame to flame, feather to feather – to the death.

I did not like this at all! They must not do it.

Or rather, we are to fight to the ultimate death. There will be no rebirth from a phoenix duel.

My breath froze in my throat. It felt like my heart was beating so hard it was going to stop.

Easy now. Easy.

I told myself to breathe. I had to keep breathing. There had to be a way to stop this. And if there wasn't, passing out and missing it all was not an option. If Kazmerev could be here for me until the end – well, could I not do the same for him?

We can flee. Which is what we were doing before the rope worker just had to stick his nose in things.

We spiraled around Triumph Square, the horrific statue of Judicus's father growing larger as we descended. In the distance, I could see the dark armies closing in on the city, growing steadily closer. Ahead of them was a wall of darkness. Stryxex, I realized.

We couldn't afford phoenixes to fight phoenixes – not with Stryxex to fight, too.

Maybe Judicus was right. Maybe we should try to talk to them.

You can't talk if they won't greet you. It's a terrible breach of protocol!

He's not wrong, a feminine phoenix voice joined in. I was relieved to see Huxabrand flying to join our spiral, a resigned-looking Gundt on her back. He looked no better than Judicus, battered and dirty, but whole. *If they did not greet you then it is war.*

But no. I didn't accept that.

Hadn't Kazmerev just been going on about humility? Maybe humility broke protocol. Maybe it didn't pridefully defend its honor but was willing to eat the insult and try for peace a second time.

That isn't our way.

But maybe it should be. Wasn't he the one who said that humility must be woven through goodness? Wasn't he the one who said I didn't understand how nuanced goodness was? Then maybe honor was nuanced, too. Maybe it was time to bend a little.

Maybe it is. To my surprise, that voice was the booming voice of Grevankin. *Maybe there is wisdom in this small Fledgling's voice.*

Prexav's face from the back of his phoenix looked hard and unbending. But after a moment, he shook his head and swung Gravankin in closer to us.

"Ask them to speak to us at the monument," Prexav called over to Judicus. "If we have any hope of being listened to, it will be there."

Judicus nodded sharply, clearly satisfied that everyone was falling in with his plan, and called back with his voice amplified by his rope work.

"Meet us at the statue in Triumph Square. What better place to negotiate peace than where it was bought with blood?"

And then we were descending again, hurrying to beat out the other phoenixes and the closing Stryxex and I'd been right. There was a figure in the square sitting on the gallows as if she cared not at all what they depicted. She wore a black dripping crown on her chestnut head, her arms crossed over her chest irritably.

Mally.

Thank the heavens, we'd found her again.

Just in time to embroil her in another battle.

142

"Well, here we are, then," Mally said when we landed. "All the trouble-makers in one place. The creeps from the temple caves, the glowing phoenixes, Judicus, the woman who killed my mother – still not brought to justice, I see – and Ceghan's brother. How lovely. You're accumulating quite the following, Sersha. It's a shame you can't pull them from a higher quality of people."

All I felt was relief. Even a cranky Mally was still Mally.

"Do we have plans to leave this place yet?" she asked. Beside her, Ceghan stood, looking worried. She clearly had not adapted yet to Mally's unique brand of general snideness.

"Where's Jensen?" Prexav asked as Grevankin settled on the ground. The smoking phoenix winked at me, and he shook a little as if he were barely containing laughter. I liked that phoenix. I hoped there wouldn't really be a duel. I didn't want him hurt.

I'm starting to feel jealous.

"Jensen heard the ship was launching without us and he ran to stop it. He left me with *her,*" Ceghan nodded at Mally. "And she put on the crown and refused to budge once he was gone."

That was Mally exactly.

"I'm not going anywhere without Sersha and I figured she'd find me if Kazmerev could help her." Mally seemed smug as she looked from face to face. When she caught my gaze, she winked. And the thing was, she wasn't wrong. If she'd gone without me, I might have missed her but by putting on the crown, she gave us all a chance.

"Did you break the sky, Mally?" Judicus asked. He looked exhausted. I held on to him even though we've landed, certain he needed my arms to hold him up.

"I might have." Her lip trembled a little. She hadn't meant to.

"Are you manipulating luck so that weird things keep happening around the city?" he pushed.

"Not intentionally." She rolled her eyes.

He nodded as if all of this was completely normal. But it was nice to have him here understanding.

I think he understands, Kazmerev said dryly.

I could finally tell him that we needed to get Mally to the raider islands to stop something that was making Stryxex from destroying the world.

Kazmerev repeated that back in my mind.

"We need to what?" Gundt's head whipped around and so did Prexav's. They were staring at me.

Well, the Grand Hadri had seen it, too, which is why he'd sent me to them. To get his spies to help. They'd been seeing indications that there was a big problem only the ai'sletta could solve. Now we knew what it was. This – whatever it was – hole in the earth or magic well or something that was spewing out dark magic. She needed to stop it and only she could. I'd promised him I'd do it.

Kazmerev relayed my thoughts crisply.

Prexav responded by cursing quietly but Grevankin seemed unconcerned. He rolled his head as if trying to scratch an itch. I wished I could be as calm about this as he was.

Gundt cleared his throat, listening as Kazmerev relayed it all to them. "Why would you promise that, Sersha?"

Well, I hadn't promised exactly. I hadn't said anything, but the Grand Hadri had taken my silence as a promise, and it felt like a promise now that I'd found Jensen like he'd said.

The Grand Hadri took her silence as a promise. Now that he's dead, she feels obligated to keep it.

"Whoa," Prexav said, blowing out through his mouth dramatically.

"I think maybe you should tell the rest of us what's going on," Ceghan said pointing at the sky. "Before the Flamerarch gets here."

"It seems that Sersha promised the former Grand Hadri that she would bring the ai'sletta to the islands of the Hand of the Rat to destroy a threat to mankind," Prexav said.

"Former Grand Hadri?" Gundt said at the same time that Judicus said "Promised?" and Mally grunted a laugh and rolled her eyes. She suspected this. Sometimes I wondered how much smarter she was than she appeared.

But none of them were able to do more than that. The Flamerarch was here, drifting down around us like red leaves from a maple in the Fall. And in there, in the center of the square, was the bronze casting Judicus couldn't look at. Mally was perched on it like the guest of honor, head held high, crown black and burning and eyes even blacker and more fiery.

"I'm not sure it really is me who is twisting fate, Sersha," she said, laughing. "I think it might be you."

As the last phoenix plunged to the earth and settled, shaking out its plumage, even Mally fell silent as the Flamerarch raised their wings together, as one, arching over us in fiery condemnation.

Who is it who has asked to speak rather than fight? one of them asked. His words boomed in my mind.

And while I was sure that all of us were thinking of Judicus, we didn't want to say his name. A minute passed in which windows around the square opened as citizens peered out into the night at the assemblage of bright phoenixes and we grew more nervous and then one of the phoenix riders spoke,

"You are declared traitors and as such, we will take the humans into our custody and the phoenixes will fight to the death as is custom."

"Again, Reichus?" Judicus said softly, and the man leading the phoenixes gaped as the rope worker disentangled himself from my hold and slipped down from Kazmerev's back to stride to the center of the square and place his hand gently on the foot of the casting of his dead father. "Once you declared a man a traitor who had done nothing but fight for you and your loved ones and all who lived in this city. Now, you do it again with me. I am here to help, but you only see my blood. We are here to save, and you only see that we are not you. Our enemies gather beyond the gates, and you are busy fighting those who would stand with you. Where is your goodness, rider of flame? Where is the righteousness of your cause and quest."

"It's here," Reichus said.

"Then forget this nonsense of phoenix fighting phoenix and countryman, countryman and stand up on this memorial to the worst day of my life and reason with me and if I cannot sway you with my thoughts and heart then you can kill me as he was killed. But if I can sway you, then we will stand together instead of apart and cleanse the black mark on the name of Flamerarch."

And I wanted to call to him to come back, that this wasn't going to work, that we were just going to lose him, too. Or failing that, I wanted to give him one last word of encouragement, but I had nothing to give him but a grim smile to meet his kind one when his eyes flickered to mine for just a moment before he mounted the gibbet and stood beside the casting of his doomed father to beg for peace.

143

The Flamerarch were showy, dressed in dark leathers with highly polished bands of metal around their wrists and ankles. They wore wide girdles of brightly polished metal around their middles and heavy torques hanging over their collarbones. It was not hard to see that they used their dress to reflect the flames and smoke of their phoenixes as a way to make themselves appear grander. Beside the bright creatures, or atop them, these men and women dazzled. Their heads were capped in fitted metal helms with black plumes running like rooster combs along the top and down to the nape of the neck.

I didn't like the pageantry. I didn't like that it made their phoenixes look like props. Kazmerev grunted in my mind in agreement, clearly not willing to say anything they might hear.

I disliked that even more. Why did their phoenixes not speak? They acted more like mounts than independent beings and if there was one thing Kazmerev had taught me since I met him – it was that phoenixes were most certainly not mounts.

He shuffled under me and then bent his head back in a way I hadn't seen him do before. It let him rub his flaming cheek against me affectionately and to my surprise, tears welled up in my eyes and my arms went out automatically to hug him closer, tighter. My nose was full of woodsmoke and cedar, of hot sparks and heavy musk, and for just a moment I let the scent of my burning phoenix comfort me for what was to come. It would be fine. He was here. And he always rose again.

We would rise from this, too.

The leader of the Flamerarch – or whoever it was that was willing to negotiate – dismounted and strode to join Judicus at the statue. He walked stiffly. A frisson of worry tickled the edges of my focus. A man didn't walk like that if he felt confident. Or if he felt merciful. A man walked like that if he was on edge – afraid or angry or vicious.

I gritted my teeth against the worry that automatically whipped to the surface, but Judicus lounged easily against the statue. Every eye was on him as he slowly looked up at the man approaching him.

"I am Judicus Franzer Irault," he said calmly, looking first at the man approaching him and then letting his gaze sweep over the others ringing us. He looked like a man choosing a fish for dinner from a stall, not a single man facing up against a ring of enemies. He hardly seemed to mind the bandage covering one eye, though on that intent face, it only made him look more dangerous. "A rope worker and the leader of this coterie."

Prexav moved uncomfortably at the word "coterie." He likely resented being included in that, but this wasn't the time to mention the finer details.

"We know who you are, Son of Chaos," the Flamerarch representative said coldly.

"And you have no introductions to offer?" Judicus asked, picking at one of his fingernails absently.

The other man bristled. "None I'd give to such as you."

"Hmm," Judicus said, looking up from his nails.

It's a strange certainty that if a man appears very casual in a tense situation, every eye goes to him. Every mind wonders if he knows something they do not. That was what was happening here, and I realized after a heartbeat that it must be deliberate, because as he had been drawing all their eyes, Mally and Ceghan had left the statue and joined us a little back from it. Ceghan slipped up on Grevankin's back with her brother and Mally was suddenly right beside me, meeting my eyes with a look that said she expected trouble and didn't like it but wasn't sure what to do about it.

I was right there with her. I didn't know what was coming, either, but I hoped Judicus had a plan.

Judicus cleared his throat. "Well then, Reichus, if you will not offer the names of your friends, then please know that we have no quarrel with you and wish only to depart your city in peace."

"That's no longer an option." The man representing the Flamerarch – Reichus – was short and stocky, at least fifty by my guess, with pouches under his eyes and a shock of thick grey hair. I wondered if he had children our age, but then remembered that Kazmerev had said phoenix riders rarely married. If only I could talk to my phoenix without us being overheard. He would certainly have observations to share.

Judicus was speaking again, hands spread out as if to reason with the other man. "Why pit brother against brother? Why pit phoenix against phoenix? We would all lose, and for what?"

"You're in the wrong, Irault. You and your coterie. You're a danger to the city and the nation of Calicarn. The best thing for everyone is if we subdue you and put you under guard for the judgment of the Grand Hadri."

"My sister?" Judicus asked mildly.

The man flinched at that.

"Was she asked if she wanted to be Grand Hadri?" His mild voice had a dangerous edge.

"We all must do our part."

"Indeed. And the part she will play was forced on her in the most unchivalrous fashion. But leaving that aside, and leaving aside that I would be in my rights as her brother to call the court to account, there are Stryxex outside the walls and they're bent on the destruction of all phoenixes. Each one of you to fall will be one less to hold them off. And each one of us to fall is another less in that good fight. The best for Calicarn requires every phoenix and every person available to fight with all their strength. And it demands we put aside our differences – me, my revenge, and you, your prejudice."

"They aren't here for us," the man said, but he was playing with his metal wristband almost unconsciously and I thought he was nervous. "We don't need your help. And your claims of being owed vengeance are null now that your sister wears a crown. No one has ever made a case *against* becoming Grand Hadri."

"They Stryxex are here for everyone. If you think otherwise, you're twice the fool. But I care not for your folly. If you don't want us in your city, that's fine. My coterie and I were just leaving."

"I can't allow that. You're as much a danger without as you are within."

"We'll fight our way out but we'd rather not." Judicus's lounging suddenly seemed to look more like a predator on a branch of a tree waiting to fall on its prey than a man taking his ease. "We'd rather talk. After all, everyone here is associated with phoenixes and they can only associate with the good. That means we all think our causes are just. Can we not come to some agreement? Can we not find something in common in all this goodness?"

The other man looked uncomfortable. I felt uncomfortable, too. What would happen if Judicus couldn't talk us out of a fight? Could we possibly win against them?

No. Kazmerev sounded very certain.

Not even with Mally?

No.

But it could work if she removed the crown. Kazmerev shuffled under me uneasily. But what if that broke the sky even more? What if he couldn't come back ... ever?

Exactly.

I swallowed down a burst of worry. No need to fret about what-ifs when I had so much to worry about right in front of me.

Hope that Judicus talks them into peace.

Around us, the ring of phoenixes seemed to ripple as if responding to Kazmerev's words. I hoped they were responding favorably.

"Would it help if I told you we're following the wishes of the last Grand Hadri?" Judicus said, seeming to weigh his words.

He was looking for any argument. Any wedge in the man's determined refusal to simply let us leave. But we *had* to leave. Unless Mally went on the quest assigned her by their dead leader, utter destruction would be unleashed upon the earth.

The other man's eyes flashed up to Judicus, his brows rising in disbelief. "You, Son of Chaos? You would work for the man who took your father's life?"

"My uncle," Judicus reminded him.

The other man scoffed. "I don't believe you care about blood as much as you do revenge. I need an act of good faith if I'm to take you at your word."

"My word is yours. That should be enough," Judicus said.

From across the square, I saw Gundt dismount as the man scoffed again.

"Your word is nothing, Son of Chaos. I need a hostage. How about the pretty girl with the angry eyes?" He pointed at Mally.

"Is my word nothing, too, Reichus?" Gundt asked, swaggering up to them. "Will you not trust me? We were friends once, I think."

"Greensleeve," Reichus acknowledged. "I know you, but the Greensleeves are not to be trusted, either. Your hearts are not with us. Your strange cult cares only for a bygone time. So, no, your word is not enough."

"Then take *me* as your hostage," Gundt said.

Huxabrand made a sound like a sheep bleating.

"I think you'd make a poor hostage, Gundt, bastard that you are. There are none who care whether you live or die, though if I am not mistaken, that is your half-sister across the back of your phoenix, and no one will be going anywhere unless she is given over to us."

Gundt and Judicus exchanged a look.

"Of course," Gundt said after a moment. "You are welcome to take her as hostage."

"No," Reichus said. "We take her as is our right as enforcers of the law of Bricatorre which outlaws kidnapping."

"Does it really?" Judicus asked in mock surprise. And no wonder. Was his sister not the victim of kidnapping?

Reichus ignored him, continuing on, "And we will take a real hostage on top of that."

Judicus shot Mally a look and shook his head, which I found hilarious. She would never offer herself and only Judicus would have so much faith in her good heart that he thought that was possible.

"Prexav, perhaps, since you don't like Gundt," Judicus offered.

I didn't want him to offer himself. I didn't want it, and yet I was surprised he did not.

A leader is not worth much set on the sidelines, Kazmerev offered. And that was true enough, but I wondered how much of that was because he was worried about being used against his sister.

Beside me, Prexav snarled. "Neither myself nor my sister will be hostages of the Flamerarch. We are free people."

"I am already reconsidering," the Flamerarch said. "It's better, perhaps, to take all of you back to the palace. Dead or alive."

Take them all, the Flamerarch phoenixes said with one mental voice. I flinched from it. It was so – uniform. As if they couldn't think for themselves. As if they didn't want to. I swallowed down horror.

Mally had to get out and away from people like that. She needed to go to the raider's islands. She needed Prexav and his spy ring to hire the ship and know where to sail it. She needed Judicus to guide her and Gundt to protect her. And they all needed to be far, far from these terribly similar Flamerarch phoenixes. What she didn't need – what none of them needed – was me.

I took a deep breath.

Tell the others that they need to get her to the islands, I told Kazmerev.

Wait.

Sersha.

And then I stepped forward.

No!

There was no one else. I was the only one expendable enough to be a hostage.

144

No, don't do this.

But just like he'd said he was not my pet, I was not his pet, either. I could choose to sacrifice for the people I loved if I wanted to. Or, in this case, if I thought it was the only way forward.

I took the first few steps slowly enough that though every phoenix was looking at me, no one else seemed to notice at first.

I salute you, mighty heart, Grevankin said in my mind, his booming voice blocking out everything else and then every Flame Rider looked at me and Judicus hissed in a breath as he saw what they were looking at and focused on the grim expression on my face.

His eyes flicked from me to Mally and back to me again. I could tell he know what I was doing – that I was giving myself so the plan could go on. He could tell how I'd reached the conclusion that he should have reached – that I was the one person here, except for maybe Ceghan, who they could afford to offer up. Gundt would have done the job, but they'd already said no to Gundt. My allies didn't need Kazmerev and me for this job. They did need everyone else.

I took another step and drew in a breath to steady myself.

But the look in Judicus's eye was almost too much for me. He looked as if someone was ripping him down the middle. His utter loyalty was touching. His absolute dedication to keeping his word – to being there for me, and providing for me, and keeping me out of danger just because I was in his coterie – it made my heart ache just a bit. Where else in all the world was there a man of character like Judicus? And how had he learned to be like that in a world that had only ever used and betrayed him?

He didn't even have a phoenix.

Behind me, my own phoenix keened sadly, quietly, just on the edge of hearing as if he was trying to suppress it and just couldn't.

I looked over my shoulder and met his eyes.

Bright and liquid, they were so full of hurt that it felt like a physical blow. I flinched from it, aching with what I was doing to both of us. But if I didn't choose this, then what? Did he want to fight and lose and … die? Did he want to watch our friends die around us? Did he want to see the ai'sletta die before she could save us all? Did he want to watch phoenixes fall one by one with no one to stop the targeted attack against them?

No.

It was such a little word to hold so much emotion.

But how can I see you sacrifice yourself and not be gutted by it?

I wasn't going to die. And neither was he. Not now. Not with this sacrifice of my freedom for a little while.

I took another step and met Judicus's eye again.

"The Flame Rider?" Reichus asked. "Yes, she'll do, I suppose. I can see she's dear to you and that's the key. A hostage is only worth what she's worth to the one you must control. Why doesn't she speak?"

"She's voiceless," Judicus said, and it was almost a gasp as his eyes stayed on mine. His eyes were exact reflections of Kazmerev's with exactly the same pain in them.

He didn't ask if I was sure. He didn't try to pretend it wasn't my decision to make or that he would take my place. We both knew he couldn't. We both knew it would be the wrong choice. He just stood there, his face drained of its last dregs of color, his eyes burning with regret and pain. His mouth hung open between words, as if he didn't remember how to shut it, or as if he was in the kind of pain you couldn't close your lips over.

"We keep her for as long as you are gone. Return to the Flamerarch when you're done saving us from this threat you claim exists and she'll be yours again," Reichus said grimly. "Refuse to leave her with us, and we fight right now. And she'll die with her phoenix along with all the rest of you. You know us, Irault. You know we are warriors of flame and smoke. The best of the best. You will not survive if we want you dead."

"Yes," Judicus said grimly.

And then, to my shock, he stepped forward and drew me into a hug.

He was warm as a phoenix, his heart hammering so fast I was worried for his health, and his arms trembled as he held me against him as gently as a boy might hold a wounded songbird.

He whispered into my hair, "Hold on and we will return for you. You and my sister. Be brave. I will not abandon you."

I looked up at him and I wanted to say, "Don't stop until you've saved the world. Don't die while you're doing it. Ask the spies to watch out for you while you're on the ship because seasickness makes you miserable."

But I couldn't say any of it.

He knows, Kazmerev said.

And the look in Judicus's eyes told me he did.

And then strong hands ripped me from him and Reichus said, "Be gone by the count of twenty, or the deal is off."

Judicus reached out, and to my utter shock, his fingers found the side of my cheek, and his touch – light as a breeze – was half a last caress and half as if he wished he could cling to me, and then he turned and strode to Gundt's side. Lady Lightland had already been pulled from Huxabrand's back and left on the ground and Mally was hurrying to join them – three to a phoenix. Gundt and Prexav didn't have my limitations.

Gundt saluted me, his face hard as stone, and then he kicked off into the air with his two precious passengers. Grevankin leapt up behind him, bearing Prexav and Ceghan.

And my friends were gone just like that.

I watched them sailing up, up, up, above me, ashes and sparks gently fluttering down in their wake until it was only me, surrounded by my enemies, with only my dear phoenix with me, still keening his sad song.

145

I still had my heart.

I still had Kazmerev.

He shifted uncomfortably, unable to speak without being heard by the other phoenixes, but clearly, he wished he was flying away, too.

We waited in silence, Reichus watching to be sure that my allies were truly away, his hand held up until the last glimmer of their flames were gone.

His men relaxed their tight formation, melting into casual knots and speaking quietly together. It bothered me that their phoenixes remained in a stiff ring – unwilling or unable to disperse as the humans had. What kept them so tight and unbending. Were they not free? Had they been enslaved in some way? The idea of it horrified me.

Perhaps it was not only Stryxex who would have to be stopped.

Above us, the darkness of the sky rippled, and I thought I saw the edges of Stryxex in the distance, settling in over the city. The barest suggestion of them made my blood feel cold in my veins. I hoped I was wrong – that it was only my imagination, that I was working myself up over nothing.

I see them, too.

Kazmerev was so quiet. And it felt so unlike him to be that quiet. I ached for him to speak freely, to tell me what he was thinking. Did he feel betrayed by my choice to sacrifice ourselves?

Never. We are one in this.

I closed my eyes for a moment, letting relief fill me. He was more gracious than I had been. If we were together, we could face whatever came next.

"Gather in your phoenix," Reichus told me. "You will not be permitted to ride him."

I couldn't. Not with Stryxex all around and the future so uncertain. I caught

Kazmerev's eye, and I couldn't tell what he was thinking but he seemed agitated, looking at the sky and then the other phoenixes.

Do not forget, one of them said suddenly, and I did not like the wooden sound of his voice. *This could still end in a duel.*

Kazmerev's feathers seemed to crackle with renewed sparks and his eye glittered as he said to me, *Do as the man asks.*

I closed my eyes and tried to relax and trust and gather him into my heart.

I failed.

I couldn't relax. Not when I didn't know what was going to happen.

I couldn't be calm. Not when I was worried for him.

What if he didn't come back?

I will always come back for you.

What if they did something to prevent it?

No one can prevent it.

Reichus made an annoyed sound in his throat. "Has he not assured you enough? Are you a child that you cannot go a moment without being cossetted and caressed?"

My face flamed hot.

Do not fear. I –

And then Kazmerev's voice cut off.

I gasped, blinded by the sudden light of gold and pink dawn. Around me, shouts of alarm told me I was not alone. Mally must have taken off the Dark Diadem. When my eyes adjusted, there was nothing but lingering smoke where Kazmerev and the other phoenixes had been.

I swallowed, clutching my hand to my chest as if I could keep all my fears bottled up with him. But I was worried. What if the sky was stuck again? What if night never returned?

Beside me, Reichus cursed.

He didn't know how bad it was if that was the only curse he could muster. But I did. I could see the edges of the Stryxex around us. I could see them gathering over the city. Light did not affect them. The dawn did not dismiss them.

And while the Flamerarch around me was still reeling from the sudden change from night to morning a Stryxex dropped down in the square, seemingly unconcerned by the Flame Riders. It screeched like an angry raven, shrill and furious. Any attempt to look at it made my eyes roll away, my head aching behind them from the way the edges of the great bird turned light away and tangled its shape into mirror-like darkness and nothingness.

From the back of the impossible creature, a figure leapt, ripping the veil from its face.

The red-headed Stryex rider. I nearly choked at the sight of him.

"The girl is ours," he said coldly. "Hand her over."

146

I froze, paralyzed by his demand. I tried to will my knees to work, to run, to … anything. But they weren't listening to me.

To my shock, Reichus shoved me roughly behind him. "I don't think so, stranger. Who are you who comes flying in here, mounted on an aberration and making demands?"

The red-haired man sneered, and his boney face looked almost skeletal with the expression.

"I'm the one with the mount when yours are nothing but memories. I'm the one whose people now rule this city. I'm the one to whom you will bend, and all your play authority will melt away like fat crackling over a fire. A few loud protests, and then it's gone leaving only a stink behind."

If Reichus was worried, he didn't show it. And neither did his Flame Riders, who, to my surprise, moved light as phoenix feathers as they surrounded us. I had expected harsh treatment and angry demands. I had not expected defense. I found the sudden consideration almost overwhelming.

Tears pricked my eyes when one of the Flamerarch reached out to clasp my arm for just a moment. I shot the rider a furtive look and saw it was a woman of maybe forty, her hair cut very short and shot with silver threads, and her leathers under the polished metal flare, worn with hard use. The look in her eyes was both firm and kind, as if she were trying to reassure me.

The raider laughed.

"Wrong girl," he said, and the twist of his mouth was so mocking that for a moment I couldn't seem to grasp what he meant, and then his men were hauling Lady Lightland to her feet.

I gasped.

"To think," he said, laughing even harder, "that you would have the ai'sletta with you and not even know it."

"The ai'sletta?" Reichus asked as warily as I would have, if I had a voice.

"She turns fate just by being near. Just by being in the same city as you. How do you think we found the Grand Hadri when he tried to flee us? How do you think we took your city? Look." Behind him was the sound of marching boots across cobbles and as I looked out at the streets surrounding Triumph Square, I realized the enemy had come through the gates at last and was taking the city without resistance. "We are here without a drop of blood spilled, our ruler installed without a voice raised in protest, our ai'sletta has made it all possible. And now, with her help, we will do what the ai'sletta was always meant to."

"And what is that?" Reichus asked, and for the first time since I met him, his voice wavered.

"We will perform the Great Transformation. We will turn men into gods and phoenixes into Stryxex. We will open the bowels of the earth and let forth her wrath to purge the land and the air and make what was weak and temporary become strong and eternal."

And I did not like those words at all. They sounded religious, worshipful. It sounded like he believed every one of them. A flickering memory of fleeing down the underground passage with the Grand Hadri washed over me. I realized, suddenly, what I had seen. Phoenixes. Being made into Stryxex.

I looked at the Stryxex before me – the terrible inverting of everything a phoenix was – and my heart froze within me.

The mural.

I should have realized.

The great evil on the other side of the ocean. The thing the Grand Hadri had been warned of. It was all the same thing. And it had come to our shores. It had come after our phoenixes.

I swayed and the steady Flame Rider beside me caught my arm in her firm grip, keeping me upright.

How had I not seen it?

How had I not known?

Casanetta Lightland shook herself as her bonds were cut and she looked through the Flamerarch, her eyes sparkling with triumph until they met mine. She winked. She knew as well as I did that she was no ai'sletta. And she knew I could tell no one.

"Keep a hold of them," she told the red-haired rider, her voice ringing out as if it was meant to carry to us more than to him. "When the sun sets, we'll turn their phoenixes. They might even survive the process."

She rested a hand lightly on his shoulder and then leapt onto his Stryxex as if it were hers.

"Let's go, Andretti, the soldiers will mop them up for us. I'll let you be the one to turn them."

She snapped her fingers, looking past me and I spun to see that while we had been distracted, a cart had drawn up. A cart with a large cage on it as if to hold mythic lions within. But the door was being opened and the soldiers that spilled into the square were all looking at us.

It dawned on me what the cage was for – who it was for. And I wished I could speak to negotiate with them. I wished I could fight. But there were hundreds of bodies pressing quietly in, weapons drawn. We couldn't fight them all. Not without our phoenixes.

"Seize them," Cassanetta said lightly. "And be sure none of them die. It would be a shame to lose a phoenix."

EPISODE THREE: "ENDLESS DAWN"

SEASON TWO

147

Being trapped in a cage is worse when the world around you is suspended in an endless dawn. Keeping track of time was impossible and it dragged on as we were silently confined and then our cage slowly dragged by oxen out of the city and up to the hillside beyond.

There was little to see in the city beyond what I already knew. Briccatore had been overrun by her enemies. Oh, it wasn't what they were saying. The Grand Hadri's guards were on every street corner, urging citizens to stay inside while the Grand Hadri "restored order" and assuring them that this was "for their safety." But I saw far more raiders than I saw guards in livery, and the sky was so full of Stryxex it was like looking up at a school of silverfish.

A feeling of tension pervaded, tight lines in the faces of every guard, tight movements in the bodies of the raiders – even those leading our cart and oxen. Tight worry echoed in the glimpses of faces I saw staring out windows.

War had been averted, perhaps, but the people were hostages in their own homes, their families trapped with them. Hostages of their own Grand Hadri – who, though they didn't know it, was now a young girl, even more a captive than they were. Even the guard must realize it was not them or their sovereign who ruled Briccatore right now. It was the dark-clad raiders, their faces covered so that it was impossible to tell one from another, who were the law in the city.

If there was any doubt of that, you need only hear the muffled cries of the few citizens resisting their new rule. For any man who dared step out his door was quickly subdued by a knot of a dozen or more raiders, beaten until he lay moaning on the ground and then abandoned there. No one dared to leave their houses to help or even to drag the poor souls back into their homes. The one person I saw who tried shared the victim's fate.

Anger and fear mixed in a toxic brew in my heart, the only release the hot wash of tears on my cheeks.

Just watching this madness created silence in our cage as the Flamerarch seemed to grasp the dire situation we were in. They stood around the sides of the cage, gripping the bars, and looking without, not saying a word.

I thought, at first, that they were stoic, able to accept hardship better than most, but when we finally reached the edge of the city – a feat that took hours by my guess, for the oxen were very slow – and I saw their shoulders begin to sag and their expressions tighten, that I realized they had been expecting the day to progress – that dawn would leak into morning and from there blossom to noonday and wax into afternoon only to wane into evening as the sun sank to the night. They had hoped that eventually, the night would fall, and their phoenixes would rise.

For if they rose, then we would stand a chance fighting together. We couldn't all survive an escape attempt – even with our phoenixes whole and hardy. But we could fight hard enough that some of us would make it out.

They'd been relying on that.

Now, they were realizing, as I had, how foolish it was to think anything could be depended on. Even day and night were subject to the whim of the creator and in his sovereign power, he had apparently offered that dominion to the ai'sletta. Mally. A girl who had her own opinions of how things should be.

I could only hope that Judicus would talk some sense into her and convince her to wear the crown and make it night eventually. And I could only hope she was safe and with friends and that they would take her where she was needed.

Part of me wanted to feel a little sorry for myself, stuck in this cage while my friends went free, but I fought that urge. I'd chosen this, and it was a good choice. Even if it made me afraid right through to my core.

As we left the city, the Flamerarch began to sit, one by one. The more stubborn of them stood standing, faces set with fury or determination. But those who sat looked resigned or sad instead. It was then that they began to speak. Quietly, at first. Then more normally when it seemed our captors didn't care.

"Look," Reichus said from where he stood close to the front of the cart. "That's one of General Vicombe's armies arrayed on the hill by the city. They're just sitting there."

There was a dark murmur from around the cart.

He was right. I caught sight of men in regimented ranks drilling in the field while others washed uniforms and cooked and worked as farriers for horses. They seemed easy and unalarmed. Meanwhile, streams of raiders poured up and down the road that ran alongside their camp.

Their whole purpose was to defend against this. They barely even looked up.

"And that is General Ferdown's army there," he pointed at another hill, his voice sharp with bitterness. "Do you remember how only yesterday the Grand Hadri's counselors told us they were on the northern border?"

"Maybe that *is* the northern border now," someone said grimly.

Reichus snorted and someone made a sad sound in the back of his throat.

Their observations carried on through what was likely the afternoon and early evening, though there was no way to tell. For us, it was an endless dawn as we were ever-so-slowly transported out of the city and up to a hillside past where the armies were camped.

In the end, I was able to draw my own conclusions from their comments. The Grand Hadri's counselors – most if not all of them – and a few of their generals had toppled the government, installed their own puppet Grand Hadri, and taken the city while the armies were held back and the raiders – their allies used against the populace to hold them down and back.

"It's genius," Reichus said eventually. "Utterly ingenious."

"Do you think Castan was in on it?" one of the others asked and after that, they were all silent for a long time.

"I hope not," Reichus said when the silence had grown so thick you could use it as a blanket. "If he was, then all phoenixes are doomed."

Which they were, already. Though he hadn't believed us when we told him.

"The Flamerarch would never agree to this," he said, and it sounded like he was trying to convince himself of that.

I tilted my head curiously and the short-haired woman in her forties noticed me doing it.

"We are only a small number of the Flamerarch," she murmured to me. "The Flamerarch is large – a hundred phoenixes in total. We guard the realm and the people. But we are not all in Briccatore at once. There were maybe ten more of us stationed here."

I was grateful for the information. I felt lost in this world of people and politics I did not know.

When, at last, our wagon stopped, only Reichus remained standing.

The raiders offered food and water and chamber pots in complete silence.

Together, we shared the horror of realizing we were not going to be let out. Not even to take care of basic needs.

Humiliated, we managed as best as we could.

I huddled against the bars when we were finished. I had always felt apart because of my voicelessness, but now, alone among strangers in a strange land, unable to speak, unable to escape, without friends or security of any kind, I felt very, very small.

I was keeping tears back. Barely. But I wasn't sure how long I could last without breaking down.

It was at that moment that I felt a hand on my shoulder. I looked up into the face of the woman with the short hair.

"Can I ask you a question?" she said.

148

How did she expect me to answer? I shrugged. But I wanted to hear the question. I wanted anything that would distract me from what I feared was coming next. No one treated people like beasts unless they planned to give them a beast's end.

"Do you, perhaps, know the Sumanian sign language?" she asked.

I blinked at her. There was a language of signs?

Her hands flew as she spoke, making signs I did not know. I looked up from them to her face which was smiling but pink with a rosy blush behind her dark skin.

"I know, of course, that most who have no voice have signs of their own that they use to speak with family and friends and I'm sure you have those signs of your own, and I don't mean to insult you or your language."

She had the worried look of someone trying very hard. But what was she trying to do and why did it have her flushed like a summer rose? She seemed too old to blush easily. She smiled again, hopefully, little crow's feet appearing around her eyes as her hands danced before her.

"I learned it in my youth, and while I'm a little rusty I've found it handy through the years. There are few who speak it and few who need to, but if there is any language that is almost universal around the world this is it. You can speak to others of many languages with the signs and ... even better ... you can speak to those with no other voice."

I envied her this and watched her deft hands with wide eyes. Her movements were fluid, and I could tell she had slowed them for me. It would be a gift, indeed, to be able to speak to others that way and have them actually understand. Although, they might be like Mally, and just refuse to watch.

"Of course, when your phoenix rises, you can speak to us all you want," she said.

I looked back at her bright eyes, at her open, hopeful expression. It was so different from the stony look of the Flamerarch in the square when they'd taken me as their captive. I risked a glance behind her and realized the others had settled into small knots of twos or threes. Some slept. Reichus seemed to be standing guard, watching all around the cage. Two others had dice out and were playing a game.

"We have nothing else to do, and who knows how long the sun will be still in the sky or we will be stuck here," she said looking a little abashed. "Would you ... I mean, if it's not insulting ... could you see yourself wanting to learn?"

I felt my jaw drop. She was offering to teach me.

I was nodding before I'd even thought it through, and I smiled back as her grin grew larger.

"My name," she said, annunciating clearly and making slow signs with her hands, "Is Ishta Ukandian."

I tried to copy her. *My name.*

I left off with a shrug and she smiled. "We'll get to that. I'll teach you letters, and you can spell it for me."

I felt my face fall.

"Or not," she was quick to say. "We can give you a nickname until we know your real one. An easy sign. How about this?"

Her hands slowly made a double flower with her fingers spread. "It means Fire Flower. Would that be okay for now?"

I nodded.

My name is Fire Flower. I signed and her encouraging grin made me blush.

We kept it up well into what would have been night, Ishta moving from speaking aloud to quiet murmurs, to eventually speaking only to me with simple phrases in signs between our yawns. And eventually, when she slipped into sleep, curled up on her balled-up jacket, I leaned against the bars and drifted off, too, satisfaction finally drowning out enough of my anxiety to allow it.

We woke to a baton dragged across the bars. The sound barely warned me in time to jerk back from the bars, saving my face. One of the others yelped. He had not been as fast.

We were on our feet before the man with the baton had finished snickering.

"I'll be taking one of you with me," he said, and my belly plunged with fear. It was sure to be me. I was the youngest and smallest. That's usually who people chose if they wanted to make others break.

I held my chin high, refusing to show my fear.

"You," he said, pointing to one of the men whose name I did not know. A pair of other raiders joined him and one of them raised a crossbow, speaking in their guttural language. The original speaker waved him to silence. "We'll take the big one. The rest of you line up along the bars. If you so much as move a hand, my friend here will shoot the person beside you. Do you like your friends? Don't move or their deaths are on your hands."

We lined up, all but Reichus.

"Take me," he said. "If you want someone, I know the most. I'm the most senior. It's me who should go with you, not my men."

"Is that you asking me to shoot one of them?" the raider asked from behind his back. "I thought I was clear. Line up. Don't move. Disobey and someone else dies. I'll add to that, now that you've brought it up. Give advice and someone else dies. Speak at all, and someone else dies."

We were silent then – as I always was – and we stood in line, our hands on the bars, our backs to each other and the center of the cart.

I could hear the raider moving a key in the lock and then the door opening. I felt the breeze of the raider's passage as he walked behind me. I wanted to shiver and didn't dare. I kept feeling like he might touch me at any moment – kill or hurt me. It made me feel like everything inside me had become liquid.

And I wished for Kazmerev. I wished for nightfall. I wished for someone – anyone – to come and save me. And I was so, so glad I couldn't speak because I might have tried, and someone might have died. Beside me, Ishta suppressed a moan of fear. It came out as an aching gasp.

I kept my eyes forward, afraid that if I met hers, we would both lose our ability to stand still.

Footsteps shuffled behind us.

The door swung shut and the key clicked in the lock.

We were silent and still a very, very long time until Reichus whispered, "They're gone."

We dropped our hands, all of us craning to watch where the last figure of a guard slipped through the trees. We had a view of the city from our hilltop, and of the armies between us and them. The raiders had set a camp just out of our earshot. But it was not to that camp that they'd taken our compatriot but up a trail that led into the forest on the north side of the hill.

I could sense the fear in everyone now, and something else – guilt perhaps?

"Marchas was a good man," one of them said eventually.

"Was?" Reichus sounded furious.

"You know it as well as we do," the speaker said with a sigh.

There were no more dice games that night.

Everyone remained silent, their heads tilted as if they were straining their ears for some sound of Marchas. None came.

Eventually, Ishta began to sign again, going through what she'd taught me the night before and adding in new words with whispers to explain them. We worked furtively, as if we were afraid of disturbing the others in their silent vigil. I almost felt guilty learning something so valuable while someone else was being ... what? Tortured? Killed? I did not know. But the worry in Ishta's face lessened when she was working with me and every now and then another of the Flamerarch would glance in our direction and offer a very small, very sad smile. It was for those smiles that I didn't stop.

We worked late into what must have been the night a second time. And even then, I barely managed sleep.

I had always preferred the dawn with its golden promise and pink innocence. Now, I hated it. Perpetually filling the sky, it barred me from my phoenix, from my purpose, from my life. And I wished Mally had never found the Dark Diadem and worn it. But I had to wonder I it was her fault or mine. Perhaps it was only meant for one wearer. Perhaps it was when I wore it, that it broke the sky. We'd been in the tunnels. We had no way to know who was at fault.

These gut-aching thoughts did not help with my rest and after what could only have been an hour or two, I woke and miserably ate the food and drank the water left for us. Reichus offered my portion to me with a bracing clap on the shoulder.

"Don't fear, fledgling. We have you under our wing now."

But though I knew that was meant to be encouraging, it felt anything but. He couldn't stop the raiders anymore than I could. He couldn't force the sun to vacate the sky. He was as helpless as I was.

149

They came for a second member of the Flamerarch not long after that. It was the same as last time – two crossbowmen and one other raider. No one from their nearby camp even looked in our direction as they approached us, as if we were just animals in a pen.

"What are you doing with our friend," Reichus asked when the raiders approached. "Where is he?"

They silently took their places, crossbows aimed up.

"Hands on the bars. Line up. Silence, or death," the leader of the three said, jingling his keys.

Fear sawed through me as I took my place against the bars. The iron was cold against my cheek. It smelled of rust. I could barely breathe. Would we have to endure this day after day as they took us one by one? It was impossible. Intolerable.

Reichus's face was bright red as if swallowing all his protests to stand in place quietly was choking him. He waited, trembling in his place closest to the door making little huffing sounds. I'd noticed him hovering there since yesterday as if daring them to take him next.

This time, I was on the side of the cage that could see everything. Was it cowardly that I wished I had my back to it all like last time? Ishta was behind me. I wished I could see her signing to me, comforting me with her smooth motions.

My heart was in my throat as the cage door swung open, squealing on hinges that needed care, and the raider stepped inside. He made it a single step into the cage when Reichus tackled him, bearing him to the ground. His hands were around the guard's throat.

Something whistled through the air and then one of the Flamerarch was done with a cry of agony.

So much was happening at once that I couldn't catch it all. On the ground,

Reichus struggled with the raider, tearing the key ring from his hands and smashing him in the face with it again and again. The man who had been beside him in line thrashed on the ground, the bolt inside his chest.

I should get to him. I should help him. But I could see the bright bubbles in the blood from his wound. Lung shot. He'd be dead before I could reach him.

I'd barely thought that before the door beside me was blocked by bodies. The rest of the Flamerarch charged the door. The first man through was hit by a second crossbow bolt straight to the throat. But the next two – no three – were out and running at full speed across the grass to the crossbowmen. It takes time to reload a crossbow. Time the raiders didn't have. They were still fumbling with them when the escaped Flame Riders dove onto them, attacking with hands and feet.

Reichus grunted and when I spun to where he was, he had the first guard's throat between his hands. I choked down bile, looking for Ishta. She wasn't there.

I spun back to where the Flamerarch fought the two crossbowmen and found her there, but to my horror, the nearby camp had noticed the commotion and raiders poured from their tents, hastily covering faces and grabbing weapons.

We had but moments.

I should join them, but a moan distracted me, and I found Reichus lying on his back, panting hard as blood bubbled between his lips. The raider beside him was dead. The first man shot by the crossbow was dead. The Flame Rider who'd left our cage first was dead, but Reichus wasn't yet. A knife protruded from his abdomen and he clutched it, panting and gasping.

I hurried to his side, hoping I could help. But I didn't have experience with knife wounds to the abdomen and I had a terrible knowledge of what organs must have been struck by the blade and how unlikely it was that anyone could recover from that, even if they had a proper healer, and a bed, and herbs to use.

Swallowing, I reached to examine him. One bloody hand reached up and grabbed my wrist.

"No," he gasped. "Run. For your life. Go."

I shuddered. He shouldn't die alone. No one should.

His eyes, glassy and unfocused, forced themselves to concentrate on me and with a sudden sharpness he said, "Run!"

To my shame, I scrambled to my feet and stumbled out of the cage.

I didn't pause to try to see what my friends were doing, who was alive, who was dying. Instead, the word "run" filled me and I rushed toward the treeline, stumbling and slipping in my panic.

I didn't reach it.

Forceful hands grabbed me from behind, flinging me to the ground. I hit it hard, wrist twisting under me painfully and head knocking against the ground, and then I was pulled to my feet, one arm forced behind me, screaming in pain at the position.

"Every one of you will pay for this," the voice behind me snarled as I was marched to the cage again and flung inside.

I caught myself on the bars and managed to turn and scramble out of the way as they threw a second Flame Rider in. A man whose name I did not know.

The door slammed behind him, and the key turned in the lock.

"See what your defiance has cost you?" the voice behind the veil growled. "See what you have done?"

And then he was stalking away, leaving us with the dead.

I threw myself at the bars, straining to see. What had happened to the rest of them?

I scanned the ground, counting bodies. There were almost as many raiders down as Flamerarch. Had none but me and this one other man survived?

My heart froze in my chest.

Where was Ishta?

I had to catch my weight on the bars when I finally found her. They were marching her between two of them down the path where the other man had disappeared yesterday.

I choked on a sob. I had no words for what I felt then. Not in my head and not in my hands. And that felt right because no words could be enough.

150

There's no dignified way to lay out bodies in a cage, but we did our best, retreating to the other end of it when we were done. The last of the Flamerarch gathered up the ashes in Reichus's hand and put them carefully in a handkerchief and into his pocket. Reichus's phoenix would need a new heart to rise in. The thought made my throat tight.

The raiders did not come for their own dead. Not the man in the cage, nor the crossbowmen on the grass, though the others killed closer to their camp were gathered up and taken away. What kind of monsters didn't see to their own dead?

They didn't come with food or water, either.

They just left us there in the horror of the remains of what and who had happened.

My guts were painful knots and I had already cried until my eyes were puffy when, after what must have been many hours, the last of the Flamerarch spoke to me.

"I'm Luca," he said in a calm voice, his brown eyes finding mine. He was probably double my age. Calm and gentle. Not at all what I'd expected when I'd met them in the square with their demands and delays.

I wondered if Reichus had regretted taking me as a hostage after how this turned out. He was a good man, I thought, so he probably had. He was also a smart man. He must have realized, as I did, that if he hadn't taken Lady Lightland from Gundt, then it would be my friends who were surrounded and captured by these raiders and not him and his people.

My hands began to quiver at the thought of "his people." Ishta had been so kind to me. In a time when anyone ought to be terrified out of their minds, she had taken me under her wing and spent every spare moment offering me a gift. And now she was out there somewhere, and I didn't know what they were doing to her.

I felt my jaw begin to quiver before the first tear fell.

"Here now, little sister," Luca said, sounding worried. "Here now. Keep courage."

There were worry lines etching his forehead and a deep one between his brows, but he managed a small smile of encouragement for me.

"What nickname did she give you? I heard her saying something about that."

I made the sign for Fire Flower and he imitated it.

"I like that. It makes me think of my Bromingaard. My phoenix," he added as if he needed to explain that. He kept my gaze as he spoke, gentle and kind, like a parent trying to draw a shaken child back out of themselves. "I was a farmer before I met him. Our land was rocky and unproductive and there were too many mouths to feed from it. I think I was twelve. Young, even for a Fledgling. We saw a bright light fall from heaven. My mother and step-father thought it an ill omen, but I was not afraid. I climbed through the oak forest and up the bluffs and I found him there – dying. Poor man. Baffler, they called him. Bromingaard doesn't like to talk much about him, it still makes him sad, but that much I know. He was old. It was his heart, I think. His last words were a plea that I care for his friend and then he shoved the ashes into my hands as his eyes glazed over. I was still looking for his friend, worried there was someone else dying on the edge of the bluffs, when Bromingaard bloomed in my heart."

He paused, smiling past me with an expression of such longing sadness at the never-ending dawn sky.

"You know how that is. How it changes you. I went to the city, and I found the Flamerarch. They took me in, impoverished though I was, and all for Bromingaard. All for him. They have been my family and my home."

Now, he turned his gaze to me.

"We would have been kind to you. I hope you know that. Reichus had hoped to protect you in the escape attempt. He told us to shield you if we could."

I swallowed, touched that they had cared even then. They must have planned it while I slept.

"If you get the chance to flee, then go," his eyes hardened. "Don't worry about me. Don't come back for me. Just go. Find the Flamerarch. I swear they will guard you. Our hostility to the Son of Chaos shouldn't cloud your eyes to how we care about other phoenixes."

If I could have spoken, I might have asked why they insisted on dueling mine if that were the case, but it was turning out that in this – as in so many things – Kazmerev was right. There were layers to people. They could be good and still not see eye-to-eye with me. They could be nuanced. It would be easier if they were not.

"If you find them. Tell them ..." he paused, not sure how to go on. "If you can find them at night so your phoenix can speak, tell them you are claw-marked. It means you have fought side by side with the Flamerarch. It means you're under our protection. Tell them it's been granted by the authority of Luca Lightheart and Reichus Klazmetti. They won't deny us, and so they won't deny you, either. You understand?"

I nodded and he reached out to squeeze my shoulder. The gesture was so like

Reichus's that I almost burst into tears. I managed to hold them off until after Luca had fallen asleep.

And then it was just me, alone in a never-ending, aching dawn, watching as kindhearted people gave me the last things they had to give – instruction, comfort, hope. And I could give them nothing in return.

I put my face in my hands and sobbed in silence.

151

They came for Luca when we woke. He clasped my shoulder and whispered his farewell while they were still approaching.

"Keep hope, little sister. At any time, night may fall."

I sucked in a silent sob, and he gripped a little harder.

"Courage."

And then they were there, and he stood in front of the door with his hands above his head, offering himself in my place. And I hated myself for not being able to save him, for not knowing how to help, for not knowing what to do.

They took him away in silence.

They did not leave food or water. My throat ached with thirsting. And the bodies of friends and enemies buzzed with flies.

I put my face in my hands, and to my shame, I gave in to despair.

It was likely hours later – though I had no way to judge – that I hear a whispered hiss.

I ignored it at first. There were no good surprises in this place. Perhaps a snake was entering the cage, and if this was the case, then I could only hope that its venom killed quickly – and if it did, then I hoped it would bite me soon.

The hissing came again, more insistent this time.

What a demanding snake. I sighed and looked up.

"Sersha." The sound was barely even a whisper. It was coming from the bars behind my back. "Don't turn. Don't move."

I did not move.

But I knew that voice.

My lower lip began to quiver with hope I didn't dare feel. I couldn't have seen him even if I'd turned around. My eyes were too glassy with sudden, aching relief.

Judicus was here. Everything would be fine. He always made everything fine.

"It's very hard to hide in endless dawn. Listen. In a moment, I will open the door to your cage. And then we will have to run as you've never run before. I have a little place prepared – a hiding place, but we have to get to it, and we have to be both fast and also leave no trail. Can you run?"

I nodded my head.

"Head due east. I will be behind you, guarding your back. Do you know where the east is?"

A silly question in an endless dawn. I just had to head directly for the golden glow in the sky.

I nodded. I couldn't believe he was here. I couldn't believe he had come for me. He was meant to be with the ai'sletta. He was meant to be protecting her.

And yet he'd come for *me.*

And the weight of that – the sheer incredibility that I might be saved out of this – made it hard to breathe.

I heard a sound that sounded like vomiting behind me. And then his voice – a little unsteady – whispered, "Are you ready?"

I nodded again.

A black rope shot out like the snake I thought I'd heard, and the lock clicked and the door fell open.

I found my feet immediately, scrambling for the door. I was out of it, dropping to the ground in a shot and spinning to find the east.

And there he was.

His eye was still bandaged. He'd scrubbed the blood and grime from his face, but his loose black hair was wild and his face ghostly pale, purple shadows under the eye that wasn't bandaged, and grim lines around his set mouth. They softened when he saw me, and his single eye burned with some emotion I couldn't read.

I had the strangest urge to throw myself in his arms.

And then he was shoving me behind him with a whisper of, "East. Run."

There was a shout in the camp.

I ran.

Judicus's medallion bounced on my chest. My throat ached, dry, and raw, and agonizing.

And I ran.

I hit the forest with a crash, tree limbs dragging against me, shouts behind me. But I did not look back. If I didn't trust Judicus knew what he was doing, we would both be dead. I pelted through the woods, barely managing not to hook a toe in a root or find myself tangled in the creeping undergrowth that filled this forest. All those days of my childhood running free in the forest with Mally and her siblings were finally benefiting me. I found a rabbit trail running east and stayed on it, swift as I could be.

The shouts behind me had turned to screams, barely muffled at all by the dense forest.

I did not dare to stop running, even when the screams cut off one by one and all I could hear was my own crashing through the forest and my agonized breath sawing through my raw throat.

Worry gripped me.

What if one of those screams had been Judicus?

What if he was even now lying on the ground back there, his single eye staring up at the dawn, thinking of me abandoning him.

I couldn't take it anymore.

I looked over my shoulder.

He was right there. Only paces behind me. I stumbled and he somehow crossed the distance and caught me, keeping me upright and steering me with him off the rabbit path. We ran under coniferous trees wide enough to have enough clear space beneath them to keep the pace.

There was another shout from behind us and a call in return.

They were giving chase.

We ran – sometimes side by side, sometimes one before the other.

I couldn't go on much further. I could feel my body faltering. No water in more than a day. No food. I was weak. It was showing.

With all my stubborn strength, I willed myself to keep going, to push through the pain in my limbs and throat.

But the shouts were getting closer and Judicus showed no signs of slowing.

They would overtake us.

I could feel them behind me, feel their ill intent crawling up my spine.

And then suddenly Judicus grabbed my hand, and his words were gasps. "When I say, jump, you must."

And then a heartbeat and we were still running, ducking under the clawing limbs of a massive conifer.

"Jump."

And even though it seemed silly, I did, only to find that the ground on the other side of the tree disappeared in a cliff, and we were sailing over the cliff, the wind snatching at us, a scream stuck in my throat, my legs and arms clawing uselessly for purchase.

And then something like a wide belt snatched at me and I was yanked backward.

I waited, ready to find my skull cracked against the rock wall.

Instead, we were pulled into a crevice that became a shallow cave and I found myself nestled against Judicus in safety, trying to catch my breath while his black ropes of magic held us tight against the rock, safe from view.

Above us, our pursuers were cursing. And I didn't dare breathe.

152

We were perfectly still for so long that my joints began to stiffen in our awkward position. I was pushed right up against Judicus, and I could feel his every angular edge pressed against me. He was too thin. He needed to eat more and vomit less.

His breathing eventually slowed from gasping, frantic breaths to something slow and steady. My own breath slowed to match his. He was warmer than I'd expected and after the cold days in the cage, the warmth and the soft *wuffs* of his breath soothed me to the point that I began to drowse, my head dropping to my chest just before he coughed awkwardly.

"I think they're gone," he whispered. "They must believe we plummeted all the way into the ravine. I'm going to unweave the ropes and set you free."

He'd already set me free, though. Just when I thought I was sure to die horribly.

I blinked and held in a trembling sob that insisted it wanted to come out. Now was not the time to cry. Not now that I was somewhat safe. It made no sense to break down *afterward* when I'd been strong during it all. But now it was all coming back to me, feeling like a punch to my middle. My guts clenched inside, singing with nerves. What about Ishta? And Luca? Was it too late to go back for them?

The ropes unwound slowly, and I fought against the silent tears dripping down my nose.

It was probably too late. But what if it wasn't, and I left them there?

There was a whole army back there. If we went back, we'd both be killed, too.

I bit my lip, concentrating on the smell of the small depression in the rock – dank and fecund, the scent of earth and moss. Familiar smells. Smells of forest and safety.

Closed my eyes and focused on the sound of wind shaking the leaves on the trees above the bluff, their shallow clatter familiar.

Felt the cold as Judicus disentangled himself from me.

Heard his gasp, his face so close to mine that I felt the air suck past as he inhaled.

My eyes shot open to find him leaning in from beside me, sheltering me from the drop with his own body. Worry stretched the skin of his face tight as he reached up and swiped a tear from my face with the pad of a thumb.

"Did I hurt you?" he whispered. "I didn't mean to."

I shook my head vehemently.

"But something did." He bit his lip and dragged a hand through his hair. "Come. I have a place for you to rest."

He slowly moved past me, careful not to touch me, despite the tightness of the space, one hand was held out as if to ward against it – or to reassure me that he meant no harm. How broken did he think I was?

Better question, how broken was I?

I was realizing, to my deep chagrin, that what I'd thought of as a harsh childhood of washing dishes, sleeping in the back in a tiny space carved out from among my cousins, being teased for being voiceless, generally being overlooked – well, it turned out it was actually quite a sheltered life. Compared to this. Compared to how bad things could go.

I'd made friends and watched them die.

I'd made friends and watched them give themselves trying to protect me.

My own Aunt Danna gave herself for others.

And here was Judicus giving himself for me. Who had he left behind to come to my rescue? He hadn't even risked it all for his own sister. Why had he done it now, when he must have known it was the wrong choice?

I bit my lip so hard I tasted blood.

Stop being so self-absorbed, Sersha.

Judicus had been working while I fretted, moving rocks I thought were part of the bluff, but were actually disguising a deeper cave behind this depression.

"Here," he murmured when he was done, offering me a hand as he led the way into the opening he'd created.

It was very tight.

Tight enough that it squeezed against my hips, and I had to wriggle to get through the entrance and follow him into a crack of rock that turned abruptly and began to descend. The air of the cavern was cold on my face. The scent of it was an unfamiliar mineral smell that turned my belly.

I stopped. My heart raced so tight in my chest I was afraid it would burst. I had never liked tight spaces. I was going to be trapped. I was going to die like a fly caught in honey.

"It's okay, Sersha. It's just tight here. It opens up in a moment," Judicus murmured.

I clutched his hand, gulping down air to steady myself, and willed my steps forward. At least in the dark, no one could see me cry.

At last, when I wiggled forward, I reached a spot where the rocks no longer squeezed me, though the ground made me feel unsteady.

"Wait here," Judicus whispered, planting my hand against a rock.

My breath sawed in my lungs. I couldn't. I couldn't wait in the dark.

"I'm not going anywhere. Don't panic. I just need to light the lantern," Judicus whispered. "Here, I'll speak to you while I work. Then you'll know I'm near. I found the cave with my ropes while I was looking for a place to hide you. We can't outrun pursuit right now and they're sprawled out across the countryside – armies upon armies. The logistics must be a nightmare. And the people of Briccatore are broken. They don't dare stand up against such numbers. It's a nightmare. Which is why I knew that if I could free you, we'd have to hide for a bit – holed up somewhere secret. It's nearly impossible to get into this place without knowing it's here, so I think we'll be safe."

He was striking his flint as he whispered, and he sighed in relief as the spark finally took and he lit the wick.

"What do you think?"

153

He lifted the lantern high, his smile as nervous and broken as my answering one must be, but his light illuminated a space in the rock that was almost a room. On one wall, water flowed in a slick coating that could possibly be caught and contained if one was very patient. It flowed in a runnel and then out a crack, forming a sluggish stream. The roof was too high up to see, the mock-room being far taller than it was wide. The floor laid out in layers of shallow steps, none wider than I was, leading up from where I stood. On the uppermost one, a pack was set with a few supplies around it.

"We'll have to share, I'm afraid," Judicus said. "I didn't have time to gather anything. If the old man hadn't offered me his pack, we'd be in real trouble.

The old man?

"He said his name was Jastomen," Judicus explained. He looked awkward and his smile was a little too tenuous, a little too bright as if he was trying to talk a child from falling off a ladder they should never have climbed. "I left the ai'sletta with them on their ship. I hope you don't think I abandoned her." He ran a hand through his hair, momentarily looking guilty instead of worried. "I suppose I did abandon her. But I abandoned her to Gundt and the spies of the Grand Hadri. Together they should be able to protect her, hide her, get her far from here. And she can put on the crown any time and Gundt can summon his phoenix so – well, the fact that they haven't done that must mean everything is fine. Sorry. I babble when I'm nervous."

Why would he be nervous?

He was staring at my hand. It was still right where he left it on the wall.

Oh.

I was scaring him. Probably because I was still weeping silently, and I hadn't moved. If there was one rule that all men followed it was that weeping women made them nervous.

I drew in a long breath and took a stumbling step forward. He caught me by the elbows and carefully steered to me a step-like ledge that formed a smooth seat. Someone had stacked wood beside it. It looked as if a giant had ripped the wood apart and I was about to wonder about that when he absently began to pile it up for a fire – using his ropes to work instead of his hands.

My eyebrows rose and he noticed enough to flush.

"Oh. Yes. I'm feeling better. It took a while, but my strength is coming back. You didn't meet me at my best. I mean, not just that I was mourning, but I wasn't at full magical strength. I was surviving on the dregs. It takes something out of a man to nearly die, if you know what I mean."

I stopped crying then because my eyes were so wide.

Absently, I made the gestures Ishta had taught me to say, *"I hadn't thought."*

Judicus dropped the wood and let out a huff of breath that tickled my ears in a funny way. He seemed pleased.

"That's Sumanian sign language."

Now it was my turn to take a surprised breath, but he was grinning boyishly, dropping the wood, and scrambling to the pack. He pulled out a small book and hurried over to show it to me, his face so flushed that his translucent skin almost had life in it.

"Look. Jastomen gave it to me, too. 'You'll be wanting this,' he told me. Generous man. I can never thank him enough."

He opened the book, and I didn't need to know how to read to see what he was showing me. Every word in the book had a picture beside it – a picture of the signs Ishta had been so carefully teaching me.

"How?" I signed.

And Judicus laughed with apparent delight. "Oh, he had four trunks of books with him on the ship already. And he was moaning that he had only had time to gather his emergency stash. He pulled this one out from the top trunk. I thought he was wasting time I didn't have – and so did Prexav – until he showed it to me." His bright cheeks were almost purple now, he was flushing so hard. And this time, his hands moved as he spoke, making the signs of each word he spoke – proving he knew even more signs than I did. "The hillside where they kept you captive wasn't far. I should have been able to reach it the first day. Everyone knew where you'd been taken. It was no mystery. But it took time to move without being seen. To gather food. To gather information. And without the cover of night, it was even harder. I had to hide where I could. And I had to pass the time while I waited. I read the book. I hope you're not angry. I swear, I didn't delay."

I shook my head. *"No. No need for ..."* I paused, not knowing the sign.

"Guilt?" he asked, making a complicated gesture.

"How can you know so many?" I signed.

He grinned again and then schooled his face and ducked his head as if he was ashamed of himself for his delight.

"I have a very good memory," he admitted. "If I read a thing, I can recall it exactly. I read the whole book."

He read the whole book.

I stared at him, my mouth dropping open.

Shyly, biting his lip, he looked up, and then he tried a hopeful smile. "I did it so I can hear you. I hate not knowing what you want to say."

"Thank you," I signed. And I had so much to say and not enough ability to say it all, so I tried the thing most on my mind. "You should not have come for me."

His smile faded. But it wasn't guilt that replaced it, or hurt, or anything else I expected. It was a deep burning look I couldn't read at all – certainty, perhaps?

"I don't take my vows lightly, Sersha. When you joined my coterie, I vowed to protect and provide for you."

I shook my head. The idea was too big for words. The commitment too strong.

"Listen," And now he did sound a little flustered and he busied himself with fixing the wood he'd been piling and lighting a fire instead of looking at me. "Most people would probably say I did the wrong thing. I understand that. I should have stayed with the ai'sletta. You were right that you were the most expendable member of our party." He glanced at me guiltily but pressed on, lighting the kindling for the fire. "It made sense to let you offer yourself to the Flamerarch as a hostage. You were right to choose that. But I was also right to come back for you. It's not just that you are owed my fidelity – though you are. I do not take my vows lightly, Sersha, I am not that kind of man. My father died standing on principle and I will die the same way."

His teeth snapped while he said that as if someone was going to run him through right there. I leaned back from the intensity of it. The first flames of the fire leapt up, excited to warm us and fill the small cave with light. Smoke wafted up into a crack I hadn't noticed over the fire.

"But it's more than that." His eyes met mine. And they burned more than any phoenix ever had. "I am your friend, Sersha. And I couldn't bear the thought of someone like you being ripped apart by your enemies, peering out into the dawn waiting to be saved, and having no one come for you. I just couldn't. And if you don't like that, then I don't care, because it's what I chose."

I made a sign.

"That one's not in the book." His jaw was set, and his eyes looked glassy. He wouldn't look at my face.

I made it again.

His face slumped like he was barely holding himself together.

"*Your name,*" I signed. I'd made a fist with another hand holding it. To me, that's who he was. The person who held other people together.

He met my eyes and I signed again, this time with tears in mine.

"*Thank you,*" I signed and then I signed the name I'd given him. "Thank you for my life."

His answering breath was a shuddering inhale, but he nodded and stared at the fire until he could control his face again and meet my hopeful smile with one of his own.

154

We planned to wait three days in the cave.

Fortunately, Judicus had planned for everything, including a small cave to the side with a very tight squeeze and a wide crack running through it that could be used for relieving ourselves.

He had gathered enough firewood that if we were very, very careful and kept our fire small it should last until the end of the three days. That's how long he thought it would take to throw any pursuers off our tracks. With the fire so small, we had to huddle close together, but neither of us seemed to mind.

Judicus shyly shared the bread and dry fruit he had stolen, his expression downcast when he admitted to pilfering both things from abandoned carts in the city.

"I could hardly pay a shopkeeper who was not there, but it still wasn't mine to take," he said sadly.

And he held me the first night when I cried and cried for Ishta, and Luca, and Reichus.

"I knew Reichus," he said into my hair, guessing easily why I was distressed. "He wasn't my favorite person, but he was a loyal man. He stuck with those he gave his commitments to. Did he protect you?"

At my nod, he held me a little tighter. "In some ways, he was a *good* man."

It seemed like a concession, like he didn't want to admit it but was doing it for my sake.

"*What happened to your eye?*" I asked in sign, when I was done sobbing my heart out. I had been worried about it since the moment I saw it. What if he'd lost the eye? Would it affect his rope work? Was he suffering because of it?

He looked away and then back at me, biting his lip. "Does it look bad?"

It looked terrible. I just nodded and offered to change his bandage.

I unwound it gently while he told me what happened.

"The Stryxex rider got a lucky strike in while I was strangling his mount. I think I killed the thing, but I don't know."

Was that the one I saw, I wondered, or did the rider have a new mount by then? I didn't mention it. I didn't want him to think he'd been injured for nothing.

"Gundt says it will heal. He thought so, at least. He stitched it. Did you know he was good with a needle? I didn't expect him to be so clever with it. The wound hurt, but I was too worried about other things to worry about it at the time. I can still see through the eye."

He was rambling. I'd noticed he did that when he was nervous.

Remarkably, the blade really hadn't hit his actual eye, though the wound above and below it was deep, and I could see why it had been bandaged. The relief I felt at that was profound. I cleaned it with care while Judicus rambled about wounds he'd seen that had gone bad and then I bandaged it again.

He was going to have a very pronounced scar. Provided it really did heal well.

There was a good chance it would. Gundt had stitched it well.

I patted him on the arm when I was done and signed, "*All good.*"

He seemed nearly as relieved by the news as I had been when I saw his eye was whole.

After that, we settled into practicing our Sumerian sign together.

"My father was a duke," he said, signing the words as he spoke to reinforce them for both of us. "He was well respected and served the Grand Hadri, but over time, he began to realize what horrors that man wreaked upon his people. He did not treat the common people with justice, nor anyone else if he could help it. Corruption was rife. There were no challengers to his authority and no way to replace him with anyone better. My father could have lived easily. As a favorite of the Grand Hadri, he had everything we needed. Wealth. Estates. Horses and ships. Everything. He could have raised us in peace."

"But he did not?" I asked with my hands.

Judicus smiled slightly. He was very happy that I could speak back to him, now, but the smile washed away into something more wistful as he looked into the distance.

"He gathered like-minded people and paid others. They fought and won. He risked everything to topple the Grand Hadri and wrest control of his lands from him. My father sacrificed so much. He even lost the respect and loyalty of his younger brother. He was Grand Hadri for exactly one year, and in that time, he turned back a dozen assassination attempts including one from his own younger brother. I still remember the look on his face the night he returned home from imprisoning my uncle – the one you may remember as Captain Rackham." He spelled Rackham out in sign letters. I still struggled with those and only caught a few of them. Judicus had drilled me on them that morning and while I could associate the signs with letters, that didn't mean I could blend them into words. "Rackham became a catalyst for everyone who wanted my father's rule to end. My father was a favorite of the common folk, finally judging their cases justly and removing any officials who took bribes or imprisoned their rivals, but he made things harder for important people. Worse, it turned out that most people like injustice in the end. They like corruption. They don't want to suffer the pinch of doing things honestly. A single year of purging that was enough for his enemies to sway the crowds. They broke my uncle out of prison, overthrew my father, and executed him in a single day."

He stared at the fire for a long moment, and I realized he was controlling his breathing, slowly bringing it in and out. How young had he been when he first was forced to learn that trick?

"They spared the family. At my uncle's insistence."

Another long pause as his face twisted with grief and fury and then his long slow breaths brought him back to calm.

"And so began the life I have now. A life of carefulness, hiding my true thoughts and hopes, dedicated study to become the very best, friendlessness, and sometimes hopelessness. I have known since I was eleven years old that my mother and sister might be killed at any moment. One wrong word, one slip, one failure to smile could be their end. They have been nothing but bargaining pieces for my uncle, convenient to keep – for now. I came looking for the ai'sletta in the hopes of freeing them. If I found her and brought her to my uncle, he would have to free them. And he would be bound to give me a coterie and the freedom to do as I pleased. A greater law than his would compel him. It was worth risking everything for. Worth dying for."

This pause was even longer than the others, but I sat very still as he mulled on his own thoughts. He had always given me the gift of trying to listen to me. I could surely do the same for him.

"But you know that, Sersha," he said, finally looking back at me as his hands flew through the signs. "Don't you? It's why you left Landsfall with me. You wanted freedom, too. You wanted to be more than a playing piece for your aunt."

I nodded and he ran his hands through his hair the way he did when he was upset.

"We have that in common," he said. "Don't we?"

"*We have that in common,"* I agreed in sign.

His fingers caught in his hair, and he laughed ruefully. "How are you at cutting hair? This has been growing for a long time.

"*Do you have ..."* I shook my head and tried to show a sign for scissors.

He was already shaking his head looking amused. "No. Only a knife."

"*I can try,"* I signed back. I did not think I could manage it with only a knife, but he looked so miserable that I had to try.

Which was how I found myself with his large belt knife and a piece of wood, laying the hair over the wood and sawing it with the knife. In the end, I didn't get it very short. But the tangles were gone, leaving it to his shoulders and though the cut was not terribly even, the wildness of it seemed to suit him.

"Thank you," he said.

"*You are welcome,"* I signed, pleased to be able to do it.

I was so pleased, that as we settled down for the night – forced to share his single blanket with our backs to one another – I realized I would be happy to stay here in this cave forever, even if it meant eating nothing but dried fruit and old bread. And I wondered if there would ever be a world where people like Judicus and me could live in peace, and work side by side, and talk together without the constant knowledge that soon we must fight and maybe even die to save the world from the people so bent on breaking it.

It was a hopeful thought and I clung to it as I drifted off to sleep to the sound of Judicus's even breathing.

155

A lot can be said in three days.

I told Judicus about living in Landsfall. About what I liked about it – the freedom of running in the woods and along the shore, the warm fires in midwinter, the smell of cedars, the way the pebbles on the beach felt in my hands, and the way the villagers sang Frostcome songs. And what I hated – raiders threatening our village, hard winters, drought in summer, chapped skin from washing dishes, uncertainty about my future, being overlooked.

He told me about training as a rope worker. About endless drills and merciless masters – stories that were more interesting to hear about than to live through, like the time he had to spin a rope and walk balanced along it over the school's great hall before he was allowed to set foot in it again. It was where every meal was served, and it took him four days to manage the feat. Even then, he was the fastest among his cohort.

He told me about being sent with the military to provide rope work service as part of his training – I hadn't expected that at all. About serving aboard ship and how ill it made him. He looked green just describing it – and not only when he told me about vomiting day and night for three weeks, his nose filled with the brine of the sea and scent of rotting fish – but also when his voice went quiet, and he told me about being asked to hold the mast together with his ropework after it was broken by a ship with a catapult aboard. How he'd had to keep it stationary for three long weeks as they sailed to port.

He spoke of his father and how he missed him, barely able to choke out the words as he stared into the fire. About his constant, gnawing, never-ending worry about his mother and sister.

He'd had no real friends, I realized. As he spoke of his loneliness, my own childhood with my cousins began to look better. A least I'd had light teasing and warm hugs, endless labor, but laughter at the end of a hard day. Mally frustrated me, and manipulated me, and used me – but she was also funny, and clever, and interesting to share a room with. He'd had none of those things. And while my future had always seemed bleak, I'd had a place to live, and food to eat, and no true worry for my family except the worry of raiders. I'd lived almost contentedly.

Judicus, on the other hand, had been ill with worry for most of his life, and just ill for the rest of it, the burden of his family thrust onto his shoulders the moment his father died.

It gave me a new appreciation for him – for how he treated us as his coterie, for the respect he showed everyone, and the kindness he showed me. I was starting to realize that his firm certainty and listening ear were hard-won traits born of a life of having to bend to others, and never having his own voice heard.

He could have been so much less than this. And he wasn't.

It was the evening of the second day, all talk of our pasts behind us, that Judicus sat by the fire, playing a game on his hands with his magical ropes. It looked like a game of cat's cradle, but he made it with ever increasingly difficult knots, and twists, and weavings, practicing his dexterity with it.

"It seems to me, Sersha," he said after a few minutes at it. "That you want to save the world. And that nothing anyone else does will prevent it."

He looked up and I licked my lips. *Did* I want to save the world? I didn't know.

He waited, watching me. And I felt my cheeks grow hot as – for the first time in my life – I was required to give an answer beyond a nod, or head shake, or shrug. I did not want to answer. It would be so easy to deflect his question with a shield of words. I could say "Do you not want that?" or I could say "What do you want?" or I could say "What kind of person would I be if I didn't?"

And if I did that, it would neatly turn aside his question and he'd have to press me for an answer. It would be so easy. I'd watched people do it all my life.

My lips parted and my breath hitched as I prepared to do it, too, but at the last second, I dropped my hands.

I finally had a voice. I finally had a way to communicate. And that meant I would be – in his eyes – the sum of my words. Did I want to begin by beating him back and fending him off? Or did I want to begin by letting him inside my heart?

"It's fine, Sersha," he said after a moment with a sad smile on his face. "Just because you can speak to me now doesn't mean you owe me answers."

I shook my head immediately. I did owe him answers. But I didn't know what answer to give.

I hugged myself as I tried to think it through.

Did I really want to save the world? I wanted to save the phoenixes because that meant Kazmerev, too. That alone was heavy enough. But did I want to save the whole world? I didn't know. But I owed it to him to know.

"Please, don't push yourself," he said, but his eyes were cooler now as he studied his tiny ropes, spinning them and tangling them to form patterns and knots.

This wasn't working!

Silence, I realized, when you had the option of breaking it, was its own answer.

Deliberately, I kneeled to join him at his level. He was propped up in a sitting position, ankles crossed and knees high with his hands between them as he hunched over his work.

I put my hand on his wrist and his ropes fell and faded to nothing.

His eyes met mine and his head tilted to the side.

"*Please,*" I signed. "*Please, hear my heart.*"

He wetted his lips and then caught one between his teeth and it looked like he was controlling some kind of emotion.

"I am listening, Sersha."

"*I do not know what I want,*" I signed. "*But I owe you better than that. I owe you what is in my heart.*"

He opened his mouth. Probably to tell me again that I didn't have to say anything. I lifted my hand to stop him. I did need to say something.

"*I know that I want ...*" I paused here. I didn't have a word for phoenix. I tried to make one, showing a fire and a bird. It was frustrating to work with a limited number of words. "*...phoenixes to be safe.*"

He nodded, following along. He'd lost the coolness in his expression, falling into an engrossed expression.

"*I know I want your sister to be safe,*" I signed, reminding him I was with him in his goals. The corners of his mouth lifted slightly but he still seemed sad.

"*I know I want my cousin to be safe.*" Although whether Mally could ever be kept safe was another matter. Surely, if she were locked in a secure tower, she would find a way to immediately cause a problem within that made it a trap and not a defense.

He nodded seriously to that.

"*I know I want Judicus to be safe,*" I said and my cheeks flushed at that. Would he consider that not my business?

"You don't have to be worried about that," he said, waving a hand dismissively.

But that was the thing about words. You could let them fail without achieving their purpose. But that was its own kind of cowardice.

I took a deep breath and I signed, "*I will always worry about that.*"

He swallowed and gazed at me for a long time before he nodded.

"*I just don't know what I will have to do to make these things happen.*"

He nodded in understanding. And I thought that might be because he felt the same way, because, like me, he was starting to see that we might not get everything we wanted and that the cost for just one piece of it might be too high.

"Then we need to plan for what comes next," he said quietly. "And I think that if you want to save phoenixes, and my sister, and your cousin, then you are aligned with me." He blushed a little and gave me a chagrined smile when he said. "I want to save the world – as arrogant as that sounds."

"*You do?*" I signed.

"My father gave his life to make things fair for just a year. Who would I be if I wasn't willing to try for at least that?"

I swallowed. His words felt heavy. They sat on my chest like rocks.

"But these things aren't done without plans. We know where the players are – Mally, the raiders, the puppet Grand Hadri, and the ones holding her strings. We know that they have some idea for allying the raiders to the people here and the

Stryxex. But that seems needlessly complex. What do they need all these pieces for if their only goal is power? Why kidnap the Flamerarch and kill them? Why take Briccatore? Why kill the phoenixes systematically?"

Oh. And that was when I realized that I had the words now to tell him about the mural we'd seen in under the temple of the Cult of Tattered Ribbons.

Even with a limited number of words, it made a chilling tale.

When I was finished, he let out a long, gusting sigh, ran his hands through his shortened hair, and looked at them in surprise when they fell through more quickly than usual.

After a moment of staring at them as if they didn't belong to him, he met my eyes and said, "Try to remember. What did the place in the mural where they were making the phoenixes look like? Was there a building? A spire? An altar?"

I wracked my brains, trying to remember. I hadn't noticed. There had been a rent in the earth. I relayed that, but he waited, hoping, I supposed, that there might be something more. I screwed up my face and thought and then I paused. There had been a marking on the tree beside the raider holding the newly birthed Stryxex, hadn't there been? The same symbol I'd seen on hands and knuckles of the raiders tattooed there. The same symbol I'd seen on some of their clothing when they raided Landsfall, though I didn't remember seeing it since.

Carefully, I took a piece of kindling, and in the ashes on the edge of the fire, I drew it as best as I could remember.

Beside me, Judicus gasped.

"Well," he said. "Well then."

And his stunned silence was like the silence beside a death bed.

156

"*What is it?*" I asked, my hands flying through the signs. It was such a relief to get to ask in moments like this instead of having to wait for information to be volunteered or for someone else to voice the question. "*Judicus? What is it?*"

He opened his mouth about to answer and then he gasped, shrinking back and I spun to follow his gaze. Something small and dark slid across the floor.

I leapt to my feet, glad I couldn't shriek and give us away. I was terrified of snakes.

My eyes danced around the cave, as if I could find something high to get up on, as I slid my feet backward, catching my bottom lip between my teeth.

Please don't notice me. Please.

It wasn't until Judicus stood, hand thrust out before him and a look on his face of indecision, that I realized it wasn't a snake at all.

It was a rope slinking into our cave. A rope just like the ones he wove, searching, questing.

I swallowed and rushed to where the blanket was crumpled by the fire. We'd have to run. We'd need the blanket and the pack.

My movement drew its attention and it raced toward me.

Judicus cursed and began signing rapidly.

"*If I touch it with my ropes, the,*" something, I didn't know this sign, "*will know. Worse, if he's ever met me before, he will know that it is me. I must not speak. If it touches you, do not breathe.*"

Well, there were other ways to deal with things than using magic. He might have forgotten that.

I flung the blanket over the rope as if it were a real snake. That should confuse it for a moment. I ran to the pack, scooping it up. Fortunately, Judicus was so tidy that he returned everything to the pack the moment he was done using it.

I flung the straps over my shoulders and spun just as the rope finally disentangled from the blanket and began to work its way to me.

"Try not to move too quickly," Judicus signed.

But I couldn't just stay still. Not when all my instincts were screaming at me to run. I edged around the cave, slowly, the rope following me as if it could sense me, and Judicus following us both. Ropes tangled and sprang from his hands just to tangle again as if he were desperate to put them to use and barely restraining himself.

The rope of magic extended itself suddenly, racing across the floor toward me and then twisting around my ankle. I froze and gasped. What if it climbed up and dove down my open mouth? I shut it with a click.

The rope released my ankle and swayed upward like I imagined snakes would do in my worst daydreams. It slowly reached my waist, my chest, and when it was at the level of my face it swayed forward, almost kissing my nose. I watched it, ill with the thought of being touched by it, too afraid to move.

And then Judicus struck like a pouncing cat, grabbing the rope with his hand and flinging it aside. He stumbled forward, grabbed my arm, and hauled me behind him, through the crack in the rock that led to where we'd been relieving ourselves.

Behind us, I heard a distant cry.

Whether the maker of the rope knew who we were or not, he knew that someone was here. And he was coming for us.

Our breath sawed through our lungs.

"Jump here," Judicus said. He'd had the sense to bring the lantern, but it jangled wildly, the light bouncing around the room making terrible laughing shadows, leaping lights, and cloaking the crevices, changes in the grade of the floor, and obstacles.

I jumped, my dark shadow long and grasping in front of me as Judicus followed me with the light. I wanted to ask where we were going and if there was a way out. There was no time to stop and sign.

"Someone hunts us," he said, and he sounded shaken. "Someone powerful. If I'd touched his rope with mine, I might have known who, but then he'd certainly know who I was. This way, I might as easily be a mountain cat as a man."

Were there mountain cats here? And if there were, could we avoid them?

I wasn't sure I wanted an answer for that.

"There's a back door through here, but it's going to be a tight squeeze. Here. Hold up."

I waited as he opened the pack on my back and shoved the blanket inside. It wasn't like him not to fold it, but his eyes were wide and his hands fumbling.

"He's sure to have others with him. And even if he doesn't, he will try to capture us. We can't afford to let him. If he gets close, I'll attack him and you ... well, run as best as you can. You need to promise me you will."

He was done securing my straps.

I made a quick sign. *"No. I will not leave you."*

"You might have to." We were pressed together in the tight squeeze between the rocks, his breath gusting over me. It smelled faintly of the dried fruit he'd eaten that morning. "I'm going to squeeze past you. It gets tricky further in and whoever leads needs the light and the ability to catch themselves if they make a wrong step. My ropes can do that for me. Watch me carefully. If I start to slip. Make sure your footing is sure."

"Judicus," I signed, but he held up a finger.

"No. No self-sacrifice. Do you hear me, Sersha?"

I nodded and to my surprise, he took my face in his hands and said, "If all the world falls apart and I die alone, it will keep my heart warm to know that someone like you still lives. If you want to give me something, give me that. Not your life. Not your freedom. That."

And then he was wiggling past me, taking the lead, our bodies pressed tightly together in the narrow crack of rock until he squirmed to the other side. He looked back, flushed.

"Are you hurt?"

I shook my head.

"I apologize for passing you in such an undignified fashion."

I snorted a laugh and he looked confused.

"We're being hunted." I signed. *"We could die. I don't care about ..."*

I didn't know how to sign "undignified," but he must have understood because he nodded briskly, his face bright scarlet in the lantern light, and then he turned and began to thread his way carefully through the cracks of rock.

"This will spit us out on the other side of the Fraren River. The rocks pass under the Falls. It's going to get muggy in here. I'll try to warn you but don't panic if we see water streaming in. I felt my way through with my ropes before I chose this spot and I thought there was enough room for people to get through."

He thought? He wasn't sure?

My heart started beating even faster. All I could see was his back and the dancing flickers of light above it.

I couldn't swallow down the lump of fear in my throat. I was pretty sure it was my heart trying to claw its way out.

157

It seemed to take a long time to pick our way through the crevice. I wanted to ask Judicus if it was a long way to go. I wanted to ask if he was using his ropes to feel the way. I wanted to ask him to hold my hand.

I was glad he couldn't see my hands, so I wasn't tempted to make a fool of myself.

He checked over his shoulder now and then and if he smiled to reassure me, I didn't see it. My night vision helped a little in these caves but not enough. All I saw was the stark outline of his head in the glow of the lantern and everything else was lost in shadow.

I was beginning to worry about whether the lantern might run out of fuel. Should I tap Judicus on the shoulder and remind him to refill it from the flask in the pack?

A drop of something cold hit my forehead and slid down my cheek. I reached up and felt for it. Water.

I could smell it, dank and slightly mineral, as if it was trying to be a living thing and failing. One of my feet slid on the wet rock of the path and I barely caught myself on the walls to either side of me.

My palms came away slimy, and I shuddered.

Ugh.

What might live here in this cave? What might be all over my hands?

I was not cut out for underground excursions. If we ever escaped this dreadful place I was going to stay solidly above the earth or in the air like a sensible human.

"Sersha?" Judicus' whisper was faint. "Tap my shoulder if you are still with me."

I tapped his shoulder, realizing that the tunnel had grown so tight now that he had turned sideways. I wiggled the pack off my shoulders and turned my own body sideways just in time. Once I'd reached the point where he had been, I had to turn sideways, too.

If I was worried before, I was doubly worried now. Not only were my back and front getting coated in slime, the pack felt tight as I dragged it behind me. What if it got stuck?

What if I got stuck? The weight and depth of the rock above us seemed suddenly very real. The immovableness of the rock to either side felt absolute. And the certainty of the rock under my feet felt tenuous.

What if Judicus got stuck? If there was somewhere he couldn't go, then I certainly wouldn't be able to go there. He was thinner than anyone else I knew. Could I even pull him loose if he was wedged? Not in this position.

My heart beat in my chest like a panicked drum.

In the distance, echoing through the cave was the sound of something sliding.

I reached out and grabbed a handful of Judicus's shirt.

He reached back and took my hand, pressing it reassuringly in his grip.

Had he heard the sound, too?

Was that why he was silent?

We slid onward, the slime easing our tight passage. It was a good thing I'd had so little to eat lately. One big meal and I wouldn't have fit.

Just the thought of that made me ill.

I was going to start vomiting. Fear clawed through me so hard that I had to shut my eyes between steps, clutching at my own breath in an effort to keep the rhythm of it.

I didn't dare panic. I didn't dare start to breathe in that too-fast way people did when they'd lost reason and let their mind run away. But I could feel I was close to it. I could feel it.

It was only the pressure of Judicus's hand on mine that held me together.

My blood roared in my ears for what felt like hours.

I'd lost track of any sounds behind me.

And then I realized that what I'd taken as the roar of my blood was actually the roar of water up ahead.

So much for trickles.

The slime on the wall in front of me changed from slime to a steady flow of cool water seeping down the stone. It stank of dead plants and earth, but it was still just a slick of water, not a rushing falls.

What if Judicus didn't see a drop or his foot slipped on all this water and he plummeted, taking me with him?

An echoing voice, loud enough to be heard over the loudness of the Falls drove that fear away and I pushed closer to Judicus.

The water was louder, so loud that I didn't think I would hear him if he spoke. He couldn't turn his head to look back at me and I couldn't turn mine to check the pack. We were sandwiched between rocks, danger behind, danger ahead, only our wobbling light to offer us any hope of pressing on.

And then the light went out.

Judicus pulled me into him, and I thought he was trying to say something, but his voice was lost in the rushing sound of water.

And I was trying not to rush away in my mind, to pretend I was anywhere but here, to not panic completely and freeze to the point where I couldn't move or just sob and sob until I died of starvation.

I didn't dare allow it. I didn't dare.

His palm was still around mine, warm and toughened by work. How odd. What work did a rope worker do? Did handling magic ropes do that to a palm the way a real rope would? I forced my thoughts to stay on his palm as he began to pull me along after him again.

I didn't need to think of the rushing water I heard as the tight crack opened up and I lost the feeling of the wall that had been pressed against my belly, sliding now, at the direction of his palm, against the wall behind me. I didn't need to think of the mist that kept washing over my face and neck and hair or how my shuffling feet kept sliding on the slick rock below me. I didn't need to think about the flood of sound or the smell of water and water pounding out its will on the rocks.

I just needed to think about that palm in mine.

I just needed to think about the things it had done over the years, making cats' cradles with power beyond my imagining, working magic aboard ships or for the army, clinging to my phoenix's back, solving problems, offering me maps and food, signing words to me.

As long as I had that hand, I couldn't be lost. How can you be lost when there's nowhere you want to be except for beside the one you're with?

I clung to that certainty the same way I clung to him, and then the roar began to recede, and a dull glow pierced the darkness – so dull that at first, I thought I was imagining it until it outlined Judicus's profile in faint charcoal, lightening to dove grey and then to white and we emerged on a rocky shelf above a rushing river.

Judicus turned and smiled at me, his grin so broad and his face so ridiculously smeared in green and black that he looked like a merry goblin who had climbed up from the depths.

I began to smile back when something caught my foot.

I clawed at the air, dropping my pack, as I was yanked backward, a black rope around my foot.

158

I kicked and fought against the pull, but it was dragging me backward, inch by inch, into the darkness and no amount of flailing or fighting could stop it.

Judicus cursed and then I felt something like a burst of pain starting where the rope held my ankle and shooting up my whole body. I clenched my teeth in a rictus and forced my eyes open. Above me, Judicus was outlined – a black silhouette – ropes falling from his hands and tangling past me.

I was shaken violently, like a rag knot ripped back and forth by an enthusiastic puppy. I fought to keep my arms over my head to keep it from being smashed into the rock. Pain flared in my elbows and hips and chest and then – as sudden as it had come, it ended and I was left, breathing raggedly on the ground.

Everything hurt.

I couldn't seem to open my eyes or even move.

"Kentinius," Judicus whispered as he gently drew my arms from around my head. "I felt him when I shook his ropes from you."

That was him? The bruises I'd just gotten were going to be brighter than summer flowers. Everything hurt.

"Can you move?" he asked, worriedly.

I nodded, swallowing. I could move. I just didn't want to.

"He'll send more ropes next time."

I was on my feet before he'd finished the words. I didn't want to wait around for next time. Once was enough.

"We'll have to be careful when we surface. He won't be alone. He'll have help. And they'll be hunting us."

He blew out a breath and ran his hand through his hair. His mouth was twisted like he was thinking thoughts I wouldn't want to hear.

"We have to stay together," I signed. *"If night ever falls, Kazmerev can help."*

"They'll expect us to head for the sea to try to escape." He chewed his lower lip.

"We must do the opposite of what they expect." He softened slightly. "At least it will bring us closer to our goal."

"*Our ...*" I stumbled over the word "goal," but he signed it quickly for me.

"Goal. Here, let me take the pack. We need to move."

I let him take it. I hoped nothing was broken inside it. No bones were broken in my limbs, but they ached and flared with pain as I moved, and I worried that the things in the bag might have fared just as poorly.

Judicus took my arm, helping my first stumbling steps and we made our way back to the light as he murmured his thoughts quickly to me.

"You should know this anyway. In case we're separated, or something happens to me."

I didn't like where that was going. I didn't want to think of Judicus shaken like that with no one to help him. I winced.

"Listen," that sign you drew in the ash – I know it. It's the sign of the Tattered Ribbons cult. The one with the temple we hid inside. They have a plinth in the eastern foothills of the Crown Peak Mountains. That symbol is carved on the plinth and it has an odd dish-shaped top. No one knows why they made it. Most of the cult was killed soon after in the Scavenge Wars, but it's there. And when I was younger, studying rope work, I studied a lot of other things, too, and I saw that symbol on a plinth almost exactly the same as that one but the second plinth was said to be located beside a rent in the earth on the islands inhabited by the Hand of the Rat."

A chill shot through me.

"That must have been what the mural showed you."

I nodded, intrigued even as I felt suddenly worried – as if this all carried more weight than I understood.

"You realize that we need to go find the plinth in the Crown Peak Mountains, right? The spies will no doubt figure out that they must bring Mally to the first plinth. But what if the two are connected? What if something needs to be done on the plinth over here? What if she risks everything to get to the one on her side of the sea, only for this plinth not to be ready for her? What then?"

I swallowed because he was right. But what would we do when we got there? We didn't know what was necessary. Would we flee from this Kentinius in a desperate attempt to get to the mountains only to end up standing useless, staring at a rock?

"*How will we know what to do?*" I signed, letting go of his arm to ask the question.

"I don't know," he said, looking worried. "I know someone I could ask. But if we arrive on his doorstep, we might put him in danger."

"*More danger than the end of the ...*"

"World?" Judicus asked, making the sign. I repeated it, trying to work it into my memory. "Your point is valid. But before we can get to it, we need to get out of here."

We'd emerged on the rocky ledge again, looking down at a rushing river.

Judicus opened his hands, a look of fierce concentration on his face, and then he was cat's cradling so fast I couldn't see all the motions until he had a weaving between his fingers of fierce complexity. He lifted it and closed his eyes, screwing up his mouth and I gasped as the ropes grew and lengthened, the knot he'd woven replicating out from itself to form a net over the river. It spanned clear to the other side.

Judicus breath came in puffs like he'd been running for hours, his face flushed bright and the shadows under his eyes deepening.

When, after a very long moment, he opened his eyes, he looked worn.

"Now that," he said with a rueful smile, "takes a lot out of a man." He drew in a long steadying breath and then addressed me, his body leaning forward, all his features sharpening. "You have to go first because the moment my feet leave the bridge it will be gone. As we cross, keep an eye out for archers or anyone else. Try to move quickly. It will sway and move and feel like walking through deep sand. I can't make it firmer when it's this wide. Try not to let that worry you. Just focus on moving quickly. Understand?"

He waited, as he always did, for me to nod my assent and then he stepped onto the network of ropes.

"Now, you join me and move past me onto the bridge."

I took a deep breath, all his warnings readying me for a nerve-wracking journey, and stepped out.

159

The ropes were worse than slippery. They were worse than soft. It felt like wading through bread dough. It wasn't just thick, it felt like it was intentionally trapping me, pulling me down to the knees, forcing my every muscle into effort to fight the way it slid under me like ice. I gritted my teeth, fighting with every muscle of my body to keep my feet under me. I was aching and sweating by the third step.

Underneath me, the river rushed, loud and gurgling, throwing up mist that coated my legs and made my bones ache. I shuddered, trying not to look down at the bubbling, frothing water, broken up with jagged rocks like the teeth of an angry shark.

"Hurry, Sersha!" Judicus gasped, barely over a whisper.

I made the mistake of trying to look back at him. I nearly lost my balance, my arms pinwheeling as I tried to regain it. I managed another stumbling step and then one more, my thighs and back aching from the effort to stay upright. I could feel Judicus right behind me, feel the warmth of his body even though he wasn't touching me. I had to hurry. I was holding him back.

A shout rang out from behind us.

"Fontellrae, Duke of Chignov," Judicus said, suddenly.

I looked back at him, confused, and he reached out to catch my hand and steady me, leaving both of us swaying wildly for one awful moment.

"That's the person I know who might understand what the plinth was for. If we get split up, you'll need to find him. His estates are east of here. You can ask anyone, and they can point you toward Chignov. Hurry, now, hurry!"

Why was he telling me this?

Another shout. I forced myself forward, pushing with everything in me, but the harder I pushed against the ropes, the deeper I seemed to sink, making movement more difficult.

Something clattered on the rocks ahead.

We were almost there!

It glanced off and I realized an arrow had hit them. A second arrow struck close to the first, sinking into a clump of moss.

Oh no.

They were shooting at us.

I was almost to the shore. Just a few more steps. I pushed hard, every muscle of my body screaming.

Behind me, Judicus gasped, and then gasped again, and the second gasp was more of a painted cry.

And then, quick as the sun hiding behind a cloud, the webbing of the bridge was gone, and I was tumbling through the air.

I landed with a splash, so close to the bank of the river, swift as it was, that I was caught in the branches of a cedar that had fallen over the river. I sank my hands gratefully into the fragrant branches, trying to catch my breath. Nothing felt broken. I was more shaken than hurt.

I spun, trying to find Judicus.

My eyes landed first on the archers on the far bank, a man dressed crisply in a short cape and a wide-brimmed hat standing there with them, looking down on us. He opened a palm and a rope started to roll out from it.

Instinctively, I ducked under the tree, swimming hard to clear the branches and come out on the other side. I scrambled to shore, staying low, careful to avoid making a profile, and then popped up when my feet were both on rock.

The dark rope lurched toward me and then was caught by another rope that dragged it away like a fox dragging a groundhog from its hole. It thrashed and the new rope rolled and tightened.

I followed it with my gaze to find Judicus spinning in the frothy water, the backpack behind him floating high in the water, pin-cushioned with arrows, and the rope in his hand dragging the other rope away from me.

A heavy thunk, and another arrow landed beside me. I caught Judicus's eyes with mine and he mouthed to me, "Run."

160

The week that followed was the longest of my life. I emerged from the river drenched and terrified, running for my life with arrows falling around me. That none of them struck me was either a miracle or the work of Judicus.

And I didn't dare turn around and go back for him. Not when I'd promised him I would not.

Leaving him there – possibly injured and in the grip of the water – was like a nightmare come to life. Every rustle of a tree branch or crack of a stick gave me hope. Would he be there when I turned around? Or was he drowning under the weight of the pack, pierced all through with arrows, strangled by a black rope of magic? Images of his possible deaths haunted me, playing in my mind again and again.

I was grateful it was warm. If the chill of autumn had been in the air, I would not have survived the first night – if that's what you could call it when dawn still it the sky. As it was, I collapsed under a pine tree when my energy left me, sleeping fitfully for only hours before waking again, setting my face to the sun, and hiking onward.

I found a road eventually. It was maybe a day later. Maybe. It was hard to tell with the sun stuck in place. The road smelled of the chives growing along it, and I followed it in a distraught haze until I ran into a wagon – literally into one.

I stared at it, blinking. Exhaustion clouded my thoughts. Oh yes, I was going east. Alone.

"Who is this now, Beatran?" an old man asked, his voice lilting and querulous.

"Just a traveler, grandfather. Go back to sleep."

The younger voice was closer and when I looked up, it belonged to a woman only a few years older than me. Her dark hair was tied back, and she wore a canvas apron over her dress. Beside her, her grandfather drowsed, his white-bearded chin dipping and bobbing against a well-padded chest. The wagon she drove was pulled by a pair of oxen, the sides of it worn down from what had once been elaborate carvings.

"Do you prefer your own feet, mistress or would you like to keep me company?" the woman asked me in an open, friendly manner. "There's room to sit on top of the wool and I could use the chatter until we reach Chignov."

My eyes must have lit at the name "Chignov" because she smiled and said, "Well then, up with you" and in the space of a moment, I was on the wagon seated behind her and her grandfather on a pile of bundled sheepskins. The wagon was an odd contraption – the bulk of it enclosed with a door set in the rear, but the front had an overhang to shield the driver's bench from rain and behind the bench – piled with neatly bundled sheepskins – was a window wide enough to be a door that led into the main wagon. Pots and pans – copper and bright – hung within, clattering at the same pace as the very slow oxen. A wide assortment of other things was hung, or strung, or bundled all through the small wagon.

Peddlars, I realized. They both lived in the cart and sold goods from it. A tidy setup, but these kinds of goods were rich for rural places. I was surprised to see no guards or strapping young lads to help them fend off predators or either animal or the human kind.

Beatran, it turned out, while disappointed when she realized I could not speak, seemed more than happy to carry on the conversation by herself.

It was through her I discovered that the smaller cities surrounding Briccatore and up the coast all the way to Wildrock had fallen to the Hand of the Rat. That the Grand Hadri in Briccatore had announced they were "brothers" and welcome in all of Calicarn.

Beatran and her grandfather were so nervous at the news that they packed up the oxen immediately and began to travel. They hadn't gone very far yet. The oxen, though very strong, were impossibly slow. So slow that I thought often of leaving them, but any thought of it was quickly squelched by Beatran's generosity.

She offered me a dry dress when we'd been traveling less than an hour together. Helped me wash and beat my old dress on rocks when we stopped for a bite to eat. Helped me hang it to dry inside the wagon, offered me food and water, and when the oxen stopped for a break – "for the night" she said, though it certainly was not that – and we strung hammocks in the wagon and helped her grandfather into one, she offered to let me sleep on the sheepskins.

Three times, soldiers rode by, passing us in the road. Once, the Hand of the Rat marched by in a ragged group. They did not stop once, ignoring the cart and the three of us entirely. It didn't stop me from flinching inside, my heart racing at the sight of them.

The first village we stopped at both confirmed my fears and gave me hope. A woman there whispered to Beatran to watch for strangers on the road.

"The soldiers are looking for someone," she said quietly as I helped another customer by cutting lengths of ribbon for her purchase. "A young man – tall, dark-haired, thin. They say he's dangerous."

Judicus. I felt a flush of relief. They hadn't caught him yet.

"And a mute girl in a silk dress with a phoenix."

Beatran nodded gravely. "I'll keep my eyes open, mother, but I think I'll know a phoenix if I see one."

"I'd be more worried about the man," the woman said dryly. "A girl like you could get in trouble with a young man. I'm young enough to remember how attractive fellows are when they're tragic and doomed to death."

I snorted through my nose, startling the other customer, but Beatran merely nodded again, still very earnest. "I'll watch myself."

"See that you do."

It was to Beatran's credit that she didn't ask me about what the woman said. She met my eyes just once and then returned to her work. Even that night, when we set camp and made our evening meal and then retired, she still didn't ask.

And the silk dress she'd washed for me mysteriously found its way to a spot under the sheepskins.

I was almost at the point where I thought that perhaps I could travel all the way to Chignov this way, when on the seventh day we turned a corner abruptly on the road to find the group of the Hand of the Rat who had passed us on the road. They were in a rough circle around someone bound spreadeagled to four stakes, her mouth gagged and eyes wild.

And the moment I saw her I knew – without knowing how I knew – that she was a Flame Rider just like me.

161

I gasped.

But before I could do anything, to my utter surprise, "grandfather" grabbed my arm in an iron grip. Something tickled my ribs and I looked down to see a short knife, barely longer than my longest finger, pressed against my ribs.

"Don't move. Don't look," he whispered. His voice had lost every trace of its querulous lilt.

I swallowed.

"Look down."

I obeyed.

And I was furious. Who was this man I had traveled with? And how dare he force me to look away while someone just like me was tortured or even killed.

"Ease the oxen along now, Beatran," he said quietly.

Their pace was too slow for words. Was it possible they were slower than they'd been before?

My heart was thundering as the moments drew out and every detail etched itself into my mind. The feel of his fingers gripping my arm too hard until my fingers on that hand felt too thick.

The knot in the wood I was staring at as the wagon swayed and jolted over the road.

The smell of oxen – fermented grass. Dung. Sweat.

The smell of Grandfather – cumin and sweat.

The dawn sun barely enough to warm me as the breeze rustled through the trees and the wagon's hardware creaked and someone tried to scream through a balled-up cloth.

I was going to be sick. I was going to faint.

The raiders spoke in their harsh tongues, but they said nothing to us, letting us roll along the road beside them until – by my muddled reckoning – we had almost curved entirely around them.

"Hold, wagon!" a voice called in a thick accent. The sound of footfalls jogging up to us made the muscles at the base of my neck clench so hard they could have stood in place of rocks. "Do you sell lengths of leather?"

"Rawhide or tanned?" Beatran asked, her voice light and cheerful.

I gritted my teeth. I knew not to blame her for it. She just didn't want to die like everyone else. But it was hard to walk by and do nothing while someone suffered – worse, to be friendly or indifferent to her torturer.

"Tanned," he said, the word garbled in his unfamiliar throat. "A strap broke and needs repair."

"I have tanned in its natural color and tanned dyed a dark brown," Beatran offered.

The oxen were still now – which was barely slower than when the oxen were moving.

"Dark brown, if you please," the raider said. I didn't need to look up. I could imagine his scowling eyes without needing to. I could imagine the cloth covering his face and the hood over his hair. Beside me, Grandfather stiffened as if the color of the leather had made this all more serious. "And choose a solid length for me. I need it to last until we reach the hold of this territory."

"Oh aye," Beatran agreed, scrambling past me into the wagon.

I risked a peek upward. The raider was looking away from me and I couldn't see his face behind the covering. I looked away in disgust. If every member of the Hand of the Rat woke up as dead as their namesakes when we poisoned the grain for them, I would not shed a single tear. There was something a little familiar about his eyes. Perhaps he'd been one of the raiders in the camp who had tied me to a tree and planned my death.

The knife poked my ribs a little harder and I turned my face down long enough to catch some kind of sign the raider's hands formed but not longer than that. The sign looked so much like the "house" sign in Sumerian sign language that for a moment I wanted to watch to see if it was intentional or if it was merely a trick of chance, but the knife dug hard enough to pierce the dress and into my skin – not badly, just enough to bleed.

I kept my gaze on the knot in the wagon floor. I didn't need to die just to assuage my curiosity.

"Here it is, good sir," Beatran said, climbing past me a little roughly. I felt the knife prick again as she rocked me against her grandfather. "The length is enough to fix a strap. Oh no, keep your coin. It's a pleasure to serve."

And then the oxen creaked forward again but the knife did not ease until long after the sweat of fear had run down my temples, wetting my hair.

162

Grandfather kept the knife to my ribs until we were well clear of the Flame Rider. By the time the knife eased away from my ribs, I was almost ready to scream with frustration. Someone needed to help that poor woman. Someone like me. I could go back. I could help her.

And then suddenly grandfather was whispering in my ear, "Stop it. Stop moving. Stop panicking. It's being handled."

He didn't sound old at all. I looked into his eyes. They weren't as lined as I'd thought. Now that he had a sharp look in them, he wasn't old-looking at all.

I squinted at him, wondering what else I had missed.

"The old mill is not far, Beatran," he murmured. "We'll part ways there, I think."

That calmed me down. If we were going to part ways soon, then I could go back for the Flame Rider. I didn't know what I could do alone against a whole group of raiders, but I also didn't trust him that it being "handled" meant the Flame Rider would be unharmed. And I couldn't leave her. Not another Flame Rider. What if one of them killed her and took the ashes of her phoenix? What if he awakened, only to die forever because the heart he was born into was evil?

No, I couldn't just walk away.

The Flamerarch hadn't walked away from me. And I wouldn't walk away from her.

I clenched my jaw, determination filling me. I'd just have to bide my time and wait. Grandfather had said we'd reach the mill soon.

But when we turned another corner, we found the river where a watermill squatted, holding firm as the water turned its wheel. Belts coming from it sawed boards for the four sweating men busily working beside it, but grandfather's little pig-sticker was back in my ribs the moment we saw them.

"Hop down now, Sersha," he said quietly, and I was forced to follow as he nodded in friendly acknowledgment to the sawmill workers and then waited as Beatran saddled a horse she found behind the mill and helped him set me on its back with grandfather straddling the mare behind me.

Betrayal stabbed through me knife-sharp and bitter. I'd thought Beatran was a friend and when she'd hidden my dress, I thought she might even be an ally. Instead, she was in on this kidnapping.

Beatran lashed my hands together quickly, never once looking in my eyes.

"This may feel like a betrayal now," she said calmly. "But you'll thank me for it eventually."

I would not. In fact, I would never forgive her, not that it was likely I'd see her again. I tried to put all of that into my glare, but she never once looked up to meet it.

"Until next time, grandfather," she said with an ironic grin to the man behind me as our mare walked away.

"My thanks, Beatran.

"Anytime," she muttered and then we were trotting up a narrow forest path, leaving the road behind and not a single sawmill worker had even blinked as if this kind of thing happened all the time.

Maybe it did.

I wanted to be sick. But I waited. At the mill, if I fought, it would have been six against one. If we got out of earshot first, I'd have an even chance against this man.

The horse moved quickly over the trail as if familiar with it, heading down a long hill where the trail split in two. She took the right-hand path with hardly any guidance, whickering happily as she bounded up the other side to a trail that hugged farm fields. Buildings in the distance picked out the farms, one after another, all rich with wide black fields of earth freshly tilled. My eyes widened at the sight. In Landsfall, a field a tenth this size was considered a wealth of soil. This estate must be very wealthy, indeed.

But it also meant barns and washing lines and gardens – places I could hide and find food and other clothing. In my current dress and canvas apron, I was easy to identify.

Now, when no one was watching, was my best bet.

I balled my tied hands into fists and twisted suddenly, my joined fists swinging like a club.

Grandfather caught them easily with one hand, and my mouth dropped open as I saw what he's been doing as we rode. His beard was gone – it had been false, covering salt-and-pepper whiskers. His hat and wig were gone, too, revealing a balding salt-and-pepper crop of hair. He'd scrubbed his face with something, and healthy color showed now where pallor had made his face look papery before.

"Hello, Sersha," he said with wry amusement. And I realized, with a sudden feeling of ice running down my spine, that it was the second time he'd said my name, and I'd never given it to him. "Judicus Franzer Irault said you'd be a fighter, but if you don't mind, I'd rather untie you and ride to my home quietly. If we cause a scene here, it will only trouble my tenants."

I didn't think my jaw could fall any further. I shut it with a snap.

I held out my hands and he drew out his small knife and sawed the leather cord.

"And before you decide to leap off the horse and going running to the aid of that poor Flame Rider you can't help, you should know it's your ropeworker friend who is helping her. If you trust him to do the job, then maybe you'd like to avoid interfering."

I nodded reluctantly and he smiled in a way that made me think of a wolf. Before I could shudder, he said, "It's nice to meet you. I am Fontellrae, Duke of Chignov."

163

I rode the rest of the way with him in stunned silence. I would have been silent anyway, but I wouldn't usually feel like I'd been hit with a hammer. To go from on the run and afraid to finding sudden friends, to then being in the hands of an actual ally who had treated me like a prisoner. It made my head spin.

The only thing that could be better would be if the sun would finally set.

We reached a large stone house some time later. The endless dawn was starting to really bother me. It was impossible to judge the passage of time without the sun, impossible for my body to determine when it was day or night or when I ought to eat or rest.

Fontellrae seemed eager to be home. He pushed the mare hard to get there and she arrived huffing and sweating. Men and women in livery poured from the big house to take his horse and to my surprise, one of them offered me a hand down.

I took his hand and slid from the mare, not sure if I should be wary or grateful.

"Lady Sersha is my guest," Fontellrae said, waving at me. Lady? "Give her a room, Steward, and send clothing and a bath."

A stern-looking man with no hair at all – not even eyebrows – gave me a quick look up and down before snapping his fingers. A maid, dressed just like me in a plain dress and canvas apron, jumped at the snap and hurried forward.

"The East corner, I think, Rose," the steward murmured to her and before I even had my bearings, the girl was leading me through the press of bodies toward the great house.

Behind us, I heard anxious questions.

"Is there really a new Grand Hadri, Your Grace?"

"Is it true that the Hand of the Rat is moving inland?"

"Should we call up our tenants and shore up defenses, Lord Duke?"

"Did you find us any allies in court, Your Grace?"

We were nearly at the door when Fontellrae announced, "In a few hours' time,

I expect another guest. He'll help me explain everything. How many bells until we sup, Steward?"

"Two, Your Grace."

"Then in two bells, you'll hear all you need to hear," the duke said. "For now, I'll speak with Grantham."

And then their voices faded as Rose led me into the great house – Fontellrae House, she called it – and through a bustling kitchen with a pink-cheeked, "Sorry my lady, but it's quickest," and then up two flights of stairs to a room as large as the entire back of the Hog's Head Inn.

Before I knew it, a pair of men had brought in a brass tub and then a series of girls brought up steaming buckets to fill it and Rose vanished and returned with a cunning midnight blue dress of fine-woven wool, fresh underthings, stockings, and tall boots, and then left again as the last bucket was sloshed into the tub.

And I was alone.

I looked out the arched window. Black, freshly-tilled fields surrounded the great house and from this vantage, I could see the river rimmed in fluffy green trees and bushes, the foothills of the mountains, purple in the distance to the east, and the cleverly laid roads and clusters of houses and village centers for the tenants of the duke's lands.

I felt two things at once.

On the one hand, this place charmed me in a way that nowhere in our travels had yet touched my heart.

And on the other hand, I felt aching, hands-in-ice-water pain at the knowledge that evil was bearing down on them.

Reluctantly, I pulled myself away from the view of the window and hurried to the bath. It was thoughtful. And it had taken so many people so much work that it would be terribly ungrateful not to enjoy it.

I stripped and cleaned myself in guilty enjoyment. Hot water was one of the gifts of the heavens. It cleaned and soothed, comforted, and loosened the thoughts.

By the time I was done, I was thoroughly clean and ready for the fresh clothing. Rose had guessed my size perfectly and by the time I was dressed, my wet hair pulled back in a tidy braid, she was back and offering to show me the way to dinner.

They ate all together in a long hall made of stone with solid wooden tables and benches in two long lines except for a table at the head of the room. Behind the head table, a massive fire danced in its own place, its mantle decorated with weapons. I recognized sabers, common from the sea cities I'd traveled through, a thick whip, a short spear, and the curving sword of a raider.

The walls were also decorated with weapons and colorful tapestries showing farming scenes – wheat bundled at harvest, dancing fields of barley, sheep in all their wooly glory, and – to my utter surprise, a shepherd fending off a mythic lion in defense of his sheep.

I stared at that one for too long before Rose tugged me to a place beside her.

"We all eat together, my lady, except those who are serving."

And in that egalitarian spirit, I ate stew and barley bread with her and ate entirely too much for the first time in so long that I couldn't remember.

I was drowsing in my place, so gloriously full that I could barely move, when a shout went up.

I straightened, startled as the door slammed open, making the whole hall shudder.

And there, to both my dismay and complete relief, was Judicus stumbling through the door, the rescued Flame Rider draped over one shoulder.

He was dressed as a raider, the mask hanging around his throat.

He started to speak, his voice harsh and terribly familiar. The raider who had asked for the leather strapping. I felt the blood drain from my face. How had I not known?

Why had he not indicated to me that he was *right there* in front of me when he'd bought the leather?

And then he cleared his throat, and his old voice was back.

"A healer, if you would, Fontellrae," he said, and his eyes met mine across the room as he smiled nervously.

164

He was alive.

I checked him over, trying not to make it obvious. There was something wrong with one of his legs. He was holding it oddly.

I didn't even realize I was out of my seat until I was halfway across the hall, hurrying to join him. Relief made me tremble. I hadn't even realized I was worrying so much until the worry fell like a stone wall in a storm.

"*You're safe. You're safe,*" I signed.

Judicus stumbled, falling to one knee, but those closer to him were already there, relieving him of the burden of the hurt Flame Rider and easing his pack to the ground. An old man in green robes flew into the room, his eyes bright, a serving boy at his side.

"Let me through," he ordered, thumbing the woman's eyelids back immediately and then giving sharp, cracking orders to bring her to his infirmary.

She was gone before I could register more than that she was alive and older than us. Her wrists were raw with angry abrasions and her face had been bruised.

I turned my attention to Judicus. No one had seemed to notice his leg.

He stood, dusting himself off, but that leg was wobbly, and – I realized belatedly – his trousers were soaked along that leg. Was that blood? How badly was he hurt?

I bit my lip, moving toward us, but he caught my hand before I could reach for his injury.

"Later, Sersha," he murmured to me. His eyes lifted and he spoke to Fontellrae. "I've brought nothing good to your house, Your Grace."

"I'll determine that, Judicus Franzer Irault. It was a boon to meet you on the road, knowing as I do that you have apt insight into the court and these times."

His words were friendly, but there was something in his tone that suggested more behind them than I understood.

"Insight I can share. Knowledge, I can offer," Judicus said and then he ran his hand through his hair, looking weary. "But I cannot keep your people or your hold safe and nothing I can tell you can save you now."

A gasp went up from the people surrounding us. They didn't speak, though, their eyes stayed on either Judicus or their lord.

"Speak then, for I have promised my people answers."

Fontellrae looked grim and I wondered for one flickering moment what kind of man rode around his own countryside dressed as an old man being drawn along by oxen. A clever one, perhaps. One who knew that people do not say everything before dukes. Or a foolish one who simply liked playing the trickster. I didn't know which one this Fontellrae was.

Judicus paused and then drew a long breath, his eyes running along the banners on the wall and then the people in the hall as if studying them and committing them to memory in this moment.

"Rackham, Grand Hadri, is Dead."

A gasp ran raggedly through the room and Fontellrae leaned forward, hands planted on the table.

"His advisors consorted with the Hand of the Rat to hunt him down, snatch him from his guard and dispatch him. I saw them take his lifeless body away myself."

A murmur of curses and pleadings to the heavens for mercy were stilled by the raised hand of Fontellrae.

"And now?" he asked, his face lined with worry.

"A puppet Grand Hadri has been set up in place of Rackham." Judicus paused here. "My sister, Kristiana."

"So young," Fontellrae murmured, looking pained and I realized that he – like Judicus – assumed she would not live long as their puppet.

"And the Hand of the Rat has been turned loose on the countryside. Their allies ride on the backs of Stryxex – an ancient evil born from the depths." Those words triggered something in my memory, but I couldn't quite grasp it. Born of the depths. There was something to that. "They have been hunting down and killing every Flame Rider they can find after trying to extract the phoenix from their hearts. The Flame Rider I brought to you was barely snatched from them before she was killed in the process."

Fontellrae clenched his jaw. "And they squat just outside my lands."

"Yes."

"And the sky?"

Everyone looked up at that.

"The ai'sletta has found the Dark Diadem and with it, she bids the sun come and go at her command."

"Nonsense," Fontellrae brushed that away with a hand. "The rest is plain. But that can only be rumor."

"Ah," Judicus said and didn't correct him. He fiddled with a string that had come loose from his jacket, looking away absently.

I watched the pair of them curiously, wondering why he let that falsehood stand.

"But I'll hear the rumor," Fontellrae said after a moment.

Judicus cleared his throat self-consciously and then in a tone clearly chosen to be careful and not offend, he said, "I went out on the Hunt, and I found the ai'sletta some weeks ago, born in a small coastal village in Wildrock. I was beset by Casanetta Lightland who stole the ai'sletta away with the help of the Hand of the Rat, and by the time I recovered her, it was too late for the Grand Hadri, but not too late for the ai'sletta. She is with his inheritors now and they have promised to help her towards the goal of hamstringing this assault on our people."

That was an interesting way to present it. Not wrong, exactly, but – careful.

"Hmm," said Fontellrae and he lifted an eyebrow. "And what brings you to our duchy? Were you so goodhearted as to act as messenger boy?"

And now his mouth turned into a wry line and his eyes had a cynicism in them I had not seen before.

"I'm here for your library," Judicus said, hands spread in peace. "Which is truly the best private library in all of Calicarn."

To my surprise, Fontellrae barked a laugh. "The nation is in turmoil, your own blood endangered, the peace of three hundred years threatened, magical creatures hunted to the death, and you have come here to read."

Judicus nodded gravely.

And now everyone was chuckling, the moment of fear broken.

Fontellrae rolled his eyes. "At least eat something first and then I'm sure we can accommodate you. Why not read away your last moments while the world burns?"

This time, the laughter had a hysterical edge.

165

Judicus ate.

And I squirmed inside.

I wanted to look at his leg, but every time I so much as glanced at it, he gave me a warning look, and once even the smallest head-shake, no. I finally gave up when he started to look annoyed.

Fine. If he didn't care he was wounded, then I didn't care either.

But I'd been worried about him and fretting and now he was here again, and he was barely acknowledging me, and it bothered me. He was supposed to be my friend and my ally. We were supposed to be close. So why was he suddenly distant, talking only to Fontellrae while I waited impatiently on the sideline?

I sighed and stood up. I might as well go back to the room assigned me as sit here and listen to Judicus talk with Fontellrae and ignore me. At least there I could get some rest. Or I could see if the healer needed help with the Flame Rider. Maybe she'd like a fellow rider nearby.

I took a single step and then Judicus pitched his voice a little louder.

"If you'd wait a moment, Sersha, I will require your help in the library. I have many volumes to sit through and little time."

I stopped and he still hadn't even glanced at me. It felt like I was nothing more than his servant. My face went hot.

I'd never heard him talk like that before. So cold and arrogant and ... noble.

And I hated it. I hated it.

But why wouldn't I be treated like a servant? I was a member of his coterie, not a friend. That we'd acted like friends for a while didn't change our official roles. I was *literally* meant to serve him. And on top of that, I was a rural girl from a foreign land who couldn't even read, and he was equal to a duke whose opinions were sought after.

"Perhaps I can help you narrow down the book, Judicus," Fontellrae said.

"Mmm," Judicus said. "Do you have any pieces on unusual monuments? The fountain in Je'swanda, perhaps, or the plinth in the foothills."

Fontellrae's eyes lit. "I do, in fact. I have Svarden's treatise on the wonders and he has a passage on each of those. I'll show it to you myself and you can let Lady Sersha get some rest."

"No, no," Judicus said, rising and gathering his small pack. "You have defenses to plan and people to consult. Who knows which way the Hand of the Rats might strike? I'm sure that between myself and the lady, we can find the book. Let's leave our host to his work, Sersha."

He walked past, sweeping me into his wake, and I followed, feeling more adrift than ever. Where had flustered, worried Judicus gone? Where were his boyish smiles and kind attention?

He felt like a stranger, but still, I followed. Where else would I go?

We stalked down the corridors – his limp pronounced, and pack dragging at one shoulder. I noticed it was dotted with small tears. I swallowed down a memory of the arrows striking it as we both fled.

When we finally got to a wide pair of double doors, he pulled the nearest one open and limped inside. I followed him into a wide room ringed in bookshelves. A rug and an empty fireplace with a pair of chairs laid out before it, were set to one side, a reading table with parchment and pens, and a lectern to the other. Every other surface was stacked with bound books in marvelous tooled leather. Their spines were stamped and engraved, their covers smooth and well-cared for. I'd thought Prexav had a bounty of them, but this place made his treasure trove look like a drop in a pig trough. Never had I seen so many books in my life. They were enough to fill the common room of the Hog's Head Inn and more besides.

I was so astonished, that I hardly noticed when Judicus closed the door behind us, but I did notice when he immediately slumped against it, face in his hands.

He groaned and I sprang to him, pulling the pack from his hands and kneeling to look at his leg.

He groaned when I tried to lift his trouser leg.

For the love of flying things!

There *was* an arrow in there!

I glared up at him, but his face was still cradled in his palms, his breath *wuffing* unsteadily, and his long deft fingers threaded through his hair.

"I know," he gasped. "I know."

I scooped up the pack and steered him toward the rug. I could hardly work on his leg here in the doorway.

To my surprise, he threw the bolt in the door first.

I didn't care who came in or out. I only cared about his injury. He was insane walking around like this. Insane.

Clicking my tongue, I cut his trousers up to the wound and gasped at the sight of a badly sawn-off arrow, the shaft still embedded in the flesh. It must have hit bone. And it did not look good. The wound was crimson and angry with little red spider legs reaching out from it.

Infected.

It had been in here too long.

And he'd been eating and drinking and carrying people around like this! What had he been thinking? How had he even managed to do it?

"Wait. Sersha," his words were gasps. "Wait."

I paused, hands hovering over his leg.

"Listen," and his voice was gentle through the pain. This was the voice I'd missed in his coldness in the banquet hall. "I'm so sorry, but we aren't safe here."

I tilted my head to one side.

"Fontellrae is ... not a bad man. A friend – sort of." He was sounding like himself again. The normal, overly thoughtful Judicus. "We are friendly. We agree on some things. But he owes us no loyalty and he'd never risk himself for us. You can't trust him not to sell you out if it will help his people, because he will. He'd sell me, too. He'd sell his own mother. This place is his heart and being the duke here is his life. Do you understand me?"

I nodded briskly and signed reluctantly, "*I was very worried about you.*"

He signed back. "*I was worried, too. More than I was for myself.*" And then switched back to speaking, seeming tired from that minimal effort. "When we are done here, I need to go back to being the brusque, powerful ropeworker. People believe their own eyes. They won't bother you, or me, if they think that's who I am. And they'll bother you less thinking you are merely an associate of mine and not a friend. Not someone they can use to manipulate me, you understand? I couldn't bear to have you hurt."

"*Judicus,*" I signed, using the fist cupped in the hand that I'd given him for a name, and I didn't know if I was saying that was who he was, or I was hoping that was who he would be for me.

His cheeks went hot, and he looked around the room, biting his lip, before meeting my eyes. "I apologize for how I treated you, Sersha. It was a necessary deception, but I'd be put out if a friend treated me as coldly as I treated you." He paused. "When I saw you with Fontellrae in the wagon, I wanted to say something to you so badly, but I was worried even then. He had that dagger drawn on you. I told him you were a lady, so he'd be more careful."

That explained a lot.

"*How?*" I signed.

"I used signs. If he'd let you look up, you would have seen them."

Which meant Fontellrae knew Sumerian sign. And he could have spoken to me with it and allowed me to speak back but he hadn't bothered to. Why did that make me so much angrier? Maybe because, like so many nobles, he just didn't bother to listen to those he didn't have to listen to and he hadn't thought I had anything important enough to say.

"And then now, when I saw you," Judicus said, "All I wanted to do was tell you how glad I was that you escaped, how I never would have left that poor Flame Rider to the mercies of the Hand of the Rat, how I desperately needed your help with this arrow, but I just couldn't."

He bit his lip, looking frantic but also a little pale. I touched his brow, cautiously at first, but firmly when he allowed the touch. He was feverish. Enough with trying to assuage my feelings. We needed to deal with his leg.

"*I understand,*" I signed. "*And I agree.*"

He sagged with relief.

"*But now I must tend your leg and it's bad.*"

"I know," he agreed. "I shouldn't have left it, but I didn't have a choice."

"*You could lose the leg.*"

He blanched.

I tried to sign but I didn't have a sign for infection.

He provided it, saying it and signing it both at once. "*Infection.*"

I nodded.

"I can't afford to lose consciousness yet. Especially if it's infected. A fever could sweep me away and then it would be too late and we'd lose this chance. I really do need to look at these books. We have to learn what they're doing, Sersha. Why is the Hand of the Rat torturing Flame Riders? Why are they hunting them? What can the ai'sletta do to save us all? And what do we need to do to help her?"

I nodded. Of course, we needed to know those things, but I had my own priorities.

"*We heal you first.*"

He leaned forward and to my surprise, he grabbed me by both shoulders and spoke through gritted teeth. "This is more important than my life."

I made a calming gesture. I was worried about the look in his face. Was he delirious?

"If there's a chance I might lose consciousness, then we have to look for the books I need first." He hauled himself to his feet and stumbled to the reading desk before I could stop him, sinking into the chair and fumbling for a sheet of parchment and the inkwell sitting close by. He unstoppered it with trembling hands and dipped a pen, writing quickly. "I need you to bring them to me. We'll deal with the arrow afterward."

I crossed my arms, shaking my head. This was a terrible idea. He'd already waited too long. What if we waited longer and I couldn't help him.

I didn't want to lose him.

Not again.

"*Judicus,*" I signed.

"Please, Sersha." His eyes were tight with strain. "Please work with me on this."

I shook my head and spread my palms wide. I hated the plan, but it didn't mean I wouldn't do it.

His worry collapsed into a boyish grin. "You don't have to be able to read to help. Just look along the spines of the books for the titles I've written here. If the letters are the same, bring the book to me."

I worked quickly, finding books from his list, and then going back for more as he wrote out more titles. Judicus was absorbed in the task, flipping through pages quickly, his finger flying along the lines of text as he scrawled on the parchment and then stacked the books to the side.

I impatiently looked for book after book in the library, finding some, not finding others, as he focused and cursed and exclaimed to himself.

I wanted to be done this task. Every minute it took was a minute we didn't have. I worried for him. Worried that he was feverish. Worried I was going to be too late.

And I was just as worried about the noises I heard from outside the library. What had started as an occasional echo or shuffle of feet, quickly morphed into a steady hum and the sound of footsteps walking turned into the sound of running feet, running first one way and then another. Murmured voices became calls which turned to shouts.

And all the while, Judicus read and read, his eyes straining in the soft dawn light.

"I think this is it," he said after a clatter outside made me nearly leap from my own skin. "Look at this, Sersha. Can you see where the artist has tried to depict the ropes? Obviously, this pattern is wrong, but the ropeworker adjusts the designs of the plinth. It starts as the Cult of Tattered Ribbons symbol, but it morphs into something else. It's built somehow with rope and not rock at all. It's ... well, I wouldn't have thought it possible."

From outside the library door, someone screamed. I looked up, alarmed, but Judicus tugged on my arm, his eyes wild.

"I think they both have to be tuned. But how could you possibly arrange that? And what pattern do you make? The text isn't clear. But look at this one," he drew another book over and flipped it open. "Look."

A picture was precisely picked out in ink. A picture of someone screaming while another person pulled something from their chest – not their heart, which would be grisly enough, but rather a flame.

"They're stealing her phoenix. And now look. They warp it with the plinth and with something that comes from the tear in the earth. Something with tentacles. No wonder the Cult of Tattered Ribbons is involved in this. I *think* and I could be crazy. But I think this is how they make Stryxex."

My heart sunk. Not because what he said was crazy, but because I thought what he was saying might be true.

"Do you know what this means?" he asked, his eyes burning and this time when I touched his forehead, he was burning up – hotter than before, completely swept up in fever. I clucked my tongue. "It means all our problems are the same problem. The threat to phoenix riders. The conspiracy against the Grand Hadri that's trapped my sister. What the ai'sletta is needed for – it all has to do with these plinths and this rent in the earth, but Sersha, I would have to weave a pattern at both plinths to stop it, and I don't know what the pattern is."

And I didn't know, either.

"We have to find the pattern," he said, standing. And then, like a tree felled by a powerful axe, he fell over, insensate on the rug.

I let a frustrated sound escape through my teeth. Only Judicus would study despite an infected injury right up until the point of collapse.

The sounds in the hall had grown louder. No. Wait. It was the sound of something outside the stone house. I ran to the window and looked out.

Black-clad figures crawled across the earth like ants, firing the buildings they reached one at a time all through the gorgeous landscape we'd ridden through.

Oh no.

Judicus had said that Fontellrae would sell us out if he was pressed. And now he was being pressed.

A heavy hand knocked on the door.

My heart fell through my chest.

166

No. No. No.

Judicus got us into this mess and now there was no way he'd get us out. I scanned the room for another exit even though I knew there was nothing but the window. That was obviously not an option. Even if Judicus had been able-bodied, it would have just revealed us to our enemies.

The knock sounded again, more urgent this time.

"Open this door! Open it now!"

No. No.

I crouched over Judicus and put my hands on him. I couldn't heal him without my phoenix being manifested – I didn't think. Just like I couldn't shoot fire without him or fly without him. But that didn't keep me from trying. I clapped a hand on his leg and gritted my teeth, trying to will warmth into his leg.

When I opened my eyes, nothing had changed.

Pounding on the door resumed.

"Open in the name of the Duke!"

Not a chance. They'd throw us to the raiders.

Maybe I couldn't heal him because of the arrow. I needed to pull it out. But if I did and I couldn't heal him, what if it bled too much? Or what if the arrowhead chipped off into the bone. I needed better supplies.

I gritted my teeth.

And then another voice spoke through the door – Fontellrae himself.

"Sersha. I assume it is you who has locked the door. By now Judicus would have come out at our request. He knows what is happening and what his life is worth, which means he's as injured as I thought he might be and cannot come to the door."

Fontellrae was still cleverer than I'd believed. I needed to stop underestimating the man.

I bit my lip.

I couldn't help Judicus locked in here. Even if I tried, raiders were on their way. They'd take this stone house. And even if they couldn't break down the stone door, then what? We'd just sit in this room until either we died, or we opened the door and were killed. We were trapped.

Which meant I might as well open the door and risk dealing with Fontellrae. Perhaps, he could at least be reasonable. Perhaps, he could give them only me and spare Judicus.

I swallowed down a wavering fear that made my hands tremble, laid a hand on Judicus's shoulder in goodbye, stood up, and unlocked the door. I opened it just as the guard in Fontellrae's livery was about to knock again. His hand stayed frozen for a moment mid-knock before he lowered it.

Behind him, Fontellrae cleared his throat and the man stepped out of the way.

I put a hand on my chest and then pointed out the window toward the raiders.

"Yes, they are coming," Fontellrae said tightly. "And there are too many for us to defend against." He looked past me and cursed. "And the rope worker is wounded. We'd hoped for his help."

He cursed again, louder, a wild look in his eyes, and then he grabbed me by the shoulders and shook me and I was certain he was going to knock my head against the wall or kill me or something, but instead he spoke, the words tearing out of him painfully.

"I can't save all my people, do you understand?"

I nodded. He was going to tell me now about how he would trade us to save who he could. I braced for it.

"It's too late. We both misjudged. We both thought we had more time." His eyes drifted to Judicus and he took a deep breath, as if steadying himself, and then his words came out in a rush. "But I spoke vows when I was made a duke. Vows to defend them, but also to defend all of Calicarn. And that means I have to guard her resources, including Judicus Franzer Irault – a curse be on his father's name – and the Flame Rider he brought to us. There's a secret way out of my home and you're going to take them out that way and run, do you understand? Flame Riders and Ropeworkers are too valuable to lose in a single fight. No matter how personal that fight might be."

I nodded. I didn't understand any of that except that he wasn't killing me, and he seemed to want to keep Judicus alive, and that would have to be good enough for me. He shoved a small book into my hands – about the size of my palm.

"The book is for Irault if he ever wakens. I think he was looking for it. I can only buy you minutes. Go with Frandtz here," he said, nodding to the big guard in livery who hurried into the library and slung Judicus over one shoulder. "Hurry," and now his voice turned bitter, "and may you succeed where the rest of us bleed and die."

And then he left, almost fleeing down the halls of his own house and I was left gaping and stunned.

He hadn't sold us out.

He'd done the exact opposite.

Judicus was wrong.

"Come on, lady," Frandtz murmured.

I scooped up Judicus's bag and followed him down the cold halls of the stone house and I wondered if Fontellrae was really going to die and what made him decide to save us first. Could it really be as simple as he said – that he had said vows and thought Judicus would be a strong resource? Or could it be something more?

I clutched his book and realized I was crying as we fled down a long stone staircase into the heart of what had once been a happy, safe home.

167

I kept hoping that Fontellrae and his people would win against the flood of raiders as if wishing for it could make it so. As we fled through a warren of passageways and past a secret door in a cellar where others were queuing up to flee it kept washing through me like a prayer.

"There are tunnels for those who can flee, but that's not where we're going," Frandtz said nodding at the line with a grunt. Judicus was probably heavier than he looked. Which wasn't saying much since he looked like he could blow away in a strong wind. "Follow me."

The place he was leading me to descended another flight of stairs. I began to get a sinking feeling in my gut.

We reached the landing. On either side, torches danced, lit bright and surrounding a towering archway carved to look as if it were made of bones. Through the arch, I saw the shelves, stacked five high and sorted by size of bones, skulls grinning down from the top shelf and each shelf beneath curated with great care and precision, femurs with the femurs, tibias – of assorted sizes – with the tibias, and so forth.

Family crypts.

I'd heard whispered stories of such things on Hallowed Night and other times that elders dredged up spooky stories to scare children with. And always when they spoke of crypts, there were crypt keepers.

I gritted my teeth and tried not to think of that as we stepped into the crypt.

I might have succeeded, except that the moment we stepped within, a gaunt figure emerged. A man – old and thin, his wispy beard so light that it drifted and floated with every movement of his head – stood in the yawning mouth of the crypts, a skull clasped between his open palms as if he was consulting it in matters of great importance. Perhaps he was.

"Frandtz," he said, and his eyes were very wide as he laid the skull onto a nearby shelf with trembling hands.

Frandtz's eyes followed the skull, and so did mine. It hadn't been placed with its kind. It was with fibulas. That seemed very out of character for this place. When my eyes returned to the old man he was trembling, gripping the shelf with one clawed hand.

"Dear heavens," he said, his voice barely more than a croak. "So, it has come."

"His Grace thinks so," Frandtz said, a deep sadness in his voice.

"And you were chosen to lead them out?" the old man asked.

"It's my honor," Frandtz said, but he sounded more like he was bidding a last goodbye than any honor, like he expected to be stacked on these shelves soon.

"But these are not who I expected. Who is this?"

"He who was spoken of in the words of Clarinfas, the Sighted," Frandtz said.

"Oh, dear. We must hurry."

And then we were hustling down the shelves of bones with no one telling me anything. None of what had been said made any sense to me except for this one thing – that the Duke of Fontellrae had not been entirely honest with me. He was not just protecting Judicus. He was following some prior plan.

We turned a corner to find two more guards in livery bearing a litter where a white-faced Flame Rider lay.

"It's as you said, Sergeant," the old man said, his voice mournful. "Frandtz was sent with the boy, too. And now you must hurry. I will defend this crypt with my dying bones, but there is little I can do beyond covering your tracks."

"We are honored, Bone Keeper," the guards said, almost as one, bowing reverently, and then they were hustling through another bone-carved doorway – this one smaller – and I was rushing with them. Inside, a pair of large carts were hitched to two donkeys apiece. They were piled high with what I thought must be supplies. Judicus and the Flame Rider were quickly added to them, and I wondered what would happen if I just hung back.

I wouldn't, of course. I'd never leave Judicus like this. But no one had mentioned me, and I was beginning to wonder if I'd become invisible – a ghost walking among the living – until the old man grasped my elbow in his boney hand and whispered to me.

"You, too, dearie. You're a part of this, too, like it or not. Fontellrae keeps the old ways and the old prophecies and even I can see you're ai'sletta touched."

I gasped and he laughed. "The luck sticks somewhat, you know. Once it touches you. It sticks like black tar bubbling up from the ground. But now, be off with you. You've a part to play and it would be a shame to be stacking up your bones when you've not yet played it."

In the distance, I heard a crash, and my heart seized in me.

The old man pushed me, and I stumbled forward into Frandtz. He didn't even grunt, just scooped me up and tossed me onto the cart as if I weighed no more than a bag of flour.

"Whatever happens next, don't look back," the old man said and then he slammed the skull door behind us and there was no light left but the lights of the torches at the front of the wagons.

We started forward with a low rumble and the creak of gears and I tried to convince myself that the sounds I heard were only creaks and echoes of creaks and not the screams of those above dying.

But I was not good at lying.

Even to myself.

168

I did not know how far we went, only that the way began to slope upward through the dank-smelling cavern and the close walls occasionally scraped the sides of the carts, triggering falls of loosened earth that made the cartwheels bump and jangle. And then the dank smell began to smell of woods and water and soon the earthen passage was balked with timber and still we rose up and up.

The air was cold on my arms, raising little prickles of gooseflesh along them. I pressed close to Judicus, feeling his hot forehead. I was worried about him – more than worried. But I could do nothing to help as the earth beneath the wheels of the open cart turned to the crunch of loose rock, and then to hard, uneven slabs of rock, and a moment later the faint light of dawn poured around us and we emerged.

I hated the dawn. Where once it had lit my heart with hope and fresh ambitions, now it tasted like ashes in my mouth.

But there were also ashes in the air, drifting in the strong wind, clouding everything with a heavy smell of fire that made my hair stand on end and bid me flee. I coughed on the ash. Around me, the armsmen of Duke Fontellrae coughed with me, and to my relief, Judicus coughed, too.

And then the ash cleared just enough to see where we were, and I wished we were back among the bones again. We had traveled far further than I'd thought.

We were in the foothills of the mountains east of the duke's estates. Not very far into them, but far enough that it was clear we'd exited from an old mining shaft on the road that would lead up farther into the hills. Far enough that we had an unobstructed view of the plains and then forest to the west. Far enough that I could see the stone house burning, the farms burning, the trees along the river burning, and the beautiful dark tilled fields speckled with soldiers.

I felt like I might be ill.

Beside me, Frandtz breathed a prayer and one of the others cursed.

And then the smoke cleared just a little more to show what they were doing with the prisoners below us, and this time I was very violently sick.

To my surprise, Frandtz held my hair for me, chanting the same prayer over and over in a ragged voice while I vomited again and again.

"They've seen us," one of the other guards said when I was finished. "We have to move."

"Donkeys won't be fast enough," his friend said. His voice was not fearful, but rather heavy with sorrow. "We can't outrun that."

"We can never outrun what we've seen," Frandtz said in a broken voice before burying himself in his prayer again.

I wanted to say it with him.

I wanted to sink into it until there was nothing but that prayer forever.

"Maybe we can hide, if we get far enough up and in," the first guard said again, clicking his tongue to the donkey.

A cloud of smoke washed over us once more, and I coughed, choking on it. But I was grateful for it. It clouded everything so I didn't have to see.

And the donkeys seemed to decide that they wanted to escape the smoke. They forged ahead faster than ever. And we walked with them – a group emerging from the crypts more stricken than the funerals that must have gone down into them over the years.

In some places, they say that smoke cleanses. I didn't believe it. But I was willing to try.

The climb became rough as the hours passed, and we wove into the winding switchback of the road that turned from a road two-carts wide to one-cart wide to a pair of furrowed tracks.

We stopped for a break at a time I would have guessed as the middle of the night though the endless, aching dawn made it impossible to know for sure. We'd been silent for hours, nothing but the squeak of harness and jingle of tack, our harsh breathing made rough by exertion and emotion, and crunch of stones under feet to break up the quiet. I was walking beside Judicus's cart, his hand clasped in mine.

If we would die, we would die together. If we lived through this endless dawn, I would try to save his leg. And if we were about to be captured, I would offer myself in his place. Even knowing ... the things I wished I didn't know. A wave of illness passed over me again and my eyelids dropped against exhaustion.

And then from below us on the hill, we heard whispering.

Frandtz made a desperate gesture to silence us – not that I needed it.

Raider words, harsh and impossible to discern, drifted up.

They were close. One bend below us, perhaps. At the speed the donkeys walked, they could be on us in minutes. How had they caught up this soon? Even with the slowness of our beasts, I didn't expect them so soon.

And then, like someone throwing a rope to a dying man, the sky went black.

I gasped. Night! Finally, night!

Something hot and wonderful pulsed in my breast.

And I was choking again – but this time on unspeakable joy.

The light flicked to the blare of full noon, and Kazmerev slipped through my heart like water through fingers, gone as quickly as he'd been there. I doubled over, hands on my knees, gasping as if I'd been struck.

Gone.

Gone.

Almost there and then gone.

My head spun, belly reeling. I was going to be ill.

There was a cry from below and the sounds of excited frenzy. They'd seen us.

Frandtz squared his shoulders and drew his weapon, one of the other guards creeping back to join him at our flank. The path was narrow enough that he could barely squeeze past the carts. One side of the track was cliff going up, the other side cliff going down. And all that was in between was this narrow rut as wide across as a donkey cart.

In the bright light of noon, tinged with peach and rose smoke, it was easy enough to see that the grass on the hill below was aflame and the fires were licking toward us.

Even if we fought off the raiders, we could not fight off the flames.

We were well and truly trapped.

I swallowed.

And the light flickered again and for a bare moment all was dark and I heard for half a heartbeat, *Little.* And then it was bright again and then dark, *Hawk.*

It was like someone passing their hand through a candle flame. Flick. Flick. Flick.

And it was bright again.

And this time when it went dark, the raiders charged up to us, screaming at the top of their lungs.

They were too late.

Kazmerev leapt from my breast, shooting up into the sky like a flower whose bloom cycle had been compressed into a single moment.

I leapt onto the cart so I could stand higher than Frandtz and his fellow guard, spread my palms wide, and let those flames pour from them into the rushing attackers, at the same moment that love poured up from me into my phoenix.

Kazmerev.

Sersha.

That moment was thinking you'd lost everything only to gain it back.

It was losing the whole world only to find it.

I couldn't even see clearly, my vision was so glazed over. Couldn't hear what the guards were calling up to me. Didn't care.

My Kazmerev was back. He was *back,* and I was whole.

I think they're all dead now, Little Hawk.

I stopped the flames, turning as he landed on the back of the cart and burying my face into his feathers. He smelled of pitch and happiness, of fragrant burnt spices and hope. And I loved him as I loved my own life and I was home.

169

What's happening?

I hardly seemed to know, myself.

But I did know one thing. My Kazmerev might not stay for long and as long as he was here, I needed to use the power he lent me for good.

Could he help me? Could he help me save them while I still could?

Of course. I can have answers later.

Gratitude washed over me as I scrambled over to where Judicus lay in the cart.

"We need to get moving again," Frandtz said, and his voice felt far away.

"What was that?" another of the guards asked.

"A miracle," Frandtz grunted. "It even burned the grass between us and the blaze below, buying us time to escape – but only if we take it."

They must not have seen that the fire came from me. Just like they wouldn't see my phoenix even now.

I shook my head vehemently. We couldn't leave yet. This had to be dealt with first. I scrambled to rip Judicus's trouser leg back so I could find that nub of arrow again. Would I have to pull it out of the bone, or could I burn it up with the healing?

I don't know. Kazmerev's tone was anxious. *How long has he been like this?*

Too long. I grasped the arrow and tugged. Nothing. It was wedged too firmly.

"Lady, we have to go," Frandtz said again, clapping a hand on my shoulder.

I looked into his worried eyes. They were bright in the full moonlight and the edges of him glowed with silver light. I motioned to him to help me pull the arrow out.

He shook his head. "No, lady. We need a solid place for him to heal before you do that. And a proper healer. Or he'll die. And His Grace was very specific that we were to keep the rope worker alive."

I let go of the arrow and grabbed his hand, trying to plead silently with him.

"No, lady." This time his expression shut down. He would not be moved.

Fine. I couldn't move it myself. But I couldn't leave Judicus like this.

And I could disappear at any second. Mally is not to be relied upon. Do what you must, Sersha.

"Frandtz?" one of the other guards called, sounding panicked. "I don't think the Flame Rider looks good. Oh no. "

He cursed.

"Can you help?" Frandtz asked me, his voice tight. The look in my eyes told me he expected a denial.

I scrambled up the cart toward the donkeys and then jumped off on one side, lifted my skirts, and pressed forward to the second cart.

"Help her down, Gerhardt," Frandtz whisper-shouted to the nearest guard, but the cart ahead had stopped, both guards leaning anxiously in over the Flame Rider.

She didn't look good. They were right to be worried. They'd bandaged her back at the stone house, but she was still ill and feverish, her face deathly pale and slick with sweat. The jostling and hurry hadn't helped and now her breathing was uneven, missing breaths. The pulse in her throat stuttered wildly when I felt for it and I couldn't tell what bones she might have broken or splinted or what herbs the healer might have given her. All I knew was that she was in terrible shape – maybe even dying as the guard feared.

I laid a hand on her and shared my warmth, my hope for her, my certainty that she could be well again. This had to work. It had to.

By the time I opened my eyes, she was opening hers, too, blinking up in surprise, and then it was my turn to gasp and stumble back as a bright white phoenix burst up from her heart. The fresh phoenix and Kazmerev both fell over themselves trying to get their greeting out.

Flame to flame I greet you, ancient fire. I am Kazmerev, Bright Flame, Bound in Oath and Heart to Sersha of Landsfall.

Flame to flame I greet you, ancient fire. I am Lilophrensa, Dazzling Star, Bound in Oath and Heart to Flara of Briccatore.

The white phoenix was small – maybe half Kazmerev's size – but she was so bright I could barely look at her.

I was grateful for something else to look at when Flara sat up, breathing out a long breath as if grateful to be using her lungs. Perhaps they had been damaged, too.

Gerhardt was there, helping her to sit up, before she could say a word. "You should rest, my ladies. We must travel through the night, but you've been through a lot."

"Thank you," Flara said carefully, looking at me.

"She doesn't speak," the guard said, apologetically, tugging his forelock to me. "Meaning no offense, lady."

I was not offended, but I wished I could tell them to stop fussing over us. I shook my head to dismiss his apology.

They're good men and they neither see your phoenixes nor realize you've healed Flara.

Instead, they wrung their hands looking worried as Flara assured them she was doing much better.

"We should keep moving, then," Gerhardt said.

You can try to heal Judicus now and see if it takes for him, too.

I bit my lip, worried. Had I used all my strength here? Would there be any left for Judicus?

I'd been a fool not to consider it before I acted.

Judicus Franzer Irault? the white phoenix asked, sounding stunned.

The very same, Kazmerev said. He sounded proud in a way that made my heart warm. I reveled in the feeling of it – until the white phoenix spoke again.

We've been looking for him for months.

170

W*hy are you looking for Judicus?*

"We don't need to talk about that," Flara muttered, but when I hopped down from her cart, she followed, and I couldn't help the stab of jealousy I felt when she did. She was maybe ten years older than I was with a serious, no-nonsense expression and a generous figure. I recalled suddenly, very exactly, that Judicus had risked his life to save hers even when he hadn't told me who he was.

Something with deep wicked claws sunk into me at that and I felt my face grow hot even as my belly twisted within me.

She'd been looking for him.

He'd saved her.

I was such a fool for thinking ... well, what had I been thinking? That he was a good friend? A good leader of my coterie? I couldn't have been thinking of more than that. It would be ridiculous.

Calm down, Little Hawk.

Of course, it was ridiculous. I had no right to think of anything more than that. He owed me nothing. He certainly didn't owe me – I swallowed, wishing I wouldn't have to admit it even to myself, but where was my courage if I couldn't even do that? – a *romantic* attachment.

I felt ill. I was such a fool.

Calm down.

"What is she so upset about?" Flara asked coolly, following me as I hurried back to Judicus's cart.

"You can't all ride in here," Frandtz grumbled as I leapt into the cart.

I glared at him, and even in the darkness, he must have seen enough to close his mouth with a snap.

I was going to heal Judicus if I could. I just had to hope I hadn't wasted all of our energy on Flara. *Flara*. Who wanted to know what I was upset about. Who didn't even say 'thank you.'

Calm down.

I did not feel calm, and I didn't know why. It was probably just that I was worried about whether I could help Judicus. That arrow was in there deep.

I scrambled down to his feet checking his pulse. He was getting worse. The red lines were past his knee now. I had to tear his trousers up past there, too, following the lines. Right up the veins. That meant infection in his blood.

"Sersha," he muttered thickly, though his eyes were still shut. He must realize it was me here with him. I clicked my tongue reassuringly.

He'd be fine. I'd find a way. I had to.

Kazmerev fluttered beside me, leaning in close.

He looks rough.

He did. He didn't look like a man being transported by a cart, but more like one who had been run over by one.

"Oh, he's not looking so good," Flara echoed my thoughts and I shot her the same glare I'd shot Frandtz. It didn't have the same effect. She ignored me, finding a seat on the baggage near Judicus's head. "Not bad looking, though, is he?"

I'd never felt the urge to push someone off a moving cart before. I felt it now. I had to grit my teeth to hold it back and hold myself in check.

I have missed you, Sersha. My thoughts are far too bland without you in them.

He could miss me when he was dead? I looked up at his flickering flame feathers, feeling a lump in my throat that had nothing to do with how much Flara was bothering me.

I can miss you always.

Warmth bloomed in my heart at that. I let it settle through me, easing whatever angry beast stirred so appallingly within. I clung to the reminder that Kazmerev was mine – my friend for life.

For life.

I had missed him, too.

And that's why I could do this.

All my needs were met. I did not demand anything from Judicus except what was best for him.

I nodded my gratitude and then closed my eyes, laying one hand on the phoenix and one on Judicus. And I thought of my love for them both, my two good friends – my brain hiccupped slightly at that – and my hopes that they would be safe, and my need to see Judicus healed, and I channeled all the warmth and heat in my heart towards Judicus.

I heard him gasp and opened my eyes in time to see the shaft of the arrow burn away and the wound close up, the spider lines of red on his leg vanishing with it.

"Sweet heavens," Flara gasped.

I sighed in relief.

But Kazmerev shifted worriedly as if he wasn't as relieved as I was.

Kaz?

The arrowhead would not have burned off.

But the shaft had, and the infection was gone, the red spider legs disappearing completely, so he probably wouldn't die tonight, right?

That's a good thing, Kazmerev agreed but he still sounded reserved. Why? *I have never had steel stuck in my bone, but I think it would hurt very much. Maybe every time I moved. And if that's so, you'll have to cut him open and draw it out before it ever gets better.*

He was right. I knew he was right. It still stung to know I hadn't succeeded.

You've succeeded in keeping our friend alive, Sersha. And it is so good to hear your warm heart again.

The cart lurched forward over a bump and Judicus grunted, coming awake with the movement of the cart. It lurched again and he hissed through his teeth.

I grabbed his hand and he clutched mine in return but to my horror, Flara grabbed his other hand. Something in my belly went from flopping to sour and spitting like a cat that fell into a pail of bad milk.

In the back of my mind, I thought I heard the echo of a laugh from Kazmerev.

"Sersha," Judicus whispered. "What's happening?"

But his eyes were closed tightly in pain, and it was too dark to sign everything, so I just squeezed one hand and patted his cheek gently with the other.

"We're in the foothills of the mountains," Flara said gently.

Judicus frowned as if he didn't like what he heard, his entire face twisting up.

"Sersha?" he gasped.

I gripped his hand a little tighter, my only response.

"Are we safe?" he asked in a thready voice.

"Yes," Flara said. "And when you awaken I have so many things to tell you."

And now that sour milk was creeping up my throat.

"Is Sersha safe, I mean?" There was a terrified edge to his voice. But I squeezed his hand again and feathered my fingers through his hair, combing it back from his face the way one does with little children when they aren't feeling well.

"She seems fine," Flara said innocently, as if she couldn't see that the poison in my throat had come right up to sparkle in my eyes.

He sighed in relief.

"Then if you don't mind, I'm afraid I might need to pass out," he mumbled, the words growing thicker until the end and then trailing off into silence.

I bit my lip and worried. How much time had I bought him? The night? A day? I'd hoped for better than that.

And now I had a bigger problem right in front of me. A woman who was edging a little closer to Judicus, patting his hand with her spare one.

I wanted to ask her what she had planned for him. I wanted to ask her what she meant when she said she had been looking for him. I tapped her on the shoulder and tried to sign a question, but she smiled gently.

"I'm sorry, I don't speak in signs," and then she turned back to Judicus, fishing a handkerchief out of her pocket and dabbing at his sweat-slicked forehead with it – which was *my* job.

Is it? That's interesting.

Kazmerev's words brought me up fast. It wasn't my job, was it?

I was being a fool.

And if Judicus knew what a fool I was, he might not want to have me in his coterie anymore. My face was hot as I very gently put his hand down – it wasn't mine to hold, was it? – and turned my back to look out behind us as the cart plodded onward. Kazmerev tucked in tight beside me.

I'm happy to be home, Sersha. Safe with you again. Why don't you sleep?

But though I held him and breathed in his hot pitch and smoke smell, I could not seem to relax as the hours melted one into the other. Instead, I told Kazmerev all that had happened while he was gone and he very quietly listened, speaking little so as not to be overheard and nuzzling me often with his great beak as if he really was delighted to have me back.

And still, Judicus slept, and still, Flara waited beside him, and still, I ached in a way I didn't understand until – to my surprise – dawn came. A real dawn.

It flared through me like an arrow shot through the heart, bringing back all my fears and terrors as Kazmerev was ripped away from me again, far too soon.

"Almost to our goal, lady," Frandtz said quietly, as if he, too, was afraid of what dawn meant, even a seemingly natural dawn. "If you look ahead, you can see it. The Untold Plinth."

I followed his finger to where it pointed there in the distance to a huge standing stone that looked very much like a pillar with no roof.

"There it is," he said, and I gasped. Because as the dawn hit the pillar it didn't look like a pillar to me at all. It looked like a glass bottle tipped upside down, larger than a silo, and filled to the brim with the screaming, panicked spirits of phoenixes.

Despite myself, my eyes met Flara's and we shared one thing in common, it seemed, because both of us were wordless with horror at what only we could see.

EPISODE FOUR: "PILLAR OF SOULS"

SEASON TWO

171

If someone had ordered a small fortress built in the foothills of the Crown Peak mountains and then ordered that it be shaped as if naturally formed of the rock and not of human hands, this, perhaps, would be the result.

The track we were following wound up around the base of it and then split off. One branch – the more well-traveled of the two – ascended further up the mountains. The other branch – grown over by scant weeds – ascended to a low, sharp peak. The peak was surrounded on three sides by steep drops, far too vertical for anyone to climb. To my surprise they were formed in such a way that they looked like sawn boards set on end in a cluster – if boards were made of granite and higher than three castles stacked one upon the other.

I'd never seen such a thing before. It gave me an unsettled feeling in my belly as we wove our way slowly up the path. This path was no natural trail widened by man as the other had been. This was formed of chisel and hammer into the planes and edges of the strange cluster of standing stones. Even if it had not led to the terrible plinth, I would not have trusted the footing of it – especially when it went over a wide crack between the standing rocks, wide as my hand and deep as the peak itself, descending into blackness.

I glanced around at my companions, wondering if they were as wary as I.

Flara looked ahead with a set jaw and determined face, as if she had known all along that we would take this path. Without her glaringly bright phoenix, she looked smaller – more like the woman recovering from grave injuries that she was and less like a fearsome thing that might steal what I loved from me.

The guards – Frandtz, Gerhardt, and the other whose name I still did not know – looked grim. Had they seen the phoenix souls trapped within the plinth, or had they seen only a dark pillar reaching up into the sky? Why did they think we were coming to this place and how had they known to come here? I had thought they were only fleeing with us as they had been ordered to do by Duke Fontellrae, to escape the Hand of the Rat gobbling up his territory and the lives of his people.

But this was not the path to safety. This was the path to the goal Judicus and I had chosen.

I wanted to ask them what they were thinking, but with Judicus passed out in the cart and the phoenixes dead for the day, none among them could understand my signs or mental voice.

I swallowed down fear and exhaustion and watched the path ahead. From where we were on the path, I couldn't see much of the plinth rising above us, and for that, I was grateful. I didn't want to see the souls trapped within or whatever puzzle might lie without.

We were, perhaps, about halfway up the chiseled rock trail, when it widened and formed a sort of shelf in the side of the hill. There was a single path leading up from the shelf to the plinth and it was rough and narrow, cut in steps rather than smoothly, not nearly wide enough for a donkey and barely wide enough for a man.

"This is as far as the carts go," Gerhardt said, soberly.

"Defensible," Frandtz remarked, looking around him, and I realized he was right. A natural rocky wall about as high as my chest blocked the shelf from the open side of the cliff, hiding the carts and donkeys from view below. The only path up was the difficult vertical one we'd taken. The shelf butted up to it so you could stand on the edge of the shelf and be at the level of someone's head coming up the path. A tiny force could likely hold off a larger one from this spot – provided they had the food and water to last.

"We'll rest here, then?" Gerhardt asked.

"No fire," Frandtz agreed.

The others seemed to shudder at that, looking over shoulders toward the lands of Duke Fontellrae which we had fled. High as we were, scraps of clouds blocked our view of the valley below and even if they had not, the thick smoke in the air would have made too great a haze to see through. But we all remembered the fires. By the scent of smoke hovering in the air, they likely still burned, consuming the lands of Fontellrae and the hillside beyond.

I swallowed down misery at the thought. My misery would be nothing to that of the men with me who had friends, and maybe even family, below.

"We'll set a watch. You ladies should sleep," Frandtz said gruffly. "We can't travel without rest, and you will have to walk some, so sleep while you may."

He murmured to the other guards, and they passed around a flask of water and some hardtack to eat, and then Frandtz went to stand by the trail to keep watch. Gerhardt tended the donkeys, unhitching them, and the third guard bedded down on the rock under one of the carts.

To my annoyance, Flara laid herself out beside Judicus and shut her eyes. There was no room for a third in the cart.

I watched them, uncertain what to do, but after a breath, I realized I was being a fool. Flara was unlikely to hurt the sleeping rope worker. After all, he'd saved her life, and she had as much right to share the cart as a bed as I did.

I slipped down from the cart, took the blanket Gerhardt nodded to when his eyes caught mine, and bedded down beside the cart as Gerhart was doing on the other side.

I was just Sersha again. Just Sersha sleeping on the ground. And though it ached to remember it, the fact remained - without Kazmerev and Judicus, I was always just a girl from a little fishing village who could not read or speak, who had no value on her own, and no connections. And I felt hollow when I remembered that and hollower still when I remembered that right now, they both needed my protection and care and I seemed to have none to give.

172

I woke to the sound of someone softly crying and jerked up to sit. Where was I?

Oh yes. The natural fortress in the hillside. Frandtz was still standing watch. He glanced back at me and then back to the perimeter. He didn't look like he was the one crying. Both of the other guards were on the ground fast asleep on the other side of the cart from me. One was snoring. Or maybe both were. It was hard to tell.

That left only the cart.

I stood up, rubbing my eyes blearily. I felt ill in the way one does when they haven't slept enough and now are awake again – an aching head and enough nausea that all I wanted to do was lie down again.

Someone snuffled like they were crying silently.

I leaned over the cart. Flara and Judicus lay back to back. She was curled up like a sleeping cat on one side. It was him who was making the noise. As I watched, he sobbed silently, shaking, his face screwed up and eyes sealed shut against his tears.

I hovered over him, unsure what to do.

He drew in a shuddering inhale.

Throwing caution to the wind I laid my hand on his shoulder and his eyes sprang open. He saw me, recognition flashing in his eyes, and then he closed them in what looked like relief and he took my hand in his, drawing in a shuddering breath.

We stayed like that for a long moment, and I wished with all my heart that I could murmur empty words of compassion over him and sing him back to sleep. It was a gift I could not give, and I felt a pauper to come to him with empty hands that could offer nothing. I settled for grasping the hand clutching mine with my other hand so his was encased in both of mine – a pitiful comfort but the best I could give.

If I could speak, I would tell him that we would soon go after his sister. That she would be safe. That I would get the arrowhead out of his leg when he was ready, and it would heal properly. That he didn't need to fear because he wasn't alone anymore, bearing an entire family on shoulders too narrow for the task. He had me and Kazmerev to help now.

I could tell him none of that, but I tried to pour it into my touch as if I could speak with the warmth of my hands where words would not spark.

After a moment, he let my hands go and opened his eyes, his cheeks flushing as if he'd been caught at something. He sat up quickly and gasped in pain.

"Your leg," I signed. *"Some of the arrow is still in the leg."*

"The arrowhead," he gasped, nodding his head in understanding. He closed his eyes and stayed like that for a few breaths, the blood draining from his face and leaving it white as mist, before whispering, "Help me down."

I helped him ease himself out of the cart. His leg didn't want to bear his weight.

"We need to see what we are dealing with," he said, shaking his head as if to clear it. He glanced over his shoulder at Flara sleeping in the cart. "Is she still ill?"

I shook my head. I'd healed *her* properly, at least.

"Then what's she doing sleeping beside me?"

I gave him a wry look. Surely, he must know why. How could he expect me to know what went on between the two of them?

He reached down and felt his leg, hissing. "Can you cut it out and heal it again?"

"When the sun sets," I mimed. I didn't want to tell him I was worried it wouldn't, even though the sun had crawled a little further into the sky.

"We can't just sleep until then," he griped, as if we'd been lying in bed relaxing instead of barely catching a few hours' sleep. "Come on, let's go investigate the plinth."

"Are you ..." I began, realizing I was missing the next sign.

"Sure?" he asked, and he sounded irritable before he caught himself and blew out a long breath. "I apologize, Sersha. You're likely exhausted. Please. Go back to sleep."

He hopped forward. Then another step. I let him go, arms crossed over my chest. Was he really going to *hop* all the way up that treacherous path?

Another hop and now Frandtz was hurrying over.

"My lord rope worker," he said in a low but slightly frantic tone. "Please, my lord, you'll do yourself a harm."

I sighed and scooped Judicus's pack from the cart, slung it over my shoulder, grabbed one of the waterskins, and hurried to catch up with him as he hopped forward again.

"My name is Judicus Franzer Irault," Judicus said with a mild smile, made mysterious by his one bandaged eye. "I'm not a lord anymore. What's your name?"

Frandtz seemed to swallow down whatever he was going to say, shaking his head and eventually just answering. "I'm Frandtz of the house of Fontellrae, sworn in service to the Duke."

"Are you standing watch for those sleeping?"

"I am."

"Then I thank you," Judicus said, hopping past him.

Frandtz hurried to get back in front of him.

"Please, sir, you need rest."

"Do you have orders concerning me, Frandtz?"

Frandtz nodded, trying to keep his voice low. "My orders are to keep you alive, sir."

"I'm not a sir, but I appreciate it," Judicus said mildly. "I can't get far out of your reach going up this path. You'll still have the trail up the hill in sight, and if anyone comes to do us harm, you'll see them."

"That's not what I'm worried about, my lord."

Judicus ran a hand over his face. I recognized that from his dealings with Mally. Impatience. Annoyance.

"If you stop fussing like a mother hen, Frandtz, then I won't interfere with your orders. Does that seem reasonable?" he asked, and to my surprise, there was steel in his voice. "If it doesn't seem reasonable to you, then I will walk down from this mountain without you or your men and there will be nothing you can do to stop me."

Frandtz swallowed down whatever retort was on his lips, nodded his head once in jerky fury, and strode past and back to his watch spot.

What had gotten into Judicus? What had made him so ... raw?

I thought of his sharp words – so unlike him. I thought of him sobbing in his sleep.

His sister. It had to be his sister.

I slipped my arm under his and he sagged gratefully onto my shoulder.

"Oh good," he said, his voice absent as if he was trying not to show me something under the surface. "You have the pack. We'll need my notes to figure out this plinth. Up for a hike?"

I nodded and ignored it when his face went scarlet. Whatever he didn't want to tell me was not sitting easily with him. The least I could do was pretend I didn't see it.

It was going to be a long morning.

173

The hike was even longer than I'd anticipated and by the time we reached the top I was grateful for the waterskin and Judicus was pale and cursing. I could imagine why. Every bit of weight he put on that leg must feel the bite of the arrowhead – an enemy within – and as much as I was supporting him, it was still hard to climb a near-vertical trail while leaning on someone else. Even with two good legs, I was on all fours at least half the climb.

In the glare of noon – muted by the peach-colored smoke that filled the air – I could no longer see the trapped spirits within the plinth. We arrived, huffing and puffing, to a simple inverted bottle of a plinth, a single design carved on its multi-faceted surface – that same design of the Cult of the Tattered Ribbons.

We circled it tiredly and when we reached the far side, I saw another symbol etched into the plinth, but this symbol was ... odd. It moved when I looked at it, like a woodland animal trying to be invisible on the forest floor. The harder I tried to catch a glimpse, the quicker it skittered away. I squinted harder, giving myself a headache, and had to turn my back so that my eyes could rest as my temples throbbed from the effort.

But when I turned my back, I had the horrifying sensation that the symbol was going to reach out and grab me. I settled for standing with my side facing it so that I didn't have my back to it but also didn't have to look at it.

"They call that Reiven's Syndrome," Judicus said a little hoarsely. He was still looking at the symbol, his face twisted in his usual mix of interest and pain. "When you can't look at a thing but can't look away. They teach us to tie knots for it, but this knot is stronger than anything I've seen before. I'm not sure how to pick it apart. Or what to do with it if I do."

I cocked my head to the side in question.

"Yes, well, I can't just leave it there," he said with a wry smile, running his hand through his hair and then looking at it with a puzzled expression when he forgot again that I'd cut his hair. "If you untie a ropework knot and just leave it, it doesn't go away. It just claws out like tentacles, snatching at anything or anyone who comes near."

He looked over the edge of the sharp cliff as he spoke and then threw himself backward.

"You said something about a rent in the earth on the tapestry?" he asked with a gasp. His back was pushed against the plinth in a way that made me queasy.

I nodded and stepped forward to see what had bothered him.

My breath stuck in my chest as I looked down a long, long drop – far too long for the height of this hill. It sank into a dark gap in the rock. Clinging to the walls of the gap were stone creatures. Octopi, crabs, things that had four long legs and a long prehensile nose. They were built with careful detail and memories surfaced as I watched them – memories of a stone octopus killing everything in its reach in the valley near the Temple of the Tattered Ribbons cult and of the stone creatures that rose from the sea and walked with our island on their backs – the Creatures of Sydonon. And now, here there were more stone creatures. They didn't seem to be moving. But when I turned from them to Judicus, I got Reiven's Syndrome all over again.

The skin on my back crept like it was covered in bugs. Surely those things must move. They must, even now, be scaling the wall. They must be about to grab us.

I turned back and glared – quickly so I would catch them. They were still in place.

"It's the same either way," Judicus said with a shiver. "No matter where you put your back, it feels like something's watching you. What if we sit so that we're both facing opposite directions? We could watch each other's backs."

I nodded quickly and helped him sit to face the plinth while I sat to face the edge of the cliff. I'd notice something immediately if it moved.

"It's going to be tricky to figure out what to do with this knot. I feel like I need to tie it into a new knot as soon as it's untied from this one – but what knot? What does it do?"

I rummaged into my bag and handed him the small book that Fontellrae had given me, and he took it.

"What's this?" he asked. We were sitting side by side with our backs to opposite dangers, but we were in front of each other enough that he could see my hands as I signed.

"The duke gave it to you."

"Fontellrae?"

"He thought it could help."

Judicus opened it. "Did you know this was written in his own hand?"

I shook my head as he read, looking up from time to time to check the plinth. The minutes passed slowly and when he looked up, I expected him to talk about the plinth. Instead, he spoke.

"Thank you for saving my life, Sersha. Can I assume you've seen Kazmerev?" he looked shy as he said that. Though why he'd be shy, I couldn't fathom.

I nodded.

"Is he well?"

I nodded again. He flushed hard.

"You must have healed Flara, too?" he was looking at the book again when he said that, and I realized he knew her name.

My own cheeks were hot when I replied, "*Yes.*"

"Thank you," he said simply, graciously, and then left it at that so he could return to his book. He read very well for a man with one eye covered.

I sat and watched the edge of the hill and if my eyes stung a bit, I had every right to let them. After all, I'd been through a lot. And there was smoke in the air. Who wouldn't have stinging eyes under those circumstances?

It certainly wasn't because I thought my heart might be bruised. Because I should have learned a long time ago that people like me aren't the ones people want to love and marry. We're the useful ones. We're the reliable ones. And I should be happy with that. I shouldn't be remembering a dark cave and hours spent signing and a friend I hadn't realized I'd grown so close to. I shouldn't be remembering any of that.

174

"This book is written in Fontellrae's own hand," Judicus said again, squinting as his fingers skimmed over the thin paper – a wonder all its own. "It is begun some time ago. Hmmm. Did he say why he was giving it to us?"

"*He said it would help,*" I signed when he looked up.

"It ... does not seem relevant at first glance," he said, glancing up at the plinth and then back at the book. "It cites a prophecy from someone named Clarinfas the Sighted. He speaks of a man seeking a sign and climbing up into these mountains. It's your typical prophecy-type thing – vague. Lots of references to everything being destroyed by fire."

He coughed awkwardly and I raised an eyebrow and sniffed. Everything literally *was* being destroyed by fire in the valley below. And what could we do to stop it?

"I see your point," he agreed, reading further. "There's something about honored banner men and women who will find the Seeker of the Sign and help him to 'return the stones to dust and that which is not a flame to the fire.' Now we are getting somewhere. The Stryxex are 'not a flame.' I still don't see what they have to do with the plinth."

"*Judicus,*" I signed, but he wasn't looking up. I laid a hand tentatively on his knee and when he startled, I tried again. "*Judicus. When it was still dark and then at dawn, we saw something within.*"

"Within the plinth?" his eyebrows rose, and he tapped his chin with his forefinger. At my nod, he followed with a second question. "Who is 'we'?"

I pointed behind us and he ran his fingers through his hair.

"You can't tell me a name. Yes. Was it one of the guards?"

I shook my head.

"Flara, then. The other Flame Rider. What did you see?"

I didn't have a word for souls, so I tried, *"Phoenixes."*

"Phoenixes? Trapped in the plinth?" He frowned, scrutinizing it, and then looked back at me.

I made a helpless gesture. I had no words for what I'd seen.

"Their souls, perhaps."

I nodded.

"They, certainly, would want to be returned to the fire. So, we read on."

He seemed to be in his element as he opened the book again and read. I, on the other hand, felt a cold chill over my back. Behind me, trapped somehow by magic, were the souls of phoenixes and before me in the open pit were the strange stone creatures and to my sleep-starved mind, it seemed as though they might come alive and begin to move at any moment.

I shivered, edging a little closer to Judicus. He seemed not to notice.

"He finishes chronicling the prophecy and then he makes notes here that can be skimmed over. This one is about a sacred trust to his family and duchy to protect the way to the plinth. Odd. This one is about the need to keep strangers from it. Which is even stranger since he has allowed *us* access. And another prophecy. Oh dear."

His face had gone white. I watched him intensely as he fell silent, his lips shaping words but no sound coming from them. He flipped through a few more pages before I grew impatient and tapped his knee.

He looked up, blinking, like a creature from under a rock after the stone has been lifted.

"Oh. Yes. Sersha. You wouldn't believe this. His ancestors believed that the day someone came to them asking for knowledge of symbols and mentioning the plinth their lands would be razed and their home destroyed, and none could save them."

His eyes met mine in shared horror.

"He knew the moment I arrived and asked. He knew and he gave us the library, and the men, and his hospitality."

He looked like he was going to be ill and then, true to form, he scrambled to all fours, moaning in pain as the movement hurt his leg, and then leaned over the edge of the cliff and vomited.

I still didn't know how he kept enough food in him to live. He seemed to always be ill from something.

I made my way cautiously to him, patting his back reassuringly and offering him the waterskin.

"Thank you, Sersha. You must think I'm forever sick."

The thought had certainly crossed my mind.

"It's not ... it's just ... I mean those poor people."

He made his way back to sit again and I waited for the pain to ease on his face before I signed.

"It is not wrong to care."

He looked at me miserably, "I care about all of it, and sometimes it feels like I can't do anything about any of it. And every time I try, I make it worse. I went to find the ai'sletta, who was prophesied about, so I could free my family. Now, my sister is trapped worse than ever before. I came to find this place – which turned out to be prophesied – so the ai'sletta could succeed, and look? All those poor people, dead. Their homes burned. I hate prophecies. I never want to see another one." He looked forlornly at the book. "Perhaps, we should stop here. Perhaps it's better if we just don't do anything."

We sat in silence for a long time, sharing a heavy feeling of guilt and misery. Because I agreed. And he was right.

He looked up, after long minutes. "What do you think?"

I swallowed, weighing my thoughts, and then began to sign.

"I think that once you have brought the bear into your house you can't decide you don't like excitement."

I struggled with "bear" and "excitement," but I thought my hasty renditions worked.

Judicus blinked twice and then burst into laughter. Had I ever seen him laugh? He was so serious always.

"What?" he asked.

"We say that in my village," I signed, smiling, but under my merriment was a bitter certainty that it was true. We were in a mess. Terrible things had happened. People had died as a result of our choices to be propelled along this path. And it didn't matter that they probably would have died anyway and that the Hand of the Rat and their evil countrymen were the true hands behind this evil. Because now the bear was in our house, and we had to deal with it one way or another.

Judicus's laughter faded. "Then I guess we deal with the bear." He opened the book again and kept reading. "There is some speculation on what sign the Seeker will be looking for and what it might do." He looked up and met my eyes with a crooked smile. "Well, we at least know where to put the sign, don't we, Sersha? Though what might happen once it is set – that troubles me. What if it doesn't free those phoenixes at all? What if it ignites the stone creatures below? I don't like any of this."

I shrugged, shaking my head in shared worry. What other choice did we have?

He read on as the afternoon bled away and as the immediate horror of where I was sitting began to fade, I fought off sleep.

I was drifting off when he slammed the book shut.

"Well. Well, then." He looked at the plinth, but his eyes were unfocused, drifting. "So much to think about, and yet no answers at all. There were symbols and suggestions – guesses, mostly. Nothing firm and certainly no understanding of what they might ... do. I'm at a loss, Sersha. And if we can't find the right path then perhaps, we should take no path at all. To change the symbol might set anything in motion and I'm afraid I've already set too much alight. Everywhere I go, flames follow and people I love are hurt."

I reached out and took his hand and he looked down at our hands, blinking furiously as if he wasn't sure how we came to be touching.

"If only I knew the right symbol and if only I knew *why* it was right," he said with a sigh.

Behind me, a soft voice spoke, and gravel crunched under a boot that had been very, very quiet sneaking up on us.

"I know the symbol, Judicus Franzer Irault. It's why I've been looking for you."

175

"Flara?" Judicus said, tipping his head to the side as he did when presented with an interesting puzzle. The edge of his eye-bandage was coming undone and it flopped slightly when he moved his head, reminding me that he was stronger than he looked – strong enough to bear up under severe injuries.

I pressed my lips firmly together and placed my hands calmly in my lap.

I did not turn around.

Somehow, I'd been expecting this.

"You're the one who was prophesied," she said, and she sounded breathless. "We started looking for you months ago."

"Me?" Judicus sounded confused. "I'm afraid there's some kind of misunderstanding. There have been no prophecies about me."

"You're reading them. I heard you talking about them."

She'd been eavesdropping on top of everything else. I felt my face grow hot with annoyance. I clenched my jaw until my teeth hurt. I still hadn't turned around. I knew there was something wrong with me. I shouldn't dislike a person so much. Hadn't I wanted to stop and save her when Fontellrae forced me to go on without her? And yet here I was feeling my temperature rise at just the sound of her voice.

I stood carefully, controlling my breath, and offered them both a smooth smile before moving to the other side of the plinth and picking my way toward the path.

Behind me, Judicus was still protesting. "Anyone could be called 'the Seeker' it just means someone who is looking for something, and I wasn't looking for this until a few days ago. You might as well be excited to see the librarians in Briccatore. They're looking for these things, too. They always are."

"It's different," she said, and I caught a look at her bright eyes as I passed. I hadn't seen that look since Gundt found Mally. It bordered on worship. It made me feel all twisted up inside. "Look!"

She pulled up the sleeve of her shirt and revealed a tattoo on her skin – an intricate knot with no ends. It wove in on itself.

"What is that?" Judicus asked, grimacing as he pulled himself to his feet and limped over to take her forearm in his hands and examine it. The move brought him very close to her.

Flara looked triumphant. This – whatever this was – was exactly what she wanted.

I left them to it, making my way to the other side of the hill and leaning over the edge in the last rays of the afternoon sun. Below, down the narrow track, Fontellrae's armsmen had started a fire and were cooking something, one of them still on watch by the wider trail.

Far past them, the foothills rolled into the thick smoke below that cloaked the landscape so thickly that I couldn't make out any details. All I could see were rising pillars, or waves of smoke, like the sea had grown furious and burnt itself into this horrific landscape.

The sun hung somewhere along the horizon, crimson in shared grief as it shone through the thick smoke.

I watched it and let my mind tumble. If Flara could help Judicus with this knot, then maybe that was for the best. Maybe they were the ones who could do this together. Maybe I wasn't needed here.

So, what? What else would I do?

I could go back for Judicus's sister myself. Just me and Kazmerev.

It was a silly thought.

How could I manage that by myself?

Another voice inside my mind reminded me that if the Flamerarch were still in Briccatore then I could tell them about Reichus and they might listen to me. Or they might not. Or they might not be there. They might have been dragged away, one by one, by the raiders.

I could go help Mally. I could make my way across the sea. I could – what? What could I do for her?

I felt foolish. Why was I even thinking about this? I'd developed an overblown sense of myself. I was no more useful than the donkeys who had brought us here. I had use, but I was not the hero of this journey.

It was in the middle of this self-doubt that the sun sank and Kazmerev sprang to life in my heart, bright and bold, a flower blooming into the sky, licking flames dancing with fresh life, bringing with him the scent of charcoal and sulfur and fresh grass.

I sighed with relief. He was here.

Little Hawk. Let's fly!

My heart leapt. If there was one thing I wanted to do right now, it was fly.

Jump.

I jumped, and he was under me immediately. Warmth and the scent of burning pine sap filled my nose and I buried my fingers into his spirit feathers – black and purple, edged with bright scarlet and sparks of gold. I leaned forward and buried my face into his feathers, so grateful for his warmth, his strength, his closeness. I hadn't realized how lonely and untethered I'd felt until I suddenly wasn't anymore.

Gratitude washed through me, a welcome tide.

We whirled upward like a flame loosened from the tip of a bonfire and shot into the sky and for one glorious moment, it was just me and my friend of flame, just the two of us in the wide, open sky. As we dove up into the height of the sky, the smoke cleared and the stars emerged, shining in merry delight and we corkscrewed up and up and into the beauty of it and I felt Kazmerev's thoughts cradling mine, his firm certainty filling in the holes in my confidence, his strong conviction bolstering my shaky hopes.

We were so high up now that I'd lost sight of Judicus entirely. I felt a pang of worry for him and then stifled it. After all, he had Flara, and she seemed very keen on being close to him.

Aren't you a bitter thing? You taste like spring onions.

Fair enough. And I was glad we were so high up because I did not want Flara's phoenix eavesdropping on us.

Lilophrensa, he corrected.

I needed his good judgment. He always saw clearly.

We soared, the cold air brushing my hair back and soothing my pounding head and his warm body keeping me toasty warm at the core as I poured out my heart and our problem out to him.

It's been a long time since I was young, he said when I was done and there was a sound of laughter in his mental voice.

I didn't see what that had to do with anything.

Have you considered that you are jealous of Flara?

I didn't know what I'd be jealous of.

Then you aren't falling tail over beak for that sickly rope worker?

My cheeks were hot – likely from his endless heat and not anything else. I was not falling for anyone. And besides, Judicus was not sickly, I'd just met him during a difficult time.

He's courageous and pure-hearted and clever. But he's sickly. Even I can see that. If a phoenix was forever spewing fire everywhere the way that boy spews his food, we'd think he was about to take the last death.

Well, Judicus wasn't. Not if I could help it and not if I could fix his leg. Which we needed to do now that Kazmerev was well.

I care not whether you acknowledge it. But you should know it's affecting your judgment.

Then it was up to him to keep me on the right path. He seemed pleased at that.

I think if the Lilophrensa's rider has a knot he can try, then he should try it. After you heal him. We don't have a lot of time. Stryxex are everywhere. Phoenixes are disappearing. The time of caution has passed. We need this puzzle solved and a way to get the duplicate puzzle to Mally, and that means he needs to try something.

I agreed.

And you need to rein in your jealousy. If you won't admit you're fond of the boy, then at least admit you need self-control around the other girl. That she is not an easy fit for you.

That was certain enough.

If you love someone then you do what's best for them, even if it's hard for you. It is not easy for me to keep my memories of the riders I had before. I could pretend they never existed. Instead, I honor them with my memories. I don't let my emotions prevent something important. You should do the same. Your emotions are a barking dog. Teach yourself to keep them on a short tether.

As always, he was right.

I could hear the song of his satisfaction as he drifted down from the sky, and I let him enjoy the moment. We'd been apart too much of late. It was so, so good to have him back.

176

We descended through the lavender dusk, the smoke around us obscuring the shape of the land below until we were almost upon the plinth.

As it came into view, a gasp tore from my chest. I could see them again. Hundreds of lights battering against the inside of the plinth like trout put in a barrel, smacking their noses forever against the side in an attempt to swim free.

I swallowed down bile, barely able to contain myself for a second time.

What madness is this? Kazmerev's voice echoed in my mind and even he sounded shaken. *This is an abomination. It must be stopped.*

And as we grew closer the sound of something that sounded almost like a very low keening – or singing? – met my ears and to my shock, I saw Flara's very bright white phoenix nestled so her forehead was against the plinth, and it was she who made that sound. I found it deeply unsettling.

Easy now, Little Hawk. Remember. Spring onions.

I was not bitter. I just didn't like what I was seeing. Before the plinth, Judicus had his head bent low over Flara's arm, studying her tattoo with his usual fervor and her other hand drifted over his head as if it might come down in a caress at any moment.

I rolled my eyes.

No, that's certainly not jealousy. Not at all.

I bit my lip as we descended. I definitely did not want Judicus to know I was jealous.

See? You are *jealous.*

My cheeks were hot as I leapt from Kazmerev's back.

I strode forward and tapped Judicus on the shoulder, ignoring Flara's look of affront.

He looked up, knocking her hand on his head and then startling, falling onto his injured leg and wincing terribly.

"Sersha. Gah, that leg hurts! Sersha. I was just wondering where you were. Have you seen this? She has this knot tattooed right on her arm and from what I can tell, it's a freedom knot. It should release something."

I glanced uneasily at the souls bumping against the plinth. Beside me, Kazmerev shuffled, shying away. I noticed Flara was not looking at the plinth. Maybe the souls made her too uncomfortable.

"I think we should try it." He ran a hand through his hair and bit his lip, his eyes glued to the plinth.

"Can you see what is inside the plinth?" I signed.

He shook his head.

"What's she saying? We don't have time for her signs," Flara said irritably. "We must work this immediately. With the Hand of the Rat swarming across the plains we may have little time."

I ignored her.

"We should heal your leg first, Judicus," I signed. *"While my phoenix is here."*

I didn't have a sign for Kazmerev. I needed one.

I am too great for any sign, Kazmerev said in my mind. *Though I would be open to seeing your suggestions.*

I'd attend to that directly. After we healed Judicus. And decided on what to do with the plinth.

"Umm," Judicus said, looking from Flara to me uncertainly.

"The leg," I signed again, more emphatically. If this knot didn't work and we had to run again, or if the raiders came and we had to run again, or if Mally decided to go crownless, and we lost the chance we would regret not acting now.

"We must do this immediately, Seeker," Flara said, her eyes burning with a combination of firmness and devotion.

I could just nudge her off the mountain. Her phoenix would catch her.

Unkind, Sersha.

My face burned hotter still. He was right.

"Flara is right," Judicus said, smiling awkwardly at me. "I need to do this while I still can."

"There's no hurry," I signed. It wasn't entirely true, but I was worried about him. We needed to help him first.

"I think, Judicus," Flara said sweetly, "That you can make your own choices without input from those without your experience. Look."

She pointed out behind her where the descent of night cut through the smoke enough to show us the fires burning in the distance.

"We only have so much time. The fires are behind us. And so is the Hand of the Rat."

Self-control, Kazmerev hissed in my mind. I unclenched my fists, taking in big breaths. Yes. I had to control myself.

"But stay close, Sersha," Judicus said, smiling at me as if nothing was going wrong. "We'll do your thing as soon as this is done."

My thing? Healing his leg from what could cripple him for life and was causing him enormous pain right now was somehow *my thing*?

Big breaths. Wow. It turns out you are more like Mally than I gave you credit for. That's quite the temper.

If he said anything after that, it was lost in the big breaths I was trying to take as Judicus leaned so that one hand was on the plinth and the other could trace Flara's tattoo with a long forefinger. She winked at me over his back. And I finally understood the term "bristled."

Self-control! It's like you came out of the egg today. You are not newly hatched.

Flara's weird phoenix was swaying now as its keening song accelerated in rhythm and I was pretty sure Judicus couldn't see it, or he'd be as creeped out as I was.

Perhaps we should fly again. You need space from this.

Someone was going to ...

I didn't finish the thought. Judicus crossed his eyes, flung his head back, and then the rock under my feet shifted to something that didn't feel like rock at all. It felt like I was standing on a living creature. I leapt for Kazmerev, catching him in a hug as he slid under me.

I was only just in time. The rock under where I was standing cracked and slid away, bouncing down the mountainside with a terrible series of quieter and quieter crashes.

Judicus didn't even notice. His eyes were still fixed above him at the strange knot on the side of the plinth, his finger still tracing the knot on Flara's arm.

Flara's eyes widened but she didn't so much as flinch. Maybe she really did believe all this. Maybe Judicus really was a religious figure to her. The thought made me feel like ants were crawling under my skin.

From the edge of my hearing, I heard the cry of a bird.

We hunt! Kazmerev said and without a word from me, we were in the sky, gaining height, his neck stretched forward and wings beating at the air as one might beat out an errant flame.

In the distance, something twisted at the corner of my eye, and I swallowed down a curse.

Flara hadn't been wrong. We had very little time after all.

The Stryxex had found us.

177

Ready yourself! Kazmerev told me, and there was an element of excitement in his focused voice.

I bit my lip and buried one hand in his feathers, the other ready for throwing fire or whatever else we must do.

They're vulnerable down there and we're their only protection while they do this thing, Kazmerev said and it seemed to me that all his energy was focused on this, that it thrilled him to be on the hunt again. I hadn't realized how much he was born for this.

We circled over the hill, defensive in our spiral. Below, Judicus and Flara worked without looking up and Liliphrensa continued her odd swaying dance.

I strained my eyes, looking for the armsmen. There they were at their little fire and guarding the pass. Whatever had made the hill above spongey must not have affected them or they'd be more alarmed. Were they under threat of attack?

I saw no small figures creeping up the hill, though it was hard to be certain.

Eyes up!

His warning was just in time. I jerked my eyes up as the Stryxex closed on us. My eyes met the narrowed eyes of the veiled rider and at that moment a gust of wind struck us both so hard that our mounts wavered and shook, blown slightly off course in the same direction. The rider's hood was ripped away and his red hair shone like a beacon.

Him again!

I felt Kazmerev's mental growl deep in my own chest.

The Stryxex dove, claws and beak outstretched, a shriek in its throat that sliced through the air like a knife slices through a melon, and then they were upon us.

I raised my hand and poured fire from the palm, but the Stryxex was fast. It rolled, bringing its rider to the side and then under it, almost falling, before righting itself underneath us. My flames passed over it harmlessly.

Kazmerev arched up and then dove down, head-first, like a fish spitting the hook. My hand in his feathers clung to him but the magic kept me tight against his back, even – impossibly – when I was in a place that surely I must fall away or be ripped from his grasp.

Sweat broke out across my brow as we followed the Stryxex, serpent-like in our slide through the air. He was making for the pillar directly and we were hot on his tail.

Something was happening below us. The symbol on the plinth seemed to be clawing out, dark arms whipping out from it like an angry squid – like the stone octopus that we'd fled at the temple of the Cult of Tattered Ribbons. He must have begun to loosen the knot and those must be its loose ends waving wildly as if they might catch him and claw him apart.

My heart felt heavy as a rock. I should snatch him back from that.

He won't thank you for it.

I needed to get to him before the Stryxex.

Too late!

And he was right. The Stryxex was ahead of us, roaring towards Judicus. The rider produced a wicked-looking javelin.

Without thinking at all, I whipped my arm as if I was throwing something and to my surprise, a ball of fire flew from my hand and splashed across the back of the Stryxex.

It keened loudly, tumbling off course and down the side of the mountain.

Nice work!

Kazmerev shifted, adjusting his course so we were chasing the fall of the creature. Wind rushed around my face, streaming around me as we plummeted.

Keep up the pressure on him!

I threw a second ball of fire and the Stryxex bucked, tumbling now in a terrible roll. The javelin fell away, and the rider clung to his mount's back with both hands, his legs spread wide and whipping out as he tumbled like flags flapping in the wind.

We were dropping so fast we were nearly to the stone creatures. They were remarkably life-like and from this close, I could see patterns picked out across them like a madman had been set loose with a chisel and hammer and told to be creative.

The Stryxex leveled out, seeming to right itself.

One more! Come on now!

But this time when I flung a ball of fire, it was smaller, weaker. I tried again, and the ball of fire materialized and then winked out.

Your energy fades.

Kazmerev's voice was tight. I felt my own chest seize with fear.

Oh no.

The fireballs had been too much – too much show and too much energy and now how would I defend Judicus?

My breath was coming too fast, and I lowered my hand to grip Kazmerev for the comfort he could offer, just as something below moved, shifting.

It was one of the stone beasts.

It reached up and snatched the Stryxex from the air, flinging the rider from its back, and to my horror, stone jaws opened, and stone jaws shut over the fluttering Stryxex like a frog eating a moth. An apt description, since the creature looked like an elongated frog with crab-like claws for hands.

My mouth was still open in horror as Kazmerev corkscrewed past the creature at top speed.

If you want a prisoner, catch him ... now!

The red-headed raider fell right in front of me, and I snatched for him to keep him from sliding from Kazmerev's back. He was smoking and burned from my fireballs, patches of his clothing entirely gone, leaving only red blistering skin. And he was out cold.

What was I supposed to do with a prisoner?

Better question – what are we supposed to do with these?

We were climbing again, nearly vertical as Kazmerev fought for immediate height. I glanced down and bit my own tongue in surprise. Below us, the entire rift in the earth was crawling like a kicked anthill, stone creatures emerging from it to crawl – sometimes over one another – in a desperate attempt to get out. Something bright flowed through them like a thin river of light.

This was not good.

This is really not good.

We agreed on that, at least.

178

We gained height quickly, fast enough that we were close to level with Judicus on the hillside when I finally thought to look up.

I was so stunned by what I saw that for a moment I didn't know what to do.

Judicus had his arms in front of him spread out, a look of shocked overwhelm on his face like he couldn't believe what he was seeing. His hands fought physically with the flapping, clawing edges of the knot he'd untied as if he could force it into place manually.

He was not succeeding.

With a roar, he screwed up his long face and flung his narrow shoulders forward, wrestling the rope work with ropes of his own, springing from his hands like tendril roots from a great oak as he thrashed against the tentacle-like strands.

Something trickled from the plinth – something that looked like bright light – in a narrow stream down the side of the plinth and down the cliff.

Beside him, Flara's eyes glowed – literally glowed – shading her smile until it looked otherworldly, and no one needed to tell me that her eyes shouldn't be doing that and as they grew brighter and brighter her swaying, trance-like phoenix's form began to dull from the white brightness it had before as the light sucked out of it. It twisted, and what had looked like a bright phoenix inverted to a Stryxex before my eyes.

Kazmerev screamed a terrible bird-like phoenix scream and I thought I might be screaming with him.

I was fooled! Tricked!

And then the top of the plinth split like the cracking of an egg and I realized what the trickle had been before as the spirits that were within flowed out in a river, screaming just like Kazmerev had screamed as they flowed like molten honey and poured down the side of the mountain into the tear in the earth where the writhing stone creatures leapt and struggled toward them. It was the spirits raising them to life. I knew it without knowing how.

I couldn't form a coherent thought. I didn't know what to do.

And then Flara took a step back from Judicus and I knew exactly what to do.

Kazmerev! We need to grab Judicus before she –

I didn't even get to finish the thought.

Flara leaned forward, kissed Judicus chastely on the lips, and then pushed him into the grappling tentacles of the rope work knot he'd been fighting.

The air seemed to suck out of the world and I couldn't breathe.

The living knot wound around him, tightening, throttling, strangling.

We dove toward them. Not fast enough. Not fast enough.

I could feel the scream of Kazmerev's flames stretching toward our goal.

Flara was faster than we could be. She leapt from the cliff, was caught by her Stryxex, and spiraled upward into the darkness of the night.

She'd be back. I knew that without having to guess. She'd come for the red-haired man I held captive. How could she not when they were both Stryxex riders?

That could not be my concern, not now.

I needed to get to Judicus.

Kazmerev dove to where I could leap from his back. It wasn't easy to sustain his physical presence to hold the prisoner while I wasn't on his back, but I did it as I leapt to the unsteady, spongey mountaintop, grabbed Judicus's bag and retrieved his belt knife from within. I threw the pack strap over one shoulder, stood, and slashed at the arms of magic clamped around Judicus's throat.

They held him in inky strands like the cords of a muscle or a thick ship's rope, one wrapped twice around his neck, while others branched around his midsection, both arms, and one leg. They weren't just single strands but rather each one was tied in knots upon knots upon knots. Judicus's own root-like ropes had vanished, and his face was red, mouth open, choking as he gasped for breath, eyes rolled back into his head.

My own gasping sobs filled my ears as I hit the knife against the ropework, but it didn't penetrate them, didn't sink in, didn't even scratch the surface of the magic holding him.

He had seconds, if that.

Stop attacking the arms and get the heart.

The heart? Where was the heart on a knot?

I wanted to sob with the frustrated despair clamping over my heart.

Where is the knot held to this pillar?

Somewhere behind Judicus, I was sure.

I sank to my knees and tried to see if I could see any kind of opening to where the knot was attached to the wall. No chance. The knot had Judicus sealed across itself, pulled tighter with every breath.

I stood, frustrated but beyond terrified by the sounds coming from him as the ropework pulled tighter.

This was a terrible way to die.

I'd only have one shot at stopping it. I stepped close, and quick as I could, I wiggled one hand behind his lower back and pulled him toward me with all my strength – making just enough room for the other arm to slip in. It was a deadly hug. I wiggled the tip of my knife into the center of the knot and *pushed.*

I felt the moment it found a soft spot and sank in and like a broken bowstring, the arms snapped away from Judicus and fell limp along the plinth.

He fell, heavy, into my arms.

The knife fell from my grasp as I stumbled backward, trying to hold his whole weight in my arms. He sank against me, head over my shoulder, shoulders drooped against my chest.

My boot heel lost its grip and I slipped hard to one side, falling into someone who smelled of pitch and smoke.

Relief shot through me – but only for a moment. The mountain was trembling again.

Shift so I can wiggle under you.

But what about the prisoner?

Keep Judicus in that hug and lift one leg. I'll slip in from the side and keep the unconscious man ahead of you.

It wasn't a certain plan, but it was the best we were going to get.

Heart in my throat, I lifted a leg, putting all my weight and Judicus's on one limb.

My muscles screamed their protest.

Kazmerev ducked under it, and for one wild moment it felt like I was sitting on nothing at all and my belly dropped out through my bottom, and then, suddenly, he was solid and we were lifting up, unsteady and shaky, but lifting, lifting, leaving the trembling pillar behind.

I sucked in a long breath, and clung to Judicus, willing him to breathe, to please breathe, and coughing on the smoke in the air.

The smoke had gotten worse, I thought.

Below us, the stone creatures rolled up out of the tear on the earth flooding into the ravine between the rocks. They did not pause, did not stop, did not turn aside no matter what the terrain in front of them, just kept rolling over the jagged landscape.

And I could see them in my mind's eye, rolling across the devastated lands of Fontellrae's people, and over the river, and up toward the people of Briccatore shut in their homes, and my throat seemed like it was closing up, too.

What had we done?

179

We soared shakily over the broken plinth, the knots hanging out of it looking like a fish half-gutted for dinner.

I shuddered.

Somewhere safe, Kazmerev was muttering in my mind, *we have to find somewhere safe.*

But we couldn't leave the men who had come with us. We had to warn them. And their carts could carry the prisoner and Judicus as they healed, for soon it would be morning.

Yes. This is best.

I was surprised to hear the note of worry in his mind. He was always so calm.

I don't like the idea of leaving you like this. Not with those stone creatures out there. Not with that terrifying Stryxex rider.

She'd gone somewhere and he was right, she could come back at any time. Her Stryxex had not been wounded.

How had we mistaken it for a phoenix?

I don't know.

And this time he seemed shaken to his core. I put a hand on him to try to reassure him. Something magical had happened there – something involving powers beyond us, something that had taken hours yet felt like mere minutes.

None of the other Stryxex have ever had a voice. None of them have spoken to me or greeted me as a phoenix. It was ... like touching a flame only to find it was icy cold. It was ... It was not right.

I didn't like hearing him panic. He was the strong one! He was the one who was always sure.

In all my centuries I've never seen anything like it. It makes my bones feel like they rot within me.

He didn't even have bones.

Maybe I do now and maybe they are rotting.

But the time to reassure him had passed. We'd arrived at the donkey carts below to where three armsmen stood clustered around the hitched donkeys, weapons in hand, and worried lines in their foreheads.

"We felt the mountain shake," Frandtz said with a trembling voice. "And now here you are on the back of a phoenix. Have you always been a Flame Rider, too?"

The others mirrored his uncertain look.

I nodded firmly and waved him closer. I would need help getting Judicus on the cart.

He leapt forward and so did Gerhardt, leaving the last guard – whose name I still didn't know – tending the donkeys. They all shot me uncertain looks as if they'd seen a rabbit transform into a wolf before their eyes.

"Here, let us help you," they said, but to my surprise they pulled the red-haired Stryxex rider down first, being very, very careful to avoid touching Kazmerev. They watched him with huge eyes, ducking their heads respectfully any time my phoenix's black eye caught theirs.

See? This is how humans are meant to regard phoenixes.

He couldn't be that worried if his arrogance was showing this strongly.

I can afford both emotions.

"A prisoner?" Gerhardt sounded a little breathless. "Were you attacked, then?"

I nodded but it was hard to do. Judicus felt heavier by the moment.

Relief filled me when they pulled him from my arms and helped me to lay him in the cart. They scrambled back to the prisoner and trussed him up as I checked the leader of my coterie.

Judicus was breathing. But there were dark bruises circling his throat. He'd likely find it as hard to speak as I did for the next week. His leg, and arms, and waist were likewise bruised, blotchy and terrible to look at. And I did not have the strength to heal him. I'd wasted all of it on the fireballs.

And so, we left the mountain the same way we ascended it – with Judicus passed out in the cart and a Stryxex rider in the other cart, danger all around, and all of us in silent agreement that things were very bad, indeed.

Frandtz had tried to insist we wait for Flara but eventually, with hand gestures from me and a lot of spitting and angry strutting from Kazmerev, they'd been persuaded to leave without her.

"It would be handy if you could speak," Frandtz had muttered and I agreed, but there was nothing for it but to push them to do something that went against their natures.

"We could go up after her?" the one whose name I did not know suggested, but it sounded more like a question.

"Better not to," Gerhardt had muttered, shooting a side look at me.

They were silent until we reached the bottom of the hill where it had branched from the main road over the pass. The trail was worn with tracks, but whether they were old or new, I couldn't tell, and neither could the men with me.

"I don't know where we should go," Frandtz said, staring at the trail. "To go back down the mountain is to find the raiders and their fires. But they may have followed us and be further up the trail."

All of their gazes drifted to me. I took a big breath and then pointed toward the mountain.

I didn't know what lay in that direction. I didn't know if these carts had enough supplies to get us there. I didn't know how we could possibly stop a stone army from rampaging across the land or do anything about those molten souls from the plinth, but I knew two things for sure: we could not go down to the valley with Judicus unconscious – none of us would survive that – and we could not stay here with Flara lingering somewhere nearby.

Upward was the only direction left.

I gritted my teeth as the carts rumbled upward and when, minutes later, Kazmerev dove back to my heart like a meteor falling to earth and the sun rose across the smoke-filled panorama, I clutched Judicus's hand, and wondered where we'd gone wrong.

180

We found a small spring around midday and stopped there under the gnarled cluster of trees that surrounded it. The three guards and I were all exhausted and only partially from the climb. We'd been looking over our shoulders for hours, expecting to be discovered and set upon at any moment.

Even now, hidden by these trees, we felt vulnerable, and it showed in our hunched shoulders and lack of a fire.

"We have provisions to take us to King's Hold," Frandtz said quietly, and I nodded as if that meant something to me. "As long as we aren't discovered. Grabbing the raider prisoner was clever of you. Perhaps the nobles of King's Hold can get some information out of him."

I hadn't even thought of that. I'd thought only that this man had dogged our heels from the moment Judicus had found us. On top of that, he had been part of Lady Lightland's plot to seize the ai'sletta and the kingdom. He wasn't just anyone. He was a pin holding everything together. Just keeping him out of it was justification for keeping him with us.

I wished I could leave him to rot, but he was still a human, so I bandaged his burns and dribbled a little water into his mouth, working to make him as comfortable as possible in the cart.

Judicus was another matter. We were finally somewhere safe enough to dig the arrowhead out of his leg and I did not know if we'd have a chance at it again. He'd been in and out of consciousness since we'd left the plinth and I'd held his hand and smoothed his hair as his eyes opened and then rolled back into his head more than once. But conscious or no, it had to come out and *I* had to get it out.

Carefully, I boiled water, gathered bandages and a sewing kit, and cleaned the sharpest knives I could find. The armsmen spoke to me as I worked.

"His Grace will be disappointed. I think he expected the rope worker to save us all," Frandtz said sadly.

"Why would he think that?" Gerhardt asked, poking the fire up for me to keep my water at a boil. I smiled at him in thanks.

"He's been keeping those prophecies forever and he was so sure that they meant our salvation. It was the charge of his father and his father before him to guard that plinth and to bring the one foretold to it no matter what the cost. I think he'd hoped it would mean something – would do something. I'll tell you, though I wouldn't tell many, that I'd hoped so, too."

"It'll be alright, Sergeant," the third guard said. His eyes were on Judicus. "You can't always see a thing working. Maybe he did do something. You know how a seed works. It grows slow and subtle in the ground, and you never know what it might be until it breaks through the soil."

Frandtz grunted. "Maybe so, Conwer, maybe so."

Which is how I learned the third guard's name.

I learned it again when I readied Judicus's leg and began to cut through the flesh, sure and certain.

Conwer's hand shot out and caught me at the same moment that Judicus's eyes shot open. I touched Judicus's shoulder gently with my other hand and then pressed it a little more firmly, making calming, shushing noises as he moaned and Frandtz barked.

"Let her work on him, Conwer. You're no healer."

"I don't think she is either," he said grimly. "She's cutting unmarked flesh."

"She's what?" Frandtz said, springing forward.

"Arrowhead," Judicus gasped, his voice raw and mangled and barely more than a whisper. He paused, coughing and gasping and I put down the knife, offering him a little water. "Arrowhead."

And then his eyes rolled back in his head, and he passed out again.

"Is there an arrowhead stuck in there?" Frandtz asked me.

And to my relief, they believed my nod and even helped me extract it when the job proved too much for me. It was bloody work, and I knew it would hurt when Judicus awoke, but when I was done, and the leg was stitched, I felt better. If night fell tonight, I'd heal it. And if it didn't, this was still better than leaving it in there.

"Maybe we should stay the night here," Frandtz said uncertainly when I was done. "We could all use the rest. It's been a trying few days."

And so, we prepared to spend the night, taking the time to make a small fire and tea and food. We slept in shifts through the afternoon, and I tended my two patients with care.

The red-haired Stryxex rider would have filled me with fear were he conscious. Even now, when he was bandaged nearly from head to foot and each breath was a rasping inhale, he made my hands shake. I was certain not to leave anything like a weapon near him and we kept his wrists bound despite his condition.

If I was being honest, I wasn't sure he would wake. The burns were severe and extensive, and they made my stomach lurch every time I tended them. I had done that to him. Me. And even though he was my enemy, it made me wonder if it were ever right to do this to someone else. Even someone bent on your death and the destruction of all your friends.

I bit my lip hard and fought to save him if I could.

Judicus slept on, tossing and crying out occasionally. In his case, I was worried. It didn't make sense to me that he hadn't regained consciousness. He should have by now. My hope was that his body was simply so weary, it was conserving its energy to heal him. But I worried that might be wishful thinking.

To my vast relief, night fell, and with it came Kazmerev.

He blossomed like the blooming of a fire on oil, springing up with a bright flash of heat and light.

To my even greater relief, he immediately took charge.

You're somewhere safe, he told me immediately. *And wrung out like a rag on the point of collapse. You need sleep and you need it now.*

But I would heal Judicus first.

He shuffled uncertainly. *You may not have the strength for that. You wore yourself out yesterday. You need to restore what was depleted.*

I would heal Judicus first.

Stubborn fledgling, he said, but he sounded affectionate. *Perhaps you should lie down beside him, then if you pass out from the effort, you won't have far to fall.*

I wasn't going to lie down beside him. I flushed at the thought. What would Frandtz and the others think? I wasn't Flara.

Just the thought of her name sent a chill through me and made Kazmerev blaze with sudden fury.

Now you know why she hovered over him and kept you at a distance. She must have meant to thwart him all along. It was the pattern on her skin he followed. Trusting her like a loyal dog.

I didn't like that comparison, apt though it was. We had both trusted her. We had both made a terrible mistake to touch that plinth at all. I'd gone into it as willing as he had.

But it was not you who did the deed.

It didn't need to be. My heart was with his when he did it, so I was equally guilty. And come to think of it, Kazmerev had thought it was a good idea at the time, too.

Hmph. Well, we all learn as we go.

I sat down heavily beside Judicus, laying a hand over his leg, and I thought of heat and warmth to fill him, to heal him, to erase his wounds. I closed my eyes, and I pushed all my heat and warmth into him.

I opened my eyes, but my vision was blurry, the world tilting terribly from side to side.

I told you it was too much, Kazmerev said in my mind as my vision narrowed and narrowed and then grew dark and I swayed, losing my balance and hitting the earth.

I'd just stay here for a moment. Just for a moment.

Sure, you will. And maybe next time you won't be so stubborn. Sleep, Little Hawk. I will spread my wing over you.

Warmth and softness were my last sensations before my mind drifted into sweet sleep.

181

"Sersha." The whisper in my ear was familiar as my own heartbeat. I felt Judicus's breath wash over me. "Sersha, I've been waiting for hours, you have to be awake by now."

I opened my eyes to see Judicus squatted over me with a lantern in his hand, his dark hair mussed and long face pale in the lantern light. He was shivering. I was not. Kazmerev made a very warm companion.

He slept off and on since you healed him. And he gave you his blanket.

I sat up and motioned for him to join me under the blanket, but he shook his head adamantly.

"We need to talk before the others wake up."

My head was still thick and heavy with something.

That "something" is called overexertion and it's going to catch up to you if you keep being so pigheaded. I hope I don't have to warn you not to heal the burned man. Not until you're somewhere safe enough to pass out again and maybe not even then.

I really did need to do that.

It will knock you on your heels, like healing Judicus did – maybe even worse since he's so much more injured.

I should have healed him first.

And why would you do something like that?

Because, objectively speaking, he needed it more.

I never think like that. What is closest to your heart is always that which is most important. Without personal good, there is no greater good. And besides, you barely had enough strength to heal the rope worker. Look at the scars you left on him.

I ran a hand over my face to clear my thoughts and stood, peering at Judicus. Kazmerev was right. I reached out instinctively and then paused, not quite daring to touch the deep ropes of scarring on his throat. He'd removed the bandage over his eye, and it had thick scars to either side, too.

Judicus caught my hand. "Whatever you did to heal my throat healed the rest of the eye, too. Or maybe it healed before when you fixed the leg the first time – I didn't think to check. Don't worry about the scars. Scars are lines on a map of where you've been, and I'd like to remember my road." He paused, his pale face grim. "I should be thanking you. I should. But Sersha." He cursed vehemently and I pulled back, but he held on to my hand, taking a step forward as I took one backward. "Sersha, what have we done?"

He dropped my hand like he had only just realized he was still holding it and his fingers spread wide, his hands moving jerkily in a double wave before he drew in a deep breath and tried again.

"We need to talk. And not where we can be heard. Gerhardt was on watch, and he fell asleep at it. This is our best chance."

If you don't go with him, he won't rest, Kazmerev said, a note of humor in his mental voice. *I'll just stay here and watch over the sleeping humans.*

I nodded my agreement to Judicus, and he led me past the sleepers to where the spring trickled in the fading moonlight and the dancing gold of the lantern. He sat on a fallen log beside it – a log so weather-beaten it was grey and the edges fraying. I sat beside him and wrapped the blanket around his shoulders.

He looked at me gravely, his eyes saying more than his words. "Thank you."

His voice was burred, despite the healing, as if his throat was as permanently scarred as his neck was. I hoped, for his sake, that he wasn't.

"*You should not ...*" I stumbled in my signs, not sure of the word I needed. "*You should not say this is you. We chose to try together. We had reason to think the phoenix was true.*"

I hated having a limited sign vocabulary. It made me feel like a child.

When he replied, his hands danced in the signs at the same time, helping me learn.

"It's entirely my fault, Sersha." My heart still leapt a little when he used the sign for my name. Probably because it had been given to me in someone's last hours. "I was arrogant. I thought I could contain any problem that arose. I thought I could see clearly what the solution was. Instead – I don't know if you saw what poured from that plinth, but I think it was the souls of phoenixes ripped asunder from their ashes and trapped within. That part, at least, was necessary – what kind of horror is that, trapping a soul in the physical realm?" He shuddered. "But I don't know what happened next. Maybe they dispelled or maybe they are trapped somewhere else. And whatever I did both freed those stone creations, and also broke the plinth. No one can put it back. And if the ai'sletta needs the pair of them to be tuned the same knot, then I've ruined everything. She can't succeed. The world can't be saved. And all because I was so certain. All those people talking about prophecies." He shook his head, hanging it low. "What a ghastly fool I was for beginning to think I could be something for someone. I'm an idiot. A completely ridiculous idiot."

I realized – to my chagrin – that he was crying. His tears, hot and fat, splashed onto the ground in front of his feet and his head was ducked so low that his face was hidden from me.

"I don't know why I let myself think otherwise, or why I dragged you along for it. I don't know if you can forgive me. Every time I turn around, I've mired you worse and worse and you just keep believing in me and sticking by me and ... uh." The sound was like an agonized groan. "You shouldn't, Sersha. You shouldn't keep trusting me."

His voice was so close to breaking.

And I didn't know what came over me, but I just wanted to tell him somehow that he was worth so much and I regretted nothing, but I didn't have the signs to say it and I just ... I needed to stop him. I needed to make him see.

I reached out, letting the blanket slip from my shoulders, and took his face in both my hands drawing it up to look at me. He stared back at me miserably, guilt and confusion warring in his eyes.

And no. He needed to know. He needed to see and there was only one way to show him.

I leaned forward and I kissed him. As slow and soft and sweet as I could. I didn't really know what I was doing, but he didn't seem to care. He melted into me with a gasp that sounded more like pain than anything, but his palm came up to hover over my lower back – just close enough that I could barely feel the feather touch, more gentle than a child saving a moth from the flame. His lips were warmer than I expected, and so much softer, but though he responded to my kiss with a kiss of his own, that, too, was feather-light and gentle and when we parted, he tucked a stray lock of my hair behind my ear.

I let my fingers feather over the scars around his eye, memorizing how his face had changed.

His lips stayed parted and he blinked at me like he'd been stunned by something and didn't know what to do.

I gave him my sternest look and signed, *"Judicus is my friend, and you need to stop telling me he is not good."*

"If you wish it," he whispered, and his eyes were full of wonder and his pale cheeks hot and red.

"We are in trouble." I agreed in sign. *"And we do not know how to fix it. But you are key to fixing it and we must have you ..."* I hesitated. *"Bright."*

"If you wish it," he said again as if he didn't know what to say, and the look in his eyes melted from shock into something that looked very much like wanting.

And then Kamerev was there, popping into visibility so that Judicus startled, and the moment was lost.

I sense something in the trees, he said in my mind.

He was still talking when a black rope slithered past us on the ground and snatched up a toad, squeezing it tight in the rope's grasp and then leaving it flattened on the ground as it slid onward.

I grabbed Judicus's arm, holding my breath in fear as he whispered, "Kentinius."

182

We scrambled back to the camp, avoiding the rope. I made Kazmerev invisible again so he could soar up and scout for us.

He broke through the trees at full speed, as on edge as I was. Could he see anything yet?

I see the camp. The hills. It's nearly dawn. I hate this part, Sersha. I don't like leaving you. It guts me every time and I never know if you'll be safe while I'm gone.

He didn't need to fret. I had Judicus, after all.

A kiss from you can't turn a frog into a prince no matter what the stories say and he's still the same boy who vomits constantly and then absentmindedly destroys massive landmarks.

That was unfair.

I'm not in a fair mood. I don't think you should be kissing boys while you're running for your life.

Then when, exactly, would I do it? I was always running for my life these days.

That's fine with me. Never is just fine with me.

We stumbled into the ring of sleeping bodies and I began to kick out the fire as Judicus reached for Frandtz.

"Frandtz, Gerhardt, Conwer!" he whispered, shaking each guard in turn.

I see them! Kazmerev crowed. *They're behind you on the trail leading down the mountain. Not far. They've made camp in a narrow pass and ... oh no Sersha, you need to know this. She's – "*

His words cut off as the sun cut through the darkness, carving a long golden line through it like a man carves a winter gourd.

I hurried to gather the last of our things and throw them in the carts, dodging the scintillating arm of black rope as it twisted its way through the camp, searching, searching.

Fortunately, we'd bedded the prisoner in one of the carts, so he didn't need to be moved. He woke as the men scrambled to hitch the donkeys, jarring the cart. The red-haired Stryxex rider moaned through clenched teeth, and I hurried to his side, offering water from a water skin.

He knocked my hand aside, shooting up and grabbing me by the throat.

I was so stunned I didn't know what to do. My vision was filled with his half-burned face and then he began to laugh as I fought for breath.

His laughter cut off as a black rope shot out and grabbed his arm, ripping it backward and away from my throat until he screamed.

"What is with you people and choking? Is it the only thing they teach you?" Judicus asked irritably.

The Stryxex rider laughed, wheezing painfully through his burned lungs. Judicus released his arm and he flexed his fingers before collapsing back to his bed.

"You're all dead, you five fools." His voice was barely more than a croak. "They're almost upon you and when they arrive you will wish I'd strangled the life out of you so you wouldn't have to live through what they'll do to you. You'll wish you'd offered up your phoenix and your ropework and all your allies. You'll be willing to offer up your own mother if it means the death you will beg for."

"Who is us?" Judicus asked precisely but the man was laughing again and then choking, and coughing, and coughing through his damaged lungs.

I offered him the waterskin again and he knocked it to the side, leaving me to scramble to stopper it. We had water from the spring, but we didn't have time to refill the skins and we couldn't afford to waste it.

"Which way?" Frandtz whispered from the head of the donkey.

"Up the trail," Judicus said with a clenched jaw. "There's nowhere else to go."

"There never was," the Stryxex rider rasped. His dancing eyes met Judicus's. "There never was for you. You've been our creature from the beginning though you didn't know it. Driven by our plan to go out to the wilds to scoop up the ai'sletta for us. You've been managed by our Lady Lightland like a dog set to the hunt, and then driven back to Briccatore and used to herd up the Flame Riders, driven to poor mad Duke Fontellrae with his ridiculous secret everyone knew – a cult in his family line for generations. So easy to turn. So easy to twist. We hardly even had to try, and you fell for all of it." He paused to wheeze a laugh. "Where will we make you dance next, do you think? Even if you escape us now and go over the mountains will you ever know for sure that we haven't sent you there to do our bidding like we sent you everywhere else? You're a hound Judicus Franzer Irault. A hound to be used by clever hunters and nothing more. The more you think to set out on your own the more our leash tightens, and we'll let it tighten and tighten while you serve our purposes, until it chokes you."

A muscle in Judicus's jaw clenched as he met the man's stare. He was walking beside the cart, just like I was. We couldn't go faster than the donkeys could move.

The guards ahead of us, leading the pack donkeys, had stiff spines and I knew they were hearing this. Were they being inspired to doubt, too? Did they wonder if all their sacrifices and all their loyalties were just as futile as this man said ours were?

"And who are you, exactly?" Judicus asked calmly. He looked as if he hadn't even heard the man's tirade. I was impressed. It had shaken me.

"I'm your doom. Your end. Your final opponent."

We were hurrying as fast as the donkeys could go over land dappled by that hated lavender and blush pink of dawn and interspersed by the darkest of velvet shadows.

"It would help to have a name to put on your monument if it comes to that," Judicus said calmly. "But if you prefer, I could name you. Fritzen, maybe. I had a cat with that name. What do you think, Sersha? Will that do?"

He looked at me and I froze for a moment, stumbling on the rough path, before nodding. I was not as good as he was at ... finesse? Is that what this was? Diplomacy? Perhaps he'd read a book on it. Perhaps even now the pages were passing before his eyes. Or, more likely, he was following in the footsteps of his self-sacrificing father who had stolen a kingdom with brash determination.

"I am Derries son of Fahtran of the Hand of the Rat and Kiessa of Briccatore and I ride the great shadow souls brought up from the depths."

My belly twisted at those words. Knowing Stryxex were a created abomination was one thing. Hearing the man admit to it was another. I shivered as we passed through the shadow of a rock three times my height. It stood like a jagged tooth in the center of the trail, forcing us to ease around it.

"I am versed in the old ways, soaked in the lore, the maker of prophecies, the crafter of dooms and I have been training all my life for this single task."

"And what task is that?" Judicus asked calmly. His face was free of all expression. Even his gait seemed smooth.

We emerged from the shadows into a bright patch of light and the warmth of the rising sun hit my face, totally incongruous with this dark conversation.

Derries snarled. "I will destroy every phoenix alive so that my people may roll over this land like a tide and sweep away every living thing in the name of our dark king. We will sow the land with the creatures of the stone and rock and twists of soul."

"How pleasant," Judicus said, a distasteful note to his voice. "I can see why you're willing to sacrifice yourself for it."

"I have fulfilled my tasks to the letter," Derries said, leaning back against the bundles in the cart with a groan.

"He also makes an excellent distraction," a voice said and from the long shadows of the rocks in front of us. From their depths, stepped three figures. At the sight of them, my heart froze in my chest.

Lady Lightland.

Flara, the fake phoenix rider.

And with them was a dark-clad, extremely thin man about Judicus's age that I knew without having to ask must be rope worker Kentinius.

"I knew I'd see you again," Lady Lightland said, shaking her cloak out. "If only to say goodbye."

183

I knew two things immediately.

First, that these three outnumbered us, even if it didn't seem like it at first glance. The ropeworker was uninjured, Flara had her Stryxex hovering somewhere nearby and he did not disappear in the daylight, and Lady Lightland always had a trick or two.

Second, that I must not let them take me captive. I had seen what happened to Flame Riders who were taken captive. I'd seen those poor phoenix souls trapped in the plinth and while I couldn't connect one to the other, I knew they were connected and I knew that if I loved Kazmerev at all, I must not let that happen to him. My own death was preferred to that.

We stood there, staring at each other for a full breath.

Out of nowhere, Derries launched himself up and hurtled into me.

I crashed to the ground, my shoulder hitting hard, and his weight fell on me in a second blow. The breath was knocked from my lungs, leaving me gasping and choked.

I scrambled, trying to get out from under his weight, but he shifted and shuffled to keep me pinned, uncaring that our scuffle must be pulling his bandages askew and exposing his open burn wounds.

Somewhere above me, a scream ripped through the air – Gerhardt, I thought – and then another scream and then a splintering sound. A donkey bellowed and the cart that Derries had been riding on collapsed beside us spilling supplies across the ground and on top of both Derries and me.

I struggled harder, managed to get head and shoulders out from under him, only to be slammed back to the earth, my chin striking hard and painfully against the ground.

I moaned, but I didn't dare give up.

I twisted sharply in his grip and slipped out just long enough to catch one glimpse of the wild scene around me. Judicus stood atop the fallen cart, hands spread wide as black ropes poured from them, spilling out across the ground, and rippling to fight as quickly and brutally as a nest of vipers. They fought against another set of black ropes, tangling and knotting and hen slipping away.

On the ground, Gerhardt lay in an unnatural position, his eyes wide and empty of life. Two of the donkeys sprawled the same way.

Oh no. My heart stuttered over the look on his face. He'd been kind to us. He'd been a constant reminder that there were kind people out there trying their best.

As I watched, Flara's Stryxex dove down, snatched the second cart up in its talons. The donkeys dragged up, up, up into the air with it, and then the Stryxex released it, smashing cart, and supplies, and donkeys all at once onto the rocks below.

A heavy weight sank into my chest.

And then Derries landed an elbow to my belly and my focus was drawn abruptly back to him. Even with his hands bound, he was too strong for me. He reached up with both hands, forcing my chin back, jamming my head back and down into the earth. He was on top of me, in a heartbeat, grabbing a handful of my hair and slamming my head against the ground. Every rock and stick on the ground stabbed painfully into my skin and no matter how hard I fought I was pinned under his weight.

He was making a horrible sound and it took me a minute to realize was laughter. His hand slid down from my jaw to wrap around my neck. I tried to reach to pull his hands away as I choked, gasping for air, feeling it not coming as panic welled up in me. I couldn't even reach to stop him. His heavy shoulders and forearms fended me back despite the burns covering them, and I was glad – so glad – that I hadn't healed him because if this was how strong he was when he was injured, what would he have been like if he were whole?

And then all thought was gone as I thrashed mindlessly, my body taking charge in a last attempt to breathe.

My hand caught something and grabbed it, managing to grip somehow and bash it against his exposed ribs. Again. Again.

My vision was narrowing. Little stars danced across my vision. He had yet to waver.

I moved the item in my hand higher, crashing into his shoulders now, and though he hissed in pain, I could barely get my arm up. I was losing consciousness with the never-ending scream of agony in my lungs. I pled in my heart for air the way one pleads for a stolen loved one.

Something told me I had one last chance and then the only thing left for me would be death.

I seized that chance, pulling my arm up as high as I could and crashing whatever I held down onto him with all my fading might. My muscles screamed and two fingers throbbed in agony from the strike, but his grip had loosened.

I wiggled and scrambled for all I was worth and managed to slide out from under him.

My vision was returning. Air sucked painfully through my lungs, making me dizzy and making my vision dance like a traveling entertainer. I blinked hard and saw that I'd hit him in the skull. Red blood poured from the wound, but he shook himself like a dog and as I was still trying to find my equilibrium, he charged, roaring as he sprang back toward me.

Panic took over, propelling me forward as I crashed what I was holding – a rock the size of two of my fists – into his head again and again until he stopped trying to attack me, stopped moving, stopped breathing.

I was still trembling, still terrified when I realized what I'd done. I scrambled backward on all fours like a crab, the rock falling from my horrified hand.

Oh no.

Guilt bubbled up in my chest.

There was no time to digest the rest of the horror of it, I was yanked to my feet by a rough hand and had a pack thrust into my hands. I just had time to catch sight of Frandtz's blunt face, blood-streaked and earnest.

"I haven't lost hope," he said between gritted teeth. "We weren't wrong. Now, run girl."

And then he shoved me off the path and spun, sword in hand as Lady Lightland leapt toward him, her blade out and stained with blood.

Of Conwer there was no sign.

Judicus remained on the wagon, his features clenched in concentration as he turned back rope after rope from Kentinius and also countered attacks from Flara's Stryxex.

I couldn't run and leave them like this. There had to be a way to help.

In the distance, a rumbling sound triggered some sense in me that we were in danger – as if I needed that with all of this going on right in front of me.

I stumbled backward in time to witness Judicus leap from the cart, execute a perfect forward flip and then leap toward Flara.

Neither she nor the ropeworker were expecting it. Kentinius's ropes missed Judicus at the same moment that he cleared the distance. He landed right in front of Flara, lifted her and her Stryxex with ropes of his own, and flung her away from him toward the rocky slopes beside me. She flew through the air, but he didn't wait to see what happened to her. He plowed past where she had stood to where Kentinius was reeling in his ropes, his eyes wide.

My eyes were on Flara, though, as she hit the rocks beside me with a loud crack and slid to the ground beside me. Her arms were bare and there was no tattoo on either of them. I sucked in a breath at the sight of that. What had happened to the sign she used to trick Judicus?

She was senseless, though not dead, and therefore not a threat to me, but she did have something I wanted – no needed – if I was going to help Judicus and Frandtz – because I couldn't leave them, no matter what Frandtz ordered.

There was no time to take her knives from each spot on the belt I spotted. It was new – something she'd acquired since I'd seen her yesterday. It was a brass-buckled belt wider than my hand studded with multiple knives of various lengths and a large pouch the size of both my hands set side by side.

I unbuckled it quickly and slung it around my own waist, securing the buckle before I drew her largest knife.

No, I definitely wasn't going to run and leave them, as if my life was more valuable than theirs.

I spun, knife out, and charged toward Lady Lightland.

Too late.

Frandtz was battling her back, pace on pace, forcing her to fight in the defensive. He was twice her size and had the training of an armsman.

I followed behind him, ready to help but not sure how to do it.

Out of nowhere, a black rope shot out and struck him like a punch to the side. He flinched.

It was all the opening Lady Lightland needed. Her blade flicked out, piercing through him and appearing like the tongue of a snake through his back, red with his heart's blood.

I had to act. Now. No time for hesitation.

My hands shook, but without waiting for him to fall or her to extract her sword, I dove forward, danced around the side of him, and stuck my knife into Cassanetta's side. She gasped, looking at me with wide eyes. Her hands left the sword hilt and she collapsed under Frandtz's weight.

I gasped, staring at the knife in my hand. And I couldn't pretend it was an accident this time or that I hadn't meant it because I'd known exactly what I was doing when I planted that blade in her side.

184

The ground under my feet shuddered and I stumbled away from the bodies, trying to catch my balance. I caught myself against one of the ruined carts and found Conwer's body there, trapped beneath the broken cart, his eyes closed and limbs still.

I reeled back in horror at the same moment that Kentinius ran past me, narrowly missing colliding with me. His eyes were fixed on what was behind him. As I watched, he danced to the side, spun, and lifted his hands, fingers spread wide as a pair of black ropes twisted out from them and formed complex knots.

A black rope snaked out and snatched one of the knots, circling it, tightening, and then shaking it as a terrier shakes a rat. The wave of motion ran up the rope and through Kentinius's arm. I heard his teeth chatter and crack and then he was flung back.

He caught himself on a net of black rope as the first pair he'd woven dissolved in the air and stabilized. With a gasp and a huff, he charged forward again.

Judicus's face was steady and determined. His eyes caught on mine and then he looked behind me and stiffened, his eyebrows rising.

He was too distracted.

Kentinius's hand jerked up and I pointed at him. Judicus barely registered my sign in time, barely dodged. The rope slid along his arm, shooting faster than an arrow and he cried out as his jacket and shirt both ripped leaving a thumb-thick line of rope burn along his bicep.

He didn't pause.

He leapt.

But not to Kentinius and not away from him.

He leapt, instead, to the cart beside me, reached down, grabbed my jacket without so much as a word, and hauled me up to the top of the cart.

I was still gaping at him like a fish pulled from the water when it struck me that the noise was louder.

Was it a rockslide?

It swallowed up a shout from Kentinus in a wall of sound, and then Judicus dropped his hold on my shirt, grabbed my hand instead, and mouthed, "Jump with me."

I kept my eyes on him and then a rope slid out and fastened around my waist. I panicked, swatting at it like it was a wasp. It gripped harder.

And before I could do anything else Judicus yelled "Jump!" and though I could barely hear it I jumped as the first figure burst through the trees.

A black rope shot from his other hand, hooking around the neck of the stone creature. It charged forward like the tiger it was formed to mock, and we leapt up in the air, aided by Judicus's ropes, and before I could so much as scream, we were jerked in the air halfway through our jump and thrown onto the stone tiger's back, gasping and terrified, clinging to each other and the slick surface like a pair of sailors hauled up from a shipwreck.

The black rope around my waist snapped, searing my side with a rope burn.

And even if I could have spoken, I would not have known what to say, as the creature crashed up the trail, flattening any tree or shrub or smaller rock in its path. Its fellows ran behind and before and on either side of it. We were moving on a wave of stampeding, living rock.

I craned my neck, looking behind me but already all I could see were stone backs and there was no sign of Kentinius, of the carts and donkeys, or of the evil deeds I'd done to stay alive.

185

I have heard the tales of wild rides on the backs of monstrous beasts but never had I imagined a ride like the one we took that day. The stone creature careened up the mountain path, heedless of height, or slope, or anything else that might deter a beast of bone and flesh. Its balance was uncanny, and the speed with which it ran among its fellows put any horse to shame.

We had no way to hold on, except by gripping the rope Judicus wove around the beast, and no way to get off without being trampled to death. I clung to the rope, and clung to Judicus, and he held on with me, white-faced as the hours bled one into the next. We tried to speak, but my hands were too full trying to hold on, and his voice could not be heard over the thunder of the herd's hooves.

In the end, we rode in deafening noise, teeth gritted, heads and bodies aching with the exertion.

Our best hope was nightfall. If we could just wait until the sun sank behind the clouds, then Kazmerev would appear, and when he did, he could rescue us.

That was what I thought on most as we fled.

Kazmerev.

Kazmerev.

My last and best hope.

But he wasn't the only one I thought of. I also thought of the terrible deeds I'd done. Over and over, I relived the moment of jamming my knife into Lady Lightland's side, of her eyes going wide, of the rock crushing into the Stryxex Rider's skull and his dim eyes when I was done.

I clenched my jaw hard, and I worried. Because evil people couldn't be Flame Riders. What if Kazmerev didn't come back because of this? What if my actions – self-defense, though they were – were enough to lose him forever? I would never forgive myself.

I shouldn't have worried. The afternoon progressed as it always does, the strange stone muscles of the creatures beneath us bunching and releasing, rocking us back and forth in a terrifying fashion. We clung until my fingers went numb and the muscle in my jaw felt like it might burst. But eventually, dusk swept through the sky and the sun sank, and as it did, Kazmerev bloomed through my exhausted heart and leapt bright and fiery into the sky above us.

Kaz, I gasped with my mental voice as he appeared. We need your help, my friend. We need your help.

He was there before I even lifted my exhausted gaze, all warmth and light and love. He ducked under me and with shaking hands, Judicus released the rope of magic and we slid from the moving stone beast onto Kazmerev's back.

For one stomach-dropping moment, we fell through the air, and then he caught us in his warmth. We were both shaking, chilled to the core, our muscles unable to relax after hours and hours of tension.

Kazmerev soared upward into the thick clouds and mist rolled over my face, refreshing me. For just one tiny precious moment, I could forget everything that had happened. For just one precious moment I could.

What are they? Kazmerev asked, and I had to come back to reality and back to a world where we'd just clung to the backs of moving stone creatures for an entire afternoon.

Are they not the stone creatures that came out of that tear in the earth? I asked him in my mind.

I think so, he agreed. *But there's more. They're ... I don't know how to say this. I feel as though I sense the souls of those phoenixes trapped now within these shells and gone mad with the terror of it.*

I thought I might be ill. Of course, that was what had happened, wasn't it?

Right on cue, Judicus leaned over Kazmerev's side and vomited.

"I think I might pass out, Sersha," he mumbled. "I'm so sorry. I've only held a knot that long once before – on the ship with the broken mast. But that was different. I wasn't holding on for dear life about to fall at any moment." He gasped. "It was different."

I patted him on the shoulder, trying to commiserate, trying to show him he wasn't alone.

But I didn't know what to do. Could we land somewhere safe just for long enough to rest? Was there anyone on our tail, about to snatch us from the air?

Were you followed, then?

I didn't know. It didn't make logical sense to follow us. I thought only Kentinius survived, and if that was true, wouldn't he have to be back there picking up the scraps of his friends and ... and ... but here my imagination failed me.

I hadn't seen the Stryxex die. It might still follow.

I do not sense it.

I hadn't seen Flara or Lady Lightland die, but they were gravely injured when the stampede came through. I couldn't imagine them avoiding those stomping feet.

In that case, it may only be my wild imagination telling me there was someone right behind us and that slowing would bring them right down on my head.

I think it is your imagination, Little Hawk. And even hawks must rest sometimes.

He soared and I closed my eyes, one hand buried in his feathers and one on

Judicus. I didn't dare let go of either of them, and yet I could barely keep my eyes open.

Fear not, Little Hawk. I have you now.

I did not know how long we flew like that, but eventually, he set us down in something that seemed like a very high meadow away from any clear road. I didn't ask questions, didn't even want to know. All I wanted was the promised oblivion of sleep.

I half dismounted, half fell from his back.

"Fire," Judicus gasped. "Need a fire."

But neither of us was up to building one. Instead, I made Kazmerev visible - I could still do that at least. Perhaps, he could make a fire.

"No need. I am here to warm you. Rest, Little Hawk. Rest."

I sat down, drawing Judicus with me and we leaned against Kazmerev's burning feathers. His warmth cupped my heart like a hand holding a baby chick and I leaned into it with all my heart.

Keep me safe, noble fire, I thought, and Judicus and I fell asleep in a heap beside my beautiful phoenix, sharing the warmth of life only he could offer.

"Sersha," Judicus said as sleep began to claim him. His hand twisted around mine as surely as any rope. "Sersha, I feel you holding guilt tight to your heart, but remember this - you did not ask to fight for your life, and you did not try to kill. They came to you. They offered you no choice."

And usually, his words soothed me and helped me, but this time they only made me ache as if I might never recover.

186

I woke to the cold of a missing Kazmerev and the iron cold rock of guilt in my belly.

There was no one beside me. Judicus was already awake, squatting against a rock, bent over something small between his hands.

When I sat up, he startled, flushing with something that looked like guilt.

"Sersha. I'm so sorry. I looked in the pouch on your belt for a flint to make a fire. And I found it, but I also found this. Did you take it from one of our enemies in the fight?"

I nodded and he squinted, looking off into the middle distance as if he was working out a problem.

"Flara," he said eventually. "She landed close to you."

I nodded again. His memory was always excellent.

"I found this and completely forgot the flint. I was curious. And now, I wish I'd never picked it up."

I took the flint from where he'd left it on the ground beside him. We could use a fire, even if he was too distracted to light it.

Patiently, I gathered up fuel, little tufts of dried grass, and the remains of dried out saplings, long dead from the fury of the sun beating on this mountain top and the harsh winds constantly blowing them. They were small and gnarled, and they made me worry that perhaps I wouldn't be able to light them at all. We were in for a brisk day if I did not. The wind had already picked up and without Kazmerev we'd have difficulty getting down from this peak or getting warm at all. I clenched my jaw at the thought. Best not to think too deeply about it. I didn't want to fall back into nerves about whether Mally might decide to put her crown on again or take it off. She was far from here - maybe far enough that she wasn't affecting things here anymore - and there was nothing I could do about it anyway.

I looked up to check on Judicus, and frowned when I saw he was still staring off into the middle distance.

He blinked and met my gaze, shaking his head slightly as he inhaled, as if he was coming back to this world after drifting off into another world.

"This is ... Sersha, I can't believe what this is."

"What is it?" I signed, pausing for a moment before returning to light the fire.

"It's another book of prophecies. written by yet another hand." He let a wry laugh rip from his throat, but it sounded midway between laughter and despair. "I think there are notes at the very back that might be Flara's - but they are brief and cryptic. It's the rest that worries me. It matches prophecies in the book that Fontellrae kept so carefully, and it matches prophecies I've seen about the ai'sletta. But Sersha - it's all upside down. It's ... I don't know how to say this but it's all wrong. If this is true - "

He cut off, making a strangled sound in his throat and I paused in striking the flint to speak in sign again.

"Calm down. Explain it to me."

He took a deep breath, nodding. "Yes, there will be time to panic later. Time for all of us to panic."

My stomach tumbled at those words, but I gritted my jaw and kept trying to coax a flame from the tinder I'd set. If he'd discovered something awful, well, we'd deal with it. But we needed a fire first. And maybe in the pack that Frandtz had shoved into my hands, there might even be water and tea leaves and maybe we could have a cup of tea and calm down. Everyone felt better after a little tea.

"If it's true - and I don't know, maybe it is! - then it explains so much. It explains why Flara was looking at me. Why she had that tattoo."

I interrupted him to sign again.

"The mark," I signed, unable to say 'tattoo,' *"It was missing from her arm. I saw when she passed out."*

"Gone?" he asked, his face pale. "How ... no, I won't ask. You couldn't know either, but Sersha, I think she was deceiving us - deceiving me from the moment I met her. I think her torture was staged to draw me in and make me trust her. And the way she was edging closer and closer to me all the time - I knew that was odd. Perhaps she was using that to gain my confidence."

Doubtless. Though it was very Judicus to only realize it now, and also very Judicus to have barely realized the girl was acting oddly when she cozied up to him in the first place. I sometimes wondered if there were whole worlds in his head that he was occupying instead of joining us here in this one.

"It makes sense of some of her notes in the back, too."

"*Tell me about these prophecies,"* I signed, and he looked up, agonized.

"Sersha, they stand everything I've been thinking all along upside down. Do you remember this prophecy? Listen. '*Evening and morning will come swift on each other's heels, the black fox chasing the white fox until they pause in their chase for her advent, they pant and wait and look to see her arrival, they anticipate the end of an age.*'"

It sounded familiar. A spark finally caught on my tinder, and I held it gently in my cupped palms, blowing it into flame.

"We believe that means we are trying to catch the ai'sletta – both us and Lady

Lightland and the Hand of the Rat. And they think that, too, but their prophecy keeps going. Listen to this. '*And those who think they are of the light will catch her and when they think their position is secure a bright light will fall from the heavens and blind their eyes and confuse their minds with a better pattern – the pattern of the Rat and like the Rat we will wait as they unravel their hopes and tie up their own destruction.*'"

He looked up at me, white-faced, and I paused from my work of gently tenting small twigs over the licking flames.

"Sersha," he said, agony in his voice. "That was me. I am the one who unraveled the plinth and tied up the knot with the pattern she showed me on her arm. The one you said was missing later."

My hands flicked through the signs. "*Her false flame bird was bright white. So bright I could not look.*"

Judicus's throat bobbed visibly as he swallowed and looked away. His hands flipping idly through the pages of his book.

"Every note in here mirrors the notes in Fontellrae's book. They show how phoenixes can be made into Stryxex. But Fontellrae didn't have all the extra notes. The ones that tell how just a piece of this would be given to his ancestors to guard in sacred trust. The part that explains how they'd be careful to only give him part of the knowledge so that he'd see it one way while they saw it another. You never touched that plinth, did you, Sersha?"

I shook my head.

"If you had," he said ruefully, "Kazmerev might have been ripped from your heart and imprisoned within it."

I froze for a heartbeat and then flinched, pulling my hand back from where the licking flames had caught it. I stuck my finger in my mouth before returning to building the fire. It *was* hard to coax flame from this gnarled wood and there was no point in bemoaning what could have happened but didn't. Any number of terrible things *could* have happened so far.

"By releasing the original knot, I broke that particular trap and set the phoenixes' souls free, but they slipped out, still weakened and broken, and we saw where that led."

I nodded, still working at the fire.

"And the second knot – that was the problem. It's a knot of their devising."

"*Why didn't they just tie it themselves?*" I signed.

The fire was burning better, but the wind whipped at it from every direction and if I didn't build it up more it would be snuffed right out.

"The book suggests that tying it would take a rope worker of uncommon strength." I glanced up to see him blushing furiously. "But the thing is, that might not be true. It might just be what they believed. A lot of ropework is in the mind. If you think you can't do a thing, then you can't do it."

I tried to keep my expression neutral as I nodded, but a smirk played behind it. He was clearly a strong and capable rope worker. Constantly denying a thing didn't make it less true.

"So they lured me in and used me. And it makes me feel awful because I should have known. But there's worse, Sersha."

"*Worse?*" What could be worse than being manipulated like that to go against your own ethics?

"Well, if this is to be believed – and I think I believe it – then they used Fontellrae's family, too, back for generations upon generations. They planted this idea in their family. They fed it. They left them to defend a trust that was a lie. His death and the deaths of his people were for nothing."

His voice cracked at the end, and I felt the pain with him. It was hard to blink away memories of his dead – the prisoners I'd seen, the armsmen who had traveled with us. I'd grown fond of them. It felt like broken glass in my chest to think of them broken on the ground.

"That means this plan – these people enacting it, the text here with the prophecies ordaining it – it's all generations old. Older than our grandparents. People have been plotting the deaths of others for their own benefit and following the signs of these prophecies for that *entire* time, Sersha. Can that even be possible? Can people be that ... rotten?"

I left the fire and came to kneel beside where he crouched so he could see my heart in my eyes. It was aching with him, broken and miserable with him. I didn't hide it or disguise how I felt. Instead, I let him look deep into my eyes and I hid nothing. We sat for a long moment, gazing deep into each other before I finally signed.

"*Was it not your uncle who killed your father?*"

"Yes," he said, and his breath hitched.

"*Was it not the people who stood behind him?*"

"Yes," he turned his eyes away, his breath trembling in his chest and his hands shaking.

"*Was it not his ... people who talk ... who conspired to overthrow him?*"

"Counsellors. Yes."

"*Then how can you doubt? People are evil. Many of them. More than we think.*"

He met my eyes again. "But how do you stop an evil that has been planned from so far back? Every eventuality has been plotted out. Every hope we have can be twisted against us. The people won't join us to fight this. They would think we were crazy if they heard us speak of it. There are too many conspirators to stop. Even if I were willing to die in an attempt to stop it, to throw myself at the leader in a gamble that I could take his life before I was killed – even then, what? There are so many of them they could simply choose another leader, and nothing would change. We cannot flee – not only because my sister is trapped and I won't abandon her, but also because there is nowhere to go. This details the people in this plot, and they span nations and creeds. The ai'sletta is already on her way to the other plinth, which I am certain must be a trap, and even were we to follow her today, we would be too late."

He paused long enough to draw in a shuddering breath.

"We're already too late."

"*It's never too late to fight for what is good,*" I signed.

"And why did they need me to do any of this. Why couldn't they have used Kentinius? He's as powerful as I am."

I doubted that, or we would have been dead back there with the others, but I didn't say that. Instead, I fell back on one of my aunt Danna's favorite sayings.

"*The devil can create nothing of his own. He can only warp what we create,*" I said.

He sighed nodded and then looked at me again with those piercing eyes.

"Sersha," he said very firmly. "I am taking a new path. I am no longer going to be obeying orders or following my nation's creeds. I will not honor the dying wishes of my uncle or respect the hopes of those who follow prophecies. I will not be aligned with any nation or ruler or way. I will be a lone hand playing this game for my own ends and purposes."

"*And phoenixes?*" I couldn't help but ask.

"I have no quarrel with them."

I nodded.

"But I will chart my own course to reverse what's been done and to prevent a fulfillment of their prophecies. I will set myself up against them, so that they must fight me at every turn and rue the day that they ever made me their enemy."

His eyes were grim and deadly, but the effect was somewhat marred when he stood hastily and stumbled to the side bushes to vomit miserably, his body shaking with the effort.

When he returned, his eyes were still lit with the fire of determination.

"I don't have the right to ask, but I will anyway, Sersha. Are you still with me?"

And of course, I was.

187

"I'm *with you to the end,"* I signed, and he sagged with relief.

"I don't mind admitting," he said with a furtive glance at the bushes over his shoulder. "The whole thing makes me ill. What is one – or two, I suppose – people supposed to do in the face of dozens – maybe hundreds – of conspirators who have planned and nudged and directed until thousands of people bend to their every whim? How can we oppose it? They have already planned to kill us, tried to kill us, and they certainly will succeed in killing us if we drop our guard. So, we can't attack them directly. There's no clear individual or groups of individuals responsible."

I thought of Lady Lightland's face when I jammed my knife in her side. Had she died? Would Gundt mourn her?

I shook my head.

"You see the problem," Judicus said with a sigh, sinking beside my fire.

I opened the pack, found water, and a small camp pot, and tea in a canister, and began to brew a pot. There was little in the way of food – a small packet of dried meat and trail bread – but enough coin we could buy more if we ever saw other people again. Tea, it was.

"So, what do we do? If we cannot fight, if we cannot flee – what?"

"Say no," I signed.

"That doesn't work. We've done that." He stared glumly into the flames.

"There is a bird," I signed. *"Sometimes we have to … word … hurt? … no … something, boys in the village because they put a stick in its beak. A little stick. Wedged just right."*

"Discipline," he murmured, making the sign.

I nodded. *"Yes. Then you have to catch the bird to get it out. Just a tiny stick. But it will kill the bird if it sticks."*

He nodded, "But how can we stick in their craw?"

I made the sign of a crown on my head.

"Mally? Her luck?"

I shrugged.

"It's a possibility," he agreed but he was troubled. "We'll need allies, too. People who can fight with us or help us at least stand up to the ones who arranged this plot. And I need to understand it better, to try to figure out if there's any indication of who is behind it. Or how we can find them. Anything at all. I feel like I'm a blind man stumbling in the dark or a mute man trying to call for ... oh, I'm so sorry."

He looked at me, aghast. I waved his worry away. I was perfectly cognizant of my limitations. And he was right. This was a massive obstacle. But just like my voicelessness, it wasn't impossible. With a friend who could understand me and a new language, I could still speak. We needed the same thing.

"*Friends,*" I signed.

He nodded, putting his head in his hands.

We spent the day like that, sipping tea, napping here and there. He read the book and read it again, cursing that the prophecies were obscure and difficult to understand, frustrated that they showed no clear hand behind what was happening.

And then he taught me to read. The sounds Gundt had taught me had stuck and Judicus showed me how to string them together in my mind, how to form the words in my mind.

"The hard part is the words that break the rules," he told me. "That's what's going to trip you up later. Here, try with this passage."

I read it in my mind.

From our heart, ... burst, flesh made stone and from our heart, they seek and flatten, ... and ... and from our heart, ... will be the banner of victory, our ... will, our ...

And then he read it aloud so I could see the words I missed.

"From our heart, they burst, flesh made stone and from our heart, they seek and flatten, strike and waste and from our heart, they will be the banner of victory, our granite will, our stone triumph."

I nodded, glad for the lesson, but there was a key here, wasn't there?

"Stone animals?" I signed. Could that be the "they" in this prophecy? And if it was could there be a clue here?

Judicus shrugged. He didn't know any more than I did.

But despite being on the run, despite the guilt we shared at our failures, and the horror that this whole murderous thing we'd lived through over the past few weeks had been planned by someone, the day was not unpleasant. It thrilled and relieved me to be able to read, even slowly and with difficulty. It opened a new world to me. And it seemed to please Judicus to teach me, as if this one thing we could accomplish together was of more value than just teaching me a new skill.

I asked him about it.

"If you're right," he said shyly. "If our enemies make nothing new and only warp what we've made then every un-warped, pure thing we create is a wall against them, don't you think."

I hadn't thought of that.

"Sersha?" he asked absently as the sun grew close to setting. "We might have to part ways."

I stiffened. There was no need for that.

"Not that I want to," he said, his eyes intent on mine. "But we need allies, and I am best suited to speak to other nations and find us new friends. And we need the ai'sletta and you are best suited to fly with Kazmerev out across the sea to the lands of the raiders where she will be and bring her back to us. I'm not saying we need to separate immediately. I'm just saying it might be practical. Don't you think?"

"*No,* I signed. "*I don't think so.*"

He laughed wryly. "Why do I think you'd say that no matter how I presented the situation?"

"*Because you know me,*" I signed.

"I think I'm starting to," he whispered, and I hadn't realized how close he was sitting to me until his lips touched mine.

I reached up to touch his face, my fingers very gentle on his thick scars.

Our kiss only lasted a moment. The sun flared scarlet and disappeared and then Kazmerev was there.

Ewwww, I wish you wouldn't, he complained, and the moment was gone.

188

Everything we'd thought was a lie. That was what I had to get through to Kazmerev. All the guidance, all the ideas of what was happening in the world – it wasn't what we thought.

Not everything, he objected. *Not the important things. What we have together has not changed. Our friends have not changed. Our loyalties have not changed.*

Yes. He was right. Yes. That had not changed.

"Have you asked him what he thinks?" Judicus asked in his slightly burred voice. He had pulled back from me and begun to carefully pack our things. He glanced sideways at Kazmerev, eyes bright. "Will he go with us over the mountain pass to look for allies?"

Evendun? Over the mountains? I went there once with Vella. Her people lie in that direction. There aren't many phoenixes that way. Not many people who like phoenixes either.

I wondered how he found Vella if her people didn't like phoenixes.

I don't want to talk about that. It remains too painful.

I would never push him to talk about what hurt him.

I'll go where you go, Little Hawk. And I admit I don't know where else he could go for help. But I don't know that I want to go to Evendun. There are strange rumors about that place.

What kind of rumors?

If I tell you, you will think I'm crazy.

"*He'll go,*" I signed to Judicus. "*But he doesn't like it.*"

Judicus waved a hand. "The Golden Salamanders are a myth. He should know that."

I had no idea what he was talking about. I looked back and forth between them but neither one so much as flinched a muscle.

I'll go. That should be enough.

"*We will go,*" I signed and Judicus nodded stiffly.

"We should make haste," he said, grimly. "We are always outnumbered and a step behind."

That was how I felt, too, and as we packed everything up and Judicus set the pack on his back and helped me onto Kazmerev's back – not that I needed help, but it seemed to settle him a bit.

I thought about Kentinius out there, perhaps even now racing ahead of us or searching for us through the mountains, and I thought of the thundering stone animals and wondered what would happen if they reached a town or a city. How could you stop something like that? How could you prevent it from trampling everything you owned to dust – and maybe everyone you loved? Would sledge-hammers be enough or would it take an act of magic? Judicus could probably swipe one of those creatures to the side – maybe more than that, maybe as many as half a dozen. But even that kind of power couldn't stop a whole stampede of them.

We rose into the air, and my heart leapt with joy at the feeling of lifting up above the ground to where we were free, where we could fly anywhere and see anything, where we could escape danger and leave confines behind. For that first moment, I could always close my eyes and feel the world and its cares sink away.

My moment was interrupted by Kazmerev's worried voice.

I think I see them, Kazmerev said, tilting uncomfortably side to side as he always did when he was worried.

What did he see?

The stone creatures, creeping across the ground. Look.

The night was bright with moonlight and as I peered down from our height, it caught across the landscape. I watched and watched.

There.

Movement.

And a little farther along, more movement.

It looked as if the rocks and the ground itself were moving.

I tugged Judicus's sleeve and pointed down.

We were silent for long minutes until he stiffened.

"I see them. Oh no, this is worse than I thought! They're ... they're ... oh no."

I felt fumbling behind me.

"Can I put this pack on your back?"

And then it was being eased on my shoulders and my arms were being tugged as he shuffled the bag onto my back. I bore with it as patiently as I could.

These creatures are everywhere. How many of them were there?

He'd seen as well as I had. We'd both been there when they crawled out of the tear in the earth.

There were maybe a dozen then. There are ...hundreds now. Can Judicus stop them?

Judging by the cursing behind me I rather thought not.

There was the sound of something scraping against something else and then a flare of light. I tried to turn but he hissed, "Don't move or I'll drop the flint."

He was lighting a *lantern*? On the back of a *phoenix*?

I'm insulted.

So was I. He could have just asked, and I could make Kazmerev visible.

Well.

Well, what?

Well, we'd be very obvious, and we are trying to hide, aren't we? In case there are Stryxex or rope workers watching the sky?

We were obvious with a lantern wobbling on his back.

"Hold this for a moment, would you?"

The flint was dropped in my hand. I tightened my fist over it and gritted my teeth. For the love of flight, what was he doing?

A lantern is less visible than a gorgeous phoenix. Like comparing a spark to a wildfire.

Fair enough. But we'd better keep a lookout for Stryxex.

Behind me, I heard the sound of rustling paper.

"There was something about this. Something about the ground. It's here somewhere."

More rustling. Was he looking at our enemies' prophecies?

That was so Judicus.

"Here it is. I knew there was something about this. Listen," he said, and then it was clear he was reading. "*The rocks themselves will rise up and guide us and lead the vanguard of the fight, they will crush our enemies before us and make straight paths for us. And a sign will come from the heavens, a symbol that our time has come. Darkness for five long days and nights. Darkness and the winds of the west rushing over our shores to the edges of our enemy's land and they will taste the bite of winter out of season and know our victory is sure.*"

I didn't feel any winds or see any snow.

The wind is westerly.

And since there was always a one in eight chance of that, it proved nothing at all. It was as silly as saying the sun had risen in the east. Besides, we all knew Mally could stop the sun with her crown. If the night lingered, that would be her doing, not a prophecy.

But they wouldn't know that. They would think it was time to attack their enemies.

Well, we were worrying about it, but night had only just fallen in a completely natural way. There was no reason to believe it wouldn't continue to follow the normal course of things.

It's deviated before. It could again.

I refused to give this book of prophecy any credence.

"*And when the time has come and we fall upon our enemies in an avalanche,*" Judicus went on, picking up on a different page, "*Then the enemies of the tattered ribbons will seek a single word and they will seek to speak it, but they must not speak the word or bow beneath it. They must be prevented from the knowing of it for with a word the world was made and with a word it can be broken.*"

Ominous.

I started to turn but Judicus stopped me again.

"No, don't turn. I'm juggling too many things on my lap. But you see it, don't you? They'll certainly take this army as proof that their prophecy is speaking the truth. And when they do, we will know where they are headed. They'll be trying to prevent some kind of word. And we're the ones who need to make sure that their plans don't succeed. We have only one hope, Sersha. We have to get to the passes of the Crown Peak mountains right into Craven Pass where King's Hold is, and we have to plead with the leaders there to listen. And we need to get there tonight We don't have time to dally or wait or these creatures will get there first, and heaven help any town or home they find before we arrive there."

Agreed, Kazmerev said.

And I found that I, too, agreed.

189

I'd heard of people following prophecies before, putting their hopes in them, trusting them, even achieving victory by them. I'd heard of people fighting against the predictions of prophecies. But I'd never heard of anyone fighting them and winning.

Once Judicus packed his precious book away into the pouch on my belt, he let me turn and the words poured out in my signs.

"How can we fight this?"

"Well, we have a plan," he started but I made a fast gesture of negation. I didn't have the words to explain but I had to try.

"If it was meant to be? If it is more than us?"

"Oh, because it's a prophecy?" he asked, his eyebrows rising sharply and his narrow face pale in the lantern light.

Tell him to put the lantern out.

I signed Kazmerev's request and Judicus snuffed it, looking chagrined.

"Just because something is foretold doesn't mean it comes from good, Sersha," Judicus said and the passion in his words made them tight and fierce. "You know this. Phoenixes are good to their fiery cores, and who do these people want dead beyond all others? Phoenixes. There must be some power they have that these people fear. It's all through their writings, *'Beware of the flame.' 'But the fire shall rise up and the flames shall burn away the beauty,'* and more like that. Over and over, it warns against fire and I'm certain they mean phoenixes because that's who threatens them. It's the good in them. That's the one thing these conspirators can't handle."

He paused, sawing in a gasping breath. I didn't realize he was this upset. He was trembling with emotion. He went on, his voice rising and his hands trembling as he tried to stow the lantern back in the pack.

"That's what I'm trying to say – that just because someone foretells something doesn't mean it comes from heaven or from anything else that's good or noble. It might just be a thing they want – and evil people so often want power and control over the lives around them as if our very freedom and joy is of personal offense to them – and then they set about fulfilling these prophecies they've made and that gives them legitimacy by bringing them to life."

His voice rose again, his words tumbling one on top of the other as if his mind were tumbling down a hill, picking up speed as it bashed against one thought only to tumble and strike the next.

"And who is to say there's anything good in that? I haven't seen anything good in the people who were killed for no reason, and the phoenixes sent to the beyond, the city overthrown, my sister betrayed, my uncle assassinated, and this terrible stone army marching on our neighbors. What happens when they reach them? What army can withstand this? And before you ask, no I can't stop them like I stopped those other stone creatures. Those were tied to something, and I found the threads and cut them and I'm not finding threads attached to these ones at all, it's like they have something entirely different inside powering them and, oh sweet heavens, Sersha," he was gasping now between breaths like he was going to cry or scream or something. "I don't know what to do. *I don't know what to do.*"

I grabbed his hand, trying to squeeze reassurance into it.

I hope he doesn't vomit again. I feel like a nursemaid when he does, and it doesn't suit me at all.

But I knew the difference. This wasn't the trembling of airsickness or of nerves. This was the desperate clawing of panic and fury and despair crawling across him and shaking him in its grasp. I tightened my hold on his hand and he closed his eyes tight.

The frustrating thing about speaking in sign is that people can just refuse to watch. They can block me out like I don't exist.

But there are some things that are hard to block out.

So I leaned back and I wrapped an arm around his waist. He startled with a little squeak sound I had *never* expected to come out of a man – but why not, wasn't he allowed a moment to be vulnerable, too? Wasn't he allowed a moment to be scared, too? Wasn't he allowed the desire – just for a little while – to have someone take care of *him?*

And I leaned in and against his tightly pressed lips, I set my own and tried to push into them every certainty and hope that I had. Because I hadn't lost my hope.

In a world where phoenixes existed, there could never really be no hope. In a world where friends stood for each other and came back again and again to save each other, there could never be full despair. And in a world where Judicus lived, evil would never win, because he would refuse to bend in the face of it no matter if it blew at him with the force of a hurricane. And I … I realized this with a solidity like discovering bedrock under your feet … I would be sure that he wouldn't break.

Ahem.

Was I forgetting something?

You're forgetting who will carry you both.

My phoenix would.

He flared bright and hot, and I didn't care that there might be Stryxex about. I didn't care that they might see us racing to the mountain pass. Sometimes you needed to make hope visible. Sometimes you needed to raise a flag of defiance. Sometimes, you needed to set your teeth and dare the world to knock you down – not for you, but for everyone who was sinking into the mud of despair and heartbreak.

I made my beautiful Kazmerev visible and when I broke my kiss, Judicus gasped, his eyes flying open. And I didn't know if the look of wonder in his eyes was for the phoenix or the kiss but either way, it was worth it.

It's for the phoenix. I would think that was obvious.

"We can do this," he whispered, and I forced myself to smile as confidently as I could and to feed every care and anxiety to the fire beneath and the fire within.

You can do this, Kazmerev echoed, and his fires burned hot, hot, hotter than the hottest ache of fear in my chest.

190

We soared over the writhing stone ground, dipping lower and lower.

Lower means we won't be as easily seen. Plus, I can keep an eye out to be sure that we have a place to set down away from these rock creatures when the sun comes up.

Judicus had grown ill hours ago – I'd known it had to happen eventually – and fallen asleep on my shoulder.

His weight was comforting. I felt, so often, like I bore the weight of the world on my shoulders but having Judicus's actual weight lessened that feeling.

It felt like it should be dawn by now, a feeling that made the hairs on the back of my neck stand up just as they did to Kazmerev. Both of us felt it coming like one feels the shift in the air that calls for a storm.

Perhaps, she's wearing the crown, Kazmerev said eventually.

I thought he might be right. The hours wore on and I was heavy from exhaustion by the time Judicus woke and took the pack from me.

"There," he said muzzily, still nauseated from the flight. "I see Craven Pass. And there is King's Hold straddling it."

He was right. In the distance, lights shone – just barely discernable from so far away, but steady and growing brighter as the minutes passed.

I wondered how they could have built such a big city up in the mountains.

It's not as big as it looks at night. They burn fires on the walls that make it look bigger. It's a tenth the size of Briccatore.

Which was still enormous.

Can you ask Judicus if we have a plan?

Night or fake night, there was still a moon and that made it possible to talk with my hands.

"*Judicus?*" I signed and he shivered at his name. I pressed on. "*Do you have a plan? Where are we going?*"

"There's a tower right in the center where the lord of King's Hold resides. We need to set right down in the courtyard," he said confidently. "We need to speak to someone in charge right away."

In a foreign nation? You'll be shot from the sky by archers!

I conveyed his concern.

"The alternative is waiting – an hour, a day, any amount is too much with those stone creatures right behind us. Think of them, Sersha. Think of them crashing through the pass flattening everything and everyone in their path. We're talking hundreds of dead – the innocent with the guilty. The hold would fall. And the land behind it will fall quickly afterward with no warning and no hope to escape. How far do you think they are behind us?"

I looked back. We'd lost them some hours ago.

At least a day by the time we reach the pass.

I conveyed that, too.

"Barely enough time," Judicus said grimly. "But we'll risk what we must to warn them."

We flew and flew, the city growing larger as the hours passed. We stopped once in a lonely spot to take care of necessary business and stretch out stiff muscles for a few moments, eat, drink, and then we were back, flying again.

"Heroism is all very well," Judicus complained, "but why does it always seem to involve some kind of travel? Why can't it be done from a comfortable chair with a warm fire and a good book."

Trust me, it's worse to carry him than to be carried, Kazmerev replied darkly.

I did not translate.

And I was too busy worrying to complain. What if the city didn't listen to us? What if the people couldn't flee in time?

Or what if they tried to fight and were killed?

I looked often at the moon, wondering what had happened to Mally that had her wearing the crown all the time. That couldn't be practical in a foreign land.

Just be glad we're stuck in night instead of in the day. This way, I can watch over you.

This was definitely better.

But there was little to do but worry and I made sure to do my fair share of that. And I held Judicus's hand in mine whenever he let me because I had a terrible feeling that this might be my only chance.

When he'd said the word "hero," I'd been reminded of a terrible truth. Heroes didn't live very long. They were always asked to sacrifice something. And this attachment that was growing between us would certainly be one of those things. Because there could be no way to save the phoenixes and turn a prophecy on its head and rescue his sister and still keep *this*, could there? It seemed like asking for too much. And I know not to push what little luck we had.

The journey seemed to be too long and too short all at once and by the time my legs were screaming for relief, and my hand was still ready to keep holding on for a few days more, we were close enough to the walls to see the guards on watch over a stone door built across the pass, four banners whipping in the wind atop the gate.

The wind stirred them up in swirls and gales, gathering and growing ominously at our backs, and whatever words the men on guard called to us as they pointed were lost in the howl of the wind and the dark of the night.

I thought I saw crossbows being snatched up, but by the time they had them in hand, we had passed.

A bell began to ring, long sonorous tolls filling the night sky. It was as clear and sharp as the chilly air had become around us, piercing enough to carry over the howling gale, and it stirred up people in the city the way that same wind would stir up dried leaves, leaving them scattered and frenzied.

"Follow my lead," Judicus called into my ear as the tower appeared and Kazmerev began to descend. "And whatever you do, don't tell them anything."

191

Bright in the light of many lanterns, the courtyard before the tower was already full of scrambling people when we dove down into it. It was indeed a tower, but it was not just a cylindrical spire. The base of the tower sprawled so that it stood more like an elongated castle than a single tower.

Judicus leapt from Kazmerev's back almost before he should have, and I clenched my teeth at what must have been a shin-aching landing. His cloak flapped wildly behind him in the rising wind, and I didn't notice the dirt and wear on it. All I saw was how it made him look bigger and bolder.

Kazmerev's flames – visible right now – whipped in the wind raggedly, little tongues of flame dancing along his length and breadth that snapped one way and then the other.

"Men of King's Hold," Judicus called in a loud voice. "I must speak to your leader. Calamity rides at our heels."

I had thought that they would run to get someone immediately – or worse – shoot us on sight. Some of them held crossbows, but they didn't even raise them. One of them spat on the ground.

"Only one of you, Calicarn? Don't think your flame beast frightens us."

I don't frighten them? Kazmerev sounded appalled.

"Be off with you. You've stirred the pot and woken good people from their sleep, but you'll find no inn will take you, no home will house you, no tavern feed you, so turn back and fly away." The spokesperson appeared to be a gravelly-voiced grey-haired man in uniform. His skin was darker than mine and his form short and somewhat squat and his fellows matched him.

"Such hospitality," Judicus said with a twist of his mouth. "I don't know how you can spare it."

"We'll spare more if you don't leave," the same man said. He stepped forward, singling himself out. "Spare you a whipping."

"What's this now Flargard?" a man's voice boomed out as the door of the tower opened and he stepped out. He was clad in heavy furs, carrying a staff with the head of a lizard carved in the top of it.

"Rabble, Lord Panziar. We were sending them away." To my surprise, the mocking voice had changed to one of respectful subservience.

The man stepped a little closer, frowning. His face was wide and bluff and darker than my own brown face. So dark that the details of his expression would be hard to see without my night vision.

"Rabble? One mounted on a phoenix and the other ... is that the visage of an Irault I see before me? Is that the face of a man set in bronze in Briccatore? The great traitor? The scourge of Calicarn? The Lord of Chaos? I know that long jaw and those mad eyes."

Judicus didn't flinch. He simply said, "Yes."

"And why are you on our doorstep? Are you here to betray your people as your father betrayed them?"

Judicus visibly stiffened, and I knew why. He wanted to tear into them. Wanted to tell them who his father was, and what he'd done. It was with masterful self-control that he responded calmly. He raised his voice, as dramatic as he had been the first time, but careful and measured.

"King's Hold stands as a house of power in the mountains, an eagle perched and waiting for the unwary."

I was surprised to see that the men in the courtyard seemed to stand a little straighter at that. Perhaps, in this place, words had greater power, and the more dramatic the words the more captivating the power. If it was true, Judicus would know. It could take a lifetime to find out everything he held inside.

I have heard that they set great store by words in this land.

Judicus continued, "But even the eagle cannot stand if the mountain rises up against him. Even your great hold cannot repel the rocks."

"Is that a threat?" Lord Panziar snapped.

"It's a warning," Judicus said boldly. "I come to you like a raven screeching in the storm. I bring a warning dire and immediate."

"Then you've warned us," the man said and there was a note of mockery in his tone. "You've warned us that the rocks are on the march. What think you, men, should we catalog the rocks and note their places so we can fend off any attack?"

The men around us snickered and I felt my heart fall. They weren't going to listen.

"The kabba bird mocks from its seat in the trees," Judicus said carefully. "Until the Kestrel snatches it."

"I thought you weren't here to threaten," Panziar said grimly.

"Is that a threat?" Judicus asked. His voice was all innocence. "Perhaps it is the Lord of this castle who should decide."

"And what if that is me?"

Judicus laughed without humor. "We both know that it is not. You are the Speaker for the Tower. That's why you carry the staff with the head of the salamander on it. An honored role – right hand to the Lord of the Castle himself. But you are not the final authority here. You bend your head to another."

The courtyard was still, each person waiting as if they expected something violent to happen.

Even Panziar seemed frozen, his eyes fixed on Judicus. He neither agreed nor denied this claim. It was as if everyone but me knew something more was coming.

"I demand the honor of the word and the blade," Judicus said.

And I thought they'd laugh again, but to my shock, they were even more still than they had been before. Silence dragged out so that only the howling of the wind was left and then Lord Panziar banged his staff on the flagstone – twice, three times.

"The honor has been called for and will be granted," he announced, and then in a quieter voice he said, "If your companion will observe, she must dismiss the bird and follow."

Bird? Now I'm insulted. It's like they want mysterious fires started around the place.

His griping was comforting, but not enough to wash away the dread I felt at the idea of asking him to return to my heart. Maybe he could circle around above us instead.

Take courage. I will warm you from within.

I swallowed, slid from his back, and drew him back within my heart.

To my surprise, Judicus handed me our pack without even looking back.

"Lead on," he told Lord Panziar.

192

To my surprise, Lord Panzier led us within the wide door of the tower. The ceilings within were so high and domed that I could have brought Kazmerev with me. He hovered in my heart – present enough that I could feel him, but too absent to comment in my mind. Maybe I would learn, someday, to still be able to talk to him when he was hidden there. Maybe it would make me feel less lonely. I buzzed with the tension of his absence as a hive buzzes with bees.

I couldn't catch Judicus's eye. He was in front of me, and we were escorted single file, the soldiers from the courtyard surrounding us in a tight formation. One of them had been sent ahead to warn of our coming. It worried me to be forced back into silence, surrounded by strangers.

The tower was barely furnished or decorated, maintaining only the most basic necessities – plain, backless wooden benches where seating was needed, the occasional stand or shelf for containing important items. Mostly, it was simply stone and more stone, undecorated, undressed, rough stone.

We tromped through the halls, my anxiety creeping upward as doors were slammed shut before we could pass. All I saw beyond the soldiers escorting us were the fleeing backs of people, or the edges of their clothing as they hurried away.

What could make them fear us that much ... or hate us that much? Were these two nations so deeply at odds with one another as that? There had been no rumors of war up in Landsfall, but then again, would we have heard of tensions from so far away?

Judicus seemed unbothered, simply striding forward as though none of this concerned him at all.

I tried to adopt a similar carefree attitude, but I thought that anyone who looked at me would see it was a bluff. Especially, if they noticed me brushing down my clothing with my palms and trying to straighten my mussed hair.

Whoever we were going to see must be as cold and unyielding as the fortress he ruled, and I was worried he'd see only that we were ragged and tired and not that we bore a severe warning.

We reached a wide door at last – closed to us and heavily guarded.

"This one has demanded the honor of the word and blade," Lord Panziar said without inflection.

"All who pass must don clarity and truth," the men at the door intoned. I was already feeling ill at ease in their strange tower and the way they spoke in unison and opaquely was not helping.

One of the guards strode forward bearing a pair of heavy bronze carcanets. Lord Panziar held out the first one to Judicus.

He did not take it.

"You asked for the honor. Now you wear the ritual carcarnet or you pay the price of failure."

I didn't like the sound of that.

Judicus took the carcarnet and put it over his head. It felt all wrong on him as if it somehow made him shorter.

"Sersha will not wear one," he said calmly.

The man's eyes flicked to me and back to him.

"Can your servant not speak for herself? Or is she a raven with no croak?"

Judicus stiffened at that, but his words were calm.

"This is Sersha of Landsfall, a member of my coterie and due all the same honors as I am. She does not speak."

Lord Panziar raised an eyebrow and held the carcanet out to me. "Then she will receive the same honor."

Judicus met my eyes and he seemed to be trying to tell me something with just his eyes. Whatever it was, I didn't understand it. Reluctantly, I dipped my head and let the big man put the necklace over my head. It was too heavy, and it made me feel terrible – lonely and cold in a way I didn't understand.

The way Judicus bit his lip made me worry I'd made the wrong choice.

I didn't have time to regret it.

Already, Lord Panzier was striding to the door and the guards there were opening both sides of it in an elaborate movement that involved some of them kneeling and others bowing and still others sweeping their polearms out in a quick, practiced movement.

Well. They certainly were a dramatic people. And they seemed very good at drills. I wished I had Kazmerev here to explain it all to me.

I wished – I didn't know what I wished, only that it felt like I was once again mounted on a stone creature with no way to leap off. And I did not like that feeling of helplessly hurtling toward an unknown goal.

I had expected a throne room through the doors. Once again, I was wrong.

We entered a long hall with a fire running down one side. The hearth over the fire was carved in a frieze of wolf heads and lizards. Before the fire, sat a long, heavy table made of some kind of thick, dark wood bearing light stripes within that could not possibly belong to this area in the wind-thrashed mountains.

At the center of the table, seated on a high-back wooden chair with a howling wolf's head over her head, was a woman who could be the sister of Lord Panziar. She was stacked with furs – red fox, mink, and something curly that made me think of mountain sheep but dyed a bright blue – and she wore a thick bronze coronet in her grey-streaked black hair. A scar ran down her dark face on one side and it quirked up when her mouth turned down in irritation.

"This is the singing cricket that begs for the word and the blade?" she asked in a quiet voice as the doors behind us closed with a shuddering boom.

"It is, Great Lady," Lord Panzier said, bowing low.

I felt my eyebrows creeping up as Judicus made his own small bow and I scrambled to follow suit.

She smiled, and it was not a smile I liked the look of.

"You know the rules, then, foreigner or you never would have demanded the honor."

"I do," Judicus said and there was something about his voice that worried me.

"And your companion?"

"Is only here to watch."

"Are you sure?" she sounded almost as if she were taunting him. "She has blood to offer, too, I think."

Blood? No, I didn't like this.

I took a step forward, but Judicus flung a hand up, his eyes meeting mine. He shook his head and mouthed the words, "One day."

I swallowed and stopped. He was going to let them do ... something ... to him and all because he cared about *their* citizens. All because he wanted *them* to be safe and the Creatures of Sydonon were only a day behind us. It was heroic. And it made me furious at the same time.

The lady drew a long, slender knife from her boot and leaned over the table.

"Place your hand on the table and speak the words," she said, and there was hunger in those words only matched by the hunger in her eyes and in the eyes of Lord Panziar beside us.

193

Judicus spread his hand wide on the table, leaning forward so there was less than an arm's length between his face and the lady's.

"I invoke the honor," he intoned and like lighting striking, her hand shot out and she buried the slender knife through his palm between the first finger and the thumb right through to the table, pinning him.

My hand shot up, covering my mouth.

Judicus's head turned, and he met my eyes again and there was no uncertainty there.

"Calm," he mouthed to me.

Even that warning was barely enough to keep me settled. I felt my blood speeding in my body and my breathing racing to catch up. Keep it together, Sersha, keep it together.

I almost reached for Kazmerev but I hesitated. He was right. If we insulted them they wouldn't listen and then how many innocent people might die?

Already, Judicus was speaking, his words coming out of him like a flood.

"Enemies march on your lands. You have just one day to remove everyone in King's Hold and get them somewhere safe. It won't be enough time. You must leave now. Stone creatures, powered by magic, are crawling across the ground as we speak. We got out in front of them only because we could fly. They can't be stopped. I don't know if they can be destroyed. They are living stone and they will crush all that stands before them."

He stopped for a breath and the lady spoke.

"I won't interrupt you. You buy your chance to speak with your words. But you come to me as a strange bird migrating from somewhere else. You come as the chick of egg-stealers claiming to want to line my nest. Why would I believe you?"

"I am Judicus Franzer Irault," Judicus said, taking in another long breath and I thought that maybe I saw in him echoes of a man who had been the undoing of a ruler. "My father is known to you. He toppled a king for what he believed. He did not lie. I come to you as his son. You know exactly who I am. There is no guessing here."

She barked a laugh. "A madman is your proof? We did not mourn the chaos in Calicarn, but that does not mean we wish to nurture it here."

"Your politics are your own," Judicus said. "And I care not what they are. I am here with this grim warning. Chaos is nipping at our heels. Great rock creatures, larger than horses. They pour up the mountainside like a backward avalanche and if you don't flee, you will be crushed under them. Maybe you will even if you flee. I do not know how fast you can move, only that you must move now. Now! Before it is too late."

"And where did these stone creatures come from?" She sat in her chair, crooking one knee over an arm, entirely at her mocking ease. Her light tone stood in stark contrast to his emotion-laced passion.

The first drip of Judicus's blood fell from the table and splashed on the stone of the floor.

I gritted my teeth. If these rulers weren't listening, we needed to move on. Or we would be crushed here, too. Maybe we could warn the next city. Or the next.

Those bees in the hives of my mind were buzzing more furiously.

"From a tear in the earth," Judicus said. "From a broken plinth in the foothills below."

"And who set all this in motion?" she asked, quirking her mouth.

"I fear that I had a hand in it," Judicus said.

She tapped the table, looking at him with disdain. "You?"

"Please. For the sake of your people." His words were edged with terrible sadness. "Please."

"I don't listen to madmen," the lady said, looking at her fingernails as if she barely cared about what he was saying. "I have a people to defend and a trust to guard. I am not – "

Her words cut off as the doors opened and a man in black stumbled in, a carcarnet around his neck, just like ours. My breath caught in my throat. We hadn't been fast enough.

He pushed past the guards on either side of him and pushed past Lord Panziar who objected with a growled, "Hold, now!"

He threw his hand on the table, drew his own dagger, plunged it through the flesh, and then ripped his hood from his head before any of us could gasp.

It was Kentinius.

I felt something like a stone sinking in my stomach.

Judicus, on the other hand, ran a hand through his hair like he was just too tired for this.

"Now, *I* speak," Kentinius said.

"That's not how it works. You ask for the honor and you claim it, but it must be granted by the Great Lady," Lord Panziar growled.

Kentinius didn't answer. He reached in a satchel thrown over his shoulder and brought out something that looked like a large jar. He slammed it on the table.

Perhaps it was opaque to the naked eye, like the plinths had been, but to *my* eye the jar was transparent and inside it was swimming with phoenix souls. They screamed and screamed until my ears ached from the sound.

I bit down on my tongue so I wouldn't cry out. My eyes were fixed on the jar. They wouldn't pull away. My hands were sweaty and that cold feeling in my heart was growing colder even as my heart raced faster and faster.

Enough.

I needed my friend and we needed to *run*.

I reached within for Kazmerev. He would know what to do. He always did.

I found nothing.

I was too far on edge. I needed to relax.

Sucking in a breath, I closed my eyes and tried again.

Nothing.

Panicked, I grabbed for the necklace just as rough hands grabbed me from behind and my wrists were thrust into hard metal.

My eyes sprang open, and to my surprise, Lord Panziar was right in front of me, breathing hard.

"Anyone who tries to interrupt the ritual must be bound until it is complete," he said in a low voice. "So must anyone who tries to remove the carcarnet. That's you."

But the carcarnet kept Kazmerev away!

I fought his grip, struggling to get to my knives but he only held me tighter. The metal was locked around my wrists. It didn't matter. I could still get this collar off. I reached up toward it and the cuffs jerked down, pulling me with them enough to rip at the muscled in my shoulders.

"None of that, now," Lord Panziar whispered and I watched in horror as he flicked the chain in his hands that extended to my cuffs.

I stole a glance at Judicus but he wasn't looking at me. He was looking at Kentinus. I clanked my wrists together to get his attention, but he didn't notice. He was fixed on the face of his enemy.

"By now these traitors will have come to you with wild stories of moving stone and a need to flee," Kentinius was saying. He must have flown on the back of a Stryxex to get here as quickly as us. "They are squawking gulls. Their cries are as endless and meaningless as the words of the wind. But they are not wrong that these creatures come. I was sent as an ambassador of the newly crowned Grand Hadri with a request to capture Judicus Franzer Irault and his companions. They evaded my grasp and washed up here on your shores. But not before they let loose a hurricane of trouble, for they awakened an ancient magic that comes up these mountains toward your hold. Surely, you noticed they knew too much about this disaster and yet had no way to stop it. Would anyone but a guilty man be so certain?"

"And what makes you any different from him?" the lady asked, tapping her fingers on the table. None of them were looking in my direction. There was no one to warn, no one to plead with.

"I will give you this opalesnascant," Kentinius said with a smile, tapping the jar. I flinched when his finger struck it. "It opens and sends out a shield for every man, woman, and child within your gates. When the creatures come, it will turn them back to Calicarn, without any of you lifting a hand. Look at the letter tied to the opalesnascent and you will see for yourself."

The lady extracted the letter from a small leather cylinder tied around the jar and began to read.

I fought with renewed energy against my bonds, but Lord Panziar threw an efficient punch at my gut, doubling me over and making me see stars. I grunted with the pain of it and a hand wrapped around my mouth, blocking any other sound I could possibly muster.

Someone needed to tell them what that was. Someone needed to tell them he was lying. That jar was full of the extracted souls of living things. I didn't know what it would do, but I knew it was no protection.

But I couldn't free myself even a little, I couldn't even straighten from my agonized collapse or pull myself free of Panziar's grip on my mouth, and not a single eye looked at me except the guard beside me and the very effective Lord Panziar.

Even Judicus was too fixed on the task at hand.

"Would you risk your people to unknown tinctures?" my leader asked in a low voice. "Would you trust something that might harm them?

"It seems like a reasonable offer," the lady said, scratching her chin as she looked from one of them to the other. "This letter is authentic, sealed with the seal of the Grand Hadri and signed by a full counselor to the crown. I do not doubt this ropeworker's words. But why would you be so generous? What would you have of us?"

"Not much," Kentinus said with a gracious tilt of his head. "Just these two troublemakers. We in Calicarn, wish to tidy up our own messes, as I'm sure you can understand."

"Mmm," the lady said, reading the letter once more. "I've a mind to grant you what you wish, but only once we see for certain that your opalesnascent does as you have promised."

"And until then?" Kentinus asked and he looked so calm you'd think this was the exact outcome he had wanted all along.

"Until then, you can open it for us and apply your help to our people. These two will be held for you. I think the raven cages will do until you're ready for them, don't you think?"

And now, for the first time since he'd arrived, Kentinus smiled and ripped the dagger from his hand.

"Bound in words and blades," he said.

And around us, the ritual words were repeated.

I felt my heart fall as Judicus's shoulders sank, and with them, my hopes.

He looked back at me at the same moment that the guards rushed him, ripped the dagger from his hand, and shoved his wrists in cuffs – just like mine. And the carcarnet must hold his ropework back just like it held Kazmerev back because judging by the fury in his eyes he would fight them all if only he could.

Our gazes held in shared horror, and this time when his lips moved his eyes were full of shame.

"Forgive me," he mouthed. "Forgive me."

EPISODE FIVE: “DARKEST HOPE”

SEASON TWO

194

King's Hold maintained the ancient and gruesome practice of crow cages. There were two on the wall facing the pass back down the mountains toward Calicarn and it was in these crow cages that they deposited Judicus and me. They took care to place locks so that we could not remove the carcanets that kept Judicus's magic and my phoenix unreachable, and they moved our manacles to the front of our bodies.

In the terrible cold of the mountains, the cold metal had bit our skin like an angry immobile snake. I flinched from it but I could not escape it.

The crow cages had been on the wall for long enough that rust stains streamed from where they were bolted down the pale stone of the wall. Whoever had made these terrible devices had cared as little for the guards stuffing prisoners into them as they did for the prisoners. That they were still used suggested that their lady cared just as little. I half expected one to fall to his death.

Our captors struggled to force us into the cages, wobbling as two of them balanced on either side, one foot and hand on the cage and the other clinging to a rope hanging down from the top of the wall. These guards levered the tops of the cages upward and then another pair of guards manhandled us over the edge of the wall and dropped us unceremoniously into the cages.

Fear seized my heart as they shoved me over the edge of the wall – fear so sharp and toothy that it seemed to rip me from throat to navel. I couldn't breathe, could barely keep myself from muted wailing. I landed in the cage, but their aim was true and I hit the bars of the cage-bottom shoulder-first.

Pain blossomed through my shoulder and raced to every extremity. I gasped, blinking back tears, feeling so disoriented that by the time I regained my sense of where I was, came to realize I was still living, and blinked back enough of the agony in my right side to see clearly again, the guards had slammed the top of the cage down again and locked it into place.

It swung wildly from the chains that held it – two wide chains from two separate anchor points to leave room for the door in the top. Even with two points, the cage wobbled so badly that I had to fight to focus my vision and gather in details without growing nauseated.

Judicus and I were close enough that we could have called to one another – if I could call, which of course, I couldn't. Close enough that he could see my signs if I made them – which, with my hands tied, I couldn't. Close enough that I could see Judicus's face was very pale as they dropped him into the cage and locked the door. He lay on the floor of the cage with his face pressed against the bars beneath us. If I'd been closer, I was sure I would hear him breathing too quickly. For someone who was paralyzed by heights, this was a terrible place to have been put.

This cage was horrible even if heights didn't quite bother you. Cold wind whipped the cage so hard that the iron squealed. The cage rocked in the throes of it so that the cold of the bars pierced through my clothing in unexpected places as different areas came in contact and out of contact with the bars. I was protected from the worst of it. As a Flame Rider, I was abnormally warm all the time and the core warmth in me kept me warmer than any normal person would be. And even *I* was shivering already. Judicus must be absolutely miserable.

I couldn't hear any sounds from him over the howling wind and squeal of the chains, but I was sure he'd be gasping against nausea in his rocking cage and shuddering against the cold.

Which meant we couldn't stay like this. He might not survive the night.

And if that happened, I'd lose more than a friend. Judicus was my whole future. Being part of his coterie gave me a purpose bigger than myself. Following his lead gave me a guidance into what was right and good. And when things went badly for me, he rescued me. Kazmerev was my strength and his encouragement nurtured me, but Judicus was my heart and my purpose.

I couldn't lose him.

Which meant I just wouldn't.

I closed my eyes and focused. I couldn't get the manacles off my wrists. I couldn't get the carcanet off. Could I wriggle my neck out of it? No. It was too tight. It would never get over my head.

But I was not willing to just give up. A simple piece of jewelry should not be enough to block my friendship with Kazmerev. It was just metal. It was made by men. It should have no hold over a being like him.

But though I told myself that over and over, I could not find him within. I righted myself in my cage, curling around myself so that I was upright, keeping Judicus in my view.

As the hours passed, he looked worse and worse. At first, he started off watching me, trying to tell me something with his eyes that I couldn't grasp with both our cages swinging in the wind. But it wasn't long until he was being miserably sick and then curling in on himself so far that his face was hidden in his knees. Even with the shaking of my cage, I could see him trembling in the cold.

I drew in a long, steadying breath. I needed to think. Judicus wouldn't live very long like this. And what could I possibly do to help him? I couldn't even speak to encourage him. I ran my hands through my hair, the cold manacles scraping against my cheeks. I had no ideas.

I peered out into the darkness – still moonlit and dark as if it were midnight instead of a couple of days since the sun went down. Mally was on the move somewhere. She was alive and doing something or the days would be back to normal. I had to hold onto that. And I had to hold on to love and hope. I couldn't lose them – not now. Because if I did and we died in these cages then who would warn these people? Their leaders had trusted the wrong people and only we were left to warn them, now. And we were here in these cages, slowly freezing to death.

If I was going to die, I didn't want to die like this. Defeated. Miserable. Bitter.

I wanted to die a different way. With love in my heart. With hope in my mind.

I stole another look at Judicus. He'd stopped shivering. That could not be good.

I smacked the bar with my manacle, trying to get his attention, but the wind was too loud. Snow began to fall in wild light swirls, stinging my face and hands with the sharp ice of the minuscule flakes. I flinched back from it, fighting to force myself back to love and hope.

I closed my eyes, and I thought of a flame in my heart – the place where Kazmerev was gone, where he probably was right now. Maybe, even now, he was feeding my heart with his endless hope. This, too, we could defeat. This, too, we could survive together.

Maybe in a world where prophecies lied and those in power had manipulated everyone's lives for years and years, maybe in a world like that the only thing you could know for sure was real was what you'd seen and heard yourself and I'd heard love every time when Kazmerev woke in my heart and offered me his unconditional devotion. I'd felt hope when Judicus came back just for me, and planned to keep me safe, and followed me to be sure I really would be. I'd found charity when the Flamerarch had taught me signs and given themselves one by one for me. And I'd found trust when the Grand Hadri gave me his plans with his last breaths and entrusted to me the work of his life.

A strange sadness, wistful but warm filled me. Perhaps that meant I was freezing to death. They said that the feeling of cold turned to a strange warmth toward the end.

I just wished I could hold Judicus's hand again. I'd loved that. Just the memory of it made me feel tingly and warm inside. I held onto the feeling, letting myself remember the warmth of his long, slender fingers and reassuring palms. Letting myself dwell on his gentle kiss. If these were to be my last moments, then I would use them to remember. I just wished I could do both those things just one more time.

I sniffled, realizing I was close to tears – foolish girl. Tears would only ache in this cold. I shook my head violently to keep them back.

But the warmth was building in my chest, and I clung to it, feeding every scrap of love I'd felt in my life into that feeling. Channeling into it all my hopes and desires.

And now my heart was so hot, I had to breathe shallowly and carefully to keep from being overwhelmed by the heat.

I opened my eyes and gasped. Something had changed.

The ground before me was moving. The Creatures of Sydonon had moved faster than we had predicted. They were here.

195

So, this, then, was the end. I didn't want to watch it. I'd close my eyes and grit them tight while these walls came down and buried me.

I stole one last glance at Judicus. I wouldn't get a chance now to tell him how I felt. Maybe he knew. Maybe the kisses had been enough to tell him. He was still huddled in a ball.

My cheeks felt hot watching him. It still would have been an amazing experience to tell him and get to watch his face and maybe he would have liked it. Maybe he might even have wanted it.

I came back for this?

I gasped.

How was this possible. It seemed too amazing, too impossible.

I pulled myself to my feet as he emerged, bursting from my heart as painfully as he had the first time. A cloud of ash burst in front of me, washing over me as a weight fell from my neck and hit my toe. I danced back, smarting, my eyes tearing up. The movement sent my cage swinging wildly and I had to grasp the bars to keep steady.

The scent of ashes was in my nose, and I didn't care. I wanted more. I inhaled long and deep, letting the scent burn through me.

He was here. He'd survived – and somehow, he'd broken the carcanet, and set himself free. My Kazmerev. My phoenix.

It was too wonderful.

It wasn't me. It was your trust, your grounding in gratitude and thankfulness and love. It reaches to something above both of us, something deeper than our hearts, something that flows in the veins of the world and beats in the center of her orb – something, or maybe someone, who wants *good to triumph and love to succeed.*

I just stared at him, marveling. This wasn't my imagination? He was real and here?

I felt as if I could feel his smile in my heart and then he swelled, glowing brighter.

Do you hear that?

And very, very faintly, I heard a voice.

I spun to look at Judicus, but he was still collapsed in on himself.

The words tickled the very back of my mind.

Kazmerev! Kazmerev! Sersha!

Who could be calling us?

It's far away. So far ...

My cage stopped suddenly and then lurched in the other direction. I forced myself to look down to where the ground was trembling beneath me.

Horns blasted and then a yell loud enough to be heard above the wind sounded from the wall. I looked up to see soldiers lining the wall, pointing down past my crow cage. They'd seen the creatures. They knew they were coming. Would they let Kentinius work his evil magic?

I swallowed, worried.

Make me visible. Let's get you out of the cage!

I wanted to, I really did. And we needed to get Judicus. But every soldier they could muster for the tops of the walls were crowding in looking right past us. They'd see an escape.

Be courageous! You have little time. You woke me at the last possible moment.

I hadn't realized I could wake him at all. I'd failed and failed before when I tried.

You should have known better. In the end, nothing – not even death – can truly separate us.

The line of creatures was ragged and strung out, chaotic. The lead stone creature looked like a scuttling lizard with pinchers for arms. It surged forward so quickly that it reached the wall first, flinging itself at the stone.

The cage jarred in response and my teeth clashed together.

In the other cage, Judicus collapsed.

Oh no. Oh no, no, no, no.

How sick was he if he was passing out instead of leaping to his feet?

I hear humans are susceptible to cold and the air is frigid. I think he may have succumbed.

I didn't have time for what-ifs. But I didn't know what I was doing or how we would escape even if my phoenix was helping. I bit my lip, looking back and forth between them, torn between uncertainty and fear.

There was nothing to do but trust. I took a deep breath and made Kazmerev visible.

He flared to life like a gout of fire when oil is thrown on it, flaring up bright gold and scarlet. His eyes blazed.

And my heart soared with him. Just the sight of his beauty eased some of my fear.

Above me, I heard a scream and then a soldier fell, striking the top of the cage before sliding off and falling again, arms and legs windmilling until I lost sight of him below me. My heart stuck in my chest. My fault. I'd scared him. His death was my fault.

Kazmerev! The faint call came again.

Over here! My phoenix called and then turned his attention to me, tipped his head to one side, and said very clearly. *Do you trust me?*

I did.

Close your eyes.

And though there were screams from the wall above us, I did.

Think your fieriest thoughts.

I did.

Be warm inside at the love you share with me – your second heart and flame, with your other friends, your family, your world.

I did.

Now focus with all your strength.

I did.

There was a feeling like a bubble bursting and a shattering sound like a broken glass pane and then screams. So many screams.

And I was falling.

And I was sinking into feathers that smelled of sulfur and cinnamon, and I buried my face into them, and burrowed into the warmth of them, and only then did I open my eyes.

Above me, the cage I'd been in was shattered, the top part of it still dangled from chains, but the bars ended in elongated threads as if they had melted and then as they dripped down, frozen in place.

I peered down to see the other half shattered on the ground at the same moment that the lead stone creature threw his body a second time at the wall. A boom shuddered through the air as a crack formed in the masonry, running up and toward Judicus's cage.

Could we do that again? I held my breath, waiting for his reply.

We could, but Judicus wouldn't survive it. Not unless he was sheltered somehow by the flame. But I could set you down on the top of his cage.

It was locked. I'd never get inside.

Or – and this could be very difficult – but you could try to cut the chains suspending it with streams of fire and then make me solid enough to catch the cage as it falls. But Sersha, I worry you won't have the strength.

I worried about that, too.

Below us, a second stone creature joined the lizard-like one. Then a third. A fourth.

I thought they'd all throw themselves against the wall, but to my horror, the first creature climbed on the backs of the newly arrived stone creatures. How much could they plan? How well could they coordinate?

I risked a glance behind my shoulder. Innumerable stone figures crawled across the surface of the ground, ignoring roads or trees or rocks, undaunted by drops or cliffs of mud. They simply moved, walking ever onward.

Even if this wall held against them, they'd just pile up and climb over it.

I bit my lip and decided. We'd try to burn him free.

I caught something on the edge of my mental voice, but it was gone almost before it began and then we were rising upward.

An arrow flew past my face, and another seemed like it was coming toward me, only to be blown by the wind that clawed and tore at me or to go wide when the archer struggled to see me in the swirling snow. I gritted my teeth, held on tight, and refused to be afraid. I would either die or I wouldn't, but I wouldn't leave Judicus.

Judicus's cage swam into view and my stomach flipped at the sight of him collapsed on the floor, motionless. Were we too late?

No sense worrying about it now. We have chains to fire!

I lifted my hand and aimed it at the nearest chain, calling on Kazmerev's fire, my teeth gritted with the effort. My vision swam and my head grew light, but the fire came, hot and bright and white, cutting the bubbling, melting chain in a jagged tear, and then it severed. The loose end above flapped in the wind and the loose end below fell with a crash, sending the crow cage spinning akilter from the second chain.

One more. Come on! The faster the better. Those arrows are flying fast and furious.

I nodded, biting my lip hard as we bobbed and dipped in the howling wind. The snow lashed so hard I couldn't see and if there were arrows flying, I couldn't see them either.

Everything was moving, the rock creatures below, the wall as it started to pile up with them, the soldiers on the wall, the eddies and spirals of snow, the cage as it wobbled – even the moon and stars were spinning. I bit my lip and tried not to be ill.

My hurt shoulder twinged suddenly, painfully. I must have moved it badly. I bit my lip and sealed my eyes shut just for a heartbeat.

One more.

I rallied. Something very wrong seemed to be happening inside me. I didn't know what, only that my head wasn't right, wasn't focusing. But I brought my hand up and I funneled all my strength into the fire, and it came again, searing, burning, cutting.

The cage fell so suddenly that my heart was in my throat as we tore through the air after it.

We have to catch it. Make me solid, make me solid!

It wasn't working. He was solid, but his talons couldn't grip, couldn't grab.

Panic clawed up my throat, warring for attention with the pain in my shoulder, and then we were plummeting together through the frigid air as the snow bit our cheeks like a thousand furious dogs.

We were losing him. Oh, merciful heavens!

Our fumbling attempts failed. Failed again.

My heart was screaming, screaming, screaming – my hand extended, my mind struggling and slipping as it tried to will my phoenix solid.

And then, abruptly, we were still falling and the cage was not.

Something hot brushed my cheek that wasn't Kazmerev and a voice rang in my head, full and deep.

I knew that voice! I knew it!

"*Let me help you with that,*" Grevankin said.

And I sobbed into Kazmerev's feathers, trembling with relief as the massive phoenix lifted the cage up and away from the wall, far from the fury of the archers and the stone creatures and up, up, up toward the shining crescent moon.

The moon made me think of a phoenix, bright and strong and smiling.

I think there's something wrong with you.

A beautiful phoenix.

Oh no. I think you've been shot.

196

You can't pass out. You can't. Focus.

The panic in Kazmerev's voice was unlike anything I'd heard from him before.

I can't land anywhere safe. The land crawls with stone creatures and their trampling feet. The city is full of your enemies. Grevankin carries the heavy cage and Huxabrand is weary to the extreme. Her rider has not slept in three days.

Three days? I knew that was important, but the thought just sat on the edge of my mind, a wrapped package I didn't have the energy to open.

Keep talking to me, any thoughts, any feelings. You just can't slip away. Come on.

I didn't have any thoughts except a burning in my shoulder and a whooshing feeling in my head that made me want to be ill on a Judicus level.

Yes, good. Think of him. We'll need to get him out of that cage.

Cage?

I saw it there, swinging beneath the massive phoenix, swaying back and forth. Judicus looked like a small, bedraggled songbird within. And around him, hail flew through the air.

Not hail.

Arrows. Ha. That's why they called it a "hail of arrows."

You're crazy when you're in pain. But keep going.

Someone bent low and furious over Grevankin's back. He looked child-sized compared to his huge phoenix. He must hate that.

Actually, I think Prexav feels safer because his phoenix is so large.

He does! Grevankin laughed in my mind. *I give him great stability. Oh, come now, Prex. The fledgling has a thorn in her wing. We must keep her mind sharp, or she will fall to the earth.*

I snorted a half laugh and didn't know how I could do that at a time like this.

If you can't laugh during terrible times, then you've lost a precious gift. Grevankin's voice boomed in my mind. *Laughter keeps the heart sane.*

I felt my mind drifting.

Focus! Kazmerev demanded.

I focused on the ground below us. It crawled like a mud field in a rain, the worms coming up from the ground and spilling out over it. How could it ever be stopped? It was as if the rocks had risen up against us.

We will find a way. Good always conquers evil because the one who made this world was good and put goodness into every fiber of every bit of it. All we have to do is find that and bring it back to the surface. Grevakin sounded very certain. I glanced over at him, and he winked at me with his great, fiery eye. *Yes, yes, Prexav. I am looking.*

What was Prexav looking for?

There was a pause. No one answered.

What could be so terrible that they wouldn't tell me? And hadn't someone said something about Huxabrand? I tried to look over my shoulder and darkness swam over my vision.

No! Look forward. Grip my feathers. No sudden movements. We will get you somewhere safe. Huxabrand is here. She's saying ... no, Gundt is saying not to worry about them. To hold on and focus ahead. We're out of arrow range now. The city grows small beneath.

Yes. I could see that now that he mentioned it. A part of my heart was leaping with joy – Gundt was here. He would help Judicus. But part of me was screaming that he shouldn't be here. That he was supposed to be somewhere else. I couldn't remember why.

My eyes drifted over the city, and I stiffened. I shouldn't be able to see individual people from here, and yet somehow, I saw little golden glowing points and to my eye, they seemed to be howling in agony, and in their midst, I was certain I could pick out a man in black, flowing robes.

Kentinius and the phoenix souls. He must have released them to hold the Creatures of Sydonon back, just as he promised.

But that didn't look like a defense. It looked like a terrible act of evil magic.

And it is. No one has the right to thwart the soul of another. And now souls are trapped and suffer on both sides of this conflict.

I swallowed and darkness danced over my eyes again.

Hold on just a little longer. Hold on!

Tell her to take deep breaths. That was a feminine mental voice – Huxabrand.

I felt Kazmerev preen under it. She always affected him too strongly. But the advice was good. I took deep breaths in and out.

My world shrank to the awareness of his warm feathers, the warmth creeping into my chilled bones, the breathing, deep and long, and the sound in my mind of phoenixes conversing. And perhaps I was too far gone in my injury to see clearly, but it seemed to me that they had taken over.

We need to set down somewhere before she passes out. Kazmerev.

I can catch her if she does. Probably. Huxabrand.

Those are well-warranted assurances, Grevankin broke in, *And yet I worry for the human in this cage. I can bear him to safety, but Prexav thinks he is too cold – close to death, even. He tells me this snow stings the skin of the humans and chills them to the core unless they hold fast to us.*

Can Mally hold on long enough to keep us here? Kazmerev sounded almost panicked. Was something wrong with Mally? The thought slipped through my head and then left again. I couldn't hold it.

She is very strong for a young human, Huxabrand said. *She will hold.*

Perhaps there? My phoenix's voice wavered as my mind fought to stay strong.

Blackness washed over me and a sense like I was falling and then I sucked in a deep, cold breath as ice washed over me and my eyes snapped open, and something caught me in the air.

Not good! You passed out for a moment. Focus! Please!

It sounded as if he was coming from far, far away. I tried to hold on to the sound of his voice. But my head was spinning. Where were we? I hoped we were close to a bed. I needed to lie down.

Please, Little Hawk!

And then the blackness washed over me, and his voice was gone.

197

I blinked awake. Cold air slapped me in the face and pain seared across my arm.

I gasped.

Kazmerev! You're back!

She must be conscious.

Kaz, tell her to stop thrashing.

I calmed before my phoenix could say anything. I didn't feel the familiar bloom in my heart, what I felt was more like a burning tether between us.

My vision flickered. I was looking at someone's knee while someone else moaned.

And then, abruptly, it was gone again.

I didn't know how long I lingered in darkness.

My eyes snapped open, breath hitching. The pain in my shoulder was agonizing. I gritted my teeth and clawed at the ground under me.

Ground. Good. That was good, I remembered.

Harsh cold met my grip, tearing at my fingernails. Little flakes of ice bit my face and neck and arms.

Kaz. Kaz.

Here. I'm here. Hold on to me, Little Hawk. I won't let you go.

Someone was keening a terrible, high-pitched moan that went on and on, braiding itself into the howl of the wind so that all I could hear was a primal wail of agony.

I forced myself up to my knees and slipped, falling onto my chest and bruising my chin. I tried again.

She's trying to stand. Tell her to stay put. Gundt will help as soon as he can. Huxabrand sounded panicked. Huxabrand.

What could be so bad that it had sliced through her arrogance and disdain?

If she was that upset, I certainly couldn't stay put. Every person would be needed.

I blinked back waves of blackness, forcing my feet under me and wobbling up to standing. My head swam, my limbs were heavy as a phoenix.

Technically, we weigh nothing.

Fine. Heavier than something much more heavy than a phoenix.

I forced my wandering eyes to focus. To one side of me, Mally was huddled over herself, crown on her head, rocking back and forth with eyes closed. She was the one keening as if she were dying. I gaped at her.

Not the urgent thing here.

She wasn't?

Huxabrand glowed pinkly, wrapped around Mally, keeping her warm enough. I didn't see any injuries. But she looked broken.

I didn't say she wasn't. But that's not our most urgent issue.

If we were dealing with something worse than the ai'sletta losing her mind – and what was she even doing here? – then ... well, that wasn't good.

Losing her mind?

Did she say losing her mind? Huxabrand asked in my mind. And her mental voice sounded like a squeal.

Easy. Easy, Kazmerev said, as if trying to calm both of us. *She's not thinking straight.*

I forced my exhausted head to turn and scan. There was Gundt, Prexav and Grevankin with him, leaning over the crow cage where Judicus still lay on the floor in a frozen rictus.

They were hitting the lock with something – an axe? – trying to get into it. Judicus's skin looked almost blue.

No. No. Sweet heavens, no.

I stumbled a step forward and another. Okay, my legs worked even if my head didn't. I wobbled badly, my brain trying to figure out which way was up and failing miserably.

Kazmerev paced beside me, and I put out a hand to steady myself against his neck. His head came down, nuzzling me.

Lie back down. You can't do anything here.

But if I didn't, he'd die.

And I'd only just realized that if he died, I would die, too.

What?

I was too wrapped up in him. It had happened without me realizing it.

No! You're my Flame Rider. Attachments like this aren't safe. They can threaten our bond. You can't let anything threaten it.

Since when was anything we did safe? Since when was anything not threatening?

He flared bright and golden, his hackles rising as he reared up.

What's wrong, Kazmerev? Grevankin boomed in my mind.

Nothing, Kazmerev said, but he sounded miserable.

Now is not the time for secrets, young friend! the bigger phoenix scolded.

She claims she will die if the frozen ropeworker dies, Kazmerev said reluctantly.

There was a long silence in which I managed two more wobbling steps.

She seems ready to kill herself already. She should be resting, Huxabrand said.

Kazmerev snorted his irritation in a cloud of steam. They were all talking as if they didn't think I was there. I was surprised the human men hadn't noticed.

Oh, they notice. But they're busy doing actually helpful things rather than making dramatic statements. Kazmerev tossed his head as he spoke, dramatic and annoyed all rolled into one. He was the dramatic one, not me. He was the dramatic – wait, I'd already thought that.

Maybe she means it. Grevankin sounded like an uncertain mountain shaking. *Maybe it's true. Have you thought of that? I was paired with a girl who fell in love once. It was a searing thing. Changed her – deepened her. I found it painful, but in the way that dawn is painful, or the call of the nightingale. In the way the center of the fire is painful as it calls to your soul. A reminder that we were made for more than this.*

Now who is being dramatic? Kazmerev grouched.

Her name was Lavendar. She married and had children. I liked them. They pulled on my feathers and laughed and listened to my stories.

Kazmerev paused. *They could hear you?*

They had a little sliver of their mother in them. They heard me to varying degrees.

I felt something like a pang of longing from Kazmerev and they were all silent as the story settled in. I managed three more steps. Nearly there. Nearly there.

I have always thought I would like children, Kazmerev said wistfully.

I would enjoy them again, Grevankin rumbled solemnly.

I hate to be the voice of reason in all this dreaming, Huxabrand said, and her voice was acid sharp. *But we are on a rocky ledge on a mountain. Below us, a city is being savaged, her people destroyed, and three of the five humans in our care are close to death. Could we speak of the charms of young humans at a later date? She does not look like she's going to give birth right now.*

I felt my cheeks grow hot against the cold wind. Of course, I wasn't giving birth! I was not the one who had brought up children. I hadn't even thought of children! But now, inevitably, I was thinking of it. A quick vision flashed across my eyes of a small, ridiculously thin child with long dark hair, and grave eyes, and a terribly uncertain stomach. My cheeks grew hotter.

I stumbled the last step and fell, catching myself on the bars of the cage and gripping them tightly in my firsts.

"It's not budging!" Prexav yelled over the wind.

Gundt shared a look with him and then lumbered to my side, squatting down.

"You can't help here, Sersha," he yelled over the wind. "You need to hunker down with Kazmerev and Huxabrand. Hux will keep you warm if you pass out again."

Pfft, Huxabrand added irritably. She would probably do it for him, but she certainly wouldn't like it.

I shook my head. They weren't going to get that lock open.

Then what will you do? Kazmerev asked. *If they can't get the lock open, then what? And don't you dare say you'll melt the bars. That will kill him for sure.*

I was going to warm him, so he didn't die.

I could almost feel Kazmerev rolling his eyes.

You are getting under my feathers, Little Hawk. I do not like seeing you care so little for your own needs. The sickly ropeworker is not the only one who needs you whole.

Gundt looked past me to my strutting, furious phoenix.

"What's going on, Kazmerev?" he called, and the wind grabbed and snatched at his words.

She's insisting on warming him up, Kazmerev said. There was a sulky sound to his voice.

Gundt shook his head. "Try to keep her warm!" he yelled and then he turned to me. "I thought you were dead, fledgling. And now that you're back, we're not going to let you die. You matter to us. Do what you must, but please don't push yourself past the brink of what's reasonable."

"That's what I keep saying."

I nodded, but I wasn't going to give up before I'd even tried. My belly knotted itself as I fell to my knees and reached my good arm as far as I could through the cold iron bars. I managed – with difficulty – to reach Judicus's hand.

It was stone cold.

198

I closed my eyes, and felt deep, deep, deep inside me, and pulled all the warmth I could out, channeling it into Judicus.

Be warm, I thought. Be warm.

It felt like running uphill. It pulled my energy out, sucking me dry so that all I felt was the pain in my shoulder. I blinked back tears, my jaw trembling, as the pain hit my raw mind hard and heavy.

I felt searing warmth as Kazmerev settled behind me and I wasn't sure if it was his physical warmth cradling me or the warmth of his acceptance in giving up his fury and helping me that was so comforting to me now, but I felt grateful. So, so grateful.

I sank into that feeling as the energy lessened. I could still feel it trickling out, but whatever healing was done now. I was tired. I wanted to just sleep.

And I didn't dare.

I forced my eyes to flicker open. I'd ended up flat on the frozen rock, my cheek stuck to the ground. I was shivering, but Kaz was there, and as my eyelashes unstuck enough to open despite my frozen tears, I saw Judicus blink awake, a flush of pink in his cheeks.

"Sersha," he whispered – too quiet for me to hear, but I could read his lips.

He smiled, slow and sweet, his deep, deep eyes widening at the sight of me until I thought I'd fall down into their depths.

Seriously. This is nauseating.

I like it, Grevankin said, shuffling closer to us. *Prexav doesn't. He told me to stop encouraging you.*

"Oh no," Judicus mouthed, his jaw falling open. He dropped my hand like it was red hot and sprang up on his feet, hurrying to the bars and peering out at me. "You're shot!"

He looked, wide-eyed – between me and Kazmerev and back.

"Why is no one helping her?" he yelled over the wind.

I could feel Kazmerev's eye roll again.

Grevankin must have noticed. He shuffled again and then Prexav climbed down from the top of the cage and hurried to the bars.

Prexav motioned to Judicus, beckoning him.

Judicus looked torn, but he ripped himself away, fighting the wind to get to Prexav. I fell back on the rock. My energy was flagging.

Darkness swam before me.

Not yet, Little Hawk. Don't pass out yet. You should think of yourself more and stop spending yourself for everyone else.

I would never.

Don't I know it.

Time didn't trickle the way it should. It seemed to be measured by my agonized breaths.

Judicus's long face swam into view. It was drawn, and a line formed between his eyebrows.

"Sersha," I saw his lips form my name but whatever else he said was lost as my eyelids sagged and I had to fight to open them again.

He was out of the cage. The collar was gone. Gundt and Prexav must have got it off of him and then Judicus must have used his ropes. Of course. I always forgot how strong he was with those.

My eyelids shuddered again. He'd be fine now. Just fine. I could afford to sleep now, perhaps.

I fought against the desire, my instincts telling me it wasn't safe yet.

Gundt and Prexav were on either side of Judicus, looking down at me. Gundt's lined face looked more tired and weathered than usual, his eyes glassy with what I thought might be exhaustion. Beside him, Prexav's honey-colored hair blew in the wind. He looked five years older. I had just enough time to wonder where his sister was when their voices grew dim, and I lost the stream of events again for a moment or two.

When I woke, they'd turned me on my side and Judicus was in front of me, holding my shoulders. He leaned down and brushed my hair from my face as my eyes batted open.

"We're getting the arrow out!" he yelled over the storm.

They shouldn't do that now. They needed to go somewhere safe.

There is nowhere safe, Kazmerev said grimly. *Don't worry yourself about it. The ill ropeworker is as distraught by your situation as you were by his. He'll take care of you.*

That's not what was worrying me.

She's right, you know, Huxabrand said. *We need to get moving. There will be no rest here.*

Yes. They couldn't afford to wait for me. They couldn't.

My thoughts went fuzzy again and the faces and voices swam together and then pain flared in my shoulder and I screamed.

Pain. Pain. Teeth-on-edge pain.

And then darkness pulled me under.

I thought I woke once, but it might have been a dream. I thought a pair of arms were around me, carrying me. I thought someone kissed my brow and whispered comforting things to me.

"Easy now, Sersha. Sleep. The pain will be better in the morning."

I thought that might be a lie.

And then something cold was pressed against the flaring agony of my arm and something hot was against one side.

A murmur of voices. A high keening. I was heavy. So, so heavy. My head was heaviest of all. Black waves washed over everything, and I lost my thread again.

When I woke again, it was to a terrible scream and a bright light.

199

I blinked awake. Everything hurt, hurt, hurt from my jaw to my calves. Every muscle. My head was heavy as lead, my shoulder a mass of angry, murmuring pain.

I had been warm. I knew that because the warmth was suddenly missing, the cold rolling over me with howling teeth.

I had been cuddled against someone. I knew that because Judicus was up on one arm beside me, twisting to look while the rest of his body lay facing mine as if he had been lying there only a moment ago, guarding me with his narrow form.

We'd all been sleeping. My consciousness was coming back slowly, but I could see that by the warm, clear patches around us where phoenixes had been a moment ago. Prexav was still on the ground, lifting himself on his elbows even as I watched and trying to lift a tired head.

Gundt was bent over an unconscious Mally, her head and arms slumped over his shoulder and her crown on the ground beside her.

It must have been her who screamed and the crown falling that brought the light. Thin sunlight filtered down through swirls of rainbow-edged snow. I shivered without meaning to.

"Is she hurt?" Judicus croaked, and I realized the wind had calmed enough to hear him. His voice sounded rusty as if he'd worn it out already but was still forcing it out. Was he hurt anywhere else? I'd thought I'd healed him, but if his voice was still raw, maybe I'd only healed him from the cold.

"Badly – but not in the body," Gundt said miserably. "It's her mind."

I sat up, rubbing a hand over my face. I didn't know how long we slept for – only that it wasn't enough.

"The dawn is not our friend," Prexav muttered, hobbling over to a pack on the ground and rummaging inside. "We'll be trapped here until dark."

Gundt grunted. He laid Mally out on the rock as Prexav brought him a blanket and, together, they tucked it around her and balled a cloak under her head.

They both looked weary beyond the point of functioning. Just wrapping her up seemed to take all their energy. They sat beside her when they were done, mirror images as they sank to the rock. I got the impression they'd been working together like that, caring for her, for so long that it had become habit.

I struggled, trying to get to my feet, but the movement made me suddenly weak and faint. My vision danced and I gasped as strong arms drew me down again.

"Easy, Sersha," Judicus said gently. "You're badly hurt, and we can't heal others like you can. Sit here with Gundt while I make a fire."

I nodded dully, blinking at the light, trying to summon enough energy to think. It was a bad idea. Thinking made me immediately panic. I sucked in a deep breath and forced myself to *stop* thinking. I gazed at the snow falling through the bright sunbeams, fanning out crystal and bright, stabbed through with shafts of pale gold. And I steadied my breath as Judicus knelt in front of me.

"Do you still have the flint, Sersha?" he asked gently, and I felt in my pocket and brought it out for him.

He smiled slowly and it was a sign of how tired we all were that no one flinched when his ropes rolled out of his hand and down the mountain and long, long minutes later they brought up bits of gnarled wood.

He lit them with care, and then without even asking, he found Gundt's pack – and it must have been Gundt's because he always carried good tea – and found what was necessary to brew us all a pot of tea.

Gundt got up for long enough to recover the Dark Diadem and set it on the ground beside me and then fall heavily back to the earth.

Eventually, as the kettle was settled into the coals of the little fire, he spoke.

"I'm grateful you're both still alive," he said, coughing awkwardly. "Maybe that should have been said earlier."

"Saving our lives said it clearly enough," Judicus said. He poked the fire, gathering the sticks in as they burned. There weren't many of them and they made for a sulky fire.

"*I'm glad they are alive, too.*" I signed,

"Sersha says she's glad you're both alive." Judicus rubbed his forehead wearily. "And so am I. I don't remember to say things like that, but it's true."

Gundt nodded slowly. "We have a lot to tell each other. Prexav and I are bone tired, you should know. Don't take our lack of enthusiasm for unfriendliness. We've both been awake for four days straight. Five maybe – hard to tell with the sun the way it is. We had a nap or two, but a phoenix can't fly long with a burden of three people – even if the rider is very powerful – and we had to cross an ocean straight without stops. Mally couldn't nap at all. Couldn't afford to make it light out. That's part of her problem, I think. Hope. I've been hoping some sleep will fix her up."

His hand hovered over her as if he wanted to touch her and comfort her but didn't think he should. Prexav looked at him balefully and he snatched it back as if guilty.

"We could have stopped when we reached the coast, but they were upon us immediately, chasing us until we reached the mountains," Prexav said dully. "We saw not a single phoenix. Saw not a single Flamerarch. Tried one of the hidden caches only to flee when it was spilling out with Stryxex. Didn't catch a single whiff of another phoenix until we crossed Kazmerev's trail down in the foothills. We've lost it all. All of Calicarn. Maybe all of the world."

"Have some tea," Judicus said carefully, pouring it out into a small wooden cup and passing it to Prexav.

Their eyes met – sorrow greeting like sorrow.

Prexav took the tea and cradled it in his hands, staring into the cup as if there might be answers there. He was not the Flame Rider I'd met at the inn – all arrogance and mystery, nor was he the boyishly delighted Flame Rider who had welcomed me into his eclectic home. This Prexav was hollowed and bitter.

I swallowed at the sight of him. It was as if he'd aged in just weeks.

"Things always look dark before salvation comes," Gundt said, but his heart was not in it.

Judicus poured him a cup of tea and passed it over, asking, "Did you make it as far as the plinth in the islands of the Hand of the Rat?"

"What plinth?" Gundt asked bitterly.

200

"The one you were supposed to find," Judicus said with a pained look on his face. "The one you crossed an entire *ocean* to find."

"It was gone by the time we arrived," Prexav said hollowly. "The top of it missing, the edges fragmented. Something sticky had poured out of it and coated the ground. We found it – after being hunted for days and barely arriving at all – and nothing. Nothing after all of that. The rest of our people melted into the shadows. It was their best chance to survive the chaos."

"And you?" Judicus pressed, his eyes darker than usual, a deep storm brewing in them.

"The ai'sletta did not react well to the plinth," Gundt said, staring into his tea. He had yet to sip it and he was trembling as if cold – but I thought perhaps it was for another reason. "She's been like that ever since." He nodded to where Mally slept, kicking fitfully, her head and hands jerking. "They came for us as she was screaming on the cliff, rocking back and forth and we didn't know what to do. There was no time for a ship. No time to hide. Our only option was flight. We flew over the ocean. But that meant we needed night for days on end as we flew. She had to be awake for all that time."

"Impossible," Judicus said, crossing his arms over his chest.

I took a sip of tea, looking from one to the other. It tasted like Gundt smelled – of cardamon and something like sandalwood.

"She has a will of iron," Gundt said, shifting so his body was bent between Judicus and Mally. I frowned. He might have been tired, but he was awake enough to notice my expression. "Please, don't look so judgmental, Sersha. I swear to you this is nothing inappropriate. I recognize how young your cousin is and how old I am. I simply feel protective of her. She's tried, and tried, and done the impossible even after we all failed. I just ... if I don't watch after her, who will? Her mother is dead. Her family cannot help her or hide her. She thought she had a purpose – a reason to keep going – but we were too late. That she is losing sanity now, is no surprise. That she is brittle, is also no surprise. But I still believe she can change everything. I do."

Prexav snorted derisively but he said nothing.

"On that front," Judicus said carefully, "I have some terrible news."

And so, he laid it out for them – the conspiracy. The prophetic texts planted. The political games played. The phoenix souls trapped in the plinth that flowed out and awakened the Creatures of Sydonon. The bid to get the ai'sletta. Everything.

They listened in dull resignation in the way people listen to someone explaining they're doomed when they are already resigned to death.

"So, there's no reason to keep going," Prexav said calmly.

"*Where is his sister?*" I asked Judicus.

"Sersha wants to know where your sister is," Judicus relayed.

"She's with the other spies. Safe for now, I suppose," Prexav said. "They were planning to return to Briccatore and help the lady Kristiana. After all, she's Grand Hadri now and we are sworn to her."

Judicus whistled silently, gaze turning inward. If they succeeded, even I could see how that might be useful. I was sure he could see a thousand other reasons it could be, too. But that assumed they succeeded and weren't just killed outright. By the tense look in Prexav's eyes when they met mine, I thought it was reasonable to think he was wondering the same thing.

"So, to summarize, some dark mysterious people – who we do not know – have hijacked history and at least two nations to enact their will on the world and they aren't just happy to rule what they've taken, they want more," Gundt said.

"That's accurate," Judicus agreed.

"And we can't find them because they're hidden in shadows, and we wouldn't even know where to start looking."

"Yes," Judicus said mildly.

"Then I don't know what to do," Gundt said, lowering his head into his hand, his tea spilling from the cup in his other hand. I inhaled sharply at that. It was a sign of distress deep for Gundt to treat his tea as if it didn't matter. "I don't know what to do. We're hunted on every side. We can't protect her. Our days are measured in hours, not weeks. We will be shredded apart with none to save us, and I can't find a way out."

"We can't do anything about Calicarn then either," Prexav said, misery thick in his tone. "You can't stop a shadow. You can't stop something that's everywhere. It's like trying to end sunlight. It can't be done."

"*That's not the full truth,*" I signed but no one was looking at me.

"I don't know what to do," Judicus admitted. "Every direction I look in sees us fleeing or dead. Our only viable option is to succumb and do as they say. But I can't live like that. I can't."

"*There's another option,*" I signed again, catching his eye this time.

"What other option?" he asked, and his eyes were so dull that they made my heart ache.

"*A trap,*" I said but he cut me off.

"Some ideas aren't worth considering," he said coldly.

"Have you held something back, Son of Chaos? Prexav asked, his face set and grim. "Are you sharing a secret with the fledgling?"

Judicus didn't answer, he watched me as I tried to explain, my face growing hot.

"Our enemies want her badly. All we need to do to discover their identities is to let them know we have her, set a trap, and wait."

Judicus shook his head, looking troubled as he translated for me.

"You can't possibly mean you'd use her as bait," Gundt said, fixing his furious regard on me. "You'd have to know it would mean it was my duty to kill you."

Judicus met his eyes, face pale and slightly green, but his voice was cool.

"Threaten Sersha again, Gundt, and you'll strain my friendship." He pulled back the neck of his shirt, exposing the broken skin from where the plinth had strangled him. "I could give you a matching collar if you want, friend. Now, what was your pledge as a Greensleeve?"

Gundt paused for a long time, looking between us.

"Doesn't he realize I would never hurt Mally? I asked Judicus.

"He does, but he's stubborn. And his trust has been put on of late," Judicus replied. "What was your pledge as a Greensleve, Gundt?"

It was for long minutes that Gundt scrutinized us. It was Prexav who broke the stalemate.

"His pledge is to seek out and aid the ai'sletta, to give himself entirely to her protection and service, that her enemies would be his enemies and her friends his friends, her fate his fate, her world his world."

That was a lot.

"And what in that pledge says she can't be risked or used?" Judicus asked in a low tone. Gundt's jaw gnashed so loudly that Prexav jumped up putting a hand on either of their chests.

I started signing rapidly and Judicus pointed at me, translating.

"Why don't you trust me? Why do you think I'd hurt her? I've shown I care for her all along and I will help," I said. *"But we cannot win if we do not fight. We cannot fight if we do not know our enemy. We cannot know our enemy if we do not take this ..."*

"Risk," Judicus said, filling in the final word. "She's right. We all must see that, tired or not. We have so few, and they are so great an enemy. We're going to die separated and hunted to the ground unless we stand together and strike one decisive blow."

For a full minute, all that could be heard was gasping breaths and then – to my complete surprise – it was Prexav who broke the silence again.

"She's right." At Gundt's raised eyebrow he spoke more forcefully. "She is. You saw the corpses just like I did. You saw our friends broken in heaps below that cliff, their ashes taken, their bodies left behind. My heart breaks just thinking about it." His face screwed up and I didn't know if it were tears or fury he was holding back. "And whatever was in that plinth broke your ai'sletta."

"Phoenix souls," Judicus said.

"What?" Now Gundt was pale.

"That's what was in the plinths. Sersha could see them. Couldn't you?"

"The plinth was broken when we arrived," he said, pale with shock.

"They migrated into the Creatures of Sydonon," Judicus said grimly. "Did you see them within the stone?"

Prexav was shaking his head. "We were a little busy saving you."

"Under the sea," Gundt gasped. "Remember the strange ripples?"

He jerked his head at Prexav who flinched.

"I told you that was important," Gundt said. "Could they have wakened something beneath the waves? The plinth was right on the shoreline, the sticky residue dripped down the cliff into the water."

Prexav and Judicus cursed in unison, and I felt the blood draining from my face. We had twice the problem we thought we did.

"Fine," Gundt said with a sigh. "Tell us about this plan to trap the creators of the conspiracy."

201

I didn't really have a plan. I looked at Judicus and licked my lips and to my relief, he spoke as smoothly as if we'd discussed it first.

"We have to let them know we have her, and we have to let them know we can defend her in such a way that they can't just bring an army to take her or smash across our defenses with stone creatures. We have to offer up a ransom – a price for her. They'd have to send someone to offer the price. It wouldn't be them, but it would have to be someone they can trust and that means someone they know – someone who knows them."

"Ransom?" Gundt's voice came out as a squeak.

"Don't lose your nerve now, Flame Rider," Judicus said easily, brushing his hair from his face.

He turned away, opening his palm, index finger thrust outward and pinkie curving in to drop one of his black ropes and fling it out over the cliff edge. It returned while they were still contemplating, laden with twisted sticks and gnarled saplings which he fed furiously into the fire.

Prexav strolled in the other direction, pacing back and forth, rubbing the small of his back, and cursing.

Gundt, for his part, stayed close to Mally, watching her with a wen between his brows and chewing his lip. His beard had come in while he was gone and it hid the subtleties of his features, but he was clearly upset.

I drank my tea. There was nothing else to do. We would die or we would win. We could only do the latter with a plan, and I didn't have a better plan than the one Judicus had proposed.

I looked up to see him regarding me with calm seriousness. "You need to go easy on the shoulder, Sersha. You should be resting with your cousin."

I nodded, but I didn't move. Everything felt better the more still I was. And I was happy enough here watching the fire and watching Judicus's long lines as he fed the fire and poured me more tea.

"It's good for you," he murmured, looking at me from under the fringe of his long eyelashes and I wondered how I'd ever thought him plain and average when now every look of his sharp eyes pierced right to my heart and set it tingling.

I sipped the tea and thought. If we took this gamble it might be the last we ever made. Life after would never be the same one way or another. Even if we won and bought everyone else their freedom, we might find ourselves outlaws, hunted and harried. More likely, we would just be dead. Which meant we were already living the last days or weeks of our lives.

I swallowed.

I should tell him. He deserved to know.

"*What is wrong?*" he signed where no one could see but me.

"*Nothing. Everything,*" I signed back with a wry snort.

"You're not telling me something."

I felt my cheeks flaming hot and I looked down, nervous about meeting his eyes. My shoulder stung. I shrugged it slightly, trying to pretend that was all that was bothering me.

"Sersha," he whispered, and I looked up at his anxious face, his lips parted in pleading and his hands flashing. "*When we were in those cages, I kept thinking we would die there. Especially toward the end. And I didn't want to die before I told you.*"

"Told me what?"

"That it hurts more to think of losing you than it does to think of dying. That I don't know if we'll live the week out, but I want to spend whatever time I have with you. And if we do live past this week." He paused and I held my breath. How was it possible that he was telling me exactly what I wanted to tell him? *"If we live past this week I don't ever want to be parted."*

His eyes burned as he signed, and it seemed ridiculous that he was saying all this to me with everyone watching and that I couldn't just fling myself over the fire separating us and throw myself in his arms.

I started to smile, a little tremulously, my eyes glassing with happy tears and his lower lip found its way between his teeth as he tried a hopeful smile. I lifted my hands to reply but I didn't even form the first sign before Gundt stepped between us.

"I'll do it," he said gruffly. I blinked hard, trying to remember what it was he was going to do. "Besides, it seems someone needs to keep an eye on you two. I don't know what those hand signs mean but one of you is going to teach me and right fast. I won't have you speaking over my head. Or under it."

"Glad to have you aboard," Judicus said, cool as the snow still drifting around us.

"I'm in, too," Prexav said irritably. "I don't like it. I can see a thousand ways it can go wrong, but I'm in. I'm loyal to the Grand Hadri. Sworn to him personally. And they killed him. I can't sit aside when I could revenge his death. Where do we start?"

"The elves," Judicus said quietly. "Veela's kin."

"The what?" Gundt gasped and then they were arguing loudly that he was insane, that it wouldn't work, that the elves were not our friends and as they ran themselves up into red-faced frustration while Judicus sipped his tea, I caught his eye and shyly began to sign.

"Judicus," I signed, and his face went hot with a blush at the sign of his name. *"I do not wish to be parted from you, either."*

The look on his face – the look of swelling joy and triumph made my own heart soar higher than any phoenix ever could and it was good we were on this mountain because if we were anywhere else, I was certain I would glow so hard that our enemies would find us easily.

"It has to be the elves," Judicus said, his eyes never leaving mine. Gundt and Prexav quieted, listening. "They're underground. So, they can't be trampled. They hate humans, so it won't be them at the bottom of this. They'd rather never see our kind again. They will be impartial. And they can be bargained with."

"And if they can't be?" Gundt asked, his voice tight.

"Then we'll think of somewhere else," Judicus said. "But I think they are our best bet."

"So do I," said a quavering voice and everyone fell silent as Mally sat up, pulled the blanket around her, and said with all the imperiousness of my aunt Danna. "And I think I'd like some of that tea."

202

"Ai'sletta!" Gundt gasped, crouching beside her. "Your mind is back."

Mally looked at him coolly and then looked right at me and rolled her eyes. "It's been back for a while. Well, maybe not entirely. But the sleep helped. The keening just happens when you've looked into the depths and hurt your heart. Mine is still hurt. It might be hurt forever but I've decided to live for now anyway. Where's that tea?"

I offered Judicus my empty cup and he filled it and offered it to Mally. We were all unnaturally silent. Perhaps the others felt, as I did, that anything we said might push her back into madness.

"What happened, ai'sletta?" Gundt asked carefully. "You saw something at the plinth and then ... you went mad, I thought."

"Mad is a good way to put it. Accurate. Descriptive," Mally said, fussing with her tea before taking a sip. "Oh, it's Gundt's tea. Why does it always taste like disappointment?"

Gundt shifted uncomfortably and Prexav laughed. "Because Gundt is disappointed with us all. He's disappointed with me for not being more dedicated to the cause and with you for not being the glorious savior he expected."

"If you have to explain a joke it isn't very funny, Prexav." Mally was enjoying herself. She always did when all focus was on her. "That plinth was a horror. Thank the heavens someone had the sense to break it. Too bad they couldn't have finished the job before I arrived and then maybe I wouldn't have had to see ... things."

I stole a quick glance at Judicus whose thoughts had turned inward.

"Did anyone else look inside?"

"*Inside?*" I signed.

"Not everything valuable is on the outside, Sersha," Mally said. "Some of us know to look within."

She was trying to get me riled up and I wouldn't give her the satisfaction. She was getting enough of it from Prexav and Gundt. Besides, the corner of her mouth ticked up and her eye twitched with it. She'd never had a tick like that before. It happened again before she took a long sip of tea.

"I looked down the pillar," she said eventually. Her hand was shaking, the tea sloshing back and forth. She put her other hand over it and her knuckles went white with clenching. "It was hollow, and it went down, down, down into the depths of the earth. It wasn't black in there. It was fire. And in the fire, I saw things. I don't want to get into what. So don't press me because I won't."

Gundt's mouth had opened. He shut it with a click.

"Good," she said after a long silence. "I'm not the hero type and I don't want to be. But I also don't want to see that again. I'm not right inside after seeing that." And this was the truth. I saw it reflected in her eyes. I saw it in the way they went glassy as she swallowed twice before she could speak again. "And I don't think I will ever be right again. So. We go to these elves. And we set this trap. And we see if they can negotiate a murder."

"I wouldn't call it that," Gundt said nervously, twisting his knuckles around themselves. He was looking older. Old enough to be our father – all of us. And the way he looked around the ring of us, I was afraid he saw it that way, too. Like we were somehow all his responsibility and he didn't know what to do with us.

"What would you call it?" Mally asked, looking at him over the rim of her cup before she took another sip.

"Assassination?" Prexav said nervously.

"We're talking about killing someone," Mally said. "Whether we say it in a fancy way or bluntly. It is exactly that. I'm not embarrassed about it. Whoever this is has robbed hundreds – maybe thousands – of their lives. They win no matter what happens. They've already won. We're just trying to stop them from winning more."

I was nodding grimly.

"It's like when a bear comes into town before winter is over," Mally said, and she seemed so unflappable after being so insane for what sounded like days. I didn't know how to take that. Maybe this was just a new kind of crazy. Her eye twitched again. "It's not its fault that it's hungry. Not its fault that the temperatures played games with its hibernation. But it starts killing. First it's livestock. But it will be people after that. Remember Old Man Gavin, Sersha? Remember what the boys found at his house?" I shivered. "Gandy couldn't eat meat for a week after they buried him. And everyone in the village went out and hunted the bear and dad brought him down in the end with a spear. And the others piled in and helped. It was murder. We meant to kill it and nothing else. We were clear about it because it was the bear or us. And what we are dealing with here is worse than a bear, worse than the Hand of the Rat raiding our villages. Worse than the Grand Hadri."

Prexav cleared his throat.

"Oh, did I offend you?" Mally asked but her tone was mocking. She paused to sip her tea and then she looked up. This time both her lip and her eye twitched and there was something dark deep in those eyes that had never been there before. "Let's just be clear. We're using me as bait to set a trap to kill a terrible person or persons. That's what we're going to do, and I agree to do it. Maybe just don't tell your phoenixes."

"You have our loyalty, ai'sletta," Gundt said humbly.

She laughed, looking ill. "Do I? How charming."

And then she tossed the empty cup at Judicus – who fumbled the catch and barely managed to keep it from the fire – and then she reached over Gundt, scooped up the Dark Diadem, and jammed it firmly on her head and the world went black again.

203

We took the time to sleep before we set out and I took time to try to heal Mally.

"I don't need anything from you, Sersha," she'd said irritably, trying to shake off my hand, but her hands were still shaking, and her tic hadn't left. I persevered, gripping her shoulder hard, and when I was done – exhausted and worn, she looked a little less haunted. I decided I would count that a success.

"Happy?" she'd asked with raised eyebrows before slinking away.

I was not happy, but it was as much as I could manage.

None of us had had enough sleep. We cuddled into the warmth of the phoenixes.

You are keeping something from us, Kazmerev had commented.

We had told them we planned to set a trap. We had told them we planned to use Mally for bait.

None of them liked it.

We could flee, Huxabrand had suggested. *There will be places no Stryxex has been.*

Whatever Gundt had said to that made her sniff, beak in the air.

We can bring the ai'sletta with us and keep her much safer far from trouble.

Trouble will only come to us, Grevankin had rumbled. *And I am fond of these humans. I've a mind to stand with them, though how they will capture their enemies, I know not. Elves? I mistrust elves.*

The mention of elves had made Kazmerev smoke.

The elves were not kind to Veela, he snapped.

She was an elf, I had reminded him.

All the more reason that they should have supported her and rallied to her.

But eventually, they'd agreed to come with us.

The humans are set on it and we are set on them, Grevankin had said, finalizing their objections. None of them suspected we meant to murder the people who had set us up like this. And I held that intention deep in my heart, only the guilt spilling over from it.

Whatever troubles you, you can tell me, Kazmerev had said

I tried to assure him it was nothing as I drifted off to sleep but I did not think he believed me.

We slept as long and deep as we could, greedy for every moment of it, before Judicus brewed more tea and we all loaded onto our beloved phoenixes to fly east.

Prexav led us on the back of Grevankin, his scarf streaming out behind him like a black flag.

On his right were Gundt and Mally on Huxabrand. On his left, Judicus and I rode Kazmerev.

The storm had cleared below us, leaving drifts of white to highlight everything below. We peered down with the small amount of light the moon afforded us.

Before we'd left, Judicus had drawn me aside behind Kazmerev's back and very gently, very cautiously, as if he thought I might bite, had brushed my hair back and then let his warm fingers linger in it as he leaned down, brushed his nose against mine and sweetly kissed my lips.

When he drew back, his finger came down to brush the chain of the necklace he'd given me.

"Mighty though small," he whispered shyly. "When we're somewhere safe, I'll give you a ring. A nice one."

He looked worried about that, as if nice rings were difficult to find.

I was too busy being shocked to say anything to that. He was gone a moment later, hurrying to consult with Prexav on the best route.

I stared after him. So we were ... what ... pledged to be married? Is that how he saw that conversation?

I think you should save important conversations for when I'm awake, Kazmerev said in my mind. He shuffled irritably before adding, *Then you won't have to wonder what they meant because I could tell you.*

Because I didn't have my privacy compromised enough. I climbed on his back and tried to look calm and unflappable so that no one else in our party would guess. This was a secret between Judicus and I, and all the more dear for being secret.

If you marry, that affects us both. Surely, you know that. If you've promised yourself to him, then you've promised my future, too, and that's something you should have consulted me on.

Promised? Grevankin asked, flaring brightly in his excitement.

From his back, Prexav directed a very pointed scowl at me at the same moment that Gundt's head snapped around to look at me and blink twice before returning to his work picking through Huxabrand's feathers.

So much drama, the female phoenix said, preening her feathers. *I could do without it. We have intrigue and war ahead and we don't need humans making cow's eyes at each other and dreaming about fat babies.*

I hope you aren't suggesting my human will be a liability, Kazmerev said, springing suddenly to my defense and springing physically, too. He hopped forward and then shook himself and I had to hold on and try not to black out as the pain in my shoulder flared to life. He froze close to panic. *I'm sorry, I'm sorry.*

Both of you get over yourselves. Grevankin's rumbling voice was the sound of wisdom. *Huxabrand, this has nothing to do with you, so stop needling Kazmerev. Kaz, you are hundreds of years old. I think you can manage to settle yourself for the lifetime of a single human. She's hardly been cautious and sedate so far and she's unlikely to start doing it now with a scheme and a battle on the way. Remember she's fragile and be grateful she's still alive to hold your hope.*

And that was the end of all of it except my red face. Well, I might not know if Judicus considered us promised to each other, but the phoenixes had decided it was the case, and their grousing had decided the humans. I settled for not looking at anyone until hours later when we were well on our way.

By then, we were soaring past King's Hold. Or what was left of it.

Perhaps the people had fled in time. Perhaps they'd put up a defense and somehow won. Perhaps.

But from the air, it was hard to believe. The wall from which our cages had hung was nothing but tumbled rubble dotted with broken Creatures of Sydonon and dark dots that perhaps were corpses. I refused to look closely enough to confirm it.

The tower, likewise, was nothing but ruin, the city between wall and tower looked like a box of pottery that had fallen off the back of a cart.

There were, perhaps, survivors. We did not see them or their fires. There were many broken stone creatures, so something Kentinius had done had broken them, but what? And was it enough of them?

It was hard to track them over stone roads and stone mountains, but I hoped for the peoples' sake that they had fled, that they were sheltered somewhere in the mountains resting by campfires, that they would return and rebuild that place someday. Or something. Anything that didn't mean they were dead under piles of rubble.

After that, we diverged from roads and passes and we flew right over the jagged crowns of mountains, silent as the stars themselves and just as unbending. We flew, and flew, stopping only briefly to stretch legs and make tea – no one had food to share – before getting back on and flying again.

If we hadn't been riding phoenixes we would have frozen to death. It was only their warmth that kept us alive, and we frequently buried face and hands and feet in their smoldering feathers.

For their part, they seemed unbothered by that, though Kazmerev grumbled for hours when Judicus finally succumbed to airsickness.

How would you feel? I wondered. What if you got ill flying?

Only the weakest of souls could be ill from something as natural as flying, was his argument.

Eventually, we left the mountains and stumbled into a hamlet on a mountain plain north and far east of King's Hold. A beautifully carved wood sign proclaimed it was "Snowflett." We landed in quiet exhaustion and Mally pulled the crown from her tumbled curls to reveal a sunrise.

Gundt looked around the little town, announced, "We'll sleep here" and before

I knew it the four of us had purchased two rooms at the inn and were making our way up to them.

I shared mine with Mally.

She snored.

And I found I did not care.

We carried on like that for four more days, though more comfortably after the first day. Prexav went out and bought food and extra clothing. To our delight, he also found a floral tea. And so we continued fueled by nerves, anxiety, and something that tasted floral.

To my horror, we saw distant armies twice – both marching toward the pass we'd left. They swarmed like ants over the ground, dark and scuttling, and so numerous they made my eyes ache. Judicus took careful notes when we saw them, his little charcoal flying over the page making marks. He'd taken the book back from its pouch on my belt and it was in the last pages of it that he made these tallies.

"Too soon, too soon," he muttered often and when he showed the book to Prexav and Gundt they seemed to agree. None of them so much as hunched after that, unwilling to relax even that much.

Mally, on the other hand, was looking more comfortable.

"As long as they're far from me, I don't care what they do," she said, studying her nails. "Maybe they'll all gather in one place and fight, and we'll never have to see them again."

I tried to sign to her that they were people's brothers and sons, but she wouldn't watch.

"Save your signs for the rope worker, Sersha. I don't want to think about how my enemies might be human. They certainly haven't bothered to think that about me."

She was doing better, it seemed. Less haunted. More snappish. But snappishness from Mally was a good sign. She still had those tics, though, and they worried me.

On the fourth day, we dove down into a wide canyon far from any human town or civilization. As the walls rose around us, my anxiety grew. I did not like being underground. Part of me was still huddled in the last cave system we left where the Grand Hadri had been murdered before our eyes. I couldn't help but think that the same thing was going to happen again.

We settled in front of a gaping entrance three phoenixes wide, decorated around the edges with jagged carved teeth as if it were the mouth of some giant, angry creature. We pulled up, abreast of one another, looking nervously back and forth.

"Do we enter mounted?" Prexav asked.

No, Kazmerev said. He was bristling as he had been since we entered the canyon, every feather sticking up on end.

"Not if we want them to talk to us," Gundt said quietly.

Not if you don't want me to eat them, Kazmerev said.

You don't eat people, I reminded him.

I will make an exception. When I was hatched in Veela's heart they told her to never return. They robbed her of everything – her birthright, her future, her family. And all because of me.

He was trembling so hard that I was afraid he'd shake apart, so I dismounted and hurried to his head, putting a hand on either cheek and leaning my forehead against his great beak.

Kazmerev. You have my heart. We will not honor those who have hurt the one you loved. We will not betray your faith. Return to me at next dusk and my heart will be waiting.

He warmed in agreement and then I drew him within my chest as Judicus yelped and fell to his bottom on the ground.

Oops. I'd forgotten he was on Kazmerev's back.

I shot him an apologetic look, but he hardly seemed to notice. He didn't even dust himself off as he wandered forward, eyes on the carved teeth, hands spread wide to drop ropes out on every side of him. They rolled out like living things, feeling and questing like roots of a tree to help him discover what we were getting into.

"Remember," he said, "These elves are not our friends."

204

"I think now would be the time to remove the crown, Mally," Judicus said carefully, his eyes wandering over the carved teeth.

Behind him, we fell into a ragged group, the phoenixes disappearing one by one.

"Is it wise not to bring our flaming friends?" Gundt asked in a low tone.

"Wiser, I think," Judicus said with care.

Mally pulled her crown from her tumbled curls and held it in both hands, spinning it nervously as the night faded to a blood-red sunset.

"I don't think I like this place," she said nervously, her eye tic making an appearance, and I couldn't help but agree. I didn't like it, either. Something about the way the wind howled into the open mouth made me feel like I was about to be swallowed.

"Here's where we prove we're men," Prexav said grimly.

"I," Mally said precisely, "am not a man."

She batted her eyelashes at him in a way that made me blush and made Gundt step between them just as Prexav muttered, "Tell me something I don't already know."

"The ai'sletta," Gundt said firmly. "Will walk in the middle. Perhaps you'll guard the rear, Prexav."

I didn't dare look, certain that I'd burst out laughing because I knew exactly how Mally would waggle her eyebrows at that comment. The strangled noise Prexav made was confirmation enough.

"And if anyone so much as steps out of line, you should know I'm carrying the food stores and I don't mind keeping you from your supper." Gundt sounded more like an exasperated parent than anything else, but soon we were following a silent Judicus into the gaping mouth.

I had never liked the sensation of earth above me – especially not so much of it

– and I didn't like it now. It made me duck unconsciously and steal furtive glances backward until I made Prexav so annoyed that he said, "What?" and reminded me to keep my eyes forward.

We were not very far into the black hole of a tunnel, and I had only just begun to wonder if maybe we should have lit the lantern, when a light bobbed toward us, slowly revealing that the tunnel was lined in a bas relief of crisscrossing speckled strands that looked almost like octopus arms. I shuddered. What was with people in the south and octopuses? I failed to see the charm.

And then the lantern lifted and revealed its holder and my mouth snapped shut.

The elf – for that was the only thing she could possibly be, looked so much like Veela that I stumbled – same bright eyes, same pointed ears, same grey-ish skin, same sleek black hair. The difference was that this one wasn't dying as I tended her.

I felt something stir within me and wondered if Kazmerev had somehow rolled over from where he was hiding within.

The elf raised a glowing orb suspended from a lantern pole and regarded us without expression.

"Humans."

"We greet you in tongue of man and ageless respect, in the acknowledgment of moons and of the great seams of the sky," Judicus said formally.

"Pretty words, weak human," the woman replied, her lip curling.

"I am Judicus Franzer Irault of Calicarn," he said calmly.

"We have heard of you even in these halls, Son of Chaos."

Everyone had heard of Judicus and it seemed none of them were capable of seeing his worth. For one small moment, I allowed myself satisfaction. I really shouldn't. It wasn't comely to be proud. But *I* had seen what they had not. *I* knew what they overlooked. Judicus was a treasure among men and anyone who had the chance to be near him came away better for it.

"I come with peace in hand, my weapons sheathed. I prostrate myself before the Law and Hammer and seek to speak to the Golden Gargantuan."

The elf woman snorted a laugh at that. Her lips curled in a cat-like manner and she held her hands at her side as if they were ready to draw a weapon at any moment.

"Do you now, child of men. How interesting. Fortunately, it is not my place to accept or deny you this. Come with me. Bring your companions. We have no desire to leave them to stir up trouble while we are gone."

She led us down the dark passage to where it ended abruptly in a section of floor that was carved like the roaring face of some type of lizard. Chains ran up from each corner of the section of floor and into the darkness above and to my surprise, the dead-end corridor was surrounded by rock polished so much I could see my reflection in it.

The elf strode to the rear corner of the carved floor section, directly over one open eye of the howling creature, and placed her hand on a hanging cord I had not seen initially.

"Are you coming?" she asked, her tone mocking as the light from her lantern danced over the polished wall where her contempt was reflected again and again.

"Be sure to stand as close to the center of the tile as you can," Judicus warned us in a whisper before hurrying to join her.

He stood on the other eye, but Mally – to my relieved surprise – took his advice and stood at the exact center, leaving room for Prexav, Gundt, and me to take our positions around her. It put me in line with the elf who smirked at me.

"Never seen an elf before, girl?" she asked.

And it was something about how she said it that rubbed me so wrong that I answered her in sign.

"I helped one die."

She watched my hands – I could give her credit for that much – but when I was done. she just shrugged with a single arm as if she could not understand, but she turned her eyes from me. And I couldn't be certain that she hadn't understood. There was something about her that suddenly seemed more tense.

"Don't step near the edges," she said wryly. "Or do, what do I care."

And then, without warning, she pulled the cord, and the platform descended so swiftly that my belly dropped to my knees, and I was afraid I might lose my lunch. At his place by the chain, Judicus's eyes were fixed steadfastly upward, and his face was white as the moon when it is full.

I followed his gaze to see we were sinking so fast that the mirror walls were gone, and the rock was rushing past like a river.

I screwed my eyes shut to avoid seeing more. I supposed I knew we would have to descend into the earth. I just hadn't reckoned on it being so dramatic.

205

The walls opened so suddenly that I gasped as fresh air rushed into the tunnel – or new air, I supposed. It smelled anything but fresh. It smelled lived-in and cooked-in and any number of other-things-in that were equally liable to wrinkle the nose.

The platform settled with a clanking sound and then the elf escorting us barked, "Don't move."

We froze.

"A word about the lifts," she said coolly. "Enter and exit them promptly. They can be called away on a moment's notice and if they are, you could lose a leg, an arm, or everything else."

I gasped.

But we all took her meaning, exiting the lift quickly to the small room that was laid out around the lift.

I noted one more tile like it and one terrible empty pit that was perfectly square and may very well hold a lift that had gone down below.

The room we'd entered felt odd – unlived in – lacking any personality at all. It was simple stone and fitted with wooden furnishings that would look as much at home in a farmer's kitchen as anywhere. But though they were not dusty, they looked as if no one had ever sat in them or placed anything on them.

"You may sit," the elf said. "The Fratzern has been called."

"Fratzern?" Prexav asked.

"The one who is the public elf. The one who speaks to outsiders," our escort said, rolling her eyes. She was exactly like Mally, if Mally had grey skin and black hair and looked like she'd been hewn from stone.

"You don't speak to outsiders?" Prexav pressed.

"I guard the mouth. I am the one who calls the proper elf at the proper time.

Were you on four legs instead of two, then the elf who wrangles animals may have been called."

And as if that was all there was to say, she glided to the side, set her light into a bracket in the wall, and then stood in a very awkward-looking one-legged pose against the wall, shut her eyes, and did not speak again no matter how much she was questioned.

Once we'd determined she wouldn't be speaking, we explored the room and settled down to wait. There was little to see in this room. It was hewn of the rock and the rock seemed to be etched in the shape of overlapping, interwoven octopus arms. At the very center of the room was a small waist-high pillar made of swirling, grasping octopus arms carved from a pearly stone. A mother of pearl sphere balanced on a golden needle that rose from between the arms. Something about it warned me not to touch it, to avoid getting anywhere close to it. It made the hair on the back of my neck rise up.

Judicus leaned over it immediately, studying it with intensity.

"What's this?" Prexav asked, snatching the sphere and bouncing it on his palm. Gundt gasped, Mally giggled, and I froze.

Against the wall, the guard's eyes had snapped open.

"Mally," Judicus asked with great care. "Would you be so kind as to retrieve that sphere from Prexav and place it on the needle again?"

"There's writing on it," Prexav said.

"Indeed," Judicus agreed.

"Can you read it?"

"As a matter of fact, I can."

"Well," Prexav said, "What does it say?"

"I shall tell you," Judicus said, running a hand through his hair, "when you hand it over to Mally."

"Why?" Prexav asked, tossing it to Gundt instead. Mally smirked, sidling in beside me as Gundt examined the ball.

"Because I'm asking," Judicus said, and I saw the muscle in his jaw tense as Gundt nodded to Mally and then offered it to her.

"Fetch that for me, would you, Sersha?" she asked lazily.

Frowning, I stepped over to Gundt and took the orb. His gaze locked onto mine as if trying to tell me something significant and as my hand wrapped around the sphere, I gasped.

Awareness filled me – awareness of this room – of the rock that lined the walls, of the seams in the rock, and then diving down, down, down into the earth as if following a vein of that awareness I felt something tremble as if it were coming awake.

Carefully, without betraying anything, I brought the orb to Mally. She studied it in her pale palms, looking from ball to needle as if wondering how she could possibly rebalance it back on the golden spike. I thought that, perhaps, she felt it, too. That perhaps she realized, as I did, that something powerful was linked to this thing. Her eye tic went wild for a moment, but her features remained calm.

"It says," Judicus told us in a grim tone, "Whoso shall remove this full moon, he and his companions shall never again see the light of the moon, lest he or they hang the moon once more in the heavens."

Gundt cursed.

So, it was a trap. A trap for guests. A trap for visitors. A trap for the unwary.

Prexav looked very pale, but Judicus and the guard both watched Mally with identical expressions of interest. Judicus wondered if she could do it. The guard wondered the same. But me, I knew. I knew without having to watch.

I was proved right when Mally laughed and set the sphere back onto the needle effortlessly before then gliding over to the elf.

"Where can I get clothing like that?" she asked, gesturing to the elf's odd clothing. It did look very interesting. She wore a long pair of flowing pants gathered at the cuffs and wrap-leather short boots that ended in broad straps which had been crisscrossed up her calves and tied just above the knees. Her upper body was swathed in what looked like a carefully wrapped scarf that left a pair of tails running down her back and her neck, ears, and bare arms were heavily ornamented in thick jewelry. It made her look both intimidating and feminine and it occurred to me that the outfit would suit Mally perfectly. "I'm thinking turquoise," Mally said.

The elf did not reply, but I wasn't prepared for what she did next.

She left the wall, marched promptly to one of the lifts, and pulled the cord. The lift dropped, immediately, and she was out of sight before my eyes went back to my cousin.

Mally met my eyes and winked. Even here, even with another species, she knew exactly what to say to rile them up.

"Ai'sletta," Judicus said, running his hand over his face, "If you don't mind, might I suggest that you take care with your words? I would like to remind you we are not among friends."

206

"How perceptive of you," said a low voice, and from the shadows, as if by magic, a second woman stepped out. She was dressed as the guard had been but in black, richly embroidered with silver thread. Her face was hidden behind a red veil and her eyes were very large and very intent. I got the impression that she was older than the guard had been. Older than Gundt, even. Leather wrist guards protected her hands and a variety of curving half-moon axes hung from her belt and along a bandolier across her chest. Most were no larger than her hand.

From an inner pocket, she produced an hourglass and set it on one of the plain chairs.

"You have until the sands run out," she said.

But we said nothing. Who in the world was this?

"Nothing to say?" she asked. "And yet one of this party balanced the yggrindaal on the needle. A sign, twice a sign, and half a sign. Such a thing is meant to be impossible. It *is* impossible without magic. So, the sign has come. And which side will you choose to trust? You must decide immediately for on your decision, the weight of the world hangs."

Beneath us, the earth trembled as if highlighting her words. My stomach clenched and trembled with it, unnerved by the earth shaking when I was buried beneath so much of it.

"*Why does every decision have to be so important?"* I signed wryly.

"*Just our luck,"* Judicus signed back without seeming to look at me. His eyes were on our new friend, but I flushed with pleasure that he was still willing to share thoughts with me.

He cleared his throat.

"You would speak?" the elf asked.

"With respect, honored elf," he said carefully. "Why should we trust you?"

"With respect, prophesied guest, what other choice do you have?"

We stared at her in silence for a heartbeat.

"I don't trust prophecies," I signed.

"I don't either," Judicus agreed in sign. *"Not anymore."*

To my shock, the elf signed as she spoke, *"No one with any sense trusts prophecies, and yet, if you fear them, you'd best join us and not the other side."* She snatched up the hourglass and reverted to speech only. "We will contact you at the right time, if we think you are trustworthy. Be prepared to answer."

And then she leapt to the empty pit where the lift was missing, grabbed the chain, and slid down it out of sight just as the first lift returned with the gate guard and the public face of elves.

"Ominous," Mally muttered, her eye mouth and eye succumbing to a tic. "I used to like drama but I'm starting to find it boring."

The public face of elves rose until the lift clicked into place, not noticing the swaying of the chain the female elf had used to flee. He strode toward us, his eyes taking us in one by one and dismissing us just as quickly. I wanted to sign my thoughts to Judicus, but if one elf understood our sign, wouldn't more elves know it?

"This human balanced the yggrindaal?" the public face asked. He was so thin he made Judicus look fleshed out but only as tall as I was. He seemed to be vibrating all over – whether from nerves or because the ground was trembling, I did not know.

"She did, honored Fratzern," the guard said pointing to Mally as she left the moving tile.

We tightened around Mally, instinctively, and I heard her snort at that as if she couldn't take it seriously.

"Funny way to run a place," Mally said. "Cold as day-old tea one minute and then hot as a boiling kettle the next."

"This human will be seen by the confessor," the thin elf said. "This party of humans will follow this public elf."

The way he spoke made them feel less personal – as if one could easily be replaced with another. It made my blood boil. I didn't like these elves. I'd expected them to be like the stories – vibrant with stories, rich in clothing and weapons, beautiful and cultured. Instead, they reminded me of the raiders – only darker and smelling more of earth.

"This party will follow," the Fratzern said, gesturing to us to follow.

A little stab of trepidation shot through me. I didn't want to go further into the ground. I wanted to return to the surface. I wanted to forget this plan and do something else. All at once the idea of us – us! – laying a plan to trap the powerful felt ridiculous. We'd never get away with it. We were going to be overwhelmed and imprisoned beneath the earth the moment it was suggested.

I saw the guard steal a look at the chair to where the small hourglass had been only moments ago. She frowned, looking around the room and I thought I could see a single grain of sand on the chair. Could she notice something that small? Really?

The guard caught me watching and tapped her chin thoughtfully before signing in signs so small that I barely caught them at all.

"Watch yourself."

I didn't want to attract any more attention. I snapped my gaze forward and followed with the others without so much as acknowledging her signs. That was two elves speaking in sign now. Could they all do it?

My heart raced as I followed the others. Part of me wished I could just stop this and go back to the surface and the rest of me scolding myself for being a coward. No one else was having second thoughts. Mally and Prexav looked bored, Judicus and Gundt respectfully attentive. I was the only one who couldn't breathe properly. I just needed to get through it and it would be fine. I couldn't ruin everything just because I had a bad feeling about it.

The lift descended once we were all on the tile, and my heart fell with the lift even though Judicus – who was closest to me – brushed the back of my hand with his in solidarity.

"It's all as it should be, Sersha," he whispered in my ear and I closed my eyes and held onto his words for a full breath before I sucked in a breath and forced myself to be brave again.

The polished stone of the last vertical shaft had been replaced in this shaft by more of those long squid-arm carvings. They grew more defined and precise the further down we went until eventually, the lift lowered into a huge open room. We clustered around the center, avoiding the edges as the walls fell away and the lift descended on heavy chains through open space.

On every side, glowing oblong orbs hung like over-large insects lighting the vast cavern and as my eyes adjusted to the light, I saw what must be – what could only be – described as a large stone squid. It was as large as the cavern and picked out across it. On the ground to which we were descending, its open maw was wide and threatening, and reaching out from it, like a very violent flower, were its long arms that crawled up, up, up the sides of the massive cavern depicted in perfect, terrifying perfection, gilded on the edges, and so large they dwarfed us to the size of ants.

Around it, smaller stone squids and octopuses were picked out in the stone with the intricate work of true craftsmen. There were more of them than I could count in every shape and pose.

My eyes grew bigger and bigger as we were lowered toward the giant squid mouth. Eventually, it became apparent that the mouth was half-buried in jet black stone shaved perfectly level and polished until it gleamed. On that floor, thousands of elves milled as if they were not conducting their lives on the face of a carven squid, nor made miniature by its terrible towering appendages.

It felt entirely like being swallowed up by a terrible monster. It made every inch of my skin creep and crawl. Seeing the elves so blithely ignore it did nothing to calm my terror.

There was too much to see in this great cavern, and too little light to see it with, despite my night vision. But one thing I did see and that was something that looked like a chair built into the very center of the squid's terrible mouth. But this chair had straps to keep its guest secure. I shuddered at the sight of it and the ground shook again in sympathy.

I wanted to bring Kazmerev back. I wanted it so badly that I almost reached for him before Gundt put a hand on my good shoulder. The other shoulder twinged painfully at his touch. The long time on my feet was catching up to me and the arm was swelling and hot, leaving me feeling light-headed. Even after so many days it wasn't as healed as I would have liked.

When I looked back at Gundt, he shook his head in warning. I must not bring my phoenix back here. He wasn't and Prexav wasn't and I could be patient, too.

I nodded to him to tell him I understood, but his face was wary at my nod. Maybe he could tell that my shoulder was bothering me.

The ground trembled a second time.

By the looks on the faces around us – faces varied but all still cast in the same elf-like shape and color – it did not normally do that. Feet rushed and movements moved from flowing and graceful, to jerky and harsh. I did not want to label their careful rush "flight," but it seemed nearer to that than to anything else.

"Honored elf," Judicus asked carefully. "Are these tremors normal."

"Did one of you touch the yggrindaal?" the Fratzern asked, turning to give us a condemning look.

"Your guard surely told you," Judicus said with care.

"And would that person happen to be one of those terrible aberrations – a human who holds another creature within?"

"What?" Prexav asked.

"Do you have a phoenix?" the elf snapped.

"Perhaps," Prexav muttered.

The elf went pale. "One of you should have said so when you begged entrance to this place."

"We begged for nothing," Judicus said mildly.

"You should have declared it," the elf said, clearly agitated. His voice rose louder with each thing he said.

"And what will happen now that we have not?" Gundt asked.

"Their foul blood wakes things long asleep. Whichever of you holds this horrible revenant must not call it up. To do otherwise is to pay in pain before we take your final breath."

Oh. How nice.

"And they cause the tremors?" Judicus asked, pressing.

"They wake them up," the elf said, his breath sawing in quickly. He was just as panicked as those around us and trying desperately to hide it. "They wake up the monsters."

207

If he had been worried about one person with a heart filled with phoenix touching the yggrindaal, I wondered what the elf would think if he knew three who held phoenixes had touched it.

Perhaps it explained the continued rumblings of the earth.

Dust rained down on us – enough that it made my belly flip flop and my heart race. I reached out and caught a hand, desperate for some kind of reassurance.

To my surprise, the hand I caught had been Mally's. She smirked at me. She'd hidden her crown somewhere again, though I couldn't tell where. She was a wonder at hiding things on her person. If I'd tried to hide it, you'd see a crown shape sticking out somewhere, but Mally just made things vanish between her fingers like a street performer and she always had been that way. Maybe it was her luck twisting things. Maybe that was what she was counting on now that kept her laughing and smirking while worry ate me from within.

"I've often wondered what it would be like to take a dust bath like a bird," she said. "I don't think I like it."

I did not like it either, but the elf we were following seemed intent on following protocol. He led us carefully down a path, ignoring the fleeing crowds, the terrified voices, and the shaking ground, keeping one foot in front of another despite the fact he was trembling head to toe. He carried on right up until a knot of elves rushed up to us, stopping him.

"Fratzern," the elf in the front of the group barked. He was slender and powerful, tall for an elf, with long red hair that looked jarring with his grey face.

I knew I shouldn't try to think of all elves as being the same. They were as varied as humans, after all. Kazmerev had been very fond of Veela who had turned her back entirely on this world and she had been as much an elf as they were, and yet it was very hard not to think of them as the same. They moved with the same formality as if every movement had been practiced and chosen beforehand. They spoke with a stiffness as if reading from a parchment.

This elf was a little different and not just because of the hair. He wore a polished and gilded breastplate that shone in the dancing orb lights of the cavern and his head was decorated with golden plates that clipped into his hair. Gold greaves, a wide gold belt, and golden ornaments for his forearms completed the look so that he seemed more statue than elf.

"My lord prince," Fratzern said, lowering himself to one knee and nearly toppling as the ground rocked under us again.

The elves behind the prince – guards I realized – fanned out impressively, extending their polearms in salute. They did not wear gold, but golden tentacles were stitched on the breasts of their grey tunics like a uniform. I looked uneasily at the large squid carved into the ground and hoped it really had been carved, that it was not some remnant of an earlier time in the world when a squid this large might have been buried in bubbling rock only to be unearthed centuries later by elves who wished to set a city on its face.

"Where are you taking these prisoners?" the prince asked.

"They are visitors, my prince," Fratzern said breathlessly as the prince regarded us.

His lip curled when he realized we had not sunk to one knee as Fratzern had.

Should we? I considered it and began to bend my knee by Mally pulled my hand upward and glared at me. Of course she would bow to no one. Of course.

"Forget the Confessor, Fratzern. Forget protocol."

"Forget protocol, my prince?" Fratzern sounded as if he might die on the spot with the horror.

The prince spoke through gritted teeth. "Have you failed to notice that the ground shakes, Fratzern?" He turned to his guards. "Bring them."

"My lord prince," Judicus started to say, and then – utterly without warning, a whip appeared in the hand of the prince, slashing hard against Judicus's face.

Bright blood welled up along the cheek just under his injured eye and I couldn't help it. I didn't want to help it. I lunged forward, stopped only when strong arms caught me from behind and held me in place.

Mally cursed in my ear. "Would you calm down, Sersha. You're going to make this worse."

But I wasn't looking at her. My eyes were on Judicus, on his slender hand cupping his cheek, on his rigid posture. And then his eyes met mine and his free hand flicked words to me.

"Calm. Later. Calm."

Was he kidding? There was no reason to be calm now. Sure, we were surrounded by armed elves, but we had three phoenixes and by the tight way Prexav and Gundt held themselves, I was certain they were as ready to spring as I was. Judicus was no slouch with rope work and Mally always had a trick or two. We could flee right now before this got out of hand.

But he only shook his head as if warning me and then tipped it toward one wall.

What did that mean?

I studied the wall as the prince said.

"I thought as much. You will be docile until you can be inspected by my father, Lord of all Elves, Majesty over all that sparkles, the Golden Gargantuan."

The guards closed in and began to urge us forward and I walked, pulled along by a muttering Mally, but I was still watching the wall. What had Judicus been trying to show me? And why had he allowed them to hurt him?

And then I saw it. One of those massive tentacles appeared to be trembling. Not in time with the ground, oh no, for it kept vibrating even when the ground was still.

I caught my breath and ripped my eyes away.

"This place looks like the Temple of the Tattered Ribbons," Gundt said casually to the guard beside him. The man stayed eyes-forward and impassive, but the prince spoke.

"That horrific travesty was a joke. A mockery of our people and our ways. But we wiped them out utterly and we will again if any human dares to imitate what we have built within this mountain range."

Interesting.

But even more interesting was that I was pretty sure the guard marching beside me was the woman who had spoken to us in the waiting room – the one who had suggested there might be another faction here within the mountain. When I looked at her – dressed in uniform just like the others – I could have sworn I saw her wink.

208

We were marched as a group into a yawning doorway that filled me with relief since it was not the maw of the wakening squid or anywhere near its tentacles, but I might have relaxed too soon.

The door led to a wide staircase with a low ceiling barely taller than the top of Judicus's head of the polearms the elves carried. The edge of each stair was edged in a line of gold that shone in the light of orbs hanging at uneven intervals on either side of the staircase, but it was not the orbs or the stairs or the low ceiling that worried me. It was what was between the orbs.

The first face took me by surprise – took us all by surprise and we froze without meaning to before the face of a frozen salamander made entirely of onyx and gold. It was the size of a large phoenix and at first, I thought it must be alive, the details were so lifelike and the carving done in such a way that seemed to have merely paused in a search for prey.

Our captors snorted derision, prodding us onward and it was in that moment that I saw the rest of them.

The stairway was lined with these golden salamanders, each presented in a different attitude, high head on the alert, low head close to the earth, eyes watching, eyes shut, head turned abruptly to the side, head cocked looking at the sky, and a hundred other poses.

Literally a hundred.

I counted at first. One. Two. Three.

But soon I'd reached a dozen, and then thirty, and then forty-six, and it was somewhere near there that I stopped counting. The air had grown colder. The rumbling had grown harsher and it came regularly as if it were breath in the lungs breathing in and out and in and out and with each breath the entire earth heaved as the chest heaves when one breathes.

I shivered in time with it, and Mally laughed an uneasy laugh, and Prexav sucked in breath like he was trying to inflate himself and float away.

Surely now was the time to wake the phoenixes. Surely now.

But each time I thought that, Judicus flicked his fingers to me.

"Easy. Calm. Wait."

"The rope worker has a plan," Gundt whispered to a quivering Prexav.

"It had better be a good one," Prexav had whispered back. Our guards had dispersed to behind and before leaving us grouped together in the middle and while they could doubtless hear us, it gave me a sense of safety to communicate.

"If it isn't, then I have another one," Mally said with a smirk, and the smile she wore worried me. She was just the kind of person who would collapse this whole place right on herself if she felt like she could get revenge on someone who had wronged her – or even disrespected her.

"Remind me again why we're here," Prexav asked grimly.

"Because we believe," Gundt said, and he sounded like he meant it. "Against all evidence. Against all odds. Against the girl herself, we really believe that she will right wrongs and turn the tide on evil itself and that even if we die in the process, it will have been worth it all."

"Oh, yes, that," Prexav said, and I couldn't tell if he was being cynical or if he really did believe that, too, but I realized that despite myself, despite knowing Mally, I believed it almost as much as Gundt did. Next thing I knew, they'd be giving me green sleeves.

Beside us, I could have sworn the salamanders were shifting, moving with the breathing of the earth and the terrible flicker of the lights.

Just my imagination.

As usual.

And then the stairway opened to another vaulted cavern, but this cavern was lit with a thousand upon a thousand candles, their dripping wax mingling with the mineral build up of natural stalagmites and stalactites, creating what I first took to be the equivalent to an underground forest but realized belatedly was so much worse than that. It was a throne room. The throne room was bright and glittering, lit with light upon light. A huge throne lined with candles rose up from the morass of wax and sediment at the far end.

There was a figure seated on it, dressed much like the prince, but even more gloriously, a crown of gold spires and stalagmite glittering peaks crowning the head of the figure. On either side of him, elves clad in loose gossamer robes studded with crystals swayed back and forth in sweet rhythm, their raised hands full of crystals. None of them seemed to even notice that the room was breathing, heaving up and down.

Their gazes were fixed on a central orb made of pure ropes of magic, weaving and unweaving so that sometimes all you saw was a knitted side and at other times there were gaps and holes twice the size of a man's head. It took the entire descent of the stairs for me to catch a proper look inside the orb. And by the time I did, my brain was already screaming at me to flee, to fight, to do anything but walk docilely forward.

Because within the orb they were cursing or blessing, or whatever they were ding in their trance, within that orb of shifting magic was a man I thought had been killed, crumpled and heaving as if he were undergoing agony after agony in rapid succession.

It was Judicus's uncle.

The former Grand Hadri.

Gundt barely caught Prexav when he stumbled. Both his hands were over his mouth as if to keep from crying out.

And it was all I could do not to look, not to flinch, not to let them know that we knew what they had.

209

I'd thought he was dead. I'd been so certain of it. Hadn't Judicus and I seen him carried past, his blank eyes staring off into the distance, his chest still and lifeless?

Hadn't we?

We'd been wrong.

Fear gripped my heart.

And it grew as I saw who else stood around the steps of the throne.

Men and women swathed in black, their mouths and noses covered by thick scarves. The Hand of the Rat. They were here. They were waiting. There were no guards surrounding them the way they surrounded us.

And I felt like such a fool for thinking I could trick these people – for thinking I could set a trap for them when they so plainly had set one for *us*.

Why hadn't I gone back when I had that bad feeling up above? Why hadn't we fled when we realized the whole world had been taken over by a conspiracy planned at the very top? Why had we gone on?

My breath caught in my throat and I spun quickly in place, seeing the archers up on the walls, their crossbows pointed down into the assembly, seeing the men hanging from chandeliers I had thought were only stalactites and candles but were actually the perfect place to put hidden assassins, seeing the salamanders ringing this room, vibrating as if they might come to life. Why had I ever tricked myself into thinking they were coming alive when they were nothing but precious metals and stillness, nothing but over-done décor in a rich man's hiding place?

I couldn't trust my own judgment anymore.

I felt sick. And that was before I saw who was on the other side of the throne – the face I never thought I'd see again.

Cassanetta Lightland.

A thick bandage was swathed around her head, and she stood in a way that favored her side. She should. I'd put a knife right there.

But the smile that blossomed on her face as her eyes locked onto Mally made me feel even more sick. I'd brought my cousin right back into her hands. I'd given her – once again – the means to break the world. I'd done it with my arrogance. I'd done it by not being willing to walk away.

Beside Cassanetta, a man with a thick white shock of hair and long sideburns stood and his smile was close-lipped and self-satisfied. I'd never seen him before, but he looked over us as if he'd just bought us at the market.

Over them all, the Golden Gargantuan, king of the elves, rose, lifting his hands high toward the stalactites above and then arcing them downward in a single, fluid movement.

At his motion the chanting stopped, the guards circled us in a ring, spears pointed inward, and the prince began to laugh and laugh and laugh. He strode to the dais and mounted the steps and took his place at the right hand of his father.

"Before you even think about calling up your phoenixes," Lady Lightland said from her place on the steps, "you should know that the presence of even one phoenix in this place will bring this entire cave down on your heads and no one – not you, or that phoenix, or your precious ai'sletta, or anyone else will survive."

And I could tell she was right by the pain in my chest and the certain knowledge that it was the beating of our hearts with our phoenixes in them that was making this entire place shake and writhe.

"Maybe that would be worth it," Prexav growled. His eyes were still on the Grand Hadri's contorting form and his face was flushed dark.

But before either of them could say more, Judicus was striding forward. He did not bow to the throne – to my surprise – or acknowledge Lady Lightland, his old rival, or gesture to his uncle and ask what was happening, or even confront the Hand of the Rat.

Instead, he walked forward until he was within easy earshot of the man with the white hair. No one tried to stop him, but when Gundt moved to follow, the spears around us bristled at the height of his neck, keeping him in place.

"It seems a trap has been sprung," Judicus said, loudly enough to be heard throughout the throne room.

And this, it seemed, would be how we would die. Because I knew I was about to call my phoenix. And from the looks Gundt and Prexav threw my way, they were going to do it, too.

"It's a clever trap, do you not think, Son of Chaos?" the man with the white hair said. There was something strangely familiar about his voice.

"I thought so," Judicus said, and it sounded more like he was pleased with himself than afraid.

I raised my hand to my breast and nodded at Mally who fished her diadem out of its hiding place without batting an eye.

"I don't feel much like dying," she muttered as we met Gundt and Prexav's eyes. Prexav looked grim but he nodded at Mally and Gundt opened his mouth, looked at the spears circling his throat, and then shut it promptly. His hand also rose to his chest.

We were ready. We would call the phoenixes and if we died, then at least we died together.

We nodded together, trying to be subtle about it, but before Mally could lift the crown the female elf slipped in between us.

"Now, you decide," she whispered. "Before it's too late."

Beyond us, another conversation was still going on.

"You thought to lay a trap for me, it would seem," Judicus said to the man with the white hair. "Prophecies? Hints? Kidnapping my uncle and forcing me to stay on this continent to free my sister?"

"And it worked," the man said. "You are exactly where we need you to be."

"Decide," the woman said, snapping me back into what was happening before my eyes. "Are you with us?"

I signed to Mally that I needed her to speak to the elf.

She smirked at us both, but she was the only chance I had at it.

"*Who are you and what do you want*?" I signed back, surprised to realize that the spears were easing back, and the eyes of the guard were all on the female elf while their prince's back was turned.

Mally opened her mouth to translate but the woman waved a hand as if she didn't need a translation. She really did understand my signs.

"You'll have to take both on faith. It's either us or the ones on the dais."

I looked from them to me and back again as I heard Judicus say, "And you are exactly where I need *you* to be."

"Do you have it worked out then, boy? Have you discovered who has been calling the shots? Who has been twisting the world, who has been orchestrating your entire life?"

"What would you have us do?" Mally whispered the female elf. "We're not servants to jump and run at a word from you."

The elf smiled tightly. "We'll have your promise that you're on our side before we tell you anything. Because once this starts, it can't be stopped."

"Once what starts?" Gundt whispered, hands held high to keep the spears back from his throat.

"Revolution," the female elf said and then ropes flowed from Judicus's hands, snaking across the room toward the man with the white hair at the same moment that Mally jammed the Dark Diadem onto *my* head.

210

"I'm on no one's side but my own," Mally said, predictably. "But maybe our sides align."

I was too busy blinking, stumbling at the weight on my head, and feeling the power of it as somewhere out in the world the sun winked out.

My eyes met Gundt's as Kazmerev bloomed in my heart. Gundt's eyes widened. A quick flick of a glance and I saw a mirror look in Prexav's eyes. And then three phoenixes were blooming – invisible to all but us – filling the cavern with bright flame and burning righteousness.

What madness is this?

I wasn't even sure which of them spoke. I was too preoccupied with how the moment the phoenixes emerged, the salamanders surrounding us and lining the stairs began to glow as if lit from within.

The female elf's jaw dropped, her eyes flicking frantically around the room. We were going to lose this chance. Everything was going to fall apart unless I did something right now.

I grabbed the female elf's arm to get her attention.

She flinched and for just a moment I feared she might throw me off and follow it up with a blow, but instead she pulled herself together enough to pause and wait.

Grateful, I signed quickly. *Let us make a bargain.*

She cocked her head.

We stand with you now. You stand with us after. You need us in this fight under the ground. We need you for the fight above. And you need it, too. The world is doomed if this goes on.

She was nodding.

But first, I signed, *I need your name.*

"What?" she asked, confused.

"Oh, for the love of creepy underworld lizards," Mally interrupted. Her eye tic went wild as she spoke. Above us somewhere a grinding noise filled the air. "Just give her your name! Just both agree. Don't you see what's happening here? Why is Sersha even the one making this agreement? She's nobody."

"She wears the crown," the elf said.

"Of course," Mally said, rolling her eyes. "It's all about crowns to all you people."

"I am Verdaine of the Hanging Spears Sect and I speak for my sect in a promise of truce with you," she said breathlessly.

Our hands met and I hoped I was doing the right thing. We knew nothing about these people. I only knew that my enemies stood with her ruler, and she said she stood against him. We were natural allies – as long as she had honor.

"I don't know how our kingdom is still standing," she said through gritted teeth. "The presence of a single phoenix should bring it down, never mind three."

To my surprise, she was looking up over our heads. She could see our phoenixes.

"I'm lucky like that," Mally said easily.

I looked around frantically, but she was the only one who saw them. I wondered what that meant.

No one else was even looking at us, our guards, or our phoenixes. They didn't even seem to notice the glow in the salamanders. Our entire agreement and the awakening of the magic around us had been silent and secret in the middle of the crowd, at the center of the throne room.

I drew in a long breath and steadied myself. It had all taken only moments. Moments where my heart raced and pulse thundered. Moments where I was certain I'd made a mistake.

"Wait for my signal," Verdaine whispered to us. "All who are with us know what to look for. We've been planning this for longer than you've been alive."

That long? Then why now? Why with us?

The earth breathed in and out and I noticed the salamanders slide a little bit forward. Still, no one seemed to notice their movement as if their very familiarity disguised them.

It was only now that I could take a breath that I was able to turn my gaze to Judicus and my mind to Kazmerev.

This is bad! This is so bad! Kazmerev said the moment he had my attention. *Ally with golden salamanders? They were supposed to be myths!*

So was he! In the background, I could hear the other phoenixes frantically speaking to their riders. I had to concentrate and focus to only hear Kazmere's voice.

Not the same thing! I don't trust them. They don't have their own souls. They're like those creatures of Sydonon only worse.

Worse in what way?

Worse because they are full of souls, but not trapped phoenix souls – the souls of these elves' ancestors were trapped willingly. They wake in our presence as if it brings them back to life just as we resurrect ourselves.

That sounded *better.* At least these souls wanted to be here.

But they are conscious, Sersha. They know what they want. They have minds. I can feel them.

Which made them valuable allies.

I heard his annoyed sound, and I knew the other phoenixes were having the same discussions with their riders. I'd just been blocking them out.

I met Gundt's eye, and he shrugged helplessly.

Still, we hadn't been noticed by the court. And no wonder.

Judicus and the man with white hair were locked in a silent struggle, Judicus's black ropes tangling, twisting, then being thrown by a set of ropes from the other man but these ropes were odd. I'd only ever seen black ropes of magic, but these ones pulsed with golden light.

They were an even match. Every knot achieved was undone by the other, every snake-like strike countered, each unraveling quickly knit back into place.

Unlike our phoenixes, the ropes were visible, and the courtiers and elven royals were up on tiptoe as they watched the duel of rope on rope on rope.

We should act now.

No! All three phoenixes spoke at once.

Why not?

Don't you see? Kazmerev asked. *Look carefully at the ball in the middle of the room.*

The sphere of ropework that had held the Grand Hadri was unspooling slowly, the threads opening and unraveling as the two ropeworkers wove against one another. But as the strands spun out, what was feeding them became apparent.

I gasped as I saw ripples of gold running through the stone all around us and leading to that central spot where they fed into that tangle of magic. Threads of gold ran like veins of precious metal, but I'd seen this kind of gold before. It reminded me of molten honey.

Souls. Kazmerev said. *Trapped souls – not like the ones in the salamanders. These are not willing. These are trapped like the phoenixes were. I don't even know what they once were, so wild and unfurled they are.*

And then the Golden Gargantuan spoke, and every eye turned to him.

"As pleasing as this display of pugilist spirit is to the crown, your efforts are misdirected, Son of Chaos. Show him, my prince."

And he smiled at his prince as Verdaine gripped my arm and hissed, "Here it comes!"

211

His son laughed and then lifted his hands.

"You came to stop the people you have now realized control your world. Instead, you will witness the finalization of those prophecies. Today, a pact is made. A promise of marriage and alliance between the Prince of Elves and Casanetta Lightland, lady of Briccatore."

Casanetta smiled, stepping around the man with the white hair and then joining the Prince, their hands clasped together.

"We are joined by our brothers of the Hand of the Rat," the prince said as the king smiled down in pleasure. "And we welcome them to the blessing of this covenant. Three lands united. Three realms joined in peace under one rule."

Five masked men and women detached themselves from the group at the base of the throne and joined him on the gilded steps leading up to his father.

"And together – we, the Elves of the Underland, you, the sons and daughters of the Hand of the Rat, our old disciples who have come so far from their origins as the Cult of Tattered Ribbons, and Occulan, Lord Adventurer of the Guild of Rope-workers – we offer to the gods this last gift to show our certainty and promise that a new era has come."

The prince raised his hands and his father stood and raised his with him. Beside me, Verdaine stiffened.

"That's it!" she hissed.

And then, with a sound like a thunderclap, the sphere of ropes was gone, replaced by a cloud of mist, the Grand Hadri shattered and disappeared in mist and light, and the golden ropes reformed weaving themselves up, up, up to the ceiling and then solidifying into a wide, golden mirror.

"Now, Occulan!" the prince called.

"Now, Flame Riders!" Verdaine yelled.

But I was frozen in place. I couldn't move. I saw every tiny thing in slow motion as the white-haired man smiled, lifted his hands a little higher, and then the gold seams from the floor ran across the marble floor and pooled at his feet – fast as lightning – and his ropes glowed brighter as he redoubled his weaving, pushing at Judicus with all the might of his tangled magic.

My beloved fought wildly, his face screwed up in concentration. He fell back a step and his eyes sought mine with one sudden panicked look and I realized that for the first time since I'd met him, he was overmatched.

Kaz! I called in my mind. Please!

He was under me before I finished the thought, and we dove forward. I didn't know if I'd made him visible or not – didn't care. All I could think was that this terrible golden ropeworker and his stolen souls were going to overpower Judicus unless I helped him.

Someone was screaming behind me – Gundt maybe? – And someone had seized me around the waist but instead of pulling me back, that someone had been snatched up onto Kazmerev's back and was flying with me. I both didn't know who it was and didn't care. I forced all my concentration into fire and opened my hand, willing it toward Occulan.

Flames bloomed from my hand, pouring out in a straight stream.

Someone screamed.

I didn't turn to look.

I didn't care, I just had to get to Judicus. I had to stop his enemy. Judicus stumbled back another step and then my fire hit Occulan full in the chest.

And nothing happened.

He didn't flame. He didn't smoke. Nothing.

It was as if it hadn't happened at all. I stared at my hand, shocked, and then I pulled it back to me, shaking it like I'd been burned. But no, no time to figure out why.

It shouldn't have done that.

Kazmerev sounded as focused as I did. Fire was only one of our tricks.

We didn't have to talk back and forth to know what we wanted. He was already reaching his talons as he dove. We'd pick the rope worker up and throw him aside.

I stiffened, waiting for the feeling of Kazmerev's talons digging into flesh, and then suddenly we were tumbling, end on end, and it was all I could do to hold on as Mally screamed from behind me, her hands tightening on my waist until I thought I wouldn't be able to breathe.

My talons went right through him!

We righted and spun, and the world spun in my vision. All around elves were leaping onto the backs of salamanders as they shook themselves, rubble shedding from their backs and legs. The courtiers had fallen free of their trance and were running, screaming, the guards hurrying to fill the voids.

I caught only that much before my eyes found Judicus. He was bent onto one knee, hands spread high and wide as his ropes worked furiously, but the golden ropes were barely an arm's length away and they were faster than his, tougher than his.

If we couldn't grab his adversary, we'd need to catch him before he was overwhelmed.

On it.

I'd never expected Judicus to meet his equal in ropework.

We all meet our equal someday. You can't expect to be the best forever.

We wheeled and Kazmerev let out a bird's shriek as we turned in the air, fire edging his wings and tail, and curling around our bodies. Smoke and fire danced deadly on our path as we plunged back toward where the fighting had begun.

"Treachery!" someone cried and then a horn sounded – long and deep – so deep that it seemed to make every hair of my body quiver with it.

As we dove for Judicus, I realized that the floor wasn't shaking anymore. The earth had stopped breathing.

Gundt and Prexav were pinned down on the backs of Huxabrand and Grevankin, wrapped up in ropes sprouting from the hands of the elven king and prince.

And suddenly everything began to make sense.

Behind Occulan, the throne began to rise. But I didn't dare try to see why that might be. I could only focus on one thing – Judicus.

He looked toward me suddenly, as if he'd heard my name and one hand flicked fast as the wind.

"Flee. I will follow."

But I would not flee. Not even when he went back to fighting. Certainly not when it was obvious he was being beaten, that unless we helped him *now,* he would never follow. We'd been trapped by the very people we'd hoped would help us set a trap. We'd been tricked and used and caught like fools. And even now we were pinched between two warring factions. We were right at the heart of the conspiracy against man. A conspiracy that had been hatched generations ago.

Occulan's rope work pushed Judicus another step backward. He was flush with the magic mirror, his narrow form reflected exactly, but exaggerated, made taller and thinner still in the golden mirror. The gold rope work forced his ropes back until barely an inch was between him and them.

We had maybe a heartbeat left.

And he should have kept fighting it. He should have fought with all he had.

But he didn't.

Instead, he dropped his ropes and chose to sign to me. And before we could reach him, the golden ropes gave him a tiny shove and he fell as one falls from a high cliff into the golden mirror and disappeared in a flash.

I gasped, horrified, unable to do anything but stare at where he'd been, the look of desperate intensity in his eyes still ringing in my heart as I replayed his signs again and again in my mind.

"I love you, Sersha."

He was gone.

212

"Sersha! Sersha!" Mally screamed in my ear as we sailed past the gold mirror. It fell to the ground, shattering into a thousand pieces. I caught one piece as it fell, slicing my hand. Blood made it slick as I forced it into my book pouch on the belt. Blood kept flowing. I scrambled for a handkerchief and wound it around my palm, blinking against the pain – not the pain of the hand, I'd barely felt that. I was still surprised to see the blood flowing from it. It was the pain at what I'd seen – at what I'd lost – that was ripping me apart.

Where had he gone? Where did that mirror lead? And how would I ever get him back now that it was broken?

I didn't want to think.

I didn't want to be here.

I just wanted to take it all back to the point on the mountain when he'd promised me a ring. That part had been good. Could we go back to that? And not to this?

Below me, people – elves – were trampled under golden feet. Swords were shedding blood. I didn't even know which ones I should be cheering for – or if I should cheer for anyone. Maybe it would help the world if no one left this cavern alive.

I swallowed hard, fighting back a sob as Mally screamed in my ear, "For the love of light, Sersha, you fool, you have to fight. Look! The octopuses!"

I looked up, numb. Thick. Slow. I wasn't hearing right. Wasn't seeing right. Everything was a blur.

Barely a moment had passed, but the throne was still rising and under it, a great golden octopus surged upward, easily the equivalent to the squid out in the other cavern. The king sat on his throne, looking imperious and powerful as the eldritch creature bore him upward. His hands twisted with the effort of keeping

Grevankin imprisoned and in the distant far reaches of my brain, I heard Grevankin's voice.

If she could just blast him, Kazmerev, that would be very helpful.

I can't get through to her, she isn't listening! Kazmerev said, panic filling his mental voice.

I gasped. I needed to shake out of this.

And then hands were around my neck choking me and Mally was yelling, "Listen! You stupid girl why won't you listen?"

She let go of me and I gasped and twisted to look at her.

"Him!" she yelled, pointing past me at the Golden Gargantuan. "Go and get him and hope my luck holds!"

We need to help them! Kazmerev said with her.

Yes. Yes, we did.

I felt relief through his mental link as I shook myself, ignoring the searing pain in my heart, and leaned over Kazmerev's fiery neck, focused on where we were flying.

The first legs of the giant octopus clawed through the floor, splitting it down the middle. From the split, a thousand smaller stone octopuses and squids scrambled up, elongated, and then compressed as they went through the narrow crack and then out again.

I felt ill.

No! Focus.

I focused. King.

The prince and Casanetta had scrambled up to the base of his throne and were clinging to it as the Prince wove more ropework.

The king, Kazmerev said certainly, keeping me from distraction.

I felt nothing.

I couldn't seem to care.

So, I let him lead me, let him take the figurative reins and guide us to the king. I held out my hand and let the fire flow and flow and flow through me and this time nothing turned it aside, nothing severed it as we streaked toward the throne.

To my astonishment, the king went up like a torch, his ropes falling and vanishing, his screams pouring from a charred throat even as his son reached up and indifferently yanked him from the throne and threw him down the side of the stone octopus.

The prince met my eyes for a heartbeat and something inside me turned to ice. He'd meant this all along.

The Golden Gargantuan fell, screaming, burning, bounced once on the octopus's side, and then hit the ground with a smack only to be crushed under a tentacle that had just wiggled free.

I didn't feel anything as I watched, though I should have. It was too hard to care with Judicus gone. One hand drifted to the pouch on my belt.

STOP! Kazmerev said and he sounded panicked. *Stop this at once! You can't despair. You can't. When hope fades from your heart I will be gone forever. So. Cut. It. Out.*

I swallowed. I didn't want to hope. Hope could carve me up a thousand different ways.

But I need you to, please Sersha, please. We'll find a way to get him back. We will. We just have to make it through this fight and then we will.

I was about to answer when Mally steered my head by grabbing both ears and pointing it where she wanted me to look.

"You're only half done!" she roared. "Finish the job!"

In the chaos below, it took a moment to see what she was pointing at. Elves mounted on Salamanders skittered over the tumbled floor, crushing bodies beneath them and then ripping into the small octopuses with snapping jaws. Other elves had scrambled onto those small octopuses, clinging to them as they shot bows or fought with swords or simply tried to avoid the waving, grasping arms of their mounts.

It was a moment before I made out Gundt, still tangled with Huxabrand in rope work. He made a choked cry and then collapsed. As he did, Huxabrand faded, and the rope work dissolved, and Gundt fell to the ground.

Gundt! I cried in my mind and Kazmerev dove, feet first, sliding through the air, screeching as he put everything he had into this dive.

We had only moments. Moments or he would be trampled.

I held my breath and clung to my glorious phoenix, and I tried to find hope, though the only hope I could find was tattered beyond belief.

213

Gundt went under, slipping like a ship under the waves of a storm. I clenched my jaw, refusing to accept it. I'd already lost Judicus. I would not lose Gundt, too.

Dive, Kaz! Dive!

I clenched my wounded hand, feeling the hot sticky blood in my palm, and I gritted my teeth as Mally's hands grew tighter on my waist. And then we were down among the grappling figures, searching.

Kazmerev swept to the left, barely avoiding a grasping gilded tentacle the size of a large oak bole.

He reared up, flowing over the tail of a gold salamander, flowing like a creek in spring melt. We slid over the cracked, broken ground where sparkling sediment poured down into the cracks like sand from an hourglass, and just like that sand, it marked how little time we had.

No mortal could stand on this ground anymore. It was too furrowed with cracks and fissures, too broken and crumbling like old bread between the fingers. A stalactite broke free from the ceiling above us, slamming down into the head of a golden salamander and pinning him to the crumbling earth. He squirmed, miserably, and then collapsed.

And *still,* I did not see Gundt.

No! There! A hand, reaching up from under the collapsed salamander. Was that him?

Can you see him? Grevankin called.

I think so. Kazmerev's voice was tight.

Then get him. We will look for a way out.

The staircase?

Have you looked at it lately? The squid from above sits in it like a cork in a bottle.

The very thought made me ill, but there was no time for sickness. I dodged the scramble of a tentacle, hands digging in tightly to Kazmerev's feathers.

We were close enough to the hand to almost reach it. Kazmerev leaned in a little closer and Mally caught the waving hand, pulling, her muscles straining. I leaned in to help her, ignoring the pain in my flayed hand, ignoring the terror gripping my heart. Was it even him? Was it even –

Yes! We'd pulled him free enough to see his face. He wasn't wedged, he was just very heavy.

I let go of his arm and leapt from Kazmerev's back.

No! Stay with me!

But if I did that, then we'd never pull him up. I threw myself into the shadow of the salamander and grabbed Gundt under the shoulders and with all my strength I pulled, and he slid entirely out from the salamander.

I paused, chest heaving as I gasped for breath.

He was alive. I felt the beat of his heart. He was pale and unconscious and probably hurt but he was alive.

Get back on my back! Quickly!

Not yet. Not until we had him safe.

The ground trembled under my feet, feeling like that bridge Judicus had made of ropework. It couldn't hold me. I was going to sink through.

I tried to lift Gundt, barely budging him, falling backward so we both collapsed on the ground. He was so heavy. Gasping, I pulled myself to my feet and heaved him up again. This time it wasn't as far.

"Stupid girl!" Mally was beside me before I could try again, shouting over the cacophony of sound. "You could just ask the bird to grab him with his feet."

I am not *a bird.*

Now was hardly the time to quibble. Mally threw her strong back into our next heave and Kazmerev – irritated though he may be – rolled to accept the burden. I gasped, trembling in every muscle with relief. We had him.

Get back on! Hurry! Hurry!

Mally was already scrambling up into Kazmerev's back.

Yes. We had to go. Go anywhere but here.

I took a trembling step forward and then something knocked me, picking me up off my feet and flinging me backward and my eyes widened as Kazmerev and Mally shrunk in my vision, and I flew up and away through the air.

It was shockingly peaceful to soar up through the air, tumbling as I went.

I caught sight of the tentacle that had struck me, saw Kazmerev execute an amazingly graceful leap and roll that kept Gundt and Mally on his back while avoiding the tentacle.

Spun to where I could see that the golden salamanders were being formed into something that seemed like a line, a dozen elves on each back. I saw a pair of elves in uniform drag a pair of elven children and an old woman onto the back of the salamander under them.

Spun once more. Our opponents were forming a line on the stone octopuses but these creatures were stacked one on the other on the other in an enormous wriggling mountain of stone life and at the apex sat the great stone octopus bearing the uprooted throne, the elf prince and Casanetta standing on it's back, hands interlinked as the prince's hand reached out and ropes fell and swelled from his hand, snatching one of the salamanders from their line and dragging it to the rent in the earth where it fell, elves dripping from its back like rain in the wind.

I spun again, beginning to fall now. Certainly, the fall would kill me. But if these were my last moments, I was going to live them. I wasn't going to say it hadn't all been worth it. I wasn't going to give up hope.

I just prayed that someone else could pull Judicus out of the mirror.

Kazmerev's eye caught mine as he raced toward me.

Sershaaaaa!

I smiled.

My sweet phoenix. Brave and righteous to the end.

I closed my eyes, the wind whistling around me.

And then I smacked against something, back first. The scent of pitch filled my nose and scaled my lungs and all my focus was on clearing my lungs as I coughed and coughed and heaved.

Come now, Grevankin's deep voice boomed. *I don't smell that bad!*

He smelled glorious. He smelled like life and hope and love and ... my eyes popped open as Kazmerev pulled up beside me and I felt us – all of us – me and Mally and Prexav, Grevankin and Kazmerev and maybe even Gundt – breathe a sigh of relief together.

I'm glad you're safe, little hawk, Kazmerev said.

We all are, Grevankin agreed.

We were all still alive. All of us.

The phoenixes spiraled upward, dodging pieces of ceiling as they fell toward the ground.

But we couldn't just wait for a hole to form. There were miles of stone above us.

There will be a way. If elves got in here, we can get out, Kazmerev reassured me as he dodged to one side to avoid a falling stalactite.

In the distance, I saw one of the elves on the back of a gold salamander stand up on its back and wave to me. Verdaine. She was signing.

"Behind you."

I spun but all I saw was Prexav. His eyes widened.

"Are you hurt, Sersha?" he asked.

And then a black rope – glowing gold – wrapped around his neck and tightened so quickly I didn't have time to gasp.

I heard a snap.

And then I was falling again, as Grevankin winked out of life forever.

214

Spin yourself upright. I'm going to catch you!

I fought the air, trying to get upright, and then he was there, coming up from under me, catching me on his back so I was sitting right behind Mally where she was holding onto Gundt.

"Good thing that crown is so tight," she said hoarsely when I landed.

I reached up numbly and touched it. Still there.

Hurry! He's after us, too.

I glanced behind me to where Occulus was climbing up the heap of octopuses, his ropes helping him like long extensions of his own arms. I'd never felt anything like the hatred that clawed at the inside of my chest at the sight of that white-haired man. I wanted to kill him back – for Prexav. For Grevankin. For Judicus. My lungs felt like they were burning.

But no. I still had Mally and Gundt and Kazmerev to keep safe.

We needed to go in opposite directions. Surely, those ropes had a limit. Surely, we could get out of their range.

Maybe.

We sped as fast as we could, and I looked over my shoulder at where Prexav had fallen. There was no sign of him. Should we go back for Grevankin's ashes?

It's a kind thought but by now they'll be too scattered to collect.

He should head toward Verdaine. She'd warned me about Occulus – even if it were too late.

Kazmerev tilted slightly and we veered closer toward the line of salamanders and Verdaine riding on their right flank.

We reached her at the same moment that she reached down and pulled a young man up, flinging him behind her on the back of the salamander.

"All is in readiness, Commander, just give the order!" he called to her.

"Consider it given! Tell Tereman to hold the line no matter what it costs," she called back, and then she turned her eyes up to us. "We need you to come with me! If this phoenix is lost, too, then our golden salamanders will not survive. They will chill and freeze where they stand, and our revolution will be lost."

I didn't sign to her that her revolution meant nothing to me. Didn't sign that we just wanted out of there, that we'd already paid too steep a price. I felt like a loaf of bread inside. Bland, thick, vulnerable.

My hands were shaking. I didn't even realize I was weeping until I saw little sizzles where my tears were hitting Kazmerev's feathers.

We hung back, following Verdaine's salamander as it skittered up the wall into the forest of stalactites as if it knew exactly where it was going. And it turned out, it did. A small tunnel – just wide enough for a single salamander opened in the ceiling.

Verdaine's salamander wriggled into it, leaving us to follow.

Sersha?

I didn't know if I should follow. Were we safe to trust her? Should I risk Mally, and Gundt, and my Kazmerev?

I think we should follow.

Then we should.

I felt so numb. I prodded the feeling, looking for a heart that wasn't there anymore. I couldn't go on. I just couldn't make it even one more step. Maybe I should pull out that shard of mirror and try to fall through it with Judicus.

Please, stop, Sersha, please!

It seemed like he was crying, too.

Of course I'm crying! Who will grow ill on my back now? Who will tell me how marvelous it would be to play with human children? Who?

We shot into the tunnel after Verdaine, Kazmerev's feathers bright, lighting the way as we soared through. I was shaking so hard I couldn't tell if the tunnel was shaking, too, or if it was just me.

And that was how we traveled, far, far, far into the tunnel and then up into a wide dark cavern that I didn't even realize was wide and dark until we were well up the winding path that spiraled around it and I looked down to see a hundred golden salamanders following us.

Whoever was holding the line against the octopuses was giving us time to escape.

It should be us.

How? Occulus was immune to our fire. He would break our necks like he broke Prexav's.

I choked on a sob.

I'm sorry my Sersha. I'm sorry. There's no happy ending right now. We just have to keep pushing. We have to get out of here. We have to make Grevankin and Prexav's sacrifice worth it. We have to help Gundt and keep Mally safe. And I will be here with you for all of it. I can't keep you from the fire, but I can stand with you in the flames. And I always will.

I clung to his words for hours upon hours as we fled together and just when I thought that even they couldn't sustain me anymore, Mally turned in her seat and looked at me. I thought she might slap me or poke me or rage at me, but to my surprise, she was crying, too. She turned and hugged me as fiercely and furiously as she did everything and as we cried together in our embrace, she whispered to me.

"I'm going to bring them all down, Sersha. Every one of them. And we'll save the skinny rope worker. And this poor loyal fool, Gundt. And then I think I'd like to be queen because the world will owe me. Don't you think?"

And I didn't know if I should cry or laugh or just be glad that I hadn't lost her, too.

EPISODE ONE: "FOR THE LOST"

SEASON THREE

215

Mally was still hugging me tight when we finally landed – hours later – in the rippling hills above the elves' home.

Kazmerev fell like a star, landing hard on the ground, his chest heaving. I hadn't realized he could grow physically tired like this. I had thought that a magical phoenix who was reborn in my heart with every sunset would be unaffected by extreme physical effort.

I hadn't reckoned with grief. He spoke into my mind through our silent connection, and I clung to his voice as Mally and I fell tiredly from his back and worked together to bring Gundt's unconscious form down.

Our losses sear me to the core. Grevankin has been a friend for a long time, and I had grown fond of Prexav and your ropeworker.

I'll get him back, I told him with my mind, but my heart was aching, too, every beat painful.

His silence made my heart lurch. He didn't believe me. But Judicus wasn't dead. He couldn't be. He'd fallen into that golden mirror and been trapped and then the mirror shattered, but that wasn't dead. I hadn't seen him fade and die, right? I could find a way to get him back, right?

I dashed tears from my eyes as we laid Gundt out. Tears would not help.

"Would you take that crown off already?" Mally asked grumpily. "I can't see a thing."

I glanced at Kazmerev.

You should do it. I will be with you again when darkness falls. I always will.

Reluctantly, I pulled the crown from my head, and around us, light sprang up, the sun high in the sky, glaring down on the sparse landscape. We'd laid Gundt on a bare patch of land, his face was pale and immobile, but he was breathing. A nasty wound on his forehead had bled everywhere and I realized – with a sudden hollow feeling – that Judicus had been the one with the pack and we'd lost all of our supplies when we lost him.

"I need to heal Gundt," I signed to Mally. "But I can't yet."

The fire of my phoenix gave me the power to burn hurt and illness away, but after flying for hours and hours and fighting an intense battle, I didn't have the strength to light a candle right now.

"You're too weak for that right now," she said, shaking her head. "We need sleep before we do anything."

I looked around us at those who were fleeing with us. We were all slumped in exhaustion, paused here in the sudden sunlight. Hundreds of elves – men, women, children, elderly – were huddled next to the golden salamanders who had carried them away from their homeland and up into this desolate world above. They looked as lost as I felt, as bone-weary, and streaked in dirt, and thirsty as I was.

Our pursuers had stopped chasing us somewhere underground. For now. Who knew if they were regrouping and beginning to follow again?

For all that we rode magical creatures, we were still people made of flesh and blood, and flesh and blood needs rest.

"I'm going to sleep," Mally said, utterly unconcerned with the mob of refugees all around us. Their worried murmurs made my stomach squeeze and tremble, but she lay down beside Gundt, cradled her head on the crook of her arm, her other hand tangled around the crown I'd removed, and she was fast asleep before I could say anything.

I tried to ease the flow of blood from Gundt's headwound with my handkerchief. It soaked through quickly, but I had nothing else to use. I bit my lip, only looking up as footsteps approached.

Around us, the elves seemed to have the same idea we had. They were collapsing in family groups and huddles, worn out and wracked with grief just as I was. I saw more than one stoic face crumple into weeping as they settled into the dust.

Verdaine's hard face met my gaze when I finally looked up. Her fine elven features were traced in dust and sweat and her clothing was rumpled and askew.

"We will rest here only briefly," she said, authority still in her rough voice. "We must seek a place of shelter for the people. Some place with water."

I nodded but she didn't say anything else, just stood staring, hands on her hips as if she expected something.

Guidance, I realized after a moment. She'd left her underground world for the surface where humans ruled, and she was looking to me – a human – to tell her where to go.

She raised a single eyebrow.

"*When the sun sets,*" I signed to her and then stopped. I didn't know the signs to say that I would heal Gundt and he would have ideas. I didn't even know if that was true.

I licked my dry lips, but it seemed to be enough for her.

"Stay here in the center of the camp. We need your phoenix – sleeping as he may be – to stay close so that our salamanders do not fade."

And then she was gone, and I fell into the dust on the other side of Gundt from Mally, and hoped our body warmth and the bright sun would be enough to keep him alive until we could do more. I shouldn't have been able to sleep with grief and turmoil filling my heart, but I closed my eyes for only a moment and exhaustion swept me away.

216

I woke to sunlight. I couldn't have slept long, but Verdaine was there shaking me awake.

"We've decided to move the moment your phoenix reemerges," she said as my eyes flickered open.

I blinked at her muzzily before what she was saying made sense and then I nodded. We couldn't tell how hot on our heels pursuit might be. I knew Lady Lightland would pursue us to the ends of the earth and beyond. Likely, their traitor prince would do the same. Which meant we couldn't stop to rest for long.

My eyes flicked immediately to Gundt. He was still breathing, though his face had gone grey.

The sun hung low on the horizon, melting from bright white into a brassy puddle. The sun would set soon and the moment it did, and Kazmerev returned, I would heal him and then we'd see if I had enough strength to carry all three of us wherever we were going. Maybe Gundt would be strong enough to ride Huxabrand.

I sat up slowly and wished I had water. My mouth was dry as old parchment. I wasn't alone, I was sure. Faint cries of infants and complaints of small children drifted to me from the huddles of fleeing elves gathered around their resting salamanders.

I looked from group to group, watching families struggling to care for small children with limited supplies, watching red-rimmed eyes and shaking hands, watching vigilance in every eye and weapons in the hands of everyone not caring for a child. I was looking at the last of the free elves. And they were depending on me to get them somewhere safe. The intensity of that weighed heavily on my shoulders. I hadn't asked them to flee their home – but I'd brought phoenixes there and destroyed it. I hadn't asked them to rely on me – but I'd made a deal to fight alongside them. They were my responsibility now because of those decisions.

Just like Mally. Just like Gundt who found me and adopted me as a Fledgling. Just like Kristiana who had been raised to a throne because I couldn't keep her uncle alive. Just like Judicus trapped in a mirror.

I reached in my belt pouch and touched the fragment of mirror I'd gathered up. Still there. My last link to him. But how could I possibly find a way to take a shard of mirror and carve a path back to the man who had entered it? Was that even possible now?

Mally blinked awake beside me and sat up suddenly.

"It's almost sunset," she gasped, excitement in her voice. She must want to get moving, too.

She fumbled in her belt pouch as I checked over Gundt. He was sweaty and far too pale and my bandage for his head was soaked in blood and mostly useless. I hoped I had slept enough to have the strength to heal him. I'd have to give whatever I had and just hope it was enough.

I felt the cold of darkness closing in as the last ray of the sun disappeared and Kazmerev burst from my heart.

"*What is this?*" he asked, sounding shocked – though why he'd be shocked when my purpose was obvious, I didn't know. Gundt's life was hanging by a thread.

I didn't have time to answer. I screwed up all my concentration into healing, put my hands onto Gundt's chest, and closed my eyes. I thought of light and warmth and good things. This had to work. It had to.

"*Mally? What have you done?*" Kazmerev sounded shocked. I could see the whirl of his flames growing hot from the corners of my eyes, but what I was doing was too pressing.

Whatever she'd done would have to wait.

"I caught the ashes when they were falling," she said, and she sounded smug.

Of all the times to cause drama, did she have to do it while I was trying to heal a man with a mortal injury? I closed my eyes. No distractions.

With all my strength, I pushed my heat and light into Gundt. I wanted him healed. I wanted him whole. We could do this. Together. Searing heat and light filled my mind and for a moment I could hardly breathe, hardly think.

I breathed deeply as Huxabrand's voice filled my mind.

"*Kazmerev? What the ... is Gundt hurt?*"

"I'm ... I'm not hurt," he said in his rumbling baritone, and he seemed to be in as much wonder as she was. "I think Sersha has healed me."

I shuddered, the exhaustion of healing washing over me. Everything hurt. Everything tingled. But he was fine and Huxabrand was back. We'd be able to keep going. Between two phoenixes, we could certainly carry three people. I breathed out a relieved sigh.

"*Whose egg is that?*" Huxabrand's mental voice was small.

My eyes popped open. Mally stood before me looking awkward, her hands spread before her and covered in ... dust? Ash. And within them was a dusky orange egg streaked in smoke. As I watched, it cracked open and flame poured out like hot honey, dripping down from the egg to the ground below and then forming a phoenix.

"*Well, this is awkward,*" the phoenix said. He was the size of a large eagle, rather than a fully grown phoenix. Orange and so smoky he looked shaggy. He put his head under one wing as if afraid to look at us.

But that low, deep voice was familiar.

I felt my eyes widening even as Kazmerev let out a fiery gasp.

"Oh?" Mally asked, dropping the fragments of egg as the small phoenix hopped to her hands from the dusty ground and then back again as if agitated.

Mally crossed her arms over her chest, glaring at him while Huxabrand and Kazmerev exchanged a quick worried look that made them look like falcons about to strike.

"And what exactly is awkward about it?" She lifted her nose in that way she always did when she was put out. "I'm pretty sure you were dead – and about to be dead forever. So, I grabbed a handful of your ash as it was falling. I would call that quick thinking, not 'awkward.'"

I glanced around us and hurried to my feet as I realized that the elves all around us were staring.

We all needed to calm down.

"How is this possible?" Gundt asked in wonder.

"I thought you were the Guiding Flame or whatever," Mally said, shooting him an annoyed look. "Shouldn't you be the one telling us how this works?"

"*Grevankin?*" Huxabrand asked gently.

"*It would appear I am reborn,*" the small phoenix said, shaking himself and billowing smoke. "*What an enormous surprise. You caught me, Blazing Queen?*"

Oh, of course now Mally smiled. He'd chosen the perfect nickname for that.

"I did," she said with a very satisfied look on her face.

"*I'm reborn in your heart.*"

"And now I'm not the only one without a phoenix anymore," she said belligerently – but I could see what the others could not.

I could see how she was melting inside by the way that she stuck her jaw out. I could see that she was touched by the nickname by the way she couldn't quite look at him. She'd have to soon. He was growing larger by the moment as if he could regain his full size in a single hour.

I was shaking my head with everyone else, but at the same time, I was filled with delight that he had survived. I'd had no idea she had caught his ashes. How had she managed that in the chaos? Lucky. She was lucky as only the ai'sletta could be.

"*I am equally delighted, Little Hawk,*" Kazmerev said. "*Though it does not ease the passing of Prexav, it is a joyous thing to have our brother reborn.*"

"*I've never seen another phoenix hatched,*" Huxabrand said, wonder in her mental voice. "*Oh, do be quiet Gundt. I know she's the ai'sletta. No, I'm not going to forget.*"

"*Forget what?*" Kazmerev asked and Huxabrand almost rolled her eyes.

"*He's worried we'll forget that we're here to protect her now that she has a phoenix of her own.*"

"*On the contrary,*" the small Grevankin said, and I smiled because his mental voice was still big and rumbling even though he was currently half his normal size. "*You'll be happy to have an extra hand to help you.*"

I peered at him, worried, as Mally set a hand carefully on his feathered head as if worried she might be burned after all. He seemed ... unharmed. But that wasn't right. Kazmerev had mourned and mourned for Veela and he hadn't been right for days.

Kazmerev coughed awkwardly, letting loose a tiny ball of flame.

"Well, as to that, Little Hawk, you forget that Grevankin is far older than I and has a better rein on his feelings. Do not doubt that he mourns."

Grevankin's orange head turned to me and the black smoke around him thickened, and for the first time, I saw the easy-mannered phoenix flare with annoyance.

"I will carry the memory and heart of Prexav with me until the day I am nothing but a memory, too. Never fear that, little human. Your children and their children will be told tales of Prexav and his mighty sacrifice. But though I am fresh and new and cannot yet bear a rider, we must be off. Prexav's sacrifice for the ai'sletta must not be in vain. And his enemies must be avenged."

"Vengeance is one of my favorite things," Mally said happily.

"Heavens give me strength," Gundt muttered, mounting Huxabrand as Verdaine hustled toward us.

"What part of leaving with the sunset was unclear?" she asked, and we scrambled to mount our phoenixes and get into the air.

But though I was exhausted from healing – and harassed by Mally who kept insisting that she ought to guide Kazmerev, who didn't need or want guidance, because after all, she was a flame Rider now, too – my eyes kept drifting to the slowly growing Grevankin flying just behind us. I thought of Prexav in the world beyond this and how he used to look at Mally. Was he watching now? Would he be glad to know that his companion in life now accompanied her? I buried my fingers into Kazmerev's feathers and every time I met Grevankin's eye my heart trembled just a little.

217

"Sarcoda," Gundt said when we stopped at midnight. We'd found a spring and those with water skins were filling them while everyone else drank as much as they could.

We'd been silent on the flight here, looking often behind us, fearing that our enemies would catch up. How would we defend ourselves with children and elderly to protect?

When we stopped at the spring, Verdaine gathered her leaders and joined us. Dirty, battle-weary, some of them wounded, and all still with weapons in hand, they looked grim and determined in equal measure. The first words out of Verdaine's mouth were a challenge.

"We will be your allies. We will fight alongside you. But you must do your part," she said, tossing her head.

"And what is that?" Gundt had asked mildly.

"We need to resupply. We need a defensible position. You need to give us a place like that. You know this territory. You have connections."

Sarcoda was his response.

"It's a fortress in the hill country not far from here," he said, pointing northwest.

"Then why have you not offered it up before?" she pressed.

He crossed his arms over his chest. "When I was unconscious or when you were herding us into the sky?"

She sighed. "Your point is taken. And yet, I still feel hesitance within you."

He nodded, and he did seem reluctant. "It will have been taken over by our enemies by now. The Stryxex have been systematically finding and destroying every stronghold or hidden cache belonging to Flame Riders and this particular stronghold belongs to the Flamerarch. They operated an academy of sorts out of

Sarcoda. The Stryxex will have certainly overwhelmed it and taken it by now. We will have to take it back."

Verdaine exchanged looks with her leaders.

"We have vulnerable people to defend. Children. Elderly. We want a place to defend, not a fortress to attack."

"And I want a hot bath and to sleep in a bed tonight," Gundt said with a sigh. "I want my nation back, this battle over and the rest that comes from the other side of conflict. We can wish all we like but it doesn't change the fact that any good fortress is in the hands of someone else and we will have to take it."

"What about the stone creatures?" I signed, speaking the words with my mind, also, so Kazmerev could hear. "There is no place safe from them."

"What stone creatures?" Verdaine asked, her sharp eyes flicking from me to Gundt and back.

He shrugged, looking awkward. "Their salamanders can defend against them Creatures of Sydonon if we find them in our path. They will be equally matched."

One of Verdaine's advisors said something in elven and she nodded, her mouth twisting unhappily.

"Duendaine makes a strong argument for your proposal," she said, "but if our success requires the salamanders, then we require phoenixes to stay near. We can't have you slipping off somewhere while we establish this hold on a fortress."

"We have a country to take back and an enemy to overthrow," Gundt said. "We came to your lands to ask for help, only to find that our enemy was already within."

One of the elves spoke in their language again and Verdaine sighed. "Look around you, Flame Rider. We are refugees swept up in chaos and destruction. Hunted and hounded. We can't help you on your journey. We can hardly help ourselves."

"All the more reason that we must part ways soon," Gundt said grimly. "The ai'sletta ..."

"Wishes to go with them," Mally said smoothly, joining us suddenly. She'd been off to one side whispering to Grevankin and she looked almost settled as if just being near him tempered her. I felt my eyebrows rise.

But don't I do that to you, too? Kazmerev said. *Don't I settle you down?*

This coming from the phoenix who told me he had to keep flying forever and never stay in one place. The phoenix who was upset because I had fallen in love because it might mean establishing a family of some kind. He needn't worry about that now.

I would not have let him fall through the mirror if I could have helped it. I miss him, too.

Go gentle on her, Grevankin advised from his place on the side. *It's hard on a human to lose a mate. Sometimes they don't recover.*

Kazmerev looked back and forth from Grevankin to me and then snapped his fiery beak to Huxabrand's laughter.

I ignored them all, trying to concentrate on what was being said by the elves.

"If the ai'sletta says we will help you, then we will," Gundt was saying. "Let's talk about what we might find."

I didn't need to be there for that. Whatever we found, we'd have to fight it. We'd have to attack Stryxex and see people die again. I just didn't seem to have the heart for any of it anymore.

I slipped off to the spring to wash. I was dusty and dirty, bloody from tending Gundt, and utterly demoralized. I found a stone to sit on close to the spring after I'd drunk and gathered water for washing. Slowly, I set about cleaning myself, stealing glances at elven children as they played, their elders chiding them or feeding them, or settling them. For just a brief time I'd thought that kind of future might be for me. How silly. I was still Sersha. Voiceless. Valueless without Kazmerev. Only Judicus would ever have looked at a girl like me and imagined a future and only because he was so oblivious to practicalities.

I let a single tear slip before dashing it to the side. It wasn't a possible future I missed. It was *him*. I missed his interesting insights. I missed the casual way he had of making the world make sense. I missed his certainty. How he always knew exactly what he needed to do.

I reached into my belt pouch and pulled out the sliver of golden mirror I had salvaged. It was the size of my palm and jagged. Sniffling, I looked into it. He'd disappeared somehow into this thing when it was whole. Had it killed him? And if it hadn't, then where did it take him? And how would I ever get him out when the only magical person I knew was him?

I was going to miss him so much.

A little breath shuddered from me as I gazed into the shard.

I almost dropped it when through the glass, someone looked back.

218

I would have known that slightly-green face anywhere. A hand shoved back long dark hair and his mouth formed an "o" of surprise and then his hands began to flick into signs as a smile lit his face.

My expression must have been shocked, too.

He was still alive! Still alive and in the mirror. I bit my lip, forcing back tears of relief. We still had a chance. Somehow, I still had a chance to free him. As long as he was alive, we had that chance.

"*You have a shard of mirror!*" he said. "*Clever, clever woman!*"

We might only have moments together. I set the shard carefully against a rock, sitting in front of it so he could see my signs.

"*You're alive! How do I get you out?*"

"*I don't know yet,*" he signed quickly, and his smile was growing as our eyes met as if he was somehow happy just to see me. "*This is a weaving I have not seen. There might be notes in Occulus's study.*"

"*Where is that?*" I asked.

He seemed to speak to someone I could not see and then he signed again. "*He has a tower south of Briccatore. If you can reach it, we can look together.*"

"*Are you safe?*" I signed. I wasn't sure how to ask what I really meant – would he die or be lost forever before I ever got to the tower? "*Are you ... in mortal danger? Do you have food? Water?*"

"*I don't know,*" he signed back, and I couldn't tell what was behind him. Everything was glowing gold as if we were just in an endless sunbeam. His face went from green to a bright blush and he glanced to the side before biting his lip and leaning closer and signing, "*But I know I love you. I will find a way back to you. Hold on, Sersha.*" As if I were the one in trouble. "*Don't rush into anything. Listen to your phoenix. Stay safe.*"

"I love you, too," I signed back shyly, and I was surprised to realize that I did.

His eyes lit at that, growing slightly misty as if my confession had touched some new emotion.

My hand reached up and clutched the necklace he'd given me. Mighty though small. That was my love for him. Small, but mighty.

He smiled in a way that felt so certain. So real. *"I have to go. This communication drains my energy. But I think I'll know if you look for me. Watch for me again soon."*

And then the mirror faded until it was only gold.

I hugged it to my chest. My chin felt wobbly. I drew in a shuddering breath.

So, the rope worker has survived, Kazmerev said.

I looked up to see him settle beside me and begin to preen his fiery feathers. From time to time, he looked up at the salamanders on the other side of the spring, glaring at them as if they were living things and not sculptures powered by the souls of the dead. They were eerily motionless as they waited, as if someone had transported a group of statues from a palace to the wilderness in the blink of an eye.

Would Kazmerev agree to help me rescue Judicus now that he'd seen him? Would he understand why it was so important to me? More important than this plan to take a fortress or Mally's plan to take over the world?

I was the one who told you that personal is always more important. Of course, I understand.

Sersha can't abandon us now, Kazmerev, Huxabrand put in. I was surprised to see her flutter over to us. She was usually so close to Gunt that she might as well be a goat on a string. *Our resources are few and she's needed. I thought she said she was loyal to the ai'sletta?*

The ai'sletta has her own phoenix now. Grevankin will guard her, Kazmerev shot back.

It's hard to guard someone with such a prickly skin, I must say. That was Grevankin. He hopped along the ground to us, joining the other phoenixes. He had grown to three-quarters size now which made him as big as the others and smokier than ever.

But he will guard her. And so will Gundt. Kazmerev shifted uncomfortably. *My duty is to my own rider. She needs this. We will find this tower of Occulus and we will find the key to rescue her ropeworker.*

There was a mental sound like a snort and then an actual snort and I looked up to see Mally glaring down at me with her arms crossed over her chest.

"Enough, Sersha, you're bothering the phoenixes," she said. "If I'd known you were ruffling their feathers all this time, I would have said something long before now."

I was doing nothing of the sort.

Kazmerev shot out a burst of annoyed fire, scalding the ground beside Mally and leaving a black streak where the earth had burned.

"Tell him I'm not impressed," Mally said without even flinching. "I've been watching you and I know that Flame Riders can't be hurt by fire so he's just making empty threats."

I shook my head at her. Flame Rider Mally was even harder to bear with than ai'sletta Mally.

"Sersha," she said in her scolding tone. "If you think I will just leave Judicus to die, then you don't know me very well."

I opened my hands wide as if to say, "After everything you've done of course that's what I think."

She shook her head. "I think I've proved lately that I'm taking my job seriously. And I owe Judicus for helping me leave that miserable village we grew up in. Imagine, I could be married already." She shivered dramatically."

You are a Flame Rider now. That's as much commitment as a marriage is. But fear not! I will show you that commitment can be a noble thing! Grevankin interrupted.

Fortunately, he was preening, so he didn't notice when Mally rolled her eyes at me before continuing.

"So. I will help you get to that tower and get whatever magic spell or item or whatever that you need. *And* we'll go rescue Judicus from the depths of hell or wherever it is he's chosen to go. Whatever he signed to you before he was thrown in there had better have been 'There's a treasure buried in my backyard worth a king's ransom' and not 'Oh Sersha, how I love you, let me count the ways,' or I'm going to be mad. And after that, we'll *also* go help his sister wiggle out from being queen – because frankly, I think that should be my job. But we won't do any of that until after we help Gundt take this fortress for the elves. Why, you might ask, does the ai'sletta think we need to do that? Why does she think she should have a say that overrules the almighty Gundt and grand-phoenix-rider Sersha, and three fiery birds that keep looking daggers at me?"

We are not birds, three phoenixes said at once in my mind. I winced from the mental volume.

Mally threw her hands up. "Fine. Not birds. Even though you look *exactly* like birds and fly like birds and caw like birds when you're mad, but not birds. Fine. Back to the point. I saw things, Sersha. In case you don't remember. I saw things in that broken pillar. Things that drove me mad. Things I can't push back and forget, and I plan to act on them. None of you seem to have the backbone to get anything done now that the ropeworker is gone, so it's going to have to be me. So, stop sulking over here about your boy, clean yourself up, and get back to where we're working up a plan, because we need you functional and consenting by dawn."

She strode away, leaving me staring after her. No backbone? No ability to get anything done? Had she not noticed everything I'd done over these past months?

I don't think she notices much, Kazmerev said.

"I notice when a big flame bird preens too much!" Mally called over her shoulder.

I was *not* going to like having her privy to the things in my head.

We shall work on her manners, Grevankin rumbled. *I once had a rider who I frequently had to rescue from taverns in the middle of the night. I found that a quick dunking in a nearby pond did the trick.* He paused before saying in a tone that betrayed he was on the verge of laughter. *No, Blazing Queen, I do not plan to curtail my stories.*

I just stared at Kazmerev until he ducked his head in what looked a great deal like a shrug.

I think we must wait to go after your ropeworker, Little Hawk. But we will be quick as we can.

I just hoped it would prove quick enough.

219

It was decided that Kazmerev and I would scout ahead of the rest. We could fly slightly faster than the salamanders and before we arrived to attack the fortress, we needed information. What were we up against? How many would we be fighting? Were there any weaknesses?

Obviously, Mally could not be risked and she required someone to protect her. Just thinking about leaving her made Gundt straighten his back and frown and made Huxabrand snarly and difficult. We volunteered immediately. Besides, the faster we got them there, the faster we could find this tower to the south and hunt for clues to set Judicus free.

We hadn't seen our pursuers since we fled above ground, but just in case, sleeping was kept to a minimum and we set out immediately after we'd rested. I was hard-pressed not to check the mirror, but I didn't want Judicus wasting what power he had just to give me the joy of the sight of him.

"Don't take any unnecessary risks," Gundt warned as I mounted Kazmerev, still yawning at the short sleep. Mally had put the crown back on so I could leave at noon instead of waiting for nightfall. "Move quickly, take note of what you see, and try not to be noticed."

Because flaming phoenix didn't draw any attention, of course. Not at all.

You know we can be sneaky. Make me invisible! We haven't had a chance to stretch our wings in a while.

We'd only been fleeing enemies for days.

This is different. It isn't fleeing – it's questing!

And then we were up in the sky with the wind streaming through my hair and in minutes the voices of Huxabrand and Grevankin faded away. It was just me and Kazmerev and finally, my mind could run free, my heart could grasp the wind, and I didn't have to pretend I was strong and fine. I could be sad about Judicus and anxious about the future without an internal dialogue to explain myself. But I found I didn't have the strength to be sad right now, only the strength to let the wind howl around me and brush my hair from my face, to let the darkness engulf me, and the ripple of the earth beneath lull me until it was only flight and our spirits drifting out over the land.

I didn't know what we were looking for, but Kazmerev had been there before.

It's a butte of sorts with many caves in the sides where phoenixes can enter like doors in the walls. Like a pigeon cote, I suppose.

I did not point out the bird aspect of that.

It's very defensible. Only one door where non-flying people can enter, and it can be closed off by thick stone doors. There's a well within and food stores. It would make it nearly impossible to siege for most people – but we have three phoenixes and the salamanders, and they have displayed they can climb vertical walls, so this is an option for us.

Even knowing that, I was worried. If this place had been taken by Stryxex there could be a lot of them there and I was in no mood to meet those creatures again.

Be calm. You and I can out-fly them, out-fight them, and out-wit them any day. We'll be fine, Kazmerev said, but I wasn't as confident as him.

We flew for what felt like a day and a night before we paused for a break. Mally must have been wearing the crown because I fell asleep and woke again for only a very short time and yet it still remained dark. I wondered if her constant tweaking of the sun was going to have a poor effect on the earth.

It will be on the harvests. Plants need sun. Or so I hear.

It certainly made it easier to travel with a phoenix. It was around what I would have guessed as noon the next day when a butte rose up in the hill country, far away in my darkened vision.

It was at that moment, that the Stryxex struck.

Three of them whistled down from the sky, talons outstretched and visible only with my enhanced vision in the depths of moonless night.

Kazmerev!

I see them.

We dipped suddenly, swooped hard to the left, and then he flapped vigorously and gained height rapidly, trying to pop up and above them.

The nearest Stryxex flew past so closely that I felt the air of his passing sweep over me and heard his rider curse in a language I didn't know. I caught a single glimpse of a face behind a black leather mask and then he was beneath us, trying to pull out of the dive.

The Hand of the Rat was here.

We were still climbing, and thank goodness for that, because one of the Stryxex behind us managed a flip in the air, and then he was climbing, too, hot on our heels, his absence-of-light wings visible against the black of night. I was so distracted by the loud shouts of his rider that I didn't notice the others until it was too late.

Air and Ashes! Kazmerev gasped, and then we were diving again, falling under the breast of a Stryxex as it screamed and tried to bite us. His beak skimmed my arm – just enough to cut through the fabric and draw blood – those things are sharp! – but not enough to cut me badly. I clamped my teeth down hard on a cry and held on.

My breath was sawing in my lungs, but my faith was in my phoenix. I held my courage tightly.

We raced under them, the butte coming up fast – faster than I'd expected. Kazmerev corkscrewed through the air suddenly, knocking a surprised gasp out of me that would have been a yelp in anyone else, and forcing me to cling to his feathers.

Something fell from one of the caves on the side of the butte. I sucked that breath in, horrified at what looked like a ball of cloth – or a person – falling, falling, falling.

And then the wind caught it and I sighed in relief. Only cloth, flapping in the wind.

Flags. They're flags. Memorize them. I can't look properly.

Memorize them?

A red bird maybe – hard to tell in the darkness – on a white background. Below it, a flag divided diagonally with white on the top and blue, perhaps, below. Below that a field of yellow with a blue dot in the center, or maybe black. Below that, two black flags and then a white flag and then a flag whose color I couldn't discern with a crown on it.

I recited the list again and then one more time.

Just about have it? Kazmerev asked and his voice was tight.

I thought I did.

Good. We need to get out of here.

He spun, diving as he turned and dropping us below another Stryxex. Its claws struck his wing, sending up a gout of flame, and then we fell farther, nearly brushing the ground with the tips of Kazmerev's wings as he fought for speed, wings flapping like great oars sculling through the sea.

Was he hurt?

I am not hurt. Hold on.

I clung to his feathers as we rushed between the trees and high bushes, clinging to the dark land as if it could cover us from the enemy. Maybe it could.

Branches brushed close to my leg and waved behind and before, making me nauseated with their nearness.

How many did you count?

I went back in my mind, thinking of them in the clumps I'd seen. Three at first, then that scattered group of four, the single one later, and that patch of three ...

Maybe twenty that I'd seen. In that short, short moment of time.

That squares with my guess.

What did we do now? It didn't seem like enough information. There could be more of them. There could be a way in we didn't see.

The flags are a message. Chances are Gundt will know what they say, Kazmerev said as we fled. We were zigging and zagging around hills and low bushes, trying to shake the Stryxex chasing us.

I just hoped he was right. If there were twenty outside, I didn't want to guess how many might have been inside that butte and every one we found would be just as bent on our deaths as those ones had been.

You worry too much, Little Hawk. We phoenixes are tough. We will take this fortress, just watch and see.

220

Gundt, it turned out, agreed with Kazmerev.

"Tell us again what you saw," he said when I returned to them. They'd made a more permanent camp to house the children and the vulnerable while the rest of us were gone and divided the force into two.

The elves, it turned out, were masters at making camps out of almost no resources and a few statue-like salamanders. We landed in camp, sat down beside one of the many campfires and I bid Kazmerev goodbye. He was finding it hard to go.

I will not be alive and yet I will worry about you with the Stryxex so near.

She'll be fine. You need to be less like a mother hen about her, Huxabrand had advised with a toss of her head. *Do you see me carrying on about Gundt?*

Gundt is not so precious as my Little Hawk, he'd said and received a sharp peck for his troubles.

Mally had taken the crown off reluctantly when I returned, and the sun was about to come up on the horizon as we settled down around the fire with the elders and Verdaine.

"There were flags," I signed. *"Someone threw them out the window on a rope. And there were at least twenty ... dark birds."*

I didn't have a sign for Stryxex but when Verdaine translated my words, Gundt said, "Stryxex?" and I nodded.

He made a kissing sound out of one side of his mouth, anxious about the numbers.

"Could you see the flags?"

I nodded and Verdaine looked at him quizzically.

"The Flamerarch communicates with flags. Maybe the invaders just threw the flags out at random, but it's also possible that there's a message attached to them. Can you tell us what you saw, Sersha?"

I nodded and signed to Verdaine.

"The first had a red bird on a white background."

Gundt's eyes widened at the translation.

"That's the sign for the Flamerarch," he said. "Could it be possible that they held out? Without anyone realizing? But we can't be the first to check."

"Perhaps these Stryxex drove off anyone else who came looking. How long has your land been overrun?" Verdaine asked.

He shrugged. "A couple of weeks."

"And how long could you hold out in that fortress?"

"Months, if you were well supplied."

"And they are well supplied."

"Yes," he agreed. "What else, Sersha?"

"A flag divided diagonally blue on the bottom, white on the top," Verdaine translated my signs. "Below that, a yellow flag with a dot that might be blue or black. Two black flags. A white flag. A flag with a crown."

"What color was the crown?" he asked.

"She doesn't remember."

"Hmmm," Gundt sounded thoughtful, rubbing his chin. "And the dot, could she make out whether it was blue or black?"

I shook my head no.

"Does it mean something?" one of the elders asked, her long ears flicking like a rabbit's.

"It means they were attacked from the air but held fast. They are in distress, requesting help from the crown. Or it might be telling us not to help them, but that seems unlikely. I wish I knew what color that dot was."

"Why would someone go to all that trouble to tell you *not* to help them?" Another elder asked wryly and Gundt shrugged.

"Perhaps they do not know your kingdom has fallen, your people are scattered and invaders feast on the bones," Verdaine said grimly.

"This is an ill place to have journeyed to," the twitchy elder said.

"We had no choice," Verdaine said, but she couldn't meet the elder's eye. "It was this or be devoured by the stone octopi."

"You don't know that," the elder said. "It looked that way, but the Prince – fool that he was – would not have sacrificed all of our people. Surely, some remain."

"Some. Would that have included us?" another elder asked. "We could not know."

"I don't think the prince was in control," Verdaine said grimly. "His actions led to the death of the Golden Gargantuan. I suspected he had ambitions – but to marry a human?"

There was a rumble of agreement and shaking heads.

From behind them, Mally smirked at me. She thought this whole thing was funny. How you could think the collapse of two nations was funny was a question only she could answer.

Verdaine sighed. "At least, if we take this fortress, this Sarcoda, then we can keep those we did rescue somewhere safe. Somewhere with allies. We can regroup.

We can decide what comes next. It's in a hill, out of the sun – a place like our home."

"What comes next is to take back Calicarn, isn't it?" Mally asked lightly.

No one looked at her and Gundt looked pointedly away.

"Isn't it?" she pressed and then her eyes grew wide as Gundt ran a hand over his head.

"I don't know. Maybe we need to focus on keeping together what we can, ai'sletta. Maybe everything else stops here. It's my solemn oath to protect you but ... none of this has gone as I had hoped. I'm starting to think we should stay with Verdaine and her people. That all of us should start over again."

Mally threw up her hands. "Well, isn't that great! Everyone is deciding for me all over again."

I felt the same way. Silently – of course – I reached into my belt pouch and felt for the shard of mirror. When I found it, I clutched it so hard that I felt pain in my fingers. We'd get him back. We had to.

I clenched my jaw as they kept talking over my head, until I heard Gundt say my name.

"Sersha got close before. She can get there again. This time, she can sneak in and tell them that we're coming and what the signal is so that they can come charging out from hiding while we attack from the outside. It will be hard to attack even with the salamanders – how do you fight birds in the air with ground creatures? So we need everybody we can find."

I signed to him quickly and Verdaine translated. "How will they hear me."

He waved a hand. "We'll send a note."

"And if they have no one to send to help?" she interpreted again, graciously, I thought.

"There will be someone. Someone put that banner out."

I wasn't so sure. I didn't like the light in his eyes or the matching light in Verdaine's. They were both set on this course. And they were both despairing of finding any other way out. You couldn't live like that for long – not and stay yourself. They both had the look of people willing to start doing desperate things and I didn't want to be around when that started.

Maybe sneaking back into that butte guarded by Stryxex would be less dangerous.

I huffed a sigh and nodded. I should probably consult Kazmerev, but I already knew what he'd say. He'd never leave phoenixes in danger if we could help them.

No one noticed when I slipped away, found a place to curl up on a sun-drenched rock, and lay down on my side, slipping out my shard of mirror. There was no face in it this time. It was hard not to worry as I hid it away again and fell into a troubled sleep.

221

I woke to Mally shaking me.

"Gundt says it's time for you to leave," she said rolling her eyes.

The sun had sunk below the horizon and as she spoke, I let Kazmerev bloom in my heard and leap out like a blossoming star. Beside him, Grevankin did the same. He was full-sized now, and utterly enormous. Even bigger than he'd been when Prexav was his rider.

"Listen," Mally said, whispering now, "And if you phoenixes are listening you'd better not rat us out to Huxabrand."

She flung a belligerent look over her shoulder at Grevankin.

"Don't worry about Gundt and all his 'joining the elves and starting a new nation' nonsense."

The thought of us starting a new nation made me nauseated. I sat up and rubbed my eyes hastily, sipping water from a skin Mally thrust toward me.

"Just do this little job for him and when you're done, if he still wants to stay with them, you and I will slip off together and go find this tower. We don't need an old cranky-pants like him anyway."

Surprisingly, her talk put the bounce back into my step. I managed a smile and leaned in to hug her, but she shook me off.

"Ugh, who do you think I am, Sersha? Your ill rope worker? I'm just offering to help you put me on the throne as Grand Hadri, or Queen, or Empress or something. That doesn't require all this ... whatever it is."

But I could tell she was pleased. If there was one thing Mally liked, it was other people knowing how valuable she was.

"Just don't forget that I'm willing to help get you what you want, and I'll be expecting the same from you."

Of course.

With those sage words in my mind, I mounted Kazmerev and we leapt back into the sky.

I think Mally might make a good Flame Rider after all, he said in my mind, stunning me.

Then maybe next time *she* could fly off and do the impossible.

It won't be impossible. I have a plan.

We flew silently until the butte was in sight once more, this time highlighted by natural moonlight.

Now what?

Now, you make me invisible and see if you can do the same for yourself.

What?

You can, if you try hard enough.

I should have been practicing that the whole time if it were possible! Besides, if Flame Riders could do that, why hadn't any of the Flamerarch done it to escape?

It's an old practice. They probably don't know how.

Then how did he know?

I don't. I just thought that since you keep doing the impossible ...

He expected me to do it again?

Well, you've picked up healing and no one thought you'd be able to do that.

I didn't know what to say.

Your mind is your limit. Just try it.

If he'd told me this was the plan, I would have come up with another one.

Why do you think I didn't tell you?

He was already invisible and – cleverly – flying low to the ground where I might be harder to spot. I screwed up my eyes and tried to think of becoming invisible, too. What if it worked and then I couldn't make myself visible again? I would never be able to communicate again.

Calm down.

What if I ...

But there wasn't time for more what-ifs.

A camp opened up suddenly in front of us among the bushes. A camp with no fires. A camp where everyone was masked and hooded.

A scream caught in the back of my throat even as Kazmerev flapped wildly to gain height. There was a shout from the camp and then another and then an arrow whistled close to my face.

I guess it is not working, Kazmerev said tightly.

It definitely wasn't working!

I gripped his feathers tightly in both hands. Should I send fire back at them?

It would be a good idea.

Gritting my teeth, I spread a hand behind us and shot a stream of fire at a Stryxex leaping from his perch close to the ground. It struck him hard in the chest and he let loose a bird-like scream as his rider leapt from his back and both of them tried to roll across the dusty ground to beat the flames out.

There was no time to revel in my victory, another Stryxex loomed in front of me. I shot out a second lance of flame, this time in his direction. He dodged it neatly as his rider raised a spear.

Uh oh. I could tell he was going to throw it before it flew. Then it was our turn to duck and roll and come up searching for enemies again.

We didn't have far to look.

Stryxex rose up on every side, leaping into the air from the ground like bats descending from a cave ceiling, only in reverse. The sound of their wings flapping filled the air.

I think there are more than twenty.

There were so many more than twenty.

I think there are more than fifty.

There were definitely more than that.

I think this might be all the Stryxex there have ever been.

And that sounded just about right.

Kazmerev sped up, his wings a blur as he pushed forward, hard, hard, with every scrap of energy he had. To me, it was a blur of a racing heart, sawing breath, and all the fire I could throw.

I wish you could have been invisible.

I wished for a lot of things. But I was willing to settle for "still alive in an hour."

Right now, the chances of that looked very slim.

Hold on, Sersha, it's about to get rough!

About to get?

He leapt – suddenly – to the side and then we were falling, falling, my heart in my belly, swooping down and then using the momentum to climb right into a wave of Stryxex as Kazmerev spun and wove and corkscrewed, trying to keep sharp beaks and sharper talons away from us while their strange wings – not quite bird wing and not quite bat – scraped and fluttered against us.

I held my breath and then we were on the other side and darting right for the face of the cliff wall. My eyes were frozen open in terror, and then to my shock, at the very last second, the face of the rock shifted, a hole opened, and we plunged through.

We landed hard on the rock on the other side as behind me the sound of rock booming on rock filled the air.

There's the door!

Kazmerev skidded and my grip slipped. My arms windmilled as I tried to catch my balance, but I was too late. I fell from his fiery feathers to the floor in an inglorious lump, shook myself, and then stood. To my utter embarrassment, we were being assessed by a hundred sets of eyes.

"Who are you?" one of them said and my eyes widened as I saw what they were wearing. These were the uniforms of the Flamerarch. And that arrogant voice could only belong to one of them.

By the authority of Luca Lightheart and Reichus Klazmetti she is clawmarked, Kazmerev said mentally.

And I hoped they could hear. I hoped they'd understand. What I'd never even considered hoping for was what they did.

They all fell to one knee.

222

What was this? I was not someone to bow to.

It seems they think you are *someone to whom they must bow.*

I swallowed. There were so many of them. Even as I gaped at them the rest of the corridor filled with people rushing in and joining the kneeling crowd. They all glowed slightly – as if they had phoenixes burning within them.

They do. Kazmerev said in wonder.

But where were they?

Trapped. He sounded horrified. *Trapped within.*

Then how will they hear me? I hadn't been sent with a letter. Hubric had been certain I could speak to any phoenix rider through Kazmerev.

A woman close to the front stood and lifted her face and I had to hold back my gasp from the bright red scars that ran down her cheek – fresh as if they were only a few weeks old. Had she received them while fleeing to this place?

"I am Shasamen Lady of Lowhills, Flamerarch," she said quietly. "We heard echoes that the ai'sletta was coming, bound now to a phoenix."

I shook my head firmly. This was not going well. I needed them mobilized and ready to fly, not mistaking me for Mally.

Bad news. I don't think they'll be flying anywhere. I hear only echoes of their phoenixes, too, as if they are a long way off.

"You are not the ai'sletta?" she looked confused and then she pointed at the medallion around my neck. It had slipped out from my collar. Again. "Everyone knows the sign of Judicus Franzer Irault. That's his medallion. Who else would he give it to but the ai'sletta ... or a sister perhaps, but his sister has been named Grand Hadri. We know her face. She is not you."

Well, they had a strong point there, but there was no telling them that Judicus seemed to do whatever he wanted. He'd given this to me long before I could lay claim to him. Had he known then how many people would recognize it and make note that I wore it? Every time I turned around he seemed to be more well-known than I'd given him credit for. I felt my cheeks blushing and turned to Kazmerev. He seemed – was he pale?

"Whoever you are, if he gave that to you – did he give it to you?"

I nodded and a sigh rippled through those kneeling.

"Then we owe you our allegiance."

How would we tell these people what was happening without Kazmerev's voice? This was all slipping out of control.

I tried to sign to Shasamen but she shook her head. "I don't know Sumerian sign, and if you want to say goodbye to your phoenix you should do it now."

Goodbye? She must be mad.

Kazmerev shifted uncomfortably and Shasamen's face hardened.

"We tried to warn you away with the flags. Did you not understand them?"

I shook my head grimly.

"I think they have us all now – every Flamerarch who remains alive – trapped here in Sarcoda – two hundred of us."

My eyes must have given me away at that. I felt them widen as I met Kazmerev's gaze.

I feel strange. He said and a burst of fear filled my heart. Fear like I hadn't felt since I watched Judicus drop his defense to say goodbye to me. Instinctually, I reached for Kaz, burying my hands in his feathers.

Behind Shasamen, the Flamerarch began to stand.

"They lured us in one by one. It is a safe place – well stocked, defensible. We all had the same idea. Rally here. Regroup where it was safe. Where we could plan and launch a counter-attack on the invaders who were hunting us down and killing us. But they put a thing here – a thing that traps our phoenixes within us and we can neither move it nor smash it to bits. We cannot free our friends and we cannot escape this place without them."

"We hardly wish to," another woman whispered from beside her and when my eyes swept over the crowd they caught on a sad man with a beard.

"Would you leave your phoenix?" he asked me mildly, his eyes deep pools of sorrow.

I shook my head and they all seemed to nod in agreement. No true Flame Rider would abandon their phoenix. It would be like ripping your own heart out.

"So, here we sit," Shasamen said.

"We cannot fight the Stryxex without. We cannot bring our phoenixes back. We don't have the heart to leave them here."

I tilted my head to the side in a question.

Shasamen sighed. "It was a cleverly laid trap. Every Flamerarch who could make it to this place flew here. Either directly, or after finding Stryxex everywhere else. Lone Flame Riders came here, too. We have perhaps another hundred of those with us. They funneled us here. Cut off every other means of escape. Infiltrated every other safe haven before they attacked. We'd heard reports of safe places overrun but we didn't understand why. And then they left the trap here – and once you're in you can't get out again. And now you are here with us."

I looked around her and saw resigned confirmation in every face.

My eyes darted to Kazmerev and to my horror he turned his face to me, and I realized I could barely see him now.

Sersha, he said clearly. *When I have faded, you must flee without me. Do not let me sink you as these others have been sunk. Run on foot. Find Mally and Gundt. Save Huxabrand and Grevankin from this fate.*

No! Kaz, no!

I tried to wrap my arms around him, and they sank through.

I love you! I love you! I was still trying to tell him as he faded to nothing.

Always.

And then he was gone, and I couldn't even sob because two hundred people were staring at me.

223

Sarcoda was massive. They hurried me through throngs of staring, worried-looking people to take me to where the trap had been laid, and even then, it took three flights of carved steps to get to the large room at the top of the cavern system.

"It doesn't matter that you aren't the ai'sletta," Shasamen said as she led me grimly upward. "You're wearing that medallion which means you mean something to the brother of our Grand Hadri. And that means if we can find a way to get you out, you'll know where to find him. Are you Gundt's voiceless Fledgling?" At my nod, she nodded, too. "I thought so. We'd heard rumors of you in the city." She meant Briccatore of course. Mally hadn't exactly helped me keep a low profile there. "If we all had our phoenixes, you could tell us all about it, but the echoes are too hard to hear unless they're all focused on the same thing."

Echoes! I'd almost forgotten she'd said that. I closed my eyes for a moment, focusing, and for just a second I thought I heard the barest *Kazmerev ...Kaz... Kazmerev* as if his name was being echoed by dozens of voices. I tried to hear more but I stumbled and Shasamen had to catch me.

"Don't try to listen while you walk, or you'll fall down the stairs."

"Should we really show her this?" someone from behind Shasamen asked. He peered up and around, standing on tiptoes and the worry in his face gave me little shivers of shared anxiety.

"Why wouldn't we? We need her to get out there to sneak past the enemy and get her friend back here to help us. They say Judicus Franzer Irault is the most powerful ropeworker of his generation. Maybe even stronger than Herowan the Great, and you know he built Zanziverda with his ropework. It was nothing but a small desert oasis and he transformed it into the most mighty city of the Salt Age in a single decade."

He did?

"She won't leave. She'll feel the pull like all of us."

Shasamen muttered under her breath, but she didn't correct them. Maybe she thought it was unlikely, too, but any dock will do when a squall has your boat. I knew – without knowing how – that the man behind us was right. I couldn't leave Kazmerev here anymore than I could leave my own body and fly without it to another place. If he was stuck here, then I was stuck here with him.

No wonder so many people were kettled up in this place. What were the Stryxex waiting for? They could charge in here and kill them all in a moment.

Unless that was the point. This place was a magnet for every single person who might want to go against their reign from the sky. Anyone who wanted phoenixes to fight back would come here eventually looking for the missing Flamerarch, or even just a hiding place. Anyone who knew about this place would want to bring civilians here to shelter, or armies here to prepare. And if the Stryxex had it bottled up then it functioned just like a prison – but a prison that attracted more and more prisoners without any effort from the guards.

I swallowed down a sick feeling and reached into my belt pouch to feel the edge of the mirror. It was still there. I wasn't alone.

I knew what we were going to see before we cleared the last steps and caught a glimpse of it. I knew by the molten-honey glow. But I still had to see it with my eyes.

We emerged from the stairs into a room at the very top of the cave structure and in that room, a transparent pillar stretched from floor to ceiling. There was a rim around both top and bottom etched with engravings that looked an awful lot like the knot Judicus untied on the pillar – or would have if I'd been able to look directly at them. Just like those knots, they turned my gaze aside so that I could not form the pattern clearly in my mind.

Behind them, in the pillar, golden phoenix souls screamed in what looked like eternal flames and for just a moment, I thought I saw Kazmerev. I stumbled forward without meaning to and someone caught me.

"Don't touch it," the rough voice warned – the man from before. "If you touch it, you'll go in, too. And your body will die here without a soul to animate it. I've buried five Flame Riders like that so far. All of them doubted my words. All of them thought they could snatch back their phoenixes from the grave – and all of them were wrong."

I clenched my jaw hard against a cry of frustration, or a moan of despair, or tears, or whatever it was that was trying to claw up my throat and make a sound. I dared not let it sweep over me. All problems had solutions. All but death. And this wasn't death, so there was a solution. I just had to figure out what it was.

"You look at it like it's a mystery to be solved," Shasamen said. "Trust me, it's not. It's a deadly warning. And it needs a rope worker to fix it."

She took me by the shoulders and turned me to look at her face – middle-aged, worn, drawn with worry, and deeply scarred.

"Will you do this for us? Will you tell Judicus Franzer Irault of this?"

I nodded. I certainly would. He would need to know why he was now doomed, too. If I couldn't get out of here, then he couldn't get out of the mirror shard.

"Do you know where he is?" she pressed.

How to answer that? I tried a bobbing head shake as if to say that I was not certain.

"But you'll try to get to him?"

That was easy to nod to. It was the only thing I wanted in the world right now. To bring him to me or to go to him. Well, not the only thing. I wanted Kaz free, too. I *needed* both those things.

"And will you do it soon?" she asked me.

I nodded, but despite their worried expressions, I sat on the stone floor studying the pillar. Judicus would need every detail I could give him.

"Is she just going to sit there? She needs to run through the ground door and go for help!" a younger voice demanded.

"At least wait for the Stryxex to calm down," someone else hissed. "They'll have seen her go in and expect her to come out right away. If you push her, they'll snatch her off her feet the moment she clears the door."

Ah. A voice of reason. How nice.

"Well? Is she just going to sit there?" the younger voice prodded.

I didn't know how many of them had followed me up the steps. They all couldn't have, but it seemed that plenty enough of them had. I ignored them and focused on the pillar. I needed them to leave. I needed to do this without them watching.

"Let her be," Shasamen said after giving me a long, hard look. "She'll go when she's ready. Let her make her peace with it." She laid a hand on my shoulder and then smiled when I startled. "Take your time. When you're ready, there's food and water below. We'll feed you before we send you off again."

I nodded, but my eyes were on the pillar. I didn't care that they were all staring at me like their great hope. I couldn't do anything about that. I didn't care that they seemed worn and thin – well, I did care, but I couldn't worry about that either.

I could only worry about one thing at a time and the thing I was worried about was Kazmerev. I'd flown him right into a trap and now I'd better get him out or I'd break his trust and lose him forever.

224

I waited until the last footstep echoed down the steps and then I waited some more until I couldn't hear breathing anymore and someone got bored and slipped away. And then I looked all around, and snuck to the edge of the stair, and looked over the edge, and when I was absolutely sure no one was watching, I drew the mirror shard from my belt pouch and peered into it.

There was nothing but gold mirror for long moments and then to my utter relief, Judicus appeared.

He scrambled up from where he seemed to be sleeping back to back with someone who was coughing.

"Sersha!" his smile was slowed by a long sigh of relief. "You're still alive."

His smile was twisted, and he ran a hand through his hair like he was worried.

I nodded and hurried to prop the mirror against a wall so I could speak with my hands. The moment I set it in place, he hissed.

"What is that?"

The pillar was right behind me, and he could see it in the mirror shard, I realized.

"It sucked Kazmerev right in," I said, biting my lip.

"Are you in Occulus's Tower?"

I shook my head miserably.

"It's fine, don't cry." I hadn't realized I was crying. He held up a calming hand. "It's fine. We can hold on here." He glanced over his shoulder and lowered his voice. "I think you'd better tell me everything."

Quickly, I sketched out what had happened – being chased and the elves promising to help retake Briccatore and free his sister but only if we found a safe place for their people. Gundt insisting on Sarcoda. The flags – which we clearly misread. Mally's promise to go with me to Occulus's tower the moment we secured

Sarcoda. The Stryxex gathered outside, and then me arriving and Kazmerev being stripped away.

He nodded along, not interrupting. He'd always been a good listener even though I didn't speak with sound.

"We need to get Kazmerev and the others free," he agreed when I finished. "Once that happens, you can destroy the Stryxex, save my sister, and free me from this mirror."

I huffed a silent laugh. If only it were so simple.

Judicus was looking off into the distance, twisting his mouth up the way he did when he solved a puzzle.

"First things first," he said. "I think I know what I did wrong last time when I untied the knot. I've been reading the books again."

He pulled out the book of prophesy we'd had all along and then the other one that showed how we'd been duped and how our enemies believed the prophecies meant something else entirely. I'd forgotten he was holding onto those before we reached the elven city. He must have tucked them into a boot or belt.

"I think if instead of untying it," he said, tapping his chin with a single finger, "I could modify it just a little, then I could open the flask without spilling it everywhere. No, I see your doubt, but that wouldn't just send the soul out loose to inhabit anything and it wouldn't transform them into Stryxex like the Hand of the Rat does – or did, before their pillar broke. Do you think I let all those souls loose into the Creatures of Sydonon when I broke the other pillar?"

I nodded.

"So do I." He looked embarrassed. "But I think that our enemies must have set this new one up here before they attacked the city. How long do you think that would take? Do you think they did it months before they ever took Briccatore?"

I shrugged.

"You should find out," he said, his eyes meeting mine, and then they seemed to catch for a second and he stopped talking and sucked in a breath before flushing and huffing a laugh. "No. No time for distractions. We need to do this now before we lose this connection, and you lose my help. Are you ... do you think you can focus?"

I nodded briskly.

"Fine. Yes. Good. I can too. I'm pretty sure."

The sideways look he shot at me made my cheeks fire hotter than ever. He was distracted by *me*? Now, I was the one who couldn't focus.

"There's a thing that can be done." He looked guiltily over his shoulder like someone might be listening. "You're not supposed to do it. No one is. But it *can* be. And frankly, a Flame Rider is going to be more susceptible because you're used to someone inhabiting your mind space, so you could let another person in if you have to."

I tilted my head in question.

"Yes," he said gravely. "I should get to the point. Sersha, would you be willing to let me try to practice ropework using your brain and body as a conduit? Bearing in mind that it might either free Kazmerev, or lead to his death, the deaths of hundreds of phoenixes, and likely yours and mine as well?"

What a very Judicus question.

225

If there was one person in this world – other than Kazmerev – who I trusted, it was Judicus.

"I trust you," I signed to him. *"And whatever happens, I will not be sorry that we try."*

He was nodding, his mouth screwed up in concentration.

"Leave the mirror where it is but back up just a little and to your left," he said, his mind clearly on the task now. "I need to see both the pillar and you. One moment."

He reached for something and came back with his stolen book, looking from the pillar to the text as if trying to check something.

I waited patiently and after a few long minutes his eyes caught on mine, and he seemed to shake back into awareness.

"Oh, my apologies. I was caught up in the problem and I forgot to keep talking to you about it."

I offered him a patient smile. It was more important that he do this right than that he tell me how.

"I believe I'm ready to make the attempt," he said, putting down the book and visibly drawing himself up as if he were about to do some sort of physical work. "There are three things we are doing – first, I'm going to try to slip into your mind from across an unfathomable distance. I have read texts on how to accomplish this, but I have never tried it as it is considered so horrifically offensive to every culture that has ever discovered it to be possible, that each one has its own terrible punishment prescribed."

"What is ours?" I signed.

He waved a hand as if swatting a fly. "Better not to say. It's the perpetrator who suffers it, not the one used to channel consciousness. Just ... perhaps it would be best if you told no one?"

I nodded adamantly and was rewarded with a ghost of a smile. He must have been as nervous as I was.

"The next thing I must do is try to grasp the threads of the universe through you and weave them into ropes. This requires knowledge – which I have – but also a natural mental affinity. We won't know how much you have until we get there. The level of affinity you're born with will determine what we can accomplish. It's like balance. Everyone has a little. But you want to have quite good balance if you plan to walk a ridgepole."

"So, if my affinity isn't good, then we can't do this?" I signed, and my heart was racing.

We couldn't afford to see me fail at this. Absolutely everything depended on getting the phoenixes free – the lives of my friends outside, my ability to find a way to free Judicus, our chance to chase the Stryxex and Hand of the Rats from our home, and the hope of overthrowing the conspiracy that had destroyed the elven kingdom and all of Briccatore.

"I think," Judicus said carefully, "that we shall try it regardless. But it will be ... more difficult and much riskier if you have little affinity for this." He bit his lip. "I will be marching you to your death. I ... should I not be doing this?"

I shook my head and signed quickly. *"You must do it."*

He sighed. "That's what I was afraid of."

And then for a moment, he paused to smile at me, as if the smile were a hug and could impart his strength to me.

Then he said, "At least the third part should be simpler. I've had more time to think than I prefer – which is saying something since if I had my way, I would spend my days drifting away on tangled thoughts – but I've had a lot of time to think, and I believe I have worked out what I did wrong last time. I think I can fix it ... so that is the easy part."

He'd thought it was simple then, too. I tried not to let that worry show on my face.

He shook himself, as if we were aware he was drifting again, gave me one last smile, and asked, "Ready?"

I nodded.

"You can face the mirror or the pillar. Your choice," he said. "I'm working through here, and though I'll be in your head, I won't see from your eyes so you can look at what you want."

In that case, I would look at him. I wouldn't know what I was looking at if I stared at the slippery knots of the pillar, and I wouldn't want to search the screaming souls within for Kazmerev. Better to keep my eyes focused on my beloved.

I smiled serenely.

"It might help at first if you closed your eyes," Judicus said. "But you can open them whenever you want to. Just try to stay still. This part is going to be challenging."

And then his eyes shut, and his face screwed up in concentration, and he started to hum, his tone and pitch changing very slightly from moment to moment. I wasn't sure why he was humming, but I wouldn't have been able to ask even if I had known, so I sat calmly and did what I did best – waiting silently while someone else was busy. I had a whole lifetime of getting good at that.

The minutes stretched until I was almost sleepy from the humming. Not almost. I was sleepy.

I was drifting. My eyes went unfocused and drifted shut.

And then, like a kiss that wakes a princess, I felt a flutter in my mind. My cheeks went hot. And I didn't even know why because I'd invited him in and what could he really experience from there anyway ... right? But it felt ... it felt intimate. Like maybe he could read my thoughts.

Just a little.

Oh. My. No. My eyes flew open again.

You did say it was fine.

Oh. Oh. Oh.

I blinked and forced myself to look through my eyes instead of within and I could see him looking back at me through the mirror, pale and worried, his forehead wrinkled with doubt. Warmth welled up in my chest and I nodded. I did agree to do this. I did give him permission to do it.

It worked! I can hardly believe it.

It had indeed and he was in my brain, reading my thoughts. I focused on him in the mirror instead of that. On his noble, concentrating expression.

But now *his* cheeks were on fire.

Don't look at me like that.

Like what?

Like you love me. Like I'm ... not me. I don't look like me *in your mind.*

Well, how did he look, then? My cheeks were hot, too.

He visibly swallowed in the mirror. *Like ... don't make me say it.*

I thought that perhaps he'd better say it, or we were both going to catch on fire and burn to a crisp.

His eyes went wide and then they focused and his mouth screwed up like he was gathering his courage and he said, *Like a hero.*

I breathed out a sigh of relief. Oh. That. Well, he was a hero, so that was fine, then.

It's not fine! I'm not a hero!

You want to save the world, I reminded him, practically.

That doesn't make me a hero!

Well. Did he really think I'd agree to marry a man who wasn't? Not that I'd agreed exactly. But he'd assumed and I'd been fine with that.

His mouth fell open.

I assumed? I ... oh, no. His lips formed that with his thoughts. *Oh no. I was supposed to ask. Didn't I ask?*

Could my cheeks get any hotter? Seriously. He didn't need to ask. He just needed to make sure he lived to do it.

He was nodding as his thoughts came through. *Yes. Yes, of course. And to do that we both need to stay on track. Maybe – possibly – do you think you could possibly look at the pillar? I'm finding it so very hard to focus when you're looking at me.*

I did something almost Mally-like. I gathered all my courage and winked at him and before I could die of embarrassment, I spun around and looked at the pillar.

I heard him clearing his throat awkwardly and when he spoke in my mind again, he sounded slightly strangled.

Well, it seems you actually do have quite a bit of latent potential, so that is good. I should be able to access it. Had you been born to wealth and power in Briccatore, they would have trained you up and you would have been quite a formidable ropeworker.

Me?

Yes. Erm. Could you possibly raise your hands, palms facing forward? I could do it for you but that feels like a violation.

I raised my palms.

Excellent. Ready, then?

As ready as I'd ever be.

And then he was silent in my mind, and I bit down hard on my lip and tried not to let my eyes grow too wide as black ropes shot out from my palms and fell to the ground, growing, thickening, tangling as they branched out, writhing toward the pillar.

His work was so quick that I could barely follow where the ropes narrowed and stretched, three of them shifting at once. They fell upon the knots before me like a woman picking out stitching and as one ribbon of the knots was loosed, the echo of the phoenix voices grew louder.

I could almost hear Kazmerev in their masses as Judicus picked apart the knot. I could almost pick out his scream of raging agony. It shuddered through me like an earthquake, unsettling every shred of me until I wasn't sure I was even sitting on solid ground. They grew louder and louder and I heard footsteps on the stairs joining them.

I risked a look over my shoulder at Judicus. His face was slick with sweat and his eyes narrowed in focus.

Eyes ahead, he reminded me, and I snapped my gaze forward, just as he forced the knots in the pillar into a new design, his ropework pouring through my hands seeming to bulge and strain against the waving ends of half-loosened knots.

I was gulping in breaths as if I'd run all the way here from Briccatore. My heart pounded in my chest to match the feet on the stone steps. My mouth was dry, arms were screaming, eyelids heavy, as if I were the one wrestling these ropes instead of just sitting here while he did the work.

"Your friends have arrived on golden salamanders and the Stryxex are tearing them to pieces! Come quickly!" a young male Flamerarch said as he climbed the last steps. He paused at the top and it was only then, with him here, that I saw how bright the pillar had become. I couldn't even look at its bright flare. Neither could this man. He threw an arm over his face with a gasp and then scrambled to draw his sword. "What is this?"

Judicus forced something else and then the phoenix screams became so earsplitting that I couldn't tell if the Flamerarch man in front of me was screaming, too, except his mouth was open. I didn't realize he was raising a weapon to crash down on me until Shasamen leapt into the room from behind him and caught his arm.

And then the world went silent with a sound like a *pop* and the pillar wasn't glowing anymore. The ropes that had extended from my hands fell to the ground, disappearing before they touched the earth, and in my mind, there was no more Judicus. Instead, all I heard echoed over and over and over were the same words.

Flame to flame, I greet you, ancient fire!

And there was Kazmerev right in front of me spitting out the words as fast as he could. And here was a small smoky phoenix with little hints of blue in his flame and a red crackling one with a missing eye and their voices rushed one over the other as they tried to say the words before someone attacked.

Flame to flame, I greet you, ancient fire!

I turned around, snatched up the shard of mirror – empty now – and carefully wrapped it in my handkerchief before putting it back in my belt pouch.

I hadn't even gotten to say goodbye. Had it been too much for him? Or was he only resting after such a great feat? And what would he think now that he'd been in my mind?

"You've saved us!" Shasamen gasped as the phoenixes continued their formalities. "Saved us."

She grabbed me by the arm and pulled me up, but all I could think about was Judicus in my mind, Judicus saving everything with his magic, Judicus gone all over again. The world wouldn't be whole until he was back in it.

226

Sersha, Kazmerev said in my mind the moment Shasamen let my shoulder go. *Sersha, we must fly.*

Kazmerev. Relief filled me as I reached for him, wrapping my arms around his fiery neck, and pulling his head down so I could rest my forehead against it. His flames licked at me, unable to touch me, but still greeting me in their own way.

He was safe. He was well. I felt no echoes of the agony he'd experienced in the pillar. He shivered, though.

For how many years was I contained?

Years? Not even an hour, I didn't think. Well, maybe an hour.

So small a time. He sounded shocked, almost haunted. *So small.*

I patted him awkwardly, not sure what to say or how to say it.

He shook himself, spitting sparks and little flickers of smoke.

I must not let it drag me back into its depths.

There were phoenix voices all around us. I could barely hear him over the babble, but what I heard most clearly was the undertone of shock and grief in their voices – fury in some – frustration and misery, too. All of a sudden, Kazmerev stiffened. His head went up and my embrace broke as he shook out his flaming feathers.

We must fly. Now.

I leapt on his back without asking how we'd do that in this tiny room. He barely fit inside it with the other phoenixes there embracing their riders. But I didn't need to know. I trusted him. I leaned forward over his back and he plunged forward.

Hold on tight. It will be hard to squeeze through.

And then my face was pressed into his feathers, and I felt my back and shoulders prodded and pushed and heard annoyed voices in my mind as we squeezed between flaming phoenixes. When I opened my eyes, cheek still pressed against Kazmerev, all I saw was a blur of bright flames and the occasional snatch of a human face or figure.

Can you hear her?

Her, who? I could hear a thousand hers, it seemed. Though Shasamen had said there were hundreds, not thousands.

Mally. I hear her – or at least I hear Grevankin. Close. And in pain.

I renewed my grasp on his feathers as fear gripped my heart. Oh no. We needed Mally! We needed her to stay alive. And more than that, she was a friend.

Kazmerev squeezed through one last knot of phoenixes and I felt someone's elbow catch my head and someone else's shoulder knock the breath out of me, and then we rebreaking free from the cavern and out into the open air and I could breathe again.

Night washed around us in thick darkness. Kazmerev took advantage of the cover and plunged high into the air.

We needed to go back and get Shasamen to organize an attack. We needed to band together and hit the Stryxex strategically. We needed some groups to flank the mass of them while others took them head-on and still others defended our ground allies. We didn't dare go off on our own right now.

Yes, we do dare!

We were just one phoenix and one girl!

You forget, the Flamerarch are Flame Riders of war. They are highly coordinated. They have heard from me – and are still hearing from me – that the ai'sletta is out there in danger. They will coordinate faster without us than with us. They will arrange themselves in ranks and divisions and it will take only minutes to achieve what could take us an hour. They'll issue orders to the independent phoenixes present and they will be heard. What they need from us is a direction. We're familiar with Mally and Grevankin. We can give them that.

Oh.

Hold on tight.

And then we were plunging down through curiously empty air. I did not see a Stryxex anywhere. Were they so convinced of their safety with us trapped in the cave system?

It would seem so.

But I couldn't hear Grevankin. Or Huxabrand.

Their voices are faint.

We rushed over the landscape, Kazmerev's wings flapping urgently. We flowed over it and up a small hillock and on the other side, my gasp was ripped from my lungs.

The bushes here were on fire, the smoke melting into the black sky, the flames carving swathes into my vision. Right in front of us, a golden salamander rose on hind legs, the small elven figures on his back brandishing weapons, and then a Stryxex fell from the sky, talons stretched out. It ripped an elf from the salamander's back, tossing the poor person to the ground, and then plunging further to grab the salamander by the neck and shake it.

Kazmerev shuddered as if it were happening to him. I'd never felt him like that before.

The memories. Claws in my flesh. Flame burning me right to the core ... they're hard to shake.

And then I could hear Grevankin's voice.

Can't hold out for long, Kazmerev. He gasped in our minds. *Need your help. Fast as you can. Please. She's giving out on me.*

Mally? Giving out? How bad was this predicament? Mally never gave out.

We all give out eventually. I ached at the hollowness of Kazmerev's voice. But there was nothing I could do to help him right now. I agreed with him. It would take death for Mally to give up on anything. If she was giving out now, then we had to get to her immediately.

Kazmerev was silent as we plunged forward. I brought up my hand and willed a blast of fire into the Stryxex trying to tear the salamander to bits. It crumpled under the heat of my flames, thrashing, dying ... giving out.

But Mally couldn't be dying. She couldn't be. Right?

Why was Kazmerev so quiet? My heart tumbled in my chest.

A knot of Stryxex surrounded another salamander, diving and ripping as the elves on the salamander's back fought valiantly with blade and bow.

An arrow struck one of the Stryxex riders, followed by three more. He toppled from the back of his Stryxex. It flew wide as if avoiding its fallen rider – something a phoenix would never do – and Kazmerev seized it in his jaws, snapping its neck and tossing it to the ground while I harnessed his fire and blasted a second Stryxex right in the chest. It crumpled, its rider leaping to the ground just in time to be swallowed whole by a golden salamander.

An arrow shot past me, and I gasped. I hadn't even seen where it came from. Below, one of our elven allies crumpled as an arrow struck her in the throat. I spun in my seat and found the Stryxex rider with the short bow who had let the shot loose. I sent a stream of flame toward him, but he wasn't the only one shooting from the sky. Arrows sliced through the air from every direction, it seemed, but all from above.

And then it was a blur of action – flinging balls of flame, avoiding grasping claws and the weapons of Stryxex riders. Kazmerev arched sinuously around one attacker so he could snatch another, biting it behind the neck while I seared its rider with flame. I didn't like the feeling of doing that, but as the Stryxex collapsed, two elven warriors dropped from its talons, landing neatly on the earth, and rolling to the side before the corrupted creature collapsed. It was war. And if I did not fight, our people would die.

Hurry!

Grevankin's voice was a wail.

Kazmerev beat his wings, but we were low – his belly nearly grazing the ground – and I couldn't see where to go. All around us, Stryxex tore into elves on salamanders. Silhouettes of battle were picked out in the light of my phoenix, or the light of the moon, as inky darkness reigned around us. I fought down panicked breaths. There was no time to be afraid.

Don't panic. I see them now. Do you see their light?

And there they were! Huxabrand and Grevankin hovering back-to-back. Gundt sent off a rapid succession of fiery darts at Stryxex after Stryxex as they rushed toward him. Mally slumped over Grevankin's back. Gundt's hand was on her shoulder, propping her up as he fought.

But as I watched, she collapsed onto him, and he caught her.

Oh, n –

We all hit the ground at once. The breath knocked hard out of my body. The world spun. I didn't think I was hurt. I couldn't tell.

Light blinded me – bright, flaring morning light. Or afternoon light, perhaps. I was too rattled to remember what time it was supposed to be.

A golden leg – large as a thick tree – set down right beside my head, gleaming painfully in the sunlight, and something pulled me to my feet. I looked up into the gritted teeth of Verdaine.

I blinked hard, trying to force aside the black patches in my vision from the blinding sun but they wouldn't be dislodged. Verdaine's black eyes were screwed up tight, too.

I would have said thank you, but my hands were shaking too hard. Instead, I nodded sharply to her – not even sure she could see the nod, and shook off her hand. She let me go but her eyes were still tightly closed. I hoped she wouldn't be the only one.

Gasping, heart aching with the pain of how fast it was pounding, I sprinted around her salamander, narrowly avoiding its swiping tail.

I needed to get to Mally.

They were forming a rough ring around her, salamanders stuck in place where they had frozen and elves calling to each other over the chaos, their eyes squinting nearly shut. But there would be no relief from phoenixes – not unless darkness could be restored. I could only hope that they had been close to the ground or still organizing when Mally fell.

I shoved my way between two salamanders, stone still and cold to the touch and vaulted over a tail to where Gundt sat, huffing from exertion, his arms around Mally, and a stunned look in his eyes.

The moment his gaze met mine, relief flooded through them. I didn't stop to try to talk. I wrenched the crown from my cousin's brow and jammed it over mine, only breathing a sigh of relief when darkness flooded over the earth again and Kazmerev flared brightly.

I blinked hard, even more blind now that it was night again, white lights behind my eyelids dazzling me. I needed to check Mally. But I couldn't see.

Gundt fell to the take the brunt of it for her, Huxabrand was saying to Kazmerev. *But we need to get her on one of our backs. I see the Stryxex regrouping.*

Gundt was still sitting there, his face confused as if he'd forgotten something. I gripped his shoulder and drew him up to standing and he let me.

Could we get Mally onto Kazmerev's back?

I'll get low.

It worried me that Gundt hadn't said anything yet.

Worried me that he wasn't objecting as I took the weight of my cousin against me instead and guided him to help me ease her onto Kazmerev.

Gundt? Huxabrand asked. But I was busy settling Mally, checking her for wounds. I didn't see anything. No arrow. No sword slash.

There's an arrow, Huxabrand said tightly. *Look closer.*

She was right. There it was. In her side. Snapped off. I could heal that.

Not right now! Kazmerev warned. *It will drain you dry, and you need me here. Need your fire here.*

I turned to see if Gundt had any advice just in time to see his eyes go glassy and see him slump. I tried to catch him, stumbling under his weight, and falling to the ground hard.

Huxabrand popped out of sight like a snuffed candle.

My eyes met Kazmerev's as we shared a thought.

Oh no.

227

"Form a ring!" I heard Verdaine shouting from somewhere nearby. And then her words changed to elven and I lost their meaning, though the tone was the same. Orders being barked. Elves asking terse questions in voices close to panic. The sound of gold scraping rock and sand as they repositioned. I had time for none of it.

I couldn't move Gundt onto Kazmerev's back. He was too heavy for me. But I could check him. An arrow protruded from his back. My hands trembled as I felt it there. Don't jar him, Sersha!

I eased him carefully to the ground and slid out from under him. I couldn't do anything else. And here we were back at the beginning again – Gundt hurt. Me without the resources to heal him when he needed me.

There was a sound like a bird scream from above me. Instinctively, I stood over Gundt, raised my hand above me, and was firing a column of flame upward before I had even looked. The Stryxex diving down toward me lit up like a flame and fell. I didn't have time to think. I threw myself over Gundt, trying to cushion the blow as the heavy creature collapsed on us in a fiery wreck.

Sersha! Kazmerev said and then everything went dark.

I hadn't lost consciousness. I could feel the rib-crushing agony of weight on me.

Hold on. I'm right here.

Could feel a tugging of some kind.

Could feel Gundt under me – still there but alive? I didn't know. He was warm. Everything was warm.

Because it's all on fire.

But Gundt and I would be protected from the flames as all Flame Riders were.

The elves are not so inflammable.

Keep them back! I urged. We didn't need more dead.

I'm trying. Hold on. I'll shift him.

The sounds above me were too muffled to hear but I felt a tug and then gasped my relief as air filled my lungs. My hand went to my crown, keeping it pinned on so that the night would not escape, and I wouldn't lose Kazmerev.

Almost there.

And then I could move fully. I pushed myself up to all fours, gasping, trying to catch a full breath, my arms wobbling under my weight. I was shaky as a newborn foal.

Strangely, I wasn't afraid. I was too bone-weary, too worried for everyone around me, to be afraid.

Hand up!

I reached a hand up just in time. Screams filled the air around me and Kazmerev was ripping a Stryxex rider from the back of his creature and flinging him aside, only to turn to another while I tossed a ball of fire at the twisted darkness that was the Stryxex. The creature screamed and fell.

Shouts surrounded me as I struggled to my feet.

Were there more? I couldn't leave Gundt.

You might have to. We're being overrun.

And we were. I spun but there were enemies in every direction, elves falling under their vicious talons and merciless swords.

Not far from me Verdaine fell to one knee, blood leaking from the corner of her mouth. Her sword met a Stryxex Rider's blade with a clang. I flung a fireball at a second Stryxex lunging for her.

We should have waited. We should have planned better.

Mount up! Kazmerev sounded tense.

But Gundt …

We have the ai'sletta. He'd want her safe.

I couldn't do it. I'd left too many people. I couldn't leave one more.

I could feel his frustration, but he didn't say anything to me he just called into the mental space we shared.

TO ME! TO ME!

It was like his mind wove a rope to mine and without thinking, my legs were moving. I abandoned Gundt, leapt around the burning remains of Stryxex, and climbed onto Kazmerev's back behind Mally.

Tears of guilt blurred my eyes as I caught a last look of Gundt lying there in the dirt. I was leaving him. And his death would be my fault.

Nonsense.

What? He sounded so calm. No one had the right to sound that calm right now.

Don't be silly.

Silly? Verdaine fell backward, the elf beside her flung in the opposite direction by an eye-turning Stryxex. The scream caught in his throat as Kazmerev bunched up about to launch into the air.

There was nothing silly about any of this!

And then, just as I was about to tell him what I thought of that, bright flame filled the air and hidden phoenixes revealed themselves.

It was as if dawn had come – but the dawn of rising hearts. They fell from the sky like flowers raining from trees in the springtime, bright and lovely. And as they fell, our enemies melted to nothing but shadows and the dead.

My mouth was still hanging open when Shasamen dropped down beside me on her smoky phoenix with the dancing blue flames.

"Is that Gundt Hellebrand?" she asked briskly. "He needs a healer."

I nodded, utterly stunned.

Why do you think I called them? I said, 'To me.'

I'd thought he was calling me.

Little Hawk – much as I worry for you, I would never force you to act against your will. You've forgotten that our friendship doesn't work that way.

I felt my cheeks flare hot at that. He was right. I *had* forgotten.

And you've forgotten something else.

What was that?

Weren't you going to heal some people who might die without your help?

My hand flew to my mouth and my eyes flew to Mally. This was no time for embarrassment or wonder. He was right. It was the time to heal.

228

Mally was first, of course. I stumbled to where she was braced on Kazmerev's back and I didn't look to where the clashes and roars of flame still gouted all around us, instead, I placed my hands on her. The arrow was right in her torso – the liver, I thought. A killing shot, though it would take a long time to die of it.

I clenched my teeth and broke the arrow fletching off and then pulled it through the wound. Blood spurted out immediately and I didn't hesitate, I put both hands on her, closed my eyes, and brought all my strength and warmth to bear. Heat flared through me, snatching away the last shreds of my energy and leaving me gasping and clinging to Kazmerev. I felt his head curve around to clutch me close, to keep me from stumbling or falling.

I blinked my eyes open and came face to face with a surprised Mally.

"Oh," she said. "So, you aren't dead then."

I shook my head.

Streaking up from her heart came a bright, smoky pillar and then Grevankin was there crowding in.

Mally! Are you badly hurt? Speak to me.

He sounded like a worried mother with only one babe.

Mally rolled her eyes. "If I were dead, you wouldn't be here, so I think the answer is obvious. Would you get off me Sersha? You look like you're trying to kiss me and well ... your breath isn't what it could be and that's me saying it nicely."

Blushing, I backed up, swaying the moment I moved. My head rattled like a pot with a pebble in it.

Gundt. I needed to heal Gundt next.

Not a chance. You can barely stand as it is.

He could barely live as it was. He needed help.

I stumbled to where he lay, just beside the flaming heap of Stryxex. The edges of his clothing were scorched and the arrow in his back had leaked so much blood.

Fear shot through me, cold and hard. He was in worse shape than I thought, despite what I said. I thought he'd be like Mally.

Doubt chewed at my edges. What if I didn't have the strength to heal him after healing Mally? After throwing all that fire.

You absolutely don't have the strength.

Behind me, I heard Shasamen introducing herself to Mally.

"What does that matter to me?" Mally asked scornfully. "Go be an amazing Captain of the Flamerarch somewhere else. We're a bit busy here, if you didn't notice."

I couldn't spare a glance up. I was teetering. I fell to my knees beside Gundt, kicking up ash and dust. I didn't even have the energy to look up when I heard Mally exclaim.

"Oh, for pity's sake, would you get up? Stop kneeling! There's work to do. Wounded to patch up. Fleeing Stryxex to chase down and murder. None of that can be done on your knees."

You're going to kill yourself trying to do this.

Trying to do what? Grevankin was there suddenly, his huge wings curving to shelter me from one side while Kazmerev sheltered me from the other side. Shouldn't he be with Mally?

This is her moment. She should enjoy it. It's not every day a hundred Flamerarch kneel to you, and she does enjoy the attention. You do, don't snap at me. I'm helping Sersha."

If only he could help me. I put a hand on Gundt's chest. His heartbeat. Where was it?

Panicked, I put my fingers in front of his mouth and felt a tiny exhalation. Still breathing, then. Finger to his neck – a pulse. Okay. He was alive, but both his heart and lungs seemed weak, and my own vision kept blacking out.

I tucked my head down and tried to catch my breath. An arrow in the back. Two others in the side. The one in the back was the worst. It was through a lung at least – maybe even knicking the heart. He wouldn't survive being moved with that. I had to take that out and deal with it. I didn't dare not try – even if I passed out doing it.

Yes, Kazmerev said, but he sounded nervous.

The Flamerarch will keep her safe, Grevankin encouraged him. *Listen to Speiledos. He's been trying to talk to you this whole time. He swears they'll watch her.*

I don't care about Speiledos. I don't care about any of them, Kazmerev snapped. *I care about Sersha and she runs herself too ragged.*

Easy, Grevankin soothed him. *Easy now. You aren't helping. Sersha?*

Was he talking to me? My head felt thick.

I am talking to you, Grevankin's larger-than-life mental voice boomed. *You can draw strength from me, too. It may be enough. Mally can't help, but if you're touching me you should be able to draw on my strength if your cousin allows it.* He paused as if listening. *Tsk, Mally. Selfish. Selfish. Remember, I will be with you for the rest of your life, and I will remember these little moments. On top of that, every phoenix here can listen to me talking to you. Yes, they most definitely heard that. No, I won't take it back. She'll do it, Sersha. Don't mind her harsh tongue.*

I didn't need to hear more. I would try this thing. But one arrow at a time.

I broke off the fletching of the arrow that went through Gundt's chest, flinching at his unconscious moan. With a jerk, I yanked the arrow through the other side and then grabbed Grevankin's wing with one hand and spread my hand flat against Gundt's chest with the other, closed my eyes, and pulled every scrap of warmth and strength that I could. I pulled and pulled – but this time, the world felt cold. It felt as though there wasn't fire enough for what I was trying to do. Wasn't heat enough. Wasn't light enough.

I felt myself wavering, heard Kazmerev and Grevankin's worried voices in the back of my head.

Should be done by now.

No, that's not how it normally goes.

Losing her.

Losing ...

Darkness encased me. And this time it was the darkness of the unconscious.

229

I woke to the sound of something dripping as a light so dim that I could barely see filled my vision. Even that much light made my head feel as though it were splitting in two. Beside me, a pile of ashes smoked. I was chilled right through and getting colder by the second. Shivering, I forced myself up and was surprised to realize my head had been pillowed on Mally's lap.

She was holding the crown in one hand, looking at it grimly through strands of soaking wet hair as the rain ran down on her and the Dark Diadem with no care at all for what it touched.

"Don't look so surprised," she said without looking at me. "Once the Stryxex were down or fleeing, I had to take it off. You can't wear it forever, and they needed daylight to hunt the rest properly. And to move the elves to that cave stronghold. And to move Gundt. I voted for you and me staying here, and they thought I was mad, but you know how it is. No one moves Mally if Mally doesn't want to move. And Grevankin was gone by then and the bossy one who promised Kazmerev he'd take care of you. Actually, I might have taken the crown off just to get rid of him. He was trying my patience and you know I don't have much of that." She glanced down at me finally. "They shouldn't rely on this thing, anyway. What do they think will happen if it ever runs out of power the way you do? They were just lucky that I was close enough to snatch it from you and jam it on my head before anyone died falling from a phoenix."

I tried to sign Gundt and she snorted.

"Gundt. Fool man. He cares too much. That's his problem. They took him to the fortress in Sarcoda. And I'm guessing you want to fly over there right now and heal the rest of his arrow wounds. That sounds like you. Even though Verdaine's healer says they'll heal on their own in a few weeks. Even though he says any poison in the body is being burned off by his Flame Rider qualities. You never told me about all these special qualities. If you had, I would have snatched up some ashes ages ago."

She sounded so glib. I hoped Grevankin never heard her talk like that.

"Let me guess," she said dryly. "You're wondering why I didn't bring you up to Sarcoda – or why Verdaine didn't. After all, you shouldn't be sleeping in the rain after passing out, right?"

I nodded. The shivering was so bad that I couldn't get warm.

Mally sighed. "I didn't think about dry clothes and that's on me, but when our phoenixes return we won't need them – the heat of those big birds will warm us completely.

They don't like the name bird, I signed.

Mally rolled her eyes. "You're too serious, Sersha. That's your problem. That and a lack of foresight. Why do you think we're sitting out here in the pouring rain with you passed out, no shelter, and a sodden bag I acquired with almost nothing in it." Here she held up a small leather bag. "Why do you think I demanded that you stay here instead of returning to Sarcoda? Why do you think I let them take Gundt?"

I shrugged and I had the feeling she was only barely holding herself back from sighing again.

"I'm going to forgive you for being so dim, Sersha, but only because apparently you spent yourself healing me. Or so they tell me. Listen. Do you want to see Judicus again?"

I nodded determinedly.

"Yes. And so do I. Why? Because I've run this out in my brain a million different ways and every time I do, this fails and we all die unless we have Judicus. So. We need to retrieve him."

I swallowed. I wanted to go and get him. Certainly. I wanted to do it right now. But there was Gundt to heal and Mally was the ai'sletta. She couldn't just slip away.

"I'm not sure if you noticed but I rather had a moment while you were busy stealing the show with that dramatic faint," she carried on. "Everyone knelt and then after you passed out, they gave me their allegiance. Well, sort of. Technically the Flamerarch is sworn to the Grand Hadri but the ai'sletta sits at the right hand of the Grand Hadri, so they swore to me, and we all agreed to go save Judicus's sister and take back the city – which works fine for me because I'm pretty sure that then I'll be owed the place."

She was always so glib about that.

"And in a few moments, they'll return. And the elves will install their people in Sarcoda and whoever can be spared will come with us to fight. And the Flamerarch will be ready to seize Briccatore and someone will remember to contact our spies inside the walls, and it will all start to snowball into the world's biggest battle. And I'm fine with that, because that's when you really need an ai'sletta. But. And this is important. But, they won't let us slip away and just go get him. And that's why I kept you out here in the rain while they mop up Stryxex like a dirty inn floor. You and I need a plan and we need to have it before they get back."

230

"What we do," she told me as she pulled me to my feet and began to trudge across the plains, "is we run. Not yet, obviously. We wait until after they talk tonight – and they will, trust me. They'll make some kind of grand alliance and I'll be part of it, and I'll smile and nod and then we'll agree, and everyone will go to bed – but not you and me. We'll get some dry clothes on and grab a few supplies and the moment no one is looking, we'll sneak out and fly just as far and as fast as we can to get to Occulus's tower to get him free. Understand?"

"*And Gundt*?" I'd signed, though his name was just 'old man' in our family sign.

"It can't be helped," she said waving a hand. "We'll leave him here. After we get Judicus we can find him. We'll all need to meet then to take the city."

As if it was that simple to "take a city." As if we could just say we were going to do it. As if we hadn't worked so hard to get all these allies just to fly away now.

"But for this to work, you have to *agree*, okay? You have to."

I gave her a puzzled look. We were making good time over the rain-soaked landscape. Heaps of rumpled cloth and ashes marked the fallen. Fortunately, there weren't many of ours. I tried not to look at them. I had to think that Verdaine and Shasomen would have checked to make sure none of them were our wounded.

"I mean you have to agree with them," Mally said. "Just nod along to whatever they say so they don't suspect anything. I know you. You always think you know best, and you'll be trying to carve some path of moral righteousness out of their plans. Don't do it. Just trust me."

I nodded along. Good practice, I guessed.

Agreeing to everything? That should be easy. I felt so tired. I felt like I could barely stand up. I should be horrified and mourning for the battlefield around me. I should be worried about how few allies we had even after rousing the elves to our side and gathering up these Stryxex. I should be .... Something. I couldn't remember what. I was too tired to remember.

Mally dug into her pocket and pulled out a silk scarf and for a moment I thought she was going to try to shield herself from the trickle of rain but instead she spread it wide in front of her and stopped. I stumbled to a stop beside her. The silk was printed with a map.

I looked a question at her.

"Clever, isn't it?" she asked me, waggling her eyebrows. "I won it in a game of shreds with the elves. Don't ask. It's like a stones game but with little parchment cards. I loved it and I had to do something while you were all jaunting off into danger. It's not fun being the ai'sletta and being treated like porcelain. We're here." She pointed to a place in the mountain foothills. "Any idea where Occulus's tower is?"

I pointed towards the rough place Judicus had explained in the south.

"We'll need better directions when we get there, but that's fine for now," she said, nodding happily. "We'll stick to the mountains. Nowhere for anyone on land to chase us and the phoenixes and Stryxex are all tied up right now, so our only fear will be those Creatures of Sydonon and we should be able to see those huge rock things lumbering past. I would hope."

She was so confident. I wished I could borrow some of her strength. I wished it even more when we finally reached the fortress on foot, and I collapsed gratefully before a roaring fire. Someone gave us soup in wooden bowls and someone else pointed the way to the storerooms where we could find dry clothes and wool blankets.

Mally winked at me twice – once when we were told and once when we were hastily dressing. I didn't need her reminding me that she'd been right, but I didn't care. I was so tired that I barely managed to shrug the clothes on – finer than anything I'd ever worn before because the Flamerarch lived in style – and then stumble back to the hearth to fall asleep directly in front of the fire like a dog after a long run.

When I was shaken awake again it was definitely night.

I knew because I awoke to a blossoming Kazmerev and a furious Grevankin.

Would you stop teasing me, Mally? Would you? he said, annoyed. And I couldn't believe she'd shaken the most laid-back phoenix I'd ever met.

I was still blinking awake when I felt confusion through Kazmerev's bond and then it hit me. We needed to keep what we were going to do a secret from our phoenixes. One wrong thought from them and every other phoenix in the place would know what we were planning. Mally, it would seem, was managing that by annoying Grevankin so much he didn't want to speak to her. I didn't think I'd need to resort to that.

Did Kazmerev remember what things were like when we first met Gundt on the ship and I didn't trust the new Flame Rider?

I can.

Could he remember how he had to keep his thoughts neutral so that Huxabrand couldn't hear?

I can.

Could he do it again?

For you, always.

Good. Because I didn't want to annoy him like Mally was annoying Grevankin.

Spare me that.

"If you're awake, Sersha, I think you should go visit Gundt," Mally said coyly. "I have meetings ... of course."

I tilted my head in a question.

"Turns out you're lucky today," she said quietly. "They only asked for me. Maybe you can take care of my bag for me. They all look the same and I don't want to lose it."

She handed me her pack and then slipped away. It was full to the brim with everything we might need. I tried not to look too suspicious as I slung it over my shoulder and made my way to where they'd put Gundt in a small room – or cave – of his own as he healed.

I slid into the room, looking in every direction.

There had been phoenixes everywhere. So many that I was overwhelmed. Phoenixes in the kitchen and the halls, perched up on chandeliers in the great halls or cuddling around the edges. Some close to their Flame Riders, some off on their own. Some preening or coughing little bursts of fire. Some with heads cocked in curiosity and some giving me wicked glares. They were bright white and hard to look at, yellow and dazzling like the sun, orange and bursting with joy like an autumn bonfire, red as the reddest rose and curving with sinuous pleasure, smoky and clouded and hard to see, puffing white clouds of steam, some with blue edges, and some with black, and some that rippled from color to color like heated metal.

I was so dazzled by them that I was lucky to have Kazmerev urging me on, or I would have forgotten where I was going.

Gundt, he reminded me, when I slowed. *You want to see him before it is too late into the night.*

He was right, of course, and by the time I made it to Gundt's room, I was not just physically tired, but mentally tired, too. I swayed in the doorway and the elf leaning over him saw me, nodded to me, and then quickly left – to give us privacy, perhaps.

I made my way slowly to Gundt's side and his eyes opened.

"Mmph. Sersha."

I nodded again, looking him over worriedly. My hands hovered over, longing to heal him but hearing Mally in the back of my mind warning me not to do it, to save my strength.

"No need," he gasped. "They tell me you saved my life from an arrow in the back. These other wounds can wait. Or they can heal on their own. They hurt, but they are not going to kill me. You saved me from what might do that."

She owed you that much, Huxabrand said from the corner. Her eyes narrowed as she looked at me and I couldn't help the way my cheeks flamed at her words because I was about to abandon him.

I felt Kazmerev shift at that, but he was careful. He said nothing to me. If he could just hold on, he would get the answers he needed. He shifted again and Gundt's eyes went from me to his phoenix to Kazmerev and back.

"Hux," he barked, and her eyes snapped to him. "Say nothing."

She looked furious, but I heard nothing of her mental voice.

Gundt looked at Kazmerev and said, "Not you, either. Silence, the pair of you." His eyes found mine. "You're planning something. Tell me no details. Is it a good thing?"

I nodded.

"Going to save us all?"

I nodded again.

"Means you'll have to leave before I'm healed up?"

I couldn't help it, my eyes were misting, but I wouldn't lie to him. I nodded a third time and he grunted.

"Then don't stand her wasting time. Do what you must. Don't tell me what it is, or it will be everywhere before you can blink with all these phoenixes here. I'll follow when I can."

I hesitated by his side, but he batted at my hovering hand.

"Go. Go now before I lose my resolve."

I turned on my heels and fled. Not because I was worried about his resolve but because I had no confidence at all in mine.

231

Mally caught my arm on the way out of the room and was marching me down the hall before I could even look behind her for Grevankin.

"I put him away," she whispered as she sped up. "He's too dramatic."

He was too dramatic?

"I told them I needed a private moment and left a note telling them what I expected from them with one of the elves. Do you know how hard it is to find a pen and parchment in this place?" It was good that she wasn't looking at me because my disbelief would be obvious. "I asked her to wait an hour to give it to them, but how much do you want to bet she reads it and goes running in there like a girl telling her mom on us?"

I wouldn't bet against that, and Mally didn't wait to hear if I would. She had us down three flights of stairs before she paused, back against a wall, huffing – not from exertion, I didn't think, but from nerves.

We were moving again before I could try to sign to her, slipping past the guards at the little ground-level door. They were still escorting elves inside Sarcoda. No one was looking at who was going out as they tried to wrangle golden salamanders into place before the sun came back up and they were stuck in place.

"They had a messenger arrive just before battle. One of the scouts the elves left behind," Mally said as we sidestepped a salamander and slipped past the last of the trailing elves.

I kept my eyes averted from their sad gazes. This was no homecoming for them. Their lives were in ruins behind them. Their futures as uncertain as ours. And they had small children and the elderly with them. At least Mally's sisters were back home where they could be kept safe. Uncle Llynd would keep them out of trouble. I tried not to think about whether he was still waiting for my Aunt Danna to return home or how long he would look for Mally and me before he finally realized none of us were ever coming back.

"Don't look so grim," Mally whispered to me. "They aren't coming this way. He said our pursuers were making a beeline toward Briccatore and they hadn't even bothered to give us chase. All this looking for a fortress and panicking about who was behind us and the whole time they were never even bothering to give chase."

I swallowed. That wasn't as good of news as she seemed to think. Briccatore was already almost impregnable, overrun with Stryxex and the Hand of the Rat. With the prince's elves joining in, how could we possibly overthrow them?

I felt small at her words. Too small. I couldn't stop this. I was just one girl in a huge world.

"Seriously, that expression is making *me* want to cry and that takes effort. Buck up," Mally said, pulling me behind a huge boulder. "Okay. Phoenix time. Where has yours been hiding?"

Kazmerev flashed into visibility beside me, still careful to be silent so he didn't alert anyone.

He could see, I was sure, that we were running away – well, not away but toward. He must realize we were going to get Judicus and he must realize we had to go alone. And he must approve, or he would have blown our cover. Right?

I looked at him and he returned my gaze, steady and kind as always, a rock in the storms of life.

I will hold you fast no matter what comes. If storms are our future, we will ride them as the eagle rides the wind. We will not be torn apart when we are together.

Warmth filled me at that. We could do this. We could.

"Why don't you braid each other's hair while you're at it?" Mally said scornfully, but she closed her eyes and sighed, and then a furious Grevankin exploded from her heart and into the air.

If you ... he started but he was interrupted by Kazmerev who said very firmly.

Flame to flame I greet thee, ancient fire.

Grevankin looked at him and then back at Mally and then, in a frustrated tone he said, *Flame to flame I greet you, ancient fire,* as if he were trying to speed past a formality.

Mally leapt onto his back before he was finished with the greeting and I climbed onto Kazmerev's.

Grevankin said, *Mally,* only to be interrupted a second time by Kazmerev as my phoenix spoke to him while leaping into the air.

I am Kazmerev, Bright Flame, Bound in Oath –

What are you – Grevankin tried to say but Kazmerev ran right over him with the formal greeting.

– and Heart to Sersha of Landsfall.

Grevankin was in the air now, too, chasing Kazmerev as he rose, rose, rose and he looked utterly perplexed as he was forced to return the greeting.

I am Grevankin, Smoke Cloud, Bound in Oath to Prex – to Mally of Landsfall.

"Nice save," Mally said as we climbed side by side.

You are not seeing me at my best, my dear girl, Grevankin complained, *and this is mostly because you are running me ragged. Why –*

Just a moment, Kazmerev said, and I looked over my shoulder to see understanding finally dawn in Grevankin's eyes as we flew hard and fast as we could toward the south.

And then, finally, we were out of range of the minds of the phoenixes at Sarcoda and Kazmerev seemed to breathe a sigh of relief as he said sharply, *Next time, have a little faith, Sersha! I can keep a secret!*

But I hadn't known all the details, only that we were going to run and get Judicus.

Well, of course, we are going to rescue Judicus!

Judicus? Grevankin asked as he dodged a scrap of cloud lit brightly by the moonlight. *I'm fond of the boy and he's the only hope of the little humans riding on our backs. Is that what this has been about? But why provoke me, you deranged girl?*

Whatever Mally said, I couldn't hear over the sound of the wind in my ears, but I did hear Grevankin's laugh.

Be glad it is I who you rescued, or this would go much harder for you, Blazing Queen I am the most tolerant phoenix you will ever meet, the most forgiving, and the most good-natured. Anyone else would be nursing a grudge as large as Sarcoda after your treatment tonight.

He's not exaggerating, Kazmerev agreed. *Anyone else would burn her to cinders.*

232

By the time dawn was almost upon us, Kazmerev was forced to keep me awake by telling me tales of his previous life. There wasn't an ounce of energy in me as we settled on a bank of grass in the predawn coolness. I set a fire while Mally unrolled blankets.

"I'm too tired for a tent," she said, but she fetched water for tea while I built up the fire.

You need to keep watch, Kazmerev warned.

Let them sleep. There's nothing for miles, Grevankin argued.

Mally was already cuddling in her blanket, not even waiting for the tea she wanted. He lay down behind her to keep her warm as she drifted off.

There's nothing right now. Who knows what may come? Kazmerev warned.

A breath later, the sun came out and he winked out.

I had meant to keep watch. I really had. But as the sun came up, I gathered my blanket around me to keep warm and put my back against an obliging tree, and before the tea water came to a boil I had drifted off.

I woke with a start, disoriented and uncertain. My face felt warm in the hot sun and Mally's snores drifted toward me. The fire had burned low.

A stick cracked and suddenly I was alert. I swallowed, trying to determine which direction the snap had come from. We'd settled on a hill with a worn path running over it, but judging by the earth, no one had wandered it in weeks. Just our luck that someone was walking down it now.

I pulled myself to my feet, blanket wrapped tight around me, but when no one emerged from the trees or came down the path, I fed the fire and put the water back on it. I could use some tea and a bite to eat, and Mally should be awake by now. I judged it to be late afternoon.

I turned to look for the food and froze. Someone was sitting at our campfire. I sucked in a breath, frozen in place, and then his hands flashed, and I huffed a gasp of relief.

It was Jastomen, the Grand Hadri's spy who had flown to the raider lands with Mally. I would never have recognized him way out here and wrapped in a cloak.

"*Did you come from – S – A – R – C – O – D – A?*" he signed and my mouth fell open. How could he know? His smile was wry but welcoming as if he were speaking to an old friend. "*It's the only reasonable place this path could have come from. Was it full of the enemy?*"

"*It was,*" I signed back, feeling honored that he had also learned the signs from the book he gave to Judicus. "*But it is no longer. Friends are there. Flame bird.*"

I didn't have a word for "Flamerarch" but he nodded and when I gestured to my ears he asked aloud, "Elves?"

I nodded.

His expression turned inward.

"I had hoped to find someone – anyone – to bear a message to whatever allies we could muster. The Flamerarch perhaps. Other nations. And it seems I'm on the right path. They are in Sarcoda?"

I nodded and he glanced over at Mally.

"And the ai'sletta is with you instead of with them. She was ... not well when last I saw her."

I shrugged at that. She seemed well now, but who could say how deep her wounds went? Mental wounds might fester just as physical ones sometimes did.

"But where is Gundt?"

Hurt, I signed.

"And Judicus Franzer Irault?"

Lost.

He flinched. "That is a heavy blow. I'd hoped to find him with you. Is he ... dead, then?"

I shook my head.

"Captured?"

A nod.

"Well, then. Well. Is he retrievable?"

"*We shall see,*" I signed as the kettle whistled. I added tea leaves with care and extracted the wooden cups Mally had brought, offering him a little brew as I took the other cup.

"Then you go to rescue him?" he asked me with a burning gaze, and for just a moment I felt fearful of those eyes turned on me.

I nodded, but slowly, with care.

He held up a hand. "I won't tell you your business. I won't tell you where to take the ai'sletta. We tried ... we failed her when we tried to steer her. Is she ... she's perhaps recovered?"

I nodded but in a way that suggested uncertainty. That seemed to be enough to reassure him. He sagged a little and sipped his tea.

"Prexav?"

I didn't know how to sign dead. Didn't know if there was a better way to do it. My eyes pricked with tears and I startled when he took my hand.

"I was very fond of the boy, too," he said with a hitch in his throat. "His sister will not take the news well. She struggles to find hope already. Briccatore has always been their home and the ... the way it is being driven not the ground right now – like a spike hammered into clay – it hollows those who love the city. I must return to her when my message is delivered. I don't suppose you could wait?"

I shook my head, but I didn't let go of his hand. He nodded his understanding and sat with me against the tree. We both put our backs to it, which left us facing two different directions. I didn't mind. He seemed to understand the things I couldn't say.

"When you rescue him," he said, and I clung to the word "when." He paused and started again. "When you rescue him, please tell him that they tore down the statue of his father's execution, and in its place, they are erecting a great pillar. It should fill Victory Square, they tell me, and be completed by the end of the month. I have seen the beginnings of it, as well as the rope workers they have employed who weave 'round the clock. That kind of effort ... that is an immense work. A working the likes of which we have not seen since Herowan the Great. I fear the pillar looks much like one I've seen before – the broken one that drove the ai'sletta mad for a time. Do you follow me?"

I nodded and he wasn't looking at me, but it didn't seem to matter.

"It feels wrong to tell him that when I know what it will compel him to do – and how can just one ropeworker destroy such a working when so many of his profession toil over it day after day? And yet, I know no other I can tell. He is just a man. But so am I. And you are just a woman. And yet in this troubled time, in this fraught age, we are all that stands between mankind and destruction. It is too small a wall, too narrow a dam." He was silent for a time, his breath sawing in and out like he, too, was struggling to keep his heart from crumbling. When he found words again they were heavy. "We cannot help but fail, and yet if we do not try, can we live knowing we let it come to pass?"

It seemed we were thinking the same thing.

We sat, then, in silence until the sun began to sink low in the sky, and Mally stalked loudly to where we sat and proclaimed, "I swear, Sersha, I can't sleep even a few hours without you picking up a new lover. It's embarrassing, is what it is."

233

To our relief, Jastomen was able to give us better directions to Occulus's Tower.

"It's a well-known landmark, though no one with sense would go there," he had said mildly as he carefully showed us the spot on Mally's map with comments about the towns, main routes, watering holes, and where to expect opposition along the way. "I suppose that includes us now that the world has gone mad. Fortunately, flying will give you an advantage. If you can avoid anyone on the way, it might be best. Informants are being paid double and there's a bounty for the heads of Flame Riders."

That had sent a chill down my spine.

"I don't want to see anyone, anyway," Mally had said. "So that will be just fine."

"How did you escape the city?" I asked him.

"You won't be able to get in the way I got out," he said, and he said it in the kind of haunted way that survivors of battles speak, so I didn't push him further.

I'd been sorry to part from him. His presence had been like a warm breeze on a cold day – it didn't fix the problem, but it made it somewhat more bearable.

"Hurry if you can," had been his parting words. "I fear what they will do when the pillar is complete."

And then we were gone, flying away into the night, and leaving him by our small fire.

I don't like the sound of this pillar, Kazmerev had said when we were well into the air and soaring across the land.

Grevankin agreed. *They are trapping phoenix souls and they are transforming them into Stryxex.*

Or trapping them in the pillars until they flow out like what happened to those stone creatures of Sydonon, Kazmerev agreed.

But they must be nearly out of phoenixes to trap, Grevankin said, and sorrow was heavy in his voice. *You and I both have seen how few there are, how our safe places are overrun. Those we left behind could be the last.*

Two hundred is not a number to sniff at.

Grevankin grunted at that. And then paused. *A valid thought, Blazing Queen. Perhaps it could be done, but I certainly would not know how.*

What does she think? Kazmerev had asked.

What can be taken away can be given back. Perhaps the key is not to destroy the pillar but to use it to take back the souls that have been transformed into Stryxex and spilled out into the stone creatures.

And then what? Leave them trapped forever in a pillar? That sounds like a fate worse than death. Kazmerev's voice was uneasy and there was no more said on the matter, but I thought Mally might be right. We had no weapons of our own to use against our enemies, why not turn their weapons back on them?

It was close to the end of the first night when Mally noticed it and told Grevankin. He cleared his mental throat awkwardly.

Have you noticed all the fires? He asked us.

Of course, Kazmerev said.

Have you noticed that they make lines across the land?

Hard to miss it.

Would you say ... perhaps ... that they follow what were once roads? That they might be villages and towns?

There are gaps in the lines, Kazmerev said, but he sounded like he was making the argument because someone needed to be hopeful, not because he actually was.

The fires there have likely burned themselves out. All the ones we see are dull – old – embers and not flames.

We were quiet for a long time after that. I was glad that my night vision was not good enough to penetrate through the darkness far enough to see the remains of the countryside surrounding Briccatore. I didn't want to know what the Hand of the Rat had done here. I didn't want to have to imagine the suffering and devastation. But my mind went there anyway, and it played it out a thousand different ways until my heart was heavier than a stone.

You can't do that.

Do what?

Take on the weight of all the tragedy of the world.

Not all the world. Just the part of it that I've failed.

How can you call it failure? His voice in my mind was kind. *You've done all a single human can do. You've pushed yourself beyond what you thought you could bear, and still, you are here, still, you are fighting. You didn't run away, even though you could. You didn't save yourself all this pain, even though you could. Instead, you chose to stand shoulder to shoulder with us and endure the heat of the flame and the scorching pain of violence afflicted on our people and ourselves and you haven't flinched, you haven't looked away, you haven't given up. That's not failure, my Little Hawk. That's the best any of us can hope for.*

But if I'd succeeded, they'd all have their homes. They'd all live in peace.

If they'd all stood up like you did, then we wouldn't have any of this.

But how could they? They were all just people. With children and responsibilities. What if one of them tried to stand up and was stopped by the others? What if a few tried and they were just killed by the Hand of the Rat?

Would you say that they had failed? Would you despise them for it?

Of course, I would not.

Then don't despise yourself.

We set down before dawn, Kazmerev insisting on it.

"I don't know why we can't fly until you fade," Mally said crankily, but her complaint was interrupted by a yawn.

I didn't object. I was tired, but I knew that wasn't why Kazmerev wanted us below the trees before the predawn light. He wanted to spare me seeing more than I had already.

You would be easier to manage if you weren't so perceptive, he agreed, but he wrapped his wing around me and despite my melancholy, I cuddled up against his warm feathers and fell asleep, trying very hard not to think of how many other people might be sleeping on the ground with no tent and no fire.

I was only one girl, and I could only do so much. But if I could get to Judicus and set him free, then maybe he could do more because somehow it always seemed like he was more than just one man, as if all his intense focus and certainty could make him three men all working at once. I couldn't be that. And I wouldn't have to be. I just needed to free him to do it.

It was with that last, longing thought, that I drifted off to sleep.

234

I woke to a rumbling sound, rattling deep in my chest and growing louder by the second and then something slammed into my torso, knocking out my breath.

My eyes popped open to see Mally on top of me.

"Follow fast," she said and then jumped up, running, pack slung over her back.

I pulled myself to my feet, disoriented, not sure what had happened. Something knocked me from behind before I could orient myself. The rumbling ran up my legs, so powerful now that the stones bounced under my feet. I fell forward, barely breaking my fall as I skidded on the dirt, and tried to stand again as the world shook, throwing my sense of balance off. Small rocks bounced on the ground around me. Leaves shook from trees and bushes.

I couldn't hear a thing over the earsplitting rumble and crash of rock on rock. Was it a landslide? An earthquake?

I'd lost sight of Mally already. Which way to flee? None of the trees around us was very large and if I tried to climb one, it might topple under the force of falling earth. I stumbled forward again, choking on clouds of dust, and felt something brush my back a second time. This time I spun around awkwardly only to swallow a scream.

In front of me, running like a herd of goats or horses, the creatures of Sydonon raced by, stone body after stone body, their feet chewing up the ground, churning green things under, stamping flat anything living.

I didn't stay to watch. It didn't matter where Mally was, only that I had to get away from these things. I fled, racing in the other direction, scanning for any kind of landscape I could find to shelter me. There was a large boulder up ahead. It didn't seem to be moving, though the face I could see was sheer - unclimbable.

I raced toward it anyway and hurried into the lee of the rock. The edges here were seamed and a cut in the rock made it possible to climb. I scurried up it fast as I could, shaking loose small stones in my hurry.

I found Mally standing on the top, looking out over a sea of moving rock bodies, her arms lifted above her head as if she had conjured them up. They parted around our lookout, like water rushing past a stone.

My heart was in my throat as I watched them pass, grateful to have been woken in time to flee, grateful not to have been smashed into the earth by stone feet.

But mostly just stunned by so much moving rock, pulverizing everything in its path. As I watched, trees toppled, folded, and were smashed to sawdust.

"So, I can thank Judicus for this, can I?" Mally asked. She shook her head in an annoyed fashion and then, to my utter shock, she put the pack down on the smooth rock, pillowed her head on it, and went to sleep in the center of the chaos, as if she found shelter from herds of running rock creatures every day and she'd like to sleep now, thank you.

I could not be so easy around them.

I waited, my mouth dry and hands sweaty, heart in my throat as the thundering herd passed by. I prayed they would not knock our boulder loose or decided to climb up it instead of flowing around it.

When the last creature ran past, his feet sending up puffs of dust into the hot afternoon air, my ears were ringing from the sound of their passing. It was long minutes before I could finally hear Mally's snoring. I sat down hard on the rock, breathless, stunned, and opened my belt pouch with trembling hands. I pulled out the mirror shard. It shook in my grip. I had to be careful. Even if he wasn't there, I just needed to hold it, just needed to know that he *could* be there.

An eye met mine through the glass and I gasped as the owner backed up and I saw Judicus's face – darker than it had been as if he'd been in the sun. On his cheeks and chin were wispy bits of beard. But he hadn't been in there that long, had he? Behind him, everything was so bright that I still couldn't make out where he might be.

"Sersha," he said my name with a gasp, tears filling his eyes as if he thought I were dead and come back to him.

I set the mirror hurriedly against Mally's sleeping leg and backed up so he could see my hands.

"*Judicus,*" I signed, breathing my own sigh of relief. "*You're still there.*"

"I was afraid I'd killed you," he said in a voice that shuddered. "All these months ..."

"*Months?!*" I signed.

"Hasn't it been months?" he asked, rubbing the long hairs on his chin. I didn't think he could grow a beard – even a thin one.

"*Days,*" I signed back. "*I would have tried sooner but we've been busy. After you released the phoenixes, we had to fight Stryxex on the first day, and then Mally and I had to sneak away to try to get to Occulus's Tower. On the second day, we met Jastomen and he told us that our enemies are erecting a huge pillar in Victory Square – one like the one you destroyed. It's the third day now.*"

I had to spell the words "victory square" but he seemed to understand.

"It's only been three days?"

I nodded but his face was screwed up in concentration.

"*Your sister is still Grand Hadri,*" I said, and he met my eyes again and smiled a tiny, worried smile.

"She lives, then," he said, and he let out another long, shuddering breath. "Then things are not as bad as I feared. And you are on your way to Occulus's Tower."

"*As fast as we can fly.*"

There was a glimmer in his eye – like hope was reigniting.

"I was sure I'd ... Sersha, I've barely been able to live with myself thinking I'd killed you. Maybe," he bit his lip. "Maybe you shouldn't go to Occulus's Tower. Maybe you should go somewhere safe."

This wasn't like him. He never held me back.

"*There is nowhere safe,*" I signed, thinking of the lines of dull glowing embers, thinking of the phoenix souls in the charging Creatures of Sydonon, thinking of the nobles and government that had banded together to crush all phoenixes and now this pillar that would finish the job. "*There's nowhere safe for anyone. All I can do is try.*"

Kazmerev had been right about that.

"You're risking yourself," he said, running his hands through his hair. "And you're risking Mally. All to get me back. That's not right, Sersha. You should go and rescue my sister instead. Rescue someone valuable."

Now, this really wasn't like him. He was always the one trying to change things, fighting to win, not afraid of the odds or of getting me involved in them. I clamped down on a wave of anxiety. What was happening to him to break him down like this? And how bad would it get before we could reach him? It was like I was watching him fall apart right in front of me.

I put my fists on my hips and gave him a look, but I couldn't keep it up and talk at the same time, so I had to lower them.

"*You are valuable. And you will help us rescue your sister when we come and get you. And you'll tear down that pillar.*"

"Someone else can do all of that," he said grimly. "I must no longer ask things of you. You must ... you must move on without me, Sersha."

I looked through his eyes and saw the shattering behind them.

"*Stop,*" I signed, but he was looking away. Why wouldn't he look at me?

"I can't bear that you might die trying to save me. I don't want to live in a world that you aren't in."

"*Stop,*" I tried again, but he still wouldn't look at me. His eyes were clouded with unshed tears but mine were falling like furious rain.

"If I knew I was the cause of that – well, I'm too selfish to live like that. You have to go. Flee as far as you can and keep yourself safe. Take whatever phoenixes you can."

Enough of this.

I clapped my hands together hard, and he looked up with a start.

"*Stop it right now,*" I signed. "*I am coming for you, whether you like it or not and you are not sending me away. You promised you were going to marry me. I'm going to make you keep your word. And only you can tear down that pillar. Jastomen said so. And also, you can't tell a girl you love her and then tell her you have to be apart forever. It doesn't work like that."*

What had happened in that mirror to make him so despondent? Worry gnawed at my heart. Could he make it the few more days we needed to get to the tower and rescue him? What about the other figure who had been there with him?

He opened his mouth to object and then suddenly the mirror was snatched from in front of me and I looked up at Mally with wide eyes. She took one look at the shard, rolled her eyes, and then held it out at arm's length so she and I could both see Judicus at once.

"Are you kidding me? He's crying? What is this, one of those tragic stories of two lovers separated by time and space? No, don't tell me, I'd rather not know."

Judicus scowled and he looked a lot better scowling than he had trying to warn me away. But my heart clenched at her mockery. His tears had been for me and that made them precious. She had no right to judge.

"If you were within reach I'd shake you, Judicus Franzer Irault," she said. "What's the matter with you? Can't you see that you're breaking her to pieces?" Mally shook her head and made a *tsk*ing sound. "No, don't talk. I think I've heard enough. She's not running away. I'm not letting her. You're not going to keep trying to nobly sacrifice yourself. We're on our way to your precious tower and when we get there, you'll need to have a cool, problem-solving head because there's work to be done, so stop with the pity party and get yourself together. Sersha needs her sleep, or she'll be no good to anyone tonight and we need to fly far. We'll talk to you again when we get to the tower. Right, Sersha?"

I nodded, but my hands were faster.

"*I love you,*" I signed. "*I miss you.*"

"*I'm sorry,*" he signed back. "*I'm so sorry for everything.*"

"*So am I,*" I hurried to say.

"*Please take care of yourself,*" he signed. "*You are my heart.*"

And then the mirror went dark, and he was gone again.

"Now," Mally said, shoving the mirror back at me. "I want some proper sleep. No more sending magic messages to people. No more making a huge scene crying. And for the love of clear skies could you be quiet?"

She sank back down, turned her back to me with a huff, and was soon snoring.

I'd never been told to be quiet before. The thought of it made me want to laugh. I clamped a hand over my mouth, not sure if it was laughter or tears I was trying to keep penned in. It took me three long breaths to put the feeling aside enough that I could tuck the little mirror back into my pouch.

Sleep did not come easily to me. I was worried. Worried about those long wisps of hair and the fine lines around his eyes. How long had he been in the golden mirror? What price would we pay for my delays in getting to him?

I slept fitfully and dreamed that I opened the mirror only to discover there was no one there and that the over-worked, over-worried man I loved had vanished forever.

235

Our remaining days of travel were a blur of flying hard and fast at night and sleeping fitfully in the day. We ate and drank, gathered water and berries, and we worried in silence together until I began to miss Huxabrand and her snide remarks. The phoenixes tried to keep our spirits up, but our anxiety permeated them, too, until they were twitchy with it.

"Not far now," Mally would mutter when we stopped. "Not far now."

Until, just before dawn one morning, we finally found the tower. We settled down on a hill not far away and watched it.

"So," she said, looking at me as I stared at the pale spire reaching up into the night sky. "What do we do now that we're here?"

What, indeed.

We need to go inside. There are large windows at the top of the tower. We might as well just fly in, Kazmerev suggested.

And if it is guarded? Grevankin asked. *I once had a rider who was a guard for a tower. Not this one, of course. He would keep me hidden, and then when he needed me, I would spring into action. There could be others who guard in this way.*

I don't sense any other phoenixes.

There could be Stryxex.

Kazmerev grunted and sparks shot from his mouth. *They aren't that clever.*

I thought we should wait. Wait and watch the tower. See if there were guards coming in and out. It was an oddly lonely tower, situated beside a lake but with no village nearby, no recent traffic on the small road that led from the main thoroughfare to the tower. How did they get supplies – whoever they were who owned this tower?

Occulus has been away. Perhaps he is the tower's only occupant, Kazmerev suggested.

That seemed unlikely. You'd need servants to maintain such a large house. And people had talked about it like it was more than a place for one person. Perhaps it was a school of some kind.

I think you're just tired from a long journey and that inflames worry. It looks unoccupied from here. Best to go in while Grevankin and I are here to protect you both.

"I agree with the phoenixes," Mally whispered – but I noticed she whispered rather than spoke. "There's no point waiting until they're gone and then getting in trouble. We should go in right now while they're awake and then we can flee if it goes badly."

I wanted to ask Judicus what he thought. I started to sign it, but Mally whispered, "I can't read your signs in the dark."

She says she wants to ask Judicus, Kazmerev said.

"What good will that do?" Mally asked, sounding annoyed. "Is he here? Can he see anything? No."

Maybe he'd been here before. I hadn't asked him. Maybe there were well-known things about the place, like who lived here or what we were looking for. Maybe we should go in prepared instead of just rushing in like fools.

Kazmerev started to translate but Mally shook her head.

"None of that is going to help. It doesn't matter who was here before. It matters who is here now, and we need to get inside and find out who that is, and if they know how to free Judicus. You have to dig your hands into a problem before you can make a plan to solve it."

That makes sense, Grevankin said gravely. *And I will keep the ai'sletta out of trouble.*

It would take an army of phoenixes to do that.

I don't see any movement, Kazmerev said, shifting side to side nervously. *No fire glows. No animals around the base of the tower in the pasture or otherwise. Nothing but a lonely dark tower and a lake.*

And that was why I didn't like it. Maybe there was a monster in the lake. Maybe there was a whole host of people hiding in the tower.

If there were a host of people hiding, who would they be hiding from? We are the ones outnumbered and fleeing.

"Enough," Mally whispered fiercely. "We're wasting time and everyone's counting on us."

And then Grevankin leapt, and they were in the air, soaring toward the tower in his wreaths of black smoke, her mahogany hair whipping in the wind behind her. Kazmerev leapt, too, and I clung to his fiery feathers, trying to focus on them instead of the sick feeling in my belly.

I think you're worried about nothing, he said to me.

I didn't want to go into the tower. Not like this.

Then what? You want to watch for a day and night outside the tower and go in then when it is still silent and unmoving? Mally is right. We'd be wasting time that no one has.

Was it a waste to be cautious? I wasn't so sure.

Trust us, Sersha. We all are worried. We all want to come here, free Judicus, and get back to things. Besides, you told me he looked like he'd been trapped more than a week. Maybe time passes differently there. How long can he live in whatever place that is? A delay of a day here might mean weeks to him there.

And, of course, he was right, but it didn't help the feeling in my belly like it had dropped right to my knees and wasn't going to go back into place any time soon. I clung to his feathers and hoped they all were right.

236

Cold drifted from the tower and wrapped around me – or so it seemed as we winged our way forward. Gravankin and Mally were ahead of us, and Grevankin was trying to keep my spirits up.

Ho now, good Sersha! Chin up! Wings full of wind! It will be well, and all will be well, and you will feel well in the end.

It sounded like a quote. I let it wash over me and take some of the anxiety, but it was fighting against that cold tower, and it seemed as if it could barely balance the ominous feeling I kept getting from that spire.

The tower was built of smooth granite and wide enough at the bottom that it likely boasted an enormous great room for guests plus kitchen, scullery, storage, and whatever else right there on the ground floor. There were various entrances from surrounding stables and gardens, the lake, and of course a great gated entrance at the front to welcome guests. From the base, the tower narrowed, swooping upward gracefully until it reached a crenelated top.

I could easily see this place being a school or a fortress. Likely, water was piped in underground from that lake and the storerooms below ground could be extensive. An armed group could hold out here for months. Vines grew up the lower floors of the tower, wrapping around the narrow windows, and cradling the tower like respectful hands. They gave the place a friendly feeling that was terribly at odds with the rest, but I could imagine young men sitting beneath the vines reading large tomes and practicing their ropework over the dark lake.

And yet, not a single person moved below, not a single animal, not even a squirrel or a songbird, and as we reached the tip of the tower, my heart was flipflopping within me like a live fish.

Around the tower, just before it ended in ragged crenellation, three large, open windows left the top floor of the tower exposed to wind and sun – so exposed that one could easily fly a phoenix into the open room – empty of anything except a cluster of three bells.

And what would they be for? Warning nearby villagers? I saw none. Signaling prayers? This was no monastery? There was a warm glow to their surfaces – faint but there, and it made the hairs on the back of my hands stand up.

We set down in the bell tower and Mally dismounted, looking around.

"There's a ladder and door to the top," she said pointing to the ladder bolted to the wall. It ended in a trapdoor and just looking at it made me nervous. To mount it, you'd have to climb between two open windows.

"Oh, and there's a trap door to go below," she said, pointing to a hatch just beside my feet.

I buried my hand in Kazmerev's feathers, mouth suddenly dry, ears prickling.

Calm, Little Hawk. I'm with you. I'm not going –

Bong! I jumped as the bell rang, the sound filling the belfry and hitting my head like a wave of the sea.

Anywhere.

Bong!

Kazmerev disappeared, his fire winking out at the bells tolled again. Across from me, I just registered Grevankin's shock as he was ripped away in a puff of smoke.

Bong!

My mouth fell open. I reached for Kazmerev, trying to claw him back ... but ... nothing.

My eyes found Mally's at the same moment that hers narrowed and her lips pressed together, and then she yanked on the trap door.

Bong!

It opened soundlessly.

"We might as well – "

Bong!

"– go inside."

Bong!

She hurried in, ignoring my sign to stop, and with a desperate glance around me, I followed her down the ladder. The bells were deafening, and without our phoenixes, there was no way to leave the tower except through the hatch. It was the sensible thing to do ... wasn't it? So why was my heart pounding like a drum?

We reached the bottom of the ladder in the dark, dark room. There were slits for windows all around, and through them, stark moonlight poured into the circular room. I could make out very little except for a large ... chair, perhaps? ... in the center of the room.

Mally kicked something, cursing at what sounded like a stubbed toe.

"There's a door!"

Bong! The bells were quieter here, but still loud enough to drown out everything else.

"Locked."

I hadn't moved. With care, I drew my tinderbox and belt knife from the pouch at my side. My hand brushed the shard of mirror, but now wasn't the time to bring it out. That would come later.

There was no bong, and the silence of it almost made me jump.

"How are we supposed to get out if the door is locked?" Mally asked aloud.

I struck my flint with my knife and was lucky when my little bit of tinder lit. Quick. A candle. I shoved the wick from my stubby candle into the flame and it lit.

I pushed everything else back into the pouch and lifted the candle. Maybe there was another door.

I didn't get a chance to look. The dark shape in front of me was a chair after all.

A tall, wing-backed chair.

And it was occupied.

"Welcome," said Occulus. "I wouldn't bother with the door, ai'sletta. It's locked and you don't have the key."

I stumbled backward and grabbed for the rungs of the ladder.

"And I wouldn't bother to try escaping out the belfry," he said to me. "Your phoenixes will not return while you reside in my tower."

"That won't be for long!" Mally said boldly.

"Ah, but that is where you're wrong. I can keep you in my pocket. Forever. Did you know that? It's a clever trick," Occulus said, and then his ropes spat out and began to weave, fast as lightning and just as golden and before I was three rungs up the ladder, he had woven a great golden mirror in the empty room.

Before I was four rungs up, he was on his feet, lunging toward me. I kicked down hard and connected with his mouth, but he dragged me from the ladder, his strong arms holding both my legs so that all I could do was pummel him with my weak fists.

A second later, golden ropes twisted around me, subduing my fight and leaving me heaving, breathless, and scared as a rabbit in a snare. He glared down at me, and his mouth opened to speak when something interrupted that sounded like shattering glass. We both spun, looking in the direction of his golden mirror. Mally stood over the shards, the winged back chair in her hands.

"Make more and I'll smash them, too," she said, her chin thrust out in defiance.

He stepped toward her, but his ropes were still squeezing me. I couldn't help her, couldn't stop him, couldn't even breathe.

The world started to shrink as my vision grew darker and darker. But I couldn't let it. I had to save Judicus. I had to get Kazmerev back. I had to keep Occulus from getting anywhere near Mally.

I had to ...

Darkness flooded over me as something in the distance crashed to the floor.

EPISODE TWO: "OCCULUS'S TOWER"

SEASON THREE

237

My face hurt. I blinked awake to see Mally leaning over me, face screwed up in concentration and hand raised as if she were about to slap me.

I groaned.

"Good, you're awake," she said grabbing my hand and pulling me to my feet. My hand found my smarting cheek and I looked at her hand. "Yes, I slapped you awake. Would you rather I left you unconscious on the floor in the few moments we might have to escape?"

She was already moving around the room, hands passing over the wreckage as if looking for something.

"Occulus knocked you out with his strangling ropes and then he threw me against a wall and left. The door's locked, so I'm thinking he'll be back soon, and when he returns it can only go worse for us. Especially since he's promised to 'keep you in his pocket forever.' I don't think I'd like that much. Who knows what else a man like him keeps in there? Used handkerchiefs? People's ears? Poisonous frogs? Yesterday's breakfast?"

I shook my head, but her list had cleared my head and I joined her in searching the room. There was no way out except the ladder leading up to the roof and the locked door. I didn't think we'd get far on the roof without our phoenixes. Not unless we wanted to die falling from it.

Mally seemed to agree, shaking her head at me when she saw me considering it.

"You want to go up there and see if there's a way out other than falling to our deaths? Be my guest. Take the crown up there with you. I don't want it to be easy to find."

She jammed it into my hand.

"*What are you going to do down here?*" I signed, but she was already back to searching the rubble. There wasn't much to search. The golden mirror Occulus had made was smashed into shards and the chair and any other furniture in the room was bashed into splinters no larger than my finger. She wouldn't find a weapon in that.

I climbed the ladder, pausing when my vision darkened and little spots danced across it. My throat hurt, and my head was muzzy and splitting with pain. Being strangled until you pass out was not something I'd want to try again. I made it to the top and through the hatch to the belfry where I paused, catching my breath. The world below seemed far away – like a foreign land you'd only ever seen on a map.

I took a second long breath and then made my way to the other ladder. It was bolted to the stone wall between huge openings and the thought of climbing it made my head spin even more. But who knew what was at the top? Ropes, perhaps. Some way to get down the side. Would I have the courage to scale down the side of a tall tower using a rope? I would if it were that or another visit with Occulus.

Gritting my teeth, I climbed the second ladder, finding the top with shaking hands and gasping breaths and collapsing on the open stone of the top of the bell tower. It was crenelated along the top with a wall that didn't reach higher than my knees. After all this time riding a phoenix, you wouldn't think that I'd have problems with heights, but it's one thing to fly with a friend who will catch you if you fall and another thing to be alone on a wavering tower that moves slightly as the wind blows.

I clung to the floor and slid across the ground until I could look over the edge at the lake and trees below. There was no one in sight for miles around. No buildings, no people, no flocks or herds. I drew in a shuddering breath and backed up, disappointed. There were also no ropes or banners or conveniently abandoned weapons. The floor looked as if it had been swept.

With a sigh, I left the Dark Diadem tucked in next to the wall and eased my way back down the two ladders, pausing often to clear my head. The pain had not lessened, though I was getting fewer dark episodes obscuring my vision.

By the time I had returned to the ruined room I was shaking all over.

"Sersha," Mally said, her voice excited enough that I spun to look at her. "I think this is a list of names."

She was holding a book that she couldn't read. But when I stumbled across the ruined room, she shoved it into my hands.

"There's nothing here we could use as a weapon. Everything is too smashed, but there was also a pen and spilled ink and this book. Can you make out anything on the list?"

My finger traced slowly down the list of what had to be names, and though I wasn't much of a reader, I found one I recognized.

Cassanetta Lightland.

Mally was right. I flipped backward in the book until I found the first entry and above it were the words, "Honor Roll."

It came halfway through the book, but the rest of the book seemed to be chronicles of what Occulus had done and where he had been. A journal, perhaps? But journals were usually small, and this book barely fit on my lap.

Mally took it back from me and with a swift motion, she ripped the pages from their bindings, folded the list twice, and then jammed it down the front of her dress, cocking an eyebrow at me.

"Don't look so shocked. If we escape this place and I become Grand Hadri, I'd like to have a list of the people I can't trust."

I nodded, as she shut the book and jammed it under the rubble heap that used to be a chair just as the door creaked open a crack, and black and gold ropes tumbled inside.

238

"We can see your rope things," Mally said, her words mocking. "And I've certainly seen better. Best you can do?"

I backed up, tripping over a chunk of chair leg and sprawling backward. If the fall hurt, I didn't notice. Everything in my body was screaming at me to flee, leaving no room for any other thought as I backed up from the questing rope, skidding over shards of mirror. It curved sinuously like a snake seeking an opening and as I was still scrambling backward, it shot forward and wrapped around my neck, drawing close so that it brushed the skin all around.

I clenched my jaw tight, fighting hard against the panic that sought to steal my vision and my breath. The memory of being choked to unconsciousness was too fresh, too raw. I couldn't take it again. I couldn't. My heart was hammering in my chest, breath sawing in and out over raw lungs as the magic noose drew me up to my feet and urged me forward.

I stumbled along where it forced my feet to go, knocking accidentally into Mally who was doing the same, her face screwed up in concentration and her hands gripping the black rope surrounding her throat.

Before we'd reached the door it crashed open and Occulus stood there, one hand open, the ropes spooling from that hand while a look bordering on indifference painted his face. He was every inch the evil ropeworker we knew him to be, as if he'd read a description of one and was making an effort to match it. And he knew this was his tower, his place, his domain. The knowledge of it seemed to radiate from him like heat.

"I'm ready for you now," he said as if he had summoned us to clean his chambers. "This shouldn't take long."

Killing us? Yes, it wouldn't take long at all. He already had us entirely in his power.

"Ready for what?" Mally asked, her voice raw with fear masked in belligerence.

Occulus's lip curled. "I didn't set this little trap for you so I could be subjected to questions – ai'sletta."

That a pause there for a moment where he probably expected gasps and questions, but we were both too occupied with trying to breathe while ropes tangled around our throats.

After a moment, he grunted and turned back the way he came.

"If you fall, I won't catch you. Keep up and keep a hand on the wall."

And then I was being pulled forward again by the rope. I couldn't look down to see my own feet, not with the way it held my head, but I knew we'd reached the stairs when Occulus's head bobbed downward. He wasn't bothering with lights. Perhaps he had Flame Rider night vision like us, or perhaps he was a creature of darkness – like the snake he acted like – and didn't need them. Either way, we were drawn down the spiral staircase in near-darkness, hands on the wall as he'd ordered.

Mally was ahead of me, and she cursed every few moments.

"I can see why you're alone here," she said after the first few moments. "Hard to find help when you live like this."

She paused, clearly waiting for a reaction. I was too busy trying not to fall down the stairs, my hands feeling the worn brickwork of the wall, my feet trying to anticipate the next step.

"Maybe it's better with the lights on. But maybe you keep them off because your face is so hideous. Is that it?"

If Occulus cared about her insults, he showed no sign.

"You know that if you kill me, then you can't use my luck, right?" she said next. "And that's pretty valuable stuff. It's ruined things for you more than once. Maybe you should think about winning me over to your side rather than trying to scare me into helping you."

Still nothing.

"I went willingly with Cassanetta Lightland at first. She was much better at the whole persuasion thing than you are."

That received a grunt. I was surprised. Maybe her luck really was holding if it had swayed him with that argument. It was certainly preventing her from falling down the stairs.

We passed through a floor into a large room that was lit by long windows and filled with racks of weapons and suits of armor covered in a thick layer of dust. The center of the room had a circle painted on the floor with other circles and lines painted through it. Some kind of weapons training room would be my guess, though it hadn't been used in a long time.

"Did you study here?" Mally asked, clearly picking up on the same clues I had. "Do you think of your old school as home?"

Still nothing.

We were descending again, our spiral stairs wrapping around the edge of the training room and then dropping through the floor again, this time into a room twice the height of the last room and lined with bookshelves. Slit windows between the shelves lit the room and dust motes danced in the beams of light that picked out reading stands and tables in the center of the wide room. There were trails in the dust leading from shelf to shelf. Someone had used the library – but hadn't bothered to clean it first.

"I can see why you'd come here again. One last goodbye before you launch your master plan. You should definitely say a good one. You'll die here among your memories if you don't let me go."

Only Mally could taunt one minute, breathe threats the next, and try to manipulate in a third breath all while half-choked by a magic rope. I admired her attempt. It wasn't going to make a difference.

We continued to descend, floor after floor, passing from the library to what seemed like a great study hall with dust-covered seating, to floors with long halls and many doors – sleeping quarters, perhaps – and then a massive dining hall, and at last the ground floor – as high as two of the other floors with gargoyles peering down from rafters, weapons crisscrossed over the walls – though none were in reach. There were many massive statues – more than weapons and gargoyles combined – of men taming or perhaps fighting fanciful creatures and one another, ropework depicted in stone braiding itself between them. At either end of this floor, were massive oak doors. An entrance, then.

My eyes kept straying to the door, only for the ropework holding me to jerk forward every time they did. Once, my frantic gaze met Occulus's, but his grim features only hardened at the touch and his mouth turned down in a frown.

"And what do you have in your cellars?" Mally asked in a mocking tone as he led us behind a statue to where the stairs dipped below the earth, but I knew from her tone of voice that she didn't like this new development any more than I did. Occulus and his creepy tower were bad enough above the ground. Who knew what horrors he kept beneath it?

239

The kitchens, it turned out, were kept below ground. And the empty servant's quarters, and cavernous storerooms. Which showed an inhuman disregard for the needs of those who would have served here. I felt my stomach flip at the thought of working all day for someone like Occulus and then having to come down here below the surface of the ground where everything smelled like earth and mildew and having to sleep here. I shuddered, and Mally's gaze caught mine. She shook her head as if warning me about something. About what? She broke eye contact without telling me what it was.

These stairs below ground were lit with hanging lanterns spaced far enough apart that my vision didn't quite adapt to the darkness, but I could see just enough to avoid pitching forward and knocking Mally and Occulus both down the steps with me.

I had a sinking feeling about going down these steps. With each new floor reaching into the earth, I couldn't help but wonder if this would be my very elaborate grave.

I stopped wondering when we reached the final floor because I knew. I would certainly die here.

"Saved the best for last, I see," Mally said in a choked voice when we reached what seemed like the bottom of the stairs, only for Occulus to raise a closed trap door.

Light flooded up from beneath us, and as he led us through and down the last set of stairs, the light burned against my eyes and blinded me. I stumbled on a step and the hands that caught me were Mally's.

"Shh," she breathed in my ear – as if I could make a noise. As if I wouldn't be begging for mercy if I could. I didn't have her nerve. I couldn't stop the panic rising up my throat at what we were looking at.

It was one of the pillars. Only this one didn't look like stone, and it didn't quite look like the one Judicus had freed the phoenixes from. This one looked as if it were made from a woven golden mirror and the inside glowed such a bright white that it dazzled the eyes. I thought I saw swinging cages – like something you might keep a massive bird in – ringing the cavern around the pillar, but it was hard to see in such bright light.

The pillar was the height of three floors of the tower, and we descended the stairs slowly, legs tired from going down, down, down from the very top to these utter reaches beneath the earth, and eyes blinded by the pillar. And with every step, I grew more panicked, but I could not stop the pull of the black rope around my neck. I felt along it as far as I could, but the rope was stiff as if it had been woven of metal and there was no give, no bend, no chance of escaping, as it drew me down step by step toward this terrible fate. Because, surely, he would not bring us here just to show off. If he was the bragging kind, he would have risen to Mally's bait. He could only have brought us here for one reason. He was going to put us into the pillar.

"Marvelous, don't you think?" he said suddenly, and I almost jumped. I hadn't expected speech after so much silence. "I hope you like it. It will be your home now, for ... oh, eternity, I suppose. Unless I unleash you and then you'll wish you could go back to this melting pot for the soul. You'll wish to return to the agony of cosmic breakdown if only to escape the purposes to which I will set your soul, willingly or unwillingly."

"Our souls?" Mally asked, choked up as we reached the ground. She gave me a subtle shove, making me stumble to Occulus's left, even as she moved as far as her tether would take her to his right.

My vision was beginning to adjust, and I could see her face as her eyes met mine. She winked.

Winked? Right now, of all times?

"Oh yes," Occulus said and finally there was human emotion in his words – satisfaction. "Your bodies are young and healthy and my faithful will be happy to inhabit them. Don't worry, the switch is fast, though it isn't painless."

"*The mirror,*" Mally signed to me, and I barely caught the words, I was so shocked. When was the last time she signed? She usually pretended not to see my signs or not to understand them. "*Take it out.*"

She meant the mirror in my belt pouch. But what could Judicus do for us now?

"Young?" she said, a cat-like smile curving on her lips as she met Occulus's eyes while her fingers flicked to me. "*Be ready.*"

"Very young," Occulus agreed.

"Healthy?" she asked, quirking an eyebrow. Was she ... flirting with him? Only Mally would try that.

There! I had the shard of mirror. I pulled it free. I could feel the edge slice my finger at my incautious handling of it, but no matter.

"*Hold it up and don't flinch.*" Mally signed. Don't flinch from what.

"If you uncollar me, I'll be a good girl," she said to Occulus and he grunted a laugh.

"I doubt that," he laughed, "but I will have to bring you close to make the exchange."

"Keep him between us," Mally signed, and I didn't think Occulus even saw her subtly moving hands When had she learned to sign so well?

"Come here," he said, lifting the hand holding out ropes and drawing her toward him. It made me twitch as it pulled me closer, too, but I kept myself angled so that he was between us. "And if you behave, we'll do this with less pain."

She stepped forward. One step. Two. And then her hands signed. *"Hold steady!"*

And she shoved him hard.

240

I gasped, but I didn't flinch. I held the shard of mirror steady in my hands. Did Mally think I was going to stab him with it? It was facing the wrong way for that, the flat golden surface facing Occulus.

He stumbled backward, arms pinwheeling, and Mally was dragged after him as the noose on her neck tightened.

I gritted my teeth as he fell right toward me, arms out, a tiny shard of mirror the only thing to break his fall.

And then, with a sudden flash of light, he slammed into the mirror and was gone. I felt the tiniest shock in my arms from his weight hitting them – and then nothing. I gasped as the ropework around our necks fell and faded.

My eyes met Mally's and she smirked.

"You flinched. I saw it," she said.

And yes, she was very clever. She'd dispatched our enemy. But now he was in the mirror with Judicus. And how would my ropeworker fare with his mortal enemy suddenly foisted on him? I turned the shard to look into it, but there was nothing there. Nothing but a cloudy golden surface.

"This golden pillar is pretty awful," Mally said casually. "Do you think it's connected to the shard of mirror?"

I blinked back moisture in my eyes and didn't answer. It was easy enough for her to be casual about whether this would work. It was not so easy for me.

Someone cleared a throat. I looked up and Mally rolled her eyes at me.

"Seriously? Tears to get my attention? I know you want your precious Judicus back but staring into a mirror shard isn't going to do that. We need to find something in this deathtrap that will give us some clues about what to do next. And I'm going to guess that standing around crying is not it."

Someone cleared their throat again, but I was looking at Mally and it wasn't her. Her eyes widened and mine went straight to the shard like a flower turns to the sun.

Nothing.

It was still cloudy and all I saw was a distorted view of my own face.

"If you need answers, it is possible that I can help you," a heavily accented voice said from above us.

"There's someone in the cages," Mally said, horror in her voice.

She began to walk carefully around the pillar, checking one cage after another. I spotted the right one first. Living things had living needs. This living thing had two buckets hanging from ropes dangling from his cage. One, I would guess, was for food and water. The other for waste.

My stomach was already turning over when he leaned down from his perch to look at us. His cage was dangling about ten feet from the ground – though the cages were at all different heights and distances. Far up toward the ceiling there seemed to be a beam-and-pully system holding them, but I wasn't worried about that.

The golden light of the pillar kept the room perpetually bright, and though the cages cast dark shadows, the man's face was easy to see when he peered over the side. Or at least, the part that wasn't swathed in a leather covering was easy to see. The lower part of his face was wrapped in a leather cowl and his hood was pulled up and over his head so that when he spoke his voice was muffled.

"Not very wise of you to push the keeper of the tower into his own trap," the man said, following his words with a rattling laugh. He sounded ill. There was a whistle in his lungs. I'd heard that before in the elderly and it was never good.

"You're one of the raiders," Mally said, crossing her arms over her chest. "The Hand of the Rat. It's a goofy name. If I was naming an organization, I'd pick a better thing than a rat. Maybe the Talon of the Eagle or the Tooth of the Bear."

"It wasn't I who picked it," he said mildly but his laugh rattled out again when a small head poked out over the side of the cage with him.

Mally drew back in disgust from the snuffling rat nose above us.

"Not much stops rats," the man said confidentially. "Not locking them up. Not starving them. Not hanging the food ten feet above the ground. A rat always finds a way."

"And the Hand of the Rat?" Mally asked.

"Also finds a way."

"And would you, perhaps, have a way to destroy this pillar?"

"The Golden Column?" he asked, and I could hear the capitals. He squinted at me. "Why doesn't she talk?"

"She's talking. You just can't hear her," Mally said, raising an eyebrow expressively. "The column?"

"They found that. Didn't build it." His accent was so thick I had to concentrate to understand. It didn't help that he was muffled and distant as he spoke. "Found it. About three hundred years ago. Made copies in my homeland and one somewhere around here. I don't know where. Somewhere. They're connected. All connected. And do you know what they connect to?"

"Oblivion." She couldn't keep the tremble out of her voice, and I had a feeling that under his mask he smiled.

"Precisely. Precisely that. Only not. The long rot of the decaying soul. Or rather, of hundreds of decaying souls all gathered together and ... fermented."

"I'm going to smash it," Mally said crossing her arms over her chest.

"No, you won't. Because if you do that, you'll destroy the world. And you'll free the rope worker you just shoved in there because that shard of mirror you just put him into channeled him straight into the Golden Column."

This time, it was I who gasped.

241

I had so many questions. Was this Golden Column the place of torment he seemed to think it was? Because Judicus was in there, too. Whatever happened to Occulus within the pillar was happening to him, too.

I raised my hands, but Mally grabbed them before I could sign, dragging me behind her, away from the cage.

"Where are you going?" the man called to us.

"Back in a moment!" Mally called over her shoulder.

"Don't leave me here to die!"

"We'll be back!" she replied but she already had me hustled away and to the stairs and was dragging me up them as he wailed behind us.

My breath was sawing in my throat, and it had nothing to do with the climb. I was panicking and I knew it, but I couldn't stop. The moment we reached the top of the stairs and crossed up into the storehouses, I ran, taking the steps two at a time. I needed to get out. I needed Kazmerev. I needed ... I needed Judicus, but I couldn't have him, so I needed a breath of air.

I reached the door at the main level – the massive, oaken barrier – gripped the iron handle, and pulled. It was locked. I could hear the bolt rattle but there was no latch or bar on this side, only a keyhole. No matter. There would be other doors. I found one on the other side of the great hall – a servant's entrance, clearly, with quick access to a door that led to a ramp to the kitchens below. It was smaller than the grand entrance, but it, too, was locked.

A quick look around showed no windows at the ground level that were large enough for a person to slip through. There were many of them, but each was a slit no wider than my arm.

Mally found me, slumped against a statue of a man with raised hands, the marble sea rising around him in swirling fury. He looked the way my heart felt.

"We're locked in," she said baldly.

I looked at her through a gap in my fingers, as I buried my face in my hands. If she saw my tears, she'd mock me.

"Don't be like that. I couldn't have known the place was locked like a strongbox or that he'd keep the key with him. I had to act fast, and the mirror thing was brilliant. I bet you didn't think of it."

I had not thought of it.

"There will be some other way out. If nothing else, we can rig some kind of bedsheet nonsense from the belfry," she said, waving a hand as if none of it mattered. "Or, more likely, we can use a cable hanging the cages below. Or something. We aren't going to die here. I won't allow that. But I did need to get you away from our friend Rat down there. I just didn't expect you to run all the way up to the door. Give me some kind of hint next time before you act."

As if she ever gave me one.

But I pulled my hands from my face and looked up at her.

"The real question, is whether you're willing to negotiate with him. And whether we can trust what he says."

"*We have to talk to him,*" I signed.

She nodded, but she looked uncertain. "We could try our own thing without him. What if we let him free and then he kills us? His price to work with us is his freedom."

"*What if the key is with the others?*" I signed.

Mally barked a grim laugh. "It probably is."

We shared a look and I signed as an idea dawned on me.

"*Then the only way to get him out would be to put him in the mirror, too.*"

"No one who understood what that is would agree to it," she said, shaking her head, and then she sat down beside me and leaned her head back against the marble waves as she thought.

"He would have to trust on us to free him again with Judicus," I signed. "*Which would mean he would have to give us a real answer.*"

"I like how you think," Mally agreed. "Let's see if there's anything to eat.

There proved to be cheese and smoked sausages in the kitchen, a little water, and not much else. Occulus, it seemed, kept no servants in his eerie tower and was not living a life of luxury. We took the food with us when we descended to the lowest level a second time.

This time I watched the pillar as we descended. I couldn't look at it directly, but there were small swirls in the light. Eddies and ripples as if it were as much water as light. It reminded me of the pillar that held the trapped phoenixes. I shuddered at the thought.

"You're back," the man said hoarsely when we reached him. "I knew you'd come back. I'm the only answer to your puzzle."

"How do we get them out?" Mally asked, finger pointing toward the pillar.

"You don't want that. I promise you, you don't." He leaned his face against the bars.

"And why is that?" she asked.

"Living people won't come out. Only the souls of the dead. I saw it happen when they first had me imprisoned here - maybe eighty or ninety years ago."

"You can't have been here that long," Mally said, crossing her arms over her chest. "You're lying to us."

His laughter made me feel ill. It wasn't right. It was barely human. After a moment he began to cough, harsh and rattling, and the laughter faded out.

"You won't want to free them. Whoever is the most powerful among them will lead and what if you can't control that soul? You'll have an army of spirits haunting you forever. And what about after that? You're no ropeworker. You can't put them back in the pillar. Are they to roam the earth forever? No one knows how to send them away. No one. And their powerful leader will drive them across the earth like a general with a conquering army."

"Powerful as in magic?" Mally asked.

"Powerful as in strength of will," the man said. "Occulus' master – the ropeworker who had this tower before him – tried to free just one soul last time. Do you know how impossible that is? He learned. It was not just his dead ai'sletta who slipped out of the pillar. It was a dozen of the dead, led by a woman who hated him. It took the lives of almost everyone in this tower to put them back into that pillar."

"Ask him his name," I signed.

Mally rolled her eyes.

"What does she say with her hands?" the man said.

"She wants to know your name."

"I lost it a long time ago. It is gone to me now, forever."

How sad.

"Ask him why they imprisoned him," I signed.

"Could we just get on with it?" Mally asked, annoyed. "We don't need his life story. We just need to know if he knows how to get souls out of that pillar."

"Don't you think it matters if we're going to free him, too? He could be as bad as Occulus."

"He wouldn't tell us if he was very evil," Mally signed back. *"Would he?"*

But at the same time our nameless man was speaking again. "Of course I know how to get them out. Why do you think I was put in this cage?"

"I think you'd better tell us everything," Mally said.

242

"I was inducted into the Creed when I was a young man."

"The Cult of Tattered Ribbons," Mally said knowingly. He made a brushing sign with his hand.

"We call it the Creed and it is how the Hand of the Rat will finally orchestrate revenge against our enemies and justice for the nations. We will topple the leaders and plant our own on every throne, destroy their creatures of magic and flame, and replace them with creatures of our own design."

I shivered but Mally rolled her eyes.

"I think we can skip the recruitment speech. Get to the point. You and Occulus should be friends with all that creed stuff in common. Why are you in this cage?"

"I, alone of all my countrymen, began to see the truth – that the Creed was not what it seemed – not about promoting the Hand of the Rat and our justice, but about bringing a small knot of people into power not just over our islands, not just over some countries of their mainland, but over every nation and creed known to man or beast."

"Cute. You're a revolutionary. So, you see through it all, but Occulus or his master – or whoever – catches you because he's one of these people who get to inherit the earth, and then they put you in a cage. And this is eighty years ago, and you've been here ever since. And in all that time they didn't launch their big plan, so you have just been sitting there getting your food in a bucket. Am I right?"

She put food in the clean bucket for him as she spoke, but my eyes were wandering, trying to pick out details in the room. I thought I could see how this room had been carved from the rock, how the pillar had, indeed, been excavated. And whoever had done it had scribed runes into the rock around the base of the pillar. I couldn't read them. I wandered closer anyway, squinting at them.

"She won't be able to read those," the man told Mally. "No one can. If they carry a hint about how to stop this – or how to make it work for the person who finds the pillar – then the language is too old to discern."

"And what, everyone who ever died is in there?" she asked, jutting out her chin like she always did when she was very upset.

His laugh was as dry and hollow as ever. "I doubt it. It seems to only be those thrown into it when a ropeworker taps the golden light and weaves a door for it."

"Well, that can't be too many."

He laughed again. "I've seen at least a few hundred ushered into it with my own eyes. I've seen grown men beg for a death of torture instead. Watched them offer to eat their own ..."

"I think we get the point," Mally said quickly, and I was glad she cut him off. I didn't want to hear these terrible things. And Judicus was in there? For all this time? I should have been faster. I should have tried harder. "And you've seen it opened."

"Yes."

"Which means you can tell me how to do it."

"I will not. I have seen no good come of opening the pillar."

"Then I have bad news for you, masked man," Mally said grimly. "Because we accidentally put Occulus into the pillar with the keys in his pocket, and we can't get you out of that cage unless we push you into the mirror just like we did to him, and if that happens, then the only way you get *out* of the pillar again is if everyone does. Still want to keep your mouth shut?"

243

It's hard to talk over someone screaming curses at the top of his lungs, but eventually, Mally got me far enough away to say her piece.

"He'll come around," she said breezily. "He'll realize we won't be staying here to feed him, we can't get him out of the cage without a key, and starving to death alone is worse than whatever the mirror will do."

I wasn't so sure.

"We need to explore the rest of the tower and see if there's anything else we can use in case we need it. I'm good at judging that kind of thing, but I can't read much. Cassanetta taught me a little – enough to catch a few names, but that's it. So, I vote you go to the library and look around and I'll go everywhere else."

I tried to sign that I couldn't read much either, but she just shook her head.

"We work with what we have," she said grimly. "Even I what we have is you."

This time, it was my turn to roll my eyes. But I made my way to the library anyway and I was still there when she found me a few hours later, lit lamp in hand.

"I found nothing except a few trinkets of Occulus's that I can't see a purpose for, and that book from the upper room," she said. "The food situation is grim. That cheese and sausage were all he had. Which begs the question, who feeds the man downstairs when Occulus is galivanting about?"

Maybe he was left to starve. It was a sad thought. Or maybe he had a way to live off magic. There was likely quite a bit of it trickling from that pillar.

"As to the bedsheet theory – it won't work. Occulus used a single blanket and there's not another one to be found. He lives like a tramp. Did *you* find anything?"

I shook my head. I'd found many books on geography with carefully drawn maps. Histories of the various Grand Hadris of the past, with more volumes coming from other countries – some of which I'd never even heard of before. There were shelves of herb and animal identification. Some with ingredients for medicines and potions, tonics and poisons. There were books on metalwork and crop rotation, on the great lords and their genealogies, on ship-building and seafaring, and every other topic one could think of. There were books on rope work theory and practice and the history of the talents and trainings of ropeworkers. Those, I would have liked to indulge in. But there was nothing for our purposes. Nothing about the pillar or its triplets. Nothing about building new pillars or taking them down.

"I brought the book he had," she said, handing me the massive tome. "See if there's anything in there."

We settled into two chairs over a low table, setting both our lamps on the table and opening the book between us.

The early entries were about Occulus's younger years. His time as a student. His work learning ropework. It was only as the years of entries passed that he became more cryptic and mysterious in his writing.

"*They inducted me into the Great Secret today,*" one entry stated. "*Showed me the wonders and mysteries. Took my blood and oath. I am one of them now.*"

There wasn't much more about that for several years. I paused. It would take days to go through this book.

"Maybe you should try starting at the end and going backward," Mally said with a raised eyebrow.

But that didn't help us, either. The later entries were written in some kind of code, impenetrable to the uninitiated.

I flipped through hundreds of pages of code before I finally found an entry in plain speech again.

"*To open the pillar – to seize the spirits banked within and finally spend them for the cause. I long for the day. It will take sacrifice. It will take death. And it will not be my death used to open it.*"

I signed the words to Mally and her eyes widened.

"Well, that's useful," she said, her gaze turning inward. "Handy, too. After all, we have someone downstairs who will have to die one way or another."

"*That's murder!*" I signed. "*That's wrong!*"

But she was already on her feet and scooping up her lamp.

She didn't even see me signing, "*You can't do this! We can't!*"

There was no use. I grabbed the huge book – I had to hug it to my chest to carry it, which was ridiculous for a journal – and I hurried after her, nearly tripping on the steps and colliding with her before she finally slowed and spun to look at me.

"I don't want to hear your objections, Sersha. I don't want to hear that it's wrong because I don't care. A lot of things that are wrong have been done lately, and for once, I want to be the one doing them. And I want to be the one winning."

And what was there to say to that?

244

I was down on the entry level when I realized that killing the man in the cage might be harder than Mally expected. We had no bow or arrows. If she wanted him dead, she'd have to build some kind of pile of debris or find a ladder and get up to his cage and then use one of the weapons in the hall above us to skewer him through the bars. I wasn't sure she had the reach to do that fast enough before he simply dodged out of the way. Besides, she'd gone down empty-handed. And what if she needed to get his body to the pillar? He was locked in a cage, which was the whole problem. None of it was likely to happen immediately.

I did the only thing I could think of and pulled the shard of mirror from my belt pouch, desperately hoping Judicus would be there. Desperately fearing what woes he might be suffering in that place of oblivion and the fermenting of souls – whatever that meant.

Please be there. Please be there.

An eye met mine and a gasp. I placed the mirror hastily against a stone statue of some war-like man on the back of a stallion, a sword brandished in one raised hand. Quickly, I drew backward as the person on the other side drew backward as if we were mirror images of one another.

But it was not Judicus. It was his uncle. Captain Rackham. The former Grand Hadri. A man I had been sure was dead and then saw writhing in a golden cage.

I gaped at him, glad I was not holding the mirror. I might have dropped it in my surprise. What would I do now?

"Sersha," he said. He knew my name? He'd heard it, of course, but in life, he'd been an arrogant man. The kind of man who would forget the name of a commoner. "My nephew is ... away ... at present."

I didn't like how he said "away." It sounded far too much like "dying."

"*Where is he?*" I signed. "*Is he hurt?*"

But Rackham shook his head. "I can't read your signs, but I have a warning for you. It's urgent. Do you understand?"

I nodded.

"Don't send anyone else through this mirror. That's the warning." He looked over his shoulder into the bright light behind him and then back at me. "No one. Understand?"

And that's when it occurred to me – for the first time, and why was this the first time when it should have been obvious? – that if I could not bring Judicus to me then I could go to him.

I tapped my chest and pointed to the mirror and Rackham lifted his palms up, shaking his head immediately.

"No. Certainly not you. Promise me you won't try."

I tried to indicate a "why" but he seemed oblivious.

He leaned forward, breathing hard as if this were taking effort. "It's important that you do not do that."

I shook my head, frustrated that he wouldn't give me more information than that. Were they prisoners, then? Was this place truly the "oblivion" the others talked about? Without answers, how could I know? Perhaps, if I went through with Occulus's book, then Judicus could figure out how to get out. The chance that I could lose my life over that seemed small compared to that chance – especially since the other alternatives were starving to death in this tower, leaping from the top, or murdering the man in the lower levels.

I shook my head, frustrated.

"Look," Rackham said, trying to mollify me. "I might be able to keep talking to you for a little while. Why don't you go about your business and keep this channel close and then when my nephew returns, he can hear whatever you're trying to say."

He sounded boyish. More boyish than I'd ever heard him, and I squinted at his image and realized the lines of his face had smoothed a little. Was there something about that place that had made him younger?

I nodded my head and scooped up the mirror, holding it so Rackham could look at what I was looking at.

"Oh! You're in Occulus's Tower," he said matter-of-factly. "I gave him that statue of Adoniram to celebrate the school's hundredth year. The tower was called Briarlake then. Before all that messiness."

That explained everything and nothing all at once. It was a good reminder that the former Grand Hadri had played both sides. He'd been kind to Judicus, but he'd also killed his father. He'd stood against the raiders, but he'd also bolstered Occulus. I shouldn't trust him too much.

I descended into the kitchens and the storerooms as he chattered about gifts given to the school and the celebration he'd attended. I wasn't listening. I was worrying. Where had Judicus gone? Were we responsible for whatever had happened to him because we put Occulus in the mirror? And why wouldn't his uncle tell me that, if it were true?

I was barely listening to him when I stepped through the last floor and down the steps into the final pillar room below and Rackham said, "Oh yes, the pillar. I remember he showed us that."

Shocked, I turned the mirror back to me and looked into his eyes.

"Oh, yes," he said wryly. "And I think I would have been less excited by it if I'd realized I'd be stuck in it now."

I turned the mirror so that he could see the nearest hanging cage.

"The cages. They were there then, too. I don't know what you'd keep in them. Nothing that large lives beneath the ground."

I turned the mirror back to me and lifted an eyebrow, which he ignored as if he didn't know full well that they were made for humans. If the man below wasn't lying, and he'd been there eighty years, then he would have been there when they showed the pillar to the Grand Hadri.

But why would they have done that unless they were trying to recruit him to their cause?

"I thought it was just a fool's dream," Rackham said quietly. "I thought it was just an intellectual problem they were playing with. That they couldn't really take over the world and they were just a ... foolish little group of academics." He met my eyes then. "They seemed harmless."

He had the grace to flush and look away.

Whatever they were, it had not been harmless, and the fact that they had a man in a cage should have been proof of that. I was not feeling particularly sympathetic.

I would have signed that to him – even if he couldn't understand me – but a scream pierced the air, high and desperate.

Mally.

245

I began to run before the thought had even registered, as if my legs were linked directly to my ears with no brain in between them. I scrambled down the steps, hardly even listening as Rackham called from the mirror.

"Slow down, you fool girl! You're going to fall. You're going to break the mirror!"

That slowed me. I didn't dare break it. Not when it was my key to reach Judicus again.

I descended the last few stairs at a normal pace and only began to run again when I reached the ground. I hardly had to look up, Mally's screams guided me to the right cage, and I found her there, her shadow black and streaming out behind her as she hung from the cage, her hair gripped in the prisoner's hand, his arm and head stuck out between the bars.

A long knife lay on the ground at her feet.

"Are you planning to kill me, too?" he asked me harshly.

I tried to sign him dropping her, but he wasn't watching, his full attention on Mally whose hands gripped his arm as she screamed curses from where she dangled.

"She tried to stab me!" he cried wildly. "Tried to kill me! That's not how you open it, you fool girl. I said death – yes – but you'd have to put me in the pillar, and how would you get me out of the cage?"

See? I'd guessed that.

"There are knots all around the bottom," the Grand Hadri said from my mirror. "A ropeworker could pick them apart."

"Ha!" the prisoner said, giving Mally a good shake like she was a misbehaving kitten. She gnashed her teeth at him. But he didn't look up. Did he not care that someone was talking to him through a shard of mirror? "You'd have to have the luck of the ai'sletta to make that work. Choose the wrong knot and who knows what will happen? Implosion, demolishing the pillar and this whole tower? Possible. A sudden extermination of all the souls inside? Possible. An end to ropework and the threads of magic entirely? Pretty likely. The death of all living things? I'd bet on it."

"You're. Awfully. Talkative. Suddenly," Mally said through gritted teeth.

"The prospect of death does that to a person," the prisoner said.

"You. Were. Already. Dying. Just. Slower."

"So are you," he said and gave her another shake.

"I know you," Rackham said suddenly. He sounded shocked. "You're Questur the Ragged. That cult leader from the Forbidden Islands. They locked you up here in my father's time. They say that no one living has ever seen your face."

"What else do they say?" he asked, pausing to look at the mirror. Mally took the opportunity to pull herself high enough to bite his arm. He yelped and dropped her. "What was that for?"

"What do you think?" she muttered, dusting herself off.

"They said you nearly murdered my father. That you tried to assassinate him in his bath. That you nearly succeeded," the Grand Hadri said.

Questur, if that was his name, shrugged. "Who hasn't done a little light assassination. I heard you had your own brother killed. And no one put you in one of these cages for the act."

"No," Rackham said quietly. "They put me in here."

"Surely you must see why you have to die my way," Mally broke in, her breath still huffing in her lungs. She was pale in the bright light and swaying, but she wasn't about to give up. "You will die in that cage anyway. Of starvation or of dehydration after we leave. There won't be anyone to bring you food and water. It's better to die quickly."

"It doesn't work that way. But I suppose I will tell you how it does work once you put me into the shard with the delightful dead ruler and his memories," he said snidely. "I don't trust you not to mangle me with a dull knife and leave me here dying over days if I don't agree, so fine. I agree. I'll go in the pillar. Never call me a liar."

"He doesn't look dead to me," Mally said, peering at the mirror shard, but the man only smirked. "Fine," she said and before I could stop her, she ripped the mirror from my hand, jumped on the debris she'd piled under the cage, climbed up the teetering mass of wrecked furniture and old stone, and jammed her hand through the cage. "You want in? Get in."

Without even a single look or pause, Questur leapt, feet first, into the shard of mirror and disappeared.

246

"I *thought he said men begged not to go in the mirror,"* I signed.

Mally didn't answer.

"I thought he'd rather die than go in."

Still no answer.

The mirror clouded and Mally came down from the cage and thrust it at me.

"When it settles down and he can talk, he'd better spill everything, or one of us will have to die up close to the pillar. I need a nap."

And then she stalked away, back up the steps leaving me in the empty, echoing room alone with nothing but the shard of mirror left in my hands.

I made my way as close to the glowing pillar as I dared to go, and sat down with the mirror on the ground in front of me, stunned. I pillowed my head in my hands. It didn't clear. Not then, and not even when, eventually, Mally trudged back down from above with our pack, a brocade coverlet embroidered in sigils I did not know, and Occulus's journal.

"Something to keep you occupied besides pulling all your lovely hair out with worry," she said, thrusting the book at me, and then without saying another word, she put our pack under her head, wrapped the coverlet around herself, and went straight to sleep.

I wished I could fall asleep so easily. I watched the mirror like a hawk, my belly churning and rolling with anxiety. With both Occulus and Questur pushed into that mirror shard, I was nervous. What if they overwhelmed Judicus and Rackham? What if it was all our fault that I never saw my kind, exhausted ropeworker again?

But even worry can't keep a girl awake forever, and I was just beginning to drift off when I heard a voice – hopeful, rough, and anxious all in one.

"Sersha? Are you there?"

My heart almost broke for joy.

Judicus.

Hastily, I plucked the mirror from the floor so he could see my relieved face.

His own held a disbelieving smile. There was a new scar on his cheek, red and raw and untreated. My hand flew up to cover my mouth of its own accord.

"You're alive." He ran a hand over his face in what looked like relief. "Alive. When that man came screaming through and died at our feet, we thought ..." He died? Oh no. "Um. My uncle is here, and he says you've been talking." He blushed a vibrant red at that. Was his uncle a secret he'd been keeping from me? But why would he be a secret? "We thought that something terrible might have happened to you."

Carefully, I set the shard of mirror against my foot, angled up so he could see my hands move.

"*We are fine,*" I signed. "*Mally and me, both. The way your uncle spoke made me think you were ... hurt.*"

He shrugged and looked abashed.

"We had a little trouble," he signed. *"Actually, we've had quite a lot of trouble. But ... is it true that you've found a pillar like the other ones in the roots of Occulus's towers?"*

I nodded and turned the shard for him to see it. His eyes lit with wonder.

"Can you turn me so I can see the knots at the base?" he asked, smiling gently as I nodded.

I turned the mirror, still propped up by my foot, and let him consider in silence. I knew, now, not to take offense when the minutes dragged out. Could he find the solution to opening it, or had Questar's death ended that? Mally shouldn't have pushed him to jump into the mirror shard. She shouldn't have tried to kill him. He would have told us eventually. I was sure of it.

"Oh," he said at last. "Oh, well that *is* clever."

"*What is clever?*" I signed.

"The knotwork requires two people present. One at each side of the pillar touching the knots while they unravel them in tandem. No wonder no one ever managed it before. You'd need to really trust the other person – and be very lucky. If you got it wrong there'd be no second try. It would be ..."

"The end of everything?" I signed, lifting an eyebrow. That's what Questur had indicated. Questur, who was now dead. I felt bad for not feeling bad about that. I only felt worried.

"Yes, I think so," Judicus said simply. "Was there a reason that the dead man came through the mirror?"

"*He was to tell you how to open the pillar.*"

Judicus clucked his tongue. "That's a pity. One look and a trained rope worker would know ... well, perhaps it's more than that. But anyone who had studied Ancient Fa'quareeline could read the inscription along the bottom of the pillar plain as day. Poor old fellow must not have known."

"*Would you say many people can?*" I signed gently.

"Oh, at least three or four," Judicus said as if that were half the country. "And they wrote it very plainly. Of course, even with instructions, you'd need to be enormously powerful and able to work with another enormously talented rope worker like two hands playing a piece on a harpsichord." He paused and looked up at me. "You might need to find more ropeworkers. Is that possible? Powerful ones?"

I shook my head sadly. "*We're trapped here with food for maybe a few days,*" I signed. "*We might be able to find a way to scale down the tower but there are no ropes or tools, so we'd be tying strips of cloth together.*"

"Likely better than starving," he agreed sagely. "But perhaps ... well, we could try something else. It's just ... well, we'd have to be quite lucky to pull it off."

"*Lucky like last time?*" I asked with a smile.

"Exactly like," he agreed but now his eyes met mine and crinkled around the edges as his gentle smile deepened. "*Are you whole still, dear heart?*" He signed.

"*I am.*" I signed back. "*And you?*"

"*Whenever I am with you.*" He paused. "*And when I have a puzzle to solve. I hope that is not a problem?*"

His eyes widened with worry on the last bit, and I laughed. Only Judicus would both admit that the woman he loved was matched by a puzzle and feel entirely embarrassed by the fact.

"*It's not a problem for you to be Judicus,*" I said, and as always, he blushed at his name in my hands. "*It will be a problem if I find you have stopped being Judicus.*"

"*Well then,*" he said, biting his lip and smiling all at once. "*Don't be angry when I tell you what I want to ask Mally.*"

"*Let me guess,*" I signed. I was getting good at guessing. "*You want to ask her to stand at one point of the pillar and me at the other with this mirror propped somewhere that can see both points and you're going to try to do ropework through both of us at once and hope her ai'sletta luck holds, and that you're more powerful and skillful than any other ropeworker in existence so that we all survive the incident and open the pillar.*"

His mouth fell open but stunned as he was, his hands danced. "*When you put it like that ...*"

"*I think that's the only reasonable way to put it,*" I signed. "*And it is also the only possible plan.*"

He nodded, looking worn and tired suddenly.

"*Can you do it?*" I asked him.

"*I must,*" he signed. "*And therefore, I will.*"

247

Mally did not like the plan. Which wasn't surprising.

"You want me to let him do *what?*"

"I'll reach through the mirror and into your mind," Judicus said, patiently.

"No."

"If there's any latent ability to weave ropework, then I'll use it to work and use Sersha's ability on the other side of the pillar. With intense concentration and cooperation, perhaps we can open the pillar."

"No." She crossed her arms over her chest.

"You were willing to murder someone to do the same thing," I signed. *"Nothing has changed. We can't open the door or get out of the tower."*

She refused to look at me.

"She was going to murder someone?" Judicus asked, appalled.

"The dead man who came through the mirror," I signed. *"She was going to murder him. He says that if you kill someone you can open the pillar."*

"Oh, I wouldn't do that," Judicus said coolly. "If you opened the pillar by killing someone then anything that came out would be tainted by that. You'd end up with a dozen or so spirits tumbling out of the pillar and all of them bent on tearing you to pieces. No, that's a terrible idea."

"It's no worse than the idea of having *you* in my mind!" Mally countered. "Surely there's a law against that!"

Judicus looked abashed. "Well, yes there is. And yet, I still don't recommend that you kill any other prisoners."

"There are no other prisoners," I signed.

Judicus's jaw dropped, a look of horror in his eyes as his gaze darted back and forth between me and Mally.

"Shut your mouth or you'll catch flies with it," Mally muttered miserably. "That wisp of a beard is bad enough."

Judicus shut his mouth and rubbed his beard self-consciously before clearing his throat and offering a very credible glare.

"I may be trapped in this mirror, Mally of Landsfall. But I will not be trapped forever. And if you hurt Sersha, I will cause such furor to rain down on you that no amount of ai'sletta luck will save you. You will learn regret until it is etched upon your bones."

I felt my eyebrows creeping up slowly as he spoke, but Mally just scoffed.

"It's a weak threat coming from a man trapped in a mirror."

"I could offer others."

"Fine!" She threw her hands up. "I'll do it. But no funny business."

Judicus coughed. "I'll also have to ask that you keep what is done here a secret."

"Well, obviously. People would tear you to pieces if they knew you could do that. I swear, Judicus, you should be ashamed of yourself. Ashamed. You know that, right? A mind is a sacrosanct place, Judicus. No one is supposed to enter it."

"That's an excellent word you acquired, Mally." He said mildly, eyes drifting to the pillar as he spoke. "Have you been saving it for me?"

She stared at him as if he'd grown a second head, but I snickered. *"It's a joke."*

"I know it's a joke," she said, looking horrified. "But *he* shouldn't tell them. They don't suit him at all. Let's just do this thing before I decide to go back to the killing Sersha plan. Should I sit on the far side of the pillar?"

"Yes," Judicus said tightly. "And if you can prop my mirror up for me, Sersha. I need to be able to see both of you at once."

As soon as she was out of view his hands flew in sign. *"Will she really kill you?"*

I shook my head. I knew Mally would do a lot of things. Murdering a relative wasn't one of them ... I thought.

"I will be here with you every step of the way. If this is our last adventure, then I'm glad to share it with you."

"I feel the same," I signed after I placed the mirror on the ground, leaning against the pack. *"You are my heart."*

"Would you two stop mooning over each other? This floor is cold," Mally called.

"Can you see her?" I asked Judicus.

"Turn it a little to your right," he said. "Then there will be a way to see you both."

"How will you see clearly enough from so far away? How can you control the ropes so minutely?"

He clenched his jaw, the only sign of his anxiety, before he looked up and smiled at me.

"Never fear, Sersha. I will manage just fine."

He always spared me a smile, no matter how hard things were. That made my heart warm every time. Hurriedly, I took my seat on the other side of the pillar. I couldn't see Mally from here, but I could still see Judicus in the mirror.

"Make sure your seat is comfortable," he called to us. "This might take a while."

"Just get on with it, rope worker!" Mally growled.

I adjusted my seat, crossed my legs, and set my palms easily down on my knees.

We'd done this once before. We could do it again.

Judicus was in my mind before I blinked.

Sersha?

Judicus.

My heart.

Excuse me, I can hear that.

And Mally was in there with us, too.

If you could both try to calm your thoughts, Judicus said.

Calm this, ropeworker, Mally said.

Rude mental pictures are entirely unnecessary. Judicus sounded tired.

I closed my eyes and concentrated on calming my thoughts. My breathing slowed. My heart slowed. Everything slowed except my love for this tired man. That, I let permeate my thoughts.

Ewww, seriously, Sersha? I don't need all that heartwarming nonsense.

Mally, please, Judicus interrupted, *I have a task for you. Concentrate on the markings below the pillar and try to pick one.*

I don't know what they say.

I'm hoping that will actually help. Maybe if you don't know which to pick, your luck will guide your choice.

There was silence for a while and then Mally said, *I pick the one that looks like a shooting star.*

Thank you, Mally, Judicus said. *Both of you, please raise your hands.*

I lifted my hands and his ropes flowed from my palms. It had begun.

248

It seemed like a long time before anything happened, the ropes hovered and slowly branched, and then tangled outward to the rhythm of my beating heart. They spread along the base of the pillar and reached along the glyphs and then it happened all at once. The ropes began to weave at a lightning speed – so fast that I could barely keep track of the weaving. I wondered how Judicus could manage to do that in two different directions. It must take enormous concentration. There were at least six different strands of rope weaving from this side and likely just as many from Mally's side.

It was impressive.

Shhhh, Sersha, he's trying to concentrate.

I gritted my teeth against her mental whisper and tried to still my thoughts so I wouldn't distract him.

I could help, Mally said. *I was a dab hand at braiding my sisters' hair.*

She actually was. But just as she said that, the ropes shifted, settling into the shape he'd woven and seeming to firm, and then slowly, like tea steeping in hot water, a golden color infused them and flowed outward and down the ropes.

My breath hitched in my throat.

"Easy, Sersha," Judicus said from the mirror. "I have to draw on that golden thread or this won't work. It is not evil in itself. You only see it as evil because of what it has been used for. For the trapping of humans and their souls."

"Yeah, easy Sersha, it's just a deadly poison that killed a ton of people," Mally said wryly. "Why would that worry you?"

But her voice shook, too.

And then the ropes were entirely taken over by gold with only the tiniest threads of black around them. I found I was sweating. I was seeing that the ropes were made of hundreds – no, thousands – of tinier threads, and the threads were woven within the ropes as well as in the pattern Judicus had laid out. Each thread was no thicker than a hair of my head.

I was beginning to tremble. How long had we been here? I'd lost track of time as I traced the threads and the knots. Something about them drew the attention – or perhaps Judicus was drawing my eyes there to aid in his work. Hadn't he said he wouldn't look through my eyes? But that was before. Maybe it was different now.

It is not the work of a moment, my heart.

We've been at this for hours, Mally agreed. *And I drank too much earlier to sit here much longer.*

Lovely thought, Mally.

It's a true thought, she shot back. *So maybe finish up with opening a portal to the netherworlds so I can go ease the tension, would you?*

We are close ... he said in my mind, and he sounded exhausted, like he might collapse from the effort.

And then, without warning, the ropes tightened and all at once Judicus's mind was snatched out of mine. My eyes went straight to the shard of mirror. There was some flurry of movement in it – but what it was I couldn't make out and then the surface clouded.

"Uh oh," Mally said.

I heard my heart beat once – too loud and hard – and then the pillar shattered as if it were made of glass.

I didn't look. I didn't wait to see what would happen. I had a sudden instinct to save the shard of glass that was my only connection to Judicus. I was on my feet while it was still shattering – while pieces were still flying. They scored my face, my arms, cut through my dress and into my legs, but they mostly hit my side and back as I ran and made it just in time to snatch up the shard of glass before something caught me like a wave and carried me – helpless – toward the rocky wall of the cavern. It was like being caught on a wave of the sea. I was carried outward and upward until my shoulder crashed against the wall. Quick thinking brought my free hand up in time to protect my head.

The wave of – whatever it was, I still couldn't see because my back had been to the pillar – ebbed and released me enough that I fell back to the cavern floor. Behind me, Mally was cursing in a way that sounded more terrified than angry.

I shoved my shard of mirror into my belt pouch and spun to see what was happening.

I came face to face with a bearded man missing an eye and both ears.

I opened my mouth to scream, and a hand clamped over my mouth – and then kept going, seeming to pass right into my flesh.

The scream stuck in my throat, my panicked breath stuttering as I looked into the face of the thing whose hand was somehow passing right through me. He was made of bright golden light, brilliant, and beautiful, and terrifying.

A spirit, I realized. A captured spirit freed from oblivion. Just as we were warned.

And behind him, the cavern was so full of them that they reached from edge to edge as far as the eye could see.

"He did it wrong!" Mally said scornfully from what felt like the other side of an ocean of spirits. "He failed somehow. This can't be right!"

There was a flurry of motion through the sea of spirits, like the path of a shark cutting through the waves. And then one of them ripped the one-eyed man out from in front of me and shook him with the words, "You don't touch her."

He was taller than he had been in life and broader in the chest. And he glowed gold. And there was something about the way the light caught his brow that looked almost as if a golden circlet had been set there, though it could only be seen from the corners of my eyes.

"I didn't fail, Mally," he said, and it was still *his* voice. It was still his eyes looking into mine, even though they were the golden, bright eyes of a spirit. "I never promised that the souls caught within would reenter bodies. Only that they would be free of their cage."

And I couldn't help the sob that caught in my throat because I'd never really let myself believe that he was dead until that moment.

249

Behind him, there was a sound like a pop and then a terrible scream.

He spun, arms up and gold ropes flowed from his hands and outward. My heart caught in my throat. Gold. Like Occulus had woven. This wasn't right. My ropeworker wove black strands.

But the gold wove outward at the same moment that violence rocked through the bright spirits which filled the cavern from side to side as wide and deep as the lake outside. Through the center of the mass of them, some kind of current bubbled up, erupting. I had to blink twice against the brightness of their collective bodies before I realized what I was seeing.

A small knot of spirits fought as it pushed through the rest. They fought with spirit hands and teeth, rending and ripping to the choked screams of the others. The man at their forefront wove golden ropes, ripping the spirits in his path with choking, tangling golden ropes.

Occulus.

He had survived and he was fighting against those who had been freed with him. The other spirits disappeared when they were ripped apart like shreds of mist before the sun. Was that ultimate death, then? Or something else? Would they reappear? Here? Or perhaps in another pillar?

And then my Judicus was leaping forward, his own ropes tangling outward and snatching Occulus's away from the neck of an elven spirit nearby – there seemed as many elves in the crowd as humans.

"Occulus!" he snarled in a way that didn't sound like Judicus at all, and the way he leapt forward – coordinated and powerful – seemed unlike him, too. It made something in my chest feel heavy.

"Son of Chaos!" Occulus cried in return. "You shall not hold us!"

And then his words were snatched away as Judicus charged forward, his ropes tangling outward like tree roots over the centuries, tangling with Occulus's, ripping and snatching and rending.

The spirits with Occulus hadn't stopped and the edges of the sea of spirits rippled on either side as the rebel spirits carved a way to the stairs, fighting for every step.

I lost sight of Judicus in the push of golden spirits. Only his ropes tangling upward with the ropes of Occulus rose above so many heads.

And I was powerless to help because what did you do against a spirit?

I heard Mally snarl in the distance, her progress impeded by bodies she could step right through if she wanted to.

And then they'd reached the stairs and I could see them again – Occulus at the rear of his contingent as they scrambled up the spiraling steps, his hands thrust outward to weave his ropes against Judicus.

Judicus, with his own ropes plucking and pulling, trying to drag Occulus back down into the morass.

"You won't hold me!" Occulus's voice boomed out across the room. "You might have the strength to hold them, but you won't hold me. You're not to my level yet, Judicus Franzer Irault. I will go out into the world with my followers, and I will rend it apart and you will be left chasing my tail like a puppy chasing the wind. You will not catch me. You will always be too late, and so will I rip your heart out and your spirit will die like an oak when the trunk is hollowed."

He threw out a burst of ropes to punctuate his words. Judicus countered with his own twisting ropes, but Occulus had sent too many and while Judicus deflected the two aimed at his throat and the one jabbing toward his midsection, he missed the rope that tangled around his ankles and sent him falling backward down the stairs.

Occulus's ropes fell and faded as he gave Judicus a mock salute and darted through the closed door above.

Judicus righted himself, looked toward the empty stairs, and then seemed to look right at me before he barked an order in a tongue I did not know, and a dozen spirits charged past him and up the stairs.

"He's slipped the noose," someone said. "We won't catch him now."

Judicus ignored them, though he must have agreed because to my utter surprise, he pushed through the sea of spirits, not headed up to chase Occulus but instead, sliding through the crowd to join me.

"Sersha," he whispered, and his bright eyes looked into mine and they were all wrong. They were all wrong. He wasn't supposed to be dead. He hadn't been dead in the mirror. "Sersha. Please stop crying."

"Shouldn't you be chasing him?" I signed.

"This is more important."

I drew in a long breath and made myself stop. I wasn't helping anyone. Judicus needed to be chasing the escaped ropeworker, not coming back for me.

"It's not. I'm not."

"You are. Always."

He bit his ghost lip and tried to reach for me, but his hand passed right through me, and I sucked in another sob, fighting hard, so, so hard not to just give in and weep my heart out.

I loved him and he was here.

And yet.

I wouldn't be marrying Judicus after all. I wouldn't be living a life with him, cooking his dinner, or mending his clothes. Ghosts didn't marry. They didn't wear clothes. I'd never feel his embrace again. Or his kiss. And his kisses had been treasures. There wouldn't be children to play with Grevankin. I felt as if I couldn't quite breathe.

"Would you make space, you hideous creatures? Space! Go chase those other spirits if you have nothing to do!" I heard Mally bellowing, but I couldn't catch my breath. I couldn't so much as sign to her. Not right now. Not like this.

"Sersha," Judicus said, and his tone nearly broke my heart. He'd known. I could tell that he'd known all along. He should have said something.

He tried, again, to touch my cheek and his fingers slipped through my flesh as a distinct look of agony twisted his long, fine features. His wince hurt me. Hurt like a slash to my skin.

And then suddenly there was an arm around me – warm and thick and trembling and Mally was beside me, hugging me into her large bosom. She was slashed and streaked with blood from the broken pillar, just as I realized I was. She shouted at the top of her lungs as only Mally can.

"If you weren't already dead, I'd gut you, you terrible excuse for a man! You went into my brain. MY. BRAIN. And you rummaged around in there. And I let you. And all that time I should have known you were a no-good little cheat. Why didn't you tell her?"

"Mally, I – "

"Why?" she demanded, and I realized, to my utter shock, that she was crying, too, her face vivid red and her whole body trembling almost as much as mine was. "It's not like we wouldn't have freed you anyways. It's not like we wouldn't have come and got all these people and made sure they could go on to the afterlife. Even knowing that Occulus would get free. Again."

"Mally," he said, and this time it was gentle, like he was a father and not our friend. My – oh, make it stop. It hurt too much to think.

"Judicus," she spat back. "Don't even start with some high-brow explanation. We set you free and I'm not an idiot. I can see that you are in charge of this army of the dead."

That got my attention. My head snapped up and I truly saw – not just my broken betrothed but the men and women who were golden ghosts. They had arranged themselves in ranks behind … him. The ones he had ordered had disappeared up into the night because he had told them to. These spirits were behind Judicus, and every eye was on him.

I felt my mouth forming an "O" as Mally kept on talking, plowing over any attempt by Judicus to get a word in edgewise. Her curls under it were mussed, and she looked for all the world like a goddess come down to judge us all.

"And I can also guess that the bunch of you can pass through walls just like you pass through bodies. Which means you'll be through the walls of this tower and off onto the road to seek your revenge and win back your sister's country before I can so much as blink, never mind come up with a way to leave this hope-forsaken tower. You don't care about us!" Judicus squared his sloping shoulders at that, chin coming back in offense. "You don't care about *her*!" Mally spat, pointing at me. "All your fine words to her were nothing but mist."

"Shut that mouth of yours, Mally!" Judicus said and the air whuffed out of my chest because I'd never heard him so furious. "Has it never occurred to you that with sufficient bravery you could have left this tower at any time?"

"I'm as brave as anyone," Mally said, thrusting out her chin. But she was holding back tears, too. I knew it.

"Fine," Judicus said, batting the question aside with a ghostly hand. He was remarkably still like himself even now that he was noncorporeal. "Then sufficient intelligence."

"I'm just as smart as you are, Judicus Franzer Irault."

"If that were true," he said coldly, "then you would have realized at once that as long as you were wearing that crown you've stashed away somewhere, and trusted your phoenix, all you had to do was leap from the tower and he would appear to catch you and wing you to safety."

Oh.

That was so ... obvious. And I hadn't thought of it.

I felt like a fool.

"And if you were sufficiently smart, Judicus Franzer Irault," Mally spat back, "then you'd realize that none of it matters since you've gone and broken my cousin's heart!"

And with that she let me go and stormed away and up the stone steps. The crowds of ghosts parted for her to pass, and I heard her cursing even as Judicus softly said, "Yes."

And his eyes stayed on me as I crumpled against the wall and curled in on myself. And I should care that I was distracting him from chasing Occulus's ghost. I should care that I was taking his attention when he had an army to lead. But I found I could care about nothing except his life, lost forever to this golden half-life before me. Someone should mourn it. Someone should care. And I was the one who was going to do that.

250

I really was trying not to sit down and cry like a child. I was trying to get a hold of myself, but I was exhausted and worn, and I had flown or run or ridden from one danger to the next for months and now to find that there was no happy ending – not even a chance of one. I just couldn't do it right now. I wished I was as strong as Mally, screaming and venting my anger and then storming away. But I wasn't her and the only thing I had the strength to do was curl down around myself and try to pretend it was all over and that I could just stay in this little ball forever.

"Sersha."

The room had grown quiet. So quiet that his whisper sounded like a shout. When had that happened?

I looked up to an empty, dark cavern. The wreckage of what was once a pillar still glowed softly, but it barely lit the room now. And the glowing ghosts were all gone except the one sitting beside me with his back to the wall just like mine.

"I sent them above," he said awkwardly. "Occulus is gone. Those who followed could not even catch a glimpse of which way he went. But there were only a few of them and I think I can keep them from the full depths of what they could do even now that they are apart from us ... me." He paused and bit his lip. "So ... you and I have time to talk."

I looked into his eyes, sorrowful. Aching.

He cleared his throat and if he'd been alive, I'd be certain he was holding back tears.

"I didn't know for sure. I didn't tell you because I didn't know."

"You don't have to explain yourself," I signed. *"You're the one who is ... "*

I stuttered over the word *dead.*

He looked off into the darkened distance. "Until the pillar broke, I kept thinking that maybe I would walk out with my body whole and unbroken like I walked in."

"Did you feel dead when you were in there?" I signed, pausing to wipe tears and blood from my face. What a mess.

He shook his head. "I ... I don't know. I don't know what I felt. Worried, I suppose. Strained. But I was feeling that before I went into the mirror. I was happy whenever I saw you. I thought ... I thought ... I thought we could still be together. That I would still marry you. That I'd protect you and guard you and carry you through this life. That I just had to right the wrongs first."

"All of them?" I signed.

"Yes."

That was so Judicus.

"And you know, get my sister to safety."

"You can do those things," I signed.

He nodded, still looking off into the distance. "Yes. Yes, I can. But I'd trade them all – "

I smacked the flat of my hand against the ground and he jumped, turning to look at me with startled eyes. His weedy beard had disappeared. His ghost was neat and tidy – or as neat and tidy as Judicus ever was. Even tidy he looked rumpled as if he'd spent the night reading instead of sleeping.

"You wouldn't trade them," I signed. *"Doing the right thing is who you are. And you still can do it."*

His eyes met mine and his lower lip was trembling and that made my tears start again, silently.

"I don't want you to be dead," I signed.

"I don't want to be a spirit while you live," he whispered and he leaned his ghostly head down so that its bright light was almost cradled on my shoulder without actually touching it while he sobbed. His light flickered like a campfire in a high wind. And I couldn't put my arms around him and that hurt so bad, but I brushed my lips along where his cheek should be, and when he looked up at me, his bright eyes fluid and deep and aching, then I brushed them along where his lips should be and he parted them and gasped, letting out a shuddering sob. I couldn't feel a bit of it. All I felt was where he wasn't.

"I will not marry another," I signed. *"I don't know what this ghost-life will be like or how long it will last, but as long as you are here, I will be by your side, and when the fight is over, if you remain, you will come and fly on Kazmerev with me and we will see the world and I will turn the pages of books for you so that you can read and I will take you to places I have never been, and tell you what the food tastes like, and just as you have given me sign words and with them a voice, I will give you touch and taste with those signs."*

He nodded briskly and stood and he seemed to be gathering his composure as he straightened.

"My precious Sersha, my heart of hearts," he said. "I will take that offer, my sweet girl."

And he smiled that sweet, selfless smile he always gave me. The one that gave far more than it ever took and then he gestured, and I stood, too.

Gently, he said, "I hope you grow to like reading, because we'll be doing that a lot."

And I did my best to smile for him, because I could not soothe him with a gentle touch or a warm blanket or a cup of tea. A smile was all I had to offer. Then, carefully, our hands not touching but rather passing in and out of each other, we climbed the stairs to the floor above. We were almost at the top when he stopped and cleared his throat awkwardly.

"I hope you don't mind, but I'll have to lead the army."

I nodded. He was somehow the most powerful among them, wasn't he? Hadn't the raider prisoner said the strongest would lead them?

"Things in the abyss were ... unusual," he said, and I could almost swear his golden cheeks were blushing. "And in the end, I had to choose to seize leadership or watch the unwatchable happen. I hope you can forgive me."

"Forgive you for what?" I signed.

His smile was rueful. "For taking the reins. I'm pretty sure that's how I lost my body."

And then we were moving again, and I was trying to breathe through lungs that just couldn't take another shock.

251

The rest of the army of the golden dead had arranged themselves on the main floor between the statues and to my surprise, they seemed to be arguing. They stopped when they caught sight of Judicus.

"The ai'sletta has bolted the door to the upper levels," a woman with elaborate braids announced. She was a full head taller than me, though what coloring she might have had in life was erased in death now that she was formed of honey-colored light. There was something familiar about her, though she looked like no one I knew in life.

"You said you thought you could manage her," a man said, stepping out from the orderly ranks.

I gasped. It was the former Grand Hadri. Captain Rackham. A honey-gold ghost like the rest of them. I felt a pang at the sight of him – not because I cared particularly for Judicus's uncle, but because he'd been alive when last I'd seen him – just like my beloved ropeworker, and now here he was just as much a spirit. He looked younger than he had in life and thinner, as if he were less burdened in death than he had been in life.

He offered me a kindly grimace as if he could see my thoughts on my face.

"What I said," Judicus said carefully, "And what I was very clear to communicate, was that the ai'sletta is both a friend and ally of mine, and she will work with us and with her cousin, Sersha," here he gestured to me, "to rid this land of the last reaching grasp of the Creed. I was precise in my words and promises. If more can be done, that can be considered, but the one aim we agreed to – all of us agreed to – was to rid this land of the Creed and to smash, forever, their ability to create the Pillars of the Abyss and trap souls living and not quite dead within the morass there. I cannot promise more, and I do not pretend to possess more power than I have."

But the power he had was plenty. He'd smashed the pillar below and no one was going to convince me that it hadn't been utterly brilliant work done under extreme pressure.

"Our loyalty remains, Weaver," the woman said, and I tilted my head in a question.

"It's what they called ropeworkers a thousand years ago," Judicus told me looking slightly embarrassed even in his golden, glowing form. He leaned in close, and I missed the warmth I used to feel when he did that. "Do you think you can convince Mally to open the door? Take all the time you need. We need to get organized here."

I nodded and then crossed the room, careful to keep my hands to myself as I walked between the gathered spirits. I didn't want to accidentally slip a hand through someone else's ghost hand. The idea gave me the creeps. They eyed me gravely, each one I passed turning to watch me. They were an impressive lot, quiet though they were. I had to squint at their brightness to make out details and the loss of color made it harder, but I thought I was seeing modes of dress and armor long forgotten. Weapons and raiment like I'd never seen before. And those who bore them stood straight and proud as if they had been something in life.

They made me nervous, but their leaders who were gathered around Judicus treated him with deference. They respected him. I was impressed by that. What would it take to win over this group and what – exactly – had he done to achieve it?

By the time I had reached the solid oak door at the top of the steps, I was convinced I'd need to hear the story.

I rapped on the door.

"Go away." A pause. "If that's you, Sersha, then rap once to tell me you're an idiot who left the journal and our bag below and twice if you are going to surprise me by remembering."

I rapped once.

"Go get them and when you get back rap the number of brothers and sisters that I have, or I won't let you in."

I wasn't sure what she thought the door was preventing. I was the only person left in the tower who could be blocked by doors. But it seemed the spirits were willing to respect her barrier, so maybe she wasn't entirely crazy.

I hurried to gather our things, passing Judicus twice. He had arranged six ghosts around him and was sketching something out for them as they leaned around where he made rope patterns on the floor. Apparently, he could still weave the ropes even if he couldn't touch physical things, and he was using them to create a map of the area. Watching them put a lump in my throat. I had yet to resign myself to the fact that a great barrier now divided me from Judicus and nothing could restore us again.

His leaders seemed to hold him in very high honor and the rest of the army of the dead followed suit. They stood in silent ranks at attention while their leaders spoke. The former Grand Hadri, the woman with the braids, a burly man with a bald head, a twin pair of hooded and masked men as narrow and thin as Judicus – those were his inner circle.

On my trip back from the depths, I glanced at them jealously as I walked past, my arms full of book and pack. They had what I would never have again. Closeness to my beloved. A future with him.

I couldn't shake the gnawing misery at that as I climbed the steps and rapped five times on the door. Mally threw the bolt, grabbed me by the collar, and yanked me inside, slamming it behind me and throwing the bolt again. She was wearing her crown again on top of her mussed hair.

I rolled my eyes at her.

"They have yet to prove they can walk through walls," she said, jaw thrust out. "And until they do, I'm keeping them out."

Her hands were shaking.

I met her eyes and saw the fear swirling there – and the pity. Her face and hands were clean and she shoved a pitcher and a rag into my hands. The rag looked clean.

"I stole these from Occulus's room. You can clean your face and hands," she said but when I wasn't fast enough she snatched the cloth back with a sigh. "I'll do it."

She had me clean in a few breaths. All my little cuts tingled.

"You look a fright," she muttered. "You'd think you were the one who was dead and not glow-boy."

At the sight of my welling eyes, she rolled her eyes and threw the rag on the floor.

"Well?" she asked.

I shook my head, confused.

"Well, don't you want to look at the library before we leap to our likely deaths? If there's some way to restore your fool man back to his body, then it must be written down somewhere. I thought you might want to look for it before we go off adventuring again."

252

"There has to be something here," Mally said for the hundredth time, breathing over my shoulder.

I looked back at her and shook my head, irritated. There was nothing. I'd looked through all these books already – well, not really, but I'd found their categories and some titles before and there were thousands of books. There wasn't a category for "How to Free Your Betrothed From a Magic Mirror When He's Become a Ghost" so I was adrift in a sea of books. It was easy to eliminate the biology, the history, the geography, and other topics like that, but what was I to do about biography. Might this have happened to someone else? The books of magic were even worse. I tried to sift them by title, but I couldn't be sure which I could truly eliminate. Something like this could be slipped in anywhere.

I'd almost given up when Mally said in a curious tone, "Oh ho, I bet you didn't look here."

And I certainly hadn't. Because I hadn't tipped over a stuffed chair, ripped up the rug, and levered open a floorboard. How had she even known to look there?

"I can't read the title," she said as I came down from the library ladder and took the small volume from her hand. "What does it say?"

It was written in a spidery hand, making it hard to read, but the title was "Of the Uncommon, Dark & Deadly."

I tried to sign it and she just sighed, "You need a bigger vocabulary. Let's just agree you should take the book."

I nodded my agreement.

"And now, I think we fly away. If you have the guts to leap from a tower and the faith to really believe you won't be smashed flat when you hit the ground."

I swallowed. I wasn't as queasy at heights as Judicus was, but I'd never had to leap from a tower before.

"Don't tell me you're scared, Sersha. For crying out loud. You're in love with a dead man. Surely a little jump won't stop you."

And that was enough to make me find my inner strength and follow her out of the library and down the stairs.

"Ready to go? Or are we going to stand around all day?" Mally called from the top of the stairs.

Below us, Judicus and his inner circle broke out of their ring and looked up at her attentively.

"Right, then," she said. "I'm going to leap from the tower – or let Sersha do it first, I haven't decided yet. But it would be nice to be sure you lot can get out of here first. Care to demonstrate?"

Judicus nodded at one of the ghostly figures – Captain Rackham, I realized – and he promptly marched through the oak doors as if they weren't there, disappearing from sight.

"Well, that's unnerving."

"Happy?" Judicus asked her.

"Happy enough, I suppose," she said indifferently. "That's not Sharma Lighthammer, is it?"

She pointed to the woman in braids.

"Yes," Judicus said tightly.

"And Haroon the Deathknell?" she asked, pointing now at the hulking bald man.

"Obviously," Judicus answered.

"And Varsheen and Vashally?" she pointed at the twin elven men in masks.

I felt my eyebrows rising. Those were all ... heroes. The characters of folktales told by the fire. Only Mally would ask if these people were them. But she was ... right? That was crazy!

"I do believe I explained that this is an army of heroes," Judicus said calmly.

"You skipped that part," Mally said dryly. "But since they're all heroes, they'd better get ready. By the time I make it off that tower I'm going to be ready for them to start proving they can live up to their reputations."

Judicus huffed a laugh, but he seemed unconcerned.

"If you want to say goodbye to Sersha before she leaps to her death," Mally said, sounding indifferent again, "then I'd suggest you do that now. We're flying this coop."

To my surprise, Judicus extricated himself from the people around him and took the stairs two at a time to reach me. He was more graceful as a spirit. Fluid. Not clumsy at all. I missed his clumsiness.

He met me on the top step.

"I'd like your thoughts on what we will do next," he said mildly.

"After the jump," Mally said firmly. "After we see if we live through it."

He nodded gently. He was always gentle in how he spoke to me and how he touched me ... oh dear. I was going to cry again.

"Are you ready for this, Sersha?"

"*Yes*," I signed, blinking those tears fiercely away. I wasn't really. But there was no point in admitting that. There was only one way out of this tower and that was it. I couldn't be a coward about it. I'd just have to do it.

"In death, I find myself looking for you at each turn – a living beacon to my unmoored soul," he signed to me, his eyes burning with more than just his golden glow.

That hurt. I didn't like the idea of him unanchored, looking only to me to keep him safe.

He put his ghost hands on either side of my face, and I wished I could feel them, but at least I could see his bright lips move as they formed his whispered words and the dent in his bright forehead as his worry still showed itself there.

"I love you to death and beyond," he whispered to me. And then he kissed my brow – though I could not feel it, smiled sadly, and turned to walk back down the stairs and I turned, too, to follow Mally back up. She rolled her eyes at me.

"Look at you two," she muttered. "So tragic. So miserable. I'm dying to get the phoenixes back so we can have some sense around here again."

But even as she said that she shoved the small black book of Uncommon and Deadly things back into my hands.

"I feel like it's out of character for me to remind you that there's still hope, but I guess Grevankin has been a bad influence after all," she said. "Let's get up to the top of the tower and let him do it in person."

I jammed the book into my belt pouch and hurried to follow her. I didn't feel much hope right now. I'd have to share hers until I could.

253

By the time we reached the belfry, the golden army of the dead were arranged on the lawn below, glowing in the darkness produced by Mally's crown. While the moon limned the trees and hills, shining off the lake like a mirror, the host stood out golden and bright as lit torches. They certainly would not be a stealth army.

Worse, they were all watching us.

"Ready?" Mally asked and I shook my head before I had even thought her question through.

I was not quite ready. I believed Kazmerev would catch me wherever I fell – if he bloomed fast enough – but what if he wasn't there? What if the guess that they would appear the moment we left the tower wasn't true? What if they were gone forever? I'd leap and die and all of it right in front of Judicus, who loved me. It didn't seem right. It wasn't a good idea. It was –

Something hit me hard on the back and I stumbled, clawing desperately for something to catch my fall. There was nothing but air for my hands to grasp. I tumbled from the stone edge of the tower into a yawning depth, falling, falling, my heart in my chest, my head pounding, my limbs flailing. The host below grew brighter and closer, and I caught Judicus's gaze from so far away and nearly squeezed my eyes shut against his wide eyes, when suddenly red fire burst up from my heart and coalesced.

Kazmerev gave a great cry – a mix of a bird's squawk and a human sound of horror – and then he flared bright scarlet with plum, and suddenly he was under me, catching my fall moments before I hit the earth, his wings spread wide, his head thrown up and back, tail fanned out and streaked with bright flame.

Warmth engulfed me, snatching away my breath of relief.

He'd caught me.

He was here.

Of course, I'm here. What happened?

So much.

And then suddenly Mally was calling out, "Catch me, you fiery fool!" and throwing herself off the tower top, arms spread wide like she thought she'd take off like a phoenix, too.

Kazmerev wheeled in a circle, clearly willing to catch her despite her insults, but he wasn't needed.

Grevankin was there quick as thinking, spreading his wide, smoky wings and giving a similar shriek to Kazmerev's.

I let my gaze fall to the earth to find Judicus's and of course, he was looking at me. Of course, there was pride and pleasure on his face. Of course, he was pleased. And all the "of courses" hurt so much.

Why? What has happened? Kazmerev asked at the same moment that Grevankin roared.

"Is he dead?" He sounded appalled. "Give me a moment to catch up, Mally. And a little explanation, if you would."

Quickly, I let my own thoughts spill out to tell Kazmerev what had happened.

So, Occulus is under their power then? He asked first.

Yes.

And there is no current threat to you?

There was not.

When did you last eat and sleep?

Was he not listening? Judicus had been rendered a spirit. There was nothing left of him but power and golden light!

I'm not sure if you've noticed, Sersha, but the same is true of me.

But I could touch Kazmerev. I could revel in his warmth. He was as real to me as anyone.

Are you saying Judicus is no longer real?

Of course I wasn't! But there was a chasm now between him and me. And it was a chasm too great to cross.

Kazmerev snorted. *Don't be silly, Sersha. We've done a thousand impossible things by this point. I'm sure we can manage just one more.*

We certainly can, Grevankin agreed. *Especially if it means small humans. There will be small humans if we find his body again, won't there?*

My cheeks felt very hot when I answered. Yes, there would be.

She says there will be, Kazmerev said.

Then hang on, Sersha, Grevankin said, sounding as confident as ever. *The Blazing Queen and I will help you restore him. We love small humans.* He paused. *Of course we do, Mally. We are good people.*

And I couldn't help but laugh at the scowl Mally sent my way or the worry on Judicus's face as we finally landed.

He ran his hand tiredly through his ghost hair. He hadn't lost that tendency even in death.

"I was hoping to talk to you about plans for what comes next."

"To us?" Mally feigned mock surprise.

"To Sersha," he said with a wry smile, "but I suppose I will take your advice with hers, Mally."

Mally waited until he was looking at me before sticking her tongue out at him and in the back of my head, I heard Grevankin's rumbling laugh.

"*How can we help?*" I signed and he smiled kindly.

"That's what's so special about you, my Sersha," he said. And again, he looked like it hurt him to say this. "You always – even when you are hurting beyond hurt – you always want to help other people. You have the biggest heart."

"And she has black hair," Mally said, shaking her head. "Can we get to the point?"

"I was actually wondering how we could help *your* plans," Judicus said. "While I've been in the ... mirror." He was so careful not to give details of that place and it worried me. "You have been out here recruiting allies for us. The faithful elves. The Flamerarch. Have you had success?"

"*Some, but not enough,*" I signed. Behind me, Kazmerev rumbled his agreement and Grevankin bobbed his fiery head.

"That's what I thought," Judicus said, his mouth set in a grim line. "It occurs to me that we can't win army against army. Not like this. Not when we are spirit, and they are flesh. Not when our numbers are small and theirs are great."

I nodded, my heart sinking. I'd hoped he'd have some brilliant plan. He was Judicus. He always had a plan.

"Which is why it is my hope to send this army of mine out in hundreds of small pieces to raise the people of Calicarn from their crofts and homes, their dells and valleys, their hidey holes and fortifications, and bid them come together and fight for the heart of our land. And then, for my army to go farther and see what other allies they might find to send to us."

I swallowed looking at the golden spirits assembled behind him. Could they truly not fight?

Not if they are spirits, Kazmerev offered. *They don't have the physical ability to kill anything other than other spirits, nor to detain a living person, nor to build walls or carry arms. Only those with rope working skills will even be able to touch our world.*

I felt a pang at that.

Please, he urged. *Please hold onto hope. Don't despair.*

It is never the right time to despair, Grevankin rumbled from where he stood. Mally rolled her eyes dramatically.

"*That's wise,*" I signed.

Judicus smiled mildly. "I plan to ride with you, of course. If Kazmerev will have me. And some of my army will meet us at Briccatore."

He'll be easier to carry this way. Light. Less prone to making a mess, Kazmerev said, and I couldn't help my smile at his words.

"*Kazmerev says you'd be welcome.*"

Judicus smiled with me, and his smile was the brightest, most beautiful thing in the world.

"Well then, it's settled," he said.

"And I wasn't consulted once," Mally reminded him. "But it's no matter. I don't need your army. I have luck."

"You certainly do," Judicus agreed. "And I have the greatest reverence for that."

He actually looked reverent when he said that, and it seemed to mollify her because she offered him a real smile.

"I suppose we should get to it, then," she said.

Judicus turned and nodded sharply to his army. They seemed to know exactly what he meant by that. Without so much as a word, they scattered, groups moving out in every direction. They broke immediately into a full run – so fast they could match a galloping horse if they wanted to – and were gone before Mally could think of something smart to say.

"I suppose I should give him credit." She sniffed loudly. "He's more useful dead than he ever was alive."

I clenched my jaw at her words, but Judicus seemed utterly unconcerned.

"Are either of you ready to fly?" he asked mildly. "Maybe you could take it in turns, one carrying the other? I think we need to get to Bricatorre as quickly as possible, or death will not be our greatest concern."

"If you make me fly without a proper rest after I had to jump from the top of a tower then yeah, death won't be your worst outcome," Mally agreed.

"I think that means she needs you to fly the first round, Sersha. Do you feel up to it?" He offered me a tired smile.

"And what will you lot do," Mally challenged him.

"I'll come with you."

I nodded my assent and he seemed pleased.

"*I love you,*" I signed. Because maybe I wouldn't get another chance to say it. Maybe this was the last time. And I wasn't going to miss that chance again.

"And I love you, my Sersha."

"Yeah, yeah, yeah, let's just get to the revenge part," Mally said grumpily. "I'm tired of all the mushy bits."

254

Do you remember the story of the first phoenix? Kazmerev asked me as we flew. *"Judicus's talk about your big heart reminded me of it."*

Mally was seated just behind me, her head slumped against my back as she slept. To my utter surprise, Judicus slept, too, in front of me, slumped back against me. I couldn't feel his weight, couldn't wrap my arms around him but he was there. Kazmerev had simply shrugged when he dozed off, reminding me that he grew weary, too, and he died every night.

The living do not get to have everything to themselves, he'd said.

His words now drew me back to sitting with Olliman and drinking tea in the sunshine. Where was he now that death had taken him? Had he moved on to a better place? With my parents? With Prexav? Is that what Judicus longed for, or would he rather stay here with me?

The story Olliman had told me was so tragic that it seared itself onto my heart. The first phoenix had been a father protecting his son, shielding him from fire with his own body. He stayed with the boy even after he died, as a phoenix, reborn in his son's heart.

I choked up a little just remembering it.

So do I. Every time. But think about it a bit, Sersha. Death is not the end. I die every morning, only to live again.

Yes, but we weren't all phoenixes. Judicus was only a man.

He has died and he lives again.

Not like Kazmerev. Not like Grevankin.

There is a life beyond the grave – beyond the final death that even phoenixes die. I believe it with all my heart. That one day all this will be but a memory and we will be reunited under bright, free skies. And I will see the sun again.

I winced at that thought. I sometimes forgot that he never got to see the sun, that it was always night for him.

I do not miss the day any more than you miss having a voice. It simply is who I am. But I will rejoice one day when I am whole – when the sun shines on my feathers.

And then what?

And then who knows? Another adventure? A deeper love? A chance to do it all right this time? I don't know. But I have faith to believe that this life is not all there is. It is too complex, too delicate, and yet so significant that it cannot stand alone without a story that follows. There's a sequel somewhere for all of us, Sersha.

I buried my hands in his feathers. I had faith in that, too. I believed that Kazmerev and I would find that place. And Judicus, too. But what about now? What about what was happening to Judicus *now*?

I wished I could tuck him in my heart with Kazmerev, safely tethered there to rise each morning.

I've never heard of a heart holding two phoenixes, Sersha. No heart is big enough.

I didn't feel like that. I felt like I could hold them both and not love either any less.

If any mortal could do so, it would be you, Little Hawk. But I fear your big heart is not the solution to this problem.

But there had to be a solution somewhere. I wasn't giving up my mirror shard until I was certain I couldn't use it to go back in somehow and draw Judicus out.

Is that what you are stewing on? I think if that were a possibility, your Judicus would have told you. He's a clever human. If it could be done, he would have thought of it. We should focus on what we can do. Somewhere ahead of us an army has formed around Briccatorre and they are building a terrible device to trap the souls of others and force them into slavery. Our allies are few. Our friends in peril. If we hurry, we may yet stop them. And after – if there is an after for us – then after all this you can find a way to restore your ropeworker if such a thing is possible.

And if it wasn't possible? If I'd fought through all of that and made it to the end and by some miracle we won and the world was saved, what then? Was I to ... what? Just miss him forever? Or live with his ghost, forever broken by our half-life together?

Is this a half life, what you and I share?

It was true friendship.

Who knows, then, what it will be for you and the rope worker. Put the thought aside and think of what is next. We have battles to fight. It's not as simple as flying forward and arriving at the city and then just winning. We need a plan. We need to focus.

But no plan was coming to me. My mind felt like a hot pan that someone had dropped a dab of grease into. Each thought skittered loudly across the surface, leaving nothing behind but echoing silence.

I was tired. That must be it. Just so tired.

It felt like hours later when Judicus finally woke with a yawn and turned to me.

"I slept," he said, a look of wonder on his face. It was quickly replaced by a frown. "I slept. That makes no sense."

Clearly, this was as curious a thing for him as it was for me.

"With the way Sersha snores you should be glad you slept while she was the one awake," Mally said from behind me before she took her head from my shoulder and straightened. "We should set down and stretch our legs and I'll wake poor Grevankin. He'll have to suffer with us when Sersha passes out."

Is Mally advanced enough to carry you?

I wasn't sure. But Kazmerev's concern was valid. She was still new at this. It had taken me some time before I could carry another rider.

"We need to make a choice," Judicus told me as we landed. He still smiled when his eyes caught mine and my heart ached with every glance. "Do we press straight toward the city and try to sneak in on our own, or do we swing up and north and join your other forces."

"Why don't we flip for it?" Mally asked with a yawn. She still hadn't fully woken from her nap. She slid from Kazmerev's back and Judicus and I joined her on the ground. She opened a hand, and Grevankin burst into the air, bright and smoky and spinning like a top.

A little gentler next time, perhaps, hmmm?

I was about to sign my opinion, when both Kazmerev and Grevankin came alert, straightening suddenly. Their mental voices cried out in unison.

Flame to flame I greet thee, ancient fire!

And far, far in the distance, I heard the reply, *Flame to flame I greet you, ancient fires.*

I knew that annoyed voice – but right now there was an edge of anxiety tinging it. I found myself lifting to my toes, ears pricking, even though the sound had been in my mind.

And a few breaths later she was there, settling down in our midst, her bright fire tinged with pink.

Huxabrand. She flared wildly.

And on her back was Gundt, leaning forward, barely clinging to her at all. He pulled his head up enough to look at me, blood trickling from his mouth.

I was moving before Kazmerev even flared his reaction, but I could see the brighter light as he and Grevankin flared in fear, their mental voices a loud chatter as I hurried to Gundt's side and put my hands on him.

What happened? Kazmerev demanded while Grevankin asked, *Has he flown the whole way like that?*

Behind us, Huxabrand gasped. *Stryxex. And a rope worker. Chasing us.*

I blocked her out and focused, letting Kazmerev's heat fill me and push through my hands and into Gundt, I felt him arc under my hands and gasp, but my eyes were screwed up tight and I saw nothing. I focused on the warmth, leaned into it, and let it flow, flow, flow until someone shook me.

"It's done," Gundt gasped when my eyes opened. "I'm fine. Fine now."

And he did seem fine, though he was gasping in breaths, his face flushed and hands shaking.

I tilted my head in a question and he shook his head, confused.

"I'll never get over that," he said with a tremble in his voice. "That you can just heal me. It's wild."

Wild or not, we must fly, Huxabrand interjected. *Now!*

255

S*ersha is too worn,* Kazmerev said, his voice laced with worry. *She hasn't slept and she just healed Gundt.*

I was feeling foggy. I stumbled slightly, my head heavy.

We need to go fast. Can she stay conscious? Huxabrand asked, anxiously dancing from foot to foot. *And would you mount up, Mally?*

We cannot carry her, Grevankin said in his booming voice, *though the thought is a generous one. You are not yet able to carry another rider, Mally.* A pause. *Because you're new at this.*

I shook my head. I could ride. Probably.

I reached for Kazmerev and he rolled his eye at me worriedly as I moved into place to mount. Was that a rumble I felt in the earth?

"What's happening?" Judicus asked at the same moment that Kazmerev spoke mentally.

Huxabrand? Are those the creatures of Sydonon?

I climbed tiredly onto his back and signed for Judicus to climb on with me.

Yes. They run under the Stryxex. I think the ropeworker is directing them.

Great.

"Are they worried that you might fall because you've spent so much energy?" Judicus asked me in a whisper.

He was looking from one phoenix to another, unable to hear them, but he must know they were convening about something. Their heads were all close together and Mally and Gundt looked agitated on their backs, looking over their shoulders constantly as if the Stryxex rider would pop into view at a moment's notice.

I nodded my reply.

"Neither Mally nor Gundt can take you with them?"

I shook my head. "*Gundt is exhausted from his injury.*"

"And there's more," he said, certain in his assessment.

I nodded and began to sign quickly.

"A rope worker and a ... not phoenix."

I didn't have a sign for Stryxex.

"Stryxex," Judicus muttered.

"Yes. Are chasing Gundt. Beneath them run the stone creatures."

"Why isn't Mally .... Oh. She can't carry you because she's too new to riding a phoenix?"

I nodded.

"I should have thought of that." He sounded anxious. I'd made a ghost anxious. I must have been very tired because that struck me as funny, and I laughed.

Shhh, Little Hawk. Easy now. Kazmerev shifted. *She's going to fall. She's too tired.*

Judicus must have sensed their conversation. "Tell them I have an idea."

"The mighty ghost has an idea," Mally said dryly. "And he thinks we're all deaf and can't hear him."

"Ghost?" Gundt said, his eyes suddenly locking on Judicus.

"You didn't notice he glows?" Mally asked. "Or that his hands pass through things? Although for some reason he doesn't pass through Kazmerev and can ride him. Which makes no sense."

"I can hold her up with rope work as long as she can keep from falling asleep," Judicus said, interrupting their comments.

Beneath us, the rumble was growing louder.

Yes, and let's get in the air. Now! Huxabrand demanded. *We saw a deer back there that the creatures had trampled. Or at least I think it was a deer. There was still an antler left. And that was it. So, I suggest – strongly – that we have this discussion in the air!*

The lady makes a strong point. To the air! Grevankin cried and with a surprised squawk from Mally, he leapt.

"I've got you, Sersha," Judicus whispered, and then his ropes wrapped around me, and I sagged into them as Kazmerev rose into the air, too, and I didn't mean to, but I was crying because I could feel his ropes and they were like the embrace I couldn't have.

He must have realized it at the same time, because I heard a gasp from him and then one of his ropes reached up slowly and swept across my cheek, running over my hair like a caress.

Huxabrand rose beside us suddenly and a worried Gundt leaned out from her back.

"Are you truly dead, brother? This is not some magical effect of your rope work?"

"I'm truly dead," Judicus said wryly. "Though still useful for now."

Gundt shot me a look that was brittle from behind a gentle smile.

"I have sent out an army of the dead to find us allies and those willing to fight from every nook and hideaway of Calicarn and beyond."

Gundt snorted. "Which is a noble thing indeed, but useless unless we can find a way to stop these stone creatures before they trample everything into paste beneath their feet."

And with that, he rose further into the air and joined Mally.
A moment later she cried out and I followed where she was pointing.
A dark shape crossed the moon. The Stryxex was here.

256

We fled, winging as quickly as the phoenixes could fly, following Gundt.

There's another to the left! Kazmerev warned as we turned. *No, I see three shapes.*

Three. We were outnumbered.

I fear we are being herded, Grevankin's great voice rumbled out. *I make four more Stryxex in front of us.*

We wheeled, Grevankin leading now over the silver snake of a river below.

Something stirred in the trees surrounding the river and even from two phoenixes back, I heard Mally curse.

I hope you're ready to stay mounted for some time, Grevankin said. *The ground creeps with the stone creatures. Okay, Mally. It does not creep, it thunders. Better?*

How many followed you here? Kazmerev asked tersely.

I wasn't exactly counting. Huxabrand's voice was strained. *I was pretty sure Gundt was dying. I was just trying to find you and find Sersha. The fool man set out on his own, knowing he wasn't healed. I will call you a fool, Gundt Helebrand for that is what you are. Do not snip at me.*

Calmly now, we must be calm, Grevankin quelled her. *Fighting amongst ourselves will not solve this problem. We must keep flying and let them herd us until we reach a place we can stand and defend, or we must outfly them and get far enough ahead to loop around somehow.*

We won't outfly them, Kazmerev said.

We shall see.

"The phoenixes seem agitated," Judicus whispered, and I startled. I forgot that he both couldn't hear them and couldn't see through the darkness. His golden ghost glow lit everything close by, though, so I signed to him.

"*We're surrounded on three sides. They're herding us. The phoenixes are trying to outfly them or find a defensible place to rest.*"

"How many?"

"At least eight. Plus, the ground is covered in the creatures of Sydonon.

"Hmmm."

Ask him to keep you awake, Kazmerev urged. *I feel your eyelids going heavy even in this dire flight.*

"Can you talk to me?" I asked Judicus. *"Can you tell me about the army of the dead you brought out from the pillar?"*

He was quiet a few moments – a heavy kind of quiet that suggested he wasn't going to answer. I yawned, fighting to stay awake. And then his words came out all in a rush.

"They called themselves my banner men and women after I won them over. And they call me the Weaver and the Seeker of the Sign."

"What sign?" I asked.

"I was asking them who could tell me how to free them from the pillar, who could tell me what knots to tie and weavings to make to set them free into the life beyond. For a long time, my uncle was unconscious, and I stood over him and defended him from all attackers. And any who came to me, I asked if they knew the way to destroy the Stryxex and set the souls of the phoenixes free. And I .... I asked them what the word was."

"The word?"

He seemed embarrassed and when I glanced back his cheeks were a brighter gold than usual.

"Remember Flara's book? The one that twisted around all the prophecies about the phoenixes?"

"The one that made it so that everything we believed wasn't true." I signed sadly.

"That's the thing. I don't think it meant that after all," he said quietly.

"You don't?"

"I think it took a true thing and twisted it. I think they built a whole conspiracy around their twisting. Around how they'd subject everyone and all magic and make it subject to them. About how they would trample us all beneath their feet. But I think the prophecies – the ones Fontellrae copied down so carefully, and the others kept hidden – I think those were true and they just ...warped ... them."

"You do?" I asked.

"I do. And the warped book – Flara's book – kept talking about how it feared the enemy who came 'seeking a single word.' I wish I still had that book."

Shyly, I reached into my belt pouch and produced both of the books.

"Oh! You have them! Oh. Sersha. I ... could you open them for me? Could you open Flara's?"

I offered him a gentle smile over my shoulder and shifted so he could see around me as I opened the book and started to flip pages.

Eventually, he said, "Stop! Right there. Do you see it?"

And there it was on the page:

"The enemies of the Tattered Ribbon will seek a single word, but they must not speak the word or bow beneath it, for with a word the world was made, and with a word it can be broken."

I shifted a little, trying to free my hand to sign and Judicus adjusted his rope-work immediately, pinning the books down for me so that I could speak.

"I thought they didn't like being called the T A T T E R E D R I B B O N," I signed.

He waved a hand. "There are all kinds of names. The Tattered Ribbon, the Creed, the Order. They all mean the same thing but from different angles. They work hand in hand, trying to bring the world to heel."

He paused, looking thoughtful. "Anyway, I kept asking them for the word and eventually, they came to me, and they told me that to earn their allegiance I must pass a series of trials. And when they were complete, they revealed to me that they were the banner men and women of prophecy who had been waiting for me, the Seeker of the Sign so that they may serve in the last battle of the earth."

"That's dramatic," I signed.

Beneath me, Kazmerev snorted his agreement.

"Well yes, rather," Judicus said and when I glanced over at him, his cheeks flushed a bright gold.

"So, you are someone special to them," I signed. He looked away, uncomfortable until I waved a hand in front of his face, and he turned back. *"Don't look away. I can't touch you to get your attention or speak to you."*

"My apologies, Sersha," he said, and if anything, his cheeks were brighter still, but he met my eyes and didn't look away until I signed again.

"You're someone special to me and you would be even if you didn't have an entire army at your beck and call." I offered a teasing smile, and he huffed a laugh with me.

"But what are these?" I asked, pointing to a sketch in Flara's book. It looked like a map with circles on it and all the circles led to a central circle.

"I hadn't really noticed them," he muttered to himself.

"I've seen them before," I signed and then I twisted my bag around from my back and fished out Occulus's journal.

I opened it before me and Judicus, obligingly, drew the other books out of the way, still held in place with his ropes as he took over holding this bigger book, too.

Hurriedly, I flipped through, looking for the spot.

"Did this belong to Occulus?" he asked almost reverently from behind me. Startled, I looked back at him, and he offered me a smile. "You're a wonder, Sersha, to have found and kept this."

"It was Mally's idea," I signed.

You never give yourself enough credit, Kazmerev scolded.

What credit does she need? Huxabrand asked and her voice sounded forced. *Credit for being a fool looking at books while we flee for our sun-doomed lives?*

Credit for knowing how to stay awake when we need her to after hours of being up on the most stressful day of her life, Kazmerev scolded.

I tuned them out and flipped through until I found the diagram.

"See?" I signed.

"I do see," Judicus said, and he sounded floored. And then he did what he always did and blocked out the whole world as he used his ropes to flick through the pages. I might have felt overlooked, except one rope slid around my hand and clung to it as he worked. My eyes pricked with tears at the touch of what should have been his warm hand instead of a slightly scratchy magical rope.

"Look," he said eventually. "He's written it all down, though he hasn't explained his source. Clearly, he did his research. He found out how the Stryxex work. How the creatures of Sydonon could be made. He worked on it with an apprentice. Kentinius, unless I miss my guess, and they started erecting pillars in other places. This, I think, is a diagram of them. These larger circles are the ones they uncovered that were already there. These smaller ones that appear only in his book are the ones that they added and connected later. You can see the one in the territory of the Hand of the Rat that drove Mally insane. And over here is the one Flara convinced me to smash. And here is the one in the basement of his tower. But. Oh dear."

I saw it at the same moment he did.

"All the lines don't lead to Occulus's tower. They all lead here," he said, moving his finger along the connecting lines. "To the heart of Briccatore."

"Do you know what this means? This is why they needed the city so badly. This is why Calicarn is at the heart of their machinations. It doesn't begin and end in Occulus's tower at all. It begins and ends right here."

"*Then what are the other pillars for?*" I signed and he shook his head.

"I don't know. They clearly trap souls, don't they? They trapped me. And when I smashed that one it created the creatures of Sydonon. And you released the phoenixes for the Flamerarch."

"*With your help.*"

"But I don't know what they do beyond that. Only that the key is in the heart of Briccatore. No matter how hard we fight, it seems to always lead back to that. I just wish we had his source book. It would have been about Uncommon magic. You didn't happen to see it lying about, did you?"

I huffed a laugh and reached in the bag a second time, drawing out the book that Mally had found under the floorboards.

I set it in front of me as Judicus made room a second time. It must be convenient to have all those ropes working like arms. I'd seen a creature once that the fishermen brought home who had eight arms. Judicus was just like them.

I opened the book and the first page bore its name. *Of the Uncommon, Dark & Deadly.*

Judicus hissed in excitement. "This is it! But how did you know?"

"*Mally knew,*" I signed.

"Who would have thought she'd be so useful."

"*Don't say that where she can hear you.*"

He opened the book randomly but then froze when Kazmerev suddenly jerked to the side. There was a scream from up ahead and Mally cursed loudly and then chatter filled the mental space.

Gundt says that ruin looks defensible, Huxabrand said.

Ruin? What ruin? That was Kazmerev.

Don't ask questions, just dive! Grevankin sounded like he was yelling.

They've surrounded us, Kazmerev told me. *Books away!*

And I don't know how Judicus knew, but he grabbed the small books, jammed them into my belt pouch, threw Occulus's tome into my backpack, and then snapped the book I was reading shut with a *fump* and pulled it behind me.

All while, Kazmerev dove from the clouds like a duck intent on landing on a pond.

I'm not a bird! He complained in my mind, but I wasn't thinking of that. I was thinking of the scrap of writing I'd read before Judicus slammed the book shut. The scrap that said, "*He came out again as a spirit and it took some convincing to retrieve his body. Though we did eventually succeed, it is not recommended that anyone else enter such a mirror or exit by a different door.*"

And I could hardly breathe at all I was choking so hard on a hope I shouldn't have.

257

We dove through the darkness, Huxabrand, and Grevankin falling ahead of us like blazing stars.

"We must be headed for that ruin?" Judicus asked in my ear.

I nodded.

"The phoenixes think it's defensible?"

I nodded again and Judicus cursed.

It's the best we can do, Kazmerev said. *We can't outfly them forever and we can't stop in a town further up the river, or the citizens of the town will be slaughtered by the Stryxex. We can't try for Briccatore because we have no allies there. We've tried to outfly them and failed. You can barely keep your eyes open. Soon you will fall, and I will wink out and it will be two phoenixes trying to carry three people while they try to fly even faster and while one is ridden by a fledgling. We can't do that.*

I knew we couldn't.

Judicus was muttering to himself, studying the ruin from above as best as he could with his human vision.

"Three entrances that I count. One from the river. Used to be a fortress. Is this Greenheart? I've read about it, but no one goes there anymore. The road is on the other side of the river. There should be access to water. No food but what you brought. Hmm. If we enter it, we'll be trapped inside. Under siege. Or at least, you will be. I might be able to sneak out and find your allies. Bring them to rescue you."

Something snaked beside us and then Kazmerev shrieked a cry and tumbled forward in a somersault. I clung to his feathers, teeth gritted and behind me, I heard Judicus grunt and then hiss in concentration.

We were falling, falling, falling and then finally my phoenix unfurled, spread his wings wide, and caught us on the wind enough to glide over the water and catch enough air to rise toward the ruin.

Behind me, Judicus was cursing, low and intense as if he were concentrating, and when I risked a look over my shoulder, I almost bit my tongue.

Someone behind us was weaving ropes. Fast and hard, trying to catch Kazmerev and Judicus was beating them back with his own ropes, a look of intense concentration on his ghostly face.

Was Kazmerev hurt?

Yes.

Could he make it to the ruin?

Almost there.

That wasn't an answer. He needed to tuck into my heart. Now.

We were over land, flying up stone steps. He needed to drop us. Right now. He needed to climb into my heart to heal.

Almost there.

What's happening? Huxabrand broke in, her mental voice wild with anxiety. *Is it mortal?*

Was it mortal? My heart was in my throat.

I'll live. I'll be born again, Kazmerev's mental voice was tight and flinty, and I didn't think he was as confident as he was trying to sound and then he winked out and I fell into the ground, hard, the breath knocked out of me.

I choked on the spasm of my diaphragm, feeling for a moment as if I were going to die, and then with a *whoosh,* the air returned to my lungs and I blinked up to see a glowing Judicus, face twisted in concentration, weaving rope upon black rope of magic as he stood over me, swatting his opponent's workings aside.

I scrambled to my feet, checked my pack – still there – and hoped Kazmerev would be reborn when he had recovered. He would, right?

There was no answering mental voice to reassure me. With my Kazmerev gone, would I hear Huxabrand or Grevankin, or would their voices be mute to me?

Where are you? Huxabrand burst into my brain and relief filled me. I could still hear her.

I was coming. I was on my way.

Where are you? We want to bar the doors!

I didn't think she could hear me without Kazmerev. Maybe it meant he wasn't dying permanently, that he would heal in my heart.

I scrambled up the steps, Judicus backing up beside me, his attention focused outward, but his eyes occasionally flicking to me to judge our pace. I wished I could seize his jacket and pull him along.

We reached the closest entrance at a painfully slow pace. There was no door or gate in the empty frame, though a broken mess of metal and wood lay on the ground on the other side.

Everything, from stone to wood to rubble was blanketed in thick green moss and painted with washes of lichen. This ruin was ancient. It was so returned to the forest that from the outside it looked like tumbled boulders and trees, rather than anything built by man. If they'd found doors to bar, then they were lucky.

We slipped through the first gaping door and into a courtyard open to the sky. Not much help defending against Stryxex, then.

Judicus was still fighting off threads of magic. Had he still been alive I would have expected him to be slick with sweat. He wove and dodged and leaned forward with hands spread wide and then hissed as he was forced back, all the while keeping a measured pace backward as I led him over tumbled rubble and around small hillocks formed of debris.

Eventually, I found an inner door hanging on its hinge. I gave it a shove and it didn't budge. Shoved again and it opened just enough to slip in, as long as I took off my pack. I shoved the pack through first and then wiggled in myself. Judicus walked backward through the closed door and looked around, his golden glow the only light in the dim interior.

The ceiling went up, up, up into a vault that had looked like a natural hill from outside. There were no windows, and shadows clung heavily in every corner, scattering only when Judicus walked near.

"I don't think it will fall down," he said as the ropes that had been battling him faded out.

I let out a sigh of relief as he shook out his ghostly arms.

"Strange that I can tire though I'm dead," he said with a nervous laugh, running a hand through his hair.

"Strange, indeed," a familiar voice answered, and then, slipping through the crack I'd wiggled through, Kentinius joined us in the room, hands open, robe somehow flowing around him as if it were alive, and malice lighting his face.

258

Judicus launched himself in front of me, hands spreading like phoenix wings and ropes pouring from them in a way that made me think of what it would look like to watch grass root at a thousand times its usual speed. The ropes unfurled, and branched, and branched again, multiplying into hundreds of waving tendrils no longer than a thread, and lit with the glow of Judicus's non-corporeal body.

Where are you? Huxabrand's voice echoed futilely through the ruin. Something smacked the rock above and the room shook, sending little rains of dust and debris down.

"Find the others," Judicus said in a voice ha was eerie in its calm.

Kentinius's low laugh was an ominous counterpoint. And then, fast as lightning, his ropes unfurled, bright and golden just as Occulus's had been.

"I've been saving the best for last. Wasn't that the smug thing you said when we trained together, Judicus Franzer Irault? 'Always save the best for last, Kentinius. Then, they'll under-estimate you.' Well, you've underestimated me. Best of your generation, they called you. Unparalleled. 'Ignore his roots,' they said. 'Focus on what he could be.' As if the rest of us from proper families, those *without* the blood of king killers in their veins were nothing but second-class versions of you and your wondrous power."

"It wasn't like that," Judicus said calmly. Some wind I could not feel was rippling through his spirit hair, making him almost seem as if he were facing into a storm. He smiled, oh so slightly, and then his woven ropes collapsed, reemerged, and reformed into a fine net spread out in front of him, shielding us. Would it be enough?

"The victors write the histories, Son of Chaos," Kentinius said, twisting his wrists and neck in the same movement that made it look like he was trying to see the room upside down. "And I am the ultimate victor. I know it, for I saw my former master Occulus running like a fox with his tail on fire, and lo and behold but he was a ghost. Just like you. Just like any of those who thought they were my betters."

Sersha! Where are you? Get to the core of the ruin! Huxabrand was beginning to get irritated. But could I leave Judicus here on his own?

"Then why bother to confront me at all?" Judicus asked, his voice deceptively calm. His net was doing something again. Growing. Expanding.

"Oh, it's not you that I'm here for, Judicus Franzer Irault. It's that ai'sletta you've had in your back pocket. She made you lucky. I saw it with my own eyes. And I'm going to need that luck slanted my way now. So, I'm here to collect her."

Judicus looked over his shoulder, caught my eyes, and nodded at the door leading further into the ruin.

"*I can't leave you,"* I signed.

"Wherever you go, I will always follow," he said simply.

Kentinius clearly thought he was talking to him because he replied, but Judicus's eyes were on me, and his smile was for me alone.

"*I love you,"* I signed and then I sprinted out the door as Kentinius spoke.

"Follow all you want. What's one more ghost haunting me when I have so many? I'm practically collecting them now."

It was too dark without Judicus. The halls were wreathed in shadow, the only light available being the light of the moon and stars that shone through cracks and holes in the roof and walls. Even that light was eclipsed again and again.

Around me, the walls shook again as something heavy struck them. And in the distance, I thought I heard a scream.

I clenched my jaw hard, put my head down, and ran.

I fell often, scraping knees and palms on the rough stone, or sliding on moss that failed to pad my falls and slips. I skidded down a staircase and then scrambled up the remains of another. I did not know if it were all one great building I was clambering through or a series of buildings with debris forming awkward halls between the collapsed walls, but it seemed that the further I went into the maze of the structure, the greater the shuddering in the ground grew until I took a last step and found myself wobbling on a shelf above a great cylindrical room.

There had been stairs here, long collapsed now. I looked down from the ragged landing to Huxabrand and Grevankin far below. The enormous phoenixes were standing back to back, their riders astride them. Gundt threw balls of fire one after another, after another, as Mally screamed in utter frustration. I remembered those fledgling days. Those days when the heat of the fire seemed inaccessible. How could I help them? I didn't know how to fight. Not like this. Not with no Kazmerev of my own to provide the fire.

I scanned the ruins around me for a way down, but all I saw was the broken stairs – rubble now on the floor below – and the creatures of Sydonon pouring into the high-ceilinged room below. Gundt was flinging bursts of fire as fast and hard as he could, but what good were fireballs against stone? Huxabrand and Grevankin crept slowly higher up the walls – able to perch on almost nothing more than a crack in the masonry as they fought with talons and beaks to rip the stone creatures from the ground and fling them into other creatures.

A shower of mortar and dust rained down on them and when I looked up, I bit back a cry. A hole had formed in the roof and as I watched, a Stryxex eye peered into the room and then drew back as hit strange there-but-not-there talons reached through and ripped at the wooden beams holding up the cone-shaped roof. This must have been a peaked tower at some point – still sound because of its shape despite how decrepit the structure had become. It would not be whole for long.

Roof tiles fell, narrowly missing Grevankin. Mally cursed again and Huxabrand's voice ripped through my mind.

I don't know where she is. Kazmerev must have died. I can't hear her voice at all. A pause. *Well, she can't very well call to us, can she. She could be right here, and we wouldn't know.*

Grevankin's rumbling voice rippled on top of hers. *No, we aren't leaving her here, Mally. Not if we can help it. You could try calling for her.*

"Sersha!" Mally called. I rolled my eyes. I was right here. "Sersha!"

I opened my mouth, about to call out when someone grabbed me from behind, hand over my mouth, and dragged me from the edge.

Judicus, I thought at first, before remembering he couldn't touch me anymore. Before realizing he would never be so rough.

"And now I have something she wants," Kentinius's voice grated in my ear and my heart fell.

259

I hated being a captive. I'd been one too many times before.

It never went well for captives. Already, Kentinius's ropes choked around my neck. Already, they lifted me up off the ground so that I had to grab at them to try to catch a breath, choking and gagging, my vision fading in and out, my hands unable to find purchase on the slippery strands.

I would die like this, I was sure.

"Do you want your Sersha?" Kentinius called as his ropes suddenly lurched forward and held me over the room. A ceiling tile fell, barely missing my head, slamming into his ropes and tightening them suddenly across my windpipe in lurching agony. "Do you want her alive? Deliver the ai'sletta to me immediately!"

There she is!

Who is that?

Grevankin and Huxabrand spoke over each other so that I could barely distinguish one from the other until Huxabrand said, *Well, of course, we won't give her up Gundt, but we also don't need to wait around here either.*

If they were wise, they would flee. Now. While they could.

"You have to the count of five!" Kentinius boomed out.

We'll try to get to her by another path.

If you can hear us, Sersha, then hang on! That was Grevankin. How long did he expect me to hang on with my life on the line?

"One!" Kentinus called.

Something roared below but I couldn't see it now, my sight restricted only to what Kentinius allowed me to face.

Another ceiling tile fell, and above us, a Stryxex screamed.

My sight narrowed and opened again and then narrowed a second time, landing on an ancient window, shattered and vine-filled now. It had been stained glass, I thought, before it was destroyed. I could barely make out the shapes that had once been a story before the vines destroyed it. The moon outside was too dim, and the phoenixes inside too bright, but it's funny how being strangled to death focuses the mind. For some reason, my mind focused on the window and saw – or thought it saw – the face of a woman, turned up to the sky, hands held high, the world at her feet, and in her heart such a jumble of flames, as if she held a half a dozen phoenixes inside her all at once.

"Two!"

A cry from above and a boom and then a muffled scrape.

"Three!"

Another cry from above as the last of the ceiling tiles and the upper quarter of the tower let loose all at once and plummeted to the ground. I was snatched back from the edge just in time to avoid being crushed. The window was gone. The tower rocked drunkenly.

"Four!"

I heard nothing below but the scrape of stone on stone.

"Five!"

I gasped a final, choking gasp, and then suddenly I fell, my arms and legs windmilling before I was caught once more – but this time on a web of black hair-fine ropes. The web drew me back toward the lip of the ruined staircase and away from where the Stryxex screamed. They faded suddenly, and I slammed into the stone, my face hitting hard and flaring with pain.

I couldn't stay down. Not with Kentinius right there.

I forced myself up, my head swimming, heart pounding like a drum, vision flashing in and out.

The world rocked around me, and my knees buckled.

Groggy, I began all over again, stumbling until I hit a wall that was blessedly solid. I turned, putting the wall at my back, and leaning all my weight on it to keep me upright. It shuddered and the feeling went right through my bones.

This was not good. None of it was.

My vision cleared, and there he was. Like an angel guarding me, Judicus stood with his ghost body between me and Kentinius, his ropework turning back attacks as fast as they came.

"Every moment you fight me is life you give up," Kentinius warned him. "I read the books Occulus gave me. I know you can skip death for a time. And, more wondrous yet, your magic goes with you. But for every bit of it you use, it drains your ghost life and you've been using an enormous amount to fight me. How much more until you puff out of existence? How much more until – "

I never found out what he meant to say. To my utter surprise, a creature of Sydonon crested the lip where the staircase had been, climbing as easily as if it were still there. The creature was caked in rubble, but that, too, did not stop it as it paused, seemed to sniff the air with its stone nose. I plastered myself against the wall as the stone creature burst into an unstoppable leap, bashing into Kentinius and sending him rolling into the wall, and passing through Judicus as if he were a fine mist, leaving me gaping in its wake.

Judicus spun to meet my eyes.

"Run, Sersha," he mouthed.

I stumbled forward, turned in the direction the creature had gone, and ran.

260

Behind me, Kentinius cursed and Judicus's voice echoed softly as he tried to reason with him. Of course he did. That was so Judicus. But both were lost in the sound of stone on stone. I couldn't go back down to that courtyard. If the Stryxex could get through the roof of a tower, they could certainly pluck me from a place open to the sky.

I searched for another way – a hall or door – and found one. I turned into it, not even breaking my stride, not even caring what might be down the narrow-enclosed stairs. I stumbled on a crumbling stair edge but caught myself on the walls. They were so close I could catch myself on both at once. This must have been a servants' back staircase. It opened at the bottom into what might have been a vast kitchen. There was a huge open fireplace at one end, fire-blackened from a time long ago but now filled with nesting materials from small animals. A long oak table was still intact with benches on either side, but they were worn with weather – and no wonder. One wall was completely missing, the masonry tumbled down in a heap and covered in creeping vines.

I almost turned to run back the way I came, but a bright glow flickered and then a door was tugged open on the other side of the room, and Grevankin barreled through and into the kitchens with Huxabrand hot on his heels.

"Sersha!" Mally cried from his back. "There you are! Get on Grevankin's back!"

You can't carry two, Mally! Grevankin sounded out of breath and as I watched he flickered and faltered, disappearing for a moment before reappearing. I didn't think phoenixes got out of breath. He must be truly close to collapse.

"You can't carry Sersha," Gundt called back from where he was barring the kitchen door. He spun, panting and I pointed at the open wall. His disappointed grunt filled the room. "I guess we die in the kitchens. There are worse places to make a final stand."

"Die?" Mally shrieked. "Die? I don't die here. And neither does Grevankin!"

He ignored her, running a tired hand over his face. It was streaked with soot and blood. Nothing serious, I didn't think. His face and hands had small abrasions from flying chunks of mortar – which explained the blood.

"It would take a miracle to escape," he said tiredly. "I'm sorry, girls. I tried. And I was starting to think – against all odds – that we could actually win. But ... well, thank you for letting me guide you on the journey. Thank you for letting me try to defend you and work with you. It's been an honor."

His eyes met mine and we shared a sad smile.

It was interrupted by Mally striding to stand between us.

"You are both a pair of hopeless fools." Her voice changed as she mocked us. "'Oh, I had such a lovely time dying with you.' 'Oh, me, too! Aren't we a tragic pair!'" She snorted. "It's not over yet. And I'm lucky, right? Lucky. That's what everyone says. So, I'll just use my luck and get us out of here."

"It's a nice thought, Mally," Gundt began but his words were drowned out but the sound of something hitting the door he'd barred. It crashed in a second time. And then a third.

Mally ignored it, finding a rusty poker from a heap of rubble and poking around the devastated kitchen with it.

Huxabrand, to my astonishment, made an elaborate movement that looked like a bow and said, *It's been an honor to fly with you all.*

And then she fluttered forward and took up a place in front of the trembling door.

An honor, Grevankin agreed, his rumble sounded – oddly enough – both resigned and somehow triumphant as if death itself were only one more adventure. He executed an identical bow and took his place on the other side of the room, facing the deadly open sky before us.

I raised my hands to speak and then to my shock, Gundt broke into a run, shoved past me, and slammed the door to the stairs shut behind me. I turned in time to see him throw the bolt, a flickering ghost of a Judicus sprawled at his feet.

"*Judicus,*" I signed, running to him.

"Sersha," he gasped, and then faded again, seeming to scatter into glowing shreds of mist before reforming. "Run."

"There's nowhere else to run," Gundt rumbled. "We will die here in this kitchen together. There are worse ways to lose your life, ropeworker. We will start the next great journey together."

"I'm fading," Judicus said, and he sounded ill. His eyes were shut, hands clutched in fists. I wanted to gather him to my chest and hold him there.

The whole room shook with a blow from outside.

They've seen us! Grevnkin warned from his place by the open wall.

"I have loved you with all my heart, Sersha," Judicus said between clenched teeth. "I didn't look for it or expect it. It just came over me slowly like discovering you've grown old. I just realized one day that without meaning to I'd turned my whole heart toward you."

"I love you, too," I signed, realizing he was saying goodbye. I swallowed back hot tears and reached for him, even though I knew I could not hold him.

He vanished, and then returned, and vanished again. This time when he came back, he forced his eyes open even though his face was in a rictus of pain.

"Goodbye, sweet girl," he forced out, and then he flickered again.

And I wasn't going to stand for this. I just wasn't. Not again.

I reached my hands into his mist, and I didn't know what I thought I was going to do about it, only that if I could heal ills, could I not heal this, too? But though I poured all the heat of my phoenix heart into what shreds of him were left, nothing happened. I closed my eyes against the tears falling down my cheeks and wished with all my heart that I could draw him in with my Kazmerev and keep him safe in my heart, that there would be room for him, too. That, despite all evidence to the contrary, a person could hold two phoenixes in one heart, but when I opened my eyes, there was nothing there.

"Oh!" Mally said, startling me out of my sorrow.

"Oh!" Gundt's word was more like having the breath knocked out of someone.

261

I had fallen to my knees at some point. I wavered there for a heartbeat and then I opened my eyes and had to clutch the rocks tightly to keep myself from shattering. There was no more ghost of Judicus before me, only empty rock.

The bar on the door splintered at another heavy blow.

But everything was still glowing brightly.

I looked up and saw Gundt staring open-mouthed at something behind my shoulder. Turning as I stood, I felt my own jaw drop.

There, in the courtyard, rising on a circular stone platform as it emerged from tumbling rocks and sprays of earth, snapping vines, uprooting grass, and wildflowers as it pushed upward, a pillar flared as bright as the sun. It was twice the size of the one back in Occulus's tower and I'd guess it was just as old or older. Slowly, it filled the courtyard outside the crumbled wall of the kitchen, displacing even the cobbles and stones that had fallen there as it rose into the black sky. The stone of its platform was of a different kind than the stones of the ruin – pure ivory white and etched with runes, making it both ancient and pristine in its emerging glory.

"What did you do, Mally?" Gundt asked in a strangled voice.

"I pushed a stone," she said. "At random. You know, for luck."

"For luck," he repeated.

It's pulling on us. Huxabrand said in a strangled tone.

"It's pulling on everything," Mally whispered, and her words were full of wonder.

And then the platform on which the pillar was set rose even further and at the base was an open door.

"Now that," Mally said, "looks defensible."

She leapt into a run toward the pillar. At the same moment, the door behind us burst open.

I opened my mouth – perhaps to scream – but Gundt was already running, throwing me over his shoulder as he passed as if I was nothing more than a pack he needed to carry. I bounced against his shoulder, my breath knocking out of my body with the heavy blows of shoulder to torso. Behind us, the door hit the wall, shattered, and fell on a broken hinge as a surge of stone creatures tore through the gaping opening. The closest looked like a bear crafted by stone and it glowed slightly golden as it surged forward, its stone paws scraping on the cobbled floor.

From above us, a Stryxex screamed, and I felt something brush close to me – like the feeling of moth wings on your face. Gundt cried out – a sound like terror ripped from unwilling lips.

And then suddenly everything was bright, and I blinked against unexpected sunlight flooding the ruins, dwarfing them before the power of day and as I blinked in the sudden light, I was thrown to my feet again and shoved hard into darkness – into the doorway at the base of the platform, I realized.

"Hurry!" Mally yelled as I tried to stand and there was a sound like stone hitting stone – which I realized was the stone door being shut behind us – and then everything was black.

"I hope you haven't locked us in our own tomb, ai'sletta," Gundt grumbled.

"I'm not dead yet, Gundt," she snapped. "And I don't plan to be so don't give me that down-in-the-mouth misery. I still have a city to conquer and a country to rule."

He laughed in the darkness, but I didn't feel like laughing. I felt like my heart had been left outside, fading on the cobbled floor. My pack shifted and the edge of the book inside jabbed into my back, and it brought back the words I'd read.

"He came out again as a spirit and it took some convincing to retrieve his body. Though we did eventually succeed, it is not recommended that anyone else enter such a mirror or exit by a different door."

Maybe he wasn't gone yet. Maybe I just needed to look for him in the right place.

I'd have to hold to that hope. Because without hope I'd lose the chance to get him back, I'd lose my beloved phoenix, and I'd most certainly lose myself.

EPISODE THREE: "CREATURES OF SYDONON"

SEASON THREE

262

I clung to Gundt's arm in the darkness. I should let go. I should let him do … whatever he thought was best to do in a dark stone room at the base of a magical pillar with stone creatures battering at the stone door trying to break it down. But I couldn't seem to make the grip of my hands on his arm relax, not even when he kindly put his heavy hand over mine in a comforting gesture.

"It's okay, Sersha. Quiet your breathing," he murmured as Mally cursed in the darkness. "Mally took the crown off. That's why the phoenixes are gone. They'll be back. You're fine now. Just fine."

It was a croon to a distressed child.

I hadn't even thought of why the phoenixes were gone. I'd been so taken up with Judicus fading away — a ghost used up and now really dead — and with my attempt to restore him failing so spectacularly, that I hadn't thought about why the world had suddenly gone bright right before Gundt ripped me off my feet and ran in here.

"Of course, I took the crown off," Mally said, her voice distorting strangely in the enclosed space. "First of all, it was an excellent distraction. Secondly, the phoenixes would never have fit in this room, and thirdly, we don't know what power this pillar might have. The last one Sersha encountered sucked the souls of phoenixes inside and trapped them there. I was hardly going to risk that, was I? Especially with no almighty Judicus Franzer Irault this time to free them all."

My heart twinged painfully at that, but I forced the thought from my mind. I didn't dare dwell on losing him or I'd be no good for anyone else. There would be time later to mourn. Time later to ask Kazmerev what to do when your heart had been ripped out. He would know the answer. He'd been through it himself.

"Are you over there sulking, Sersha?" Mally asked as if she could see me instead of being just as blanketed by thick darkness as the rest of us. "You'd better not be. The skinny rope worker deserves better than that, don't you think? If he were here, he'd be poking around just like me. You haven't even tried to ask how I found out the whole story of what you did with that pillar full of phoenixes."

"How would you know what she's saying, Mally?" Gundt asked tiredly. "You can't see her hands in this darkness. Sersha, I'm going to let go of you to see if I can light a waxed cloth with my flint. Perhaps there is another way out of here."

"What do you think I've been looking for?" Mally asked and then, a little louder, "I asked Grevankin and he knew about the pillar," Mally said. "He's great at ferreting out information when no one is noticing. Don't ask me where he got the whole story. The phoenix collects gossip like a child collects bright things."

She sounded distracted as she rambled like she was busy with something.

I heard the sound of Gundt striking flint and there was a spark and a curse, but not enough of one to light anything.

"How about this?" Mally muttered and then suddenly stone was sliding on stone and I clenched my jaw against the painfully loud sound as a bright blade of white light cut into the room.

The stone parted to open a door further into the base, white light flooding into the room we were standing in. It lit Mally as she stood in front of it with a triumphant look on her face and the Dark Diadem hanging from one wrist like an oversized bangle. It lit Gundt crouched on the floor beside me, flint and knife frozen in hands as he looked up at the opening door. It lit the small dark room —clearly an entrance or antechamber of some kind. The walls were completely embossed with images of guardian animals and birds, some kind of runic writing I couldn't read bordering the top and bottom of the bas relief. If Judicus were here, he would likely be able to read it and think that was normal for everyone.

It was a wonder Mally found the door from feeling these images. They were so complex and interwoven that it would be almost impossible to find the catch to open a door even with full light — never mind in the dark. It was her luck again— the luck we were going to need to win against an overwhelming enemy.

"Don't look at me like that, Sersha," she said breezily when the scraping of stone on stone finally faded. "It's not like I raised the dead or anything." She smirked at me in a way that was slightly charming even while it stung and then without another word she stepped into the brightness beyond, leaving Gundt to lurch to his feet with a cry.

"Mally, wait!"

And leaving me to roll my eyes because at least in a world full of heartbreak and twists and turns I didn't expect, there was still Mally acting exactly like herself no matter what else happens.

I did the practical thing and took a moment to examine the door we came through before following them, but I found no cracks or flaws that would allow our enemies to get inside it — and also no mechanism to let us back out. Not a handle, a switch, or a toggle. Had either of them considered that when they shut us into this pillar?

I swallowed down a wave of fear as my mind stuttered over an image of the three of us trapped and starving to death here beneath the glowing pillar while outside everything we'd worked so hard for melted away. I shivered and then forced myself to calm. There was no point panicking over that right now. I could panic later when I had the time for it.

"Sersha? Are you still back in the entrance?" Mally called. "You have to see this!"

With a sigh, I turned to face whatever the next setback was going to be.

263

The light filling the room came from the bottom of the pillar that extended into these strange rooms at the pillar's base. Something swirled within the light —trapped souls, perhaps, but they were too bright for the eye to see, though they emitted a kind of a roiling emotion that washed over me uncomfortably. There, hanging beneath the bottom of the pillar, suspended in the light, was a book.

"Don't touch the —," Gundt started to say, but Mally was too quick.

Fast as lightning, she reached the book and flipped through the pages.

"What does it say, Sersha?" she asked me as I craned my neck up and looked into the pillar from below.

How many souls were trapped within all that light? How many phoenixes — or even people? How long had this ancient pillar been buried here in the earth, designed by a people so ancient only three people in the world knew their language, a people so powerful that they made materials we could hardly fathom, a people who had somehow collapsed their own culture and left the ruins of it to scavengers like us? Were their souls in there, too?

"Forget the book, Ai'sletta," Gundt said wearily. "How will we get out of here? I don't dare have Huxabrand manifest so close to this thing — but it was noon outside when you took the crown off and that means it's just hours until she returns. We need to be out of here before then, if we can be, or resign ourselves to risking our phoenixes if we cannot."

"I'm sure there will be some kind of a way," Mally said absently. "There always is. An underground river, or a magical creature, or a network of caves. My life just works like that."

Gundt grunted and I took a careful step toward the book. I was just as worried as he was about our phoenixes being snatched into that pillar — even more worried since it had happened to me before and this time I had no Judicus to free them again. My heart lurched at the pain of that thought, but I reached for the first page, anyway. If he were here, he would want to read the book.

If he were here, he would...

...he would see that same symbol with the circles and the lines between them — only this one was off just a little.

I reached into my belt pouch and drew out the books and spread them at my feet and then pulled Occulus's book out of my bag, opening it to the same diagram and then the book of "The Uncommon, Dark & Deadly" and opened it up, too.

Anyone who has ridden on the back of a phoenix would have seen immediately what was happening between these images. I was used to seeing the land spread out below me like a rug and that made it easy to see how this book that hung magically in the air before me had the original locations of the pillars. Easy to see how the ones uncovered by Occulus and others matched this map completely and just as easy to see how the ones they had tried to erect later were placed where they thought the other past pillars had been. Pillars that must be gone now, because my eyes could see the discrepancies, could see a slight difference in the angles between one line and another, a slight difference in the line lengths that led to the new pillar being in an entirely different spot.

My eyes found a paragraph in Occulus's book that seemed unintelligible unless you were looking at this same puzzle.

"*Rivers and valleys and mountains move,*" it read. "*And diverting them takes the work of many skilled men. But how precise is it necessary to be? We put one close though not exact, and it drew them in like moths to the flame. I think exactitude is not as necessary as my peers dictate. I prefer results to perfect alignment.*"

If Judicus were here now, he'd be elated.

I clamped down on the pang at that thought and studied the original map. The main pillar was still in Briccatore. The lines still all led to the city – but they seemed to be connected, somehow, as if they were plant stalks that all shared a single set of roots.

I frowned and leaned in closer.

"And now Sersha is absorbed in it, too," Gundt complained as he ringed the large room, feeling the walls.

I should be helping him search for a way out. Instead, I was utterly engrossed in the book.

"*The hearts of men,*" it said on the next page,"*are easily entrapped in simple arguments, in the application of comfort, and the elimination of grievance. And as they are trapped, so they may be tapped and used for better schemes than they would have planned for themselves. And the creatures and temples and the stones that live will all feed the source until we have grown the light to fill all the world and a new dawn will come – an endless dawn that will never see noon. The dawn of the strong overtaking the weak and those with great knowledge outshining the masses of mankind.*"

Pleasant. So, these people were just like Occulus and Kentinius and all the others. They wanted to make mankind serve them, to dominate the other humans of the world. And someone had stopped them before. But could we stop them again? Now, when the population was too afraid to fight, and every level of our government was intent on keeping things exactly as they already were?

"And anything trapped in one vessel can be moved to another, provided it has the room," the book went on to say. *"A vial, perhaps, could hold a few souls to be poured out into new vessels. A great pillar — even more. We are already fashioning vessels carved of stone to house what we can. We have buried them deep in ravines and in many storehouses — ready for the moment they are needed. We shall make full use of them. But what else could house the spirit of another? The heart of man? Well, that is still untapped. For are we not spirit contained in one body? But there is no limit on how many spirits might occupy one space. And is the body not a space? The heart not a doorway? And what will you let in? For the word is gate, and by it we see the truth — that both man and creature can cross through a gate and move from here to there and from there to here, but who is the gate and who would sacrifice themselves to offer such a thing? Surely it would crumble the mighty, and bring to foolishness the wise, and break into many pieces those who were once whole."*

"I can't make this out at all," Mally said, frustrated. "I'd be better off running my hands over the walls hoping something popped."

"Which is what you should be doing instead of reading a book when you can't read," Gundt muttered.

"Sometimes, I think," Mally said, pitching her voice for his ears. "That things were better when you held me in awe."

"Sometimes, I think that things were better when I thought you'd save the world," Gundt said and I looked up at that and met his eyes with a question in mine. "Yes, I've lost my faith, Sersha. Or rather, I've seen what faith has done to others."

"I did tell you that faith was a waste of time," Mally said dryly. But she sounded somewhat forlorn as she moved to run her hands over the complicated bas relief carvings on the walls. They were, I realized, gates. And things and people parading in and out of the gates. And I thought of Judicus the Seeker of the Sign and how he'd wanted just one word. Was this it? Had it been "gate" all along? And what did it mean if I'd found it?

"He should not lose his faith," I signed to Mally but she looked away with a blank expression as if she couldn't see me.

"I think you must be signing about my loss," Gundt said to me. "The fact of the matter is, it's not a complete loss. I think I still have some faith in her – but it's in Mally the person. And perhaps in us for working with her. It's not in the great ai'sletta anymore. I don't think an ai'sletta and luck maneuvered by great men and women to do as they wish is the savior I once thought she would be."

"You don't say," Mally said dryly.

"But I'd still give my life to defend her," Gundt said. "Because she's Mally. Because she's my friend and a fledgling - my charge."

It was a sobering thought.

"The Greensleeves will disown me if they hear about it. But they've never watched evil hearts try to turn a thing to get what they want. They haven't seen how prophecy and good intention have been warped. They haven't seen what has happened over these last months and how a regular girl has watched her mother die for her, her land ripped apart, been tortured and abused, and then gone mad with trying to save everything only to have to keep on going. They haven't seen what it means to be the chosen one — and they haven't seen what it isn't. Because it's not glamorous or a thing of virtuous rules and actions. It's just doing your best as a person every day and not giving up hope."

"My goodness, Gundt," Mally said dryly. "Your fallen faith is so beautifully melancholy. You'll teach it to me, won't you?"

Gundt snorted.

"Or maybe you could think about turning it to something worthy," she said and there was a bite to her tone now. "God, perhaps. Or even something a little lower than him. Just don't put it all on me ever again."

Gundt cleared his throat awkwardly.

"Because it's good that you know now that I'm just a person, but it would be even better if you could find it in your heart to treat me as one instead of acting like I'm the gateway to all you've ever wanted."

A gate.

A person as a gate.

I chewed my lower lip in thought.

"I will," Gundt sounded a little hoarse. "But you should know that I'm not going anywhere. That I might not hold you in reverence anymore, but I still hold affection for you. I still feel responsibility and loyalty. And if you're going to try to save the world even when you aren't some kind of supernatural promised one — well, I'm going to try to save it right along with you."

"That's nice," Mally said indifferently. "Come and look at this carving."

But I wasn't looking at the carving. I was flipping frantically through the glowing book for more references to a gate as a chill crept into my bones. Because it couldn't be so simple, could it? It couldn't have been such an obvious thing all along? Could it?

264

Whoever had written the book had taken the time to scrawl illustrations on the pages. Some were like the diagram of pillars, others were coastlines which we likely knew now by different names, cities which had long since crumbled, and the ornamentation on staves and thrones which looked both foreign and very obsessed with birds.

Wait. Not birds.

I felt my eyes widen.

Phoenixes. These people were obsessed with phoenixes.

These were phoenixes carved into their thrones and topping their staves. Phoenixes set into their stained glass. And here was a sketch of the window I'd seen in the ruin — the window depicting the woman with three phoenixes in her heart. And here, a little further on, was a gate again. A gate opening into a pillar and phoenixes pouring into it like rain fills a creek. Well, that was not what I wanted to happen. Had they used these pillars to capture phoenixes and put many of them into one person's heart?

I shook my head. That wasn't right at all. It was — morally unthinkable, right? An insult to the sacrifice a phoenix made for his or her rider. But the text near the illustration didn't specifically say that. It was more of that opaque discussion about hearts and doorways.

"*It is easiest to gather up these soul flames from inside their human hosts,*" the text read, and I shivered. "*For the hearts of these humans are already gates. Already vulnerable. Already open and waiting for a strong hand to push them open and to draw out the treasure within. And if we can gather them up through these gateway hearts, then can we not channel them out into any gate we please? A creature of stone, perhaps? A statue? Some contraption made of wood or metal or potter's work?*"

I gasped and drew back. The creatures of Sydonon had been no accident, then. Flara had been guiding Judicus to create an old thing. A thing of the past. But if these ancient people had done this before, then surely there must be some way to stop them, because hadn't we found the original creatures of Sydonon beneath the sunken island and in the gorge beside the mountain pillar? And they had been inert at first, woken only when the actions of humans stirred them up and – in the case of the ones at the pillar – filled them with life again.

And if souls could be put into them, couldn't souls be pulled out of them? I flipped to a page that showed a stream of phoenixes going into the gateway heart of a woman and then funneled straight into a pillar. Yes, that. Couldn't I do that with the creatures of Sydonon? Couldn't I funnel them back into the pillar if my heart was a gateway?

I froze. When had I started to think I would do this myself? And wouldn't it be evil to rip a soul from a thing and stash it away like a used robe? Or was it more evil to leave it in a stone creature and let it trample people to pulp?

And who should be making these kinds of decisions? Should it really be a voiceless girl from a tiny fishing village?

It should be Judicus. Judicus, who had read so many texts that he knew all the possible outcomes. Judicus, who was so respected that a spirit army followed him. Judicus, who had spent his whole life wanting to undo the wrongs of this world. But he wasn't here.

I bit my lip to keep it from trembling.

He wasn't here and I was.

And so was this book. I flipped furiously through the pages, barely hearing it when Gundt exclaimed, "Again? If I took you out mining for gold, I could retire with what we found on the first day."

"If I were after gold, I wouldn't bother mining it," Mally said lightly. "Let other people do the hard work. I have empires to topple."

They'd found another door. It opened with a *whoosh.*

"Are you coming, Sersha?" Mally asked.

I reached for the book. It didn't budge. Whatever suspended it in light kept it stuck in place. I fought against the hold. It didn't so much as tremble. Only the pages could move at all. Ingenious. And terribly inconvenient.

But I wasn't done yet. Not until I discovered how they learned to use the heart gates to move souls. And how I could, too. Because if I could do that, I could save all the souls trapped in these pillars. And I could save the ones trapped in the stone creatures. And I could save Judicus.

And no amount of moral quandary was going to keep me from that.

265

"Oh, sweet merciful heavens," Gundt gasped from the other room. But I was focused on the book, flipping frantically through the pages.

There had to be some indication of how, right? They wouldn't just state that all this could be done without telling how?

I was back to the diagram again. This time the one I studied was elaborated with wide arching curves and dotted circles as if to show some sort of border that extended out from the pillars and then connected them in a way that was separate from the solid lines linking them.

I followed the lines, squinting at them.

"Does this do what I think it will do?" Mally asked in a hushed tone. "Is it a gate?"

At that, my head snapped up.

A gate?

"I think the map shows that it somehow connects one place to another," Gundt said but he sounded uncertain.

"Well, obviously," Mally agreed. "And you're looking at the places it connects to."

"Some of them are just blackness."

"Well, if this map is true then that black one you're looking at is the pillar on the Forgotten Isles. And that one behind you is the one that Judicus broke. I really wouldn't recommend traveling to them. Whatever is on the other side would probably eat your soul."

They were going to go through a door? Were they insane?

With a last agonized glance at the book, I threw my books back into my belt pouch and backpack and rushed through the hidden door they'd opened. It was a double door, reaching outward as if to embrace the one entering. Inside, a map was tiled into the floor in tiny mosaic tiles the size of my fingertips. Gundt's head was bent as he studied it, but Mally was looking around her in wonder at the walls.

They looked like a series of arches forming a round room. But inside each arch, a scene showed as if it were a window to the outside and each window faced a different scene. The scenes wavered and jumped as if they were born of memory rather than of reality. The one directly facing me showed the inside of a cave lit with an eerie glow. Two more were broken somehow, nothing but blackness revealed through those doorways.

Instinctively, I moved to the center of the room. I did not want to fall through one of those black doorways.

One showed a series of friezes decorated in bas relief much like the room I just left, another showed a mountain scene, still another showed what looked like a throne room with people moving through it in a strange sleep-like manner, but their features and clothing were like none I'd seen before and a lazy animal sleeping at the foot of the throne was enough like a dragon that my eyes widened to twice their normal size.

"Which one should we go through?" Mally asked in wonder.

My quick "*no*" in sign was accompanied by a desperate shake of my head. Whatever we did next, we should not go through one of these doors. Who knew where they went? What time or place?

"I don't know if you can go through them," Gundt said absently. "I think they probably are just windows. We should look for another exit from the tower or prepare to fight our way out through Kentinius and the Creatures of Sydonon."

At least someone was speaking sense.

Mally's mouth thinned at that and carefully she drew the Dark Diadem from her arm and jammed it on her head and to my shock, the lit windows or doors, or whatever they were that faced the mountains and the throne room went dark as night.

"Mally, no! The phoenixes!" Gundt yelled.

I felt Kazmerev bubbling in my heart – and something else, something odd – and then he was gone as Mally ripped her crown off again.

"Don't do that," Gundt said hoarsely, clutching his chest. "It's dangerous."

"I was just checking to see that the windows led to our world right now," Mally said with a beatific smile. "They do. So, tell me, Gundt. Based on that map, which one is closest to Briccatore?"

"Our phoenixes could have been sucked away into the pillar," he gasped, still shaken.

"Well.. they weren't. So pick an arch."

I was shaking my head before she could finish her sentence. No one should go through those gates. No one.

"Stop it, Sersha," Mally said, crossing her arms. "I'm not going back outside where the creatures of Sydonon and the bad rope worker are. If I can leave this place through this nice little travel room, I'm going to."

I let my exhale out in a huff and hurried back into the book room. Maybe there would be something there to show her how unsafe her idea was.

"I think it would be that one that shows the cave," Gundt said a bit absently.

"But I don't think we should try going through. Sersha's right. It's far more dangerous than going back outside again. Besides, the map might not line up with the doors. Or maybe they've shifted over time. All of this is very old. Ancient magic of the most mysterious sort."

I ran to the book and began to flip pages, trying to find the words "gate" or "door" as I flipped. There were so many of them. And all of them seemed more like a figurative door.

"What about this one with all the books? It could be a room in a castle," Mally said.

I kept flipping.

"*The gate would have to be wide open. But still, it would need to protect itself or it would collapse,*" I read. Nothing about those gates out there.

"*The gate breathes out the sorrows and pains and breathes in the calm.*"

That wasn't helping either.

"I like the book one. I think I'll choose that one," Mally said firmly.

A loud creak made me freeze as I flipped another page.

"What was that?" Gundt asked.

And then the distinctive sound of rock on rock rang out and I spun to see the entrance door opening and the silhouette of a man in the doorway. His clothing flapped in a way that made me think of a Stryxex rider and from behind him, I heard one of their ripping cries.

"Sersha?" Gundt called even as I leapt forward, jumping around the book and toward the open arms of the door they'd opened. If we could get it closed it would be hard to open, wouldn't it? But Kentinius had opened the main tower base door and I'd thought that was impossible, too.

"Sersha?" the man echoed in a voice I didn't recognize.

From behind him, I heard the sound of stone feet on stone floor and my heart was in my throat as I grabbed the carved door and tried to pull it closed behind me. It didn't budge.

"Grab her, Gundt. She's impossible," Mally hissed and then something pulled me off my feet and I was half dragged, half steered toward my cousin, who threw an arm around me from the other side and hustled me to the center of the room. "We'll go through the doorway into the room with the library!"

The doorway. The library. I caught a glimpse of it and froze. All the books were illuminated. Why hadn't I noticed this the first time when those two were staring at it deciding which archway to enter? We were looking at the room from a vantage point of the inside of one of the pillars.

And I knew, suddenly, with a complete certainty that I couldn't have explained, that if I went through that door and into that room then I would be trapped within a pillar. Forever.

266

With a terrible wrench, I ripped myself from Mally and Gundt's grasp, and I barrelled forward, knocking into the surprised Stryxex rider and right past him into the body of a great stone creature.

Behind me, Mally screamed in frustration, and then the doorways went dark as she jammed her crown on her head. I gritted my teeth and did the only thing I could think of as I felt Kazmerev streaming into my heart. I forced him back. I shut him away. There was a strange sensation and I shut that away with him, with my own self, and with all my dreams and loves and sorrows. I opened my heart up as if it were a door. I opened it to the pillar above the book. I opened it to the stone creature I was touching, and I willed myself to be a gate.

Gate, I thought, *Gate, Gate, Gate.*

But nothing was happening. I wasn't doing it right. I breathed in a long breath, willing myself calm, willing myself to accept as the creature I was touching thrashed and jerked, smacking against carved walls and chipping the careful phoenix engravings. There was a sudden, sharp, stabbing agony, a scream in my mind. It burst into my heart – not like Kazmerev did with joy and a blossoming, but like a vein bursting open, spurting its sorrow and pain into me. I let out a shuddering, agonized breath, a breath so barbed it seemed to stick in my lungs and catch and pull. When it finally released the bursting pain my heart released with it and I felt it happen – like breaking a beaver's dam – just a trickle at first and then a rush as the gate opened and the soul trapped in the Creature of Sydonon roared through my heart, searing it hot, and then rushed up into the pillar.

Was I a villain then? Was I a monster to have ripped it from the stone creature and imprisoned it again? Was I … I felt then, my own spirit trying to flood through my body again instead of being crammed into a tiny space, and with another exhale of agony, I let it fill me, swell into all my parts. It felt both right and uncomfortable, as if my body were no longer the correct size for me.

Behind my own spirit, I felt the flood of Kazmerev's spirit flow with it and – desperate for his comfort – I opened my heart and let him flood through, blooming into existence in front of me just in time to rip the shocked Stryxex rider from the ground and fling him into the carved frieze so hard that I heard the crunch of his bones.

Huxabrand and Grevankin popped into bright life between me and Gundt and Mally but before I could so much as think about how cramped this space suddenly was with three phoenixes and a stone statue, another spirit was following Kazmerev, blooming in my heart – this one like warm honey-sweet, slow, and almost kind. It welled up and up and I felt as if I could barely contain it when it finally flowed from my heart into the room in front of me.

My gasp was so huge that I thought I might accidentally suck him back in. And my eyes must have been wide because his spirit eyes were the widest I'd ever seen, his spirit mouth hung open in shock, and his spirit hair was a rumpled mess. He brought his hands up to the sides of his head – either because he was checking to see if it was there or out of some shocked reaction, I couldn't have said which, and then his hands flew in sign.

"*Sersha! How can this be? Did you put me in your heart with your phoenix?*"

But I heard his words in a double echo inside my mind, and with them the sudden shocked alertness of three phoenixes turning all at once to look at us. I thought my cheeks might be on fire. Or maybe I was crying, or possibly smiling, and I just didn't know what to think or feel at this sudden wonder.

Because he wasn't gone.

He wasn't dead – well, he was, but his ghost was still here which meant it wasn't over. I hadn't lost him completely.

And somehow, he was in my heart.

I love you, I said with my mind and the look of wonder on his face was extremely gratifying.

Sweet stars and skies, get them out of my head! Huxabrand wailed.

This is amazing, Grevankin said. *Amazing. A gift from the heavens. And we get to be here for all of it! I'd squeal if my mouth could make that sound!*

"What's happening?" Mally demanded.

And my head swiveled to Kazmerev – sure I'd see disappointment there in the middle of all this silence from him. Sure I'd see jealousy or even fury. But to my absolute surprise, he looked me in the eyes, and then very deliberately he winked.

I told you that you have a big heart, he said.

267

"You stopped it," Mally said – unable to contain the awe in her voice. She rushed past me and put her hands on the frozen creature of Sydonon – a lion carved of snarling stone. "What did you do, Sersha? Can you do it again?"

"No time for that, Mally!" Gundt called, rushing past her and toward the door.

He made it three steps before a second creature rushed into the anteroom, stone feet scrabbling on the stone floor. This one looked surprisingly like an ox. It tossed its horns back and forth, threatening us. Fortunately, it was so large, that nothing else could get in the room from behind it. I heard a far-away Kentinius's cursing between the ear-splitting strike of stone on stone.

I didn't dare open my heart as a gateway. Not with Judicus and Kazmerev right there. What if it sucked them in, too? I'd have to draw them in tight, and hold them in a safe bundle out of the way, along with everything about myself and I wasn't sure if I could do it fast enough. My breath sped up but before I could panic, Judicus was there leaning in front of me and whispering.

"Don't do anything yet. Take a breath. Gather your thoughts."

And then he was stepping in front of me, lightning-quick, ghostly glowing hands held up before him and dark ropes slithering from them like questing snakes. They fell from his hands, darted forward, and caught the creature of Sydonon, forcing the ox back through the entrance. Gundt danced to the side, avoiding the thrashing stone creature as it kicked out in every direction, its stone hooves scraping along the mosaic floor looking for purchase. I heard more cursing from somewhere outside the door before Judicus called out.

"Gundt! Get ready! The moment I throw it through, I need you to close the door!"

Gundt grunted in acknowledgment and then Judicus's ropes flung the bucking creature through the doorway and Gundt slammed the door shut. Judicus's ropes broke, faded, and then reformed, tangling and weaving to hold the door tight even as something from outside pounded against it.

"We're never getting out that way," Gundt said, sagging against the door. "We need to pick one of those arches immediately and leave through there."

My head was shaking before he could say more. But I didn't need to offer an argument because Kazmerev and Grevankin were roaring one before I could.

Don't do it!

Don't go in there!

"Wait," Judicus said turning to look at Gundt and Mally, and he looked pale even for a ghost. "You weren't honestly going to go through one of those arches, were you?"

"They look like a good way out to me," Mally said, caressing the lion statue that remained now that its spirit was gone. "Not sure if you've noticed but the other way out is blocked by raging stone creatures, flying Stryxex with insane riders, and a ropeworker with a vendetta against us. Is it really so crazy that we thought of using a back door, ghost boy?"

Judicus ran his palm over his ghostly face. "Let me guess. You didn't ask Sersha. Or you did, and she said no, and you ignored her."

Mally's cheeks went pink. "Sersha never wants to make bold moves."

"Bold moves, in this case, being where you get stuck in a pillar with the other trapped spirits for all eternity? It's clearly a trap for the unwary. It's clearly meant to keep the pillar safe. How could you be fool enough to fall for it?" Judicus asked, shaking his head.

"A trap set in a hidden room?" Mally's voice went higher. He'd rattled her.

"A hidden room is precisely where you should set a trap for the kinds of people who might break into the base of a magical pillar," Judicus said in a measured tone. "Besides, you wouldn't want anyone to fall in it by accident. You only want to catch the misbehaving in your little trap. How could you not see that, Ai'sletta? And why haven't you learned to listen to Sersha yet?"

Mally shrugged. "I'm not the one who's in love with her."

"I'm not the one ignoring her good advice," he shot back but his narrow cheeks were flushed.

"Well, at least I haven't died dramatically on her *twice* – no, make that three times," Mally said flippantly. "Besides, I don't know another way out of here."

"I think that perhaps I might," Gundt said but his face was pinched and tight. "Can you freeze the rest of them like this, Sersha?"

He ran a hand over the flank of the stone lion creature that was now nothing more than a statue.

I had sucked his soul back into the pillar.

Kazmerev gasped and flickered.

What? Huxabrand demanded. *What did she say?*

Judicus turned slowly to face me, and it seemed to me that he was moving with deliberate slowness so as not to frighten me. His face was very calm, very carefully calm.

You sucked the soul out of the stone creature and put it back in the pillar? Kazmerev asked and his mental voice sounded tight.

It was my only option. That or go through the pillars with Mally and Gundt and then where would we all be?

Dead, Grevankin agreed, but Huxabrand rolled over him. *Stupid, foolish girl! Evil. Evil. Evil.*

"Easy now, Huxabrand," Gundt said, but he looked at me in an uneasy manner.

"Why shouldn't she?" Mally asked, jutting out her chin. "If they can do it, why shouldn't she? The soul was trapped in a stone creature. What difference does it make if it's trapped there or in a pillar? Trapped is trapped. And in the pillar it isn't trampling us to death."

The pillars are torture, Kazmerev said mentally, and I couldn't meet his eye because he'd told me that. He had. And I should have listened.

"Well, maybe if she puts them *all* back in, then she can figure out how to make the torture stop," Mally suggested. "She's very concerned about that kind of thing and she's sure to find a way."

You must not do it again, Kazmerev said. *No more souls must be put into those pillars. No more souls of man or phoenix or any other creature.*

My face flared red, but I nodded sharply. I didn't know how else we'd deal with an army of stone creatures set against us, but if he told me I must not do it ... well, I'd have to find some other way.

My chest hurt – like it wasn't big enough for my heart, like it couldn't keep up with the way it was racing.

"What about Stryxex, Kazmerev?" Judicus asked carefully, "If Sersha managed to free a trapped spirit within a Creature of Sydonon, then she might be able to suck them into the pillars, too."

I think that might be just as bad, Kazmerev said, but he sounded uncertain.

"Wait. You aren't really saying that we finally found a weapon and you aren't going to use it, are you?" Mally asked.

"What about trying to turn them to our side – to direct them?" Judicus pressed Kazmerev. He ran his glowing hand through his ghost hair as if considering the project, pursed his lips, caught sight of me long enough to smile shyly, and then went back to shoving his hair back as he thought.

"Seriously? We're not going to *use* it?" Mally asked, but no one was listening to her. "You don't win wars by being squeamish."

That ... seems acceptable. Kazmerev looked anxious, shifting from foot to foot.

Acceptable? I should say. It's a miracle! Grevankin roared. *If you could manage that we could turn the tides of this war.*

I wouldn't go so far as that, Kazmerev said.

But even Huxabrand was peering at me with a hopeful look in her eye.

I felt my cheeks grow hot and I couldn't ... I just wanted to talk to Judicus. Just to him.

The door shuddered again as something heavy crashed against it.

"*I don't know how,*" I signed, my hands shaking as I met his eyes. "*I can move the spirits back to the pillar – by becoming a gate. But the turning of the hearts of these stone creatures – I don't think I could. I don't know ... I don't know how.*"

"You don't know how?" Mally asked, exasperation in every syllable. "Then just put them in the pillar and enough of this moral back and forth. Who cares?

We're fighting a war against evil. Who cares how we defeat it, only that we do! You can worry about freeing souls once the battle is over and I am Grand Hadri."

"*You* as Grand Hadri?" Judicus asked with a lifted eyebrow. "I'm fairly certain that is my sister's role."

"A role she doesn't want. And if any role could use my luck, I think it would be that one, don't you?"

He didn't reply but he looked pensive.

"*Tell me about this gate,*" he offered instead.

"*It's in the book,*" I signed. "*The one just here.*"

He turned hungry eyes on the tome as I showed

"There's no time for him to read the book," Gundt said quietly. "And frankly, the ai'sletta is right. The door is being battered down. We are surrounded by stone enemies. If we force our way through the door, we'll be set on by stone creatures, attacked by the ropeworker with them, and overwhelmed by the Stryxex. But the Stryxex are souls, too. If you can take the spirits out of the stone creatures, then you can take them out of the Stryxex. If we try to leave without this talent of yours then we will be right back to where we were before we fled into this room – only worse off because we will have to battle through a small door just to leave. But, if you could pull the Stryxex souls into the pillar – well, we could flee. No ground force could keep up with phoenixes in flight. Do you have to touch them to be this gate?"

I shrugged.

"Do you have to be able to see them?"

I shrugged again. What did I know?

"Then we'll just have to hope that you can do it without touching them," Gundt said with finality in his voice.

It was a nice idea in theory, but I could only become a gate if I kept both Kazmerev and Judicus hidden within me. Otherwise, I was pretty sure they'd be sucked in.

Do you know for sure that you must keep us hidden? Kazmerev asked. *Neither me nor Judicus can be outside your heart when you reach for these souls?*

I didn't know for sure – but I didn't dare risk it. If something happened to them... If anything happened to them...

I worried my lip between my teeth.

"All will be well Sersha, do not concern yourself," Judicus said with a gentle smile.

If she has to keep them in reserve, it will be much trickier, Huxabrand said, shifting worriedly. *Perhaps she should sneak out in the day and then they won't expect it and she'll know for certain that Kazmerev is safe.*

It hadn't worked until Mally had put the crown back on.

Ah, but did you try it before she put the crown on? Kazmerev asked.

I hadn't.

Best not to risk it, Huxabrand said. *But perhaps she could carry the crown and we could open the door and trick them into running in here. While they are distracted, she could slip out, jam the crown on her head and do what she does to suck the Stryxex into the pillar. And while she does that, you can manifest Grevankin and me and we'll carry the rest of you to safety – safe once the Stryxex are gone.*

Except we wouldn't be safe from the rope worker, Grevankin rumbled.

We would be safe as soon as we were far enough away – and with no Stryxex to carry him, he'll quickly be left behind.

I don't like it, Kazmerev said. *It leaves her too vulnerable. It leaves* all *of you too vulnerable. And what if it doesn't work? What if she can't affect the Stryxex like she does the Creatures of Sydonon?*

"Then give in on the Creatures of Sydonon souls," Mally suggested. "If she sucked all of those out and put them in the pillar, that would give us a similar edge."

I can't, Kazmerev said tightly. *You weren't in there. You don't know what it's like!*

"*Don't I? What did I gaze into? What stole my sanity for three days?*"

Enough, Kazmerev said, but he was troubled.

"Then this is the one thing we can do," Mally said firmly. "And it is what we *must* do. Even if it has little chance of working, it's the only chance left. Or would you rather decide to do it three days from now when we're starving and weak?"

She's right, Grevankin boomed.

"She's right," Gundt agreed.

I see no other option, Huxabrand agreed. *The Stryxex are not phoenixes any more than a ghost is a human.*

She didn't look at Judicus when she said that, but I did, and I saw him flinch and the flinch was like a stab to my heart. Neither of us wanted him to stay a ghost, but could I draw him from that mirror shard? Could my heart be that kind of gate?

I ached to think of it.

Gently, I took his hand and drew him to the book. He watched me with opaque eyes as I flipped through it and found the illustration of the girl with the phoenixes in her heart.

What matters is what Sersha wants, Kazmerev pushed. *What does she think of this?*

I tapped on the word "Gate" and looked at Judicus.

"*It's the word you were looking for,*" I told him with my mind. "*Gate. And I think I can be the gate. The gate to free all of them. It looks like death, but it will be freedom.*"

His eyes were sober when he signed. "*There is no peace in that pillar. No freedom.*"

"*Can I not find a way to send them beyond? If you were channeled into a stone beast and set loose to trample innocent people, how would you feel?*"

His face twisted with guilt, and he hung his head.

Sersha? Kazmerev pressed. *What do you want?*

I wanted to save the souls in the creatures. I wanted to return the Stryxex to the pillars. I wanted to defeat our enemies and bring Calicarn into a time of peace again.

Those are worthy goals.

My heart would just have to be big enough to hold them all.

Them all? Judicus's head snapped up, puzzled.

Kazmerev should tell Gundt that I'd do it.

She'll do it, Kazmerev said as another strike rocked the walls around us.

"Then we should hurry," Gundt said, and he sounded excited.

"Give me your pack," Mally said, rushing to my side. "You'll need to be unburdened when you dodge stone animals to get out there. Don't forget, concentrate on the Stryxex and on drawing their souls back into the pillars."

She should go out on my back – initially, Kazmerev said. *I can drop her down in a clear spot before she starts her work. Somewhere that she can see the Stryxex from.*

Too visible, Huxabrand disagreed. *We all need to be tucked away until she's out the door. There needs to be room in here for the humans to draw those Creatures of Sydonon into the trap.*

And then we conquer! Grevankin agreed.

But even as they discussed it and Mally took my pack, my eyes were still on Judicus. He hadn't lifted his head.

I snapped my fingers and his gaze shot up, looking wracked with something a lot like guilt.

"Judicus," I signed.

"Sersha," he whispered, his cheeks flushing as they did anytime, I signed his name.

"Judicus, what is it?"

"You're going to burn yourself out," he signed. *"I see it like a storm on the horizon. Inevitable. Devastating."*

"It will be okay."

He shook his head, and his distress was plain.

"I don't have words," he signed, frustrated. *"I don't have words for what I fear and I'm afraid that if I try to say what I do have words for, that saying them will make them happen – like a ropework of the mind."*

"Then don't say them." I signed, feeling suddenly as bold as Mally. *"Just trust me. Just put your future in my hands. I will keep you safe. I will keep you whole. And in the end, I will restore you. Somehow."*

"I fear you'll do it at the expense of yourself."

"I would consider that a fair trade."

"That's what I fear most." The look in his eyes was aching. *"Promise me you won't do something crazy. You'll only try to trap the Stryxex and if it doesn't work, you'll retreat right back here. Nothing more."*

"Just kiss her and let's get going," Mally said, rolling her eyes.

It was a good idea. I leaned forward, reaching for him even though I knew I wouldn't be able to touch him. Before I'd moved more than a hair, Mally ripped off her crown in a sudden movement, the phoenixes winked out, and Judicus disappeared with them.

A curse bubbled on the tip of my silent tongue.

"Ooops," Mally said. "I swear I didn't think he'd go, too."

"Simplifies things," Gundt said as Mally shoved the crown into my stunned hands. "Don't put that crown on yet, Sersha. Let's get into position."

"Wait," I signed. *"We need a plan with details."*

"After you, Flame Rider," Mally said boldly, ignoring my signs even though I knew she could read them perfectly

"We need a proper plan!" I insisted.

"Don't look so sad, Sersha," Mally said, still ignoring my signs. "By the time we're done here, you'll be such a hero that they'll write ballads about you. If we survive, that is. Where should we stand, Gundt? I was think – "

But she didn't get to finish her sentence as the door burst open with a boom and a terrible stony crunch.

Oh no.

Judicus's ropework had disappeared with him. And the moment it was gone, the pounding of the stone creatures had broken the hinges on the doors. I was pretty sure Mally hadn't considered that.

Her lips formed a surprised, "O" and I did the only thing I could think of, running up beside her, pressing my back to the wall, and steeling myself for what I would have to do.

This had better work.

268

"Outside, Sersha!" Gundt whispered loudly as he threw himself against the wall beside us. We pressed tightly against the carved frieze as the stone creatures flooded into the tower base, rampaging past us in a blur.

How was I supposed to get through that?

I took a step toward the door only to be nearly trampled by a Creature of Sydonon with the longest neck of anything I'd ever seen. It was bent nearly double just to get through the door. Mally yanked me back just in time. We pressed together against the wall, huffing in terrified breaths.

"This isn't going how we planned," Gundt said between clenched teeth as the room around us shook, the sound all but drowning out his voice.

"You don't say," Mally looked sour. "Can you feel the Stryxex without looking at them, Sersha?"

I reached, trying to feel something — anything — with my mind. Nothing greeted me in the depths beyond.

I shook my head.

"Listen," she hissed as a horse-shaped Creature of Sydonon thundered past. "New plan. Before this place is so full that we're crushed to death by moving rock. You put on the crown, Sersha, and we'll carve a way through so you can try your trick outside where you can see them. And we'd better all hope that you don't need to touch those things to make this work or we're in real danger of ending this life trampled into the ground."

I nodded briskly.

She had no patience for agreement. "Jam that crown on your head and let's go!"

I hurried to obey, shoving the crown in place and blinking as the light shining through the door went suddenly black. I felt Kazmerev and Judicus trying to rise in my heart. Dutifully, I bundled them up and pressed them carefully aside. It hurt me to do that — like ignoring a friend's greeting.

Gundt gave a loud grunt and then Huxabrand appeared in the air and threw herself at the first creature to barrel through the door, grabbing him in her thick talons and dragging him out of the way.

It felt strange not to hear her mental voice. Even when Kazmerev was dead and waiting to be reborn, I could usually hear her. Apparently muffling him, erased the voices of the other phoenixes from my mind.

I gritted my teeth, tried to push that thought aside, and readied myself for my chance.

The second that the first creature was clear of the door, Grevankin rushed into the space the creature had filled. Mally was on his back almost as soon as he materialized. Her hand reached out and fire poured from it, splashing off the creature, but seeming to blind it. It thrashed in every direction as Grevankin reached out, caught a leg in his beak, and hurled it backward toward the congregated bodies of its fellows.

I gasped as it smacked with the terrible percussive sound of stone hitting stone.

Run, Sersha, I told myself. You have to go.

And with a massive inhale, I raced forward, leaping in behind Grevankin and outward to the spot he'd cleared. To my surprise, Huxabrand followed right behind me, leapfrogging me to grab the next creature and send it spinning into the mass of its fellows.

Gold ropework snaked over their backs toward her as above us a Stryxex shriek tore the air. It made the small hairs on my arms and the back of my neck stand up.

The Stryxex was here. Time to enact the plan.

There was no time to linger. I mashed my back against the ruined door frame and tried not to think of the mass of stone bodies in front of me, barely held back from crushing me entirely.

I could see the Stryxex swirling above us in a wild whirlpool of light-twisting bodies, their riders dark, twisted silhouettes against the night sky. Fear welled up inside my heart but there was no time for it. It must be dealt with later. For now, I drew in a long breath and began, trusting Grevankin and Huxabrand to keep me safe as I worked.

I exhaled and out went the chaos and terror. Inhaled in peace and calm. Exhaled anxiety and fury. Inhaled certainty and purpose.

And this time when I thought of a gate, my heart snapped open into one almost without instruction from me.

I hoped I was right. I hoped I could do this. For all of our sakes.

Like a hole in a dam, the gateway I formed with my heart opened first with a trickle and then with a flood.

I hadn't expected this. I hadn't planned for it. I fell back at the spiritual onslaught, grateful when the stone door frame held me against the power of that internal roar.

Wait.

No.

Sensations rushed through me so quickly that I lost my senses. The battle beyond me vanished along with the cries of my friends. I did not hear the crash of stone on stone or smell the sun-warmed grass. Instead, I felt only an agonizing pressure and a roil of emotions as souls poured into me like water rushing from a reservoir. I was full and overflowing and it was all I could do to hold onto myself, to not lose myself entirely in the rush that filled me.

But these weren't the Stryxex. I reached for *them* and felt nothing, nothing at all. I was a gate chock full, jammed so full that nothing more could pass, but not with the spirits I had reached for, but with something else?

A burst of panic filled me. This wasn't right. It wasn't supposed to work this way. Was this what Judicus had feared? That I wouldn't be able to control what came in the gate? An open gate drew in everything. Everything.

I stumbled, feeling as though I had been feasting and had eaten to overflowing and past that. I felt ill. My head was swimming. I could hardly hold a thought.

Something had filled me — was filling me still — but it wasn't leaving, it was just flooding in, in, in. It was supposed to be the Stryxex. If it wasn't them, then Mally and Gundt couldn't escape, and we were all trapped.

I fought back waves of clawing panic.

It had to be them.

I reached again, staring at the nearest light-twisting creature that I could find and willing, desperately, that he be sucked from the sky and into my gate, but though I broke out into a cold sweat, nothing happened. Nothing to the Stryxex, at least. My gate widened. And into the margin, more souls flooded in from the Creatures of Sydonon that were surrounding me.

I leaned against the smooth stone of the wall behind me, my weary body slumping, letting my head rest against the cold surface and feeling the cold on my face. I'd failed. Worse, I had Kazmerev's creatures within me and no place to put them now.

They can't stay here! My mind begged me. I couldn't hold them. But where else would I put them?

I swallowed, opened my eyes, and by the light of the moon, I saw them – rank upon rank of still creatures. Motionless. It was as if some mad sculptor had filled a field with depictions of every beast dreamed of in this world and also the lands of tale and myth. They were posed as they'd been in life – some in the midst of swiping with claws or talons. Some lunging forward, others crumpled over themselves.

I could ... possibly ... put their souls back into those stone containers. Couldn't I?

I blinked, still too full of souls to move more than to let my eyes roll directionless over the masses until a scream from above drew my gaze upward.

Two phoenixes – so bright and glorious that they made my heart hurt – swirled in the sky, tossing fire at their dark, inverted opponents. But the light-twisting Stryxex outnumbered them, harrying them from every side. I reached for their souls again, and again I found nothing.

Huxabrand – bright and lit with pink, dropped suddenly, diving toward the ground, and Grevankin darted after her. They were coming toward me, I realized.

Probably coming to get me now that they'd seen I couldn't disable the Stryxex as we'd hoped.

I swallowed a wave of despair. This was not the time. I needed to think. Why couldn't I think?

I swallowed and pushed myself out from the stone wall awkwardly. I was still not mistress of my own limbs. I managed a wavering step forward as my allies skimmed toward me, phoenix bellies touching the ground as they flew.

"Sersha!" Mally screamed, pointing at me.

And then something caught me from behind and the crown was ripped from my head.

Light flooded the world before me, and lightness flooded my heart as if a weight so heavy that it was crushing me had finally been lifted. I gasped as Mally and Gundt tumbled to the ground, their phoenixes gone. They hit hard, and I tried to run to their aid only to be dragged backward, lifted off my feet entirely.

Something was pulled over my head, blocking out the light, and then my arms and legs were immobile, wrapped in something strong and tight, and my stomach lurched as the sensation of being drawn upward filled me, and all I could think was that I didn't dare panic. Not with so many living beings within me. Because if I panicked, I might lose my hold on them and on myself, and then there would be no chance of saving any of us.

269

I was held in place for so long that I thought my limbs may never wake up again. For my part, I drifted in and out of sleep because even though I knew I was a captive and knew I was likely going to be killed, I was still exhausted from far, far too little sleep and the long periods of darkness and immobility made me drift in and out. I heard snatches of incomprehensible conversation. Heard a whir like dragonfly wings. Felt the sun beating on me and the wind catching at my clothing. Beyond that, I was senseless. Sleep was an intermittent mercy.

When, eventually, the bonds released, I couldn't move anyway. I waited as waves of pins and needles ran over me and eventually, I was able to pull the sack from my head and sit up.

I was sitting in a rough circle of people eating beside a hasty fire. Kentinius was one. A handful of Stryxex riders made up the rest. No women, I noticed. Odd. But had I seen a female Stryxex rider in all this time? I didn't think so. Except for Flara. And she was … an anomaly. None of these people had half her flare.

On the horizon, the sun dipped low. Sunset was coming soon.

None of them seemed to care that I'd taken the sack off my head. Perhaps they were waiting for that. Like a sign to them to move to the next thing. I swallowed down a shiver of fear and tried to look dauntless. No need to let them know how terrified I was to be in the hands of the enemy.

Kentinius had the Dark Diadem in his hands, and he was turning it round and round.

"This will make it night if we put it on a head, yes?" he asked and I nodded, even though it wasn't precisely true. It would be night if he put it on *my* head. And that was not the same thing.

"Will it do the opposite?" he asked me. "Can you use it to make it day?"

I shook my head.

He watched me, tapping his chin as the light-eyed Stryxex rider beside him muttered an oath. The man stood abruptly, pacing around the makeshift camp. They were not traveling in comfort. The pot they had on the fire was alone. No kettle for tea. No tents erected. This wasn't even a very promising spot. I couldn't see past our small party, the trees here were so thick. It was not a hilltop with a view or the edge of a river. Was there a reason for that?

"They'll catch up, then. In the night," the Stryxex rider said grimly, his head whipping back and forth as he tried to look in every direction at once. "Unless we keep flying. Those phoenixes cover ground quickly. And we'll need to keep an eye on her. The minute the sun sinks in the sky, she'll have her phoenix here and ready to rip us to shreds."

I wished that were true. I wished I didn't have to keep Kazmerev locked down and held tight. I didn't dare risk letting him free unless the other souls I carried now had a place to go. But with the pillar far behind us and the stone statues they'd been in left behind with it, how could I ever release these spirits? And what would they do when I finally succumbed to my own pity and refused to play jailor to the innocent?

"What do we do when her phoenix shows his flame?" the light-eyed rider asked and Kentinius raised an eyebrow.

"Don't you think I can handle one sorry phoenix? After all you've seen?"

The Stryex rider grunted. "Let's just make this fast. I don't like being out so far from the rest. Not right now. Not like this. There are phoenixes amassing in the mountains. We saw them ourselves. We might show well against a handful of strays but even you couldn't defeat hundreds of the creatures, Kentinius."

"You underestimate me." Kentinius's face went cold and I stiffened. He had the look of violence in his eyes.

"That army has to be every remaining phoenix still alive. It's a powerful force."

"As am I." Kentinius's voice snapped like a whip.

"Arrogance will get you killed."

"That's what I told my predecessor," Kentinius said with a cruel laugh and his eyes were on me. Did he mean Occulus, his mentor, or Judicus, the student who ranked above him?

I couldn't tell, but either way, it spoke ill of Kentinius. He wore his jealousy like an open wound.

"We were only ordered to accompany you for a short mission. This has extended and extended, rope worker," the Stryxex rider said. "Best to return to the fold and make an end of it. We've been ordered to be there before the wedding and we'd best be quick."

Wedding? Who could possibly be important enough to be getting married at a time like this?

Kentinius grunted.

Good. They were allies but not friends and they rode roughly beside one another. If I could find a crack between them, perhaps it would give me a chance of escape.

They grew quiet. Eating, Setting a watch schedule.

I tried to ask for food, or water, or a moment to use the necessary, but none were given to me. I stood, meaning to find a convenient bush on my own, but golden ropes whipped out and shoved me back to my knees with little regard for which way limbs should actually go and I ended up with a twisted knee, smarting eyes, a heaving chest, and a firm understanding that there would be no niceties where I was concerned.

"Let her at least use a bush," the Stryxex rider muttered. "Do you want her to soil your robes the next time you're carrying her tied up in front of you?"

Eventually, Kentinius relented on that point, but my brief break was not enough to reveal any paths to escape, and the light-eyed rider stayed near me the entire time. I didn't know if his concern meant he had a little compassion or that he was merely practical. Either way, he didn't look me in the eyes, merely escorting me to and from the area they had set aside for such things.

When the sun set, the rider grew agitated, watching me like a hawk watching a mouse, and shifting position often. He didn't need to worry. Though my heart ached, I was no fool. I kept Kazmerev and Judicus bundled deep inside.

I ached to have them with me, to advise me, to comfort me. To just listen. It would be nice to know if Mally and Gundt had escaped their enemies. Maybe with me gone, the Stryxex and Kentinius would have left them alone. I'd disabled many of the Creatures of Sydonon before I was stolen away. But had it been enough to keep them from being stampeded into the earth?

The terrible feeling of being full to overflowing — of my seams under pressure and my skin about to burst — returned with the night. I felt as though I could feel the weight of all the souls I had let into my heart. Heavy, uncomfortable — painful, even — they filled me in a way that made me ill.

Left to my own thoughts, I found it impossible to sleep. The same worries chased round and round inside my head. I needed to be alert. There would be a way out if I could find it.

But no way out presented itself. We were all shaken awake a few hours later, the campfire extinguished and the Stryxex mounted. Kentinius bound me in ropes and set me in front of him, returning the sack to my head as if my sight were a deadly weapon and for a long half a night and well into the morning, I rode between him and the light-eyed rider.

I was almost grateful for the ropework holding me in the saddle. With the discomfort of my heart too full of life, I could barely stay upright on my own.

"Did you drug her?" the rider had asked Kentinius.

"What good would she be drugged? Maybe she's slow. She can't talk, after all."

"Maybe it's a head wound," the rider had replied. "A solid knock to the head can do that to a person. Just don't let her vomit on me."

I had not vomited, though I would have liked to. I had the feeling it might ease the too-full feeling I couldn't shake.

When morning came, even with a bag over my head, all I felt was relief. I napped on and off despite my confines, the pure ecstasy of relief filling me.

I had not considered the implications of taking all those souls within myself. I had thought that if it were possible, I would hardly feel it. I hadn't known I could take in Judicus until I did and I hadn't felt him until he emerged. But it turned out taking in this many was different, and here I was, filled to overflowing and it was making me feel feverish and disoriented. I needed a sharp mind and a plan to escape my captors. More than that, I needed a plan to purge all these souls. And I had none. And I was losing my ability to think up a solution with every hour that they weighed on my mind. Dawn came like light and life, lifting that exhausting burden, if only for a day.

I needed a plan. I needed to think.

We stopped for only a short half-hour to manage our business, refill the water skins and eat and then we were back aboard the Stryxex again. I hated the creatures. They felt like riding an oil slick and even when you were not on their backs their scent and coating seemed to fill the nose and be impossible to clean from the hands. They smelled like fish left out too long and the scent — overpowering at first — did not mellow with time. Instead, it became worse and worse with each added exposure.

I thought hard as we flew. What could I do with these souls? Should I just let them out and let them decide where they ought to go and if that meant creating a wandering miserable army of the once dead, then so be it? Would they not just be like the ones Judicus had accidentally freed or Mally had seen freed and flow until they found something to animate? But if there were no stone carvings to fill, then would they animate rocks and trees? Would a forest rise and march on Briccatore? I sounded crazy even to myself.

What other alternative did I have? Could I channel them into a pillar? And if I did, would that mean that Kazmerev and Judicus were ripped away into that pillar, also? Could the way I'd wrapped them up separately be enough to save them when so many souls battered me on their way out? They battered me now, and I was only a container.

Or, perhaps, it might be possible to channel them into a flask as I'd once seen Kentinius hold — a jar of souls. But how was that different from a pillar, and would Kazmerev ever forgive me if I did that?

My thoughts were a whirl.

When — at long last — night fell again, I forced back my friends from being reborn, and fought with my self-control as the masses within me bucked and swelled, heaving my body as if I were wracked with illness. I would not last long like this.

We landed on a hilltop and pitched a hasty camp. I was shown a place and told not to leave it, and since they set their camp around that spot, it would be impossible not to be caught if I ignored their instructions.

I swore I could hear the edges of voices within my own mind. Perhaps, this was how Mally went mad. Perhaps the souls in her broken pillar had tried to colonize her.

I drifted off to the thought of that and woke to a voice in my head.

Sersha? Can you hear me?

270

I gasped in the darkness and then clamped a hand over my mouth. I wasn't used to my mouth giving me away. The irony was not lost on me, though I did not have time to dwell on it.

Judicus? Is that you?

I felt the bubble of his bemused laugh in my own chest and looked around furtively.

My captors were asleep except for a single man who stood watch. He was dressed in Stryxex-rider leathers, his face masked in the way that made them nearly impossible to tell one from another. He was not looking at me. I stayed very still in hopes that he didn't decide to change that.

This is the oddest sensation, Sersha. I neither see nor hear and yet I do both.

Could you explain that? It sounds impossible to believe.

I fear I cannot. I've read nothing about this. He sounded unaccountably irritated at that. *Perhaps, if I had a library close. Or that book you found in the bottom of the pillar.*

I did try to take it.

Again, I felt a ghost of a smile within.

There are many reasons I respect you. This is one of them.

I felt my cheeks warm at his thought and a pleasant sensation of pride fill me. It trickled away a breath later when I remembered that I could neither bring the book for him, nor restore his body back to him in a way that would let him flip the pages.

I desperately needed him, though.

Have you been listening all along? I asked him.

Only when it's night. I can hear you then – and see, but I can't seem to move.

Are you seeing through my eyes? I asked, a little aghast.

No. I'm looking out from your body, I think, but not from the same level as your eyes, and my vision is fixed. I can't turn my head to follow movement or look at anything I'm not facing, but I've seen enough. You've been taken by Kentinius and Stryxex riders.

Yes! I breathed. The one watching the camp was moving, circling his sleeping comrades. I tried to breathe normally so as not to attract his attention.

And you're flying to Briccatore.

Yes.

And Mally and Gundt are chasing you, they're but far behind because they can only fly at night.

Judicus?

Yes? He seemed to be pausing mentally, as if I'd led him off the track his brain had been running in.

Can you feel Kazmerev in there?

He paused. *No. But a phoenix is dead and must rise in the heart of his rider.*

It's night. I would think you would feel him.

Now he seemed nervous. *Are you saying that you can't feel him inside you?*

No ... I ... yes, but only because I'm being battered so hard that I can't feel much of anything.

Battered? He repeated, seeming somewhat thick for Judicus who was usually so perceptive. I didn't like communicating like this. I liked to be able to see him. To watch him chew his lip or run a hand over his face or through his hair when he was anxious.

I'm being battered b*y the souls I sucked in with you,* I replied.

You ... you did what?

Don't you feel them in there?

I sense only you.

I swallowed. *I opened myself as a gate and all the souls in the nearby Creatures of Sydonon flooded me until I could carry no more.*

That left him silent for a long breath. When he spoke again, he sounded measured, controlled.

I am not surprised by that from so great a heart. But, Sersha, now what will you do with them?

I felt like my mental voice was small as I replied. *I was hoping you could tell me.*

Again, I felt his mental laughter - wry this time.

Did you, now? An apt thought.

Are you teasing me? At a time like this? That didn't seem like him at all.

He sobered. *I apologize. I was so relieved to awaken when I thought I was dead — and now, all over again, that it makes me almost giddy.*

The man on watch was making his circuit again, his leather boots creaking as he passed. They were just one sound among many - the rustling of the wind in the nearby trees, the rush of small creatures through the grasses.

Would it always be like this now? Judicus close here in my heart, close as my own soul, and yet with a distance between us that kept us from ever holding? Ever touching?

He was sober again when he answered me.

That's the question, isn't it? Find an answer to the problem of the souls that came out of the creatures and we might find an answer to that, too. He paused, and I had the feeling that if I could see him he'd be chewing on his lip. *It's very like you to give of yourself so generously, Sersha. In your heart, they are safe and well, unlike the torture of the pillar.*

I took that in quietly. Had he been tortured then? Was he referring to his own experience when he mentioned theirs?

I feel the troubled thoughts in your mind, Sersha. Rest easy. What was endured was only for a time. Here with you, I am at ease. But I must turn my mind to your problem. I must consider with you how to lay these spirits to rest. Can you speak to them?

I shuddered at the thought.

They are chaos within me.

He was quiet as he considered. Eventually, he spoke again, his mental voice as gentle as it would have been had he still been a living man before me.

You are exhausted and overcome. And you are a prisoner. Rest tonight. You must take care of yourself how you can. I will sing you to sleep and then take time to consider what we might do next. You do not need to carry this burden alone.

To my surprise, I blinked back tears at those words.

Eyes closed, now.

I closed my eyes.

Rest easy. Deep breaths.

I did as I was told. Relaxing first into the sounds of the nighttime forest, and the squeak of my captor's boots, and then, into the silent song Judicus sang to me. He did not have much of a singing voice. But I found I did not care. His rough voice was full of comfort rather than skill and kindness rather than beauty and I sank into it with gratitude.

271

I woke to arguing. It was still dark.

Easy. Draw no attention to yourself. Judicus sounded tense.

"It's that or risk them catching up," the light-eyed Stryxex rider was arguing. "They're right behind us. Gaining. I can feel it."

"They can't gain on us," Kentinius was scornful. "We can fly days and nights and we've been flying all day and half the night. They can't hope to catch up with less time to fly."

"They're faster. Surer. They can catch up. I feel them behind us, practically breathing down our necks."

"You feel it," Kentinius mocked. "Have you seen it? Can you show me the glow of a phoenix in the sky behind us?"

I'd never thought of it like that, but I supposed you could see a glow if they were flying visibly, and wouldn't Mally have to fly that way? She was too new a fledgling to have mastered flying invisibly. Wasn't she?

I shifted my weight. The spirits within me were stretching and moving, making me feel painfully full and pained. Even shifting didn't help with the discomfort. It was growing worse.

Don't look, Judicus said in my mind. *It will only alert them to the fact that you are awake — a thing you should disguise so we can gather more information.*

I swallowed. He had good advice. I wished I could hold his hand right now - for strength and support.

So do I. A —

He went silent as Kentinius spoke again. "We could use the old ways, but you said you didn't like the way they feel. You can't have it both ways. Either you creep underground and do it without complaint, or you fly in the sky without complaining. But either way, I'm done with this endless whining."

"This endless whining — as you call it — has been what has kept you from danger more than once."

Kentinius grunted — all the acknowledgment he was likely to offer. "Make a choice and then leave off. What's it to be? The skies or the earth? Get it over with, Heja and then we can travel in peace."

Heja — it was nice to have a name to go with his growling voice and light eyes — cursed, kicking at the grass under his feet for a moment before barking out.

"Earth."

He was storming away before Kentinius could reply, but the rope worker's only reply was a vicious laugh.

My heart was pounding in my chest already. I did not want to go beneath the earth in these "old ways." The last time we'd been in caves under the ground it had been a harrowing thing and I'd been glad to escape with my life.

Worse, the spirits in me were roiling at the thought, rolling through me, round and round, like a never-ending wave. My head swam, my belly heaved, and I scrambled up to all fours to heave with my stomach. Vomiting did nothing to help, though I heard Judicus in my mind, comforting me.

Easy now. Easy. It always passes. Trust me.

He would know. He was always sick.

Exactly. I have a great deal of experience with being ill.

But not anymore.

He was quiet for a long beat after that and he sounded deeply troubled when he replied. *I miss being ill. Who would think you could miss a thing like that.*

Trust me. You don't want it.

I was hot all over. Feverish. Heaving again.

"Ugh," a voice said over me. "The prisoner is ill."

"We don't have time to accommodate that," Kentinius said. I couldn't look up to see him. The best I could manage was to wipe my mouth with the back of my hand and not pass out in my own mess. "Get her on her feet."

I was hauled up hastily, still reeling. The world spun and I was grateful that it was night. With less to see, it was easier not to be dizzy.

"Bring her with us, Cared," Kentinius ordered.

The man holding me said something about his Stryxex and Kentinius snapped at him, but I couldn't pay attention to that. For me, the world was entirely internal right now — the heaving and writhing and now — out of nowhere — internal screaming of the souls within me. Did they realize, somehow, that we were headed underground? Was this a reaction to that choice?

I couldn't tell. Even with my thoughts entirely focused inward, I could not sort out any meaning behind the chaos within me.

"They're right there!" Someone yelled, and they seemed to be right beside me.

I forced my eyes open. The camp was already packed. Men were shoving last items hastily into the bags they had slung over shoulders or strapped to those sick-making Stryxex. I forced my swimming vision to focus and follow the finger pointing beside me.

There, in the distance, a pair of glowing dots grew larger. They looked as if someone had thrown fireballs from very far away. They looked like angry campfires about to rain upon the earth.

My friends.

They were so close.

But could they possibly be close enough?

"Now, will you be convinced to hurry?" Heja asked Kentinius. There was tension in his voice. His eyes darted to me, but I couldn't hold his gaze. The spirits inside me twisted, churning my belly.

Kentinius gazed at the sky, never looking away from it. "A little longer, Heja. What is the point of a trap if you don't bait it properly?"

"You want to draw them in?" Heja threw up his hands in disgust. "I've told you before, They talk to each other. And there are hundreds of the things not far from here. If they get close and tell the others, we'll be surrounded and destroyed. Better to run hard and fast and get to Briccatore in time for the wedding. The Grand Hadri has ordered all loyal subjects there. You know that the same as I do. Do you want to be painted with a brush of treason?"

"The Grand Hadri will understand," Kentinius drawled, his hungry eyes still on the phoenixes beyond us. "Judicus Franzer Irault is out there somewhere, dead though he is. He fought me in the ruins and he'll be with those phoenix riders. Don't you think the man deserves to be at his sister's wedding, ghost or not?"

My head snapped up and inside me, I thought I could feel an echo of that in Judicus.

I started to sign before I realized what I was doing.

"*Who is she marrying?*" I signed. It felt as if Judicus was holding his breath in my lungs.

"I can't read your signs, girl," Heja said, glancing at Kentinius who was ignoring us both. "But the Grand Hadri is marrying the Prince of the Elves."

What? The horror in Judicus's eyes must have been matched in my face because Heja shrugged in a way that suggested that life was not in fact fair.

"*I thought he was marrying Lady Lightland,*" I signed, unable to help myself, even though no one could read what I was saying.

"So did I," a voice said from the trees. "We were both wrong, I suppose."

And to my absolute shock, Lady Lightland herself emerged from the thick trees, a band of armed men and women at her back including one who glowed a bright gold and had a hint of sadistic pleasure in his smile.

"Your watchstanders need training, Kentinius," she said scornfully. "They didn't see an entire armed party or a ghost that glows gold, did they Occulus?"

"They did not," Occulus's ghost said dryly.

Could your actual eyeballs fall out of your head from surprise? I thought mine might.

"Put your eyes back in your head, Sersha," Lady Lightland said as if she could read my thoughts. "There's nothing all that surprising about us both being here, is there? We're always at the heart of the action."

272

My sister? Ask her why my sister is marrying. Judicus sounded like he was being strangled. Worse, the spirits in me responded to Lady Lightland's presence with renewed fury, battering at my mind and heart in a way that made my head spin and thoughts scatter.

With difficulty, I signed, "*Why does the Grand Hadri marry?*"

Lady Lightland strode right up to Kentinius, ignoring my question. She studied the Stryxex riders surrounding him without seeming to before sniffing in dismissal. They held their mounts as the shadow creatures bucked and reared. Something about the woman set everything living on edge. She swayed when she walked, her boots heeled and rising to over her knees. She ought to attract — and yet she repelled. Also, how did she walk through the forest in those boots? She was clearly a woman of many talents.

"Going somewhere, rope worker?"

Kentinius drew himself up, shoulders back. His expression was poisonous. "Threatening me, Lightland? As if I don't know who your true masters are?"

"Who are they then?" she asked, smiling as if he were an amusing child rather than a rope worker of great power.

"Occulus for one," he said, raising an eyebrow.

"The ghost?" she asked, lifting a brow and then a beckoning finger. To my surprise, Occulus followed her call, joining her in front of Kentinius, his head bowed in silence.

That was ... unexpected.

It certainly is, Judicus agreed. *And her arrival is good. This is our chance, Sersha.*

Kentinius was still speaking in the background. "We're needed in Briccatore, Lady Lightland. As I'm sure you are, too. Or have you renounced your loyalty to the Grand Hadri now that she has taken the pretty golden prize you dug up from an elven mine?"

Our chance for what? What was Judicus talking about? I saw no opportunities in the arrival of our greatest enemy, only danger.

We are surrounded by enemies, our allies outnumbered and far away. We have no way into Briccatore or to the palace to free my sister, he reminded me. *And it seems that task is more urgent than ever. We must act. Now.*

His tone brooked no argument. Part of me felt like I should argue anyway - that something about the way he was saying it made this seem unwise, but with the spirits in me swelling like a broken ankle, I could barely handle what was happening within. I had nothing extra to make decisions about what was happening outside myself.

"I've renounced nothing," Cassanetta Lightland said airily. "And who am I to object if the Grand Hadri wants my leftovers. I enjoyed the company of the Prince of the Elves for a time, it's true, but they do grow boring in time, don't they? So rigid in their views of morality and power. He was hardly going to be adaptable for a long ... friendship, was he? Much less a marriage."

Prepare yourself.

Judicus sounded like he was gritting his teeth. Against what? Could he not explain? He was worrying me.

Oh. I'm so sorry.

I almost breathed a sigh of relief. That sounded like the old Judicus. My Judicus.

But then he said, *Yes, I should explain. We need to kidnap Lady Lightland. Right now. Before they can drag you down those paths. And then we'll use her to get to Kristiana.*

Wait. He never asked for this kind of thing. He didn't.

It's my sister.

But did that make it right?

Does my young sister being forced to marry a villain justify kidnapping? He paused, as if actually considering. *I think so.*

Even as we circled the idea of kidnapping someone more powerful than me in front of dozens of other people more powerful than me, Kentinius circled Lady Lightland, speaking thoughtfully.

"You want moral adaptability, do you, Lady Lightland?"

"I would consider it chief among virtues, yes," she agreed and again her tone was light.

"You want someone able to bend and twist with the vagaries of fate?" he asked, his voice heavy with some new thoughtfulness.

"Perhaps," she agreed. "Or perhaps I want someone to twist fate with me."

My head was swimming. Nausea turned my stomach as every part of me felt like it was going to burst. I couldn't form an argument or even think of one. If this was what Judicus thought was best, maybe I should just let him get on with it. But how in the world did he think that I — a captive — was going to kidnap a woman who was currently the center of attention and then convince her to do anything?

Leave that to me.

I glanced over my shoulder to where the two burning lights flew ever closer. I hadn't realized that Lady Lightland had turned, too, until I heard her gasp, "And what have we here, Kentinius. Have you been clever enough to lay a trap for the ai'sletta?"

He laughed and it was not a kind laugh. "I've outpaced even you, Cassanetta Lightland. I've chosen just the right bait and when I get her to the capital, I will have the ai'sletta, and two phoenix riders to offer the Grand Hadri as a wedding present. Do you think she'll like them? And here you have nothing to offer."

"Oh, I doubt that," Casanetta said lightly. And then — before I could blink — she had an arm snaked around my throat, the other reaching up to grip my jaw and turn my face to him. "I came for just this dainty entrapment. Why do you think I learned to read her sign words? With this trophy, we can turn not only the ai'sletta but the army lurking for us just north and east of the city, too. She may be a silent thing, but her capture will speak volumes and every word of it will be about me."

Kentinius snarled, but when he raised a hand to work his ropes, Occulus stood between them, raising his own hands silently and letting gold ropes pour out of them.

"Or ..." Lady Lightland let the word hang in the air.

"Or what?" Kentinius asked, and it sounded like a curse.

"Or we could work together. Wouldn't that be nice?"

Now! Judicus called in my head.

Now what?

Now, you let your spirits out to do what they must.

273

He couldn't really mean that he wanted me to let them out, could he?

Just don't let go of Cassanetta.

He meant it. I … I couldn't … I didn't know what they would do.

"I don't think we'd make a very good team, Cassanetta," Kentinius said grimly. "We want different things."

Sersha? Judicus lost the hardness to his voice. It caressed my mind like a gentle breeze. *Sersha, are you still with me? It's okay to be afraid. It's okay to feel nervous. Just talk to me.*

"On the contrary, Kentinius," Cassanetta said, shoving me a step forward and making me wince as her grip tightened. "We want the same thing. It's just that we each want it for ourselves."

Sersha? Judicus sounded like he was trying — and failing — to be patient.

He was trying so hard. I was just … what if it was the wrong choice? What would Kazmerev say? He'd be so angry. He'd be so …

My thoughts cut off as Cassanetta forced me to my knees. "Decide, Kentinius. Are you with me or against me?"

Sersha. Judicus's tone was urgent, *It has to be now. Can you do it?*

I didn't think I could.

There was a pause and then his mental voice, all kindness despite what had to be a disappointment. *It's fine. We can only do what we can. Big breaths now. We'll find another way.*

But what other way could there be? I was on my knees, a captive, unable to do anything at all to keep myself safe and I couldn't even free my allies without setting the spirits free with them. My head pounded and my skin stretched too tight over the bulk of life I was holding in. But no, I wouldn't cry. I wouldn't.

"I need assurances," Kentinius hedged, eyes darting from Cassanetta to Occulus and back. "A place in whatever you're building."

Cassanetta sounded pleased when she replied, though I couldn't see her face from the position she had me forced into. "Occulus — dear ally that he has been — will not live as a spirit forever. I need a rope worker. Dependable. Loyal."

Kentinius hissed.

"And in return, I can be loyal, too, can't I, Occulus?"

The spirit of the powerful rope worker grunted.

"I can offer you a place at my right hand, Kentinius," Lady Lightland said easily.

"The right hand of nothing is still nothing," Kentinius replied, snapping his fingers. Around him, the Stryxex formed up, their riders taking their places on their backs. "Without you, I have my own Stryxex riders, the power of rope work, and access to a river of souls to power stone armies. What is your right hand compared to that?"

"I aim to be the next Grand Hadri," Lady Lightland said quietly.

I felt Judicus's gasp of shock inside and my own echoed it. There was only one way for her to claim that position.

"A tough target to hit when that place is already full. If you really wanted it, you would have married this elf prince yourself."

Lady Lightland snorted. "Why marry for position when I can kill for it?"

Behind Kentinius, several of the Stryxex riders gasped, though I couldn't tell if the sound was horror or admiration.

My heart sank. This was exactly what I feared. Inside, Judicus's emotions flooded through my own. I hadn't realized they could do that. They left me gasping as rage and terror and sorrow whipsawed through me morphing from one to the next so quickly that I couldn't keep up.

There had to be a way to stop it. There had to be.

"If you could kill for it, then why are your rivals still living?" Kentinius sounded unimpressed.

"Because unlike you, Kentinius, I have perfect timing. Why would I eliminate useful tools when I still have need for them? The time to execute my wishes is yet to come."

No, I couldn't allow it. There had to be some way out of this. I opened up my heart, seeking answers, seeking Judicus, fear and sorrow blinding me as I sought help.

And just like that, my heart was a gate again.

Oh no.

With a quick inhale, I tried to pull it back, to close the gate, but like a dam with a leak, a trickle poured past me and then grew, fighting against me as I tried to close in the walls.

It all happened so fast that I couldn't form a thought. One moment, I was listening to Lady Lightland brag about her plans to kill Judicus's sister, and the next moment souls were slipping out. One moment, I was open to the world and the next I was snapping shut faster than a willow snaps up when its branches are released from the snow.

But in that brief window, spirits had fled me. They flowed across the ground, slow as honey, bright as gold.

I felt Judicus's hiss of indrawn spirit breath, felt my own match his.

"Agreed," Kentinius said, as if he couldn't see the souls slipping past him and fanning out. "I'll be your right hand. I'll do this with you. We can combine our strengths."

As if he couldn't see the souls meet the feet of the Stryxex and then rush up them like fire up the side of a heap of dry grass.

I held my breath as the Stryxex lit like bonfires.

Pfft. Pfft. Pfft.

Cries filled the air as the creatures went from the light-turning aberration of a Stryxex to the blazing warmth and light of a phoenix and then —almost as quickly as they ignited — to a pile of dust on the ground.

So that's it! Judicus said.

I felt like I'd swallowed my own heart and it was stuck in my throat. My eyes were huge. And I wasn't alone. The riders, splayed out on the ground where they'd fallen with their gear from the backs of Stryxex, Cassanetta's soldiers, even Occulus's ghost — everyone, it seemed — was frozen in place, mouths open in shock.

Kentinius whirled around, looking for answers in every face.

Something hurt. Something was burning.

A sensation like a fireball lodged in my chest overwhelmed me, stealing my vision and rendering me frozen, thoughtless, emotionless. I was nothing but pain and more pain, clawing desperately upward.

Hold on, Sersha. I'm right here with you!

I clung to the voice of my beloved as the world went black.

274

I woke to shouts and jostling, tried to lift my head, and was smacked hard for my trouble.

"Stay still," a voice growled. Heja, I thought. I was bouncing on his shoulder and it jammed into my belly with each thudding step he took. That he could jog with me slung over his shoulder was amazing in itself. He must be very strong.

Above us, the sky was fading from the thick black of night to the pale dove grey of morning. I saw it in shivery glimpses from the corners of my eyes.

My head was pounding, my stomach swimming with nausea. The feeling of fullness had not lessened, despite the spirits I'd let slip. If anything, I felt more confused, more swirling with uncertainty than before.

Judicus? I called in my mind. Are you there?

With a surprising suddenness — the sun sliced across the horizon in a melon-yellow dawn. Bright light blinded me for a moment and the second it hit me, my sense of the souls within was snatched away and with it, the nausea-inducing roiling of being overfull of souls.

I let out a long, shuddering breath, grateful, relieved, and sorrowful all in one. I would have liked to talk with Judicus. I would have liked to get some sense of what was happening. Had I only returned to consciousness with the dawn? Did that mean that nightfall would overwhelm me again?

That the Stryxex had been reverted back to their original form and set free to die as phoenixes did not seem to be a bad thing. Kazmerev would certainly not judge me for it. But what of those souls who had been extraneous to that? Had they gone with their brethren to the place beyond or were they wandering in the forest, lost and afraid?

I needed answers to those questions before I dared let more souls out. I let out a sigh of worry and tried to peer around my captor to see if any escaped souls might linger near.

"We're close. Keep quiet," Heja whispered. And then we were moving more slowly and voices whispered loudly back and forth.

"You can stop whispering," Cassanetta Lightland said irritably. "Wherever those phoenixes are, they can't catch up to us in the daylight. Quick, climb aboard. We'll run the river through the day until we reach the spot. And then someone is going to tell me what happened to your Stryxex."

"Tell you?" The speaker punctuated his words with a string of curses. "We don't know ourselves and the loss is severe."

So, they didn't know it was my efforts that lost them the Stryxex, and Cassanetta had come here by boat and planned to return to the boat to flee. That made sense. The river ran to Briccatore and then to the sea. Everyone would be able to rest as she let the current carry her and only a skilled skipper able to steer the riverboat away from shoals would be necessary.

Good news for Cassanetta. Bad news for me. Mally and Gundt would fall behind, forced to wait for night to fall before they could chase after us. And what if they lost our trail now that we had no Stryxex for Huxabrand and Grevankin to smell in the air? Would they think to look for a boat, or would they look down that underground passage Kentinius had wanted to take? I wished I had a way to communicate with them. Wished I could leave a message somehow. If Judicus were here, he'd have an idea.

"The ai'sletta is on our heels. You told us that," one of the riders said to Lady Lightland. "Could her luck have destroyed the magic?"

"We're vulnerable without them," another muttered.

Occulus's ghost leaned in and whispered in Cassanetta's ear.

She looked up coolly and said, "We will discuss the details once we're aboard. We'll solve nothing losing time here."

Murmurs greeted her change of mind, but no one spoke out against it.

"We'll need more of them and quickly," one of the masked riders whispered to Heja as he passed. He hefted his short spear irritably. "We're at the whim of rope workers and nobility until we get back our status."

Heja grunted and I huffed a breath as he finally let me down to the ground but my relief did not last long. He leaned in close, his angry breath gusting in my face.

"I do not buy their excuses about ai'slettas, and bad luck, and places of ancient power. I think you are the one who stripped my phoenix from me, girl. And you did it after I urged the ropeworker to be kind to you. I will not forget. You have made an enemy for life."

And before I could respond, he grabbed my wrist, forced it behind my back and upward until every part of it from wrist to elbow to shoulder ached, and then he marched me forward to climb a narrow gangplank with the others and wobble my way across to the low-slung riverboat.

"Place her in the center," Lady Lightland ordered, looking at my disheveled state with apparent satisfaction. She was still perfectly groomed, despite a run through the woods at night, and in her hands, she held the Dark Diadem. She turned it over and over, watching me slyly, and then with raised eyebrows, she placed it on her brow.

I couldn't help the smirk that painted my face when nothing happened. I shouldn't have done that. The look of fury in her eyes told me that much. The backhand across my cheek reinforced it.

"Make sure she can't leap over the side," Cassanetta ordered, no longer looking at me. "We have a use for her and I will see it carried out."

"News from downriver," one of the sailors told her as he grabbed my arm and I was forced to wait with my cheek stinging and tears fresh on my cheek as he reported. "The army of phoenixes they sighted has swung east and south, circling the city. They've avoided the armies of Generals Ferdown and Viacombe quite neatly, but we might see them before we reach the city."

"Not in the day," Cassanetta said definitively. "And it's no concern of ours, Farris. Is it, Andretti?"

I turned to see who she was speaking and ice ran down my spine as a familiar raw-boned redhead smiled at Casanetta in the most vulpine way I'd ever seen.

"Certainly not," he agreed before returning to rummaging in a chest on the deck of the riverboat.

"You were hired to sail, Farris. So, sail. I will handle strategy. We are neither as weak nor as craven as you seem to think we are."

"As you say, my lady."

And so I found myself tied securely to Andretti's heavy chest. Whatever discussion they were having about what had happened to their Stryxex was happening on the other side of the boat, the words snatched away by wind and waves. They occasionally glanced at me, but no one came to question me or punish me for what I'd done. They must not be sure. Perhaps, even Occulus had not realized what had happened, even though he must suspect. After all, he'd read the books - or most of them. He'd been in the pillar. Worry at being found out by them gnawed at me — but exhaustion bit harder and though I tried to keep my eyes open as the trees passed on either side, sheer tiredness overtook me, and I soon drifted off to sleep.

It was still day when rough hands shook me awake and untied me, forcing a water skin and bread into my numb hands.

"Eat," Andretti said, his eyes narrowing as he watched me. He crouched down before me and I gaped at how much he looked like Derries - the Stryxex rider who had ridden us down, confronted us, and been wounded and then killed.

He watched me as I obeyed and when I was finished he said, "I won't ask you if you knew my twin, Derries. But by the look of recognition on your face when you saw me, you most certainly did. I also won't ask if you were part of his death. That he has passed is certain, or he would have returned here by now. But I will tell you that you've gained no friend in Heja and you have no friend in me. If you survive whatever Lightland's trap requires, I will buy you from her, and slit your throat in the presence of my brethren, and we will paint our Stryxex with your lifeblood and revel in the end of you."

Well. Wasn't that nice.

"Get up now," he said, taking the water skin from me. "We are at our destination."

I'd been so riveted by his words that I hadn't noticed that the boat was no longer moving. As I watched, men tied long cables to trees and made the gangplank stable. It ran out to a rundown dock, aged by sun and wind and waves and twisted by weather.

Stryxex riders and warriors began to hurry over it even before it was fully secure, their hands full of weapons, bags of supplies slung over their shoulders. They must mean to stay awhile. In their midst, the glowing spirit of Occulus disembarked, too. Where were those he led from the pillar, I wondered. Would they meet us soon, reinforcing his ranks with more just like him? I couldn't so much as look at him without trembling and he was dead now and I'd watched him die. You'd think I would not be so frightened of a man I knew for such a short time, and yet I was bone-terrified of him.

Lady Lightland was already on land, I realized, barking orders with the Dark Diadem still displayed on her head. I needed that crown. I needed to get it back to Mally. And I needed it to keep her and Gundt in the air, even if it cost me in pain.

I set my jaw and considered if there might be a way to get it back. I felt my eyes narrow as I watched her, wondering if a bargain, a trick or a threat would work best. I had little to threaten, less to bargain, but perhaps her own fears could trick her.

When her gaze met mine, it skittered away as if she were already afraid — and afraid of me, at that. Strange.

And then Andretti was prodding me in the back and it was my turn to cross the gangplank. I shivered at his poke in my back. It could just as easily be a knife. He could slit my throat just as he promised right here before everyone.

"Move, girl," he growled and I moved, stepping neatly onto the plank and keeping my balance just fine as I was marched across.

Lady Lightland called his name and beckoned him with a crooked finger, and once again my wrist was grabbed, my arm jammed up behind me, and I was forced to walk before him as he hurried to her side.

"Dress her in this," Lady Lightland said, shoving a red gown at him. "She needs to be visible and red draws the eye. There's no use having bait the prey can't see."

"And the crown," I signed awkwardly with one hand. She refused to acknowledge the comment, so I signed again, *"Crown."*

"This is not for your benefit, Sersha," she said acidly but then she paused and I saw her realizing what I was suggesting. If she wanted to use Mally's desires against her to trap her, then she might want me back, but what she wanted even more was that crown. With a snarl of annoyance, Cassanetta dragged the diadem from her head and shoved it roughly into Andretti's hand. "And put that on her head. Sweeten the pot."

He grunted in reply and to my surprise, he steered me away from the boat and where the others were organizing together and directly off the worn path by the river and into the underbrush.

This couldn't be right. But when I glanced over my shoulder, Lady Lightland only lifted a single eyebrow as if daring me to challenge them. She meant me to be shoved into the forest then.

Confused, I let Andretti guide me, but it all became clear after hard minutes of hiking uphill through dense growth. We emerged on a hillside crisscrossed with slender fallen trees. A storm had passed through this spot at some point, downing everything in its path and leaving a wide swath right across the crown of the hill that could be seen for miles around on land — especially from the river — and most certainly from the air.

A lone rock stood at the peak of the hill and it was to this rock that I was directed and then Andretti put the gown in my hands.

"Dress," he said curtly.

The gown wouldn't go over my jacket, but I certainly wasn't going to strip in front of him. I wiggled free of my jacket, tunic, and belt pouch, dragged the gown over my undershirt and pants and boots, and then made haste to fasten my belt over top of the gown.

He grunted derisively but waited until I was done. When I reached for the jacket he yanked it away.

"No jacket."

I mimed shivering.

But he only repeated, "No jacket" and wrenched it from my grip, and then, before I could say anything more, he finished cinching the rope he'd brought around the rock, shoved me so that I stumbled and fell against the boulder, and then followed through, wrapping the rope around me and cinching it tightly around the rock so that I was pinned by the waist to the rock. He followed that up with a tie around my hands and then another rope pulling them up and over my head to the other side of the rock.

Effective. And ridiculously uncomfortable.

He waited until the very end to pick up the Dark Diadem from where he'd left it and as he moved toward me with it, my heart was galloping faster than wild horses.

His mouth twisted unhappily, and then, without ceremony, he jammed the crown on my head and the sky went black.

275

Where is Cassanetta? Judicus's voice asked almost at the same moment that my awareness of him returned. I gasped a sigh of relief. He was still there. I hadn't lost his spirit when I let out the souls that filled the Stryxex.

But his arrival returned with other sensations. Kazmerev was trying to be reborn — a thing I must still prevent for his sake and mine — and the spirits still within me were expanding and filling me until I bulged inside and ached from the pressure. It was worse than the worst headache, a terrible, stretching pain that went on and on. I needed them out or they would wear me down to nothing.

But now I knew one way to let them safely pass by me — I could release them into Stryxex. Provided I didn't pass out every time I let just a few out. How many times would it take to let them all out when just a handful had knocked me out entirely?

Has she left already to kill my sister?

I shared his stab of fear at the thought. But she wasn't there yet. First, she was using us as bait for the ai'sletta. I told him what I knew as quickly as I could.

So we are waiting, then. But they have no Stryxex with them anymore. Nothing to challenge our allies by air?

Only two powerful ropeworkers. They had them in their favor.

I could feel his tension within me. He wanted to be out here, meeting rope work with rope work and keeping his allies safe with his skill and magic.

Easy now. Don't fret. You said there's an army of phoenix riders coming this way. Perhaps they will arrive in time to save Mally. And if not, it still gives us time to solve this puzzle. Difficulty, misery, defeat —they're all just puzzles to be solved.

I should have tried to let out the souls when he asked me to. I should have grabbed Cassanetta like he told me to and run.

Judicus was —wisely — silent on that point as I looked grimly at our options.

It was night, at least, giving Mally and Gundt the advantage. And though I was tied to this rock and out in the open they wouldn't be foolish enough to fly right to me and into this trap.

Won't they?

Mally wouldn't be.

But Grevankin would. And so would Gundt. They would put your welfare over their own.

I gritted my teeth against my frustration, because of course he was right. They would put me first. And I had no way to warn them ahead of time. I couldn't even call out.

They could win ... perhaps. He sounded thoughtful. *There is no record that I know of containing a description of two phoenixes fighting head-to-head against two rope workers. It's possible that their speed and mobility could counter the power of the rope workers. The rope worker must stay on the ground in a fixed place, weaving ropes and spitting them out after our allies. Would the ropes be fast enough to catch a phoenix who was purposely avoiding them? Would it be possible to shoot fire through a rope? I haven't noticed it happening, but most battles we've fought have been chaotic and I was focused on my own fight. The phoenixes have always been my allies. What if the rope were weakened because the one weaving it was trying to use too many strands at once? Perhaps, that would make it vulnerable to a phoenix flame. Or what if the ropes tangled a phoenix and were bringing him down, only for him to flame the ropeworker in place? That could work. And with two of them, they should be equally matched. It will certainly be a fight worth recording for those who follow.*

Judicus?

Oh, my apologies, Sersha. It seems my speculations leak across my mental channel from time to time. I should guard against that.

I rather liked it. It was just that I was shivering with my hands tied above my head and I didn't really sound as enthusiastic as I felt.

He made a mental sound a lot like clearing the throat and I thought that perhaps I sensed embarrassment. *I should have remembered that. Where are your captors?*

I let my gaze — enhanced by the fire of my phoenix — scan the edges of the forest around the clearing. It was hard to see from here, since I was at the peak of the hill, but I thought I could make out figures moving furtively along the edges.

To my surprise, one broke away from the rest and strode across the tangle of fallen trees toward me. His arms were full of something and I doubted that whatever it was was my missing jacket.

I shivered as I watched him pick his way across the ankle-twisting ground. Above us, a cloud passed before the moon, darkening the landscape, and then to my surprise, it opened up and cold rain began to mist down, coating my already chilled flesh with freezing rain. I gritted my teeth against it, glad that I had the inner fires of a phoenix rider to take the worst of the edge off.

I feel as though I should remind you that while you are in a very physically vulnerable place right now, Judicus began, sounding a bit apprehensive. *You are dearly loved within. Both by your phoenix Kazmerev, and,* here he rushed as if embarrassed, *by me. Of course.*

I pressed my lips together, my mind skittering between flushing at his words and fear at the approach of the enemy. I wanted to thank him for his sweet words, but I wasn't sure how to say the words.

Take heart. Inwardly, you are strong and beloved.

I swallowed down a lump in my throat.

By the time the silhouette in the rain had reached me, I could pick out the cold features of Heja. His hood was pulled up against the drizzle and he laid his burden nearby and began to build a fire with the logs and dry grass he'd brought.

I wanted to say something to provoke an answer from him, but with my hands tied above my head, it was impossible.

"Don't think this is for your comfort," he muttered shooting me one sharp glare and then refusing to meet my eye. "This is to show *them* where you are."

Actually, that made perfect sense. If it was going to rain, then I doubted that Mally and the others would so much as see me here on the hill, never mind realize what they were seeing.

His fire kindled — the wood having been very dry before the rain began and still mostly protected from the worst of it — and he had a decent bonfire built in no time. What I hated most about it was how it blinded my vision. I could no longer see my enemies in the trees. Even when Heja snuck off again, I lost sight of him quickly, my eyes blinded by the bright flames nearby.

It was warm — which cheered my heavy heart — but I felt deeply disadvantaged by my loss of sight. Even as I peered upward into the clouds, I could not see a spark in the distance that might be Mally or Gundt and I couldn't see how the clouds were swirling or moving across the moon.

The rain intensified, pouring down in drenching sheets, making the fire dance before it, and soaking my gown until it hung heavy from me as a blanket of snow.

The fire flickered, wavering in the rain, almost snuffed out by a sudden fierce gust of wind and in that momentary darkness, my sight returned and I saw them. They swirled overhead like a school of fish. They billowed and blew and expanded and ... it was really them. More than I could possibly count right now in the dark.

And just the sight of them sent my heart galloping and my breath racing it, until I could barely catch it at all.

Sersha? What is it?

Stryxex. All the Stryxex you could possibly imagine. But what were they doing here?

Can you open your gate? Judicus asked.

I had to. I reached for a calming breath but at that same moment, Heja arrived in a swirl of lashing rain, throwing fuel on the fire with a curse. I reached again for calm and it skittered away.

"Come on! Come on! Make a flare. Let them see you," Heja cried and I knew he wasn't talking to me. His eyes flicked from the sky to the fire, the fire to the sky and back again, and then to my utter surprise, he yanked his mask down to blow on the reluctant flames and I caught sight of a boy not much older than me — a boy with a pretty rosebud mouth and two scars reaching from one side of his mouth and spreading across the right side of his face.

My breath caught in my throat. He was so young.

I should be thinking about opening the gate and filling the Stryxex with my spirits. I should be working on freeing us, but all I could think about was those scars on that pretty, boyish face, and what might have caused them, and what else might be hidden beneath the masks the raiders wore. Perhaps, they were as complicated as I was under all those layers. Perhaps, they, too, had voiceless among them and sickly scholars and angry cousins.

I blinked back sudden tears.

And for just a moment my breath was stolen away until Judicus reminded me, *Sersha. Can you open your gate?*

I swallowed and tried to find it, tried to open my heart but the sight of Heja's face and his burning eyes as he looked at me kept making my heart stutter.

I flinched when I felt Judicus's mental voice, certain he'd rebuke me, but his voice was soft - almost gentle.

It might be helpful to think of how he is indeed like you — only instead of a beloved phoenix, he rides a cruel bird of darkness, bent on rending the world apart. You could save him from that.

How could Judicus be so full of understanding when I was so weak?

I, too, am often weak. And over and over, you have helped me overcome that. We wouldn't have your gate if your heart were not so big. And we wouldn't have this new puzzle without that great strength.

He was right. This was my strength. I dare not let it become my weakness. I gritted my teeth together. I would not be weak today. Focus, Sersha, I told myself, and in my mind, I saw a gate and the rush of heat and I opened my heart and then —

Red light painted the backs of my eyelids as Judicus and the spirits were snatched away with a suddenness that stole my breath, and when I opened my eyes there was the furious face of Heja, the crown in his hand. His hair was plastered to his face, his mask back up, and the delicate diadem between his palms.

"She won't like this," he said grimly. "But it's not her who gets to make this choice."

And then, with a terrible wrench, he broke the crown in two and threw the halves to the ground as I stared at him, my mouth gaping open.

The rain hit again, in a sudden burst as hard and breath-snatching as a wave of the ocean. It didn't matter that it was day once more, the rain was so heavy I couldn't see more than the length of two men from me in any direction. I was still fighting for breath when suddenly the Stryxex were descending, dropping all around us, rain pouring off their light-twisting forms. Heja threw down the branches he'd been carrying for the fire and leapt onto the back of the nearest one with a whoop of delight, arm raised above his head in a fist. A roar came from the trees and I knew without having to look that it would be the rest of the Stryxex riders with him, overjoyed that they had mounts again.

I swallowed, looking at the ground where the Dark Diadem had been torn in two and this time, when my cheeks were wet, it was not solely because of the rain.

276

I had always considered compassion to be my greatest strength. But when I needed to be the strongest, it had weakened me. Ruined me. Made me useless.

I sucked in a long, shuddering breath, trembling in the frigid wind, staring helplessly at the broken ruin of a crown — the crown that had been our greatest advantage all this time — making both our phoenixes, and now Judicus, accessible whenever they were needed. How could I have been so foolish as to pause when I saw a similarity to myself in my enemy? Hadn't I known all along that they were just like me, only making different choices?

But no. They were not just like me, right? Not anymore. Because the series of choices I had made had changed who I was. They had made me courageous where before I had been hesitant. They had carved a deep rut of compassion in my heart and a deep trench of fortitude. And if their choices had been cruel enough to bring Stryxex into this world, then they had carved the opposite things into themselves. We may have started the same with all the same potentials for weakness or love. But we were not the same now.

And if I was not like them, then I would not feel guilt for being different from them — for hesitating when I needed to consider the best choice rather than just taking what I wanted. I would not feel despair because someone else had snatched what was valuable to me and shattered it. All of this — everything we'd endured together — had made me into something more than that.

And so I squared my shoulders, and I watched the Stryxex and the position of the sun. Day could not last forever, and the moment that the night rose and filled the sky, I would open my big heart up and become a gate, and the Stryxex would wink out like stars past their time.

I balled up my fists, cold and numb from being above my head for as long as they had been, and I promised myself I would be ready.

The rain settled into a steady drench but still, the Stryxex swirled. Some with riders, some without. Any time they flew close to me, the wind of their passage stirred up the rain even worse, flooding me again and again. I was miserable in the torrent.

But more miserable when I realized what had occupied my adversaries.

It was well into the afternoon when Heja set down his brand new Stryxex nearby and hefted a heavy burden from its back. He tossed the heap of cloth from the back of the snapping bird-like creature and then leaped down after it. It wasn't until he stooped and lifted his burden a second time, that I realized it was no heap of cloth but a man. A man I knew well.

They had Gundt.

Heja dragged him to the boulder and dumped him at my feet.

Was he breathing? I watched his sides anxiously. Perhaps that was movement? Perhaps he yet lived. Heja was certainly trussing him as if he were likely to escape.

"With both of you here, the ai'sletta will not be far behind," he said grimly. "And then Andretti has promised to purchase you from Lady Lightland and show us what we do to people who try to take our Stryxex from us."

I should have been trembling — perhaps somewhere inside I was — but for now, my concern was with Gundt and Mally. How injured was my friend? Had they hit him on the head or stabbed him in some place I couldn't see?

And what about my cousin? Could she evade them for an entire day until Grevankin was born once more? Or would she try something terribly brave and rush out here to her captivity and eventual death?

If I were a betting woman I would bet on the latter and that left me biting my lip, the tightness of anxiety twisting my belly. I would have to find some way to indicate to her not to come here. But what could I do with my hands tied and no voice? What?

I wiggled and struggled against my bonds, hoping I could get free enough to check on Gundt. My throat was dry and my belly rumbled hollowly. The storm cleared and the sun came out, strong and powerful and blazing, making my wet clothing steam with its intensity. Gundt had not moved. Miserably, I watched him lying there, unconscious, as the hours ticked away.

The tree line was busy with comings and goings of Cassanetta's people and Kentinius's. I saw those primary figures arguing before a group of Stryxex, hands gesturing as they laid out a disagreement I was too far away to hear. They must have chosen to stay the course because as the sun began to drift to the horizon, they had not untied me or moved their people. Everyone continued to wait in place except for the Stryxex who went up in small flights and then returned.

They were looking for her. All signs pointed to that.

And what would they do when they found her? The ai'sletta luck was not so easily turned to one's advantage. I certainly knew that. Though I also knew that had she been here the Dark Diadem would likely still be whole and we would all be flying off to some other place.

I was glad she wasn't here. Glad she'd had the willpower to resist this trap because despite her bold words and objections, I knew that if Mally saw me like this she wouldn't easily walk away. She had a soft heart she kept in a tight grip behind that hard exterior.

I watched the sun — as much as one can without going blind — and anxiety ate me away. The moment it sank, I would try again.

The moment it sank, I would let the spirits out and if they tore through me and rendered me useless and broken — well, then that is what would happen.

It was nearly dusk when I heard a cry from the edge of the clearing. My heart leapt — fear and hope warring side by side within it.

They must have found Mally. She must be here. Was she whole? Would they bring her to where I was?

But no.

The woman they eventually dragged across the littered clearing — working hard to lift her over the crisscrossed fallen trees — was one I did not recognize. Her face and clothing were smeared with mud. She bore no weapons, but by the look of the loops on her belt, she'd had weapons before my enemies had captured her. A gash on her forehead and bruising on her face told me she had not been brought down easily.

They dumped her at my feet with dark looks.

"It seems that when the sun sets, we'll find a second use for you," Andretti said as he wiped his hands on his pants. "And here I thought you were only ai'sletta bait."

The man beside him grunted a laugh. "They won't know what hit them. They always think they own the skies."

Own the skies?

I looked again at the bruised face of the woman at my feet. She looked familiar, but I couldn't say where I had known her or if it was only a resemblance to someone else I had known.

Along the tree line, Kentinius's Stryxex rider allies were bringing their Stryxex in from the skies — including the many riderless ones — and tucking them under the cover of the trees. The wild Stryxex fought against their control, sending the trees shaking and causing tremors in the ground.

But I hardly noticed that because my heart was in my throat. That they were tucking them under the cover of the trees just before dusk could only mean one thing — they expected an air attack. And that meant phoenixes close by.

I swallowed, looking again at the mud-smeared woman. A phoenix rider, perhaps?

"Don't look too excited," Andretti said and there was a hungry look in his eye. "We outnumber them two to one. They don't know we're here. And by the time they do, the trap will close and we'll have them all as ready for the slaughter as you are. My brother's killer will pay. One way or another."

I wanted to sign to him to ask him why he thought one of us had killed his brother when he had no proof that the brother was even dead. I wanted to sign and say he was crazy. I wanted to warn them not to go up into the air on their Stryxex or they would fall to their deaths. But my hands were tied above my head and all I could do was flinch when he slapped my face, fighting back tears and choking on all the warnings I ought to be able to give him.

"We'd better hurry," the other man said, "It's nearly dark."

"We have lots of time," Andretti answered, his eyes fixed on mine. He waited for me to shudder before he turned and followed the other man back to the tree line.

For my part, I watched the sky and hoped for darkness to come quickly.

277

Darkness fell with a now-familiar wave of agony as my spirit felt the pressure of millions of other souls rushing into me.

I refused to be bowled over by them this time. Instead, I kept my eyes open, my jaw set, ready to act. Which was why I saw them come alive all around me in the trees. Bright balls of fire bloomed as shouts and curses echoed across the leveled hilltop.

I gaped, glancing down at the woman painted in mud at my feet.

Mud.

They'd disguised themselves. And infiltrated the forest. And now the cries and shouts all around and the bright flares of fire proved there were Flame Riders in the forest in among the Stryxex riders. So much for their trap. The riders had known and had set a trap of their own.

But even in that first wave of knowledge, I watched as one bright light flared and was immediately winked out. They were outnumbered. They were going to be overwhelmed.

No time to think more about it. It was time to act and to act now. Could the spirits reach Stryxex so far away? I could only hope.

Sersha, I do hate to interrupt such a useful line of thought.

I nearly leapt from my skin at the sound of Judicus's voice in my mind. I felt my face flush with excitement that he was back and near and then felt it get worse knowing he could feel that, too.

And now, I seem to have certainly distracted you. Forgive me. But to the point, perhaps, when you open your gate you could attempt to ... point it? ... in the correct direction, given that the distance is so far?

It was a reasonable suggestion.

If he could hold my mental hand, I'd ask for that right now.

I'm here. I can't wait to see this.

I closed my eyes. I bundled up the essence of who he was, and the essence of Kazmerev who I missed in a way that made me feel hollow for a moment. And then I opened my heart up as a gate.

And nothing happened.

How could nothing have happened? I could feel them there, bulging just under my skin, desperate for release. Go! Get out! I release you!

I inhaled sharply.

Nothing.

Was I doing it wrong?

"You're doing it wrong," someone whispered.

I jumped and nearly laughed all in one motion. A garbled gasp came from my lips and Mally snickered from somewhere close by.

"That's not how to be a hostage. You're supposed to look romantic and languid, not like a drowned rat."

I needed to focus. I needed to open the gate.

There was a sound like something sawing and then suddenly my hands slipped free, falling to hang like dead things on either side of me. They had no feeling in them and they were purple and swollen from where the rope had choked them.

"I can't carry either of these two on Grevankin," Mally hissed, as she bent over Gundt, checking him. What did she think she could do for him? She'd never paid much attention to how to nurse the sick or tend the wounded. But, then again, I didn't remember watching her practice freeing hostages, and yet here she was, doing an admirable job.

"Call up Kazmerev," she demanded as the sky grew brighter with painful suddenness.

No, not the sky.

The area around us was lit for a breath and then a ball of fire splashed to one side, blackening fallen trees and debris. If everything had not been so thoroughly soaked it would be on fire now.

"Hurry!" Mally hissed.

But I could no more call him up than I could shout. Not unless I could free these souls within me. But how could I do that? Why would they not release?

Could I make a small suggestion?

Yes!

And please, don't take this the wrong way but was your gate open when you made it? It felt a bit ...rigid.

I ... I didn't know. I —

"Sersha!" Mally hissed. "Stop standing there looking stupid and help me! Or did they break your wits along with the crown?"

She had the fragments of the dark diadem in her hands and was shoving them hurriedly down the front of her bodice.

I took a deep breath, trying to be patient. After all, she'd just rescued me.

I was just thinking, Judicus said in my mind, *that the other times when you opened your heart you did it with no real purpose in mind. You didn't think you'd be gathering the souls into yourself. You didn't realize they could slip into the Stryxex. It was unconscious. Perhaps, you should just try to open up without forcing anything.*

"If you're talking to that rope worker somehow, I'm going to grind your wrist bones," Mally said through clenched teeth, with her usual perceptiveness.

I lifted my hands to try to sign my thanks to her, but my hands were all prickles, refusing to respond to my urging.

"Don't bother, Sersha," Mally said, annoyed. "Just get Kazmerev over here. We need to move. Now. They've started the assault. Look!"

She pointed to where phoenixes ripped up between the trees, fire blazing from the hands of their riders in streams or flung in balls of flame. Swirling around them rose swarms of Stryxex, some with riders directing them, some wildly diving and attacking, ripping at anything in their path, some ripping bright feathers from a phoenix, others in the way of the tangling gold ropes reaching around them toward our fellow Flame Riders.

Urgency welled up within me and a desperate need to help. They'd come for the bait — for me — and this was how they were rewarded — with death and horror.

But there would be no Kazmerev until I rid myself of souls. And I couldn't force that. I'd have to try it Judicus's way and hope it worked.

Experience suggests it will, but be cautious. We are in unknown territory.

He sounded almost excited. I shouldn't be surprised. If there were two things Judicus loved, they were puzzles and knowledge.

And you. I love you.

And with the warmth of those words burning in my heart, I closed my eyes, opened my gate, and let go.

278

"You'd better be calling Kazmerev, Sersha!" Mally said. "Oh. Oh no. I think Terese is dead."

I didn't dare respond. I kept my eyes closed and my gate open and then — like a dam bursting, they started to pour out of me, souls like hot liquid honey. I felt a scream building in my throat and a hand clamped over my mouth.

"Quiet! Quiet! Of all the people I thought I'd have to warn to be quiet, I never thought it would be you!"

But I wasn't paying attention to her. I was trying to keep calm and not pass out as the spirits poured from my gate and outward. Pain seared me to the very edges, filling up every pore of my being, drowning out Judicus's mental voice and even the sounds of battle beyond me.

I opened my eyes in time to see golden souls pouring from my numb hands. They flooded out across the broken ground of the clearing, sliding between and over the husks of fallen trees, through the tangles of dead branches, outward. I gasped at the pain building, building, and then darkness stole me away.

I woke to Mally's face, her nose almost touching mine she was leaning in so close.

"You're awake." She said it like a curse. I could barely hear the words above the screams and wails in the distance — not far enough in the distance. Behind Mally's sweat-smeared face, I caught sight of the towering boulder. It was no longer close by. Mally — strong woman that she was — must have dragged me all the way here. Dragged *us* all the way here. An unconscious Gundt lay beside me, still breathing, though raggedly.

A feeling of emptiness — like having just purged everything from your body — filled me, leaving me trembling from top to bottom.

Before I could so much as work my dry mouth she grabbed my gown by the neckline, yanked me up to a sitting position, and pointed to the trees.

There were fewer phoenixes in them. So few. Just a few flares of bright red light.

If there were fewer Stryxex, I could not tell. They swirled in the air like a whirlpool that never ended and never ebbed, diving, ripping, attacking, but then rising again to join their school of soulless husks.

"Whatever you did. Do it again," Mally said fiercely.

There was no arguing with that. I opened my sore mind and heart, formed a gate, and barely managed a breath before my gate was flooded with souls rushing through.

This time, I was able to keep my eyes open for long enough to watch the honey-bright souls flood across the ground and wash across the trees, and branch upward until they touched the twisted ranks of the Stryxex, whirling with the flock of not-birds and twisting around and into them like reaching roots until they winked to brightness one by one and then burst into puffs of dust. It was like watching flowers bud and blossom and wilt in a single second instead of a season — a whole garden of them, one after another. It went on and on and I felt as though I had the entire sea rage through me, wash me clean, and leave me empty and sagging.

I was still heaving and shaking when the world tipped and darkness swept over me a second time.

I woke to a slap, my hand clutching my stinging cheek.

"No time for that now. Get up."

If nothing else, Mally was persistent. But it wasn't "nothing else" was it? Because she'd dragged us even further, sweating and huffing though she was, coated in mud, soaking wet, and arguing loudly to Grevankin who was clearly invisible or our enemies would have been here in a heartbeat.

"Don't talk to me about gentleness. If there was another way to do this, don't you think I'd do that?" She bent over me, her chest heaving with her breath. "Sersha, for the love of life, get up on your feet."

She grabbed my arm, but her grip was light, and when she tried to pull me up, I could tell she was at the end of her strength. Usually, when Mally touched me, tried to force me to do something, or tried to force a reaction, she was firm and strong and it hurt. This pull barely registered.

I drew in a long breath, trembling with my own exhaustion, and then forced myself to my feet, swaying there with her. She nodded approval and looked down at Gundt, seeming to sigh at the sight of him.

I saw everything double. Double Mally's staring at me. Double Gundts lying like lumps on the broken ground. I swallowed down bile. My head rang with the echo of voices no longer there. My heart howled silently at the souls that had fled.

And above me, the whirlpool was just gone. Disappeared as if it never was. I looked up at the twinkling stars, blinking owlishly.

"Almost out of allies," Mally gasped.

And I followed her wavering hand to the sky where two last phoenixes flew, bright like flags of hope in the sky. My heart lurched as they were chased through the air, not by Stryxex but by tangles of lightning-fast ropes.

"Stryxex," I tried to sign, fumbling the word.

Mally shook her head tiredly. "Your last ... whatever ... destroyed them. Every one of them. Whatever that was, can you do it to rope workers?"

I shook my head and almost fell over as I lost my balance.

"That's a pity. It happened maybe a minute ago. Unless you have another trick up your sleeve, I'd guess we have less than a minute before they run out of phoenixes and come for us. No, Grevankin, I have not forgotten you. But as you've pointed out, we're limited to what I can do with your strength, and right now, I'm not sure I have the strength to sit down without collapsing."

Her legs trembled as if to emphasize that point.

But she was right. I was not out of tricks yet.

Forcing my heart open was like forcing a frozen muscle to move anyway. With a lurch, I felt it cave and I gasped. After being full for so long, the emptiness within was almost painful. I could breathe again but breathing left me feeling raw and ragged. Gently — with careful slowness — I reached for where I had wrapped Kazmerev up tight and close. To my relief, the merest touch and he blossomed from my heart, rolling out in flame and life.

I kept him invisible, but his advent opened my eyes to Grevankin as the two phoenixes greeted each other and looked at their fellows in the sky.

"Now, grab Gundt, and let's go help," Mally gasped.

I stumbled into Kazmerev, wrapping my arms around his fiery body. Was he hurt from being dead for so long? Was he ill or broken or ...

I live. I breathe. I am unharmed. But what is this about holding me back?

He seemed concerned, perhaps even furious. But I was not done yet — not when I could still see those ropes flung across the sky. They tangled around one of the phoenixes, dragging it down from the heights.

I closed my eyes, took a deep breath, and reached with all my heart.

And there he was.

I opened my eyes and Judicus burst to life from my heart, a golden, glowing ghost on a mission.

He spared me a warm smile. "Sersha. Perfect timing."

Those few words held a thousand others. Before I could guess at all the meanings behind them, he leapt forward, hands opening wide before anyone even needed to tell him. A pair of black ropes leapt from his hands and spooled out, fast as striking snakes. They were already grabbing and ripping at his opponent's ropes before I climbed onto Kazmerev's back.

"Always up to me in the end," Mally muttered and as I turned toward her I was surprised to see she already had Gundt most of the way up Kazmerev's back.

I reached to help her, and with a violent pull, we found him a place on my beloved phoenix's back. I leaned back, swaying, deeply grateful that he was here. That he was back.

Are you injured? Something feels off about you but I can't say what it is...

I wasn't injured, but I certainly felt unwell — as if those souls had left fingerprints all over the inside of me. What did that matter beside his return?

It matters to me.

"Let's see if my luck holds," Mally said, her chin thrust out, and then she was rushing to Grevankin's back and leaping with him into the air.

Hold on tight! Kazmerev roared in our mental channel. *I will want an accounting of what's been done while I was gone, but for now, I'd better grab that rope worker and get him closer to our brethren. No more phoenixes will see ash today!*

And then we were in the air again, rising, and as we rose, so did hope rise in my heart.

279

Grab him! Kazmerev called as he flew low, sailing in behind Judicus, his flame-edged wings flickering with every movement.

My ghostly betrothed barely noticed us, hands held out, eyes focused on his work as it wove and spun, cutting off threads formed by the other rope workers, every movement outlined in his golden glow.

I leaned out from Kazmerev's back, heart in my throat, trying hard not to disturb Gundt's balance from where he lay belly-down across my legs. This felt precarious. Did Kazmerev really want me to try to sweep him off his feet?

I have you! You won't fall. Just get a strong hold on the rope worker.

Wait. But Judicus was a ghost. I wouldn't be able to hold him.

Oh. I had forgotten.

Kazmerev sounded slightly embarrassed and then he swerved slightly, changing the angle of his swoop, ducked his head, and before I could gasp, Judicus was rolling over Kazmerev's head and across his purple and red feathered back and then sailing right through me in a way that stole my breath and froze me all at once, and as my head turned to follow his progress, he caught Kazmerev with a strand of rope work and settled himself on the phoenix's back behind me. I felt a memory of his warmth from when he was alive, of the way that his breath used to gust on my neck and it was laced with sadness.

My mouth was still open in surprise when he said courteously, "My thanks, Kazmerev. An excellent solution," and then turned his attention back to his rope work as if he'd been offered nothing more than a chair to sit on.

I am not a chair.

Of course not. I didn't think my mind was working quite correctly. I felt so ... hollow.

Hold on tightly, Sersha, Kazmerev said, shooting forward with a great stroke of his wings. *You've done your part. Let us do ours.*

Yes, echoed Judicus.

We gained height with astonishing speed. Ahead of me, I saw Grevankin roll in the air and shoot suddenly to one side, narrowly avoiding a coil of rope work. I searched below and above, only to see one of the phoenixes we were rushing to save pulled down from the sky, completely tangled in ropes like a bird in a fowler's net. It flickered. Its fire went out. Kazmerev cursed and his pain pulsed through me more powerfully than ever.

I don't fully know what you've woken me into, Sersha, but there are two rope workers below and we can both see what wickedness they weave. And also ... hmmm. Aim for the one at the bottom of that magnificent tree!

He swerved enough that I could see the tree and I aimed my hand, drawing in his warmth and fire as the great tree grew closer. I meant to let out the flames, but felt, instead, a pool of warmth filling my soul as if I'd accidentally opened my heart like a door again. I shook my head, trying to clear it before I tried again. This time, I let loose a stream of fire, aiming for the base of the tree and it went up in flames like a torch.

Whatever you did has left you exhausted and empty.

Souls. I'd brought in the souls of the creatures of Sydonon and when Kazmerev found out he'd be so angry.

You just told me.

People swarmed out from under the flaming tree — dark silhouettes running in the flickering light of the fire. It was not them I was looking at but the figure at the base of the tree. He hadn't so much as flinched when the tree caught fire and now he aimed his hand upward and golden ropes shot out, tangling just ahead of us. Mally screamed as they caught her from Grevankin's back, her phoenix flapping wildly, trying to stay under her.

Occulus! My fire hadn't so much as touched him.

I risked a glance behind me at Judicus. He gave me a brief nod, acknowledging that he saw it, before flicking a rope in the direction of my screaming, furious cousin and shaking the magic loose from her, but it was all he could manage before his ropes returned to their original target.

Kentinius stood out from the tree line, perched on the tall root bole of a fallen tree, his hands spread wide and ropes dancing into the sky. Beneath him, on the clearing floor, I caught a glimpse of Lady Lightland forming up what was left of her ragged group into a defense surrounding him. She moved stiffly, protecting one side as if she'd been injured.

I wasn't good at secrets when I was this worn at the edges. And now — in the middle of all this, I'd have to confess to Kazmerev that the souls I'd drawn in went into the Stryxex and made them phoenixes again and then winked out forever into ashes and dust.

They did?

To my surprise, he sounded ...touched. Warm. Almost proud.

Is that so hard to believe? I do not condemn you, Sersha. You saved my people — many of them. Both those whose souls were ripped from them and those who were nothing left but empty husks and energy. That they faded to ash means they died the final death. They're safe from all that man could do to them.

Oh.

It's a good thing.

I watched helplessly as Kentinius grabbed the remaining phoenix I didn't know and twist it in his ropes. I gasped, hand flying to my throat, breath caught, but then the rope worker lost his grip as Judicus snatched Kentinius's magic away with ropes of his own and the phoenix fell free of the ropes, spiraling downward.

I have my own secret to confess. Kazmerev sounded tense.

I clenched my jaw, worried about what he might have to say but more worried about the battle. Kentinius and Judicus were a close match. Made closer by the need for Judicus to switch his attention back and forth between Occulus and Kentinius. At least the Stryxex were gone. All of them. I scanned the sky looking for them and then the ground, too, and what I saw made my stomach lurch. Broken figures littered the ground or were caught in trees. Stryxex riders. Men who had been aloft when I let loose the souls I had contained and ripped out their mounts from beneath them. My heart was in my throat at the results of my work.

"Can we get in closer, Sersha?" Judicus asked, sounding strained. "Can you ask Kazmerev for me?"

Could we?

Yes.

But before he could shift our direction, I caught sight of Kentinius, and saw the wicked gleam in his eyes as he reached into his coat, drew out a bottle, and poured its honey-gold contents across the rocks. The bottle of souls. We'd seen him with it before. My heart was in my throat as they rolled out across the ground, but where would they go? There were no statues here to animate. There were no ... oh no. Not that. No.

The liquid touched a fallen Stryxex rider and he began to rise, slowly, his broken limbs pulling themselves under him and his awkwardly bent head jerking wildly side to side, and I knew, without knowing how, that I must not allow this to happen.

Kazmerev needed to land. Right now. Right now.

"We need to stay in the air," Judicus said to me, glancing at me, suddenly desperate.

"He's raising the dead," I signed. *"I have to stop him."*

As I spoke, Kentinius finished pouring out the bottle, threw it over his shoulder, and ran at the same moment that the last Phoenix drew in side by side with Mally and Grevankin and together they sailed toward the last remaining soldiers, even as the resurrecting ones began to gather.

That's not quite the last Flamerarch phoenix, Kazmerev said, but I wasn't listening, I was twisted in the saddle, trying to convince Judicus with only my expression that we had to land. Now.

"Yes," Judicus gasped, swallowing visibly at the look in my eyes. "I understand."

Please, Kazmerev, I began to think.

And then to my shock, Judicus leapt off of Kazmerev's back, landed perfectly on the ground, dodged the grabbing hands of a resurrected body, and darted past — not toward a fleeing Kentinius. Not toward Occulus throwing ropes at his back, but directly toward Lady Lightland, flinging her guards aside with his ropes as if they were no more than playing cards standing in his way and not men at all.

He wrapped her in his rope work at the same time that we smacked the ground, jostling Gundt.

He woke, blinking and I hauled him from Kazmerev's back, sliding down with him.

"What is this?" He asked in a tiny voice at the same moment that Huxabrand manifested with a roar and a keening shriek. Something caught her around the neck and flung her backward — a golden rope. But I couldn't think of that. Couldn't think of how close it came to grabbing Kazmerev instead. I had to focus.

For what I'm about to do, I am sorry, I thought.

If it stops my people from animating corpses, then do what you must, my phoenix said, turning his trusting eyes on me. *But there is something I need to tell you.*

Could it wait?

He looked to the sky. *Yes. For now.*

I nodded briskly, and then I laid a hand on his head, closed my eyes, and opened my gate, drawing him back within. I felt a heartbeat of peace and harmony as his soul settled in mine, a heartbeat of frustration from Judicus as he was drawn away from his battle and back into my heart, too, and then a maelstrom of emotion as I drew in the spilled souls, forcing them to abandon their host revenants and enter the gate of my heart. There was a feeling like a pop and my eyes opened to see golden ropes fade from a bristling Huxabrand. I turned, slowly, shakily.

There was no more ghost of Occulus behind me.

Turned back, still shaking, to see Gundt laying a hand on a shaking Huxabrand. And just past him, I saw Mally rolling across the ground with an agitated Grevankin hovering over her as she wrestled Lady Lightland into the hold of a rope - a real one, not a magic one. Around them, the ground was littered with the dead and the last phoenix who wasn't one of ours landed, huffing and flickering beside Mally. Her rider swayed in the saddle, an arrow sticking from one shoulder. If Kentinius doubled back, we'd be as easy to pick off as new-hatched chicks.

But we'd won. We'd won against overwhelming odds. How was that even possible. Was it only the luck of the ai'sletta, or was it something more? Some kind of blessing from the heavens themselves upon our cause. I felt a stab of hope and then winced at how it hurt to hope with Kazmerev tucked far away.

Was dawn close already? That couldn't be possible - could it? But at some point, as we'd been fighting, the sky had lightened. And it was growing lighter by the second.

I stood, swaying, hand shading my eyes as I peered upward. To my shock, what had just looked like a brightening was coalescing into shapes — many, many, many glowing fiery shapes.

"There came after all," the other Flame Rider said, a smug smile on her face.

That's what I've been trying to tell you.

I couldn't count how many there were. A hundred at least. They flew towards us, speeding like fallen stars. My heart was in my throat at the sight of them. Too late, and yet, here they were. The last of the Flamerarch just as Lady Lightland had discussed. I almost thought I could see Shastomen at their head.

I blinked away tears of relief at the sight of so many reinforcements. They were really here. They were really going to stand with us. We weren't alone.

"They're here," Gundt gasped, saying with words what my heart was acknowledging. "We're saved."

I spread my hands to say something to Gundt who was stumbling — grey-faced — across the uneven ground. But as I did that, something jolted inside me — almost as if the souls inside me were not just filling me too full, but had begun to storm within me, to fight or battle, or something. The sensation stole all my senses, flooding my mind with pain, and stealing the light.

I pitched forward and the last thing I remembered was the feeling of Gundt catching me, falling with me, and whispering, "Hold on. I'll call Mally. Just hold on."

EPISODE FOUR: "FOR THOSE REGAINED"

SEASON THREE

280

The world tilted horribly when I sat up, clutching my head. I felt like I was underwater. No. Underground. No, perhaps under fire. Could you go under fire?

My thoughts weren't making sense.

I blinked through mental fog and the world settled into focus in the blazing brightness of noon. I had been placed on a rocky outcropping along the river. Beside me, Gundt sat with his head in his hands, a thick bandage swathed around it and a cup of something steaming in his hands. He looked up blearily at me and smiled. His smile was deeper and harsher than it had been before, but I couldn't tell if it was the dirt on his face that made his smile lines pale or just the events of the last few days and weeks that had left him looking so hollow.

I wondered, for the first time, what it had been like to be Gundt before this all began. Discredited, his only home with the independent Flame Riders and among the Greensleeves. No family. No home. Had he always been looking for a purpose like this, or had he been happy to drift along the breeze taking life as it came? I knew him so well — could guess how he'd respond to anything that came up, knew his loyalty and kindness were unbendable, like that of a phoenix, and yet I knew nothing of his life before he found me and the ai'sletta. I'd like to ask him more about it. Maybe when my head stopped hurting.

"You're awake," he rumbled in a gentle undertone. "I was starting to worry. Mally kept insisting that you be awake before the council, but no one believed you'd find consciousness that soon. This thing you do to fight for us all takes a lot out of you."

I reached up to feel my own head. There were no injuries, though I was terribly thirsty. It must have been simply the efforts of drawing in all those spirits that knocked me out. How many might have been flowing across the ground when I drew them in? More than before? Or did it only feel like that because I'd already been so exhausted? I wished Judicus or Kazmerev was there to help me figure out what to do with them. I squeezed my eyes shut, breathing harshly, and then suddenly an arm was around me. I stiffened at the pressure, opened my eyes in surprise, and saw Gundt's concerned face inches from mine.

"You're not alone, Sersha," Gundt said. "You always think you are when Kazmerev is hidden but you aren't. Why do you think Mally made them wait for you? She has insisted that you be part of things. Why do you think I waited here beside you? I didn't want you to wake up alone. You aren't the only one who cares or who will work for our common cause. You need to start to trust us. When you need it — I'll be here for you. I swear it. Mally isn't the only one I want to protect."

I felt myself melt at his words and he removed his arm awkwardly with a cleared throat.

"You can trust me," he said grimly. "It's hard for me to put aside everything I've ever believed sometimes, too. But if I can give up my faith in a creed, you can give up your refusal to have faith in people, don't you think?"

I nodded in understanding, meeting his eyes with a wry smile. He had, after all, given up the idea that Mally was the savior of the world. And his whole life had been about that. He tipped his head and I followed the gesture, snorting in surprise at what he was showing me.

We weren't alone along the river's edge. Flame Riders stood in little huddles or gathered around fires eating or mending gear and weaponry along the banks. They were dressed in the manner of the Flamerarch — with uniformed precision. Even the faces that I thought I recognized from among Shasamen's people were in uniform now. It was the same clothing that the poor woman who had died at my feet — Terese — had been wearing.

It was strange to see them like this. The only other times I'd seen more than a few of the Flamerarch they'd either been imprisoned with me, awaiting their deaths with dignity, or imprisoned in the mountain hold of Sarcoda and anxious for my help to free them.

When emotions are high, you get one kind of impression of a group of people. When they're working efficiently at what they love you get another. I was fascinated now to see the precision with which they worked together and the clear, calm way that they spoke. There was a hierarchy that I didn't understand at work in how they deferred to one another but even then it was with a crisp factuality that I found appealing. I couldn't have been one of them. Kazmerev had a wild heart that couldn't be tamed to stay put or work for a long time with those who did stay put and my voicelessness would make that kind of cohesion impossible, but it still fascinated me.

In the distance, far enough that the river drowned her voice, Shasamen stood speaking with a carefully groomed older man with a short beard. There was something familiar about him that I couldn't place. I thought, at first, that Gundt was pointing them out, but after a heartbeat, the man shifted and revealed Mally standing behind him with Lady Lightland held beside her, a length of rope extending from where her fists were tied together to Mally's hand.

Lady Lightland — our old enemy and Gundt's half-sister. Were his words about beliefs referring to her, too?

"Mally thinks Cassanetta Lightland is the key to sneaking in and rescuing Judicus's sister without being caught," Gundt whispered, looking around furtively before he added, "They won't like that if they find out."

By "they" he clearly meant the Flamerarch. But then, why risk whispering when they might hear? Why not wait until he could tell me mind to mind? I stiffened. Oh. I'd almost forgotten. The moment night fell, and our phoenixes emerged, these phoenix riders would hear all their thoughts. And perhaps they would hear Judicus's too, just as I could.

I clenched my jaw in worry. How would we get around that?

"We'll make a plan after their council," Gundt assured me, but at that moment, Mally's eye caught on mine and there was a look of urgency in hers that chilled me to the core.

She sauntered past Shasamen, directing Cassanetta to pick up food and water as she walked and when they reached us, she turned to Lady Lightland and said, "Feed them and give them water."

"*Are we pets, then?*" I signed.

"Don't be silly, Sersha," Mally said lightly. "Pets are there to be decorative. I'd hardly say you were qualified for that role."

That was Mally for you, offering reassurances and insults in the same breath.

She leaned in closer.

"Say nothing," she whispered to me, eyes dancing with some suppressed secret that made me very nervous. "We'll talk when the council is over."

And then, to my horror, she flicked her rope, and Cassanetta winked at me.

281

The man with the short beard was named Flamerarch Castan and he was — apparently — the highest-ranking living member of the Flamerarch and the man leading this group of Flame Riders. Something tickled the back of my memory at his name, but whatever it was refused to surface. I'd heard that name somewhere before. But where?

Shasamen was serving as his right-hand lieutenant. No one bothered to tell me what the position was actually called and I didn't try to ask Mally. It didn't matter. What mattered was that the remaining Flamerarch led by Shasamen had been joined by a few dozen others brought to them by information Jastomen had gathered in the city of Briccatore. Together, they formed our army against the invaders. Our entire army.

Generals Ferdown and Vicombe had survived with their armies intact, but they were part of the conspiracy against the original Grand Hadri, the Flamerarch, and the populace of Briccatore, and they led the only living remnants of Calicarn's army. That made them our enemies. Anyone who was living side by side with traitors and doing their bidding to suppress anyone fighting against this evil takeover was an enemy. I'd seen how the soldiers and conspirators had treated the people of Briccatore. I'd been there as they took the Flamerarch away one by one to their evil purposes. I knew that those who had helped me were dead at their hands and just thinking about it made fire run through my veins and roar in my head so that I could hardly think.

"We should liaise with them," was Flamerarch Castan's great idea. "See if we can win their hearts back to the good."

"*I don't trust this bottom-feeder,*" Mally signed to me. I was so stunned that she was bothering to communicate with me that my eyebrows rose involuntarily. She never did that unless it was important.

I agreed with her thoughts, though. There was something about this man that was untrustworthy, beyond even his desire to find harmony with our clear enemies.

"What are you doing?" Flamerarch Castan asked her smoothly, his eyes on the signs. His words seemed mild, but to me, his expression appeared to be threatening.

Beside me, Gundt stiffened and my eyes flicked to Lady Lightland, still tied up and now standing behind Mally, her head bowed. She watched me through the veil of her hair. Whatever possessed her to learn Sumarian sign? She could betray us in a heartbeat.

"I'm translating for Sersha," Mally said easily. "She deserves to be part of this. She has a phoenix, too."

If anything, Flamerarch Castan's face grew even stonier. "We do not offer votes to every fledgling who comes to us."

"But hopefully you will humor the ai'sletta," Mally said casually. "If you want my help you will, anyway. It's come to my knowledge that you might need more of it than you're letting on. I've heard the prophecies the same as you have. I've heard the histories, too. The ai'sletta has always been a tool for the use of others. And she always dies. What purpose are you planning for this tool, Flamerarch Castan? I think I can guess. You can't fly into the city, can you? Not now that they've started building the pillar. And with every day that it grows stronger, your reach towards the city grows smaller. Cross the line and it will suck your phoenixes up into its grasp and you will lose any might you have. Or are you as adept at fighting on your feet as you are in the sky?"

She said it all with sugar sweetness. A sure sign — if anyone knew her at all — that she was feeling prickly.

"And how would you propose to help with that?" Flamerarch Castan asked coldly. Her speech about tools had not moved him at all. "Your phoenix is as much at risk as ours are."

"I can sneak in under the cover of day and disable the pillar while my phoenix is safe," she said confidently. I did not share her confidence. In the day, we wouldn't have Judicus and we needed him to unravel the pillar. "I have ways you know nothing about."

Again, my eyes flicked to Lady Lightland who stood with her head bowed. Is she the one from whom Mally had learned of the limitations on the phoenixes entering Briccatore? Was she the source of these "ways" Mally claimed to have? It made me nervous seeing them together. It was like watching a dog fight a snake. At any moment Mally might break her neck and we'd lose whatever we could gain from having captured her, but just as easily, she could bite my cousin, infect her with venom and destroy all our hopes.

"Don't I have secret ways, Sersha?" Mally asked with raised brows, signing the words over-dramatically as she said them as if I were particularly difficult to communicate with. It took all my effort not to roll my eyes. Instead, I nodded, my expression as neutral as I could manage.

"We'll bear that in mind," Flamerarch Castan said in a quelling tone. "But for now we need to discuss amongst ourselves." He turned his back to her as much as he could while still addressing the rest of the Flamerarch gathered around him.

"We are divided — half of us here and half on the other side of the city. Should we go and treat with the generals, knowing we are at half-strength, or should we wait to hear from our fellow Flame Riders that they have found a firm position first?"

Well, that explained why I was only counting just over one hundred Flame Riders assembled on the low rocks along the river. It was a good place to meet on this shore of a river bend. The river was quiet and slow-moving here. Arranged like this, in a swell of the river that formed a bay, even a group this large could easily see one another and be heard when they spoke.

"We should go immediately," Shasamen said. "It will take time to turn hearts and minds. Besides, I would like to go together before this additional army that the ai'sletta claims is coming arrives. Things will only grow more complicated the moment anyone takes the field in earnest."

Had Mally told them that we were waiting for the ghost army to return? She was offering our information rather freely if she had. I felt my lips pursing together in judgment.

"We should wait," another voice spoke but I wasn't paying attention as they debated. I couldn't stop thinking about the name "Castan." I'd heard it somewhere before. Whatever I'd heard made my nerves all buzz with worried attention and made me very, very nervous about sharing anything we knew.

"*Why do you have that look on your face?*" Mally asked me, pretending to interpret.

I'd heard his name from another Flame Rider, hadn't I? But could I remember who it was or what had happened? I felt my brow furrow as I tried to think.

It came to me all at once with a memory of his face. Reichus! The Flamerarch who died for me, who had tried to protect me. He'd speculated then that Castan might have conspired against him.

My eyes flicked up to Castan as Mally signed, "*You'd better tell me what you're hiding.*"

"*Has he tried to talk to Cassanetta?*" I signed subtly, trying to hide what I was doing.

"*He, who?*"

"*C - A - S - T - A - N,*" I signed as she rolled her eyes.

But she took the question seriously, giving me only the faintest hint of a shake of the head.

"*I think he was one of the people who ...*" I paused, fumbling for a word that might mean 'conspirator.' "*Who made the Grand Hadri's death.*"

Both of us glanced worriedly at Cassanetta. To my surprise, she still hadn't looked up. That was so unlike her. I was pretty sure that meant she was plotting something. Something that probably would result in her trying to kill us.

"*We need to get out of here faster than I thought,*" Mally signed.

"*I thought you needed them,*" I signed. "*To defeat the enemy, drive them from our shores, and take your place as ruler.*"

"*I will do all those things,*" Mally agreed. "*But I will do them without these fussy bird riders.*"

Cassanetta choked on something, bursting into a coughing fit. Well, at least she was still paying attention if she could laugh at Mally's jokes.

"And what makes you think Cassanetta won't rat you out?"

"I have something she needs that Castan can't give her."

Fair enough. Cassanetta seemed to run on what was best for Cassanetta. And who would understand that better than Mally who ran on what was best for Mally?

I shook my head in resignation. I could only flow with these currents. I could not stop them.

"But we also need to stay here," I argued, trying once more even if I knew Mally would be unmovable. *"Shasamen is not evil and neither are most of these Flame Riders. We need their help to take the city."*

"They can't even enter the city while the pillar is there."

"Then we need a signal to tell them when to come — when the pillar is down and they are safe. We need a plan."

"If we make a plan, they'll just tell our enemies," Mally said, a cool smile on her face as if she were only passing on the words of the Flamerarch as they debated whether to join with their allies before confronting the generals. *"We'll leave a note."*

"What is with you and notes? That's always a bad plan! Besides, if they think they can turn the Generals to their side, then maybe they can. Maybe we could get their help to take back Briccatore. Flesh and blood humans won't be in the same danger as the phoenixes are."

"Do you hear yourself? You trust Castan — a man you say conspired to kill your rope worker's uncle — to tell you who might listen and join us? It's far more likely that he'll turn his Flamerarch allies over to those generals."

I hadn't thought of that.

"*Besides,*" Mally signed and I could tell by her smug smile that she was about to make a point I couldn't argue with. "*We only have three days until the Festival of Moons which is the date of the wedding and your rope worker will never forgive you if you let his sister marry a monster.*"

"And how would we prevent that?" I signed, frowning. The Flame Rider nearest me backed up a step as if he thought I was that frustrated looking over the plan to ration food supplies rather than my inability to save a girl from an unwanted wedding.

"*Cassanetta knows a way. Don't you?*" Mally signed and she gave a sharp tug to the rope holding Cassanetta as she tossed her hair at the same time so that anyone watching would only notice the brilliant chestnut hair rather than see the subtle cruelty of the gesture.

I watched in stony silence. I didn't like pettiness, but Mally had every right to let out a little frustration with the woman who had murdered her mother, and if she wanted to get back a little of her own this way I didn't think I had the energy to stop her. I needed to focus on bigger things — like bringing down an entire ruling class, two armies, a whole breed of magical creatures, and a massive magical monument they were building. We could worry about pettiness after that.

Cassanetta met my eye and smiled in a way that made me shudder. She'd been following the whole conversation. And she'd convinced Mally to listen to her. But I didn't think we should trust this enemy. Not even if she promised us the entire world on a platter.

"We need to go — immediately. Start puking. I need an excuse to leave this meeting," Mally said, smiling graciously as she pretended to translate.

"You're kidding." My eyes were still on Cassanetta's rock-cold gaze. What was she going to us? How would she betray us this time and who would suffer the consequences?

"Stop staring at my pet. I have her fully declawed and she can't hurt you," Mally signed, but I didn't believe that for a second. *"Now, think like your rope worker and ... vomit."*

I swallowed down a protest. It wasn't actually that hard to look ill when I felt so terrible. Besides, I was starting to realize that this was one of those situations where Mally was going to do whatever she wanted and there was nothing I could do to stop her. Better to go with her now than chase after her later. But maybe we could find a better way than a note. Maybe we could tell Gundt and he could stay behind and make everything work out.

I relaxed my iron control, let my knees sway and my head spin a bit. I hadn't even realized I'd begun to fall yet when Gundt caught me, directing my weight against his chest.

"I need to take my friend away where she can be ill," Mally said gracefully.

"You made us wait all this time for her and now you're going to leave?" Flamerarch Castan snapped.

"I suppose she could stay and ruin this discussion being ill. I didn't bring a change of clothes. Do any of you have extra? When she gets ill it can be violent."

Really? She couldn't have chosen a less humiliating lie? I felt my face growing hot, but Gundt took me by the elbow, steering me through the gathered crowd. Most of them offered him sympathetic looks and avoided my gaze. And no wonder. I must look a sight. How long had it been since I'd bathed or had fresh clothing to wear? How long since I'd slept in a bed or eaten hot food? Far too long.

Mally's voice faded into the distance. When, finally — the last Flamerarch was behind us, and the shore had grown lonelier and steeper, and I really was starting to think I'd collapse if I didn't sit down soon — Gundt pulled me close and whispered.

"Whatever fool thing she's planning — count me in."

Which, I supposed, was exactly what I'd expected him to say.

282

Mally caught up to us and didn't pause to say a word. She grabbed my other arm and pulled me hard and fast toward the forest.

"Everyone keep up," she huffed between breaths, forging through the undergrowth as if she knew exactly where she was going.

Apparently, she did. She shoved her way through the thick brush, knocking light branches so that they whipped back and hit me in the face or the arms, stinging my skin. I wasn't fast enough to catch them, I was so dazed.

"Whatever trick you have that lets you destroy those enemy souls is awfully convenient," she huffed at me, totally ignoring Gundt who was doing his best to support most of my weight. He caught a stinging branch in the face and grunted. "But I wish it didn't leave you so weak afterward. I already have to drag Cassanetta with me. I wish I could count on you to be at full strength."

I ignored her grumbling, focusing instead on keeping one foot in front of the other and not accidentally stepping on Casanetta's heels. She was between Mally and me, led by the short piece of rope.

There was no point in arguing with Mally. She just needed to air her frustrations. She had to know that the ability to defeat an army of Stryxex was worth hollowing out my strength.

Gundt checked over his shoulder frequently.

"I hope your plan involves a good place to hide, Mally," he said in an undertone. "The way you left was extremely suspicious and someone will certainly follow."

"I hid our supplies right here," she said, stopping in front of a tree that grew right into a steep incline. Its roots tangled and wrapped around a few larger rocks and it was between two of the rocks that she reached and yanked out a pair of packs. "I had to stash yours here, too, Gundt."

She shoved one at him and he grunted in thanks or approval — I wasn't sure which.

"And no, we aren't hiding. We're running. As fast and as far as we can. Don't look at me like that, Sersha. We aren't abandoning the cause. We're hurrying it up. You want to save Judicus's sister from this elf prince? Well, it's going to take us at least a day, maybe two or even three to get to Briccatore and that will leave very little time to figure out how to get into the city and rescue her. It's hardly the moment for delays. We can't afford to wait for night and our phoenixes and even worse, we can't count on the folks back there not to do their best to get in our way, whether intentionally because they have evil designs in this, or unintentionally by trying to help and keeping us back from this."

She was moving again, dragging a huffing Cassanetta along behind her. I blinked hard and pushed even harder, trying to take more of my weight on my own. Gundt still held my arm, catching me when I stumbled. I was lightheaded and thirsty. I was not going to manage a whole day of walking, but there was no one to hear my concerns, so I'd just have to go until I gave out.

We had been hiking parallel to the river and as it turned we emerged at the ancient dock where Lady Lightland's riverboat had been moored. I'd forgotten about it entirely in the madness. If I'd had to guess, I would have expected someone to flee on the craft or sink it in the chaos. Lady Lightland must have thought the same thing. The moment she saw it through the trees, she laughed in a way that sounded almost despairing.

"When I told you that you could be part of my plans, Ai'sletta, I did not mean literally."

"Neither did I," Mally muttered, but it was definitely to the boat that she led us, leaping onto the gangplank without a moment's hesitation. Cassanetta's balance was just as good and she followed even with her hands tied.

I would have expected the Flamerarch to post guards here. That's what I would have done. Unless they didn't realize it was here. I peered worriedly into the trees.

"Stop delaying, Sersha. The faster you get on board, the faster Gundt can learn to steer the boat."

"*Gundt* can learn?" Gundt echoed, sounding wary.

"You have the thickest arms," Mally said, as if that was enough explanation.

To my relief, Gundt helped me across the gangplank and led me to the stern of the boat, propping me against the rail but out of his way as he examined the tiller.

"I've never steered a boar before," he told me in an undertone. "Unless you count a rowboat."

I shook my head. I was pretty sure a rowboat didn't count.

"I'm going to cast off," Mally said easily. "Then we can talk."

She was already dragging the gangplank off the deck and throwing it into the river with a splash by the time Gundt had his hands on the tiller, his eye on the channel, and a solemn expression on his lined face.

"They say that you can run aground fast on a river," he told me. "And I'm not sure what you do to prevent that."

I motioned with my hands, trying to convey that maybe he should stay where it was deep.

"Won't the current be strongest there?" he asked, but all I could do was shrug. I was no more experienced with riverboats than he was.

I could tell the moment Mally cast off because the boat started moving and Gundt screwed up his face in concentration.

"I'd say, 'Quiet now so I can focus,' but you're always so attentive that I'm sure you can see that," Gundt said, sparing me a brotherly smile before turning his full attention to his work. "I'll admit, I've enjoyed working with you, Sersha. You're a restful person to be around. I hope you heal as we travel."

I appreciated his sentimental mood, but I was distracted by worry. We were going to have to float right past all those Flamerarch on the shores and we didn't even have a plan.

I tried to focus my foggy brain on that.

I waved to Mally and she sauntered over with Cassanetta on a leash.

"I think you can untie me now," Lady Lightland said coolly.

"Not until we're past the assembly on the shore," Mally said, not even looking at her captive. Her eyes were on me and she looked worried. The afternoon was hot and thick. It was that time of day before the sun started to sink. "Otherwise you'll try to jump in, won't you? And take your chances with someone else. I think I know you by now. You take whatever chance will get you higher and you don't count the cost of burning your bridges."

Cassanetta snorted. "When you hear what I have to say, you'll agree this is better. And you'll agree to untie me."

"I will, will I?" Mally sounded unconvinced.

"Even my bitter half-brother will agree," Cassanetta said, but if she'd hoped for a reaction from Gundt, she didn't get one. Gundt's attention was fully on his task as he moved us to the center of the river.

"We shall see," Mally said, hands on her hips. Her eyes studied the shore, which was why she couldn't even see me signing that we should hide. I tried again and she sighed. "I do have peripheral vision, Sersha. I can see you frantically moving those hands. And no, we aren't going to hide. We'll let them watch us sail right by."

I groaned.

"They can't hope to catch us with the current so strong and no other boats nearby. There aren't even horses. What are they going to do, swim for it?"

I swallowed, nervously, eyeing the sun.

"The sun will set eventually, Mally," Gundt reminded her in an undertone.

"Will it, though?" My cousin's words were so faint they were almost indistinguishable.

The shore rose up alongside us so quickly that I couldn't help my indrawn breath. One moment we were floating between dark trees shading darker water and then in the next we had turned a bend in the river and the shore on the left was packed full of people — the Flamerarch, of course — all staring at us open-mouthed. I swallowed nervously at the sight of them.

We were frozen as if all sharing the same nightmare, hoping someone else would bring us back to our senses, and then someone on shore pointed and yelled and the spell broke.

Mally clenched her jaw and shoved Cassanetta to her knees on the deck placing her rope in my hands.

"Hold on to our pet, would you, Sersha?"

And then she strode across the deck as I exchanged a look with a smug-looking Lady Lightland. My eyes narrowed and I tightened my grip on the rope. She was definitely planning something.

"I've known you since you left that backwater rural fishing town," Cassanetta said calmly. "I know you're of no consequence or power. You just happen to be related to the ai'sletta along with a gaggle of other rural people. Once the ai'sletta hears what I have to say she will work with me and you can go home to your fishy-smelling home."

I raised my eyebrows in disbelief. I had not forgotten the terrible ice-cold feeling in my gut when Cassanetta Lightland had killed my aunt Danna right in front of me. I had not forgotten her many cruelties to us, to Judicus, to his former rider Veela who had likely died at her hand, too. This was not a person I wanted to work with. Or spend any time with. What did it take for Mally to be so cool in her presence? Unless, perhaps, my cousin planned to use her first and then get revenge later. That, I could believe. A merciful Mally was a much greater stretch.

"So don't do anything hasty," Lady Lightland breathed. "Or you'll regret it."

Her words were bold — but was that just a hint of fear she was hiding under them? Perhaps she wasn't so confident as she pretended.

"Sersha never acts hastily," Gundt said from the tiller. "But I do. And I have half a mind to throw you over the stern."

Cassanetta stiffened. Perhaps she knew Gundt well enough to know he didn't make idle threats. I took the opportunity to look past her as we floated past the last of the Flamerarch. A few of the most enterprising among them had found their short bows, but not quickly enough. An arrow flew, falling well short and then washing away in the current. Someone else had leapt into the water and my heart was in my throat as one of the arrows struck the current beside him. He almost caught our boat before the current swept us further away.

I was breathing out in relief when something hit the side of the boat, echoing hollowly. I looked forward to see a dripping Shasamen hauling herself up onto the deck right in front of Mally. We froze, like children caught out in trouble, and she wrung the water from her hair as the current carried us around the bend and away from the sight of the rest of the Flamerarch.

"Explain yourselves," she said, icily. "We gathered an army. We found you. We have a plan. Why have you run off like unruly children? And in the *day* when I have to swim a river and climb up a boat to get your attention. I am not your parent. I should not be forced to chase after you. Now, turn this boat immediately to shore and get off."

"Your plan is to wait outside the city," Mally said, crossing her arms over her chest. "Your plan is to wait while the Grand Hadri is married off to a strange elf with terrible ambitions of his own, and that hellish pillar is built and activated making phoenixes more in danger than ever before."

"*Tell her about Castan,*" I signed.

Mally ignored my plea.

"And how are the three — four — of you charging into the city a better idea, Ai'sletta? Gundt, did you not hear me when I spoke? Have you no gratitude for how we helped you when you were injured only days ago? Turn this craft to shore!"

"*Castan,*" I signed urgently. "*Tell her about Castan!*"

"We aren't turning, Shasamen," Mally said, drawing her shoulders even further back. "Your phoenixes can't go into the city. Yet. Wait here, and then when we see to the disabling of that pillar, then we'll signal you and your phoenixes can come pouring over the walls. In the meantime, use this charm of yours to talk those two armies into disbanding or joining us. If you can get that side of things ready, we'll open up the gates and make it possible."

"The pillar that endangers our phoenixes also endangers yours," Shasamen said, exasperation in her tone. "You can't go in there, either. Gundt, for the love of loyalty, would you turn this boat to shore?"

"I only take orders from the ai'sletta," Gundt said, eyes glued forward as he steered the boat.

"This is madness!" Shasamen said.

"*C - A - S - T - A - N!*" I signed, practically growling, I was so frustrated.

Mally rolled her eyes.

"What is your friend saying?" Shasamen asked.

"She wants me to inform you that Castan was among those who betrayed the Flamerarch in Briccatore. Those Flamerarch she was with told her that."

Shasamen gaped at me.

"*Tell her it was Reichus who told me.*"

Mally rolled her eyes. "Does the name Reichus mean anything to you?"

Shastomen's voice was hollow when she said, "It does."

"*She will need to sort it out. Quickly. Before he meets with the armies and finds allies to use against them,*" I signed, urgently.

Mally made a brushing sign. "I'm sure she realizes that, Sersha. She's a grown woman. She won't let him meet up with the evil generals or keep leading things now that she knows."

"I —" Shasamen sounded tongue-tied.

"Listen, we'll give you a signal from the city," Mally said. "Clean house. Get rid of Castan. Firm up your people. Level those armies if you can, and wait for the signal."

"Level the armies?" She sounded like she might be currently having a heart attack.

"Judicus sent a ghost army out to recruit people from the countryside. They should trickle in soon. When they get here, they can help with that."

"You want me to level armies with farmers and merchants?"

"And ghosts. Keep up. But yes, and then come to the city when we're done our part."

Shasamen shook her head, seeming to come to her senses. "You have no authority to order me."

"Only the authority of the truth," Gundt said quietly from his place at the tiller. That made her pause, going a little green. "And the authority of necessity. If not you, then who?"

And now he met her eyes and something I couldn't quite read passed between them. Something that looked like resignation and maybe pain and just a tinge of hope.

"Can you do it?" he asked quietly.

"I don't know," she was shaking her head. But her tone had changed now that she was addressing him and not Mally and she sounded calmer, more reasonable, and infinitely sadder. "How can I know this is even true? How can I —?"

Gundt's words were even and careful. "Sersha saved your phoenix from the pillar back in Sarcoda. You saw it with your own eyes. Without that, you'd still be trapped. Now, either trust her and me and do this, or don't. It's time to decide."

Shasamen nodded her head, thoughtfully.

"And it's also time to jump. See you in a few days if we all live that long," Mally said, and then she shoved Shasamen backward and the woman stumbled overboard and slipped into the river with a loud splash.

She emerged, sputtering, calling out, "How will I know the sign?"

"You'll know!" Mally called back and as we turned another bend in the river, the last thing I saw was Shasamen's scowl.

283

"Alright then," Mally said, returning to where we were in the stern. She had a small ball of twine in one hand and as she sat heavily on the deck, she began to fish pieces of the Dark Diadem from her bodice. "Start at the beginning, Lady Lightland, and make it good."

She arranged the crown on the deck before her, tying the twine to one piece, and then weaving it through and around the pieces as the lady spoke.

"You're the ai'sletta. But you know what you are least of anyone."

"You had a lot to say about it," Mally said dryly, fitting one piece of the crown against another with a look of concentration in her eyes.

"I did. I told you I would make you powerful."

"And then you killed my mother," Mally said lightly.

Gundt stiffened at the tiller. We'd told him that, hadn't we? I couldn't remember, but I supposed that even if you knew, hearing it said so easily by Mally was a bit of a shock.

"I set you free of your past. I should have worked harder," Lady Lightland said, shooting a glance at me. "And then we wouldn't have had to go through all of this."

"We?"

"We could have gone to Briccatore together and deposed the Grand Hadri together, and avoided all this conflict. Thousands have died because you were so headstrong."

"Scolding me isn't going to get you what you want," Mally said. There was a careful edge to her voice and I could tell she was trying to disguise deep emotion behind it.

"Throwing your mother's fate in my face isn't going to get you what you want, either," Lady Lightland countered. "From the moment we realized you were the ai'sletta, you were marked for a certain end. There was no stopping it. The only question was who would benefit."

"Oh?" Mally asked, one eyebrow raised.

"But you know that, don't you?" Cassanetta said coyly. "Surely someone told you. Not my bastard brother over there steering the ship, obviously. He and his kind believed they could side-step fate. They thought they could protect you. Thought that they could avoid the fate the rest of us knew was inevitable."

"What fate?" Mally pressed, tugging the knot she was tying much more tightly than she needed to.

"Don't play coy. Didn't the Grand Hadri tell you? Or Judicus? Or one of the others you've seen along the way? Those sneaky agents in Briccatore, perhaps?"

"Tell me what?" And my cousin's tone was dead cold now. I could almost feel Gundt straining over his tiller in the back, trying to be quiet so he could hear every word.

He had the look of a man with a secret that was about to slip out.

"That you have to die," Cassanetta said, cool as a spring morning. "It's always been inevitable from the moment Judicus Franzer Irault found you."

284

"Don't be ridiculous," Mally said, fumbling at her weaving so she had to pull out her knots twice before one fit the way she was trying to make it work.

"Your words say one thing but your shaking hands say something else," Cassanetta said and there was a barb in her tone, like she was enjoying this. "Haven't you noticed that all the former ai'sletta's died?"

"Because they lived a long time ago," Mally said, yanking hard on her twine.

"They did. But they didn't die of old age."

"No," Mally said bitterly. "People like you squabbled to control them — to steal their luck and use it to conquer kingdoms, sway battles, and find treasures beyond the wildest imaginings. That's how they died. Torn between two sides. But that's not happening this time. This time, I have Gundt."

Gundt grunted in agreement.

"And I have Sersha and her miserable rope worker." I almost laughed at how she said that, as if we both mattered and didn't matter all at once. "And I have Grevankin." At least with her phoenix she sounded respectful. "And they're going to protect me from that." I felt my eyes widening at how her voice shook. She sounded small when she said it like that, and she must have realized that because she lifted her chin and said, "Besides. I'm not waiting around to be used. I've grabbed you and you're going to get us into the city to stop this marriage."

"Yes," Lady Lightland said easily.

"Yes?" Mally's voice was stern.

"Yes, of course, and then you are going to step into that pillar they built all on your own, because all that luck tucked up inside you is actually the ends of the threads of all the rope work in the world. The pillar goes down into the threads of the world and you hold the end of those threads. You're going to burn those threads to nothing and end rope work, and phoenixes, and Stryxex, and flowing evil souls in Creatures of Sydonon. You're going to end them forever."

"No."

She went on, unrelenting. I did not realize Lady Lightland was a true believer. I had thought her to be purely mercenary. Had something changed along the way or had I always misunderstood her?

"It's going to kill you, but you'll do it anyway, because by the time you get there you'll realize that unless you do it, the rope workers rule the world, and they are terrible tyrants who grind everyone under their boots. And you are just self-sacrificing and moral enough that you'll decide to be the one to do something about it, won't you? You'll remember the stories you've heard about fathers giving their lives for sons, and mothers for daughters, and sweethearts for each other, and you'll look at your cousin and Gundt and feel that twinge in your heart, and you'll step in there and give yourself for the whole world."

"And leave the world to you?" Mally raised a single brow.

Lady Lightland shrugged. "You'll have saved it from the worst things. You can't save it from everything. This has been prophecied from the start. Everyone knew. Everyone was betting on it. It was only you who went in blind."

"You're mad," Mally said.

"I'm right," Lady Lightland said. "Think about everything that's ruined your life. Think about the raiders who will stop coming when their religion has ended. Think about the Cult of Tattered Ribbons that will be over. The Stryxex who can never tear apart those you love. The rope workers who will never bend your life again by their magic. Think about it all, and by the time we get to Briccatore, you'll agree that it's worth it. I know you. And I know Gundt." She looked at me. "I don't know her, but I have a feeling she's the type who would die doing the right thing. She has that look in the way she holds her chin. Am I right? She chased you halfway across the world and no one would do that out of fondness. I found that out. Anyways. Think about it. Until then, maybe you should start preparing for what you're going to do when the sun goes down. Those Flame Riders you left behind will be a problem. They'll be after you so fast you might as well have just given up and gone with them."

She nodded at the sun which was slowly creeping toward the horizon and then, to my surprise, she settled down on the deck of the ship, closed her eyes, and pillowed her face on her bound hands.

"That, at least, won't be a problem," Mally said, tying the last knot around her crown and then stuffing it upside down on her head. It looked odd there with the points facing down instead of up, but she smiled happily and sauntered down to the other end of the boat.

I waited for the sun to go down. Nervous as I was about pursuit, I was anxious to see Judicus and Kazmerev again. I wanted to ask Judicus if any part of what Lady Lightland said had been right. Did people really expect Mally to die? Had *he* expected that? It bothered me to think he might have.

But though I waited and waited and Gundt yawned beside me, exhausted from concentrating on steering, the sun didn't so much as budge.

After what I reckoned to be about an hour, I went looking for Mally and found her staring out to sea.

"Do you really think I'll have to die, Sersha?" Her voice was so un-Mally-like that it shook me. I carefully placed an arm around her only to be more appalled when she leaned her head on my shoulder and blinked back tears. She must be very upset to accept comfort from me. "I don't think I want to die. I think I want to be Grand Hadri. I think I want to put Cassanetta in the pillar instead and see how she likes it. And I'll tell her it was fate and it was prophesied and it's not my fault that she never heard about any of this. And that maybe she should pay attention if she didn't want to miss stuff like this."

That got a snort of a laugh from me. I couldn't even imagine the expression on Cassanetta's face if that really happened. It would be gratifying.

"I miss Grevankin," Mally said with a sigh. "And I miss my family." She grew so quiet that I could barely hear her whisper. "Do you think I'll see them again?"

"*I think you'll see wonders they never dreamed of,*" I signed, "*I think you'll be bolder than your lion of a mother, and more immovable than your rock of a father, and make your brothers and sisters proud.*"

"But do you think I'll live?"

I hesitated before answering.

"*I'm not sure any of us will.*"

"That's what I thought." She looked off into the distance with the saddest expression I'd ever seen on her face until eventually she took a long breath, pushed my arm away, and said, "How great is this crown? I bet you never thought of flipping it upside down to make it forever day."

I had not.

"People should trust my genius more."

And then she was stalking back to the stern of the boat leaving me picking at a bit of wood on the railing and wishing I knew what was best.

285

Both Lady Lightland and Mally were fast asleep, despite the bright light of a false noon. Lady Lightland hadn't moved from her place curled around her bonds. Mally had found a blanket in her pack and curled up close by as if she could guard her prisoner in her sleep.

I wanted to join them, but Gundt was barely holding on, his head falling to his chest only for him to shake himself back awake. I set down the books I'd been studiously poring over, shoved them back into the pack Mally and I shared, and then joined Gundt and gently put my hands over his. I urged him with nods of my head to go and rest while I took the tiller. If I was no expert at it, well, neither was he, and the river seemed easy enough here. I had been around boats enough growing up to grasp the basics of what I needed to do to stay in the channel in the middle of the river.

"Do you believe she really has to die?" Gundt asked me as he gave over the tiller, his face lined with sorrow. His eyes wandered to where I'd stowed the books.

I wanted to tell him she'd be fine. I wanted to say that she was Mally. She would succeed where anyone else had failed. But I'd been searching the books for answers to that question and I hadn't found any. I shook my head, not in negation but in confusion.

"That's not what the Greensleeves believe," he said, mouth set in a straight line. He wasn't really one of them anymore - not if he didn't believe in her, was he. "We always thought we could keep her safe. That she would save the world, but that it would be by living. By great acts of generosity and power."

I made a gesture I hoped he could interpret — a sort of a shrug with a questioning gaze. We'd traveled with him all this time and we'd never met another Greensleeve. Where had they been for all of this? For a secret society bent on keeping the ai'sletta safe, they had certainly been scarce.

He flushed and looked away. "I didn't tell them about her. I should have, but at first, we were all swept up in danger and trouble and there wasn't a way to get them a message, and then ... well, then I knew her. And I started to wonder if there might be a similarity between protecting something and controlling it. And I wondered if maybe she was protected enough."

I felt my eyes prick with tears and I blinked them away. That was ... incredibly touching. All this time I'd been seeing Gundt as somewhat one-dimensional when in fact he'd been going through this complicated mental puzzle about how to best protect the girl who was the "chosen one" in his beliefs without seeing her hurt by that very protection. I wasn't sure what to make of that, only that I was touched by a kindness that quietly sacrificed where no one could see it.

I gestured toward Briccatore and he nodded.

"Yes," he said. "There might be other Greensleeves still alive in the city and yes, I could probably find them. I still don't know if I should. And I feel like a traitor to everything I called important."

I shot a pointed look toward Lady Lightland and Mally. Tied up or not, Cassanetta was a threat and she'd be more of one the closer we got to the city. We'd need any allies we could find. Any at all. Even ones who practically worshipped my cousin like a goddess.

"I'll think about it," he said and then he gave me a kind smile and made his way to the bow to sleep.

I reached into my belt pouch with one hand and touched the mirror shard, wishing I could call up the night and bring Judicus to tell me what we should do. I didn't dare. Not while we were fleeing the Flamerarch. They'd catch up with their phoenixes in no time and then it would be all waiting and no action and who knew how things went when Shasamen challenged Castan — or if she'd even won in that battle of loyalties.

I gritted my teeth and steered the boat.

All around me there were these crises of conscience. Friend pitted against friend. Neighbor against neighbour. Not in a war of easy-to-see us against them, but in a war of differing ideas of what was good. Cassanetta thought it was good to kill Mally to end all magic and phoenixes. I thought it was good to end the people who wanted that to happen. Gundt and his Greensleeves disagreed with each other on how to uphold the ai'sletta and even the books of prophecy fought to push their own preferred end.

I sighed and wished things were simpler. That people could just see what was plainly the truth.

But maybe truth wasn't a thing you could find for yourself. Maybe it had to find you.

The banks grew tamer and then villages began to pop up along the banks and curious eyes on the shore where people washed clothing or fished or mended nets, turned to watch our riverboat pass. And as the hours passed, the river grew more crowded, as I shared the space with fishing boats and skiffs, with small barges hauling upriver against the current, and with the houseboats of traders and peddlers.

The journey was taking too long. This one long, long day was taking too long.

What if the Grand Hadri married despite the days not turning? What if we arrived too late?

I stared at the river and the banks with tired eyes and tried to imagine how we'd get into the city and into the palace. I'd been inside once before with Judicus and Prexav. Could we go in the same way? But we'd found ourselves immediately lost in a maze of corridors. Perhaps Lady Lightland could lead us through the palace. And then what? Did we dare make it night and release our phoenixes near a pillar so strong it could snatch them from us? If the Flamerarch couldn't get close then neither could we. We'd need help. We needed Jastomen. But how would I find him in the city? Especially if it were still as carefully shut down as it had been when I was carted away with its citizens stuck in their homes and patrols everywhere?

We needed a much better plan than what we had. I tried out at least a dozen in my mind as the banks of the river grew thicker and thicker with people and then I realized that the edges of the city were coming in sight.

I looked over at where Mally was sleeping, wondering if there was a way to wake her without abandoning the tiller. Her place was empty. I looked around, worried, and then jumped when I found her right at my shoulder.

"Ease in to the first wharf or dock you can find," she whispered. "Before we reach the city gates. And then help me with Lady Lightland. We're going to leave Gundt right here. He'd never leave if I asked him to, but we don't need to risk his phoenix, too."

My eyes widened in comprehension. She rolled hers.

"At some point, I'll have to make it night and when I do, you know how to protect your phoenix from emerging so he'll probably be fine, but Grevankin and Huxabrand won't be, and it's bad enough that I'm risking my phoenix friend. I won't do that to Gundt, too. Would you?"

I swallowed and then shook my head.

"Then it's settled," she said, clapping me on the shoulder. But there was sadness in her eyes as she looked toward where Gundt was sleeping in the bow and I found I was equally worried. Could we really leave our last ally behind? "Don't look so gloomy. I have a plan."

286

If she really did have a plan, she didn't bother to tell it to me. But I didn't wake up Gundt, either. She was right. He'd insist on coming in with us, and then we would have to let it be night at some point and his phoenix would rise and die. But what about Grevankin? And what about Kazmerev and Judicus if I wasn't quick enough to tamp down on them, too? Did we know for sure that the pillar would suck them in?

"We can't risk it, Sersha," Mally had hissed at me when she saw me looking back at his sleeping form over my shoulder. "Don't be a fool."

But we hadn't even had a chance to say goodbye and I had a sinking feeling that we weren't going to see him again. I bit my lip, saddened at the thought. I'd been relying on Gundt's good judgment for a while now and with Kazmerev and Judicus inaccessible, I needed him more than ever.

Mally never thought she needed anyone else's judgment. She had untied Lady Lightland once we tied up along the docks. Cassanetta had directed us to her trunk on deck and unlocked it with a key from her belt pouch. It contained an enormous supply of richly stitched clothing and those heeled boots she liked to wear. They fit Mally perfectly, but were too large for me. The clothing was mostly the same, Mally and Lady Lightland being built to similar hourglass proportions.

"We'll stand out if you wear those rags," she had said to Mally who nodded her agreement, and in minutes they had gone down below and emerged again, dressed in the fitted trousers, light blouses, and tailored jackets that Cassanetta favored with her heeled boots. I managed to wear one of her dresses with a hasty adjustment from Mally. She used the back laces to cinch the too-loose bodice a little tighter. I was not built the same as those two, and my hem was in the dirt.

"It will have to do," Mally said. And at least it wasn't that ridiculous dress they'd thrown over my clothing to sacrifice me as bait.

I felt a pang of something close to guilt at the memory of that and the rough

Stryxex rider who had forced me into the dress. He was dead now. They all were. All but Kentinius who was wandering around somewhere. I felt ill knowing I'd caused that. None of this had to happen like this, were it not for the ambitions of some people to rule over others and take from them their free will and lives.

"Hurry up, Sersha," Mally hissed as we set out the gangplank and joined the throngs along the busy dock streets. We were still outside the city walls, but the press of people was moving in that direction. Even so, they were not fast enough for Mally who had grabbed both Cassanetta and me by the arms and pulled us through the crowds like a tug pulling barges.

"They must have eased the restrictions on the population before the Festival of Moons and the wedding," Cassanetta murmured.

Mally shot her a quelling look, but it explained the crowds. It also explained how odd the crowds were. People barely made eye contact and when they did, it was nervous, as if they lived in fear of buying and selling even though they were there to do just that. The hawker carts and the fishing boats had an air of almost disuse about them, and no one called out on the streets or shouted over the city noises. Instead, everything was spoken in quiet undertones, as if the speakers were afraid that their orders for bread or fish would be overheard. Fear was everywhere, bubbling just under the surface. The eyes of everyone strayed to us, only to jerk away immediately.

The reason for so much concern soon showed itself. A patrol of the Hand of the Rat, faces covered and hoods up despite the bright sunlight and heat, arrowed through the crowd. They didn't march. They would suggest a uniformity that was not part of the Hand of the Rat. Instead, they sauntered in a group, eyes flicking over the crowd as if assessing each individual, and when each head bowed, gaze lowering, they moved on, hands prominently placed on weapons.

I hoped they didn't look at Mally. I couldn't imagine her averting her gaze even if the consequence was arrest or a painful death. But their eyes did catch on me and then on Cassanetta, and though we dropped our gazes those eyes flicked back three times before the fist of warriors moved on.

Lady Lightland had been wrong. Far from helping us blend in, her clothing was making us stand out.

"We need better clothing," Mally muttered.

"And how do you propose to pay?" Cassanetta had asked poisonously.

Mally's hand drifted toward her belt knife and she shot Cassanetta a look, but she said nothing.

Worse than our clothing was Mally's crown. Twice, hands in the crowd tried to snatch the broken crown from her head. Twice, we prevented the theft before the would-be criminal melted into the crowd, but this was getting ridiculous. It was only her sheer ai'sletta luck that had kept that group of soldiers from stopping her, I was sure of it, and I thought I saw another group of dark-clad figures moving this way.

"At the very least, I need a cloak," Mally said. I nodded fervently, eyes still on the group of soldiers. They were moving faster than I'd originally guessed.

Cassanetta sighed and led us to the first cart selling clothing. She bought the cloak with silver from her belt pouch and handed it to a frowning Mally.

"Maybe you all should wear cloaks," the cart seller said wryly, looking at my too-long dress.

"Your concern is noted," Cassanetta said shortly.

Even with the cloak, our arrival through the city gates, when we finally reached them, caused a stir.

"Lady Lightland!" The gate guard abandoned his post at the sight of her, scrambling between people to offer her a bow. He was from Calicarn, I thought, though he stood with a knot of leather-clad Hand of the Rat enforcers. "What an honor is ours. But where is your retinue?"

Cassanetta shot an arrogant glance at Mally — a reminder that while we thought we were leading her, she was certain she was leading us — and said, "I left them to other tasks. I need little protection within the walls of Briccatore with such capable guardians watching our gates."

"We do our best, Lady," he said, bowing deeply.

"And your friends?" She raised an eyebrow at the clump of Hand of the Rat men he'd left.

"The support is most welcome!" the guard said, wiping his brow of sudden sweat. "With so many new regulations to enforce, it's a relief to have help."

"I can imagine," Lady Lightland murmured before he made an awkward bow again.

And that seemed to be all there was to say because he let us through with no questioning and we were swept along by the crowds up the broad avenue and past at least a half-dozen more Hand of the Rat patrols until and eddy of the crowd pushed against us and we found ourselves in an alley trying to catch a breath.

"Which way from here," Mally asked Cassanetta. Not, "You seem very friendly with the gate guards" or "Has the Hand of the Rat been enforcing rules in Briccatore all this time?" like I would have asked.

"There's a hidden way into the palace," Lady Lightland murmured. "We just need to get nearby and I can take you directly to it. It is taking longer than expected. I don't usually travel the city on foot."

She sounded disgusted. Which was interesting. I had seen ox carts out there hauling goods, but no horses. How did she usually travel the city? Was it in one of those palanquins I'd seen carried on shoulders?

Mally nodded her agreement, jaw jutting out as it did when she was nervous.

"Then we have no time to waste. We need to get to the palace as quickly as we can," she said briskly.

Maybe we could hire a palanquin. Would that make us less or more conspicuous?

"Once we're in, finding the Grand Hadri won't be a problem," Lady Lightland said and I did not like the gleam in her eye when she said it or the way she shot a sidelong look at Mally.

"I think it will be," a voice said from the mouth of the alley. "For you *and* for her."

287

"Ceghan Bassica," Mally said and it sounded like a curse.

I could only see the black silhouette where she blocked the sunlight of the alley but the sound of her name made me freeze. Ceghan. Sister to Prexav. Who was dead because I wasn't fast enough. Who had been so faithful and so dedicated and now was dead under an elven mountain. Just thinking about facing his sister made me feel sick.

I could see him like he was right there beside me with his easy grin, sober eyes, and firm dedication.

What were the odds of her finding us in the middle of the crowds of Briccatore?

"Just my luck," Mally said. Oh. Yes. That. Somehow I always forgot that. "What are you doing here?"

It wasn't a very friendly greeting, but she had reason to worry. What would Ceghan think if she knew Mally carried her brother's phoenix? There hadn't been much love lost between her and Mally already. Who knows how grief might twist the heart. Knowing her brother's great phoenix was now in the hands of a girl she didn't much care for might turn her into our enemy and we already had enough of those.

"Ai'sletta," Ceghan said, acknowledging my cousin. "I could ask you the same. Why are you back in Briccatore and why do I hear the name of our Grand Hadri on your lips while you keep company with her who is our enemy?"

She thrust a jabbing finger at Lady Lightland.

"If you mean me, then you can call me Cassanetta," Lady Lightland said coolly as if she lounged around in alleys with people who hated her all the time.

Both Mally and Ceghan ignored her, but I kept my eyes on Lady Lightland. Just because they had differences to settle between the two of them did not make Cassanetta any less dangerous. She could be chained to a stone and thrown into the sea and still be dangerous.

"You left us on the island," Ceghan told Mally, bitterness in her tone. "You flew away and left us. We had to make our own way home."

"I wasn't in my right mind," Mally said in a brittle tone.

"Most of us died. *I* almost died," Ceghan accused, her voice getting louder.

"You need to calm her down," I signed to Mally. *"People are going to notice."*

"She has every right to be angry, Sersha," Mally told me in the sugar-sweet tone her mother had always used when she was particularly irritated.

I tried not to sigh. I missed Judicus. He'd been the one person I could depend on to listen when I tried to communicate.

"I'm not sure if you've noticed," Mally went on, turning to Ceghan now and using a tone so arrogant that I wanted to slap her myself. "But the world is on the brink of collapse. I feel like this petty squabble about who had a worse time in foreign lands can wait, don't you?"

Ceghan's face flushed so red I thought it might verge over into purple and her hands shook with emotion, but her voice, when she spoke, was incredibly controlled.

"I serve the Grand Hadri, as you well know. I don't plan to change that, no matter who is crowned to that place. And so, Ai'sletta, that means I must take charge of you. Any threat to my ruler — no matter who that threat might be — is a threat to all of us and it will be destroyed one way or another."

"Listen this time," I signed desperately catching Mally's angry gaze. *"Tell her you are not a threat. Tell her you've come to save the Grand Hadri. We want the same things."*

"Let me guess, you're taking me to Jastomen," Mally said boldly and I sighed my disappointment but I was still watching Lady Lightland and I found myself frowning at her expression. Was that ... hope? Excitement? Why would she be excited at the mention of the name of a spy she should not know?

"Jastomen?" Ceghan's face twisted in disgust. "Why would I — don't you realize? Oh, this is rich. You haven't heard that he's your enemy?"

I felt my heart plummet at the same time Mally went deathly pale.

"What do you mean?" she asked.

288

Ceghan's laugh was harsh.

"You didn't know. You didn't realize who separated you from your rope worker friend right before our journey by giving him a book to talk to *her* with?" The bitterness in her tone when she pointed to me chilled me. "Let me guess. Judicus Franzer Irault dead now, right?" I swallowed. Because he was. "Just like the former Grand Hadri who Jastomen was supposedly the spymaster for. Dead. Jastomen manipulated him. He drove him to his death. That obsession with finding the ai'sletta? That was all Jastomen." She paused for a ragged breath before jabbing her finger at Mally's chest. "Didn't you see how Jastomen pointed you and my brother toward that pillar? How he assured you he'd take care of the new Grand Hadri and all you had to do was just one impossible task first? Why do you think he did that? Why do you think he came back here and found the last of the phoenixes and sent Castan to them? Castan. Who alone survived the purge of the Flamerarch in Briccatore. Why was he allowed to survive when every other Flame Rider was laid bare, their souls reaped for harvest?"

I felt like I might be ill. I had helped him find Shasamen and the last of the Flamerarch. I had sent him down the right path for that.

Ceghan felt the same way, apparently. Her tirade over, she stumbled over the closest wall and vomited noisily. Half sobbing as she did it, like she alone had carried the burden of these words, and now that they were coming up everything else was coming up with them.

"Who is this madwoman?" Lady Lightland asked, picking at a bit of lint on her sleeve as if it made no difference to her. But I could see the tension in how she held herself. Like so many others, she'd forgotten that she could speak in more than just words. Her body screamed worry even while her words were honey smooth. "And shouldn't we be hurrying? There's a wedding coming soon and if you wish to stop it, we'll need time to break into the palace."

"Break in?" Mally asked, and she sounded alarmed. "I thought you said there was a secret way."

At the same time, Ceghan spat, "Madwoman? You dare say that to me? You, who has been his toy all these years? His hound sent to the north? His hand set against us."

She said all that while still leaning her head against the wall as if she was too upset to look up.

"My brother is dead and it's his fault. Your fault. All your faults."

How did she know that? I tried to meet her gaze to offer some comfort but she refused to look at me.

"I know he's dead. I knew when Jastomen found me so he could pretend to console me. That's when I realized he was lying to me. That's when I started digging to find out more. How could he have known when he wasn't there? But he didn't have to be. He'd gotten word from his pawn, Lady Lightland. Once I realized how deep his corrupt roots went, it all began to make sense."

Lady Lightland smirked. But still, she was speaking in two languages.

"We don't have time for this," she said in a droll tone.

But her pale face and the slight tremor in her hand confessed for her.

I swallowed as Mally looked sharply from face to face, her expression full of confusion.

"Why would you trust the woman who killed your mother?" I signed to her, nodding at Lady Lightland. *"You should listen to Ceghan."*

"Why would you distrust the one who taught your rope worker those fancy new signs?" She asked back, meaning Jastomen.

"This is all irrelevant," Lady Lightland signed to us both with a smug look on her face. *"If you want to save the Grand Hadri, then we need to leave right now and forget this distraction."*

And I wasn't sure why I acted — or even how I moved so fast — but one moment she was signing, and the next I had both hands wrapped around her throat as I slammed her against the wall.

Ceghan looked up from her rest against the wall, her mouth falling open in surprise. Why hadn't I noticed before that she seemed so ragged and worn? She was threadbare.

Behind me, Mally barked a laugh. "I swear, Sersha. That rope worker is rubbing off on you. You've never been such a violent creature."

But she sounded shaken, too.

"Should I assume you aren't working with Jastomen anymore then, Ceghan?"

"I don't work for evil," Ceghan said, wiping her mouth. Her face looked hopeless. "And I won't work for you either. You're the ones who told him about the elves."

"Elves?" Mally asked with a raised eyebrow.

I froze. I told him about the elves. That they were at Sarcoda with the phoenixes. When he told me how to get to Occulus's ... tower ... which would have been suicidal for anyone who wasn't the ai'sletta. I clenched my jaw. How could I be so wrong about a person?

"Does the name 'Verdaine of the Hanging Spears Sect' mean anything to you?" Ceghan asked. "It's what they wrote under her cage."

"What cage?" Mally pressed. She looked shaken.

"The one they hung from a branch of the pillar in Victory Square. They announce her name from the walls every morning and taunt her people to come for her before the wedding. They're going to execute her after the ceremony. You know. For luck."

Could eyes fall right out of your head? Mine felt like they might and Mally's matched them.

I let go of Lady Lightland with one hand and signed with the other.

"Ask her how she came here. How did she find us?"

"It's awfully convenient that you just found us here, don't you think?" Mally said casually.

"Convenient?" Ceghan said, snorting. "I've been looking for you."

"To get revenge?" Mally asked.

Ceghan's mouth twisted in a way that told me she wished she could say yes, but wasn't a liar.

"No. Because I thought you'd try to kill the Grand Hadri. I guess I was wrong about that."

"We want to save her from a wedding she didn't ask for to a wicked man. And we want to get her out of the city to somewhere safe, like her brother wanted," Mally said quietly.

Ceghan nodded, looking down. "Then it's probably your luck that brought you to me. After all, if you want the Grand Hadri, I know where to find her."

"In the palace."

She snorted again.

"No. At vigil the night before her wedding in the crypts beneath the city."

"Gross." Mally's face twisted up. "They sit in the graveyard before they get married? Oh ugh."

Ceghan gave her a blank look. "It's yet another lucky thing for you. Because I know the way in. And I know how to navigate the crypts. And she won't have many guards under there."

"Define not many."

"Less than fifty, I would think."

Mally gasped a disbelieving laugh.

"You didn't expect it would be easy to steal a ruler, would you? Do you want to give up now?'

"No. You'd better take us to her."

Ceghan gave her a rueful look. "You'd better make it night." She pointed to the crown. "Or there might not be a vigil."

Mally felt her patched-together crown, her mouth thinning to a straight line.

"Not until the last minute," she muttered.

Ceghan shrugged. But she looked satisfied.

"What should we do with her?" I signed, pointing at Lady Lightland.

"We can't leave her here. And we probably shouldn't kill her. Yet," Mally said. "We bring her for now. And if she so much as flinches you cut her throat, Sersha.

And don't give me your big-eyed innocent stare. You had no problem leaving Ceghan's brother for dead. You should have no problem killing an enemy."

I shook my head in denial, my cheeks flaming, but Ceghan was already shooting me a look of death. Thank you so much, Mally. Of course, I felt guilty about Prexav. Of course, I missed him. But did she really feel it was helpful to lay his death at my feet when we needed to work with his sister?

"Where are these crypts anyway?" Mally asked.

"Close to the center of the city," Ceghan said, eyes still trained on me. "But there's an entrance close by. We'll have to get you out of those eye-catching clothes, though. You can borrow some of mine."

"If you had to pick a landmark in the city that was above the crypt where the Grand Hadri might be, where would you place it?" Mally said carefully.

Ceghan shrugged. "Victory Square, perhaps?"

All roads, it seemed, were headed there.

289

The tension in our little party was so tight you could rig a ship sail with it. Ceghan led us silently to her room beneath a wine cellar, inside a smaller wine cellar. Half the space was filled with large stamped barrels and the rest was a small pallet, a crate with clothing, and another with books. Ceghan reached into the clothing crate and began to pull out threadbare hose and tunics for us. Cloaks followed.

"Let me guess, you'll be keeping our finery," Lady Lightland said and to my surprise, Mally snapped at her.

"Keep your mouth shut or I will shut it."

If it had been tense before, it was twice as tense after that. I kept glancing at Mally. Maybe she was just worried about what came next. Just like I was. Just like Ceghan was. But it wasn't like Mally to be nervous. And it wasn't like her to snap now when she'd already moved to the more dangerous sugar-sweet voice.

"*We could leave her here,*" I suggested in sign. "*Tie her up.*"

But Mally shook her head. "We still might need her. For barter if nothing else."

My eyebrows rose. Barter?

"Don't look so innocent, Sersha," Mally scowled. "We seem to make no end of enemies. Maybe they'll want her back. Maybe they'll trade for her."

I didn't think that was likely. Cassanetta didn't seem to make many friends.

Fortunately, Ceghan cut off further discussion by reappearing with a small cold meal, lanterns, extra oil, knives for the three of us, and a pack.

"We'd better start immediately," she said. "Maybe they'll decide to go down to the crypts for vigil early, anticipating night coming eventually. Even if they don't we should get into position before you make it night again."

Mally nodded. "How far away is this entrance?" Mally asked.

Ceghan smirked and then threw her shoulder into one of the barrels, slowly, it rolled to the side, revealing a low entrance.

"Close," she said, and lit a lamp.

Crypts, it turned out, were not the kind of place you want to go with two people who hate you. The looks I got from Cassanetta were bad enough. The ones I received from Ceghan when she didn't think Mally was looking were worse. We'd been down for at least an hour when I began to count my steps in a hope that we'd soon reach our destination.

Whoever had designed this place seemed to have done it on the spur of the moment, adding new passages and carving new crypt beds at random, sometimes adding a room full of shelves, other times just lining long halls with shelves for bodies. If they were grouped in a known way, it hadn't been labeled.

I held my limbs close, held my lantern high, and tried not to touch the shelves on either side — or the bones on those shelves — for every space was occupied and sometimes with more than one resident. If you were a heavy eater, you wouldn't be able to pass through here without making very good friends with the dead.

"You're sure you know the way?" Mally asked Ceghan for the hundredth time.

"Yes." The answer had shortened each time, starting with explanations about curiosity and lonely journeys with a scrawled map to eventually becoming this one, steady monosyllable.

"And you didn't keep the map?"

"No."

"Hmmm."

"Look, do you want my help or not."

"Don't you serve the Grand Hadri?" Mally's voice echoed more than I liked. "And isn't it in her best interest to be saved from an unwanted marriage?"

"How do you know it isn't wanted?" But Ceghan, though arguing, was only doing it half-heartedly.

"Give me one reason a woman like her would want to marry a creepy old elf who loves octopuses."

"Octopuses?"

"Yeah, those things with eight legs. What was that?"

Ceghan had muttered under her breath. "Nothing."

"I distinctly heard something."

"I said, your luck had better be worth this."

Mally laughed. "Trust me. It is."

It was at moments like this that I missed having a voice the most. It's ridiculously hard to stop people from quarreling when you can't get their attention. But Ceghan was leading, lantern high, flinching occasionally from a scurrying rat. Mally was next to "bring the luck" as she put it. Lady Lightland was after that "where Sersha can keep an eye on you" and I got to be last and to feel the icy darkness reaching at my back from behind and trying to creep into my bones.

"Is it close yet?" Mally asked.

"Soon."

"Everything looks the same."

"It's not."

"That skull is grinning at me the exact same way one of them grinned five minutes ago. Are we going in circles?"

"No."

"Are you sure?"

"Yes."

"Look! It did it again."

"The skull is not grinning at you Mally," Ceghan said a little testily. "How are *you* the ai'sletta? It could have been someone well-bred, or serious-minded, accomplished, powerful, or sensible. I could keep listing traits all day."

"That's what I've been saying," Lady Lightland said dryly, under her breath. But in the echoey crypts, everything —even that — could be heard by everyone.

"I think maybe it's not about those things," Mally said after a long moment, and there was steel in her voice when she said, "I think it's about how I haven't given up. Not when disaster has struck and the people I love are killed, my allies driven mad, or sucked into pillars, or just plain slaughtered in front of me. The only other person like that is Sersha. None of you notice her because she's quiet. And all of you think I'm a fool because I'm not quiet. But we two are the only ones who haven't given up, or given in, or even taken a single break while we try to save the world, so, you know, you're welcome. Even if you haven't said thank you. And maybe you should think about how you value all the wrong things because do you know who *is* well-bred, and serious-minded, and powerful, and accomplished? Yeah, it's the traitor walking behind me who killed my mother in front of me."

Silence reigned after she said that. Not a single sound but the scurry of rats and our muffled footfalls in the dusty crypts. It was the kind of silence that echoed differently for everyone. I didn't know if the others were feeling shame or guilt or anger. I was just feeling sad. Sad for all our losses. Sad that they might be for nothing. I slipped my hand into my belt pouch and felt the shard of mirror, swallowing down a lump in my throat.

I walked into Lady Lightland's back and she made a sound like she was biting back a yelp. Everyone was frozen, lanterns held still, the flickering light flickering just a little less.

And then I heard whatever sound had made them freeze. The sound of echoing footsteps. A lot of them.

And then a voice.

"If you will step this way Honored Grand Hadri, the chamber has been prepared for your nuptial vigil."

We'd found the right place. I could hardly breathe. I hadn't realized that I didn't really think we would until just this moment. And now we were here.

Ceghan made frantic motions and we extinguished all the lamps but hers. She hooded the lantern, leaving only a single narrow slat open to guide our way as we crept forward. We worked our way toward the sounds echoing through the halls, taking a series of turns in near silence.

Something brushed my arm and I bit my own tongue when I realized it was a femur sticking out too far from its resting place. I eased myself back and we tiptoed forward. The hall ahead seemed to end abruptly in darkness, but then I saw dancing lights beyond — faint and flickering, casting washed-out shadows.

I drew in a little closer behind them and then Ceghan slipped to one side and Mally to the other as the hall opened. Mally grabbed Lady Lightland roughly and pulled her to the side with her, signing a reminder.

"I'll cut you if you talk."

But I wasn't watching their small drama. I was gaping at the way the hall ended in a steep drop like a balcony with no railing. It fell below to a massive, cylindrical space lined with bone-filled halls just like this one that were bathed in shadow and the occasional flickering diffuse light from lanterns below. I peered over the edge and saw a statue below — a terrible statue of what looked like a stone octopus holding birds in its tentacles. No, not birds, phoenixes.

It was one of four monstrous statues — each of a tentacled creature. One stone-carved creature held struggling men and women in its grasp, one poor man dangling from its beak. Another held a sword in each tentacle and it straddled the backs of four horses. I could not see the fourth easily, because at the center of the statues was a great, cloudy pillar — like the pillar at Occulus' tower, only this pillar did not glow golden, it pulsed with darkness, a murky cloud filling it and the light of the lanterns nearby seeming to be absorbed by the pillar in the way that light usually overcomes the darkness — scattering it completely.

At its base, the form of a woman, veiled and clad in flowing white, kneeled before the statue, and surrounding her were rank upon rank of Briccatore guards.

I felt like a thief surveilling the prize she meant to steal — and the impossible obstacles to getting to it. The very sight of the living darkness of that pillar filled me with a knee-trembling terror.

And I raised my hands to ask Mally a question, catching her eye, but before I could suggest a cautious approach, she shrugged, gave me a wry smile, and tugged the crown from off her head, spinning it in the air with one hand and then jamming it back onto her brow right side up.

290

Howling pain hit me like an avalanche. I stumbled and Ceghan caught me, whispering a frantic, "shhh" in my ear. I didn't think I'd made a sound, but even the scrape of a boot on earth was loud here in the crypts. She steadied me, swaying, and it took a full breath before I realized she'd caught me just before I'd pitched right over into the open cavern below.

Inside, my world was boiling. I clenched — everything — trying to bundle Kazmerev up tight, trying not to let the souls slip out the gate with the pillar so close.

Across from me, Mally's face was screwed up tight, and then she opened her eyes, panic tightening her features, and Grevankin bloomed, spinning out bright and then immediately disappearing. I swallowed down bile, hoping that he hadn't been sucked away, that she'd just made him invisible. Mally turned deadly pale, ripped her crown off again, spun it, and jammed it back down.

I gaped at her in horror.

"What?" She whispered.

And the echo vibrated through the chamber below.

What ... what ... what ... what.

A harsh command was issued below and then the sound like something snapping, once, twice, three times, and I realized it was the guards below executing some kind of drill formation, where their spears were readied, their formation cinched up until they surrounded the Grand Hadri in a tight, three-deep ring. I swallowed. How in the world would we get her out of that?

"Ready? Let's try again," Mally whispered.

Again ... again ... again.

I gaped, trying to show her with expression alone that she was a mad woman. Beside her, Lady Lightland was hyperventilating as if she wasn't our enemy but a co-conspirator as locked into this foolhardy behaviour as I was. Mally simply frowned and then quickly reversed her crown, snapping it into place.

I clamped down hard on my gate, but maybe it was the whipsaw of back and forth or maybe it was the pillar. or maybe it was something else, but my spiritual grip on the souls within me slipped and everything came pouring out my gate in a golden flood. I was glued to the floor and wall, only Ceghan's hands keeping me upright. I heard her gasp in my ear but my vision was completely flooded with gold as the souls poured free from my heart, running down my body, down the stone, over the edge, and into the cylinder. One pulled free from the mass, shaking himself like a dog coming out of the water and stepping into the crypt in a low crouch.

Every line of Judicus's ghostly face was sharp and focused, his hands flung out, eyes looking everywhere at once. I wanted to sign to him what was happening, to tell him I needed his help, but then suddenly a second bright figure leapt from the mass and hit him, square in the chest, bowling him over. The spirits might not be able to touch us, might slide right through walls and closed doors, but they could touch each other — hurt each other.

Judicus sprawled backward, face a rictus of pain, hands thrown up and golden ropes spiraling out of his palms to tangle just in time with the ropes coming at him from the second figure. I gaped as I recognized Occulus. But how ...? He'd been at the base of the tree when I'd sucked up the souls Kentinius had poured out. I must have sucked his spirit up with them. Had he been inside me this whole time? Horror filled me, thick and powerful, coating my mouth and sliding down my throat.

And then another spirit leapt from the mass, rushing forward just as Judicus leapt back to his feet, his rope work pushing Occulus back a step.

This spirit rushed up in a feeling like joy and new birth. Flames bloomed from my heart, washing over me hot and powerful as my phoenix hatched, rose, and burst forth like a spring of flame and life, and my heart soared up with him.

Opposite me, Mally's teeth were still gritted, and then suddenly Grevankin was free, too, bursting out hot, smoky, and howling.

Howling.

Kazmerev was howling, too.

He was being tugged toward the pillar. I fought, frantically, to tug him back and felt it when the pull from the pillar and the pull from me evened out and held him fluttering there, trapped between the two. The Flamerarch had been right. The pillar was trying to take him. I risked a glance at Mally, locked in the same desperate battle. Sweat formed on her forehead as she argued with herself.

"It's the only way down," she muttered. "The only way to get her right in front of her guard's noses."

She was winning, I thought. Her sheer force of will dragging Grevankin back bit by bit.

And then suddenly she was flying over the edge, arms pinwheeling as she fell, fell, fell.

I stumbled to the edge, trying to catch sight of her. A golden rope sailed past and then Grevankin rose, Mally on his back, a golden tether of rope work holding him back from the pillar like a horse harnessed for the carriage.

Relief washed through me.

I'd lost track of Ceghan. I was too focused on Mally's fall. I glanced over my shoulder but she wasn't there.

Sersha! Kazmerev's panicked cry snapped my gaze back to him. He was sliding toward the pillar. I reached out as if I could catch him physically, both arms flung forward, my gate fighting with all my strength to draw him back.

I was losing him. He was slipping.

I heard a cry from beside me — high pitched and terrified, and then something knocked my legs so hard that my knees collapsed sideways, and I fell into the wall of the crypt, nearly toppling into the abyss below. My heart was in my throat, breath sawing through my lungs. I gasped, close to panic. Something swiped at my leg again, and as I looked, it slid away. It was a hand, I heard the fading scream of Ceghan falling over the edge of the cliff and down to the people below. There was a sudden roar of surprise from the soldiers and the scream snuffed out with a *thump.*

Sersha, get back from the edge! Sersha!

Kazmerev sounded like he was fully panicked.

I pulled myself up on trembling legs as he slipped even further in my grasp. My eyes skittered over Lady Lightland, lunging toward me, back to where Judicus fought rope against rope as he battled the grunting ghost of Occulus. One of Judicus's hands was fully occupied with the thick rope tether holding Grevankin in place. His eyes snagged on mine just for a moment — just long enough for me to see the terror and horror in equal measure in their depths — and then he was eclipsed by Lady Lightland, stalking toward me, a grim expression on her face.

"I wanted to use you," she said, frowning. "But if I can't do that, then it's best to be rid of you."

My heart was ice. I was going to die right here. She had already pushed the other girls. She would push me, too. I fumbled for my knife.

Sersha! Kazmerev called to me, but he couldn't help. He couldn't get close enough to catch me. He couldn't stop what was coming.

Sersha! Judicus's mental cry echoed his and I could feel the strain as he tried to get close to me, held back by his battle with Occulus.

I pulled the belt knife out and got it up in front of me. I couldn't dive past Lady Lightland to flee. She was blocking the way out. And I couldn't jump unless I wanted to die like Ceghan. There was no one who could rescue me this time. The knife was my last resort.

"You don't really think you can beat me in a knife fight, do you?" Cassanetta asked, and she had the exact same look on her face that she'd had when she murdered my aunt. The same look she'd had when she stole Mally away and done — whatever she'd done to her that Mally wouldn't talk about. The same look when she'd watched me and the Grand Hadri surrounded by enemies and conspirators before Mally found the Dark Diadem. The look that told me a murder was about to take place. Had already taken place.

My heart twinged at the realization that Ceghan had died so quickly and brutally, but I didn't dare dwell on it. Not now.

I clutched my knife and tried not to shake. Maybe if I could maneuver her so that she let me slip by into the hall ...

She had her own belt knife out now, and when I tried a sudden lurch to one side, she slashed at me in that direction and I had to ease back. I was no expert at this. Suddenly, the idea of trying to stick a knife into someone seemed a lot more complicated than it had before.

Sersha. Kazmerev's voice was tight. I didn't dare risk a look over my shoulder at him.

"Your phoenix isn't looking too good," Lady Lightland said, widening her eyes as she tried to tempt me to look. "Mally's phoenix is holding him with his talons, but I don't see that lasting for long. Shouldn't you be worried about helping him, too? Or are you as heartless as you are silent?"

I lunged forward, trying to stick my knife into her chest. She batted my arm aside so hard that my knife slipped from my grip. But I wasn't through. I kept driving toward her, weaponless though I was. My hands reached for her throat. I felt the sting of her belt knife somewhere in my ribs, and then she was on the ground and so was I. I tried to grapple with her, but she was fast, leaping to her feet and grabbing my hair, dragging me forward. I swiped at her hands and then clung to them, trying to slow the movement as she dragged me along by the hair, trying to flip over onto my belly so I could find my feet.

I succeeded at neither. I could feel when the cold air of the room below hit my scalp.

I could hear the mental voices of Judicus and Kazmerev screaming together, "*Noooo!*"

So this was the end.

At least I would die trying.

And then suddenly the pressure on my scalp was gone. I rolled with all my strength, leaping to my feet the moment I could get my legs under me.

Cassanetta. Where was she?

She was gone.

I looked up just in time to see a pink blur of fire shooting out from where I was standing, on its back was a dark silhouette gripping a struggling figure in his powerful hands.

Gundt.

Riding Huxabrand.

He must have followed us and been back there in the crypts somewhere. And Huxabrand must have materialized and he'd leapt on her back and been sucked toward the pillar — and scooped up Cassanetta on the way past. I caught one glimpse of his face as he looked over his shoulder, nodded briskly to me, and then hit the pillar at full speed.

One moment there was a phoenix and two humans speeding through the air.

The next moment, there was nothing.

Nothing but a searing memory of Gundt, saving me and saving Mally one last time.

And my eyes were prickling with tears and I couldn't stop shaking. I was losing my hold on Kazmerev. Grevankin slipped, and Kazmerev tore toward the pillar.

A gasp of terror wrenched from my lips.

And then he stopped, caught by a lasso of golden rope and I looked back to see the spirit of Judicus standing on *top* of a trussed-up spirit Occulus, a rope in each hand like a chariot driver holding two reins. His teeth were gritted and his untamed, wild hair streamed behind him as if it was just as unmanageable in death as it had been in life. He strained, his lean arms bulging with effort as he pulled in both phoenixes against the powerful grasp of the pillar.

We need to get your sister, I said with my mental voice but those weren't the words in my heart. The words in my heart were the ones he said to me.

I love you, he said in my mind, meeting my eyes with all the mixed sorrow and tenderness of this terrible, tight moment on his face, and then his eyes wandered to the pillar and I couldn't see him anymore because the tears were too much. Because Gundt had loved me, too. Enough to give up himself to save me.

I drew in a shuddering breath, and then Kazmerev was there, drawing in close, and so was Grevankin, and we were all drawn back together toward Judicus in an action that was both desperate and like a massive embrace all rolled into one.

We didn't know what to say. Or at least, I didn't. We just huddled there together for a heartbeat, trying to breathe. I pressed my forehead to Kazmerev's fiery one and breathed in Grevankin's smoke and felt Mally shivering beside me and looked deep into Judicus's worried eyes for a long, drawn-out breath.

We will sort this out, Sersha, Kazmerev rumbled from deep inside. *We will sort this out. It's not over yet. We are still here.*

But Gundt was not. Huxabrand was not. I still couldn't believe it.

But Judicus's sister is still here and we still have our goal — to get her back. To save her. To destroy this pillar so our phoenix allies can come and take back the city.

But what if he got sucked into it, too? What if I lost him. I didn't think I could lose him. I'd already lost J —

I arrested my thoughts, gaze flicking to Judicus, not wanting to hurt his feelings. He gave me an apologetic half-smile.

I don't judge you for being afraid of losing Kazmerev, he said gently, running his ghostly hand through his hair in a way that was so familiar that I could almost feel again what those hands were like when I could hold them, when I could touch him, when I could ...

I blinked away tears.

I don't judge you for mourning the passing of my physical life, either. I also mourn it. And I mourn the life with you that could have been.

There will be time to mourn later, Kazmerev said gravely. *And then I will mourn with you and together we will honor our lost and the lost futures we would have had with them, but for now, let's save the living like we planned to do.*

"My sister is still down there," Judicus whispered, biting his lip and bringing his ghostly forehead close as if he wished to lean it against mine. "And I cannot rescue her from this fate without your help."

Mally cleared her throat, crossing her arms and looking at Judicus.

"I suppose you think you're in charge now?"

It seemed to take him a moment to recover himself before he turned from me to address her.

"Well, I am holding the reins," he said mildly.

"Maybe so, but I'm the one wearing the crown."

And there was no arguing with that.

291

"Buck up, Sersha," Mally said in a hoarse whisper. "Your ghost-lover is right. If we don't hurry, the Grand Hadri be gone before we can blink, and we'll miss this chance. We'd better go right now." She turned to Judicus. "Loosen your hold on the phoenixes enough to let them dive down close to the pillar. We'll try to hold off the guards below with flame, and then whoever gets close to the Grand Hadri first scoops her up, we give the signal, and you pull us back up with those golden ropes like we're barrels coming from the belly of a ship. Ready?"

"Wait," Judicus gasped. "I think there's a flaw to the plan."

"No flaw. Let's go. Brace yourself, Sersha!"

"What if my sister doesn't go with you?"

Mally stared at him, silent for just long enough that we could hear the echoes of shouts and orders being barked down below. Someone was cursing loudly between shouted orders until the sound of feet slapping on stone drowned out his furious tirade.

"Let's just hope she does. Are you coming?"

"I have to stay here to hold the ropes," he said but he looked torn, like he wanted to come and was being physically forced to stay back.

She nodded tightly and was already mounting her phoenix. I scrambled to get on Kazmerev's back, surprised when I saw Judicus's ghostly hand laid in an approximation of where it would be if he'd put his hand on my leg in farewell. I bit my lip at the bittersweetness of the caress I could not feel.

"Be careful," he whispered. "One word from you and I'll reel you up."

I nodded and offered him the best smile I could manage.

"*I love you,*" I signed and then he blurred for a moment as Grevankin shoved into the space where he'd been, bumping into Kazmerev, and I had to tighten my grip to stay on my phoenix's back.

Watch it! Kazmerev objected.

Mally, do you think we could skip the dramatics and get to work now? Grevankin asked politely and then we were racing down the cavern toward the lip, the golden rope reins spooling out behind us and my heart was in my throat.

Get ready, Sersha! Kazmerev reminded me. *About to leap ...*

We flew through the air and weightlessness took me, plunging over the edge and into the wide cavern. I felt my breath freeze in my throat as it all came into view — the yawning depth, the scurrying bodies in careful co-centric rings around one kneeling figure in white, the thick pillar rising up through the rock ceiling and swirling with dark, angry clouds.

If the souls that had poured from my gate had troubled them, there was no sign of that now — not in the darkened cavern, lit only by the lamps of the soldiers and the dull glow of the pillar — and not in the dark, roiling pillar.

We dove, and Kazmerev's fiery flames wrapped around me as I spread my fingers wide.

Whatever happens next, please know that I am so proud of you. Even Veela could not have done more than this, Sersha.

I gasped, and then Mally sent out a fireball. I froze for a moment, not sure if I was ready to unleash violence before our enemies did. Then I saw the broken body of Ceghan in the light of Mally's splashing fireball and my spine stiffened and jaw clenched in readiness.

Mally's first shot hit in front of the ranks of soldiers — a warning shot, clearly, meant to tell them to stay back.

There was a shout, and one of the men close to the Grand Hadri pointed at us with his sword. I let Kazmerev grow visible at the same moment that Mally must have done the same with Grevankin because shouts and curses filled the room. They must not have had bows because no arrows flew. An order was barked and they all turned, facing inside instead of outside. We dropped like lead weights into the very center of the soldiers and I could see the whites of their eyes as we drew near — the surprise mixed with readiness.

"By order of the Grand Hadri, you are to surrender!" their captain demanded. He was marked with a red cloak and plumed helm and he thrust his sword toward us without hesitating.

I clenched my jaw as we landed on either side of the kneeling figure in white, expecting to be rushed by soldiers, expecting to be throwing fireballs ... not expecting to be met by a calm ring of men who did nothing to threaten me.

This doesn't feel right, Kazmerev said, warily.

Should I pull you back up? Judicus asked from above.

I ... don't ... know.

"We're here to rescue you," Mally said, leaping from Grevankin's back and hurrying to the kneeling figure.

I wheeled on Kazmerev's back, trying to look in every direction. This felt ... wrong ... too easy. Too ... something.

"Surrender!" the captain demanded again, pointing his sword straight at me. "Now!"

"Grand Hadri?" Mally asked, kneeling down beside the small figure in the white gown and veil.

My heart was in my throat as the captain took a step forward. The moment he did, the soldiers all moved one step inward with him. Their single step echoed in a sharp note of steel on stone and a flash of panic whipped through me.

I'm reeling you back in! Judicus said at the same moment that the Grand Hadri finally moved — but not in the confused, or grateful way I'd expected. She shot upright in a flash, snatched the crown from Mally's head, and broke it over her knee so fast that I could barely gasp as I fell from Kazmerev's back and hit the hard stone.

Judicus, Kazmerev, and Grevankin winked out of existence.

Mally rocked back on her heels, only to have the Grand Hadri's hand shoot out and grab her by the collar, drawing her in with one hand as she whipped off her veil with the other.

The Captain's sword was already at my throat when I saw the face the veil revealed — not the sweet innocent face of Judicus's sister, but the face of Jastomen the spymaster.

"I expected something like this," he said with a sly smile, "but not from you, Ai'sletta. Maybe you aren't the only lucky one around here."

He made a sharp gesture with a hand and the guards hurried forward, grabbing Mally's arms and dragging her to her feet and then mine, too.

"Bring them along," he said grimly. "They'll make an excellent wedding present for tomorrow."

292

They led us up through the crypts, though this way was laid with wide stairs and halls wide enough for horses to bear litters down. Between the shelves of the crypts, more bronze statues stood in poses ranging from the peace of eternal sleep, to the rage of a beast falling beneath a weight of arrows. I did not have much chance to contemplate them. The guards marched on either side of us, a veritable host of guardians, and I caught only glimpses of our surroundings between their uniformed bodies.

Someone had been sent as a runner out ahead of us and by the time we emerged to the light above, arrangements had been made. A wide cage — horribly reminiscent of the cage they had put me in with the other phoenix riders — emerged, and within it, a weakened Verdaine of the Hanging Spears, our elven ally, lay slumped in one corner.

I swallowed down a gibbering terror as the door was opened and we were propelled toward the cage.

Jastomen met us at the entrance, a goblet in his hand. He poured a draught into it and handed the bottle back to one of the guards.

"You're to be my gift to the Grand Hadri and her new husband on the occasion of their wedding," he said with a cold smile. It did not touch his eyes at all. They were like black holes into nothing and I felt my face twist with the confusion I felt. He'd been so kind to me. He'd tried to make me feel comfortable. He'd been gentle in my sorrow. "You, Mally, are thinking that you only have to wait a few hours until sunset, and then you can escape me because you think I did not note that you rode a phoenix down to try to rescue the Grand Hadri from her own guards," he said dryly. "And you, Sersha, are wondering how this can be me when it was also me who was gentle and welcoming to you and gave you such grave and kind words. As if a man can only be one thing. As if I can't want to end magic and the users and products of magic forever but not also be kind to a mute girl. I can do both. I am no monster. I'm merely a man with a very specific vision. Did you not watch Prexav suffer and eventually die for the love he held for a creature not of this world? I had a brother just like him. A young man with the blossom of life still fresh in his heart. He gave it all to a vision — a specter — a firebird made of magic and wishes. It ate him up until he was nothing but a Flame Rider, not a brother, not a friend, not even human anymore. I pity all of you for that — worse, it spreads like a disease. Mally here was not infected only a short time ago, but now here she is, as ruined as you are, Sersha. It's time to end that. It doesn't make me evil. It makes me conscientious."

I shook my head, but he wasn't looking at me anymore.

"Open their mouths," he ordered and strong arms grabbed me, holding me tightly in place and forcing my jaw open.

Jastomen poured sticky, sweet liquid down my throat, dulling my senses even as it was still going down. It filled my nose with an overpowering scent, making my head spin and swirl. The strength faded from my limbs until the men who had been holding me down were now holding me up, and carrying me into the cage. I watched with glassy eyes I couldn't seem to shut as they laid Mally beside me, closed the door of the cage, and began to drag it away.

She moaned something incomprehensible, and I tried to turn my head to her. It wouldn't move. I could only stare past her hip to the slumped figure of Verdaine — drugged just like us, I would guess — and past her still, through the bars, to the courtyard that soon became decadent palace. Then a heavy drape of fabric was thrown over the cage, and it was wheeled into a loud room and left there.

No one peeked under the cloth. No one checked to make sure we were still there. We were simply set aside and left and the hours passed before me and the room grew dark, and then pitch black, and I was tired and hungry and miserable and I could not move a single inch. If night fell and my phoenix came with it, then I missed it, for I soon fell into a drugged sleep and did not wake again until the rumble of the cage woke me.

My eyes opened, but it was still too dark to see, the movement of the cage jostling me against the floor and bars, moving me slowly until my legs bent and folded under me and I was powerless to prevent the awkward angle or the way I was shoved up against Mally, my face smeared into her back.

Eventually, the cart stopped. Murmurs from beyond it quieted and then grew loud again. I heard the sound of horses trotting over cobbles and then a shout and a reply and then a murmur of voices. One was high-pitched and anxious. Another low and calming.

And the draping over the cage was lifted and my drugged eyes saw a lantern and the face of Jastomen peering into the cage. From behind him, another face emerged into the lamp light and if I could have gasped, I might have. It was Judiucus's sister, the Grand Hadri, clutching her cloak around her and chewing on her bottom lip. She looked so young.

"You're sure that's her?" she whispered.

"Of course. I told you I've met her many times."

"And do you this is the right thing to do?"

"Of course, my dear, of course." Jastomen offered her a fatherly smile. "Who would not want the ai'sletta there on their wedding day?"

"It won't hurt, will it?" Kristiana asked, worriedly.

"You have a kind heart. But no. It won't hurt her. It will be over quickly. Her soul will be given to the pillar, as it was prophesied in ages past. And by this means, the scourge of magic will cease and we will build on the rubble a new empire. An empire of people. Of hard work and dreams. Not one where a few with access to a world beyond can tip the balance - a world where everyone has an equal chance."

She nodded along, looking pleased. To my eye, she looked young for her age and she couldn't have been more than sixteen. "But does she really have to die?"

"If not here, then somewhere," Jastomen said gently. "It speaks well of you that you wish to spare her. But it cannot be. The ai'sletta must sacrifice herself. Everyone has always known that. You will see. In the end, she will do it willingly."

I would have scoffed at that if I could. I could feel Mally's breath hitch in her back. She was listening, too.

"And these others? Can we not spare them?" Kristiana asked, her eyes sad when they met mine and I felt a shock at how they looked when they met mine. She looked surprisingly like her brother.

"You won't want that," Jastomen said sadly. "I didn't want to tell you this, but these people had a hand in the death of your brother, Judicus Franzer Irault. They could have saved his life and they did nothing. They admitted as much to me, face to face."

She nodded and I felt ill with shock at how Jastomen was twisting what I'd confided in him.

"Look at how this one wears your brother's trinket, bold as a lion. It's not hers to wear is it?" he asked, reaching into the cage and grabbing hold of the tiny "small but mighty" necklace Judicus had given me. My heart twisted as he tangled his fingers in the chain and wrenched it from my neck with a snap.

He straightened and offered it to Kristiana who took the medallion, trembling and pale-faced. I wanted to cry. My frozen eyes burned with the need of it. That medallion was the last physical thing I had of Judicus and they'd just snatched it from me.

"You're right. You're always right, Jastomen. I wish my mother could have seen this," she said sadly. "I wish she could have known that we would avenge him."

"How sad it is that she was taken from us the very night I went to secure her safety," Jastomen said and I reeled at the glint in his eye. Oh no. Judicus's mother. I felt sick as I watched him place a kind hand on Kristiana's shoulder and look into her eyes with false consideration. I had no doubt who had ended her mother's life. It was this man offering platitudes now. "She will be so proud of you when she looks down on your wedding. When she sees you cement your power forever."

I tried to force my hands to move, to be able to make a single sign of negation. A shake of the head — anything.

"And my brother," she said sadly. "I almost thought I saw him the night I was made Grand Hadri."

"A trick of the light," Jastomen murdered. "As I told you, he perished in the northeast. That you have the ai'sletta in time to offer to the pillar on the very day your alliance is sealed is thanks to his brave sacrifice."

And now I was screaming inside, screaming my denials inside a mute body, a frozen body, a prison within a prison. If Judicus were here he'd tell his sister the truth — that she'd been lied to and manipulated. That we were his friends. That he'd given me that medallion as a tiny piece of him because he loved me.

But I couldn't so much as twitch as they lowered the cloth again and left.

It was another hour, at least, before I could twitch a finger.

Another hour after that before I could turn my head.

Another hour after that before I could hear Mally's whispered curse.

When she finally flopped herself over so that our eyes met I was in full agreement with the whispered stream of curses coming out of her.

"Sersha," she managed, in a garbled, thick voice. "We're going to kill Jastomen."

I tried to nod but I couldn't tell if she could see.

"And then we're going to stuff him into that pillar."

I tried to nod again.

"I'm going to use every scrap of ai'sletta luck to end them all."

I thought that sounded like a great idea.

"And then I'm going to kill that elf prince."

"No."

If I could have jumped at that voice I would have. I had thought that Verdaine was dead, but clearly she was only drugged just like us.

"I get that honor," she said thickly. "My last great work. You owe me that for betraying our hiding place."

We did owe her that.

"Okay, but you have to make it good," Mally said, slow and halting. "And then we conquer this city from the inside out and destroy our enemies forever."

And I didn't know if the spasm rolling through me was laughter or tears at the sheer ridiculousness of that comment.

293

Destroy our enemies forever.

What did that even mean?

I pressed my face to the cold floor of the cage — there was little else I could do with it when I couldn't move more than to turn my head — and utterly unbidden, my tears swelled and fell and pooled under my face.

I saw in my mind a memory of Landsfall, of my Uncle Llynd nursing a drink by the door while my Aunt Danna ordered the inn to perfect harmony. I saw Mally giggling as she served drinks with a wink to the boys who came in with a fresh catch. I saw Judicus the first time he smiled at me — sickly and miserable and yet so kind. I saw Kazmerev emerge from the flame egg, bright and devastating. Gundt, the first time we met him, so earnest, so full of faith. And I choked now on a harsher sob. Huxabrand, pink as a bright blossom in her vibrant flame. She always made Kazmerev stutter over his words, like he couldn't quite hold them smooth around what he saw as phoenix beauty. The first time we flew — him and me — soaring up into a dark sky. The first time Judicus kissed me. So achingly sweet. The moment I realized he was gone to another realm forever.

And I felt the book digging into my side through my belt pouch.

"I think I do have to die," Mally said eventually in a thick mumble.

"I think we all will," Verdaine said. She was sitting now, head balanced against a bar so it wouldn't loll over her neck. Her gaze was distant. She had a handful of the fabric covering the cage in one hand. I thought she might have been trying to pull it down and off the cage, but she didn't have the strength. "I think we'll all die in a few hours. I just want to take them with me."

Did I want that? I didn't think I did. I didn't want more death. I didn't want more misery. I just wanted all the innocent people to be safe.

"If I'm going to save them, I think I have to die," Mally said and I tried to shake my head but it wouldn't shake. "Don't look at me like that, Sersha. Don't. I think it should be obvious. They know it. The book hinted at it. It was always coming to this. They want to put my soul into that pillar. They want to use me — my luck — to open that gate once and for all and destroy all the phoenixes and suck all the magic out of the world and trap it in there where only they can access it, where only they can control it. And then the people here will never have any way to say no. They'll live like this with their heads bowed forever."

I wanted to ask why she'd cared. She'd never cared before.

"And Gundt's sacrifice will be for nothing. All his faith. All his hope — in me. It was so so stupid and it will be for nothing."

I realized, with a horror so heavy that it choked me for a moment, that she meant that. Was Mally — my cousin, Mally, the girl who cared only for herself — was she having a moment of clarity and unselfishness? Why did it have to be *now?* Why did it have to be about *this?*

I sat up like a shot. I didn't even know I had it in me.

The world swayed terribly, rocking side to side, my vision darkening and then brightening, but I shoved it all away while I signed.

"No," I signed, *"No, no, no. You can't just die."*

Mally sighed. "I can't stay here and let them use me like that. How long until their rule spreads? How long until it affects my dad? My sisters? My brothers?"

And she sounded so un-Mally-like.

"Why did you have to pick right now to be unselfish? " I signed and I was still crying and I couldn't stop.

"I've always been the most unselfish person I know," Mally said, sounding noble and brave and like she actually believed that. "I've always done everything for the good of someone else."

"You have?"

"Obviously. It's the best thing for everyone if I'm in charge and I get what I want."

I began to laugh. Silently, of course, but also hysterically. Why not? Why not her, too? After all, everyone else I loved was dead. Why not Mally, too?

I was shaking my head as I choked on my sob, eyes sealed shut now with helpless tears. I felt her arms wrapping around me, not just tight but way too tight, like she was going to wring the last drops of her life right out of my body. It was so Mally to hug too hard. Where it would be a comfort from someone else, it was a challenge coming from her.

"You've been a good cousin, Sersha. I like being around you. And most of the time you don't steal the spotlight. And you're the perfect foil to all my talents and good qualities. You have this great way of looking stupidly at me like you don't know what I'm going to do just before I do something utterly genius. Yes, that's the one right there. I'm going to miss you. I would have liked to see the rest of the world with you. Do you think it would have been nice? Maybe there would have been a boy for me. Not a sick one. That's really more your thing."

I was crying so hard that my whole chest was heaving. She began to rock me a little back and forth like I was her little sister.

"And that, Sersha, is why you're going to put me in the mirror shard you carry around."

I pulled back. I was going to do what? I blinked hard trying to clear my vision. Mally thrust her chin out determinedly, her eyes narrowing.

"Because either they kill me and use me, or you let me stroll on in there with your boyfriend, out of the way where I can't cause trouble. I'm all luck. That's the point of the ai'sletta. To twist things the right way. If I'm in there in the world that connects to that pillar and then *it* connects to all the threads of the world, maybe I can twist it. Maybe I can make it twist out away from evil and twist back to what is good. Just by being willing to go there. Just by showing up. Or maybe I'll think of something even more genius when the time comes."

I felt my mouth drop open.

"And then when you go rescue Judicus you can come get me, too. Don't look at me like that," she said as I shook my head violently. "We both know you won't rest until either you die or you get him out. Well, I'm betting on those odds. For whatever reason, things seem to work out for you. I think you really will find a way to save him. And when you do, you'll save me, too."

I was still shaking my head when I felt her pulling at my belt pouch. I rubbed my eyes hard, trying to clear them. They were still blurry as she extracted the shard. I'd only just cleared them when she shoved it into my hands.

"I hope you're amazing at figuring this out because I'm going to be a terrible ghost and if you don't bring me back, I'm going to haunt you forever and say embarrassing things at exactly the wrong time until you're jumpy as a squirrel," she said grimly and then she dove toward me and I gasped as she disappeared into the shard of mirror and a flash of light.

"I guess that simplifies things," Verdaine said groggily from her place beside the bars. "I really am dreaming, after all. Want to dream with me, silent girl? It's better than the alternative."

But none of this felt like a dream at all. It felt like a nightmare. I stared in horror at the shard of mirror in my hands. And then I looked out at the cloth covering the bars, hiding me from the world beyond. My death was scheduled for later this morning. My cousin was gone. And I'd never felt so lost or so alone.

294

I could finally stand up by the time the area around the cage began to fill with people. I stood with the shard of mirror hidden in my belt pouch and my hands shaking so hard on the bars that I couldn't seem to catch my breath. Last time I'd been trapped in a cage, Judicus had come for me. He'd rescued me and kept me safe and taught me to speak with him with my hands.

This time, it was just me and Verdaine, and the elf had first slipped into some kind of meditative trance and when she was done that, she began to speak to me very fiercely without looking me in the eye.

"They've timed it for the day so they can get you without the phoenix."

More likely because people preferred to marry in the day, but even if I could speak I wouldn't have interrupted her. I was too lost in my own worries. I felt too helpless in the face of this.

"They might not open the cage. They might kill us in here with spears or arrows. We might have no chance. But. If they do come in here, we charge. Do you understand? I'll go first. I will be like the sky itself has opened on them in fury. I don't expect much from you, but if we survive long enough to get out of the cage, and if I get close to the newly married royals, the Prince's throat is mine to tear out, you understand?"

I gave her a very worried smile and nodded. I wasn't going to be tearing any throats out. But I also didn't want to die. I had a plan before. But that plan relied on all my friends and they were all gone now. There was no one but me and a dehydrated, furious elf who terrified me.

I had no plan. I had nothing to work with. And if I didn't figure out how to survive this, then Kazmerev, Mally, and Judicus, and everyone else would be without help and without a hope of ever getting back into this world and it would all be my fault.

It was hard not to panic with the fate of the world resting on me.

Verdaine tugged uselessly at the cloth one last time as the noise around us went from a slow trickle to a roar. Voices layered upon voices upon voices and soon I could barely hear myself think. The occasional snatch of conversation broke free and kept me standing.

"... be here soon ..."

" ... elves ..."

" ... wedding ..."

And then, finally, a hush fell over the crowd and a voice cried out, "The Grand Hadri and her wedded husband, Prince of Briccatore!"

There was a sound of fabric rustling and then I gasped as the cover was wrenched from our cage, landing in a heavy thump and the brightness of the noonday sun blinded me.

My heart hammered in my chest, my breath sawing out of me in startled gasps. I could hear Verdaine's grunt of frustration and then my vision began to clear.

I knew this square — Victory Square. The last time I'd been here, I'd been taken by the Flamerarch and then we'd all been imprisoned together.

The last time I'd been here, there had been a horrific statue of Judicus's father — of the current Grand Hadri's father, I realized belatedly. It was gone now and in its place, the pillar had been erected. Dark, swirling anti-light filled the crystal surface. Around the base of the pillar, bronze cast sculptures had been placed — crude and rushed, perhaps, but still clear in their subject matter. Immortalized in bronze, a ring of phoenixes trampled under the feet of men with swords raised to fight.

I felt ill at the sight, but even more ill at the sight of the young Grand Hadri, crown on her head, shoulders thrown back under her light, filmy wedding dress, one hand resting on the arm of an elf clad in diamond-plate armor, lacquered in green, the edges bright with gilding. His proud face was cruel and he was flanked by a row of elves dressed just like him, while on the Grand Hadri's other side her guards flanked her.

Surrounding them, the people of Briccatore were packed into Victory Square like fish dried and barrelled. And I could not tell if they were noble or common, man or woman, because they were all bent on their knees, foreheads resting on the ground.

Something deep inside me twisted at the sight. No free people should bow like that. And these people should be free.

It twisted again when Jastomen rose in front of us, the edge of the cloth that had covered the cage still in his hand.

"In honor of your wedding and as an auspicious gift, the Grand Hadri bids me present her husband with a gift — the ai'sletta of Calicarn!" he announced, spreading his hand toward us.

He froze, jaw dropping at the same moment that the Grand Hadri made a strangled sound in the back of her throat.

They were all staring at us.

I began to shake under their regard.

If only it were night. If only I could call my Kazmerev and Judicus. If only I had any idea what to do.

"Where is she?" The elf prince asked in a hard voice.

A murmur rose from the people still bent in obeisance, a hushed, worried terror like a tremor that runs through a herd of farm animals when they sense the presence of a predator.

"What manner of jest is this?"

"She's here," Jastomen said smoothly, reaching through the bars and gripping my arm so hard, pulling me forward so quickly, that I stumbled against his jerk and crashed into the bars, my lip and nose stinging where they collided. His hand had clamped right over the site of my old arrow wound and pain from that joined the sharp feelings in my face and nose. "She is ready to be fed to the great pillar of your might, and open the gate to receive the souls of all our enemies."

He made a dramatic gesture to highlight his words.

"This slight woman is the ai'sletta of prophecy?" the prince pushed, skepticism bathing every word. "But I saw this woman in the city under the earth. And it was another who was named ai'sletta then."

"A ruse," Jastomen said easily. "A way to hide the identity of the true ai'sletta to ensure her safety."

"She rode a phoenix," the prince said, sounding uncertain.

"Which is why she has been kept caged," Judicus's sister said easily. "With this great alliance we have made, signed in blood and marriage, witnessed by your people and mine, binding us under one family through vow and magic, we have done something never done before, and now with this gift of the ai'sletta I do something new once again. I seal our reign and the reign of our children for all eternity."

And her words seemed to mollify him because he left her side with a look in his eye like a wolf stalking a fluffy yellow chick, he strode across the courtyard, unmindful of those he trod on or over in his effort to reach us.

Beside me, I felt Verdaine stiffen with hope. But I didn't think she would get her chance. The Grand Hadri had moved with him, and they were both ringed by their guards even now when their citizens' bowed forms were under their feet in an ultimate image of dominance and submission.

"Open her cage," the prince breathed with delighted anticipation. He was, perhaps, an objectively beautiful being, but here and now facing us with sadistic cruelty on his face, he was uglier than anyone I'd ever seen. "Let us not delay. The pillar thirsts and I will quench that thirst."

295

I shouldn't have been surprised when Jastomen made a quick gesture and it brought Kentinius forward — but I was surprised.

Kentinius's eyes glinted with malice and though he was washed and dressed for the wedding, he had a smudge on his neck where he'd missed a bit of road dust when he was washing. He couldn't have arrived at the city much sooner than we had — maybe not even as soon — but already he was back in the thick of things.

His arms spread wide, rope work spilled from his hands, and then the ropes reached up and I expected them to unlock the door or open it with their magic tendrils, but instead, they spiraled around the bars like reaching vines and wrenched them apart with a loud squeal. Reaching inward, Kentinius plucked us up with strands of rope work and I had to clench my teeth against my distaste as he pulled us through the bars like a squid drawing out prizes from a poorly set trap.

As he drew us out, the elven prince and the Grand Hadri mounted the steps to the pillar, hand in hand, arranging themselves to stand over the bronze casting of the defeated phoenixes. Their stance was garish and so unbelievably arrogant that a part of me felt like it was watching a nightmare slowly unravel rather than an actual event taking place.

"Have the people stand," the elven prince said, and I thought I caught a flicker of annoyance on his new wife's face. After all, these were her people and he was ordering them around right in front of her, but Jastomen spread his arms graciously as he and Kentinius arranged themselves just below the prince and the Grand Hadri. Their guards fanned out around them, and then Kentinius raised his hands and we were jerked upward, floating above the crowd by lines of black rope work.

My heart was in my throat, my hands flexing and unflexing, my gaze skittering over the hundreds gathered below us.

Don't panic, Sersha. Don't you dare panic or you'll miss an opportunity if it comes.

But as I was raised ever upward, I realized it wasn't just hundreds of people, it was thousands — lining every street around the square and hanging from the windows of every building — watching this spectacle as Kentinius lifted us higher and higher.

And now I was high enough that I felt like I could see the whole city laid out around me, and on the very edges of it, I felt as though I could almost see a glow.

"Behold!" The prince called. "Behold the gifts given to me by my new bride! The ai'sletta. The rebel leader who thought to bring down the elves. And the city of Briccatore and all her bounty! I will offer these gifts to the beyond and seal for us power for a thousand generations!"

There was a pause, and then there must have been some kind of signal because the silence dissolved into a roar that sounded either of approval or of desperate fear. I didn't know what was in the hearts of the citizens, but as we were lowered down again, I knew what was in the eyes of the Grand Hadri, because her eyes were bright with fear and excitement.

"Shall we offer up these gifts?" the prince called out.

My mouth was dry at the resounding roar. My eyes flicked from face to face. And some were hungry as they watched me with wide greedy eyes. And some had clenched jaws and clenched hands as though they thought they might hold back trouble from themselves if it would only come to me instead. There was relief in those eyes and I recognized that, too, the sheer and utter relief of knowing that the person suffering today wasn't you.

I cast a last glance at the sun. It was too far from the horizon. Too far. Night wasn't going to come in time. I was going to die as the mistaken ai'sletta, my blood let to flow on the pillar. And then who knew who they might feed to it next? By the slightly panicked look in the eyes of Judicus's sister, I thought she might know.

The moment our feet hit the ground, Verdaine leapt. And I didn't fault her for it. She'd told me she was doing exactly that. What else could she do? She leapt with a roar toward the prince, her athletic body tensed and intent, her lips curling back in fury, hands reaching forward.

She didn't manage a single step. The loop of rope work that had held her a moment before twined upward, wrapped around her, and snapped her neck in a single motion.

I gaped, horrified.

Clearly, I would not be trying a mad leap.

Jastomen nodded to Kentinius — so subtly that I could hardly credit it, but the rope worker was fast — deadly fast — and as I watched, he wrapped me in fresh bonds, drew me forward, and forced me to my knees.

So then.

This was the end.

I'd thought that before but this was truly it.

I was sweating more than I'd imagined I would at the end of my life.

And I was less scared than I'd feared I might be. That was a relief. I'd worried I'd embarrass myself.

Jastomen stood, lifted his hands for quiet, and from his belt he drew out a book. I was going to be treated to a speech before they killed me. It should have been a relief since it was buying me time. Instead, it just made my stomach twist.

I didn't have any ideas.

I was flat out.

I'd only ever been a simple girl who a blazing phoenix chose. And now I was going to die without ever getting to say goodbye. The thought of it broke something in my heart. Some door I'd been braced against to hold me safe and tight.

And then I heard a voice in my mind.

Sersha?

296

Judicus?

It couldn't be.

And yet I could feel him there, inside my mind. I trembled at the sheer joy of it, at the comfort it brought me even now when everything was falling apart just to have him with me in this moment. I was held steady only by the rope work pinning me in place on my knees.

"You have seen with your own eyes the abomination of day when there should be night and night when there should be day — a sign given to us that judgment is at hand if we do not act," Jastomen said loudly to the crowd.

Sersha, what's happening? Judicus's mental voice whispered in my mind. *My last memory is of Jastomen dressed as my sister. Have you found her?*

How was he here? It wasn't night. It was day. I gasped in a breath but I shouldn't be wasting my time with these thoughts. I only had moments to tell him goodbye.

"This great pillar of power — connected to ancient artifacts that span the earth — will put an end to this today in your presence," Jastomen said, raising his book. "It is a gate to our future."

Jastomen made a gesture and Verdaine's limp body was carried to the pillar.

But I wasn't focused on her. This was my last chance to say goodbye.

Goodbye? Judicus sounded startled.

He had made these last weeks of my life sweet. And though he was dead already and I was going to be dead soon, too, I wanted him to know that the gentle love and understanding he'd given me had filled my heart. I loved him. Treasured him. And even now as I looked up at the bright glare of the sun I knew that there were doors beyond me and beyond death and I knew enough now to know I didn't know everything, that I could rule nothing out. That there might be a gate I could walk through and find him on the other side. We always called the heavens merciful. Perhaps there would be mercy for us.

Why are you saying goodbye to me? Sersha? Sersha, if Mally is in there with you, tell her to get as close to the pillar as she can. We're going to need her luck to unravel it and for that, we need her close and focused on that pillar!

Kentinus's grip shifted, turning me slightly so that my eyes fell on Kristiana dressed to the hilt as the Grand Hadri in swathed cloth of pale cream and white and wearing a lace and diamond headdress.

"Sacrifices must be made," Jastomen said in a ringing voice.

But now neither of us was listening to him because I could feel Judicus's shock at the sight of his sister, at the way she watched coolly as Jastomen nodded and the men laid Verdaine's body next to the pillar and leapt back just in time as it disappeared. At the way she had her hand on her new husband's arm.

Kristiana? Judicus's mental voice sounded small. *No.*

It was denial and plea all rolled into one.

Has she turned to evil, then? Kazmerev's voice asked and I gasped again.

Kazmerev! My great fiery friend! He was here, too, though it was day.

I could hardly believe it, but I choked down my disbelief and reached for him with my heart. I would not have to leave him without a goodbye either, and the thought of it made me tremble with gratitude. I hoped someone would take his ashes. I hoped they would bring him new life.

I do not hope for that, Sersha. If this is the end, then I want an end. I want you to be the last Flame Rider to hold my heart. We've flown well, my girl. We've done all we could. Death comes when it must. It is only losing love that makes it so bitter. But I believe we will not lose each other. I believe the Almighty holds us in his hands and that he has a special place for Flame Riders and their phoenixes in a place that never gets dark again.

"For the good of Calicarn!"

There was a cry and then, to my shock, a group of five men surged toward us, bellowing, belt knives in their hands, but no other weapons. They had shoved up their sleeves and under them, they wore green bracers. My heart seemed to be stuck in my chest. My breath hitched in my throat and my eyes clouded with tears as the Greensleeves rushed the guards who outnumbered them ten to one. They thought I was the ai'sletta. They were throwing themselves at my captors in a brave attempt to save me. It hurt to watch as they were cut down. Hurt even more as it triggered memories of Gundt's brave last charge. Alone, in a crowd of silent subservience, these men had clung to what they believed. Alone, in a nation oppressed, they had not bent. And I was choking on tears as their resolute steadfastness leaked out of them with their lives.

Jastomen turned, acting as if nothing had happened.

"For the good of Briccatore, and the world!" Jastomen he shouted, ignoring the last screams of the dying Greensleeves. He held his arms up, and like it was a signal, Kentinius's rope fell from me and shot out like a thrown javelin, catching the elven prince in the chest and knocking him straight into the pillar.

He flailed, his hand catching at Kristiana's dress.

Kristiana! Judicus cried.

I leapt forward, catching her other arm and stabilizing her as her new husband's grip ripped away and he hit the pillar in a burst of not-light. Something within it flared up — bright in a way that wasn't light but still seared the backs of my eyelids — as if it had grown stronger with his absorption.

There was a hush over the crowd and then Jastomen said simply, "In a world without magic we need no allies from other lands. Are you ready to do what you must, Grand Hadri? Are you ready to take the life of the ai'sletta?"

And then he turned and looked right at the Grand Hadri and Kentinius pushed a dagger into her hands and Judicus's sister swallowed, facing me, hands trembling as she raised the dagger before me. Kentinius's ropes swirled around my legs and held me there.

What are you doing, Kristiana? Judicus cried in my mind. *Sersha! The mirror! Put her in the mirror!*

I fumbled in my belt pouch.

"Sacrifices must be made!" Jastomen. "Lead us into the future, Grand Hadri!"

There was a roar from the crowd as Kristiana steeled her spine and took a step toward me. But none of this felt real. None of it.

"He tells me that you killed my brother," Kristiana whispered in an undertone as she lifted her dagger just a touch higher. My hand closed around the mirror shard, trembling. "And I saw the medallion you stole from him."

I gave it to her. Because I love her, Judicus's whisper in my mind was faint with hurt.

"I don't think I'll be a murderer if I kill the one who killed him," Kristiana said clearly.

Please, Judicus pled in my mind and I thought he was saying it to her, but it could just as easily be me or anyone. *Please, please, please.*

It was like a prayer.

Kristiana shook. The crowd went nearly silent as they waited for her to kill me right in front of them.

"If it wasn't you, then deny it," she said between clenched teeth.

I shook my head, violently.

"Say it. Tell me it wasn't you who killed my brother." She dropped her voice to a whisper. "I know you are not the ai'sletta, that she has escaped somehow. Your life could be spared if you would just say it was not you who took his life."

And though I shook my head she merely sighed and shifted her stance.

"So be it," she said.

Use the mirror! Kazmerev called in my mind. The mental sound Judicus made was so despairing that I did not know if he wanted the same thing or something different. Maybe he wanted his sister to kill me and be safe herself. Maybe he wanted to be attached to someone — anyone — who wasn't me and all the problems I brought with me. I didn't know. But I did know that if I let her kill me then our futures died with me.

I slammed outward with my shard of mirror at the exact moment that her dagger came down, sliding along my hand and arm and downward, slicing flesh to the elbow.

I was already screaming as the shard shattered in my hand and my hand passed through Kristiana's fading torso, and in the blink of an eye, she was gone.

I looked down at my fistful of ruined glass.

Looked up at the pain and horror on Jastomen's face.

Heard the gasp of horror from the crowd.

Saw the ripples of Kentinus's ropes spitting outward to quell any voices of dissent. Most of them were wrapped around members of the elven guard.

Looked down again. Oh no.

I'd been so sure that when all this was over I could go into that mirror and bring them all out. That I could find a way where no one else had. I'd been counting on it.

But now the mirror was smashed to little bits.

How could there be a chance when there were only shattered fragments?

I must have started to cry.

I could hear Kazmerev and Judicus in my mind whispering together, *It's fine, Sersha.*

It will be fine, Judicus corrected, but he sounded gutted — like a man who had just watched the sister he loved try to kill his bride-to-be only to die in the exact same way he had.

You did the right thing, Kazmerev assured me.

You did your best, Judicus agreed and I could feel that he was trying to be brave for me and he was holding back his true feelings as Jastomen narrowed his eyes and drew his own dagger.

My last hope was that when I died, I would go to be with them, wherever they were.

I could hold onto that at least.

I closed my eyes and made my heart a door one last time. A door for me to walk through this time. A door for a voiceless girl who had the very best friends anyone could ask for.

I made my heart a door and let it sweep me away.

The world went white.

Sersha? Sersha! Open your eyes!

Kazmerev sounded like he was choking, gasping.

My eyes flew open at the same moment that he flew from my heart, bursting bright scarlet and gold and blossoming to fullness. The moment he was fully back, he opened his mouth and swallowed Jastomen whole.

EPISODE FIVE: "FOR THOSE WE LOVE"

SEASON THREE

297

My gorgeous phoenix had just burst from my heart, gold and scarlet and beautiful. The moment he emerged he opened his great beak and swallowed Jastomen whole.

My mouth fell open, but there was no time to react. Not even when I didn't know that was possible. I'd never seen a phoenix eat anyone or anything before.

Good will always swallow up evil in the end.

I blinked twice, and then pain ripped through me as my gate opened, opened, opened, and the magic pillar beside me seemed to swell with the intensity of what was happening, the dark not-light within it tumbling outward from the pillar.

To my shock, Judicus leapt from my heart, pausing to swipe his lips across my cheek and even though I couldn't feel it, his proud smile made my heart ache, and then he was sliding in front of me, hands flying open to do battle with his rope work while more spirits poured from my gate.

Thank you for my sister.

Judicus's voice in my mind was sincere but aching all at once. Because if she went into the mirror shard then she was as lost as he was, right? She was a spiritual, insubstantial ghost just like him. My heart hurt at the thought of it, at the way I still felt helpless in the face of her accusations and violent misunderstandings.

But there was something odd about Judicus's ghost. He flickered wildly like a flame in the wind, his whole body shimmering and shivering. I hoped he was not fading. I desperately needed him here. Could he deal with the knot on the pillar? Could he unravel it as he had before?

Ropes ripped from his hands and grabbed hold of the ropes clinging to my feet, ripping them aside and shredding them as a strong man might shred a linen sheet. I felt my feet come free, pulling me forward and then releasing suddenly.

I stumbled forward, falling after him, but then Kazmerev was there, blaring red and hot as a forge fire. I dove into his warmth, both arms stretched out in relief. He was here. I wouldn't have to do this alone.

We're here. Let the flames rise into the sky once again! We will not rest until the world is put to right.

But it was day! How could he be here in the day?

Perhaps it is the end of the world and all the rules are breaking. Or perhaps you've found that your gate can open into places we didn't think possible.

He sounded so earnest, so strong. And yet, my eyes were still riveted to where the pillar beside us was boiling upward. A loud screeching sound like a kettle coming to a boil made me flinch and then a huge disk that looked like a cap flew from the top of the pillar, spinning up into the sky as dark clouds boiled upward.

Too much was happening at once. And my arm throbbed with pain from the deep slash Kristiana had made down the inside of it. Little spatters of blood trailed everywhere I went but I had nothing to stem the flow with.

Beside me, someone screamed so close to us that it felt like it was right in my ear.

I spun and saw a man go down in the crowd, stomping feet clambering over him. Another scream and I couldn't help it, I looked there, too, just in time to see a guard ripped apart by a pair of Elven guards. The elves had formed up back to back in pairs and they were slashing and hacking through the crowd — or what they could reach of it as the people scrambled for cover in ever direction. I watched as a woman pushed a man from one of the upper windows of the buildings nearby — perhaps he had been trying to scale the walls? He fell into the masses with a shout and more shouts echoed in the wake of his crash. Everywhere I looked were scenes of human chaos.

But I couldn't afford to let it distract me. Not when I could hardly breathe. My breath hiccuped out of me because the sensation of my gate was growing greater by the second and getting worse. I could feel it in a way I hadn't felt before. It drove me to my knees, hands clutching at my head. Then, as the pain hit hard and fast and I sucked in a long breath and clung to Kazmerev, I could see in my mind's eye how this time my gate had opened and connected to the pillar, and this time, that pillar was connected to *every* pillar through the ropes that ran through the whole earth.

I hovered on the edge of passing out both from pain and from how my mind felt like it was being stretched too wide and too fast.

Don't pass out! Stay with me.

Kazmerev's voice in my mind was hot and ragged. Had he really eaten Jastomen?

Yes.

Really?

Yes.

He could do that?

I want to gain height to keep you safe from the fighting, but I'm afraid that if I do and then you pass out you'll fall to your death.

Just hold onto me. Just don't let me go.

I clung to his neck, his molten feathers brushing me, at once far too hot and yet comforting. The very heat of them was an anchor and I tied my heart to it as the strength of my gate shook me like a flag in a high wind, throttled and agitated until the wind began to fray the edges.

He rolled slightly and came up under me so that now I was on his back, still clinging to fistfuls of feathers. I breathed into his sulfur smell, letting the sharp blast of it clear my head just a little.

I tried to relax into the terrible pain. To let it roll me and toss me over its waves like the current sweeping an unwise swimmer away from shore. Maybe then I wouldn't pass out.

Maybe.

Hold on.

And then suddenly Judicus was vaulting onto his back, too, hands outstretched as ropes spooled out of them and my breath caught as the great central pillar pulsed, and then ghosts began to pour from me, dripping from my hands in thick golden honey and then bubbling up into the golden glowing silhouettes of people.

They were snatched, almost immediately, from my grasp and pulled toward the pillar like tiny shells drawn out by a receding tide — the strength pulling them as inexorably as the pull of the horizon on the sun at the end of the day.

Mally and Grevankin emerged — both glowing gold — and there was no time to hear what she was shouting before more spooled out, hundreds, no — thousands of ghosts — a second army of the dead. I lost hold of Kazmerev, reaching for Mally and Grevankin's ghosts trying to pull them back by sheer willpower.

A loop of golden rope shot out, reeling them back, but there was only one Judicus and he couldn't catch the rest of the ghosts as they sprang from my gate and flew in a head-long collision toward the pillar.

"Trying to hold the reins again, Judicus Franzer Irault?" Mally asked from somewhere nearby.

"Be glad I threw you a rope, ai'sletta," he replied and I didn't have to see him raise an eyebrow to know he was doing that.

Can you hold the souls back? Kazmerev begged me.

But I couldn't. They were pouring out so fast that I couldn't shut the gate and with no Dark Diadem we couldn't force day or night or do anything else to destroy the pillar. Not that it seemed to matter. Nothing was playing by the rules right now.

My head hurt too much, the pain was too severe, and still hundreds of souls a second poured from my hands — but I didn't think I'd had that many!

"We have to disable the pillar," Judicus said firmly. "I don't suppose you still have the book from the pillar, Sersha? I would expect it to have the pertinent information — if any exists."

He said it so casually, but as he spoke, he flung out a rope and snatched a soldier out of our path. The man had his weapon raised, murder in his eyes one moment and fear the next as he was flung up into the sky. I didn't watch his trajectory. My eyes were on the next man sprinting toward us at the head of a knot of guards — all one in purpose. They crashed toward us and I raised a hand, willing Kazmerev's fire to scorch through my hand and spray toward them.

They lit up like torches, screaming as they fled and my heart was ice within me.

Don't mourn them, Sersha. They were trying to kill you!

But to burn like that ...

They would have killed not just you but all of us. Do I not matter to you?

Of course he did.

Does Judicus not matter to you?

Of course he —

Our conversation was cut off as Occulus dripped from my hand, spinning toward us for a heartbeat and then sprinting outward as if he knew that a moment's hesitation would leave him trussed up again by bonds of magic.

He was gone as fast as a blink, but it wasn't an end to the souls spiraling through my gate. I felt so odd — like I was both a girl and a wide yawning cavern, open, open, open.

"I had the book last," Mally said through a tight grimace. I risked a glance in her direction just in time to see her open a ghostly hand and fling a spirit fireball at a pair of elves slashing toward her. I expected it to go right through them, but to my horror, flames licked them up, lighting them like torches.

I muffled a gasp.

"Sersha, the book," Mally said tightly.

I couldn't believe she was still alive — sort of. I lifted my hands to sign and tell her so and she made a scoffing noise.

"If you're going to tell me how amazing it is to see me, trust me, I know. Save it for later. Go and get the book!"

I'd slid halfway down Kazmerev's back before Judicus said tightly, "I've got it, Sersha."

And then the backpack we'd had was flying toward me on the end of a rope. I caught the bag, opening the mouth and spilling the contents out until I found the book and drew it out, clutching the heavy tome to my chest.

My head spun, the pain mounting.

I risked a look above me and saw that the top of the pillar was still spouting up, up, up, the roiling black, not-smoke, not-light rising up into the sky — a black pillar of spirit that dwarfed the manmade crystal pillar beneath.

Darting toward it from every direction were the eye-bending figures of the Stryxex.

298

I stared for a full heartbeat, my mouth dry, my limbs shaking.

But then the pain in my head seared harsh and intense and I had to squint my eyes closed against it.

"What's wrong with her? Open your eyes, Sersha! You're the only one who can turn the pages!" Mally called.

"Mally," Judicus sounded like he was barely leashing his temper. "Spirits are pouring through her like a gate right now. Her pain and disorientation are intense."

"She'll see intense if we don't find a way to cap this pillar again. Do you see what it's doing? It's manufacturing more of those things. Can't you cap it, rope worker?"

"I can see the knot to unravel, Mally, but if I do it wrong it will just kill us all and the pillar will remain unaffected."

My eyes snapped open and my heart was in my throat as I realized Mally was telling the truth. Stryxex were not just darting *toward* the pillar, they were bubbling up from the smoke billowing out of the top as if it were making them. Mind-bending and light twisting, they rippled and twisted and made me want to close my eyes for the next year to make my head stop pounding.

"This is worse than I could have imagined. I thought that if they didn't feed me to it it couldn't get worse!" Mally complained.

It's the gate, Kazmerev said with a trembling mental voice. *Sersha's gate. All the souls not just from within her but from — wherever they are coming from — are pouring into that thing and somehow it is manufacturing Stryxex from them.*

"Great. Just amazing, Sersha. Do you think you might want to close that gate?"

I tried to squint at her, to shoot her a dirty look for complaining when I was doing my very best, but I had to hold my head in my hands to turn it and when I looked at her, she wasn't even facing me. Bold as you please, she stood on

Grevankin's back, hands flinging forward as she threw balls of ghost fire at the men and women trying to swarm us. Her spirit fire, like Judicus's spirit ropes, had physical effects, knocking the enemy back even though she wouldn't have been able to touch them if she'd tried to let loose a physical blow.

I turned, gasping, wondering if anyone else was seeing this, only to realize that Judicus was keeping them off our other flank, weaving ropes and tossing our enemies as quickly as an energetic farm wife plucks weeds from a garden.

I gasped, facing forward as Kazmerev leaned out and snapped, snatching an elven warrior as he screamed toward us and swallowing him in a single gulp.

I had no idea he ate people.

No idea that he even could.

I felt frozen.

"Well, if you can't stop it, then at least read about it!" Mally snarled at me.

"Mally!" Judicus scolded. "Give her a moment. We are none of us at our best when everything we love is threatened."

"No one makes those excuses for me," Mally grumbled, but she said nothing more as I opened the book and turned the pages.

Concentration felt impossible. For every word I read, another spew of ghosts flew through my gate and poured from my fingertips, snatched away toward the pillar like sticks in an overflowing river.

"There," Judicus said after a moment. "Can we pause and look at that page."

I glanced back at him to see his forehead furrowed in concentration and his pale face — even paler in his ghost form — whipping back and forth between his battle against all those attacking us and his gaze on the book.

Fire is the enemy. I caught a glimpse of the page. *Fire burns to the core and cleans to the soul itself, it burns away the lie and leaves only the truth and who can live on so barren a thing as truth? We need our lies to cover us, our platitudes to comfort us, our carefully crafted images to shape reality as we wish it to be. And for every gate that opens, a million possibilities are created and if we only follow the truth then those possibilities die. Guard against the flame, for it unleashes what we have carefully bound and licks away what has been carefully assembled, and sears the soft heart of all our plans.*

There will be no leashing of spirits if they go on to heaven above, no use for that which we have carefully harvested if it is stripped away before we can compel it.

"There's nothing in there about knots," Judicus said, frustration in his voice.

"Then can you just guess?" Mally pushed.

"Last time that ended in disaster."

"I thought you were good at guessing!" she pushed.

"The only thing it mentions is a fire. But how would that work? And wouldn't the knot need to be undone somehow for it to matter?"

"You can't set a pillar on fire," Mally said. "And if you could, don't you think it would be engulfed by now?"

She nodded to the pillar and I followed her gaze to where her fireballs fell at the base of the pillar, sending screaming soldiers scattering, but not doing so much as even smudging the surface of the crystal column.

Fire made sense. Hadn't I read that in one of the prophecy books? *"And healing will come in flames and the darkness will be burnt in the bright light of a new dawn."*

I lifted my hands to sign, but the spirit that poured out of my heart at that moment made my hands drop in shock.

Kristiana. The Grand Hadri.

She poured out in a river with the others, but unlike them, Judicus snatched her back, lifting her up with his golden ropes, his mouth falling open in pain and his gaze growing heavy with sorrow.

"Sister," he said and it was like a eulogy in a single word.

Her ghost looked from him to me and back again and then she spoke in a small, wavering voice.

"Judicus?"

299

"They killed you," she said, the words tumbling out as she pointed to me and then to Mally. "They killed you and left you without burial."

"No," he said, gentle as he always was, even while it looked like his heart was breaking.

"Pay attention!" Mally snarled and I followed her gaze to where a group of guards broke through his distracted attention and were nearly upon us.

I opened my hand and let the fire fall from it, burning them up in a blink of an eye and when I did, I felt a tug on my gate and I could have sworn I saw them among the ghosts falling from me and pooling on the ground and rolling toward the pillar.

"These women are your enemies," Kristiana's hollow voice was growing shrill. She reeled back from Judicus even as a golden rope arched towards her. Judicus caught it and shredded it.

"What happened to our mother?" he asked calmly — the kind of dead calm that told me he was burning inside.

"Jastomen found her dead," Kristiana said.

He blinked back tears, his ghost eyes red-rimmed suddenly. "You buried her?"

"He did."

"They're going to overwhelm us," Mally protested. "Try to light the pillar on fire, Sersha!"

I snatched my gaze from the reunited siblings and back to the problem at hand. I sent out a rolling pillar of flame toward the pillar, but just like hers, it did nothing, not so much as touching the pillar.

It seemed smoky, though, more smoky than before. Beside me, Mally coughed.

"We need to get out of here. We aren't doing any good," she said. "There has to be some way to use my ai'sletta luck here. Think, Sersha, think!"

"Our uncle?" Judicus asked Kristiana tightly. Was he pushing to see what she'd been part of? We knew how her uncle had died.

"Dead," Kristiana said coolly. "Everyone is gone but me. I had only his spymaster left to help me."

"And a husband," Judicus said grimly and if it were possible for a ghost to grow paler, then she did.

"Enough of the family reunion. We need to get into the sky!" Mally cried.

In the middle of that? Kazmerev protested but when I looked up toward the Stryxex I couldn't see a thing. The world above us was filled with smoke. I sucked in a breath, coughed, and realized the air around us had grown smoky, too.

"It's that or burn in a fire," Mally said. "Am I the only one who is noticing that it's becoming a problem?"

She wouldn't burn, she was a ghost.

"And before you mention that most of us are ghosts or phoenixes, must I remind you that Sersha is not and she's our last hope?" Mally pressed.

Wow. I was very touched by that. Mally was thinking about me.

And as if that was a bell ringing in the town square, Kazmerev leapt into the sky, bringing Judicus and me up with him. I clung to the book as the air whipped around my face, coughing and choking as I tried to suck in a breath. I could hear Judicus still speaking beside me, but I couldn't see his sister or Mally.

"You tried to kill my betrothed."

"Who?"

"Sersha. The Flame Rider I am sitting behind."

"Betrothed?" his sister sounded aghast. "You can't marry her!"

"I can't marry at all, sister. We are as dead as all the rest."

"Dead —?" Was that a sob I heard at the end of her word? I swallowed down a wave of grief. Because he was right. She was dead. My Judicus was dead. My cousin was dead. And I was flying right now in the middle of a family of ghosts — echoes of people who had been.

More than that, Kazmerev said gently. *They are more than that and always will be. But I think you and I will lay them to rest now. If we can cap this pillar and stop the flow of spirits through you.*

But how could we do that when Judicus couldn't see a way and he was the most likely to see it of anyone alive or dead?

We have to hope that we'll find one.

And as he said that we drew up above the smoke and when I looked down where we had been, all I saw was a city in flames. Lines of orange fire ran down the streets in every direction from Victory Square. If anyone was fighting the flames, I could not see it in the smoke. What I did see were billows of white and black, and trails of people fleeing the city as fast as their legs would take them.

"Well, if fire is the key you've certainly set the biggest one possible, Sersha," Mally said, still completely unaffected by the argument going on between Judicus and his sister.

But it wasn't me who started that fire!

Mmmm, rumbled Grevankin and I could hear the disbelief in his tone.

Well, I don't think she meant to, Kazmerev said. He didn't think I *meant to?*

Yes, that likely counts for something, Grevankin agreed.

This was madness. If that fire was my fault, then it was me who needed to put it out! It had traveled so far now, that I could see the supine curve of the river outlined in scarlet flame as the fire hit the bank of the river, consuming docks as it arrived. People were packed into every boat and craft, fleeing already out to the expanse of the river and I couldn't believe this was happening so quickly. Couldn't believe the city had gone up in flame, couldn't believe it was my fault.

I felt like I couldn't breathe.

How could I ever fix this?

Despair clawed up my throat and I choked, gasping.

"Sersha?" The voice behind me was mild. I spun, anxiety making my movement jerky as I clung to the book and looked through spilling tears to Judicus's gentle face. He was balanced behind me, his sister behind him and her face held disbelief that was almost comical beside his gentle concern. "Surely you don't think this is your fault?"

The phoenixes did. And how was I going to fix this now? I had fire at my disposal but no water. I had only one phoenix. I couldn't even pluck people and carry them to safety fast enough. The fire would rage and burn and kill people and burn their homes and it was all my fault and there was nothing I could do.

I could hardly see through my swimming tears. I dashed them away angrily. They were no help at all.

I coughed again, choking on despair. A sick feeling in my belly that told me I deserved to choke. This was all my fault.

"It's the fault of those who captured you and tried to unleash this great evil on the world," Judicus said gently. "It will only be our fault if we contribute to it rather than stopping it. So stop panicking, and let's think about how to disable the pillar. All of us. Together. You don't have to do this alone."

You really don't, Kazmerev agreed.

"Well, technically she's the only one of us still alive, so it might have to be her," Mally said wryly.

But we'll be there with you to the very end, Grevankin agreed.

I bit my lip and nodded sharply.

Can you get me to the pillar again? I asked Kazmerev. *I think I have an idea.*

300

There's no way through, Kazmerev gasped after the third Stryxex in as many moments tore past, talons extended, barely missing my face.

I held his feathers in one fist, the book in the other.

Grevankin flew with Mally on his back, tucked in far more tightly than any living phoenix could have managed, his ghost wings often passing right through Kazmerev's living flame. He burned a strange golden green that seemed both like him and unlike him at the same time and I missed the thick smoke that always wreathed him in life.

Behind me, Judicus held both himself and his sister in place, his ropes twisting to rip whatever Stryxex he could from the sky, but even as a ghost, he was only one man. He could only weave so many ropes at a time. Even if he no longer sweated from effort or bled from wounds, he was still held by mortal limitations of concentration and acuity.

We continued to climb, first in an effort to rise above the choking smoke, then in an effort to outdistance the swirling Stryxex. They fought like swarms of bugs or schools of toothy fish, attacking in clumps, concerted in their efforts.

My head felt as though it might split in half as I clung to Kazmerev, shooting off spikes of fire or flinging balls of flame whenever they came close to me and trying to catch a breath in between.

We were high up now to where the air had grown cold and below us, the city was laid out like a map — a map made of smoke and fire.

It was only our position so high in the air that revealed how terrible things had become.

Black moving dots — or long black ribbons where the roads were — showed groups of citizens fleeing the city in a torrent. To the south of the city, the two armies we'd heard about were positioned on the surrounding hills, and they, too, were in chaos. Even from so far away, we could tell they were fighting. Who they were fighting or how — we couldn't guess. There were no Stryxex there, but now at the height of noon, there were no phoenixes either. Whatever had granted me the ability to open my gate and hatch my beloved Kazmerev had not opened for the Flamerarch — or if it had, then the phoenixes they rode had not survived long enough for us to see them now.

I tried not to think about what that meant as fear ricocheted through my heart.

There was no one to help. There would be no one to ride to our aid.

But there were also few clear enemies left of the physical kind. As the flames grew hotter and more intense, even the Grand Hadri's guard, the Hand of the Rat, and the evil elves had begun to flee. Out there somewhere, Occulus's ghost and Kentinius were still a problem. But I could not see either one from here. It would be hard to see Occulus anyway in the daylight. The ghosts flickered more then, and were so bright that they faded a little in the heat and light of midday.

It would mean sure death to dive down into that, Kazmerev said through a strained voice.

We were going to have to do it, though. We didn't have a choice.

Are you sure? he pressed. *Perhaps they can be defeated from far away?*

But I didn't think so. I only had one idea — fire. But not in the sense where I planned to set it alight. My plan was wild. It would take every scrap of luck we had for it to work.

If we go down there, even if you succeed we may never escape. The enemies are too thick. The flames too high. We might die before we even get there.

But I had to try. Or when night fell every Phoenix everywhere would be sucked into that pillar and made Stryxex.

This would never end. New enemies would rise up to take advantage of the power of the pillar. New men would use it to crush the populace and eradicate phoenixes. And anyone who stood up to stop them would face the same danger as we did, face the same obstacles. But they couldn't possibly have our resources. I was here with the greatest rope worker of his generation and the ai'sletta. I was here with two powerful, brave phoenixes in all their glory. And I had a secret weapon, too. Something no one but Kazmerev and I had.

What do we have?

The ability not just to sever, but to mend.

There was a long silence and then Judicus whispered. "Do you really think it's possible? Do you really think you could ... heal ... the pillar? That's what you're planning, right?"

Of course he figured it out. I couldn't keep secrets from him. His guesswork was perfect.

"I can't sever the knot or untie it because I don't know what shape it needs to take and we both learned what happens if you just guess. What happened at that other pillar with Flara is only a tiny taste of the disaster that would happen here at the apex of all this power and all these threads. I can't possibly solve this puzzle and ... well, this sounds arrogant but please don't take it the wrong way. If I can't solve it then no other rope worker can."

Behind him, his sister snorted but I nodded, keeping my eyes on his. He knew that I needed to try this. That we didn't have any other options.

"But healing a person can knock you out flat," he said, his ghostly brow wrinkling. He rubbed worriedly at the thick scar that ran above and below his eye. "What will happen if you heal this pillar? Without you, we all disappear. There will be no one to catch you and save you."

"She can't destroy it!" Kristiana hissed. "It's our future."

Judicus turned very deliberately and spoke with careful enunciation. "Kristiana. You are my sister. And I forgive you for all you have done. But my future is not this element of evil. My future — if I get to have one — is Sersha and all the good she is seeding into this world." He paused and he was trembling more than the flickering would have caused. "I will take your hand and bring you into it with us if you will let me. And I will pay what price I must to buy forgiveness for you. But our future is not with the power crafted by man or the ability to oppress the weak. Our future is supporting the voice of the voiceless and the healing of rifts that run through generations. Our future is the faithfulness of phoenixes and the pursuit of understanding so that good may be birthed into a dark world and light into a shadowed one. And I think that right now, before we go any further, you need to decide if you're with us. I've fought and fought to save you and free you. I came too late to rescue your body. But I will save your soul if it is possible. And if it is not, then I will not let you endanger anyone else's."

And there was a kind of tooth to that last threat that made me shiver with the intensity of it.

She was silent for a long time and then she gasped out her answer.

"I'm sorry. I'm so sorry. I've been such a fool."

Tell her that we all have been, Kazmerev said gently.

And as Judicus repeated the words, Mally butted in. "Except for me. I've been an absolute genius through this whole thing and you'd better not forget it."

301

We dove.

I clenched my teeth and hugged the book to my chest as Kazmerev spun in a sinuous circle, thrust his beak forward, pinned his wings back, and tilted forward.

His feathers clutched with one hand, my face buried into their flames, and inhaling his scent of woodsmoke and sulfur, we descended. Fear gripped my heart and danced along every nerve, but I leaned into my Pheonix and into his certainty and friendship and let the fear wash over me and drift away.

Beside me, Grevankin stretched, too, seeming to be invigorated by our fall from the heights.

I'll distract them, he rumbled, *It's been the greatest of honors to serve with you, Kazmerev. And of course with you, Sersha.*

"And with me," Mally said so loudly I could hear her even over the wind of our descent.

Always, Ai'sletta.

And then he shot away and straight toward the Stryxex whirling up toward us. He and Mally struck the mass right in the center so that for a heartbeat it looked as if those non-light, non-living creatures were swirling around them intentionally. And then fire blazed from both Mally's hands at once and the Stryxex scattered in every direction, wheeled, and came back toward my wild cousin and her steady friend.

Now! Now! Grevankin cried and I thought I heard Kristiana shriek from behind me as we dove directly at Grevankin and Mally, through the clear path they'd carved for a moment, brushing almost right through their ghostly golden forms and streaking toward the ground below.

A Stryxex struck us suddenly from behind, knocking my breath away and drawing another squeak out of Kristiana.

"Hold your nerve," Judicus mumbled and I wasn't sure if he was talking to her or me, but his ropes flung out like extra arms as he ripped the Stryxex away, still holding onto the reins he'd made for Kazmerev and Grevankin and Kristiana and even himself, to keep them all from being sucked immediately into the pillar.

We were getting close now, I thought, though it was hard to see with the clouds of smoke bubbling up below us in their charcoal fury. I gritted my teeth, squinted my eyes, and reached for the pillar with my gate.

I still had golden souls trickling from me like hot honey, slipping out before I could even see what they looked like and trailing into the pillar, so even if I couldn't see it, I knew it was beneath me.

Another Stryxex struck us and Kazmerev tumbled slightly to the side. My balance threw me backward and the book fell from my grip. I clawed toward it, too slow as it fell, pages falling from the ancient binding. Judicus clawed out for it with a rope, too, a cry wrenching from his lips.

In the moment of distraction, he didn't see the snake-like rope that wrapped around my waist and snatched me from Kazmerev's back.

I was in the air, yanked back like the end of a rope breaking under tension, and flying through the flames and smoke to crash down on the cobblestone square below.

I tried to catch my breath, but something was broken inside. I gasped, curling in on myself against the stabbing pain in my side. But I didn't dare pass out. I didn't dare slip away from consciousness. Not with so many people depending on me. I forced my eyes open, forced myself to breathe.

Sersha! I heard Kazmerev's strangled mental voice in my mind, but I was still blinking away stars and it took me a moment to realize he wasn't speaking into my mind from close by. He wasn't hunched over me protectively like he usually would be. He wasn't scooping me up out of danger with his burning talons.

Instinctively, I forced myself onto all fours, choking back a sob of pain. Something was very wrong with my ribs. But when I managed to lift my pounding head the air was knocked out of me entirely.

Kazmerev dangled in front of me, tangled up in black ropes like a cocoon. He hung from a thread of ropework, and holding the rope was Kentinus, black fury painted on his face as he swung Kazmerev back and forth within inches of the pillar. As I watched, mind-numbing terror filling me, a gold rope wrapped around me like a reaching vine and ripped me from the ground and to my feet before pulling me upward, wrapping around me, and ensnaring me in the same stomach-lurching way.

The fierce ghost of Occulus met my eyes as he stepped up beside Kentinus and growled.

"And now we dispatch the last of our enemies and claim this burning city, my apprentice. And never again can you say that I do not offer you excellent gifts."

I gasped, despair washing away even the fear I felt as Kentinus swung Kazmerev closer to the pillar.

Sersha, he said again in his strangled mental voice.

And then it echoed, *Sersha.* But this time in Judicus's voice as he dashed out of the smoke and drew up short before his enemies.

"One flick of a rope and they're both as dead as you are," Occulus warned him.

302

Judicus's eyes widened and though his hands were flung outward, he bit his golden glowing lip and looked at me as vulnerable as the very young man he still was despite everything that had happened. In his eyes was a look of apology, and then his fingers flicked so quickly that I doubted anyone else would be able to read the signs he was sending me.

"I will love you long past death," his signs told me. *"And meet you again on the other side."*

And then, before he was done signing, a scream tore through the air and Kristiana leapt onto Occulus's back. To my utter shock, her hands wrapped around his throat as she shook him with all her ghostly strength. His ropes whipped backward toward her as if he could dislodge her, but she held on, bucking and kicking as Judicus's ropes spun out toward Kentinius.

He'd always been more powerful than the other rope worker, but Kentinius had the advantage of being alive and physical. It lent a vitality to him that a ghost simply couldn't match. They danced, ropes shooting out and meeting, tangling, pulling, wrapping, and then vanishing as they grappled, each one trying to get a hold on the other, to stop their power and strength.

But though they might not be fully equal, fighting Kentinius head to head left Judicus unable to help his sister. Occulus shook her off, his ropes around Kazmerev faltering for only a moment, and then whipping back into place.

My phoenix burned hot and bright.

Hurry! he urged, and at first, I thought he was speaking to Judicus but the answer came from Grevankin.

For righteousness! he called in my mind and I heard the echo of Mally's voice behind it, *Really? Righteousness? Could we not pick something more ... me?*

And then there they were, hurtling down from the sky like a fireball with a twin core. Grevankin had always been large for a phoenix — now he seemed gigantic and my heart ached that he wasn't black smoke and scarlet flames but was instead white light and golden glow, but none of that mattered when his spirit claws sunk into Occulus. He lifted the ropeworker into the air, Kristiana still hanging off his back.

Sersha, Mally called desperately, as if she were racing to say this. *I'm going to focus every bit of my ai'sletta luck on your healing plan.*

I didn't think it worked like that.

It works how I say it does. Judicus said it himself. When all else is stripped away, that's when you can access rope work. I'm going to do a great work and direct my luck to your efforts. No matter what happens next, you can count on it.

Golden ropes spun out from Occulus's hands — but he wasn't fast enough. A single flap of spirit wings, and then Grevankin smashed straight into the pillar, Mally's ghost on his back, the ghost of Occulus in his talons, and Kristiana dangling below. They hit the pillar with a flash of light and the four of them disappeared, the echo of their passing ringing loud and agonizing through my battered heart.

I must have let out a mental yelp because Kazmerev was speaking in my mind even as his bonds fell apart with Occulus's passing.

I'm here. I'm here.

Mally. Her last promise rang heavy in my mind.

Kazmerev tore toward me at the same moment that Judicus's gaze flicked to what was happening and then his rope shot out, wrapping around Kentinius's bonds around me and wrenching them backward, forcing them to unwind. He gave me a tiny nod and just a flicker of a smile and then his eyes were back on his rival. Kentinius seized the opportunity, his face twisting as he hit Judicus with everything he had and Judicus stumbled backward, and stumbled again.

My bonds fell, dropping me hard on the cobbles. I lost track of Judicus as Kazmerev landed beside me, supporting me with a fiery shoulder as I scrambled to my feet, swallowing a scream of pain as my ribs flared in pain. I couldn't bring in a full breath. I clutched my phoenix with both fists, not able to stand on my own, not able to take a single step, but I had to get to the pillar. I couldn't waste all their sacrifices.

I have you. I have you. Lean on me.

I leaned hard on him as he dragged me forward. I couldn't seem to make my feet do more than catch me as I stumbled along, but I kept myself close to Kazmerev, arms shaking as they bore the full weight of my body.

Almost there. Almost there.

He turned slightly, and then I saw Kentinius fly past in a blur of black, choking on a rope wrapped around his neck, his face dark and swollen as he clawed out with his fingers, trying to catch something, anything that might save him from this plunge into death. His eyes were desperate black holes.

He hit the pillar, shuddered, and then dissolved into it, creating a ripple of non-light and bubbling smoke. But before he dissolved, his rope pulled hard, and on the end of it, my glowing ghost beloved was yanked after him into the maelstrom.

I caught his sorrowful gaze for a half a beat, caught a last glimpse of his affection and the barest whisper of his mental voice like an escaping sigh.

Sersha.

And then he was gone.

We reached the pillar a moment later and I couldn't help the sobs that were shaking me. I couldn't help how they throttled me like a large dog shaking a stick. They sent flashes of agony out from my ribs as the ragged breaks rubbed bone on bone and still I couldn't stop it, or stop the harsh gasps that took the place of breath, or stop the way my sight blurred and blinded me.

I clung to the burning side of my phoenix and felt as he bore my weight and took on himself as much pain as he could. He angled me just right, and I set my hands against the monstrous pillar and hoped I hadn't been wrong about what this might achieve.

Are you ready? he asked in my mind.

I wasn't ready, but I hadn't been ready for any of this.

Your life has been precious to me. If this is your death, then it is precious to me, too, and I will join you in the journey beyond.

And with his sweet words echoing in my mind, I closed my eyes and reached for his fire. And in that moment, I thought I felt something reaching back to touch me — something green and vibrant and bright as spring. Something that made the edges of my consciousness sparkle like dancing sunbeams, something that felt like watching a smile form. Mally was keeping her promise. She was reaching back through death and beyond with her ai'sletta luck.

303

The pain left first. That was my first sign something was happening.

That terrible agony in my head just stopped and my gate slammed shut — or maybe slammed open in the other direction? — I couldn't tell.

But I could feel the heat searing through me and going on and on and on. I opened my eyes and saw the smoke growing fainter, tipped my head up, and saw the Stryxex being sucked into the pillar and vanishing.

I felt the gate in my heart open, and then as if the tide had turned, the souls that had been flowing, flowing, flowing through me in one direction reversed course and went the other way, dashing through my door and out to — where?

To the beyond, I think, Kazmerev said quietly, reverently.

He didn't feel as hot as usual. But I felt hot as a glowing cinder. I bit my lip hard and opened my gate as wide as I could.

This is good, Sersha. It's so good.

And then it wasn't just the ghosts of the pillar whipping through my mind fast as a summer storm, it was ghosts being sucked right through the city, dashing past us into the pillar and then through my gate. I saw the faces of Judicus's friends from the world of the dead as they passed, saw the faces of the ancient heroes who had gone out at his command. I wished them well as they rushed past me and out to the great beyond.

Maybe they'd find peace there. Maybe we all would.

We will. You're doing so well and I'm so proud.

The ghosts rushing by must have been terribly loud because his voice sounded quiet in comparison.

It felt like it had been hours when the smoke finally dissipated completely and the pillar became clear. Beneath my feet, the bronze depictions of phoenixes and men melted and ran down the cobbles and across the square.

So proud.

And then the heat began to recede. And the ghosts faded away and my gate closed slowly, leaving only a mad ringing in my mind.

So proud.

A burst of something like white flame shot upward into the sky and then rippled out from the pillar, clawing out in searing bright arms of flame and I couldn't help it, I remembered the prophecy of Clarinfas the Sighted — that fire would go out and claw across the land and destroy evil. Duke Fontallrae had died trying to see that prophecy realized. He hadn't been wrong after all. Just like the Greensleeves hadn't been wrong and Gundt hadn't been wrong. My heart burned at the thought.

Kazmerev sounded like he was quoting when he spoke in my mind, so softly I could barely hear him at all, *"For healing comes from hope reborn and all things are made new in the giving of ourselves for the heart of another." I'm so proud.*

I startled when the pillar shattered, raining crystal down to the ground until it was nothing but a mound of shattered fragments without a flicker of life to them. They left little cuts across my palms and face and my hands fell to my sides. And this time when I took a breath, I heard myself inhale.

I looked over at Kazmerev, trying to smile for him. Trying to show him how grateful I was for all he had done but to my horror, he was gone.

I gasped. My gasp echoed across the square, hollow and lonely.

I turned around in place. Had I simply missed him? Had he gone somewhere else?

But there was no one there. Not Kazmerev, and not anyone else. The entire square was blackened from fire. Around the dais, in the center, a lake of molten bronze had bubbled and spread and then solidified and the edges were blackened and charred with what it had dissolved under its spreading heat. And in the middle, there was nothing but this heap of crystal rubble.

I sat down heavily, ignoring the smarting of my hands and face, the pain from the slash in my arm, and the agony in my broken side. I pillowed my face on my arms, and sobbed and sobbed, until there were no tears left to spill.

I hadn't had to do it alone. Not even at the very end.

But now, here, with the pillar destroyed and all the spirits set free, and the most evil of men removed from the world, right here I was utterly alone.

I'd lost Mally and Grevankin.

I'd lost Judicus.

I'd lost Kazmerev.

And as the sun sank in the west, it felt like I was sinking with it, and not even the bright flames popping up across the horizon and shooting up into the sky could soothe the aching hollowness of my empty heart.

They found me like that, hours later. A dozen phoenixes setting down all around me, and for the second time, Shasamen bowed in front of me, and those with her sunk to their knees, too. And I couldn't find the signs to tell them to get up or the strength to find my own feet and I wasn't even sure that I wanted to.

304

"You were right about Castan," Shasamen said as she came up out of her bow. "You were right about all of it." She paused like she was taking in the fact that she and the last remaining Flamerarch were bowing to me — a torn, roughed up girl sitting at the base of a ruin. "I realized after you left that he had always ridden with one of us. His phoenix was gone — it left when his heart turned evil. We deposed him and gathered together, but there were still not enough of us to take on two full armies of our own countrymen. Lucky for us, an army of spirits found us. They brought help."

I looked up at her then, and met her eyes, saw the glassiness there as she spoke again, her heart full and her tone echoing that.

"We fought alongside farmers and carpenters, fishermen and carters, beggars and innkeepers, the old and the young. They came at the call of one Judicus Franzer Irault. I don't suppose you know where he is?"

The corner of her mouth quirked up and I felt my pulse quicken. His army had come after all. His army of simple people who had come to fight alongside dead heroes and take back what had been stolen from them all.

I gestured sadly to the rubble heap and she nodded, her head bowing down as if she were carrying a great weight.

"The city continues to burn." She glanced up at the sky as she said that, though it was too dark to see the waves of smoke that had been there before. There was a faint orange glow to the sky, as if the smoke or clouds reflected the fire in the city. "The phoenixes can fly through it, but their riders suffer. Where is Kazmerev?"

I gestured to the rubble again and there must have been something wrong with me, because I couldn't even cry. The ache in my chest was too great.

"Did you do that, then? Smash the pillar? Destroy the phoenixes? Draw our ghost allies back into the world beyond?"

I nodded and she was quiet for a moment.

"Then you are our hero."

I snorted.

She paused again for a long, silent moment and I thought she might leave but instead, she shuffled her feet and spoke again.

"Sometimes, when a great act of power has been done by a Flame Rider using the strength of her phoenix, it can take many days for that Phoenix to return. The power saps their strength and they need that strength to resurrect. I'm sure you've seen times when Kazmerev took a day or two to reappear. Give it time. I heard that when Kardonian purged the Dread Waters it took a full month before his phoenix rose again in his heart. But you have to keep your hope burning or he will not come."

I wanted to tell her that phoenixes were only born in good hearts and I wasn't sure mine was good anymore. I wanted to tell her that this was different. That everyone I loved had been swept away and into that pillar and there was no hope of ever finding them again, that even my mirror shard had splintered into tiny pieces. But she didn't speak my language, and even if she did, she wouldn't know what to do any more than I did.

So I said nothing, merely hung my head down, and let the weight of all that had happened rest on my shoulders.

"You should come with us," she said. "We have food. A camp nearby. You can rest."

When I said nothing she murmured something and I heard a shuffling — the other Flamerarch rising from their long tribute to me, I supposed. It was an honor. And yet, I found I could not care about honors.

"If you stay here there will be no one with food or water for quite some time," Shasamen said gently. "The city is in flames or burned out. Your Flame Rider abilities keep you safe — you do not burn and smoke does not char your lungs. But everyone else will wait outside the city where it is safe. Already, the army who came and fought for us is setting up camps and sharing food with the city's survivors. They will stay outside the city — those who remain — until it burns down enough to recover what they can." She paused. "I doubt they'll find much. Briccatore is no more. A memory of a memory. Calicarn will rebuild itself and another city will take its place as capital, another person its place as ruler. Perhaps that's for the best, but there's no point waiting around here. There will not be a Briccatore again in our lifetimes."

I looked up at that, and saw the sorrow in her face. She'd lost almost everything, too, I thought.

"Come with us." This time when she spoke, it wasn't the formal offer of before, it sounded like the heartfelt plea of one human to another. "Come with us, and fly with us. We'll rebuild the Flamerarch somewhere else. There are thirty-two of us remaining. We could use a thirty-third. You would have a family among us and a place of honor for your sacrifice." She paused. And it was her next words that broke my heart. "Even if your phoenix isn't reborn."

I choked on a sob, a silent, chest-shaking sob, but when she took a step forward I held up a hand. I didn't want comforting. I wanted to grieve. I wanted to honor them all with this aching tremble in my heart. I wanted to honor them by not denying how much their passing *hurt*.

Shasamen stopped and this time when I looked up, eyes blurry with my pain, I shook my head and she sighed.

"The offer is open for when you want to take it, but I can't linger," she said. "There are others who need us. Those who survived need someone to guide them to safety."

I nodded. I couldn't tell what she might be thinking. My vision was too blurred and my heart ached too much to clear my eyes.

"Let us at least tend your wounds before we go."

I didn't respond to that, so lost was I to grief, but I didn't brush their hands away as they cleaned my wounds, sewed up my arm and wrapped it in linen strips, and then bound my broken ribs with thick cloth. Everything hurt and I couldn't bring myself to care.

I sat, letting sorrow wash over me and break me apart, and eventually, Shasamen and the others left — all except one who slunk over to the other end of the square, seeming to examine the rubble. I felt an ache in my heart at the sight of him there, calmly pacing the perimeter, resting a hand from time to time on the limping red phoenix at his side. Every so often, the great creature would look over at me with its piercing eye, and I'd catch sight of the flickering flames and twisting smoke at the ends of each feather and I'd break into sobs all over again.

Shasamen had said not to lose hope or I'd never Get Kazmerev back. And I believed her. But I couldn't help the pain that hope stirred up. Because for every thought I had that maybe I could get him back, I also felt the fear that he might be gone forever, and if he was, I didn't think I could bear it.

305

I didn't know how long I sat like that, in the rubble of what had been my last battle. Certainly all night. There were rays of sunshine creeping through the city when I pulled out the little book of prophecy in my belt pouch and read the last entry.

"And when all has come to pass the sojourner will set out and look for the sun and find it. For healing comes from hope reborn and all things are made new in the giving of ourselves for the heart of another."

I choked on that. Kazmerev's last words to me rang again and again in my empty head. All things made new. Healing from hope reborn.

But he was my hope and I was terrified he would not be reborn.

This book had been twisted by those who interpreted it as a manual to seize power for themselves. If it had been the sacred trust that those guarding it thought, then it had been long warped and used by our enemies. Could there still be truth in it despite that? Did I dare to hope in so uncertain a thing as written words?

I shut the book and put it back into my pouch with my precious mirror fragments, curled up in the ashes and rubble, and sobbed myself to sleep.

I slept a long time.

The sun was red and setting in the sky when a gentle hand shook me awake and I did not know if I had slept away one day or many days. I felt hollow and terribly thirsty.

"It's her! We've found her," the relieved voice said.

I blinked awake. Though I must still be dreaming. That voice was familiar, but from a time that felt like it was a lifetime away.

"Sersha?" the voice asked kindly. "Sersha? Can you hear me?"

That couldn't possibly be ... no, it couldn't be, could it?

"Those phoenix people said she'd be here but they didn't say she was half dead. Maybe they should have done something instead of just watching." This voice was familiar, too. The note of annoyance in it as familiar as my own name. Fon?

My eyes snapped upward to see my burly cousin Gandy frowning down at me with concern across his open face, one hand on my shoulder. Behind him, my cousin Fon stood with slumped shoulders, an axe in one hand stained with red, his clothing torn and filthy.

I tried to lift a hand to sign something but before I could move I was hefted upward and the person lifting gave a familiar grunt. I gasped in pain as my ribs protested, knocking both breath and thought away to replace them with pain. Even so, I tried to turn to look at who it was, still stunned by this strange dream — because it had to be a dream, right? My cousins wouldn't be here all the way from Landsfall — but I found I didn't have the strength to turn my head.

"Rest yourself, Sersha. We've got you now." But that was definitely my Uncle Llynd's voice. And that was his gasping grunt as he carried me out of the rubble.

"You're too old to be carrying her, Da, hand her to me," Gandy said and then there was a transfer of me from one to the other — painful enough when it shifted my ribs that I had to bite my lip to keep from screaming. I was still weak as a newborn kitten. I couldn't so much as move my head.

"They should have told us she was half dead," Fon complained. "All they said was that she needed us."

"And that Mally was dead. Gone. That we were too late for her," Gandy said and there was a deep sorrow to his words.

"Yes, they were full of happy news," Fon said bitterly and he sounded so much like his sister that my heart ached with it.

"Let's just get her back to camp. It's a long walk to the mules yet," Uncle Llynd said. And I wished I could ask questions because we didn't own mules and why were they camped here and how had they gotten here at all?

But in my weakened state, I could not move, so I listened to their grumbles and huffs and gentle assurances as I flickered in and out of awareness.

"That phoenix rider in the black has been shadowing us," Fon complained.

"I see it," his father agreed.

"It's like he doesn't trust us."

"Oh, he's probably been told to keep an eye on her. She's a hero to them."

"They bow when we pass with her," Gundy said in an undertone. "I saw one man trying to paint a picture of her on a phoenix. He told me he'd sell it to me for five silver."

"Five silver! That's a fortune." Fon sounded horrified.

"Like I said," Uncle Llynd reminded him. "A hero."

"I wouldn't want to be a hero to them if this is how they treat their heroes."

I faded out and when I came back to consciousness I was being placed on a bed of straw in the back of a cart and there were new voices.

" ... any water?" Uncle Llynd was asking and then a reply from someone I did not know.

"We're getting low, this is all there is. Need to get back to camp."

"Yes. Let's go," he agreed. But they stopped and wet my tongue for me before the wagon lurched forward and the mules, I assumed, carried me over the rough rubble-strewn, fire-blackened road out of Briccatore.

From the mule cart we found a boat, and from the boat we made our way upriver, tracing the path I'd once taken with Mally from the underground river to Briccatore, and then we were deposited along the bank and I was helped up onto my shaky legs, barely able to stand as my ribs screamed at me, and led to a tent in a sea of tents where a woman I didn't know spoke anxiously with my uncle, spooned broth into my mouth and then wrapped me in a blanket and told me to sleep.

And I slept.

And there were no dreams and there was no phoenix.

And I slept again.

And there was still no Kazmerev when I rose on the second morning since they'd brought me here and found I was strong enough to stand and with great care, to make my way out of the tent on my own.

The generous woman who had been caring for me had cleaned me up and had washed my dress. It was hanging from the center of the tent, mostly dry now. I tugged it on which was a hero-like task all on its own when I couldn't lift my arms over my head. I found when my boots had been cleaned and left to the side and my belt and pouch folded neatly over them.

Something hard and heavy clenched in my throat at the thought that I might have lost it while I was asleep. I dressed with trembling hands and I didn't stop shaking until I'd pawed through the pouch and assured myself that I still had those delicate fragments of mirror.

When I was finally dressed, I stumbled out of the tent, and found them there, gathered around a fire sipping tea. A wave that looked like relief passed through them as I looked around the circle. My uncle Llynd and cousins, Fon and Gandy. And the woman whose quiet murmurs had been nursing me to health. They were clean now, bandages where blood had been, weapons set aside. And they all watched me with worried eyes and slightly anxious expressions.

"*Thank you,*" I signed and Uncle Llynd waved my thanks away.

"You're family," he said simply, and then I was waved to sit down on the bench, and a hot cup of tea was pressed into my hands and I listened as they spoke to me.

"We know about Mother and Mally," Gandy said. He'd always been affable like his father, but he ran a weary hand over his face now. "So, you don't need to tell us about that."

That, at least, was a relief. But what were they doing here?

"The war raged all along the coast," my uncle said after a moment. "Don't know if you knew that. Raiders everywhere. Had to learn to fight them. Not our favorite thing to do." My eyes must have been wide with surprise because he added, as if the extra explanation was all that was needed, "No extra school for Fon. Couldn't send him away in the middle of that."

Fon kicked the fire grimly, but he nodded with my uncle. "Probably no school left to attend now."

"Probably not," my uncle said and he didn't sound too concerned about that. He folded his hands over his belly and pursed his lips before continuing. "The ghost of Haroon the Deathknell came to Landsfall. Asked that all able-bodied warriors gather and follow him to Briccatore."

The ghost army had gotten that far that fast? I wondered if Judicus had ever guessed they could spread out so quickly. My uncle must have mistaken my surprise for disbelief.

"It was definitely Haroon. Fon quizzed him on his great acts just to make sure, and he answered clearly. Maybe Fon will write down some of the extra stories he told on the way here. Haroon sent someone to every farm and village and hamlet along the way and it felt almost like some kind of magic carried us. We moved too fast, traveled too far in a day, — like we weren't bound by the limitations of time or bodies. Oddest thing."

"Because it was magic," Fon said dryly.

His father ignored him. "But not so odd as his stories."

"I might not need a school if I write them down," Fon said, kicking the fire again. "I'll be known everywhere as the greatest storyteller who ever lived."

"Not much money in stories," Uncle Llynd said easily. "Better do it from the inn so you can eat, mmm?"

I wanted to laugh. Their conversation was the sound of home. Their easy acceptance of this insane story — this thing that was bound to become a legend in the telling, passed down from generation to generation — made it all feel less painful somehow.

"Maybe Sersha will have some things to add to your story," Gandy suggested.

"I doubt it," Fon said. "Clearly, Mally was the hero of the story. That phoenix rider said she sacrificed herself and her phoenix to save us all."

"Imagine Mally on a phoenix," Uncle Llynd said wistfully. "I would have liked to see that. It would suit her so well."

"So that makes her the hero," Fon said with confidence. "They were calling her the ai'sletta and saying she was chosen to save them all. And she did. It was very generous of her to find a way to save Sersha's life while she was at it."

"Well, Sersha's family," Uncle Llynd said easily.

I wanted to laugh at their interpretation of what had happened. But I paused, because weren't they right in a way? Mally *had* been the chosen one, the ai'sletta, the one whose luck had kept helping us and helping us. It might have been the thing that made healing the pillar even possible in the end. I'd felt her luck tangle with my healing flames, reaching out to me as I reached in, just like she promised she would. Together, we'd mended the ropes that held the world together. I was pretty sure that's what we'd done. The pillar cat cut one or more of them and left them raw and exposed, sucking in life wherever they could. We — together — had fused those broken ends back together.

But Mally was more than that. She was the one who drove us forward into all the places we had to go. The one who ended up fulfilling the prophecies and saving us all in the end with her sacrifice. I blinked back tears. I wished Gundt would have lived to see this. Would it have restored his faith to see that all *his* sacrifices and the faith of the Greensleeves hadn't been misplaced? I bit my lip at the memory of his death, giving himself for Mally and for me, even though he didn't believe anymore that she was the key to saving everything, even though he thought he was just doing it for a pair of girls he'd begun to feel responsible for. It made what he did even more noble, somehow.

"Well," Uncle Llynd said, breaking into my reverie. "If you're all done your tea, we'd better get up and going. We have a lot of miles to cover today."

I looked up at that and he offered me a contented smile. "We're headed home now, Sersha. Go check on the girls. Make sure the Inn is still standing. What do you say?"

And I nodded. Because there was nothing else left for me than to go back to the village where I was the voiceless cousin and niece. And right now, I was grateful for even that.

306

Shasamen had been right. People had come to Briccatore from all the surrounding area and they didn't like talking about how they arrived so quickly. If someone mentioned it casually or tried to laugh at how much longer it would take to get back, he was met with only stony silences.

"They don't like magic," Gandy told me with the confidence of someone who didn't care, as we loaded packs with their tent and food and supplies. "I don't either, really." He laughed, rubbing the back of his neck with one hand. "When we get back I'm never leaving again. Wish we'd been here in time for Mally, though."

By midday, the people camping around the city had broken up and scattered outward like a kicked ant hill. I could only assume that the few remaining groups around the city planned to stay and rebuild, but they were few and scattered. If any elves had survived, I did not see them here in the ruined outskirts of the city. Hopefully, they had remained in Sarcoda. Maybe they could even build something there.

If Kazmerev had been here, maybe we would have gone to help them. We could have told them about Verdaine's courage and what an honor it was to fight side by side with her.

As it was, we paused on the first big hill and looked back, watching all the other groups spreading out across the landscape. From here, I could see an organized camp of a few dozen people — the remaining Flamerarch, I would guess. Everyone else was ragged and disorganized. They broke into friend and family and village groups to return home.

Our group had a half dozen men and older boys from Landsfall outside of my cousins and uncle. They spoke quietly and little, content to watch.

"I'll be happy to get home," Gandy said when we made camp that night. "Too many people here."

It was at the first camp that the men around me finally began to admit to wounds and aches and I found myself busy silently tending them after Uncle Llynd mentioned I had experience in "the healing work of women."

And so, I slipped back into the life I'd had before, tending wounds silently into the small hours of the night, and there was no flicker of fire in my heart, no hope of anything more.

I broke down that first night, crying silently in my borrowed blanket. Should I just give up then, and return to my old life in the tiny town of Landsfall? Already, listening to the men talk about catches of fish, about re-thatching the roof this year, about the price of nails — it felt foreign and small. I used to fly over buildings that needed thatch. I used to rescue the people whose actions influenced the price of nails. And now, I couldn't buy a single nail on my own if I were pressed to do it.

For a moment, I almost despaired. But I couldn't let myself do that, could I? To stop hoping would be to betray Kazmerev. What if he really did heal in a month or two months, and he rose, ready to be born, only to find my heart had lost hope and there was no place for him?

But hope hurt. It ached inside me, growing more painful by the hour because to hope was to not accept that my happy life with him was over. To hope was to keep thinking that this awkward fit among those of my village and those traveling in the same direction was only temporary. As long as I kept hoping for more, I was caught between the two, neither one nor the other.

If my relatives found my long face odd, they didn't mention it. They simply kept traveling day after day as we watched those with us melting away to their homes and villages.

At night, I read the prophecy books in my pouch when I wasn't tending wounds or illnesses for the travelers around us or the villages and crofts we visited, but I'd lost the book we found in Occulus's tower. It had fallen from Kazmerev's back. And I didn't have the book that had suggested there was another way out of the mirror shard. And so, I was as trapped as my friends inside that mirror world with no way out.

I puzzled over the possibilities as I wrapped bandages and cleaned out infection, as I boiled water, and silently sterilized tools. People rarely spoke to me as I worked. My silences seemed to keep them away and any mention by my cousins that I was voiceless garnered me only pitying looks.

Those looks hollowed me out.

Only days ago, there had been people in my life who did not pity me, but depended on me. Who saw value in me beyond a voice and now I was right back here again with people who couldn't look past this one small disadvantage. I ground my teeth when they couldn't meet my gaze and I tried as hard as I could to hold onto hope.

My family was kind to me in their way. I had no reason to complain. And yet, this life fit me as poorly as if I'd tried to wear Gundt's clothing. I missed Gundt. From the moment he met me he'd never seen me as anything other than capable.

On the fourth day, we traveled along the edge of a cliff and stopped there to eat. I set up five stones stacked one on another — my tribute to Gundt. It was in this that I felt my silence most strongly because he deserved to have his tale told, to be recognized for the hero he was. But who would ever hear it from the lips of a voiceless girl?

It was on the tenth day that I decided I wouldn't stay in Landsfall. I would bring my family there, but I would go on. Where I would go, I did not know. I knew only that it was no longer home, and I couldn't go back to stay. It would be full of memories. Of Aunt Danna and Mally. Of Judicus stumbling out of the inn with ropes flying from his hands. Of Kazmerev blooming in my heart.

My cousins and uncle mourned Mally. I could see it sometimes in their silences and surly replies. And when they mourned her, they were extra kind to me, as if they could give me the kindness they could no longer offer her. But I couldn't make a home with them again.

On the fourteenth day, we camped in a wide clearing. There were maybe fifty of us still headed in this direction. We'd taken a small branching road that was not the most direct route, but we had to spread out. With so many people traveling away from Briccatore it was hard to buy food or find places to sleep at night and spreading to less direct paths helped to even the burden out.

We didn't regularly set watches, so when everyone else fell asleep and I wandered along the edge of the trees and sat down by a burbling brook, there was no one watching me. I contemplated the water and pulled out one of the tiny shards of mirror and tried to will it to open for me, or to show the face of one of those I loved.

But after gazing in it for an hour or more, I saw nothing more than the moon. With a sigh, I shoved it away. It was almost dawn. Almost time to begin to walk again.

And then I froze as I felt something I hadn't felt now in two weeks. Was it my imagination? Was I simply overtired?

But no, I felt it again.

It was almost like the sensation of Kazmerev rising in my heart but fainter, further away.

I tried to reach for it, but at that moment the sun came up and the feeling melted away.

It had been there, hadn't it? I hadn't just imagined it.

I clung to that hope all day as we traveled.

What if he'd been there? Did I dare to hope he had been? And what if I hoped and then tonight when the sun set nothing happened? My instinct was to protect myself, to refuse to surrender to hope. But if I did that, then I might lose him entirely.

Reluctantly, fearful of the pain, I let the hope build instead, let expectation swirl inside me tumultuous and insistent. There must have been some shred on my face because Uncle Llynd pulled me aside as we were setting up camp.

"Are you holding up, Sersha?"

I nodded.

"You look often to the trees and you look like you expect something." He let that sit for a moment. "If you see trouble you'll tell me?"

I nodded again.

"You don't need to be afraid. You have a place with us."

And he pulled me into an unexpected hug and I found myself hugging him back. Maybe, even if Kazmerev never rose again, I should still embrace hope. Maybe there were unexpected kindnesses out there and hope could only foster them and make them bright. I shouldn't give up yet.

I smiled at my uncle and got to work, content for the first time since leaving Briccatore as I wrapped bandages and checked on sores from the road. And when the last cut was cleaned and wrapped and I stood up with an aching back to stretch, the sun dipped down behind the horizon and fire raced through my veins as hope overwhelmed me.

Would it be now?

Could he be rising even now?

My hands tingled with anticipation.

But even hope could not have prepared me for the fire that washed through me.

It burned away every shred of doubt, every scrap of worry, leaving me with nothing but a bright engulfing flame inside — and a gorgeous phoenix rising outside, bursting up through my heart and into the world, his bright feathers scarlet with little licks of purple flame at their hearts, and tiny curls of black smoke at the edges.

And he was the most beautiful thing I'd ever seen. My heart soared within me as my body froze, insensible, before this shock of hope reborn.

Sersha? he said in my mind, sounding uncertain.

I collapsed to the ground, covering my face with my hands as I sobbed with relief.

Sersha! he said again, and then he was there, tucking me under his flame-covered wing, and holding me close to his body so that I could feel the intensity of his fire, and smell his campfire and cinnamon scent.

And I thought hope could only hurt you when it wasn't realized. I had no idea it could sear you to the core with absolute joy when it was finally realized.

307

I had been so afraid that I'd lost him.

Never.

We'd lost so many others.

Not forever, only for a time.

I laughed at that, at how strong his hope was in the face of all of it.

Your hope is strong, too, or I wouldn't be here.

I buried my face in his feathers and just breathed, letting long breaths fill me.

But where are we? Where are we going?

Ha! W could go somewhere else now. We could fly out into the world as he'd once asked me to do. We'd search for adventure, the two of us. And he'd show me all the places I'd never seen before.

But what of Mally and Judicus? What of Grevankin? I thought you had some idea of saving them from the mirror.

I pulled back so I could look him in the eye to deliver the news. I'd lost the book. I didn't know how to get them free. I'd lost everything and only barely received my own phoenix back.

You might have lost the book, but you haven't lost your gate. Didn't you see at the pillar how you could open it different ways? Can you open it to the shard?

I hadn't tried. Without Kazmerev, it had felt as though magic had left the world entirely. I still couldn't believe he was here. Here!

I am so happy to be back with you, my Flame Rider. But I know you. You need more than just me.

I felt his mental smile bathing me with love but then he shook out his feathers.

Your gate, he reminded me. *You need to open your gate.* And when I hesitated he leaned in close. *I am reborn, Sersha. I am not going anywhere again. I'll be here with you for every step.*

And it was just like hoping for him all over again, allowing it — even a little — hurt. It made me feel as though I had my throat laid bare to a knife.

If the gate does not open and they remain in the mirror, you will still have me. I will not abandon you, Little Hawk.

I smiled at his pet name for me. And he was right. I did not have to go back to the old life that didn't fit me anymore. I didn't have to go back to being voiceless and ignored. I didn't have to lose my life and self all over again, because he was back.

But did I dare ask for more? Did I dare open myself up to crushing disappointment for the hope of regaining my cousin and my beloved rope worker? Could I even call it love if I wouldn't risk that much?

And what if I opened my gate and Kazmerev was snatched away again and I was back to where I was only minutes ago, brokenhearted and alone? I couldn't bear the thought of losing him again. Especially now when I'd only just received him back from the dead.

I grimaced at my own lack of courage, and then my phoenix was there, butting his forehead against mine.

You tend so many wounds, but you don't see your own. You don't realize that you've sacrificed in this, too. Others gave their lives, and with them their futures. You gave your heart and your future, too. You sacrificed just as they did for the sake of others.

I hadn't realized that. I hadn't tried to sacrifice anything or be a hero. I just did the only right thing at the time.

Of course you did. He sounded like his words were melting him, though phoenixes did not melt. *That's who you are. But now, be reasonable. Do you chastise a man for the battle wound you tend? Do you berate him for the broken arm he gets in a fall? Of course you don't, Sersha. You treat their injuries and have compassion for their situation.*

I swallowed down a burst of feeling. His words made so much sense. I clung to them, feeling my eyes tearing up with the relief of being known. I was crying too much these days. I had to stop somehow.,

You are injured, too, Sersha. Injured in your heart and mind. You fought a great battle. You faced fear and tragedy and the very worst happened — you were left by everyone you loved, alone and desolate.

He really did understand. I pressed my forehead in tight to his and let my tears spit and evaporate as quickly as they could fall in the heat of his flames.

You had to fight for hope. You had to hold it close to your heart when everything tried to snatch it away. That takes strength and courage.

And now I was really crying — but with relief that someone understood.

And that's why I know you can do this again. You can find the hope to try. You can find the courage to open up your heart again and open up the possibility that you might lose everything.

He was right. Perhaps *this* was my fight. Fighting my own fears and worries. Being willing to sacrifice my happiness for the possibility that I could restore happiness to others. It felt too big for me. It felt like too much. But maybe sacrifices always did. Maybe I just needed to step out and into it without knowing what came next.

Would he stay by me while I tried? My mental voice sounded weak and shaky to me, but his boomed out with confidence.

Always.

I sank to my knees, closed my eyes, and let myself feel all his fiery warmth for a full breath and then I reached into my belt pouch and brought out the fragments of mirror I'd been carrying. I arranged them in front of me, making sure I had them all, took a deep breath, and opened the gate of my heart as wide as I could.

308

Nothing happened.

Disappointment tore through me hard and fast as a knife cut and I choked in it for a moment before Kazmerev's voice cut through my mental noise.

It's only your first try. Don't give up so easily. It's a wonder that you held out hope long enough for me to be reborn.

I'd always hope for him.

But not Mally? Not Judicus?

I felt my cheeks flaming at that.

Try it another way. You've only ever opened one kind of gate. Can you think of them and maybe try something more ... specific?

It was worth a try. Could he help me?

I...I never considered that. I suppose that I could try.

I opened my heart again. And this time, I let Kazmerev's fire fill me at the same time, as if I was going to heal a person — or a pillar. I could feel him there with me, his fire strengthening what I pulled from him, his intent strengthening mine.

I thought of my friends specifically and thought of the mirror that Judicus had stumbled into and the shard that Mally had leapt through, and I thought of how they weren't meant for that plane of existence, but for this one. What I needed to do was heal the gap between where they were and where they were meant to be. I needed to heal this broken mirror so they could cross through. I needed to heal their hearts and souls that had come detached from their bodies in the mirror and slipped out like ghosts.

I closed my eyes tight. And I let that healing fire flow through me. Once again, I felt that strange flickering, as if something was tangling out to meet me halfway.

And when my eyes flicked open again, I gasped. The mirror was whole. Not just a whole fragment again, but really whole. I glanced over my shoulder quickly. Was anyone watching?

No, we were hidden from casual view behind a tent and everyone had gravitated toward the cook fires. I swallowed and edged my way toward the mirror, Kazmerev coming with me, his fiery head level with mine. We shared a worried look and then turned back to the mirror.

Perhaps you need to go inside?

I didn't like the thought of that. Anyone who went in couldn't come back out again.

You're different than just anyone, he reminded me. *You have the ability to make a gate with your heart. What if this gate is wide open and they are on the other side but they don't know that it is open, so they never try to come out?*

What if I stepped through and it closed and we were all trapped?

Then we will be trapped together. He paused. And then spoke again. *What is the alternative? We can hardly go riding off after the sunset and leave them here.*

And I *had* felt that indescribable flickering that seemed an awful lot like Mally's luck. But I could have imagined that.

I turned to him and gave him a fond look. Riding off after the sunset was *exactly* what he'd wanted me to do in Landsfall when raiders had attacked my home.

I've changed, I think. I've been around you so long that I am starting to think like you. He sniffed. *It happens to phoenixes. It's nothing to be ashamed of.*

But that meant this was my responsibility, too. If it was my attitude infiltrating him that made him like this, then if he came with me and we both got stuck that was my fault, too.

He shrugged his great fiery shoulders.

In the end, we all bear guilt for a hundred possibilities where we could have gone left but went right, where we could have acted but didn't, or did when we should have left it alone. We cannot know the future. We can only do the best we can with the present.

He was right. I pressed my lips firmly together and clenched my fists and looked toward the gate with determined purpose. Alright. I would step into the gate. And whatever came next, we'd deal with that.

Would he go with me?

I'll go with you anywhere.

Perhaps I could try to put just my head inside. Everyone I'd watched had fallen or been pushed inside. I'd never seen anyone try to go only halfway.

Whatever you do, we're a team and I'll do it with you.

I paused, drew in a long breath, pressed my forehead to his, and said in my mind, *Thank you, friend.*

If this was to be the last journey for us, then I was glad that we were making it together.

I stepped forward and he stepped forward with me, and then —very deliberately — I checked to be sure my heart was still wide open and I plunged my face into the mirror.

Bright light filled my vision, searing my eyes so that I couldn't see. I blinked in the intensity of it. I seemed to be looking at a ledge on the side of a cliff. Below was nothing but cloud. Above, nothing but cloud. Like an island midway to the sky.

I tried to open my heart-gate further and I called with my heart, *Judicus? Judicus!*

And then something crashed into me and I stumbled backward, my face pulling free of the mirror.

Whoa! Easy now!

I blinked against the sudden darkness of the night as I stumbled into Kazmerev's steadying hold.

I have you.

And then the heavy thing that had hit me moved and I jumped, surprised. It rose, shook itself, and as I blinked, trying to see, I heard the flurry of a second phoenix arriving.

Flame to flame I greet you, ancient fire! Kazmerev spat out, fast as lightning.

Flame to flame I greet you, ancient fire! Came the gravel sound of Grevankin's deep rumbling voice, laughter twisting through it like threads of gold through a rock. And now I didn't need to wait to see who had thrown me back through the gate. I leapt forward and wrapped my arms around Mally and drew her into a huge hug.

"What took you so long? It felt like I was waiting for weeks. Stars and skies, I'll have to find a new companion in these adventures if you can't shape up, Sersha."

But, despite her grumbles, she turned and hugged me back — fiercely and deliberately, like everything Mally ever did.

"Well, what are you waiting for? I heard you calling your rope worker. You'd better go back in for him, too."

Were all the trapped souls who had gone into the mirror in there?

No, no, Grevankin said reassuringly. *Only those who went in the gate made by Occulus's magic, or the shard that you carried with you. When the other souls were freed from the pillar, we remained. Mally, myself since I am her shadow and flame, Judicus, and one other.*

Kristiana, obviously. So, I just needed to go in and get those two, too, I supposed.

They are deeper within the mists, as they were put into the shard earlier.

But wouldn't that mean the heroes were trapped in there, too? Since Judicus had communed with them before he came out of the pillar the first time.

You sound just like him, Grevankin grumbled. *And trust me, it is getting old. If I have to hear one more long rambling speculation about how the mirror works, and how to replicate it, and how to avoid trapping people for all eternity, I am going to lose my flame.*

And what about Occulus?

I ate him, Grevankin said smugly. *It was Kazmerev who gave me the idea.*

"Stop bragging," Mally said, but she was smirking when she said it.

It made the rope worker vomit. I didn't think ghosts could vomit.

And just like that, the need to go back in and find my rope worker burned in me like a fire all its own.

We'd better hurry before Mally learns her family is here and runs off, Kazmerev said in my mind.

"My family?" Mally asked, crossing her arms over her chest.

Oops.

She was already gone, striding across the ground like a ship through the surf.

Grevankin rolled a huge eye at him and shook his smoking head and then he was gone, fluttering after her, stirring the tents the way storm winds make them flap and tear.

Ooops, I heard him echo as one of them flew into the trees, but I had no time for that.

My mouth was dry and my hands were clammy as I stepped toward the mirror a second time.

Are you ready? Will you do this with me a second time? I asked Kazmerev.

I told you, Little Hawk. Where you go, I go. To the ends of the earth.

309

We plunged back into the mirror.

I hadn't realized I was shaking until the bright light hit me and I had to close my eyes against it and clasp my shaking hands. I wouldn't have been able to sign if I'd wanted to.

Judicus? I called. *Judicus!*

And then we waited.

And waited.

Judicus!

It was a long time before Kazmerev said, *We might need to step inside.*

I didn't like the idea of that. What would keep the gate open?

Perhaps, I could fly in and you could hold it open?

But it had only worked when the pair of us worked together. If one of us were gone, I didn't think the gate would hold open.

We're so close. I can feel it.

And it wasn't enough. I choked on the realization.

I'm going to try. I can't bear to see you heartbroken like this.

He slipped in further until all that was left in the real world was the tip of his tail. He shuffled forward, but the second his whole tail slipped into the gate, it began to close.

Kazmerev! I screamed in my mind, and then he leapt back and the gate opened wide again and we were both left breathing hard, looking at each other in the painful white light.

Well, he said, *I guess that won't be the answer.*

Was that movement I saw on the horizon through the clouds?

I suppose we'll have to draw back and regroup.

Was that — it couldn't be, could it? Was it the figure of a man striding through the clouds with nothing under his feet and a burden carried on his shoulders?

Perhaps if Grevankin helps us, Kazmerev mused. *If you are more able to open the gate with the help of one phoenix, surely the help of two will push it over the edge.*

But no, he wasn't walking on nothing — he was walking on the finest woven bridge of rope and as he stepped forward, it spooled out in front of him as if he were weaving it as he went out of the very thinnest, most fine-spun threads of magic and reality. He was fashioning a bridge of reality out of nothing as he walked.

I only knew one man who could do that.

It's not over yet, Sersha, but I think we need to accept that it's over for now.

And then the clouds parted and there he was, long dark hair mussed and tangled, new lines on his narrow face, and a slight woman slung over his two shoulders, legs down one side, arms and head down the other, as my Judicus stumbled under her weight.

"No faith in me, Kazmerev?" Judicus asked and he sounded confident, a man returned home, a hero back from slaying a dragon, but as he drew nearer, I noticed his face was slightly green and his breath slightly hitched.

I … I … I

I'd never heard Kazmerev rendered completely speechless before. It made me want to laugh. Just seeing Judicus at all made me want to laugh. And cry. Both at once.

And I realized I'd already started on both as he stumbled forward, and I caught him in my arms, and to my surprise, I stood up on my toes and kissed him full on the mouth. His kiss back was wild and desperate, like he thought he would only have this one kiss and he planned to make the most of it.

When he drew back he whispered, "Take me home, sweetheart."

I clasped his hand in mine and drew him back through the gate.

310

Are there more in there? Kazmerev said the moment we stumbled back from the gate.

Judicus glanced over his shoulder, his eyebrows rising when he saw the full golden door but his voice was low and final when he said, "There are no other souls trapped within. Close the vile door and free us from the fear of ever being sent there again."

I hurried to comply, shutting my gate with something that felt like a slam. The door dissolved into nothing, leaving only the fragments of crushed mirror I had picked up from the ground back at the pillar. I looked at them for a heartbeat, trying to decide what to do with the fragments, and then to my shock, Kazmerev stooped down and ate them, quick as a heron gulping down fish.

"Are we going to talk about where things go when you eat them?" Judicus asked him.

No. Could Judicus still hear his mental voice?

"Are we going to talk about where *people* go when you eat them?"

Still no.

Judicus turned to me. "I'm guessing that's a no."

He couldn't hear Kazmerev anymore. And he couldn't hear me. And he was right here in the flesh again. It was too wonderful.

His eyes were full of affection and something that looked like relief. It lasted for a full, beautiful moment while I drank in the sight of him, the warmth of his hand which was still clinging to mine like a lost child clings when he's found again, and then he swayed slightly, went paler than before and fell to his knees, his burden tumbling to the ground behind him.

I sank with him, trying to stabilize him, to keep him from falling. A smile flickered across his face and then he passed out and I barely caught him in time to help ease him gently to the ground.

"Well," Mally said from behind me. "We've come full circle, I guess. You, with a sick rope worker to tend. Me, with my family here and all the world spread before me."

But she said it in a way that shook, that sounded uncertain and not at all secure.

"And the Grand Hadri is still following me around like a lost dog," she said acidly and I followed her gaze to Judicus's burden and gasped. It really was his sister, her face long and pale just like his, her eyes closed in his familiar swoon."

"Gather them up and I'm sure Sersha will nurse them through the night," she ordered her brothers and father. "It's what she does. And in the morning there had better be a kingdom offered to me and an unbroken crown or I'm going to be seriously testy."

You know she isn't going to be offered a kingdom, right? Kazmerev asked Grevankin as my cousins and uncle helped me settle Judicus and the Grand Hadri in the tent we'd been sharing up until now. I didn't know what was wrong with either of them. Hopefully, nothing that rest couldn't cure because that was basically all I had to offer. I hovered over them like a nervous bird over her eggs.

Try telling Mally that, Grevankin replied, but he sounded amused.

What happened to Judicus's sister?

There was a long pause before Grevankin said, *She's been like that since she went into the shard, as far as we can tell. Judicus is worried. He thinks it's his fault for begging Sersha to put her in the mirror.*

"It's not his fault," Mally said in an irritated voice like they'd been over this before. She had stormed back into the tent with a bucket of water and a pair of clean cloths to put on the brows of those we were tending. "You know I'm missing my family reunion to do this, right Sersha? Missing it. You owe me so much."

And I wanted to laugh at that, because of course I owed Mally. We all owed Mally and for much bigger things than this, and yet it was this she wanted gratitude for. Without realizing what I was doing, I spun and grabbed her into a hug, holding her tight even as she wiggled away.

"Don't be so needy, Sersha. No one likes someone who clings."

I do, Kazmerev said.

Mally rolled her eyes. "Of course you do, you big softy. I meant real people who aren't bound by fire and vow to keep coming back and loving someone."

And yet, we who are fake people to you, are the best friends you'll ever have, Grevankin said, unmoved by her words.

Do you have to put up with this all the time? Kazmerev asked him.

You get used to it, Grevankin said easily. *She grows on you. And you start to realize she doesn't mean a word of it. She's all flame and smoke, nothing that can hurt you.* He paused. *Now that the rope worker is back with your rider, will there be little humans? I've really been getting my hopes up about that.*

"Grevankin!" Mally complained.

What? I like small humans. They are cuddly.

Mally shook her head, looking like she'd lost her patience entirely, but I knew that look of fondness in her eye.

"It's time for me to introduce you to my family," she said testily. "And no talk about small humans. And no eating anyone."

I have eaten no one, Grevankin said. *That was all Kazmerev.*

Sure. Blame me.

It would help if you would allow that.

"You both know I can hear you, right?" Mally grumbled, but she seemed pleased as she left the tent and when she was gone, she left a quiet behind her that was full of worry.

I bathed the heads of Kristiana and Judicus, but while Judicus seemed to calm at that, his breath evening and slowing, Kristiana's breath was thready and weak.

Out in the camp, the voices of Uncle Llynd and Fon and Gandy rang, ecstatic with the joy of a sister and daughter returned to them.

Here in the tent, I was fraught with worry, only the warm presence of Kazmerev calming me.

You brought them out, he told me. *They're back in the world. You can only do what you can do.*

But I could heal her, couldn't I?

The former Grand Hadri died in that mirror. Who knows what hardships met them in there?

It was ... grueling, Grevankin murmured in my mind. *Do what you can for her, but do not take her situation on yourself. She came through a phoenix gate, through your heart and Kazmerev's. Only the good can survive that process.*

Are you saying she was not good? Kazmerev asked carefully, preening his feathers as if to avoid looking at me when he said it. The slash along my arm was mostly healed, leaving only a long red scar.

I'm saying her sacrifice helped buy our victory, that her love for her brother spurred her to action, and that in it she found a shade of redemption. But I am not the judge of souls and hearts. That is beyond me. I know only that the gate you wove burned away all that was not good and only what remained could pass through. I'm a phoenix. I was not affected by the purification of such a gate, since the same happens to us every morning and evening. Mally, too, felt little change.

Mally? Kazmerev asked. "*Mally with the harsh tongue?*"

Is good, Grevankin said, laughing. *Isn't that a delight? But it's not much of a surprise since I am born in her heart and no phoenix can be born in a heart that is not true.*

I closed my eyes then and focused my heat and warmth on Kristiana, pouring all the healing strength I could into her as they whispered in the back of my mind, but when my eyes fluttered open there was no change.

Eventually, the camp quieted and everyone found their blankets and I was alone, waiting up in the darkness, listening to the breath of the two siblings on either side of me. And I cried silent tears for what Judicus would face when he woke. My healing attempt had not taken and far from growing stronger, Kristiana's breath was slipping away.

311

He woke with a start and sat up so fast that his knee hit my chin. I'd been sitting between the pair of them where they were laid out on blankets and the impact sent me sprawling backward.

"Oh," he said, a little breathlessly. "Oh, I'm so sorry, Sersha. I didn't ... I had no idea."

He looked around the tent and swallowed, growing still for a moment and tilting his head as if listening.

"We're in a tent. It's the middle of the night. You've been up with us, taking care of us. And Kazmerev is here but invisible?"

Ooops. I quickly made Kazmerev visible and he flared to life, head in the tent, the rest of him out in the campground. Out there somewhere I heard a terrified murmur followed by the faint sound of Mally scoffing. Oh yes, I forgot. We were traveling with people terrified of magic.

Judicus bowed to Kazmerev. "It's an honor to see you again, brother. Thank you for fighting at my side. I see you have kept your Flame Rider alive. You have my deepest respect."

Well, if he keeps talking like that, he can stay. But you'd better tell him for me because now that he's flesh again, he cannot hear my voice.

"He says thank you," I signed and Judicus smiled gently.

He lifted a hand and looked at it and some deep emotion rolled through him that made his chin tremble for a moment before he got a fierce look on his face and the trembling stopped. He swallowed visibly again and then turned a gentle smile to me.

"You came for me — for us."

"For you," I signed. *"Judicus."*

And the admission seemed to break something in him, or maybe it was his sign name that brought such warmth to his eyes. He leaned forward suddenly and gathered me into his arms, leaning his forehead against mine and then pressing his nose tip to tip with my own, just breathing like that.

I closed my eyes and let the sensation of him being so near fill me up with all the feelings I couldn't let myself feel before. Gratitude welled up with it. I'd been so worried about him and Kristiana that I hadn't taken the time to be grateful. We'd retrieved them. After so long, I was starting to think it wasn't possible, and yet here he was. And he wasn't dead. And he wasn't imprisoned on another plane. He was right here with me where I could touch him and breathe him in and ... oh.

He kissed me — just a brush of his soft lips on mine and then he pulled back with a disbelieving huff of air.

"I'm alive," he said in wonder, running his hands through my tangled hair. I should have taken a moment to straighten myself. "I'm alive and with you."

And his face was such a mix of pain and relief that I longed to soothe his hurts away. I gently drew him back to me and he allowed me to do it, slowly, in wonder. I caught his face between my hands — his long, pale, serious face — and gently kissed him again, and then folded him into an embrace. And I loved his warmth and the way I could hold his hunched shoulders and feel the tension ease out of them. And I loved that he was alive and that I could feel every breath.

And I loved when he whispered, "This time we get married before it's all gone again."

And I wanted to sign to him that it wouldn't go away this time, but I didn't because I didn't know if it were true. I'd been surprised so many times that I didn't think I could know the future anymore. So, I wouldn't. I'd just hold onto him right here and right now.

Kazmerev sighed dramatically from the tent door. *If this is going to be a long, drawn-out love story, I think I'd like to go to sleep for a while.*

I thought phoenixes didn't sleep.

Daydream, then. I'd like to daydream.

But though he laid his head down and closed his eyes, there was a playfulness to it that told me he wasn't entirely serious.

Sersha, he said in my mind. *Never doubt that I want the best for you. Even if it means I have to be there for the kissy parts.*

"How is my sister?" Judicus asked and I had to unwind from our embrace to sign to him.

"*She is not well. I have tried to heal her, but I cannot.*"

He nodded gravely and moved to look at her, taking up one of her limp hands in his.

"I tried to hold onto her." He choked, shook his head, managed to pull himself back together, and then spoke again. "I knew that hope was slim. When she came through the pillar she was like this. I was busy with Occulus, but it was only for a few moments. I don't think she woke during that time. I must admit, if Mally hadn't joined us, I would have gone crazy."

I looked a question at him.

"Yes," he laughed. "Mally. Queen of biting comments and grim predictions. She was surprisingly good company once she got over screaming at me for not telling her about how the ai'sletta is foretold to die saving the world. I had to explain to her that I never believed that part — that it seemed impossible that she would ever die. After that, she settled into her normal self. There's nothing quite like a biting comment about your doomed love, or how you're too thin to live, to really buck you up when you're sure your sister is dying."

I laughed with him — that kind of laugh you do when you're close to crying.

He reached out and smoothed his sister's hair back as you do for a child.

"She's so young," he said gently. "And it was too much for her. She trusted Jastomen. *I* trusted Jastomen."

I pointed to my chest because I had, too.

"We all did," he agreed. "And with me away and my mother gone, what was she supposed to think? I should have been there."

I put a hand on his arm and shook my head.

"*They would have killed you,*" I signed. "*If you were in Briccatore they would have stormed your house and killed your mother and sister and you because you couldn't be controlled and they needed you out of the way and powerful as you are, could you have stood up to an army of Stryxex riders and rope workers all on your own?*"

"No," he agreed. "But maybe it still would have been better for her. She wouldn't have been deceived by evil people or made to be their figurehead, or left by them to die."

I shook my head, because if he'd died and they'd captured her they still would have done all of that and he wouldn't have been there with her at the very end.

"I think I'd like to sit up with her," he said and sorrow sang in his voice. "And I can see you have not slept. Why don't you rest now? I will be right here. I will wake you if you are needed."

I paused, reluctant to sleep when I'd only just received him back from the dead. Afraid to close my eyes in case he disappeared again.

He patted the blanket. "I'll be right here."

Hesitantly, I spread out across his blanket, eyes still on him.

I'm in the entrance of the tent. Trust me. No one is coming in or out except through me.

That was reassuring.

It was meant to be.

I swallowed and tried to settle, my mind still insisting that if I relaxed at all, it would all go away. But then Judicus took my hand — one hand holding mine and one his sister's — and calm flooded me and I found my eyelids going heavy as sleep claimed me.

312

I woke to the golden light of dawn and quiet tears. I stayed completely still for a moment, only opening my eyes, so as not to disturb Judicus. He was in a corner of the tent, sitting with knees drawn up to his nose and arms wrapped around his knees, his chest shaking as he sobbed.

His sister lay silent and still on her blanket. Death had come in the night. I wished it was still dark. I could use the kind of calm comfort of Kazmerev right now.

When I'd been young, I'd always thought of great defeats of evil at the hands of the good as these beautiful, triumphant things. I hadn't realized that victory is bought with great pain, that destroying evil often means watching the destruction of the people caught up with it, and that doing what is good can be a complicated thing. I knew all that now. And it still didn't take the sting out of it.

I moved quietly to his side and laid a hand on his shoulder, and though he didn't look up or speak, he took my hand. We sat like that for what felt like a long time until the tent door rustled and Mally stuck her face inside. She glanced around the tent, and then disappeared again, returning what felt like an hour later with Gandy.

"We've dug a grave," she announced baldly. "And we'll bring her to it. Why don't you follow us?"

They lifted Kristiana on the blanket — I was always surprised by how strong Mally was — and I helped Judicus to his feet as we silently followed them through the camp. The camp was utterly still as people stood out of the way, heads bowed in respect, hats in hand.

They turned to follow us as we passed, a funeral procession made up of strangers, and I wondered if they knew this had been their Grand Hadri, or if it would make a difference if they did. They were paying their respects either way. They were showing honor either way.

When we reached the place they'd cleared where a hole had been dug, my Uncle Llynd was waiting. He placed a small violet on Kristiana's chest. And that act was where Judicus broke, sinking to his knees, a hand covering his face as he cried again, silently.

We laid her gently in her grave and covered her over.

"Heart of earth take your bones, heart of heaven take your spirit," Uncle Llynd said the traditional burying words formally and everyone nodded along. It felt like too small a thing to represent all that had happened to this poor soul. But I knew no other way.

They left slowly, one by one, and Uncle Llynd and all my cousins worked to set up a marker of piled stones as I rubbed Judicus's back and sat with him.

When it was complete, he pulled himself together, rose, and ran a hand through his hair awkwardly.

"I would like to thank you for the honor you have done my sister," he said a little brokenly. "Your gift is gratefully received."

"We're going to camp here today," Uncle Llynd said soberly. "Let you say your respects as you please."

Judicus nodded. "Thank you."

"Come now, Sersha," Uncle Llynd said. "There's work to be done. Leave the man to grieve. He'll find you when he's ready for company."

I hesitated, but Judicus smiled grimly and nodded to me to go.

There's always work to be done when you're traveling, and since we were stopped not far from a brook, I worked with Mally silently washing clothing and cooking implements, gathering fresh water for all the water skins, and repairing broken equipment.

It was noon when she laughed harshly, breaking the silence.

"Doesn't it seem silly?" she said. "Yesterday I was dead, hoping that my straw-brained cousin would be clever enough to realize she could cross into the spirit world and pull me out, and not sure if she would or if she'd spend the rest of her life moping while I rotted in that place. Now, today, we're washing stains out of clothing. I'm scrubbing my brother's stockings. His stockings."

She gave me a meaningful look as if this was the most demeaning thing she could be doing.

I nodded my agreement. It was fairly ridiculous to compare the two. What would Gundt think? Would he be happy for us or would he roll his eyes at this turn of events?

"We saved the world and no one really knows it," she said, looking wistfully into the distance.

What would the elves do without Verdaine, I wondered. Without a home or an alliance to buy them one? Would they stay in their stronghold? Would they find a way to survive?

"And now what?" Mally asked. "I talked to my family. I know Briccatore is no more. There's no more Grand Hadri. There's probably no more Calicarn. No one knows who might rise to power here, but it won't be me because no one knows or cares what an ai'sletta is. There's no more Flamerarch for Flame Riders to join —

or at least there's maybe a dozen people who think they have that title but *ha!* that's not exactly an army."

It would take decades to rebuild a Flamerarch and reestablish a network to find and train phoenix riders and to have outposts where they could seek shelter. And that was assuming that someone had found the ashes of some of the lost phoenixes. What if they were gone forever? What if there would only ever be these few we had with us now?

Mally was still talking, "We don't have to worry about raiders for a while since we slaughtered them with magic. Our enemies are gone, dead and defeated. But what now? What do we do now?"

The words hung between us as we crouched together along the stream, side by side. And I was glad I had a cousin. I was glad she was Mally.

"We go on adventures," a voice said, startling us both so that I slipped and put a foot in the water. We spun and there he was. A little red-eyed. A little pale. But smiling gently at us. "There's a place called the City of the Amethyst Faces that's rumored to be to the southeast of here. It's guarded by mountains too steep to climb. I bet phoenixes could fly over them, though. I think I still remember the code to open the gate that was recorded in Prostinic's Guide to the Ancient world."

Mally laughed, a disbelieving, but delighted laugh.

"Or perhaps there is Ghar Gh'har, across the Great Ocean. They say it is the place from whence phoenixes first came. Or the islands of the Harsh Snows to the north where the birds swim. Or the deep Frondlands to the south where the light cannot reach the ground through the thick foliage. Everyone carries a long knife and must hack a path forward. But perhaps phoenixes would find a different way to get through."

And this time, Mally's laugh was very pleased indeed. "Are you saying you'll travel with us, rope worker?"

Judicus smiled and puffed out his chest. "I'm saying that *you'll* travel with *me.*"

This time it was I who laughed. It just slipped out before I could help it.

"*Will you be ... well?*" I signed and I wasn't talking about his motion sickness.

"I will be. In time," he said, his smile growing grave, but still there. "I will be sooner, if you stay with me."

"*I will stay with you forever,*" I signed.

"Stars and skies," Mally muttered. "Will the two of you just get married already?"

"Yes," Judicus said, shooting her a teasing smile. "I think we will — right now."

"*Right now?*" I signed, worried. His sister had just died. Was this really the time?

He looked at me with a heavy gaze that told me he was thinking the same thing.

"We'll wait for nightfall, so Kazmerev and Grevankin can be there, too. They won't want to miss it. The phoenixes have taught me that hope is most important when things are darkest. That love is strongest in the midst of sorrow. That faithfulness can carry you through the impossible. This is the right time to do it. I can grieve and rejoice in the same heart."

"*So can I,*" I signed.

"You two are the mushiest ever," Mally said, rolling her eyes. "You'd better go ask my dad to officiate or he's going to be an impossible grumbler.

As if she was one to talk.

But of course we did what she asked, which was why we found ourselves at sunset surrounded by strangers and the last of my living family except for my cousins who had remained in Landsfall. We stood away from the campsite in a small meadow Fon had stumbled on. It was full of wildflowers and some of the others had dragged fallen logs over to sit on around the edge of the clearing.

My Uncle Llynd stood under a spreading tree as the last beams of sunlight started to fade, his hands clasped over his belly. Mally stood to one side of him and Gandy to the other, as tradition demanded. And in the center of the circle before them all, stood Judicus and I, hands intertwined.

The moment the sun winked out Kazmerev and Grevankin flared to life, visible to everyone, their arrival met with gasps of surprise or delight or tight-lipped expressions of denial.

They're doing it! Finally! Grevankin exclaimed the moment he was made alive again. *Kaz! There will be little humans!*

I told you there would be if you would just be patient.

You always say that, but this is the first time it's been true.

They found their way to the spots we'd left clear for them on either side of Mally and Gandy and their bright scarlet and gold light was all we needed to light the wedding ceremony. Tears pricked my eyes — tears of joy at the privilege of having our wedding lit by actual phoenixes.

You deserve the world, Kazmerev said. *I'm so proud of you.*

I hoped he would be fine with this. It meant bringing someone airsick with us everywhere we went for the rest of our lives.

I'll get used to it, he said.

And if he doesn't, the rope worker can ride with me, Grevankin offered and the silent look Mally shot him told me that she did *not* agree.

I almost laughed, but then I caught Judicus's eye and his expression held so much pride, so much joy tinged by his deep sorrow that I forgot about bickering phoenixes and glaring cousins and I thought only of him.

"We're gathered here according to the traditions of Landsfall," my Uncle Llynd said, in the way every wedding I'd ever witnessed started. "Our job is to witness the binding of two of our people. If they agree to what comes next they will be one in the eyes of our community, as tightly bound as family and for all their lives nothing will permitted to separate them - not poverty or illness, not the cold of winter nor of a shoulder, not the heat of flame nor of anger, not the sharpness of the blade nor of the tongue. They will be one in our eyes. Do you wish this, Sersha and ... rope worker?"

"Judicus Franzer Irault," Mally hissed.

"Judicus something and something," Uncle Llynd said gravely.

We turned to him together, and Judicus said "Yes," his mouth twisting with laughter while I nodded.

"Say your piece then," my Uncle Llynd said and there was a happy murmur from the gathered people as I stepped back and signed.

"I vow to never leave you, to respect and honor you, to offer to you my warmth and affection, my heart and my home, my forgiveness and loyalty, now and forever," I signed the traditional vow of brides of Landsfall for as long as there had been Landsfall brides, blushing furiously over it all.

And he was blushing, too, as only Judicus could as he repeated his vow to me in sign, with only one small change, *"I vow to never leave you, to respect and honor you, to offer to you my warmth and affection, my heart and my name, my forgiveness and loyalty, now and forever."*

And while it was not a tradition of my people, I found that yes, I would like very much to take his name — a name dreaded and feared, despised and rejected, and now, at this time victorious. Judicus Franzer Irault.

"It has been witnessed and it is done," my Uncle intoned. "And now we eat."

And just like that, we were married.

313

Different places have different wedding celebrations and it seemed that phoenixes were no exception.

"I thought phoenix riders rarely married," Judicus said, sounding confused.

I couldn't help myself — I grinned. It was a somber time. There was much sorrow to consider. And yet, in this small moment, his uncomfortable expression at entering into something unfamiliar to him — at even finding something he wasn't familiar with — was utterly priceless.

Tell him that it is, indeed, exceedingly rare, Kazmerev said as I translated in sign. *And because of that, it is all the more important that we get this right. Phoenixes around the world will be asking me if we did it — and if we did it correctly — and if I do not answer them, there will be flames.*

"I'm sorry," Judicus said, running a hand through his hair and looking bemused, "but aren't there always flames around phoenixes?"

Tell him these would be different flames.

I relayed this faithfully.

We will do this right, and we will do this according to tradition. Who knows. We may be the last of the phoenixes, Grevankin and me, and a couple of dozen others. With so few it is even more important that we retain our traditions.

He sounded so sober and intense.

"*I think he really means it,*" I signed to Judicus.

Of course, I mean it!

Of course he means it! Grevankin agreed.

"Then I suppose we'll do it," Judicus said. "Umm, what is it that we are doing?"

It involves flying, Kazmerev said.

"Oh no," my brand new husband said. "I think it must involve flying."

I laughed again, my eyes closing in amusement, and then, to my surprise, my laughing lips met something soft and warm and I gasped, eyes flying open to catch a glimpse of Judicus with his own eyes closed very gently kissing my laughter. And it was so unexpected and so terribly dear that I melted into him.

See? We have to put up with this. And not just today for a wedding but all the time, Kazmerev said in my mind.

And I will be enjoying it too. Mally and I will be questing with you, Kazmerev, Grevankin declared.

I didn't say I enjoyed it! I said I had to tolerate it. Wait. You are staying with me?

If there are only a few phoenixes, then it would be a shame to split up. We will need each other to keep alive the ways of the Flame. And also, brother, you could exercise a little compassion here. How do you expect me to look after Mally all on my own? By Leaf Turn she'll be trying to take over the world and establish an empire if I don't keep her occupied. It's not the work of a single soul.

Well, that's certainly true ...

Mally! Stop it! Grevankin said. *You cannot hit a flame and you should stop trying before you pull something.*

Even though Judicus couldn't hear any of it, he was still laughing when we broke apart from our kiss.

"I think I'm ready," he said, still smiling tenderly at me. "And if I die in whatever this ritual of theirs is, I will die a happy man."

Kazmerev glowed brighter for a moment — like a phoenix version of clearing the throat — and then leaned down low.

Both of you mount on my back and hold hands.

We hurried to comply and then he shot into the air like a rocket, a very excited, whooping Grevankin chasing hot on his tail. He'd forgotten Mally in his excitement and I heard her down below calling fruitlessly to him.

We sped up into the clouds and then Kazmerev circled once, still with Grevankin swirling around, and said, *Let's see if your bond remains unbreakable. Hold each other tight.*

I didn't have time to sign. I just grabbed Judicus's wrists with both my hands. He clasped my wrists and turned pale.

"I don't think I'm going to like th...I...s...s...s!"

Kazmerev dropped us and we fell through the air, hair and clothing whipping around us. My heart was in my throat, and Judicus's face was a picture of terror — worse than I'd ever seen despite all our adventures. He let out a very unmanly keening sound like he couldn't quite even manage a scream and then suddenly we were caught in a pillow-soft flurry of feather and hot flame. Scarlet and gold and deep purple surrounded us and the sound in my mind was of phoenix laughter as Kazmerev drifted to the ground with the pair of us clutching each other on his back.

With our blessing, the phoenixes said together, fly together through soaring days and falling times, cling tightly together, and may nothing tear you apart!

It took a long minute of staring wide-eyed at an equally wide-eyed Judicus before I could manage to translate the sign.

We were still laughing very shakily when Mally stormed over.

"Really? You two are not flying off without me ever again! I'm already regretting letting you get married."

Judicus rounded on her so suddenly and violently that it made me jump, but to my delight, he said, "Mally, there is a legend that in the Hinduran Mountains that look out over the Great Growling River a crown of emeralds and light is hidden in a series of caverns. Each is guarded by a riddle and none but the most devious may venture through them and claim the crown, but whoever does will be Queen over all the Seas of the Earth and may command whales and storms and unleash her fury upon the land."

"Are you offering to go get it for me?" she asked, tipping her chin up boldly.

"Oh, I hardly think I'm devious enough to capture it," he said with a twisting smile. "But I'm offering to tell you everything I know about it on the way there, so that you'll be prepared when you go in after it and attain the crown no one else has ever been determined enough to acquire."

Mally sniffed. "I suppose it will have to do. We've wasted most of the night on this wedding. We could have found five lost crowns by now. We'll have to leave tomorrow night, I suppose."

And I realized, with a sinking feeling, that she was right. In my joy and excitement, I hadn't realized that there would have to be hard goodbyes in the morning because Mally and I were never made for staying in Landsfall. And Judicus most certainly wasn't.

"Out there somewhere," Judicus said waving a hand like he was already showing it to us, "The whole world waits. They called me Son of Chaos before. Once I unleash Mally of Landsfall, I will truly earn the title."

I was still laughing and Mally still frowning when the sky above us lit with flaring red and gold and before our eyes, a dozen bright spots coalesced and descended. I heard the shouts of alarm from our relatives and fellow travelers from where they were feasting at the campfires, but I knew immediately who had come — who Kazmerev had not told me were near as they enacted their phoenix wedding tradition.

The last of the Flamerarch had come to my wedding.

The phoenixes quickly offered their greetings as the Flamerarch landed in a ring around us, dressed once more in their Flamerarch finery, Shasamen directly in front of us, and to my complete embarrassment, they fell to one knee as they dismounted. Shasamen bowed for only a moment before striding forward. Her eyes were wide with wonder.

"Judicus Franzer Irault, Son of Chaos," she murmured, "You live." Her eyes strayed down to where our hands were still clasped together. "We witnessed your marriage in the sky."

Kazmerev shifted smugly behind me as if to remind me that it had been his idea and a good one.

"Ai'sletta," she whispered, seeing Mally standing with arms crossed over her chest. "What marvels are these?"

"If you've come to ask us to return to Briccatore you're going to waste your breath," Mally said boldly. "We didn't find we were at all welcomed there."

I wanted to laugh at her gross understatement, but I had to keep myself steady. I might be the only one here capable of a clear head right now.

"We sought Sersha of Landsfall," Shasamen said warily. "Our hearts went out to her for her great loss and our gratitude overflows for the gift she gave in saving Briccatore, Calicarn, and the world."

Mally snorted. "Sure. And destroying them while she was at it."

Discomfited, Shasamen looked back and forth from her to me. "We sought to find her and offer her refuge among us, what luxuries we could find, safety from enemies — as much of what she had earned as we could offer."

"Have you decided to rebuild Briccatore?" Judicus asked quietly. He plucked a stick from the ground and squatted down, drawing idly with it in the dirt. Nothing could look less threatening, and yet Shasamen stepped back.

"Yes."

"Are you sending Flamerarch to the surviving cities of Calicarn to establish control over them and cement the nation again?"

"Of course," she sounded annoyed by his question.

"Will the Flamerarch rule Calicarn, then? As you are the only remaining organized group who still retains your magic, the rope workers hunted and destroyed by Kentinius and Occulus and the other phoenixes destroyed by the same?"

"Who else will take on such a great burden?" There was a bite now to Shasamen's words.

"And will you cross the sea when your reign here is firmly established? Will you take, too, the lands of the Hand of the Rat as they were foolish enough to come here and challenge us with their twisted perversions of magic?"

"There has been talk," she hedged.

He looked up and smiled.

"Then let me tell you my plans, too, Shasamen of the Flamerarch." He stood, and in that moment, I was reminded that I was looking at the most powerful rope worker alive. "I will not let you take my wife to be your prisoner." He lifted a hand and there was a sharp bite to his tone. "In fact, if not in name. Don't insult me by pretending you are trying to do otherwise. I have matters of my own to attend. As does my wife, the Lady Irault." I thrilled a little at the title he'd given me. "As does the honored ai'sletta who ought to be held in deepest esteem for all she has given to Calicarn. We will be gone for a time. But my ears reach long, and my memory longer. My power is not restricted to saving lands. It can be turned against them, too. And the phoenixes with me are free phoenixes, subject to no laws but that of the wind and the sky. If it reaches my hearing that you are not using your newfound power well, trust that I will return and set that right. And if ever again you come after my wife," and here his eyes narrowed in a way that made me shiver, "consider your life forfeit and the lives of all those with you today, human or phoenix. I see your heart, I recognize your ambitions, and if necessary I will check you at every turn."

No one was bowing now. They were moving slowly, mounting their phoenixes.

"You leave, you say?" Shasamen said in a falsely light tone. "Soon, I hope?"

"Very soon," Judicus said.

"Then we wish you well. May we meet again in peace."

"May we, indeed."

And then they launched into the sky and we watched them go until they were nothing but spots on the horizon. Mally let out a long, shuddering breath.

"If they were going to hold Sersha as a prisoner, I can only imagine what they would have done to you and me, ropeworker."

"Indeed."

"I think I'd like to find a crown of emeralds instead."

"Yes, I think that would be preferable, Mally. And now, if you don't mind, I think I'd like some time with my wife."

And to my utter surprise, he kissed me again, this time tenderly and as if he had the rest of the night to make it perfect. At some point, Mally left with a snort of disgust and the phoenixes winked out, and it was only the two of us in a small forest clearing warmed only by each other and our shared love and it was enough — more than enough — so much I ached with the fullness of this happiness and I never wanted it to end.

In the morning, we said goodbye to our fellow travelers and goodbye to Uncle Llynd and my cousins. They left us with what supplies they could spare, a meager assortment of things, but enough to make it to the next town. And they left us with their best blessings and a demand that we return home as soon as possible.

"Don't forget us, now!" Uncle Llynd had said.

"I know a place where we can gather what we need," Judicus said as we sat around a campfire. There was no point going anywhere before sunset.

"That sounds terribly convenient," Mally said. "Are you sure there will really be supplies for the taking there?"

"Not supplies, no. But books. Lots and lots of books. My family's country estate was barred to us for the past few years but it's likely empty now, and if it isn't we can still sneak in and take the books. It's not stealing when they're yours."

"Books?" Mally asked, horrified.

"Well, once you're Queen of the Sea you might decide to be Queen of the Air and Queen of the Earth, too, and we'll have to read to figure out how to make all of that happen," he said, spreading out on his back on the ground as I laughed beside him.

"That's true," Mally agreed, sounding contemplative. "Fine, we'll get your books. And supplies. And then we're flying off into the sunset, all three of us and our phoenixes. Agreed?"

"Agreed," Judicus said.

"*Agreed,*" I signed.

"Oh, and Mally?" Judicus said as he closed his eyes and she rose to leave. She paused. "Stop pretending you can't see Sersha's signs. It's disrespectful."

"Who's pretending?"

"If you do, I'll take your voice, and then you'll be forced to see what it's like."

"There's no way you could do that," she said, but she didn't sound very confident. "If you could, you already would have."

"I guess you'll find out."

She shot me a death look, but I just shrugged. I had no idea if he could do that, but I was certainly finding the pair of them amusing.

She stalked off and after a few minutes, Judicus opened one eye.

"Is she gone?"

I nodded.

"Good," he said with a laugh and caught me into a cuddle on the grass. "I have been teasing her a lot, but I want to tell you a bit about what I have to offer you, Sersha my sweet love, and it is not emerald crowns."

And so he told me about the places we would visit, and the things we would see and the peace we would restore everywhere we went, until we both drifted off to sleep and when the sun set low in the sky, orange and scarlet and gold, we packed up our few things and stood together with Mally in the clearing until the first star of night rose in the sky and our phoenixes rose with it.

To adventure! Kazmerev said the moment he was born again.

Onward! Grevankin agreed as we mounted them, but he spoiled the effect by mentally whispering, *and there will be little humans, right? I thought there would be some by now.*

It takes time, Kazmerev reproved, as Mally burst into laughter.

"The worst part of this is being unable to hear the jokes," Judicus whispered in my ear, but his arms were around me and I liked it that way, so I didn't turn to reply, I just sank into his warmth behind me and Kazmerev's warmth below.

Who knew what we would find in the world beyond? What adventures we'd have, what sorrows we'd share, what sacrifices would need to be made. We'd left so many behind who should have gone with us. But for this moment, as we rode off together, I was perfectly happy.

THE END

BEHIND THE SCENES:

USA Today bestselling author, Sarah K. L. Wilson loves happy endings, stories that push things just a little further than you expect, heroes who actually act heroic, selfless acts of bravery, and second chances. She writes young adult fantasy because fantasy is her home and apparently her internal monologue is stuck in the late teens

Sarah would like to thank **Melissa Wright & Eugenia Kollia** for their incredible work in beta reading and proofreading this book. Without their big hearts and passion for stories, this book would not be the same.

Sarah has the deepest regard for the talent of her phenomenal artist Luciano Fleitas who created the gorgeous cover art that accompanies this book. Without her work, it would be so much harder to show off this story the way it deserves!

Thanks also to the Noble Order of Female Fantasy Authors who keep me sane – sort of. And for my beloved husband, Cale and sons Neville and Leif who are endlessly patient as I talk to them about bookish passions.

And a HUGE THANK YOU to my patrons, **Mike Burgess, Jennifer Wood, Victoria Hamilton, Ken Baker,** and **Carly Salsbury** for their support. I couldn't do this without readers like you!

Visit Sarah's website for more information:
www.sarahklwilson.com

www.ingramcontent.com/pod-product-compliance
Lightning Source LLC
Chambersburg PA
CBHW020533310726
48979CB00014B/2323/J

* 9 7 8 1 9 9 0 5 1 6 3 4 4 *